HIPPOCRENE STANDARD DICTIONARY

Revised Edition

POLISH-ENGLISH
ENGLISH-POLISH

with Complete Phonetics

HIPPOCRENE STANDARD DICTIONARY

POLISH-ENGLISH
ENGLISH-POLISH

DICTIONARY

with Complete Phonetics

IWO CYPRIAN POGONOWSKI

Revised Edition

HIPPOCRENE BOOKS
New York 1990

Second revised edition, 1990
Fifth Printing, 1990

Hippocrene Books, Inc.
171 Madison Avenue
New York, New York 10016

Printed in the United States or America

Library of Congress Cataloging in Publication Data

Pogonowski, Iwo Cyprian, 1921–
    Dictionary, Polish-English, English-Polish

    1. Polish language—Dictionaries—English.
    2. English language—Dictionaries—Polish.
    I. Title.
PG6640.P54   1982   491.8′5321   82-9211
    ISBN 0-87052-908-0 (hb)   AACR2
    ISBN 0-87052-882-3 (pbk)

To my wife, Magdalena

CONTENTS
SPIS TRESCI

Introduction

The Polish-English part of this dictionary contains about 16,000 entries. The unique feature of the work is the way in which ordinary English pronunciation is used to convey the approximate sound of the Polish word. There is no need, therefore, to learn the complicated phonetic symbols which are often a stumbling block in the everyday use of dictionaries by non-scholars.

Unlike English, the Polish language has an abundance of grammatical forms. Changes in endings of nouns, adjectives and verbs correspond to their function in a sentence, their gender, their number and their tense. Thus Polish declensions call for seven different endings, for each gender, in the singular and in the plural. The number of Polish words is further increased by the multitude of augmentatives and diminutives.

Unlike English, Polish pronunciation is consistent and clear. Polish achieves the size of its vocabulary by use of prefixes and suffixes to a greater extent than the English language. Thus English has some 120,000 root words, about double the 60,000 root words in Polish. Yet the many variants in the Polish language provide a vocabulary of half a million words, about the same as in English.

Spoken by over 50 million people today, the Polish language, with its logic, finery and elegance will continue to serve well abstract thinkers such as mathematicians and philosophers, as well as novelists and poets, thus contributing to the pluralistic culture of the world.

EXAMPLE OF NOUN AND ADJECTIVE DECLENSION IN POLISH LANGUAGE

DOBRY DOM = GOOD HOME, GOOD HOUSE

SINGULAR:

NOMINATIVUS	= MIANOWNIK	DOBRY DOM	GOOD HOME
GENETIVUS	= DOPEŁNIACZ	DOBREGO DOMU	OF A GOOD HOME
DATIVUS	= CELOWNIK	DOBREMU DOMOWI	FOR A GOOD HOME
ACCUSATIVUS	= BIERNIK	DOBRY DOM	A GOOD HOME
INSTRUMENTALIS=NARZĘDNIK		DOBRYM DOMEM	BY A GOOD HOME
LOCATIVUS	= MIEJSCOWNIK	W DOBRYM DOMU	IN A GOOD HOME
VOCATIVUS	= WOŁACZ	O DOBRY DOMU!	OH! GOOD HOME

PLURAL:

NOMINATIVUS	= MIANOWNIK	DOBRE DOMY (2,3,4)	GOOD HOMES
		DOBRYCH DOMOW (5...)	GOOD HOMES
GENETIVUS	= DOPEŁNIACZ	DOBRYCH DOMOW	OF GOOD HOMES
DATIVUS	= CELOWNIK	DOBRYM DOMOM	FOR GOOD HOMES
ACCUSATIVUS	= BIERNIK	DOBRE DOMY (2,3,4)	GOOD HOMES
		DOBRYCH DOMOW (5...)	GOOD HOMES
INSTRUMENTALIS=NARZĘDNIK		DOBRYMI DOMAMI	BY GOOD HOMES
LOCATIVUS	= MIEJSCOWNIK	W DOBRYCH DOMACH	IN GOOD HOMES
VOCATIVUS	= WOŁACZ	O DOBRE DOMY!(2,3,4)	OH!GOOD HOMES
		O (PIĘC) DOBRYCH	OH! (FIVE)
		DOMOW! (5...)	GOOD HOMES

NOTE: (2,3,4) = Small Polish plural of two, three and four.
(5...) = Large Polish plural of five and more.

DIMINUTIVES: SING.: DOBRY DOMEK - PLUR.: DOBRE DOMKI (2,3,4)
                                          DOBRYCH DOMKOW (5...)
                        DOBRY DOMECZEK   DOBRE DOMECZKI (2,3,4)
                                          DOBRYCH DOMECZKOW (5...)
AUGMENTATIVES: SING.:DOBRE DOMISKO PLUR.:DOBRE DOMISKA(2,3,4)
                                          DOBRYCH DOMISK (5...)

XII

EXAMPLE OF CONJUGATION OF A VERB IN THE POLISH LANGUAGE

CZYTAC (chi-tach) = TO READ

- PAST TENSE -

PERFECT FORM = SINGLE TIME COMPLETED OCCURENCE

MASCULINE	"I"	(JA)	CZYTAŁEM	I READ
FEMININE	"I"	(JA)	CZYTAŁAM	
MASCULINE	"YOU"	(TY)	CZYTAŁES	YOU READ
FEMININE	"YOU"	(TY)	CZYTAŁAS	
		(ON)	CZYTAŁ	HE READ
		(ONA)	CZYTAŁA	SHE READ
		(ONO)	CZYTAŁO	IT READ
MASCULINE	"WE"	(MY)	CZYTALISMY	WE READ
FEMININE	"WE"	(MY)	CZYTAŁYSMY	
MASC.PLUR.	"YOU"	(WY)	CZYTALISCIE	YOU READ
FEM. PLUR.	"YOU"	(WY)	CZYTAŁYSCIE	
		(ONI)	CZYTALI	THEY READ
FEM.& NEUTER		(ONE)	CZYTAŁY	

CZYTYWAC (chi-ti-vach)=TO READ (OFTEN)

IMPERFECT FORM = MULTIPLE INCOMPLETE OCCURENCE IN THE PAST

MASCULINE	"I"	(JA)	CZYTYWAŁEM	I USED TO READ
FEMININE	"I"	(JA)	CZYTYWAŁAM	
MASCULINE	"YOU"	(TY)	CZYTYWAŁES	YOU USED TO READ
FEMININE	"YOU"	(TY)	CZYTYWAŁAS	
		(ON)	CZYTYWAŁ	HE USED TO READ
		(ONA)	CZYTYWAŁA	SHE USED TO READ
		(ONO)	CZYTYWAŁO	IT USED TO READ
MASCULINE	"WE"	(MY)	CZYTYWALISMY	WE USED TO READ
FEMININE	"WE"	(MY)	CZYTYWAŁYSMY	
MASC.PLUR.	"YOU"	(WY)	CZYTYWALISCIE	YOU USED TO READ
FEM. PLUR.	"YOU"	(WY)	CZYTYWAŁYSCIE	
		(ONI)	CZYTYWALI	THEY USED TO READ
FEM.& NEUTER		(ONE)	CZYTYWAŁY	

EXAMPLES OF WORDS DERIVED FROM THE VERB "CZYTAC"= TO READ

DOCZYTAC, DOCZYTAC SIE, DOCZYTYWAC, DOCZYTYWAC SIE,
NACZYTAC SIE, NACZYTYWAC SIE, OCZYTAC SIE, ODCZYTAC,
ODCZYTYWAC, POCZYTAC, POCZYTAC SOBIE, POCZYTYWAC, POCZY-
TYWAC SOBIE, PRZECZYTAC, ROZCZYTAC SIE, ROZCZYTYWAC SIE,
WCZYTAC SIE, WCZYTYWAC SIE, WYCZYTAC, WYCZYTYWAC, ZACZY-
TYWAC, SIE, ZACZYTAC SIE describe all the possible ways
and conditions of reading with the exception of "reread-
ing" which can not be translated into Polish in one word.
Besides the twenty three verbs are nouns: CZYTANKA, CZY-
TELNICTWO, CZYTELNIK, CZYTELNIA, CZYTELNOSC, ODCZYT, POCZY-
TALNOSC, NIEPOCZYTALNOSC, POCZYTNOSC, and adjectives as:
CZYTELNY, NIECZYTELNY, OCZYTANY, NIEOCZYTANY, POCZYTALNY,
NIEPOCZYTALNY, POCZYTNY etc.

XIII

Przedmowa

Angielsko-polska część słownika zawiera około 20,000 haseł. Wymowę słów angielskich podano w języku polskim, a nie w symbolach fonetycznych, które często przysparzają trudności w codziennym użyciu słowników.

Bogactwo polskich form gramatycznych nie ma odpowiednika w angielskim. Język angielski bogatszy jest w wyrażenia zwyczajowo-idiomatyczne; więcej też jest w nim przyimków i zaimków.

Ogólnie biorąc język polski ma więcej form rzeczownikowych, przymiotnikowych oraz czasownikowych. W angielskim natomiast prawie każdy rzeczownik bez zmiany pisowni może być użyty jako czasownik, a nieraz także jako przymiotnik. Polskie zasady gramatyczne i fonetyczne można wyrazić słowami "zawsze z kilkoma wyjątkami," angielskie zasady gramatyczne i fonetyczne są bardziej płynne – mówi się w nich "często," "czasem" i "nieraz." W angielskim przewazają wyrazenia i fonetyka zwyczajowe.

Hasła wybrano z uwzględnieniem słownictwa używanego obecnie w Polsce i Ameryce; są wśrod nich ważniejsze wyrażenia potoczne. Język angielski, bogaty, energiczny i stosunkowo nieskomplikowany gramatycznie, jest obecnie językiem swiatowego przemysłu, handlu i wiedzy scisłej, i liczebnie na świecie dominuje.

Język polski, oparty na pięknych tradycjach, elegancki i logiczny, dobrze służy myśli abstrakcyjnej i literaturze pięknej, wnosząc znaczne walory do pluralistycznej kultury świata.

XV

POLISH-ENGLISH

a (a) (as"a" in car) conj. and; or; but; then: at that time

a to (a to) conj. and so

abażur (a-bá-zhoor) m. lamp shade; a device to screen light

abdykować (ab-di-kó-vaćh) v. abdicate, abdicate the throne

abecadło (a-be-tsá-dwo) n. A.B.C., alphabet

abonament (a-bo-ná-ment) m. subscription, season ticket

abonent (a-bó-nent) m.subscriber, holder of a season ticket

abonować (a-bo-nó-vaćh) v. subscribe to a periodical etc.

absencja (ab-sén-tsya) f. absence, non-attendance

abstrakcja(ab-strák-tsya) f. abstraction; abstract

absurd (áb-soord) m. absurdity

aby (á-bi) conj. to; in order to, in order that, only to

ach ! (akh) excl.:oh ! ah!

aczkolwiek (ach-kól-vyek) conj. though; although, albeit, tho

adapter (a-dáp-ter) m. record player, adapter; pick-up

administracja (ad-mee-ñees-tráts-ya) f.administration; (management) authorities

admirał (ad-mée-raw) m.admiral

adres (ád-res) m.address

adwokat (ad-vó-kat) m. lawyer

afera (a-fé-ra) f. swindle

aferzysta (a-fe-zhis-ta) m. swindler: confidence man

afisz (á-feesh) m. poster

afiszować (a-fee-shó-vaćh) v. advertise; flaunt: parade

agrafka (a-gráf-ka) f. safety pin; hist.: buckle; brooch

agrest (ág-rest) m.gooseberry

aha ! (ákh-a!) excl.:oh yes...

a jakże ! (a-yák-zhe) excl. oh yes...; yes indeed!

akacja (a-káts-ya) f. acacia; locust tree: black locust

akcja (ák-tsya) f. action; share; plot ; campain

akord (ák-ort) m. chord; piece work ; contract work

AK (a-ká) f. Polish Home Army (W.W.II) (Armia Krajowa)

akowiec (a-kóv-yets) m. soldier of the Polish Home Army (W.W.II)

aksamit (ak-sá-meet) m. velvet

akt (akt) m. deed; act; cer-tificate; painting of a nude

akta (ák-ta) pl. documents; deeds; dossier; files; records

aktualny (ak-too-ál-ni) m. timely; current; up to date

akumulator (a-koo-moo-lá-tor)m. battery: storage battery

akuszerka (a-koo-shér-ka) f. midwife: accoucheuse

akwarela (ak-va-ré-la) f. water-color; painting in water color

albo (á-lbo) conj. or; else

albowiem (al-bó-vyem) conj. for; as; since;because; on account of

ale (á-le) conj. however; but; still; yet; not at all; n.defect

aleja (a-le-ya) f. avenue: alley

aleź (á-lesh) conj. why (yes)

alfa (ál-fa) f. alpha

alfabet (al-fá-bet) m. alphabet

alfons (ál-fons) m. pimp; cadet

alimenty (a-lee-mén-ti) pl. alimony for separated wife

alkohol (al-kó-khol) m. alcohol

alpejski (al-peý-skee) adj. m. Alpine: of the Alps

aluzja (a-looz-ya) f. hint: allusion; insinuation: dig

ałun (á-woon) m. alum

amant (á-mant) m. lover; beau

ambasada (am-ba-sá-da) f. embassy; ambassador and his staff

ambicja (am-beéts-ya) f. ambi-tion: aspiration: self esteem

ambona (am-bó-na) f. pulpit

Amerykanin (A-me-ri-ká-ñeen) m. American: man native of America

Amerykanka (A-me-ri-kán-ka) f. American: American women

amerykański (a-me-ri-kań-skee) adj. m. American: of America

amnestia (am-nést-ya) f.amnesty

amory (a-mó-ri) pl. flirtation; courting; love affairs

amortyzacja (a-mor-ti-záts-ya) f. depreciation; amortization

amperomierz (am-pe-ró-myesh) m. ammeter: meter of amperes

amputować (am-poo-tó-vach) v.
amputate ; to cut off
amunicja (a-moo-neets-ya) f.
ammunition; munitions,
analfabeta (a-nal-fa-bé-ta) m.
illiterate ; an ignorant
analiza (a-na-lée-za) f. analysis ; parsing
analogia (a-na-lóg-ya) f. analogy; parallelism; parity
ananas (a-na-nas) m. pineapple;
rascal ; rogue; blighter
andrus (an-droos) m. rough kid
andrut (ánd-root) m. wafer
anegdota (a-neg-dó-ta) f.
anecdote; story; theme
aneksja (a-neks-ya) f. annexation; rape of a country
anemia (a-ném-ya) f. anemia
angażować (an-ga-zhó-vach) v.
engage; undertake; hire;bind
angielski (an-gél-skee) adj.
m. English; English language
ani (á-ñee) conj. neither; nor;
no; not; or; not even
anielski (a-ñel-skee) adj. m.
angelic; cherubic; angelical
animusz (a-ñeé-moosh) m.
courage; verve; vigor; zest
anioł (á-ñow) m. angel
aniżeli (a-ñee-zhé-lee) part.
rather; than; rather than
ankieta (an-ké-ta) f. poll;
inquiry; questionnaire
anons (a-nons) m. advertisement in a newspaper; ad
antybiotyki (an-ti-bee-yó-ti-
kee) pl. antibiotics
antyk (an-tik) antique
antypatyczny (an-ti-pa-tich-
ni) adj. m. repugnant
apartament (a-par-tá-ment) m.
residence; suite of rooms
aparat (a-pa-rat) m. apparatus;
appliance; camera; gadget;gear
apel (áp-el) m. appeal; roll-
call; appeal; muster; parade
apetyt (a-pé-tit) m. appetite
apostolski (a-pos-tól-skee)
adj. m. apostolic; missionary
aprobować (a-pro-bó-vach) v.
approve; endorse; sanction

aprowizacja (a-pro-vee-záts-ya)
f. food supply; provisions
apteczka (ap-téch-ka) f. first
aid kit; medicine chest
apteka (ap-té-ka) f. pharmacy
arbiter (ar-bée-ter) m. umpire;
arbitrator; moderator; mediator
arbuz (ár-boos) m. watermelon
architekt (ar-khée-tekt) m.
architect
arcydzieło (ar-tsi-dzhé-wo) n.
masterpiece
arena (a-ré-na) f. arena; stage
areszt (á-resht) m. arrest; jail
argument (ar-góo-ment) m.
argument; reason; contention
arkusz (ar-koosh) m. sheet
armata (ar-má-ta) f. cannon
armator (ar-má-tor) m. shipowner; skipper; charterer
armia (árm-ya) f. army; array
arogancja (a-ro-gán-tsya) f.
arrogance; insolence; conceit
arteria(ar-tér-ya) f. artery
artykuł (ar-tí-koow) m. article
artretyzm (ar-tré-tizm) m.
arthritis; gout
artyleria (ar-ti-lér-ya) f.
artillery; gunnery; ordnance
artysta (ar-ti-sta) m. artist
arytmetyka (a-rit-mé-ti-ka) f.
arithmetic
as (as) m. ace ; A flat
asceta (as-tsé-ta) m. ascetic
asekuracja (a-se-koo-ráts-ya)
f. insurance; assurance
aspiryna (as-pee-rí-na) f.
aspirin
astma (ást-ma) f. asthma
asygnata (a-sig-ná-ta) f.
order (of payment)
asymilować (a-si-mee-ló-vach)
v. assimilate; absorb; liken
asystować (a-sis-tó-vach) v.
accompany; attend; court; assist
atak (á-tak) m. attack; charge
(fit); spasm; offensive
atlas (át-las) m. atlas
atleta (at-lé-ta) m. athlete
atłas (át-was) m. satin
atmosfera (at-mos-fé-ra) f.
atmosphere; air; climate; tone

atom (á-tom) m. atom
atol (á-tol) m. atoll
atomowy (a-to-mó-vi) adj. m. atomic
atrakcja (a-trák-tsya) f. attraction; high light
atrament (a-trá-ment) m. ink
atut (á-toot) m. trump
audycja (aw-díts-ya)f. broadcast; program; pop
aukcja (áwk-tsya) f. auction
autentyczny (aw-ten-tích-ni) adj. m. authentic; genuine
auto (áw-to) n. motor car
autor (áw-tor) m. author
autostrada (aw-to-strá-da) f. superhighway; freeway
awans (á-vans) m. promotion; advancement; preferment
awantura (a-van-too-ra) f. brawl; fuss; row; scandal
azot (á-zot) m, nitrogen
aż (ásh) part. as much; up to; til ; until; as far as
ażeby (a-zhé-bi) conj. that; in order that; so that
ażurowy (a-zhoo-ró-vi) adj. m. lace-like; transparent
ba (bá) excl.:hey ?; nay; indeed..; and even; what more
baba (bá-ba) f. woman (old, simple); grandmother; rammer
babiarz (báb-yash) m. lady chaser; ladies' man
babie lato (bá-bye lá-to) n. Indian Summer; lass;chick;cake
babka (báb-ka) f. grandmother;
babrać (báb-rach) v. smear; stain; dabble; soil; fumble
bachor (bá-khor) m. kid; brat
baczność (bách-noshch) f. attention; care
bać się (bach shán) v. fear
badacz (bá-dach) m. researcher
badać (bá-dach) v. investigate; examine; research ; explore
badyl (bá-dil) m. stem; weed
badylarz (ba-dí-lash) m. marketing gardener (slang)
bagatela (ba-ga-té-la) f. trifle ; easy matter
bagaż (bá-gash) m. luggage

bagażowy (ba-ga-zhó-vi) m. porter; adj.m. baggage-; luggage-
bagnet (bág-net) m. bayonet
bagno (bág-no) m. swamp; morass
bajka (báy-ka) f. fairy-tale; gossip; scandal; story; fable
bajoro (ba-yó-ro) n. muddy pool
bak (bak) m. gasoline tank; side whisker; bacteria;
bakterie (bak-tér-ye) pl.germs
bal (bal) m. ball; bale; log
balet (bá-let) m. ballet
balia (bál-ya) f. wash tub
balkon (bál-kon) m. balcony
balustrada (ba-loos-trá-da) f. railing; hand rail; guard rail
bałagan (ba-wá-gan) m. mess; disorder; disarray; confusion
bałamucić (ba-wa-moo-tseech) v. lead astray; loiter; flirt; coax
bałwan (báw-van) m. snowman; ass; breaking wave crest; blockhead; fool; nitwit; fetish; idol; lump
banał (bá-naw) m. stock phrase; tag; banality; truism; triviality
banan (bá-nan) m. banana
banda (bán-da) f. band; gang
bandaż (bán-dash) m. bandage
bandera (ban-dé-ra) f. flag
bandyta (ban-dí-ta) m. bandit
bank (bank) m. bank; pool
bankiet (bán-ket) m. banquet
banknot (bánk-not) m. banknote
bankrut (bánk-root) m. bankrupt
babtysta (bap-tís-ta) m. baptist
bar (bar) m. bar; barium
barman (bár-man) m. barman
barak (bá-rak) m. barrack
baran (bá-ran) m. ram;tup; idiot
baraszkować (ba-rash-kó-vach) v. frolic; gambol; romp; caper
barbarzyńca (bar-ba-zhiń-tsa) m. barbarian; savage; vandal
barczysty (bar-chis-ti) m. broad-shouldered; square built
bardziej (bár-dzhey)adv.more; (emphatic "bardzo"); worse
bardzo (bár-dzo) adv. very
bariera (bar-yé-ra) f. rail; barrier; hand rail; obstacle
barki (bár-kee) pl. shoulders
barłóg (bár-woog) m. litter bed

barszcz (barshch) m. beet soup
barwa (bár-va) f. color; hue
bary (bá-ri) pl. large
  shoulders; parallel bars
barykada (ba-ri-ká-da) f.
  barricade; barrier
baryłka (ba-riw-ka) f. barrel
basen (bá-sen) m. pool; tank
bastard (bás-tard) m. bastard
baśń (baśhń) f. fable; myth
bat (bat) m. whip; lash
bateria (ba-tér-ya) f. battery
bawełna (ba-véw-na) f. cotton
bawialnia (ba-vyál-ña) f.
  sitting room; parlor
bawić (bá-veech) v. amuse;
  entertain; recreate; stay
bawidamek (ba-vee-dá-mek) m.
  ladies man; gallant
bawół (bá-voow) m. buffalo
baza (bá-za) f. base; basis
bazgrać (báz-grach) v. scribble;
  scrawl; scratch; daub; splotch
bażant (ba-zhant) m. pheasant
bąbel (bówn-bel) m. blister
bądź (bownch) v. be this
bądź (bownch) conj. either-or
bąk (bównk) m. horse fly;
  blunder; vulg.: fart
bąkać(bówn-kach) v. mumble;
  hint; mutter; hum
bebechy (be-bé-khi) pl. guts
beczka (béch-ka) f. barrel
bednarz (béd-nash) m. cooper
befsztyk (béf-shtik) m. beefsteak
beksa (bék-sa) f. cry baby
beletrystyka (be-le-tris-ti-
  ka) f. fiction; letters
belka (bél-ka) f. beam; bar
bełkot (béw-kot) m. mumbling
benzyna (ben-zína) f. gasoline
berbeć (bér-bech) m. small kid;
  toddler; brat; dot
berek (bé-rek) m. tag play
beret (bé-ret) m. beret; cap
besztać (bésh-tach) v. scold;
  rebuke; chide; rebuke;trounce
bestia (bés-tya) f. beast
beton (bé-ton) m. concrete
bety (bé-ti) pl. bedding
bez (bes) prep. without

bez (bes) m. lilac;prep.without
bez-(bes) prefix = suffix less
beza (be-za) f. meringue
bezbarwny (bez-bárw-ni) adj.
  m. colorless; plain; drab; dull
bezbłędny (bez-bwáñd-ni) adj.
  m. faultless; correct; perfect
bezbolesny (bez-bo-lés-ni) adj.
  m. painless
bezbronny (bez-brón-ni) adj.
  m. defenseless; helpless;unarmed
bezcelowy (bez-tse-ló-vi) adj.
  m. aimless; pointless; useless
bezcenny (bez-tsén-ni) adj.m.
  priceless; invluable; inestimable
bezchmurny (bez-khmoó-rni)
  adj. m. cloudless; serene; clear
bezdomny (bez-dóm-ni) adj. m.
  homeless; houseless; shelterless
bezdzietny (bez-dzhét-ni) adj
  m. childless; without offspring
bezdźwięczny (bez-dzhváñch-ni)
  adj. m. soundless; voiceless
bezecny (be-zéts-ni) adj. m.
  wicked; infamous; ignominious
bezgotówkowy (bez-go-toov-kó-
  vi) adj. m. without cash
bezgrzeszny (bez-gzhésh-ni)
  adj. m. sinless;inocent; chaste
bezkonkurencyjny (bez-kon-koo-
  ren-tsíy-ni) adj. m. unrivaled
bezkrwawy (bez-krvá-vi) adj.
  m. bloodless; free of bloodshed
bezkształtny (bez-kshtáwt-ni)
  adj. m. shapeless; formless
bezład (béz-wat) m. disorder
bezmiar (béz-myar) m. immen-
  sity; boundlessness; vastness
bezmyślnosć (bez-miśhl-noshch)
  f. thoughtlessness; wantonness
beznadziejny (bez-na-dzhéy-ni)
  adj. m. hopeless; desperate
bez ogródek (bez o-groó-dek)
  adv. bluntly; unequivocally
bezokolicznik (bez-o-ko-leech-
  ñeek) m. infinitive (mood)
bezowocny (bez-o-vóts-ni) m.
  fruitless; vain; unsuccessful
bezpieczeństwo (bez-pye-cheñ-
  stvo) m. security; safety
bezpłatnie (bez-pwát-ñe) adv.
  free of charge; gratuitously

bezpłciowy (bez-pwchó-vi) adj.
m. sexless; neutral; insipid
bezpodstawny (bez-pod-stáv-ny)
adj. m. groundless; baseless
bezpośrednio (bez-po-shred-ño)
adv. directly; directly
bezprawny (bez-práv-ni) adj.
m. lawless; illegal; illicit
bezprzedmiotowy (bez-przed-myo-
tó-vi) adj. m. aimless
bezprzykładny (bez-pzhi-kwád-
ni) adj. m. unprecedented
bezradny (bez-rád-ni) adj. m.
helpless; baffled; at a loss
bezręki (bez-rán-kee) adj.m.
armless; handless (cripple)
bezrobotny (bez-ro-bó-tni)
adj. m. unemployed
bezrolny (bez-ról-ni) adj.m.
landless; with no land
bezsenny (bez-sén-ni) adj. m.
sleepless; restless; wakeful
bezsens (béz-sens) m. nonsense
bezsilny (bez-sheel-ni) adj.
m. powerless; weak; helpless
bezskuteczny (bez-skoo-téch-
ni) adj. m. to no avail;
futile; ineffective; nugatory
bezsporny (bez-spór-ni) adj.
m. incontestable; undebatable
bezsprzeczny (bez-spzhéch-ni)
adj. m. indisputable; evident
bezstronność (bez-strón-noshch)
f. impartiality; fairness
beztroski (bez-trós-kee) adj.
m. care-free; careless;jaunty
bezustanny (bez-oos-tán-ni)
adj. m. ceaseless; endless
bezużyteczny (bez-oo-zhi-téch-
ni) adj. m. useless; idle
bezwartościowy (bez-var-tosh-
chó-vi) adj. m. worthless
bezwarunkowy (bez-va-roon-kó-vi)
adj. m. unconditional; utter
bezwładność (bez-vwád-noshch)
f. inertia; torpor; decline
bezwstydny (bez-vstid-ni) adj.
m. shameless; lewd; flagrant
bezwyznaniowy (bez-viz-na-ño-
vi) adj. m. nonsectarian
bezwzględny (bez-vzglánd-ni)
adj. m. ruthless; despotic
bezzębny (bez-zánb-ni) adj. m.
toothless; edentate

bezzwłoczny (bez-zvwóch-ni)
adj. m. immediate; prompt
bezzwrotny (bez-zvrót-ni) adj.
m. not to be refunded
beż (besh) m. beige
bęben (bán-ben) m. drum; kid;
brat; barrel; cylinder;tumbler
bęcwał (bánts-vaw) m. nincompoop; dullard; chickle head
bękart (bán-kart) m. bastard
biadać (byá-dach) v. moan
białaczka (bya-wách-ka) f.
leukemia
białko (byá-wko) n. egg white;
protein; white of the eye
biały (byá-wi) adj. m. white
biba (bée-ba) f. drinking spree
biblia (béeb-lya) f. Bible
biblioteka (beeb-lyo-té-ka) f.
library; bookcase; book series
bibuła (bee-boó-wa) f. blotting
paper; illegal political
publication; literary trash
bicz (béech) m. whip; whiplash
bić (béech) v. beat; defeat(etc)
biec (byets) v. run; trot; flow
bieda (byé-da) f. poverty; want;
trouble; distress; evil days
biedny (byéd-ni) adj. m. poor
bieg (byeg) m. run; race; course
biegle (byé-gle) adv. fluently
biegun (byé-goon) m. pole;
rocker; spindle; trunnion
biegunka (bye-goón-ka) f.
diarrhea; dysentery
biel (byel) f.whiteness; white
bielizna (bye-leéz-na) f. linen
bielmo (byél-mo) n. cataract
bierny (byér-ni) adj. m. passive
bieżący (bye-zhówn-tsi) adj. m.
current; flowing; running
bieżnia (byézh-ña) f. runway;
track; racecourse; tyre tread
bigos (bée-gos) m. hashed meat
and cabbage (Polish style)
bijatyka (bee-ya-tí-ka) f.
fight; brawl; tussle; scrimmage
bila (bée-la) f. billiard ball
bilans (bée-lans) m. balance
sheet; balance; rest; outcome
bilet (bée-let) m. note; ticket
biodro (byód-ro) n. hip; huckle
biszkopt (béesh-kopt) m.
biscuit; sponge cake; cracer

bitny (beet-ni) adj. m. valiant

bitwa (beet-va) f. battle;fight

biuro (byoo-ro) n. office

biust (byoost) m. bust; breast

biustonosz (byoos-tó-nosh) m.
  brassiere; bra; bust bodice

biżuteria (bee-zhoo-tér-ya) f.
  jewelry: jewels

blacha (blá-kha) f. sheet
  metal; cook top; tinware

blady (blá-di) adj. m. pale

blaga (blá-ga) f. lie; bluff

blankiet (blán-ket) m. blank
  form; printed form: blank

blask (blask) m. flush; luster

bliski (blées-kee) adj. m.
  near; imminent; near by;close

blizna (bleéz-na) f. scar

bliźni (bleéźh-ñee)m. fellow
  man; twin: identical; neighbor

blokować (blo-kó-vach) v.block;
  blockade; obstruct; stall

blondynka (blon-dín-ka) f.

blonde (girl); fair haired girl

bluzka (bloóz-ka) f. blouse

bluźnić (bloóźh-ñeech) v. curse;
  blaspheme; talk nonsense

błahość (bwá-khoshch) f. trifle

błagać (bwá-gach) v. beseech

błazen (bwa-zen) m. clown;
  buffoon ⌠mistake; lapse

błąd (bwownt) m. error; slip-up;

błąkać się (bwówn-kach śháñ)v.
  wander; stray; roam; rove

błękit (bwañ-keet) m. blue;
  azure; blue pigment; sky

błocić (bwo-cheech) v. get
  muddy: soil with mud; spatter

błogi (bwo-gee) adj. m.bliss-
  ful: delightful; sweet

błogosławić (bwo-go-swá-veech)
  v. bless: praise; exalt; thank

błona (bwona) f. membrane; coat;
  film; tunic; velum; web

błonie (bwo-ñe) n. meadow;·
  plain; public grassy land

błotnik (bwot-ñeek) m.(car)
  fender; mudguard; splash board

błoto (bwo-to) n. mud: muck

błysk (bwisk) m. flash; flare

bo (bo) conj. because; for; or;
  as; since; or else: but then

bochenek (bo-khé-nek) m. loaf

bocian (bó-chan) m. stork

boczny (bóch-ny) adj. m. lateral; side ; collateral (line)

boczyć się (bó-chych śháñ) v.
  sulk; be angry; look askance

bodaj (bó-day) part. may be;
  should be…; would be...;

bodziec (bó-dźhets) m. stimulus

bogactwo (bo-gáts-tvo) n.riches;
  wealth; means; fortune; plenty

bogaty (bo-gá-ti) adj. m. rich

bogobojny (bo-go-bóy-ni) adj.
  m. pious; devout; church going

bohater (bo-kha-ter) m. hero

boisko (bo-eés-ko) n. stadium;
  field; threshing floor;gridiron

bojaźń (bó-yaźhñ) f. fear; fright

boja (bó-ya) f. buoy ; beacon

bojkot (bóy-kot) m. boycott

bojownik (bo-yóv-ñeek) m.
  fighter; militant; champion

bok (bok) m. side; flank

boks (boks) m. boxing; stall

boleć (bó-lech) v. pain; ache

bolesny (bo-lés-ni) adj. m. sore;
  painful: sad; woeful; dismal

bomba (bóm-ba) f. bomb; sphere

bombowiec (bom-bó-vyets) m.
  bomber ; bombing plane

borykać się (bo-rí-kach śháñ)
  v. cope; struggle; wrestle

bosak (bó-sak) m. boat hook

boso (bó-so) adv. barefoot

bosy (bó-si) adj. m. barefoot

bowiem (bó-vyem) conj. for;
  because; since; as; hence

boży (bo-zhi) adj. m. God's

Bóg (book)m. God

bój (booy) m. fight; battle

ból (bool) m. pain; ache; sore

bór (boor) m. forest; wood

bóść (booshch) v. gore; sting

bóźnica (boozh-ñee-tsa) f.
  synagogue: house of prayer

bractwo (bráts-tvo) n. fraternity; brotherhood; guild

brać (brach) v. take; hold etc.

brak (brak) m. lack; need;want;
  scarcity; shortage;absence;fault

brama (brá-ma) f. gate; gateway;
  front door; wicket

bransoletka (bran-so-lét-ka) f.
  bracelet; wristlet; bangle
brat (brat) m. brother; mate
bratać (brá-tać) v. unite;
  fraternize; chum up
bratanek (bra-tá-nek) m. nephew
bratanica (bra-ta-ńée-tsa) f.
  niece
brednie (bréd-ńe) n. nonsense
brew (brev) f. eyebrow
brewerie (bre-vér-ye) n. brawl
brezent (bré-zent) m. tarpau-
  lin; canvas
brnąć (brnównch) v. wade
broczyć (bró-chich) v. bleed
broda (broda) f. beard; chin
brodzić (bró-dźheećh)v. wade
broić (bró-eećh) v. make
  mischief; frolic; romp;gambol
brom (brom) m. bromine
brona (bró-na) f. harrow
bronić (bró-ńeećh) v. defend
bronz (brons) m. bronze
broń (broń) f. weapon; arms
broszka (brósh-ka) f. brooch
broszura (bro-shóo-ra) f.
  pamphlet; folder; booklet
browar (bró-var) m. brewery
bród (broot) m. ford
brud (broot) m. dirt; filth
bruk (brook) m. pavement
brukiew (bróo-kȩv) f. turnip
brulion (bróol-yon) m. rough
  draft; notebook; exercise book
brunatny (broo-ná-tni) adj. m.
  brown; tawny; tan colored
brunetka (broo-nét-ka) f.
  brunette
brutal (bróo-tal) m. brute
bruzda (bróoz-da) f. furrow;
  groove; deep wrinkle; streak
brwi (brvee) pl. eye brows
brykać (brí-kaćh) v. prance
bryła (brí-wa) f. lump; mass
bryzg (brizk) m. splash
bryzgać (bríz-gaćh) v. splash
brzeg (bzhek) m. shore; margin
brzemię (bzhe-myáń) n. burden
brzęk (bzháňk) m. clink; chink;
  rattle; ping; buzz; hum:drone
brzuch (bzhóokh) m. belly; abdomen; stomach; tummy; guts

brzydki (bzhíd-kee) adj. m.
  ugly; unsightly; hideous; foul
brzydzić się (bzhi-dźheećh sháń)
  v. feel disgust; loathe; abhor
brzytwa (bzhít-va) f. razor
buchać (bóo-khaćh) v. squirt;
  spout;burst forth; flare; blaze
bucik (bóo-cheek) m. shoe; boot
buda (bóo-da) f. shed (stall)
budowa (boo-dó-va) f. construction; erection; framework
budowla (boo-dov-la) f. building (large); edifice;structure
budynek (boo-dí-nek) m. building; edifice; house
budzić (bóo-dźheećh)v. wake up
budzik (bóo-dźheek)m. alarm
  clock; alarum clock
budżet (bóo-jet) m. budget
bujać (bóo-yaćh) v. rock; lie
bufor (bóo-for) m. buffer
bułka (bóow-ka) f. roll (breakfast); bread roll; loaf
bunt (boont) m. mutiny
bura (bóo-ra)f. reprimand
burak (bóo-rak) m. beet
burda (bóo-r-da) f. scuffle;row;
  brawl; disturbance; rough neck
burmistrz (bóor-meestsh) m.
  mayor
bursztyn (bóor-shtin) m. amber
burta (bóor-ta) f. ship's side
bury (boo-ri)adj. m. dark gray
burza (bóo-zha) f. tempest;
  storm; wind storm; rain storm
burżuazja (boor-zhoo-áz-ya) f.
  bourgeoisie; middle class
busola (boo-só-la) f. compass
but (boot) m. boot; shoe; sabot
buta (bóo-ta) f. arrogance
butelka (boo-tél-ka) f. bottle
butny (bóot-ni) adj. m. arrogant; insolent; overbearing
buzia (boo-zha) f. face; mouth
by (bi) conj. in order that;
  (conditional)as if; at least
byczy (bí-chi) adj. m. 1. bull's
  2. very good; glorious
być (bich) v. be; exist; live
bydlę (bíd-láň) n. beast; brute
byle (bi-le) conj. in order to;
  so as to; pron. any; slap-dash

były (bi-wi) adj. m. former
bynajmniej (bi-náy-mňey) adv.
by no means; not at all
bystrość (bist-roshch) f.
swiftness; shrewdness
byt (bit) m. existence
bytność (bit-noshch) f. stay
bywać (bi-vach) v. frequent
bywalec (bi-vá-lets) m.patron
frequenter; man of the world
bzdura (bzdoo-ra) f. nonsense
bzik (bźheek)adj. m. crank;
loony; crazy; m. fad; craze
bzyknąć (bzi-kach) v. buzz
cackać się (tsáts-kach shán)v.
fondle; pamper; humor;coddle
cacko (tsáts-ko) n. jewel;
trinket; plaything;toy;beauty
cal (tsal) m. inch
całka (tsáw-ka) f. integral
całkiem (tsáw-kem) adv.quite;
entirely; completely; totally
całkowity (tsaw-ko-vée-ti)
adj. m. total; complete
cało (tsá-wo) adv. (in one
piece) safely; safe and sound
całować (tsa-wó-vach) v. kiss;
embrace; give a kiss
całus (tsa-woos) m. kiss
cap (tsap) m. billy goat
cąber (tsówn-ber) m. rump;
fillet
cążki (tsównzh-kee) pl. small
tongs; pliers; pincers
ceber (tsé-ber) m. bucket
cebula (tse-bóo-la) f. onion
cech (tsekh) m. trade; guild
cecha (tsé-kha) f. feature;
mark; trait; stamp; character
cechować (tse-khó-vach) v.
mark; characterize; calibrate
cedr (tsedr) m. cedar
cedzić (tse-dźheech)v. strain;
filter; percolate;sip;trickle
cegielnia (tse- gél-ňa) f.
brickyard; brick factory
cegła (tség-wa) f. brick
cel (tsel) m. purpose; aim
cela (tsé-la) f. cell
celnik (tsél-ňeek) m. customs
inspector; customs officer
celować (tse-lo-vach) v. aim;
excel; exceed

celuloza (tse-loo-ló-za) f.
celulose
cembrować (tsem-bró-vach) v.
case(well); timber (a shaft)
cement (tsé-ment) m. cement
cena (tsé-na) f. price; value
cenić (tsé-ňeech) v. value;rate;
esteem; prize; evaluate
cennik (tsén-ňeek) m. price
list; price catalogue
centnar (tsént-nar) m. hundredweight
centrala (tsen-trá-la) f. head
office ; main office ; exchange
centrum (tsént-room) n. center
centryfuga (tsen-tri-fóo-ga) f.
centrifuge; separator
centymetr (tsen-ti-metr) m.
centimeter __ blockhead
cep (tsep) m. flail; darn; mend
cera (tsé-ra) f. complexion
ceramiczny (tse-ra-meéch-ni)
adj. m. ceramic; earthenware
cerata (tse-rá-ta) f. oilcloth
ceregiele (tse-re-ge -le) n.
fuss; petty formalities
certować sie(tser-to-vach shan)v.
pretend;stand on ceremony;fuss
cewka (tsév-ka) f. spool
cęgi (tsán-gee) pl. tongs
cętka (tsánt-ka) f. dot
chałat (khá-wat) m. lab.coat
chałastra (kha-wás-tra) f. mob
chałupa (kha-woo-pa) f. hut
cham (kham) m. roughneck; boor
charakter (kha-rák-ter) m.
disposition; character
charczeć (khár-chech) v.
wheese; snort; be hoarse
chata (khá-ta) f. hut; cabin
chcieć (khchech) v. want
chciwiec (khchee-vyets) m.
greedy man; grasping man
chełpić się (khew-peech shán)
v. boast; brag; bluster;vaunt
chemia (khém-ya) f. chemistry
chemiczny (khe-meéch-ni) adj.m.
chemical
cherlak (khér-lak) m. weakling
chęć (khańch) f. wish; desire
chędogi (khán-do-gi) adj. m.
neat; clean; tidy; orderly

chichot (khee-khot) m. giggle;
laughter ; chuckle; titter
chimera (khee-me-ra) f. whim
chinina (khee-ñee-na) f. quinine
chiński (kheeń-skee) adj.m.
Chinese
chirurg (khee-roorg) m. surgeon ; sawbones (slang)
chlapać (khla-pach) v. splash
chleb (khleb) m. bread
chlew (khlev) m. pigsty;pigpen
chlor (khlor) m. chlorine
chluba (khloo-ba) f.glory,pride
chlubić się (khloo-beech shań)
v. boast; flatter oneself
chlusnąć (khloos-nowńch) v.
splash; fling; spout; spurt
chłeptać (khwep-tach) v. lap up
chłodzić (khwo-dżheech)v. cool
chłonąć (khwo-nowńch) v. absorb;
devour; drink in; inhale
chłop (khwop) m. peasant; man
chłosta (khwos-ta) f. lashing
chłod (khwoot) m. cold; freshness ; coolness; iciness:shiver
chłystek (khwis-tek) m. squirt
chmara (khma-ra) f. swarm
chmiel (khmyel) m. hop; hops
chmura (khmoo-ra) f. cloud
chociaż (kho-chash) conj.albeit;
even if; though, tho'; while
chociaż = chocby = chociazby
choć (khoch) conj. at least
chodnik (khod-ñeek) m. sidewalk; pathway; stair carpet
chodzić (kho-dżheech) v. go;
walk; move; creep; pace;attend
choina (kho-ee-na) f. fir
cholera (kho-le-ra) f. cholera
excl.:damn ! hell! the devil!
cholewa (kho-le-va) f. boot
chorągiew (kho-rowń-gev) f.
flag; standard; ensign
choroba (kho-ro-ba) f. sickness
chory (kho-ri) adj. m. sick;
ill; ailing; infirm; unwell
chowac (kho-vach) v. hide
chod (khoot) m. gait; walk
chor (khoor) m. choir
chow (khoof) m. breeding
chrabąszcz (khra-bowshch) m.
beetle;May —bug

chrapać (khra-pach) v. snore
chroniczny (khro-ñeech-ni) adj.
m. chronic
chronić (khro-ñeech) v. shelter;
protect; quard; shield; fence
chropowaty (khro-po-va-ti) adj.
m. rough; callous; coarse;harsh
chrust (khroost) m. kindling
chrupać (khroo-pach) v. crunch
chrypka (khrip-ka) f. hoarse —
ness; sore throat
Chrystus (khris-toos) m. Christ
chrzan (khzhan) m. horseradish
chrząstka (khzhowńst-ka) f.
cartilage; gristle; copula
chrząszcz (khshowńshch) m.
May bug; beetle; cockchafer
chrzcić (khzhcheech) v. baptize
chrzest (khzhest) m. baptism
chrześcijanin (khzhe-shchee-
yá-ñeen) m. Christian
chrzęst (khzháñst) m. clatter
chrzęscić (khzháñ-shcheech) v.
clank; jangle; grate; crunch
chuchać (khoo-khach) v. puff
chuchro (khóokh-ro) m. weakling
chuć (khooch) f. lust
chudnąć (khood-nowńch) v.lose
weight; grow thin; lose flesh
chuligan (khoo-lee-gan) m.
hoodlum; ruffian; roughneck
chustka (khoost-ka) f. handkerchief; kerchief; scarf
chwacki (khvats-kee) adj. m.
brave; plucky; gallant; rakish
chwalić (khva-leech) v. praise
chwała (khva-wa) f. praise;
glory; splendor; pride
chwast (khvast) m. weed
chwiać (khvyach) v. waver
chwila (khvee-la) f. moment
chwycić (khvi-cheech) v. grasp
chwyt (khvit) m. grasp; grip
chyba (khi-ba) part. maybe
chybotać (khi-bo-tach) v. rock
chybić (khi-beech) v. miss
chylić (khi-leech) v. bow
chyłkiem (khiw-kem) adj.
stealthily; on the sly
chytry (khit-ri) adj. m. sly
chyży (khi-zhi) adj. m. swift
ci (chee) pron. these; they;
part.: for you

ciało (chá-wo) n. body; substance; frame; anatomy;corpse
ciarki (char-kee) pl. shudder
ciasnota (chas-nó-ta) f. tightness; narrow-mindedness
ciastko (chast-ko) n . cake;pie
ciasto (chás-to) n, dough
ciąć (chównch) v. cut; clip
ciągnac(chówng-nównch)v.pull
ciągnik (chówng-ñeek) m. tractor; agrimotor; crawler
ciąża (chówn-zha) f. pregnancy
ciążenie (chówn-zhe-ñe) v. gravitation;tendency
cichaczem (chee-kha-chem) adv. stealthily; on the quiet
cichnąc (cheekh-nównch) v. quiet down; subside; abate
cicho (chee-kho) adv. silently; noiselessly ; softly;privately
cichy (chee-khi) adj. m. quiet; still; low;gentle; calm; serene
ciec (chets) v. leak; flow
ciecz (chech) f. liquid
ciekawy (che-kav) adj. m. cute; curious ;interesting;prying
cielak (che-lak) m. calf
cielesny (che-les-ni) adj. m. carnal; bodily; sexual
ciemię (che-myań) n. crown of the head ; septum of the skull
ciemiężenie (che-myań-zhe-ñe) n. oppression ; subjugation
ciemnia (chém-ña) f. dark room
ciemno (chém-no) adv. darkly
ciemny (chém-ni) adj. m. dark
cieniowac (che-ño- vach) v. shade ; modulate; grade
cienisty (che-ñees-ti) adj. m. shady ; shade giving
cienki (chen-kee) adj. m. thin
cień (cheñ) m. shade ; shadow
cieplarnia (che-plár-ña) f. greenhouse ; hothouse; stove
ciepło (che-pwo) adv. warm
ciepławy (che-pwá-vi) adj. m. lukewarm ; tepid
ciepły (chép-wi) adj. m. warm
cierń (cherñ) m. thorn;pricle
cierpiący (cher-pyówn-tsi) adj. m. suffering ; ailing;ill
cierpieć (chér-pyech)v.suffer; anguish; be troubled; endure

cierpki (cherp-kee) adj. m. tart; acid;surly;acrid;sour
cierpliwosc (cher-plee-voshch) f. patience; endurance
cierpliwy (cher-plee-vi) adj. m. enduring; patient; forbearing
cierpnąć (cherp-nównch) v. grow numb; creep; go to sleep
ciesielstwo (che-shel-stvo) n. carpentry (in construction)
cieszyc (che-shich) v. cheer
ciesla (chesh-la) m. carpenter (constr.);wood worker;shipwright
cietrzew (che-tzhev) m. blackcock; black grouse; grey hen
ciesnina (chesh-ñee-na) f. strait
cięcie (chañ-che) n. cut; gash
cięciwa (chañ-chee-va) f. chord; bow string; string; subtense
cięgi (chañ-gee) pl. lashing
cięty (chañ-ti) adj. m. sharptongued; biting;dogged;incisive
ciężar (chañ-zhar) m. weight; burden; gravity; onus; duty;task
ciężec (chañ-zhech) v. grow heavy; become a burden;encumber
ciężki (chañzh-kee) adj. m. heavy; weighty: bulky; oppressive
ciężko (chañzh-ko) adv. heavily
ciocia (chó-cha) f. auntie;aunt
cios (chos) m. blow; stroke; hit ; shok; ashlar; block; joint
cioteczny brat (cho-tech-ni brat) m. cousin
ciotka (chót-ka) f. aunt
ciosac (chó-sach) v. hew; chop out
cis (chees) m. yew
cisawy (chees-ávi) adj. m. chesnut (horse)
ciskac (chees-kach) v. fling;cast; throw; hurl: sling; plunk;let fly
cisnąc (chées-nównch) v. press; squeeze; bear; urge; pinch;crowd
cisza (chee-sha) f. calm; silence
cisnienie (cheesh-ñe-ñe) n. pressure ; blood pressure; thrust
ciuch (chookh) m. used clothing
ciułac (choo-wach) v. hoard
ciurkiem (choor-kem) adv. in a trickle; with big drops
ciupa (choo-pa) f. jail; clink
ciupasem (choo-pá-sem) adv. under convoy under armed convoy

ciżba (chéezh-ba) f. crowd
ckliwy (tsklée-vi) adj. m.
  qualmy ; sickly; faint;sloppy
clić (tsleéch) v. collect
  custom duty ;lay a custom duty
cło (tswo) n. customs
cmentarz (tsmén-tash) m. cemetery ; burial ground
cmokać (tsmo-kach) v. smack
cnota (tsnó-ta) f. virtue
co (tso) pron. part. what;which
codzień (tsó-dźheń)adv. daily
cofać się (tsó-fach shań) v.
  back up ; remove; withdraw
cokolwiek (tso-kól-vyek) pron.
  anything ; whatever; somewhat
comber (tsom-ber) m. saddle
  (of mutton);rump;loin; haunch
coraz (tso-raz) adv. ever
coś (tsosh) pron. something
córka (tsoor-ka) f. daughter
cóż (tsoosh) pron. what then
cuchnąć (tsóokh-nownch) v.
  stink foul ; smell foul
cucić (tsóo-cheech) v. revive
cud (tsoot) m. wonder; miracle
cudzołożyć (tsoo-dzo-wó-zhich)
  v. commit adultery
cudzoziemiec (tsoo-dzo-źhe-
  myets) m. alien; foreigner
cudzy (tsóo-dzi) adj. m.
  someone else's; alien;foreign
cudzysłów (tsoo-dzi-swoof)m.
  quotation marks
cukier (tsóo-ker) m. sugar
cuma (tsóo-ma) f. mooring
cwał (tsvaw) m. full gallop
cwaniak (tsva-ñak) m. city
  slicker; sly dog;crafty guy
cwany (tsva-ni) adj. m. sly;
  cunning; crafty; artful
cyc (tsits) m. nipple (vulg.)
cyfra (tsif-ra) f. number
cygan (tsi-gan) m. gipsy;
  cheat; Gypsy;swindler; liar
cykl (tsikl) m. cycle
cylinder (tsi-leén-der) m.
  cylinder; barrel; top hat
cyna (tsi-na) f. tin
cynamon (tsi-ná-mon)m.cinnamon
cynober (tsi-nó-ber) m.vermil-
  ion

cyngiel (tsin-gel) m. trigger
cynik (tsi-ñeek) m. cynic
cynk (tsink) m. zinc; tutenag
cypel (tsi-pel) m. cape; tip
cyprys (tsi-pris) m. cypress
cyrk (tsirk) m. circus
cyrkiel (tsir-kel) m. compass
cysterna (tsis-tér-na) f.
  cistern; tank car; vat
cytadela (tsi-ta-dé-la) f.
  citadel; fortress
cytata (tsi-tá-ta) f. quotation
cytryna (tsi-trí-na) f. lemon
cywil (tsi-veel) m. civilian
cyzelować (tsi-ze-ló-vach) v.
  engrave; carve; elaborate
czad (chat) m. carbon monoxide
czaić się (cha-eéch shań) v.
  lie in wait; lurk; stalk;crouch
czajnik (cháy-ñeek) m. tea-pot
czajka (cháy-ka) f. gull
czako (chá-ko) f. shako
czapka (cháp-ka) f. cap; pileus
czapla (cháp-la) f. heron
czaprak (cháp-rak) m. horse
  blanket; caparison; trappings
czar (char) m. spell; charm
czarno (chár-no) adv. blackly
czart (chart) m. devil; deuce
czas (chas) m. time; duration
czaszka (chásh-ka) f. skull
czaty (chá-ti) pl. watch;
  lookout; wait; ambush
cząstka (chównst-ka) f. particle
czcić (chcheéch) v. adore;
  worship; idolize; venerate
czcigodny (chchee-god-ni) adj.
  m. honorable; revered; venerable
czcionka (chchyon-ka) f. type;
  character; letter in print
czczo (chcho) adv. empty (stomach) ; emptily; vainly; idly
czego (che-go) conj. why? what?
czek (chek) m. check (in banking)
czekać (che-kach) v. wait;
  expect; waste time; be in store
czekanie (che-ka-ñe) n. wait
czekan (ché-kan) f. pickhammer
czekolada (che-ko-lá-da) f.
  chocolate; slab of chocolate
czeladnik (che-lád-ñeek) m.
  apprentice; journeyman

czelność (chel-noshch) f. impudence ; effrontery; nerve
czeluść (che-looshch) f. abyss; gulf; precipice; depths [to what?
czemu (che-moo) part. why?what
czepek (che-pek) m. bonnet; hood ; night cap; caul; calyptra
czepiać się (chep-yach shan) v. cling; hang on; peck at
czereda (che-re-da) f. gang; throng ; crowd; swarm; pack
czerep (che-rep) m. shell; skull; fragment; splinter; shard
czereśnia (che-resh-na) f. cherry; cherry tree; gean
czernić (cher-neech) v, blacken ; black; paint black
czerń (chern) f. black color
czerpać (cher-pach) v. scoop; draw, ladle; derive (benefit)
czerstwy (chers-tvi) adj. m. stale; robust(man); firm
czerw (cherv) m. worm ; grub
czerwienić się (cher-vye-neech shan) v. blush (redden)
czerwony (cher-vo-ni) adj. m. red ; scarlet; crimson; ruddy
czesać (che-sach) v. comb ; brush
czeski (ches-kee) adj. m. Czech
czesne (ches-ne) n. tuition
cześć (cheshch) f. honor; cult; respect ; adoration; good name
często (chans-to) adv. often
częstokroć (chan-sto-kroch) adv. often ; repeatedly
częstość (chans-toshch) f. frequency ; recurrence
częstotliwość (chan-sto-tlee-woshch) f. frequency; recurrence
częstować (chan-sto-vach) v. treat to something ; regale
częsty (chans-ty) adj. m. frequent ; repeated often
częściowy (chan-shcho-vi) adj. m. partial ; fragmentary
część (chanshch) f. part : share
czkawka (chkav-ka) f. hiccups
człon (chwon) m. element; segment ; link ; member; clause
członek (chwo-nek) m. limb; member; man's sex organ
człowiek (chwo-vyek) m. man ; individual; chap; somebody

czmychnąć (chmikh-nownch) v. bolt; steal out; whisk away
czochrać (chokh-rach) v. tousle; ripple; hackle ; scratch
czołg (chowg) m. tank (military) ; reptile
czołgać (chow-gach) v. crawl
czoło (cho-wo) n. forehead
czop (chop) m. peg; plug; pin
czosnek (chos-nek) m. garlic
czterdzieści (chter-dzhesh-chee) num. forty
czternaście (chter-nash-che) num. fourteen
czteropiętrowy (chte-ro-pyan-tro-vi) adj. m. four stories high ; four storeyed
cztery (chte-ri) num. four
czub (choop) m. tuft; crest
czucie (choo-che) n. feeling; smelling ; sense perception
czuć (chooch) v. feel; smell
czujka (chooy-ka) f. sentry
czułość (choo-woshch) f. tenderness ; affection; caress
czuły (choo-wi) adj. m. tender; affectionate; sensitive; keen
czupurny (choo-poor-ni) adj. m. pugnacious; boastful; defiant
czuwać (choo-vach) v. watch; nurse ; look-out ; stay up; tend
czwartek (chvar-tek) m. Thursday
czwarty (chvar-ti) num. fourth
czworobok (chvo-ro-bok) m. quadrilateral; square; tetragon
czworokąt (chvo-ro-kownt) m. quadrangle; quad; tetragon
czwórka (chvoor-ka) f. foursome; crew of four; good mark
czy (chi) conj. if; whether
czychać (chi-khach) v. lurk
czyj (chiy) pron. whose
czyjś (chiysh) pron. somebody's
anybody's; someone else's
czyli (chi-lee) conj. or; otherwise; that is to say
czym...tym (chim...tim) adv. the sooner... the; the more the...; the less... the...
czyn (chin) m. act. deed
czynsz (chinsh) m. rent
czynić (chi-neech) v. do; render ; act; amount; cause

czyrak (chi-rak) m. boil; furuncle ; boil; anbury; rising
czynnik (chin-ñeek) m. factor
czysto (chi-sto) adv. clean
czysty (chis-ti) adj. m. clean
czyszczenie (chish-che-ñe) n. cleaning ; brushing;diarrhoea
czyscic (chish-cheech) v. clean ; scour; brush; rub;purge
czysciec (chish-chets) m. purgatory ; woundwort
czytac (chi-tach) v. read
czytelnia (chi-tel-ña) f. reading room ;lending library
czytelnik (chi-tel-ñeek) m. reader ; reading individual
czytelny (chi-tel-ni) adj. m. legible ; readable
czyz (chish) part. if; whether
cma (chma) f. obscurity; swarm; night butterfly ;night moth
cmic (chmeech) v. obscure; dim; darken ; eclipse; smoke; sicken
cwiartka (chvyart-ka) f. one quarter : one fourth of a liter
cwierc (chwyerch) f. one fourth (of a liter etc.)
cwiczenie (chvee-che-ñe) n. exercise ; instruction; drill
cwiek (chvyek) m. nail ; stud
cwikla (chveek-wa) f. beetroot with horseradish (salad)
dach (dakh) m. roof ; shelter
dac (dach) v. give ; pay;result
daktyl (dak-til) m. date
dal (dal) f. distance; remoteness : far away; aloof
dalece (da-le-tse) adv. further; by far; so far;(so)much so
dalej (da-ley) adv. further; moreover : further on; so on
dalmierz (dal-myesh) m. range finder ; telemeter
dalszy (dal-shi) adj. m. further;farther ; later; another
dama (da-ma)f. lady ; partner
dana (da-na)adj.f.given (data)
danie (da-ñe) m. serving; dish ; course
danser (dan-ser) m. dancer
dane (da-ne) pl. data
dar (dar) m. gift ; present
daremnie (da-rem-ñe) adv. in vain ; without success

daremny (da-rem-ni) adj. m. futile; vain; idle; ineffective
darmo (dar-mo) adv. free; gratuitously; to no avail
darowac (da-ro-vach) v. give; forgive; overlook; spare
data (da-ta) f. date
datek (da-tek) n. small gift
dawac (da-vach) v. give (often)
dawno (dav-no) adv. long ago
dąb (domp) m. oak tree (wood)
dąc (downch) v. blow; resound
dąsac się (down-sach shañ) v. sulk; be in the pouts; mump
dążyc (down-zhich) v. aspire; tend; aim; be bound; trend
dbac (dbach) v. care;set store
dech (dekh) m. breath; gust
decydowac (de-tsi-do-vach) v. decide; resolve; determine
decyzja (de-tsis-ya) f. decision; ruling; resolve
delikatnosc (de-lee-kat-noshch) f. delicacy; gentleness; tact
defekt (de-fekt) m. defect
demaskowac (de-mas-ko-vach) v. unmask; uncover; denounce
demokracja (de-mo-krats-ya) f. democracy,
denerwowac (de-ner-vo-vach) v. bother; make nervous; irritate
dentysta (den-tis-ta) m. dentist
depesza (de-pe-sha) f. wire; telegram; cable; dispatch
deponowac (de-po-no-vach) v. deposit; put in safe keeping
depozyt (de-po-zit) m. deposit
deptac (dep-tach) v. trample; tread; pace up and down;stain
derka (der-ka) f. rug; blanket
desen (de-señ) m. pattern; design; decorative design
deska (des-ka) f. plank; board
desperacja (des-pe-rats-ya) f. desperation; despair
deszcz (deshch) m. rain
detal (de-tal) m. retail; detail; trifling matter
determinacja (de-ter-mee-nats-ya) f. determination
dewiza (de-vee-za) f. foreign money ; motto; slogan; device

dębina (dăn-beé-na) f. oak
wood; oak bark
dętka (dănt-ka) f. pneumatic
tire; tube; air chamber
diabeł (dyá-bew) m. devil
dieta (dye-ta) f. diet;regimen
dla (dla) prep. for; to;towards
dlaczego (dla—che-go)prep. why;
what for
dlatego (dla—te-go)prep.
because; this is why; and so
dławić (dwa-veech) v. choke;
squash; throttle; strangle
dłoń (dwoń) f. palm of the
hand; hand; metacarpus; quart
dłubac (dwoo-bach)v. groove;
poke; tinker; pick one's teeth
dług (dwoog) m. debt; obligation
długi (dwoo-gee) adj. m. long
długo (dwoo-go) adv. a long
time; a long way; long before
dłuto (dwoo-to) n. chisel
dłutować (dwoo-to-vach) v.
chisel; cut with chisel
dłuźnik (dwoozh-ńeek) m. debtor
dmuchać (dmoo-khach)v. blow
dniówka (dńoov-ka) f. day's
work; work by day; time work
dno (dno) n. bottom; utterness
do (do) prep. to; into; up;till
doba (do-ba) f. 24 hours
dobić (do-beech) v. deal
a death blow; drive home
dobierać (do-bye-rach) v.
match; take more; select
dobitny (do-beet-ni) adj. m.
expressive; emphatic; distinct
doborowy (do-bo-ro-vi) adj. m.
choice; select; picked
dobosz (do-bosh) m. drummer
dobór (do-boor) m. selection;
assortment; choice;assortment
dobra (dob-ra) n. riches
dobranoc (do-bra-nots)(indecl.)
good-night
dobrany (do-bra-ni) adj. m.
matching; becoming;accordant
dobre (dob-re) adj. n. good
dobro (dob-ro) n. good; right
dobrobyt (do-bro-bit) m. well-
being; prosperity; welfare
dobroczynnosc (do-bro-chin-
noshch) f. charity; works of
mercy; philanthropy

dobroć (do—roch) f. kindness
dobroduszny (do-bro-doosh-ni)
adj. m. kindhearted ; kindly
dobrodziej (do-bro-dżhey) m.
benefactor ; his reverence
dobrotliwy (do-bro-tlee-vi)
adj. m. kind; good natured
dobrowolny (do-bro-wol-ni)
adj. m. voluntary; gratuitus
dobry (dob-ri) adj. m. good;
kind; right; hearty; retentive
dobrze (dob-rze) adv. well;
O K; rightly; properly ;okay
dobudówka (do-boo-doov-ka) f.
building extension
dobyć (do-bich) v. pullout
dobytek (do-bi-tek) m. belongings; effects; livestock
doceniać (do-tse-ńach) v.
duly appreciate; value
docent (do-tsent) m. associate
professor ; lecturer
dochodzenie (do-kho-dze-ńe) n
investigation; inquiry
dochodzić (do-kho-dżheech)v.
draw near; investigate; reach
dochód (do-khoot) m. income;
revenue; profit; returns
dociąć (do-chownch) c. sting;
taunt; fit by cutting off
dociec (do-chets) v. find out
dociekać (do- che -kach) v.
search; investigate; find out
docierać (do-chye-rach) v.
draw near; reach; reduce
friction ; rub up; get at
docinek (do-chee-nek) m. taunt
doczekać (do-che-kach) v. wait;
live to see; wait 'til
doczepiać (do-chep-yach) v. fix
append; attach; hitch; link
doczesny (do-ches-ni) adj. m.
temporal; worldly; mundane
dodać (do-dach) v. add; sum up
dodatek (do-da-tek) m. supplement; addition; fixture; extra
dodatni (do-dat-ńee) adj. m.
positive; advantageous; active
dodawanie (do-da-va-ńe) n.
addition
dogadać się (do-ga-dach shăn)v.
come to terms;communicate well
dogadzać (do-ga-dzach) v.
please; accommodate; satisfy

dogladać (do-glówn-dać) v.
supervise; tend; oversee
dogmat (dóg-mat) m. dogma
dogodny (do-gód-ni) adj. m.
convenjent; suitable; handy
dogonić (do-go-ńeećh) v. catch
up; overtake; bę in hot pursuit
dogryzać (do-gri-zaćh) v. vex;
tease; finish munching;disturb
doić (do-eećh) v. milk; fleece
dojarka (do-yár-ka) f. milk
maid; milking machine
dojazd (do-yazt) m. access;drive;
approach; means of transport
dojechać (do-yé-khaćh) v. reach;
arrive; approach; bang; hit
dojeżdżać (do-yézh-jaćh) v.
commute; be coming; pull in
dojmujący (doy-moo-yówn-tsi) adj.
m. acute; piercing; sharp;keen
dojrzały (doy-zha-wi) adj. m.
ripe; mellow; mature; adult
dojrzeć (doy-zhećh) v. glimpse;
notice;;ripen; be ripe;mellow
dojście (doy-shćhe) n. approach
dok (dok) m. dock
dokarmić (do-kár-meećh) v.
nourish additionally
dokazać (do-ká-zaćh) v. prove;
achieve; accomplish;do the trick
dokazywać (do-ka-zí-vaćh) v.
frolic: gambol; romp and play
dokąd (do-kównt) adv. where;till
whither; where to ? how far?till
dokładać (do-kwa-daćh) v. add;
throw in; pay more; give moore
dokładny (do-kwád-ni) adj. m.
accurate; exact; precise
dokoła (do-ko-wa) adv. round;
round about; all round
dokonać (do-ko-naćh) v. achieve;
accomplish; carry out;fulfil;do
dokończenie (do-kon-che-ńe) n.
conclusion: completion; end
doktor (dók-tor) m. doctor
dokręcać (do-krań-tsaćh) v.
tighten; screw tight; turn off
dokuczać (do-koo-chaćh) v. vex;
annoy; nag; bully; sting;trouble
dola (do-la) f. fortune; lot
dolar (dó-lar) m. dollar
doliczyć (do-lee-chićh) v.
count up; add; charge more

dolina (do-lee-na) f. valley;
dale; glen; coomb; pocket
dolny (dól-ny) adj. m. lower
dołączyć (do-wówn-chićh) v.add;
join; enclose; affix; tack on
dołek (do-wek) m. dimple; pit
dom (dom) m. house
domagać się (do-ma-gaćh sháń)
v. demand
domiar (do-myar) m. additional
assessment; surtax;on top of it
domniemany (do-mńe-ma-ni) adj.
m. supposed; assumed; alleged
domostwo (do-mós-tvo) n. household; homestead; farmstead
domownik (do-mow-ńeek) m.
inmate ; housemate
domowy (do-mó-vi) adj. m.
domestic; homemade; private
domysł (do-misw) m. guess
doniesienie (do-ńe-she-ńe) m.
denunciation; report; news
doniosły (do-ńo-swi) adj. m.
significant; far reaching
donosiciel (do-no-shee-ćhel)
m. denunciator; informer
donosny (do-nósh-ni) adj. m.
resounding; renging; loud
dookoła(do-o-ko-wa) adv. round;
round about; all around; around
dopaść (dó-pashćh) v. catch up;
overtake: reach at a run;seize
dopalać (do-pa-laćh) v. after-
burn; finish burning; burn up
dopasować (do-pa-só-vaćh) v.
fit; adapt; adjust; match;tone
dopatrywać (do-pa-tri-vaćh) v.
see to it; find out; keep an eye
dopełnić (do-pew-ńeećh) v.fulfil;
fill up; complete ; make up
dopędzić (do-páń-dźheećh) v.
catch up with; overtake;gain on
dopiąć (do-pyówńćh) v. attain;
buckle up; button up; obtain
dopiero (do-pye-ro) adv. only;
just; hardly; barely; not till
dopilnować (do-peel-no-vaćh) v.
see something done ;supervise
dopisek (do-pee-sek) m. postscript; foot note
dopłata (do-pwa-ta) f. extra
payment; surcharge;extra fare
dopływ (do-pwif) m. tributary

dopomagać (do-po-má-gać) v.
help; be of assistance
dopominac się (do-po-mee-nach
shán)v.put in claim; demand
dopóki (do-poóki) conj. as
long; as far; while; until;till
dopóty (do-poó-ti) conj. 'til ;
until ; so far; up to here
dopraszac się (do-pra-shach
shán) v. solicit; beg; insist
doprawdy (do-práv-di) adv.
truly; indeed; really
doprawiac (do-práv-yach) v.
add (to taste); replace
doprowadzić (do-pro-va-dźheech)
v. lead to; cause; provoke
dopust Boży (do-poost Bo-zhi)
m. calamity; scourge;act of God
dopuszczać (do-poósh-chach) v.
admit; allow; permit; be open
dopytać się (do-pi-tach śhán)
v. find out; inquire; question
dorabiać (do-ráb-yach) v. make
additionally; replace; finish
doradca (do-rád-tsa) m. adviser; counselor, ; guide
dorastać (do-rás-tach) v.
mature; grow; grow up; reach
doraźnie (do-ráźh-ńe) adv.
(immediately) on the spot
doręczyc (do-rán-chich) v.
hand in; deliver; transmit
dorobek (do-ró-bek) m. acquisition; rise to affluence
dorobkiewicz (do-rob-ke-veech)
m. upstart; parvenu
doroczny (do-róch-ni) adj. m.
yearly; annual; recurring yearly
dorodny (do-ród-ni) adj. m.
handsome; fine-looking; shapely
dorosły (do-rós-wy) adj. m.
adult; grown up; mature ;grown
dorożka (do-rozh-ka) f. cab
dorównywac (do-roov-ni-vach) v.
match; equal; catch up with
dorsz (dorsh) m. cod (fish)
dorywczy (do-riv-chi) v.
occasional; improvised; fitful; off-and-on; hit-and-run
dorzecze (do-zhe-che) n.
river basin; drainage area
dorzeczny (do-zhéch-ni) adj. m.
reasonable; sensible; efficient;
adequate;acceptable;logical

dorzucac (do-zhoó-tsach) v.
throw in; add; throw as far as
dosadny (do-sád-ni) adj. m.
forceful ; expressive; crisp
dosiadać (do-śha-dach) v.
mount (horse); bestride
dosięgać (do-shán-gach) v.
reach.attain; catch up with
doskonalić (dos-ko-na-leech)
v. perfect; improve; cultivate
doskwierac (do-skvye-rach) v.
pinch; gripe ; trouble; worry
dosłowny (do-swóv-ni) adj. m.
literal ; verbal; textual
dosłyszec (do-swi-shech) v.
hear well; catch a sound
dostać (dos-tach) v. get;
obtain ; reach; take out
dostarczyć (dos-tár-chich) v.
provide; supply ; deliver
dostateczny (do-sta-téch-ni)
adj. m. sufficient ; adequate
dostatek (do-stá-tek) m. abundance; wealth; affluence
dostawca (do-stáw-tsa) m.
supplier ; provider
dostawa (do-stá-va) f. delivery
dostawać (do-stá-vach) v. reach;
receive ; be attended to
dostęp (do-stáńp) m. access
dostojnik (do-stóy-ńeek) m.
dignitary; notable of high rank
dostosować (do-sto-so-vach) v.
accommodate; subordinate;fit
dostroic (do-stró-yeech) v.
tune up ; conform; adapt
dostrzec (do-stzhets) v. notice;
behold ; perceive; spot; spy;see
dostudzić (do-stoo-dźheech) v.
cool off ; plenty; sufficient
dosyć (do-sich) adv. enough;
dosztukować (do-shtoo-kó-vach)
v. piece on; eke out; sew on
dosc (doshch) adv. enough
dosrodkowy (do-shrod-kó-vi)
adj. m. centripetal;concentric
doświadczyć (do-shvyád-chich) v.
experience ; sustain; feel
dotarcie (do-tár-che) n. reaching; overcoming friction
dotąd (do-tównt) adv. up till
now; here to fore ; hitherto;
thus far; so far; yet; by then;
till then;still;not...as yet

dotkliwy (dot-klee-vi) adj. m.
painful ; keen; intense; severe
dotknąć (dot-knównch) v. touch
dotknięcie (dot-kña´n—che) n.
touch; contact; feeling;stroke
dotrzeć (do-tzhech) v. reach;
overcome friction ; rub up
dotrzymać (do-tzhi-mach) v.
keep; stick to one's
commitment ; adhere;redeem
dotychczas (do-tikh-chas) adv.
up to now; hitherto; to date
dotyczyć (do-ti´-chich) v.
concern; relate; regard; affect
dotyk (dó-tik) m. touch;feel
dowcip (dóv-cheep) m. wit;
joke; jest; gag; quip; sally
dowiedzieć się (do-vye-dzhech
sháñ) v. get to know; learn
dowidzenia (do-vee-dze-ña)
good bye,; see you later
dowierzać (do-vye-zhach) v.
trust; have confidence in
dowieść (do-vyeshch) v. prove
dowieźć (do-vyeżhch) v.
1. supply 2. drive to
dowodzić (do-vó-dżheech)v.
conduct;keep proving
dowolnie (do-vol-ñe) adv. at
will ; optionally; freely
dowolny (do-vól-ni) adj. m.
optional; any; whichever
dowód (do-voot) m. proof;
evidence ; record; token
dowódca (do-vood-tsa) m.
commander   delivery
dowóz (do-voos) m. supply;
doza (dó-za) f. dose
dozbroić (do-zbró-eech) v.
rearm; supplement weapons
dozgonny (do-zgón-ni) adj. m.
lifelong ; lasting 'til death
doznać (do-znach) v. go through;
undergo ; endure; feel ;suffer
dozorca (do-zor-tsa) m. caretaker; watchman; overseer
dozorować (do-zo-ro-vach) v.
oversee; supervise; attend
dozór (do-zoor) m. surveillance
dozwolić (do-zvo-leech) v.
allow to happen; let happen
dożynki (do-zhin-kee) pl.
harvest festivities

dożywocie (do-zhi-vo-che)n.
life estate; life pension
dół (doow) m. pit; bottom part
drab (drap) m. ruffian; scamp
drabina (dra-bee-na) f. ladder
dramat (dra-mat) m. drama
drań (dráñ) m. scoundrel; crumb
drapacz (drá-pach) m. scraper
drapać (dra-pach) v. scratch)
drapieżnik (dra-pyezh-ñeek) m.
beast of prey; plunderer
drastyczny (dra-stich-ni) adj.
m. drastic; rough; violent
dratwa (drát-va) f. pitched-
thread; shoemaker's twine
draźliwy (drazh-lee-vi) adj.
m. touchy; irritable; ticklish
draźnić (drazh-ñeech) v. tease;
irritate; whet; vex; annoy; jar
drąg (drównk) m. pole; bar
drążyć (drówn-zhich) v. hollow
out; bore; torment ; fret;gnaw
drelich (dre-leekh) m. denim
dren (dren) n. drain (pipe)
dreptać (drép-tach) v. trip-
trot; toddle; totter; patter
dreszcz (dreshch) m. chill;
shudder; thrill; flutter; shiver
dreszczowiec (dresh-chó-vyets)
m. thriller (novel or movie)
drewno (drév-no) n. piece of
wood; timber ; log; xylem
dręczyć (drań-chich) v. torment
dretwieć (dran-tvyech) v. grow
numb; grow stiff; stiffen
drgać (drgach) v. tremble;
vibrate; quiver; throb; wobble
drobiazg (dró-byazk) m. trifle;
detail; trinket; small fry
drobina (dro-bee-na) f. particle
drobne (dró-ne) n. small
change; petty cash ; small coin
drobnica (drob-ñee-tsa) f.
small goods; packages
drobnostka (drob-nóst-ka) f.
trifle; small matter; trinket
drobny (dró-bni) adj. m. small;
tiny ; trivial; petty; slight
droga (dró-ga) f. 1. road;
2.journey ; 3.adj.f. dear
drogeria (dro-gér-ya) f. drugstore ; drysaltery

drogi (dró-gee) adj. m. dear;
expensive; costly; beloved
drogowskaz (dro-góv-skas) m.
road sign; signpost
drozd (drozt) m. thrush
drożdże (dróżh-je) pl. yeast
drożeć (dró-zheć) v. grow
dear; rise in price;appreciate
drożyzna (dro-zhíz-na) f. high
cost of living; high prices
drób (droop) pl. paltry
dróżka (dróózh-ka) f. path
druciany (droo-ćha-ni) adj. m.
of wire; made out of wire
drugi (droó-gee) num. second;
other; the other one; latter
druh (drookh) m. buddy;
companion; friend; boy scout
druk (drook) m. print; printing
drut (droot) m. wire
druzgotać (drooz-go-taćh) v.
smash; shatter; crush to pieces
drużba (dróózh-ba) m. best man
drużyna (droo-zhí-na) f. team
drwal (drval) m. lumber jack
drwić (drveećh) v. mock;deride
drwiny (drveé-ny) pl. mockery
dryg (drik) m.knack; flair for
drzazga (dzház-ga) f. splinter
drzeć (dzhećh) v. tear; pull
drzemka (dshem-ka) f. nap
drzewo (dshe-vo) n. tree
drzeworyt (dshe-vo-rit) m.
woodcut; wood engraving
drzwi (dzhveé) n. door
drżeć (drzhećh) v. shiver;shake
dubeltówka (doo-bel-toóv-ka) f.
double barrel gun; shotgun
duch (dookh) m. spirit; ghost;
state of mind ; intent; life
duchowieństwo (doo-khov-yeń-stvo)
pl. clergy ; priesthood
dudek (doó-dek) m. 1. hoopoe;
2. dupe; fool; dolt; booby
dudnić (doód-ńeećh) v. resound
dudy (doo-di) pl. bagpipe
dukat (doo-kat) m. ducat
dulka (doól-ka) f. oarlock
duma (doó-ma) f. pride ; epic
dumać (doó-maćh) v. meditate
dumny (doóm-ni) adj. m. proud
dupa (doó-pa) f. ass (vulg.)
dur (door) m. typhoid fever

dureń (doó-reń) m. fool; ass
durzyć (doó-zhićh) v. fool;
infatuate; bewilder; dupe
dusić (doó-śheećh) v. strangle
dusigrosz (doo-śheé-grosh) m.
penny pincher; niggard
dusza (doó-sha) f. soul;psyche
dużo (doó-zho) adv. much; many
duży (doó-zhi) adj. m. big;
large; great; fair-sized
dwa (dva) num. two
dwakroć (dvá-kroćh) num. twice
dwanaście (dva-náśh-ćhe) num.
twelve
dwieście (dvyéśh-ćhe) num. 200
dwoić (dvó-eećh) v. double
dwojaczki (dvo-yách-kee) pl.
twins ; double pot [the two;
dwoje (dvó-ye) num. two;in two;
couple ;two(fold);two(ways)
dwór (dvoor) m. country manor
dworski (dvór-skee) adj. m.
courtly; manorial; of court
dworzec (dvó-zhets) m. (railway) station ; depot
dwukrotnie (dvoo-krót-ńe) adv.
twice ; twice over
dwunastka (dvoo-nást-ka) f.
twelve ;(team)of twelve
dwustronny (dvoo-stron-ni)adj.
m. two-sided; bilateral
dyg (dik) m. curtsy ; bob
dygnitarz (dig-ńeé-tash) m.
dignitary; high- ranking man
dygotać (di-go-taćh) v. tremble
dykta (dík-ta) f. plywood
dyktator (dik-tá-tor) m.
dictator ;absolute ruler
dylemat (di-le-mat) m. dilem-
ma; perplexity; fix
dym (dim) m. smoke; fumes
dymić (dí-meećh) v. smoke
dynamit (di-na-meet) m. dynamite; W.W, II German ersatz bread
dyndać (dín-daćh) v. dangle
dynia (dí-ńa) f. pumpkin
dyplom (dí-plom) m. diploma
dyplomacja (di-plo-máts-ya) f.
diplomacy; policy; tact
dyrekcja (di-rék-tsya) f.
management ; headquarters
dyrygent (di-rí-gent) m.
orchestra conductor

dyscyplina (dis-tsi-plee-na) f.
discipline; branch; line
dysk (disk) m. disc; discus
dyskrecja (dis-krets-ya) f.
discretion; management
dyskusja (dis-koos-ya) f.
discussion; debate
dysponować (dis-po-no-vach) v.
dispose; control; order
dysputa (dis-poo-ta) f. dispute; debate; controversy
dystans (dis-tans) m. distance
dystyngowany (dis-tin-go-va-
ni) adj. m. distinguished
dysza (di-sha) f. nozzle;
blast pipe; snout; twyer
dyszeć (di-shech) v. gasp;pant
dywan (di-van) m. carpet; rug
dywidenda (di-vee-den-da) f.
dividend
dywizja (di-veez-ya) f. division
dyżurny (di-zhoor-ny) adj. m.
on call; on duty; orderly
dzban (dzban) m. jug; pitcher
dziać się (dzhach shan) v.
occur; happen; take place
dziadek (dzha-dek) m. grandfather; nut cracer
dział (dzhaw) m. section
działacz (dzha-wach) m. acti-
vist(in politics, religion etc)
działać (dzha-wach) v. act;
work; be active; be effective
działka (dzhaw-ka) f. parcel
działo (dzha-wo) n. cannon
dziarski (dzhar-skee) adj. m.
brisk; lively; swinging; rakish
dziąsło (dzhown swo)n. gum
dzicz (dzheech)pl. savages
dzida (dzhee-da) f. spear ;pike
dzieci (dzhe-chee) pl. children
dzieciństwo (dzhe-cheen-stvo)
n. childhood; boyhood;infancy
dziecko (dzhets-ko) n. child;
baby; trot; brat; kiddie; kid
dziedziczyć (dzhe-dzhee-chich)
v. inherit (property,features)
dziedzina (dzhe-dzhee-na) f.
realm; area;sphere ; domain
dziedziniec (dzhe-dzhee-nets)m.
yard; court; backyard

dziegieć (dzhe-gech) m. tar
dzieje (dzhe-ye) pl. history
dziejowy (dzhe-yo-vi) adj. m.
historical; historic
dziekan (dzhe-kan) m. dean
dzielić (dzhe-leech) v. divide;
share; split; distribute
dzielnica (dzhel-nee-tsa) f.
province; quarter; section
dzielny (dzhel-ni) adj. m.
brave; resourceful; efficient
dzieło (dzhe-wo) n. achievement; work; composition
dziennik (dzhen-neek)m. daily-
news; daily; journal; diary
dzienny (dzhen-ni) adj. m.
daily; diurnal; day's
dzień (dzheń)m. day; daylight
dzień dobry(dzheń dob-ri)good morn-
dzierżawa (dzher-zha-va) f. ing
lease; rental; holding
dzierżyć (dzher-zhich) v.
wield (power); hold; grip
dziesiątka (dzhe-shownot-ka) f.
ten;(team of)ten
dziesięć (dzhe-shańch) num.
ten
dziewczyna (dzhev-chi-na) f.
girl; lass; wench; maid
dziewica (dzhe-vee-tsa) f.
virgin; maiden
dziewięć (dzhe-vyańch) num.
nine
dziewiętnaście (dzhe-vyańt-
nashche) num. nineteen
dzięcioł (dzhań-chow) m.
woodpecker
dziękczynienie (dzhańk-chi-
ńe-ńe)n. thanks-giving
dziękować (dzhań-ko-vach) v.
thank ; give thanks
dzik (dzheek) m. boar; tusker
dziobać (dzho-bach)v. peck
dziób (dzh-oob) m. beak; bill
dzisiejszy (dzhee-shey-shi)
adj. m. today's ; modern
dziś (dzheesh) adv. today
dziupla (dzhoop-la) f. (tree)
hollow(in a trnk)
dziura (dzhoo-ra) f. hole
dziurawy (dzhoo-ra-vi) adj. m.
leaky; full of holes
dziw (dzheef) m. wonder

dziwactwo (dżhee-vats-tvo) n.
crank; fad; craze; peculiarity
dziwić (dżhee-veech) v. astonish
dziwny (dżheev-ni)adj.m.strange;
dzwon (dzvon) m. bell; chime
dźwięczeć (dżhvyań-chech) v.
ring; sound; jingle; clang
dźwięk (dżhvyánk) m. sound
dźwig (dżhveek) n. crane
dźwigać (dżhvee-gach)v. lift;
hoist; raise; heave; erect;carry
dżdżysty (j-jis-ti) adj. m. wet;
rainy ; drizzly (weather)
dżem (jem) m. jam; fruit jam
dżet (jet) m. jet
dżinsy (jeen-si) pl. blue
jeans (pants)
dżokey (jó-key) m. jockey
dżudo (joo-do) m. judo (sport)
dżuma (joo-ma) f. plague
dżungla (joon-gla) f. jungle
echo (ekho) n. echo; response
edukacja (e-doo-kats-ya) f.
education; schooling;instruction
efekt (e-fekt) m. effect
efektowny (e-fek-tóv-ni) adj.
m. showy ; striking; attractive
efektywny (e-fek-tiv-ni) adj.
m. efficient ; effective; real
egida (e-gee-da) f. protection;
auspices ; protectorate
egoista (e-go-ees-ta) m.egotist
egoistyczny (e-go-ees-tich-ni)
adj. m. selfish; self seeking
egzamin (eg-za-meen) m. examination; exam ; standing a test
egzekucja (eg-ze-koots-ya) f.
execution ; seizure; flogging
egzemplarz (eg-zem-plash) m.
copy (sample); specimen
egzystencja (eg-zis-ten-tsya)
f. existence; livelihood
ekierka (e-ker-ka) f. set
square ;draftsman's triangle
ekipa (e-kee-pa) f. team;crew
ekonomia (e-ko-nom-ya) f.
economics; thrift; economy
ekran (ek-ran) m. screen;shield
ekspedient (ex-pe-dyent) m.
salesperson ; clerk;salesman
ekspedycja (ex-pe-dits-ya) f.
1. dispatch 2. expedition

ekspert (ex-pert) m. expert
eksploatować (ex-plo-a-to-vach)
v. exploit; sweat; utilize
eksponat (ex-po-nat) m. exhibit
ekspozytura (ex-po-zy-too-ra)
f. agency; branch office
ekwipować (ek-vee-po-vach) v.
equip; fit out; provide with
elaborat (e-la-bo-rat) m. study (elaboration)
elastycznosć (e-las-tich-noshch)
elasticity; resilience;flexibility
elegancja (e-le-gants-ya) f.
elegance; fashion; style
elektrociepłownia (e-lek-tro-
chep-wov-ña) f. steamplant
elektrycznosć (e-lek-trich-
noshch) f. electricity
element (e-le-ment) m. element
elementarny (e-le-men-tar-ni)
adj. m. fundamental; primary
elewator (e-le-va-tor) m.
elevator ; hoist
emalia (e-mal-ya) f. enamel
emeryt (e-me-rit) m. retired
person; pensioner; pensionary
emigracja (e-mee-grats-ya) f.
emigration; exile; emigrants
emisja (e-mees-ya) f. emission
emocja (e-mo-tsya) f. thrill
entuzjazm (en-tóoz-yazm) m.
enthusiasm; rapture
energia (e-nerg-ya) f. energy
energiczny (e-ner-geech-ni)
adj. m. energetic; vigorous
epoka (e-pó-ka) f. epoch
epitet (e-pee-tet) m. epithet
era (era) f. era; epoch
erotyczny (e-ro-tich-ni) adj.
m. erotic; sexual
eskadra (es-kad-ra) f. squad-
ron; aerial fleet: flight
eskorta (es-kór-ta) f. escort
estetyczny (es-te-tich-ni)
adj. m.esthetic; in good taste
etap (e-tap) m. stage (of development) ; halting place
etatowy (e-ta-tó-vi) adj. m.
permanent (job): full time
eter (e-ter) m. ether
etyczny (e-tich-ni) adj. m.
ethical; moral

etykieta (e-ti-ke̱—ta) f. label;
etiquette; formality;ceremonial
ewakuacja (e-va-koo-a-tsya) f.
evacuation
ewangielia (e-van-gél--ya) f.
gospel; gospel truth
ewangielik (e-van-gé—leek) m.
protestant,; Lutheran
ewentualnosć (e-ven-too-al̯-
nośhćh) f. possibility
ewentualnie (e-ven-too-ál-ñe)
adv. possibly; if need be
ewidencja (e-vee-dén-tsya) f.
records; list; files ; roll
ewolucja (e-vo-loo-tsya) f.
evolution; development
fabryczny (fa-brích-ni) adj.
m. manufactured
fabryka (fa-brí-ka) f. factory
fabuła (fa-boo-wa) f. fable;
plot of a novel etc.; story
facet (fá-tset) m. guy
fachowiec (fa-kho-vyets) m.
expert; specialist;connoisseur
fajdać (fáy-dać) v. shit (vulg.)
fajans (fáy-ans) m. earthenware
fajerka (fa-yér-ka) f.cook-top
unit; stove lid
fajka (fáy-ka)f. pipe (for
smoking); wild boar's tusk
fajtłapa (fayt-wá-pa) m. all
thumbs guy(awkward,clumsy man)
fakt (fakt) m. fact
faktor (fák-tor) m. broker;
agent; factor; intermediary
faktycznie (fak-tích-ñe) adv.
in fact;actually; indeed; truly
fala (fa-la) f. wave; tide;surge
falisty (fa-lées-ti) adj. m.
wavy; rolling; corrugated
falochron (fa-ló-khron) m.
breakwater: pier; jetty; mole
falsyfikat (fal-si-fée-kat) m.
forgery; counterfeit; fake
fałd (fawt) m. fold (wrinkle)
fałsz (fawsh) m. falsehood
fałszować (faw-sho-vaćh) v.
falsify; fake; forge; sing flat
fama (fa-ma) f. fame; rumor
fanaberie (fa-na-bér-ye) pl.
whims; fads; frills; ostentation
fanatyk (fa-ná-tik) m. fanatic;
enthusiast; bigot; maniac

fanfaron (fan-fa-ron) m.
braggart; coxcomb; swaggerer
fantastyczny (fan-tas-tích-ni)
adj. m. fantastic; wild; odd
fantazja (fan-taz-ya) f. dash;
imagination; fiction; whim
fara (fá-ra) f. parish church
farba (fár-ba) f. paint; dye
color; dyeing; blood
farbować (far-bó-vaćh) v. dye
farsa (fár-sa) f. farce;mockery
farsz (farsh) m. stuffing
fartuch (fár-tookh)m. apron
fasola (fa-só-la) f. bean
fasonować (fa-so-no-vaćh) v.
fashion ; shape; mold model
fatalny (fa-tal-ni) adj. m.
fatal ; ill-fated; awful;fateful
fastryga (fas-tri-ga) f. tack;
basting; baste; tacks
faszyzm (fa-shizm) m. fascism
fatyga (fa-ti-ga) f. trouble;
fatigue ; trouble; bother;pains
fatałaszki (fa-ta-wash-kee) pl.
knik-knacks; frippery; trinkets
febra (féb-ra) fever;the shakes
faworyzować (fa-vo-ri-zo-vaćh)
v. favor, play favorites
felczer (fél-cher) m. male
nurse : medical assistant
federacja (fe-de-rats-ya) f.
federation ; union
feralny (fe-rál-ni) adj. m.
unlucky; ill fated; hapless
ferie (fér-ye) pl. holidays
ferma (fér-ma) f. farm ; ranch
ferment (fér-ment) m. ferment
festyn (fés-tin) m. festival
fetor (fé-tor) m. stench
figa (feé-ga) f. fig ; nix
figiel (feé-gel) m. practical
joke ; prank; trick; ill turn
figura (fee-góo-ra) f. figure;
shape ; form; image; big wig
fikcja (feek-tsya) f. fiction
filar (feé-lar) m. pillar
filatelista (fee-la-te-leés-ta)
m. stamp-collector
filc (feelts) m. felt
filia (feél-ya) f. branch
(store); branch-office
filiżanka (fee-lee-zhán-ka) f.
cup ; cupful; coffee-cup

film (feelm) m. film

filolog (fee-ló-lok) m. philol-ogist; linguist

filozof (fee-ló-zof) m. philos-opher

filtr (feeltr) m. filter

filut (fee-loot) m. jester; rogue; sly boots; joker

finanse (fee-nán-se) pl. finances; finance; funds

finisz (fee-ńeesh) m. end (of a run); the finish

fiołek (fyo-wek) m. violet

fiołkowy (fyow-ko-vi) adj. m. purple; violet; of the violet

firanka (fee-rán-ka) f. curtain; drapery

firma (feer-ma) f. business; firm; name of a firm

fisharmonia (fees-har-móń-ya) f. harmonium

fizjognomia (feez-yo-gnóm-ya) f. face; external aspect

fizjonomia (feez-yo-nóm-ya) f. face; physiognomy

fizjolog (feez-yo-lok) m. physiologist

fizyczny (feez-ich-ni) adj. m. physical; bodily; manual

fizyk (fee-zik) m. physicist

flaczki (flách-kee) pl. tripe

flaga (fla-ga) f. banner; flag; ensign; standard

flaki (fla-kee) pl. bowels

flakon (fla-kon) m. vase

flanela (fla-ne-la) f. flannel

flaszka (flásh-ka) bottle

flama (fla-ma) f, lady-love

flądra (flówn-dra) f. flounder

flegma (flég-ma) f. phlegm

flejtuch (fléy-tookh) m. slut

flet (flet) m. flute

flirt (fleert) m. flirt

flisak (flee-sak) m. raftsman

flora (flo-ra) f. flora

floret (flo-ret) m. foil

flota (flo-ta) f. navy; fleet

fluksja (flooks-ya) f. tooth-infection swelling

fluid (floo-eet) m. fluid

fochy (fo-khi) pl. blues; whims; sulks; pouts

foka (fo-ka) f. seal

folgować (fol-gó-vach) v. slacken; relax; indulge; abate

folklor (fólk-lor) m. folklore

folusz (fo-loosh)m.fulling mill

folwark (fól-vark) m. farm

fonetyczny (fo-ne-tich-ni) adj. phonetic

fontanna (fon-tán-na) f. fountain ; spurt ; waterworks

foremny (fo-rém-ni) adj. m. shapely; handsome; symmetrical

forma (for-ma) f. shape; mold

format (for-mat) m. size

formularz (for-móo-lash) m. (application) form ; blank

formuła (for-móo-wa) f. formula

fornir (for-ńeer) m. veneer

forsa (for-sa) f. (money); dough; bread; tin; chink

forsować (forso-vach) v. force; strain ; urge; exhort;overcome

fort (fort) m. fort; stronghold

forteca (for-té-tsa) f. for — tress ; citadel ; stronghold

fortel (for-tel) m. stratagem; trick ; ruse; subterfuge

fortepian (for-té-pyan) m. grand piano; piano

fortuna (for-tóo-na) f. fortune

fosa (fo-sa) f. moat

fosfat (fós-fat) m. phosphate

fosfor (fós-foor)m. phosphorus

fotel (fo-tel) m. armchair

fotograf (fo-tó-graf) m. photographer

fotografia (fo-to-gráf-ya) f. photograph ; snap shot; picture

fracht (frákht) m. freight

fragment (frág-ment) m. frag-ment ; episode; excerpt;scrap

frak (frak) m. evening formal

framuga (fra-móo-ga) f. recess (structure); bay; embrasure

frant (frant) m. sly dog; knave

frasunek (fra-sóo-nek) m. worry; grief; sorrow; care; trouble

fraszka (frász-ka) f. trifle

frazes (fra-zes) m. platitude

frekwencja (fre-kvén-tsya) f. attendance ; turnout; frequency

frędzla (frándz-la) f. fringe

fresk (fresk) m. fresco
front (front) m. front ;face,etc
froterować (fro-te-ró-vach) v.
  rub ; polish ; wax (floors)
frunąć (froo-nównch) v. fly
  away ; fly about; flee
frymarczyć (fri-mar-chich) v.
  barter ; trade; traffic
fryzjer (friz-yer) m. barber;
  hairdresser ; beautician
fujara (foo-ya-ra) m. & f. all-
  thumbs; nincompoop; pan-pipe
fukać (foo-kach) v. scold
fundacja (foon-dáts-ya) f.
  foundation ; endowment
fundament (foon-da-ment) m.
  foundation; substructure
fundusz (foon-doosh) m. fund
funkcja (foonk-tsya) f.
  function; office ; duties
funt (foont) m. pound
fura (foo-ra) f. cart; wagon
furgon (foor-gon) m. truck
furia (foor-ya) f. fury; rage
furiat (foor-yat) m. madman
furman (foor-man) m. carter
furora (foo-ró-ra) f. sensation
furtka (foort-ka) f. gate
fusy (foo-si) pl. grounds
fuszer (foo-sher) m. bungler
futerał (foo-te-raw) m.
  (gun)case; holster
futro (foo-tro) n. fur
futryna (foo-tri-na) f. door-
  frame ; window-frame
futrzarz (foot-zhash) m.furrier
fuzja (fooz-ya) f. fusion;
  rifle ; shotgun
gabardyna (ga-bar-di-na) f.
  gabardine
gabinet (ga-bée-net) m. study;
  (ruling)cabinet; office
gablotka (ga-blot-ka)f.showcase
gad (gat) m. reptile;mean guy
gadać (ga-dach) v. talk; yak;
  prattle ; talk nonsense
gaduła (ga-doo-wa) m. clapper
gaj (gay) m. grove
gala (ga-la) f. gala
galanteria (ga-lan-ter-ya) f.
  haberdashery
galareta (ga-la-re-ta) f. jelly

galeria (ga-ler-ya) f. gallery
galimatias (ga-lee-mat-yas) m.
  gibberish; hotchpotch; mess
galon (ga-lon) m. gallon
galop (ga-lop) m. gallop; run
galwaniczny (gal-va-neech-ni)
  adj. m. galvanic ; voltaic
gałąź (ga-wównzh) f. branch
gałgan (gaw-gan) m. rag; rascal ; good-for-nothing;scamp
gałganiarz (gaw-ga-nash) m.
  ragtagman; ragpicker
gałka (gaw-ka) f. knob
gama (ga-ma) f. scale
gamoń (ga-moń) m. lout; oaf
ganek (ga-nek) m. balcony
gangrena (gan-gre-na) f.
  gangrene; depravity; corruption
ganić (ga-neech) v. blame
gapa (ga-pa) f. sucker
gapić się (ga-peech shań) v.
  gape; star-gaze ; moon; stare
gapie (ga-pye) pl. gapers
garaż (ga-rash) m. garage
garb (garb) m. hunch; hump
garbarnia (gar-bar-ña) f.
  tannery ; tan-yard
garbować (gar-bó-vach) v. tan
garbaty (gar-ba-ti) adj. m.
  hunch-backed; humpy; uneven
garbus (gar-boos) m.=garbaty
garbić (gár-beech) v. stoop
garderoba (gar-de-ro-ba) f.
  wardrobe; dressing-room
gardło (gard-wo) n. throat
gardłować (gard-wo-vach) v.
  v. talk big; clamor; cry for
gardłowy (gard-wo-vi) adj. m.
  guttural; punishable by death
gardzić (gár-dźheech)v. scorn;
  despise; have in contempt
gardziel (gar-dźhel) f. throat;
  fauces; choke; gorge; jaws
garnąć (gar-nównch) v. gather
garncarz (garn-tsash) m. potter
garnek (gar-nek) m. pot; potful
garnirować (gar-ñee-ro-vach) v.
  garnish; trim (a dress etc.)
garnitur (gar-ñee-toor) m. set;
  suit; suite; assortment
garnizon (gar-ñee-zon) m.
  garrison

garnuszek (gar-noo-shek) m. cup

garstka (garst-ka) f. handful

garsć (garshch) f. handful

gasic (ga-sheech) v. extinguish; quench ; put out;eclipse

gasnąć (gas-nownch) v. die out

gaśnica (gash-nee-tsa) f. fire-extinguisher

gastronomiczny (gas-tro-nomeech-ni) adj. m. gastronomic

gastryczny (gas-trich-ni) adj. m. gastric

gatunek (ga-too-nek) m. kind; quality; sort; class; species

gawęda (ga-van-da) f. chat

gawiedz (ga-vyedzh) f. mob; rabble ; populace; gaping crowd

gawron (ga-vron) m. rook

gaz (gas) m. gas; open throttle

gaza (ga-za) f. gauze

gazeciarz (ga-ze-chash) m. newspaperboy ; newsstand

gazeta (ga-ze-ta) f. newspaper

gazolina (ga-zo-lee-na) f. gasoline; gasolene: petrol

gazomierz (ga-zo-myesh) m. gas-meter

gazownia (ga-zov-na) f. gas-plant: gas works

gaźnik (gazh-neek) m. carburetor

gaża (ga-zha) f. wage; salary

gąbczasty (gownb-cha-sti) adj. m. spongy; squashy; mushy

gąbka (gownb-ka) f. sponge

gąsienica (gown-she-nee-tsa) f. caterpillar; band; track

gąsior (gown-shor) m. gander; jar; demijohn; ridge tile

gąszcz (gownshch) m. thicket

gbur (gboor) m. rude; boor

gburowaty (gboor-ro-va-ti) adj. m. boorish; rude ; churlish

gdakac (gda-kach) v. cackle; yak

gderac (dge-rach) v. grumble

gdy (gdi) conj. when; as; that

gdyby (gdi-bi) conj. if

gdyż (gdish) conj. for; because

gdzie (gdzhe) adv. conj. where

gdzie indziej(gdzhe-een-dzhey) adv. elsewhere

gdziekolwiek (gdzhe-kol-vyek) adv. anywhere ; wherever

gdzie niegdzie (gdzhe-neg-dzhe) adv. here and there; in places

gdzieś (gdzhesh) adv. somewhere ; somewhere round

gejzer (gey-zer) m. geyser

gen (gen) m. (biol) gene

genealogia (ge-ne-a-log-ya) f. genealogy; origin

generacja (ge-ne-rats-ya) f. generation

generalny (ge-ne-ral-ni) adj. m. general ; widespread

generał (ge-ne-raw) m. general

genetyczny (ge-ne-tich-ni) adj. m. genetic

geneza (ge-ne-za) f. origin; genesis ; birth

genialny (ge-nal-ni) adj. m. ingenious; genial ; great

geniusz (ge-nyoosh) m. genius

geodezja (ge-o-dez-ya) f. geodesy

geografia (ge-o-graf-ya) f. geography

geologia (ge-o-log-ya) f. geology

geometra (ge-o-met-ra) m. surveyor ; land surveyor

geometria (ge-o-metr-ya) f. geometry ; geometry book

georginia (ge-or-gee-na) f. dahlia

germański (ger-man-skee) adj. m. Germanic

gest (gest) m. gesture ;motion

gestykulowac (ges-ti-koo-lovach) v. gesticulate

getto (get-to) n. ghetto

gęba (gan-ba) f. mug; mouth; puss ; snout; muzzle; face

gęgac (gan-gach) v. cackle

gęś (gansh) f. goose

gęsl (ganshl) f. lute

gęstosc (gan-stoshch) f. density; thickness; closeness

gęstwina (gan-stvee-na) f. thicket; array; accumulation

giąc (gyownch)v. bow; bend

gibki (geeb-kee) adj. m. pliant; flexible; limber

giełda (ǵew-da) f. stock-
exchange; money-market
giez (ǵes) m. gadfly; breeze
giętki (ǵ ant-kee) adj. m.
flexible; nimble; elastic
gigant (gee-gant) m. giant
gilza (geel-za) f. (cartridge)
case; shell; cigarette tube
gimnastyczny (geem-nas-tich-
ni) adj. m. gymnastic
gimnazjum (geem-náz-yoom) n.
high-school; middle-school
ginąc (gee-nównch) v. perish
ginekolog (gee-ne-ko-log) m.
gynecologist
gips (geeps) m. gypsum
gitara (gee-tá-ra) f. guitar
glazura (gla-zoó-ra) f. glaze
gleba (glé-ba) f. soil
glejt (gléyt) m. safe-conduct
ględzić (glań-dźheech)v. talk-
through one's hat; talk-
nonsense;twaddle; blather
gliceryna (glee-ce-rí-na) f.
glycerin
glin (gleen) m. aluminum
glina (glee-na) f. clay; loam
glista (glées-ta) f. earthworm; ascaris; nema
glob (glop) m. globe; sphere
gładki (gwad-kee) adj. m. plain;
smooth; sleek;even; level;glib
gładzic (gwa-dźheech)v. smooth;
(put to death);mangle; stroke
głaskac (gwás-kach) v. caress;
fondle; stroke;pet; tickle
głaz (gwas) m. boulder; rock
głąb (gwównp) f, depth
głąb (gwównp) m. stalk
głębia (gwánb-ya) f. depth;
deep; interior; intensity
głęboki (gwań-bó-kee) adj. m.
deep; distant; remote; intense
głębokosć (gwań-bó-koshch) f.
depth; profundity; keenness
głodny (gwód-ni) adj. m. hungry
głodowac (gwo-do-vach) v.
starve; hunger; lay off food
głodzic (gwo-dźheech)v. starve
(somone); underfeed; deprive
głos (gwos) m. voice; sound;tone
głosowac (gwo-so-vach) v. vote

głosnik (gwósh-neek) m. loudspeaker;public-address system
głosno (gwósh-no) adv. loud
głosny (gwósh-ni) adj. m. loud
głowa (gwó-va) f. head ; chief
głowic się (gwo-veech shań) v.
beat one's brains out;puzzle
głod (gwoot) m. hunger; famine
głog (gwook) m. hawthorn
główka (gwoo-vka) f. pinhead;
knob; tip; top; boss; heading
głownodowodzący (gwoov-no-do-
vo-dzown-tsi) m. commander-
in-chief
głowny (gwoov-ni) adj. m.
main; predominant; foremost
głuchy (gwoó-khi) adj. m. deaf
głupi (gwoó-pee) adj. m. silly;
stupid; foolish; asinine
głupiec (gwoop-yets) m. dumb-
head; fool; idiot;loony; goof
głupota (gwoo-pó-ta) f. stupidity;imbecility; foolishness
głupstwo (gwoop-stwo) n.
nonsense; trifle; blunder
głuszec (gwoo-shets) m. grouse
gmach (gmakh) m. large building
gmatwac (gma-tvach) v. tangle;
embroil; mix up; complicate
gmerac (gme-rach) v. rummage
gmin (gmeen) m. populace
gmina (gmeé-na) f. county
subdivision ; parish
gnat (gnat) m. bone (slang)
gnębic (gnań-beech) v. oppress
gniady (gna-di) adj. m. bay
(horse); dark brown horse
gniazdo (gnaz-do) n. nest
gnic (gneech) v. rot; decay
gnida (gneéda) f. nit
gniesć (gneshch) v. squeeze
gniew (gnev) m. anger; wrath
gnieździc się (gneźh-dźheech
shań) v. nestle ; cluster
gnilny (gneel-ni) adj. m.
putrid; of rot; septic
gnoic (gno-eech) v. putrefy
gnojówka (gno-yoóv-ka) f.
liquid manure; manure pit
gnój (gnooy) m. manure; dung;
stinker (vulg.); lousy bum
gnusny (gnoósh-ni) adj. m.
sluggish; lazy; idle ; listless

godło (gód-wo) n. emblem
godność (gód-noshch) f. dignity; name; pride; self-esteem
godny (gód-ni) adj. m. worthy
gody (go-di) n. nuptials; mating
godzić (go-dzheech) v. reconcile; hire; square; engage
godzien (go-dzhen) adj. m. deserving ; worth; worthy
godzina (go-dzhee-na) f. hour
godziwy (go-dzhee-vi) adj. m. proper; suitable; just; fair
goić (go-eech) v. heal; cure
goleń (go-leń) m. shin-bone
golić (go-leech) v. shave
golonka (go-lon-ka) f. pig's feet dish ; knuckle
gołąb (go-wownp) m. pigeon
gołoledź (go-wó-ledzh) f. glazed frost ;frozen dew
gołosłowny (go-wo-swóv-ni) adj. m. unfounded; proofless; vain
goły (go-wi) adj. m. naked
gonić (go-ńeech) v. chase; hunt
goniec (go-ńets) m. messenger
gonitwa (go-ńeet-va) f. chase
gont (gont) m. shingle
gorąco (go-równ-tso) n. heat
gorący (go-równ-tsi) adj. m. hot; sultry; warm; hearty;lively
gorączka (go-równch-ka) f. fever; shakes; excitement; heat
gorczyca (gor-chi-tsa) f. mustard; charlock
gorętszy (go-rańt-shi) adj. m.hotter; fervent; intense
gorliwiec (gor-lee-vyets) m. zealot; ardent supporter
gorliwy (gor-lee-vi) adj. m. zealous; keen; eager; devout
gorset (gor-set) m. girdle
gorszy (gor-shi) adj. m. worse
gorszyć (gor-shich) v. demoralize; scandalize; shock;deprave
gorycz (go-rich) f. bitterness
goryl (go-ril) m. gorilla
gorzałka (go-zhaw-ka) f. brandy spirits ; booze; spirit
gorzec (go-zhech) v. be ablaze
gorzej (go-zhey) adv. worse
gorzelnia (go-zhel-ńa) f. distillery ; still
gorzki (gozh-kee) adj. n.bitter

gospoda (gos-pó-da) f. inn
gospodarczy (gos-po-dar-chi) adj. n. economic;farm; charring
gospodarka (gos-po-dar-ka) f. economy;housekeeping; farming
gospodarny (gos-po-dar-ni) adj. m. economical; thrifty
gospodarstwo (gos-po-dar-stvo) n. household; farm; possessions
gospodarz (gos-pó-dash) m. landlord; host ; farmer;manager
gospodyni (gos-po-di-ńee) f. landlady; hostess ; manageress
gosposia (gos-pó-sha) f. housekeeper; maid; servant
gościć (gosh-cheech) v. receive; entertain; treat; stay at
gościna (gosh-chee-na) f. visit; stay at sb house
gościnność (gosh-cheen-noshch) f. hospitality
gość (goshch) m. guest;caller
gościec (gósh-chets) m. gout; arthritis
gotować (go-tó-vach) v. cook; boil; get ready; prepare
gotowość (go-tó-voshch) f. readiness; willingness
gotowy (go-tó-vi) adj. m. ready ; done; complete;willing
gotówka (go-toóv-ka) f. cash
gotyk (gó-tik) m. Gothic
goździk (gózh-dzheek)m. carnation ; clove; gilly-flower
góra (goó-ra) f. mountain
góral (goó-ral) m. mountaineer
górnictwo (goor-ńeets-tvo) n. mining ; mining industry
górnik (goor-ńeek) m. miner
górnolotny (goor-no-lót-ni) adj. m. lofty ; soaring;gaudy
górny (goór-ni) adj. m. upper
górować (goó-ro-vach) v. prevail ; excel; dominate ; rise
górski (goór-skee) adj. m. mountainous ; mountain
górzysty (goo-zhis-ti) adj. m. hilly ; mountainous
gówniarz (goóv-ńash) m. (vulg.): shitass; whipster
gówno (goóv-no) m. shit (vulg.)
gra (gra) f. game ;sham; acting
grab (grap) m. hornbeam; hardbeam

grabarz (gra-bash) m. grave-digger;sexton; burying beetle

grabić (gra-beech) v. rake; plunder ; rob; sack; rake up

grabie (gra-bye) n. rake

grabież (gra-byesh) f. plunder

graca (gra-tsa) f. scraper

gracja (grats-ya) f. grace

gracować (gra-tsó-vach) v. scrape; rake; mix mortar

gracz (grach) m. player; gambler; double-dealer; sly fox

grać (grach) v. play; act; gamble ; pretend; pulsate

grad (grad) m. hail; volley

grafika (fra-fee-ka) f. graphic art ; graphics; art of writing

gram (gram) m. gram

gramatyka (gra-má-ti-ka) f. grammar; grammar book

gramofon (gra-mo-fon) m. record player; phonograph

gramolić się (gra-mo-leech shan) v. clamber;climb

granat (gra-nat) m. grenade

granatnik (gra-nát-ñeek) m. mortar ; howitzer

granatowy (gra-na-tó-vi) adj. m. navy blue ; of grenades

granda (gran-da) f. swindle

graniastosłup (gra-ña-stó-swoop) m. prism

granica (gra-ñee-tsa) f. boundary; limit; border; range

granit (gra-ñeet) m. granite

granulować (gra-noo-ló-vach) v. granulate

grań (grañ) f. (mountain) ridge; crest; edge; razor's edge

grasować (gra-so-vach) v. roam about; prowl; maraud; stalk

grat (grat) m. run down furniture (or man) ; crock; trash

gratis (gra-tees) adv. free of charge; something given free

gratka (grat-ka) f. windfall

gratulacja (gra-too-láts-ya) f. congratulations;felicitation

grawer (gra-ver) m. engraver

grawitacja (gra-vee-táts-ya) f. gravitation

grdyka (grdí-ka) f. Adam's apple

grecki (gréts-kee) adj. m. Greek

gremialnie (grem-yal-ñe) adv. in-a-mass; completely;altogether

grobla (gró-la) f. dike; dam

grobowiec (gro-bóv-yets) m. tomb ; sepulchre ;family vault

grobowy (gro-bó-vi) adj. m. grave ; deathly; gloomy;dismal

groch (grokh) m. pea; pea plant

grom (grom) m. thunderclap

gromada (gro-má-da) f. crowd; throng; community; team

gromadzić (gro-má-dźheech) v. amass; hoard; gather;attract

gromić (gro-meech) v. storm; rout ; reprimand; defeat

grono (gro-no) n. bunch of grapes ; cluster; group;body

gronostaj (gro-nó-stay) m. ermine

grosz (grosh) m. penny (copper)

groszek (gró-shek) m, green pea(s) ; spotted pattern

grot (grot) m. dart; spike

grota (gro-ta) f. grotto; care

groza (gro-za) f. dread; horror

grozić (gro-źheech)v. threaten

groźba (gróźh-ba) f. threat

grób (groop) m. grave : tomb

gród (groot) m. (fortified)town

gródź (groodźh)f. bulkhead

grubiański (groob-yań-skee) adj. m. rude ; coarse; obscene

grubość (groo-boshch) f. thickness ; girth; size; grist

gruby (groo-by) adj. m. thick; fat; stout; big;low-pitched

gruchotać (groo-kchó-tach) v. shatter ; batter; rattle;crash

gruczoł (groo-chow) m. gland

gruda (groo-da) f. lump; clod

grudzień (groo-dźheñ) m. December

grunt (groont) m. ground; soil

grupa (gro´o-pa) f. group ; class

grusza (groo-sha) f. pear-tree

gruz (groos) m. rubble ; ruins

gruzeł (groo-zew) m. clot

gruzy (groo-zi) pl. debris

gruźlica (grooźh-lee-tsa) f. tuberculosis; consumption

gryka (gri-ka) f. buckwheat

grymas (gri-mas) m. grimace

grypa (gri-pa) f. flu;influenza

grysik (gri-sheek) m. grits

gryzoń (gri-zoń) m. rodent

gryźć (griżhćh) v. bite;torment

grzać (gzhać) v. warm;thrash

grządka (gzhownd-ka) f. flower bed ; patch ; (hen-)roost

grząść (gzhownshćh) v. wade

grząski (gzhown-skee) adj. m. quaggy; slimy; slushy; miry

grzbiet (gzhbyet) m. back; spine ; ridge; butt; edge;rib

grzebać (gzhe-baćh) v. bury; rummage; dig;rake up; fumble

grzebień (gzhe-byeń) m. comb; crest of a wave; ridge;teaser

grzech (gzhekh) m. sin; fault

grzechotka (gzhe-khot-ka) f. rattle; flapper; clapper

grzechotnik (gzhe-khot-ńeek) m. rattlesnake

grzeczność (gzhech-noshćh) f. politeness; favor; attentions

grzęznąć (gzhanz-nownćh) v. get stuck;wade; flounder;sink

grzmiący (gzhmyown-tsi) adj. m. thundering; booming;fulminatory

grzmot (gzhmot) m. thunder; hag

grzyb (gzhip) m. mushroom; fungus; snuff

grzywa (gzhi-va) f. mane

grzywna (gzhiv-na) f. fine

gubernator (goo-ber-na-tor) m. governor(general)

gubić (goo-beećh) v. loose;ruin

gula (goo-la) f. knob; bump

gulasz (goo-lash) m. meat soup

gulgotać (gool-go-taćh) v. gurgle; bubble; gobble

guma (goo-ma) f. rubber

gumno (goom-no) n. barn (yard)

gust (goost) m. taste; palate

guz (goos) m. bump; tumor

guzdrać się (gooz-draćh śhań) v. dawdle; dally; waste time;lag

gwałcić (gvaw-ćheećh) v. rape; violate; compel; coerce;force

gwałt (gvawt) m. rape; outrage

gwałtowny (gvaw-tov-ni) adj. m. 1. outrageous 2. urgent

gwar (gvar) m. hum; noise

gwara (gva-ra) f. dialect; slang ; jargon; lingo; cant; 'patter ; colloquial language

gwarancja (gva-ran-tsya) f. warranty; guarantee; pledge

gwardia (gvar-dya) f. guard

gwarny (gvar-ni) adj. m. noisy

gwarzyć (gva-zhićh) v. chat

gwiazda (gvyaz-da) f. star

gwint (gveent)m.thread (mech.)

gwintować (gveen-to-vaćh) v. cut thread ; tap; rifle

gwizd (gveezt) m. whistle

gwoli (gvo-lee) conj. for the sake of ; because of;in order

gwóźdź (gwoożhdżh) m. nail ⌐to

gzyms (gzims) m. molding cornice; mantelpiece

habit (kha-bit) m. monk's frock ; habit ; nun's frock

haczyk (kha-chik) m. small hook ; barb; snag; catch

hafciarka (haf-char-ka) f. embroideress

haft (khaft) m. embroidery

haftka (khaft-ka) f. clasp

hak (khak) m. hook ; clamp

hala (kha-la) f. (sports) hall

halka (khal-ka) f. petticoat

halny wiatr (hal-ni vyatr) Tatra wind (foehn)

halucynacja (kha-loo-tsi-nats-ya) f. hallucination

hałas (kha-was) m. noise; din

hałasować (kha-wa-so-vaćh) v. make noise ; be noisy

hałastra (kha-was-tra) f. mob; rabble; riff-raff; ragtag mob

hałaśliwy (kha-wash-lee-vi) adj. m. noisy ; loud; rowdy

hamak (kha-mak) m. hammock

hamować (kha-mo-vaćh) v.apply brakes; restrain; hamper;curb

hamulec (kha-moo-lets) m. brake

hamulec ręczny (kha-moo-lets rańch-ni) handbrake

handel (khandel) m. commerce

handlarz (khand-lash) m. mer-chant;shopkeeper; peddler

handlować (khan-dlo-vaćh) v. trade; deal; be in business

hangar (khan-gar) m. hangar
haniebny (kha-ńeb-ni) adj. m.
  disgraceful; dirty; foul; vile
hańba (khań-ba) f. disgrace
hańbić (khań-beech) v. disgrace
haracz (khá-rach) m. tribute
harcerstwo (khar-tser-stvo) n.
  scouting
harcerz (khár-tsesh) m. boy
  scout
hardy (khá-rdy) adj. m. haughty
harfa (khár-fa) f. harp
harmider (khar-mee-der) m.
  hullabaloo; clatter; din; row
harmonia (khar-moń-ya) f. harmony; accordion; harmonics
harować (kha-ró-vach) v. toil
harpun (khár-poon) m. harpoon
hart (khart) m. fortitude;
  hardness; sternness;temper;grit
hartować (khar-tó-vach) v.
  temper; harden; anneal;quench
hasać (kha-sach) v. frisk;
  frolic; romp;gambol; dance
hasło (kha-swo) n. password
haubica (khau-bee-tsa) f.
  howitzer
haust (khaust) m. gulp; swig
hazard (khá-zard) m. risk;
  hazard; the gaming table
heban (khe-ban) m. ebony
hebel (khé-bel) m. plane
hebrajski (kheb-ráy-skee) adj.
  m. Hebrew
heca (khé-tsa) f. fun; fuss
hegemonia (khe-ge-moń-ya) f.
  hegemony
hej (khey) excl.: hey! ho!
hejnał (khéy-naw) m. trumpet-
  call; bugle-call; reveille
hektar (khék-tar) m. hectare
hełm (khewm) m. helmet; dome
hemoroidy (khe-mo-róy-di) pl.
  piles;hemorrhoids
hen (khen) adv. far; away
herb (kherp) m. coat-of-arms
herbaciarnia (kher-ba-chár-ńa)
  f. teahouse
herbata (kher-bá-ta) f. tea
herbatnik (kher-bát-ńeek) m.
  biscuit
heretyk (khe-ré-tik) m. heretic

herezja (khe-réz-ya) f. heresy
hermetyczny (kher-me-tich-ni)
  adj. m. air-tight; hermetic
heroiczny (khe-ro-eech-ni) adj.
  m. heroic
heroizm (khe-ró-eezm) m. heroism
herszt (khersht) m. ringleader
het (khet) adv. far; away
hetman (khét-man) m. commander
hiacynt (khyá-tsint) m.hyacinth
hiena (khee-é-na) f. hyena
hierarchia (khye-rár-khya) f.
  hierarchy
hieroglif (khye-ró-gleef) m.
  hieroglyph; illegible writing
higiena (khee-ge-na) f. hygiene;
  sanitation; hygienics
hinduski (kheen-doos-kee) adj.
  m. Hindu
hiperbola (khee-per-bó-la) f.
  hyperbola; hyperbole
hipnotyczny (kheep-no-tich-ni)
  adj. m. hypnotic; mesmeric
hipochondryk(khee-po-khon-drik)
  m. hypochondriac
hipokryta (khee-po-krí-ta) m.
  hypocrite; pretender;dissembler
hipopotam (khee-po-pó-tam) m.
  hippopotamus
hipoteka (khee-po-téka) f.title;
  mortgage; records office
hipoteza (khee-po-té-za) f.
  hypothesis; assumption
histeria (khees-ter-ya) f.
  hysteria; hysterical fit
historia (khees-tór-ya) f. story; history; affair; show;fuss
hiszpański (kheesh-pań-skee)
  adj. m. Spanish
hitlerowiec (kheet-le-ró-vyets)
  m. hitlerite
hodować (kho-dó-vach) v. breed
hodowca (kho-dov-tsa) m. breeder; grower; farmer;cultivator
hojny (khóy-ni) adj. m. generous; lavish; liberal; profuse
hokej (khó-key) m. hockey
holenderski (kho-len-der-skee)
  adj. m. Dutch
holować (kho-lo-vach) v. tow;
  haul; drag; tug; haul; truck

hołd (khowd) m. tribute
hołota (kho-wó-ta) f. riffraff
honor (kho-nor) m. honor
honorarium (kho-no-ıar-yoom)
  n. fee; honorarium
horda (khor-da) f. horde; throng
horrendalny (kho-ren-dal-ni)
  adj. m. awful; horrible
hormon (khor-mon) m. hormone
horoskop (kho-ros-kop) m.
  horoscope ; prophesy ;prospect
horyzont (kho-ri-zont) m.hor-
  izon; vistas; prospects
hotel (kho-tel) m. hotel
hoży (kho-zhi) adj. m. brisk;
  handsome; comely; fresh
hrabia (khrab-ya) m. count
hrabina (khra-bee-na) f.
  countess
hrabianka (khra-byan-ka) f.
  countess (miss)
hrabstwo (khrab-stwo) n. county
hreczka (khrech-ka) f. buckwheat
hreczkosiej (khrech-ko-shey)
  m.country bumpkin
hubka (khoob-ka) f. tinder
huczeć (khoo-chech) v. roar
hufnal (khoof-nal) m. horse-
  shoe nail
huk (khook) m. bang; roar
hulać (khoo-lach) v. carouse;
  riot; make merry; run wild
hulajnoga (khoo-lay-no-ga) f.
  scooter (without motor)
hulaka (khoo-la-ka) m. carous-
  er; debaucher; rioter; rake
hulanka (khoo-lan-ka) f. riot;
  debauch ; junket: carouse;revel
hultaj (khool-tay) m. libertine;
  rascal; rogue
humanista (khoo-ma-nees-ta) m.
  humanist ; classical scholar
humanitarny (khoo-ma-nee-tar-
  ni) m. humane ; humanitarian
humor (khoo-mor) m. humor
hura (khoo-ra) f. hurrah !
  cheers ! long live !
huragan (khoo-ra-gan) m. hurricane ; cyclone
hurmem (khoor-mem) adv. in
  swarms ; in a mass; altogether

hurt (khoort) m. wholesale
humus (khoo-moos) m. humus
husarz (khoo-sash) m. Polish
  winged-armor cavalryman (hist.)
hustać (khoosh-tach) v. swing;
  rock; dandle; toss up and down
hustawka (khoosh-tav-ka) f.
  swing ; seesaw ; swing boat
huta (khoo-ta) f. metal or
  glass mill ; smelting works
hutnik (khoot-neek) m. metal
  or glass(man)worker ;metalurgist
hycel (khi-tsel) m. dogcatcher;
  rascal ; good for nothing
hydrant (khid-rant) m. hydrant
hydraulika (khi-drau-lee-ka)
  f. hydraulics ; plumbing
hymn (himn) m.anthem; hymn
i (ee) conj. and; also; too
ichtiologia (eekh-tyo-log-ya)
  f. ichthyology
idea (ee-de-a) f. idea ; aim
idealista (ee-de-a-lees-ta) m.
  idealist ; dreamer; visionary
idealny (ee-de-al-ni) adj. m.
  ideal ; perfect; visionary
identyczny (ee-den-tich-ni)
  adj. m. identical ; similar
ideologia (ee-de-o-log-ya) f.
  ideology ; world view
idiosynkrazja (ee-dyo-sin-kráz-
  ya) f. idiosyncrasy
idiota (ee-d-yó-ta) m. idiot
idiotka (eed-yot-ka) f. idiot
iglaste drzewo (ee-glas-te
  dzhe-vo) m. coniferous tree
iglica (eeg-lee-tsa) f. spire
igła (eeg-wa) f. needle
ignorancja (eeg-no-ran-tsya) f.
  ignorance; lack of knowledge
igrać (eeg-rach) v. play; trifle
igrzysko (ee-gzhis-ko) n.
  spectacle (games); contest
ikra (eek-ra) f. spawn; roe
ile (ee-le) adv. how much
ilekroć (ee-le-kroch) adv.
  every time; whenever ; when
iloczas (ee-lo-chas) m. quantity (of a vowel or syllable)
iloczyn (ee-lo-chin) m. (multiplication) product
iloraz (ee-lo-raz) m. (division)
  quotient

ilościowy (ee-losh-cho-vi)adj.
m. quantitative; numerical
ilość (ee-loshch) f. quantity
iluminacja (ee-loo-mee-nats-ya)
f. illumination; floodlight
ilustracja (ee-loos-trats-ya)
f. illustration; figure;picture
iluzja (ee-looz-ya) f. illusion
ił (eew) m. loam
im (eem) conj. the more...
imać (ee-mach) v. size upon
imadło (ee-mad-wo) n . (shop)
vice ; chuck; holder ; vise
imaginacja (ee-ma-gee-nats-ya)
f. imagination; empty fancy
imbir (eem-beer) m. ginger
imbryk (eem-brik) m. teapot
imieniny (ee-mye-nee-ni) n.
name-day; name-day party
imiennie (ee-myen-ne) adv. by
name; personally; individually
imiennik (ee-myen-neek) m.
namesake
imiesłów (ee-mye-swoov) m.
participle
imię (ee-myan) n. name (given)
imigracja (ee-mee-grats-ya) f.
immigration; the immigrants
imigrant (ee-mee-grant) m.
immigrant;foreign settler
imigrować (ee-mee-gro-vach) v.
immigrate;settle in a new land
imitacja (ee-mee-tats-ya) f.
imitation; counterfeit; fake
imitować (ee-mee-to-vach) v.
imitate; mimic; simulate
impas (eem-pas) m. deadlock
imperialista (eem-per-ya-lees-
ta) m. imperialist
imperium (eem-per-yoom) n.
empire
impertynent (eem-per-ti-nent) m.
arrogant; pert,impertinent man
impet (eem-pet) m. impetus
imponować (eem-po-no-vach) v.
impress; impose on sb; dazzle
import (eem-port) m. import
impregnować (eem-preg-no-vach)
v. impregnate; make waterproof
impreza (eem-pre-za) f. enterprise; spectacle; show; stunt
improwizować (eem-pro-vee-zo-
vach) v. improvise; extemporize

impuls (eem-pools) m. impulse
inaczej (ee-na-chey) adv. otherwise; differently; unlike
inauguracja (ee-na-goo-rats-ya)
f. inauguration; opening
inaugurować (ee-na-goo-ro-vach)
v. inaugurate; initiate
in blanko (een-blan-ko) adv.
in blank ; blank,check
incydent (een-tsi-dent) m.
incident; happening; event
indagacja (een-da-gats-ya) f.
investigation; questioning
indeks (een-deks) m. index
indemnizacja (een-dem-nee-
zats-ya) f. indemnity
indukcja (een-dook-tsya) f.
induction; generalized reasoning
indyk (een-dik) m. turkey
indyczka (een-dich-ka) f.
turkey-hen
indywidualny (een-di-vee-doo-
al-ni) adj. m. individual
inercja (een-erts-ya) f. inertia ; inaction; inertness
infekcja (een-fekts-ya) f.
infection; contamination
infiltracja (een-feel-trats-ya)
f. infiltration
inflacja (een-flats-ya) f.
inflation
influenza (een-floo-en-za) f.
influenza ; flu ; grippe
informacja (een-for-mats-ya) f.
information ; intelligence;news
informacyjny (een-for-ma-tsiy-
ni) adj. m. information (office)
informować (een-for-mo-vach) v.
inform ; instruct; post up
ingerencja (een-ge-ren-tsya) f.
interference; meddling
inhalacja (een-kha-lats-ya) f.
inhalation; breathing in
inicjał (ee-neets-yaw) m. initial (letter); ornate letter
inicjator (ee-neets-ya-tor) m.
originator ; mover ; founder
inicjatywa (ee-neets-ya-ti-va)
f. initiative; enterprise
inkasować (een-ka-so-vach) v.
collect (money); get a blow
inklinacja (een-klee-nats-ya)
f. inclination ; liking

inkwizycja (een-kvee-zíts-ya)
f. inquisition ; investigation
innowacja (een-no-vats-ya) f.
innovation ; novelty
innowierca (een-no-vyer-tsa)
m.dissenter; heretic
inny (eén-ni) adj. m. other;
different; another (one)
inscenizacja (een-stse-ńee-záts-
ya) f. putting on stage
inspekcja (een-spék-tsya) f.
inspection; review; inspectorate
inspekty (een-spék-ti) n. hotbed ; glass covered frame
inspiracja (een-spee-ráts-ya)
f. inspiration ; breathing in
instalacja (een-sta-láts-ya) f.
installation ; plumbing, etc
instalator (een-sta-la-tor) m.
plumber; fitter; electrician
instrukcja (een-stróok-tsya)
f. instruction ; order;training
instrument (een-stroo-ment) m.
instrument; tool; deed;appliance
instynkt (eén-stinkt) m. instinct ; aptitude; knack
instytucja (een-sti-toots-ya) f.
institution ; establishment
insynuacja (een-si-noo-áts-ya)
f. insinuation; innuendo
integralny (een-te-grál-ni)
adj. m. integral; whole; entire
intelekt (een-té-lekt) m. intellect; intelligence; mind
intelektualista (een-te-lek-
too-a-lées-ta) m. intellectual
inteligencja (een-te-lee-gén-
tsya) f.intelligensia ; intelligence;(quick)understanding
inteligentny (een-te-lee-gén-
tni) adj. m. intelligent
intencja (een-tén-tsya) f. intention ; purpose; view;finality
intensywny (een-ten-siv-ni)
adj. m. intensive; strenuous
interes (een-té-res) m. interest; business;store; matter
interesowny (een-te-re-sów-ni)
adj. m. selfish; greedy
interesujący (een-te-re-soo-
yówn-tsi) adj. m. interesting
internat (een-tér-nat) m. boarding school

interpretacja (een-ter-pre-
táts-ya) f. interpretation
interwencja (een-ter-vén-tsya)
f. intervention ;interference
intratny (een-trát-ni) adj. m.
lucrative; profitable ;paying
introligator (een-tro-lee-gá-
tor) m. bookbinder
intruz (eén-troos) m. intruder
intryga (een-trí-ga)f. plot;
intrigue ; machination
intuicja (een-too-eéts-ya) f.
intuition ; insight; feeling
intuicyjny (een-too-ee-tsiý-ni)
adj. m. intuitive
inwalida (een-va-leé-da) m.
invalid; disabled (soldier)
inwazja (een-váz-ya) f. invasion
inwencja (een-vén-tsya) f. in-
ventiveness; invention
inwentarz (een-vén-tash) m.
inventory; stock ; list
inwestycja (een-ves-tits-ya)
f. investment ; capital outlay
inżynier (een-zhi-ńer) m.
engineer (with college degree)
inżynieria (een-zhi-ńer-ya) f.
engineering
ircha (eér-kha) f. suede-
leather; chamois ; shammy
irlandzki(eer-lańdz-kee) adj.
Irish
irys (ee-ris) m. iris
ironia (ee-ro-ńya) f. irony
irygacja (ee-ri-gáts-ya) f.
irrigation ; watering
irytacja (ee-ri-táts-ya) f.
irritation ; vexation; chafe
iskać (eésk-ach) v. v. seek
lice; cleanse of vermin
iskra (eés-kra) f. spark
istnieć (eést-ńech) v. exist
istnienie (eest-ńé-ńe) n.
existence ;being; entity
istny (eést-ni) adj. m. real;
veritable ;downright; sheer
istota (ees-tó-ta) f. being ;
essence ; gist; sum; entity
istotny (ees-tót-ni) adj. m.
real; substantial ; vital
istotnie (ees-tót-ńe) adv.
indeed; truly ; really;in fact
iście (eésh-che) adv. indeed;
truly ; really ; in truth

iść (eeśhćh) v. go; walk
izba (eéz-ba) f. room; chamber
izba handlowa (eéz-ba khan-
dló-va) f. Chamber of Commerce
izolacja (ee-zo-láts-ya) f.
isolation; insulation; seal
izolator (ee-zo-lá-tor) m. insu-
lator; non-conductor
izolacyjna taśma (ee-zo-la-tsiy-
na táśh-ma) f. insulating tape
izoterma (ee-zo-ter-ma) f. iso-
therm;line of equal temperature
izotop (ee-zo-top) m. isotope
izraelicki (eez-ra-e-léets-kee)
adj. m. Israeli; of Israel
izraelita (eez-ra-e-lee-ta) m.
Israelite; citizen of Izrael
iż (eezh) conj. that(literary)
iżby (eézh-bi) conj.m. in order
that; in order to; lest
ja (ya) pron. I;(indecl.):self
jabłecznik (yab-wech-ńeek) m.
apple cider; apple pie
jabłko (yáp-ko) n. apple
jabłoń (yá-bwoń) f. apple tree
jacht (yakht) m. yacht
jachtklub (yákht-kloob) m.
yacht club
jad (yat) m. venom; poison
jadalnia (ya-dál-ńa) f. dining-
room; mess; mess-hall
jadalny (ya-dál-ni) adj. m.
eatable; edible; dining-
jadło (yád-wo) n. food;edibles
jadłodajnia (ya-dwo-dáy-na) f.
restaurant; eating house
jadłospis (yad-wó-spees) m.
menu; bill of fare
jaglana kasza (yag-lá-na ká-
sha) f. millet-groats
jaglica (yag-lee-tsa) f.
trachoma; viral eye infection
jagnię (yag-ńań) n. lamb
jagoda (ya-gó-da) f. berry
jajko (yáy-ko) n. egg(small)
jajo (yá-yo) n. egg; ovum
jajko na twardo(yáy-ko na twar-
do) hard-boiled egg
jajko na miękko(yáy-ko na myáń-
ko) soft-boiled egg
jajecznica (ya-yech-ńee-tsa) f.
scrambled eggs

jajnik (yáy-ńeek) m. ovary
jak (yak) adv. how;as;if; than
jakby (yák-bi) adv. as if; if
jakgdyby (yak-gdi-bi) adv.
as if; seemingly; sort of
jaka (yá-ka) pron. f. what;
which; f. jacket
jaki (yá-kee) pron. m. what;
which one? that;some; like
jakie (yá-ke) pron. n. what;
which=jaki(fem.& neuter)
jakiś (yak-eeśh) pron. some
jakkolwiek (yak-kól-vyek) conj.
though: pron. somehow;anyhow
jakkolwiek (yak-kól-vyek) adv.
somehow; anyhow; however
jako (yá-ko) adv. as;by way of
jako tako(yá-ko tá-ko) adv.
so-so; tolerably well
jakoś (yá-kosh) adv. somehow
jakość (ya-kośhćh) f. quality
jakościowo (ya-kośh-ćhó-vo)
adv. m. qualitatively
jakże (yák-zhe) pron. how;sure
jałmużna (yaw-moózh-na) f.
alms; charity;(hist.endowment)
jałowcówka (ya-wov-tsoóv-ka) f.
gin; juniper-flavored vodka
jałowiec (ya-wó-vyets) m. juni-
per(Juniperus)
jałowiec (ya-wó-vyećh) v. grow-
sterile; grow unproductive
jałowy (ya-wó-vi) adj. m.
barren;sterile;arid;aseptic
jałówka (ya-woóv-ka) f. heifer
jama (yá-ma) f. pit; hole; den;
cavity; cave; burrow; hollow
jamnik (yam-ńeek) f. dachshund
jankes (yán-kes) m. Yankee
Japończyk (ya-poń-chik) m.
Japanese
japoński (ya-poń-skee) adj. m.
Japanese; of Japan
jar (yar) m. canyon; ravine
jarmark (yár-mark) m. fair
jarosz (yá-rosh) m. vegetarian
jarski (yár-skee) adj. m.
vegetarian; meatless
jary (yá-ri) adj. robust; vigorous; hale; spring-
jarzębiak (ya-zhań-byak) m.
sorb brandy; rowan-berry vodka

jarzębina (ya-zhȧn-bee-na) f.
  sorb tree; rowan;rowan berry
jarzmo (yȧzh-mo) n. yoke
jarzyć (yȧ-zhić) v. sparkle;
  glitter; glow; shimmer
jarzyna (ya-shi-na) f. vegetable ; dish of vegetables
jasełka (ya-sew-ka) pl. crib;
  Nativity play; créche
jasiek (yȧ-shek) m. little
  pillow ; bean; beans
jaskinia (yas-kee-ña) f. cave
jaskiniowiec (yas-kee-ño-vyets)
  m. cave dweller; cave man
jaskółka (yas-koow-ka) f.
  swallow; martin; harbinger
jaskrawy (yas-kra-vi) adj. m.
  glowing ; showy ; vivid;extreme
jasno (yȧs-no) adv. clearly;
  brightly ; cheerfully;plainly
jasny (yȧs-ny) adj. m. clear;
  bright ; light; shining;noble
jasnowidz (yas-no-veets) m.
  clairvoyant ; cristal gazer;seer
jastrząb (yas-tzhȯwnp) m. fal-
  kon; hawk; goshawk
jaszczyk (yash-chik) m. muni-
  tion box; ammunition trailer
jaśmin (yaśh-meen) m. jasmine
jaśnieć (yaśh-ñech) v. shine;
  sparkle; radiate; gleam; pale
jatka (yȧt-ka) f. shambles;
  butcher's shop ; massacre
jatki (yȧt-kee) pl. shambles
jaw (yav) m. reality;expose
jawić (yȧ-veech) v. appear;show
jawny (yav-ni) adj. m. evident;
  public ; open; notorious;sheer
jawor (ya-vor) m. plane tree;
  maple; sycamore;sycamore wood
jaz (yas) m. weir ; milldam
jazda (yȧz-da) f. ride ;driving
jaźń (yȧzhñ) f. ego; self;
  the I ; the inner man ; psyche
jąć (yowñch) v. seize; begin
jądro (yowñ-dro) n. nucleus;
  testicle ; kernel; core
jąkać (yowñ-kach) v. stutter
jątrzyć (yowñ-tzhich) v. irritate; fester ;vex; embitter
jechać (yé-khach) v. ride;drive
jeden (yé-den) num. one; some

jedenaście (ye-de-nash-che)
  num. eleven
jedlina (yed-lee-na) f. fir
  grove; fir and spruce branches
jednać (yéd-nach) v. conciliate
jednak (yéd-nak) conj. however;
  yet; still;but; after all;though
jednaki (yed-nȧ-kee) adj. m.
  identical; similar; equal;alike
jedno (yéd-no) n. num. one; one-
jednocześnie (yed-no-cheśh-ñe)
  adv. simultaneously; also
jednoczyć (yed-no-chich) v.
  unify; merge; join; unite
jednogłośnie (yed-no-gwośh-ñe)
  adv. unanimously; in chorus
jednokrotnie (yed-no-krot-ñe)
  adv. one time; once
jednostka (yed-nost-ka) f. unit;
  individual;entity;measure;digit
jedność (yéd-nośhch) f. unity
jedwab (yéd-vab) m. silk
jedwaczka (ye-di-nȧch-ka) f.
  only daughter
jedynak (ye-di-nak) m. only son
jedynie (ye-di-ñe) adv. only;
  merely; solely; nothing but
jedyny (ye-di-ni) adj. m. the
  only one ; the sole; unique
jedzenie (ye-dze-ñe) n. meat;
  food; victuals; feed; eats
jemioła (ye-myo-wa) mistletoe
jeleń (ye-leñ) m. stag; deer
jelito (ye-lee-to) n. intestine;
  bowel ; gut
jełczeć (yew-chech) v. grow-
  rancid :become rancid
jeniec (ye-ñets) m. captive
jerzyna (ye-zhi-na) f. blackberry
jesień (ye-sheñ) f. autumn;
  fall; the fall of the leaf
jesienny (ye-shen-ni) adj. m.
  autumnal; of autumn
jesion (ye-shon) m. ash tree
jesionka (ye-śhon-ka) f. fall
  overcoat; light overcoat
jesiotr (ye-śhotr) m. sturgeon
jestestwo (yes-tés-tvo) m.
  being ; nature; creature
jeszcze (yesh-che) adv. still;
  besides; more; yet; way back

jeść (yeshch) v. eat; feed sb
jeśli (yesh-lee) conj. if
jezdnia (yézd-ña) f. roadway
jezuita (ye-zoo-ee-ta) m. Jesuit: member of Jesuit Order
jeździec (yeżh-dżhets) m.
horseman; rider; equestrian
jeż (yesh) m. porcupine
jeżdżenie (yezh-dzhé-ñe) n.
riding; driving; tyrannizing
jeżeli (ye-zhé-lee) conj. if
jeżyc się (yé-zhich shan) v.
bristle up; stand on end
jeżyna (ye-zhi-na) f. blackberry; blackberry bush;bramble
jęczec (yań-chech) v. moan;
groan; wail; whine;complain
jęczmień (yańch-myeñ) m. barley
jędrny (yañdr-ni) adj. m. firm;
robust; strong; terse; pithy
jędza (yań-dza) f. witch; shrew
jęk (yank) m. groan; moan; wail
jęknąc (yank-nownch) v. moan;
groan; whine; bellyache(once)
język (yań-zik) m. tongue
jod (yod) m. iodine
jodła (yód-wa)f.fir tree; spruce
jodyna (yo-dí-na) f. tincture
of iodine; iodine
jon (yon) m. ion
jowialny (yo-vyál-ni) adj. m.
jovial; debonair; genial
jubiler (yoo-bee-ler) m. jeweler (store or profession)
jubileusz (yoo-bee-lé-oosh) m.
jubilee; annversary
jucht (yoo-kht) m. Russian
leather; water-proof leather
juczny koń (yooch-ni koñ) adj.
m. pack-horse; beast of burden
judzić (yoo-dżheech)v.instigate
juki (yoo-kee) pl. packsaddle
junak (yoo-nak) m. brave; swaggerer; dashing fellow
jurysdykcja (yoo-ris-dik-tsya)
f. jurisdiction;legal authority
juta (yoo-ta) f. jute;jute plant
jutro (yoo-tro) adv. tomorrow
jutrzejszy (yoo-tshey-shi) adj.
m. tomorrow's ; future
jutrzenka (yoo-tzhén-ka) f.
day-break; morning star; dawn

już (yoozh) conj. already;
at any moment; by now;no more
juzci (yoożh-chee) conj. of
course; certainly;sure thing!
kabalarka (ka-ba-lar-ka) f.
fortune teller (by cards)
kabała (ka-bá-wa) f. cabbala
kabaret (ka-bá-ret) m. cabaret
kabel (ká-bel) m. cable
kabestan (ka-bé-stan) m. cap-
stan; winch; windlass
kabina (ka-bee-na) f. cabin
kabłąk (kab-wownk) m. bow;hoop
kabotyn (ka-bo-tin) m. poser;
buffoon; second-rate actor
kabriolet (ka-bryó-let) m.
convertible car; gig
kabza (káb-za) f. purse
kac (kats) m. hangover
kacerz (ká-tsesh) m. heretic
kacet (ká-tset) m. Nazi concentration camp
kaczka (kách-ka) f. duck
kaczor (ká-chor) m. drake
kadłub (kád-woop) m. trunk;
hull; fuselage; framework
kadra (kád-ra) f. staff; cadre
kadzić (ká-dżheech)v. incense;
flatter; fart (vulg.)
kadzidło (ka-dżheed-wo)n.
incense; fragrance;frankincense
kadź (kadżh) f. tub; tubful
kafar (ká-far) m. piledriver
kafel (ká-fel) m. tile (ceramic)
kaftan (káf-tan) m. jacket
kaftan bezpieczeństwa (káf-tan
bez-pye-cheñ-stva) m. straight
jacket ;"waistcoat"
kaftanik (kaf-tá-ñeek) m. bodice; vest;jacket; caftan
kaganiec (ka-gá-ñets) m. muzzle;
torch ; oil lamp; lamp; cresset
kajać się (káy-ach shañ) v.
repent; confess with contrition
kajak (ká-yak) m. kayak;canoe
kajdany (kay-dá-ni) pl. hand-
cuffs; shackles; chains; bonds
kajuta (ka-yoo-ta) f. ship-
cabin ; living quarter at sea
kajzerka (kay-zer-ka) f. fancy
roll of bread ; kaiser roll
kakao (ka-ká-o) n. cacao

kaktus (kąk-toos) m. cactus
kalać (ká-lach) v. pollute;
 foul up; stain;befoul; sully
kalafior (ka-lá-fyor) m. cauliflower ; form of snow
kalarepa (ka-la-ré-pa) f.
 turnip-cabbage; kohlrabi
kalectwo (ka-léts-tvo) n. disability; lameness; cripplehood
kaleczyć (ka-le-chich) v. wound;
 mutilate; hurt; injure;cripple
kalejdoskop (ka-ley-dós-kop) m.
 kaleidoscope; medley;miscellany
kaleka (ka-le-ka) m; f. cripple
kalendarz (ka-lén-dash) m.
 calendar; almanach
kalesony (ka-le-só-ni) pl.
 underware;drawers;under pants
kalina (ka-lee-na) f. guelder-
 rose; cranberry shrub (tree)
kalka (kál-ka) f. carbon paper
kalkulacja (kal-koo-láts-ya) f.
 calculation; computation
kalkulować (kal-koo-ló-vach) v.
 calculate; compute; work out
kaloria (ka-lór-ya), f. calorie
kaloryfer (ka-lo-rí-fer) m.
 radiator; steam heater; heater
kalosz (ká-losh) m. rubber
 overshoe; galosh; rubber boot
kalumnia (ka-loóm-ña) f.
 calumny; slander; aspersion
kalwin (kal-veen) m. Calvinist
kał (kaw) m. excrement; stool
kałamarz (ka-wá-mash) m. ink-
 stand; ink bottle; ink pot
kałuża (ka-woo-zha) f. puddle
kamelia (ka-mél-ya) f. camellia
kameralna muzyka (ka-me-rál-na
 moo-zi-ka) chamber music
kamerdyner (ka-mer-dí-ner) m.
 butler ; valet (de chambre)
kamerton (ka-mér-ton) m.
 tuning-fork"U", shaped
kamfora (kam-fó-ra) f. camphor
kamgarn (kám-garn) m. worsted
kamienica (ka-mye-ñee-tsa) f.
 apartment house; tenants
kamieniec (ka-mye-ñech) v.
 petrify; turn into stone
kamieniołom (ka-mye-ño-wom) f.
 quarry; stone pit

kamień (ka-myeñ) m. stone
kamizelka (ka-mee-zél-ka) f.
 waistcoat; vest; camisole
kampania (kam-pá-ña) f. campaign ; drive(promotional)
kamrat (kám-rat) m. chum
kamyk (kám-ik) m, pebble
kanadyjski (ka-na-díy-skee) adj.
 m. Canadian ; of Canada
kanalia (ka-nál-ya) f. scoundrel
kanalizacja (ka-na-lee-záts-ya)
 f. sewers ;sanitation; drainage
kanał (ká-naw) m. channel; dyke;
 sewer; duct; ditch; conduit;tube
kanapa (ka-ná-pa) f. sofa
kanapka (ka-náp-ka) f. sandwich; small size sofa
kanarek (ka-ná-rek) m. canary
kancelaria (kan-tse-lár-ya) f,
 office: chancellery; archives
kancerować (Kan-tse-ró-vach) v.
 damage; mangle; lacerate; hack
kanciarz (kán-chash) m. swindler; trickster ; con man
kanciasty (kan-chá-sti) adj.
 m. angular; awkward; stiff
kanclerz (kán-tslesh) m.
 chancellor(chief of government)
kandelabr (kan-dé-labr) m.
 chandelier; street lamp
kandydat (kan-di-dat) m. candidate; applicant; aspirant
kangur (kán-goor) m. kangaroo
kanon (ká-non) m. canon (priest)
kanonierka (ka-no-ñér-ka) f.
 gunboat; patrol boat
kanonik (ka-nó-ñeek) m. canon
 (priest); monsignor; prelate
kanonizować (ka-no-ñee-zó-vach)
 v. canonize ; glorify
kant (kant) m. edge; crease;
 swindle; trick; racket; chant
kantar (kán-tar) m. halter
kantor (kán-tor) m. office;
 counter; counting office
kantyna (kan-ti-na) f. canteen
kanwa (kán-va) f. canvas
kapa (ká-pa) f. bedspread;cover
kapać (ká-pach) v. dribble;
 trickle; drip;fall drop by drop
kapela (ka-pé-la) f. (music)
 band; choir

kapelan (ka-pé-lan) m. chap-
lain(in armed forces, hospital)
kapelusz (ka-pé-loosh) m. hat
kapilarny (ka-pee-lár-ni) adj.
m. capillary
kapiszon (ka-peé-shon) m. hood
kapitalista (ka-pee-ta-leés-
ta) m. capitalist
kapitalizm (ka-pee-tá-leezm) m.
capitalism
kapitał (ka-peé-taw) m. capital
kapitan (ka-peé-tan) m. captain
kapitulacja (ka-pee-too-lá-
tsya) f. surrender; capitula-
tion ; giving up
kapitulować (ka-pee-too-ló-
vach) v. surrender; give up
kaplica (kap-leé-tsa) f. chapel
kapliczka (kap-leéch-ka) f.
shrine; wayside shrine
kapłan (ka-pwan) m. priest
kapłon (ká-pwon) m. capon
kapota (ką-pó-ta) f. long coat
kapral (káp-ral) m. corporal
kaprys (káp-ris) m. caprice;
fad; whim; fency; freak;vagary
kaptować (kap-tó-vach) v.
win over; bring over; canvas
kaptur (káp-toor) m. hood
kapturowy sąd (kap-too-ró-vi
sownd) kangaroo court
kapusta (ka-poós-ta) f. cabbage ; a dish of cabbage
kapuś (ká-poosh) m. stool-
pigeon ; informer; police spy
kapuśniak (ka-poósh-ńak) m.
cabbage soup; drizzle;mizzle
kara (ká-ra) f. penalty; fine;
punishment; correction;nuisance
karabin (ka-rá-been) m. rifle
karać (ka-rach) v. punish
karafka (ka-ráf-ka) f. serving-
bottle; water bottle; flagon
karakuły (ka-ra-koó-wi) pl.
astrakhan sheep fur
karalny (ka-rál-ni) adj. m.
punishable ;deserving a fine
karaluch (ka-ra-lookh) m.
cockroach ; black beetle
karambol (ka-rám-bol) m. collision ; cannon; carom
karaś (ká-rash) m. crucian

karat (ká-rat) m. carat
karawaniarz (ka-ra-vá-ńash) m.
undertaker: coffin bearer
karb (karb) m. notch; score;
crease; fold; nick; tally;curl
karbid (kár-beed) m. carbide
karbol (kár-bol) m. carbolic
acid ; phenol
karbować (kar-bó-vach) v.
notch; curl; tally; crimp;fold
karbunkuł (kar-boón-koow) m.
ulcer ; carbuncle
karburator (kar-boo-rá-tor) m.
carburetor
karcer (kár-tser) m. prison;
dark cell; detention
karciarz (kár-chash) m. (cards)
gambler; card player; gamester
karcić (kár-cheéch) v. reproof;
admonish; scold; castigate
karczemny (kar-chém-ni) adj.
m. rude ; vulgar; coarse
karczma (kárch-ma) f. tavern
karczoch (kár-chokh) m. arti-
choke (thistlelike plant)
karczować (kar-chóv-ach) v.
dig up (stumps); clear land
kardiografia (kar-dyo-gráf-ya)
f. cardiography
kardynalny (kar-di-nál-ni) adj.
m. fundamental; essential
kardynał (kar-di-naw) m. cardinal; prince(Catholic Church)
karetka (ka-rét-ka) f. ambulance;
(prison or mail) van; chaise
kariera (kar-yé-ra) f. career
kark (kark) m. neck ; nape
karkołomny (kar-ko-wóm-ni) adj.
m. neckbreaking ; breakneck
karłowaty (kar-wo-vá-ti) adj.
m. dwarfish ; undersized
karamel (ka-rá-mel) m. caramel
karmić (kár-meech) v. feed;
nourish ; nurse; suckle;nurture
karmin (kár-meen) m. carmine
karnawał (kar-ná-vaw) m. carnival penally
karnie (kár-ńe) adv. in order ;
karność (kár-noshch) f. discipline ; orderly conduct
karny (kár-ni) adj. m. disciplined; penal ; punitive

karo (ka-ro) n. diamonds (in
cards); square cut, décolleré
karoseria (ka-ro-sér-ya) f.
car body ; truck body
karp (karp) m. carp (fish)
karta (kár-ta) f. card; page;
note; sheet; ticket; charter
kartel (kár-tel) m.(industrial)
trust ; cartel; combine; pool
kartofel (kar-to-fel) m. potato
kartoflanka (kar-to-flán-ka) f.
potato soup; type of onion
kartograf (kar-to-graf) m.
cartographer ; map maker
karton (kár-ton) m. cardboard
kartoteka (kar-to-té-ka) f.
card index ; file
karuzela (ka-roo-zé-la) f.
merry-go-round ; carousel
kary koń (ka-ri koń)m.black
horse; horse of black color
karygodny (ka-ri-gód-ni) adj.
m. unpardonable ; guilty;gross
karykatura (ka-ri-ka-too-ra)
f. cartoon ; caricature;parody
karykaturzysta (ka-ri-ka-too-
zhis-ta) m. cartoonist
karzeł (ká-zhew) m. dwarf
kasa (ká-sa) f. cashier's desk;
cash register; ticket office
kasjer (kas-yer) m. cashier
kask (kask) m. helmet ; tin hat
kaskada (kas-ká-da) f. cascade
kasowac (ka-só-vach) v. cancel
kasta (kás-ta) f. caste
kastrowac (kas-tro-vach) v.
castrate; geld
kasyno (ka-si-no) n. casino;
club ; mess-hall; mess room
kasza (ká-sha) f. grits; groats;
cereals ; gruel; porridge;mess
kaszel (ká-shel) m. cough
kaszkiet (kásh-ket) m. cap
kasztan (kásh-tan) m. chestnut
kat (kat) m. executioner
katafalk (ka-tá-falk) m. bier
kataklizm (ka-ták-leezm) m.
cataclysm ; disaster; calamity
katalizator (ka-ta-lee-zá-tor)
m. catalyst
katalog (ka-tá-lok) m. catalog
katar (ká-tar) m. headcold ;
running nose ; catarrh

katarakta (ka-ta-rák-ta) f.
cataract; opaque eye lens
kataryniarz (ka-ta-ri-ńash) m.
organ grinder
katarynka (ka-ta-rin-ka) f.
barrel organ; street organ
katastrofa (ka-tas-tro-fa) f.
catastrophe; disaster; crash
katecheta (ka-te-khé-ta) m.
teacher of catechism
katedra (ka-té-dra) f. pulpit;
univ. dept. chair; cathedral
kategoria (ka-te-gór-ya) f.
category; division; class
kategoryczny (ka-te-go-rich-ni)
adj. m. absolute; categorical
katoda (ka-tó-da) f. cathode
katolicki (ka-to-leéts-kee)
adj. m. Catholic
katowac (ka-tó-vach) v. torture; beat cruelly; hack
kaucja (kaw-tsya) f. bail; deposit; security; recognizance
kauczuk (kaw-chook) f. India
natural rubber; caoutchouc
kaukaski (kaw-kás-kee) adj. m.
Caucasian; of Caucasus
kawa (ká-va) f. coffee
kawaler (ka-vá-ler) m. bachelor; suitor; beau; cavalier
kawaleria (ka-va-lér-ya) f.
cavalry ; young folks
kawalkada (ka-val-ká-da) f.
cavalcade
kawał (ká-vaw) m. piece; joke;
cheat ; lump; funny business
kawałek (ka-vá-wek) m. bit;
morsel; scrap; chunk;1000zł.
kawiarnia (kav-yár-ńa) f. café
kawior (káv-yor) m. caviar
kawka (káv-ka) f. jackdaw
kawon (ká-von) m. watermelon
kawowy (ka-vó-vi) adj. m. (of)
coffee; coffee-
kazac (ká-zach) v. order;tell;
preach ; make sb. do something
kazanie (ka-zá-ńe) n. sermon
kazic (ká-żheech)v. pollute;
corrupt; blemish;contaminate
kazirodztwo (ka-żhee-ródz-tvo)
n. incest
kaznodzieja (kaz-no-dźhé-ya) m.
preacher; evangelist

kaźń (kaźhń) f. execution
każdorazowy (kazh-do-ra-zó-vi)
adj.m.every;each;every single
każdy (kázh-di) pron. every;
each; respective; any; all
kącik (kówn-cheek) m. nook
kąkol (kówn-kol) m. cockle-
weed; corn cockle
kąpać (kówn-pach) v. bathe;soak
kąpiel (kówn-pyel) f. bath
kąpielisko (kówn-pye-leés-ko)
n. resort;spa; public bath
kąsać (kówn-sach) v. bite
kąsek (kówn-sek) m. bit; nip
kąt (kównt) m. corner; angle
kątomierz (kówn-tó-myesh) m.
protractor ; dial-sight
kciuk (kchook) m. thumb
kelner (kél-ner) m. waiter
kelnerka (kel-nér-ka) f.
waitress; bar maid
keson (ke-son) m. caisson
kędzierzawy (kán-dzhe-zha-vi)
adj. m. curly, curled; fuzzy
kędzior (kán-dzhor) m. curl;
lock; ringlet
kępa (kán-pa) f. cluster;
holm ; hurst; clump; tuft
kęs (káns) m. bit; mouthful
kibic (kee-beets) m. kibitzer
kibić (kee-beech) f. figure;
waist; middle
kichać (kee-khach) v. sneeze
kiecka (kéts-ka) f. frock;
skirt; petticoat (inelegant)
kiedy (ke-di) conj. when; as;
ever; how soon?;while; since
kiedy indziej (ke-di een-dzhey)
adj. some other time
kiedykolwiek (ke-di-kól-vyek)
adv. whenever; at any time
kiedyś (ke-dish) adv. someday; in the past; once;one day
kiedyż ? (ke-dish) adv. when-
then ? when on earth?
kielich (ke-leekh) m. goblet;
chalice; cup; cupful; glassful
kielnia (kel-ña) f. trowel
kieł (kew) m. tusk; canine-
tooth; fang;cutting bit
kiełbasa (kew-ba-sa) f. sausage

kiełek (ke-wek) m. sprout
kiełkować (kew-kó-vach) v.
sprout. germinate; spring up
kiełzać (k ew-zach) v. bridle
kiep (kep) m. oaf; fool; gull
kiepski (kép-skee) adj. m.
mean; bad; poor; second-rate
kier (ker) m. (cards) hearts
kierat (ke-rat) m. thrasher
kiermasz (ker-mash) m. fair
kierować (ke-ró-vach) v.steer;
manage; run; show the way
kierownik (ke-rov-ñeek) m.
manager; director ;supervisor
kierunek (ke-róo-nek) m.
direction ; course; trend;line
kiesa (ke-sa) m. purse
kieszeń (ke-sheñ) f. pocket
kij (keey) m. stick; cane; staff
kijanka (kee-yán-ka) f. tadpole
kikut (kee-koot) m. stump ;stub
kilim (kee-leem) m. rug ;carpet
kilka (keel-ka) num. a few;some
kilkakroć (keel-ká-kroch) adv.
repeatedly ;again and again
kilkakrotny (keel-ka-krót-ni)
adj. m. repeated ;recurring
kilkudniowy (keel-koo-dñó-vi)
adj. m. of several days
kilkoro (keel-kó-ro) num. some;
several ; one or two; a number
kilof (kee-lof) m. pick ; hack
kilogram (kee-ló-gram) m. kilogram ; 2.2 pounds
kilometr (kee-ló-metr) m. kilometer ; 3,280.8 feet
kiła (kee-wa) f. syphilis
kinetyka (kee-ne-tí-ka) f.
kinetics; science of motion
kino (kee-no) n. cinema;movies
kiosk (kyosk) m. kiosk; booth
kipieć (kee-pyech) v. boil
kisić (kee-sheech) v. ferment
kisnąć (kees-nówñch) v. turn
sour ; ferment; pickle; fug
kiszka (keesh-ka) f. intestine
kiść (keeshch) f. bunch; wrist
kit (keet) m. putty ; mastic
kiwać (kee-vach) v. rock; nod;
wag; dangle;fool dodge; jink
klacz (klach) f. mare
klajster (kláy-ster) m. glue;
paste ; water base glue

klakson (klák-son) m. car horn
klamka (klám-ka) f. door knob
klamra (klám-ra) f. buckle;
clasp ; bracket; fastener;staple
klapa (klá-pa) f. lapel: valve
klapsy (kláp-si) pl. spanking
klarować (kla-ró-vach) v. clarify ; filter;clear; purify
klarnet (klár-net) m. clarinet
klasa (klá-sa) f. class; classroom ; rank; order; division
klaskać (klás-kach) v. clap
klasowy (kla-só-vi) adj. m.
class ; of classes; class-
klasyczny (kla-sich-ni) adj. m.
classic ; standard;conventional
klasyfikować (kla-si-fee-kó-
vach) v. classify;sort; grade
klasztor (klásh-tor) m. monastery ; convent; cloister
klatka (klát-ka) f. cage ; crate
klatka schodowa (klát-ka skho-
dó-va) staircase ; stairway
klatka piersiowa (klat-ka
pyer-shó-va) ribcage; chest
klauzula (klaw-zóo-la) f.
clause ; proviso; reservation
klawisz (klá-veesh) m. (piano)
key;stool pigeon; jailer
kląć (klównch) v. curse; swear
klątwa (klównt-va) f. curse;
ban; excommunication; anathema
klecić (kle-cheech) v. botch
kleić (kle--eech) v. glue;
stick together; fudge; shape
kleik (kle—eek) m. gruel
klej (kley) m. glue ; cement
klejnot (kley-not) m. jewel
klekotać (kle-kó-tach) v. clatter; rattle ; chatter; prate
kleks (kleks) m. blot;ink-spot
klepać (kle-pach) v. hammer;
flatten ; prattle; pat;blab;clap
klepka (klep-ka) f. stave
klepsydra (klep-sid-ra) f. hour-
glass; obituary notice
kleptomania (klep-to-ma-ña) f.
kleptomania: impulse to steal
kler (kler) m. clergy;priesthood
kleszcz (kleshch) m. tick
kleszcze (klésh-che) n. pliers;
tongs ; claws; pincers; nippers

klękać (klań-kach) v. kneel
down; bend the knee; kneel
klęska (kláns-ka) f. defeat;
disaster; calamity
klęsnąć (kláns-nównch) v.
shrink; subside; go down
klient (klee—ent) m. customer
klika (klee-ka) f. clique
klimat (klee-mat) m. climate
klin (kleen) m. wedge;cotter
klinga (kleen-ga) f. (sword)
blade; sabre-blade
kliniczny (klee-ñeech-ni) adj.
clinic ; clinic-
klinika (klee-ñee-ka) f. clinic
klisza (klee-sha) f. (photo)
plate; printing plate
klitka (kléet-ka) f. cell
kloc (klots) m. log; block
klomb (klomp) m. flower bed
klon (klon) m. maple
klops (klops) m. meat loaf
klosz (klosh) m. glass cover;
lamp shade; dish cover
klozet (kló-zet) m. toilet
klub (kloob) m. club; union
klucz (klooch) m. key; wrench
kluska (kloós-ka) f. boiled
dough strip; dumpling
kładka (kwád-ka) f. foot-
bridge; gangway; brow
kłaki (kwá-kee) pl. oakum;
shaggy hair; matted hair
kłam (kwam) m. lie; falsehood
kłamać (kwá-mach) v. lie
kłamca (kwám-tsa) m. liar
kłaniać się (kwá-ñach shan) v.
salute; bow; greet; worship
kłaść (kwashch) v. lay; put
dawn; place; set; deposit
kłąb (kwównp) m. clew; ball
kłąbek (kwówn-bek) m. ball
(of thread); hunk of yarn
kłębić się (kwań-beech shań) v.
whirl; swirl; surge; billow
kłoda (kwo-da) f. log; clog
kłopot (kwo-pot) m. trouble
kłopotać (kwo-pó-tach) v.
trouble; disturb; worry
kłopotliwy (kwo-pot-lée-vi) adj.
troublesome; baffling
kłos (kwos) m. (corn) ear

kłócić (kwoo-cheech) v. quarrel
kłódka (kwood-ka) f. padlock
kłotliwy (kwoot-lee-vi) adj.
 m. quarrelsome; cantankerous
kłótnia (kwoo-tña) f. quarrel
kłuć (kwooch) v. stab; prick
kłus (kwoos) m. trot;jog trot
kłusownik (kwoo-sov-ñeek) m.
 poacher; trespassing hunter
kmieć (kmyech) m. peasant
kminek (kmee-nek) m. cumin
knajpa (knay-pa) f. tavern
knebel (kne-bel) m. gag
knocić (kno-cheech) v. bungle
knot (knot) m. wick;fuse;bungle
knuć (knooch) v. plot; scheme
koalicja (ko-a-leets-ya) f.
 coalition: temporary union
kobiałka (ko-byaw-ka) f.
 wicker-basket; chip basket
kobieciarz (ko-bye-chash) m.
 ladychaser; lady's man
kobiecość (ko-bye-tsooshch) f.
 womanhood; femininity
kobiecy (ko-bye-tsi) adj. m.
 female; womanish; feminine
kobierzec (ko-bye-zhets) m.
 carpet; anything like a carpet
kobieta (ko-bye-ta) f. woman
kobyła (ko-bi-wa) f. mare
kobza (kob-za) f. bagpipe
koc (kots) m. blanket; coverlet
kochać (ko-khach) v. love
kochanie (ko-kha-ñe) n. love;
 darling; sweetheart; affection
kochany (ko-kha-ni) adj. m.
 beloved; loving; affectionate
kochliwy (kokh-lee-vi) adj. m.
 easily in love; amorous
koci (ko-chee)adj. m. catlike
kociak (ko-chak) m. kitty;
 lassie; lass; pinup girl
kocioł (ko-chow) m. kettle;
 boiler; pot; encirclement
kocur (ko-tsoor) m. tomcat
koczować (ko-cho-vach) v. nomad-
 ize; wander about;be encamped
koczownik (ko-choy-ñeek) m.
 nomad; wanderer; vagrant
kodeks (ko-deks) m. (legal)code
koedukacja   (ko-e-doo-kats-ya)
 f. coeducation

koegzystencja (ko-eg-zis-ten-
 tzya) f. coexistence
kofeina (ko-fe—ee-na) f.
 caffeine; alkaloid in coffee
kogut (ko-goot) m. cock ;rooster
koić (ko—eech) v. soothe
kojarzenie (ko-ya-zhe-ñe) n.
 matching ; association; union
kojarzyć (ko-ya-zhich) v. unite;
 bind; join; link; connect
kojący (ko-yown-tsi) adj. m.
 soothing;comforting; balmy
kojec (ko-yets) m. coop ; pen
kokaina (ko-ka-ee-na) f.' co-
 caine; an alkaloid drug
kokarda (ko-kar-da) f. rosette;
 bow ; slip-knot; knot
kokietka (ko—ket-ka) f. flirt
kokietować (ko-ke —to-vach) v.
 flirt ; court; woo: coquet
koklusz (kok-loosh) m.
 whooping-cough
kokos (ko-kos) m. 1. coconut
 2. good business ; a grand thing
kokoszka (ko-kosh-ka) f. brood-
 hen; laying hen
koks (koks) m. coke; gas coke
koksownia (kok-sov-ña) f. cok-
 ing plant ; cokery
kolaboracja (ko-la-bo-rats-ya)
 f.collaboration ; collaborators
kolacja (ko-lats-ya) f. supper
kolano (ko-la-no) m. knee
kolarstwo (ko-lar-stvo) n.
 cycling ; bicycle sport
kolarz (ko-lash) m. cyclist
kolący (ko-lown-tsi) adj. m.
 prickly; thorny; spiked
kolba (kol-ba) f. (rifle) butt
kolczasty (kol-chas-ti) adj. m.
 barbed ; thorny; spiny
kolczyk (kol-chik) m. earring;
 earmark; ear tag; eardrop
kolebka (ko-leb-ka) f. cradle
kolec (ko-lets) m. thorn
kolega (ko-le-ga) m. buddy;
 colleague; fellow worker
koleina (ko-le-ee-na) f. truck;
 rut; groove; wheel trace
kolej (ko-ley) f. railroad
kolejka (ko-ley-ka) f. (waiting)
 line;narrow-gage railroad; turn

kolejno (ko-léy-no) adv. by
turns; one after the other
kolejny (ko-léy-ni) adj. m.
next; successive; following
kolekcja (ko-lék-tsya) f. collection ; things collected
kolektywizacja (ko-lek-ti-vee-
záts-ya) f. collectivization
koleżeństwo (ko-le-zhéń-stvo)
n. fellowship; comradeship
kolęda (ko-láń-da) f. Christmas
carol; song of joy or praise
kolędować (ko-lań-dó-vach) v.
sing carols; wait a long time
koliber (ko-lée-ber) m. hum-
mingbird
kolia (kól-ya) f. necklace
kolidować (ko-lee-dó-vach) v.
collide ; interfere
koligacja (ko-lee-gáts-ya) f.
(family) relationship
kolisty (ko-leés-ti) adj. m.
circular ; round
kolizja (ko-leéz-ya) f. collision; clash; interference
kolka (kól-ka) f. colic
kolokwium (ko-lók-vyoom) m.
oral examination; test
kolonia (ko-lóń-ya) f. colony
kolonista (ko-lo-ńees-ta) m.
settler; colonist; colonial
kolońska woda (ko-lóń-ska vó-
da) cologne water
kolor (kó-lor) m.color;tint;hue
koloryt (ko-ló-rit) m. coloring
kolosalny (ko-lo-sál-ni) adj.
m. colossal; vast;tremendous
kolportaż (kol-pór-tash) m.
(paper) distribution
kolumna (ko-loóm-na) f. column
kołatać (ko-wá-tach) v. knock;
rattle; beg; throb; bang;
kołczan (ków-chan) m. quiver
kołdra (ków-dra) f. quilter-
cover; quilt; coverlet
kołek (kó-wek) m. peg ;stake
kołnierz (ków-ńesh) m. collar
koło (kó-wo) n. wheel; circle
koło (ko-wo) prep. around;
near; about; by; in vicinity
kołodziej (ko-wo-dźhey) m.
wheelwright

kołowacizna (ko-wo-va-čheéz-
na) f. dizziness
kołować (ko-wó-vach) v. revolve;
confuse ; circle; stray; whirl
kołowrotek (ko-wo-vro-tek) m.
spinning-wheel; reel; winch
kołowrót (ko-wó-vroot) m. windlass ; hoist; gin; whip;turnpike
kołowy ruch (ko-wó-vi rookh)
vehicular traffic
kołpak (ków-pak) m. pointed
fur cap ; calpack
kołtun (ków-toon) m. hair.snarl;
bigot; moron; obscurant
kołysać (ko-wi-sach) v. rock;
sway ; toss to and fro; roll
kołysanka (ko-wi-sán-ka) f.
lullaby ; cradle song;berceuse
kołyska (ko-wis-ka) f. cradle
komar (kó-mar) m. mosquito
kombajn (kóm-bayn) m. combine
kombinacja (kom-bee-náts-ya) f.
combination ;union; scheme;slip
kombinować (kom-bee-nó-vach) v.
combine; speculate ; scheme
komedia (ko-méd-ya) f. comedy
komenda (ko-mén-da) f. command ; headquarters ; an order
komentarz (ko-mén-tash) m. com-
mentary ; glossary; remark
kometa (ko-mé-ta) f. comet
komfort (kóm-fort) m. comfort
komiczny (ko-meéch-ni) adj. m.
comic ; amusing; funny;droll
komin (kó-meen) m. chimney
kominek (ko-mée-nek) m. fireplace ; hearth; open fire
kominiarz (ko-mee-ńash) m.
chimney-sweep
komis (kó-mees) m. (on) commission sale; commission shop
komisariat (ko-mee-sar-yat) m.
police station : commissariat
komisja (ko-meés-ya) f. commission; board (of inquiry etc.)
komitet (ko-mée-tet) m. committee ; board
komitywa (ko-mee-ti-va) f.
intimacy ; good friendly terms
komiwojażer (ko-mee-vo-ya-zher)
m. traveling salesman
komnata (kom-ná-ta) f. chamber

komoda (ko-mó-da) f. chest of
 drawers ; low-boy;commode
komora (ko-mó-ra) f. chamber
komora celna (ko-mó-ra tsél-na)
 customs office; custom house
komorne (ko-mór-ne) n. (appartment) rent ; rental
komórka (ko-moó-rka) f. cell
kompan (kóm-pan) m. chum ;pal
kompania (kom-páń-ya) f. company ; stock company; society
kompas (kóm-pas) m. compass
kompensata (kom-pen-sá-ta) f.
 compensation; indemnity
kompetentny (kom-pe-tén-tni)
 adj. m. competent; qualified
kompleks (kóm-pleks) m. com—
 plex; group;(inferiority)complex
komplement (kom-plé-ment) m.
 compliment ;complement
komplet (kóm-plet) m. set
kompozytor (kom-po-zí-tor) m.
 composer (of music)
kompot (kóm-pot) m. compote
kompres (kóm-pres) m. compress
kompromis (kom-pro-mees) m.
 compromise ;accomodation
kompromitacja (kom-pro-mee-tá-
 tsya) f disgrace; loss of face
komuna (ko-moó-na) f. commune
komunał (ko-moó-naw) m. platitude; banality; commonplace
komunia (ko-moóń-ya) f. communion;part of Catholic mass
komunikacja (ko-moo-ńee-kats-
 ya) f. communication ;contact
komunikat (ko-moo-ńée-kat) m.
 bulletin ; communiqué; report
komunikować (ko-moo-ńee-kó-vach)
 v. inform; give news; report
komunista (ko-moo-ńees-ta) m.
 communist(advocate or supporter)
konać (ko-nać) v. agonize;
 expire; be dying;die(with greed)
konar (ko-nar) m. limb; branch
koncentryczny (kon-tsen-trich-
 ni) adj. m. concentric
koncept (kon-tsept) m. concept;
 idea; joke; plan ;brain wave
koncert (kon-tsert) m. concert
koncesja (kon-tsés-ya) f. concession; license; license to do...

koncha (kón-kha) f. shell;
 lobe
kondensator (kon-den-sá-or) m.
 condenser ; capacitor
kondolencja (kon-do-lén-tsya)
 f. condolence ;words of sympathy
kondukt (kón-dookt) m. funeral
 procession ;funeral service
konduktor (kon-doók-tor) m.
 conductor (train-ticket inspector in charge of passengers
kondycja (kon-dits-ya) f.
 condition; form; status
konewka (ko-név-ka) f.
 (watering) can; pot;jug;pewter
konfederacja (kon-fe-de-ráts-
 ya) f. confederation; confederacy
konfekcja (kon-fék-tsya) f.
 ready-made clothes (pl.)
konferencja (kon-fe-rén-tsya)
 f. conference ; meeting(official)
konferować (kon-fe-ró-vach) v.
 confer ;hold a conference
konfesjonał (kon-fes-yo-naw)
 m. confessional
konfiskata (kon-fees-ká-ta) f.
 seizure ; confiscation
konfitura (kon-fee-toó-ra) f.
 jam ; preserve ; candied fruits
konfrontować (kon-fron-tó-vach)
 v. confront ;bring face to face
kongres (kón-gres) m. congress
koniak (kó-ńak) m. brandy;cognac
koniczyna (ko-ńee-chi-na) f.
 clover ; trefoil; shamrock
koniec (kó-ńets) m. end;
 conclusion; tip; point ;close
koniecznie (ko-ńech-ńe) adv.
 absolutely; necessarily
konieczny (ko-ńech-ni) adj. m.
 indispensable ;vital;necessary
konik (kó-ńeek) m. pony
konik polny (kó-ńeek pól-ni)
 grasshopper; cricket (Locusta)
konina (ko-ńee-na) f. horse-
 meat; horseflesh
koniunktura (koń-yoonk-toó-ra)
 f. market condition ;situation
konkluzja (kon-klooz-ya) f.
 conclusion ; inference
konkretny (kon-krét-ni) adj. m.
 concrete; definite ;real

konkurencja (kon-koo-rén-tsya)
f. competition; rivalry;contest
konkurs (kón-ñee-koors) m. contest
konnica (kon-ñee-tsa) f. cavalry ; cavalry unit; horse
konno (kón-no) adv. on horseback ; sit astraddle ;mounted
konny (kón-ni) adj. m. mounted
konopie (ko-nóp-ye) n. hemp
konował (ko-nó-vaw) m. farrier;
quack doctor ; sawbones
konserwa (kon-sér-va) f. preserve; conservatists
konserwatorium (kon-ser-va-tór-
yoom) n. conservatory
konsola (kon-só-la) f. console
konspirować (kon-spee-ró-vach)
v. plot ; conspire; keep secret
konstatować (kon-sta-tó-vách)
v. state; ascertain; find
konsternacja (kon-ster-náts-ya)
f. consternation ; dismay
konstrukcja (kon-strook-tsya)
f. construction ;design; plan
konstruować (kon-stroo-ó-vách)
v. construct ;build; make
konstytucja (kon-sti-toóts-ya)
f. constitution; physique
konsulat (kon-soó-lat) m. consulate (office or term of office)
konsumować (kon-soo-mó-vách) v.
consume ; eat; drink; use up
konsylium (kon-sil-yoom) m.
consultation (usually medical)
konszachty (kon-shakh-ti) pl.
collusion; scheming
kontakt (kón-takt) m. contact
kontaktować się (kon-tak-tó-
vach shan) v. contact ;touch
konto (kón-to) n. account
kontrabanda (kon-tra-bán-da)
f. smuggling ;contraband
kontrakt (kón-trakt) m. contract enforcable by law
kontraktować (kon-trak-tó-vách)
v. contract; hire; engage
kontrast (kón-trast) m. contrast (pointing the differences)
kontrastować (kon-tras-tó-vach)
v. contrast ;stand in contrast
kontratak (kontr-a-tak) m.
counter-attack

kontrola (kon-tró-la) f. control; checking; check up
kontrolny (kon-tról-ni) adj.
m. of control;of supervision
kontrolować (kon-tro-ló-vach)
v. control; check; verify
kontrpropozycja (kontr-pro-po-
zíts-ya) f. counterproposal
kontrrewolucja (kontr-re-vo-
loóts-ya)f.counterrevolution
kontrowersja(kon-tro-vérs-ya)
f. controversy; a quarrel
kontuar (kon-toó-ar) m. counter
kontur (kón-toor) m. outline
kontusz (kón-toosh) m. split-
sleeve Polish overcoat (of old)
kontuzja (kon-tooz-ya) f. shock
kontynent (kon-ti-nent) m.
continent; mainland ;land mass
konwalia (kon-vál-ya) f. lily
of the valley ; convallaria
konwikt (kón-veekt) m. boarding school (for boys or girls)
konwój (kón-vooy) m. convoy
konwulsja (kon-voóls-ya) f.
convulsion; a fit ; a spasm
koń (koń) m. horse ; steed
koń mechaniczny (koń me-kha-
ñeech-ni) mechanical horsepower; horsepower
końcowy (koń-tso-vi) adj. m.
final; terminal; last; late
końcówka (koń-tsoov-ka) f.
ending; remainder;tail-piece
kończyć (kóń-chich) v. end;
finish; quit; be dying; stop
kończyna (koń-chi-na) f. extremity; limb; member; leg
kooperacja (ko-o-pe-ráts-ya)
f. cooperation ; acting together
koordynacja (ko-or-di-náts-ya)
f. coordination (mental&phys.)
kopa (kó-pa) threescore (60);
pile; dozens; stack
kopa siana (ko-pa shá-na) haystack ; hayrick
kopać (ko-pach) v. dig; kick
kopalnia (ko-pál-ña) f. mine
koparka (ko-pár-ka) f. excava-
tor; mechanical shovel
kopcić (kop-cheech) v. soot;
smoke; blacken with smoke

kopciuszek (kop-choo-shek) m.
Cinderella; drudge
kopeć (ko-pech) m. soot
koper (ko-per) m. dill; fennel
koperta (ko-per-ta) f. envelope; quilt-case;(watch-)case
kopiasty (kop-yas-ti) adj. m.
heaped; piled up;heaped(plate)
kopiec (kop-yets) m. mound;
barrow ; mound;heap; knoll
kopiować (kop-yo-vach) v. copy
kopuła (ko-poo-wa) f. dome
kopyto (ko-pi-to) n. hoof
kora (ko-ra) f. bark; cortex
koral (ko-ral) m. coral (red)
korale (ko-ra-le) pl. bead
necklace; coral beads; gills
korba (kor-ba) f. crank; winch
kordon (kor-don) m. cordon
korek (ko-rek) m. cork; fuse;
stopper; traffic jam; tie-up
korekta (ko-rek-ta) f. proof
korepetycja (ko-re-pe-tits-ya)
f. tutoring; private lessons
korespondencja (ko-res-pon-den-
tsya) f. correspondence;letters
korespondent wojenny (ko-res-
pon-dent vo-yen-ni) war correspondent; war reporter
korkociąg (kor-ko-chownk) m.
cork-screw; tail-spin; twist
korniszon (kor-nee-shon) m.
pickled cucumber; gherkin
korny (kor-ni) adj. m. humble
korona (ko-ro-na) f. crown
koronacja (ko-ro-nats-ya) f.
coronation; crowning
koronka (ko-ron-ka) f. lace
koronować (ko-ro-no-vach) v.
crown ; be crowned
korowód (ko-ro-vood) m. procession; pageant; train;difficulty
korporacja (kor-po-rats-ya) f.
corporation ; association;guild
korpulentny (kor-poo-len-tni)
adj. m. fat; corpulent; obese
korpus (kor-poos) m. body;
staff; (army) corps, etc
korsarz (kor-sash) m. pirate
kort tenisowy (kort te-nee-so-
vi) tennis court
korupcja (ko-roop-tsya) f. corruption; venality; bribery

korygować (ko-ri-go-vach) v.
correct; rectify; put right
korytarz (ko-ri-tash) m. corridor; passage-way; lobby
koryto (ko-ri-to) n. through;
river-bed ; channel; chute
korzec (ko-zhets) m. bushel
korzeń (ko-zheń) m. root; spice
korzyć (ko-zhich)v. humble;
humiliate ; prostrate
korzystać (ko-zhis-tach) v.
profit; gain;enjoy a right
korzystny (ko-zhist-ni) adj.
m. profitable; favorable
korzyść (ko-shishch) f. profit
kos (kos) m. blackbird
kosa (ko-sa) f. scythe; tress
kosiarka (ko-shar-ka) f. mower
kosić (ko-sheech) v. mow;scythe
kosmaty (kos-ma-ti) adj. m.
shaggy ; hairy; fleecy
kosmetyczka (kos-me-tich-ka) f.
vanity bag ; beautician
kosmetyk (kos-me-tik) m. cosmetic : makeup(skin and hair)
kosmiczny (kos-meech-ni) adj.
m. cosmic ; outer space
kosmopolita (kos-mo-po-lee-ta)
m. cosmopolite ;cosmopolitan
kosmyk (kos-mik) m. wisp ; strand
kosodrzewina (ko-so-dzhe-vee-
na) f. dwarf mountain pine
kosooki (ko-so-o-ki) adj. m.
with slanting eyes; with scowl-
ing eyes ; cross-eyed
kostium(kos-tyoom) m. suit;dress
kostka (kost-ka) f. small bone;
ankle; knuckle; die; lump
kostnica (kost-nee-tsa) f.
morgue ; mortuary ;dead house
kostnieć (kost-nech) v. grow
stiff ; ossify; freeze
kosy (ko-si) adj. m. slanting
kosz (kosh) m. basket ;Tartar camp
koszary (ko-sha-ry) pl. barracks (military); caserns
koszenie (ko-she-ne) n. mowing
koszerny (ko-sher-ni) adj. m.
kosher (clean or fit to eat)
koszmar (kosh-mar) m. nightmare ; frightening experience
koszt (kosht) m. cost ; price;
expense; charge; economic costs

kosztorys (kosh-to-ris) m.
  estimate (of cost),
kosztowny (kosh-tov-ni) adj.
  m. expensive ; costly;precious
koszula (ko-shoo-la) f. shirt
koszyk (ko-shik) f. small
  basket,; grab bag; hilt guard
koszykówka (ko-shi-koov-ka) f.
  basketball
kościany (kosh-cha-ni) adj. m.
  bone ; osseous;made out of bone
kościec (kosh-chets) m. skeleton ; framework ; frame
kościelny (kosh-chel-ni) adj.
  m, of church ; ecclesiastical
kościotrup (kosh-cho-troop) m.
  skeleton (vulg.)
kościół (kosh-choow), m. church
koścista (kosh-chee-sti) adj.
  m. bony; angular ; rawboned
kość (koshch) f. bone ; spine
koślawić (ko-shla-veech) v.
  deform ; distort; crook
koślawy (ko-shla-vi) adj. m.
  crooked; lame ; lopsided
kot (kot) m. cat; pussy cat;puss
kotara (ko-ta-ra) f. curtain
kotek (ko-tek) m. kitten ;puss
kotlet (kot-let) m. cutlet
kotlina (kot-lee-na) f. dale
kotłować (kot-wo-vach) v.whirl;
  seethe; surge; drive crazy
kotłownia (kot-wov-ña) f.
  boiler room ;boiler house
kotwica (kot-vee-tsa) f. anchor
kotwiczyć (kot-vee-chich) v.
  anchor ; lie at anchor
kowadło (ko-vad-wo) m. anvil
kowal (ko-val), m. blacksmith
kowalny (ko-val-ni) adj. m.
  malleable ; ductile; forgeable
koza (ko-za)f. goat; jail
kozioł (ko-zhow) m. buck;gambol
koźlę (kozh-añ) n. kid;goatling
kożuch (ko-zhookh) m. sheepskin
  furcoat ;coating on hot milk
kół (koow) m. stake; post
kółko (kow-ko) m. small wheel;
  small circle: (soc.) circle
kpiarz (kpyash) m. scoffer
kpić (kpeech) v. jeer; sneer
kpiny (kpee-ni) n. mockery ;
  this is preposterous ! (exp.)

kra (kra) f. ice floe
krach (krakh) m. crash
kraciasty (kra-chas-ti) adj.
  m.checquered ; grated;checkered
kradzież (kra-dzhesh) f. theft
kradziony (kra-dzho-ni) adj.
  m. stolen ; robbed
kraina (kra-ee-na) f. land;
  region ; province ;country
kraj (kray) m. country; verge;
  edge; hem of a garment; land
krajać (kra-yach) v. cut;slice;
  carve; operate; hack; saw
krajobraz (kray-ob-ras) m.
  landscape; scenery painting
krajowy (kra-yo-vi) adj. m.
  native; nationally made
krajoznawczy (kra-yo-znav-chi)
  adj. m. hiking, touring
krakać (kra-kach) v. croak
kram (kram) m. booth; mess;
  trouble; stall; odds and ends
kramarz (kra-mash) m. huckster
kran (kran) m. tap; faucet
kraniec (kra-ñets) m. border;
  edge; end; extremity; margin
krańcowy (krañ-tso-vi) adj. m.
  extreme; marginal; excessive
krasa (kra-sa) f. grace;
  beauty; loveliness ; splendor
krasić (kra-sheech) v. decorate
krasomówca (kra-so-moov-tsa) m.
  orator(very eloquent)
kraść (krashch) v. steal; rob
kraśnieć (krash-ñech) v. blush;
  grow beautiful; redden
krata (kra-ta) f. grate
krater (kra-ter) m. crater
krawat (kra-vat) m. (neck) tie
krawcowa (krav-tso-va) f.
  seamstress ;tailor's wife
krawędź (kra-vandzh) f. edge
krawęznik (kra-vanzh-ñeek) m.
  curb(stone); roof-hip
krawiec (krav-yets) m. tailor
krąg (krownk) m. ring ; ver-
  tebre; disk; range ; sphere
krążek (krown-zhek) m. small
  disk; potter's wheel;pulley
krążyć (krown-zhich) v. circulate; rotate; wander; stray
kreacja (kre-ats-ya) f. (dress)
  creation; theatre part

kreda (kre-da) f. chalk
kredens (kre-dens) m. china
  cabinet ; cupboard; buffet
kredka (kred-ka) f.crayon;
  lipstick; chalk for writing
kredowy (kre-do-vi) adj. m.
  cretaceous;chalky;made of chalk
kredyt (kre-dit) m. credit
krem (krem) m. cream;custard
krematorium (kre-ma-tor-yoom)
  n. crematorium ; crematory
kremowy (kre-mo-vi) adj. m.
  creamcolored; cream yellow
kreować (kre-o-vach) v. create;
  act; set up; institute; appoint
krepa (kre-pa) f. crape
kres (kres) m. end; limit;term
kreska (kres-ka) f. dash(line);
  stroke; hatch; scar; accent
kreślić (kresh-leech) v. draw;
  trace; sketch; cross out
kret (kret) m. mole ; schemer
kretowisko (kre-to-vees-ko) n.
krew (krev) f. blood ˥molehill
krewetka (kre-vet-ka) f. shrimp
krewki (krev-kee) adj. m. rash;
  quick-tempered; impetuous
krewny (krev-ni) m. relative
kręcić (kran-cheech) v. twist;
  turn; shoot film;fuss; boss
kręcony (kran-tso-ni) adj. m.
  twisted; curled;winding;spiral
kręgle (krang-le) n. bowling
  (ninepin)game of bowles;tenpins
kręgosłup (kran-gos-woop) m.
  spine; vertebral column
kręgowiec (kran-go-vyets) m.
  vertebrate ;animal with spine
krępować (kran-po-vach) v. bind;
  embarrass; hamper; hinder
krępy (kran-pi) adj. m. stocky;
  thickset; sturdy; short
krętactwo (kran-tats-tvo) n.
  cheat; foul dealing; shuffle
krętacz (kran-tach) m. double-
  dealer; dodger; quibbler;cheat
kręty (kran-ti) adj. m. curved;
  curly; winding; tortuous
krnąbrny (krnownbr-ni) adj. m.
  stubborn; unruly; restive;balky
krochmal (krokh-mal) m. starch
krochmalić (krokh-ma-leech) v.
  starch ; beat up; stiffen

krocie (kro-che) pl. thousands
kroczyć (kro-chich) v. stride
kroić (kro-eech) v. cut; slice
krok (krok) m. step ;pace;march
krokiew (kro-kev) f. rafter
krokodyl (kro-ko-dil) m. crocodile ; split flap (aviation)
kromka (krom-ka) f. slice
kronika (kro-nee-ka) f.chronicle
kropić (kro-peech) v. sprinkle
kropka (krop-ka) f. dot ; point
kropkować (krop-ko-vach) v. dot
kropla (krop-la) f. drop
krosno (kros-no) n. loom
krosta (kros-ta) f. pimple
krotochwila (kro-to-khvee-la)
  f. joke; burlesque; farce
krowa (kro-va) f. cow; mine
krój (krooy) m. cut; fashion
król (krool) m. king; rabbit
królestwo (kroo-les-tvo) n.
  kingdom; the realms; sphere
królewicz (kroo-le-veech) m.
  crown prince ; king's son
królewski (kroo-lev-skee) adj.
  m. royal; king's; queen's
królik (krool-eek) m. rabbit
królikarnia (kroo-lee-kar-ña)
  f. warren : rabbit warren
królowa (kroo-lo-va) f. queen
krótki (kroot-kee) adj. m.
  short; brief ;terse; concise
krótko (kroo-tko) adv. briefly;
  shortly; tersely;(hold) tightly
krtań (krtań) f. larynx
kruchy (kroo-khi) adj. m. brittle;
  frail; tender; crisp; crusty
krucjata (kroots-ya-ta) f. crusade ; action for some cause
krucyfiks (kroo-tsi-feeks) m.
  crucifix ; cross of Jesus
kruczek (kroo-chek) m. trick
kruczy (kroo-chi) adj. m. jet-
  black; raven's (color)
kruk (krook) m. raven
krupy (kroo-pi) pl. groats
kruszec (kroo-shets) m. (metal)
  ore ; metal; gold; silver
kruszeć (kroo-shech) v. crumble;
  grow brittle; repent
kruszyć (kroo-shich) v. crush;
  crumb; destroy; shatter;disrupt

kruszyna (kroo-shi-na) f. crumb
kruźganek (kroozh-gán-ek) m.
portico ; gallery; ambulatory
krwawica (krva-vee-tsa) f. hard-
won money; toil ; labor
krwawić (krvá-veech) v. bleed
krwawy (krvá-vi) adj. m. bloody;
bloodthirsty; bloodstained
krwiobieg (krvee-ó-byeg) m.
blood circulation
krwisty (krvées-ti) adj. m.
sanguineous; blood-red
krwotok (krvó-tok) m. hemorrhage : bleeding
kryć (krich) v. hide; conceal;
cover ;roof over;shield; mask
kryjówka (kri-yoóv-ka) f.
hiding-place ; hide-out
kryminalista (kri-mee-na-lées-
ta) m. criminal, crime;thriller
kryminał (kri-mée-naw) m. prison;
krynica (kri-ńee-tsa) f. spring
krystalizować (kris-ta-lee-zo-
vach) v. crystallize ; shape
kryształ (krish-taw) m. crystal
kryterium (kri-ter-yoom) n.
criterion; touchstone; test
kryty (kri-ti) adj. m. covered
krytyczny (kri-tích-ni) adj. m.
critical; decisive; crucial
krytyk (kri-tik) m. critic
krytyka (kri-tí-ka) f. criticism; review; censure
kryzys (kri-zis) m. crisis
krzaczasty (kzha-chás-ti) adj.
m. bushy; shaggy; beetle
krzak (kzhak) m. bush
krzątać (kzhówn-tach)v. bustle
krzątanina (kzhówn-ta-ńee-na)
f. bustle ; comings and goings
krzem (kzhem) m. silicone
krzemień (kzhe-myeń) f. flint
krzepić (kzhe-peech) v. brace
up; refresh; invigorate;fortify
krzepki (kzhep-kee) adj. vigorous; lusty; robust; husky
krzepnąć (kzhep-nownch) v. coagulate; gather strength
krzesać (kzhe-sach) v. strike
fire ; strike sparks
krzesiwo (kzhe-shee-vo) n.
tinder-box ; flint

krzesło (kzhés-wo) n. chair
krzew (kzhev) m. shrub
krzewić (kzhe-veech) v. spread;
propagate ; teach; graft
krzta (kzhta) f. whit; bit
krztusiec (kzhtoo-shets) m.
whooping-cough
krztusić się (kzhtoo-sheech
shań) v. choke; stifle
krzyczeć (kzhi-chech) v. shout;
cry ; scream; yell; clamor
krzyk (kzhik) m. cry; scream;
shriek ; yell; outcry; call
krzykacz (kzhi-kach) m. bawler;
crier ; shouter; agitator
krzykliwy (kzhik-lee-vi) adj.
m. noisy ; clamorous; loud
krzywa (kzhi-ya) f. curve
krzywda (kzhiv-da) f. harm;
wrong ; a sense of wrong
krzywdzący (kzhiv-dzówn-tsi)
adj. m. harmful; injurious
krzywdzić (kzhiw-dźheech)v.
harm; wrong ;damage;be unfair
krzywica (kzhi-vee-tsa) f.
rickets ;rachitis;sweep saw
krzywić (kzhi-veech) v. bend
krzywić się (kzhi-veech shań)
v. make faces; bend ; warp
krzywo (kzhi-vo) adv. crooked
krzywy (kzhi-vi) adj. m. crooked; skew; distorted;slanting
krzyż (kzhish) m. cross
krzyżować (kzhi-zhó-vach) v.
cross; thwart; crucify
krzyżówka (kzhi-zhoóv-ka) f.
crossword puzzle
ksiądz (kśhównts) m. priest
książę (kśhown-zhan) m. prince;
duke; ruler of a duchy
książka (kśhównzh-ka) f. book
księga (kśhań-ga) f. register;
large book; volume; tome
księgarnia (kśhan-gár-ńa) f.
bookstore ; bookshop
księgarz (kśhań-gash) m. bookseller; owner of a bookstore
księgować (kśhań-go-vach) v.
keep-books ;enter in the books
księgowy (kśhań-gó-vi) m. bookkeeper ; accountant
księgozbiór (kśhań-go-zbyoor)
m. book collection; library

księstwo (kshāṅ-stvo) n. duchy
księżna (kshāṅzh-na) f. princess ; wife of a prince
księży (kshan-zhi) adj. m.
priestly ;belonging to a priest
księżyc (kshāṅ-zhits) m. moon
kształcić (kshtaw-cheech) v.
educate ; train; form;school
kształt (kshtawt) m. form;
shape ; configuration; figure
kształtny (kshtawt-ni) adj. m.
shapely ; neat; nicely made
kształtować (kshtaw-to-vach) v.
shape ; form; mold ; fashion
kto (kto) pron. who ; all;those
kto inny (kto een-ni) pron.
somebody else ; someone else
kto bądź (kto bowndch) pron.
anybody ; nayone;just anyone
ktoś (ktosh) pron. somebody
którędy (ktoo-raṅ-di) adv.
which way; how to get there?
który (ktoo-ri) pron. who;
which; that ; any; whichever
któż (ktoosh) pron. whichever
ku (koo) prep. towards; to
kubatura (koo-ba-too-ra) f.
(building) volume ;cubature
kubek (koo-bek) m. cup: mug
kubeł (koo-bew) m. pail;bucket
kucharka (koo-khar-ka) f. cook
kucharz (koo-khash)m. cook
kuchenka gazowa (koo-khen-ka
ga-zo-va)f.(gas) hotplate
kuchnia (kookh-na) f. kitchen
stove; cooking range; kitchen
kucnąć (koots-nownch)v. squat
kucyk (koo-tsik) m. small pony
kuć (kooch) v. hammer; shoe a
horse; cram lessons: peck;coin
kudłaty (kood-wa-ti) adj. m.
shaggy; hairy ; hirsute
kudły (kood-wi) pl. shaggy hair
kufel (koo-fel) m. beer mug
kufer (koo-fer) m. trunk
kuglarz (koog-lash) m. juggler
kukiełkowy teatr (koo- kew -ko-
vi teatr) puppet-show
kukła (kook-wa) f. puppet
kukułka (koo-koow-ka) f. cuckoo
bird; cuckoo clock
kukurydza (koo-koo-ri-dza) f.
maize; corn; Indian corn

kula (koo-la) f. sphere; bullet
crutch; ball; globe; shot
kulawy (koo-la-vi) adj. m. lame
kulbaczyć (kool-ba-chich) v.
saddle (a horse)
kulec (koo-lech) v. limp
kulić się (koo-leech shan) v.
snuggle; crouch; cringe;nestle
kulinarny (koo-lee-nar-ni) adj.
m. culinary ; of cooking
kulisy (koo-lee-si) pl. theatre
scenes ; the inner facts; links
kulisty (koo-lee-sti) adj. m.
spherical; ball-shaped
kulminacyjny (kool-mee-na-tsiy-
ni) adj. m. culminant; climactic
kult (koolt) m. cult ;worship
kultura (kool-too-ra) f. culture ; good manners;cultivation
kuluar (koo-loo-ar) m. lobby
kułak (koo-wak) m. fist;punch
kum (koom) m. godfather; crony
kumoterstwo (koo-mo-ter-stvo)
n. favoritism; log rolling
kumulacja (koo-moo-lats-ya) f.
cumulation; merger; fusion
kuna (koo-na) f. marten
kundel (koon-del) m. mongrel
kunszt (koonsht) m. art ;skill
kunsztowny (koon-shtov-ni) adj.
m. artistic; artful; ingenious
kupa (koo-pa) f. heep; pile;
lot; excrement ; assemblage
kupczyc (koop-chich) v. bargain;
trade ; influence peddling
kupic (koo-peech) v. buy
kupiec (koop-yets) m. shopkeeper ; merchant; dealer
kupno (koop-no) n. purchase
kupon (koo-pon) m. coupon
kur (koor) m. cock; cock crow
kura (koo-ra) f. hen; hen bird
kuracja (koo-rats-ya) f. cure
kuratorium (koo-ra-tor-yum) n.
board of trustees (of schools)
kurcz (koorch) m. cramp;shrinking
kurczę (koor-chan) n. chicken
kurczyc (koor-chich) v. shrink
kurek (koo-rek) m. tap; cock
kurier (koor-yer) m. courier
kurnik (koor-ṅeek) m. chicken
house; hen house; hen roost
poultry house; hen cote

kuropatwa (koo-ro-pát-va) f.
partridge (game bird)
kurowac (koo-ró-vach) v. heal;
cure ; treat for an illness
kurs (koors) m. course;rate;fare
kursowac (koor-só-vach)v.
circulate; ferry; run; ply
kurtka (koór-tka) f. jacket
kurtyna (koor-ti-na)f. curtain
kurwa (koór-va) f. whore (vulg.)
kurz (koosh) m. dust
kurza slepota (koózha shle-po-
ta) night blindness
kusic (koo-sheech) v. tempt
kustosz (koós-tosh) m. custo-
dian; curator ; conservator
kusy (koosi) adj. m. short
kusza (koo-sha) f. crossbow
kusnierz (koósh-nesh) m. furrier
kuter (koo-ter) m. cutter
kutwa (kóot-va) f. miser
kuty (koo-ti) adj. m. forged;
shod; cunning; sly; shrewd
kuzyn (koo-zin) m. cousin
kuzynka (koo-zin-ka) f. cousin
kuznia (koózh-na) f. forge
kwadra (kvád-ra)f.quarter moon
kwadrans (kvád-rans) m. quarter
of an hour; fiftee minutes
kwadrat (kvád-rat) m. square
kwakac (kvá-kach) v. quack
kwalifikacja (kva-lee-fee-káts-
ya) f. qualification;evaluation
kwalifikowac (kva-lee-fee-kó-
vach) qualify ; class;appraise
kwapic sie (kva-peech shan) v.
be eager; be in a hurry
kwarantanna (kva-ran-tán-na) f,
quarantine; period of isolation
kwarc (kvarts) m. quartz
kwarta (kvar-ta) f. quart
kwartalny (kvar-tál-ni) adj. m.
quarterly;occuring quarterly
kwas (kvas) m.acid; pl.discord
kwasic (kva-sheech) v. sour;
ferment; pickle;embitter;be idle
kwaskowaty (kvas-ko-vá-ti) adj.
m. sourish ; acidulous
kwasy (kvá-si) pl. fusses; bad-
blood; ill humor; dissent
kwasny (kvash-ni) adj. m. sour
kwatera (kva-té-ra) f. quarters;
lodging; living accommodation

kwaterka (kva-tér-ka) f. quarter
of a liter; quarter liter bottle
kwesta (kves-ta) f. collection
(for); passing the hat around
kwestia (kvést-ya) f. question
kwestionariusz (kves-tio-nár-
yoosh) m. questionnaire
kwekac (kvan-kach) v. complain
kwiaciarka (kvya-chár-ka) f.
florist; flower girl
kwiaciarnia (kvya-chár-na) f.
flower shop; florist's
kwiat (kvyat) m. flower
kwiczec (kvee-chech) v. squeak
kwiczol (kvee-chow) m. field-
fare (Turdus pilavis)
kwiecien (kvye-chen) m. April
kwiecisty (kvye-chees-ti) adj.
m. flowery; colorful; ornate
kwietnik (kvyet-neek) m. flower-
bed; carpet bed
kwik (kveek) m. squeal; squeak
kwit (kveet) m. receipt
kwitnac (kveet-nownch)v. blossom ;grow moldy; look healthy
kwitowac (kvee-to-vach) v. give
receipt; relinquish; forgo
kwoka (kvó-ka) f. sitting hen
kwota (kvó-ta) f. amount (of
money); amount ; allocation
kynologiczny zwiazek (ki-no-lo-
geech-ni zvyówn-zek) kennel
club ; kennel association
labirynt (la-bee-rint) m. la-
byrinth; maze
laborant (la-bó-rant) m. lab.
technician; assistant chemist
laboratorium (la-bo-ra-tór-
yoom) m. laboratory ; lab
lac (lach) v. pour; shed; (spill)
lada (lá-da) f. counter; chest
lada (lá-da) part. any; whatever; the least; paltry
lada kto (lá-da kto) anybody
ladacznica (la-dach-nee-tsa) f.
harlot; prostitute; strumpet
laik (lá-eek) m. layman
lak (lak) m. sealing wax
lakier (lá-ker) m. varnish
lakmus (lák-moos) m. litmus
lakoniczny (la-ko-neech-ni) adj.
m. terse; brief; curt; laconic
stating much in few words

lakowac (la-kó-vach) v. seal
lalka (lál-ka) f. doll ;puppet
laktoza (lak-tó-za) f. lactose
lament (la-ment) m. lament
lamowac (la-mó-vach) v. laminate
lamówka (la-moóv-ka) f. trim;
 border ; edge; trimming; piping
lampa (lám-pa) f. lamp
lampart (lám-part) m. leopard
lampas (lám-pas) m.stripe;lampas
lampion (lám-pyon) m. lampion
lamus (la-moos) m.storeroom
lanca (lán-tsa) f. lance; spear
lancet (lán-tset) m. lancet ;fleam
landara (lan-dá-ra) f. jalopy;
 old crate ; rumble-tumble
lanie (la-ñe) n. pouring; cast-
ing; beating ;thrashing; licking
lanolina (la-no-leé-na) f. lanolin ; wool-fat (in ointments)
lansady (lan-sá-di) pl. pranc-
 ing gait ; skips; leaps; bounds
lansowac (lan-só-vach) v. launch
lapidarny (la-pee-dár-ni) adj.
 m. terse; concise ;curt; crisp
lapis (lá-pees) m. silver nitrate ; lunar caustic
lapsus (lap-soos) m. lapse(slip)
laryngologia (la-rin-go-lóg-ya)
 f. laryngology
las (las) m. wood; forest ;thicket
lasek (la-sek) m. grove
laska (lás-ka) f. cane ; stick
laskowy orzech (las-kó-vi
 ó-zhekh)m.hazelnut
lasowac (la-só-vach) v. slake
lata (la-ta) pl. years
latac (la-tach)v.fly;be running
latarka (la-tár-ka) f. flashlight ; torch ; small lamp
latarnia (la-tár-ña) f. street-
 light ; lantern; beacon
latarnia morska (la-tár-ña mór-
 ska) lighthouse
latarnik (la-tár-ñeek) m. lighthouse keeper
latawiec (la-táv-yets) m. kite
lato (la-to) n. Summer
latorosl (la-tó-roshl) f. shoot;
 offspring; scion; sprig; sprout
laubzega (lawb-zé-ga) f. fret-
 saw; jigsaw; scroll saw

laufer (láw-fer) m. runner;
 (chess)bishop
laury (law-ri) pl. laurels
laureat (law-ré-at) m. laure-
 ate ; prize-winner
lawa (la-va) f. volcanic lava
lawenda (la-vén-da) f. lavender ; lavender water
laweta (la-vé-ta) f. gun-
 carriage; heavy gun base
lawina (la-veé-na) f. avalanche ; shower (of words)
lawirowac (la-vee-ró-vach) v.
 veer; tack; intrigue
lazaret (la-zá-ret) m. field
 hospital(for infections)
lazur (la-zoor) m. azure; sky
 blue ; blue pigment
lad (lównd) m. 1. land;
 2. mainland; 3. continent
ladowac (lówn-dó-vach) v. land;
 disembark; go ashore; alight
leciec (le-chech) v. fly; run;
 hurry;wing; drift; drop; fall
leciutko (le-choot-ko) adv.
 bearly touching;very lightly
leciwy (le-chee-vi) adj. m.
 up in years;advanced in years
lecz (lech) conj. but;however
leczenie (le-che-ñe) n. healing ; cure; treatment
lecznica (lech-neé-tsa) f. hospital; clinic;nursing home
leczyc (le-chich) v. heal;
 treat; nurse;practice medicine
ledwie (led-vye) adv. hardly;
 scarcely; barely ;almost;nearly
ledwo ze nie (le-dvo zhe ñe)
 adv. almost; nearly; hardly
legacja (le-gáts-ya) f. legation; legacy; bequest
legalizowac (le-ga-lee-zó-vach)
 legalize; certify; attest
legalny (le-gál-ni) adj. m.
 legal; lawful;allowed by law
legat (le-gat) m. bequest;
 papal muncio
legawiec (le-ga-vyets) m.
 pointer ; setter
legenda (le-gén-da) f. legend
legendarny (le-gen-dár-ni) adj.
 m. legendary ; fabulous;storied

legia (leg-ya) f. legion
legion (leg-yon) m. legion
legitymacja (le-gee-ti-máts-ya)
f. i-d card; identification
papers; membership card etc
legitymować się (le-gee-ti-mo-
vach śhań) v. prove one's
identity; identify oneself
lęgnąć (leg-nównch) v. fall
in battle; perish; lie down
legowisko (le-go-vee-sko) n.
berth; bedding;encampment;den
legumina (le-goo-mee-na) f.
dessert; sweet dish;legumin
lej (ley) m. crater; funnel
lejce (ley-tse) pl. reins
lejek (le-yek) m. small funnel
lek (lek) m. medicine; drug
lekarski (le-kár-skee) adj. m.
medical; medicinal
lekarz (le-kash) m. physician
lekceważący (lek-tse-va-zhówn-
tsi) adj. m. disrespectful
lekceważenie (lek-tse-va-zhe-
ńe) n. disdain;disrespect
lekceważyć (lek-tse-vá-zhich)
v. slight; scorn; neglect
lekcja (lek-tsya) f. lesson
lekki (lek-kee) adj. m. light;
light-hearted;graceful; slight
lekko (lek-ko) adv. easily
lekkoatleta (lek-ko-at-le-ta) m.
field&track man
lekkomyślny (lek-ko-mishl-ni)
adj. m. careless; thoughtless;
reckless; rash; fickle
lektura (lek-too-ra) f. reading
matter; reading list; reading
lemiesz (le-myesh) m. plough-
share; blade; vomer
lemoniada (le-mo-ná-da) f. lemonade; lemon squash
len (len) m. flax;linen;
lenić się (le-ńeech śhań) v.
be idle; be lazy; shed hair
leniec (le-ńech) v. shed hair
leninizm (le-ńee-ńeezm) m. Le-
ninism;Lenin's interpretation
lenistwo (le-ńees-tvo) n. laziness; idleness; sluggishness
leniwy (le-ńee-vi) adj. m. lazy
lennik (len-ńeek) m. vassal
pledging fealty to overlord

lenno (len-no) n. fief
leń (leń) m. lazy-bones; idler;
lazy bum; sluggard
lep (lep) m. glue; flypaper
lepianka (lep-yán-ka) f. adobe;
mud hut; mud cabin
lepić (le-peech) v. stick; glue
lepiej (lep-yey) adv. better;
rather ;(feel) better
lepki (lep-kee) adj. m. sticky
lepszy (lep-shi) adj. m. better
lesbijka (les-beey-ka) f. les-
bian;homosexual women
lesisty (le-śhees-ti) adj. m.
wooded; woody; forest-
leszcz (leshch) m. bream
leszczyna (lesh-chi-na) f.
hazelnut tree; hazel grove
leśnictwo (leśh-ńeets-tvo) n.
forestry; forest-range
leśniczówka (leśh-ńee-choov-ka)
f. ranger's house (forester's)
leśniczy (leśh-ńee-chi) m. ranger; forest-ranger;forester
leśnik (leśh-ńeek) m. forester
leśny (leśh-ni) adj. m. of
forest; of forestry;forest-
letarg (le-targ) m. lethargy
letni (let-ńee) adj. m. lukewarm; half-hearted; summer
letnik (let-ńeek) m. vacationer
letnisko (let-ńees-ko) n. summer
resort;summer vacation spot
lew (lev) m. lion; lady's man
lewa (le-ya) f. left (side)
lewar (le-var) m. lever; jack
lewatywa (le-ya-ti-va) f. enema
lewica (le-vee-tsa) f. the left
(polit.); left-hand side
lewo (le-vo) adv. to the left
lewy (le-vi) adj. m. left; false
lezć (lezhch) v. crowl; creep-
along; plod along; climb;jostle
leżak (le-zhak) m. folding
(canvas) chair;deck-chair
leżeć (le-zhech) v. lie; (fit)
lędźwie (lańdzh-vye) pl. loins
lęgnąć (lang-nównch) v. hatch
lęk (lańk) m. fear;anxiety;dread
lękać się (lán-kach śhań) v.
be afraid; dread;stand in awe
lękliwy (lańk-lee-vi) adj. m.
timid;faint-hearted;apprehensive

lgnąć (lgnownch) v. adhere;sink;
stick; be partial;feel attracted
libacja (lee-bats-ya) f. drinking party; drinking bout
liberalny (lee-be-rál-ni) adj.
m.liberal; broad-minded
liberał (lee-bé-raw) m. liberal
libertyn (lee-bér-tin) m. libertine; free thinker
lice (lee-tse) n. face; cheek;
the right side; evidence
licencja (lee-tsén-tsya) f. license (ermission to practice)
licho (lee-kho) adv. poorly
licho (lee-kho) n. evil; devil
lichota (lee-kho-ta) f. rubbish
lichtarz (leekh-tash) m. candlestick ; candelabrum;candelabra
lichwa (leekh-va) f. usury
lichwiarz (leekh-vyash) m. usurer; loan shark; money lender
lichy (lee-khi) adj. m. shoddy;
shabby ; poor; mean;rotten;petty
lico (lee-tsom.face; cheek; surface ; front; outer part
licować (lee-tsó-vach) v. fit
for... ; comport;veneer; face
licytacja (lee-tsi-táts-ya) f.
auction ; bidding; the bid
licytować (lee-tsi-tó-vach) v.
auction; bid; offer; call
liczba (leech-ba) f. number;
figure ; integer; group; class
liczbowy (leech-bó-vi) adj. m.
numerical ;numeral
licznik (leech-neek) m. counter;
numerator; gasmeter; electro-
meter, etc;taximeter; register
liczny (leech-ni) adj. m.numer-
ous ; large; abundant;plentiful
liczyć (lee-chich) v. count ;
reckon;compute;calculate
liczydło (lee-chid-wo) n. aba-
cus; counter; register
liga (lee-ga) f. league ;alliance
lik (leek) m. lot ;countless
lignina (leeg-nee-na) f. lignin
likier (lee-k er) m. liquor
likwidacja (leek-vee-dáts-ya)
f. liquidation ;closing down
likwidować (leek-vee-do-vach) v.
liquidate ;do away with

lila (lee-la) adj. m. (color)
pale-violet; lily-
lilia (leel-ya) f. lily
liliowy (leel-yo-vi) adj. m.
lilac (color) ; lily-
liliput (lee-lee-poot) m.
little dwarf ; midget; pygmy
limfa (leem-fa) f. lymph
limit (lee-meet) m. limit
limuzyna (lee-moo-zi-na) f.
limousine; pilot's enclosure
lin (leen) m. tench
lina (lee-na) f. line; rope
lincz (leench) m. lynch
linczować (leen-cho-vach) v.
lynch; kill by mob action
lingwista (leen-gvees-ta) m.
linguist (specialist)
linia (leen-ya) f. line; lane
linijka (lee-neey-ka) f. ruler
liniować (lee-nyo-vach) v.
rule; line (paper)
liniowy okręt (leen-yo-vi ok-
ránt) liner (ship);battleship
linoleum (lee-no-lé-oom) n.
linoleum (floor covering)
linoskoczek (lee-no-sko-chek)
m. tightrope artist
linotyp (lee-no-tip) m. lino-
type (typesetting machine)
linowa kolejka (lee-no-va ko-
ley-ka) cable car
lipa (lee-pa) f.1.linden tree
2. fake; cheat; fraud
lipiec (leep-yets) m. July
lira (lee-ra) f. lyre
liryczny (lee-rich-ni) adj. m.
lyric; lyrical
liryk (lee-rik) m. lyrist;lyric
liryka (lee-ri-ka) f. lyric
poetry ; lyricism
lis (lees) m. fox; sly man
list (leest) m. letter;note
lista (lees-ta) f. list;roll
listonosz (lees-to-nosh) m.
postman
listopad (lees-tó-pad) m. November
listownie (lees-tóv-ne) adv.
by letter ; by mail
listwa (lees-tva) f. trim
liszaj (lee-shay) m. herpes

liszka (leesh-ka) f. caterpillar ; vixen; sly fox
liściasty (leesh-chas-ti) odj.
m. leafy ; leafed; foliaceous
lisc (leeshch) m. leaf ; frond
litania (lee-tan-ya) f. litany
litera (lee-te-ra) f. letter
literacki (lee-te-rats-kee)
adj. m. literary ; of letters
literat (lee-te-rat) m. writer
literatura (lee-te-ra-too-ra)
f. literature ; writings
litewski (lee-tev-skee) adj. m.
Lithuanian ;Lithuanian language
litograf (lee-to-graf) m.
lithographer
litościwy (lee-tosh-chee-vi)
adj. m. merciful; compassionate
litosc (lee-toshch) f. pity;
mercy ; compassion
litować sie (lee-to-vach shan)
v. have pity ;feel pity
litr (leetr) m. liter
liturgia (lee-toor-gya) f.
liturgy; religious ritual
lity (lee-ti) adj. m. massive
solid; cast; pure-
lizac (lee-zach) v. lick
lizol (lee-zol) m. lysol
lizus (lee-zoos) m. bootlicker
lniany (lna-ni) adj. m. linen;
flaxen; linseed
loch (lokh) m. dungeon; cellar
lodołamacz (lo-do-wa-mach) m.
icebreaker : ice shield
lodowaty (lo-do-va-ti) adj. m.
icy ; ice-cold; chilling;frigid
lodowiec (lo-do-vyets) m. glacier;mass of ice and snow
lodowisko (lo-do-vees-ko) n.
skating-rink ; ice rink
lodownia (lo-dov-na) f. ice-
chamber; ice-cellar; icy cold
lodowy (lo-do-yy) adj. m. of ice
lodówka (lo-dov-ka) f. refrigerator; ice box; ice chest
lody (lo-di) pl. ice cream
logarytm (lo-ga-ritm) m. loga-
rithm
logiczny (lo-geech-ni) adj. m.
logical ;consistent; sound
logik (lo-geek) m. logician;
expert in logic

logika (lo-gee-ka) f. logic
lojalnosc (lp-yal-noshch) f.
loyalty;straightforwardness
lojalny (lo-yal-ni) adj. m.
loyal; staunch; low-abiding
lok (lok) m. curl; coil
lokaj (lo-kay) m. lackey
lokal (lo-kal) m. premises
lokalizowac (lo-ka-lee-zo-vach)
localize; locate; range
lokalny (lo-kal-ni) adj. m.
local; regional;of a place
lokata (lo-ka-ta) f. investment
lokator (lo-ka-tor) m. tenant
lokomocja (lo-ko-mots-ya) f.
locomotion ; communication
lokomotywa (lo-ko-mo-ti-va) f.
train engine; locomotive
lokować (lo-ko-vach) v. place
lombard (lom-bard) m. pawnshop
lont (lont) m. fuse ;slow-match
lornetka (lor-net-ka) f. field
glasses; opera glasses
los (los) m. lot; fate; chance;
lottery-ticket; destiny;hazard
losowac (lo-so-vach) v. draw
lots ; raffle ; draw cuts
lot (lot) m. flight ; speed
loteria (lo-ter-ya) f. lottery
lotnia (lot-na) f. hang glider
lotnictwo (lot-neets-tvo) n.
aviation; aeronautics;air force
lotnik (lot-neek) m. aviator
lotnisko (lot-nees-ko) n. airport; airfield; aerodrome
lotniskowiec (lot-nees-kov-
yets) m. aircraft carrier
lotny (lot-ni) adj. m. bright;
quick; swift;sharp; subtle
lotos (lo-tos) m. lotus
loza masonska (lo-zha ma-sons-
ka) shriner's lodge
lod (loot) m. ice; pl.ice cream
lsniacy (lshnown-tsi)adj. m.
shining; bright;glossy; sleek
lsnic (lshneech) v. glitter;
shine;gleam; glimmer; shimmer
lub (loop) conj. or;or else
luba (loo-ba) f. sweetheart
lubic (loo-beech) v. like;
be fond; enjoy; be partial
lubieżny (loo-byezh-ni) adj.
m. lustful; voluptuous; lewd

lubość (loo-boshćh) f. delight
lubować się (loo-bó-vaćh śhań)
  v. take delight ; find pleasure
lud (loot) m. people; nation
ludność (lood-noshćh) f. population (of a given territory)
ludny (lood-ni) adj. m. populous ; teeming; crowded
ludobójstwo (loo-do-booy-stvo)
  n. genocide;killing of a nation
ludowy (loo-do-vi) adj. m.pop-
  ulist; popular; country
ludożerca (loo-do-zhér-tsa) m.
  cannibal ; man man-eater
ludzie (loo-dźhe) pl. people
ludzkość (loodz-koshćh) f.
  mankind; humaneness; humanity
lufa (loo-fa) f. gunbarrel
luk (look) m. hatch ;skylight
luka (loo-ka) f. gap;blank;break
lukier (loo—ker) m. sugar-
  icing ; frosting
lukratywny (look-ra-tiv-ni) adj.
  m. lucrative ; profitable
luksus (look-soos) m. luxury
lunatyk (loo-na-tik) l. sleepwalker; 2. loony
lunąć (loo-nównćh) v. rain in
  torrents;slap ;lash down;whack
luneta (loo-né-ta) f. field-
  glass ;spy-glass; telescope
lupa (loo-pa) f. magnifying
  glass ; jeweler's glass (loop)
lusterko (loos-tér-ko) n. hand-
  glass ; rear-view mirror(in a car)
lustro (loos-tro) n. mirror
lustrować (loos-tró-vaćh) v.
  inspect; review ; check; audit
lut (loot) m. solder
luteranin (loo-te-ra-ńeen) m.
  Lutheran
lutnia (loot-ńa) f. flute
lutować (loo-tó-vaćh) v. solder
luty (loo-ti) m. February
luty (loo-ty) adj. m. bleak;
  grim ; severe; bleak
luz (loos) m. clearance; play
luzak (loo-zak) m. loose (replacement) horse
luzować (loo-zó-vaćh) v. replace;
  relieve ; loosen;slacken;ease off
luźny (loozh-ni) adj. m. loose

lwi (lvee) adj. m. lion's
lżej (lzhey) adv. lighter;
  easier ; with less weight
lżenie (lzhé-ńe) n. abuse; insults;vituperation
lżyć (lzhićh) v. abuse; insult
łabędź (wa-bańdźh)m. swan
łach (wakh) m. rag ; clout
łacha (wa-kha) f. sandbank
łachman (wåkh-man) m. rag
łachudra (wa-khood-ra) m.
  ragtagman; ragamuffin
łaciarz (wa-ćhash) m. patcher
łaciaty (wa-ćhá-ti) adj. m.
  in patches ; pinto(horse)
łacina (wa-ćhee-na) f. Latin
łaciński (wa-cheeń-skee) adj.
  m. Latin; of Latin
ład (wad) m. order;orderliness
ładnie (wad-ńe) adv. nicely
ładnieć (wad-ńech) v. grow
  pretty ; grow prettier
ładny (wad-ny) adj. m. nice
ładować (wa-do-vaćh) v. load;
  charge; cram; fill
ładownica (wa-dow-ńee-tsa) f.
  cartridge pouch (or box)
ładunek (wa-doo-nek) m. load;
  cargo; charge ; shipload;burden
łagodność (wa-god-noshćh) f.
  gentleness; kindliness;suavity
łagodny (wa-god-ni) adj. m.
  gentle ;mild;soft;meek;easy
łagodzący (wa-go-dzówn-tsi) adj.
  m. alleviating; extenuating
łagodzić (wa-go-dźheech)v.
  soothe; relieve; alleviate
  attenuate; mitigate ; smooth
łajać (wa-yaćh) v. scold; chide
łajdactwo (way-dáts-tvo) n.
  mean trick;scoundrels;rabble
łajdak (wáy-dak) m. scoundrel
łajno (wáy-no) n. dung; shit
łaknąć (wak-nównćh) v. hunger
  for; thirst for ;crave for
łakocie (wa-kó-ćhe) pl. deli-
  cacies; sweets;tidbits;candy
łakomić się (wa-ko-meećh śhań)
  v. covet; lust;be tempted
łakomy (wa-kó-mi) adj. m.
  greedy; covetous; avid
łakomstwo (wa-kóm-stvo) n.
  greed; gluttony;greediness

Łamać (wa-maćh) v. break;crush; quarry;shatter; crack; snap

Łamigłówka (wa-mee-gwoow-ka) f. riddle; puzzle;jig-saw puzzle

Łamistrajk (wa-mee-strayk) m. scab; strikebreaker

Łamliwy (wam-lee-vi) adj. m. fragile;frail;brittle;breakable

Łan (wán) m. stand of wheat

Łania (wa-ña) f. hind; doe

Łańcuch (wáń-tsookh) m. chain; range; series; train;succession

Łańcuchowa reakcja (wań-tsoo-khó-va re-ák-tsya) chain reaction

Łapa (wa-pa) f. paw ;claw;arm

Łapać (wá-pać) v. catch;snatch

Łapanka (wa-pan-ka) f. roundup

Łapcie (wáp-che) n. bast sandals ; moccasins

Łapczywość (wap-chi-voshćh) f. greed; greediness; avidity

Łapczywy (wap-chi-vi) adj. m. greedy; money-grubbing

Łapka (wáp-ka) f. (mouse) trap

Łapówka (wa-poóv-ka) f. bribe

Łapserdak (wap-sér-dak) m. rogue; ragamuffin;scoundrel

Łasica (wa-shée-tsa) f. weasel

Łasić się (wa-sheećh śhań) v. fawn; fawn on sb.; toady

Łaska (wás-ka) f. grace ; clemency; favor; generosity;mercy

Łaskawy (was-ka-vi) adj. m. gracious; kind; generous

Łaskotać (was-ko-tać) v. tickle; titillate

Łaskotliwy (was-kot-lee-vi) adj. m. ticklish; titillating

Łasy (wa-si) adj. m. greedy

Łaszczyć się (wash-chich śhań) v. covet; lust

Łata (wa-ta) f. patch

Łatać (wa-tać) v. patch up

Łatanina (wa-ta-nee-na) f. patch work; bungling

Łatwo (wát-vo) adv. easily

Łatwopalny (wat-vo-pál-ni) adj. m. inflammable ; combustible

Łatwość (wát-voshćh) f. ease; facility ;aptitude; fluency

Łatwowierny (wat-vo-vyér-ni) adj. m. credulous ;gullible

Łatwy (wát-vi) adj. m. easy

Ława (wa-va) f. bench ;footing

Ławica (wa-vee-tsa) f. (fish) shoal ; sandbank; shelf; layer

Ławka (wáf-ka) f. pew; bench

Ławnik (wáv-ńeek) m. juror; alderman ; assessor

Łazić (wa-żheećh)v. crawl; loiter ; slouch about;creep

Łazienka (wa-żhén-ka) f. bathroom; toilet; bath

Łazik (wá-żheek) m. tramp; jeep

Łaźnia (wáżh-ńa) f. bath

Łażący (wa-zhówn-tsi) adj. m. dragging; crawling;scansorial

Łączący (wówn-chówn-tsy) adj. m. uniting; joining; unitive

Łącznica (wównch-ńeé-tsa) f. junction ;switchboard

Łącznie (wówn-chńe) adv. together; including; inclusive of

Łącznik (wownch-ńeek) m. hyphen; liaisonman ;link; tie; bond

Łączność (wownch-noshćh) f. contact; communication; unity; signal service; connection

Łączny (wownch-ni) adj. m. joint; combined;total; global

Łączyć (wown-chich) v. join; unite ;merge;link;bind;weld

Łąka (wówn-ka) f. meadow

Łeb (web) m. head; pate

Łechtać (wékh-tać) v. tickle; flatter ; titillate; lure

Łęk (wańk) m. saddlebow; syncline; arch; bow; pommel

Łgać (wgać) v. lie;brag;boast

Łgarstwo (wgár-stvo) n. lie

Łgarz (wgásh) m. liar; braggart

Łkać (wkać) v. sob

Łobuz (wo-boos) m. rogue; rascal; scamp; scoundrel

Łodyga (wo-di-ga) f. stem

Łoic (wo-eećh) v. tallow; beat up; wallop; curry

Łokieć (wo-kećh) m. elbow

Łom (wom) m. crowbar;scrap;junk

Łomot (wo-mot) m. crash; crack

Łono (wo-no) n. lap; bosom;womb

Łopata (wo-pá-ta) f. spade

Łopot (wo-pot) m. (sail)flutter

Łoskot (wos-kot) n. clatter; bang; din; rumble;racket;boom

Łosoś (wo-sośh) m. salmon

Łoś (wośh) m. elk; moose

Łotewski (wo-tev-skee) adj. m.
Latvian ; Latvian language

Łotr (wotr) m, vicious scoun —
drel; knave; rascal; rogue

Łowczy (wóv-chi) adj. m. hunting;, huntsman's; hunter's

Łowić (wóv-eećh) v. trap;
fish; catch; hunt; chase

Łowiectwo (wov-yéts-tvo) n.
hunting; game shooting

Łowy (wó-vi) pl. hunt; chase

Łozina (wo-żhée-na) f. wicker;
sallow; osier; osier-bed

łoże (wó-zhe) n. bed; cradle

łożyć (wó-zhićh) v. spend

łożysko (wo-zhis-ko) n.(river)
bed; (ball) bearing

łódka (wóod-ka) f. small boat

łódź (wóodżh) f. boat;craft

łój (wooy) m. tallow;suet;sebum

łów (woov) m. hunt; chase

łożeczko (woo-zhéch-ko) n.
(child's) bed; small bed

łóżko (wóozh-ko) n. bed;bunk

łubin (woó-been) m. lupin

łucznik (wooch-ńeek) n. archer

łuczywo (woo-chi-vo) n. resin-
ous kindling;resinous chips

łudzący (woo-dzówn-tsi) adj.
m. delusive; deceptive

łudzić (woo-dżheećh)v. delude;
deceive; give false hope

ług (woog) m. lye

ługować (woo-gó-vaćh) v. leach;
lixiviate

łuk (wook) m. bow; arch; bent;
vault

łuna (woó-na) f. glow (of sun
or fire)

łup (woop) m. booty; spoils

łupać (woó-paćh) v. cleave;
split; ache; give shooting pain

łupek (woó-pek) m, slate

łupić (woó-peećh) v. plunder

łupież (woó-pyezh) f. dandruff

łupieżca (woo-pyezh-tsa) m.
plunderer; looter; pillager

łupina (woo-pée-na) f. husk;
shell; peel; skin; hull;rind

łuska (woós-ka) f. scale; husk;
shell; pod; flake; rind

łuskać (woós-kaćh) v. scale;
husk; peel; pod; hull (rice)

łuszczyć (woosh-chićh) v. peel;
pare; flake off; shell off

łuza (woó-za) f. billiard
pocket

łydka (wit-ka) f. calf(leg-shank)

łyk (wik) m. gulp; sip; draft

łykać (wí-kaćh) v. swallow;
gulp; sip; bolt; gorge; drink

łyko (wi-ko) n. bast; phoem

łykowaty (wi-ko-vá-ti) adj. m.
wiry; tough; fibrous

łypać (wí-paćh) v. blink

łysek (wí-sek) m. (boldhead)
boldy; bold-faced animal

łysieć (wí-shech) v. become
bold; grow bold; lose hair

łysina (wi-shée-na) f. pate

łyskać (wís-kaćh) v. flash

łysy (wí-si) adj. m. bold

łyżeczka (wi-zhéch-ka) f. tea-
spoon; dessert spoon; curette

łyżka (wízh-ka) f. spoon;spoonful

łyżwa (wízh-va) f. skate

łyżwiarz (wízh-vyash) m.skater

łyżwowy (wizh-vo-vi)adj.of skates

łza (wza) f. tear

łzawy (wzá-vi) adj. m. tearful

łzowy kanał (wzó-vi ka-naw)
tear canal; tear duct

maca (ma-tsa) f. matzos

macać (ma-tsaćh) v. feel; grope

machać (má-khaćh) v. wave;whisk;
swing; wag; lash; flap;brandish

macher (má-kher) m. trickster

machina (ma-khee-na) f. (large)
machine; bureaucratic machine

machinacja (ma-khee-náts-ya) f.
machination; dodge; intrigue

machlojka (ma-khlóy-ka) f.
swindle; defraudation

macica (ma-chée-tsa) f. uterus;
womb; screw nut; tap root

macierz (ma-ćhesh) f. mother
country; matrix; mother

macierzanka (ma-ćhe-zhan-ka) f.
thyme ; wild thyme

macierzyński (ma-ćhe-zhiń-ski)
adj. m. maternal; mother's

macierzyństwo (ma-ćhe-zhiń-stvo)
n. maternity; motherhood

macierzysty (ma-che-zhis-ti)
adj. m. maternal; (parental)
maciora (ma-cho-ra) f. sow
macka (mats-ka) f. tentacle;
feeler; antenna; horn
macocha (ma-tso-kha) f. stepmother; not as good as mother
maczac (ma-chach) v. dip; soak
maczuga (ma-choo-ga) f. bat;
club; bludgeon; cudgel
magazyn (ma-ga-zin) m. store;
warehouse; repository; store
magazynier (ma-ga-zi-ner) m.
warehouseman; storekeeper
magia (mag-ya) f. sorcery
magiczny (ma-geech-ni) adj. m.
magic; conjuring tricks
magiel (ma-gel) m. mangle
magik (ma-geek) m. magician
magister (ma-gees-ter) m.mas-
ter (diplomat); chemist
magisterium (ma-gees-ter-yoom)
n. master's degree
magistrat (ma-gees-trat) m.
city hall; municipality
maglowac (mag-lo-vach) v, mangle; calender; bother; crush
magnat (mag-nat) m. magnate
magnes (mag-nes) m. magnet
magnetofon (mag-ne-to-fon) m.
tape-recorder
magnetyczny (ma-gne-tich-ni)
adj. m. magnetic;magnetical
magnetyzm (mag-ne-tizm) m.
magnetism;personal charm
magnez (mag-nes) m. magnesium
magnezja (mag-nez-ya) f. mag-
nesia; magnesium
magnolia (mag-nol-ya) f. magnolia (Magnolia)
mahometanin (ma-kho-me-ta-neen)
m. Mohammedan; Moslem
mahon (ma-khon) m. mahogany
maic (ma-eech) v. decorate
with green leaves
maj (may) m. May
majaczyc (ma-ya-chich) v. rave;
loom ; be delirious
majatek (ma-yown-tek) m. fortune; estate; property;wealth
majdan (may-dan) m. parade-
ground; personal junk; traps

majeranek (ma-ye-ra-nek) m.
marjoram; fragrant mint(cooking)
majestat (ma-yes-tat) m. majesty; kingship; stateliness
majetnosc (ma-yant-noshch) f.
wealth; fortune; property
majetny (ma-yant-ni) adj. m.
well to do ;wealthy; affluent
majonez (ma-yo-nes) m. mayon-
naise ; egg yoke dressing
major (ma-yor) m. major
majowka (ma-yoov-ka) f. May-
outing ; picnic; junket
majster (may-ster) m. qualified
craftman; boss; master;foreman
majstersztyk (may-ster-shtik) m.
masterpiece;greatest work
majstrowac (may-stro-vach) v.
tinker ; make (an object)
majtek (may-tek) m. deckhand
majtki (mayt-kee) pl. panties
mak (mak) m. poppy seed
makaron (ma-ka-ron) m. macaroni
makata (ma-ka-ta) f. tapestry
makler (mak-ler) m. broker
makolagwa (ma-ko-lowng-va) f.
linnet; lass; lassie
makrela (ma-kre-la) f. mackerel
maksyma (ma-ksi-ma) f. axiom;
maxim ; adage ;rule of conduct
maksymalny (ma-ksi-mal-ni) adj.
m. maximum ;top-;peak-;most-
makulatura (ma-koo-la-too-ra) f.
waste-paper;spoilage; rubbish
makuch (ma-kookh) m. oilcake
malaria (ma-lar-ya) f. malaria
malarstwo (ma-lar-stvo) m.
painting (art); house painting
malarz (ma-lash) m. painter
malec (ma-lets) m. youngster
malec (ma-lech) v. shrink;dwindle
malenki (ma-len-kee) adj. m.
very small; tiny; insignificant
malenstwo (ma-len-stvo) n. tiny
thing; little one; little mite
malina (ma-lee-na) f. raspberry
malowac (ma-lo-vach) v. paint;
stain; color; make up;depict
malowidlo (ma-lo-veed-wo) n.
painting; picture (painted)
malowniczy (ma-lov-nee-chi)
adj. m. picturesque; vivid

maltretować (mal-tre-tó-vać)
v. abuse; mistreat; ill-treat
malwersacja (mal-ver-sáts-ya)
f. embezzlement; peculation
mało (má-wo) adv. little; few;
seldom; lack; not enough
małoduszny (ma-wo-doósh-ni)
adj. m.small-minded; narrow-
minded; cheap ;fainthearted
małoletni (ma-wo-lét-ñee)adj.
m. minor; under age ;juvenile
małomówny (ma-wo-moóv-ni) adj.
m. reticent; laconic;taciturn
małostkowy (ma-wost-kó-vi) adj.
m. fussy; petty; mean
małpa (máw-pa) f. ape; monkey
małpować (maw-po-vać) v. ape
mały (má-wi) adj. m. little;
small size; low; modest;slight
małżeński (maw-zheń-skee) adj.
m. matrimonial ;conjugal
małżeństwo (maw-sheń-stwo) n.
married couple; wedlock
małżonek (maw-zhó-nek) m. husband ; spouse; consort; mate
małżonka (maw-zhón-ka) f. wife
mama (má-ma) f. mamma ; mother
mamałyga (ma-ma-wí-ga) f.
maize gruel ; hominy
mamić (ma-meéch) v. deceive;
delude ;beguile; lure;tempt
mamidło (ma-meéd-wo) n. illusion ; delusion;lure;seduction
mamona (ma-mó-na) f. mammon
mamlać (mám-lać) v. mumble
mamrotać (mam-ró-tać) v. mutter ; mumble; gibber
mamut (má-moot) m. mammoth
manatki (ma-nát-kee) pl.person-
al belongings; traps
mandaryn (man-dá-rin) n. man-
darin; Chinese dignitary.
mandat (man-dat) m. mandate;
traffic ticket ; fine
mandolina (man-do-leé-na) f.
mandolin with 8 to 10 strings
manekin (ma-ne-keen)m.mannequin
manewr (má-nevr) m. maneuver
manewrować (ma-nev-ró-vać) v.
maneuver; steer;handle; switch
maneż (má-nesh) m. riding-
school; horse-driven thrasher

mangan (mán-gan) m. manganese
mania (má-ńya) f. mania ;fad
maniak (má-ńyak) m. maniac;crank
manicure (ma-ńee-keer) m.
manicure;doing one's fingernails
manic (má-ñeech) v. deceive;tempt
maniera (ma-ñé-ra) f. manner
manierka (ma-ñér-ka) f. canteen
manifest (ma-ñee-fest) m. man-
ifesto: a public declaration
manifestacja (ma-ñee-fes-táts-ya)
f. manifestation; demonstration
manifestować (ma-ñee-fes-tó-
vać) v. demonstrate; display
manipulacja (ma-ñee-poo-láts-ya)
f. manipulation; handling
manipulować (ma-ñee-poo-lo-vać)
v. manipulate;handle; tinker
mankiet (man-k et) m. cuff;turn-up
mankament (man-ka-ment) m. defect; shortcoming; fault
manko (mán-ko) n. (acc.) shortage; allowance for cash errors
manna (mán-na) f. cream of
wheat; a godsend manna
manometr (ma-nó-metr) m. pressure gauge; steam gauge
manowce (ma-nóv-tse) pl. road-
less area; misguided direction
manufaktura (ma-noo-fak-toó-ra)
f. fabrics; manufacture ; shop
manuskrypt (ma-noós-kript) m.
manuscript(hand or typewritten)
mankuctwo (mań-koóts-tvo) n.
left-handedness;
mapa (má-pa) f. map; chart
mara (ma-ra) f. ghost; apparition; nightmare; dream; vision
marazm (ma-razm) m. sluggishness
marchew (mar-khev) f. carrot
marcepan (mar-tse-pan) m. mar-
zipan; marchpane
margaryna (mar-ga-ri-na) f.
margarine ; marge (slang)
margines (mar-geé-nes) m. margin; edge; border;minor thing
mariaż (mar-yazh) m. marriage
marionetka (mar-yo-nét-ka) f.
puppet;dummy ; figurehead
marka (már-ka) f. mark; brand;
stamp; trade mark; reputation
markotno (mar-kót-no) adv. sad

markotny (mar-kót-ni) adj. m.
peevish; moody; sullen; sad
marksistowski (mark-shees-tóvs-
kee) adj. m. Marxist: of Marx
marksizm (márk-sheezm) m.
Marxism; Marxist believes
marmolada (mar-mo-lá-da) f.
marmalade; jam; shambles
marmur (már-moor) m. marble
marniec (már-ñech) v. deteriorate; waste; decline; perish
marność (már-noshch) f. futil-
ity; flimsiness; vanity
marnotrawny (mar-no-tráv-ni)
adj. m. wasteful; prodigal
marnować (mar-nó-vach) v. waste
marny (már-ni) adj. m. poor;
meagre: sorry; of no value
marsz(marsh) m. march; walk
marsz ! (marsh) excl.: (command)
forward march; split ! get
out ! off you go !
marszałek (mar-sha-wek) m.
marshal; Polish Seym speaker
marszczyc (marsh-chich) v.
wrinkle; frown; crease; ripple
marszruta (marsh-róo-ta) f.
route ; itinerary
martwica (mart-vee-tsa) f.
necrosis ; sinter; travertine
martwic (mart-veech) v. distress;grieve; vex; worry;afflict
martwy (mart-vi) adj. m. dead
martyr (már-tir) m. martyr
maruder (ma-roo-der) m. maraud-
er; straggler; loiterer
marudzic (ma-roo-dzheech)v.
loiter; grumble; lag behind
mary (má-ri) pl. mar; bier
marynarka (ma-ri-nár-ka) f.
jacket; sportscoat; navy
marynarz (ma-rí-nash) m. mariner; sailor; seaman;jack(tar)
marynata (ma-ri-ná-ta) f. pickle
marynować (ma-ri-nó-vach) v.
pickle; marinade; side-track
marzec (ma-zhets) m. March
marzenie (ma-zhé-ñe) n. dream;
reverie; day dream; pensiveness
marznąc (márzh-nównch) v. freeze
marzyciel (ma-zhi-chel) m.
dreamer; fantast; visionary

marzyc (má-zhich) v. dream
masa (má-sa) f. bulk; mass
masa perłowa (ma-sa per-wó-va)
f. mother of pearl
masakra (ma-sák-ra) f. massacre; carnage; butchery
masakrować (ma-sak-ró-vach) v.
massacre; slaughter;butcher;
masarnia (ma-sár-ña) f. pork·
meat shop: pork butcher's shop
masarz (má-sash) m. pork-
butcher; pork meat worler
masaż (má-sash) m. massage
masażysta (ma-sa-zhis-ta) m.
masseur ; rubber
maselniczka (ma-sel-ñeech-ka)
f. butter-dish; small churn
maska (más-ka) f. mask; hood
maskować (mas-kó-vach) v.
disguise; mask;hide; screen
masło (más-wo) n. butter
masoński (ma-són-skee) adj. m.
masonic; freemason's
masować (ma-só-vach) v. massage
masowo (ma-só-vo) adv. wholesale; in a mass: in masses
masywnosc (ma-siv-noshch) f.
massiveness ; solidity
masywny (ma-siv-ni) adj. m.
massive ; solid; bulky; massy
maszerować (ma-she-ró-vach) v.
march ; march on; keep marching
maszkara (mash-ká-ra) f. monster; scarecrow; eyesore
maszt (masht) m. mast;flagstaff
maszyna (ma-shí-na) f. machine
maszynka do golenia (ma-shin-
ka do go-lé-ña) safety razor
maszyneria (ma-shi-nér-ya) f.
machinery ; mechanism
maszynista (ma-shi-ñees-ta) m.
railroad engineer
maszynistka (ma-shi-ñeest-ka)
f. typist
maszynopis (ma-shi-nó-pees) m.
typescript; typewritten copy
maść (mashch) f. ointment;
horse color; unguent
maślanka (ma-shlán-ka) f.
buttermilk ; product of churning
mat (mat) m. flat color; check-
mate (one's opponent)

mata (ma-ta) f. mat; matting
matactwo (ma-tats-tvo) n. legal
  trickery; fraudulence; deceit
matczyny (mat-chi-ni) adj. m.
  maternal ; mother's
matematyczny (ma-te-ma-tich-ni)
  adj. m. mathematical
matematyk (ma-te-ma-tik) m.
  mathematician (also student)
matematyka (ma-te-ma-ti-ka) f.
  mathematics ;science of numbers
materac (ma-te-rats) m.mattress
materia (ma-ter-ya) f. matter;
  stuff; subject;point;puss;cloth
materialista (ma-ter-ya-lees-ta)
  m. materialist
materialistyczny (ma-ter-ya-
  lees-tich-ni) adj. m. materia-
  listic (opposite to spiritual)
materiał (ma-ter-yaw) m. material; substance; stuff; cloth
matka (mat-ka) f. mother
matnia (mat-ña) f. snare; trap
matowy (ma-to-vi) adj. m. flat
  color ; dull; without luster
matrona (ma-tro-na) f. matron
matryca (ma-tri-tsa) f. matrix;
  die ; type;mold ; stencil;swage
matrykuła (ma-tri-koo-wa) f.
  register of university students
matrymonialny (ma-tri-mo-ñal-ni)
  adj. m. matrimonial;marital
matura (ma-too-ra) f. final
  highschool examination
maur etański (maw-re-tań-skee)
  adj. m. Moorish ; of Moors
mazać (ma-zach) v. smear; daub
mazgaj (maz-gay) m. crybaby
mazur (ma-zoor) m. mazurka
  rythm; Mazurian ; Mazovian
maż (mażh) f. grease;tallow
mącić (mown-cheech) v. blur;
  ruffle ; muddy; cloud;confuse
mączka (mownch-ka) f. fine
  flour;powder; dust; starch
mądrość (mown-droshch) f. wisdom; intelligence; sagacity
mądry (mown-dri) adj. m. sage
mąka (mown-ka) f. flour; meal
mąż (mownsh) m. husband; man
mąż stanu (mownsh sta-noo)
  statesman ; outstanding politician: outstanding diplomat

mdlec (mdlech) v. faint ;weaken
mdlić (mdleech) v. nauseate
mdłość (mdwoshch) f. nausea
mdło (mdwo) adv. dull; nauseating; sickening; faintly;dimly
meble (meb-le) pl. furniture
mecenas (me-tse-nas) m. lawyer
mech (mekh) m. moss ; down
mechaniczny (me-kha-ñeech-ni)
  adj. m. mechanical;automatic
mechanik (me-kha-ñeek) m. mechanic; Jack of all trades
mechanika (me-kha-ñee-ka) f.
  mechanics ;practical mechanics
mechanizm (me-kha-ñeesm) m.
  mechanism;gear ; device
mecz (mech) m. sport match
meczet (me-chet) m. mosque
medal (me-dal) m. medal
mediacja (med-yats-ya) f. me-
  diation; settling of differences
meduza (me-doo-za) f. jellyfish
medycyna (me-di-tsi-na) f. medicine: art of healing
medyczny (me-dich-ni) adj. m.
  medical; medicinal
medyk (me-dik) m. medical student; medic(hist.:physician)
medykament (me-di-ka-ment) m.
  drug; medicine (hist. expr.)
medytacja (me-di-tats-ya) f.
  meditation; thinking deeply
megafon (me-ga-fon) m. loudspeaker; megaphone
megaloman (me-ga-lo-man) m. meg-
  alomaniac;self appointed boss
melancholia (me-lan-khol-ya) f.
  melancholy; the blues;dejection
melasa (me-la-sa) f. molasses
meldować (mel-do-vach) v. report; register; announce
meldunek (mel-doo-nek) m. report; announcement; notification
melioracja (mel-yo-rats-ya) f.
  reclamation of land; drainage
melodia (me-lod-ya) f. melody
meloman (me-lo-man) m. music
  lover; music enthusiast
melon (me-lon) m. melon
melonik (me-lo-ñeek) m. bowler
  hat; derby; bowler;billycock
memoriał (me-mor-yaw) m. memorial;minutes' journal(commercial)

menażeria (me-na-zhér-ya) f.
menagerie ;animal collection
menażka (me-nazh-ka) f. mess kit
mennica (men-née-tsa) f. mint
menstruacja (men-stroo-áts-ya)
f. menstruation ; menses
mentalność (men-tál-noshćh) f.
mentality ; a way of thinking
menu (mé-noo) m. menu ;bill of
mer (mer) m. mayor fare
merdać (mér-dach) v. wag tail
merytoryczny (me-ri-to-rích-ni)
adj. m. of substance ;essential
meszek (mé-shek) m. down; nap
meta (mé-ta) f. goal; hang-out
metafizyka (me-ta-feé-zi-ka) f.
metaphysics (speculative phil.)
metal (mé-tal) m. metal
metalowy (me-ta-ló-vi) adj. m.
metallic(luster, sound etc)
metalurgia (me-ta-lúr-gya) f.
metallurgy : science of metals
metamorfoza (me-ta-mor-fo-za)
f. metamorphosis ;metamorphism
meteor (me-té-or) m. meteor
meteorologia (me-te-o-ro-lóg-
ya) f. meteorology system
metoda (me-tó-da) f. method;
metodyczny (me-to-dích-ni) adj.
m. methodical ;systematic
metr (metr) m. meter : 39.37in.
metro (mét-ro) n. subway
metropolia (me-tro-pól-ya) f.
metropolis ; main large city
metryczny (me-trich-ni) adj. m.
metric ; metrical
metryka (me-tri-ka) f. birth-
certificate;the public register
metys (mé-tis) m. metis
mewa (mé-va) f. sea-gull
mezalians (me-zál-yans) m. mis-
alliance ; improper alliance
mezanin (me-za-ńeen) m. mezzanine
męczarnia (mań-chár-ńa) f. torture; torment; anguish; agony
męczennik (mań-chen-ńeek) m.
martyr : sufferer for faith etc.
męczyć (man-chich) v. bother;
torment; oppress;tire; exhaust
mędrek (man-drek) m. smart
aleck;know all; wiseacre
mędrzec (mań-dzhets) m. sage

męka (mań-ka) f. fatigue; torment ;pain;distress; nuisance
męski (mańs-kee) adj. m. masculine; manly ; man's; virile;male
męskość (mańs-koshćh) f. manhood ; virility; manliness
męstwo (mańs-tvo) n. bravery
mętny (mańt-ni) adj. m. turbid;
dull ;dim; blurred;vague; fishy
męty (mań-ti) n. dregs; scum of
society ; underworld; raffle
mężatka (mań-zhát-ka) f. married woman; femme covert (legal.)
mężczyzna (mańzh-chiz-na) m. man
mężnieć (mańzh-ńech) v. grow
manly ; muster courage;take heart
mężny (mańzh-ni) adj. m. brave
mglisty (mgleés-ti) adj. m.
foggy; misty; dim;nebulous;vague
mgła (mgwa) f. fog; mist; cloud
mgławica (mgwa-vee-tsa) f, neb-
ula ; cloud; hazy idea; haze
mgnienie (mgńe-ńe) n. blink;
twinkle; wink; flash;jiffy;trice
miał (myaw) m. dust; powder
miałki (myaw-kee) adj. m. fine
(sugar ; sand etc.); powdered
miano (myá-no) n. name ;designation
mianować (mya-nó-vach) v. appoint ; promote; give a title
mianowicie (mya-no-vee-che)
adv. namely ; to wit ; that is ...
mianownik (mya-nov-ńeek) m.
denominator; nominative
miara (myá-ra) f. measure; gauge
yard-stick;foot-rule;amount;limit
miarkować (myar-ko-vach) v.
guess; note; mitigate one's self
miarodajny (mya-ro-dáy-ni) adj.
m. authoritative; competent
miarowy (mya-ró-vi) adj. m.
rythmic ; steady; regular
miasteczko (myas-tech-ko) n.
borough ;country town
miasto (myas-to) n. town
miałczeć (myaw-chech) v. mew
miazga (myaz-ga) f. pulp ; squash
miażdżyć (myazh-dzhich) v. crush;
squash ; smash; grind;lacerate
miąć (myownch) v. crumple ;wrinkle
miąższ (myównzhsh) m. pulp;
flesh of fruit; pomace; squash

miech (myekh) m. bellows

miecz (myech) m. sword

mieć (myech) v. have;hold; run

miednica (myed-née-tsa) f. hand washtub ; pelvis;wash basin

miedza (mye-dza) f. farm boundary strip ; bounds; balk

miedź (myedż) f. copper

miedziak (mye-dżhak) m. copper penny; copper coin

miedziany (mye-dżhá-ni) adj. m. of copper; of brass

miedzioryt (mye-dżhó-rit) m. copper engraving

miejsce (myejs-tse) n. place; location; spot; room; space; seat; employment;berth; scene

miejscowość (myey-stsó-voshch) f. locality ; place;town;village

miejscowy (myeys-tsó-vi) adj. m. local; native; indigenous

miejski (myéys-kee) adj. m. of town; of city ;urban

mielizna (mye-leéz-na) f. shoal; shallow water ; sandbank; shelf

mielenie (mye-lé-ńe) n. grinding; milling; mincing; jabber;prattling

mielony (mye-ló-ni) adj. m. ground ; milled; minced;chewed up

mieniać (mye-ńach) v. change; swap; exchange; convert

mienić (mye-ńeech) v. call; glitter; shimmer; change color

mienić sie (mye-ńeech shań) v. change one's color; glitter

mienie (mye-ńe) n. property; belongings ;estate; effects

miernictwo (myer-ńeets-tvo) m. surveying; land measuring

mierniczy (myer-nee-chi) m. surveyor; adj. m. geodetic

mierność (myer-noshch)f.mediocrity ; average range

miernota (myer-nó-ta) f. average intelligence; mediocrity

mierny (myer-ny) adj. m. mediocre; mean; moderate;indifferent

mierzeja (mye-zhe-ya) f. sand-bar

mierzić(myer-żheech) v. be disgusting; sicken;make unbearable

mierznąć (myezh-nównch) v. become disgusting; pall on sb

mierzwa (myesh-va) f. litter

mierzwić (myezh-veech) v. tousle

mierzyć (mye-zhich) v. measure; judge; try on; aim;tend towards

miesiąc (mye-shownts) m. month; moon ; lunar month ;massage

miesic(mye-sheech)v. knead;

miesięcznie (mye-shańch-ńe) adv. monthly ; every month

miesięcznik (mye-shańch-ńeek) m. monthly paper ; monthly

mieszać (mye-shach) v. mix; mingle; shuffle; confuse

mieszać się (mye-shach shań) v. meddle; become confused

mieszanina (mye-sha-ńe-na) f. mixture; compound ; medley

mieszanka (mye-shan-ka) f. blend ;mix; mixture;miscellany

mieszczanin (myesh-cha-ńeen) m. burgher ; townsman; citizen

mieszczaństwo (myesh-chań-stvo) n. middle class ;narrow-minded-

mieszek (mye-shek) m.small ness bellows; bag ; money-bag

mieszkać (myesh-kach) v. dwell; live; stay ;have a flat; lodge

mieszkalny (myesh-kál-ny) adj. m. inhabitable; habitable

mieszkanie (myesh-ka-ńe) n. apartment; rooms; lodgings

mieszkaniec (myesh-ka-ńets) m. inhabitant; lodger; resident

mieść (myeshch) v. sweep; fling

mieścić (myésh-cheech) v. contain; fit ;hold; store; place

mieścina (myesh-chee-na) f. small town, out-of-the-way

miewać (mye-vach) v. have occasionally; feel sometimes

mięczak (myań-chak) m. mollusk

międlić (myańd-leech) v. bruise; hackle; crush; hold forth

między (myań-dzi) prep. between; among; in the midst

międzymorze (myań-dzi-mó-zhe) n. isthmus : narrow strip between sea

międzynarodowy (myań-dzi-na-ro-dó-vi) adj. m. international

międzyplanetarny (myań-dzi-plane-tár-ni) adj. m. interplanetary ; of cosmic space

miękczyc (myáńk-chich) v. soft-
en; move; touch; palatalize
miękisz (myáń-keesh) m. pulp
miękki (myáńk-kee) adj. m.
soft ; flabby; limp; supple
miękko (myáńk-ko) adv. softly
miękkosc (myáńk-koshch) f.
softnes ; irresolution;pliancy
mięknąc (myáńk-nównch) v.
soften up ;relax; relent
mięsien (myáń-shen) m. muscle
mięsisty (myáń-shees-ti) adj.
m. fleshy ;meaty; pulpous
mięsiwo (myáń-shee-vo) n. meat
mięso (myáń-so) n. flesh; meat
mięsozerny (myáń-so-zhér-ni)
adj. m. carnivorous;meat eating
mięta (myáń-ta) f. mint ;trifle
miętosic (myáń-to-sheech) v.
crumble; knead ; crush up
mig (meeg) m. split second;
twinkle; sign language
migac (mee-gach) v. twinkle
migawka (mee-gáv-ka) f. camera
shutter; news in brief
migdał (meég-daw) m. almond;
tonsil ; good and tasty thing
migi (mee-gee) pl. sign language; speaking by signs
migotac (mee-go-tach) v. twinkle; flicker; waver;whisk;flit
migracja (mee-gráts-ya) f. mi-
gration; migrating (of groups)
migrena (mee-gre-na) f. mi-
graine; sick headache
mijac (mee-yach) v. go past;
pass by; pass away; go by
mijac się z prawdą (mee-yach
shañ z práv-dówn) swerve from
the truth; to be untrue
mika (mee-ka) f. mica
mikrob (meé-krob) m. microbe
mikrofon (mee-kró-fon) m. microphone ;transmitter
mikroskop (mee-krós-kop) m. microscope
mikroskopijny (m ee-kros-ko-
peéy-ni) adj. m. microscopic
mikstura (meeks-tóo-ra) f. mixture; concoction; medicine
mila (meé-la) f. mile (1609,35m)
mila morska (meé-la mór-ska) f.
nautical mile (1853,2 meters)

milczący (meel-chówn-tsi) adj.
m. silent; reticent ; mum;tacit
milczec (meel-chech) v. be silent; quit talking; be quiet
milczenie (meel-che-ńe) n. silence; keeping still; stillness
milczkiem (meelch-kem) adv.
secretly; stealthily;on the sly
mile (meé-le) adv. pleasantly;
kindly ; warmly; courteously
miliard (meel-yard) m. thousand
million; billion
milicja (mee-leéts-ya) f. mi-
litia; police; constabulary
milicjant (mee-leéts-yant) m.
policeman; constable
miligram (mee-leé-gram) m. mil-
ligram ; 1/1,000 of a gram
milimetr (mee-leé-metr) m. mil-
limeter: 1/1,000 of a meter
milion (meél-yon) m. million
milioner (meel-yó-ner) m. mil-
lionaire; a very wealthy man
milionowe miasto (meel-yo-no-ve
mya-sto) city of million people
militarny (mee-lee-tár-ni) adj.
m. military; of soldiers
militaryzowac (mee-lee-ta-ri-
zo-vach) v. militarize
milknąc (meelk-nównch) v. abate;
guit talking; die away;subside
miło (mee-wo) adv. nicely;
pleasantly; agreeably
miło poznac (mee-wo póz-nach)
glad to meet ; nice to meet
miłosierdzie (mee-wo-sher-dzhe)
m. charity; mercy;compassion
miłosierny (mee-wo-sher-ni) adj.
m. merciful; charitable
miłosny list (mee-wós-ni leest)
love letter
miłostka (mee-wost-ka) f. little
love affair
miłosc (mee-woshch) f. love
miłosnik (mee-wosh-ńeek) m.
fancier; amateur ; fan
miłowac (mee-wo-vach) v. love
miły (mee-wy) adj. m. pleasant;
beloved; likable;nice;enjoyable
mimiczny (mee-meéch-ni) adj. m.
mimic; imitative;make-believe
mimo (meé-mo) prep. in spite of;
notwithstanding ; (al)though

mimo (mee-mo) adv. pas̱t; by
mimochodem (mee-mo-khó-dem) adv.
by the way; incidentally
mimo woli (mee-mo vo-lee) adv.
involuntarily: unintentional
mimowolny (mee-mo-vól-ni) adj.
m. involuntary; unintentional
mimo wszystko (mee-mo vshist-ko)
after all; in spite of all
mina (mee-na) f. 1. facial
expression; 2. mine ; air
minaret (mee-na-ret) m. minaret
minąć (mee-nównch) v. pass by
mineralny (mee-ne-rál-ni) adj.
m. mineral;containing minerals
mineralogia (mee-ne-ra-lóg-ya)
f. mineralogy
minerał (mee-né-raw) m. mineral
minia (meen-ya) f. minium; red
lead base; red lead
miniatura (meen-ya-too-ra) f.
miniature; miniature copy
minimalny (mee-nee-mál-ny) adj.
m. minimal;the least possible
minimum (mee-nee-moom) m. minimum;adv. at the very least
miniony (mee-no-ni) adj. m. bygone; of long ago; olden
minister (mee-nees-ter) m. minister; cabinet member
ministerialny (mee-nees-ter-
yál-ni) adj. m. ministerial
ministerstwo (mee-nees-tér-stvo)
n. ministry;department of state
minorowy (mee-no-ró-vi) adj. m.
in minor key; low-spirited
minuta (mee-nóo-ta) f. minute
minutowy (mee-noo-tó-vi) adj.
m. of one minute
miodownik (myo-dóv-neek) m.
gingerbread
miodowy miesiąc (myo-do-vi mye-
shównts) honeymoon
miodosytnia (myo-do-sit-na) f.
meadbar
miot (myot) m. throw; cast; lit-
ler; brood ;animal birth; fling
miotacz (myo-tach) m. thrower
miotacz ognia (myo-tach óg-na)
m. firethrower
miotać (myo-tach) v. throw; fling;
toss ;hurl; stir; rave; storm
miotła (myot-wa) f. broom

miód (myoot) m. honey ; mead
mir (meer) m. esteem;respect
miriady (meer-yá-di) pl. myr-
iads : large numbers
mirra (meer-ra) f. myrrh
mirt (meert) m. myrtle
misa (mee-sa) f. platter; bowl
misja (mees-ya) f. mission
misjonarz (mees-yo-nash) m.
missionary
miska (mees-ka) f. dish; pan
misterny (mees-tér-ni) adj. m.
fine; delicate; subtle;clever
mistrz (mees tsh) m. master;
maestro; champion; expert
mistrzostwo (mees-tzhós-tvo)
m. championship; mastery
mistrzowski ruch (mees-tzhóvs-
kee rookh) masterstroke
mistycyzm (mees-ti-cizm) m.
mysticism;intuitive knowledge
mistyczny (mees-tich-ni) adj.
m. mystic ; mystical: occult
mistyfikacja (mees-ti-fee-
káts-ya)f.mystification
mistyfikować (mees-ti-fee-kó-
vach) v. mystify; hoax;deceive
mistyk (mees-tik) m. mystic
misyjny (mee-siy-ni) adj. m.
missionary; mission-
miś (meesh) m. teddy bear;
nylon fur coat or jacket
mit (meet) m. myth: mythology
mitologia (mee-to-lóg-ya) f.
mythology : study of myths
mitologiczny (mee-to-lo-geech-
ni) adj. m. mythologic
mitra (mee-tra) f. mitre
mitręga (mee-trán-ga) f. delay;
waste of time; delay; dawdler
mitrężyć (mee-trán-zhych) v.
loiter; waste time;dally; lag
mityczny (mee-tich-ni) adj. m.
mythical; mythic ; fictitious
mitygować (mee-ti-gó-vach) v.
quiet; appease;check;restrain
mityng (mee-ting) m. (mass)
meeting : a gathering of people
mizantrop (mee-zán-trop) m.
misanthrope ; hater of people
mizdrzyc się (meez-dzhich shán)
v. ogle; wheedle ;make eyes

mizerak (mee-zé-rak) m. poor
soul; weakling; poor devil
mizeria (mee-zér-ya) f. cucumber salad ; shabby possessions
mizerny (mee-zér-ni) adj. m.
meager; ill-looking; mean;paltry
mknąć (mknównch) v. fleet;rush
mlaskać (mlás-kach)v.lap; smack
mlecz (mlech) m. marrow ;milt
mleczarnia (mle-chár-ña) f.
dairy ; creamery : milk bar
mleczny (mléch-ni) adj. m. milk;
milky; dairy; lactic;milk-white
mleć (mléch) v. grind; mill
mleko (mlé-ko) n. milk
młocarnia (mwo-tsár-ña) f.
thresher ;threshing-machine
młocka (mwóts-ka) f. threshing
młoda (mwó-da) adj. f. young
młode (mwo-de) adj. pl. young
n.pl. the young; litter
młodociany (mwo-do-chá-ni) adj.
m. juvenile; youthful
młodosć (mwo-doshch) f. youth
młody (mwo-di) adj. m. young
młodzian (mwo-dzhan) m. young
man ; lad ; youth
młodzieniaszek (mwo-dzhe-ña-
shek) m. sprig; stripling;lad
młodzieniec (mwo-dzhe-ñets) m.
young man ; lad: youth
młodzieńczy (mwo-dzheń-chi)
adj. m. youthful
młodzież (mwo-dzhesh) f. youth;
young generation
młodzik (mwo-dzheek)m. youngster; teenager; youngling
młokos (mwo-kos) m. kid
młot (mwot) m. sledge; hammer
młotek (mwo-tek) m. hammer;
tack-hammer ;clapper
młócic (mwoó-cheech) v. thrash
młyn (mwin) m. mill; grinder
młynarz (mwi-nash) m. miller
młynek (mwi-ñek) m. handgrinder
młyński (mwiń-skee) adj. m.
mill-; of a mill
mnich (mñeekh) m. monk; friar
mniej (mñey) adv. less; fewer
mniej wiecej (mñey vyań-tsey)
more or less ; about ; round
mniejsza o to '(mñey-sha o to)
never mind that (exp.)

mniejszosć (mñey-shoshch) f.
minority; the lesser part
mniejszy (mñey-shi) adj. m.
smaller; lesser ;less; minor
mniemać (mñe-mach) v. suppose;
deem; imagine;think; consider
mniemanie (mñe-má-ñe) n. opinion ;notion;conviction
mniszka (mñeesh-ka) f. nun
mnoga (mnó-ga) num. plural
mnogi (mnó-gee) adj. m. numerous ; of the plural
mnogosć (mno-goshch) f. abundance; plurality; multitude
mnożenie (mno-zhe-ñe) n. multiplication ;increase; breeding
mnożyć (mno-zhich) v. multiply
mnóstwo (mnoós-tvo) n. very
many; multitude; swarm; loads
mobilizacja (mo-bee-lee-záts-
ya) f. mobilization ;call-up
mobilizować (mo-bee-lee-zó-
vach) v. mobilize; call up
moc (mots)f. might; great-
deal; power;vigor;strength
mocarstwo (mo-tsár-stvo) n.
strong country;(world)power
mocarz (mo-tsash) m. strong
man; potentate; powerful man
mocny (mots-ni) adj. m. strong
mocować się (mo-tsó-vach shań)
v. wrestle; exert oneself
mocz (moch) m. urine
moczar (mo-char) m. bog; marsh
moczopędny (mo-cho-pańd-ni)
adj. m. diuretic
moczowy (mo-chó-vi) adj. m.
uric; urinary: of urine
moczyć (mo-chich) v. wet;
drench; steep; soak;urinate
moda (mó-da) f. fashion
model (mó-del) m. model
modelować (mo-de-ló-vach) v.
model; shape; mold; fashion
modernizować (mo-der-ni-zó-vach)
v. modernize;bring up to date
modlić się (mód-leech shań) v.
pray; say one's prayers
modlitewnik (mod-lee-tev-ñeek)
m. prayer-book
modlitwa (mod-leet-va) f.
prayer : grace(at meal time)

modła (mód-wa) f. mold; standard; fashion; model; pattern

modniarka (mod-ńár-ka) f. milliner; modiste; hat maker

modny (mód-ni) adj. m. fashionable; in fashion;in vogue

modry (mód-ri) adj. m. azure-blue; deep blue;cerulean blue

modrzew (mód-zhev) m. larch

modulacja (mo-doo-láts-ya) f. modulation;inflection

modulować (mo-doo-ló-vach) v. modulate; inflect; regulate

modyfikacja (mo-di-fee-káts-ya) f. modification; alteration

modyfikować (mo-di-fee-kó-vach) v. modify; alter; qualify

modystka (mo-dist-ka) f. modiste; milliner; hat maker

mogący (mo-gówn-tsi) adj. m. able; capable; competent

mogiła (mo-gee-wa) f. tomb

mojżeszowy (moy-zhe-shó-vi) adj. m. Mosaic: of Moses

mokka (mók-ka) f. natural coffee : mocha: Mocha coffee

moknąć (mok-nównch) v. get wet; get soaked, drenched;be soaked

mokradło (mo-krád-wo) n. bog

mokry (mók-ri) adj. m. wet; moist ; watery;rainy; sweaty

molekularny (mo-le-koo-lár-ni) adj. m. molecular; of molecule

molekuła (mo-le-koó-wa) f. molecule ; smallest particle

molestować (mo-les-tó-vach) v. molest; annoy; vex; trouble

molo (mó-lo) n. pier; mole; jetty; breakwater ; quay

moment (mo-ment) m. moment

momentalny (mo-men-tál-ni) adj. m. instantaneous ;immediate

monarcha (mo-nár-kha) m. monarch ; sovereign: king

monarchista (mo-nar-khees-ta) m. monarchist ; royalist

moneta (mo-né-ta) f. coin ;chink

moneta brzecząca (mo-né-ta bzháń-chówn-tsa), cash;coins

mongolski (mon-gól-skee) adj. m. Mongol ; of Mongolia

monitor (mo-ńee-tor) m. monitor

monitować (mo-ńee-tó-wach) v. admonish ; monitor : check on

monogram (mo-nó-gram) m. monogram; initials in a design

monokl (mó-nokl) m. eye-glass

monolog (mo-nó-log) m. monologue; soliloquy of one actor

monopol (mo-nó-pol), m. monopoly

monoteizm (mo-no-té-eezm) m. monotheism; belief in one god

monotonia (mo-no-tóń-ya) f. monotony ; sameness : no variety

monotonny (mo-no-toń-ni) adj. m. monotonous ;drab; dull

monstrualny (mon-stroo-ál-ni) adj. m. monstrous ; horrible

monstrum (móń-stroom) n. monster ; monstrosity

montaż (móń-tazh) m. mounting; assembling;installation; set-up

monter (móń-ter), m. installator

montować (mon-tó-vach) v. install; put together; put up

monumentalny (mo-noo-men-tál-ni) adj. m. monumental

mops (mops) m. pug-dog

moralizator (mo-ra-lee-zá-tor) m. moralizer

moralizować (mo-ra-lee-zó-vach) v. moralize; discuss morality

moralność (mo-rál-noshch) f. morals; morality; ethics

moralny (mo-rál-ni) adj. m. moral ; ethical;of good conduct

morał (mó-raw) m. moral lesson

moratorium (mo-ra-tór-yoom) n. moratorium; legalized delay

mord (mord) m. murder; slaughter

morda (mór-da) f. snout; muzzle; vulg.: mug; kisser; puss; phiz

morderca (mor-dér-tsa) m. murderer; assassin;cutthroat

morderczy (mor-dér-chi) adj. m. murderous; cutthroat; deadly

morderstwo (mor-dér-stvo) n. murder; assassination

mordęga (mor-dáń-ga) f. toil; drudge; moil;fag; strain

mordować (mor-dó-vach) v. kill; torment;harass;toil;sweat;worry

mordować się (mor-dó-vach sháń) v. toil; kill oneself with work

morela (mo-ré-la) f. apricot
morena (mo-ré-na) f. moraine
morfina (mor-fée-na) f. morphine (derivative of opium)
morfologia (mor-fo-lóg-ya) f.
morphology: science of forms
morga (mór-ga) f. acre
morowy (mo-ró-vi) adj. m. pes-
tilential; clever; good buddy; fine fellow; first-rate
mors (mors) m. walrus
morska choroba (mórs-ka kho-ró-
ba) seasickness; dizziness
morski (mórs-kee) adj. m. maritime; sea; nautical; naval
morwa (mór-va) f. mulberry
morze (mozhe) n. sea ; ocean
morzyc (mo-zhich) v. starve
mosiądz (mo-shównts) m. brass
moskit (mos-keet) m. mosquito
most (most) m. bridge
moscic (mosh-cheech) v. pad
(nest); make a bed of straw
motac (mo-tach)v. reel; embroil;
entangle; intrigue; spool
motek (mo-tek) m. reel ; ball
motłoch (mot-wokh) m. mob
motocykl (mo-to-tsikl) m. motorcycle (a two-wheeled vehicle)
motor (mo-tor) m. motor
motorówka (mo-to-róov-ka) f.
motorboat
motoryzacja (mo-to-ri-záts-ya)
f. motorization;mechanization
motoryzowac (mo-to-ri-zo-vach)
v. motorize; mechanize
motyka (mo-ti-ka) f. hoe
motyl (mo-til) m. butterfly
motyw (mo-tiv) m. motif;motive
motywowac (mo-ti-vó-vach) v.
give reasons; explain;justify
mowa (mo-va) f. speech; language
mozaika (mo-záy-ka) f. mosaic
mozolic (mo-zo-leech) v. toil;
take pains; exert oneself
mozolny (mo-zol-ni) adj. m.
toilsome; strenuous arduous
mozół (mo-zoow) m. exertion
moździerz (mozh-dzhesh) m. mortar ; mine thrower
może (mo-zhe) adv. perhaps; maybe; very likely; how about?

możliwosc (mozh-lee-voshch) f.
possibility; chance; contigency
możliwosci (mozh-lee-vosh-chee)
pl. scope ;vistas; capabilities
możliwy (mozh-lee-vi) adj. possible ; fairly good; passable
można (mozh-na) v. imp. it is
possible; one may; one can
możnosc (mozh-noshch) f. power;
freedom to; free choice to
możny (mózh-ni) adj. m. potent;
powerful; mighty
móc (moots) v. (potentially)
to be able ; be capable
moj (mooy) pron. my; mine
mol (mool) m. moth
mól ksiażkowy (mool kshównzh-
kó-vi) bookworm
mor (moor) m. pestilence;
epidemic ;plague ; pest
morg (moorg) m. acre
mówca (moóv-tsa) m. speaker
mówic (moó-veech) v. speak;
talk; say; tell;say things
mównica (moov-nee-tsa) f. (pulpit); speaker's platform
mózg (moozk) m. brain
mózgowy (mooz-gó-vi) adj. m.
cerebral ; of the brain
mroczny (mroch-ni) adj. m.
dusky; gloomy ;obscure;dark
mrok (mrok) m. dusk; twilight
mrowic się (mró-veech shán) v.
swarm ; teem; be alive
mrowie (mrov-ye) n. swarm;
tingle ;gooseflesh;creeps
mrowisko (mro-vées-ko) n. ant-
hill ; ants'nest
mrozic (mro-zheech) v. freeze;
congeal; refrigerate ; chill
mrozny (mroozh-ni) adj. m.frosty;
icy ; freezing
mrówka (mroov-ka) f. ant ;emmet
mróz (mroos) m. frost ;the cold
mruczec (mroo-chech) v. mumble;
mutter ; purr; murmur; grumble
mrugac (mroo-gach) v. twinkle;
blink; wink ; flicker; flinch
mruk (mrook) m. mumbler; grumbler; man of few words;growler
mrukliwy (mrook-lee-vi) adj. m.
mumbling; sulky; gruff;taciturn

mrużyć (mroo-zhich) v. blink;
wink ; squint; half-shut(eyes)
mrzonka (mzhón-ka) f. illusion
msza (msha) f. mass (in church)
mszalny (mshál-ni) adj. m. for
mass; of mass (in the church)
mszał (mshaw) m. missal
mściciel (mshchee-chel) m.
avenger ; retaliator
mścić (mshcheećh) v. avenge
mściwy (mshchée-vi) adj. m.
vindictive; vengeful
mszczenie (mshche-ńe) n. vengeance ; retaliation
mszyca (mshi-tsa) f. mite
mszysty (mshis-ti) adj. m. mossy
mucha (moo-kha) f. fly
mufka (moof-ka) f. muff
mularz (moo-lash) m. mason
mulat (moo-lat) m. mulatto
mulisty (moo-lees-ty) adj. m.
muddy; oozy; slimy ; sludgy
muł (moow) m. ooze; slime
muł (moow) m. mule
mumia (moom-ya) f. mummy
mundur (moon-door) m. uniform
municypalny (moo-nee-tsi-pál-ni)
adj. m. municipal
munsztuk (moon-shtook) m. (bridle) bit; mouthpiece
mur (moor) m. brick wall
murarz (moo-rash) m. bricklayer
murawa (moo-rá-va) f. lawn
murować (moo-ró-vach) v. lay-
bricks ; build in brick(in stone)
murowany (moo-ro-vá-ni) adj. m.
of bricks; of stone ; certain
murzyn (moo-zhin) m. negro
mus 1, (moos) m. necessity; compulsion ; constraint
mus 2. (moos) m. froth;mousse
musieć (moo-shech) v. be obliged
to; have to ;be forced; must
muskać (moos-kach) v. touch
lightly ; skim; stroke
muskularny (moos-koo-lár-ni) adj.
m. muscular ; strong;hefty;beefy
muskuł (moos-koow) m. muscle
musować (moo-só-vach) v. foam;
froth ; bubble; fizz; sparkle
muszka (moosh-ka) f. fly; gun-
bead; face skin-spot ;bow-tie;
midge; dry-fly; patch (on skin)

muszkat (moosh-kat) m. nutmeg
muszkiet (moosh-ket) m. musket ; smooth bore firearm
muszla (moosh-la) f. shell;conch
musztarda (moosh-tár-da) f.
mustard seasoning
musztra (moosh-tra) f. (drill)
training; exercise
muslin (moosh-leen) m. muslin
mutacja (moo-táts-ya) f. muta-
tion; change; variation
muterka (moo-tér-ka) f. (bolt)
nut; female screw
muza (moo-za) f. Muse
muzealny (moo-ze-ál-ni) adj. m.
of museum
muzeum (moo-ze-oom) n. museum
muzułmanin (moo-zoow-ma-ńeen)
m. Moslem (Mussulman)
muzyczny (moo-zich-ni) adj. m.
musical; set to music
muzyk (moo-zik) m. musician
muzyka (moo-zi-ka) f. music
muzykalność (moo-zi-kál-noshćh)
f. ear for music
muzykalny (moo-zi-kál-ni) adj.
m. having ear for music
muzykant (moo-zi-kant) m. low
class musician ; bandsman
my (mi) pron. we ; us
myć (mich) v. wash
mycka (mits-ka) f. skull-cap
mydlarnia (mid-lár-ńa) f. soap-
store; soap-works; perfumery
mydlarstwo (mid-lár-stvo) n.
soap-making; soap-boiling
mydlarz (mid-lash) m. soap-maker
mydlić (mid-leećh) v. soap;
froth; dress someone down
mydlić oczy (mid-leećh ó-chi) v.
pull wool over eyes
mydliny (mid-lée-ni) pl. soap-
suds; lather
mydło (mid-wo) n. soap; soft soap
mylić (mi-leech) v. mislead;
misguide;confuse; deceive
mylny (míl-ni) adj. m. wrong.
mysz (mish) f. mouse
myszkować (mish-kó-vach) v.
covertly explore; trace scent
myśl (mishl) f. thought; idea
myślący (mish-lówn-tsi) adj. m.
thoughtful; reflective

myśleć (miśh-lech) v. think
myśliciel (miśh-lee-chel) m.
thinker;one who thinks a lot
myśliwiec (miśh-leev-yets) m.
fighter plane; fighter pilot
myśliwy (miśh-lee-vi) m. hunter
myślnik (miśhl-ńeek) m. dash
(mark); hyphen
myślowy (miśh-ló-vi) adj. m.
mental;,reflective; intellectual
myto, (mi-to) n. toll; tollgate
mżyć (mzhich) v. drizzle
na (na) prep. on; upon; at;
for; by; in;
NOTE: verbs with prefix na
NOT INCLUDED HERE: CHECK WITH-
OUT THE PREFIX "na"
nabawić się (na-bá-veech śhań)
v. bring upon oneself; incur
nabawić strachu (na-bá-veech
stra-khoo)v.frighten
nabiał (ná-byaw) m. dairy
products including eggs
nabiegać się (na-bye-gach śhań)v.
have run a lot; exert oneself
nabić (ná-beech) v. load weapon;
beat up (somebody); whack
nabiegły krwią (na-byeg-wi
krvyówn) adj.m. bloodshot
nabierać (na-bye-rach) v. take;
take in; tease; cheat; amass
nabijać (na-bee-yach) v. stud;
(repeatedly) load gun
nabijać się (na-bee-yach śhań)
v. make fun of (somebody)
nabożeństwo (na-bo-zheń-stvo)
n. church service
nabożny (na-bózh-ni) adj. m.
pious; religious; godly;devoutly
nabrać (ná-brach) v. take; take
in; tease; cheat; gather;swell
nabój (ná-booy) m. charge; car-
trige; round of ammunition
nabrzeże (na-bzhe-zhe) n. wharf;
embankment; landing-pier
nabrzmiały (na-bzhmya-wi) adj.
m. swollen ; distended
nabytek (na-bi-tek) m. acquisition ; purchase;new recruit
nabrzmiewać (na-bzhmye-vach) v.
swell;plump up; plump out
nabywać (na-bi-vach) v. acquire;
obtain; gain ; buy; purchase

nabywca (na-biv-tsa) m. buyer
nacechowany (na-tse-kho-vá-ni)
adj. m. marked; characterized
nachodzić (na-kho-dźheech)v.
intrude; (abstr.) haunt
nachylać (na-khi-lach) v. stoop;
bend; incline; lean;tilt;slant
nachylenie (na-khi-lé-ńe) n.tilt
slope; inclination;batter;slant
nacięcie (na-chań-che) n. incision; notch; cut:nick:score
naciągać (na-chówn-gach) v.
streach; draw; strain; pull
one's leg,;take sb in; infuse
naciek (ná-chek) m. infiltration; leak ; swelling
nacierać (na-che-rach) v. rub;
attack; harass,; demand
nacinać (na-chee-nach) v. notch;
cut; score; nick;hoax;dupe
nacisk (ná-cheesk) m. pressure;
stress; accent;thrust; push
naciskać (na-chees-kach) v.
press; urge ;bear on; push
nacjonalista (na-tsyo-na-lees-
ta) m. nationalist
nacjonalizacja (na-tsyo-na-lee-
záts-ya) f. nationalization
nacjonalizm (na-tsyo-ná-leezm)
m. nationalism
nacjonalizować (na-tsyo-na-lee-
zó-vach) v. nationalize
naczekać się (na-ché-kach śhań)
v. wait too long:tire of waiting
na czczo (ná chcho) adv. on an
empty stomach: unfed: fasting
naczelnik (na-chél-ńeek) m.
manager; chief; head; master
naczelny (na-chél-ni) adj. m.
chief; head; paramount; primate; principal;main;paramount
naczerpać (na- cher-pach) v.
dip up; draw (fluid);scoop up
naczynie (na-chi-ńe) n. vessel
nad (nad) prep. over; above; on
upon; beyond; at; of;for
nadajnik (na-dáy-ńeek) m.
transmitter: feeder
nadal (ná-dal) adv. still; in
future; continue (to do)
nadaremnie (na-da-rém-ńe) adv.
in vain; unsuccessfully; to no
purpose; without result

nadaremny (na-da-rém-ni) adj.
m. fruitless; vain;unsuccessful
nadarzać się (na-da-zhach shán)
v. happen; occur; turn up
nadawać (na-da-vach) v. confer
bestow ;grant; endow; christen
nadawca (na-dav-tsa) m. sender
nadąć (na-downch) v. puff up
nadąsany (na-down-sa-ni) adj.
m. sulky; sullen; stuffy
nadążać (na-down-zhach) v. keep
up with; cope with ;keep pace
nadbałtycki (nad-baw-tits-kee)
adj. m. on the Baltic ;Baltic
nadbiec (nad-byets) v. come
running up; hasten up :run up
nadbrzeże (nad-bzhe-zhe) n.
shore; coast; littoral
nadbrzeżny (nad-bzhezh-ni) adj.
m. coastal; sea-shore
nadbudowa (nad-boo-do-va) f.
superstructure ;added floor
nadbudować (nad-boo-do-vach)
v. build on ;add an upper floor
nadchodzić (nad-khó-dżheech)v.
approach; arrive; come
nadciągać (nad-chown-gach) v.
draw near; be nearing; come
nadciśnienie (nad-cheesh-ne-ne)
n. excess pressure;hypertension
nadczłowiek (nad-chwo-vyek) m.
superman ; superhuman man
nadejście (na-dey-shche) v.
coming; arrival; oncoming
nadepnąć (na-dep-nownch) v.
step on ; tread on (crushing)
nader (na-der) adv. greatly;
excessively; highly; most
nadesłać (na-de-swach) v. send
in ; forward; remit
nade wszystko (na-de vshist-ko)
adv. above all (else)
nadęty (nad-áñ-ti) adj. m.
puffed up; inflated ; superior
nadgraniczny (nad-gra-neech-ni)
adj. m. near-border ;frontier-
nadjechać (nad-yé-khach) v.
drive up; come up; arrive
nadlecieć (nad-le-chech) v. fly
in ; arrive in a hurry
nadleśniczy (nad-lesh-nee-chi)
m. chief ranger ; forest inspector: head of rangers

nadliczbowy (nad-leech-bo-vi)
adj. m. overtime; additional
nadludzki (nad-loodz-ki) adj.
m. superhuman ; divine
nadmiar (nád-myar) m. excess
nadłamać (nad-wa-mach) v. break
slightly; cause a slight break
nadmienić (nad-mye-neech) v.
mention ; allude;hint; add
nadmierny (nad-myér-ni) adj.
m. excessive; extravagant;undue
nadmorski (nad-mór-skee) adj.
m. seaside-;maritime
nadmuchać (na-dmoo-khach) v.
inflate; blow up with air
nadobny (na-dob-ny) adj. m.
handsome; comely; pretty
nadobowiązkowy (nad-o-bo-vyownz-
kó-vi) adj. m. optional
na dół (na doow) down; down
stairs; downwards
nadpić (nád-peech) v. take a
sip; start overfilled drink
nadpłynać (nad-pwi-nównch) v.
sail in; swim in; arrive
nadprodukcja (nad-pro-dook-
tsya) f. excess production
nadprogramowy (nad-pro-gra-mo-
vi) adj. m. extra; additional
nadprzyrodzony (nad-pzhy-ro-dzó-
ni) adj. m. supernatural
nadpsuty (nad-psóo-ti) adj. m.
partly spoiled; impaired
nadrabiać (nad-ráb-yach) v.
catch up with; make up; work
ahead of schedule;compensate for
nadruk (na-drook) m. overprint
nadrzędny (nad-zhánd-ni) adj.
m. superior; primary;precedent
nadskakiwać (nad-ska-kee-vach)
v. try to ingratiate oneself
nadsłuchiwać (nad-swoo-khee-
vach) v. strain to listen
nadspodziewany (nad-spo-dżhe-vá-
ni) adj. m. unexpected
nadstawiać (nad-stáv-yach) v.
expose; risk; hold out; cock
nadto (nád-to) adv. moreover;
besides; too much; too many
nadużycie (nad-oo-zhi-che) n.
abuse; excess; misuse
nadużywać (nad-oo-zhi-vach) v.
abuse; take advantage ;strain

nadwaga (nad-vá-ga) f. overweight;allowed extra weight
nadwartość (nad-vár-toshch) f.
overvalue in economics
nadwątlić (nad-vownt-leech) v.
weaken; impair; damage
nadwiślański (nad-veesh-lan-
skee) adj. m. on the Vistula
nadwodny (nad-vód-ni) adj. m.
near water; riverside; aquatic
nadwozie (nad-vó-zhe) m. car-
body; body of a car or truck
nadwyrężać (nad-vi-rán-zhach)
v. impair; strain; weaken
nadwyżka (nad-vizh-ka) f. surplus; excess amount
nadymać (na-di-mach) v. puff up
nadymić (na-dí-meech) v. fill
with smoke;make a lot of smoke
nadzieja (na-dzhé-ya) f. hope
nadziemski (nad-zhém-skee) adj.
m. celestial; heavenly;divine
nadzienie (na-dzhé-ne) n.
stuffing ; filling; forcemeat
nadziewać (na-dzhé-vach) v.
stuff;pierce with;put on; fill
nadzorca (nad-zór-tsa) m. overseer; superintendent;supervisor
nadzór (nad-zoor) m. supervision
nadzwyczaj (nad-zvi-chay) adv.
unusually; extremely; most
nadzwyczajny (nad-zvi-chay-ni)
adj. m. extraordinary; extreme
nafta (náf-ta) f. petroleum
naftalina (naf-ta-lée-na) f,
naphthalene; naphthaline
nagabywać (na-ga-bi-vach) v.
annoy; accost; trouble;molest
nagana (na-gá-na) f. blame
nagi (ná-gi) adj. m. naked;
bare ; nude; bald; empty
naginać (na-gee-nach) v. bend
down; submit to; adapt; bow
nagle (nág-le) adv. suddenly
naglić (nág-leech) v. urge
nagłość (nág-woshch) f. urgency
nagłówek (na-gwoo-vek) m. heading; caption; title; headline
nagły (nág-wi) adj. m. sudden;
urgent;instant;abrupt; pressing
nagminny (na-gmeen-ni) adj. m.
universal;usual;current;general

nagniotek (na-gnó-tek) m.
(skin) corn; callus on the skin
nagonka (na-gón-ka) f. campaign
against; hue and cry against
nagość (ná-goshch) f. nudity
nagradzać (na-grá-dzach) v.
reward; give prize;recompense
nagrobek (na-gró-bek) m. tomb
nagroda (na-gró-da) f. reward
nagrodzić (na-gró-dzheech)v.
reward; requite; recompense
nagromadzić (na-gro-má-dzheech)
v. accumulate; amass; heap up
nagrzewać (na-gzhé-vach) v.
warm up ; heat up; preheat
naigrawać (na-ee-gra-vach) v.
mock; scoff; deride;ridicule
naiwny (na-eev-ni) adj. m. naive
najazd (ná-yazt) m. invasion
najbardziej (nay-bár-dzhey)
adv. most(of all)
najechać (na-yé-khach)v.overrun;
invade; run into;ram; crowd
najedzony (na-ye-dzó-ni) adj.
m. full (of food); satiated
najem (ná-yem) m. hire
najemnik (na-yém-neek) m.
hireling; mercenary;free lance;
soldier of fortune;wage earner
najemny (na-yém-ni) adj. m.venal;
mercenary; hired labor
najeść się (ná-yeshch shań) v.
eat plenty of; eat a lot
najeźdźca (na-yeźhdźh-tsa) m.
invader; assailant; violator
najeżdżać (na-yezh-dzhach) v.
invade; run into; attack; ram
najeżony (na-ye-zho-ni) adj. m.
bristling; bristly ; beset
najgorszy (nay-gór-shi) adj. m.
worst; the worst of all
najgorzej (nay-go-zhey) adv.
worst of all : worst possible
najlepiej (nay-lép-yey) adv.
best ; best of all
najlepszy (nay-lép-shi) adj. m.
best; best of all; best possible
najmniej (náy-mney) adv. least
najmniejszy (nay-mney-shi) adj.
m. least; smallest; least of all
najmować (nay-mó-vach) v. rent;
hire; engage; lease

najpierw (náy-pyerv) adv. first
of all;in the first place
najście (nayśh-che) n. intrusion; inroad; invasion;incursion
najść (nayshch) v. intrude
najwięcej (nay-vyan-tsey) adv.
most of all (worst of all)
największy (nay-vyank-shi) adj.
m. biggest; largest; extreme
najwyżej (nay-vi-zhey) adv.
highest; at the very most
najwyższy (nay-vizh-shi) adj.
m. highest; top; utmost
nakarmić (na-kár-meech) v. feed
nakaz (na-kas) m. order ;writ
nakazywać (na-ka-zi-vach) v.
order; demand; command
nakleić (na-kle—eech) v. stick
on ; paste up; mount; post
nakład (na-kwad) m. outlay
nakładać (na-kwa-dach) v. lay
on; put on; place; set;spread
nakładca (na-kwád-tsa) m. publisher (of printed work)
nakłaniać (na-kwa-ñach) v. persuade ;induce; bring;get;urge
na koniec (na kó-ñets) adv.
finally ; at the end
nakreślać (na-kresh-lach) v.
delineate ; sketch;draft;write
nakręcać (na-kran-tsach) v. wind
up; shoot (movie);turn ;direct
nakrętka (na-kránt-ka) f.(screw)
nut; female screw; jam nut
nakrycie (na-kri-che) n. cover
nakrywać (na-kri-vach) v. cover
nakrywka (na-kriv-ka) f. lid
na kształt (na kshtawt) in form
of...;in shape of; a kind of...
nalać (na-lach) v. pour in; pour
on (liquid only,no sand etc.)
nalegać (na-le-gach) v. insist
naleganie (na-le-ga-ñe) n. in-
sistence ; urgent demand
nalepiać (na-lep-yach) v. stick
on; paste on; mount; glue on
nalepka (na-lep-ka) f. label
naleśnik (na-lésh-ñeek) m. pancake wrap around stuffing
nalewać (na-le-vach) v. pour in
należeć (na-lé-zhech) v. belong
należność (na-lézh-noshch) f.
due; ration ; charge; fee

należny (na-lezh-ni) adj. m.
due. owing; rightful; proper
należycie (na-le-zhi-che) adv.
properly; duly; suitably
należyty (na-le-zhi-ti) adj.
m. proper; right; appropriate
nalot (na-lot) m. air raid;
(skin) rush ; coating
naładować (na-wa-do-vach) v.
load; charge; cram
nałogowiec (na-wo-go-vyets) m.
addict; chain-smoker
nałogowy (na-wo-gó-vi) adj. m.
addicted ; inveterate;habitual
nałogowy pijak (na-wo-go-vi
peé-yak) alcoholic
nałóg (na-woog) m. addiction
namacalny (na-ma-tsál-ni) adj.
m. tangible; substantial
namaszczać (na-másh-chach)v.
anoint ; grease; smear
namaszczenie (na-mash-che-ñe)
n. unction ;anointing
namawiać (na-máv-yach) v.
persuade ; prompt; urge;egg on
namazać (na-ma-zach) v. daub-
over; anoint ; scrawl(scribble)
namiastka (na-myást-ka) f.
substitute; ersatz ; stopgap
namiernik (na-myér-ñeek) m.
direction finder ; pelorus
namiestnik (na-myest-ñeek) m.
regent; governor; viceroy
namiętność (na-myant-noshch) f.
passion ; infatuation; fervor
namiętny (na-myánt-ni) adj. m.
passionate ; keen; ardent;lusty
namiot (na-myot) m. tent
namoczyć (na-mo-chich) v. wet;
soak ; soak; steep; drench
namoknąć (na-mok-nównch) v. get
soaked ; become saturated
namowa (na-mó-va) f. persuasion
namulić (na-moo-leech) v. slime
up ; silt up; mud up; ooze up
namydlić (na-mid-leech) v.
soap up ; put soap lather on
namysł (na-misw) m. reflection
namyślać się (na-mish-lach shan)v.
ponder; reflect ; think over
nanosić (na-no-sheech) v.bring;
deposit; plot; track (mud)
na nowo (na nó-vo) adv. anew

naocznie (na-och-ñe) adv. by
eye; visually ; clearly
naoczny świadek (na-och-ni
shvya-dek) eyewitness;bystander
na odwrót (na od-vroot) adv.
inversely;the other way round
na ogół (na o-goow) adv. (in
general) generally; on the whole
na około (na o-ko-wo) adv. all
around; about;right round
naokoło (na-o-ko-wo) prep. round
naonczas (na-on-chas) adv. at
that time; then;in those days
naoliwić (na-o-lee-veech) v. oil;
lubricate ; grease;make slippery
na opak (na o-pak) adv. backward; perversely; the wrong way
na ostatek (na o-sta-tek) adv.
finally; in the end; at last
naostrzyć (na-os-tzhich) v.
sharpen up ; become sharp
na oścież (na ośh-chesh) adv.
wide open; opened all the way
na oślep (na ośh-lep) adv. blind-
ly; full tilt; headlong
na ówczas (na oov-chas) adv. at
that time ;then; in those days
napad (na-pad) m. assault;attempt
napadać (na-pa-dach) v. assail
napar (na-par) m. infusion;
brew ; a beverage brewed
naparstek (na-par-stek) m. thimble: dram; thimble full
naparzyć (na-pa-zhich) v. infuse
napaskudzić (na-pas-koo-dźheech)
v. soil up; make a mess; dirty
napastliwy (na-past-lee-vi) adj.
m. aggressive ;malicious;bitter
napastnik (na-past-ñeek) m. aggressor; forward center (sport)
napastować (na-pas-to-vach) v.
pester; attack; wax molest;worry
napaść (na-pashch) f. assault
napawać (na-pa-vach) v. fill up
(with feelings .panic, wander)
napatrzyć się (na-pat-shich śhañ)
v, see enough ;have a good look
napełniać (na-pew-ñach) v. fill
up ; inspire; imbue; pervade
napewno (na-pev-no) adv. surely;
certainly; for sure ;without fail
napęd (na-pand) m. propulsion:
drive;force; driving gear

napędowy (na-pan-do-vi) adj.
m. motive ;driving; impulsive
napędzać (na-pan-dzach) v. chase
in; propel ;round up;drift in
napić się (na-peech śhañ) v.
have a drink ; quench one's thirst
napierać (na-pye-rach) v. press
forward; insist ; advance
napięcie (na-pyan-che) n. tension; strain; voltage;intensity
napiętek (na-pyan-tek) m. heel
napiętnować (na-pyant-no-vach)
v. brand; stigmatize;censure
condemn as being very bad;stamp
napięty (na-pyan-ty) adj. m.
tense; taut; strained; tight
napinać (na-pee-nach) v. strain
napis (na-pees) m. inscription
napitek (na-pee-tek) m. drink
napiwek (na-pee-vek) m. tip
napluć (na-plooch) v. spit on
napływ (na-pwiv) m. influx
napływać (na-pwi-vach) v. inflow; flow in; flock;pour in
napływowy (na-pwi-vo-vi) adj.
m. alluvial; immigrant; allien
napoczynać (na-po-chi-nach) v.
start up; open; broach
napominać (na-po-mee-nach) v.
admonish; reprimand; rebuke
napomknąć (na-pom-knownch) v.
mention; hint at; allude to
napomnienie (na-pom-ñe-ñe) n.
admonition; reprimand;rebuke
na pomoc ! (na po-mots) excl.
help ! give help! please,help!
napotny (na-pot-ni) adj. m.
sudatory; perspiratory
napotykać (na-po-ti-kach) v.
run in; come across:be faced with
napowietrzny (na-po-vyetzh-ni)
adj. m. aerial; overhead-
na powrót (na pov-root) adv.
return; again; on the way back
na pozór (na po-zoor) adv. ap-
parently; on the face of it
napój (na-pooy) m. drink
na pół (na poow) adv. in half
napór (na-poor) m. pressure
naprawa (na-pra-va) f. repair;
redress: renovation; reform
naprawdę (na-prav-dañ) adv. indeed; really; truly; positively

naprawiać (na-práw-yach) v. repair: fix; mend; rectify;reform
naprędce (na-pránd-tse) adv.
hastily: in a hurry;slapdash
naprężenie (na-prań-zhe-ńe) n.
tension; strain; tautness
naprężyć (na-prań-zhich) v.
tauten; stretch;strain
naprowadzać (na-pro-vá-dzach)
v. lead in; direct to;advise
na próżno (na proozh-no) adv.
in vain: uselessly;to no avail
naprzeciw (na-pzhe-cheev) adv.
opposite: vis-a-vis
naprzec (na-pzhech) v. press;
urge : press hard; insist on
na przekor (na pzhe-koor) adv.
in despite; just to spite
na przełaj (na pzhe-way) adv.
shortcut (across obstacles)
na przemian (na pzhe-myan) adv.
alternately ; by turns
naprzód (ná-pzhoot) adv. forwards;first;in the first place
na przykład (na pzhik-wat) adv.
for instance; for example
naprzykrzać się (na-pshik-shach
śhań)v bother;molest;pester
napuchnąć (na-pookh-nowńch)v.
swell ; become swollen
napuchły (na-pookh-wi) adj. m.
swollen ;bulging; distended
napuścić (na-poosh-cheech) v.
set up ; impregnate; let in
napuszony (na-poo-shó-ni) adj.
m. puffed up; bristling;ruffled
napychać (na-pi-khach) v. stuff;
cram ;cram;fill;pack;crowd,stow
narada (na-rá-da) f. consultation ; council; conference
naradzać się (na-rá-dzach śhań)v.
consult; confer with;deliberate
naramiennik (na-ra-myeń-ńeek)
m. epaulet; shoulder-strap
narastać (na-rás-tach) v. grow
on ;increase; accumulate;accrue
naraz (ná-ras) adv. suddenly
na razie (na rá-źhe) adv. for
the time being;for the present
narażać (na-rá-zhach) v. expose
to endanger
narciarstwo (nar-chár-stvo) n.
skiing

narciarz (nár-chash) m. skier
narcyz (nár-tsis) m. narcissus
nareszcie (na-résh-che) adv.
at last : finally;at long last
naręcze (na-rań-che) n. armful
narkotyczny (nar-ko-tích-ni)
adj. m. narcotic;causing numbness
narkotyk (nar-kó-tik) m.narcot-
ic :drug for sleep and relief
narkoza (nar-kó-za) f. anesthe-
sia ; anaesthetization
narobić (na-ró-beech) v.mess up;
cause nuisance; make a mess
narodowość (na-ro-dó-voshch) f.
nationality :national status
narodowy (na-ro-dó-vi) adj. m.
national;of national character
narodzenie (na-ro-dzé-ńe) n.
birth ; a being born;the beginning
narodzić się (na-ró-dźheech śhań)
v. be born ; originate; arise
narodziny (na-ro-dźhee-ni) n.
birth ; origin; the beginning
narosl (ná-roshl) f. tumor;
growth;excrescence; wart;knar
narowisty (na-ro-vees-ti) adj.
m. restive;vicious:skittish
narożnik (na-rózh-ńeek) m. corner ;angle; cross-roads;gusset
narożny (na-rózh-ni) adj. m.
corner-; at the street corner
naród (ná-root) m. nation;people
narów (ná-roof) m. vice (res-
tivness); bad habit; fault
narta (nár-ta) f. ski; sleigh
naruszać (na-roo-shach) v. disturb; violate; injure; harm
naruszenie (na-roo-shé-ńe) n.
offense ; disturbance; breach
narwany (na-rvá-ni) adj. m.
hot-head; reckless; rash
narybek (na-rí-bek) m. small
fry; coming generation
narząd (na-zhownt) m. organ
narzecze (na-zhé-che) n. (primitive)dialect
narzeczona (na-zhe-chó-na) f.
fiancée: an engaged woman
narzeczony (na-zhe-chó-ni) m.
fiance
narzekać (na-zhé-kach) v. complain: grumble: lament

narzekanie (na-zhe-ká-ńe) n.
complaints; kick; bitching
narzędzie (na-zhań-dzhe) n.
tool; utensil; implement
narzucać (na-zhoo-tsaćh) v.
throw over; impose; shovel on
nasada (na-sá-da) f. base
nasenna pigułka (na-sén-na pi-
goow-ka) sleeping-pill
nasiadówka (na-śha-doóv-ka) f.
sitzbath; hip-bath
nasiąkać (na-śhówn-kaćh) v.
soak up; become saturated; imbibe
nasienie (na-śhé-ńe) m. seed;
sperm; semen; posterity
nasilenie (na-śhee-lé-ńe) n.
intensification; intensity
naskórek (na-skoó-rek) m. outer
skin; epidermis; cuticle
naskarżyć (na-skár-zhićh) v.
denounce; lodge a complain
nasłuchać się (na-swoo-khaćh
śhań) v. hear plenty
nasłuchiwać (na-swoo-khee-vaćh)
v. monitor (radio); listen
nasmarować (na-sma-ró-vaćh) v.
smear over; grease; lubricate
nastać (ná-staćh) v. set in;
enter; occur; come about
nastanie (na-stá-ńe) n. arrival;
setting-in; advent; coming
nastarczyć (na-stár-chićh) v.
supply enough; keep pace; cope
nastawać (na-stá-vaćh) v. insist
nastawiać (na-stáv-yaćh) v. set
up; set right; tune in; point
nastawienie (na-sta-vyé-ńe) n.
attitude; bias; disposition
następca (na-stáńp-tsa) m. successor; heir
następnie (na-stáńp-ńe) adv.
next; then; subsequently
następny (na-stáńp-ni) adj. m.
next; the next; the following
następować (na-stáń-po-vaćh) v.
follow; tread; come after; ensue
następstwo (na-stáńp-stvo) n.
result; succession; upshot
następujacy (na-stáń-poo-yown-
tsi) adj. m. successive; following; the following
nastraszyć (na-stra-shićh) v.
frighten; intimidate

nastręczać (na-stráń-chaćh) v.
afford; present; offer; procure
nastroic (na-stró-eećh) v. at-
tune; tune up; dispose to
nastroszyć (na-stró-shićh) v.
bristle up; perk up; heap up
nastrój (ná-strooy) m. mood
nasturcja (na-stoór-tsya) f.
nasturtia; lark-heel
nasuwać (na-sóo-vaćh) v. shove
up; draw over; afford; overthrust
nasycać (na-sí-tsaćh) v. satiate; satisfy; sate; saturate
nasycenie (na-si-tsé-ńe) n. sa-
tiation; saturation; satisfaction
nasycony (na-si-tsó-ni) adj. m.
satiate; saturated; replete
nasyłać (na-sí-waćh) v. send on
nasyp (ná-sip) m. embankment
nasypać (na-sí-paćh) v. pour in;
spread up (dry powder etc)
nasz (nash) pron. our; ours
naszyć (na-shićh) v. sew on;
trim with; trim
naszkicować (na-shkee-tsó-vaćh)
v. sketch; make a sketch
naszyjnik (na-shiy-ńeek) m.
necklace; neck jewelry
naśladować (na-śhla-dó-vaćh) v.
imitate; mimic; reproduce
naśladowanie (na-śhla-do-va-ńe)
n. imitation; copy
naśladowca (na-śhla-dóv-tsa)
m. imitator
naśmiewać się (na-śhmyé-vaćh
śhań) v. laugh at; deride
naświetlać (na-śhvyet-laćh) v.
explain; irradiate; expose
natarcie (na-tár-che) n.
1. rubbing; 2. onslaught; attack; offensive; advance
natarczywosc (na-tar-chi-vośhćh)
n. insistency; obtrusiveness
natarczywy (na-tar-chi-vi) adj;
n. insistent; pressing; urgent
natchnąć (nát-khnownćh) v. inspire; infuse; penetrate
natchnienie (nat-khńe-ńe) n.
inspiration; brain wave; impulse
natenczas (na-ten-chas) adv.
then; at that time; as
natężać (na-táń-zhaćh) v. strain;
intensify; strenghten; exert

natężenie (na-tán-zhe-ńe) n.
tension;strain; effort;pitch
natężony (na-tań-zho-ni) adj.
m. intense, ; strained
natknąć (nát-knównch) v. come
across ;butt; stick; stud
natłoczony (na-two-chó-ni) adj.
m. crowded; packed; huddled
natłoczyć (na-two-chich) v.
cram: pack: crowd; huddle
natłok (na-twok) m. crowd;
throng; pressure accumulation
natomiast (na-to-myast) adv.
however; yet; on the contrary
natłuścić (na-twoósh-cheech) v.
oil; grease; lubricate
natrafić (na-tra-feech) v. encounter;. come across
natręctwo (na-tráńts-tvo) n.
intrusiveness;importunity
natręt (ná-tráńt) m. intruder
natrętny (na-tráńt-ni) adj. m.
intrusive; bothersome
natrysk (na-trisk) m. shower-
bath: shower; sprying
natrząsać się (na-tzhówn-sach
śhąń)v.scoff at: sneer;poke fun
natrzeć (ná-tzhech) v. rub;
attack; harass: scold; rate
natura (na-too-ra) f. nature
naturalizacja (na-too-ra-lee-
záts-ya) f. naturalization
naturalizować (na-too-ra-lee-zó-
vach) v. naturalize
naturalny (na-too-rál-ni) adj.
m. natural; true to life
natychmiast (na-tikh-myast) adv.
at once;instantly; right away
natychmiastowy (na-tikh-myas-
tó-vi), adj. m. instantaneous
nauczać (na-oó-chach) v. teach;
instruct; tutor; train
nauczanie (na-oo-cha-ńe) n.
teaching; instruction
nauczka (na-oóch-ka) f. (pointed) lesson (unpleasant)
nauczyciel (na-oo-chi-chel) m.
teacher; instructor
nauczyć się (na-oo-chich śhąń)
v. learn: come to know
nauka (na-oo-ka) f. science;
learning; study; teaching

naukowiec (na-oo-kóv-yets) m.
scientist; scholar; researcher
naukowość (na-oo-kó-voshch) f.
erudition; scholarship;learning
naukowy (na-oo-kó-vi) adj. m.
scientific; scholarly;academic
naumyślnie (na-oo-míshl-ńe)
adv. on purpose; of set purpose
nawa (ná-va) f. nave; aisle
nawadniać (na-vád-ńach) v.
irrigate: saturate with water
nawalić (na-vá-leech) v. pile
up; fail; bungle;break down
nawał (ná-vaw) m. no end of
nawała (na-vá-wa) f. overwhelm-
ing mass; swarms; onslaught
nawałnica (na-vaw-ńee-tsa) f.
tempest; storm; hurricane
nawarstwienie (na-var-stvyé-ńe)
n. stratification
nawarzyć (na-vá-zhich) v. brew;
cook; concoct; get in trouble
nawet (ná-vet) adv. even
nawet gdyby (na-vét gdí-bi)
adv. even if; even though
nawias (ná-vyas), m. parenthesis
nawiasem (na-vyá-sem) adv. incidentally; by way of digression
nawiasowy (na-vya-só-vi) adj.
m. parenthetical; incidental
nawiązać (na-vyówn-zach) v.
tie to; refer to; enter in
nawiązanie (na-vyówn-zá-ńe) n.
connection; reference to
nawiedzać (na-vyé-dzach) v.
visit; haunt; afflict; obsess
nawierzchnia (na-vyezh-khńa) f.
surface (finish); pavement
nawijać (na-vee-yach) v. wind
up;reel; roll up; spool: coil
nawlekać (na-vle-kach) v. thread;
string ; slip on
nawodnienie (na-vod-ńe-ńe) n.
irrigation; saturation with water
nawoływać (na-vo-wi-vach) v.
call; hail; exhort to; halloo
nawozić (na-vó-zheech) v. fertilize; manure ;truck;cart; fill
nawóz (ná-voos), m. manure ;dung
na wpół (na vpoów) adv. half;
semi-: half-(finished, boiled)
nawracać (na-vra-tsach) v. turn
around; convert ; turn back

nawrócenie (na-vroo-tsé-ñe) n.
conversion; being converted
nawrót (ná-vroot) m. return;
relapse; recurrence; set-back
na wskros (na vskrosh) adv.
throughout; from end to end
nawyk (ná-vik) m. habit; wont
nawykać (na-vi-kach) v. accustom; fall into a habit
nawykły (na-vik-wi) adj. m.
accustomed; get used to...
na wylot (na vi-lot) adv. through
and through; right through
nawymyslać (na-vi-mish-lach) v.
revile; abuse; insult; invent
na wyrywki (na vi-riv-kee) adv.
at random; at haphazard
nawzajem (na-vzá-yem) adv. mu-
tually; same to you
na wznak (ná vznak) adv. on
one's back; on one's supine
nazad (ná-zat) adv. back (wards)
nazajutrz (na-zá-jootsh) adv.
next morning; next day
nazbierać (na-zbyé-rach) v.
gather up; collect; assemble
nazbyt (ná-zbit) adv. too much
na zewnątrz (na zév-nówntsh)
adv. out; outwards; outside
naznaczyć (na-zna-chich) v.
mark; fix; appoint; outline; scar
nazwa (náz-va) f. designation;
name; appellation; title
nazwisko (naz-vee-sko) m. family name; surname; reputation
nazywać (na-zi-vach) v. call;
name; term; denominate; christen
nażarty (na-zhar-ti) adj. m.
gorged; stuffed(greedily)
nażreć się (ná-zhrech shán) v.
gorge; stuff oneself (vulg.)
negacja (ne-gáts-ya) f. negation; opposite of positive
negatyw (ne-gá-tiv) m. negative
negatywny (ne-ga-tív-ni) adj.
m. negative; saying "no"
negliż (nég-leesh) m. undress;
morning dress; dishabille
negocjacje (ne-go-tsyáts-ye) pl.
negotiations; settling a treaty
negować (ne-gó-vach) v. deny
nekrolog (ne-kró-log) m. obituary notice : obituary

nektar (nék-tar) m. nectar
neofita (ne-o-fée-ta) m. convert; neophyte; proselyte
neologizm (ne-o-ló-geezm) m.
neologism; new word; new meanning
neon (né-on) m. neon light
nepotyzm (ne-pó-tizm) m. nepo-
tizm; favoritism to relatives
nerka (nér-ka) f. kidney
nerw (nerv) m. nerve; vigor; ardor
nerwica (ner-vée-tsa) f. neurosis; nervous disturbance
nerwobol (ner-vo-bool) m. neuralgia; severe pain along a nerve
nerwowosc (ner-vó-voshch) f.
nervosity; irritability; fidgets
nerwowy (ner-vó-vi) adj. m. nervous; made up of nerves; fearful
neseser (ne-sé-ser) m. dressing
case; make-up case: toilet case
netto (nét-to) adv. net (cost)
neutralizować (ne-oo-tra-lee-
zó-vach) v. neutralize
neutralnosc (ne-oo-trál-noshch)
f. neutrality; neutral status
neutralny (ne-oo-trál-ni) adj.
m. neutral; indifferent
neutron (né-oo-tron) m. neutron
newralgia (ne-vrál-gya) f.
neuralgia; pain along a nerve
newroza (ne-vró-za) f. neurosis
nęcic (nán-cheech) v. entice;
court; allure; tempt; be seductive
nędza (nán-dza) f. misery
nędzarz (nán-dzash) m. destitute
wretch; beggar; pauper
nędznik (nándz-ñeek) m. villain
nędzny (nándz-ni) adj. m. wretched; miserable ; shabby; sorry
nękac (nán-kach) v. molest; hurry;
torment; harass; annoy; worry
ni to ni owo (ñee to ñee o-vo)
adv. neither this nor that
ni stąd ni zowąd (ñee stównt
ñee zo-vównt) without reason;
suddenly ; for no reason whatever
niania (ná-ña) f. (baby's)
nurse ; nanny; dry nurse
niańczyc (ñań-cheech) v. nurse
niańka (ñáń-ka) f. nurse
niby (ñee-bi) adv. as if; pre-
tending ; as it were; like
nic (ñeets) pron. nothing; nought

nic nie szkodzi (ňeets ňe shko-
džhee) expr.: does not matter
nic z tego (ňeets z te-go)
expr.: no use: to no avail
nicość (ňee-tsoshćh) f. nothing-
ness; oblivion; nonentity
nicpoń (ňets-poň) m. good-for-
nothing; "nogoodnik"; scamp
niczyj (ňee-chiy) adj. m. no-
man's: nobody's; no one's
nici (ňee-ćhee) pl. 1. threads
2. nothing; nothing of it
nić (ňeećh) f. thread
nie (ňe) part. no ; not(any)
nie jeszcze (ňe yesh-che) not-
yet: not for a long time
nieagresja (ňe-a-gres-ya) f.
nonaggression (treaty)
niebaczny (ňe-bach-ni) adj. m.
imprudent; rush; inconsiderate
niebawem (ňe-ba-vem) adv. soon
niebezpieczeństwo (ňe-bez-pye-
cheň-stvo) m. danger; peril
niebezpieczny (ňe-bez-pyech-ni)
adj. m. dangerous; risky; tricky
niebiański (ňe-byan-skee) adj.
m. heavenly; divine
niebieskawy (ňe-byes-ka-vi) adj.
m. bluish
niebieski (ňe-byes-kee) adj. m.
blue; heavenly; of the sky
niebieskooki (ňe-byes-ko-o-kee)
adj. m. blue-eyed
niebiosa (ňe-byo-sa) pl. Hea-
vens: the visible sky
niebo (ňe-bo) n. sky
nieborak (ňe-bo-rak) m. poor
soul; poor soul; poor devil
nieboszczyk (ňe-bosh-chik) m.
deceased; dead person
niebosiężny (ňe-bo-shaňzh-ni)
adj. m. sky-high: towering
niebotyczny (ňe-bo-tich-ni) adj.
m. sky-high; sky reaching
niebożę (ňe-bo-zhaň) n. poor
soul; poor thing; poor devil
nie byle jak (ňe bi-le yak) expr.:
not just any way; not carelessly
niebyły (ňe-bi-vi) adj. m. null
and void; unexisting
niebywale (ňe-bi-va-le) adv.
unusually; exceptionally
niebywały (ňe-bi-va-wi) adj. m.
unheard-of; unusual; uncommon

niecały (ňe-tsa-wi) adj. m.
incomplete: defective; less than
niecenzuralny (ňe-tsen-zoo-
ral-ni) adj. m. indecent; un-
printable: obscene; suggestive
niech (ňekh) part. let: suppose
niechcący (ňe-khtsown-tsi) adv.
unintentionally; unawares
niechęć (ňe-khanćh) f. disincli-
nation; aversion; ill-will
niechętny (ňe-khaňt-ni) adj. m.
unwilling; reluctant: averse
niechluj (ňe-khlooy) m. grub;
sloppy; slut: dirty: sloven
niechybny (ňe-khib-ni) adj. m.
without fail: certain: unerring
niechże (ňekh-zhe) part. let
niecić (ňe-ćheećh) v. kindle;
stir up; light (a fire)
nieciekawy (ňe-ćhe-ka-vi) adj.
m. blank; void of interest
niecierpliwić się (ňe-ćher-plee-
veećh shaň) v. be impatient
niecierpliwy (ňe-ćher-plee-vi)
adj. m. impatient; restless
niecnota (ňe-tsno-ta) m. scamp;
rogue; rascal: scoundrel
niecny (ňets-ni) adj. m. vile
nieco (ňe-tso) adv. somewhat;
a little: a trifle; slightly
niecodzienny (ňe-tso-dzheň-ni)
adj. m. uncommon; unusual
nieczesany (ňe-che-sa-ni) adj.
m. unkempt ; disorderly
nieczęsty (ňe-chaň-sti) adj. m.
infrequent: not frequent
nieczuły (ňe-choo-wi) adj. m.
callous: heartless: insensible
nieczynny (ňe-chin-ni) adj. m.
inert; inactive; out of order
nieczysty (ňe-chis-ti) adj. m.
unclean; polluted: dirty; shady
nieczytelny (ňe-chi-tel-ni) adj.
m. illegible; cramped; crabbed
niedaleki (ňe-da-le-kee) adj. m.
near; not distant; at hand
niedaleko (ňe-da-le-ko) adv.
near; not far; a short way off
niedawno (ňe-dav-no) adv. recently; not long ago; newly
niedbale (ňe-dba-le) adv. carelessly; casually; nonchalantly
niedbalstwo (ňe-dbal-stvo) n.
negligence; laxity; carelessness

niedbały (ńe-dba-wi) adj. m.
negligent;untidy;lax;careless
niedługi (ńe-dwoo-gee) adj. m.
short; not long
niedługo (ńe-dwoo-go) adv. soon;
not long; before long;by and by
niedobitki (ńe-do-beet-kee) pl.
survivors; routed soldiers
niedobór (ńe-do-boor) m. deficit ; shortage; scarcity; loss
niedobrany (ńe-do-bra-ni) adj.
m. ill-suited ; ill-matched
niedobry (ńe-dob-ri) adj. m.
no-good ; bad; wicked; nasty
niedobrze (ńe-dob-zhe) adv. not
well; badly;wrong;improperly
nie doceniać(ńe-do-tse-ńach) v.
underestimate; estimate too low
niedociągnięcie (ńe-do-chown-
gnań-che) n. shortcoming
niedogodność (ńe-do-god-noshch)
f. inconvenience; drawback
niedogodny (ńe-do-god-ni) adj.
m. inconvenient: undesirable
nie dogotowany(ńe-do-go-to-va-
ni) adj. m. underdone; half-
cooked; half-raw; under done
nie dojadac(ńe-do-ya-dach) v.
not eat enough;starve
niedojda (ńe-dóy-da) m. nitwit;
bungler ; fumbler; lout
niedojrzały (ńe-doy-zha-wi) adj.
m. unripe; immature; under age
niedokładny (ńe-do-kwad-ni) adj.
m. inaccurate; inexact
niedokończony (ńe-do-koń-cho-ni)
adj. m. unfinished;incomplete
niedokrwisty (ńe-do-krvees-ti)
adj. m. anemic; anaemic
niedola (ńe-do-la) f. adversity
niedołęga (ńe-do-wań-ga) m.
blunderer; cripple;duffer
niedołęstwo (ńe-do-wań-stvo) m.
inefficiency; clumsiness
niedomagać (ńe-do-ma-gach) v.
be unwell; be ailing
nie domknięty(ńe-do-mkńań-ti)
adj. m. ajar; slightly open
niedomówienie (ńe-do-moo-vye-ńe)
n. vague hint; insinuation
niedomyslny (ńe-do-miśhl-ni)
adj. m. slow thinking

niedopałek (ńe-do-pa-wek) m.
(cigarette) butt: stub;ember
niedopatrzenie (ńe-do-pa-tzhe-
ńe) n. oversight; neglect
niedopuszczalny (ńe-do-poosh-
chál-ni) adj. m. inadmissible
niedorozwinięty (ńe-do-roz-
vee-ńań-ti) adj. m. underdeveloped; mentally retarded
niedorzeczny (ńe-do-zhech-ni)
adj. m. absurd; ridiculous
niedoskonały (ńe-dos-ko-na-wi)
adj. m. imperfect;deficient
niedosłyszalny (ńe-do-swi-shál-
ni) adj. m. inaudible
niedosmażony (ńe-do-sma-zho-ni)
adj. m. underdone ; half-raw
nie dospać(ńe-dos-pach) v.
sleep too short time; not sleep
enough; not to have enough sleep
niedostateczny (ńe-dos-ta-tech-
ni) adj. m. insufficient
niedostatek (ńe-dos-ta-tek) m.
shortage; indigence; poverty
niedostępny (ńe-do-stánp-ni)
adj. m. inaccessible;out of reach
niedostosowanie (ńe-dos-to-so-
va-ńe)n. maladjustment
niedostrzegalny (ńe-do-stzhe-
gál-ni) adj. m. imperceptible
niedościgły (ńe-do-shchéeg-wi)
adj. m. matchless; inimitable
niedoświadczenie (ńe-do-shvyad-
ché-ńe) n. inexperience
niedouczony (ńe-do-oo-cho-ni)
adj. m. half-educated
nie dowarzony (ńe do-va-zhó-ni)
adj. m. half-boiled; rough
niedowarzony (ńe-do-va-zho-ni)
adj. m. immature ;undereducated
niedowiarek (ńe-do-vya-rek) m.
unbeliever;atheist; skeptic
niedowidzieć (ńe-do-vee-dźech)
v. be short-sighted
nie dowierzać(ńe-do-vye-zhach)
v. distrust; disbelieve
niedowład (ńe-do-vwat) m. pare-
sis : partial paralysis
niedozwolony (ńe-doz-vo-ló-ni)
adj. m. not allowed;illicit
niedrogi (ńe-dro-gee) adj. m.
cheap ; inexpensive

nieduży (ńe-doo-zhi) adj. m.
small; little;not big;not tall
niedwuznaczny (ńe-dvoo-znach-ni)
adj. m. unequivocal; clear
niedyskrecja (ńe-dis-krets-ya)
f. indiscretion;indelicacy,
niedyspozycja (ńe-dis-po-zits-
ya) f. indisposition
niedziela (ńe-dźhé-la)f. Sunday
niedźwiadek (ńe-dźhvya-dek) m.
bear, cub ; Teddy bear
niedźwiedzica (ńe-dzhvye-dźhee-
tsa) f. female bear:she-bear
niedźwiedź (ńe-dźhvyedźh) m.
bear : bearskin; clumsy man
nieelastyczny (ńe-e-las-tích-
ni) adj. m. inelastic
nieestetyczny (ńe-es-te-tích-
ni) adj. m. unesthetic
nieetyczny (ńe-e-tích-ni) adj.
m. unethical; immoral
niefachowy (ńe-fa-khó-vi) adj.
m. incompetent; inexpert
nieforemny (ńe-fo-rém-ni) adj.
m. shapeless; deformed
nieformalnie (ńe-for-mál-ńe)
adv. informally; illegally
niefortunny (ńe-for-tóon-ni)
adj. m. unlucky; regrettable
niefrasobliwy (ńe-fra-sob-lee-
vi) adj. m. care-free;jaunty
niegdyś (ńeg-diśh) adv. formerly; once; at one time
niegodny (ńe-gód-ni) adj. m.
unworthy;undignified;yile;base
niegodziwy (ńe-go-dźhee-vi)adj.
m. wicked;vile;base;mean;foul
niegościnny (ńe-gośh-cheen-ni)
adj. m. inhospitable;desolate
niegrzeczny (ńe-gzhéch-ni) adj.
m. rude; impolite;unkind: bad
niegustowny (ńe-goos-tóv-ni)
adj. m. tasteless;in bad taste
niehigieniczny (ńe-khee-ge-
ńeéch-ni) adj. m. unsanitary
niehonorowy (ńe-kho-no-ró-vi)
adj. m. dishonorable; unfair
nieistotny (ńe-ees-tó-tni) adj.
m. inessential; immaterial
niejaki (ńe-yá-kee) adj. m. a;
one; certain;some;slight
niejasno (ńe-yás-no) adv. dimly:
vaguely;ambiguously;obscurely

niejasny (ńe-yás-ni) adj. m.dim;
unclear;indistinct;vague;obscure
niejeden (ńe-yé-den) adj. m.
many a: quite a number
niejednokrotnie (ńe-yed-no-krót-
ńe) adv. repeatedly;recurrently
nie karany (ńe ka-rá-ni) adj. m.
with a clean record; not con-
victed before
niekiedy (ńe-kyé-di) adv. now
and then; sometimes; at times
niekonsekwentny (ńe-kon-se-kvént-
ni) adj. m. inconsistent
niekorzystny (ńe-ko-zhíst-ni)
adj. m. disadvantageous
niekorzyść (ńe-kó-zhiśhch) f.
disadvantage; detriment
niekształtny (ńe-kshtáwt-ni)
adj. m. unshapely; formless
niektóry (ńe-ktoó-ry) adj. m.
some;one here and there
nieledwie (ńe-léd-vye) adv. all
but: almost:practically
nielegalny (ńe-le-gál-ni) adj.
m. illegal;unlawful:illicit
nieletni (ńe-lét-ńee) adj. m.
under age;juvenile; minor
nieliczny (ńe-leéch-ni) adj. m.
not numerous; scarce;rare;small
nielitościwy (ńe-lee-tośh-chee-
vi) adj. m. unmerciful
nielogiczny (ńe-lo-geéch-ni)
adj. m. illogical; nonsensical
nieludzki (ńe-loódz-kee) adj.
inhuman: atrocious;ruthless
nieład (ńe-wat) m. disorder;
disarray; confusion:mess
nieładnie (ńe-wád-ńe) adv. not
nicely: unattractively;wrongly
niełaska (ńe-wás-ka) f. disgrace;
disfavor;loss of respect
niemal (ńe-mal) adv. almost;
nearly ;pretty nearly;well-nigh
niemało (ńe-má-wo) adv. not a
few; pretty much ;not a little
niemały (ńe-má-wi) adj. m. pretty big ;fair-sized;goodly;no mean
niemądry (ńe-mownd-ri) adj. unwise; ill-judged ;silly;stupid
niemczyć (ńem-chich) v.Germanize
niemęcki (ńe-mań-kee)adj.m.unmanly
niemiecki (ńem-yéts-kee) adj. m.
German ; German language

niemiły (ńe-mée-wi) adj. m. unpleasant;unsightly;harsh;surly
niemniej jednak (ńe-mney yednak) nevertheless; all the same;none the less; however
niemoc (ńe-mots) f. impotence
niemodny (ńe-mód-ni) adj. m. outmoded; out of fashion
niemoralny (ńe-mo-rál-ni) adj. m. immoral; dishonest
niemowa (ńe-mó-ya) m.ϗ f. mute
niemowlę (ńe-móv-lań) n. baby
niemożliwy (ńe-mozh-leé-vi) adj. m. impossible
niemrawy (ńe-mrá-vi) adj. m. sluggish; tardy; indolent
niemy (ńié-mi) adj. m. dumb
nienaganny (ńe-na-gán-ni) adj. m. blameless; faultless
nienaruszalny (ńe-na-roo-shál-ni) adj. m. inviolable
nienaruszony (ńe-na-roo-shó-ni) adj. m. intact·undisturbed
nienasycony (ńe-na-si-tso-ni) adj. m. insatiable; (chem. unsaturated); voracious
nienaturalny (ńe-na-too-rál-ni) adj. m. unnatural; insincere
nienawistny (ńe-na-veést-ni) adj. m. hateful;full of hatred
nienawiść (ńe-ná-veeshćh) f. hate; abomination;detestation
nie nazwany (ńe naz-vá-ni) adj. m. unnamed; not maned
nienormalny (ńe nor-mál-ni) adj. m. abnormal; insane
nieobecność (ńe-o-béts-noshćh) f. absence; non-attendance
nieobecny (ńe-o-béts-ni) adj. m. absent; not present;not in
nieobeznany (ńe-o-bez-ná-ni) adj. m. uninformed; ignorant
nieobliczalny (ńe-o-blee-chál-ni) adj. m. unreliable; incalculable ;irresponsible
nieobyczajny (ńe-o-bi-cháy-ni) adj. m. immoral;ill-mannered
nieoceniony (ńe-o-tse-ńo-ni) adj. m. inestimable
nieoczekiwany (ńe-oche-kee-vá-ni) adj. m. unexpected
nieodłączny (ńe-od-wowńch-ni) adj. m. inseparable

nieodmienny (ńe-od-myén-ni) adj. m. invariable;undeclinable
nieodparty (ńe-od-pár-ti) adj. m. irrefutable; compelling
nieodpowiedni (ńe-od-po-vyéd-ńee) adj. m. inadequate; wrong
nieodpowiedzialny (ńe-od-po-vye-dźhál-ni) adj. m. irresponsible
nieodstępny (ńe-od-stáńp-ni) adj. m. inseparable;ever present
nieodwołalny (ńe-od-vo-wál-ni) adj. m. irrevocable; final
nieodzownie (ńe-od-zóv-ńe) adv. inevitably; absolutely
nieodzowny (ńe-od-zóv-ni) adj. m. indispensable;irrevocable
nieodżałowany (ńe-od-zha-wo-vá-ni) adj. m. never enough regretted; much regretted
nieoględny (ńe-o-glánd-ni) adj. m. inconsiderate;reckless;rash
nieograniczony (ńe-o-gra-ńee-chó-ni) adj. m. infinite; boundless
nieokiełzany (ńe-o-kew-za-ni) adj. m. unbridled; uncontrollable
nieokreślony (ńe-o-kresh-ló-ni) adj. m. indefinite;undetermined
nieokrzesany (ńe-o-kzhe-sa-ni) adj. m. rude;crude;ill-mannered
nieomal (ńe-ó-mal) adv. almost; nearly; pretty nearly;practically
nieomylny (ńe-o-míl-ni) adj. m. infallible;unerring;sure
nieopatrzny (ńe-o-pátzh-ni) adj. m. unguarded;inconsiderate
nieopisany (ńe-o-pee-sa-ni) adj. m. indescribable;excessive;extreme
nieopłacalny (ńe-o-pwa-tsál-ni) adj. m. unprofitable
nieopłacony (ńe-o-pwa-tso-ni) adj. m. unpaid;not paid for
nieopodal (ńe-o-pó-dal) adv. near by; close at hand;next door
nieorganiczny (ńe-or-ga-ńéech-ni) adj. m. inorganic;inanimate
nieosobowy (ńe-o-so-bó-vi) adj. m. inpersonal; not personal
nieostrożny (ńe-os-trozh-ni) adj. m. careless; imprudent
nieoswojony (ńe-os-vo-yo-ni) adj. m. untamed; unfamiliar
nieoświecony (ńe-osh-vye-tso-ni) adj. m. dark; ignorant

nieoznaczony (ňe-oz-na-cho-ni)
adj. m. indefinite;unmarked
niepalący (ňe-pa-lown-tsi) adj.
m. not smoking; non smoking
niepalność(ňe-pál-noshch)f.in-
combustibility;non-inflammability
niepalny (ňe-pál-ni) adj. m.
incombustible;uninflammable
niepamięć (ňe-pa-myanch) f.
oblivion; forgetfulness
niepamiętny (ňe-pa-myant-ni)
adj. m. forgetful; immemorial
nieparlamentarny (ňe-par-la-
men-tár-ni) adj. unparliamen-
tary rough (language)
nieparzysty (ňe-pa-zhis-ti)
adj. m. odd;uneven; unpaired
niepełnoletni (ňe-pew-no-let-
ňee) adj. m. minor; underage
niepewnosc (ňe-pév-noshch) f.
uncertainty; incertitude
niepewny (ňe-pév-ni) adj. m.
uncertain ;insecure; unsafe
niepisany (ňe-pee-sá-ni) adj.
m. unwritten; not in writing
niepiśmienny (ňe-peesh-myen-ni)
adj. m. illiterate;unlettered
niepłacący (ňe-pwa-tsown-tsi)
adj. m. non-paying
niepłodny (ňe-pwod-ni) adj. m.
sterile; barren; infertile
niepłonny (ňe-pwon-ni) adj. m.
well-founded ; motivated
niepochlebny (ňe-po-khleb-ni)
adj. m. unfavorable
niepocieszony (ňe-po-che-sho-
ni) adj. m. desolate
niepoczciwy (ňe-poch-chee-vi)
adj. m. wicked; unkind
niepoczytalny (ňe-po-chi-tál-ni)
adj. m. irresponsible ;insane
niepodejrzany (ňe-po-dey-zha-ni)
adj. m. unsuspected
niepodległość (ňe-pod-lég-woshch)
f. independence :sovereignty
niepodległy (ňe-pod-lég-wi) adj.
m. independent; sovereign
niepodobieństwo (ňe-po-do-byen-
stvo) n. impossibility
niepodobna (ňe-po-dób-na) adv.
it's impossible ;there is no way
niepodobny (ňe-po-dób-ni) adj.
m. unlike; unlikely ;dissimilar

niepodzielny (ňe-podzhel-ni)
adj. m. indivisible;undivided
niepogoda (ňe-po-gó-da) f. bad
weather; foul weather
niepogwałcony (ňe-po-gvaw-tso-
ni) adj. m. inviolate
niepohamowany (ňe-po-ha-mo-
vá-ni) adj. m. unrestrained
niepojętny (ňe-po-yánt-ni)
adj. m. dull(man);stupid
niepojęty (ňe-po-yáň-ti) adj.
m. inconceivable; incomprehensible; unimaginable
niepokalany (ňe-po-ka-lá-ni)
adj. m. immaculate;faultless
niepokaźny (ňe-po-kázh-ni) adj.
m. inconspicuous;modest;shabby
niepokoic (ňe-po-ko-eech) v.
disturb; trouble; annoy;pester
niepokonany (ňe-po-ko-ná-ni)
adj. m. invincible;irresistible
niepokój (ňe-pó-kooy) m. anxiety; unrest;trouble;agitation
niepolityczny (ňe-po-lee-tich-
ni) adj. m. impolitical; in-
expedient; improper;impolitic
niepomierny (ňe-po-myer-ni)
adj. m. excessive : extreme
niepomny (ňe-póm-ni) adj. m.
forgetful; oblivious
niepomyślny (ňe-po-mishl-ni)
adj. m. adverse : unlucky
niepopłatny (ňe-po-pwát-ni)
adj. m. unprofitable
niepoprawny (ňe-po-práv-ni)
adj. m. incorrigible
niepopularny (ňe-po-poo-lár-ni)
adj. m. unpopular
nieporadny (ňe-po-rád-ni) adj.
m. awkward ;helpless
nieporęczny (ňe-po-ráňch-ni)
adj. m. cumbersome ;unhandy
nieporozumienie (ňe-po-ro-zoo-
myé-ňe) n. misunderstanding
nieporównany (ňe-po-roov-ná-
ni) adj. m. incomparable
nieporuszony (ňe-po-roo-sho-ni)
adj. m. immovable; firm
nieporządek (ňe-po-zhown-dek)
adj. m. disorder; mess
nieporządny (ňe-po-zhownd-ni)
adj. m. disorderly; untidy;
messy;slipshod;chaotic

nieposłuszeństwo (ńe-po-swoo-
shen-stvo) n. disobedience
nieposłuszny (ńe-po-swoosh-ni)
adj. m. disobedient;unruly
niepospolity (ńe-pos-po-lee-ti)
adj. m. uncommon: rare
niepostrzeżenie(ńe-po-stshe-zhe-
ńe)adv.imperceptibly;unnoticeably
niepotrzebny (ńe-po-tzheb-ni)
adj. m. unnecessary; useless
niepowetowany (ńe-po-ve-to-va-
ni) adj. m. irreparable
niepowodzenie (ńe-po-vo-dzhe-
ńe) n. failure; adversity
niepowołany (ńe-po-vo-wa-ni)
adj. m. uncalled for; incompetent; unfit; undesirable
niepowrotny (ńe-pov-rot-ni)
adj. m. irrevocable; irrecoverable; beyond recall
niepowstrzymany (ńe-pov-stzhi-
ma-ni) adj. m. irresistible
niepowszedni (ńe-pov-shed-ńee)
adj. m. uncommon: exceptional
niepowsciągliwy (ńe-pov-shchowng-
lee-vi) adj. m. intemperate
niepozorny (ńe-po-zor-ni) adj.
m. inconspicuous; modest
niepożądany (ńe-po-zhown-da-ni)
adj. m. undesirable: undesired
niepożyteczny (ńe-po-zhi-tech-
ni) adj. m. useless;unprofitable
niepraktyczny (ńe-prak-tich-ni)
adj. m. impractical;unwieldy
niepraktykujący (ńe-prak-ti-koo-
yown-tsi)adj. m. noncommuni-
cant ; retired (professional)
nieprawda (ńe-prav-da) f. untruth; falsehood; lie
nieprawdopodobny (ńe-prav-do-
po-dob-ni) adj. m. improbable
nieprawdziwy (ńe-prav-dzhee-vi)
adj. m. untrue; false ;faked
nieprawidłowość (ńe-pra-vee-dwo-
voshch) f. anomaly; irregularity; falsity;incorrectness
nieprawidłowy (ńe-pra-vee-dwo-
vi) adj. m. anomalous; irregular; contrary to the rules
nieprawny (ńe-prav-ni) adj. m.
illegal: unlawful: invalid
nieprawomyslny (ńe-pra-vo-mishl-
ni) adj. m. unorthodox:disloyal

nieprawy (ńe-pra-vi) adj. m.
unrighteous; adulterous; bastard; unlawful; illegitimate
nieproporcjonalny (ńe-pro-por-
tsyo-nal-ni) adj. m. dispro-
portional;out of proportion
nieproszony (ńe-pro-sho-ni)
adj. m. uncalled for; self-in-
vited; unwelcome (guest)
nieprzebaczalny (ńe-pzhe-ba-
chal-ni) adj. m. unpardonable
nieprzebłagany (ńe-pzhe-bwa-ga-
ni) adj. m. implacable
nieprzebrany (ńe-pzhe-bra-ni)
adj. m. inexhaustible;countless
nieprzebyty (ńe-pzhe-bi-ti)
adj. m. impassable: unfordable
nieprzejednany (ńe-pzhe-yed-
na-ni) adj. m. irreconcilable
nieprzejrzysty (ńe-pzhey-zhis-
ti) adj. m. not clear
nieprzekupny (ńe-pzhe-koop-ni)
adj. m. unbribable;incorruptible
nieprzemakalny (ńe-pzhe-ma-kal-
ni) adj. m. waterproof
nieprzenikniony (ńe-pzhe-ńeek-
ńo-ni) adj. m. impenetrable
nieprzepuszczalny (ńe-pzhe-
poosh-chal-ni) adj. m. impervious;impenetrable
nieprzerwany (ńe-pzher-va-ni)
adj. m. continuous ;ceaseless
nieprzescigniony (ńe-pzhesh-
cheeg-ńo-ni) adj. m. unsur-
passable ; unexcelled
nieprzewidziany (ńe-pzhe-vee-
dzha-ni) adj. m. unforeseen
nieprzezorny (ńe-pzhe-zor-ni)
adj. m. improvident; unfor-
seeing ;wanting of foresight
nieprzezroczysty (ńe-pzheżh-ro-
chis-ti) adj. m. opaque
nieprzezwyciężony (ńe-pzhez-vi-
chan-zho-ni) adj. m. invincible ;insurmountable
nieprzychylny (ńe-pzhi-khil-ni)
adj. m. unfriendly ;prejudiced
nieprzydatny (ńe-pzhi-dat-ni)
adj. m. useless ; unserviceable
nie przygotowany(ńe-pzhi-go-to-
va-ni) adj. m. unprepared
nieprzyjaciel (ńe-pzhi-ya-chel)
m. enemy; foe ;ill-wisher

nieprzyjacielski (ńe-pzhi-ya-chél-skee) adj. m. enemy; hostile; enemy's; enemy-

nieprzyjazny (ńe-pzhi-yaz-ni) adj. m.unfriendly; inimical

nieprzyjaźń (ńe-pzhi-yazń) f. hostility; unfriendliness

nieprzyjemnosc (ńe-pzhi-yém-noshćh) f. unpleasantness

nieprzyjemny (ńe-pzhi-yém-ni) adj. unpleasant; disagreeable

nieprzymuszony (ńe-pzhi-moo-shó-ni) adj. m. free; unconstrained ; voluntary

nieprzystępny (ńe-pzhis-tánp-ni) adj. m. inaccessible

nieprzytomnosc (ńe-pzhi-tóm-noshćh) f. unconsciousness; absentmindedness

nieprzytomny (ńe-pzhi-tóm-ni) adj. m. unconscious; absent-minded ;frantic;mad; wild

nieprzyzwoitosc (ńe-pzhi-zvo-eé-toshćh) f. indecency

nieprzyzwoity (ńe-pzhiz-vo-eé-ti) adj. m. indecent; obscene

nieprzyzwyczajony (ńe-pzhi-zvi-cha-yó-ni) adj. m. unaccus-tomed: lacking of habit

niepunktualny (ńe-poon-ktoo-ál-ni) adj. m. unpunctual; late

nierad (ńé-rad) adj. m. unwill-ing; discontent : annoyed

nieraz (ńé-ras) adv. often; again and again ;many a time

nierdzewny (ńe-rdzév-ni) adj. m. rustproof ;stainless

nierealny (ńe-re-ál-ni) adj. m. imaginary; unreal; unrealizable

nieregularnosc (ńe-re-goo-lár-noshćh) f. irregularity

nieregularny (ńe-re-goo-lár-ni) adj. m. irregular ; erratic

niereligijny (ńe-re-lee-geey-ni) adj. m. irreligious

nierogacizna (ńe-ro-ga-cheez-na) f. pl. swines pl.

nierozdzielny (ńe-roz-dźhél-ni) adj. m. inseparable

nierozerwalny (ńe-ro-zer-vál-ni) adj. m. indissoluble

nierozgarnięty (ńe-roz-gar-ńań-ti) adj. m. dull; (dim-witted)

nierozłączny (ńe-roz-wównch-ni) adj. m. inseparable

nierozmyslny (ńe-roz-mishl-ni) adj. m. unintentional

nierozpuszczalny (ńe-roz-poosh-chál-ni) adj. m. indissoluble

nierozsądny (ńe-roz-sównd-ni) adj. m. unwise; unreasonable

nierozwaga (ńe-roz-vá-ga) f. inconsideration; rashness

nierozważny (ńe-roz-vázh-ni) adj. m. imprudent; inconsider-ate ; thoughtless; rush; hasty

nierównosc (ńe-roov-noshćh) f. inequality ;uneyenness

nierówny (ńe-roov-ni) adj. m. unequal; crooked; uneven

nieruchliwy (ńe-rookh-lée-vi) adj. m. slow ; unwieldy

nieruchomosc (ńe-roo-kho-moshćh) f. real estate : immobility

nieruchomy (ńe-roo-khó-mi) adj. m. immobile; fixed;still:at rest

nierychło (ńe-rikh-wo) adv. not soon: slowly: not forthcoming

nierzadko ńe-zhád-ko) adv. of-ten: now and then; not seldom

nierząd (ńe-zhównt) m. prosti-tution; anarchy ; debauchery

nierzeczowy (ńe-zhe-chó-vi) adj. m. pointless; futile

nierzeczywisty (ńe-zhe-chi-veés-ti) adj. m. unreal ;fictitious

nierzetelny (ńe-zhe-tél-ni) adj. m. dishonest : unreliable

niesamowity (ńe-sa-mo-vée-ti) adj. m. weird; uncanny : unearthy

niesforny (ńe-sfór-ni) adj. m. unruly; disorderly ;turbulent

nieskalany (ńe-ska-lá-ni) adj. m. immaculate : spotless; pure

nieskazitelny (ńe-ska-zhee-tél-ni) adj. m. unblemished; up-right ; spotless: moral

nieskładny (ńe-skwad-ni) adj. m. awkward;discordant;clumsy

nieskończonosc (ńe-skon-cho-noshćh) f. infinity

nieskończony (ńe-skoń-chó-ni) adj. m. unfinished; infinite

nieskromny (ńe-skróm-ni) adj. m. indecent ; immodest;morally offensive: improper

nieskuteczny (ńe-skoo-téch-ni)
adj. m. ineffective: futile
niesłabnący (ńe-swab-nówn-tsi)
adj. m. unabated;unflagging
niesława (ńe-swá-va) f. infamy
niesławny (ńeswáv-ni) adj. m.
infamous ;inglorious:disgraceful
niesłowny (ńe-swóv-ni) adj. m.
unreliable; undependable
niesłuszność (ńe-swoósh-noshch)
f. injustice :groundlessness
niesłuszny (ńe-swoósh-ni) adj.
m. unjust; wrong :groundless
niesłychany (ńe-swi-khá-ni) adj.
m. unheard of; unprecedented
niesmaczny (ńe-smách-ni)adj. m.
tasteless: unsavory; unseemly
niesmak (ńes-mak) m. bad taste;
disgust: repugnance;nasty taste
niesnaski (ńes-nás-kee) pl. dissension :discord; quarrels
niespełna (ńes-péw-na) adv. nearly; not all;not quite: about
niespodzianka (ńe-spo-dźhán-ka)
f. surprise : surprise gift
niespodziewany (ńe-spo-dźhe-vá-ni)
adj. m. unexpected ;unlooked for
niespokojny (ńe-spo-kóy-ni) adj.
m. restless; fussy :upset;fretful
niesporo (ńe-spó-ro) adv. slowly
nie sposób (ńe spó-soop) adv.
it's impossible :bv no means
niespożyty (ńe-spo-zhi-ti) adj.
m. durable; indefatigable
niesprawiedliwość (ńe-spra-vyed-
leé-voshch) f. injustice
niesprawiedliwy (ńe-spra-vyed-
leé-vi) adj. m. unjust ;unfair
niesprawny (ńe-správ-ni) adj. m.
ineffective; inefficient
nie sprzyjający (ńe spzhi-ya-
yówn-tsi) adj. m. adverse
niestały (ńe-stá-wi) adj. m. unsteady; inconsistent :variable
niestaranny (ńe-sta-rán-ni) adj.
m. careless;sloppy: dowdy
niestateczny (ńe-sta-téch-ni) adj.
m. unstable; fickle; flighty
niestety (ńe-sté-ti) adv. alas;
unfortunately: I am sorry
niestosowny (ńe-sto-sóv-ni) adj.
m. improper; unsuitable;unfit:
inappropriate: out of place

niestrawność (ńe-strav-noshch)
f. indigestion: dyspepsia
niestrawny (ńe-stráv-ni) adj.
m. indigestible: stodgy; dull
niestrudzony (ńe-stroo-dzó-ni)
adj. m. indefatigable; untiring
niestworzony (ńe-stvo-zhó-ni)
adj. m. unreal; nonsense
niesumienny (ńe-soo-myéń-ni)
adj. m. unscrupulous ;unreliable
nieswojo (ńe-svó-yo) adv. un-
easily;strangely; qualmishly
nieswój (ńe-svooy) adj. m. ill
at ease; uncomfortable;seedy;
strange : off color
niesymetryczny (ńe-si-me-trich-
ni) adj. m. asymmetrical
niesympatyczny (ńe-sim-pa-tich-
ni) adj. m. unpleasant
nieszczególny (ńe-shche-góol-ni)
adj. m. mediocre : so-so
nieszczelny (ńe-shchél-ni) adj.
m. leaky; not shut tight
nieszczery (ńe-shche-ri) adj.
m. insincere: double dealing
nieszczęsny (ńe-shcháns-ni) adj.
m. miserable; ill-fated
nieszczęście (ńe-shchań-śhche)
n. misfortune; disaster
nieszczęśliwy (ńe-śhchań-śhleé-
vi) adj. m. unhappy;ill-starred
nieszkodliwy (ńe-shkod-leé-vi)
adj. m. harmless; not grave
nieszlachcic (ńe-shlákh-tseets)
m. commoner: man not of gentry
nieszpetny (ńe-shpet-ni) adj.
m. fairly good-looking
nieszpory (ńe-shpó-ri) pl. ves-
pers; evening prayers
nieścisły (ńe-śhchees-wi) adj.
m. inexact: inaccurate; faulty
nieścisliwy (ńe-śhcheesh-lee-vi)
adj. m. incompressible
nieść (ńeśhch) v. carry; bring;
bear; lay; afford; drive;waft
nieślubny (ńe-śhloob-ni) adj. m.
illegitimate; out of wedlock
nieśmiały (ńe-śhmyá-wi) adj. m.
coy; shy; timid; bashful
nieśmiertelny (ńe-śhmyer-tél-ni)
adj. m. immortal: everlasting
nieświadomy (ńe-śhvya-dó-mi) adj.
m. ignorant; unaware :involuntary

nietakt (ńe-takt) m. lack of tact; slip; taktlessness

nietaktowny (ńe-tak-tóv-ni) adj. m. tactless: indelicate

nietknięty (ńe-tknáń-ti) adj. m. intact;virgin;untouched

nietolerancja (ńe-to-le-ránts-ya) f. intolerance

nietoperz (ńe-tó-pesh) m. bat

nietowarzystki (ńe-to-va-zhís-kee) adj. n. unsociable

nietrafny (ńe-tráf-ni) adj. m. wrong; missing the mark

nietrzeźwy (ńe-tzheźh-vi) adj. m. drank; tipsy;unsound

nietutejszy (ńe-too-téy-shi) adj. m. stranger; non-resident

nietykalny (ńe-ti-kál-ni) adj. m. immune; inviolable

nie tyle (ńe ti-le) adv.not so much : not exactly; but;rather

nie tylko (ńe til-ko) adv. not only ; anything but

nieubłagalny (ńe-oo-bwa-gál-ni) adj. m. implacable;irrevocable

nieuchronny (ńe-oo-khrón-ni) adj. inevitable ; inescapable

nieuchwytny (ńe-oo-khvít-ni) adj. m. elusive;evasive;inaudible

nieuctwo (ńe-oóts-tvo) n. lack of education: ignorance

nieuczciwy (ńe-ooch-chee-vi) adj. m. dishonest; foul;unfair

nieuczynny (ńe-oo-chin-ni) adj. m. unobliging; disobliging

nieudolny (ńe-oo-dól-ni) adj. m. awkward; clumsy; decrepit

nieufny (ńe-oóf-ni) adj. m. distrustful; suspicious

nieugaszony (ńe-oo-ga-shó-ni) adj. m. unextinguished; unquenchable; unsuppressible

nieugięty (ńe-oo-gyáń-ti) adj. m. inflexible;unyielding

nieuk (ńe-ook) m. know-nothing

nieukojony (ńe-oo-ko-yó-ni) adj. m. inconsolable

nieuleczalny (ńe-oo-le-chál-ni) adj. m. incurable

nieumiarkowany (ńe-oo-myar-ko-vá-ni) adj. m. intemperate

nieumiejętny (ńe-oo-mee-yáńt-ni) adj. m. inexpert; unskilled

nieumyślny (ńe-oo-miśhl-ni) adj. m. unintentional

nieunikniony (ńe-oo-ńeek-ńo-ni) adj. m. unavoidable:inevitable

nieuprzedzony (ńe-oo-pzhe-dzó-ni) adj. m. unbiased; not forwarned; not prejudiced

nieuprzejmy (ńe-oo-pzhéy-mi) adj. m. impolite; discourteous

nieurodzaj (ńe-oo-ró-dzay) m. bad harvest; bad crops;scarcity

nie usprawiedliwiony (ńe-oos-pra-vyed-lee-vyó-ni) adj. m. unexcused;unjustified; wantom

nieustanny (ńe-oos-tán-ni) adj. m. constant: perpetual;unceasing

nieustraszony (ńe-oos-tra-sho-ni) adj. m. fearless; intrepid

nieusuwalny (ńe-oo-soo-vál-ni) adj. m. immovable: irremovable

nie uszkodzony (ńe oosh-ko-dzó-ni) adj. m. unhurt; undamaged

nieuwaga (ńe-oo-vá-ga) f. inattention; absentmindedness

nieuważny (ńe-oo-vaźh-ni) adj. m. inattentive;careless

nieuzasadniony (ńe-oo-za-sad-ńó-ni) adj. m. unfounded;unjustified

nieuzbrojony (ńe-ooz-bro-yó-ni) adj. m. unarmed: disarmed

nieużyteczny (ńe-oo-zhi-tech-ni) adj. m. useless; superfluous

nieużyty (ńe-oozhí-ti) adj. m. unused; uncooperative;disobliging

niewart (ńe-vart) adj. m. not worth; unworthy; not deserving

nie warto (ńe vár-to) adv. not worth (talking):not worth while

nieważny (ńe-vaźh-ni) adj. m. invalid; trivial;null and void

niewątpliwy (ńe-vównt-plee-vi) adj. m. sure; doubtless

niewczesny (ńe-vchés-ni) adj. m. untimely; late; inopportune

niewdzięczny (ńe-vdzháńch-ni) adj. m. ungrateful; thankless

niewesoły (ńe-ve-só-wi) adj. m. sad; joyless; pretty bad

niewiadomy (ńe-vya-dó-mi) adj. m. unknown(direction, origin etc.)

niewiara (ńe-vyá-ra) f. disbelief; mistrust; unbelief

niewiasta (ńe-vyás-ta) f. woman

niewidomy (ńe-vee-do-mi) adj.
m. blind;lacking insight
niewidzialny (ńe-vee-dżhal-ni)
adj. m. invisible
niewiedza(ńe-vye-dza) adj. m.
ignorance: unawarness
niewiele (ńe-vye-le) adv. not
much; not many: little: few
niewielki (ńe-vyel-kee) adj. m.
small; little: unimportant
niewierny (ńe-vyer-ni) adj. m.
disloyal; infidel; unfaithful
niewieści (ńe-vyesh-chee) adj.
m. womanly: feminine
niewinność (ńe-veen-noshch) f.
innocence: purity: chastity
niewinny (ńe-veen-ni) adj. m.
not guilty: innocent;harmless
niewłaściwy (ńe-vwash-chee-vi)
adj. m. improper: unsuitable
niewola (ńe-vo-la) f. captivity;
slavery; bondage:servitude
niewolić (ńe-vo-leech) v. enslave; compel: oppress
niewolnica (ńe-vol-ńee-tsa) f.
slave: serf: prisoner of war
niewolnik (ńe-vol-ńeek) m. slave
nie wolno (ńe vol-no) v. not
allowed · not permitted
niewod (ńe-voot) m. dragnet
niewprawny (ńe-vprav-ni) adj.
m. unversed; unskilled; inexpert: incompetent: inefficient
niewspołmierny (ńe-wspoow-myer-
ni) adj. m. incommensurable
nie wtajemniczony(ńe-vta-yem-
nee-cho-ni) adj. m. uninitiat-
ed; outsider: not privy
niewyczerpany (ńe-vi-cher-pa-ni)
adj. m. inexhaustible
niewygoda (ńe-vi-go-da) f. discomfort; trouble: hardship
niewygodny (ńe-vi-god-ni) adj.
m. uncomfortable: awkward
niewykonalny (ńe-vi-ko-nal-ni)
adj. m. unfeasible· unworkable
niewykształcony (ńe-vi-kshtaw-
tso-ni) adj. m. uneducated
niewymierny (ńe-vi-myer-ni) adj.
m. irrational; surd
niewymowny (ńe-vi-mov-ni) adj.
m. unspeakable:inexpressible

niewymuszony (ńe-vi-moo-sho-ni)
adj. m. free (and easy)
niewymyślny (ńe-vi-mishl-ni)
adj. m. unsophisticated
niewypał (ńe-vi-paw) m. dud
niewypłacalny (ńe-vi-pwa-tsal-
ni) adj. m. insolvent
niewypowiedziany (ńe-vi-po-vye-
dżha —ni) adj. m. untold
niewyraźnie (ńe-vi-rażh-ńe) adv.
indistinctly: seedily
niewyraźny (ńe-vi-rażh-ni) adj.
m. queer; indistinct
niewyrobiony (ńe-vi-ro-byo-ni)
adj. m. raw; inexperienced
niewyrozumiały (ńe-vi-ro-zoo-
mya-wi) adj. m. intolerant
niewysłowiony (ńe-vi-swo-vyo-
ni) adj. m. ineffable
niewyspany (ńe-vis-pa-ni) adj.
m. sleepy; not slept enough
niewystarczający (ńe-vis-tar-
cha-yown-tsi) adj. m. insufficient : inadequate
niewystawny (ńe-vis-tav-ni) adj.
m. frugal; modest; simple
niewytłumaczony (ńe-vi-twoo-ma-
cho-ni) adj. m. inexplicable
niewytrwały (ńe-vi-trva-wi)
adj. m. not persistent
niewytrzymały (ńe-vi-tzhi-ma-wi)
adj. m. not enduring
niewzruszony (ńe-vzroo-sho-ni)
adj. m. unmoved ;rigid
niezachwiany (ńe-za-khvya-ni)
adj. m. unshaken ;undeterred
niezadowolenie (ńe-za-do-vo-le-
ńe) n . discontent :displeasure
niezadowolony (ńe-za-do-vo-lo-ni)
adj. m. dissatisfied:displeased
niezakłócony (ńe-za-kwoo-tso-ni)
adj. m. undisturbed :unmarred
niezależność (ńe-za-lezh-noshch)
f. independence :self-sufficiency
niezależny (ńe-za-lezh-ni) adj.
m. independent; self contained
niezamężna (ńe-za-mańzh-na) adj.
f. unmarried :single woman
niezamożny (ńe-za-mozh-ni) adj.
m. rather poor: indigent
niezapominajka (ńe-za-po-mee-
nay-ka) f. forget-me-not

niezapomniany (ně-za-pom-ńá-ni)
adj. m. not-to-be-forgotten
niezaprzeczalny (ńe-za-pzhe-
chál-ni) adj. m. undeniable
niezaradny (ně-za-rád-ni) adj.
m. helpless: resourceless
niezasłużony (ńe-za-swoo-zhó-
ni) adj. m. undeserved
niezawisły (ńe-za-vees-wi) adj.
m. independent:self-dependent
niezawodnie (ńe-za-vód-ńe) adv.
surely; without fail:infallibly
niezawodny (ńe-za-vód-ni) adj.
m. sure: never failing: safe
niezbadany (ńe-zba-dá-ni) adj.
m. unexplorable:,inscrutable
niezbędny (ńe-zbánd-ni) adj.
m, indispensable: essential
niezbity (ńe-zbee-ti) adj. m.
irrefutable; uncontrovertible
niezbyt (ńe-zbit) adv. not very
(much): none too; not too
niezdarny (ńe-zdar-ni) adj. m.
clumsy: awkward; bungled
niezdatny (ńe-zdat-ni) adj. m.
unfit: unqulified:unserviceable
niezdecydowany (ńe-zde-tsi-do-
vá-ni) adj. m. undecided
niezdolność (ńe-zdol-noshch)
f. inability; unfitness
niezdolny (ńe-zdol-ni) adj. m.
incapable; unable:unfit: dull
niezdrowy (ńe-zdró-vi) adj. m.
unhealthy: unwell:ill;sickly
niezdyscyplinowany (ńe-zdis-tsi-
plee-no-vá-ni) adj. m. un-
disciplined : unruly
niezgłębiony (ńe-zgwánb-yó-ni)
adj. m. inscrutable: abyssal
niezgoda (ńe-zgó-da) f. discord;
disagreement: dissension
niezgodność (ńe-zgód-noshch)
f. inconsistency,; clash
niezgodny (ńe-zgód-ni) adj. m.
discordant; incompatible
niezgrabny (ńe-zgráb-ni) adj.
m. unhandy; clumsy:shapeless
nieziszczalny (ńe-zeesh-chál-
ni) adj. m. unattainable
niezliczony (ńe-zlee-chó-ni)
adj. m. uncountable:countless
niezłomny (ńe-zwóm-ni) adj. m.
inflexible; firm: steadfast

niezmącony (ńe-zmówn-tsó-ni)
adj. m. unruffled:undisturbed
niezmienny (ńe-zmyen-ni) adj.
m. invariable: constant;fixed
niezmierny (ńe-zmyer-ni) adj.
m. immense: vast: boundless
niezmordowany (ńe-zmor-do-vá-ni)
adj. m. indefatigable;tireless
nieznaczny (ńe-znách-ni) adj.
m. trivial; insignificant
nieznajomość (ńe-zna-yó-moshch)
f. ignorance; unawareness
nieznajomy (ńe-zna-yó-mi) adj.
m. unknown; strange (faces etc.)
nieznany (ńe-zná-ni) adj. m.
unknown: unfamiliar: obscure
nieznośny (ńe-znósh-ni) adj. m.
unbearable: annoying:nasty;pesky
niezręczny (ńe-zránch-ni) adj.
m. awkward: clumsy;tactless
niezrozumiały (ńe-zro-zoo-mya-
wi) adj. m. unintelligible
niezrównany (ńe-zroov-ná-ni)
adj. m. matchless; incomparable;peerless: unique; grand
niezwłoczny (ńe-zvwóch-ni) adj.
m. instant:prompt: immediate
niezwyciężony (ńe-zvi-chán-zho-
ni) adj. m. invincible
niezwykły (ńe-zvík-wi) adj. m.
unusual;extreme: rare: odd
nieżonaty (ńe-zho-ná-ti) adj.
m. unmarried: single: bachelor
nieżyczliwy (ńe-zhich-lee-vi)
adj. m. unfriendly;ill-disposed
nieżyt (ńe-zhit) m. inflamma-
tion:catarrh: hay fever;colitis
nieżywy (ńe-zhi-vi) adj. m.
dead; lifeless: inanimate
nigdy (ńeeg-di) adv. never
nigdzie (ńeeg-dzhe) adv. nowhere: anywhere(after negation)
nijaki (ńee-yá-kee) adj. m.
none; neuter (gender)
nikczemnik (ńeek-chém-ńeek) m.
villain: scoundrel; wretch
nikczemny (ńeek-chém-ni) adj.
vile:abject; despicable: base
nikel (ńee-kel) m. nickel
nikły (ńeek-wi) adj. m. scanty
niknąć (ńeek-nównch) v. vanish
nikotyna (ńee-ko-tí-na) f. nicotine: poisonous tabacco extract

nikt (ñeekt) pron. nobody
nim (ñeem) conj. before:till
nimb (ñeemp) m. halo:aureole
niniejszy (nee-ñey-shi) adj. m.
　this; present; the present
niski (ñees-kee) adj. m. low
nisko (ñees-ko) adv. low
nisza (ñee-sha) f. niche;recess
niszczący (neesh-chówn-tsi) adj.
　m. destructive: disruptive
niszczec (ñeesh-chech) v. waste
　away: deteriorate: decay:waste
niszczyciel (ñeesh-chi-chel)
　m. devastator: destroyer:waster
niszczyc (ñeesh-chich) v. de-
　stroy;spoil:ruin: wreck;damage
nit (ñeet) m. rivet
nitka (ñeet-ka) f. thread
nitowac (nee-tó-vach) v. rivet
niwa (ñee-va) f. field:soil
niweczyc (ñee-vé-chich) v. de-
　stroy: annihilate: lay waste
niwelacja (nee-ve-láts-ya) f.
　leveling; survey: surveying
niwelowac (nee-ve-ló-vach) v.
　level: survey
nizina (ñee-žhee-na) f. lowland
niż (ñeezh) m. lowland;atmospher-
niż (ñeesh) conj. than ‖ ic low
niżej (ñee-zhey) adv. lower;
　below; down: further down
niższosc (ñeesh-shoshch) f.
　inferiority
niższy (neezh-shi) adj. m. lo-
　wer; inferior: shorter
no (no) part. why; well; now;
　then: just: there: there now!
noc (nots) f. night
nocleg (nots-leg) m. place to
　sleep : night's lodging
nocny (nots-ni) adj. m. noctur-
　nal; night-
nocowac (no-tsó-vach) v. spend
　night: stay overnight; sleep
noga (no-ga) f. leg : foot
nogawica (no-ga-vée-tsa) f.
　legging : trouser leg
nomenklatura (no-men-kla-tóo-
　ra) f. nomenclature
nominacja (no-mee-náts-ya) f.
　appointment : nomination
nominalny (no-mee-nál-ni) adj.
　m. nominal : face(value)

nonsens (nón-sens) m. nonsense
nora (nó-ra) f. burrow
norma (nór-ma) f. standard;
　norm: rule; general principle
normalizacja (nor-ma-lee-záts-
　ya) f. normalization;standard
normalizowac (nor-ma-lee-zó-vach)
　v. normalize: standardize
normalny (nor-mál-ni) adj. m.
　normal: standard: ordinary
normowac (nor-mó-vach) v. regu-
　late; standardize;normalize
nos (nos) m. nose ; snout
nosic (nó-sheech) v. carry;
　wear: bear :have about one
nosorożec (no-so-ró-shets) m.
　rhinoceros (with horn)
nostalgia (nos-tál-gya) f. nos-
　talgia: homesickness
nosze (nó-she) pl. stretchers
nota (nó-ta) f. note; grade
notariusz (no-tár-yoosh) m. no-
　tary public
notatka (no-tát-ka) f. note
notatnik (no-tát-ñeek) m. note-
　book: diary: notes
notes (nó-tes) m. pocket note-
　book: notebook
notoryczny (no-to-rích-ni) adj.
　m. notorious ; flagrant:arrant
notowac (no-to-vach) v. make
　notes; take notes: write down
notowanie (no-to-vá-ñe) n.
　quotation : record
nowela (no-vé-la) f. short
　story : amendment
nowelista (no-ve-lées-ta) m.
　short story writer
nowicjat (no-véets-yat) m. no-
　vitiate ; novitiate
nowicjusz (no-véets-yoosh) m.
　novice ; beginner; tiro
nowina (no-vée-na) f. news
nowinka (no-véen-ka) f. fad
nowiutki (no-vyóot-kee) adj. m.
　brand-new; spick-and-span
nowoczesny (no-vo-chés-ni) adj.
　m. modern :up to date:newest
noworoczny (no-vo-róch-ni) adj.
　m. New Year's : of New Year
nowosc (nó-voshch) f. novelty
nowotwór (no-vo-tvoor) m. tu-
　mor : new coined word

nowożytny (nʋ-vo-zhít-ni) adj.
m. (of) modern (perio
nowy (nó-vi) adj. m. new
nozdrze (nóz-dzhę) n. nostril
nożownik (no-zhov-ńeek) m.
knifer; knife-fighter
nożyce (no-zhí-tse) pl. shears;
clippers ! large shears
nożyczki (no-zhích-kee) pl.
scissors; small scissors
nożyk (no-zhik) m.pocketknife
nów (noov) m. new moon
nóż (noosh) m. knife ;cutter
nucić (nóo-cheech) v. hum
nuda (nóo-da) f. boredom
nudności(nood-nósh-chee) pl.
nausea : impulse to vomit
nudny (nood-ni) adj. m. boring;
nauseating :dull: sickening
nudysta (noo-dis-ta) m. nudist
nudziarz (noo-dźhash) m. bore
nudzić (noo-dźheech) v. bore
numer (noo-mer) m. number
numerować (noo-me-ró-vach) v.
number : give a number to
numerowy (noo-me-ro-vi) adj. m.
porter; bell-boy: hotel waiter
numizmatyka (noo-meez-ma-ti-ka)
f. numismatics :study of coins
nuncjusz (noón-tsyoosh) m. nun-
cio ; papal ambassador
nurek (ngóo-rek) m. diver
nurkować (noor-kó-vach) v. dive
nurt (noort) m. current (flowing): stream: trend; wake
nurtować (noor-tó-vach) v. fret;
penetrate ; pervade: ferment
nurzać (noo-zhach) v. dip; welter in; plunge :immerse:steep
nuta (nóo-ta) f. (sound) note
nuty (nóo-ti) pl. written music: printed music: score
nuż (noozh) adv. if; and if
nużący (noo-zhown-tsi) adj. m.
tiring :tiresome: wearisome
nużyć (noo-zhich) v. tire :weary
nygus (ni-goos) m. lazybones
nygusować (ni-goo-só-vach) v.
lounge about; loiter : loaf
nylon (ne-lon) m. nylon
nyża (ni-zha) f. niche; alcove

o (o) prep. of; for; at; by;
about; against; with; to; over
oaza (o-á-za) f. oasis
oba (o-ba) pron. both
obabrać (o-ba-brach) v. besmear
obaj (o-bay) pron. both
obalenie (o-ba-le-ńe) n. overthrow: subversion; abolition
obalić (o-ba-leech) v. overthrow :knock down: fell;refute
obarczyć (o-bar-chich) v. encumber; saddle :load: burden
obarzanek (o-ba-zha-nek) m.
round cracknel torus shaped
obawa (o-ba-va) f. fear; apprehension : phobia;anxiety
obawiać się (o-bav-yach śhań) v.
be anxious ; fear: dread
obcas (ób-tsac) m. heel
obcążki (ob-tsownzh-kee) pl.
(small) tongs : pincers;pliers
obcesowo (ob-tse-só-vo) adv.
headlong; outright :abruptly
obcęgi (ob-tsań-gee) pl. tongs
obchodzić (ob-kho-dźheech) v.
go around; evade; elude;
celebrate :inspect:by-pass
obchód (ob-khoot) m. (daily)
beat; celebration :circuit
obciągać (ob-chown-gach) v.
pull down; cover; pull tight
obciążać (ob-chown-zhach) v.
burden; charge (account)
obcierać (ob-che-rach) v. wipe
obcinać (ob-chee-nach) v. cut
off; clip :crop;chop off
obcisły (ob-chees-wi) adj. m.
tight : close fitting:clinging
obcokrajowiec (ob-tso-kra-yó-
vyets) m. foreigner : alien
obcokrajowy (ob-tso-kra-yó-vi)
adj. m. foreign : alien
obcować (ob-tsó-vach) v. associate :have an intercourse
obcowanie (ob-tso-va-ńe) n. intercourse; association
obcy (ób-tsi) adj. m. strange;
foreign :unfamiliar: unrelated
obczyzna (ob-chiz-na) f.foreign
country ; exile: foreign land
obdarować (ob-da-ró-vach) v.
bestow :lavish gifts on ...

obdarty (ob-dar-ti) adj. m. ragged;in rags: tattered
obdarzyć (ob-da-zhićh) v. bestow: lavish gifts on ...
obdzielić (ob-dżhe-leećh)v. divide; distribute;deal;endow
obdzierać (ob-dżhé-raćh)v. rip off; skin off ;strip; fleece
obecnie (o-bets-ńe) adv. at present;just now;to-day
obecnosć (o-bets-noshćh) f. presence,: attendance
obejmowac (o-bey-mo-vach) v. embrace; enfold; span; include; take over; take in; grasp
obejrzec (o-bey-zhech) v. inspect ; glance at; see
obejscie (o-bey-shćhe) n. bypass; farmyard : manner
obejsć (o-beyshćh) v. go around
obelga (o-bél-ga) f. insult; outrage; abuse: affront
obelzywy (o-bel-zhi-vi) adj. m. insulting; abusive:opprobrious
oberwać (o-ber-vach) v. tear off; cop it; pluck;get a knock
oberza (o-ber-zha) f. inn
oberzysta (o-ber-zhis-ta) m. innkeeper:owner of an inn
oberznąc (o-ber-zhnównch) v. cut off; trim; clip
obeschnąc (o-bes-khnównch) v. dry up: get dry: dry
obetrzec (o-be-tzhech) v. wipe out: dust: rub sore: skin
obezwładnić (o-bez-vwad-ńeećh) v. overpower:subdue: disable
obeznany (o-bez-na-ni) adj. m. familiar; acquainted;conversant
obfitosć (ob-fee-toshćh) f. plenty: abundance:profusion
obfity (ob-feé-ti) adj. m. abundant: ample: profuse:liberal
obgadywac (ob-ga-di-vach) v. talk ill; talk over; crab
obgryzać (ob-gri-zach) v. nibble bare: gnaw: pick a bone: bite
obiad (ob-yat) m. dinner
obicie (o-beé-che) n. upholstery; padding; chip; beating ;drubbing
obiecywac (o-bye-tsi-vach) v. promise: look forward to

obieg (o-byek) m. circulation
obiegac (o-bye-gach) v. runaround; circulate;revolve
obiekcja (o-byek-tsya) f. objection; demur
obiekt (ob-yekt) m. object; target: subject: building
obiektyw (o-byek-tiv) m.objectlens: object-glass; bjective
obiektywny (o-byek-tiv-ni) adj. m. objective;impartial
obierac (o-bye-rach) v. choose; elect; peel: pick; strip
obierzyny (o-bye-zhi-ni) pl. peelings; parings
obieralny (o-bye-ral-ni) adj. m. elective: eligible
obietnica (o-byet-ńee-tsa) f. promise: engagement
obijac (o-bee-yach) v. chip; hoop; loaf ;hurt; injure
objadac się (ob-ya-dach shań) v. gorge; overeat : cram
objasniac (ob-yash-ńach) v. explain ; make clear: gloss
objaw (ob-yav) m. symptom
objawic (ob-ya-veech) v. reveal
objazd (ob-yazt) m. tour; circuit;detour:diversion:by-pass
objąc (ob-yownch) v. embrace; assume: grasp: encompass:span
objeżdżac (ob-yezh-dzhach) v. ride; around;break in a horse
objętosć (ob-yań-toshćh) f. volume; bulk:capacity: content
obkładac (ob-kwa-dach) v. wrap; cover: line: impose:hit:buffet
oblegac (ob-le-gach) v. besiege
oblac (ob-lach) v. pour on(water)
oblekać (ob-le-kach) v. clothe; put on; cover; encase: don
oblepiac (ob-le-pyach) v. paste over: stick: post:plaster over
oblewac (ob-le-vach) v. pour on: drench: bathe; sprinkle·wash
oblężenie (ob-lań-zhe-ńe) m. siege: state of siege
obliczac (ob-lee-chach) v. count: reckon; figure out: mean
oblicze (ob-lee-che) n. face
obliczenie (ob-lee-ché-ńe) n. calculation: evaluation: count

obligacja (ob-lee-gáts-ya) f.
obligation; bond; share
oblizać (ob-lee-zaćh) v. lick
obładować (ob-wa-do-vaćh) v.
load down;heap; burden
obława (ob-wá-va) f. roundup;
posse; man hunt: chase: raid
obłąkany (ob-wówn-ká-ni) adj.
m. insane; loony; madman
obłęd (ób-waht) m. insanity
obłędny (ob-wańd-ni) adj. m.
mad; wild ; insane: crazy
obłok (ób-wok) m. cloud
obłowić się (ob-wo-veećh shań)
v. pick up a lot;make a pile
obłożnie (ob-wózh-ńe) adv. bedridden; severely (ill)
obłożyć (ob-wo-zhićh) v. cover;
wrap: line:impose: hit;buffet
obłuda (ob-woo-da) f. hypocrisy
obłudnik (ob-wood-ńeek) m.hyp-
ocrite:snuffler:dissembler
obłudny (ob-wood-ni) adj. m.
hypocritical;false: canting
obłupać (ob-woo-paćh) v. shell;
peel:bark: flay: skin
obłuszczać (ob-woosh-chaćh) v.
scale; shell: husk; flay: skin
obły (ob-wi) adj.oval;tapering;
terete; cylindrical; oval
obmacać (ob-ma-tsaćh) v. feel
about; explore with fingers
obmawiać (ob-mav-yaćh) v. slander; backbite; gossip:speak ill
obmierznąć (ob-myerzh-nównćh) v.
get sick of (something)
obmowa (ob-mo-va) f. slander;
detraction: backbiting
obmurować (ob-moo-ró-vaćh) v.
brick in; brick veneer
obmyślać (ob-mish-laćh) v. design; contrive; reflect
obmywać (ob-mi-vaćh) v. wash-
up:sponge·down·give a wash
obnażać (ob-na-zhaćh) v. denude;
bare ; unclothe:strip;uncover
obniżać (ob-ńee-zhaćh) v. lower;
sink; drop; abate; level down
obniżenie (ob-ńee-zhé-ńe) n.
decrease; reduction; lowering
obniżka (ob-ńeezh-ka) f. reduction; depreciation:drop:fall

obojczyk (o-bóy-chik) m. collar
bone;clavicle: amice:gorget
obnosić (ob-nó-sheećh) v. take
around; flaunt; parade
obojętnie (o-bo-yańt-ńe) adv.
indifferently;slang:no matter
obojętność (o-bo-yańt-noshćh)
f. indifference; neutrality
obojętny (o-bo-yańt-ni) adj. m.
indifferent; neutral
obok (ó-bok) adv. prep. beside;
next; about:close by:by:close
obopólny (o-bo-poól-ni) adj. m.
common; mutual:reciprocal
obora (o-bó-ra) f. cowbarn
obosieczny (o-bo-shéch-ni) adj.
m.two-edged; double edged
obowiązek (o-bo-vyówn-zek) m.
duty; obligation; responsibility
obowiązkowy (o-bo-vyównz-ko-vi)
adj. m. dutiful; compulsory
obowiązany (o-bo-wyówn-za-ni)
adj. m. obligated;compelled
obowiązujący (o-bo-vyówn-zoo-
yówn-tsi) adj. m. obligatory
obowiązywać (o-bo-vyówn-zi-vaćh)
v. be in force (law etc)
obozować (o-bo-zó-vaćh) v. camp;
camp out: tent:encamp:bivouac
obój (o-booy) m. oboe, (horn)
obóz (ó-boos) m. camp
obrabiać (ob-ra-byaćh) v. machine (metal, wood etc.); work-
over; fashion; shape;till:hem
obrabiarka (ob-rab-yar-ka) f.
machine tool: lathe
obrabować (ob-ra-bo-vaćh) v. rob
obracać (ob-ra-tsaćh) v. turnover; rotate; crank
obrachować (ob-ra-kho-vaćh) v.
compute: figure out; calculate
obrachunek (ob-ra-khoo-nek) m.
settlement; bill;"day of reckoning":count: reckoning
obrada (ob-ra-da) f. conference
obradować (ob-ra-do-vaćh) v.
confer; deliberate; debate; sit
obradzać (ob-ra-dzaćh) v. bear
crops; yield a crop:be plentiful
obramować (ob-ra-mo-vaćh) v.
frame:encircle; encase:hem:edge
obrastać (ob-ras-taćh) v. overgrow: grow ;grow all over

obraz (ob-raz) m. picture;
image : painting:drawing
obraza (ob-ra-za) f. affront;
offense ;insult:outrage:offence
obrazek (ob-ra-zek) m. illustration; small picture
obrazić (ob-ra-źheech) v. offend : affront; insult:sting
obrazowy (ob-ra-zó-vi) adj. m.
pictorial ; picturesque:vivd
obrażenie (ob-ra-zhé-ńe) n.
offense; injury: insults
obraźliwy (ob-raźh-lee-vi) adj.
m. offensive; touchy:resentful
obrazać (ob-ra-zhaćh) v. offend;
(repeatedly) insult: affront
obrąb (ob-równb) m. cutoff
obrąbek (ob-równ-bek) m. hem
obrączka (ob-równch-ka) f. ring
obręb (ob-rąnb) m. compass;
area;reach:extent:precincts
obrębiać (ob-rąnb-yaćh) v. hem
obręcz (ob-rąńch) f. hoop; tire;
rim: band: gridle: ring:circle
obrobić (ob-ro-beećh) v. machine
obrok (ob-rok) m. feed;fodder
obrona (ob-ro-na) f. defense
obronność (ob-ron-noshćh) f.
defense capability;defences
obronny (ob-ron-ni) adj. m. de-
fensive:fortified:protective
obrońca (ob-roń-tsa) m. defender
guard; barrister:advocate
obrośnięty (ob-rosh-ńań-ti) adj.
m. overgrown; unshaven
obrotny (ob-rot-ni) adj. m.
active; skillful; nimble:agile
obrotowy (ob-ro-tó-vi) adj. m.
turnover (tax);rotary;revolving
obroża (ob-ró-zha) f. (dog) collar: neck band
obrócić (ob-roo-ćheećh) v. rotate ;revolve :turn: go
obrót (ob-root) m. turn; turnover: revolution: slew: sales
obrus (ob-roos) m. tablecloth
obruszać (ob-roo-shaćh) v. loos-
en up: irritate; bring down
obrywać (ob-ri-vaćh) v. tear
off: tear away:pluck;wrench off
obryzgiwać (ob-riz-gee-vaćh) v.
splash; spatter

obrzęd (ob-zhańd) m. rite; ceremony . custom
obrzęk (ob-zhańk) m. swelling
obrzękły (ob-zhańk-wi) adj. m.
swollen: oedemous: tumid
obrzmiały (obzh-myá-wi) adj.
m. swollen: oedemous: tumid
obrzucać (ob-zhoo-tsaćh) v.
throw upon: hurl:pelt; fell
obrzydliwy (ob-zhid-lee-vi)
adj. m. revolting; disgusting
obrzydzenie (ob-zhi-dzé-ńe) n.
aversion: nausea: disgust
obrzynać (ob-zhi-naćh) v. clip;
cut: cut off; edge: trim;cheat
obsada (ob-sá-da) f. cast; crew;
garrison; staff: mounting
obsadka (on-sád-ka) f. penholder: small mounting
obsadzać (ob-sá-dzaćh) v. plant;
staff: set: fix: occupy;stock
obserwacja (ob-ser-váts-ya) f.
observation: remark
obserwator (ob-ser-vá-tor) m.
observer: look out man:witness
obserwatorium (ob-ser-va-tór-
yoom) m. observatory
obserwować (ob-ser-vó-vaćh) v.
watch; observe; take stock
obsługa (ob-swoo-ga) f. attendance; service: staff
obsługiwać (ob-swoo-geé-vaćh)
v. wait-upon; service
obstalować (ob-sta-lo-vaćh) v.
order (a suit of clothes etc.)
obstalunek (ob-sta-loo-nek) m.
order; a request to supply
obstawać (ob-sta-vaćh) v. insist on; hold to; stand by;
persist in; abide by
obstąpić (ob-stówn-peećh) v.
surround: form a circle;cluster
obstrzał (ob-stzhaw) m. gunfire; scope of fire; firing
obstrukcja (ob-strook-tsya) f.
obstruction; constipation
obsuwać (ob-soo-vaćh) v. slide
down; creep: lower:bring down
obsuwisko (ob-soo-vees-ko) n.
landslide : landslip
obsychać (ob-si-khaćh) v. dry
up : get parched: run dry;go dry

obsyłać (ob-si-wach) v. send
around (messengers etc.)
obsypywać (ob-si-pi-vach) v.
strew: sprinkle: shower:heap
obszar (ob-shar) m. area; range
obszarnik (ob-shar-ñeek) m.
landowner:large scale farmer
obszerny (ob-sher-ni) adj. m.
spacious: extensive:vast:broad
obsztorcować (ob-shtor-tso-vach)
v. snub; give hard time
obszukać (ob-shoo-kach) v.
search: ransack:make a search
obszyć (ob-shich) v. sew around
obuch (o-bookh) m. back of axe;
sledge: head of an axe
obudzić (o-boo-dżheech)v. wake
up;awaken; excite; stir up
obumarły (o-boo-mar-wi) adj. m.
deadened; half dead:decaying
obumierać (o-boo-myé-rach)v.
wither; atrophy:decay: shrink
oburącz (o-boo-rownch) adv.
with both hands:with both arms
oburzać (o-boo-zhach) v. revolt;
shock: provoke indignation
oburzony (o-boo-zho-ni) adj. m.
indignant; resentful
obustronny (o-boo-stron-ni) adj.
m. bilateral;mutual:reciprocal
obuwie (o-boo-vye) n. footwear
obwarowywać (ob-va-ro-vi-vach)
v. fortify; entrench: secure
obwąchiwać (ob-vown-khee-vach)
v. sniff around:smell around
obowiązywać (ob-vyown-zi-vach)
v. bind up; bandage; tie
obwieszczać (ob-vyesh-chach) v.
announce; proclaim: notify
obwieszczenie (ob-vyesh-ché-ñe)
n. proclamation: notice
obwiniać (ob-vee-ñach) v. accuse
obwisać (ob-vee-sach) v. sag;
droop: hang loosely: flag
obwodowy (ob-vo-do-vi) adj. m.
circumferential; district
obwoluta (ob-vo-loo-ta) f. wrapper; book-jacket: file cover
obwołać (ob-vo-wach) v. acclaim;
proclaim: call names
obwód (ob-voot) f. perimeter
oby (obi) part. may...;may you

obycie (o-bi-che) n. good
manners: experience;familiarity
obyczaj (o-bi-chay) m. custom
obyczajność (o-bi-chay-noshch)
f. decency; morality: morals
obyczajny (o-bi-chay-ni) adj.
m. decent; moral
obydwaj (o-bi-dvay) num. both
obyty (o-bi-ti) adj. m. familiar; easy mannered:polished
obywać śie (o-bi-vach shañ) v.
do without: dispense with
obywatel (o-bi-va-tel) m. citizen; squire:inhabitant
obywatelka (o-bi-va-tel-ka) f.
citizen: inhabitant: citizeness
obywatelstwo (o-bi-va-tel-
stvo) m. citizenship;nationality
obznajomić (ob-zna-yo-meech)v.
familiarize: acquaint;inform
obżarstwo (ob-zhar-stvo) n.
gluttony: stuffing oneself
ocalec (o-tsa-lech) v.survive
(danger)·rescue: save
ocalenie (o-tsa-le-ñe) n. rescue: salvation: escape
ocalić (o-tsa-leech) v. rescue
ocean (o-tsé-an) m. ocean
ocena (o-tse-na) f. grade;
estimate; appraisal
ocet (o-tset) m. vinegar
och!(okh !) excl.: oh !
ochędożyć (o-khán-do-zhich) v.
clean; put in order
ochlapać (o-khla-pach) v.
splash: splatter(with mud)
ochładzać (o-khwa-dzach) v.
cool; chill: refresh
ochłap (o-khwap) m. offal;
trash ; scrap of meat
ochłonąć (o-khwo-nownch) v.
calm down: get cooler: cool
ochoczo (o-khó-cho) adv.eager-
ly; cheerfully: gladly:gaily
ochota (o-khó-ta) f. eagerness;
forwardness; willingness
ochotnik (o-khót-ñeek) n. volunteer: serving of free will
ochraniać (o-khra-ñach) v.
protect; preserve: shield
ochrona (o-khró-na) f. (shelter) protection; conservation

ochronny (o-khrón-ni) adj. m.
protective; preventive
ochrypły (o-khrip-wi) adj. m.
hoarse; husky; raucous
ochrypnąć (o-khrip-nównch) v.
hoarsen; grow hoarse
ochrzcić (okh-zhchééch) v. baptize; christen; name: dub
ociągąc się(o-chówn-gach šhåñ)
v. linger; delay:put off
ociec (ó-chets) v. drain; drip
ociekać (o-ché-kach) v. drain;
drip; stream; overflow: dry
ociemniały (o-chem-ña-wi) adj.
m. blind; blind man
ocieniać (o-che-ñach) v. shade
over: protect from the sun
ocieplac (o-chép-lach) v. warm
up: make warmer: get warm
ocierać (o-che-rach) v. wipe
off; rub sore; gall; abrade
ociężały (o-chåñ-zha-wi) adj.
m. inert; (lazy) heavy; tardy;
dull; ponderous; languid:bovine
ociosać (o-chó-sach) v. hew
ocknąć się (óts-knównch šhåñ)
v. wake up (from a nap) awake
oclić (óts-leech) v. assess custom duty; levy duty;pay duty
oczarować (o-cha-ro-vach) v.
charm; enchant;fascinate:ravish
oczekiwać (o-che-keé-vach) v.
wait for; await; expect;hope
oczekiwanie (o-che-kee-vá-ñe)
n. expectation; prospect
oczerniać (o-cher-ñach) v.
slander; malign; defame; vilify
oczko (óch-ko) n. (needle) eye-
let; little eye:mesh:stitch
oczny (óch-ni) adj. m. optic
oczyszczać (o-chish-chach) v.
clean; purify; dust: clear
oczytany (o-chi-ta-ni) adj. m.
well-read : of wide reading
oczywisty (o-chi-veés-ti) adj.
m. obvious; self-evident;plain
oczywiście (o-chi-veésh-che)
adv. obviously; of course
od (od) prep. from; off; of;
for; since; out of; with; per;
by; then (idiomatic)
odbarwić (od-bar-veéch) v.
bleach; decolorize

odbicie (od-beé-che) n. reflection; bounce; ricochet; beating
back; deflection: repercussion
odbic (od-beéch) v. bounce back;
rescue; recover: reflect:print
odbiegać (od-byé-gach) v. desert; deviate; stray; digress
odbijać (od-beé-yach) v. reflect; print; put off; fend
off; recapture: leave a trace
odbiorca (od-byor-tsa) m. receiver; customer; addressee
odbiornik (od-byor-ñeek) m.
(radio) receiver: collector
odbior (od-byoor) m. receipt;
reception; collection
odbitka (od-beét-ka) f. copy;
reprint: impression: proof:slip
odblask (ód-blask) m. reflection
of light: gleam; irradiation
odbudowa (od-boo-do-va) f. reconstruction: restoration
odbudować (od-boo-do-vach) v.
rebuild; restore: reconstruct
odbyt (ód-bit) m. 1. sale
2. anus: end of alimentary tract
odbywać (od-bi-vach) v. do;
perform; be in progress
odcedzić (od-tsé-dżeech) v.
strain: strain out: drain away
odchodzić (od-khó-dżhaech)v.
go away; leave; walk off;
split;sail; retire; withdraw
odchudzać (od-khoo-dzach) v.
reduce (weight); slim:slenderize
odchylać (od-khi-lach) v. deflect; slant; slope:bend back
odchylenie (od-khi-lé-ñe) n.
deviation: declination:variation
odciągać (od-chówn-gach) v.
draw aside : retract:divert:delay
odciążać (od-chówn-zhach) v.
relieve;unburden; lighten:ease
odcień (ód-cheñ) m. shade; tint;
undertone; tinge:hue:cast: tone
odcierpieć (od-cher-pyech) v.
suffer for; expiate; atone
odcinać (od-chee-nach) v. cut
off; sever; amputate; detach
odcinek (od-chee-nek) m. sector;
segment; space; period; receipt
odcisk (ód-cheesk) m. imprint;
skin-corn; stamp:trace: squeeze

odcyfrować (od-tsi-fró-vach) v.
decipher; make out

odczekać (od-che-kach) v. wait
out: wait for the right moment

odczepić (od-che-peech) v. detach; unhook; get rid:clear out

odczuć (od-chooch) v. feel;
notice; resent; smart from

odczyn (od-chin) m. (chem) reaction: chemical change

odczynnik (od-chin-neek) m.
reagent; reacting substance

odczyt (od-chit) m. lecture

odczytać (od-chi-tach) v. read
over; take the reading; call

oddać (od-dach) v. give back;
pay back; render; deliver

oddalać (od-da-lach) v. remove;
send away; drive away

oddalony (od-da-ló-ni) adj. m.
distant; remote ;far away

oddany (od-dá-ni) adj. m. given
up; devoted ;loving; intent

oddawać (od-dá-vach) v. give
back; pay back; return:repay

od dawna (od dáv-na) since a
long time :long since

oddech (ód-dekh) m. breath

oddychać (od-di-khach) v.
breathe; take breath; respire

oddział (ód-dźhaw) m. division;
section; ward; branch; detail

oddziaływać (od-dźha-wi-vach)
v. influence; affect

oddzielać (od-dźhe-lach) v. separate; divorce; split

oddzielny (od-dźhél-ni) adj. m.
separate ;individual;discrete

oddzierać (od-dźhe-rach) v.
tear off; pull off;pull away

oddźwięk (ód-dźhvyánk) m. echo;
resonance; repercussion

odebrać (o-dé-brach) v. take
away; receive; withdraw;regain

odechcieć się (o-dekh-chech shan)
v. lose interest:cease liking

odegnać (o-dég-nach) v. chase
away; drive away; drive off

odegrać się (o-de-grach shán) v.
win back; recover;take place

odejmować (o-dey-mo-vach) v.
subtract; deduct; take away
diminish;withdraw; deprive

odejście (o-déy-shche) n. departure :, withdrawal;deviation

odejść (o-deyshch) v. depart;
go away; leave; abandon

odemknąć (o-dem-known-ch) v.
open; half open;set ajar;unbolt

odepchnąć (o-dep-khnown-ch) v.
shove away; beat back;reject

odeprzeć (o-dep-zhech) v. repel;
repulse; fight off; retort

oderwać (o-der-vach) v. tear
off; break off; detach;sever

odesłać (o-dés-wach) v. send
back: return;refer; direct

odetchnać (o-det-known-ch) v.
breathe (freely); respire

odetkać (o-det-kach) v. unstop;
open; uncork: unchoke: fall out

odezwa (o-déz-va) f. proclamation; appeal;urgent request

odgadywać (od-ga-di-vach) v.
guess: surmise; solve a riddle

odgałęziac (od-ga-wán-żhach) v.
branch away; fork off; ramify

odganiac (od-ga-nach) v. chase
away: drive off; dismiss

odgarniac (od-gar-nach) v. shove
away: rake aside: push aside

odginac (od-gee-nach) v. unbend;
fold back; straighten: curve

odgłos (od-gwos) m. echo; resonance: sound; noise; thud

odgniatac (od-gna-tach) v. bruise ; wrinkle; crease (the skin)

odgrażac się (od-gra-zhach shán)
v.talk big; threaten

odgradzac (od-gra-dzach) v.
fence off; separate; shut out

odgrodzic (od-gro-dżheech) v. divide off; fence off; shut off

odgruzowac (od-groo-zo-vach) v.
clear off rubbish from a space

odgrywac (od-gri-vach) v. play
off; perform; act; make believe

odgryzac (od-gri-zach) v. bite
off; snap off; gnaw off

odgrzebywac (od-gzhe-bi-vach) v.
dig up; rake up;unearth; turn up

odgrzewac (od-gzhe-vach) v. re-
warm; rehash; warm up (food)

odjazd (ód-yazt) m. departure

odjeżdżac (od-yézh-dzhach) v.
depart; be off; abandon;start

odjęcie (od-yan-che) n. deduction; amputation; weaning
odkazić (od-ka-źheech) v. disinfect; sterilize
odkażać (od-ka-zhach) v. disinfect (repeatedly); sterilize
odkażenie (od-ka-zhe-ñe) n. disinfection; sterilization
odkąd (od-kownt) adv. since; since when ? ever since;from
odkleić (od-kle-eech) v. unglue; unstick; detach; ungum
odkładać (od-kwa-dach) v. put aside; save; put back;put off
odkłonić się (od-kwo-ñeech shañ) v. greet back
odkopać (od-ko-pach) v. dig up
odkorkować (od-kor-ko-wach) v. uncork; unjam·(the traffic)
odkręcić (od-kran-cheech) v. unscrew; turn around
odkroić (od-kro-yeech) v. cut off; carve off; slice off
odkryć (od-krich) v. discover; uncover; lay bare;expose;notice
odkrycie (od-kri-che) n. discovery;exploration; exposure
odkupić(od-koo-peech) v. repurchase; redeem; buy ;replace
odkupienie (od-koo-pye-ñe) n. redemption ; repurchase
odkurzacz (od-koo-zhach) m. vacuum cleaner; carpet sweeper
odkuwać się (od-koo-vach shañ) v. recoup losses;forge;knock off
odlać (od-lach) v. pour off;cast
odlatywać (od-la-ti-vach) v. fly away; fly off· take off
odległość (od-leg-woshch) f. distance: remotness; interval
odległy (od-leg-wi) adj. m. distant; remote; far away:long ago
odlepiać (od-lep-yach) v. unglue; unstick; detach; ungum
odlew (od-lev) m. cast; pour
odlewać (od-le-vach) v. pour off; cast; mould; pour out
odlewacz (od-le-vach) m. founder
odlewnia (od-lev-ña) f. foundry
odliczać (od-lee-chach) v. deduct; count;reckon·off;allow
odliczenie (od-lee-che-ñe) n. deduction; allowance

odlot (od-lot) m. departure (by plane): take-off; start
odludek (od-loo-dek) m. recluse
odludny (od-lood-ni) adj. m. solitary; lonely; secluded
odłam (od-wam) m. fraction
odłamać (od-wa-mach) v. break off; sever; snap off
odłamek (od-wa-mek) m. chip; splinter; fragment;chip;stub
odłazić (od-wa-źheech) v. crawl away; get unstuck; come off
odłączyć (od-wown-chich) v. sever; disconnect; separate
odłożyć (od-wo-zhich) v. set aside; put off; put back
odłóg (od-wook) m. fallow
odłupać (od-woo-pach) v. split off; chip off; break off
odma płucna (od-ma pwoots-na) f. pneumothorax; pneumatosis
odmarznąć (od-mar--znownch) v. thaw; melt; get warm;unfreeze
odmawiać (od-mav-yach) v.refuse; say prayers; decline;recite
odmeldować (od-mel-do-vach) v. take a formal leave
odmęt (od-mant) m. chaotic whirlpool; confusion; depths
odmiana (od-mya-na) f. change; alteration;modification
odmieniać (od-mye-ñach) v. change; alter; decline ; conjugate
odmienny (od-myen-ni) adj. m. mutable; different; unlike
odmierzać (od-mye-zhach) v. measure off ;mark off
odmłodzić (od-mwo-dźheech) v. rejuvenate;make (look) younger
odmowa (od-mó-va) f. refusal; denial; saving "no"
odmówic (od-moo-veech) v.refuse; say prayers,; say "no"
odmrozić (od-mro-źheech) v. get frostbite ; get frozen; thaw
odmrożenie (od-mro-zhe-ñe) n. frostbite ; kibe
odmruknąć (od-mrook-nownch) v. mutter back; grunt out
odnająć (od-na-yownch) v. sublet
odnawiać (od-nav-yach) v. renew; renovate ; restore;reform

odnajdywać (od-nay-di-vach) v.
recover; find ; discover
od niechcenia (od ñe-khtse-ña)
adv. carelessly; willy-nilly
odniemczać (od-ñem-chach) v.
de-Germanize (language etc.)
odniesienie (od-ñe-she-ñe) n.
carrying back; reference (line)
odnieść (od-ñeshch) v. bring
back; take back ;sustain
odnoga (od-no-ga) f. spur;
branch; offshoot; river pass
odnosić (od-no-sheech) v. take
back; carry back (repeatedly)
odnośnie (od-nósh-ñe) prep.
concerning; in comparison
odnośnik (od-nosh-ñeek) m. reference; footnote(in a text)
odnośny (od-nosh-ni) adj. m.
relative; respectiye;proper
odnotować (od-no-to-vach) v.
check off ; note down; state
odnowa (od-no-va) f. renewal;
restoration ; regeneration
odnowić (od-no-veech) v. renew; renovate:reform;revive
odosobnić (od-o-sob-ñeech) v.
isolate; confine ;stand alone
odosobnienie (od-o-sob-ñe-ñe)
n. isolation ;privacy;seclusion
odor (o-door) m. reek; smell
odpad (od-pat) m. refuse; dropout ; waste; muck; scraps
odpadać (od-pa-dach)v. drop off;
fall off ; peel off; come off
odpadki (od-pad-kee) pl. waste
odparcie (od-par-che) n. repulsion; rejection ; refutation
odparować (od-pa-ro-vach) v.
parry; repel; evaporate
odparzenie (od-pa-zhe-ñe) n.
gall; scald ; chafe (skin)
odparzyć (od-pa-zhich) v. blister ; chafe one's skin
odpędzać (od-pañ-dzach) v. chase-
away; repel: expel;banish
odpiąć (od-pyownch) v. unfasten;
unbutton ;unbuckle; unclasp
odpieczętować (od-pye-chañ-to-
vach) v. unseal ;open(a letter)
odpinać (od-pee-nach) v. unbutton; disconnect; undo;unclasp

odpierać (od-pye-rach) v. repel;
refute ; force back; disprove
odpiłować (od-pee-wo-vach) v.
saw off,; file off; cut off
odpis (od-pees) m. copy
odpisać (odpee-sach) v. copy;
write back; answer: deduct
odpłacić (od-pwa-cheech) v.
repay; reciprocate;get back at
odpłata (od-pwa-ta) f. retribution ; repayment; retaliation
odpłynąć (od-pwi-nownch) v.
float away; sail away; swim
away ; put to sea ; low tide
odpływ (od-pwif) m. ebb; outflow;
odpoczynek (od-po-chi-nek) m.
rest; repose; relax from work
odpoczywać (od-po-chi-vach) v.
rest; have a rest ;take a rest
odpokutować (od-po-koo-to-vach)
v. expiate; atone; pay dearly
odpornosć (od-por-noshch) f.
immunity;resistance:hardiness
odpowiadać (od-po-vya-dach) v.
answer to; correspond to
odpowiedni (od-po-vyed-ñee) adj.
m. respective; adequate; suitable; fit; right;due;opportune
odpowiedzialność (od-po-vye-
dzhal-noshch) f. responsibility;
liability: civil liability
odpowiedzialny (od-po-vye-dzhal-
ni) adj. m. responsible; liable;
accountable; trustworthy
odpór (od-poor) m. opposition;
resistance; opposition
odprasować (od-pra-so-vach) v.
press; iron; press out ;express
odprawa (od-pra-va) f. dispatch;
rebuff;briefing; debriefing
odprawiać (od-prav-yach) v.dis-
patch; dismiss; celebrate
(mass); order away; send away
odprężać (od-prañ-zhach) v. relax; slacken; let down;recoil
odprężenie (od-prań-zhe-ñe) m.
relax; easing of tension;détente
odprowadzać (od-pro-va-dzach)
v. divert; drain off; escort
odpruwać (od-proo-vach) v.
rip off (buttons);rip away
odprzedać (od-pzhe-dach)v. resell

odprzedaż (od-pzhe-dash) f. re-
sale;sale at second hand
odpust (od-poost) m. indulgence
odpuszczenie (od-poosh-che-ne)
n.foregiveness;remission
odpychać (od-pi-khach) v. repel
odpychanie (od-pi-kha-ne) n.
repulsion; repelling
odra (od-ra) f. measles pl. ru-
beola(high fever&skin eruption)
odrabiac (od-rab-yach) v. work
off; work out; get done;undo
odraczać (od-ra-chach) v. put
off; postpone; defer; delay
odradzac (od-ra-dzach) v. advise
against; regenerate; revive
odrapać (o-dra-pach) v. scratch
up; dilapidate; scrape off
odrastać (od-ras-tach) v. grow
back; sprout again; shoot again
odraza (od-ra-za) f. aversion
odrazu (od-ra-zoo) adv. at once
odrażający (od-ra-zha-yown-tsi)
adj. m. repulsive; hideus
odrąbać (od-rown-bach) v. chop
off; hew away; cut off
odrębnosc (od-ranb-noshch) n.
distinction; individuality
odrębny (od-ranb-ni) adj. m.
distinct; individual:separate
odręczny (od-ranch-ni) adj. m.
freehand; personal; longhand
odrętwiały (od-rant-vya-wi) adj.
m. numbed; torpid : stiff
odrobić (od-ro-beech) v. work
off; work out; get done: do
odrobina (od-ro-bee-na) f. small
bit; particle· shred: a dash
odroczenie (od-ro-che-ne) n.
adjournment; postponement
odroczyć (od-ro-chich) v. put
off; delay; defer; postpone
odrodzenie (od-ro-dze-ne) m.
rebirth; renaissance
odrodzić (od-ro-dzheech) v.
regenerate :renew; revive
odróżniac (od-roozh-nach) v. dis-
tinquish; differentiate
odróżniac się (od-roozh-nach
shan) v. differ :be different
odruch (od-rookh) m. reflex
odrywać (od-ri-vach) v. tear
off; sever;separate;break off

odrzec (od-zhech) v. reply
odrzucać (od-zhoo-tsach) v.
reject; repulse; cast away
odrzutowiec (od-zhoo-tov-yets)
m. jet (plane)
odrzwia (od-zhvya) pl. door-
frame: mine prop set
odrzynac (od-zhi-nach) v. cut
off; cut away; detach: sever
odsądzac (od-sown-dzach) v.
deny; infamize;deprive of merit
odsetka (od-set-ka) f. interest
point; percentage; proportion
odsiadywac (od-sha-di-vach) v.
sit out; serve (sentence)
odsiecz (od-shech) f. rescue
odskoczyc (od-sko-chich) v.
jump off; spring back:dart away
odsłonic (od-swo-neech) v. un-
veil;expose; display: show
odsprzedac (od-spzhe-dach) v.
resell; sale at second hand
odstawac (od-sta-vach) v. hang-
loose; not fit; come off
odstawic (od-sta-veech) v. put
aside; deliver; play(dumb)
odstąpic (od-stown-peech) v.
step back; secede; cede
odstęp (od-stanp) m. margin;
space; interval; lapse (of time)
odstępca (od-stanp-tsa) m.ren-
egade; deserter; turncoat
odstępne (od-stanp-ne) n. payment for giving up a lease
odstraszyc (od-stra-shich) v.
deter; frighten away;scare
odstręczyc (od-stran-chich) v.
dissuade; turn away;repel;deter
odstrzał (od-stzhaw) m. shooting
off; firing (game, mine)
odsunąc (od-soo-nownch) v. push
away; shove away; brush aside
odsyłacz (od-si-wach) m. reference mark; footnote mark
odsyłac (od-si-wach) v. send
back; refer ;return; direct
odsypac (od-si-pach) v. pour
off (not liquid);alluviate
odsypiac (od-sip-yach) v. catch
up on sleep ; sleep off
odszkodowanie (od-shko-do-va-ne)
n. indemnity : compensation

odszukać (od-shoo-kach) v. retrieve; run down;seek out:find
odśrodkowy (od-śhrod-ko-vi)
adj. m. centrifugal
odświeżyć (od-śhvye-zhich) v.
refresh; recondition·restore
odświętny (od-śhvyant-ni) adj.
m. festive;ceremonial·showy
odtąd (od-townt) adv. henceforth; from now on; from here
odtłuścić (od-twoosh-cheech)
v. degrease; reduce weight
odtrącać (od-trown-tsach) v.
repel; jostle; knock off; deduct (charges);thrust aside
odtrutka (od-troot-ka) f.anti-
dote! counterpoison
odtwarzać (od-tva-zhach) v.
reproduce; reconstitute
odtwórca (od-tvoor-tsa) m. re-
producer; performer
oduczać (od-oo-chach) v. un-
teach; unlearn; break a habit
odurzać (o-doo-zhach) v. stun;
make dopey; stupefy;daze;dizzy
odurzenie (o-doo-zhe-ńe) n.
stupor; giddiness;intoxication
odwadniać (od-vad-ńach) v.
drain; dehydrate· dewater
odwaga (od-va-ga) f. courage
odwalić (od-va-leech) v. push
away; beat it; copy; get over
with; roll aside;remove:sham
odwar (od-var) m. decoction
odważnik (od-vazh-ńeek) n.
scale— weight
odważny (od-vazh-ni) adj. m.
brave; courageous;bold;daring
odważyć (od-va-zhich) v. weigh
odważyć się (od-va-zhich śhań)
v. dare;have the courage:risk
odwdzięczyć się(od-vdźhań-chich
śhań) v. repay (with gratitude; return; requite:repay
odwet (od-vet) m. retaliation;
retort;·revenge; requital
odwiązać (od-vyown-zach) v.
untie; unfasten; unbuckle;undo
odwieczny (od-vyech-ni) adj. m.
eternal; immemorial·age long
odwiedzać (odvye-dzach) v.vis-
it; call on; pay a visit;
pay a call; come to see

odwiedziny (od-vye-dzhee-ni)n.
visit; call; coming to see
odwijać (od-vee-yach) v. unwrap
odwilż (od-veelzh) f. thaw
odwlekać (od-vle-kach) v. put
off; postpone:delay;drag away
odwodnic (od-vod-ńeech) v. drain
odwodzić (od-vo-dźheech)v. draw
off;draw aside;dissuade
odwołać (od-vo-wach) v. take
back; appeal; refer; recall
odwołanie (od-vo-wa-ńe) n. recall; appeal;repeal;cancellation
odwozić (od-vo-zheech) v. take
back (by car); drive back
odwód (od-voot) m. reserve
odwracać (od-vra-tsach) v. reverse; turn around;invert
odwrotny (od-vrot-ni) adj. m.
reverse;opposite;converse
odwrót (od-vroot) m. retreat;
reverse; withdrawal
odwykać (od-vi-kach) v. break
a habit; loose the habit
odwzajemniać (od-vza-yem-ńach)
v. reciprocate;repay;return
odyniec (o-di-ńets) m. boar
odzew (od-zev) m. echo; reply
odziedziczyć(o-dźhe-dźhee-chich)
v. inherit; succeed(to a title)
odzienie (o-dżhe-ńe) n. clothing
odzież (o-dżhezh) f. clothes
odznaczać (od-zna-chach) v.
distinguish; decorate;mark off
odznaczenie (od-zna-che-ńe) n.
distinction;award;decoration
odznaka (od-zna-ka) f. badge
odzwierciadlać (od-zvyer-chad-
lach) v. reflect (something)
odzwyczajać (od-zvi-cha-yach)
v. break a habit;make loose a
habit
odzyskać (od-zis-kach) v. retrieve ;regain;recover:win back
odzywać się (od-zi-vach śhań) v.
speak up;drop a line:respond
odźwierny (od-dźhvyer-ni) m.
doorman ;janitor;caretaker
odżyć (od-zhich) v. come back to
life; revive;be reborn:reappear
odżywczy (od-zhiv-chi) adj. m.
nutritious;nourishing;alimentary
odżywiać (od-zhiv-yach) v.nour-
ish; feed ;supply with food

odżywienie (od-zhiv-yé-ńe) n. food ; nourishment; diet

ofensywa (o-fen-si-va) f. offensive ; push; attack

oferma (o-fér-ma) f. sad sack

oferta (o-fér-ta) f. offer

ofiara (o-fyá-ra) f. victim; offering;sacrifice; dupe

oficer (o-fée-tser) m. (military) officer

oficjalny (o-feets-yál-ni) adj. m. official;formal;reserved

oficyna (o-fee-tsi-na) f. backhouse; printing shop;annex

ofuknąć (o-fóok-nównch) v. rebuke; reprimand;trounce;rate

ogar (ó-gar) m. bloodhound

ogarek (o-ga-rek) m. candleend; stump; stub:cigarette end

ogarniac (o-gár-ńach) v. seize; comprehend;take in;grasp

ogien (ó-geń) m. fire; flame

ogier (ó-ger) m. stallion

ogladać (o-glówn-dach) v. inspect; consider; see

oględny (o-glánd-ni) adj. circumspect;moderate;cautious

oglada (o-gwa-da) f. good manners;refinement;urbanity:polish

ogłaszac (o-gwa-shach)v. advertize; declare; publish

ogłuchnąc (o-gwookh-nównch) v. become deaf ; be hushed

ogłupiec (o-gwoop-yech) v. become stupid;grow silly

ognie sztuczne (óg-ńe shtóoch-ne) pl. fireworks

ogniotrwały (o-gńo-trva-wi) adj. fireproof;incombustible·

ognisko (od-ńees-ko) n. hearth; focus; camp fire·fire place

ognisty (og-ńees-ti) adj. m. fiery;flaming; passionate

ogniwo (og-ńee-vo) n. link

ogolic (o-gó-leech) v. shave

ogon (ó-gon) m. tail;trail;scut

ogonek (o-gó-nek) m. waiting line;queue;diacritical mark

ogorzały (o-go-zhá-wi) adj. m. sunburnt;tanned;weather beaten

ogólnie (o-góol-ńe) adv. generally;as a rule;universally

ogólny (o-góol-ni) adj. m. general;prevailing; global; total

ogół (ó-goow) m. people; public

ogółem (o-góo-wem) adv. on the whole; as a whole; altogether

ogórek (o-góo-rek) m. cucumber

ogórkowy sezon (o-goor-kó-vi se-zon) slack time(season)

ograbic (o-grá-beech) v. rob

ograniczony (o-gra-ńee-chó-ni) adj. m. narrow-minded; limited

ogrodnik (o-gród-ńeek) m. gardener; horticulturist

ogrodzic (o-gró-dźheech)v. fence in; enclose;wall in; rail in

ogromny (o-grom-ni) adj. m. huge

ogród (ó-good) m. garden

ogryzac (o-gri-zach) v. gnaw away; nimble at; pick(a bone)

ogrzewac (o-gzhe-vach) v. heat

ohydny (o-khíd-ni) adj. m. hideous; gastly;abonimable:vile

o ile (o ée-le) conj. as far as

ojciec (óy-chets) m. father

ojciec chrzestny (óy-chyets khzhést-ni) godfather

ojczym (óy-chim) m. stepfather

ojczysty język (oy-chis-ti yań-zik) native tongue

ojczyzna (oy-chíz-na) f. native country; motherland;homeland

okaleczyc (o-ka-lé-chich) v. maim;cripple·lame;mutilate

oka mgnienie (o-ka mgńe-ńe) n. eye blink; split second

okap (ó-kap) m. eaves;overlap

okaz (ó-kas) m. specimen;type

okazac (o-ka-zach) v. show; demonstrate; evidence;exhibit

okazały (o-ka-zá-wi) adj. m. magnificent;stately;grand

okaziciel (o-ka-żhee-chel) m. bearer (of a check etc.)

okazja (o-kaz-ya) f. opportunity

okazyjny (o-ka-zíy-ni) adj. m. occasional; chance(acquaintance)

okazywac (o-ka-zí-vach) v. demonstrate; show ;manifest;display

oklaski (o-klas-kee) pl. applause;clapping; acclamations

oklaskiwać (o-klas-kee-vach) v. applaud ; clap(one's hands)

okleić (o-klé-eech) v. paste-
over;stick over; smear over
oklepany (o-kle-pá-ni) adj. m.
commonplace; (well) worn
okład (ó-kwat) m. compress;
hotpad ; lining;wrapping
okładka (o-kwád-ka) f. (book)
cover; book binding
okłamać (o-kwa-mach) v. deceive; tell a lie; delude
okno (ók-no) n. window
oko (ó-ko) n. eye; eye sight
okolica (o-ko-lee-tsa) f. region; surroundings;vicinity
okoliczność (o-ko-leéch-noshch)
f. circumstance; fact;occasion
około (o-ko-wo) prep. near;
about; more or less;at;on;or so
okoń (ó-koń) m. perch; bass
okop (ó-kop) m. trench
okopcić (o-kóp-čheech) v. soot
okostna (o-kóst-na) f. perios-
teum; lining of the bones
okólnik (o-koól-ńeek) m. circular; corral;poultry yard
okpić (ó-kpeech) v. pool wool
over eyes; deceive;cheat;gull
okradać (o-krá-dach) v. pickpocket; burglarize; rob
okrakiem (o-krá-kem) adv.
astraddle;with legs wide apart
okrasa (o-krá-sa) f. fat; ornament ; seasoning ;gravy;lard
okrasić (o-kra-sheech) v. adorn;
season ;add a condiment
okratować (o-kra-to-vach) v.
grate; bar (a window)
okratowanie (o-kra-to-va-ńe)
m. grating; railings; bars
okrąg (o-krownk) m. district
okrągły (o-krówng-wi) adj. m.
round; spherical;full(month etc)
okrążać (o-krówn-zhach) v. encircle; circle;revolve:detour
okres (ó-kres) m. period;phase
określać (o-kresh-lach) v.
define; qualify;fix;appoint
okręcać (o-krań-tsach) v. coil
around;wrap; turn around
okręt (o-krańt) m. ship:boat
okrężny (o-krańzh-ni) adj. m.
roundabout;indirect;devious
circuitous; circular:travelling-
pedlar's(trade etc.)

okropność (o-króp-noshch) f.
horror; atrocity;outrage
okropny (o-króp-ni) adj. m.
horrible;fearful;awful;extreme
okruch (ó-krookh) m. crumb
okrucieństwo (o-kroo-chyeń-
stvo) n. cruelty;atrocities
okrutny (o-kroót-ni) adj. m.
cruel;savage;excessive; sore
okrycie (o-kri-che) n. covering; wrap;garment;overcoat
okrywać (o-kri-vach) v. cover
okrzyczany (o-kzhi-chá-ni) adj.
m. notorious;famous;renowned
okrzyk (ó-kzhik) m. outcry
okrzyknąć (o-kzhik-nównch) v.
proclaim;declare; brand
oktawa (ok-ta-va) f. octave
okucie (o-koó-che) n. hardware; ferrule; fitting
okuć (ó-kooch) v. shoe a horse;
shackle; fit a lock and hinges
okular (o-koó-lar) m. eyeglass
okularnik (o-koo-lár-ńeek) m.
cobra;poisonous snake of Asia
okulista (o-koo-lees-ta) m.
eye doctor;eye surgeon;oculist
okultyzm (o-koól-tizm) m. oc-
cultism; hidden knowledge
okup (ó-koop) m. ransom
okupacja (o-koo-páts-ya) f.
occupation; occupancy
okupować (o-koo-pó-vach) v.
occupy;invade a territory
okupywać (o-koo-pi-vach) v. pay
ransom; compensate;redeem;atone
olbrzym (ól-bzhim) m. giant
olbrzymi (ol-bzhí-mee) adj. m.
gigantic;huge;cllossal;excessive
olcha (ól-kha) f. alder tree
oleander (o-le-án-der) m. oleander (an evergreen shrub)
olej (ó-ley) m. oil; oil paint
olej lniany (ó-ley lńa-ni) adj.
m. linseed-oil
oligarchia (o-lee-gár-khya) m.
oligarchy;the ruling persons
oliwa (o-lee-va) f. olive; oil
oliwić (o-lee-veech) v. oil
oliwka (o-leév-ka) f. olive-tree
olszyna (ol-shi-na) f. alder-
tree stand; alder wood
olśniewać (ol-shńe-vach) v.
dazzle; ravish;enchant·

ołów (owoof) m. lead;lead shot
ołówek (o-woo-vek) m. lead
  pencil;drawing in pencil
ołtarz (ow-tash) m. altar
omackiem (o-mats-'kem) adv.
  gropingly ; blindfold
omal (o-mal) adv. nearly
omamić (o-ma-meech) v. deceive
omaścić (o-mash-cheech) v. add
  fat; add butter(on bread etc.)
omawiac (o-mav-yach) v. discuss
omdlały (om-dla-wi) adj. m.
  fainted; faint; languid
omdlec (om-dlech) v. faint
omen (o-men) m. omen
omieszkać (o-myesh-kach) v.
  fail;omit;neglect·
omijac (o-mee-yach) v. pass
omlet (om-let) m. omelet
omłócić (o-mwoo-cheech) v.
  thresh out; give a thrashing
omotac (o-mo-tach) v. entangle
omowic (o-moo-veech) v. discuss
omylic (o-mi-leech) v. mislead
omylny (o-mil-ni) adj. m. fal-
  lible;misleading;deceitful
omyłka (o-miw-ka) f. error
on; ona; ono (on; o-na; o-no)
  pron. he; she; it
oni (o-nee) m. pl. they;
  one (o-ne) f. pl. they
ondulacja (on-doo-lats-ya) f.
  (hair) wave;permanent wave
ondulacja trwała (on-doo-lats-
  ya trva-wa) permanent (wave)
onegdaj (o-neg-day) adv. the
  other day;two days ago
ongis (on-geesh) adv. (arch)
  at one time;once upon a time
oniemiały (o-ne-mya-wi) adj.
  m. mute; dumb; speechless
oniesmielac (o-ne-shmye-lach)
  v. intimidate;browbeat;cow
opactwo (o-pats-tvo) n. abbey
opaczny (o-pach-ni) adj. m.
  wrong;mistaken;improper
opad (o-pat) m. (rain) fall
opadac(o-pa-dach) v. subside
(na)opak (na o-pak) adv. up-
  side down; reverse;wrong way
opakowanie (o-pa-ko-va-ne) n.
  wrapping ; packing

opal (o-pal) m. opal
opalac się (o-pa-lach shañ) v.
  suntan; tan;bronze;lie on the sun
opalanie (o-pa-la-ne) n. heating (house etc.);fire marking
opalenizna (o-pa-le-neez-na) f.
  suntan; tan; scorched remains
opał (o-paw) m. fuel for heating
opamiętac (o-pa-myañ-tach) v.
  sober down; bring to reason
opanowac (o-pa-no-vach) v.
  master;conquer;seize; learn
opanowany (o-pa-no-va-ni) adj.
  m. cool-headed;composed;calm
opary (o-pa-ri) pl. fumes
oparcie (o-par-che) n. support
oparzyc (o-pa-zhich) v. scald
opasac (o-pa-sach) v. belt;
  girdle;grid;encircle;surround
opaska (o-pas-ka) f. band
opasły (o-pas-wi) adj. m. obese
opasc (o-pashch) v. drop; sink;
  hang loose;settle;collapse;slope
opatentowac (o-pa-ten-to-vach)
  v. patent ;take out a patent
opatrunek (o-pa-troo-nek) m.
  dressing; bandage; field dressing
opatrywac (o-pa-tri-vach) v.
  fix; dress; provide;prepare
opera (o-pe-ra) f. opera; opera
  house; no end of a joke
operacja (o-pe-rats-ya) f. surgery; operation; action;process
operowac (o-pe-ro-vach) v.oper-
  ate; manipulate; act; handle
opętanie (o-pañ-ta-ne) n. obsession;demonical possession
opieczętowac (o-pye-chañ-to-
  vach) v. seal up; seal
opieka (o-pye-ka) f. care
opiekowac (o-pye-ko-vach) v.
  take care; care for;have charge
opiekun (o-pye-koon) m. guardian; curator; foster-parent
opierac się (o-pye-rach shañ)
  v. lean; base; relay;rest;defy
opieszały (o-pye-sha-wi) adj.
  m. slow; tardy; lazy; inert
opinia (o-peen-ya) f. opinion;
  view; reputation; sentiment
opis (o-pees) m. description
oplątać (o-plown-tach) v. ensnare; entangle; entwine

opluwać (o-ploó-vach) v. spit
on ;spit at; slander; defame
opłacać (o-pwa-tsach) v. pay;
bribe ;cover the cost;reward
opłakany (o-pwa-ka-ni) adj. m.
deplorable ;sad; pitiful
opłakiwać (o-pwa-kee-vach) v.
lament; deplore ;mourn
opłata (o-pwa-ta) f. fee
opłatek (o-pwa-tek) m. wafer
opłucna (o-pwoots-na) f. pleura ;membrane around the lungs
opłukiwać (o-pwoo-kee-vach) v.
rinse; wash with water
opływać (o-pwi-vach) v. sail
around; abound ;encircle;roll
opływowy (o-pwi-vo-vi) adj. m.
streamlined; streamline
opodal (o-po-dal) adv. near by
opodatkować (o-po-dat-ko-vach)
v. tax; impose a tax
opona (o-po-na) f. tire
oponować (o-po-no-vach) v.
oppose ; take exception
opornie (o-por-ne) adv. with
difficulty; arduosly
oporny (o-por-ni) adj. m. balky;
recalcitrant; refractory
opowiadać (o-pov-ya-dach) v.
tell — tale ;relate;record
opozycja (o-po-zits-ya) f. opposition ; resistance
opór (o-poor) m. resistance
opozniać (o-poózh-nach) v. delay; retard;slow down,defer
opóźnienie (o-poozh-ne-ne) n.
delay ;deferment;tardiness
opracować (o-pra-tso-vach) v.
work up; elaborate:compile
oprawa (o-pra-va) f. frame;
binding ;framework:handle
oprawca (o-práv-tsa) m. skinner;
executioner: torturer:assassin
opresja (o-pres-ya)f.oppression
oprocentowanie (o-pro-tsen-to-wa-ne) n. interest(on money)
oprowadzać (o-pro-va-dzach) v.
show around; act as a guide
oprócz (o-rooch) prep.: except;
besides : apart from;but:save
opróżniać (o-proózh-nach) v.
empty ;clear:evacuate·unload

opryskliwy (o-prisk-lee-vi)
adj. m. peevish;gruff;harsh
opryszek (o-pri-shek) m. hoodlum:hooligan:rowdy:rough-neck
oprzec (op- zhech) v. lean; base;
resist:become inffamed;inflame
oprzytomniec (o-pzhi-tom-ńech)
v. recover; collect oneself
optyk (op-tik) m. optician
optymista (op-ti-mees-ta) m.
optimist: one of cheerful views
opublikować (o-poo-blee-ko-vach) v. publish:make public
opuchły (o-pookh-wi) adj. m.
swollen; dilated
opuchlina (o-pookh-lee-na) f.
swelling ;dilatation
opuszczać (o-poósh-chach) v.
leave; omit; abandon· lower
opustoszały (o-poos-to-sha-vi)
adj. m. deserted:desolate;empty
opuszczenie (o-poosh-che-ne) n.
omission:lowering:reduction
orać (o-rach) v. till; plough
oranżeria (o-ran-zher-ya) f.
greenhouse: hothouse:orangery
oraz (o-raz) conj. as well as
orbita (or-bee-ta) f. orbit
order (or-der) m. decoration;
order(for service rendered etc.)
ordynarny (or-di-nár-ni) adj.
m. gross; coarse:vulgar:trashy
oredzie (o-rán-dzhe) n. (official) message;proclamation
oręż (o-ransh) m. weapon
organiczny (or-ga-ńeech-ni)
adj. m. organic:constitutional
organista (or-ga-ńees-ta) m.
organist :organ player
organizacja (or-ga-ńee-zats-ya)f.organization:organized group
organizm (or-ga-ńeezm) m. organism: any living thing
orgia (org-ya) f. orgy
orka (or-ka) f. tillage
orkiestra (or-kes-tra) f. orchestra: orchestra pit
orny (or-ni) adj. m. arable
orszak (or-shak) m. retinue
ortodoksja (or-to-doks-ya) f.
orthodoxy: conventionality

ortografia (or-to-gra-fya) f.
orthography;correct spelling
oryginalny (o-ri-gee-nal-ni)
adj. m. original;inventive;new
orzech (o-zhekh) m. nut;walnut
orzeczenie (o-zhe-che-ńe) m.
decision; sentence; ruling
orzeł (o-zhew) m, eagle;genius
orzeźwiać (o-zheźh-vyać) v.
refresh; brace up; invigorate
osa (o-sa) f. wasp; vixen;shrew
osad (o-sat) m. sediment; dregs
osada (o-sa-da) f. settlement
osadnik (o-sad-ńeek) m. settler
osadzać (o-sa-dzać) v. plant;
seat; settle; place;fix;steady
osamotnienie (o-sa-mot-ńe-ńe)
n. isolation;loneliness
osądzać (o-sown-dzać) v.
sentence ; judge ;prejudge
oschły (oskh-wi) adj. m. arid;
dry; cold; stiff; stand-offish
osełka (o-sew-ka) f. whetstone
oset (o-set) m. thistle;teasel
osiadać (o-sha-dać) v. settle;
subside; make a settlement
osiągnąć (o-showng-nownć) v.
attain;achieve;gain;reach
osiedlać (o-shed-lać) v.
settle;make a settlement
osiem (o-shem) num. eight
osiemdziesiąt (o-shem-dzhe-
shownt) num. eighty
osiemnaście (o-shem-naśh-che)
num. eighteen
osiemset (o-shem-set) num.
eight hundred ___ v. be orphaned
osierocić (o-she-ro-cheech)
osika (o-shee-ka) f. aspen
osikać (o-shee-kać) v. sprinkle; piss on (vulg.)
osiodłać (o-shod-wać) v. saddle ; reduce to subjugation
osioł (o-shyow) m. donkey; ass
oskarżać (o-skar-zhać) v.
accuse ;charge with;indict
oskrzela (o-skzhe-la) pl. n.
bronchia ;main part of windpipe
oskrzydlać (o-skzhid-lać) v.
outflank ;go beyond; cut off
oskubać (o-skoo-bać) v. fleece;
feather;pluck;skin; soak
osłabiać (o-swab-yać) v. weak-
en ;reduce; lessen;diminish

osłabienie (o-swa-bye-ńe) n.
weakness ; diminuation;debilitation
osłona (o-swo-na) f. shield;
cover ; protection: defense
osładzać (o-swa-dzać) v. sweet-
en ; put sugar; cheer up
osłupiały (o-swoo-pya-wi) adj.
m. amazed; aghast ; astounded
osmarować (o-sma-ro-vać) v.
besmear; libel ; run down; soil
osoba (o-so-ba) f. person
osobisty (o-so-bees-ti) adj.
m. personal; private ;particular
osobiście (o-so-beésh-che) adv.
personally ; in person
osobnik (o-sob-ńeek) m. individual ; specimen; person
osobny (o-sob-ni) adj. m.sep-
arate; private ; individual
osobowość (o-so-bo-voshch) f.
personality ; individuality
osowiały (o-so-vya-wi) adj. m.
depressed; dejected ;glum:monish
ospa (os-pa) f. smallpox
ospały (os-pa-wy) adj. m.
drowsy; sleepy; sluggish; dull
ostatecznie (o-sta-téch-ńe) adv.
finally; after all; at last
ostateczny (o-sta-téch-ni) adj.
m. final ;ultimate; eventual
ostatek (o-sta-tek) m. reminder; rest; remains; scrap
ostatni (o-stat-ńee) adj. m.
last; late; end ;closing; parting
ostatnio (o-stat-ńo) adv. of late;
lately; not long ago ; recently
ostoja (o-sto-ya) f. mainstay
ostroga (o-stro-ga) f. spur
ostrokątny (o-stro-kównt-ni)
adj. m. sharp-angled
ostrożność (o-strozh-noshch)
f. caution; prudence; care
ostrożny (o-strozh-ni) adj. m.
careful; prudent;cautious; wary
ostry (o-stri) adj. m. sharp
ostryga (o-stri-ga) f. oyster
ostrze (o-stzhe) n. cutting
edge; spike ;blade; point;prong
ostrzegać (o-stzhe-gać) v.
warn of: warn against;admonish
ostrzeliwać (o-stzhe-lee-vać)
v. shoot at; strafe ; fire at;
accustom to gun fire

ostrzeżenie (o-stzhe-zhe-ńe)
n. warning ;danger sign·notice
ostrzyc (o-stzhich) v. sharp-
en : whet;grind;put an edge
ostrzygać (o-stzhi-gach) v.
cut (hair) ; shear sheep;trim
ostudzać (o-stoo-dzach) v. cool
ostygać (o-sti-gach) v. cool
down ; chill; cool off: abate
osuszac (o-soo-shach) v. dry;
drain : dehumidifv;wipe; mop
oswobodzic (o-svo-bo-dźheech)
v. free ; liberate:rescue:rid
oswoic (o-svo-eech) v. tame;
familiarize; tame;domesticate
oszacowac (o-sha-tso-vach) v.
evaluate; estimate;appraise
oszczep (osh-chep) m. javelin
oszczerstwo (osh-cher-stvo) n.
calumny; libel; defamation
oszczędności (osh-chand-nosh-
chee) pl. savings(money)
oszklenie (o-shkle-ńe) n. glaz-
ing (of windows)
oszołomic (o-sho-wo-meech) v.
stun: daze:stunefy;bewilder
oszpecic (o-shpe-cheech) v. deface; disfigure;deform; mar
oszukac (o-shoo-kach) v. cheat
oszust (o-shoost) m. cheater
oś (osh) f. axle (axis)
oscienny (o-shchen-ni) adj. m.
bordering: adjoining: adjacent
ość (oshch) f. (fish) bone
oslepiac (o-shle-pyach) v.
blind; dazzle; strike blind
osmieszac (o-shmye-shach) v.
ridicule;deride;make fun of
osrodek (o-shro-dek) m. center
oswiadczenie (o-shviad-che-ńe)
n. declaration; pronouncement
oswiadczyny (c-shvyad-chi-ni)
pl. marriage proposal
oswiata (o-shvya-ta) f. education; learning
oswiecac (o-shvye-tsach) v.
light up; enlighten; educate
oswietlenie (o-shvyet-le-ńe) n.
lighting ;light; illumination
otaczac (o-ta-chach) v. surround;enclose;turn on a lathe
otchłan (ot-khwań) f. abyss

otępienie (o-tań-pye-ńe) n.
dullness ;stupor:stupefaction
oto (o-to) part. here; there
otoczenie (o-to-che-ńe) n. environment;setting; associates
otoczyc (o-to-chich) v. surround; enclose;turn on a lathe
otomana (o-to-ma-na) f. couch
otoż (o-toosh) conj. now
otruc (o-trooch) v. poison
otrucie (o-troo-che) n. poisoning
otrzaskac (o-tshas-kach)v.acquaint
otrząsac (o-tzhown-sach) v.
shake loose; shudder; strew
otrzewna (o-tzhev-na) f. peri-
toneum; lining of abdomen
otrzeźwiec (o-tzheżh-vyech) v.
sober up;be disillusioned;brisk up
otrzymac(o-tzhi-mach) v. receive ; get; be given;acquire
otulic (o-too-leech) v. tuck in;
wrap;wrap up: shroud:enfold: lag
otwarcie (o-tvar-che) adv.openly;
frankly; in plain words;outright
otwarty (o-tvar-ti) adj. m.
open; frank:overt;professed
otwierac (ot-vye-rach) v. open
otwor (ot-voor) m. opening
otyły (o-ti-wi) adj. m. obese
owacja (o-vats-ya) f. ovation
owad (o-vad) m. insect
owal (o-val) m. oval
owca (ov-tsa) f. sheep
owczarek (ov-cha-rek) m. sheep-dog
owczarnia(ov-char-ńa)f. sheep-fold
owdowiały (ov-do-vya-wi) adj.
m. widowed ; one who lost wife
owies (o-vyes) m. oats
owiewac (o-vye-vach) v. blow
upon;sweep over: encompass:inspire
owijac (o-vee-yach) y. wrap up
owłosiony (o-vwo-sho-ni) adj.
m. hairy; hirsute; shaggy; pilose
owo (o-vo) pron. that : that thing
owoc (o-vots) m. fruit ;fruitage
owrzodzenie (o-vzho-dze-ńe) n.
ulceration : sore: sores
owsianka (ov-shan-ka) f. oatmeal; kasha; porridge
owszem (ov-shem) part. yes;
certainly; on the contrary
ozdabiac (o-zdab-yach) v. dec-
:orate; adorn ;trim; garnish

ozdoba (oz-do-ba) f. decoration
oziębiac (o-zhan-byach) v. cool off; chill; cool down; damp
oziębły (o-zhanb-wi) adj. m. frigid ; cold; reserved; dry
oznaczac (o-zna-chach) v. mark; signify ; indicate; fix; spell
oznajmiac (o-znay-myach) v. announce ;inform; notify;state
oznaka (o-zna-ka) f. sign; symptom; badge; mark
ozor (o-zoor) m. (bull's) tongue; gossiping tongue
ożenic (o-zhe-neech) v. marry
ożywiac (o-zhiv-yach) v. bring to life; animate;brisk up
ożywienie (o-zhi-vye-ne) n. animation ;liveliness: stir
ożywiony (o-zhiv-yo-ni) adj. m. animated; lively; brisk,
ósemka (oo-sem-ka) f. eight
ósma godzina (oos-ma go-dzhee-na) eight o'clock
ósmak (oos-mak) m. eighth grader; eighth grade pupil
ow (oof) m. pron. that
owa (o-va)f. pron. that
owo (o-vo)n. pron. that
owi (o-vee)pl. m. pron. that
owe (o-ve)pl. f. pron. that
owczesny (oov-ches-ni) adj. m. the then;of those days
owdzie (oov-dzhe) adv. else-where; there
pa ! (pa) excl.: bye-bye !
pacha (pa-kha) f. armpit
pachnąc (pakh-nownch) v. smell (good) ;have a fragrance
pacholek (pa-kho-wek) m. boy; page;servant:menial; flunkey
pachwina (pakh-vee-na) f. groin
pacierz (pa-chesh) m. prayer
pacierzowy stos (pa-che-zho-vi stos) spinal column; spine
paciorki (pa-chor-kee) pl. string of beads ;short prayer
pacjent (pats-yent) m. patient
pacyfista (pa-tsi-fees-ta) m. pacifist ;believer in peace
pacyfizm (pa-tsi-feezm) m. pacifism; ideology of peace
paczka (pach-ka) f. parcel

paczyc (pa-chich) v. warp
padac (pa-dach) v. fall down
padalec (pa-da-lets) m. blind-worm; slow warm
padlina (pad-lee-na) f. carrion
pagorek (pa-goo-rek) m. hill
pająk (pa-yownk) m. spider
pajęczyna (pa-yan-chi-na) f. cobweb ; spider web;gossamer
paka (pa-ka) f. crate ;lock-up
pakowac (pa-ko-vach) v. pack; cram; wrap ; pack off; pack up
pakunek (pa-koo-nek) m. baggage
pal (pal) m. pile ; stake;picket
palący (pa-lown-tsi) m. smoker
palec (pa-lets) m. finger : toe
palenie (pa-le-ne) n. smoking
palenisko (pa-le-nees-ko) n. hearth ; fireplace; grate
paleta (pa-le-ta) f. palette
palic (pa-leech) v. burn; smoke cigarette; heat;scorch;shoot
paliwo (pa-lee-vo) n. fuel
palma (pal-ma) f. palm-tree
palnik (pal-neek) m. burner
palto (pal-to) n. overcoat
pałac (pa-wats) m. palace
pałka (paw-ka) f. stick; club
pamflet (pam-flet) m. pamphlet
pamiątka (pa-myownt-ka) f. souvenir; token of remembrance
pamięc (pa-myanch) f. memory
pamiętac (pa-myan-tach) v. re-member; recall;be careful
pamiętnik (pa-myant-neek) m. diary; memoirs; album
pan (pan) m. lord ; master; mister; you ;gentleman: squire
pan młody (pan mwo-di) m. bride-groom; man about to be married
pani (pa-nee) f. lady; you; madam ; mistress(in school etc.)
panika (pa-nee-ka) f. panic: scare
panna (pan-na) f. miss; girl:lass
panna młoda (pan-na mwo-da) f, bride; woman about to be married
panoszyc się (pa-no-shich shan) v. domineer ; boss : run the show
panowac (pa-no-vach) v. rule; reign; be master of; command;rife
panteizm (pan-te-eezm) m. pan-theism

pantera (pan-té-ra) f. panther
pantoflarz (pan-to-flash) m.
 henpecked husband·
pantofel (pan-to-fel) m. slipper;
 shoe; light low shoe
pantomima (pan-to-mée-ma) f.
 pantomime; gestures no words
panujący (pa-noo-yówn-tsi) adj.
 m. prevailing; ruling
pański (pań-skee) adj. m.
 lord's; your's
państwo (pań-stvo) n. state;
 married couple
papa (pá-pa) f. feltpaper
papier (pá-pyer) m. paper
papieros (pa-pyé-ros) m. cigarette;tabacco rolled in paper
papieski (pa-pyés-kee) adj. m.
 papal; of the Pope
papież (pá-pyesh) m. pope
papka (pap-ka) f. pulp; mash;
 pap; gruel; paste; slurry
paplać (pap-lach) v. prattle
paproć (pá-proch) f. fern
papryka (pa-pri-ka) f. red-
 pepper; paprica· paprika
papuga (pa-poo-ga) f. parrot
para 1. (pá-ra) f. couple
para 2. (pá-ra) f. steam
parabola (pa-ra-bó-la) f. parabola
parada (pa-rá-da) f. parade
paradoks (pa-rá-doks) m. para-
 dox; apparent contradiction
parafia (pa-ráf-ya) f. parish
parafina (pa-ra-fée-na) f.
 paraffin(waxy petroleum)
paragraf (pa-rá-graf) m. para-
 graph(a distinct section)
paraliż (pa-rá-leesh) m. paralysis;crippling of activities
parametr (pa-rá-metr) m. para-
 meter;element of an orbit
parapet (pa-ra-pet) m. window-
 sill; stool· rail; breastwork
parasol (pa-ra-sol) m. umbrella
parawan (pa-ra-van) n. screen
parcelować (par-tse-ló-vach) v.
 parcel out(land);cut up
parcie (pár-che) n. thrust
park (párk) m. park
parkan (pár-kan) m. fence; net;
 hoarding

parlament (par-lá-ment) m.
 parliament; national legislature
parny (pár-ni) adj. m. sultry
parobek (pa-ró-bek) m. farmhand; plough man; rustic
parodia (pa-ród-ya) f. parody
parokrotnie (pa-ro-krót-ńe) adv.
 repeatedly; a couple of times
parostatek (pa-ro-stá-tek) m.
 steamboat; steamer; steamship
parować (pa-ró-vach) v. evaporate; vaporize; cook by steam
parowiec (pa-ró-vyets) m. steamboat; steamer; steamship
parowóz (pa-ró-voos) m. steam
 locomotive : railroad engine
parów (pa-roov) m. ravine
parówki (pa-roóv-kee) pl. hot
 dogs; sausages; frankfurters
parszywy (par-shi-vi) adj. m.
 mangy; scabby; lousy; horrid
partacki (par-tats-kee) adj. m.
 bungled up; botched;fudged
partacz (pár-tach) m. bungler
parter (pár-ter) m. ground
 floor; first floor; parterre
partia (párt-ya) f. party; card
 game; political party; game
partner (párt-ner) m. partner
partyjny (par-tíy-ni) adj. m.
 party(member); party member
partykuła (par-ti-koó-wa) f.
 particle;
partyzantka (par-ti-zánt-ka)
 f. guerrilla; partisan war
parytet (pa-ri-tet) m. parity
parzyć (pá-zhich) v. scald;
 steam; burn; percolate; couple
parzysty numer (pa-zhis-ti noó-
 mer) even number
pas (pas) m. belt; traffic lane
pasat (pá-sat) m. trade wind
pasażer (pa-sá-zher) m. passenger : chap: fellow; liner
pasek (pá-sek) m. belt; band
pasieka (pa-shé-ka) f. apiary
pasierb (pá-sherb) m. stepson
pasierbica (pa-sher-bée-tsa) f.
 step daughter
pasja (pás-ya) f. passion
paskarz (pás-kash) m. profiteer
pasmo (pás-mo) n. streak; tract;
 range; traffic lane

pasożyt (pa-só-zhit) m. parasite ; sponger
pasta (pás-ta) f. paste
pasterka (pas-tér-ka) f. midnight mass; shepherdess
pasterz (pás-tesh) m. shepherd
pastwa (pás-tva) f. prey
pastwisko (pas-tveés-ko) n.
pasture ; grassland
pastylka (pas-til-ka) f. tablet
pasywny (pa-sív-ni) adj. m.
passive; acted upon
pasza (pa-sha) f. fodder
paszcza (pásh-cha) f. jaw
paszport (pásh-port) m. passport ; certificate
paść (pashćh) v. fall down;
graze ; tend cattle; feed
patelnia (pa-tél-ña) f. frying-
pan with a handle
patent (pá-tent) m. patent
patetyczny (pa-te-tich-ni) adj.
m. pathetic ; pompous; turgid
patolog (pa-to-lok) m. patholo-
gist ; specialist in pathology
patriarcha (pa-tree-ar-kha) m.
patriarch
patriota (pa-tree-o-ta) m.
patriot
patron (pá-tron) m. sponsor;
stencil; pattern ; protector
patronat (pa-tró-nat) m.patron-
age :power to grant favors
patroszyc (pa-tro-shich) v.
disembowel; gut ; draw (a fowl)
patrzec (pá-tzhech) v. look
patyk (pá-tik) m. stick
patyna (pa-tí-na) f. patina
pauza (páw-za) f. pause
paw (pav) m. peacock
paznokieć (paz-nó-kyeéh) m.
(finger) nail ; toe nail
pazur (pá-zoor) m. claw
paż (pash) m. page
październik (pazh-dzhér-ñeek)m.
October
pączek (pown-chek) m. bud
pąsowy (pown-só-vi) adj. m. red;
crimson : bright red;poppy red
pchać (pkhaćh) v. push; thrust
pchła (pkhwa) f. flea
pchnięcie (pkhñáñ-che) n. push;
thrust; jostle : shove: lunge

pech (pekh) m. bad luck
pechowiec (pe-khó-vyets) m.
unlucky fellow; lackless chap
pedagog (pe-dá-gok) m. peda-
gogue; educator: educationist
pedał (pé-daw) m. l. pedal;
2. gay; homosexual; pansy boy
pedant (pé-dant) m. pedant
pejcz (peych) m. horsewhip
pejzaż (péy-zash) m. landscape
peleryna (pe-le-rí-na) f. cape
pelikan (pe-leé-kan) m. pelican
pełnia (péw-ña) f. fullness
pełnic (péw-ñeech) v. fulfill
pełno (péw-no) adv. plenty
pełnoletni (pew-no-lét-ñee) adj.
m. adult; of age
pełnomocnictwo (pew-no-mots-
ñeets-tvo) n. power of attorney ; full powers (legal)
pełhy (péw-ni) adj. m. full
pełzać (péw-zach) v. creep;
crawl; fawn; drag: cringe
penicylina (pe-ñee-tsi-leé-na)
f. penicillin
pensja (pén-sya) f. salary;
pension; allowance; wages
pensjonat (pen-syó-nat) m.
boarding house
perfidny (per-feéd-ni) adj. m.
perfidious; double dealing
perfumy (per-foo-mi) pl. scent;
perfume; perfumes
pergamin (per-gá-meen) m.
parchment: sheep skin
period (pér-yod) m. period
perkal (pér-kal) m. calico
perła (pér-wa) f. pearl
peron (pé-ron) m. train- platform at railroad station
perski (pér-skee) adj. m. Per-
sian; Iranian; of Iran
personalny (per-so-nál-ni) adj.
m. personal; personnel officer
personel (per-só-nel) m. staff;
personnel; employees
perspektywa (per-spek-tí-va) f.
perspective;sense of pornortion
perswazja (per-sváz-ya) f. persuasion; power of persuading
pertraktacja (per-trak-táts-ya)
f. negotiation; parley
peruka (pe-roó-ka) f. wig

peruwiański (pe-roo-vyań-skee) adj. m. Peruvian: of Peru

peryskop (pe-rís-kop) m.periscope

pestka (pést-ka) f. kernel;pip; drupe; stone; trifle

pesymista (pe-si-meés-ta) m. pessimist

petent (pé-tent) m. petitioner

pewien (pé-vyen) adj. m. certain; one; a; an; some; sure

pewnik (pév-ńeek) m. axiom

pewniak (pev-ńak) m. cinch; surefooted man; certainty

pewny (pév-ni) adj. m. sure; secure; dependable· safe

pęcak (pań-tsak) m. peeled barley; hulled barley

pęcherz (pań-khesh) m. bladder

pęczniec (pańch-ńech) v. swell

pęd (pańd) m. rush; dash; run; speed;impetus;urge;shoot;sprout

pędzel (pań-dzel) m. (paint) brush; tuft of hair

pędzic (pań-dżeech) v. drive; run; lead; distill;hurry

pęk (pańk) m. bunch

pękac (pań-kach) v. burst;split; crack:go off; burst; snap

pępek (pań-pek) m. navel

pętac (pań-tach) v. shackle; hobble;knock about

pętak (pań-tak) m. squirt

pętelka (pań-tél-ka) f. loop; noose; knot

piac (pyach) v. crow ; sing

piana (pya-na) f. foam

pianino (pya-ńee-no) n. piano

piasek (pya-sek) m. sand

piasta (pyas-ta) f. hub; nave

piastowac (pyas-to-vach) v. nurse; tend; hold

piąc się(pyównch shań)v.climb

piątek (pyówn-tek) m. Friday

piątka (pyównt-ka) f. five

piąty (pyówn-ti) num. fifth

picie (peé-che) n. drinking

pic (peech) v. drink; booze

picuś (peé-tsoosh) m. dandy

piec (pyets) m. stove; oven; furnace; kitchen stove; kiln

piec (pyets) v. bake; roast ; burn; scorch; sting; smart

piechota (pye-kho-ta) m. infantry ;a variety of beans

piechotą (pye-kho-tówn) adv. on foot; (go) on foot

piecza (pyé-cha) f. care; charge

pieczarka (pye-chár-ka) f. meadow mushroom

pieczątka (pye-chównt-ka) f. seal; stamp; signet

pieczen wołowa (pye-cheń vo-wó-va) f. roast beef

pieczyste (pye-chis-te) n. roast meat; meat course; joint; roast

pieczywo (pye-chi-vo) n. bakery-goods; bread; baking

pieg (pyeg) m. freckle ;ephelis

piegowaty (pye-go-vá-ti) adj. m. freckled

piekarnia (pye-kár-ńa) f. bakery; baker's shop

piekarz (pyé-kash) m. baker

piekielny (pye-kél-ni) adj. m. infernal; of hell; hellish

piekło (pyék-wo) n. hell

pielęgniarka (pye-lańg-ńár-ka) f. nurse; hospital nurse

pielęgnowac (pye-lańg-no-vach) v. nurse; tend; care;cultivate

pielgrzym (pyél-gzhim) m. pilgrim :wanderer to holy place

pielucha (pye-loo-kha) f. diaper; baby's napkin

pieniądz (pye-ńównts) m. money; coin; currency; funds

pienic (pye-ńeech) v. foam; sparkle; cover with foam

pieniężny (pye-ńanzh-ni) adj. m. monetary; pecuniary;moneyed

pien (pyeń) m. trunk; stem; stump ; snag; stock; root

pieprz (pyepsh) m. pepper

pierdziec (pyér-dzhech) v. fart (vulg.): stink up

pierdzioch (pyér-dżhokh)m. old fart (vulg.); old stinker

piernat (pyer-nat) m. feather-bed ; bedding

piernik (pyer-ńeek) m. ginger-bread; duffer

piers (pyersh) f. breast:chest

pierscien (pyérsh-cheń) m. ring

pierścionek (pyersh-chó-nek) m. ring (small)

pierwej (pyer-vey) adv. of
first; sooner; before; first
pierwiastek (pyer-vyas-tek) m.
root; element; radical
pierworodny (pyer-vo-rod-ni)
adj. m. firstborn
pierwotny (pyer-vot-ni) adj.
m. primitive; primary;original
pierwszeństwo (pyerv-sheń-stvo)
n. priority; precedence
pierwszy (pyer-vshi) num. first
pierzchać (pyezh-khach) v. run
away;fly;flee; disperse;scutter
pierze (pye-zhe) n. feathers
pierzyna (pye-zhi-na) f.feather-
bed; eider down; quilt
pies (pyes) m. dog
pieszczota (pyesh-cho-ta) f.
caress; endearment
pieszo (pye-sho) adv. on foot
pieścić (pyesh-cheech) v. fondle;caress;pet;hug; babble
pieśń (pyeshń) f. song
pietruszka (pyet-roosh-ka) f.
parsley
pięciobój (pyań-cho-booy) m.
pentathlon
pięcioletni (pyań-cho-lét-nee)
adj. m. five year old
pięć (pyańch) num. five
piędź (pyandzh) m. palm; span
pięćdziesiąt (pyań-dzhe-shownt)
num. fifty
pięćset (pyańch-set) num. five-
hundred
piękność (pyank-noshch) f.
beauty; good looks; loveliness
piękny (pyan-kni) adj. m.beau-
tiful; lovely; fine:handsome
pieściarz (pyansh-chash) m.
boxer ; pugilist
pieść (pyańshch) f. fist
pieściarstwo (pyansh-char-stvo)
m. box; boxing; pugilism
pięta (pyan-ta) f. heel
piętnastoletni (pyańt-nas-to-
lét-ni) adj. m. fifteen years
old
piętnasty (pyańt-nasti) num.
fifteenth
piętnaście (pyańt-nash-che) num.
fifteen
piętno (pyańt-no) n. mark;stig-
ma; brand; stamp; impress

piętro (pyańt-ro) n. story;
floor ;storey
piętrzyć (pyańt-zhich) v. pile
up ; bank up;heap; accumulate
pigułka (pee-goow-ka) f. pill
pijak (pee-yak) m. drunk
pijany (pee-ya-ni) adj. m.
drunk ; tipsy; intoxicated;elated
pijawka (pee-yav-ka) f. leech
pikantny (pee-kant-ni) adj. m.
spicy; piquant; pungent; sharp
piknik (peek-neek) m. picnic
pilnik (peel-neek) m. file
pilność (peel-noshch) f. diligence; urgency;industry: care
pilny (peel-ni) adj. m. diligent; urgent; industrious:careful
pilot (pee-lot) m. pilot
pilśń (peelshń) f. felt
piła (pee-wa) f. saw; bore
piłka (peew-ka) f. ball; hand-
saw : football; socker; shot
piłować (pee-wo-vach) v. file;
saw : bore; rasp
pingwin (peen-gveen) m. penguin
piołunówka (pyo-woo-noov-ka) f.
absinth flavored liqueur
pion (pyon) m. plumb (line)
pionek (pyo-nek) m. pawn
pionier (pyo-ner) m. pioneer
pionowy (pyo-no-vi) adj. m.
vertical; upright; plumb
piorun (pyo-roon) m. thunder-
bolt; lightning shaft
piorunochron (pyo-roo-no-khron)
m. lightning-rod
piosenka (pyo-sen-ka) f. song
piórko (pyoor-ko) n. (small)
feather; pen ; plumelet
pióro (pyoo-ro) n. feather; pen
piramida (pee-ra-mee-da) f.
pyramid
pirat (pee-rat) m. pirate
pirotechnika (pee-ro-tekh-nee-
ka) f. pyrotechnics
pisać (pee-sach) v. write
pisarz (pee-sash) m. writer
pisemnie (pee-sem-ne) adv. in
writing; in black and white
pisk (peesk) m. squeal
piskliwy (peesk-lee-vi) adj. m.
shrill; squeaky; thin; strident;
piping; reedy

pisklę (peesk-lą̃n) n. chicken;
nestling; squealer
piskorz (pees-kosh) m.loach;eel
pismo (pees-mo) n. writing;
letter; newspaper; scripture;
alphabet; type; print
pisownia (pee-sóv-ña) f. spelling; orthography
pistolet (pees-tó-let) m. pistol; handgun ; gun ; spray gun
pisuar (pee-soo-ar) m. urinal
piszczeć (peesh-chech) v.creak:
squeak; screech; squeal;peep
piszczel (peesh-chel) m. shin-
bone; tibia; blow pipe
piśmiennictwo (peesh-myen-ñeets-
tvo) n. literature
piśmiennie (peesh-myen-ñe) adv.
in writing;in black and white
piwiarnia (pee-vyár-ña) f.
beer hall;beer house;saloon
piwnica (peev-ñee-tsa) f. cellar; basement; coal cellar
piwny (peev-ni) adj. m. brown
(color); hazel; beer-
piwo (pee-vo) n. beer
piwonia (pee-vó-ña) f. peony
piwowar (pee-vó-var) m. brewer
piżama (pee-zhá-ma) f. pyjamas
plac (plats) m. square; area;
ground;building site; field
plac boju (plats bó-yoo) battle
field; field of battle
placek (plá-tsek) m. cake; pie
placówka (pla-tsoóv-ka) f.
sentry; post; outpost;agency
plaga (plá-ga) f. plague
plagiator (plag-yá-tor) m.
plagiarist
plakat (plá-kat) m. poster
plama (plá-ma) f. blot; stain
plamić (plá-meech) v. blot;
stain; soil; tarnish; defile
plan (plan) m. plan; design;map
planeta (pla-né-ta) f. planet
planować (pla-nó-vach) v. plan
planowo (pla-nó-vo) adv. according to plan; systematically
plantacja (plan-táts-ya) f.
plantation
plaster (plás-ter) m. plaster;
patch; tape; adhesive; slice

plastyczne sztuki (plas-tích-ne
shtoó-kee) fine arts
plastyczny (plas-tích-ni) adj.
m. plastic; artistic; vivid
plastyk (plás-tik) m. artist;
plastic (substance)
platerować (pla-te-ró-vach) v.
plate (with an other metal)
platforma (plat-fór-ma) f. platform :truck; lorry; shelf
platoniczny (pla-to-ñeech-ni)
adj. m. Platonic;unsubstantial
platyna (pla-tí-na) f. platinum
plazma (pláz-ma) f. plasma
plaża (plá-zha) f. beach
plażować(pla-zho-vach)v.sun-bathe
plądrować (plown-dró-vach) v.
plunder; ransack
pląsy (plown-si) pl. dance
plątać (plówn-tach) v. entangle
plebania (ple-bá-ña) f. rectory
plebiscyt (ple-bées-cit) m. pleb-
iscite; people's direct vote
plecak (ple-tsak) m. rucksack
plecionka (ple-chón-ka) f. plaid
braid; wattle; basket work
plecy (ple-tsi) pl. back;backing
pleć (plech) v. weed (a garden)
plemienny (ple-myen-ni) adj. m.
tribal; of a trbe
plemię (ple-myą̃) n. tribe
plemnik (plém-ñeek) m. sperm
plenum (ple-noom) n. plenary
session; plenary assembly
pleść (pleshch) v. twist; blab;
weave;interlace; talk nonsense
pleśnieć (plesh-ñech) v. mold
pletwa (plét-va) f. fin;dovetail
plewić (ple-veech) v. weed
plik (pleek) m. bundle; sheaf
plisa (plee-sa) f. pleat
plomba (plom-ba) f. lead seal;
tooth filling; stopping
plon (plon) m. crop;yield
plotka (plót-ka) f. gossip; rumor; piece of gossip
pluć (plooch) v. spit; abuse
plugawy (ploo-gá-vi) adj. m.
filthy; squalid;foul;obscene
plus (ploos) m. plus; asset
plusk (ploosk) m. splash
pluskać (ploos-kach) v. splash

pluskiewka (ploos-kev-ka) f. thumbtack;drawing pin

pluskwa (ploos-kva) f. bedbug

plusz (ploosh) m. plush

plutokracja (ploo-to-kráts-ya) f. plutocracy

pluton (ploo-ton) m. platoon

plwocina (plvo-chee-na) f. spittle;expectoration; spit

płaca (pwa-tsa) f. wage;salary

płachta (pwakh-ta) f. sheet

płacić (pwa-cheech) v. pay

płacz (pwach) m. cry; weep

płakać (pwa-kach) v. cry; weep

płaski (pwas-kee) adj. m. flat

płaskorzeźba (pwas-ko-zhezh-ba) f. (bas) relief; bas-relief

płaskowyż (pwas-kóvish) m. plateau; table land

płaszcz (pwashch) m. overcoat

płaszczyć (pwash-chich) v. flatten; become flat;fall flat

płaszczyzna (pwash-chiz-na) f. plane;surface;area;sheet;plain

płat (pwat) m. slice; lobe

płatać (pwa-tach) v. cut; play (tricks);slice;split;fell

płatek (pwa-tek) m. flake

płatność (pwat-noshch) f. payment ; remittance

pławić (pwa-veech) v. float; wallow : duck; drown;soak

płaz (pwas) m. reptile

płaz (pwas) m. flat of sabre

płciowy (pwcho-vi) adj. m. sexual: genital; sex-(urge etc.)

płeć (pwech) f. sex; complexion

płetwa (pwet-va) f. fin

płochliwy (pwo-khlee-vi) adj. m. timid ; shy; skittish

płochy (pwo-khi) adj. m. frivolous ;shy;timid;fickle

płodny (pwod-ni) adj. m. fertile ;productive; prolific

płodzić (pwo-dżheech)v. beget

płomień (pwo-myeń) m. flame

płonąć (pwo-nownch) v.be on fire :blaze;be inflamed;glow

płonny (pwon-ni) adj. m. sterile ;useless;vain;of no avail

płoszyć (pwo-shich) v. frighten

płot (pwot) m. fence ;hoarding

płowieć (pwo-vyech) v. fade

płowy (pwó-vi) adj. m. flaxen; fair; buff; fallow; fawn

płód (pwoot) m. fetus; fruit

płócienny (pwoo-chen-ni) adj. m. linen; canvas-(sail,shoes etc.)

płótno (pwoot-no) n. linen;canvas

płuco (pwoo-tso) n. lung

płucny (pwoots-ni) adj. m. pulmonary

pług (pwook) m. plough; plow

płukać (pwoo-kach) v. rinse; wash; gargle

płyn (pwin) m. liquid: fluid

płynąć (pwi-nownch) v. flow; swim; sail; drift; go by;come

płynny (pwin-ni) adj. m. liquid; fluent; fluid;smooth;graceful

płyta (pwi-ta) f, plate; slab; disk; sheet: board;record

płyta gramofonowa (pwi-ta gramofo-no-va) f. (musical) record : disk

płytki (pwit-kee) adj. m. shallow; flat; trivial; poinless

pływać (pwi-vach) v. swim; float; navigate; be afloat; be evasive

pływak (pwi-vak) m. swimmer; float; quibler; buoy

pniak (pńak) m. stump; trunk

po (po) prep. after; to; up to; till; upon; for; at; in; up; of; next; along; about; over; past; behind : as far as

pobicie (po-bee-che) n. battery

pobić (po-beech) v. beat up; defeat ; beat in; thrash; spank

pobielac (po-bye-lach) v. whiten; tin : make white; paint white

pobierać (po-bye-rach) v. take; collect ; receive;get;draw:charge

pobliski (pob-lees-kee) adj. m. nearby ; neighboring

pobłażać (po-bwa-zhach) v. indulge; forbear ; be tolerant

pobłażliwy (po-bwazh-lee-vi) adj. m. lenient ; forgiving

poboczny (po-boch-ni) adj. m. lateral; secondary ; accessory

poborca (po-bor-tsa) m. (tax) collector : tax gatherer

poborowy (po-bo-ro-vi) m. recruit ; recruiting

pobory (po-bó-ri) pl. salary
pobrać (po-brach) v. receive;
collect; get: draw; gather
pobudka (po-bood-ka) f. incen-
tive; motive; reveille
pobudliwy (po-bood-lee-vi) adj.
m. excitable: ebullient
pobyt (pó-bit) m. stay; visit
pocałować (po-tsa-wó-vach) v.
kiss; give a kiss
pocałunek (po-tsa-woo-nek) m.
kiss; caress with the lips
pochlebiać (po-khle-byach) v.
flatter: adulate: expect:fawn
pochlebny (po-khleb-ni) adj. m.
flattering; complimentary
pochłaniać (po-khwa-ñach) v.
absorb: swallow up;engulf
pochmurny (po-khmoor-ni) adj.
m. gloomy; cloudy: overcast
pochodnia (po-khód-ña) f. torch
pochodny (po-khód-ni) adj. m.
derivative: derived
pochodzenie (po-kho-dze-ñe) n.
origin; descent; source
pochopny (po-khop-ni) adj. m.
hasty; eager; rush: ready
pochować (po-kho-vach) v. bury
pochód (pó-khoot) m. march;
procession; parade ‗vagina
pochwa (pókh-va) f. sheath;
pochwała (po-khva-wa) f. praise:
eulogy; approval: applause
pochylić (po-khi-leech) v. incline; slope: slant: droop
pochyły (po-khi-wi) adj. m. inclined; stooped: sloping:oblique
pociąć (pó-chównch) v. cut up;
slash; sting; saw up:intersect
pociąg (póch-ównk) m. train;
affinity; inclination
pociągać (po-chówn-gach) v.pull:
draw; attract;tug: attract:coat
pociągnięcie (po-chówng-ñań-che)
n. pull; move: stroke: pluck
po cichu (po chee-khoo) adv.
secretly; silently; softly
pocić (pó-cheech) v. sweat
pociecha (po-che-kha) f. comfort; joy:solace: satisfaction
po ciemku (po chem-koo) adv.
in the dark:while in the dark
pocierać (po-che-rach) v. rub

pocieszać (po-che-shach) v. console; comfort;cheer up; solace
pocieszenie (po-che-she-ñe) n.
consolation: comfort; solace
pocieszny (po-chesh-ni) adj. m.
funny; amusing;droll; comic
pocisk (po-cheesk) m. missile;
bullet; projectile
po co ? (po tso) what for ?
począć (po-chównch) v. begin;
conceive; become pregnant
początek (po-chówn-tek) m. beginning; start:outset;fore-part
początkujący (po-chównt-koo-
yówn-tsi) m. beginner
poczciwy (poch-chee-vi) adj. m.
good-hearted ; friendly ;kindly
poczekać (po-che-kach) v. wait
poczekalnia (po-che-kal-ña) f.
waiting room
poczęstować (po-chań-stó-vach)
v. treat: entertain; serve
poczęstunek (po-chań-stoo-nek)
m. treat; drinks; entertainment
poczta (póch-ta) f. post; mail
pocztówka (poch-toóv-ka) f.
postcard: picture postcard
poczucie (po-choo-che) n. feeling; sense; consciousness
poczwórny (po-chvoor-ni) adj.
m. fourfold;four times as large,
as tall;as long,as strong,as big
poczynać (po-chi-nach) v. begin
(aggressively); conceive
poczytalny (po-chi-tal-ni) adj.
m. accountable; sane
poczytny (po-chit-ni) adj. m.
popular (book):widely read
pod (pod) prep. under; below;
towards; on; in ; underneath
podać (po-dach) v. give; hand;
pass ;serve: shake (hand)
podanie (po-dá-ñe) n. application : request; legend
podarek (po-da-rek) m. gift
podarty (po-dár-ti) adj. m. torn
podatek (po-dá-tek) m. tax ;duty
podatnik (po-dat-ñeek) m. taxpayer; rate payer
podaż (pó-dazh) f. supply
podążać (po-dówn-zhach) v. make
for; draw to: make ons's way
podbicie (pod-bee-che) n. conquest; instep; lining ;ceiling

podbiec (pod-byets) v. run up
podbiegunowy (pod-bye-goo-nó-vi) adj. m. polar;near pole
podbój (pod-booy) m. conquest
podbudowa (pod-boo-dó-va) f. substructure; base course
podbródek (pod-broo-dek) m. chin ; bib; feeder
podburzać (pod-boo-zhach) v. stir up ; incite to revolt
podchmielony (pod-khmye-ló-ni) adj. m. tipsy ; in drink
podchodzić (pod-khó-dzheech)v. approach ; assume an attitude
podchwycić (pod-khvi-cheech) v. catch up ; snatch up; spot
podchwytliwy (pod-khvit-lee-vi) adj. m. captious (question etc.)
podciągać (pod-chown-gach) v. draw up ;pull up;improve;class
podczas (pod-chas) prep. during; while;when; whereas
podczerwony (pod-cher-vó-ni) adj. m. infrared
poddać (pod-dach) v. surrender; suggest ;submit; expose
pod dostatkiem (pod dos-tat-kyem) adv. plenty; enough
podejmować (po-dey-mó-vach) v. take up; entertain ;pick up
podejrzany (po-dey-zha-ni) adj. m. suspect ;suspicious; shady
podejrzliwy (po-dey-zhlee-vi) adj. m. suspicious ;distrustful
podeptać (po-dep-tach) v. tramp (under foot);bustle about
poderwać (po-der-vach) v. jerk up; pick up; weaken ;rouse
podeszwa (po-desh-va) f. sole
podginać (pod-gée-nach) v. tuck up; cock ;turn up; bend(a knee)
podglądać (pod-glown-dach) v. spy; peep ; pry; snoop
podgórski (pod-goor-skee) adj. m. foot-hill ;piedmont
podjechać (pod-ye-khach) v. drive up ;ride uphill; come up
podgrzewać (pod-gzhé-vach) v. warm up ; heat up;
podjudzać (pod-yoo-dzach) v. stir up; incite (to evil)
podkasać (pod-ká-sach) v. tuck up ; turn up; rise

podkład (pod-kwat) m. base; railroad tie;undercurrent;bedding
podkładać (pod-kwa-dach) v. lay under; put under;plant as evidence
podkop (pod-kop) m. mine; sap
podkowa (pod-kó-va) f. horse-shoe; semicircle
podkradać (pod-krá-dach) v. thieve; pilfer; creep up
podkreślać (pod-kresh-lach) v. stress underline; emphasize; accentuate
podkuwać (pod-koo-vach) v. shoe(horse) ;hopnail a shoe; cram
podlegać (pod-le-gach) v. be subject; be liable;succomb;undergo
podległość (pod-leg-woshch) f. dependence; subjection;subordination
podlewać (pod-le-vach) v. water
podlizywać się (pod-lee-zi-vach shan) v. suck up to;make up to
podlotek (pod-ló-tek) f. fledg-ling; flapper;girl in her teens
podłoga (pod-wo-ga) f. floor
podłość (pod-woshch) f. meanness
podług (pod-wook) prep. : according to;in conformity with
podłużny (pod-woozh-ni) adj. m. oblong; longitudinal; elongated
podły (pod-wi) adj. m. mean
podmiejski (pod-myey-skee) adj. m. suburban
podminować (pod-mee-nó-vach) v. undermine; sap
podmiot (pod-myot) m. subject
podmuch (pod-mookh) m. gust; blow; puff; waft; breath;blast
podmywać (pod-mi-vach) v. wash under; sap ; undermine;wash away
podniebienie (pod-ne-bye-ne) n. palate ;roof of the mouth
podniecać (pod-ne-tsach) v.flurry excite ;agitate;rouse;egg on
podnieść (pod-neshch) v. lift; hoist ;rise;elevate;rear;incerease
podnieta (pod-ne-ta) f. stimu-lus :impulse;spur;stimulant
podniosły (pod-nos-wi) adj. m. sublime ;elevated; lofty
podnosić (pod-no-sheech) v. hoist; raise; lift; take up ; elevate
podnóżek (pod-noo-zhek) m. foot-stool; ottoman ;leg rest

podobać się (po-dó-bach shãn) v. please; be attractive;like

podobny (po-dób-ni) adj. m. similar; like; congenial

podoficer (pod-o-fee-tser) m. noncommissioned officer

podołać (po-dó-wach) v. be up to;be equal to;cope;manage

podomka (po-dom-ka) f. house-robe; dressing gown

podówczas (pod-oóv-chas) adv. at that time;at the time;then

podpadać (pod-pá-dach) v. be spotted; fall under a category

podpalenie (pod-pa-le-ñe) n. arson; setting of fire

podpatrzyc (pod-pá-tzhich) v. spy; peep; find out; pry

podpierać (pod-pyé-rach) v. prop up ; support; bolster

podpinac (pod-pée-nach) v.pin; buckle up; strap;fasten;gird

podpis (pód-pees) m. signature

podpływać (pod-pwi-vach) v. swim up; sail up; row up

podpora (pod-pó-ra) f. prop

podporucznik (pod-po-roóch-ñeek) m. second lieutenant

podporządkować (pod-po-zhõwnt-ko-vach) v. subordinate,

podprowadzic (pod-pro-vá-dzheech) v. bring near

podpułkownik (pod-poow-kóv-ñeek) m. lieutenant colonel

podrażnic (pod-rázh-ñeech) v. displease; irritate;vex;gall

podręcznik (pod-rãnch-ñeek) m. handbook; textbook; manual

podrożec (pod-ró-zhech) v. go up; grow dear; rise in price

podróż (pód-roozh) f. travel; voyage; journey; passage

podróżnik (pod-roozh-ñeek) m. traveler; voyager; wayfarer

po drugie (po droo-ge) adv. in the second place; second

podrzec (pód-zhech) v. tear up

podrzędny (pod-zhãnd-ni) adj. m. subordinate; secondary

podsądny (pod-sõwnd-ni) m. defendant; the person sued

podskakiwac (pod-ska-kée-vach) v. leap; jump up;hop;skip

podsłuch (pód-swookh) m. eaves-dropping; wire tapping;listen in

podstawa (pod-stá-va) f. base; basis;footing;mount;principle

podstawić (pod-stá-veech) v. substitute;put under;bring round

podstęp (pód-stãnp) m.trick;ruse; guile; deceit;piece of deceit

podstępny (pod-stãnp-ni) adj. m. deceitful; tricky; crafty;insidious

podstrzygać (pod-stzhi-gach) v. trim the hair; shorten the hair

podsuwac (pod-soó-vach) v. push near; plant; suggest; slip under

podsycac (pod-sí-tsach) v. fo-ment; feed; fan (a quarrel etc.)

podsypywac (pod-si-pi-vach) v. pour (sand etc.);strew; sprinkle

podszept (pod-shept) m. sugges-tion; prompting; insinuation

podszeptywac (pod-shep-ti-vach) v. prompt; suggest;hint;insinuate

podszewka (pod-shév-ka) f. lin-ing ; inside information

podswiadomy (pod-shvya-dó-mi) adj. m. subconscious(mental process)

podupadac (pod-oo-pá-dach) v. decline; deteriorate;fall into decay

poduszka (po-doósh-ka) f. pillow; pad; cushion; ball (of the thumb)

podwajac (pod-vá-yach) v. double; duplicate; increase twofold

podważyc (pod-vá-zhich) v. lever up; pry up; shake(an opinion)

podwiązka (pod-vyówns-ka) f. garter; suspender; ligature

podwieczorek (pod-vye-cho-rek) m. afternoon tea; afternoon snack

podwiezc (pód-vyezhch) v. give a ride; give a lift(in one's car)

podwładny (pod-vwad-ni) adj. m. subordinate (to somebody);inferior

podwodna łódz (pod-vód-na woodźh) f. submarine (under water warship)

podwoic (pod-vo-ęech)v. double

podwozie (pod-vó-zhe) n. chassis

podworko (pod-voór-ko) n. back-yard ;farmyard; court;courtyard

podwyżka (pod-vizh-ka) f. raise

podzelowac (pod-ze-ló-vach) v. resole (shoes, boots, foot ware)

podziac (po-dźhach) v. loose

podział (pó-dźhaw) m. division

podziałka (po-dzhaw-ka) f.
scale; graduation; division
podzielac (po-dzhe-lach) v.
share; participate; concur
podzielic (po-dzhe-leech) v.
divide (into parts)
podzielny (po-dzhel-ni) adj. m.
adj. m. divisible (easily)
podziemie (pod-zhem-ye) n.base-
ment; underworld
podziemny (pod-zhem-ni) adj. m.
underground; secret
podziękowac (po-dzhan-ko-vach)
v. thank; decline with thanks
podziewac (po-dzhe-vach) v.
loose; mislay; leave somewhere
podziw (po-dzheef) m. admiration; wander
podzwrotnikowy (pod-zvrot-nee-
ko-vi) adj. m. tropical
podżegacz (pod-zhe-gach) m. instigator; warmonger; abettor
poemat (po-e-mat) m. poem
poeta (po-e-ta) m. poet
poetka (po-et-ka) f. poet
poezja (po-ez-ya) f. poetry
pogadanka (po-ga-dan-ka) f,
talk; chat; chatty lecture
poganiac (po-ga-nach) v. drive;
egg on; urge on; prod on; hustle
poganin (po-ga-neen) m. pagan
pogarda (po-gar-da) f. contempt
pogarszac (po-gar-shach) v.
make worse; aggravate; worsen
pogawędka (po-ga-vand-ka) f.
chat; chit-chat
pogląd (po-glownd) m. opinion
pogłębiac (po-gwanb-yach) v.
deepen; dig deeper; dredge
pogłoska (po-gwos-ka) f. rumor
pogniewac się (po-gne-vach shan)
v. get angry; be angry
pogoda (po-go-da) f. weather;
cheerfulness; fine weather
pogodny (po-god-ni) adj. m.
serene; cheerful; sunny
pogodzic (po-go-dzheech) v.
reconcile; square (things)
pogoń (po-goń) f. pursuit;
chase; hunt; quest; pursuers
pogorszenie (po-gor-she-ne) n.
worsening; deterioration

pogorszyc (po-gor-shich) v.
make worse; aggravate
pogorzelisko (po-go-zhe-lees-
ko) n. after fire ruins
pogotowie (po-go-to-vye) n.
ambulance service; readiness
pogranicze (po-gra-nee-che) n.
borderland; border line
pogrom (po-grom) m. rout
pogromca (po-grom-tsa) m.tam-
er; conqueror
pogrozka (po-groozh-ka) f.
threat; threatening expression
pogrzeb (po-gzhep) m. funeral
pogrzebacz (po-gzhe-bach) m.
poker (for stirring a fire)
pogwałcic (po-gvaw-cheech) v.
violate; outrage; transgress
poic (po-eech) v. water; ply
pojawic się (po-ya-veech shan)
v. appear; emerge; occur; arise
pojazd (po-yazt) m. car; vehicle
pojąc (po-yownch) v. grasp;
marry; comprehend; understand
pojechac (po-ye-khach) v. go;
leave; take (train, boat etc.)
pojednac (po-yed-nach) v. reconcile (two or more parties)
pojednawczy (po-yed-nav-chi)
adj. m. conciliatory
pojedynczy (po-ye-din-chi) adj.
m. single; individual; onefold
pojedynek (po-ye-di-nek) m.
duel; encounter; single combat
pojemnik (po-yem-neek) m. container; vessel; receptacle
pojemnosc (po-yem-noshch) f.
capacity; cubic content
pojezierze (po-ye-zhe-zhe) n.
lake land ; lake district
pojęcie (po-yan-che) n. notion;
idea; concept; comprehension
pojętny (po-yant-ni) adj. m.
intelligent; sharp; teachable
pojmowac (poy-mo-vach) v.grasp;
comprehend; conceive; imagine
pojutrze (po-joot-zhe) adv. day
after tomorrow
pokarm (po-karm) m. food; feed
pokaz (po-kas) m. display; shaw
pokazywac (po-ka-zi-vach) v.
show; point; exhibit; let see

pokaźny (po-kázh-ni) adj. m.
respectable; appreciable
pokład (pók-wad) m. deck; layer
pokątny (po-kównt-ni) adj. m.
underhanded; secret; illegal
pokłon (pók-won) m. bow; homage
pokłócić się (po-kwoó-cheech
śhän) v. fall out with; quarrel
pokochać (po-ko-khach) v. fall
in love; become fond of
pokoik (po-kó-eek) m. little
room; little cozy room
pokojówka (po-ko-yóov-ka) f.
maid; housemaid; chamber maid
pokolenie (po-kole-ne) n. generation; about 30 years
pokonać (po-ko-nach) v. defeat
pokorny (po-kor-ni) adj. m.
humble; meek; submissive
pokost (po-kost) m. varnish
pokrajać (po-kra-yach) v. cut
up; carve up; slice; slash
pokój (po-kooy) m. room; peace
pokrapiać (po-krá-pyach) v.
sprinkle; wash down (a meal)
pokrewieństwo (po-krev-yeń-stvo)
n. kinship; kindred; relation
pokrewny (po-krev-ni) m. related; kindred; akin; cognate
pokrótce (po-króot-tse) adv.
in short; in brief; concisely
pokrycie (po-kri-che) n. cover
pokryć (po-krich) v. cover
po kryjomu (po-kri-yó-moo) adv.
secretly; on the sly; in secret
pokrywa (po-kri-va) f. lid
pokrywać (pokri-vach) v. cover;
upholster; serve (mare)
pokrzepić (po-kzhé-peech) v.
invigorate; refresh; fortify
pokrzywa (po-kzhee-va) f. nettle
pokrzyżować (po-kzhi-zho-vach)
v. cross up; confound; tangle
pokup (po-koop) m. demand
pokupny (po-koop-ni) adj. m.
in demand; selable
pokusa (po-koo-sa) f. temptation
pokuta (po-koo-ta) f. penance
pokwitować (po-kvee-to-vach) v.
receipt; acknowledge receipt
pokwitowanie (po-kvee-to-va-ne)
n. receipt (liquid)
polać (po-lach) v. pour over

Polak (pó-lak) m. Polonian;
Pole; Polonius; vulg.:polack
polana (po-lá-na) f. glade
polano (po-lá-no) n. billet; log
polarny (po-lar-ni) adj. m. polar; of the polar axis
pole (po-le) n. field
polec (pó-lets) v. fall; be
killed (in battle)
polecać (po-le-tsach) v. recommend; commend; instruct; order
polegać (po-le-gach) v. rely
polemika (po-le-mee-ka) f. po-
lemics; controversy
polepszać (po-lep-shach) v. improve; ameliorate; mend; better
polerować (po-le-ro-vach) v.
polish; furbish; burnish; refine
polewać (po-le-vach) v. water;
glaze; glaze; enamel; ice
polewka (po-lev-ka) f. broth
polędwica (po-land-vee-tsa) f.
sirloin; loin; fillet(of beef)
policja (po-leets-ya) f. police
policzek (po-lee-chek) m. cheek
politechnika (po-lee-tekh-nee-
ka) f. polytechnic college
politowanie (po-lee-to-va-ne)
n. pity; compassion
polityk (po-lee-tik) m. politician; statesman
polka (pól-ka) f. polka; Polish
girl; Polish woman; Pole
polny (pól-ni) adj. m. field
polon (pó-lon) m. polonium
(chem.)
polonez (po-ló-nez) m. polonaise
(dance)
Polonia (po-lon-ya) f. Polish
colony; Polish emigrants
Polonus (po-ló-noos) m. Pole of
old; typical Pole of the past
polot (po-lot) m. elan; imagination
polować (po-ló-vach) v. hunt
polski (pól-skee) adj. m. Polish; Polish language
polszczyć (polsh-chich) v. Polo-
nize; invest with Polish traits
polszczyzna (pol-shchiz-na) f.
Polish language; Polish traits
polubić (po-loo-beech) v. get to
like; become fond; take a fancy

polubownie (po-loo-bóv-ńe) adv.
amicably; by compromise
połamać (po-wa-mać) v. break
połączenie (po-wówn-che-ńe) n.
connection; linkage;contact
połknąć (pów-knównch) v. swallow;gulp down; drink down
połowa (po-wó-va) f. half
położenie (po-wo-zhé-ńe) n.
position; situation; site
położna (po-wózh-na) f. midwife
położnica (po-wozh-ńee-tsa) f,
woman in childbed
położyć (po-wó-zhich) v. lay
down; place;deposit;fell;ruin
połóg (po-wook) m. childbirth
połów ryb (pó-woov rib) fish
catch; fishing; fish haul
południe (po-wood-ńe) n. noon;
south; midday; the South
południk (po-wóod-ńeek) m. meridian; the line of longitude
południowo-wschodni (po-wood-
ńo-vo wskhód-ńee) south-east
południowo-zachodni (po-wood-
ńo-vo za-khód-ńee) south-west
południowy (po-wood-ńó-vi) adj.
m. south; midday; southerly
połykać (po-wi-kać) v. swallow
połysk (pó-wisk) m. glitter;
gloss; luster; sheen; sparkle
pomadka (po-mád-ka) f. lipstick
pomagać (po-má-gać) v. help
pomalenku (po-ma-leń-koo) adv.
little by little; very slowly
pomału (po-má-woo) adv. little
by little; slowly; leisurely
pomarańcza (po-ma-rań-cha) f.
orange; orange tree
pomarszczony (po-marsh-chó-ni)
adj. m. wrinkled; creased
pomazać (po-má-zach) v. smear-
over; anoint; soil; scrawl
pomawiać (po-máv-yach) v. accuse; impute; charge with
pomiar (po-myar) m. measurement;
survey; surveying;mensuration
pomiatać (po-myá-tach) v. push
around; spurn; hold in contempt
pomidor (po-mée-dor) m. tomato
pomieszać (po-myé-shach) v. mix
up; mingle; blend;stir;tangle;
muddle up;embroil;mistake

pomieszanie zmysłów (po-mye-sha-
ńe zmis-woov) insanity; madness
pomieszczać (po-myesh-chach) v.
admit; contain; accomodate
pomiędzy (po-myáń-dzi) prep.
between; among; in the midst
pomijać (po-mée-yach) v. pass
over; omit; overlook; leave out
pomimo (po-mée-mo) prep. in
spite of; notwithstanding
pomnażać (po-mná-zhach) v. multiply; increase; intensify
pomniejszać (po-mńey-shach) v.
diminish; lessen;reduce;belittle
pomnik (póm-ńeek) m. monument
pomoc (pó-mots) f. help ; aid
pomocnik (po-móts-ńeek) m. helper; assistant: helpmate; aid
pomocny (po-móts-ni) adj. m.
helpful; instrumental
pomorski (po-mór-skee) adj. m.
Pomeranian; of Pomerania
pomost (pó-most) m. platform
pomóc (pó-moots) v. help; assist
pompa (póm-pa) f. pump; pomp
pompować (pom-pó-vach) v. pump
pomsta (pó-msta) f. vengeance
pomruk (póm-rook) m. murmur;
grumble; growl;purr; rumble
pomstować (pom-stó-vach) v.
curse; swear; revile;vituperate
pomyje (po-mí-ye) pl. dish-
water; hog-wash; swill; lap
pomylić (po-mi-leech) v. confound; be mistaken; mislead
pomyłka (po-miw-ka) f. error
pomysł (pó-misw) m. idea
pomyślność (po-mishl-noshch) f.
prosperity; success; happiness
pomyślny (po-mishl-ni) adj. m.
successful; favorable; good
pomywaczka (po-mi-vach-ka) f.
dishwasher; scullery maid
ponad (po-nat) prep. above;
over; beyond;upwards of;super-;
more than;over and above;besides
ponadto (po-nád-to) prep. moreover; besides; furthermore;also
ponaglać (po-nág-lach) v. rush;
urge; remind;press; urge on
ponaglenie (po-nag-le-ńe) n.
reminder; pressure
ponawiać (po-náv-yach) v. renew

ponętny (po-nant-ni) adj. m.
seductive; attractive;alluring
poniechać (po-ńe-khać) v.give
up ;relinquish; renounce;desist
poniedziałek (po-ne-dźha-wek)
m. Monday
poniekąd (po-ńe-kównt) adv.
partly;in a way; in a sense
poniesć (po-ńeshćh) v. sustain;
carry ;bear; suffer;incur;push
ponieważ (po-ne-vash) conj. because; as; since; for
poniewczasie (po-ńev-cha-śhe)
adv. too late;after the event
poniewierać (po-ńe-vye-rać) v.
kick around;slight;mishandle
poniżej (po-ńee-zhey) adv. below; beneath ;hereunder;under
poniżyć (po-ńee-zhić) v. degrade; humble;tread down
ponosić (po-no-śheećh) v. bear;
carry (away) ;suffer;incur
ponowić (po-no-veećh) v. renew
ponownie (po-nóv-ńe) adv. anew;
again ; afresh; a second time
ponowny (po-nóv-ni) adj. m. repeated; renewed;reiterated
ponton (pón-ton) m. pontoon
ponury (po-noo-ri) adj m.gloomy
dismal; sullen; dreary; sullen
pończocha (pón-cho-kha) f.
stocking
popadać (po-pá-dać) v. fall in
poparcie (po-pár-ćhe) n. support; backing; promotion;push
popasć (po-pa-śhćh) v. fall in
popatrzeć (po-pá-tzhećh) v. look
popelina (po-pe-lee-na) f.
poplin;a ribbed cloth
popchnąć (pop-khnównćh) v. push;
shove ;hastle; jostle;steer
popełniać (po-pew-ńach) v. commit ;perpetrate
popęd (po-pańt) m. impulse
popędliwy (po-pand-lee-vi) adj.
impetuous; rush;hot headed
popędzać (po-pań-dzach) v. drive
on; urge; push on; prod;spur
popielaty (po-pye-la-ti) adj. m.
charcoal-grey; ashen; gray
popielec (po-pye-lets) m. Ash
Wednesday

popielniczka (po-pyel-ńeech-
ka) f. ash-tray; ash pan
popierac (po-pye-rach) v. support; back;promote;favor;uphold
popiersie (po-pyer-śhe) n. bust
popić (po-peech) v. rinse down
popiół (po-pyoow) m. ashes;ash;
cinders; slag
popis (po-pees) m. show; parade
popisywać się (po-pee-si-vach
śhań)v.show off;flaunt;parade
poplecznik (po-plech-ńeek) m.
backer; upholder; partisan
popłatny (po-pwát-ni) adj. m.
profitable; lucrative
popłoch (po-pwokh) m. panic
popołudnie (po-po-woód-ńe) n.
afternoon
po południu (po po-woód-ńoo) in
the afternoon
poprawa (po-prá-va) f.improve-
ment;change for the better
poprawka (po-práv-ka) f. correction;amendment; alteration
poprawny (po-práv-ni) adj. m.
correct;faultless;proper
po prostu (po prós-too) adv.
simply;openly;uncremoniously
poprzeczka (po-pzhéch-ka) f.
crossbar; crossbeam;the bar
poprzedni (po-pzhéd-ńee) adj.
m. previous; preceding;former
poprzedzać (po-pzhe-dzach) v.
precede;orelude;go before
poprzestać (po-pzhés-tach) v.
settle for; be satisfied
popularny (po-poo-lár-ni) adj.
m. popular; prevalent
popychać (po-pi-khach) v. push;
shove; ill treat; hustle; jostle
popychadło (po-pi-khad-wo) n.
drudge; scapegrace
popyt (po-pit) m. demand
pora (po-ra) f. time; season
porachunek (po-ra-khoo-nek) m.
reckoning; a bone to pick
porada (po-ra-da) f. advice
poradnia (po-rád-ńa) f. information bureau;dispensary;clinic
poradnik (po-rád-ńeek) m. guide;
handbook; reference book
poradzić (po-ra-dżhech) v. advise

poranek (po-rá-nek) m. morning
porastać (po-rás-tach) v. overgrow; grow; become overgrown
poratować (po-ra-tó-vach) v.
help in distress; recuperate
porażenie (po-ra-zhe-ńe) n.
stroke; shock; paralysis
porażka (po-rázh-ka) f. defeat; set back; reverse
porcelana (por-tse-lá-na) f.
china; porcelain
porcja (por-tsya) f. portion
poręcz (pór-ańch) f. banister
poręczenie (po-rań-che-ńe) n.
guarantee; bail;warranty;pledge
poręka (po-rań-ka) f. guaranty;
pledge;sponsorship; surety
poronić (po-ró-ńeech) v. abort;
miscarry; have a miscarriage
porost (po-rost) m. growth
porowaty (po-ro-vá-ti) adj. m.
porous; full of pores
porozdawać (po-roz-dá-vach) v.
give away; pass around
porozumienie (po-ro-zoo-mye-ńe)
m. understanding;agreement
poród (po-root) m. child delivery; childbirth; partitution
porównać (po-roóv-nach) v. compare; draw a comparison; liken
porównanie (po-roov-ná-ńe) n.
comparison;equalization
poróżnić (po-roózh-ńeech) v.
disunite; divide; embroil
port (port) m. port; harbor
portfel (pórt-fel) m. wallet
portier (pórt-yer) m. doorman
portki (pórt-kee) pl. pants
(vulg.);breeches; trousers
portmonetka (port-mo-nét-ka) f.
purse; billfold; wallet
porto (por-to) n. postage
portret (pór-tret) m. portrait
portugalski (por-too-gál-skee)
adj. m. Portuguese
poruczać (po-roó-chach) v. entrust; charge with
porucznik (po-roóch-ńeek) m.
lieutenant
poruszać (po-roó-shach) v. move:
touch; sway; set in motion
poruszenie (po-roo-she-ńe) n.
agitation;movement; stir;touch

poryw (pó-riv) m. impulse; rapture; gust; onrush; elation
porywać (po-ri-vach) v. snatch;
carry off; whisk away;grab;thrill
porywacz (po-ri-vach) m. kid-
naper; abductor; ravisher
porywczy (po-riv-chi) adj. m.
rash;irritable;impetuous;hasty
porządek (po-zhówn-dek) n.
order;tidiness;regularity;system
porządny (po-zhównd-ni) adj. m.
neat; decent; accurate;reliable
porzucać (po-zhoo-tsach) v.
abandon; desert;forsake; leave
porzucić (po-zhoo-cheech) v.
abandon; give up; cast away
posada (po-sá-da) f. employment
posadzka (po-sádz-ka) f. parquet floor; tile floor
posąg (po-sównk) m. statue
poselstwo (po-sél-stvo) n. legation; deputation; envoys
poseł (po-sew) m. envoy; con-
gressman; deputy; legate
posępny (po-sánp-ni) adj. m.
gloomy; dismal; dreary; dark
posiadacz (po-sha-dach) m. bearer; holder; possessor;owner
posiadać (po-sha-dach) v. hold;
own; possess; acquire;dominate
posiadłość (po-shad-woshch) f.
estate; property; dominion
posiedzenie (po-she-dze-ńe) n.
session; conference; meeting
posilać (po-shee-lach) v. refresh; nourish; feed
posiłek (po-shee-wek) m. meal;
refreshment; reinforcement
posłać (po-swach) f. send; make a
bed; dispatch somewhere
posłanie (po-swa-ńe) n. bed;
bedding; message;dispatch
posłaniec (po-swa-ńets) m. messenger; commissionaire
posłuchać (po-swoo-khach) v.
listen; obey; take advice
posługa (po-swoo-ga) f. service
posługacz (po-swoó-gach) m. servant; attendant; commissionaire
posłuszny (po-swoósh-ni) adj. m.
obedient; submissive;docile
pospolity (pos-po-lee-ti) adj. m.
vulgar; common;commonplace

posrebrzac (po-sréb-zhach) v.
silver (plate);silver foil
post (post) m. fast; fast day
postac (pó-stach) f. form;shape;
figure;human shape;personage
postanowic (po-sta-nó-veech) v.
decide; enact;resolve;determine
postanowienie (po-sta-no-vye-ñe)
n. decision; resolve; provision
postarac się (po-sta-rach śhań)
v. procure; obtain;get;try;find
postawa (po-sta-va) f. attitude;
posture; pose;bearing; position
postawny (po-staw-ni) adj. m.
portly;handsome;well made
postawic (po-sta-veech) v. set
up; put up;set on;put on;raise
postąpic (po-stown-peech) v.
proceed; act; deal;follow;treat
posterunek (po-ste-roo-nek) m.
outpost; sentry; police station
postęp (pó-stanp) m. progress;
advance;march;headway
postępowanie (postan-po-va-ñe)
n. behavior; advance;procedure
postojowe (po-sto-yo-ve) n.
demurrage;adj.n.parking
postój (pó-stooy) m. halt;stop;
stand; parking;stopping place
postrach (pó-strakh) m. terror;
dread;scare;fright;bugaboo
postrzał (pó-stzhaw) m. gunshot;
wound;shot;rifle shot;lumbago
postrzelony (po-stzhe-ló-ni)
adj. m. wounded; crazy;cracked
postulat (po-stoó-lat) m. demand; claim; requirement
postument (po-stoo-ment) m.
pedestal; socle
posucha (po-soó-kha) f. drought
posuw (pó-soov) m. feed (of a
drill); feed of a lathe
posuwac (po-soó-vach) v. move;
shove; push on;carry;dash;speed
posyłac (po-sí-wach) v.send over
posyłka (po-síw-ka) f. errand
posypywac (po-si-pi-vach) v.
dust; pour; sprinkle (dry)
poszanowanie (po-sha-no-va-ñe)
n. respect; observance(of a law)
poszarpac (po-shár-pach) v.maul;
tear up; jag up;mangle;rend

poszczególny (po-shche-goól-
ni) adj. m. individual
poszerzac (po-shé-zhach) v.
widen;broaden;extend;ream;spread
poszewka (po-shév-ka) f. pil-
low-case ; pillow slip
poszkodowany (po-shko-do-va-
ni) adj. m. victim ;sufferer
poszlaka (po-shla-ka) f.trace:
circumstantial evidence; sign
poszukiwac (po-shoo-kee-vach)
v. search;look for;inquire;claim
poszukiwanie (po-shoo-kee-va-
ñe) n. search;quest;research
poscic (pósh-cheech) v. fast
posciel (pósh-chel) f. bedclothes sheets and blankets
poscig (pósh-cheeg) m. chase
posladek (po-shla-dek) m. but-
tock; rump; bum
posliznac się (po-shleéz-nownch
śhań) v. slip ;make a slip
poslubic (po-shloo-beech) v.
marry; take in marriage
posmiertny (po-shmyert-ni) adj.
m. posthumous (child, works etc.)
posmiewisko (po-shmye-veés-ko)
n.laughingstock;butt of ridicule
pospiech (pósh-pyekh) m. haste;
hurry; dispatch
posredni (po-shred-ñee) adj.
m. intermediate; indirect
posrednik (po-shred-ñeek) m.
go-between; intermediary
posredniczyc (po-shred-ñeé-
chich) v. mediate;be a go-between
posrod (po-śh-rood) prep. among
poswiadczac (po-shvyad-chach)
v. attest; certify;testify;witness
poswiadczenie (po-shvyad-che-
ñe) n. certificate;attestation
poswięcac (po-shvyan-tsach) v.
sacrifice; sanctify
poswięcenie (po-shvyan-tse-ñe)
n. devotion; sacrifice
pot (pot) m. sweat; prespiration
potajemny (po-ta-yem-ni) adj.
m. secret; clandestine;underhand
potakiwac (po-ta-kee-vach) v.
assent; agree; acquiesce
potas (pó-tas) m. potassium
potaż (pó-tash) m. potash

potąd (po-townt) adv. up to
here ;up to this place
potem (po-tem) adv. after ;
afterwards; then; later on
potencjalny (po-ten-tsyál-ni)
adj. m. potential ;virtual
potęga (po-tán-ga) f. power;
might ;force;impressiveness
potęgowac (po-tán-go-vach) v.
intensify ;raise to a power
potępiac (po-tán-pyach) v.
damn; run down ;condemn
potępienie (po-tán-pye-ñe) n.
damnation ;disapproval;blame
potężny (po-tánzh-ni) adj. m.
mighty ;tremendous;powerful
potknąc sie (pot-known´ch shan)v.
slip ;trip; stumble;make a slip
potknięcie (pot-knan-che) n.
slip; stumble; trip ; a lapse
potoczny (po-toch-ni) adj. m.
current; common ;everyday;daily
potok (po-tok) m. stream ;brook
potomek (po-to-mek) m. descendant ; offspring; scion
potomnosc (po-tom-noshch) f.
posterity ;future generations
potomstwo (po-tom-stvo) pl. issue; progeny; offspring;breed
potop (po-top) m. deluge; flood
potrafic (po-tra-feech) v. know
how to do ;manage;be able to do
potrawa (po-tra-ya) f. dish
potrawka (po-trav-ka) f. fric-
assee ;ragout
potrącic (po-trown-cheech) v.
knock; deduct ;poke;push;jostle
po trochu (po-tro-khoo) adv.
little by little ;gradually
potrojny (po-trooy-ni) adj. m.
triple ;triplicate;treble
potrzask (pot-shask) m. trap
potrząsac (po-tzhown-sach) v.
shake ; brandish; agitate;strew
potrzeba (po-tzhe-ba) f. need;
want;call;emergency;extremity
potrzebny (po-tzheb-ni) adj. m.
necessary ;needed;wanted
potulny (po-tool-ni) adj. m.
docile ;submissive;humble;meek
poturbowac (po-toor-bó-vach) v.
manhandle; rough up ;beat;maul
batter;knock about;ill-treat;
give a rough handling; hurt

potwarz (po-tvash) f. slander
potwierdzac (po-tvyer-dzach) v.
confirm; attest;corroborate
potwór (po-tvoor) m. monster
potykac się (po-ti-kach shan)
v. stumble; skirmish;joust
potylica (po-ti-lee-tsa) f.
occiput; back part of skull
pouczac (po-oo-chach) v. instruct; teach;give instructions
pouczenie (po-oo-che-ñe) n.
instruction;giving instructions
poufalic się(po-oo-fá-lich shan)v.
take liberties; familiarize
poufały (po-oo-fá-wi) adj. m.
intimate;unceremonious;free with
too familiar; maty;hob-nobbing
poufny (po-oof-ni) adj. m. confidential;private;secret
powab (po-vap) m. charm;attrac-
tion;lure;seduction;loveliness
powabny (po-váb-ni) adj. m. attractive; charming;alluring
powaga (po-vá-ga) f. gravity;
seriousness;dignity;prestige
powalac (po-va-lach) v. soil;
dirty ; overthrow;kill;slay
powalic (po-va-leech) v. knock
down;overthrow;kill;slay;fell
poważa (po-va-wa) f. ceiling
poważac (po-va-zhach) v. respect;esteem;have regard
poważny (po-vazh-ni) adj. m.
earnest; grave;dignified;serious
powątpiewac (po-vownt-pye-vach)
v. doubt;have doubts; be dubious
powetowac (po-ve-to-vach) v.
make up;idemnify oneself;retrieve
powiadac (po-vyá-dach) v. say;
tell; speak ;(the legend)has it
powiadomic (po-vya-do-meech) v.that
inform; notify; let know
powiastka (po-vyast-ka) f. tale
powiat (po-vyat) m. county;
district; district authorities
powicie (po-vee-che) n. swad-
dling clothes; child delivery
powidła (po-veed-wa) pl. jam;
marmalade; jam
powiedziec (po-vye-dżhech) v.
say; tell; declare
powieka (po-vye-ka) f. eyelid
powielacz (po-vye-lach) m.
mimeograph

powiernica (po-vyer-née-tsa) f.
confidante;trusted friend
powierzac (po-vye-zhach) v.
confide;charge with a task
powierzchnia (po-vyezhkh-ña) f.
surface;plane; area; acreage
powiesic (po-vye-sheech) v.
hang ;supend; hung up;ring off
powiesc (po-vyeshch) f. novel
powiesc sie (pó-vyeshch shan)
v. succeed; be successful
powietrze (po-vyet-zhe) n. air
powiew (pó-vyev) m, breeze
powiekszac (po-vyank-shach) v.
enlarge;augment;extend; add
powiekszenie (po-vyank-she-ñe)
n. enlargement; magnification
powijaki (po-vee-ja-kee) pl.
swathings;initial stage
powiklac (po-veek-wach) v.
complicate; embroil
powinnosc (po-veen-noshch) f.
duty; obligation
powinowaty (po-vee-no-va-ti)
adj. m, related; akin
powitac (po-vee-tach) v. welcome; salute; bid welcome
powlekac (po-vle-kach) v. cover; drag; coat;smear; spread
powloczka (po-vwoch-ka) f. pillowcase: envelope;covering
powloka (po-vwo-ka) f. (paint)
coat; covering;envelope; shell
powloczysty (po-vwoo-chis-ti)
adj. m. trailing; enticing
powodowac (po-vo-do-vach) v.
cause; bring about; touch off;
effect; induce; give,occasion
powodzenie (po-vo-dze-ñe) n.
success; well-being;prosperity
powodzic sie (po-vo-dzhech shan)
v. fare (well; ill);be well off
powojenny (po-vo-yen-ni) adj.
m. post-war; after-war
powoli (po-vo-lee) adv. slow
powolny (po-vol-ni) adj. m.
slow; tardy;leisurely;gradual
powolanie (po-vo-wa-ñe) n. vocation; call;appointment;quot.
powonienie (po-vo-ñe-ñe) n.
sense of smell; smell
powod (pó-voot) m. cause: reason;ground; motive;plaintiff

powodz (po-voodzh) f. flood
powoj (pó-yooy) m. bindweed
powoz (pó-woos) m. carriage
powracac (po-vra-tsach) v. return; come back;resume;recover
powrotny (po-vrot-ni) adj. m.
return; return(ticket)
powrot (pó-vroot) m. return
powroz (pó-vroos) m. rope
powstanie (po-vsta-ñe) n. rising; uprising ; insurrection
powstaniec (po-vsta-ñets) m.
insurgent(against a government)
powstawac (po-vsta-vach) v.
rise up; stand up;revolt;
powstrzymac (po-vstzhi-mach) v.
restrain; refrain; hold back
powszechny (po-vshekh-ni) adj.
m. universal; general; public
powszedni (po-vshed-ñee) adj.
m. everyday; commonplace;daily
powsciagliwosc (povshchowng-
lee-voshch) f. abstinence;
temperance; moderation;restraint
powsciagliwy (povshchowng-lee-
vi) adj. m. reserved; absti-
nent; moderate;temperate
powtarzac (pov-ta-zhach) v. say
again; go over; repeat;reproduce
po wtore (po vtoo-re) adv. secondly; in the second place; then
powtornie (pov-toor-ñe) adv.
anew; again; a second time
powtorny (po-vtoor-ni) adj. m.
repeated; renewed; second-
powyzej (po-vi-zhey) adv. above;
here in before; higher up; over
powziac (pov-zhownch) v. take
up; form ;decide;conceive(a plan)
poza (pó-za) f. pose; attitude;
sham
poza (pó-za) prep.; beyond; besides; except; apart;outside;extra-
pozagrobowy (po-za-gro-bo-vi)
adj. m. beyond the grave;
hereafter; from beyond the grave
pozbawiac (po-zbav-yach) v.
deprive ;dispossess;take away
pozbyc sie (poz-bich shan) v.
rid oneself; get rid;shake off
pozdrawiac (po-zdra-vyach) v.
greet; send one's greetings
pozew (po-zef) m. summons; writ;
citation

poziom (pó-żhom) m. level
poziomka (po-żhóm-ka) f. wild
strawberry(fruit or plant)
poziomy (po-żho-mi) adj. m.
horizontal;level;uninspired
pozłota (po-zwó-ta) f. gilding
poznać (pó-znaćh) v. get to
know; recognize;taste;acquaint
poznajomić (po-zna-yo-meećh) v.
acquaint; introduce
poznanie (po-zna-ñe) n. cogni-
tion; acquaintance; learning
pozornie (po-zór-ñe) adv. ap-
parently; on the surface
pozostać (po-zós-taćh) v. remain; stay behind;continue
pozostały (po-zos-ta-wi) adj.
m. remaining; residual;left
pozostawiać (po-zos-táv-yaćh)
v. leave (behind);bequeath
pozór (pó-zoor) m. appearance;
pretext; sham;look;mask;cloak
pozwać (póz-vaćh) v. summon
pozwalać (po-zva-laćh) v. let;
allow; permit; tolerate;suffer
pozwany (po-zva-ni) m. defendant; person sued or accused
pozwolenie (po-zvo-le-ñe) n.
permission;consent; permit
pozycja (po-zyts-ya) f. position; item; status;posture
pozyskać (po-zis-kaćh) v. gain;
win over ; conciliate
pozytywny (po-zi-tiv-ni) adj.
m. positive; affirmative
pozywać (po-zi-vaćh) v. sue;
cite; summon; cite(to court)
pożałować (po-zha-wo-vaćh) v.
repent; regret; take pity
pożar (pó-zhar) m. fire (woods,
buildings);conflagration
pożądać (po-zhown-daćh) v. desire; covet; lust after
pożądany (po-zhówn-da-ni) adj.
m. desirable; welcome;desired
pożądliwy (po-zhównd-lee-vi)
adj. m. greedy; covetus;lewd
pożegnać (po-zhég-naćh) v. bid
goodbye; see off; dismiss
pożerać (po-zhe-raćh) v. devour
pożoga (po-zhó-ga) f. fire; conflagration; ravages (of war)

pożółknąć (po-zhoówk-nównćh) v.
grow yellow;turn yellow
pożycie (po-zhi-će) v. intercourse; conjugal life
pożyczka (po-zhich-ka) f. loan
pożyteczny (po-zhi-téch-ni)
adj. m. useful;profitable
pożytek (po-zhi-tek) m. use;
advantage;usefulness; benefit
pożywić (pozhi-veećh) v. feed;
nourish; refresh;give food
pożywny (po-zhív-ni) adj. m.
nutritious; nourishing
pójść (pooyshćh) v. go; go away;
go up..;leave;fly;drift;pan out
póki (poó-kee) conj. till; un-
till; as long as;while; when
pół (poow) num. half;semi- ;
demi-;one half; mid(way);hemi-
półbucik (poow-boó-cheek) m.
half boot; low shoe
półgłosem (poow-gwó-sem) adv.
in a low voice;in an undertone
półgłówek (poow-gwoó-vek) m.
half-wit; fool; simpleton; dolt
półka (poów-ka) f. shelf;ledge
półkole (poow-kó-le) n. semicircle; half-circle;hemicycle
półksiężyc (poow-kshań-zhits)m.
half-moon; crescent;the Crescent
półkula (poow-koó-la)f. hemisphere ;half of a sphere
półmisek (poow-mée-sek) m.
charger dish; dish
półnagi (poow-na-gee) adj. m.
half naked ; half dressed
północ (poów-nots) f. midnight;
north; North; the North
północno-wschodni (poow-nóts-no
wskhód-ñee)north-east
północno-zachodni (poow-nóts-no
zakhód-ñee)north-west
północny (poow-nóts-ni) adj.
north ; Northern; Northerly
półroczny(poow-róch-ni) half-
yearly; semi-annual
półświatek (poow-shvyá-tek) m.
love industry;demimonde
półtora (poow-tó-ra) num. one
and half; a (day etc.) and half
połurzędowy (poow-oo-zhań-dó-vi)
adj. m. semi-official

półwysep (poow-vi-sep) m. penin-
sula; almost an island
póty (poo-ti) conj. as long
później (poozh-ney) adv. later
on; afterwards ;at a later date
późno (poozh-no) adv. late ;late-
późny (poozh-ni) adj. m. late
prababka (pra-bab-ka) f. great
grandmother
praca (pra-tsa) f. work; job
pracodawca (pra-tso-dav-tsa) m.
employer(employing for wages)
pracowity (pra-tso-vee-ti) adj.
m. industrious; hard-working
pracownik (pra-tsov-neek) m.
worker;emploee ; clerk;official
praczka (prach-ka) f. wash-
woman; laundress;washerwoman
prać (prach) v. wash; beat up
pradziad (pra-dzhad) m. great
grandfather; ancestor
pragnąć (prag-nownch) v. be
thirsty; desire; wish;long for
pragnienie (prag-ne-ne) n.wish;
thirst; desire; lust for
praktyczny (prak-tich-ni) adj.
m. practical;sesible;expedient
praktyka (prak-ti-ka) f. practice; usage;apprentiship
praktykować (prak-ti-ko-vach)
v. practice; be in training
pralka (pral-ka) f. washing
machine; washer;wash board
pralnia (pral-na) f. laundry
pranie (pra-ne) n. washing
praojciec (pra-oy-chets) m.
forefather; ancestor
prasa (pra-sa) f. press; print
prasować (pra-so-vach) v. iron
(linen etc.);press; print
prawda (prav-da) f. truth
prawdomówność (prav-do-moov-
noshch) f. truthfulness
prawdopodobny (prav-do-po-dob-
ni) adj. m. probable; likely
prawdziwie (prav-dzheev-ye) adv.
truly; genuinely; indeed
prawdziwy (prav-dzhee-vi) adj.
m. true; real; authentic
prawica (pra-vee-tsa) f. the
Right; right hand; right wing
prawic (pra-veech) v. talk; say

prawidło(pra-veed-wo) n. rule;
boot tree ; law; centering
prawidłowy (pra-veed-wo-vi) adj.
m. regular; correct;proper
prawie (prav-ye) adv. almost;
nearly;practically; all but
prawnik (prav-neek) m. lawyer
prawnuczka (prav-nooch-ka) f.
great granddaughter
prawnuk (prav-nook) m. great
grandson
prawny (prav-ni) adj. m. legal;
lawful;legitimate;rightful
prawo (pra-vo) adv. right;law
prawo (pra-vo) n. law; (driving) license;statute; claim
prawodawca (pra-vo-dav-tsa) m.
legislator;lawmaker;lawgiver
prawodawstwo (pra-vo-dav-stvo)
n. legislation; legislature
prawomocny (pra-vo-mots-ni)
adj. m. legal; valid
prawosławny (pra-vo-swav-ni)
adj. m. orthodox
prawosc (pra-voshch) f. honesty; integrity; righteousness
prawować się (pra-vo-vach shan)
v. litigate; sue; be engaged
in a lawsuit; be at law with...
prawowity (pra-vo-vee-ti) adj.
m. legal (heir etc.)
prawy (pra-vi) adj. m. honest;
right; rigth hand-;upright;lawful
prażyć (pra-zhich) v. grill;roast
burn; keep heavy gunfire on
prąd (prownd) m. current; flow
stream ;air flow;tendency; trend
prądnica (prownd-nee-tsa) f.
generator ;dynamo
prąd stały (prownd sta-wi) m.
direct current
prąd zmienny (prownd zmyen-ni)
alternating current
prążek (prown-zhek) m. stripe
precyzja (pre-tsiz-ya) f. precision ;accuracy;exactness
precyzować (pre-tsi-zo-vach) v.
define; state precisely ;define
precz ! (prech) adv. go away;
do away with; down with
prefabrykować (pre-fa-bri-ko-
vach) v. prefabricate

prefiks (pre-feeks) m. prefix
prelegent (pre-le-gent) m. lecturer (presenting a lecture)
prelekcja (pre-lek-tsya) f.
lecture (informative talk)
preliminarz (pre-lee-mee-nash)
m. estimate of a budget
premedytacja (pre-me-di-tats-
ya) f. premeditation
premia (prem-ya) f. premium;
bonus;bounty; prize; gift
premier (pre-myer) m. prime
minister ; premier
premiera (pre-mye-ra) f. first
night show;first night
prenumerata (pre-noo-me-ra-ta)
f. subscription(to a paper etc.)
preparat (pre-pa-rat) m. pre —
paration;concoction;specimen
prerogatywa (pre-ro-ga-ti-va)
f. privilege; prerogative
presja (pres-ya) f. pressure
prestiż (pres-teesh) m. prestige; high esteem
pretekst (pre-tekst) m. pretext;
excuse; false reason or motive
pretensja (pre-tens-ya) f. claim;
grudge;debt;pretentiousness
prezerwatywa (pre-zer-va-ti-va)
f. contraceptive sheath
prezent (pre-zent) m. gift
prezes (pre-zes) m. chairman
prezydent (pre-zi-dent) m. president; mayor; Lord Mayor
pręcik (pran-cheek) m. (small)
stick; stamen ;rod; graphite
prędki (prand-kee) adj. m. swift;
quick; rapid; fast; prompt;hasty
prędko (prand-ko) adv. quickly;
fast; 2. soon;at once
prędkość (prand-koshch) f. speed;
swiftness; velocity;impetuosity
prędzej (pran-dzey) adv. quicker
sooner; rather; with all haste
pręga (pran-ga) f. stripe; wale
pręgierz (pran-gesh) m. pillory
pręgowaty (pran-go-va-ti) adj.
m. striped ;with stripes
pręt (prant) m. rod; bar; pole;
switch;stick;wand;twig;perch
prężność (pranzh-noshch) f. resilience; elasticity;energy

prężny (pranzh-ni) adj. m.
elastic; resilient;supple
prężyć (pran-zhich) v. strain
probierczy kamień (pro-byer-
chi kam-yen) m. touch-stone
problem (prob-lem) m. problem
probostwo (pro-bos-tvo) n.
parsonage; parish; rectory
proboszcz (pro-boshch) m.pas-
tor; parish priest;parson
probówka (pro-boov-ka) f.
test-tube; test glass
proca (pro-tsa) f. sling
proceder (pro-tse-der) m.trade;
(shady)dealings; a plot
procedura (pro-tse-doo-ra) f.
procedure; legal practice
procent (pro-tsent) m. percentage; interest on money
procentować się (pro-tsen-to-
vach shan) v. bring interest
proces (pro-tses) m. lawsuit
procesja (pro-tses-ya) f. procession; moving as in parade
procesować (pro-tse-so-vach)
v. sue; be engaged in a liti-
gation ;litigate a cause
proch (prokh) m. powder; dust
proch strzelniczy (prokh
stzhel-nee-chi) m. gunpowder
producent (pro-doo-tsent) m.
producer; manufacturer; maker
produkcja (pro-dook-tsya) f.
production ;output;performance
produkować (pro-doo-ko-vach)
v. produce; grow;generate;stage
produkt (pro-dookt) m. product
profanować (pro-fa-no-vach) v.
profane; desecrate :despoil
professor (pro-fe-sor) m. professor ; teacher
profil (pro-feel) m. profile
profilaktyczny (pro-fee-lak-
tich-ni) adj. m. prophylactic
prognoza (prog-no-za) f. prognosis ; forcast(of weather etc.)
program (prog-ram) m. program
progresja (pro-gres-ya) f.
progression ; sequence
prohibicja (pro-hee-beets-ya)
f. prohibition ;forbiddind
projekcja (pro-yek-tsya) f.
projection (on a screen etc.)

projekt (pró-yekt) m. project
projektować (pro-yek-tó-vach)
v. design ;plan;lay out;draft
proklamować (pro-kla-mo-vach)
v. proclaim;announce officially
prokurator (pro-koo-ra-tor) m.
public prosecutor
proletariat (pro-le-tar-yat) m.
proletariat ;working class
prolog (pro-lok) m. prologue
prolongować (pro-lon-gó-vach)
v. prolong; extend
prom (prom) m. ferry (boat)
promieniec (pro-mye-ñech) v.
radiate; beam(with joy etc.)
promieniotwórczy (pro-mye-ño-
tvoór-chi) adj. m. radio-
active(matter, isotopes, etc.)
promieniować (pro-mye-ño-vach)
v. radiate;beam;glow;brim over
promienisty (pro-mye-ñees-ti)
adj. m. radial;radiant;rediate
promienny (pro-myen-ni) adj.
m. radiant; beaming;bright
promień (pró-myeń) m. beam;
ray; gleam;radius; fin ray
promocja (pro-móts-ya) f. promotion;conferment of a degree
propaganda (pro-pa-gán-da) f.
propaganda;publicity;boosting
propagować (pro-pa-gó-vach) v.
propagate; publicize;boost
proponować (pro-po-nó-vach) v.
propose;put forwards;suggest
proporcja (pro-pórts-ya) f.
proportion;ratio; relation
proporcjonalny (pro-por-tsyo-
nál-ni) adj. m. proportional
proporzec (pro-pó-zhets) m.
pennon; banner;streamer;jack
propozycja (pro-po-zits-ya) f.
proposal; offer; suggestion
proroctwo (pro-rots-tvo) n.
prophecy; prediction
prorok (pro-rok) m. prophet
prosić (pró-sheech) v. beg;
pray; ask; invite; request
prosię (pró-shañ) n. young pig
proso (pró-so) n. millet
prospekt (prós-pekt) m. prospect;folder;view;panorama
prosperować (pros-pe-ró-vach)
v. prosper;be prosperous;thrive

prostacki (pros-táts-kee) adj.
m. boorish; rude ;vulgar;coarse
prostak (prós-tak) m. boor; gull
prostata (pros-tá-ta) f. prostate (gland at the of male bladder)
prosto (prós-to) adv. straight;
right; upright;simply;candidly
prostoduszny (pros-to-doósh-ni)
adj. m. simple-hearted ;naive
prostokąt (pros-tó-kownt) m.
rectangle(with four right angles)
prostolinijny (pros-to-lee-ñeey-
ni) adj. m. straightforward
prostopadła (pros-to-pád-wa) f.
perpendicular ;normal; sheer
prostota (pros-tó-ta) f. simplic-
ity ; neatness; boorishness
prostować (pros-to-vach) v.
straighten; correct;revise
prosty (prós-ti) adj. m. straight;
right; direct simple;vulgar;plain
prostytucja (pros-ti-toó-tsya) f.
prostitution; streetwalking
prostytutka (pros-ti-toót-ka) f.
prostitute; streetwalker
proszek (pro-shek) m. powder
(for baking etc.); wafer
proszę (pró-shañ) please
prośba (pró-sh-ba) f. request;
demand; petition; application
proszkować (prosh-kó-vach) v.
pulverize; grind to powder
protegowany (pro-te-go-vá-ni)
adj. m. protégé
protekcja (pro-tek-tsya) f. pull;
patronage; backing;influence;push
protest (pro-test) m. protest
protestant (pro-tés-tant) m.
Protestant ; evangelical
protestantyzm (pro-tes-tan-tizm)
m. Protestantism
proteza (pro-té-za) f. artificial limb or denture
protokół (pro-tó-koow) m. record;
protocol;minutes; official record
prototyp (pro-tó-tip) m. proto-
type; archetype; protoplast
prowadzenie (pro-va-dzé-ñe) n.
management; conduct;leadership
prowadzić (pro-vá-dzheech)v. steer;
lead;conduct; guide; keep; live;
carry on ;show the way;escort;run;
manage (an institution)

prowadzić auto (pro-vá-dźheećh áu-to) drive a car

prowiant (pró-vyant) m. provisions;eatables; rations

prowincjonalny (pro-veen-tsyonál-ni) adj. m. provincial

prowizja (pro-veéz-ya) f. comission; percentage; brokerage

prowizoryczny (pro-vee-zo-rích-ni) adj. m. provisional

prowodyr (pro-vó-dir) m. ringleader; gang leader

prowokacja (pro-vo-káts-ya) f. provocation; stirring trouble

proza (pró-za) f. prose;dullness

próba (proo-ba) f. trial; test; proof; ordeal;acid test;try;go

próbka (proób-ka) f. sample

próbny (proób-ni) adj. m. experimental; tentative ;testprobować (proo-bó-vach) v. try; test; taste;put to test;offer

próchnica (prookh-ńee-tsa) f. moulder; (tooth) decay;humus

próchno (proókh-no) n. rotten wood; mould;rot; wood dust

prócz (prooch) prep. save; except;besides;apart from

próg (prook) m. threshold

prószyć (proó-shich) v. sift; flake; make dust;sprinkle;spray

próżnia (proozh-ńa) f. vacuum

próżniaczy (proozh-ńa-chi) adj. m. lazy; idle;inactive;leisured

próżniak (proózh-ńak) m. idler

próżno (proózh-no) adv. vainly; empty-;in vain; to no avail

próżność (proózh-noshćh) f. vanity; false pride;futility

próżny (proózh-ni) adj. m. 1. empty; void; 2. vain

pruć (proočh) v. rip; unsew

pruski (proós-kee) adj. m. Prussian ; of Prussia

prychać (pri-khach) v. snort

prycza (pri-cha) f. plank -bed

pryk stary (prik stá-ri) adj. m. old goat; old duffer

prym (prim) m. lead; first place; superiority;the lead

prymas (pri-mas) m. primate

prymka (prim-ka) f. chewing tobacco;plug of chewing tobacco

pryskać (pris-kach) v. splash; spray; fly;clear out;bolt;burst

pryszcz (prishch) m. pimple

prysznic (prish-ńeets) m. shower bath; shower

prywatny (pri-vát-ni) adj. m. private; personal;confidential

pryzmat (priz-mat) m. prism

prządka (pzhównd-ka) f. spinner

prząść (pzhównshćh) v. spin

przebaczać (pzhe-bá-chach) v. forgive; pardon; condone

przebaczenie (pzhe-ba-ché-ńe) n. pardon; forgiveness;remittal

przebąkiwać (pzhe-bówn-kee-vach) v. mutter ;hint;allude;mention

przebić (pzhe-beech) v. pierce; perforate; puncture;stab;recoin

przebieg (pzhé-byeg) m. curse; run ;progress;process; milage

przebiegać (pzhe-bye-gach) v. run cross ;take place;proceed

przebiegły (pzhe-byeg-wi) adj. m. cunning; sly ;wily;crafty

przebierać (pzhe-bye-rach) v. choose; sort;change clothes;sift

przebijać (pzhe-bee-yach) v. pierce; puncture;show through

przebłysk (pzhé-bwisk)m.glimpse; ray; flash; sparkle;glimmer

przebłyskiwać (pzhe-bwis-keé-vach) v. gleam ;shine;flash

przeboleć (pzhe-bó-lech) v. get over; put up with ;get over it

przebój (pzhe-booy) m. hit; success; breakthrough ; clou

przebranie (pzhe-brá-ńe) m. disguise ;being disguised

przebrnąć (pzhe-brnównch) v. muddle through; wade through

przebrzmiały (pzhe-bzhmyá-wi) adj. m. overblown; has-been

przebudowa (pzhe-boo-dó-va) f. remodeling; rebuilding

przebudzić (pzhe-boo-dźheech)v. wake up; awake ;rouse;revive

przebyć (pzhe-bich) v. be over through; surmount; ride out storm ;travel;cross;pass;dwell

przebywać (pzhe-bi-vach) v. stay; reside ;dwell;inhabit

przecedzać (pzhe-tse-dzach) v. filter;strain through a sieve

przeceniac (pzhe-tse-ńach) v.
overrate ;lower the price
przechadzka (pzhe-chádz-ka) f.
walk ;stroll;tour; airing
przechadzac się (pzhe-kha-
dzach shań) v. take a walk;
stroll ;go for a walk; saunter
przechodzic (pzhe-kho-dżheéch)
v. pass (through)
przechodzień (pzhe-kho-dżheń)
m. passerby ; pedestrian
przechowanie (pzhe-kho-va-ńe)
n. safekeeping;storage
przechowywac (pzhe-kho-vi-vach)
v. store ;preserve;harbor;keep
przechrzcic (pzhekh-zhcheech)
v. convert; change name
przechwalac (pzhe-khva-lach) v.
talk big ;overpraise;extol;puff
przechwycic (pzhe-khvi-cheech)
v. intercept; seize
przechylic (pzhe-khi-leech) v.
tilt; lean; tip; incline
przechytrzyc (pzhe-khit-zhich)
v. outwit; overreach;outsmart
przeciąg (pzhe-chownk) m.
draught; span;spell;time lapse
przeciąc (pzhe-chownch) v. cut;
cross; intersect;slice;cleave
przeciągac (pzhe-chown-gach) v.
draw; drag; delay; stretch
przeciążac (pzhe-chown-zhach)
v. overload;overburden
przecie (pzhe-che) conj. yet;
still; of course but;after all
przeciekac (pzhe-che-kach) v.
leak; ooze; drain; percolate
przecierac (pzhe-che-rach) v.
rub; wipe clear; threadbare;
fret ;polish (shoes);clear up
przecierpiec (pzhe-cher-pyech)
v. endure; bear; suffer
przeciez (pzhe-chezh) conj. yet;
still; after all; now ;though
przeciętny (pzhe-chant-ni) adj.
m. average ;ordinary;mediocre
przecinac (pzhe-chee-nach) v.
cut; intersect ;slice;cleave
przecinek (pzhe-chee-nek) m.
comma ; point (in mathematics)
przeciskac się (pzhe-chees-kach
shan) v. squeeze through ;push
through;elbow one's way

przeciw (pzhe-cheev) prep.
against; versus ;contrary to
przeciwko (pzhe-cheev-ko) prep.
against; contrary ; versus
przeciwdziałac (pzhe-cheev-
dżha-wach) v. counteract
przeciwległy (pzhe-cheev-lég-wi)
adj, m. opposite; contrary
przeciwlotniczy (pzhe-cheev-
lot-ńee-chi) adj. m. antiair-
craft(artllery, defence etc.)
przeciwnie (pzhe-cheev-ńe) adv.
on the contrary; reverse
przeciwnik (pzhe-cheev-ńeek) m.
opponent ; adversary;enemy;foe
przeciwnosc (pzhe-cheev-noshch)
f. adversity; set-back;reverse
przeciwstawiac (pzhe-cheev-stav-
yach) v. oppose; set against
przeciwwaga (pzhe-cheev-va-ga)
f. counterweight;balance weight
przecudny (pzhe-tsood-ni) adj.
m. most wonderful;just marvellous
przeczący (pzhe-chown-tsi) adj.
m. negative; contradictory
przeczenie (pzhe-che-ńe) n.
negation;negative;denial
przecznica (pzhech-nee-tsa) f.
side-street ;cross street
przeczucie (pzhe-choo-che) n.
foreboding ;presentiment
przeczulony (pzhe-choo-ló-ni)
adj. m. high-strung; over-
-sensitive ;touchy; irritable
przeczyc (pzhe-chich) v. deny;
belie; negate; contradict
przeczyszczac (pzhe-chish-chach)
v. purge; cleanse; scour ;wipe
przeczytac (pzhe-chi-tach) v.
read through ;peruse;read over
przec (pzhech) v. insist on;urge;
press on ;push;exert pressure.
impel;drive;insist;bear down;strive
przed (pzhet) prep. before; in
front of; ahead of; previous
to; from ;since;age;against
przedajny (pzhe-day-ni) adj. m.
venal ;open to bribery
przedawnienie (pzhe-dav-ńe-ńe)
n. expiration of validity
przedawniony (pzhe-dav-ńó-ni)
adj. m. of expired validity
przeddzień (pzhéd-dżheń) m. eve

przede wszystkim (pzhe-de
vshíst-keem) adv. above all;
first; first of all; in the
first place; to begin with
przedhistoryczny (pzhed-hees-
to-rích-ni) adj. m. pre-
historic;before recorded hist.
przedimek (pzhed-eé-mek) m.
article (in grammar)
przedkładać (pzhed-kwa-dach) v.
submit; refer; propose; present; prefer;give priority
przedłużać (pzhed-woó-zhach)
v. lengthen; prolong;extend
przedmieście (pzhed-myésh-che)
n, suburb;outskirts of a city
przedmiot (pzhéd-myot) m. object; subject; subject matter
przedmiotowy (pzhed-myo-tó-vi)
adj. m. objective; at issue
przedmowa (pzhed-mó-va) f. preface; foreword;introduction
przedmówca (pzhed-moóv-tsa) m.
previous speaker
przedni (pzhéd-ńee) adj. m.
leading; front; forward;
choice; fine ;foremost;superior
przedostać się (pzhe-dos-tach
shań) v. penetrate;pass through
przedostatni (pzhed-os-tat-ńee)
adj. m. last but one
przedpłata (pzhed-pwa-ta) f.
advance payment;subscription
przedpokój (pzhed-po-kooy) m.
(waiting-room) lobby; ante-
chamber; anteroom; hall
przedpole (pzhed-pó-le) n. foreground; foreland
przedpołudnie (pzhed-po-woód-ńe)
n. morning; forenoon
przedpotopowy (pzhed-po-to-pó-
vi) adj. m. fossil; antedilu-
vian; fossilized; obsolete
przedramię (pzhed-ram-yań) n.
forearm; antebrachium
przedrostek (pzhed-ros-tek) m.
prefix (in grammar)
przedruk (pzhéd-rook) m. reprint; reimpression;impression
przedrzeć (pzhéd-zhech) v. tear
up; tear through; rend ;
break through;penetrate;burst

przedrzeźniać (pzhed-zhéźh-
ńach) v. ape; mimic; mock;
take off; immitate like an ape
przedsiębiorca (pzhed-shań-byor-
tsa) m. contractor;businessman
przedsiębiorstwo (pzhed-sháń-
byor-stvo) n. business; concern; enterprise; firm,
przedsiębrać (pzhed-shań-brach)
v. undertake;embark upon
przedsionek (pzhed-shó-nek) m.
lobby; vestibule; porch;auricle
przedsmak (pzhéd-smak) m. foretaste;earnest(of future events)
przedstawić (pzhed-sta-veech)
v. present; represent;recommend
przedstawiciel (pzhed-sta-vee-
chel) m. representative
przedstawicielstwo (pzhed-sta-
vee-chél-stvo) n. agency
przedstawienie (pzhed-sta-vyé-
ńe) n. performance;show;version
przedszkole (pzhed-shko-le) n.
kindergarten; nursery school
przedświt(pzhed-shveet)m. pre-
dawn; daybreak;dawn; harbinger
przedtem (pzhéd-tem) adv. before; formerly;in advance;earlier
przedterminowy (pzhed-ter-mee-
nó-vi) adj. m. advance;
premature; done ahead of time
przedwczesny (pzhed-vches-ni)
adj. m. premature; untimely
przedwczoraj (pzhed-vcho-ray)
adv. the day before yesterday
przedwieczny (pzhed-vyéch-ni)
adj, m. eternal;primeval;ancient
przedwiośnie (pzhed-vyósh-ńe)
n. early spring
przedwojenny (pzhed-vo-yén-ni)
adj. m. prewar; before the war
przedział (pzhe-dźhaw) m. partition; compartment; section
przedzielić (pzhe-dźhe-leech)
v. divide; part;separate
przedzierać (pzhe-dźhe-rach) v.
tear down; tear up; rend
przedziurawić (pzhe-dźhoo-ra-
veech) v. perforate; puncture;
riddle; pierce ;make a hole
przedziwny (pzhe-dźheév-ni) adj.
m. prodigious; admirable; odd

przeforsować (pzhe-for-so-vach)
v. ram through;force through
przegapić (pzhe-ga-peech) v.
let slip; over look;miss
przeginać (pzhe-gee-nach) v.
bend (over); turn up;turn down
przegląd (pzhe-glownt) m. review; inspection; survey
przegłosować (pzhe-gwo-so-vach)
v. outvote; take a vote
przegonić (pzhe-go-neech) v.
overtake; drive out; drive
through; drive away;rush past
przegotować (pzhe-go-to-vach)
v. boil; overcook;overboil
przegrać (pzhe-grach) v.lose
(war; game etc.);gamble away
przegradzać (pzhe-gra-dzach) v.
partition;divide;separate
przegrana (pzhe-gra-na) f. defeat; loss;beating;licking
przegryzać (pzhe-gri-zach) v.
bite through;bite in two
przegroda (pzhe-gro-da) f. partition;division;stall;cell
przegub (pzhe-goop) m. wrist;
ball-and-socket joint
przeholować (pzhe-kho-lo-vach)
v. overshoot; rush into excess
przeistoczyć (pzhe-ees-to-chich)
v. transform; remould;convert
przejaśnienie (pzhe-yash-ne-ne)
n. clearing up;bright interval
przejaw (pzhe-yav) m. symptom;
sign; indication;manifestation
przejawiać (pzhe-ya-veeach) v.
reveal; display; manifest;show
przejazd (pzhe-yazt) m. cross—
ing; passage ;thoroughfare
przejąć (pzhe-yownch) v. take
over; seize;adopt;master;thrill
przejechać (pzhe-ye-khach) v.
pass; ride; cross; run over
przejęty (pzhe-yan-ti) adj. m.
impressed; upset; deeply
stirred ;perturbed;wrapped up
przejmować (pzhey-mo-vach) v.
take over ;seize;penetrate
przejrzeć (pzhey-zhech) v. see
through; recover sight ;revise
przejrzysty (pzhey-zhis-ti) adj.
m. transparent; clear ;sheer

przejście (pzhey-shche) n. pass;
transition;conversion;roadway
przejściowo (pzhey-shcho-vo)
adv. temporarily;provisionally
przejść (pzheyshch) v. pass;
cross; experience; go across
przekaz (pzhe-kas) m. transfer;
money order;remittance
przekazywać (przhe-ka-zi-vach)
v. transfer; pass on; send on;
transmit:deliver; direct
przekaźnik (pzhe-kazh-neek) m.
relay; repeater; transmitter
przekąsem (pzhe-kown-sem)adv.iro-
nically; mockingly; spitefully
przekąska (pzhe-kowns-ka) f.
snack; refreshment
przekątna (pzhe-kownt-na) f.
diagonal(line)
przekleństwo (pzhe-klen-stvo)
n. curse; profanity;damnation
przekład (pzhe-kwat) m. translation; rendering;rearrangement
przekładać (pzhe-kwa-dach) v.
shift; transfer; prefer; move;
translate;reach;put between
przekładnia (przek-wad-na) f.
gearbox; clutch ;transposition
przekłuć (pzhe-kwooch) v. prick;
pierce; puncture;perforate
przekonać (pzhe-ko-nach) v.
convince; persuade ;bring round
przekonanie (pzhe-ko-na-ne) n.
conviction ;persuasion;opinion
przekop (pzhe-kop) m. trench;
ditch ; tunnel;cutting;piercing
przekopać (pzhe-ko-pach) v. dig-
through ;turn over; excavate;cut
przekora (pzhe-ko-ra) f. spite
przekraczać (pzhe-kra-chach) v.
overstep; cross ;surpass
przekradać się (pzhe-kra-dach
shan) v. steal through
przekreślić (pzhe-kresh-leech)
v. cross out; delete; annul
przekręcić (pzhe-kran-cheech) v.
twist; distort(a statement)
przekroczenie (pzhe-kro-che-ne)
n. trespass;offence;transgression
przekroczyć (pzhe-kro-chich) v.
cross; trespass; exceed; offend; violate;transgress(the law)

przekroić (pzhe-kro-eech) v. cut
przekrój (pzhe-krooy) v. cross
  section; profile;review,
przekrwienie (pzhe-krvye-ne) n.
  hyperemia;congestion
przekształcić (pzhe-kshtaw-
  cheech) v. transform
przekupić (pzhe-koo-peech) v.
  bribe; buy over; corrupt
przekupka (pzhe-koop-ka) f.
  huckstress; vendor;wrangler
przekupny (pzhe-koop-ni) adj.
  m. venal; bribable
przekupstwo (pzhe-koop-stvo) n.
  bribery ;graft; corruption
przekwitać (pzhe-kvee-tach) v.
  wither; fade; decay;shed blossom
przelatywać (pzhe-la-ti-vach)
  v. fly through;cross;run;pass
przelew (pzhe-lef) m. transfusion; transfer;over flow
przelewać (pzhe-le-vach) v.
  overfill; transfer; shed
przelękły (pzhe-lan-kwi) adj.
  m. frightened ;intimidated
przelęknąć (pzhe-lank-nownch)v.
  frighten ;scare; terrify
przelicytować (pzhe-lee-tsi-
  to-vach) v. outbid
przeliczyć (pzhe-lee-chich) v.
  miscalculate; count over
przelot (pzhe-lot) m. over-
  flight; flight; passage
przelotny (pzhe-lot-ni) adj. m.
  fleeting; passing; transient
przeludnienie (pzhe-lood-ne-ne)
  n. overpopulation; congestion
przeładować (pzhe-wa-do-vach)
  v. overload; transship;reload
przeładunek (pzhe-wa-doo-nek)
  m. load transfer ; reloading
przełamać (pzhe-wa-mach) v.
  break through;break in two
przełazić (pzhe-wa-zheech) v.
  climb over ;creep across
przełącznik (pzhe-wownch-neek)
  m. switch; shift;commutator
przełęcz (pzhe-wanch) v. (mountain) pass;saddle; col
przełknąć (pzhew-known'ch) v.
  swallow; swollow down
przełom (pzhe-wom) m. breakthrough; turning point;gorge

przełożony (pzhe-wo-zho-ni)
  adj. m. principal; superior
przełożyć (pzhe-wo-zhich) v.
  transfer; prefer; shift;reach
przełyk (pzhe-wik) m. gullet;
  esophagus
przemakać (pzhe-ma-kach) v.
  ooze; get wet; be permeable
przemarsz (pzhe-marsh) m.
  marching past; march of troops
przemarznąć (pzhe-mar-znownch)
  v. be chilled ;freeze stiff
przemawiać (pzhe-ma-vyach) v.
  speak; harangue; address
przemądrzały (pzhe-mownd-zha-
  wi) adj. m. smart aleck
przemęczać (pzhe-man-chach) v.
  overstrain; overwork ;spend
przemęczenie (pzhe-man-che-ne)
  n. strain ;overwork; tiredness
przemiał (pzhe-myaw) m. grinding; milling ;meal;grist;shoal
przemiana (pzhe-mya-na) f.change;
  transformation; alteration
przemianować (pzhe-mya-no-vach)
  v. rename ; change name
przemienić (pzhe-mye-neech) v.
  change; transform ;alter;turn
przemieścić (pzhe-myesh-cheech)
  v. displace ;dislocate; shift
przemijać (pzhe-mee-yach) v.
  go by;be over; pass; cease
przemilczeć (pzhe-meel-chech)
  v. keep secret;leave unsaid
przemoc (pzhe-mots) f. force;
  violence ;constraint;compulsion
przemoczyć (pzhe-mo-chich) v.
  soak; drench ;wet;seep; sop
przemoknąć (pzhe-mok-nownch) v.
  be soaked ;be permeable;get wet
przemowa (pzhe-mo-va) f. speech;
  oration; address :harangue
przemóc (pzhe-moots) v. overcome ;conquer;defeat;master;prevail
przemówić (pzhe-moo-veech) v.
  speak up ;make a mistake(speaking)
przemówienie (pzhe-moov-ye-ne)
  n. speech ;address; oration
przemycać (pzhe-mi-tsach) v.
  smuggle (into a country,a room etc.)
przemyć (pzhe-mich) v. rinse; scrub;
  wash ;give a wash; lavage; flush
przemysł (pzhe-misw) m.industry

przemysłowy (pzhe-mis-wo-vi) adj. przepierzenie (pzhe-pye-zhe-ne)
m. industrial;manufacturing n. partition (wall etc.)
przemyśliwać (pzhe-miśh-lee- przepiękny (pzhe-pyań -kni)
vach) v. ponder; think over adj. , very beautiful; gorgeous
przemyślny (pzhe-miśhl-ni) adj. przepiłowac (pzhe-pee-wo-wach)
m. ingenious;clever;cunning v. saw through; file through
przemyt (pzhe-mit) m. smuggling przepiórka (pzhe-pyoor-ka) f.
przemytnik (pzhe-mit-neek) m. quail(migratory game bird)
smuggler; contrabandist przepis (pzhe-pees) m. 1. re-
przemywac (pzhe-mi-vach) v. gulation; 2. recipe
rinse; wash; scrub;lavage;flush przepisac (pzhe-pee-sach) v.
przeniesc (pzhe-neshch) v. 1. prescribe; 2. copy
transfer; surpass; carry over; przepłacać (pzhe-pwa-tsach) v.
remove;convey; move; retrace overpay; pay too much; bribe
przenigdy (pzhe-neeg-di) adv. przepłukać (pzhe-pwoo-kach) v.
nevermore; never ,never rinse; gargle ;scour; wash
przenikac (pzhe-nee-kach) v. przepłynąć (pzhe-pwi-nownch) v.
penetrate; pierce; permeate swim across ;row across
przenikliwy (pzhe-neek-lee-vi) przepływać (pzhe-pwi-vach) v.
adj. m. penetrating; acute; flow; float across; swim
sharp; piercing;keen;shrewd across; row across;sail across
przenocować (pzhe-no-tso-vach) przepocic (pzhe-po-cheech) v.
v. pass the night;put up sweat through ;sweat (a shirt)
przenośnia (pzhe-nosh-na) f. przepoic (pzhe-po-eech) v. im-
metaphor; figure of speach pregnate ;saturate; fill
przenośny (pzhe-nosh-ni) adj. m. przepona (pzhe-po-na) f. dia-
portable; mobile;metaphorical phragm ;midriff; stiffener
przeobrażać (pzhe-o-bra-zhach) przepowiadac (pzhe-po-vya-dach)
v. transform; modify;change v. predict ;foretell;repeat
przeoczenie (pzhe-o-che-ne) m. przepracowac się (pzhe-pra-tso-
oversight; omission vach shań) v. overwork (one-
przeoczyc (pzhe-o- chich) v. self) ;overstrain oneself
overlook; leave out;omit przepraszac (pzhe-pra-shach) v.
przepadac (pzhe-pa-dach) v. be apologize ;excuse oneself
lost; be extremely fond;vanish przeprawa (pzhe-pra-va) f.
przepalic (pzhe-pa-leech) v. 1. passage; crossing ;journey
burn through;overheat;scorch 2. fight ;incident;scene; row
przepasac (pzhe-pa-sach) v. przeprawiac (pzhe-prav-yach) v.
gird ;belt;tie;overfeed cross over ;carry across
przepaska (pzhe-pas-ka) f. band przeproszenie (pzhe-pro-she-ne)
przepasc (pzhe-pashch) f. abyss n. apology ; apologies
przepchac (pzhep-khach) v. push przeprowadzac (pzhe-pro-va-dzach)
through; pass through;clean out v. convey; lead; move ;pass
przepełniac (pzhe-pew-nach) v. przeprowadzka (pzhe-pro-vadz-ka)
overfill; cram ; over cram f. moving (form a house etc.)
przepełnienie (pzhe-pew-ne-ne) n.
overfill; crowd;excess przepuklina (pzhe-poo-klee-na)
przepędzac (pzhe-pan-dzach) v. f. hernia ; rupture
drive away; spend ;distil;stay przepustka (pzhe-poost-ka) f.
przepic (pzhe-peech) v. spend pass; permit ;liberty; sluice
on drinking ; drink away;waste przepuszczac (pzhe-poosh-chach)
przepierac (pzhe-pye-rach) v. v. let pass ;promote;leak;miss;
launder; wash clothes let slip;waste;squander away

przepuszczalność (pzhe-poosh-chál-noshch) f. permeability
przepych (pzhe-pikh) m. luxury; pageantry;splendor;ostentation
przepychać (pzhe-pi-khach) v. push through; force through
przepytywać (pzhe-pi-ti-vach) v. examine;inquire ;question
przerabiać (pzhe-ra-byach) v. do over; revise ;remodel;alter
przerachować (pzhe-ra-kho-vach) v. miscalculate; count over
przeradzać się (pzhe-ra-dzach shán) v. change (into)
przerastać (pzhe-rás-tach) v. outgrow; rise above ;surpass
przerazić (pzhe-ra-zheech) v. terrify; appal; consternation
przeraźliwy (pzhe-razh-lee-vi) adj. m. appalling; terrifying shrill ; awesome; acute;sharp
przerażenie (pzhe-ra-zhe-ńe) n. terror ;horror;dread;dismay
przerażony (pzhe-ra-zho-ni) adj. m. horror stricken
przeróbka (pzhe-roob-ka) f. revision ;reshaping; alteration
przerwa (pzher-va) f. pause; break; recess ; interval
przerys (pzhe-ris) m. tracing
przerysować (pzhe-ri-só-vach) v. trace; copy ;retrace
przerwać (pzher-vach) v. interrupt; pause; cut-off
przerzedzić(pzhe-zhe-dzheech)v. thin out ; decimate(a population)
przerzucać (pzhe-zhoo-tsach) v. throw over; shift; move; flip; browse ;transfer; ransack
przerzynać (pzhe-zhi-nach) v. cut through ;cut in two
przesada (pzhe-sá-da) f. exaggeration ;overstatement
przesadzać (pzhe-sa-dzach) v. 1. exaggerate; 2. transplant
przesalać (pzhe-sa-lach) v. oversalt ;put too much salt
przesąd (pzhe-sównt) m. prejudice; superstition ;fallacy
przesądny (pzhe-sównd-ni) adj. m. superstitious ;prejudiced
przesiadać się (pzhe-sha-dach shán) v. change(places; seats)

przesiedlać (pzhe-shed-lach) v. displace; migrate;transplant
przesiewać (pzhe-she-vach) v. sift; sieve ;screen out;riddle
przesilać się (pzhe-shee-lach shán) v. subside ;get over; culminate;overcome;overstrain
przesilenie (pzhe-shee-le-ńe) n. crisis ;turning point
przeskoczyć (pzhe-skó-chich) v. jump over;vault ;outstrip;skip
przesłać (pzhe-swach) v. 1.send ; 2. make bed over ;rearrange a bed
przesłaniać (pzhe-swa-ńach) v. screen off ;veil;cover;hide;shade
przesłanka (pzhe-swan-ka) f. premise ;prerequisite;condition
przesłuchiwać (pzhe-swoo-khee-vach) v. interrogate ;question
przesmyk (pzhes-mik) m. strait
przesolony (pzhe-so-lo-ni) adj. m. oversalted;with excess salt
przespać (pzhes-pach) v. sleep over ;fail to wake up for...
przestać (pzhes-tach) v. cease
przestanek (pzhes-tá-nek) m. pause; rest ; stop
przestankować (pzhe-stan-kó-vach) v. punctuate (written matter)
przestarzały (pzhe-sta-zha-vi) adj. m. obsolete ;time worn
przestawać (pzhe-stá-vach) v. 1.cut out; break off; 2. associate; hobnob ;keep company
przestawiać (pzhe-stáv-yach) v. displace; transpose ;shift
przestąpić (pzhe-stówn-peech) v. step over;transgress ;cross
przestępca (pzhe-stánp-tsa) m. criminal ;felon;law breaker
przestępny (pzhe-stánp-ni) adj. m. leap (year) ;felonious
przestępstwo (pzhe-stánp-stvo) n. offense; crime ;transgression
przestrach (pzhe-strakh) m. fright; alarm; fear; terror
przestraszyć (pzhe-stra-shich) v. scare; startle;alarm
przestroga (pzhe-stro-ga) f. warning; admonition ;caution
przestronny (pzhe-stron-ni) adj. m. spacious; roomy

przestrzegać (pzhe-stzhe-gach)
v. observe (rules); caution
przestrzelić (pzhe-stzhe-leech)
v. shoot through;shoot down
przestrzenny (pzhe-stzhen-ni)
adj. m. spatial; roomy
przestrzeń (pzhe-stzheń) f.
space ; outer space; room
przestworze (pzhe-stvo-zhe) n.
expanse; infinity ; space,
przesunięcie (pzhe-soo-nań-che)
n. shift ; transfer;displacement
przesuwać (pzhe-soo-vach) v.
move; shift ; shove; transfer
przesycać (pzhe-si-tsach) v.
saturate; glut; impregnate
przesyłać (pzhe-si-wach) v.
send ; dispatch; forward
przesyłka (pzhe-siw-ka) f.
shipment ; mail; parcel
przesypiać (pzhe-sip-yach) v.
oversleep; sleep away
przesyt (pzhe-sit) m. glut
przeszczep (pzhe-shchep) m.
transplant; graft; grafting
przeszkadzać (pzhe-shka-dzach)
v. hinder; trouble ;prevent
przeszkoda (pzhesh-ko-da) f.
obstacle ; hitch; obstruction
przeszkolenie (pzhe-shko-le-
ńe) n. training ; course
przeszło (pzhesh-wo) adv.
more than ; over(an amount)
przeszłość (pzhesh-woshch) f.
past ; record;antecedents
przeszukać (pzhe-shoo-kach) v.
search over ; ransack
przeszyć (pzhe-shich) v. sew-
through; pierce; gore;quilt
prześcieradło (pzhesh-che-rad-
wo) n. bedsheet; sheet
prześcignąć (pzhe-shcheeg-
nownch) v. outdistance; outdo;
do; outstrip;overtake;excel
prześladować (pzhe-shla-do-
vach) v. persecute;harass;haunt
prześladowanie (pzhe-shla-do-
va-ńe) n. persecution;obsession
prześliczny (pzhe-shleech-ni)
adj. m. most beautiful;lovely
prześliznąć (pzhe-shleez-nownch)
v. slip through;glide past
przeświadczenie (pzhe-shvyad-
che-ńe) n. conviction;certitude

prześwietlać (pzhe-shvyet-lach)
v. shine through; fluoroscope
przetak (pzhe-tak) m. riddle
przetaczać (pzhe-ta-chach) v.
1. rollover; 2. transfuse
przetapiać (pzhe-tap-yach) v.
recast; smelt(metals); melt
przetarg (pzhe-tark) m. auction
przetarty (pzhe-tar-ti) adj. m.
threadbare; rubbed through,
przetłumaczyć (pzhe-twoo-ma-
chich) v. translate ; explain
przeto (pzhe-to) conj. therefore;accordingly;consequently
przetrawić (pzhe-tra-veech) v.
digest;ruminate;etch;corrode
przetrwać (pzhe-trvach) v.
survive; outlast;remain;keep
przetrwonić (pzhe-trvo-ńeech)
v. squander,;waste;fritter away
przetrząsnąć (pzhe-tzhowns-
nownch) v. search (shake
through);ransack;comb out
przetrzymać (pzhe-tzhi-mach) v.
endure; outdo; keep waiting
przetwarzać (pzhe-tva-zhach)
v. remake; manufacture
przetwornia (pzhe-tvoor-ńa) f.
factory; processing plant
przewaga (pzhe-va-ga) f. pre-
dominance ; overbalance ;lead
przeważać (pzhe-va-zhach) v.
outweigh; prevail ; overbalance
przeważający (pzhe-va-zha-yown-
tsi) adj. m. prevailing; superior; predominant,
przeważnie (pzhe-vazh-ńe) adv.
mainly; mostly ; chiefly;largely
przewiązać (pzhe-vyown-zach) v.
bind up; change dressing
przewidywać (pzhe-vee-di-vach)
v. anticipate; foresee
przewiercić (pzhe-vyer-cheech)
v. drill through (pierce)
przewiesić (pzhe-vye-sheech) v.
sling over;hang over;rehang
przewietrzyć (pzhe-vyet-zhich)
v. ventilate
przewiew (pzhe-vyev) m. draught;
breeze; breath of air;whiff
przewiezienie (pzhe-vye-zhe-ńe)
n. transport ;transportation;
carriage; conveyance

przewijać (pzhe-vee-yach) v.
wrap up; change dressing
przewinienie (pzhe-vee-ńe-ńe)
n. offense; delinquency
przewlekły (pzhe-vlek-wi) adj.
m. protracted; lingering;lasting
przewodni (pzhe-vod-ńee) adj.
m. leading ;guiding(principle)
przewodniczący (pzhe-vod-ńee-
chówn-tsi) m. chairman
przewodnik (pzhe-vód-ńeek) m.
guide; conductor; leader
przewodzić (pzhe-vo-dzheech) v.
head; command ;lead;conduct
przewozić (pzhe-vo-zheech) v.
convey; transport;cart across
przewoznik (pzhe-vozh-ńeek) m.
ferryman;carter; carrier
przewód (pzhe-voot) m. conduit;
channel; wire;procedure
przewóz (pzhe-voos) m. transport ;freight ; cartage
przewracać (pzhe-vra-tsach) v.
overturn; turn over; upset;
toss ; topple; invert;reverse
przewrotność (pzhe-vrót-noshch)
f. perversity; perfidy;deceit
przewrót (pzhe-vroot) m. revolution;upheaval;coup d'état
przewyższać (pzhe-vizh-shach)
v. out do; exceed; surpass
przez (pzhes) prep. ; across;
over; through; during; within; in; on;on the other side
przeziębić się (pzhe-zhań-beech
shań) v. catch cold;grow cold
przezimować (pzhe-zhee-mo-vach)
v. winter; hibernate
przeznaczać (pzhe-zna-chach) v.
intend; earmark ; mean; destine; assign; allocate;design
przeznaczenie (pzhe-zna-che-ńe)
n. destiny; destination
przezorność (pzhe-zor-noshch) f.
caution; prudence;foresight
przeźrocze (pzhe-zhro-che) n.
transparency; slide;open work
przezroczysty (pzhe-zhro-chis-
ti) adj. m. transparent
przezwisko (pzhes-vees-ko) n.
1. nickname; 2. abusive name
przezwyciężać (pzhez-vee-chań-
zhach) v.overcome; conquer

przezywać (pzhe-zi-vach) v. revile; abuse; call names
przeżegnać się (pzhe-zheg-nach
shań) v. cross oneself
przeżuwać (pzhe-zhoo-vach) v.
chew;masticate; ponder over
przeżycie (pzhe-zhi-che) n.
experience; survival
przeżyć (pzhe-zhich)v.survive;
live through;outlive
przeżytek (pzhe-zhi-tek) m.
relic of the passd;old timer
przędza (pzhań-dza) f. yarn
przędzalnia (pzhań-dzal-ńa) f.
spinning mill;spinning room
przęsło (pzhańs-wo) n. (bridge)
bay; (stair) flight; span
przodek (pzho-dek) m. 1. ancestor; 2. front;heading;end;top
przodować (pzho-do-vach) v.
lead; excel; be the best
przodownictwo (pzho-dov-ńeets-
tvo) n. leadership; hegemony
przodownik (pzho-dov-ńeek) m.
leader;foreman;police inspector
przód (pzhoot) m. front; ahead
przy (pzhi) prep. by; at; near
by; with; on; about; close to
przybić (pzhi-beech)v. nail down
przybiec (pzhi-byets) v. run
up ; hasten;come up running
przybierać (pzhi-byé-rach) v.
dress up; put on; adopt;adorn
przybliżać (pzhi-blee-zhach) v.
bring near;draw near;magnify
przybliżony (pzhi-blee-zho-ni)
adj. m. approximate;very near
przyboczny (pzhi-bóch-ni) adj.
m. side(kick) ; personal (aide);
body (guard);adjutant (officer)
przybory (pzhi-bo-ri) pl. accessories;outfit; tools;tackle
przybór (pzhi-boor) m. rise
(of flood);rise (of a river)
przybrać (pzhi-brach) v. adorn;
put on; assume; adopt;rise;grow
przybrzeżny (pzhi-bzhezh-ni)
adj. m. coastal; riverside
przybudówka (pzhi-boo-doov-ka)
f. annex;addition(to a building)
przybycie (pzhi-bi-che) n. arrival;gain;growth; accession
przybysz (pzhi-bish) m. newcomer

przybytek (pzhi-bi-tek) m. increase; sanctuary;repository
przybywać (pzhi-bi-vach) v.
1. arrive 2. increase;rise
przychodnia (pzhi-khod-na) f.
outpatient clinic;ambulatory
przychodzić (pzhi-kho-dźheech)
v. come over, around, along,
to, again; turn up; arrive
przychód (pzhi-khoot) m. income;profit; takings;proceeds
przychylać (pzhi-khi-lach) v.
incline: comply; bend
przychylny (pzhi-khil-ni) adj.
m. favorable; kind;friendly
przyciągać (pzhi-chown-gach) v.
attract; draw near;appeal;lure
przyciąganie ziemskie (pzhi-
chown-ga-ne zhem-ske) gravitation; gravitational pull
przyciemniać (pzhi-chem-nach)
v. dim; darken;shade;black out
przycinać (pzhi-chi-nach) v.
1. cut; slip; 2. make fun of
przycisk (pzhi-cheesk) m.
1. pressure; 2. accent; 3. paper-weight; weight;emphasis
przyciskać (pzhi-chis-kach) v.
press; keep down;squeeze
przycupnąć (pzhi-tsoop-nownch)
v. squat down;crouch;lie in wait
przyczaić się (pzhi-cha-eech
shan) v. lurk; sulk; ambush;hide
przyczepić (pzhi-che-peech) v.
attach; fasten;link;fix;pin;hook
przyczepić się (pzhi-che-peech
shan) v. cling; pick a quarrel;
find fault; hold tight; attach
przyczepka (pzhi-chep-ka) f.
trailer
przyczółek (pzhi-choo-wek) m.
abutment; bridgehead; beachhead;fronton;frontal;pediment
przyczyna (pzhi-chi-na) f.cause;
reason; ground; intercession
przyczynek (pzhi-chi-nek) m.
contribution(to science etc.)
przyczyniać (pzhi-chi-nach) v.
add; add to; contribute
przyczynowość (pzhi-chi-no-
voshch) f. causation;causality
przyćmiewać (pzhi-chmye-vach) v.
dim; tarnish; obscure; outshine;
overshadow;darken; eclipse

przydać (pzhi-dach) v. add;
apend; lend; add weight
przydatny (pzhi-dat-ni) adj.
m. useful;helpful;serviceable
przydawka (pzhi-dav-ka) f.
attribute (gram.);qulifier
przydeptać (pzhi-dep-tach) v.
thread upon; step on
przydługi (pzhi-dwoo-gee) adj.
m. lengthy;somewhat too long
przydomek (pzhi-do-mek) m.
by-name; surname;nickname
przydreptać (pzhi-drep-tach) v.
trip along; come tripping
przydrożny (pzhi-drozh-ni) adj.
m. roadside(shrine etc.)
przydusić (pzhi-doo-sheech) v.
throttle; smother;press down
przydybać (pzhi-di-bach) v.
overtake; take unawares;nab
przydymać (pzhi-dimach) v. foot
it along; run up(slang)
przydymiony (pzhi-dim-yo-ni)
adj. m. smoky; tinted
przydział (pzhi-dżhaw) m. allotment; ration;allowance
przydzielać (pzhi-dżhe-lach)
v. assign; allocate;allot
przyganiać (pzhi-ga-nach) v.
blame; find fault with; criticize;rebuke;reprimand
przygarnąć (pzhi-gar-nownch) v.
take up; adopt;hug;grasp;shelter
przygasać (pzhi-ga-sach) v. dim;
subside; abate;go out;die down
przyglądać się (pzhi-glown-dach
shan) v. observe;look on;scan;see
przygnać (pzhi-gnach) v. drive
near; bring; run up; hasten
przygnębiać (pzhi-gnan-byach) v.
depress; deject;dishearten
przygnębienie (pzhi-gnan-bye-
ne) n. depression; low spirits
przygniatać (pzhi-gna-tach) v.
crush;overwhelm; oppress; burden; press down;squeeze; pinch
przygoda (pzhi-go-da) f. adven-
ture; accident; experience
przygodny (pzhi-god-ni) adj. m.
occasional; casual; accidental
przygotować (pzhi-go-to-vach)
v. prepare; get ready; worn ;
fit; coach; train; make ready;
pack up; turn on (the bath)

przygotowanie (pzhi-go-to-va-ñe) n. preparation;getting ready
przygotowawczy (pzhi-go-to-vav-chi) adj. m. preparatory;initial
przygrywac (pzhi-gri-vach) v. 1. accompany; 2. play(music)
przygrzewac (pzhi-gzhe-vach) v. warm up; heat up;swelter
przygwozdzic (pzhi-gvozh-dzheech) v. nail down;pin down
przyimek (pzhi-ee-mek) m. preposition(relation word)
przyjaciel (pzhi-ya-chel) m. friend;good friend;close friend
przyjaciolka (pzhi-ya-choow-ka) f. girl friend;close friend
przyjazd (pzhi-yazt) m. arrival; time of arrival
przyjazny (pzhi-yaz-ni) adj. m. friendly; amicable; kindly
przyjazn (pzhi-yazhñ) f. friendship; friendly relations;amity
przyjaznic się (pzhi-yazh-ñeech shañ) v. be friends;pal;chum
przyjechac (pzhi-ye-khach) v. come (over); arrive; come
przyjemnosc (pzhi-yem-noshch) f. pleasure; enjoyment; gusto;zest
przyjemny (pzhi-yem-ni) adj. m. pleasant;attractive;nice;cosy
przyjezdny (pzhi-yezd-ni) m. stranger; sightseer;visitor
przyjezdzac (pzhi-yezh-dzhach) v. arrive (by transportation)
przyjęcie (pzhi-yañ-che) n. admission; adoption; reception
przyjęty (pzhi-yan-ti) adj. m. customary; acceptable
przyjmowac (pzhiy-mo-vach) v. receive; accept; entertain
przyjscie (pzhiysh-che) n. arrival; coming; advent
przyjsc (pzhiyshch) v. comeover; come along; come around
przykazac (pzhi-ka-zach) v. order; tell; enjoin to do
przykazanie (pzhi-ka-za-ñe) n. commandment; injunction
przyklasnąc (pzhi-klas-nówñch) v. applaud;commend;praise
przykleic (pzhi-kle-eech) v. stick; glue; paste; stick on (stamp etc.)

przyklękac (pzhi-klañ-kach) v. genuflect; bend the knee
przykład (pzhi-kwat) m. example; instance; pattern; sample
przykładac (pzhi-kwa-dach) v. 1. apply;affix; lend a hand;
2. beat up with;.apply a force
przykładny (pzhi-kwad-ni) adj. m. exemplary; model(husband)
przykrajac (pzhi-kra-yach) v. cut off; cut out(garments etc.)
przykrawac (pzhi-kra-vach) v. cut out(garments etc.);cut off
przykręcac (pzhi-krañ-tsach) v. screw on; 2. turn tight
przykrosc (pzhi-kroshch) f. annoyance;irritation;vexation
przykry (pzhi-kri) adj. m. disagreeable;painful;nasty;bad
przykrywac (pzhi-kri-vach) v. cover; roof over
przykrywka (pzhi-kriv-ka) f. lid; cover (of friendship etc.)
przykrzyc się (pzhi-kzhich shañ) v. be bored; have nothing to do;pall on;weary;long
przykucnąc (pzhi-koots-nówñch) v. squat down;crouch; squat
przykuc (pzhi-kooch) v. 1. hammer; 2. arrest(attention);chain;grip;rivet;fascinate
przylatywac (pzhi-la-ti-vach) v. fly in; fly into (a room)
przylądek (pzhi-lówn-dek) m. cape; tip of land; headland
przyleciec (pzhi-le-chech) v. fly in; arrive;come running
przylegac (pzhi-le-gach) v. 1. fit; cling; 2. adjoin
przyległy (pzhi-lég-wi) adj. m. adjacent;adjoining;contiguous
przylepic (pzhi-le-peech) v. stick; glue on;stick to;post
przylepiec (pzhi-le-pyets) m. adhesive tape; court plaster
przylgnąc (pzhil-gnówñch) v. stick; cling; adhere;nestle up
przylot (pzhi-lot) m. plane arrival(of an airplane)
przylutowac (pzhi-loo-to-vach) v. solder on; sweat on
przyłączac (pzhi-wówn-chach) v. annex; join; add;connect;attach

przyłączenie (pzhi-wǒwn-che-ńe) n. annexation;incorporation

przyłbica (pzhiw-bee-tsa) f. visor; beaver;welder's helmet

przymawiać (pzhi-mav-yach) v. criticize;rebuke;pinprick;nettle

przymawiać się (pzhi-mav-yach śhań) v. hint around for

przymiarka (pzhi-myár-ka) f. fitting on; trying on clothes

przymierać (pzhi-mye-rach) v. starve;be half dead;be dying

przymierzać (pzhi-mye-zhach) v. try on;set to; apply to

przymierze (pzhi-mye-zhe) n. alliance; covenant; Testament

przymierzyć (pzhi-mye-zhich) v. try on; set on; apply to

przymieszka (pzhi-myesh-ka) f. admixture;addition;modicum;dash

przymiot (pzhi-myot) m. (man's) quality; trait; attribute

przymiotnik (pzhi-myot-ńeek) m. adjective (grammar)

przymknięty (pzhim-knań-ti) adj. m. half-closed; shut up

przymocować (pzhi-mo-tso-vach) v. fasten; fix; secure;attach

przymówka (pzhi-moov-ka) f.gibe; hint; allusion;scoff;jeer

przymrozek (pzhi-mro-zek) m. slight frost;ground frost

przymrużyć oczy (pzhi-mroo-zhich ó-chi) blink; narrow one's eyes; wink

przymus (pzhi-moos) m. compulsion; constraint; coersion

przymusić (pzhi-moo-śheech) v. compel;force;oblige;coerce

przymusowy (pzhi-moo-so-vi) adj. m. obligatory;coercive;forced

przynaglać (pzhi-nag-lach) v. urge; haste; push on;hustle;spur

przynajmniej (pzhi-náy-mńey) adv. at least;at any rate;anyway

przynależeć (pzhi-na-le-zhech) v. belong; be member(of a party)

przynależnosc (pzhi-na-lezh-nośhch) f.(nationality) membership;affiliation;(national)status

przynależny (pzhi-na-lezh-ni) adj. m. belonging; appurtenant

przynęta (pzhi-nań-ta) f. bait; lure; enticement; lure; decoy

przynosić (pzhi-no-śheech) v. 1. bring; fetch; 2. bear; yield; bring(profit);afford

przyobiecać (pzhi-obye-tsach) v. promise; give a promise

przyobiecywać (pzhi-ob-ye-tsi-vach) v. promise;give a promise

przypadać (pzhi-pa-dach) v. be due; fall; come ; happen

przypadek (pzhi-pá-dek) m. event; chance; case; incident

przypadkiem (pzhi-pád-kem) adv. by chance; accidentally

przypadkowo (pzhi-pad-kó-vo) adv. accidentally;unintentionally

przypadłosć (pzhi-pád-woshch) f. affliction; ailment; disease

przypalić (pzhi-pa-leech) v. singe; burn; smoke;scorch;sear

przypasać (pzhi-pá-sach) v. attach (to belt); grid on

przypatrywać się (pzhi-pa-tri-vach śhań) v. observe; look at; contemplate;have a look at

przypatrzyć się (pzhi-pá-tzhich śhań) v. observe;contemplate

przypędzać (pzhi-pań-dzach) v. 1. come in haste; 2. drive (to)

przypiąć (pzhi-pyǒwnch) v. pin; fasten;attach;buckle; pin on

przypieczętować (pzhi-pye-chań-tó-vach) v. seal up; confirm

przypisek (pzhi-pee-sek) m. note; postscript; added note

przypisywać (pzhi-pee-si-vach) v. ascribe; attribute; credit

przypłacać (pzhi-pwa-tsach) v. pay (with life; health; property etc.); pay (dearly)

przypłynąć (pzhi-pwi-nǒwnch) v. arrive sailing or swimming; come to shore; swim up;sail up

przypływ (pzhi-pwif) m. high tide; inflow;influx; high water

przypodobać się(pshi-po-dó-bach śhań)v.get into good graces

przypominać (pzhi-po-mee-nach) v. remind; recollect;resemble

przypomnienie (pzhi-pom-ńe-ńe) n. reminder; memento;souvenir

przypowieść (pzhi-póv-yeshch)
f. tale; parable; allegory
przyprawa (pzhi-prá-va) f. seasoning; spice;relish;sause
przyprawiać (pzhi-práv-yach)
v. 1. season; 2. cause a loss
przyprowadzać (pzhi-pro-va-
dzach) v. bring along; fetch
przypuszczać (pzhi-poosh-chach)
v. suppose;let approach;admit
przypuszczalnie (pzhi-poosh-
chál-ńe) adv. supposedly
przypuszczalny (pzhi-poosh-
chál-ni) adj. m. supposed
przypuszczenie (pzhi-poosh-che-
ńe) n. guess; supposition
przyroda (pzhi-ro-da) f. nature
przyrodni brat (pzhi-ród-ńee
brát) half brother
przyrodnia siostra (pzhi-ród-ńa
shós-tra) half sister
przyrodnik (pzhi-ród-ńeek) m.
naturalist;natural historian
przyrodzony (pzhi-ro-dzó-ni)
adj. m. innate;natural;inborn
przyrost naturalny (pzhi-rost
na-too-rál-ni) birthrate
przyrostek (pzhi-rós-tek) m.
suffix (grammar)
przyrząd (pzhi-zhównd) m. instrument;tool; appliance;device
przyrządzać (pzhi-zhówn-dzach)
v. make ready; prepare;cook
przyrzeczenie (pzhi-zhe-che-ńe)
n. promise; plighted word
przyrzekać (pzhi-zhe-kach) v.
promise to do(something)
przysadka (pzhi-sád-ka) f. pi-
tuitary gland; stipule
przysądzać (pzhi-sówn-dzach) v.
award; adjudge; allocate
przysiad (pzhi-shad) m. squat
przysiadać (pzhi-shá-dach) v.
sit down; crouch; sit up
przysięga (pzhi-shán-ga) f.
oath; sworn attestation
przysięgać (pzhy-shań-gach) v.
swear to do; take an oath
przysięgły (pzhy-sháng-wi)adj.
m. sworn (jury man)
przysłać (pzhi-swach) v. send in
przysłaniać (pzhi-swa-ńach) v.
shade; vail;cover up;screen

przysłona (pzhi-swó-na) f. veil;
shade; screen; diaphragm; stop
przysłowie (pzhi-swov-ye) n.
proverb; by word
przysłówek (pzhi-swoo-vek) m.
adverb (grammar)
przysłuchiwać się (pzhi-swoo-
khee-vach shań) v. listen to
przysługa (pzhi-swoo-ga) f.
service;good turn;favor;kindness
przysługiwać (pzhi-swoo-gee-
vach) v. to have right;be vested
przysłużyć się (pzhi-swoo-shich
shań) v. render service
przysmak (pzhis-mak) m. delicacy
przysmażyć (pzhi-sma-zhich) v.
roast; fry a little; brown;devil
przysparzać (pzhi-spá-zhach) v.
1. increase; add to 2. cause
(trouble);bring unpleasantness
przyśpieszać (pzhish-pye-shach)
v. accelerate; urge;speed up
przyśpieszenie (pzhish-pye-she-
ńe) n. acceleration;speeding up
przysposabiać (pzhis-po-sáb-yach)
prepare; adapt; adopt;fit;qualify
przystać (pzhis-tach) v. join;
comply;cohere;fit together;befit
przystanąć (pzhi-sta-nównch) v.
stop; pause; halt
przystanek (pzhi-stá-nek) m.
stop; station; bus stop etc.
przystań (pzhi-stań) f. small
(boat) harbor(inland); port
przystawać (pzhi-sta-vach) v.
fit; enlist; coincide; halt
przystawiać (pzhi-stáv-yach) v.
place near; set against; put
przystawka (pzhi-stáv-ka) f.
side dish; hors-doeuvre
przystęp (pzhi-stánp) m. access
przystępny (pzhi-stánp-ni) adj.
m. 1. accessible; 2. moderate
przystojny (pzhi-stóy-ni) adj.
m. handsome; decent; suitable
przystosować (pzhi-sto-só-vach)
v. adjust; fit;accomodate;adapt
przystrajać (pzhi-strá-yach) v.
decorate; adorn; dress; trim
przysunąć (pzhi-soo-nównch) v.
move near; push nearer
przyswajać (pzhi-sva-yach) v.
acquire; assimilate; adopt(ways)

przysyłać (pzhi-si-wach) v.
send;send along;send up
przysypac (pzhi-si-pach) v. cover (with earth; snow etc.)
przyszłość (pzhish-woshch) f.
future;days to come;the future
przyszyc (pzhi-shich) v. sew on
przyszykować (pzhi-shi-ko-vach)
v. prepare; make ready
przyśnić się (pzhish-neech shan)
v. appear in a dream
przyśrubować (pzhi-shroo-bo-vach)
v. screw on; screw down
przyświadczyc (pzhi-shviad-
chich) v. agree with;attest
przytaczac (pzhi-ta-chach) v.
quote; cite;wheel up;bring up
przytakiwać (pzhi-ta-kee-vach)
v. say yes;assent;acquiesce
przytepic (pzhi-tan-peech) v.
dull; blunt somewhat;dim;befog
przytępienie (pzhi-tan-pye-ne)
n. dullness; bluntness
przytknąć (pzhit-knownch) v.
place touching; set to;apply to
przytłaczać (pzhi-twa-chach) v.
overwhelm;press to earth;crush
przytłumic (pzhi-twoo-meech) v.
damp; deaden;stifle;subdue;dim
przytoczyc (pzhi-to-chich) v.
quote; cite; roll up; bring up
przytomnie (pzhi-tom-ne) adv.
with presence of mind;lucidly
przytomność (pzhi-tom-noshch)
f. consciousness;(one's)senses
przytomny (pzhi-tom-ni) adj.m.
conscious;quickwitted
przytrafiać się (pzhi-traf-yach
shan) v. happen; occur;befall
przytrzymać (pzhi-tzhi-mach) v.
hold; detain;keep in place;arrest
przytulic (pzhi-too-leech) v.
snuggle; cuddle; hug;cuddle;fold
przytułek (pzhi-too-wek) m.
shelter;alms;house;poor house
przytwierdzic (pzhi-tvyer-dzheech)
v. fasten; fix;attach;assent
przytyk (pzhi-tik) m. dig; allusion;tilt;reference;junction
przytykac (pzhi-ti-kach) v.
1. adjoin; 2. set; apply;border
przy tym (pzhi-tim) adv. besides

przyuczac (pzhi-oo-chach) v.
train; accustom an animal
przywabiać (pzhi-vab-yach) v.
decoy; allure; lure
przywara (pzhi-va-ra) f. vice;
fault;defect;shortcoming
przywiązac (pzhi-vyown-zach) v.
bind;tie;attach;hitch;lash;fasten
przywdziewac (pzhi-vdzhe-vach)
v. put on (clothes)
przywidzenie (pzhi-vee-dze-ne)
n. illusion;delusion;phantasm
przywieźc (pzhi-vyezhch) v.
import; bring; drive up;recall
przywilej (pzhi-vee-ley) m.
privilege; prerogative;charter
przywitac (pzhi-vee-tach) v.
welcome; greet;bid good morning
przywłaszczać (pzhi-vwash-
chach) v. usurp; appropriate
przywodzic (pzhi-vo-dzeech) v.
lead; bring about;remind;drive
przywłaszczenie (pzhi-vwash-
che-ne) n. appropriation;
usurpation (of rights etc.)
przywołać (pzhi-vo-wach) v.
summon; call in;signal;sign
przywozic (pzhi-vo-zheech) v.
bring (by car);import;deliver
przywodca (pzhi-vood-tsa) m.
leader ; ringleader;chietain
przywoz (pzhi-voos) m. import;
delivery ;transport;carriage
przywracac (pzhi-vra-tsach) v.
restore ;bring back;reappoint
przywrocenie (pzhi-vroo-tse-ne)
n. restoration ;reinstatement
przywyknąć (pzhi-vik-nownch) v.
get accustomed ;get used
przyznac (pzhi-znach) v. award;
admit ;allow;acknowledge;grant
przywalać (pzhi-zva-lach) v.
consent; approve ;agree;concede
przywoitość (pzhi-zvo-ee-
toshch) f. decency ;propriety
przywoity (pzhi-zvo-ee-ti) adj.
m. decent ;proper;seemly;suitable
przywolenie (pzhi-zvo-le-ne)
n. consent ; acquiescence
przyzwyczajac (pzhi-zvi-cha-
yach) v. accustom;habituate

przyzwyczajenie (pzhi-zvi-cha-
ye-ne) n, habit; custom
przyzywać (pzhi-zi-vach) v.
call in ; call sb;beckon;sign
psalm (psalm) m. psalm
pseudonim (psew-do-neem) m.
pseudonym; pen name
psiarnia (pshar-na) f. kennel
psie pieniądze (pshe pye-nown-
dze) dirt cheap; dog cheap
psikus (pshee-koos) m. prank
psota (pso-ta) f. prank; mischief; practical joke; trick
psotnik (psot-neek) m. prank-
ster; practical joker;scamp
pstrąg (pstrowng) m. trout; kelt
pstry (pstri) adj. m. 1. mottled;
speckled; 2. uncertain;freaked
psuć (psooch) v. spoil; decay;
waste; corrupt; deprave; damage;put out of order;mess up
psychiatra (psi-khyat-ra) m.
psychiatrist; shrink; alienist
psychiczny (psi-kheech-ni) adj.
m. mental(state,disease etc.)
psycholog (psi-kho-lok) m.
psychologist; behaviorist
pszczelarstwo (pzhche-lar-stvo)
n. beekeeping ; apiculture
pszczelarz (pshche-lash) m. beekeeper; apiarist
pszczoła (pshcho-wa) f. bee
pszenica (pshe-nee-tsa) f. wheat
ptactwo (ptats-tvo) pl. fowl;
birds; the species of birds
ptak (ptak) m. bird;fowl
ptaszek (pta-shek) m. little
bird; small bird; rogue
publicysta (poo-blee-tsis-ta)
m. columnist; journalist
publiczność (poo-bleech-noshch)
pl. public;community; audience
publikacja (poo-blee-kats-ya) f.
publication;something published
puch (pookh) m. down;fluff
puchacz (poo-khach) m. eagle
owl(night bird of prey)
puchar (poo-khar) m. cup; bowl
puchlina wodna (poo-khlee-na
wod-na)f.dropsy ;hydropsy
puchnąć (pookh-nownch) v. swell
puchowy (poo-kho-vi) adj. m.
downy;fluffy;eiderdown

pucołowaty (poo-tso-wo-va-ti)
adj. m. chubby cheeked
pucz (pooch) m. Putsch
pudełko (poo-dew-ko) n. box
(small); tin ; can;hand box
puder (poo-der) m. powder
puderniczka (poo-der-neech-ka)
f. powder box; compact;puff box
pukać (poo-kach)v. knock ;rap
pugilares (poo-gee-la-res) m.
billfold; pocket book;wallet
pukiel (poo-kel) m. curl;lock
pula (poo-la) f. pool;kitty
pularda (poo-lar-da) f. pou-
larde; fowl
pulchny (pool-khni) adj. m.
plump;mellow;loose;spongy
pulower (poo-lo-ver) m. pullover (sweater)
pulpit (pool-peet) m. desk;
lectern; shelf;book rest
puls (pools) m. pulse;vibration
pulsować (pool-so-vach) v.
pulsate;palpitate;throb;vibrate
pułap (poo-wap) m. ceiling
pułapka (poo-wap-ka) f. trap
pułk (poowk) m. regiment;group
pułkownik (poow-kov-neek) m.
colonel; group captain
pumeks (poo-meks) m. pumice
punkt (poonkt) m. point; mark
punktualny (poonk-too-al-ni)
adj. m. punctual;exact;prompt
pupa (poo-pa) f. behind; buttocks; bottom
pupil (poo-peel) m. ward; pupil; favorite
purchawka (poor-khav-ka) f. 1.
puff-ball; 2. grumpy fellow
purpura (poor-poo-ra) f. purple
purytanin (poo-ri-ta-neen) m.
Puritan;man of strict religion
pustelnia (poos-tel-na) f. her-
mitage;solitary secluded place
pustelnik (poos-tel-neek) m.
hermit; recluse
pustka (poost-ka) f. solitude;
empty (place);emptiness;void
pustkowie (poost-kov-ye) n.
deserted place;desert;solitude
pustoszyć (poos-to-shich) v.
devastate;ravage;lay waste;ruin
pusty (poos-ti) adj.m. empty

pustynia (poos-ti-ña) f. desert
puszcza (poosh-cha) f. primeval
  forest; wilderness
puszczać (poosh-chach) v. let
  go; let fall; set afloat; free;
  fade; drop; let out; emit; start
puszczać się (poosh-chach shañ)
  v. draw apart; let go; be a
  permissive girl; go to bed with
puszek (poo-shek) m. down
puszka blaszana (poosh-ka bla-
  sha-na) tin can; tin box
puszysty (poo-shis-ti) adj. m.
  downy; fluffy; flossy; flaky; nappy
puścić (poosh-cheech) v. let go;
  let free; release; let fall
puzon (poo-zon) m. trombone
  (one octave lower than trumpet)
pycha (pi-kha) f. 1. pride;
  2. excellent tidbit; fine stuff
pykać (pi-kach) v. puff; pop
pylić (pi-leech) v. dust; be dusty
pył (piw) m. dust; powder
pyskować (pis-ko-vach) v. be
  saucy; bark; bawl
pysk (pisk) m. muffle; snout;
  mug; muzzle; phiz; rowdyism
pyskaty (pis-ka-ti) adj. m.
  foulmouthed; saucy; pert; bawling
pyszałek (pi-sha-wek) m. boaster; braggart; coxcomb
pysznić się (pish-ñeech shañ)
  v. swagger; prance; swank; strut
pysznie (pish-ñe) adv. proudly;
  admirably; in grand fashion
pytać (pi-tach) v. ask; inquire;
  question; interrogate
pytanie (pi-ta-ñe) n. question;
  inquiry; query; interrogation
pytel (pi-tel) m. bolter
pytlować (pi-tlo-vach) v. sift;
  bolt(flour); be a chatterbox
pyton (pi-ton) m. python
pyza (pi-za) f. dumpling
pyzaty (pi-za-ti) adj. m. chubby
rab (rab) m. slave; servant
rabarbar (ra-bar-bar) m. rhubarb
rabat (ra-bat) m. discount; rebate; reduction (in price)
rabin (ra-been) m. rabbi
rabować (ra-bo-vach) v. rob;
  maraud; plunder; pirate; take
  by force; steal

rabunek (ra-boo-nek) m. robbery; plunder; holdup; spoliation
rabuś (ra-boosh) m. robber;
  plunderer; pillager
rachityczny (ra-khee-tich-ni)
  adj. m. rickety; rachitic
rachmistrz (rakh-meestsh) m.
  accountant; calculator; reckoner
rachować (ra-kho-vach) v. calculate; count; reckon; compute; rely
rachunek (ra-khoo-nek) m. bill;
  account; count; calculation; sum
rachunkowość (ra-khoon-ko-
  vośhch) f. bookkeeping
racica (ra-chee-tsa) f. cloven
  hoof; cow hoof
racja (rats-ya) f. reason; right;
  ration; propriety; correctness
racjonalizować (ra-tsyo-na-lee-
  zo-vach) v. rationalize; improve
racjonalny (ra-tsyo-nal-ni)
  adj. m. rational; reasonable
raczej (ra-chey) adv. rather;
  sooner; rather than
raczkować (rach-ko-vach) v. go
  on all fours; crawl on all four
raczyć (ra-chich) v. deign; be
  pleased; treat; condescend; stoop
rad (rad) adj. m. 1. pleased;
  glad 2. m. radium
rada (ra-da) f. advice; counsel
radar (ra-dar) m. radar
radca (rad-tsa) m. advisor;
  counselor; legal advisor
radcostwo (rad-tsos-tvo) n.
  councillorship; post of advisor
radio (rad-yo) n. radio; wireless; broadcasting (system)
radiofonia (ra-dyo-fo-ña) f.
  broadcasting; radiotelephony
radioaktywny (rad-yo-ak-tiv-ni)
  adj, m. radioactive
radiostacja (rad-yi-stats-ya)
  f. radio station
radiodepesza (rad-yo-de-pe-sha)
  f. radiotelegram
radioterapia (rad-yo-te-rap-ya)
  f. radiotherapy; X-ray therapy
radny (rad-ni) m. alderman
radosny (ra-dos-ni) adj. m. gay;
  glad; festive (day etc.)
radość (ra-dośhch) f. joy; gladness; delight; merriment; glee

radykalny (ra-di-kal-ni) adj. m.
radical;man of radical views
radykał (ra-di-kaw) m. radical
radzić (ra-dzheech) v. deliberate; suggest; advice;counsel
radziecki (ra-dzhets-kee) adj.
m. Soviet;of Soviet Union
rafa (ra-fa) f. reef;rim;ripple
rafineria (ra-fee-ner-ya) f.
refinery; refining works
rafinować (ra-fee-no-vach) f.
refine; purify; distil
raid (rayd) m.sport rally (race)
raj (ray) m. paradise; heaven
rak (rak) m. crayfish; cancer
rakieta (ra-ke-ta) f. 1. rocket; flare; 2. (tennis) racket
rama (ra-ma) f. frame;scheme;case
ramię (ra-myań) n. shoulder
ramowy (ra-mo-vi) adj. m. frame
rampa (ram-pa) f. ramp; loading
platform;bar;barier; float
rana (ra-na) f. wound;injury;sore
randka (rand-ka) f. date
ranek (ra-nek) m. morning; day-
break; break of day
ranga (ran-ga) f. rank; standing
ranic (ra-neech) v. wound; hurt
ranny (ran-ni) adj. m. 1. wounded; injured; 2. morning; early
rano (ra-no) adv. 1. early;
2. morning; forenoon;too early
rapier (ra-pyer) m. rapier
raport (ra-port) m. report; account; statement; log
raptem (rap-tem) adv. suddenly;
abruptly;no more than;all in all
raptowny (rap-tov-ni) adj. m.
abrupt; sudden;impulsive;heady
rasa (ra-sa) f. race; stock;
breed ;(plant)variety; blood
rasizm (ra-sheezm) m. racism
rasowy (ra-so-vi) adj. m. racial;
thoroughbred;purebred;racy
raszpla (rash-pla) f. rasp
rata (ra-ta) f. instalment (payment);part payment(system)
ratować (ra-to-vach) v. rescue;
save; deliver(from danger)
ratownictwo (ra-tov-neets-tvo) n.
life saving (system)
ratownik (ra-tov-neek) m. lifeguard; rescuer; life saver

ratunek (ra-too-nek) m. rescue;
salvation;help;assistance;resort
ratunkowy pas (ra-toon-ko-vi
pas) m. life belt; life jacket
ratusz (ra-toosh) m. city hall
ratyfikacja (ra-ti-fee-kats-
ya) f. ratification
raut (rawt) m. evening party
raz (ras) m. 1. one time;
2. blow; stroke; buffet
raz (ras) adv. once; at one
time; at last; time being
razem (ra-zem) adv. together
razić (ra-zheech) v. 1. strike;
2. offend; 3. dazzle; shock;hit
razowy (ra-zo-vi) adj. m. brown
(bread); whole meal (bread)
razowiec (ra-zo-vyets) m. whole
meal bread; brown bread
rażący (ra-zhown-tsy) adj. m.
1. glaring; 2. flagrant; rank
raźnie (razh-ńe) adv. cheerfully; briskly; at a lively pace
rąb (r쳐ownb) m. rim;pane;clearing
rąbać (rown-bach) v. 1. chop;hew;
2. say truth to face ; slash
rączka (rownch-ka) f. handle;
small hand; handgrip;holder
rączy (rown-chi) adj. m. swift
rdza (rdza) f. rust;mildew;blight
rdzenny (rdzen-ni) adj. m.
essential; original;specific
rdzeń (rdzeń) m. core; pith;
marrow; gist; essence; log
rdzoodporny (rdzo-od-por-ni)
adj. rust-proof;stainless
reagować (re-a-go-vach) v.
react; respond;be suscrptible
rdzewieć (rdze-vyech) v. corrode;
rust; get rusty; gather rust
reakcja (re-ak-tsya) f. reaction
reakcjonista (re-ak-tsyo-ńees-
ta) m. reactionary
reakcyjny (re-ak-tsiy-ni) adj.
m. reactionary;retrograde
reaktywować (re-ak-ti-vo-vach)
v. 1. start again; 2. reacti-
vate;bring back to life;recall
realia (re-al-ya) pl. realia;
realities
realista (re-a-lees-ta) m. re-
alist; advocate of realism
realizm (re-a-leezm) m. realism

realizować (re-a-lee-zó-vach) v.
actualize; realize;cash(assets)
realność (re-ál-noshch) f. 1.
real estate;2. reality;the real
realny (re-ál-ni) adj. m. real;
concrete; actual;genuine;true
rebelia (re-bél-ya) f. rebellion;uprising against government
recenzent (re-tsen-zent) m.critic;
reviewer (of books, plays, etc.)
recenzja (re-tsen-zya) f. review (of books, plays, etc.)
recepcja (re-tsep-tzya) f. reception;formal social function
recepis (re-tsé-pees) m. receipt; recipe;written receipt
recepta (re-tsep-ta) f. pre-
scription; doctor's order
rechot (re-khot) m. shrieking
laughter; croak(of forgs)
recydywista (re-tsi-di-vees-ta)
m. recidivist;old offender
recytować (re-tsi-to-vach) v.
recite;give a recitation
redagować (re-da-go-vach) v.
edit;draw up;formulate;draft
redakcja (re-dak-tsya) f. 1.
editing; 2. editors office
redaktor (re-dák-tor) m. editor
redukcja (re-dook-tsya) f. re-
duction(in size,price etc.)
redukować (re-doo-ko-vach) v.
reduce; lay off;cut down
referat (re-fé-rat) m. report
referencja (re-fe-rén-tsya) f.
reference; testimonial
referent (re-fé-rent) m. clerk
refleks (re-fleks) m. reflex
refleksja (re-fleks-ya) f. reflection; thought; cogitation
reflektor (re-flék-tor) m. re-
flector; searchlight;headlight
reflektować (re-flek-to-vach)
v. 1. apply for; want; 2. reflect;bring to reason;moderate
reforma (re-for-ma) f. reform
reformacja (re-for-mats-ya) f.
reformation; Reformation
reformować (re-for-mo-vach) v.
reform; reorganize
regaty (re-ga-ti) pl. boat race
regencja (re-gén-tsya) f. regency; regency style

regionalny (re-gyo-nál-ni)
adj. regional; local
regulacja (re-goo-lats-ya) f.
regulation;control;regulator
regularny (re-goo-lar-ni) adj.
m. regular; even;systematic
regulować (re-goo-lo-vach) v.
1. regulate control 2. settle
reguła (re-góo-wa) f. rule
rehabilitować (re-kha-bee-lee-
to-vach) v. rehabilitate
reja (re-ya) f. yardarm
rejent (re-yent) m. notary
public; notary; regent
rejestr (re-yestr) m. register;
file; index;roll;register mark
rejestracja (re-yes-tráts-ya)
f. registration; licensing
rejestrować (re-yes-tro-vach)
v. register; enroll;record
rejon (re-yon) m. region
rejwach (réy-vakh) m. uproar;
hullabaloo;row;hurly-burly
rekin (ré-keen) m. shark
reklama (rek-lá-ma) f. advertising; commercial publicity
reklamacja (re-kla-máts-ya) f.
complaint;demand for compensation
reklamować (re-kla-mo-vach) v.
1. complain; 2. advertise
rekolekcje (re-ko-lék-tsye) pl.
retreat;period of contemplation
rekomendacja (re-ko-men-dáts-
ya) f. recommendation;reference
rekompensata (re-kom-pen-sá-ta)
f. compensation;recompense
rekonvalescent (re-kon-va-lés-
cent) m. convalescent
rekord (ré-kord) m. (sports)
record; (world) record
rekordzista (re-kor-dzhees-ta)
m. record holder;champion
rekreacja (re-kre-áts-ya) f.
recreation;opposing action
rekrut (rék-root) m. recruit;
conscript;recently enlisted man
rekrutować (re-kroo-to-vach)
v. recruit; enlist(new people)
rektor (rék-tor) m. university
president;university head
rektyfikować (rek-ti-fee-ko-
vach)v. rectify;correct; put
right; purify

rekwizycja (rek-vee-zits-ya) f.
requisition;seizure
relacja (re-lats-ya) f. 1. report; 2. rate; relation
relatywizm (re-la-ti-veezm) m.
relativity; relativism
relegacja (re-le-gats-ya) f.
expulsion; relegation
religia (re-leeg-ya), f. religion
religijny (re-lee-geey-ni) adj.
m. religious; godly
relikwia (re-leek-vya) f. relic
remanent (re-ma-nent) m. remainder; inventiry;stock
remis (re-mees) m. (sport)draw
remiza (re-mee-za) f. engine-
shed ; engine-house; depot;barn
remont (re-mont) m. 1. repair;
2. (horse) remount
remontować (re-mon-to-vach) v.
repair; recondition;overhaul
renumeracja (re-noo-me-rats-ya)
f. renumeration;recount
ren (ren) m. reindeer; caribou
renegat (re-ne-gat) m. renegade
renifer (re-nee-fer) m. reindeer;(domesticated)arctic deer
renoma (re-no-ma) f. renown
renta (ren-ta) f. rent ; fixed
income; annuity; pension
rentowność (ren-tov-noshch) f.
profitability;earning capacity
rentgenolog (rent-ge-no-lok) m.
radiologist; roentgenologist
rentowny (ren-tov-ni) adj. m.
profitable;renumerative
reorganizacja (re-or-ga-nee-
zats-ya) f. reorganization
reparacja (re-pa-rats-ya) f.
1. repair; 2. reparation,
repatriacja (re-pa-tree-ats-ya)
f. repatriation
reperować (re-pe-ro-vach) v.
mend; repair;fix; set right
repertuar (re-per-too-ar) m.
repertory; repertoire
repetycja (re-pe-tits-ya) f.
repetition(of a lesson etc.)
replika (rep-lee-ka) f. 1, re-
plica; 2. rebuttal; 3. (theatre)cue; retort;rejoinder
replikować (re-plee-ko-vach) v.
answer back; rejoin; retort

reportaż (re-por-tash) m. 1.
account; 2. reporting; com-
mentary;coverage (of event etc.)
represja (re-pres-ya) f.
reprisal;repressive measures
reprezentacja (re-pre-zen-tats-
ya) f. representation
reprezentant (re-pre-zen-tant)
m. representative
reprezentować (re-pre-zen-to-
vach) v. represent; display
reprodukcja (re-pro-dook-tsya)
f. reproduction;copy;replica
republika (re-poob-lee-ka) f.
republic
republikański (re-poob-lee-kan-
skee) adj. m. republican
reputacja (re-poo-tats-ya) f.
reputation; (character)
resor (re-sor) m. (car) spring
resort (re-sort) m. 1. agency;
2. competence;scope;province
respekt (res-pekt) m. respect
restauracja (res-taw-rats-ya)
f. 1. restaurant; 2. restoration (of objects of art etc.)
restrykcja (res-trik-tsya) f.
restriction; reservation
restytucja (res-ti-toots-ya)
f. restitution; restoration
reszta (resh-ta) f. rest; reminder; change; residue
retoryka (re-to-ri-ka) f. rhetoric;manual of rhetoric
retusz (re-toosh) m. retouch
retuszować (re-too-sho-vach)
v. touch up; retouch
reumatyczny (re-oo-ma-tich-ni)
adj. m. rheumatic
reumatyzm (re-oo-ma-tizm) m.
rheumatism(pain in joint etc.)
rewanż (re-vansh) m. 1. rematch;
2. revenge; get back at
rewelacja (re-ve-lats-ya) f.
revelation;striking disclosure
rewers (re-vers) m. 1. receipt;
2. reverse (side etc.)
rewia (rev-ya) f. 1. parade;
2. (theatre) revue
rewidować (re-vee-do-vach) v.
1. revise; 2. search; 3. audit
rewizja (re-veez-ya) f. revision
search;audit;inspection;retrial

rewizjonizm (re-veez-yo-ńeezm)
m. revisionism
rewizyta (re-vee-zi-ta) f. return visit
rewolucja (re-vo-loots-ya) f. revolution;complete change
rewolucyjny (re-vo-loo-tsiy-ni) adj. m. revolutionary
rewolwer (re-vol-ver) m. revolver; gun (with revolv.cylinder)
rezerwa (re-zer-va) f. reserve
rezerwat (re-zer-vat) m. reservation;game preserve
rezerwować (re-zer-vo-vach) v. reserve; set aside; book
rezerwuar (re-zer-voo-ar) m. reservoir;(storage)tank
rezolutny (re-zo-loot-ni) adj. m. resolute;determined; game
rezonans (re-zo-nans) m. resonance(intesifying vibrations)
rezultat (re-zool-tat) m. result; effect; numerical answer
rezydencja (re-zi-den-tsya) f. residence;dwelling place
rezydent (re-zi-dent) m. resident(not a transient)
rezygnacja (re-zig-nats-ya) f. resignation;patient submission
reżim (re-zheem) m. regime
reżyser (re-zhi-ser) m. stage manager; (film) director
ręcznie (rańch-ńe) adv. by hand
ręcznik (rańch-ńeek) m. towel
ręczny (rańch-ni) adj. m. manual; hand made; wrist(watch)
ręczyć (rań-chich) v. guarantee
ręka (rań-ka) f. hand; arm;touch
rękaw (rań-kav) m. sleeve
rękawica (rań-ka-vee-tsa) f. mitten; gauntlet;mitt;glove
rękawiczka (rań-ka-veech-ka) f. glove(fur lined,velvet, etc.)
rękodzielnik (rań-ko-dzhel-ńeek) m. craftsman;handicraftsman
rękojeść (rań-ko-yeshch) f. hilt; handle; handgrip; helve
rękojmia (rań-koy-mya) f. guaranty; pledge; gage;warranty
rękopis (rań-ko-pees) m. manuscript; script; MS
robactwo (ro-bats-tvo) n.vermin-

robak (ro-bak) m. worm;beetle;grub
rober (ro-ber) m. (bridge) rubber (in card game)
robić (ro-beech) v. make; do;act; work; become; get;feel;turn;knit
robociarz (ro-bo-chash) m. common laborer (slang); mechanic
robocizna (ro-bo-cheez-na) f. wages;cost of labor; labor
roboczogodzina (ro-bo-cho-go-dzhee-na) f. man-hour
robot (ro-bot) m. robot
robota (ro-bo-ta) f. work; job
robotnica (ro-bot-ńee-tsa) f. worker (bee) ; operative;mechanic
robotnik (ro-bot-ńeek) m. worker; worker;operative;mechanic
robótki (ro-boot-kee) pl. needlework; fancy work
rocznica (roch-ńee-tsa) f. anniversary
rocznie (roch-ńe) adv. yearly
rocznik (roch-ńeek) m. annual; yearbook; annual set; age group
roczny (roch-ni) adj. m. annual; one year's (duration etc.)
rodak (ro-dak) m. compatriot
rodowity (ro-do-vee-ti) adj. m. native; by birth; trueborn
rodowód (ro-do-voot) m. genealogy; origin;pedigree;descent
rodzaj (ro-dzay) m. kind; sort; gender;type; race; manner;aspect
rodzajnik (ro-dzay-ńeek) m. article (definite or indefinite)
rodzeństwo (ro-dzeń-stvo) n. brothers and sisters
rodzice (ro-dzhee-tse)pl. parents;father and mother
rodzić (ro-dzheech)v. bear; procreate breed; yield (crops)
rodzina (ro-dzhee-na)f. family
rodzinny (ro-dzheeń-ni)adj. m. family; native; home(life etc.)
rodzynek (ro-dzi-nek) m. raisin; currant
rogacz (ro-gach) m. 1. stag; 2. cuckold;deceived husband
rogatka (ro-gat-ka) f. tollgate; toll bar; turnpike
rogaty (ro-ga-ti) adj. m. . horned; haughty; deceived (husband)

rogatywka (ro-ga-tiv-ka) f.
four-cornered cap(Polish style)
rogowacieć (ro-go-va-chech) v.
grow horny;become corneous
rogowaty (ro-go-va-ti) adj.
corneous ; horny
rogówka (ro-goov-ka) f. cornea
rogóżka (ro-goozh-ka) f. (door)
mat (flat,woven of straw etc.)
roić (ro-yeech) v. 1. dream;
imagine; 2. swarm; teem; run
rojalista (ro-ya-lees-ta) m.
royalist; supporter of the king
rojny (roy-ni) adj. m. teeming;
swarming(crowds etc.)
rojowisko (ro-yo-vees-ko) n.
hive; swarm;gathering place
rok (rok) m. year;a twelvemonth
rok przestępny (rok pzhe-stanp-
ni) leap year
rokować (ro-ko-vach) v. 1. negotiate 2. expect; promise
rokowania (ro-ko-va-ña) pl. 1.
negotiations; 2. prognosis
rola (ro-la) f. 1. arable land
2. (theatre) part;scroll;weight
rolka (rol-ka) f. roll; spool;
reel;runner;pulley;castor
rolnictwo (rol-neets-tvo) v.
agriculture;farming;husbandry
rolnik (rol-neek) m. farmer
romans (ro-mans) m. 1. novel;
2. love affair; laison
romantyczny (ro-man-tich-ni) adj.
m. romantic;full of romance
romantyk (ro-man-tik) m. romantic
romantyzm (ro-man-tizm) m. ro-
manticism(literary style etc.)
romański (ro-man-skee) adj. m.
Romance; Romanesque
romb (romb) m. rhomb;diamond
rondel (ron-del) m. stewpan
rondo (ron-do) n. brim; circular
plaza; traffic circle;circus
ronić (ro-neech) v. 1. shed;
2. miscarry;drop;cast;emit;moult
ropa (ro-pa) f. 1. puss; 2. crude
oil;rock oil; naphta;petroleum
ropieć (rop-yech) v. fester;have
oozing sore; suppurate
ropień (rop-yen) m. abscess
ropny (rop-ni) adj. m. purulent;
oil fired; oil-(derrick etc.)

ropucha (ro-poo-kha) f. toad
rosa (ro-sa) f. dew
rosły (ros-wi) adj. m. tall;
big frame; stalwart
rosnąć (ros-nownch) v. grow
rosół (ro-soow) m. broth;
bouillion; clear soup;pickle
rostbef (rost-bef) m. roast-
beef; baked beef
rosyjski (ro-siy-skee) adj. m.
Russian; of Russia
roszczenie (rosh-che-ñe) n.
claim; pretension; pretence
rościć (rosh-cheech)v. claim
roślina (rosh-lee-na) f. plant;
vegetable; living plant
roślinność (rosh-leen-noshch)
f. flora, ; vegetation
rowek (ro-vek) m. (small) channel; groove; gutter; rut;furrow
rower (ro-ver) n. bike; cycle
rowerzysta (ro-ve-zhis-ta) m.
cyclist
rozbawiony (roz-ba-vyo-ni) adj.
m. merry; amused;in high spirits
rozbestwić (roz-best-veech) v.
enrage;turn into a wild beast
rozbicie (roz-bee-che) n. break;
wreck;jumble;defeat;rout; hurt
rozbić (roz-beech) v. smash;
defeat; wreck;shatter;disrupt
rozbiegać się (roz-bye-gach shañ)
v. scatter; run; swarm (through)
rozbierać (roz-bye-rach) v. undress; strip; dismount; analyze
rozbieżny (roz-byezh-ni) adj. m.
divergent;different;discordant
rozbijać (roz-bee-yach) v. break
up; rout; crush;bluster;storm
rozbiór (roz-byoor) m. 1. analysis; 2. dismemberment;partition
rozbiórka (roz-byoor-ka) f. de-
molition;taking to pieces
rozbitek (roz-bee-tek) m. shipwreck person; castaway; wreck
rozbój (roz-booy) m. robbery;
piracy; banditry;highjacking
rozbójnik (roz-booy-neek) m.
bandit;robber;cutthroat;brigand
rozbrajać (roz-bra-yach) v.
disarm(a person etc.);dismantle
(a ship);appease; pacify

rozbrat (róz-brat) m. split;
disunion;break with somebody
rozbrojenie (roz-bro-ye-ńe) n.
disarmament;reduction of arms
rozbrojeniowy (roz-bro-ye-ńo-vi)
adj. m. disarmament
rozbrzmiewać (roz-bzhmye-vach)
v. resound;ring out; (re)echo
rozbudowa (roz-boo-do-va) f.
build up; extension;expansion
rozbudować (roz-boo-do-vach) v.
extend;enlarge;expand;develop
rozbudzić (roz-boo-dżheech)v.
rouse up; wake up ;excite;stir
rozchmurzyć (roz-khmoo-zhich)
v. clear up; brighten up
rozchodzić (roz-kho-dżheech) v.
1. stretch (shoes); 2. spread;
3. come apart
rozchód (róz-khoot) m. expendi-
ture; expenses; outgoings
rozchwytać (roz-khvi-tach) v.
snatch up;scramble for;sweep off
rozchylać (roz-khi-lach) v.
open; force apart, spread
rozciągać (roz-chown-gach) v.
stretch; extend;widen;expand
rozcieńczyć (roz-cheń-chich) v.
thin; dilute; rarefy;attenuate
rozcierać (roz-che-rach) v. rub;
grind;crush;spread (ointment)
rozcinać (roz-chee-nach) v.
cut up ; dissect; rip open
rozczarować (roz-cha-ro-vach) v.
disappoint;disenchant
rozczesać (roz-che-sach) v. comb
down;brush out(one's hair)
rozczłonkować (roz-chwon-ko-vach)
v. dismember;divide;break up
rozczulić (roz-choo-leech) v.
move; touch;affect;stir(feelings)
rozczyn (róz-chin) m. solution
(chem.); leaven (yeast)
rozdać (róz-dach) v. distribute
rozdarcie (roz-dar-che) n.
1. tear; 2. disruption
rozdeptać (roz-dep-tach) v.
trample out under foot;tread on
rozdęcie (roz-dań-che) n. swelling; inflation;expansion
rozdmuchać (roz-dmoo-khach) v.
fan; inflate;blow about;amplify

rozdrapać (roz-dra-pach) v.
1. scratch; 2. snatch up
rozdrażnić (roz-drazh-ńeech)
v. irritate; exaspreate; vex
rozdrobnić (roz-drob-ńeech) v.
split up; divide;crumble;morsel
rozdroże (roz-dro-zhe) n.
crossroads; parting of the ways
rozdwoić (roz-dvo-eech) v.
split; cleave; divide in two
rozdymać (roz-di-mach) v. inflate; swell;expand;puff out
rozdział (róz-dżhaw) m. distribution; disunion; parting
(hair);dispensation;chapter
rozdzielać (roz-dżhe-lach) v.
divide; distribute;set at odds
rozdzierać (roz-dżhe-rach) v.
tear up;tear asunder;rend;pierce
rozdźwięk (róz-dżhvyańk) m.
discord ;dissonance; clash
rozebrać (ro-zéb-rach) v. undress; analyze; take apart
rozedma (ro-zéd-ma) f. emphy-
sema(swelling produced by gas)
rozejm (ro-zeym) m. truce
rozejrzeć się (ro-zey-zhech
śhań), v. look around
rozejść się (ro-zeyśhch śhań)
v. split; part; separate
rozerwać się (ro-zér-vach śhań)
v. divert oneself;get torn
rozgałęzić (roz-ga-wań-żheech)
v. branch out; fork off
rozgałęzienie (roz-ga-wań-żhe-
ńe) n. branching;ramification
rozgardiasz (roz-gard-yash) m.
bustle; chaos; confusion
rozgarnać (roz-gar-nównch) v.
rake aside; part;brush apart
rozgarnięty (roz-gar-ńań-ti)
adj. m. bright; clever; sharp
rozglądać się (roz-glown-dach
śhań) v. look around;look for
rozgłaszać (roz-gwa-shach) v.
make known; broadcast
rozgłos (róz-gwos) m. publicity;
fame; renown;repute;notoriety
rozgłośnia (roz-gwośh-ńa) f.
broadcasting station
rozgmatwać (roz-gmat-vach) v.
disentangle; extricate

rozgnieść (roz-gńeshćh) v.
flatten; squash (once)
rozgniatać (roz-gńa-tać) v.
squash; flatten (often)
rozgniewać (roz-gńe-vać) v.
anger; vex; irritate
rozgoryczenie (roz-go-ri-che-ńe)
n. bitterness; exasperation
rozgoryczyć (roz-go-ri-chićh) v.
embitter; exacerbate;disgust
rozgotowac (roz-go-to-vać) v.
cook to a pulp;cook to rags
rozgraniczyć (roz-gra-ńee-chićh)
v. delimit; mark boundaries
rozgromić (roz-gró-meećh) v.
rout(the enemy);crush(an army)
rozgrywac (roz-gri-vać) v. play
one's game ;put through;carry out
rozgryzc (roz-grizhćh) v. bite
through;bite in two;crack(nuts)
rozgrzac (roz-gzhać) v. warm up
rozgrzebac (roz-gzhe-bać) v.
dig up; rake up; scatter
rozgrzeszyc (roz-gzhe-shićh) v.
absolve(of sins); forgive
rozgrzewac (roz-gzhe-vać) v.
warm up; rouse; stimulate
rozhukany (roz-khoo-ka-ni) adj.
m. wild; unruly;riotus
rozhustac (roz-khoósh-tać) v.
set swinging; set rocking
roziskrzyc (roz-eésk-zhićh) v.
start sparkle; make sparkle
rozjasnić (roz-yash-ńeećh) v.
brighten; clear up; clarify
rozjątrzyc (roz-yownt-zhićh) v.
exasperate; irritate; chafe
rozjemca (roz-yém-tsa) m. referee; arbiter; umpire
rozjeżdżać się (roz-yézh-dzhać
shań) v. disperse; part
rozjuszyc (roz-yoo-shićh) v.
enrage;infuriate; exasperate
rozkapryszony (roz-ka-pri-sho-
ni) adj. m. whimsical; fitful
rozkaz (róz-kas) m. order
rozkiełznąc (roz-kéwz-nać) v.
unbridle; unchain; let loose
rozkleic (roz-kle-eećh) v. 1.
unglue; weaken; 2. post up
rozkład (róz-kwat) m. dissolution;
decay; disposition; timetable ;
train schedule;breakdown

rozkładac (roz-kwa-dać) v. de-
compose; spread; display; stagger (hours);lay out; distribute
rozkołysac (roz-ko-wi-sać) v.
set rocking; set swinging;agitate
rozkopywac (roz-ko-pi-vać) v.
dig up; rip up; make excavations
rozkosz (róz-kosh) f. delight
rozkrajac (roz-kra-yać) v.
cut up; carve; slice; divide
rozkręcic (roz-krań-ćheećh) v.
unscrew; unreel;take to pieces
rozkruszyc (roz-kroo-shićh)
v. crush up; grind;disintegrate
rozkrzewic (roz-kzhe-veećh) v.
propagate; increase; diffuse
rozkuc (róz-kooćh) v. unshackle;
unshoe (horse);unchain;hammer out
rozkulbaczyc (roz-kool-ba-chićh)
v. unsaddle; take the saddle off
rozkupic (roz-koo-peećh) v. buy
up; buy everything;buy all
rozkwit (róz-kveet) m. bloom
rozkwitac (roz-kvee-tać) v.
flower; burst into flower;beam
rozlatywac sie (roz-la-ti-vać
shań) v. fly away; break up;
scatter;disperse;run away;burst
rozlazły (roz-láz-wi) adj. m.
slack; loose;spread out;sloppy
rozległy (roz-lég-wi) adj. m.
spacious; vast; wide;extensive
rozleniwiac (roz-le-ńeev-yać)
v. make lazy;induce to laziness
rozlepic (roz-le-peećh) v. post;
put up;paste up;stick;unstick
rozlew (róz-lev) m. flood
rozlew krwi (róz-lev krvee) m.
bloodshed;killing; slaughter
rozlewac (roz-le-vać) v. spill;
shed; pour(out);ladle out(soup)
rozliczenie (roz-lee-che-ńe) n.
settling; reckoning;settlement
rozliczny (roz-leéch-ni) adj.
m. manifold; diverse;numerous
rozliczyc (roz-leé-chićh) v.
settle up (accounts);calculate
rozlokowac (roz-lo-ko-vać) v.
put up; make at home; quarter
rozlosowac (roz-lo-só-vać) v.
allot; distribute by lot
rozluźnic (roz-loożh-ńeećh) v.
slacken; relax;unfasten

rozluźnienie (roz-loozh-ńe-ńe)
n. loosening;laxity;slackness
rozładować (roz-wa-do-vać) v.
unload; discharge(a battery)
rozłam (róz-wam) m. breach;
split;break;division;dissent
rozłamać (roz-wa-mać) v.
break (in two); split
rozłazić się (roz-wa-zheeć
śhań) v. fall apart; disperse
rozłączenie (roz-wown-che-ńe)
n. separation; disjunction
rozłączyć (roz-wown-chić) v.
disconnect;sever;uncouple
rozłąka (roz-wown-ka) f. separation (of people)
rozłożyć (roz-wo-zhić) v.
spread;lay out;disassemble
rozłupać (roz-woo-pać) v.
split; cleave; rift; slit;
crack(nuts,etc.); rive
rozmach (róz-makh) m. impetus;
dash; grand style;force;swing
rozmaitości (roz-ma-ee-tosh-
chee) pl. miscellanea; vaude-
ville theater;variety theater
rozmaity (roz-ma-ee-ti) adj.
m. various; miscellaneous
rozmaryn (roz-má-rin) m. rose-
mary (Rosmarinus)
rozmarzenie (roz-ma-zhe-ńe) n.
daydream;dreaminess;reverie
rozmawiać (roz-máv-yać) v.
converse; talk; speak with
rozmazać (roz-ma-zać) v. blur;
smear;daub; let out (a secret)
rozmiar (róz-myar) m. dimension;
extent;size;proportion;scale
rozmienić (roz-mye-ńeeć) v.
change (money);get the change
rozmieszczać (roz-myesh-chać)
v. arrange; dispose;place;put
rozmieszczenie (roz-myesh-che-
ńe) n. distribution; layout
rozmiękczyć (roz-myank-chić) v.
soften; soak;steep;make soft
rozmięknąć (roz-myank-nownć)
v. become soft ;get soaked;sop
rozmijać się (roz-mee-yać śhań)
v. miss; swerve from;fail to meet
rozmiłować się (roz-mee-wo-vać
śhań) v. take a liking to

rozminać się(roz-mee-nownch śhań)v.
miss (on road):pass each other
rozmnażać (roz-mna-zhać) v.breed;
multiply; propagate; imcrease
rozmoczyć (roz-mo-chić) v.soak;
steep; wet thoroughly; sodden
rozmoknąć (roz-mok-nownć) v.
become soaked; get soggy
rozmowa (roz-mo-va) f. conversation; talk ;discourse
rozmowny (roz-móv-ni) adj. m.
communicative; talkative
rozmówca (roz-moov-tsa) m.
interlocutor (in conversation)
rozmówić się (roz-moo-veeć
śhań) v. talk over;get understood
rozmysł (róz-misw) m. premeditation; consideration; intention
rozmyślać (roz-miśh-lać) v.
meditate; ponder how to do
rozmyślanie (roz-mish-la-ńe) n.
meditation; contemplation
rozmyślić się (roz-miśh-leećh
śhań), v. change one's mind
rozmyślny (roz-miśhl-ni) adj.
m. deliberate;intentional;wilful
roznamiętnić (roz-na-myańt-
ńeech) v. impassion; excite
rozniecić (roz-ńe-ćheech) v.
inflame; enkindle a fire;inspire
roznosić (roz-no-śheeć) v.
carry around; serve;rout;cut up
rozochocić (roz-o-kho-ćheeć)
v. make merry;enliven; animate
rozogniać się (roz-og-ńach
śhań) n. inflame; excite;flare up
rozpacz (róz-pach) f. despair
rozpad (róz-pat) m. decay;break up
rozpakować (roz-pa-kó-vać) v.
unpack(one's luggage);unwrap
rozpalić (roz-pa-leeć) v.fire up;
ignite; start a fire; set ablaze
rozpamiętywać (roz-pa-myań-ti-
vać) v. contemplate ;reflect upon
rozpaplać (roz-pa-plać) v.
blab out;divulge ; babble out
rozpasany (roz-pa-sa-ni) adj. m.
unbridled; dissolute; licentious
rozpatrywać (roz-pa-tri-vać)
v. consider; act upon ;examine
rozpęd (róz-pańt) m. impetus;
dash ;momentum; taking a run

rozpędzać (roz-pán-dzach) v. pick
up speed; scatter;disperse
rozpętać (roz-pán-tach) v. unshackle; unleash;let loose
rozpiąć (róz-pyównch) v. unbuckle; undo; stretch; set (sail)
rozpieczętować (roz-pye-chán-
to-vach), v. unseal;open
rozpierać (roz-pyé-rach) v. expand; extend; push aside
rozpierzchnąć się (roz-pyezh-
khównch shán) v. scatter
rozpieszczać (roz-pyésh-chach)
v. pamper; spoil;coddle up
rozpiętość (roz-pyán-toshch) f.
span; spread; range;strech
rozpinać (roz-pée-nach) v. unbutton; stretch; spread (sails etc.)
rozplątać (roz-plówn-tach) v.
untangle;untie(a knot);unravel
rozplesć (róz-leshch) v. unbraid;
untwine; unplait(hair);unravel
rozpłakać się (roz-pwa-kach shán)
v. burst into tears;start weeping
rozpłaszczyć (roz-pwash-chich) v.
flatten out; flat (metal)
rozpłatać (roz-pwa-tach) v.slit;
split; cleave; split in two
rozpłodowy (roz-pwo-dó-vi) adj.
m. (for) breeding; breeding-
rozpłodzić (roz-pwó-dźheech) v.
propagate;cause reproduction
rozpłód (róz-pwoot) m. propagation; reproduction
rozpływać się(roz-pwi-vach shán)v.
melt away;dissolve; flow;spread
rozpoczęcie (roz-po-chán-che) n.
start; outbreak;beginning;start
rozpoczynać (roz-po-chi-nach) v.
begin; start going; open;initiate
rozpogodzić się (roz-po-go-
dźheech shán) v. clear up
brighten up;cheer up;rise spirit
rozporek (roz-pó-rek) m. fly; slit
rozporządzać (roz-po-zhówn-dzach)
v. dispose; decree; order;control
rozpościerać (roz-pośh-che-rach)
v. unfurl; spread out;expand
rozpowiadać (roz-po-vya-dach) v.
tell tales;divulge; talk about
rozpowszechniać (roz-pov-shekh-
ńach) v. widespread; diffuse
disseminte;propagate; spread

rozpowszechnienie (roz-pov-
shekh-ńe-ńe) n. propagation;
spread;diffusion;prevalence
rozpoznać (roz-póz-nach) v.
recognize; spot; diagnose
rozpoznanie (roz-po-zná-ńe) n.
diagnosis; identification;
reconnaissance;recognition
rozpoznawczy (roz-poz-náv-chi)
adj. m. diagnostic;distinctive
rozpraszać (roz-prá-shach) v.
scatter; dispel; distract;disperse
rozprawa (roz-prá-va) f. trial;
showdown; dissertation; debate
rozprawiać (roz-práv-yach) v.
debate: argue; dispute; reason; talk at length;discuss
rozprawić się (roz-prá-veech
shán) v. settle matters;
fight out;dispose of; floor
rozprężyć (roz-prán-zhich) v.
distend; expand; dilate; re-
sile;deprive of elasticity
rozprostować (roz-pros-tó-vach)
v. straighten;unbend;stretch(legs)
rozproszyć (roz-pró-shich) v.
disperse;scatter;dispel;distract
rozprowadzić (roz-pro-vá-
dźheech) v. spread; retail;
distribute; dilute; convey;smear
rozpruć (róz-prooch) v. rip up;
open; unsew;unravel;rip open
rozprzedać (roz-pzhé-dach) v.
sell out;sell(successively)
rozprzedaż (roz-pzhe-dash) f.
sale;complete sale;retailing
rozprzestrzenic (roz-pzhe-
stzhe-ńeech) v. spread;propagate
rozprzegać (roz-pzhán-gach) v.
1. unhitch; 2. disorganize
rozprzężenie (roz-pzhan-zhé-ńe)
n. anarchy; demoralization
rozpusta (roz-poós-ta) f. debauch; riot; libertinism
rozpustnica (roz-poost-ńee-tsa)
f. rake; rip; libertine; debauchee; profligate; libertine
rozpustnik (roz-poóst-ńeek) m.
libertine; debauchee; rake;
profligate;rip; reprobate
rozpuszczać (roz-poosh-chach)
v. dissolve; dismiss; let go;
disband;thaw;melt;defrost;unfreeze

rozpuszczalnik (roz-poos'-chál-ñeek) m. solvent;pair ...inner
rozpuszczalny (roz-poos..-ch?l-ni) adj. m. soluble;dissolvable
rozpychać się (roz-pi-khach shań) v.shove aside; jostle; elbow one's way;push one's way
rozpylacz (roz-pi-lach) m. sprayer; nozzle; atomizer
rozpylać (roz-pi-lach) v. spray; pulverize; atomize
rozpytywać (roz-pi-ti-vach) v. ask for;inquire for;ask questions
rozrachować (roz-ra-kho-vach) v. settle accounts; calculate
rozrachunek (roz-ra-khoo-nek) m. squaring up accounts
rozradzać się (roz-ra-dzach shań) v. breed;propagate
rozrastać się (roz-ras-tach shan) v. grow larger; in-crease; develop; expand
rozrąbać (roz-rown-bach) v. cut asunder; hew apart;chop up
rozrobić (roz-ro-beech) v. stir up; dilute;scheme;intrigue;brawl
rozrodczość (roz-rod-choshch) f. reproduction;reproductiveness
rozróżniać (roz-roozh-ñach) v. distinguish; tell apart;discern
rozruchy (roz-roo-khy) pl. riots; disturbances
rozruszać (roz-roo-shach) v. start up; stir up; put in motion;set in motion;animate
rozrywać (roz-ri-vach) v. burst; disrupt;tear open;entertain
rozrywka (roz-riv-ka) f. amusement; recreation; pastime
rozrządnica (roz-zhownd-ñee-tsa) f. control panel
rozrzedzić (roz-zhe-dżheech) v. dilute; rarefy;thin down;weaken
rozrzewnić (roz-zhev-ñeech) v. move; touch;affect;stir(the soul)
rozrzucać (roz-zhoo-tsach) v. scatter; squander;distribute
rozrzutność (roz-zhoot-noshch) f. extravagance;lavishness
rozrzutny (roz-zhoot-ni) adj. m. wasteful; extravagant; thriftless;squandering;prodigal; spendthrift; lavish

rozsada (roz-sa-da) f. seedling; seedlings
rozsadzać (roz-sa-dzach) v. space-out;place; seat separately; blow up;explode;split
rozsądek (roz-sown-dek) m. good sense; discretion;reason
rozsądny (roz-sownd-ni) adj. m. sensible; reasonable; advisable;sound;judicious
rozsiadać się(roz-sha-dach shan)v. sit stretched; sprawl round
rozsiekać (roz-she-kach) v. cut up; slash asunder; hack up
rozsiewać (roz-she-vach) v. saw; disseminate;spread;shed
rozsiodłać (roz-shod-wach) v. unsaddle;take the saddle off
rozsławiać (roz-swav-yach) v. glorify; make famous; extol
rozstać się (roz-stach shań) v. part; give up;part with
rozstanie (roz-sta-ñe) n. parting;separation
rozstawać się (roz-sta-vach shań) v. part with; give up
rozstawiać (roz-stav-yach) v. disperse; place apart; space; spread;put at intervals
rozstąpić się(roz-stown-peech shań) v. step aside;come apart;split
rozstęp (roz-stanp) m. gap; space; slit;interval;heave
rozstroić (roz-stro-eech) v. put out of tune; upset; disarray;derange;disorder; untune
rozstrój (roz-strooy) m. upset; disorder;confusion;derangement
rozstrzelać (roz-stzhe-lach) v. 1. scatter; 2. execute by shooting;put before a firing squad
rozstrzygać (roz-stzhi-gach) v. try out; decide; fight out; judge
rozstrzygnięcie (roz-stzhig-nan-che) v. decision; settleme(nt)
rozsuwać (roz-soo-vach) v. part; draw aside;separate;expand(a compas)
rozsyłać (roz-si-wach) v. distribute; circulate; send out
rozsypać (roz-si-pach) v. disperse(a granular substance);spill
rozszarpać (roz-shar-pach) v. tear up; claw; disjoin;mangle

rozszczepiac (roz-shchep-yach)
v. split; cleave; fissure
rozszczepienie (roz-shche-pye-
ne) n. split; diffraction
rozszerzac (roz-she-zhach) v.
widen; broaden; enlarge; expand;spread out;extend;open
rozszerzenie (roz-she-zhe-ne)
n. enlargement; dilation
rozsznurowac (roz-shnoo-ro-
vach) v. unlace;loosen the lace
rozszyfrowac (roz-shif-ro-vach)
v. decode; break the code
rozscielac (roz-shche-lach) v.
spread; make the bed
rozsmieszac (roz-shmye-shach) v.
amuse; make laugh;be amusing
rozswiecic (roz-shvye-cheech) v.
light up;throw light on;shine on
roztaczac (roz-ta-chach) v. roll
out; spread;unfold;display;bore
roztajac (roz-ta-yach) v. thaw
roztapiac (roz-tap-yach) v.
melt; smelt(metal);thaw (ice)
roztargac (roz-tar-gach) v.
tear to pieces;ruffle;dishevel
roztargniony (roz-targ-no-ni)
adj. m. absentminded ; distracted; scatterbrained ; far-away
rozterka (roz-ter-ka) f. tearing
between; dissension;suspense
roztkliwiac (roz-tklee-vyach) v.
feel for; touch; move;stir
roztłuc (roz-twoots) v. smash up
roztopy (roz-to-pi) pl. thaw
roztratowac (roz-tra-to-vach)
v.run over; trample; tread
under foot;trample to death
roztrabic (roz-trown-beech) v.
broadcast; blaze abroad
roztracic (roz-trown-cheech) v.
push aside;elbow;part;jostle
roztropnosc (roz-trop-noshch) f.
prudence; thoughtfulness
roztropny (roz-trop-ni) adj. m.
wise;cautious;circumspect;politic
roztrwonic (roz-trvo-neech) v.
squander(a fortune,money etc.)
roztrzaskac (roz-tzhas-kach) v.
smash; shatter; crash to pieces
roztrzepanie (roz-tzhe-pa-ne) n.
scatterbrain; fickleness

roztrzepany (roz-tzhe-pa-ni)
adj. m. scatterbrain; giddy
roztwor (roz-tvoor) m.(chem.)
solution(colloidal,molal etc.)
roztyc sie (roz-tich shan) v.
grow fat; become fat
rozum (ro-zoom) m. mind; reason; intellect; understanding;
wit;senses; judgment; brains
rozumiec (ro-zoom-yech) v.
understand; get; perceive
rozumny (ro-zoom-ni) adj. m.
rational;reasonable; wise
rozumowac (ro-zoo-mo-vach) v.
reason; argue
rozwaga (roz-va-ga) f. thoughtfulness; prudence; reflection;
deliberation; consideration
rozwalac (roz-va-lach) v. shatter; demolish; smash; sprawl
rozwarty kat (roz-var-ti kownt)
m. obtuse angle
rozważac (roz-va-zhach) v.
1. weigh out; 2. consider
rozweselic (roz-ve-se-leech) v.
cheer up; put in good humor
rozwiac (roz-vyach) v. blow
away; blow to and fro;scatter
rozwiązac (roz-vyown-zach) v.
untie; solve; undo; dissolve;
loosen; unbind; unravel; undo
rozwiązanie (roz-vyown-za-ne)
n. solution; way out; (child)
delivery; realization;execution
rozwiązły (roz-vyown-z-wi) adj.
m. fast; dissolute;debauched
rozwidniac (roz-veed-nach) v.
dawn; be lit up;become lit up
rozwiedziony (roz-vye-dzho-ni)
adj. m. divorced(f.divorcee)
rozwierac (roz-vye-rach) v.
open wide; fling open
rozwieszac (roz-vye-shach) v.
hang about;stretch; spread out
rozwiesc sie (roz-vyeshch shan)
v. divorce; dwell upon
rozwijac (roz-vee-yach) v. unwrap; unfold; develop; spread
rozwikłac (roz-veek-wach) v.
disentangle; unravel; clear up
rozwikłanie (roz-veek-wa-ne) n.
unraveling; disentanglement

rozwlekać (roz-vle-kaćh) v.
drag out; protract; spread
rozwlekły (roz-vlek-wi) adj. m.
verbose; lengthy; long-spun
rozwodnić (roz-vod-neećh) v.
dilute; water down; weaken
rozwodnik (roz-vód-neek) m. divorced man; divorcee
rozwodowy (roz-vo-dó-vi) adj. m.
divorce-(proceedings etc.)
rozwodzić (roz-vo-dźheećh) v.
divorce(a married couple)
rozwojowy (roz-vo-yo-vi) adj.
evolutional; developmental
rozwolnienie (roz-vol-ńe-ńe) n.
diarrhea; lax bowels; open bowels
rozwozić (roz-vo-źheećh) v.
transport; deliver (mail etc.)
rozwód (roz-vood) m. divorce
rozwódka (roz-vood-ka) f. divorcee; divorced woman
rozwój (roz-vooy) m. development; evolution; growth
rozwścieczony (roz-vśhćhe-cho-
ni) adj. m. enraged; furious
rozwydrzony (roz-vid-zhó-ni)
adj. m. rampant; wild; lawless
rozzłościć (roz-zwóśh-ćheećh)
v. irritate; make angry; provoke
rozżalenie (roz-zha-lé-ńe) n.
grudge; resentment; bitterness
rozżarzyć (roz-zha-zhićh) v.
inflame; set on fire; fire
rożek (ró-zhek) m. small horn;
croissant; small corner
rożen (ro-zhen) m. roasting spit
ród (rood) m. clan; breed; family; stock; race; origin; line
róg (roog) m. horn; corner; bugle; antler; corner kick(sport)
rój (rooy) m. swarm; hive; cluster
rość (rooshćh) v. grow; age; go up
rów (roov) m. ditch; trench; trough
rówieśnik (roo-vyéśh-ńeek) m.
peer of same age; contemporary
równać (roov-naćh) v. equalize;
level; make even; smooth out
równanie (roov-na-ńe) n. equation; equalization; comparison
równia (roov-na) f. plane; level
równie (roov-ńe) adv. equally
również (roov-ńesh) conj. also;
too; likewise; as well

równik (roov-ńeek) m. equator
równina (roov-ńee-na) f. plain;
flat country; level landscape
równo (roov-no) adv. even; (equi-)
równoboczny (roov-no-boch-ni)
adj. m. equilateral
równoczesny (roov-no-chés-ni)
adj. m. simultaneous
równoległobok (roov-no-leg-wó-
bok) m. parallelogram
równoległy (roov-no-lég-wi) adj.
m. parallel to; collateral
równoleżnik (roov-no-lezh-ńeek)
m. parallel(of latitude)
równomierny (roov-no-myér-ni)
adj. m. even; uniform; steady
równoramienny (roov-no-ra-myen-
ni) adj. m. isosceles(triangle)
równorzędny (roov-no-zhánd-ni)
adj. m. equal rank; equivalent
równość (roov-noshćh) f. equality; parity; identity
równouprawnienie (roov-no-oo-
prav-ńe-ńe) n. equality of
rights(of women, men etc.)
równowaga (roov-no-vá-ga) f.
equilibrium; balance; poise
równowartościowy (roov-no-var-
tosh-chó-vi) adj. m. equivalent; equipollent
równoważny (roov-no-vázh-ni)
adj. m. equivalent; equiponderant
równoważyć (roov-no-vázhićh)
v. balance; equalize; even up
równoznaczny (roov-no-znáćh-ni)
adj. m. synonymous; tantamount
rozga (rooz-ga) f. switch; cane
róż (roozh) m. rouge ; pink
róża (roo-zha) f. rose(flower etc.)
różaniec (roo-zha-ńets) m. ro-
sary; beads; telling one's beads
różdżka (roozhdzh-ka) f. dowsing
rod ; twig; divining rod(or wand)
różnica (roozh-ńee-tsa) f. difference ; disparity; dissent
różniczka (roozh-ńeech-ka) f.
differential; small difference
różnić się (roozh-ńeećh śhán) v.
differ ; be at variance
różnobarwny (roozh-no-bárv-ni)
adj. m. many colored ; motley
różnojęzyczny (roozh-no-yán-
zich-ni) adj. m. many-tongued

różnolity (roozh-no-lee-ti) adj. m. diverse ; varied
róznorodny (roozh-no-ród-ni) adj. m. heterogeneous ;varied
róznoznaczny (roozh-no-znach-ni) adj. m. ambiguous
różny (roozh-ni) adj. m. different miscellaneous;sundry
różowy (roo-zho-vi) adj. m. pink; rosy ; ruddy ;rose color
rtęciowy (rtań-cho-vi) adj.m. mercuric(compounds etc.)
rtęc (rtańch) f. mercury
rubaszny (roo-bash-ni) adj. m. coarse ; ill-mannered
rubin (roo-been) m. ruby (red)
rubryka (roo-bri-ka) f. space; column;blank space; rubric
ruch (rookh) m. move; movement; traffic; motion; gesture stir
ruchawka (roo-kháv-ka) f. riot
ruchliwy (rookh-lee-vi) adj.m. busy; mobile; agile;active
ruchomości (roo-kho-mósh-chee) pl. movables (personal property);belongings;(one's things)
ruchomy (roo-kho-mi) adj. m. mobile ;moving; shifting,flexile
ruczaj (roo-chay) m. brook
ruda (roo-da) f. ore(metallic)
rudera (roo-dé-ra) f. run-down house ; shanty; ruin ;hovel
rudy (roo-di) adj. m. red(haired);russet;ginger;foxy;ruddy
rufa (roo-fa) f. stern ;poop
rugować (roo-go-vaćh) v. eject; oust; evict; eliminate ;displace
ruina (roo-ee-na) f. ruin,wreck
ruja (roo-ya) f. heat; rut
rujnować (rooy-no-vach) v. ruin; undo; destroy;wreck
ruleta (roo-lé-ta) f. roulette
rulon (roo-lon) m. roll;rouleau
rum (room) m. rum (drink)
rumak (roo-mak) m. charger; steed; palfrey; courser
rumianek (roo-mya-nek) m. camomile ; chamonile(tea)
rumiany (roo-mya-ni) adj. m. rosy ; ruddy; browned;florid
rumienic (roo-mye-neech) v. blush; brown; redden;color
rumieniec (roo-mye-ńets) m. blush; ruddiness; floridity

rumor (roo-mor) m. racket; uproar; rumble; clatter; din
rumowisko (roo-mo-vees-ko) n. debris ; rubble; brash
rumuński (roo-moón-skee) adj. m. Rumanian ;of Rumania
runąc (roo-nównch) v. fall down; collapse; crash; swoop;resound
runda (roon-da) f. bout; round; lap; fall (in wrestling)
runo (roo-no) n. fleece; nap
rupiecie (roo-pyé-che) n. rubbish; trash; junk; stuff;oddments
ruptura (roop-too-ra) f. hernia
rura (roo-ra) f. tube; pipe
rurka (roor-ka) f. small pipe
rurociąg (roo-ro-chówng) m. pipeline ;run of pipes;piping
rusałka (roo-sáw-ka) f. undine; naiad;water nymph; vanessa
ruszac (roo-shaćh) v. move; stir; touch; start;take away;withdraw
rusznikarz (roosh-ńee-kash) m. gunsmith (man or shop)
rusztowanie (roosh-to-va-ńe) n. scaffold ; cradle (hanging)
rutyna (roo-ti-na) f. routine
rutynowany (roo-ti-no-vá-ni) adj. m. experienced;conpetent
rwać (rvach) v. pluck; tear; pull out; pull up; rush ;burst
rwący (rvówn-tsy) adj. m. rapid; racking (pain);swift flowing
rwetes (rve-tes) m. bustle; ado; racket ; turmoil ;agitation; stir
ryba (ri-ba) f. fish; the Fish
rybak (rí-bak) m. fisherman
rybny staw (rib-ni stav) fish pond (artficially made)
rybołóstwo (ri-bo-woós-tvo) n. fishery; fishing
rycerski (ri-tser-skee) adj. m. chivalrous ; courteous
rycerz (ri-tsesh) m. knight
rychło (rikh-wo) adv. soon; quickly; early; soon after
rychły (rikh-wi) adj. m. speedy; quick; early; prompt;approaching
rycina (ri-chee-na) f. engraving; illustration;cartoon;drawing;plate
rycynus (ri-tsi-noos) m. castor oil; castor oil plant
ryczałt (ri-chawt) m. lump sum; global sum

ryczeć (ri-chech) v. roar; moo; bellow; low; growl; bray; hoot; yell

ryć (rich) v. dig; root: engrave; carve; excavate; burrow; plough

rydel (ri-del) m. spade; spud

rydwan (rid-van) m. chariot

rygiel (ri-gel) m. bolt; bar; lock

rygor (ri-gor) m. rigor; severity

ryj (riy) m. snout; phiz; mug(vulg.)

ryk (rik) m. roar; moo; low; yell

rylec (ri-lets) m. burin; graver; chisel; etching- needle; dry point

rym (rim) m. rhyme; rhyme word

rymarz (ri-mash) m. saddler

rymować (ri-mó-vach) v. rhyme

rynek (ri-nek) m. market(square)

rynna (rin-na) f. gutter; chute

rynsztok (rin-shtok) m. sewer

rynsztunek (rin-shtoo-nek) m. armor; armature; outfit; kit

rys (ris) m. feature; trait

rysa (ri-sa) f. crack; flow; fissure; scratch; rift; crevice; chink

rysopis (ri-so-pees) m. description(of a person for a passport)

rysować (ri-so-vach) v. draw; design; sketch; draft; trace; show

rysownica (ri-sov-nee-tsa) f. drawing board; drafting table

rysownik (ri-sov-neek) m. draftsman; illustrator; designer

rysunek (ri-soo-nek) m. sketch; drawing; draft; outline; cartoon

rysunkowy (ri-soon-ko-vi) adj.m. tracing; drawing; cartoon; drawn

ryś (rish) m. lynx

rytm (ritm) m. rhythm; cadence

rytmiczny (rit-meech-ni) adj. m. rhythmic; regular; measured

rytownictwo (ri-tov-neets-tvo) n. engraving; die sinking

rytownik (ri-tov-neek) m. engraver; die sinker

rytuał (ri-too-aw) m. ritual

rywal (ri-val) m. rival; contestant

rywalizacja (ri-va-lee-záts-ya) f. rivalry; competition; emulation

ryza (ri-za) f. ream; restraint

ryzyko (ri-zi-ko) n. risk; venture

ryzykować (ri-zi-kó-vach) v. risk; venture; gamble; hazard

ryzykowny (ri-zi-kóv-ni) adj.m. risky; hazardous; venturesome

ryż (rizh) m. rice

ryży (ri-zhi) adj. m. red (haired); russet; ginger; foxy; red-brown

rzadki (zhád-kee) adj. m. rare; thin

rzadko (zhád-ko) adv. seldom; thinly rarely; far apart; exceptionally

rzadkość (zhád-koshch) f. rarity; sparseness; curiosity; curio

rząd (zhownt) m. row; rank; file; line up; government

rządca (zhownd-tsa) f. administrator; ruler; land steward

rządowy (zhown-dó-vi) adj. m. governmental; government-; state-

rządzić (zhown-dzheech) v. rule; govern; control; direct; be in power

rzec (zhets) v. say; utter.

rzecz (zhech) f. thing; matter; act; stuff; deal; work; subject; theme

rzeczka (zhech-ka) f. small river; river; brook; stream

rzecznik (zhech-neek) m. spokesman; attorney; patent agent

rzeczownik (zhech-óv-neek) m. noun; substantive (grammar)

rzeczowo (zhe-chó-vo) adv. factually; terse; business like; to the point; objectively

rzeczoznawca (zhe-cho-znáv-tsa) m. expert; specialist(authority)

rzeczpospolita (zhech-pos-po-lee-ta) f. republik; commonwealth

rzeczywistość (zhe-chi-vees-toshch) f. reality; actuality

rzeczywisty (zhe-chi-vees-ti) adj. m. real; actual; virtual

rzednieć (zhed-nech) v. grow thin; become rare; scatter; thin

rzeka (zhe-ka) f. river; stream

rzekomo (zhe-kó-mo) adv. would be; allegedly; supposedly; ostensibly

rzekomy (zhe-ko-mi) adj.m. make believe; reputed; supposed; sham; alleged; immaginary; so called

rzemień (zhe-myeń) m. leather strap; leather band; leather belt

rzemieślniczy (zhe-myeshl-nee-chi) adj. m. trade; craft-

rzemieślnik (zhe-myeshl-neek) m. artisan; craftsman; tradesman

rzemiosło (zhe-myós-vo) n. (handi) craft; trade; job; business

rzemyk (zhe-mik) m. small leather
strap;chin strap; thong
rzepa (zhe-pa) f. turnip
rzepak (zhe-pak) m. rapeseed;cole
rzesza (zhe-sha) f. crowd; Reich
rzeszoto (zhe-sho-to) n. sieve
rzeski (zhesh-kee) adj. m. lively; brisk ; spry; fresh;brisk
rzeskosc (zhesh-koshch) f. vigor
rzetelny (zhe-tel-ni) adj. m.
honest; upright ; fair; real
rzewny (zhev-ni) adj. m. wistful
rzezac (zhe-zach) v. slaughter;
castrate ; circumcise
rzezimieszek (zhe-zhee-mye-shek)
m. cutpurse; thief; pickpocket
rzez (zhezh) f. carnage; massacre;slaughter ; shambles;carnage
rzezba (zhezh-ba) f. sculpture
rzezbiarstwo (zhezh-byar-stvo)
n. sculpture; sculpturing
rzezbiarz (zhezh-byash) m. sculptor;artist creating sculptures
rzezbic (zhezh-beech) v. carve;
cut;sculpture;weather(the earth)
rzeznia (zhezh-na) f. slaughter-
house
rzeznik (zhezh-neek) m. butcher
rzezwic (zhezh-veech) v. refresh
rzezwosc (zhezh-voshch) f. agil-
ity; briskness;sprightliness
rzezwy (zhezh-vi) adj. m. agile;
brisk; smart;spry;lively;bracing
rzezaczka (zhe-zhownch-ka) f.
gonorrhea
rzedem (zhan-dem) adv. in a row
rzedna (zhand-na) f. ordinate
rzepolic (zhan-po-leech) v.
scrape (on fiddle);rasp(the fiddle)
rzesa (zhan-sa) f. eyelash
rzesisty (zhan-shees-ti) adj. m.
profuse; heavy; abundant;copious
rzezic (zhan-zheech) v. death
rattle ; ruckle(in sickness)
rznac (zhnownch) v. cut,carve;
butcher; vulg.:screw;have sex
rzodkiew (zhod-kev) f. radish
rzodkiewka (zhod-kev-ka) f. rad-
ish(the pungent root eaten raw)
rzucac (zhoo-tsach) v. throw;
fling; pitch; dash;hurl; toss
rzucic (zhoo-cheech) v. throw;
cast; plunge; dash; pitch; fling

rzut (zhoot) m. throw; cast;
projection; view; sketch
rzutki (zhoot-kee) adj. m.
brisk; lively; enterprising
rzutkosc (zhoot-koshch) f.
briskness; initiative
rzyc (zhich) f. (vulg.) ass
rzygac (zhi-gach) v. vomit;
belch; spew; eject;emit
rzymski (zhim-skee) adj. m.
Roman; of Rome(church;rite)
rzec (rzhech) v. whinny; neigh
rznac (rzhnownch) v. cut; saw;
engrave; carve; butcher; bang;
play cards; (vulg.):screw
rzniecie (rzhnan-che) n. colic;
bellyache; (slang): beating
rzysko (rzhis-ko) n. stubble-
field; rye field
sabat (sa-bat) m, Sabbath
sabotaz (sa-bo-tash) m. sabotage; act of sabotage
sacharyna (sa-kha-ri-na) f.
saccharine
sad (sad) m. orchard
sadlo (sad-wo) n. leaflard
sadowic (sa-do-veech) v. place;
show to a seat; seat
sadownik (sa-dov-neek) m. fruit-
grower;fruit farmer; orchardist
sadyba (sa-di-ba) f. dwelling ;
house; human habitation; home
sadysta (sa-dis-ta) m. sadist
sadza (sa-dza) f. soot; black
sadzac (sa-dzach) v. show to
a seat; seat;make sit down
sadzawka (sa-dzav-ka) f. pool
sadzic (sa-dzheech) v. plant;
set; run; speed;stud(decorate)
sadzonka (sa-dzon-ka) f. seedling; quickset; cutling
sadzonejajka (sa-dzo-ne yay-ka)
s. fried eggs sunny side up
safandula (sa-fan-doo-wa) f.
bungler; yes-man; oaf;muff;duffer
safian (sa-fyan) m. morocco
(lather); saffian
sagan (sa-gan) m. kettle ;pot
sak (sak) m. dipnet; sack
sakrament (sa-kra-ment) m. sacrament (of matrimony etc.)
sakwa (sak-va) f. wallet;purse
money-bag; feed-bag ;nose bag

sala (sa-la) f. 1. hall; 2. audience (in a hall)

salaterka (sa-la-ter-ka) f. salad bowl; vegetable dish

salceson (sal-tse-son) m. headcheese; (mock)brawn

saletra (sa-let-ra) f. niter; saltpeter;potassium nitrate

salina (sa-lee-na) f. saltworks; saline; salt mine

salmiak (sal-myak) m. ammonium-chloride; sal-ammoniac

salon (sa-lon) m. drawing-room

salonka (sa-lon-ka) f. club car (railroad);parlor car

salutować (sa-loo-to-vach) v. salute; dip the flag

salwa (sal-va) f. volley;salvo

sałata (sa-wa-ta) f. 1. lettuce; salad; 2. cabman(slang)

sam (sam) adj. m. alone; oneself; myself; yourself; nothing but

samica (sa-mee-tsa) f. female

samiec (sam-yets) m. male

samobójca (sa-mo-booy-tsa) m. suicide; suicidal man

samobójczy (sa-mo-booy-chi) adj. m. suicidal;leading to suicide

samobójstwo (sa-mo-booy-stvo) n. suicide;act of killing oneself

samochód (sa-mo-khood) m. automobile; car;motor car

samochwał (sa-mo-khvaw) m. braggart; boaster; blow hard

samodział (sa-mo-dżaw) m. homespun (cloth)

samodzielność (sa-mo-dżhel-noshch) f. independence

samodzielny (sa-mo-dżhel-ni) adj. m.self-reliant; independent; self-contained

samogłoska (sa-mo-gwos-ka) f. vowel; vocal

samogon (sa-mo-gon) m. moonshine

samoistny (sa-mo-eest-ni) adj. m. independent;autonomous

samokrytyka (sa-mo-kri-ti-ka) f. self-criticism;self-accusation

samokształcenie (sa-mo-kshtaw-tse-ne) n. self-education

samolot (sa-mo-lot) m. airplane

samolub (sa-mo-loob) m. egoist

samolubstwo (sa-mo-loob-stvo) n . selfishness ; egoism

samolubny (sa-mo-loob-ni) adj. m. selfish; self-seeking;egoistic

samoobrona (sa-mo-o-bro-na) f. self-defense

samopas (sa-mo-pas) adv. alone; by oneself; loosely; unheeded

samopoczucie (sa-mo-po-choo-che) n. frame of mind; feeling

samopomoc (sa-mo-po-mots) f. self-help; mutual aid (society)

samorodek (sa-mo-ro-dek) m. (gold) nugget

samorodny (sa-mo-rod-ni) adj. m. autogenous; natural; virgin

samorząd (sa-mo-zhownt) m. autonomy; self-government

samotnik (sa-mot-neek) m. recluse; hermit;solitary;rogue

samostanowienie (sa-mo-sta-no-vye-ne) n. self-determination

samotność (sa-mot-noshch) f. solitude; loneliness

samouctwo (sa-mo-oots-tvo) n. self-education;self instruction

samouczek (sa-mo-oo-tchek) m. handbook (for self-instruction)

samouk (sa-mo--ook) m. self-taught (man);self taught person

samowładczy (sa-mo-vwad-chi) adj. m. autocratic; arbitrary

samowola (sa-mo-vo-la) f. license (arbitrariness);lawlessness

samowystarczalny (sa-mo-vis-tar-chal-ni) adj. m. self-sufficient;self contained;unsubsidized

samozachowawczy instynkt (sa-mo-za-kho-vav-chi een-stinkt) m. self-preservation instinct

samozapalenie się (sa-mo-za-pa-le-ne shan) n. spontaneous combustion; self ignition

samozwaniec (sa-mo-zva-nets) m. usurper; pretender

sanatorium (sa-na-tor-yoom) m. sanitorium; sanatorium

sandacz (san-dach) m. perch-pike

sandał (san-daw) m. sandal

sanie (sa-ne) pl. sleigh; sledge

sanitariuszka(sa-nee-tar-yoosh-ka) f. nurse(emergency, military)

sanitarny (sa-ñee-tár-ni) adj.
m. sanitary; health-
sankcja (sánk-tsya) f. sanction
sankcjonować (sank-tsyo-nó-
vach) v. sanction;authorize
sanki (sán-kee) pl. sled
sanskryt (san-skrit) m. San -
skrit; Sanscrit
sapać (sá-pach) v. gasp; pant;
heave; snort;puff and blow;chug
saper (sá-per) m. combat engineer;army engineer; sapper
sardynka (sar-dín-ka) f. sardine
sarkać (sár-kach) v. grumble
sarkastyczny (sar-kas-tích-ni)
adj. m. sarcastic(smile etc.)
sarna (sár-na) f. roe deer
sarnia skóra (sár-ña skoó-ra)
f. buckskin;roe-deer's hide
satelita (sa-te-leé-ta) m. satellite; attendant
satyna (sa-ti-na) f. satin
satyra (sa-ti-ra) f. satire
satysfakcja (sa-tis-fák-tsya)
f. satisfaction; compensation
sączyć się (sówn-chich śhán)
v. drip; trickle; distill;
sift ; ooze out; seep;percolate
sąd (sównd) m. judgment ; court
sądownictwo (sówn-dov-ñeets-tvo)
n. judicature ;jurisdiction
sądowy (sówn-do-vi) adj. m. judicial; of court;judiciary
sądzić (sówn-dźheech) v. judge;
think; believe; expect; guess
sąg (sówñg) m. cord (of wood)
sąsiad (sówn-śhad) m. neighbor
sąsiadka (sówn-śhad-ka) f.
neighbor; lady next door
sąsiedni (sówn-śhed-ñee) adj.
m. adjacent;neighboring
sąsiedztwo (sówn-śhedz-tvo) n.
neighborhood; nearness;proximity
sążeń (sówn-zheñ) m. fathom;
cord;approximately six feet
scalić (stsa-leech) v. integrate
scedzić (stse-dźheech) v. strain
off;decant; pour off(a liquid)
scena (stse-na) f. scene; stage
scenariusz (stse-nár-yoosh) m.
scenario; script; screenplay
sceneria (stse-nér-ya) f. scen—
ery;srage decorations;backdrops

sceptyczny (stsep-tích-ni) adj.
m. sceptic; skeptical(smile etc.)
sceptyk (stsép-tik) m. skeptic
schab (skhab) m. pork chop
schadzka (skhádz-ka) f. date
scheda (skhé-da) f. inheritance; inheritance; heirloom
schemat (skhé-mat) m. scheme;
plan;draft;outline; diagram
schematyczny (skhe-ma-tích-ni)
adj. m. schematic (drafting...)
schizma (skheéz-ma) f. schism
schlebiać (skhléb-yach) v.
flatter;wheedle;adulate;gratify
schludny (skhloód-ni) adj. m.
neat; clean;trim;slick;tidy
schnąć (skhnównch) v. dry; dry
up; wane; waste;parch;wither
schodki (skhód-kee) pl. steps
(small);small stairs
schodowa klatka (skho-do-va
klát-ka) staircase
schody (skho-di) pl. stairs
schodzić (skho-dźheech) v. get
down; go down stairs;step down
scholastyka (zkho-las-ti-ka) f.
scholasticism; Scholasticism
schorowany (skho-ro-va-ni) adj.
m. invalid;ailing;ill;sick
schować (skho-vach) v. hide;
pocket;conceal;put away; save
schowek (skho-vek) m. closet;
safe; hiding place; cubby;recess
schód (skhood) m. stair; step
schron (skhron) m. shelter;
pillbox; air raid shelter etc.
schronić się (skhro-ñeech śhán)
v. take refuge;take cover
schronisko (skhro-ñeés-ko) n.
shelter;hiding place;refuge
schudnięcie (skhood-ñán-che) n.
loss of fat (weight);slimming
schwycić (skhvi-cheech) v.
seize; catch; get hold of
schylać (skhi-lach) v. bend;
bow; incline; stoop down
schyłek (skhi-wek) m. decline
scyzoryk (stsi-zo-rik) m. pocketknife; clasp knife;pen knife
seans (sé-ans) m. seance; sitting;showing;performance
secesja (se-tsés-ya) f. seces-
sion:Secession style(architecture)

sedes (sé-des) m. toilet seat
sedno (séd-no) n. crux; core;
gist; essence(of the matter)
sejm (seym) m. Polish parliament (600 years old)
sekcja (sék-tsya) f. dissection;
section; cross-section ;division
sekret (sék-ret) m. secret
sekretarz (se-kré-tash) m. secretary;reporter; minuter
seksualny (se-ksoo-ál-ni) adj.
m. sexual; sex-(appeal,urge etc)
sekta (sék-ta) f. sect
sektor (sék-tor) m. sector
sekunda (se-koón-da) f. second
sekundnik (se-koónd-neek) m.
second -hand(of a watch)
sekutnica (se-koot-nee-tsa) f.
shrew; scold; vixen
seledynowy (se-le-di-nó-vi) adj.
m. aquamarine;willow green
selekcja (se-lék-tsya) f. selec-
tion(by elimination,natural etc)
seler (se-ler) m. celery
semafor (se-má-for) m. semaphore
semicki (se-méets-kee) adj. m.
Semitic (character etc.)
seminarium (se-mee-nár-yoom) n.
seminar;seminary;trainning school
sen (sen) m. sleep; dream
senat (sé-nat) m. senate (in Poland evolved from royal council
in XV c.);Upper House
senator (se-ná-tor) m. senator
senior (sén-yor) m. senior
senny (sén-ni) adj. m. sleepy
sens (séns) m. sense; significance;gist;drift;meaning;point
sensacja (sen-sáts-ya) f. sensation; a hit;making a hit
sensacyjny (sen-sa-tsiy-ni) adj.
m. sensational; exciting
sentencja (sen-ténts-ya) f.
maxim; dictum; pronouncement
sentyment (sen-ti-ment) m. sentiment;partiality;fondness;feeling
separacja (se-pa-ráts-ya) f.
separation(from bed and board)
separatka (se-pa-rát-ka) f. pri-
vate-room; solitary cell
separować (se-pa-ró-vach) v.
separate;isolate

seplenić (se-plé-neech) v.
lisp; have a lisp;speak with lisp
ser (ser) m. cheese
serce (sér-tse) n. heart;kindness
sercowy (ser-tsó-vi) adj. m.
cardiac ; love-(affair,secret etc.)
serdak (sér-dak) m. sleeveless
(furred) waistcoat
serdeczność (ser-dech-noshch)
f. cordiality;heartiness;caresses
serdeczny (ser-dech-ni) adj.
m. hearty; cordial;sincere
serdelek (ser-de-lek) m. small
sausage (specially smoked)
serenada (se-re-na-da) f. se-
renade (music and song at night)
seria (sér-ya) f. series;
chain; set;train (of events etc.)
serio (sér-yo) adv. seriously
sernik (sér-neek) m. cheese-
cake ; casein
serwatka (ser-vát-ka) f. whey
serweta (ser-vé-ta) f. (small)
table cloth;doily;serviette
serwetka (ser-vét-ka) f. napkin
serwilizm (ser-vee-leezm) m.
servility; humbly submission
serwis (sér-vees) m. dinner set;
service (tennis),turn of serving
serwować (ser-vo-vach) v. (tennis) serve; do services;aid;help
seryjny (se-riy-ni) adj. m.
serial; consecutive
sesja (sés-ya) f. session
setka (sét-ka) f. hundred
setny (sét-ni) num. hundredth
sezon (se-zon) m. season
sędzia (sań-dzha) m. judge; umpire; referee; magistrate
sędziwy (sań-dzhee-vi)adj. m.
aged; old;grey headed;ancient
sęk (sańk) m. knot;knag;knar
sękaty (sań-ká-ti) adj. m. knotty;knaggy;gnarly;nodose;rugged
sęp (sańp) m. vulture
sfera (sfe-ra) f. sphere;zone
sferyczny (sfe-rich-ni) adj. m.
spherical(geometry,triangle etc.)
sfinks (sfeenks) m. sphinx
sfora (sfó-ra) f. pack of dogs
siać (shach) v. sow(corn,terror...)
siadać (shá-dach) v. sit down;
take a seat;get stranded;go flat

siano (śha-no) n. hay
sianokosy (śha-no-ko-si) pl.
haymaking; hay cutting
siarczan (śhar-chan) m. sulfate
siarka (śhar-ka) f. sulfur
siarkowy (śhar-ko-vi) adj. m.
sulfuric(acid etc.)
siatka (śhat-ka) f. net; screen
siatkówka (śhat-koov-ka) f. ret-
ina; volley-ball
siąść (śhańśhch) v. sit down
sidło (śhid-wo) n. snare; trap
siebie (śhe-bye) pron. (for)
self; oneself;one;each other
siec (śhets) v. cut; mow; whip
sieczka (śhech-ka)f.chop straw;
chaff; empty head(slang)
sieczna (śhech-na) f. secant
sieczna broń (śhech-na broń) f.
cutting weapons
sieć (śhech) f. net; network;
grid;fishing net;trap;snare;web
siedem (śhe-dem) num. seven
siedemdziesiąt (śhe-dem-dżhe-
shownt) num. seventy
siedemdziesiąty (śhe-dem-dżhe-
shown-ti) num. seventieth
siedemnasty (śhe-dem-nas-ti)
num. seventeenth
siedemnaście (śhe-dem-nash-che)
num. seventeen
siedemset (śhe-dem-set) num.
seven hundred
siedlisko (śhed-lees-ko) n, seat;
abode;habitation;hotbed;nest
siedmiokrotny (śhed-myo-krot-ni)
adj. m. sevenfold
siedmioletni (śhed-myo-let-nee)
adj. m. seven year (old; lasting)
siedzący (śhe-dzown-tsi) adj. m.
sitting(posture);sedentary
siedzenie (śhe-dze-ne) n. seat;
bottom; behind
siedziba (śhe-dzhee-ba)f. seat;
abode;habitat(of an animal)
siedziec (śhe-dzhech) v. sit
(stay);be perched;be settled
siejba (śhey-ba) f. sowing; sowing time
siekacz (śhe-kach) m. incisor;
chopping knife; chopper

siekanina (śhe-ka-nee-na) f.
hash;chopping up;cutting up
siekiera (śhe-ke-ra) f. axe
siekierka (śhe-ker-ka) f.
hatchet; small axe
sielanka (śhe-lan-ka) f. idyll
sielankowy (śhe-lan-ko-vi) adj.
m. idyllic; pastoral;bucolic
sielski (śhel-skee) adj. m.
rural;idyllic; pastoral
siemię (śhe-myań) n. bird seed
siennik (śhen-neek) m. straw-
mattress;pallet;paillasse
sień (śheń) f. hallway; corridor;vestibule;entrance hall
siepacz (śhe-pach) m. (rough)
henchman;hired assassin
sierota (śhe-ro-ta) m. f. orphan;lonsome person;poor fellow
sierp (śherp) m. sickle
sierpień (śher-pyeń) m. August
siersć (śhershch) f. hair (coat)
sierżant (śher-zhant) m. sergeant (military rank)
siew (śhev) m. sowing; seeds
siewca (śhev-tsa) m. sower
siewnik (śhev-neek) m. seeder;
sowing-machine
się (śhań) pron. self (oneself;
myself etc.;of itself);each other
sięgać (śhań-gach) v. reach
sikać (śhee-kach) v. squirt;
spout; gush; piss (vulg.)
sikawka (śhee-kav-ka) f. fire
hose; squirt; fire engine
sikora (śhee-ko-ra) f. titmouse
siksa (śheek-sa) f. hussy; small
girl piddler
silnik (śhil-neek) m. motor
silnik spalinowy (śhil-neek spa-
lee-no-vi) combustion engine
silny (śhil-ni) adj. m. strong;
powerful;mighty;hefty;lusty;stiff
silos (śhe-los) m. silo;(store)pit
siła (śhee-wa) f. 1. force; might;
strength; power; 2. many; much
siłacz (śhee-wach) m. strongman
siłownia (śhee-wov-na) f. power
plant;power station;power house
sinawy (śhee-na-vi) adj. m.
bluish; somewhat blue
siniak (śhee-nak) m. bruise

sinus (see-noos) m. sine (of
an angle)
siny (shee-ni) adj. m. livid;
blue; purple;blue in the face
siodełko (sho-dew-ko) n. bicycle seat;small saddle
siodlarz (shod-lash) m. saddler
siodłać (shod-wach) v. saddle
siodło (shod-wo) n. saddle
sioło (sho-wo) m. hamlet;village
siostra (shos-tra) f. sister
siostrzenica (shos-tshe-nee-
tsa) f. niece
siostrzeniec (shos-tshe-nets)
m. nephew
siostrzyczka (shos-tzhich-ka)
f. little sister
siodemka (shoo-dem-ka) f. seven
siodmy (shood-mi) num. seventh
sito (shee-to) n. sieve;strainer
sitowie (shee-tov-ye) n. bulrush
siusiac (shoo-shach) v. tinkle;
urinate ; piss;pee;piddle
siwek (shee-vek) m. grey horse
siwiec (sheev-yech) v. grow gray
siwucha (shee-voo-kha) f. low
grade vodka; rot gut
siwy (shee-vi) adj. m. gray;
blue; grizzly;grey haired;hoary
skafander (ska-fan-der) m. diving
suit ; pressure suit;wind jacket
skakać (ska-kach) v. jump; spring;
bounce; leap; pop; skip ; dive
skakanka (ska-kan-ka) f. jumping
rope; skipping rope
skala (ska-la) f. scale;extent
skaleczenie (ska-le-che-ne) n.
cut; injury; hurt;wound
skaleczyć (ska-le-chich) v. hurt;
injure; cut;prick;wound
skalisty (ska-lees-ti) adj. rocky
skalp (skalp) m. scalp
skała (ska-wa) f. rock
skamieniały (ska-mye-na-wi) adj.
m. petrified ;fossil-;stone-
skamieniec (ska-mye-nech) v. become petrified ;turn into stone
skandal (skan-dal) m. scandal
skarb (skarb) m. treasure; treasury; riches;beloved person;hoard
skarbiec (skar-byets) m. treasury;
strong room;safe deposit

skarbnik (skarb-neek) m.treas-
urer;cashier;paymaster
skarbonka (skar-bon-ka) f.
piggy bank;money box;poor box
skarcic (skar-cheech) v. admonish;rebuke;reprimand;scold
skarga (skar-ga) f. complaint;
suit; claim; charge;grievance
skarłowaciały (skar-wo-va-
cha-wi) adj. m. stunted;
dwarfish
skarpa (skar-pa) f. scarp; buttress;slope;escarpment
skarpetka (skar-pet-ka) f.
sock;a short stocking
skarżyc (skar-zhich) v. sue;
denounce;complain;tell tales
skarżypyta (skar-zhi-pi-ta) m.
squealer; informer; telltale
skaza (ska-za) f. tarnish;brab;
blot; flaw;defect;spot;speck
skazac (ska-zach) v. condemn;
sentence;pass judgement;doom
skazaniec (ska-za-nets) m.
condemned man (to death)
skazic (ska-zheech) v. spoil;
corrupt; adulterate;pollute
skąd (skownt) adv. from where;
since when; where from?
skądinąd (skownd-ee-nownt) adv.
otherwise; on the other hand
skąpic (skown-peech) v. skimp;
stint; begrudge (food,money...)
skąpiec (skownp-yets) m. miser
skapstwo (skownp-stvo) n. par-
simony;avarice;stinginess
skapy (skown-pi) adj. m. stingy; scanty; meager; scant
skiba (skee-ba) f. clod
skinąć (skee-nownch) v. signal;
motion;nod; bow (one's head)
skinienie (skee-ne-ne) m. nod;
bow; sign ;call;gesture;motion
sklejac (skle-yach) v. glue
together;stick;paste; patch
sklejka (skley-ka) f. plywood
sklep (sklep) m. store; shop
sklepienie (skle-pye-ne) n.
vault ;vaulting; dome
sklepikarz (skle-pee-kash) m.
shopkeeper; tradesman
sklepowa (skle-po-va) f. saleslady; saleswoman

skleroza (skle-ro-za) f. scle-
rosis;hardening of body
skład (skwat) m. composition;
warehouse; store;framework
składać (skwa-dać) v. make up;
compose; piece;fold;set together
składacz (skwa-dach) m. type-
setter; compositor
składany (skwa-da-ni) adj. m.
compound; folding;miscellaneous
składka(skwad-ka) f. contribution;collection;membership fee
składnia (skwad-na) f. syntax
składnica (skwad-nee-tsa) f.
depository; warehouse;depot
składnik (skwad-neek) m. ingredient; component;element
składowe (skwa-do-ve) n. warehouse fee; storage charges
skłamać (skwa-mach) v. tell
a lie;tell an untruth; lie
skłaniać (skwa-nach) v. bend;
lean; incline;induce;impel;rest
skłon (skwon) m. slope; bow
skłonność (skwon-noshch) f.
inclination;tendency;disposition
skłonny (skwon-ni) adj. m. disposed; inclined;prone;apt
skłócić (skwoo-cheech) v. stir
up; agitate; cause to disagree
sknera (skne-ra) m.& f. miser
skobel (sko-bel) m. staple
skoczek (sko-chek) m. jumper
skocznia (skoch-na) f. ski-
jump (ramp);take off ramp
skoczny (skoch-ni) adj. m. brisk;
lively; vivacious;saltary
skoczyć (sko-chich) v. leap;
jump; spring;make a dash;hurry
skojarzenie (sko-ya-zhe-ne) n.
association; union;conjunction
skok (skok) m. jump; leap; hop
skok tłoka (skok two-ka) m. piston stroke
skołatany (sko-wa-ta-ni) adj. m.
worn; battered; shattered
skołować (sko-wo-vach) v. confound; muddle; exhaust
skomleć (skom-lech) v. whine
skomplikowany (skom-plee-ko-va-
ni) adj. m. complex; intricate
skonać (sko-nach) v. expire; die

skończyć (skon-chich) v. finish; end;stop;have done
skoro (sko-ro) conj. after;at;
since; as;quickly;soon;if;once
adv. very soon; by and by
skoroszyt (sko-ro-shit) m.
folder ;letter file
skorowidz (sko-ro-veets) m.
index; indexed note book
skorpion (skor-pyon) m. scor-
pion; Scorpio
skorupa (sko-roo-pa) f. crust;
shell;hull;incrustation;carapace
skory (sko-ri) adj. m. quick;
eager;prompt(to act); swift
skostniały (skost-na-wi) adj.
m. ossified;numb;stiff;fossilized
skośny (skosh-ni) adj. m. slanting; oblique; inclined
skotłować (skot-wo-vach) v. whirl;
bewilder;agitate;swirl; seethe
skowronek (skow-vro-nek) m.
lark; skylark
skowyczec (sko-vi-chech) v.
yelp; whipe;squeal;whimper;whine
skowyt (sko-vit) m. yelp;squeal
skóra (skoo-ra) f. skin; hide;
leather; hide;skin;coat;pelt;derm
skórka (skoor-ka) f. skin; peel;
crust; cuticle;agnail;pelt;fur
skórny (skoor-ni) adj. m. cuta-
neous; dermal;skin-(disease etc.)
skórzany (skoo-zha-ni) adj. m.
leather made; leathery;leather-
skra (skra) f. spark (poetic)
skracać (skra-tsach) v. short-
en; cut down;lessen;abridge
skradać się (skra-dach shan) v.
steal; creep up;advance stealthily
skraj (skray) m. border; edge;
brink; margin;fringe;rand;outskirts
skrajać (skra-yach) v. cut off;cut
(cloth);cut up (to pieces)
skrajność (skray-noshch) f.
extremism; extreme
skrajny (skray-ni) adj. m.
extreme;intense;utmost;ultra;utter
skrapiać (skrap-yach) v.damp;
sprinkle ;moisten; water
skraplać (skrap-lach) v. liquefy; condense;precipitate

skrawek (skra-vek) m. shred;snip; strip; patch; chip; fragment;patch
skreslić (skrésh-leech) v. sketch; cancel; jot down;delete
skręcać (skrán-tsach) v. twist; turn off; break (neck);strand
skrępować (skrán-pó-vach) v. tie up; restrict;embarrass;impede
skręt (skránt) m. twist; twisting; coil; turn; torsion
skrobaczka (skro-bach-ka) f.rasp; scraper; foot scraper(for mud)
skrobać (skró-bach) v. scrape; rasp; scratch; scale (fish)
skromny (skróm-ni) adj. m.coy; modest;unassuming;simple;lowly
skroń (skroń) f. temple
skropić (skró-peech) v. liquefy; sprinkle;water;moisten;damp
skrócić (skroo-cheech) v. abbreviate; shorten ;cut down;curtail
skrót (skroot) m. abbreviation
skrucha (skroo-kha) f. contrition; repentance;compunction
skrupulatny (skroo-poo-lát-ni) adj. m. scrupulous;precise,exact
skrupuł (skroo-poow) m. scruple
skruszyć (skroo-shich) v. crumble;crush;bring to repentance
skrycie (skri-che) adv. secretly
skryć (skrich) v. hide;obscure
skrypt (skript) m. script; mimeographed lecture; I.O.U.
skrytka pocztowa (skrit-ka pochtó-va) post office box
skrytość (skri-toshch) f. secrecy; secretiveness
skryty (skri-ti) adj. m. underhanded; secret; reticent
skrzek (skzhek) m. scream; croak
skrzep (skzhep) m. clot; coagulation(of blood);grume;thrombus
skrzepnąć (skzhep-nównch) v. clot; coagulate;set;freeze;solidify
skrzętnie (skzhańt-ñe) adv. sedulously ; diligently;busily
skrzętny (skzhańt-ni) adj. m. industrious; busy; diligent
skrzydlaty (skzhid-lá-ti) adj. m. winged;wing-shaped;winglike
skrzydło (skzhid-wo) n. wing; leaf; brim; (fan) arm;extension

skrzynia (skzhi-ña) f. chest;bin; box;hutch;case;crate;coffer
skrzynka (skzhin-ka) f. box;chest
skrzynka biegów (skzhin-ka bye-goov) f. gearbox;gear case
skrzypce (skzhip-tse) n. violin; fiddle;person playing fiddle
skrzypek (skzhi-pek) m. violinist; fiddler
skrzypieć (skzhi-pyech) v. crunch; creak; screech; grind;squeak;gride
skrzywiać (skzhi-vyach) v. bend; distort; twist;contort;put awry
skrzyżowanie dróg (skzhi-zhová-ñe droog) pl. f. crossroads;crossing;intersection
skrzyżowany (skzhi-zho-vá-ni) adj. m. crossbred; crosslegged
skubać (skoo-bach) v. nibble; pluck; pick; fleece;graze;tease
skuć (skooch) v. shackle; chain
skulić (skoo-leech) v. curl up; cuddle up; squat; lie low;crouch
skup (skoop) m. purchasing center
skupiać (skoop-yach) v. concentrate; bring together; gather
skupienie (skoop-ye-ñe) n. concentration;focussing;compression
skupiony (skoop-yo-ni) adj. m. collected; concentrated ;dense
skupować (skoo-pó-vach) v. buy; buy up ;keep buying; buy out
skurcz (skoorch) m. cramp; shrinking; spasm; twitch; systole;contraction
skurczyć (skoor-chich) v. draw in; shrink; contract; lessen;diminish
skuteczność (skoo-tech-noshch) f. efficiency; efficacy;good trsult
skutecznie (skoo-tech-ñe) adv. with good result;effectively
skuteczny(skoo-téch-ni) adj. m. effective;efficient; operative
skutek (skoo-tek) m. effect; result; outcome; consequence
skuter (skoo-ter) m. motorscooter
skutkować (skoot-ko-vach) v. have effect; work; operate
skwapliwy (skwap-lee-vi) adj. m. eager; willing;ready
skwar (skvar) m. scorching heat

skwarek (skva-rek) m. crackling
skwaśniały (skvash-ńa-wi) adj.
m. sour;turned sour; glum
skwer (skver) m. square
słabiutki (swa-byoot-kee) adj.
m. very weak(in diminutive)
słabnąć (swab-nownch) v. weaken;
grow feeble;decline;diminish
słabość (swa-boshch) f. weakness;
illness;debility;fragility
słabowity (swa-bo-vee-ti) adj.
m. weakly; feeble;fragile;puny
słaby (swa-bi) adj. m. weak;frail
feeble;infirm;faint;flimsy;poor
słać (swach) v. send; make bed;
spread(a table cloth etc.);strew
słaniać się(swa-ńach shań) v.
totter; stagger;lurch; reel
sława (swa-va) f. glory; renown;
fame; celebrity;reputation;repute
sławetny (swa-vet-ni) adj. m.
notorious;famous;ill famous
sławić (swa-veech) v. praise;
celebrate; glorify;laud;blazon
sławny (swav-ni) adj. m. famous;
glorious;celebrated;illustrious
słodkawy (swod-ka-vi) adj. m.
sweetish; slightly sweet
słodki (swod-kee) adj. m. sweet
słodycze (swo-di-che) pl. sweets
słodzic (swo-dżheech) v. sweeten
słoik (swo-eek) m. jar; gallipot;
glass;pot ;small jar;little jar
słojowaty (swo-yo-va-ti) adj. m.
grained;veined ;shownig grain
słoma (swo-ma) f. straw
słomianka (swo-myan-ka) f. straw
mat;doormat;straw plaited basket
słomiany wdowiec (swo-mya-ni
vdo-vyets) m. grass widower
słomka (swom-ka) f. small straw
słonecznik (swo-nech-ńeek) m.
sunflower
słoneczny (swo-nech-ni) adj. m.
sunny;solar(system,year etc.)
słonina (swo-ńee-na) f. lard
słoniowa kość (swo-ńo-va koshch)
f. ivory
słonka (swon-ka) f. wood-cock
słony (swo-ni) adj. m. salty
słoń (swoń) m. elephant
słońce (swoń-tse) n. sun;sunlight

słota (swo-ta) f.foul weather
słotny dzień (swot-ni dżheń) m.
rainy day; bad weather day
słowacki (swo-vats-kee) adj.
m. Slovak; Slovakian
słowianin (swo-vya-ńeen) m.
Slav
słowianski (swo-vyań-skee) adj.
m. Slav; Slavonic
słowik (swo-veek) m. nightingale; good singer
słownictwo (swov-ńeets-tvo) n.
vocabulary; list of words
słownik (swov-ńeek) m. dictionary; vocabulary; language
słowny (swov-ni) adj. m. verbal; reliable; dependable
słowo (swo-vo) n. word; verb
słoworód (swo-vo-rood) m. etymology; origin of words
słowotworstwo (swo-vo-tvoor-
stvo) n. word formation
słód (swood) m. malt
słój (swooy) m. jar; (tree)
ring;pot;vain;grain
słówko (swoov-ko) n. (little
or sweet) word;nice word
słuch (swookh) m. hearing
słuchacz (swoo-khach) m. listener; student ;hearer;auditor
słuchać (swoo-khach) v. hear;
obey;listen;obey orders
słuchawka (swoo-khav-ka) f.
(tel.) receiver; earphone
słuchowisko (swoo-kho-vees-ko)
m. radio drama;broadcast drama
słuchy (swoo-khy) pl. rumors;
(animal) ears;uncertain news
sługa (swoo-ga) f. servant
słup (swoop) m. pillar; column;
post; pole; pylon; landmark
słupek (swoo-pek) m. pillaret;
small post;stake;stud; rail
słuszność (swoosh-noshch) f.
rightness; equity; rightful-
ness; legitimacy;aptness;justice
słuszny (swoosh-ni) adj. m.
just; fair; right;pertinent;apt
służalczy (swoo-zhal-chi) adj.
m. servile ;cringing;subservient
służąca (swoo-zhown-tsa) f.
maid ;servant; cleaning woman

służący (swoo-zhówn-tsi) m.
 servant;manservant;domestic
służba (swoozh-ba) f. service
służbowy (swoozh-bo-vi) adj. m.
 official;business(trip etc.)
służyc (swoo-zhich) v. serve
słychać (swi-khach) v. people
 say; one hears;be heard
słynąć (swi-nównch) v. be famed
słynny (swin-ni) adj. m. famous
słyszalny (swi-shál-ni) adj. m.
 audible;within hearing range
słyszec (swi-shech) v. hear
smacznego ! (smach-né-go) exp.
 good appetite
smaczny (smach-ni) adj. m. tasty
smagać (smá-gach) v. lash; whip
smagły (smág-wi) adj. m. swarthy
smak (smak) m. taste; relish;
 savor;palate;liking;appetite
smakołyk (sma-ko-wik) m. tidbit;
 delicacy;dainty;choice morsel
smakować (sma-ko-vach) v. taste
smakowity (sma-ko-vée-ti) adj.
 m. savory;appetizing;tasty
smalec (sma-lets) m. lard; fat
smar (smar) m. grease; lubricant
smarkać (smár-kach) v. blow nose
smarkacz (smár-kach) m. squirt;
 snot; whippersnapper;raw lad
smarkaty (smar-ká-ti) adj. m.
 snotty; callow; raw
smarować (sma-ro-vach) v. smear
smarowidło (sma-ro-vid-wo) n.
 grease ; lubricant; ointment
smażyc (sma-zhich) v. fry
smętny (smán-tni) adj. m. melancholy; blue;doleful; dolorous
smoczek (smó-chek) m. nipple;
 pacifier;dummy;comforter
smok (smok) m. dragon
smoking (smó-king) m. dinner
 jacket; tuxedo;formal jacket
smolny (smól-ni) adj. m. resi-
 nous; pitchy;tarry
smoła (smó-wa) f. pitch; tar
smrodliwy (smrod-lée-vi) adj. m.
 rank; stinky; smelly; foul
smród (smroot) m. stench; fetor
smucic (smoo-cheech) v. sadden
smukły (smook-wi) adj. m. slender; slim; willowy; gracile
smutek (smoo-tek) m. sorrow;
 sadness ; grief; mournfulness

smutny (smoot-ni) adj. m. sad
smycz (smich) f. leash;dog lead
smyczek (smi-chek) m. (violin)
 bow; fiddle stick
smyk (smik) m.whippersnapper;
 brat; kid; small boy
snop (snop) m. sheaf; bunch
snop światła (snop shvyat-wa)
 light beam;light shaft
snuc (snooch) v. spin;reel off
snycerz (sni-tsesh) m. sculptor
sobek (so-bek) m. egoist
sobota (so-bo-ta) f. Saturday
sobowtor (so-bov-toor) m. double
sobol (so-bool) m. sable (fur)
sobor (so-boor) m. synod
socjalista (so-tsya-lees-ta)
 m. socialist
socjalizacja (so-tsya-lee-za-
 tsya) f. socialization
socjalizm (so-tsya-leezm) m.
 socialism
socjologia (so-tsyo-log-ya) f.
 sociology ; social science
soczewica (so-che-vée-tsa) f.
 lentil; lentils
soczewka (so-chev-ka) f. lens
soczysty (so-chís-ti) adj. m.
 juicy ; sappy; mellow; coarse
soda (so-da) f. soda
sodowa woda (so-dó-va vo-da) f.
 soda water
sofa (só-fa) f. lounge; sofa
sofistyczny (so-fees-tich-ni)
 adj. m. sophistical; captious
sojusz (só-yoosh) m. alliance
sojusznik (so-yoosh-neek) m.
 ally;associate joined for a
 common purpose
sok (sok) m. sap; juice
sokół (so-koow) m. falcon
solanka (so-lan-ka) f. salt
 spring; solted bread roll;brine
solić (so-leech)v.salt;add salt
Solidarność (so-lee-dar-noshch)s.
 Solidarity Labor Union;solidarity
solidarny (so-lee-dar-ni) adj.
 m. solidary; sympathetic
solidny (so-leed-ni) adj. m.
 solid; firm;sound;reliable;safe
solista (so-lees-ta) m. soloist
soliter (so-lée-ter) m. tapeworm; solitary tree; solitaire
 (gem stone)

solniczka (sol-ńeech-ka) f.
saltshaker; saltcellar
solo (so-lo) adv. solo
solny (sol-ni) adj. m. saline
solony (so-lo-ni) adj. m. salt-
ed ; corned(beef);salt cured
sołtys (sow-tis) m. village
head(officer below wójt)
sonata (so-na-ta) f. sonata
sonda (son-da) f. probe; feeler;
lead;plummet;sounding ballon
sonet (so-net) m. sonnet
sopel (so-pel) m. icicle
sopran (sop-ran) m. soprano
sortować (sor-to-vach) v. sort
sos (sos) m. gravy; sauce
sosna (sos-na) f, pine
sosnina (sosh-ńee-na) f. pine-
wood;pine tree;pine branches
sowa (so-va) f. owl
sowity (so-vee-ti) adj. m. lav
ish;ample;abundant;rich
sód (sood) m. sodium
sól (sool) f. salt
spacerować (spa-tse-ro-vach) v.
walk; stroll; walk about
spacja (spa-tsya) f. (print)
space
spaczać (spa-chach) v. warp;
pervert; twist;distort
spaczenie (spa-che-ńe) n. dis-
tortion; perversion; warp
spać (spach) v. sleep;slumber
spad (spat) m. slope; drop
spadać (spa-dach) v. fall; drop
spadek (spa-dek) m. fall; inheritance; downfall;slope;dip
spadkobierca (spad-ko-byer-tsa)
m. heir;inheritor;successor
spadochron (spa-do-khron) m.
parachute
spadzisty (spa-dzhees-ti) adj.
m. steep;sloping;precipitous
spajać (spa-yach) v. weld; solder; link;join;unite;bond
spalenizna (spa-le-ńeez-na) f.
(smell of) burning (smoke)
spalić (spa-leech) v. burn out
spalony (spa-lo-ni) adj. m.
adust; (sport) offside
sparzyć (spa- zhich) v. burn;
sting ; scald;blister;scorch

spasły (spas-wi) adj. m. fat
spaść (spashch) v. fall; fatten
spawacz (spa-vach) m. welder
spawać (spa-vach) v. weld; solder; weld metal
spawanie (spa-va-ńe) n. weld-
ing(of metals etc.)
spazm (spazm) m. spasm;convulsion
spec (spets) m. specialist;expert;
craftsman; dab hand; dab
specjalizacja (spe-tsya-lee-
zats-ya) f. specialization
specjalność (spe-tsyál-noshch)
f. specialty;peculiarity
specjalny (spe-tsyal-ni) adj.
m. special;express;particular
specyficzny (spe-tsi-feech-ni)
adj. m. specific;peculiar
spedytor (spe-di-tor) m. shipping agent; forwarding agent
spekulacja (spe-koo-lats-ya) f.
speculation; venture
spekulant (spe-koo-lant) m.
profiteer; speculator;gambler
spekulować (spe-koo-lo-vach) v.
speculate; profiteer; gamble
spelunka (spe-loon-ka) f, joint
spełniać (spew-nach) v. perform;
fulfill;comply with;accomplish
spędzać (spąn-dzach) v. round
up (cattle); spend (time);
abort;drive away;gather;pass time
spichlerz (spee-khlesh) m. gran-
ary
spiczasty (spee-chas-ti) adj. m.
pointed;peaked;tapering;sharp
spiec (spyets) v. burn;scorch;
sunblister;blush; parch;sinter
spieniężyć (spye-ńan-zhich) v.
cash(checks);sell(property)
spieniony (spye-ńo-ni) adj. m.
foamy;foaming;covered with foam
spierać (spye-rach) śhań) v.
argue;contend;quarrel;dispute
spieszny (spyesh-ni) adj. m.
hasty; quick; hurried
spieszyć się (spye-shich śhań)
v. hurry; dismount;be eager
spięcie (spyań-che) n. buckle;
short circuit;collision; clash
spiętrzyć (spyań-tzhich) v.
pile up; heap up;bank up;dam up

spiker (spee-ker) m. (radio) announcer; disc jokey;Speaker
spinacz (spee-nach) m. fastener
spinać (spee-nach) v. fasten;
pin up; clasp; spur (horse)
spinka (speen-ka) f. clasp
spirala (spee-ra-la) f. spiral;
coil;volute;helix;spiral glide
spiralny (spee-ral-ni) adj. m.
spiral;helical;involuted
spirytus (spee-ri-toos) m. spirit; alcohol; spirits
spis (spees) m. list; register;
inventory;record;roll;census
spis rzeczy (spees zhe-chi)
table of contents
spisać (spee-sach) v. record;
write down;acquit oneself(well...)
spisek (spee-sek) f. plot; conspiracy; hatching a plot
spiskowiec (spees-ko-vyets) m.
conspirator; plotter
spiż (speezh) m. brass; bronze
spiżarnia (spee-zhar-ña) f.
pantry; buttery; cupboard
spiżowy (spee-zho-vi) adj. m.
brass ; bronze; booming(voice)
splatać (spla-tach) v. braid;
interlace;interlock;plait
splątać (splown-tach) v. snarl
up; mat;ravel;confuse;muddle up
spleśniały (splesh-ña-wi) adj.
m. moldy: musty ;mildewy
splot (splot) m. twine; twist;
coil;tangle;plaitcoincidence
splunąć (sploo-nownch) v. spit
spluwaczka (sploo-vach-ka) f.
spittoon ;cuspidor
spłacić (spwa-cheech) v. pay off
spłaszczyć (spwash-chich) v.
flatten out; humble (another)
spłata (spwa-ta) f. refund; instalment payment; repayment
spłatać figla (spwa-tach feeg-la)
v. play a trick;play a joke
spław (spwav) m. rafting;floating
spławiać (spwav-yach) v. float;
get rid;shunt; raft (timber etc.)
spławik (spwa-veek) m. (fishing)
float(dipping when fish bites)
spławny (spwav-ni) adj. m. navigable (river, waterway etc.)

spłodzić (spwo-dzheech)v. beget; generate;put out;produce
spłonąć (spwo-nownch) v. burn
down;go up in flames; redden
spłonka (spwon-ka) f. percussion cap; primer;detonator
spłoszyć (spwo-shich) v. scare
away; frighten;startle; flush
spłowiały (spwo-vya-wi) adj.
m. faded (appearance)
spłukać (spwoo-kach) v. rinse;
flush;swill out;wash away
spływać (spwi-vach) v. flow
(down);drift;float(down stream)
spochmurnieć (spo-khmoor-ñech)
v. grow cloudy; gloomy
spocić się (spo-cheech shán) v.
sweat; become sweaty;prespire
spoczynek (spo-chi-nek) m. rest
spoczywać (spo-chi-vach) v. sit;
rest; lie down;be at rest;rest on
spod (spot) prep. form under
spodek (spo-dek) m. saucer
spodenki (spo-den-ki) pl.
(knee) pants; shorts
spodlić (spod-leech) v. debase;
degrade; disgrace; demean
spodnie (spod-ñe) n. trousers;
pants; slacks; breeches
spodobać się (spo-do-bach shán)
v. take a liking; take a fancy
spodziewać się (spo-dzhe-vach
shán)v.expect; hope for
spoglądać (spo-glown-dach) v.
look out; look at; contemplate
spoić (spo-eech) v. make drunk;
weld; ply with liquor
spoistość (spo-ees-toshch) f.
cohesion; compactness ; density
spoisty (spo-ees-ti) adj. m.
compact;cohesive;dense;tenacious
spojenie (spo-ye-ñe) n. weld;
joint; pubic symphysis
spojówka (spo-yoov-ka) f. con-
junctiva
spojrzeć (spoy-zhech) v. look;
glance at; gaze at;view
spojrzenie (spoy-zhe-ñe) n.
glance; look; gaze;peep
spokojny (spo-koy-ni) adj. m.
quiet; calm; peaceful;still

spokój (spo-kooy) m. peace;
calm ;quiet;serenity;placidity
spokrewniony (spo-krev-no-ni)
adj. m. related to; related
spoliczkować (spo-leech-kó-vach)
v. slap face
społeczeństwo (spo-we-cheń-stvo)
n. society; public;community
społeczny (spo-wéch-ni) adj. m.
social (evil etc.);public;welfare
społem (spó-wem) adv, together
in common ;jointly; unitedly
spomiędzy (spo-myáń-dzi) prep.
from among;;from the midst
sponad (spó-nat) prep. from
above ; from over(the top of...)
sponiewierać (spo-ńe-vye-rach)
v. abuse; ill-treat; maltreat
spontaniczny (spon-ta-ńeech-ni)
adj. m. spontaneous ; voluntary
sporadyczny (spo-ra-dich-ni)
adj. m. sporadic; occasional
sporny (spór-ni) adj. m. controversial;debatable;questionable
sporo (spó-ro) adv. good deal;
a lot of; briskly;quite a few
sport (sport) m. sport;athletics
sportowiec (spor-tó-vyets) m.
sportsman;athlete;sporting man
spory (spó-ri) adj. m. pretty
big; fast; useful; lasting
sporządzać (spo-zhówn-dzach) v.
make up;draw up; make out
sposobić (spo-só-beech) v. prepare; make ready(colloquial exp.)
sposobność (spo-sób-noshch) v.
opportunity;occasion;chance
sposobny (spo-sób-ni) adj. m.
convenient; capable; able
sposób (spó-soop) m. means; way
spostrzegać (spo-stzhe-gach) v.
notice; perceive;observe;spot
spostrzegawczy (spo-stzhe-gáv-
chi) adj. m. quick to notice;
keen;observant;perceptive
spostrzeżenie (spo-stzhe-zhe-ńe)
n. observation ;awareness;notice
spośród (spó-shrood) prep. from
amongst;from the midst
spotęgować (spo-tán-gó-vach) v.
intensify; increase ;strengthen
spotkać (spót-kach) v. come
across; meet ;run across;befall

spotkanie (spot-ka-ńe) n. meeting; date; encounter
spotwarzać (spo-tva-zhach) v.
calumniate;defame; slander
spoufalać się (spo-oo-fa-lach
shań) v. become intimate
spowiadać (spo-vya-dach) v.
confess; listen to confession
spowiednik (spo-vyed-ńeek) m.
confessor (priest)
spowiedź (spo-vyedzh) f. confession; confided secrets
spowijać (spo-vee-yach) v.
swathe; wrap ;shroud; cover
spowodować (spo-vo-dó-vach) v.
cause ; induce; set off
spoza (spó-za) prep. from
behind;from beyond;from outside
spozierać (spo-zhe-rach) v.
glance at;look;gaze at
spożycie (spo-zhi-che) n. consumption;intake (food,calories)
spożywać (spo-zhi-vach) v. consume; eat; drink; have a meal
spożywca (spo-zhiv-tsa) m. consumer
spożywcze artykuły (spo-zhiv-
che ar-ti-koo-wi) pl, n.
groceries;food products
spód (spoot) m. bottom; foot
spódnica (spood-ńee-tsa) f.
skirt ; petticoat;apron strings
spójnia (spóoy-ńa) f. bond;
union; tie; bond; link
spójnik (spóoy-ńeek) m. conjunction
spółdzielczość (spoow-dzhel-
choshch) f. cooperation
spółdzielnia (spoow-dzhel-ńa)
f., coop; cooperative
spółgłoska (spoow-gwos-ka) f.
consonant (grammar)
spółka (spoow-ka) f. partnership; company ;society
spór (spoor) m. strife; dispute
spóźniać się (spoozh-ńach shań)
v. be late; be slow come late
spóźnienie (spoozh-ńe-ńe) n.
delay; late coming;late arrival
spóźniony (spoozh-ńo-ni) adj.
m. late ;delayed;belated;tardy
spracować się (spra-tso-vach
shań) v. be tired; be exhaust-
ed ; have worked hard

spracowany (spra-tso-va-ni) adj.
m. overworked;exhausted; tired
spragniony (sprag-ño-ni) adj.
m. thirsty;thirsting for
sprawa (spra-va) f. affair; matter; cause; case;question;job
sprawca (sprav-tsa) m. doer;
author ; culprit;originator
sprawdzic (sprav-dźheech) v.
verify;examine; test; check
sprawdzian (sprav-dżhan) m.
test; gauge; criterion;template
sprawiac (sprav-yach) v. cause;
bring to pass;occasion;afford
sprawiedliwosc (spra-vyed-lee-
voshch) f. justice; equity
sprawiedliwy (spra-vyed-lee-vi)
adj. m. just;righteous;fair
sprawka (sprav-ka) f. doing;
trick; small offense; prank
sprawnosc (sprav-noshch) f. efficiency; dispatch; skill
sprawny (sprav-ni) adj. m. able;
efficient; deft; dexterous
sprawowac (spra-vo-vach) v. perform;discharge; hold; exercise
sprawowanie (spra-vo-va-ñe) n.
conduct; behavior;performance
sprawozdanie (spra-voz-da-ñe) n.
report; account;statement
sprawozdawca (spra-voz-dav-tsa)
m. reviewer; reporter
sprawunek (spra-voo-nek) m.
purchase(made while shopping)
sprężac (spran-zhach) v. compress; tense;prestress
sprężarka (spran-zhar-ka) f.
compressor; air compressor
sprężenie (spran-zhe-ñe) n.
compression;prestress;pretension
sprężyna (spran-zhi-na) f.
spring; mainspring; impulse
sprężystosc (spran-zhis-toshch)
f. elasticity; energy;resilience
sprężysty (spran-zhis-ti) adj.
m. elastic; springy; energetic
sprostowac (spros-to-vach) v.
rectify; correct; right
sprostowanie (spros-to-va-ñe)
v. rectification;correction
sproszkowac (sprosh-ko-vach) v.
pulverize; levigate;triturate

sprosny (sprosh-ni) adj. m.
obscene; lewd ;foul(language)
sprowadzac (spro-va-dzach) v.
bring; import; fetch; call in
sprochniały (sprookh-na-wi)
adj. m. rotten;decayed
sprochniec (sprookh-ñech) v.
rot; decay; moulder;grow carious
spryciarz (spri-chash) m. dodger; trickster; slyboots
spryskac (spris-kach) v. splash
spryt (sprit) m. shrewdness;
cunning; gumption; knack
sprytny (sprit-ni) adj. m.
tricky; clever;cunning; cute
sprzączka (spzhownch-ka) f.
buckle ;clasp
sprzątaczka (spzhown-tach-ka)
f. cleaning woman;charwoman
sprzątac (spzhown-tach) v.
tidy up; clean up; clear up;
pich up; take away;snatch away
sprzątanie (spzhown-ta-ñe) n.
clearing; tidying up;housework
sprzeciw (spzhe-cheev) m. objection; opposition; resistance
sprzeciwiac się (spzhe-cheev-
yach shan) v. object; oppose
sprzeczac się (spzhe-chach
shan) v. fight; argue; dispute;
squabble; quarrel;contend about
sprzeczka (spzhech-ka) f. quarrel; squable;altercation; tiff
sprzecznosc (spzhech-noshch) f.
contradiction; discrepancy
sprzeczny (spzhech-ni) adj. m.
contradictory; incompatible
sprzedac (spzhe-dach) v. dispose of; sell; trade away
sprzedajny(spzhe-day-ni) adj.
m. venal;corrupt; corruptible
sprzedawca (spzhe-dav-tsa) m.
salesman; shop keeper;dealer
sprzedawczyni (spzhe-dav-chi-
ñee) f. saleslady;saleswoman
sprzedaż (spzhe-dash) f. sale
sprzedaż detaliczna (spzhe-
dash de-ta-leech-na) f. retail;sale at retail prices
sprzedaż hurtowa (spzhe-dash
khoor-to-va) f. wholesale
sprzeniewierzenie (spzhe-ñe-
vye-zhe-ñe) n. embezzlement

sprzęgać (spzhań-gaćh) v. couple; tie; link; team up; connect

sprzęgło (spzhań-gwo) n. clutch; coupling ; coupler;attachment

sprzęt (spzhańt) m. implement; furniture; accessories; utensils; tackle; outfit; chattels

sprzyjać (spzhi-yaćh) v. favor

sprzykrzyć (spzhik-zhićh) v. get sick of; get fed up with

sprzymierzeniec(spzhi-mye-zheńets) m. ally; confederate

sprzymierzony (spzhi-mye-zhó-ni) adj. m. allied;confederated

sprzysięgać się (spzhi-shań-gaćh shań) v. conspire; plot

sprzysiężenie (spzhi-shań-zheńe) n. plot; conspiracy

spuchnąć (spookh-nównćh)v. swell

spulchniać (spoolkh-ńaćh) v. fluff up;loosen;cultivate(soil)

spust (spoost) m. release; catch; slip; trigger; appetite; drain

spustoszenie (spoos-to-she-ńe) n. devastation; ravage;ruin

spustoszyć (spoos-to-shićh) v. devastate; ravage; make havoc

spuszczać (spoosh-chaćh) v. let down; drop; droop; lower; drain

spuścizna (spoośh-ćheez-na) f. inheritance; legacy;heritage

spychacz (spi-khach) m. bulldozer; stripper

spychać (spi-khaćh) v. push down; relegate; drive away

spytać się (spi-taćh shań) v. ask; ask a question

srać (sraćh) v. shit (vulg.)

srebrnik (srebr-ńeek) m. silvercoin; silversmith

srebrny (srebr-ni) adj. m. silver; of silver

srebro (sreb-ro) n. silver

srebrzyć (sreb-zhićh) v. silverplate;silver;wash with silver

srebrzysty (sreb-zhis-ti) adj. m. silvery(glow,color etc.)

srogi (sró-gee) adj. m. fierce; cruel; severe; srict; grim

sroka (sro-ka) f. magpie

srokaty (sro-ká-ti) adj. m. piebald (horse) ;with patches

srom (srom) m. disgrace; vulva

sromota(sro-mo-ta)f.shame;ignomity; disgrace

sromotny (sro-mót-ni) adj. m. shameful; disgraceful;infamous

srożyć (sro-zhićh) v. rage; torment; storm;oppress;be severe

ssać (ssaćh) v. suck; exploit

ssak (ssák) m. mammal;mammalian

ssawka (ssav-ka) f. sucker

ssąca pompa (ssówn-tsa póm-pa) f. suction pump

stabilizować (sta-bee-lee-zó-vaćh) v. stabilize; fix

stacja (státs-ya) f. station

stacja benzynowa (státs-ya ben-zi-nó-va) f. filling or service station

stacjonować (sta-tsyo-no-vaćh) v. be stationed;be in garrison

staczać (stá-chaćh) v. roll down; fight (battle)

staczać się (sta-chaćh shań) v. roll down; go from bad to worse;be on the down grade

stać (staćh) v. stand; be stopped; farewell; ill-afford;rise

stać się (staćh shań) v.become; grow; occur; happen

stadion (stá-dyon) m. stadium

stadło (stá-dwo) n. couple

stadnina (stad-ńee-na) f. stud

stado (stá-do) n. flock; herd

stagnacja (stag-náts-ya) f. stagnation;recession;stagnancy

stajnia (stáy-ńa) f. stable

stal (stal) f. steel

stale (stá-le) adv. constantly; always; for ever;incessantly

stalownia (sta-lov-ńa) f. steelmill; steel plant; steel works

stalowy (sta-ló-vi) adj. m. steel; steely; steel gray

stała (stá-wa) f. constant

stałość (stá-woshćh) f. stability; firmness; steadiness

stały (stá-wi) adj. m. stable; permanent; solid; fixed;firm

stamtąd (stam-tównd) adv. from there; from over there;out of it

stan (stán) m. state; status; condition;order; estate; class

stanąć (stá-nównćh) v. stand up; stop at; put up; rise; set foot

standaryzować (stan-da-ri-zo-
vach) v. standardize
stanik (sta-neek) m. bodice;
bra; brassiere;waste; corsage
staniol (stan-yol) m. tin foil
stanowczość (sta-nov-choshch)
f. determination; finality
stanowczy (sta-nov-chi) adj. m.
final; positive; decided ;firm
stanowić (sta-no-veech) v. establish; determine; constitute;; decide; proclaim
stanowisko (sta-no-vees-ko) n.
position; post; status; stand
starać się (sta-rach shan) v.
take care; try one's best
staranie (sta-ra-ne) n.care;
endeavor; exertion; pains
staranny (sta-ran-ni) adj. m.
careful; accurate; nice;exact
starcie (star-che) n. clash;
collision; friction ; squabble
starczy (star-chi) adj. m. se-
nile; v.:it is enough (exp.)
starczyć (star-chich) v. suffice
starodawny (sta-ro-dav-ni) adj.
m. old time; ancient;antique
staromodny (sta-ro-mod-ni) adj.
m. old fashioned;outmoded
starosta (sta-ros-ta) m. county-
head; wedding host; foreman
starość (sta-roshch) f. old age
staroświecki (sta-rosh-vyets-
kee) adj. m. old fashioned
starożytność (sta-ro-shit-noshch)
f. antiquity; ancient times
starożytny (sta-ro-zhit-ni) adj.
m. ancient; antique ;old world
starszeństwo (star-shen-stvo) n.
seniority ; superiority
starszy (star-shi) adj. m. old-
er; elder; superior(officer)
starszyzna (star-shiz-na) f. the
elders; the seniors;the chiefs
start (start) m. take-off; start
startować (star-to-vach) v.
start; take off; make a start
staruszek (sta-roo-shek) m. old
fellow;old man;old gentleman
stary (sta-ri) adj. m. old
starzec (sta-zhets) m. old man
starzec się (sta-zhech shan) v.
grow old ;age;grow stale;go bad

stateczny (sta-tech-ni) adj.
m. stable; bouyant; staid
statek (sta-tek) m. ship;
craft; vessel;boat;steamship
statki (stat-kee) pl. kitchen
pots & pans
statua (sta-too-a) f. statue
statut (sta-toot) m. statute
statyka (sta-ti-ka) f. statics
statysta (sta-tis-ta) m. supernumerary (actor);dummy;mute
statystyczny (sta-tis-tich-ni)
adj. m. statistical; statistic
statystyka (sta-tis-ti-ka) f.
statistics ;returns
statyw (sta-tiv) m. stand;
support; tripod
staw (stav) m. pond; joint
stawać się (sta-vach shan) v.
become; grow (scarce,big etc.)
stawiać (sta-vyach) v. place;
erect; put; stand; offer; lay
down ;post; station;put upright
stawka (stav-ka) f. stake
stąd (stownd) adv. from here;
away;therefore;that is why
stągiew (stown-gyev) f. vat
stąpać (stown-pach) v. pace;
tramp;tread;plod along;lumber
stchórzyć (stkhoo-zhich) v.
show fear; shrink with fright
stearyna (ste-a-ri-na)f. stea-
rin (glyceryl tristearate)
stek (stek) m. steak; pile of...
(lies; insults etc.); pack of...
stelmach (stel-makh) m. cart-
wright;wheelwright
stempel (stem-pel) m. stamp;
prop; ramrod; punch; die
stemplowany (stem-plo-va-ni)
adj. m. cancelled; used
stenograf (ste-no-graph) m.
stenographer;sorthand writer
stenografia (ste-no-graph-ya)
f. shorthand ;stenography
stenotypistka (ste-no-ti-peest-
ka) f. stenotypist ; steno
step (step) m. steppe
ster (ster) m. helm; rudder
sterczeć (ster-chech) v. stand
out; stick out; tower; bulge
stereoskop (ste-re-os-kop) m.
stereoscope

stereotypowy (ste-re-o-ti-po-
vi) adj. m., stereotyped
sternik (ster-neek) m. pilot
sterować (ste-ro-vach) v. steer
sterta (ster-ta) f. stack
stebnować (stan-bno-vach) v.
stitch; quilt
stęchlizna (stan-khleez-na) f.
fusty smell; musty smell
stęchły (stankh-wi) adj. m.
musty; stale; foul;fusty;frowsty
stękać (stan-kach) v. moan;
groan; utter a groan;complain
stępić (stan-peech) v. blunt;
dull; take the edge off
stępienie (stan-pye-ne) n. dullness (of knife; mind etc.)
stęskniony (stan-skno-ni) adj.
m. sick for; yearning for;
hankering for;nostalgic
stężały (stan-zha-vi) adj. m.
hardened; stiff; concentrated ; solidified;coagulated
stężec (stan-zhech) v. harden;
stiffen ; coagulate;concentrate
stężenie (stan-zhe-ne) n. concentration; strength(solutions)
stłoczyć (stwo-chich) v. cram;
compress;jam;squize;pack;pile up
stłuc (stwoots) v. smash; break;
bruise;shatter;injure;beat up
stłuczenie (stwoo-che-ne) n.
bruise; break ;contusion;injury
stłumiać (stwoom-yach)v. dampen;
muffle;deaden;suppress;stifle
sto (sto) num. hundred
stocznia (stoch-na) f. shipyard
stodoła (sto-do-wa) f. barn
stoik (sto-eek) m. Stoic
stoisko (sto-ees-ko) n. stand
stojak (sto-yak) m. stand
stojący (sto-yown-tsi) adj. m.
standing; stagnant;erect;upright
stok (stok) m. slope;hillside
stokroć (sto-kroch)adv.hundred
times;a hundred times;hundredfold
stokrotka (sto-krot-ka) f. daisy
stokrotny (sto-krot-ni) adj.
m. hundredfold repeated
stolarnia (sto-lar-na) f. joiner's shop ;carpinter's shop
stolarz (sto-lash) m. cabinetmaker; joiner; carpenter

stolec (sto-lets) m. stool
(large); bowel movement
stolica (sto-lee-tsa) f. capi-
tal(of a country)
stolik (sto-leek) m. small
table ;nice little table
stolnica (stol-nee-tsa) f. molding board ; paste board
stołeczny (sto-wech-ni) adj. m.
metropolitan (taxes);capital(city)
stołek (sto-wek) m. stool
stołować (sto-wo-vach) v. board
stołownik (sto-wov-neek) m.
boarder
stołówka (sto-woov-ka) f. mess
hall; mess; cantine
stonka (ston-ka) f. potato
beetle ;potato bug;Colorado beetle
stonoga (sto-no-ga) f. centi-
pede ; wood louse
stop (stop) m. (metal) alloy;
melt;traffic sign :stop; halt
stopa (sto-pa) f. foot;standard
stopa procentowa (sto-pa pro-
tsen-to-va) f. interest rate
stopa życiowa (sto-pa zhi-cho-
va) f. living standard
stoper (sto-per) m. stopwatch
stopić (sto-peech) v. melt
stopien (sto-pyen) m. (stair)
step; degree; grade;extent
stopniały (stop-na-wi) adj.m.
molten away; dwindled;shrunk
stopniec (stop-nech) v. melt
down ;melt away;sfrink;dwindle
stopniowo (sto-no-vo) adv.
gradually;little by little
stopniowy (stop-no-vi) adj. m.
gradual ;progressive
stora (sto-ra) f. shade; blind
storczyk (stor-chik) m. orchid
stos (stos) m. (wood) pile
stos atomowy (stos a-to-mo-vi)
m. atomic pile
stosować (sto-so-vach) v. use
stosownie (sto-sov-ne) adv.
accordingly; properly
stosowny (sto-sov-ni) adj. m.
proper; convenient;opportune
stosunek (sto-soo-nek) m. rate;
relation; proportion;attitude
stosunek płciowy (sto-soo-nek
pwcho-vi) m. sexual intercourse

stosunki handlowe (sto-soón-kee khand-ló-ve) pl. trade relations ;commercial relations
stosunkowy (sto-soon-kó-vi) adj. m. relative; proportional
stowarzyszenie (sto-va-zhi-shé-ńe) n. association; club
stożek (stó-zhek) m . cone
stożkowaty (stozh-ko-vá-ti) adj. m., conical; cone shaped
stóg (stoog) m. stack (rick)
stół (stoow) m. table
stracenie (stra-tsé-ńe) n. execution; loss ; doom
straceniec (stra-tsé-ńets) m. desperado; madcap
strach (strakh) m. fear; fright
stracić (stra-ćheećh) v. lose; execute(a man);shed(teeth etc.)
stragan (strá-gan) m. booth; stand; (market) stall
straganiarz (stra-gá-ńash) m. stand owner; stall holder
strajkować (stray-kó-vaćh) v. go on strike; strike
strapienie (stra-pyé-ńe) n. worry; distress; heartbreak
strapiony (stra-pyó-ni) adj. m. worried; dejected; distressed
straszak (strá-shak) m. noisy toy pistol; scarecrow; bugaboo
straszliwy (strash-lee-vi) adj. m. horrible; fearsome;awful
straszny (strásh-ni) adj. m. awful; terrible;awesome;frightful
straszyc (stra-shićh) v. frighten; haunt; threaten; bluff
straszydło (stra-shid-wo) n. scarecrow; fright
strata (stra-ta) f. loss
strategia (stra-tég-ya) f. strategy ;generalship
strategiczny (stra-te-geéch-ni) adj. m. strategic
stratny (strát-ni) adj. m. one that lost;being the looser
strawa (stra-ya) f. food ; meal
strawić (stra-veećh) v. digest; consume; bear;stomach; stand
strawne (stráv-ne) n. food ration (in the army etc.)
straż (strash) f. guard; watch ; safe custody;strict guard;escort

straż pożarna (strash po-zhar-na) f. fire brigade
straż przednia (strash pzhed-ńa) f. vanguard ;advance guard
straż tylna (strash til-na) f. rearguard ; rear guard
strażak (stra-zhak) m. fireman
strażnica (strazh-ńee-tsa) f. guardhouse; watchtower
strażnik (strazh-ńeek) m. guard; watchman ;sentry
strącić (strówn-ćheećh) v. knock off (apples); throw down
strączek (strówn-chek) m . (small) pod ;hull;husk;legume
strąk (strównk) m. pod;hull;husk
strefa (stré-fa) f. zone ;area
streszczać (strésh-chaćh) v. sum up ; summarize;abbreviate
streszczenie (stresh-ché-ńe) n. resume; summary ;digest
stręczyciel (stran-chi-ćhel) m. pimp; procurer ; broker
stręczyc (stran-chićh) v. procure (women) ; recommend
strofa (stró-fa) f. strophe
strofować (stro-fo-vaćh) v. reprimand ;admonish;scold;chide
stroic (stro-eećh) v. dress up; tune up; make fun ;add beauty
strojny (stróy-ni) adj. m. dressed up; elegant; smart
stromy (stró-mi) adj. m. steep
strona (stró-na) f. side; page; region ; aspect; part; party
stronnictwo (stron-ńeets-tvo) n. party (political)
stronniczy (stron-ńee-chi) adj. m. partial; biased;unfair
stronnik (stron-ńeek) m. partisan; supporter;follower;henchman
strop (strop) m. ceiling ;roof
stropic (stró-peeċh) v. discourage ; confound; abash;disconcert
stroskany (stros-ka-ni) adj.m. worried; sorrowful; dejected
strój (strooy) m. attire ;dress
stróż (stroosh) m. watchman
strudzony (stroo-dzó-ni) adj. m. weary ; tired;exhausted
strug (stroog) m. plane (tool)
struga (stroo-ga) f. stream; creek ; trickle;flow in streams

strugać (stroo-gach) v. whittle
struktura (strook-too-ra) f.
structure flow; flux; jet; torrents
strumień (stroo-myeń) m. stream;
struna (stroo-na) f. string;
chord; wire; (metal) wire
struna głosowa (stroo-na gwo-
so-va) vocal cord
strup (stroop) m. scab; crust
struś (stroosh) m. ostrich
strych (strikh) m. attic
strychnina (strikh-ńee-na) f.
strychnine
stryczek (stri-chek) m. (hanging) rope ; noose; the halter
stryj (striy) m. uncle
stryjeczny brat (stri-yech-ni
brat) m. cousin
strzał (stzhaw) m. shot
strzała (stzha-wa) f. arrow
strzaskać (stzhas-kach) v.
smash to pieces; shatter
strząsać (stzhown-sach) v. shake
off; shake down; flick off
strzec (stzhets) v. guard; protect; watch; keep an eye on
strzelać (stzhe-lach) v. shoot;
fire; slap; score; blunder
strzelanie (stzhe-la-ńe) n. shooting (practice); gunfire
strzelanina (stzhe-la-ńee-na) f.
gunfire ; shots; gunplay
strzelba (stzhel-ba) f. shotgun
strzelec (stzhe-lets) m. shooter;
rifleman; sniper; gunner; scorer
strzelnica (stzhel-ńee-tsa) f.
shooting range; rifle range
strzelniczy proch (stzhel-ńee-chi
prokh) m. gunpowder
strzemienne (stzhe-myen-ne) n.
parting drink; stirrup cup
strzemię (stzhe-myań) m. stirrup
strzepać (stzhe-pach) v. brush
off; flick off; shake off (away)
strzęp (stzhanp) m. shred; tatter
strzępić (stzhań-peech) v. shred
strzępić język (stzhań-peech
yan-zik) v. wag one's tongue;
waste breath; talk nonsense
strzyc (stzhits) v. cut; clip;
shear; cut (hair); mow; trim; graze
strzyc uszami (stzhits oo-sha-
mee) v. prick up ears

strzykać (stzhi-kach) v. squirt;
spray; inject; ache
strzykawka (stzhi-kav-ka) f.
syringe; hypodermic syringe
strzyżenie (stzhi-zhe-ńe) n.
(hair) cut ; sheep shearing
strzyżony (stzhi-zho-ni) adj.
m. cropped; cut; clipped
student (stoo-dent) m. student
studenteria (stoo-den-tér-ya)
pl. students ; student folks
studiować (stoo-dyo-vach) v.
study ; investigate; peer
studnia (stood-na) f. well
studzić (stoo-dżheech) v.
cool down (one's tea etc.)
studzienny (stoo-dżhen-ni)
adj. m. well (shaft; water etc.)
stuk (stook) m. knock ; clutter
stukać (stoo-kach) v. knock;
tap; hit; rap; patter; rattle; drum
stulecie (stoo-le-chè) n. century ; an age; hundred years
stuletni (stoo-lét-ńee) adj.
m. hundred years old ; age old
stulić (stoo-leech) v. press
tight; close up; coil up
stwardnieć (stvard-ńech) v.
harden; stiffen ; grow callous
stwardniały (stvard-ńa-wi) adj.
m. hardened; hard ; sclerotic
stwardnienie (stvard-ńe-ńe) n.
hardening; callosity
stwierdzać (stvyer-dzach) v.
state; find out; confirm
stwierdzenie (stvyer-dze-ńe)
n. statement; ascertainment
stworzenie (stvo-zhe-ńe) n.
creature; formation; creation
stworzyciel (stvo-zhi-chel) m.
creator ; maker (of the world)
stworzyć (stvo-zhich) v. create : produce; set up; compose
Stwórca (Stvoor-tsa) m. Creator; Maker
styczeń (sti-cheń) m. January
styczna (stich-na) f. tangent
styczność (stich-noshch) f.
contact; tangency ; adjacency
stygmat (stig-mat) m. stigma
stygnąć (stig-nownch) v. cool
down; cool off; cool
styk (stik) m. contact; butt

stykać się (sti-kach shan) v.
contact; touch;adjoin;meet
styl (stil) m. style; fashion
stylista (sti-lees-ta) m. styl-
ist
stylistyka (sti-lees-ti-ka) f.
art of composition ;syntax
stylowy (sti-lo-vi) adj. m. stylish; of style;in a given style
stypa (sti-pa) f. wake; funny
confusion; funeral banquet
stypendium (sti-pend-yoom) n.
scholarship; stipend; grant
subiektywny (soo-byek-tiv-ni)
adj. m. subjective
sublokator (soob-lo-ka-tor) m.
lodger ;subtenant
subordynacja (soob-or-di-nats-
ya) f. subordination
subskrypcja (soob-skrip-tsya) f.
subscription
substancja (soob-stan-tsya) f.
substance; matter
subsydiować (soob-sid-yo-vach)
v. subsidize
subtelność (sub-tel-noshch) f.
subtlety; niceness; delicacy
subtelny (soob-tel-ni) adj. m.
subtle;nice;fine;refined
subwencja (soob-ven-tsya) f.
subsidy; grant in aid
suchar (soo-khar) m. dry-bread
ration; cracker; biscuit
sucharek (soo-kha-rek) m. cracker ; biscuit
suchość (soo-khoshch) f. dryness
suchotnik (soo-khot-neek) m. con-
sumptive
suchoty (soo-kho-ti) pl. consumption; phthisis
suchy (soo-khi) adj. m. dry
sufit (soo-feet) m. ceiling
sugerować (soo-ge-ro-vach) v.
suggest;allude;hint
sugestia (soo-ges-tya) f. suggestion; motion; proposal
sugestywny (soo-ges-tiv-ni) adj.
m. suggestive(speech etc.)
suka (soo-ka) f. bitch
sukces (sook-tses) m. success
sukcesja (sook-tses-ya) f. succession; inheritance; devolution

sukienka (soo-ken-ka) f. dress
sukiennice (soo-ken-nee-tse)
n. weaver's or draper's market
hall ; cloth hall
sukiennik (soo-ken-neek) m.
draper; clothier
suknia (sook-na) f. gown
sukno (sook-no) n. cloth
sułtan (soow-tan) m. sultan
sum (soom) m. sheatfish
suma (soo-ma) f. sum; total;
high mass ;entirety;whole
sumaryczny (soo-ma-rich-ni)
adj. m. summary; total;global
sumienie (soo-mye-ne) n. conscience
sumienny (soo-myen-ni) adj. m.
conscientious;scrupulous
sumować (soo-mo-vach) v. sum up
sunąć (soo-nownch) v. glide;
slide; push; move ; skim along
supeł (soo-pew) m. knot
surdut (soor-doot) m. frock
coat; overcoat
surogat (soo-ro-gat) m. surro-
gate ; substitute for
surowica (soo-ro-vee-tsa) f.
serum
surowiec (soo-ro-vyets) m.
raw material ;staple; rawhide
surowość (soo-ro-voshch) f.
severity; crudeness ;rigor
surowy (soo-ro-vi) adj. m.
severe; raw; coarse; harsh
surówka (soo-roov-ka) f. pig
iron;fruit salad;raw hide
susza (soo-sha) f. drought;
dryness ;dry weather
suszarka (soo-shar-ka) f. (hair)
dryer ; desciccator
suszarnia (soo-shar-na) f. dry-
ing shed ;drying plant;kiln
suszka (soosh-ka) f. blotter
suszyć (soo-shich) v. dry
sutanna (soo-tan-na) f. cassock
sutener (soo-te-ner) m. cadet;
souteneur ; bully ;ponce
suterena (soo-te-re-na) f.base-
ment
sutka (soot-ka) f. nipple
suty (soo-ti) adj. m. copious;
abundant ; lavish ;plentiful;rich

suwać (soo-vach) v. shove
suwak (soo-vak) m. slide rule
swada (sva-da) f. eloquence
swar (svar) m. squabble; quarrel;rife;dissension
swarliwy (svar-lee-vi) adj. m. quarrelsome;cantankerous
swastyka (svas-ti-ka) f. swastica; swastika.
swat(svat) m. matchmaker
swatać (sva-tach) v. matchmake
swaty (sva-ti) n. matchmaking
swawola (sva-vo-la) f. anarchy
swawolny (sva-vol-ni) adj. m. unruly;playful;frolicsome;wilful
swąd (svownd) m. reek; stench
sweter (sve-ter) m. sweater
swędzenie (svan-dzhe-ne) n. itch; an itch; tingle
swędzić (svan-dzheech) v. itch
swoboda (svo-bo-da) f. freedom; ease; latitude;liberty
swoboda działania (svo-bo-da dzha-wa-na) v. freedom to act
swobodny (svo-bod-ni) adj. m. free; easy;at liberty;loose;lax
swoisty (svo-ees-ti) adj. m. specific;characteristic
swojski (svoy-skee) adj. m. homely;familiar;friendly;tame
sworzeń (svo-zhen) m. carriage bolt; lug bolt;cotter;pin
swój (svooy) pron. his; hers;my; its;our;your;their;one's own
swój człowiek (svooy chwo-vyek) m. trustworthy man
sybaryta (si-ba-ri-ta) m. Sybarite;sybarite; voluptuary
syberyjski (si-be-riy-skee) adj. m. Siberian; of Siberia
sycić (si-cheech)v. satiate
syczeć (si-chech) v. hiss
syfon (si-fon) m. siphon
sygnalizować (sig-na-lee-zo-vach) v. signalize; signal
sygnał (sig-naw) m. signal
sygnatura (sig-na-too-ra) f. (official) signature
sygnet (sig-net) m. signet; seal ring; imprint;colophon
syk (sik) m. hiss;sizzle;fizzle
sylaba (si-la-ba) f. syllable

sylogizm (si-lo-geezm)m. syllogism;rozumowanie dedukcyjne
sylweta (sil-ve-ta) f. silhouette; outline;profile;figure
symbioza (sim-byo-za) f. symbiosis:living together
symbol (sim-bol) m. symbol
symboliczny (sim-bo-leech-ni) adj. m. symbolic ;symbolical
symbolizować (sim-bo-lee-zo-vach) v. symbolize
symetria (si-metr-ya) f. symmetry
symetryczny (si-me-trich-ni) adj, m. symmetrical
symfonia (sim-fon-ya) f. symphony
symfoniczny (si-fo-neech-ni) adj. m. symphonic
sympatia (sim-pat-ya) f. liking
sympatyczny (sim-pa-tich-ni) adj. m. congenial;attractive
sympatyk (sim-pa-tik) m. well-wisher; sympathizer
sympatyzować (sim-pa-ti-zo-vach) v. like; go along ; feel with
symptom (simp-tom) m. symptom
symulacja (si-moo-lats-ya) f. simulation;make believe;sham
symulować (si-moo-lo-vach) v. simulate ;feign;pretend;affect
syn (sin) m. son
synagoga (si-na-go-ga) f. synagogue
syndykat (sin-di-kat) m. syndicate;syndicat;labor union
synek (si-nek) m. sonny
synekura (si-ne-koo-ra) f. sinecure; cosy job;fat job
synod (si-nod) m. synod
synonim (si-no-neem) m. synonym
synowa (si-no-va) f. daughter in law
synowiec (si-no-vyets) m. nephew
syntetyczny (sin-te-tich-ni) adj. m. synthetic
synteza (sin-te-za) f. synthesis
sypać (si-pach) v. strew; pour; scatter (dry matter);betray secrets
sypialnia (si-pyal-na) f. bedroom ;bedroom furniture suite
sypki (sip-kee) adj. m. loose (dry);granular(substance);friable

sypki towar (syp-kee tó-var) m.
granular goods; dry goods
syrena (si-re-na) f. siren;
mermaid;hooter;Warsaw's emblem
syrop (si-rop) m. syrup
syryjski (si-riý-skee) adj. m.
Syrian; of Syria
system (sis-tem) m. system
systematyczny (sys-te-ma-tich-
ni) adj. m. systematic; neat
syt (sit) adj. m. satiate; full
sytny (sit-ni) adj. m. filling
up; nourishing; satiating
sytuacja (si-too-ats-ya) f.
situation;circumstances;things
sytuować (si-too-o-vach) v. sit-
uate ; locate; position
sytuowany (si-too-o-va-ni) adj.
m. situated ; placed;located
syty (si-ti) adj. m. satiate;
dilled up; well-fed;nourishing
szabla (shab-la) f. sabre
szablon (shab-lon) m. stencil;
pattern; model; stereotype
szablonowy (sha-blo-no-vi) adj.
m. routine; stereotype
szach-mat (shakh-mat) m. check-
mate (in a chess game etc.)
szachista (sha-khees-ta) m.
chess player
szachować (sha-kho-vach) v.
check (in chess); check
szachownica (sha-khov-nee-tsa)
f. chessboard ;checker board
szachraj (shakh-ray) m. cheat
szachrować (zhakh-ro-vach) v.
cheat; swindle; jockey
szachy (sha-khi) pl. chess
szacować (sha-tso-vach) v.
evaluate; estimate ;size up
szacunek (sha-tsoo-nek) m.
1. valuation; 2. respect
szafa (sha-fa) f. chest; wardrobe; bookcase ; cupboard
szafir (sha-feer) m. sapphire
szafka nocna (shaf-ka nóts-na)
f. night table;bedside table
szafot (sha-fot) m. (execution)
scaffold
szafować (sha-fo-vach) v. lavish ; squander;be liberal
szafran (shaf-ran) m. saffron

szajka (shay-ka) f. gang
szakal (sha-kal) m. jackal
szal (shal) m. shawl ;scarf
szala (sha-la) f. scale
szalbierstwo (shal-byer-stvo)
n. swindle ; fraud;imposition
szalbierz (shal-byesh) m.fraud;
swindler ; quack ;impostor
szaleć (sha-lech) v. rage ;rave
szalenie (sha-le-ne) adv. mad-
ly; terribly;awfully;like mad
szaleniec (sha-le-nets) m. madman; daredevil ; desperado
szaleńczy (sha-len-chi) adj. m.
frantic;mad;insane;reckless
szaleństwo (sha-len-stvo) n.
fury; madness ; craze;frenzy
szalik (sha-leek) m. scarf
szalony (sha-lo-ni) adj. m. mad
szał (shaw) m. rage;fury;frenzy
szałas (sha-was) m. tent; shanty ; shed; shelter; chalet;hut
szamotać się (sha-mo-tach shań)
v. scuffle; struggle; tussle
szampan (sham-pan) m. champagne
szaniec (sha-nets) m. bastion
szanować (sha-no-vach) v. respect; honor; have regard;esteem
szanowny (sha-nov-ni) adj. m.
honorable;worthy; dear(sir)
szansa (shan-sa) f. chance
szantaż (shan-tazh) m. blackmail ; extortion
szantażować (shan-ta-zho-vach)
v. blackmail ;make squeal
szantażysta (shan-ta-zhis-ta)
m. blackmailer ;extortioner
szarak (sha-rak) m. hare; average man of the street ;yeoman
szarańcza (sha-ran-cha) v. locust ;swarm of locust;swarm
szarfa (shar-fa) f. scarf; sash
szargać (shar-gach) v. besmear;
foul up; slander; tarnish;slur
szarlatan (shar-la-tan) m. confidence man; charlatan
szarotka (shar-ót-ka) f. edelweiss
szarość (sha-roshch) f. greyness;
drabness ;dullness; duskiness
szarpać (shar-pach) v. jerk; pull;
tear; tousle ; knock about;assail

szaruga (sha-roo-ga) f. gray,
foul weather; gray skies
szary (sha-ri) adj. m. gray;drab
szarzec (sha-zhech) v. loom;
gray ; grow dusky; show grey
szarzyzna (sha-zhiz-na) f.
grayness; drabness; duskiness
szarża (shár-zha) f. (cavalry)
charge;(military)rank; officer
szarżować (shar-zho-vach) v.
charge (recklessly);overact
szastać (shas-tach) v. squander
szata (sha-ta) f. garment;gown
szatan (sha-tan) m. satan; devil ; very strong coffee
szatański (sha-tán-skee) adj.
m. devilish ; infernal;satanic
szatkować (shat-ko-vach) v.
cut; chop ; shred;slice
szatnia (shat-na) f. locker
room; coat room
szatynka (sha-tin-ka) f. dark-
blond girl;auburn haired woman
szczać (shchach) v. piss (vulg.)
szczapa (shchá-pa) f. split log;
splint; chip ; sliver;thin man
szczaw (shchav) m. sorrel
szczątek (shchown-tek) m. remnant; vestige ;fragment
szczebel (shche-bel) m.(ladder)
rung; spoke; grade ;round
szczebiot (shche-byot) m. chatter; chirp;babble;prattle;warble
szczebiotać (shche-byo-tach) v.
chirrup ; chirp; chatter;bable
szczebiotanie (shche-byo-ta-ne)
n. chatter; prattle;chirp;warble
szczecina (shche-chee-na) f.
bristle (of hogs);stubble beard
szczególność (shche-gool-noshch)
f. peculiarity;singularity
szczególny (shche-gool-ni) adj.
m. peculiar ; special; specific
szczegół (shche-goow) m. detail
szczegółowy (shche-goo-wo-vi)
adj. m. detailed ; minute
szczekać (shche-kach) v. bark
szczekanie (shche-ka-ne) n. bark
szczelina (shche-lee-na) f. slot;
crevice; cleft ;slit; riftcrack
szczelny (shchel-ni) adj. m.
(water) tight; (air) tight etc.

szczeniak (shche-nak) m. puppy ; kid ; pup
szczep (shchep) m. graft; tribe;
seedling
szczepić (shche-peech) v. graft;
vaccinate; inoculate
szczepienie (shche-pye-ne) n.
grafting; vaccination
szczepionka (shche-pyon-ka) f.
vaccine
szczerba (shcher-ba) f. jag;
notch; gap ;nick; chip; dent
szczerbaty (shcher-ba-ti) adj.
m.gap-toothed; jagged
szczerbić (shcher-beech) v. jag
szczerość (shche-roshch) f.
sincerity ; open-heartedness
szczerozłoty (shche-ro-zwo-ti)
adj. m. pure golden
szczery (shche-ri) adj. m.
sincere ;frank; candid
szczędzić (shchan-dzheech) v.
spare ; economize ;grudge;stint
szczęk (shchánk) m. clink;clash;
clang ;jangle; rattle
szczęka (shchan-ka) f. jaw
szczękać (shchan-kach) v.
clink; clang ;jangle;rattle
szczęścić się (shchansh-cheech
shan) v. have good luck
szczęście (shchansh-che) n.
happiness; good luck success
szczęśliwy (shchan-shlee-vi)
adj. m. happy; lucky;successful
szczodrość (shchod-roshch) f.
generosity ;open-handedness
szczodry (shchod-ri) adj. m.
generous ;abundant; ample
szczoteczka (shcho-tech-ka) f.
small brush; toothbrush
szczotka (shchot-ka) f. brush
szczotkarski (shchot-kar-skee)
adj. m. brush ;brush maker's
szczotkować (shchot-ko-vach) v.
brush down; bursh;polish(a floor)
szczuć (shchooch) v. hiss; bait;
embitter against ;set dogs on
szczudło (shchood-wo) n. stilt ;
crutch
szczupak (shchoo-pak) m. pike
szczuplec (shchoop-lech) v.
slim down; reduce; diminish

szczupłość (shchoop-woshch) f. slimness; scarcity;scantiness

szczupły (shchoop-wi) adj. m. slim; slender; thin; lean

szczur (shchoor) m. rat

szczycić się (shchi-cheech shän) v. boast; take pride; be proud

szczypać (shchi-pach) v. pinch

szczypce (shchip-tse) pl. tongs; pliers; pincers; clippers

szczypczyki (shchip-chi-kee) pl. tweezers; forceps

szczypiorek (shchi-pyo-rek) m. chive

szczypta (shchip-ta) f. pinch

szczyt (shchit) m. top; summit

szczytny (shchit-ni) adj. m. lofty; sublime ;commendable

szczytowy (shchi-to-vi) adj.m. pick; culminant ; uppermost;top

szef (shef) m. boss; chief

szelest (she-lest) m. rustle

szeleścić (she-lesh-cheech) v. rustle; whisper(in the wind)

szelki (shel-kee) pl. suspenders; straps; belts; braces

szelma (shel-ma) f. rogue; scoundrel; wretch; knave

szelmostwo (shel-most-vo) n. roguery;rascally trick

szemrać (shem-rach) v. murmur; grumble;prattle;repine against

szept (shept) m. whisper

szeptać (shep-tach) v. whisper

szepnąć (shep-nownch) v. whisper; murmur; conspire; scheme

szereg (she-reg) m. row; file; series;range;chain(of events)

szeregować (she-re-go-vach) v. rank; classify; arrange

szeregowy (she-re-go-vi) adj.m. series; soldier in the ranks

szermierka (sher-myer-ka) f. fencing

szermierz (sher-myesh) m. fencer

szeroki (she-ro-kee) adj. m. wide;broad; ample; extensive

szerokość (she-ro-koshch) f. width;latitude; breath

szerokotorowa kolej (she-ro-ko-to-ro-va ko-ley) f. wide gauge railroad (Russian)

szerszeń (sher-shen) m. hornet; wasp

szerzenie (she-zhe-ne) n. spread

szerzyć (she-zhich) v. spread

szesnasty (shes-nás-ti) num. sixteenth

szesnaście (shes-nash-che) num. sixteen

sześcian (shesh-chan) m. cube

sześcienny (shesh-chen-ni) adj. m. cubic

sześciokrotny (shesh-cho-krot-ni) adj. m. sixfold

sześcioro (shesh-cho-ro) num. six

sześć (sheshch) num. six

sześćdziesiąt (sheshch-dzhe-shownt) num. sixty

sześćdziesiąty (sheshch-dzhe-shown-ti) adj. m. sixtieth

sześćset (sheshch-set) num. six hundred

szew (shev) m. seam ;stitch

szewc (shevts) m. shoemaker

szewstwo (shev-stvo) n. shoemaking;shoemaking trade

szkalować (shka-lo-vach) v. slander;defame; calumniate

szkapa (shka-pa) f. jade

szkaradny (shka-rad-ni) adj.m. hideous; ugly; abominable;nasty

szkarlatyna (shkar-la-ti-na) f. scarlet fever; scarlatina

szkarłat (shkar-wat) m. scarlet

szkarłatny (shkar-wat-ni) adj. m. scarlet;crimson; purple

szkatuła (shka-too-wa) f. casket

szkic (shkeets) m. outline; sketch; essay; study;draught

szkicować (shkee-tso-vach) v. sketch; outline; draw up;design

szkicownik (shkee-tsov-neek) m. sketch pad; sketchbook

szkielet (shke-let) m. skeleton; framework; shell; carcass

szkiełko (shke w-ko) n. small glass; pane;slide

szklanka (shklan-ka) f. (drinking) glass; glassful (of water etc.)

szklany (shkla-ni) adj. m. glass; glassy(eyes); vitreous

szklarz (shklash) m. glazier

szklić (shkleech) v. glaze;brag
szklisty (shklees-ti) adj. m.
 glassy;glazy;vitreous;hyaline
szkliwo (shklee-vo) n. enamel;
 glaze;(desert)varnish
szkło (shkwo) n. glass;pane
szkocki (shkóts-kee) adj.m.
 Scottish; of Scotland
szkoda (shkó-da) f. damage;
 harm;detriment;mischief
szkodliwy (shkod-lee-vi) adj.m.
 harmful;detrimental;damaging
szkodnik (shkod-ñeek) m. wrong-
 doerpest;nuisance
szkodzić (shkó-dźheećh) v. harm;
 injure;be harmful;cause damage
szkolenie (shko-le-ñe) n. training;instruction; schooling
szkolić (shkó-leećh) v. school;
 train;give instruction;instruct
szkolnictwo (shkol-ñeets-tvo) n.
 school system; education
szkolny (shkól-ni) adj. m.
 school; scholastic; school-
szkoła (shkó-wa) f. school
szkop (shkop) m. Kraut; Hun(vulg.)
szkopuł (shkó-poow) m. obstacle
szkorbut (shkór-boot) m. scurvy
szkuner (shkóo-ner) m. schooner
szkwał (shkvaw) m. squall;flaw
szlaban (shla-ban) m. tollgate ;
 barrier;train crossing barrier
szlachcic (shlakh-cheets) m.
 squire ; nobleman; gentleman
szlachecki (shla-khéts-kee) adj.
 m. noble ; gentle; gentleman's
szlachetny (shla-khét-ni) adj.
 m. noble ; noble-minded ;elegant
szlachta (shlakh-ta) f. gentry
szlafrok (shlaf-rok) m. house-
 robe ; wrapper; dressing gown
szlak (shlak) m. trail; track;
 border;route;band;selvage;scent
szlam (shlam) m. slime;ooze;slit
szlem (shlem) m. big slam
 (bridge)(card game)
szlemik (shle-meek) m. little
 slam (card game,bridge)
szlifa (shlee-fa) f. epaulette
szlifierka (shlee-fyer-ka) f.
 grinding machine;grinder
szlifierz (shlee-fyesh) m. pol-
 isher; cutter;grinder

szlifować (shlee-fo-vać) v.
 polish; burnish;cut(diamonds)
szlochać (shló-khać) v. sob
szmaciany (shma-ćha-ni) adj.
 m. rag; made out of rags
szmaragd (shma-ragd) m. emerald; emerald green
szmat (shmat) m. large piece;
 long way;a good bit;expanse
szmata (shma-ta) f. clout; rag
szmatławiec (shma-twa-vyets)
 m. shabby newspaper; smear
 sheet;rag
szmelc (shmelts) m. scrap
szmer (shmér) m. murmur;rustle
szmergiel(shmer-ġel)m. emery
szminka (shmeen-ka) f. lipstick; paint;rouge;make up
szmugiel (shmoo-ġel) m. smuggle;smuggling;contraband
szmuglować (shmoo-glo-vać) v.
 smuggle(goods)
szmonces (shmon-tses) m. Jewish
 quip or joke; nonsense(slang)
szmuklerstwo (shmook-ler-stvo)
 n. haberdashery
szmuklerz (shmook-lesh) m.
 haberdasher
sznur (shnoor) m. rope; cord
sznurek (shnoo-rek) m. string
sznurować (shnoo-ro-vać) v.
 lace up; lace; tie
sznurowadło (shnoo-ro-vad-wo)
 n. shoe lace;lace;shoe string
sznurowany (shnoo-ro-va-ni) adj.
 m. laced
sznycel po wiedeńsku (shni-tsel
 po vye-deń-skoo) m. Wiener
 cutlet
szofer (shó-fer) m. chauffeur;
 driver;(bus)driver;truck driver
szopa (sho-pa) f. shed;lark;fun
szopka (shóp-ka) f. puppet show
szorować (sho-ro-vać) v. rub;
 scour; scrub; wash;grate;run
szorstki(shórst-kee) adj. m.
 coarse; rough; crude; harsh
szorstkość (shórst-kośhćh) f.
 roughness; harshness;bluntness
szosa (shó-sa) f. highway;road
szowinizm (sho-vee-ñeezm) m.
 chauvinism
szósty (shóos-ti) adj.m. num.
 sixth

szpada (shpa-da) f. sword

szpagat (shpa-gat) m. string; (ballet) split;cord;twine;twist

szpaler (shpa-ler) m. double (tree) row; lane; hedge

szpalta (shpál-ta) f. (newspaper) column;(printer's)slip

szpara (shpá-ra) f. gap; slot; rift;chink;crack;slit;crevice

szparag (shpa-rak) m. asparagus

szpargał (shpar-gaw) m. scrappaper;scrap of paper

szpecić (shpe-ćheećh) v. disfigure; make ugly;mar beauty

szperacz (shpe-rach) v. ferreter; scout;sniper;searcher

szperać (shpe-raćh) v. forage; burrow;poke about;search books

szpetny (shpet-ni) adj. m. ugly

szpic (shpeets) m. spike;peak; (sharp) point;Pomeranian dog

szpicel (shpee-tsel) m. stool pigeon; informer;plainclotheman

szpiczasty (shpee-chás-ti) adj. m. pointed; tapering

szpieg (shpyeg) m. spy; sleuth

szpiegostwo (shpye-gós-tvo) n. espionage ; spying

szpiegować (shpye-go-vaćh) v. spy upon;shadow;watch;eavesdrop

szpik (shpeek) m. marrow

szpikować (shpee-ko-vaćh) v. stuff (meat);lard(meat etc.)

szpilka (speel-ka) f. pin(small)

szpilkowy (shpeel-kó-vi) adj.m. conifer; pegged (soles)

szpinak (shpee-nak) m. spinach

szpital (shpee-tal) m. hospital

szpon (shpon) m. claw; talon

szponder (shpon-der) m. flank (meat); sirloin

szprotka (shprot-ka) f. sprat

szpryca (shpri-tsa)f. syringe

szprycha (shpri-kha) f. spoke

szprycować (shpri-tso-vaćh) v. sprinkle ; syringe

szpulka (shpool-ka) f. bobbin

szpunt (shpoont) m. plug; stopper; bung;peg; tongue;feather

szpuntować (shpoon-to-vaćh) v. bung (barrel); plug;peg

szrama (shrá-ma) f. scar

szranki (shrán-kee) pl. lists; bounds; reins;tilt yard;barriers

szreń (shreń) f. neve ; frost

szron (shron) m. hoar-frost; rime; coat of rime

sztab (shtab) m. staff;headquarters

sztaba (shta-ba) f. bar;(gold) ingot ;ingot(of silver)

sztabowy (shta-bo-vi) adj. m. staff (officer)

sztachety (shta-khe-ti) pl.(picket) fence; railing

sztafeta (shta-fe-ta) f. relay (race); relay race

sztaluga (shta-loo-ga) f. easel

sztanca (shtan-tsa) f. die; stamp ; punch

sztandar (shtan-dar) m. banner

sztokfisz (shtok-fish) m. stockfish; cod; codfish

sztolnia (shtol-ña) f. gallery

sztucer (shtoo-tser) m. rifle (gun); sporting rifle

sztuciec (shtoo-ćhets) m. fork

sztuczka (shtooch-ka) f. trick; small piece; dodge;manoeuvre

sztuczne tworzywo (shtooch-ne tvo-zhi-vo) n. plastic

sztuczny (shtooch-ni) adj. m. artificial;sham;false;immitationsztućce (shtooćh-tse) pl. (table) silver;knife,fork and spoons

sztuka (shtoo-ka) f. art; piece; cattlehead; (stage) play;stunt

sztukateria (shtoo-ka-tér-ya) f. stucco work; stucco

sztukować (shtoo-ko-vaćh) v.piece; patch up; eke out; lengthen

szturchać (shtoor-khaćh) v. poke; dig; prod; jab; push; jostle

szturm (shtoorm) m. attack; storm; assault ;onslaught

szturmować (shtoor-mo-vaćh) v. storm; attack; assault; harass

sztych (shtikh) m. stab; engraving ;etching;woodcut; spade

sztyft (shtift) m. tag; pin; peg

sztylet (shti-let) m. stiletto; dagger; poniard; bodkin; spike

sztywnieć (shtiv-ñećh) v. stiffen ;grow stiff;become stiff

sztywny (shtiv-ni) adj. m. stiff

szubienica (shoo-bye-nee-tsa)
f. gallows; hanging matter
szubrawiec (shoo-bra-vyets) m.
scoundrel; rascal;rogue
szubrawstwo (shoob-rav-stvo) n.
villainy;rascally trick;rabble
szufla (shoof-la) f. shovel
szuflada (shoof-la-da) f. drawer; shunting;shelving
szuja (shoo-ya) f. scoundrel
szukać (shoo-kach) v. look for;
seek;search;cast about for
szukanie (shoo-ka-ne) n. search
szuler (shoo-ler) m. gambler
szum (shoom) m. (wind) noise;hum;
roar;uproar; scum; frost
szumieć (shoom-yech) v. buzz;
roar; froth;hum;rustle;fizz
szumny (shoom-ni) adj. m. roar-
ing; boistrous;noisy;frothy
szumowiny (shoo-mo-vee-ni) pl.
scum; scum of the society
szurgać (shoor-gach) v. shuffle
noisily;scrape foot on the floor
szuter (shoo-ter) m. gravel
szwaczka (shvach-ka) f. seamstress; needlewoman
szwadron (shvad-ron) m. squad-
ron;(cavalry)squadron; troop
szwagier (shva-ger) m. brother-
-in-law
szwagierka (shva-ger-ka) f.
sister-in-law
szwajcar (shvay-tsar) m. doorman; (Szwajcar = Swiss)
szwajcarski (shvay-tsar-skee)
adj. m. Swiss; of Switzerland
szwalnia (shval-na) f. underwear
factory;tailoring shop
szwargot (shvar-got) m. gibberish; jabber; lingo
szwedzki (shvedz-kee) adj. m.
Swedish; of Sweden
szyb (shib) m.shaft; (oil)well
szyba (shi-ba) f. (glass) pane
szybki (shib-kee) adj. m. quick;
fast; prompt;rapid; sharp;smart
szybko (shib-ko) adv. quickly;
fast; promptly;swiftly; apace
szybkość (shib-koshch) f. speed;
velocity; rate; fastness
szybować (shi-bo-vach) v..glide;
soar;tower;sail;plane

szybowiec (shi-bo-vyets) m.
glider (motorless)
szychta nocna (shikh-ta nots-
na) v. night shift
szycie (shi-che) n. sewing
szyć (shich) v. sew; sew up
szydełko (shi-dew-ko) n.croch-
et needle; crochet hook
szydełkować (shi-dew-ko-vach)
v. crochet
szyderca (shi-der-tsa) m.
scoffer; giber; railer
szyderczy (shi-der-chi) adj.
m. scoffing; sarcastic
szyderstwo (shi-der-stvo) n.
scoff;jeer;sneer;gibe;derision
szydło (shid-wo) n. awl;pricker
szydzić (shi-dzheech) v. scoff
szyfr (shifr) m. code;cipher
szyja (shi-ya) f. neck;bottleneck
szyk (shik) m. order; elegance;
(battle) array; order;formation
szykana (shi-ka-na) f. chica-
nery;vexation;difficulties;style
szykanować (shi-ka-no-vach) v.
vex; chicane; annoy; nag;pick at
szykować (shi-ko-vach) v. make
ready; prepare;get ready
szykować się (shi-ko-vach shan)
v. get ready;be in prospect
szykowność (shi-kov-noshch) f.
elegance;smartness; style;chic
szykowny (shi-kov-ni) adj. m.
smart; elegant;fashionable;chic
szyld (shild) m. sign-board
szyldwach (shild-vakh) m. sentry; military guard
szyling (shi-ling) m. shilling
szympans (shim-pans) m. chim-
panzee
szyna (shi-na) f. rail
szynk (shink) m. bar;saloon;pub
szynka (shin-ka) f. ham
szynkarz (shin-kash) m. barman
szyszak (shi-shak) m. helmet
szyszka (shish-ka) f. (tree)
cone;trobile; bigwig;topdog
ściana (shcha-na) f. wall
ścianka (shchan-ka) f. partition; bulkhead; small wall
ściągać (shchown-gach) v. draw
down or together;cheat in class;
assemble; collect (taxes)

ściągaczka (shchown-gach-ka)
f. cheat note; crib
ścieg (shcheg) m. stitch
ściec (shchets) v. drain off;
run off;trickle down; drip
ściek (shchek) m. sewer; gutter;
sink; sewage;drain;sewer;gully
ściekać (shche-kach) v. drain
off; flow down;trickle down
ściemniać (shchem-nach) v. dark-
en; dim; obscure;dim the lights
ścienny (shchen-ni) adj. m. mu-
ral(painting);wall (map etc.)
ścierać (shche-rach) v. rub off;
dust off;grind down;wear off
ścierka (shcher-ka) f. duster;
rug; kitchen towel;clout
ściernisko (shcher-nees-ko) n.
stubble field; stubble
ścierń (shchern) m. stubble
ścierpły (shcherp-wi) adj. m.
numb; gone to sleep
ścierwo (shcher-vo) n. carrion
ścieśniać (shchesh-nach) v.cramp;
tighten;narrow;restrict;close
ścieżka (shchezh-ka) f. trail;
pass ;(foot) pass; alley
ścięcie (shchan-che) n. behead-
ing; cutting off;truncation
ścięgno (shchang-no) n. tendon
ścięty (shchan-ti) adj. m.
truncated;cut off; beheaded
ścigacz (shchee-gach) m. torpedo boat;motor gun boat
ścigać (shchee-gach) v. chase;
pursue;run after;hunt;procecute
ścinać (shche-nach) v. cut off;
cut down; fell (tree);clip;clot
ścinać się (shchee-nach shan) v.
coagulate; congeal;fix;clot;fail
ściółka (shchoow-ka) f. litter
bed; litter,bedding;barn litter
ścisk (shcheesk) m. throng;press;
crowd; squeeze ;crush;clamp
ściskać (shchees-kach) v. compress; shake (hand); squeeze;
embrace;clasp;harass;hamper;hug
ścisłość (shchees-woshch) f.
exactness; accuracy; compactness; density; reliability
ścisły (shchees-wi) adj. m.
exact; precise; compact;dense

ściśle (shcheesh-le) adv. exactly; tightly; compactly
ślad (shlat) m. trace; track;
(foot) print; footstep
ślamazara (shla-ma-za-ra) f.
sluggard; slowheaded person
ślamazarny (shla-ma-zar-ni)
adj. m. sluggish
śląski (shlowns-kee) adj. m.
Silesian ;of Silesia
śledczy (shled-chi) adj. m.
inquisitional ; of inquiry
śledzić (shle-dzheech) v. spy;
watch; investigate; observe
śledziona (shle-dzho-na) f.
spleen ; milt
śledziowy (shle-dzho-vi) adj.
m. herring(oil,salad etc.)
śledztwo (shledz-tvo) n.
investigation ;inquest;inquiry
śledź (shledzh) m. herring
ślepie (shlep-ye) n. (animal's)
eye ; eye; lights
ślepnąć (shlep-nownch) v. go
blind ;loose one's eyesight
ślepa ulica (shle-pa oo-lee-
tsa) s. dead end street
ślepota (shle-po-ta) f. blindness ;cecity;lack of foresight
ślepy (shle-pi) adj. m. blind
ślęczeć (shlan-chech) v. drag
study or reading; drudge;
pore; plod; slog away; boggle
śliczny (shleech-ni) adj. m.
pretty; lovely; dandy
ślimacznica (shlee-mach-nee-
tsa) s. road access ramp;helix
ślimak (shlee-mak) m. snail
ślina (shlee-na) f. saliva
śliniak (shlee-nak) m. bib
śliski (shlees-kee) adj. m.
slippery ; slimy;scabrous
śliwa (shlee-va) f. plum tree
śliwka (shleev-ka) f. plum
śliwowica (shlee-vo-vee-tsa)
f. plum brandy;plum vodka
ślizgacz (shleez-gach) m.speed-
boat; gliding boat
ślizgać się (shleez-gach shan)
v. slide; glide; slip; skate
ślizgawka (shleez-gav-ka) f.
skating rink ;kid's slide

ślizgowiec (shleez-gó-vyets)
m. hydrofoil; gliding boat;
speed boat

ślub (shloob) m. wedding; vow

ślubna obrączka (shloób-na ob-
rówńch-ka) f. wedding ring

ślubny (shloob-ni) adj. m. nup-
tial; wedding-(ring);legitimate

ślubować (shloo-bo-vach) v. vow

ślusarz (shloó-sash) m. locksmith; ironworker;metal worker

śluz (shloos) m. slime; phlegm

śluza (shloo-za) f. sluice

śmiać się (shmyách shań) v.
laugh;chuckle;scoff;make sport

śmiałek (shmyá-wek) m. daredevil; mad cap

śmiałość (shmyá-woshch) f. bold-
ness;courage;bravery;daring;guts

śmiały (shmyá-wi) adj. m. bold

śmiech (shmyekh) m. laughter

śmieci (shmye-chee) pl. rubbish;
garbage;rag;shred;scrap;refuse

śmiecić (shmye-cheech) v. litter; throw litter about

śmiecie (shmye-che) pl. rubbish;
garbage;refuse;litter;scrap

śmieć (shmyech) m. litter; rag

śmiercionosny (shmyer-cho-nóshn-
ni) adj. m. lethal; deadly

śmierć (shmyerch) f. death

śmierdzieć (shmyer-dzhech) v.
stink; smell; reek(of nicotine)

śmiertelnik (shmyer-tel-ńeek)
m. mortal man

śmiertelność (shmyer-tel-noshch)
f. mortality; deadliness

śmiertelny (shmyer-tel-ni) adj.
m. mortal;deadly;death(throes)

śmieszność (shmyesh-noshch) f.
comic trait; the ridiculous

śmieszny (shmyesh-ni) adj. m.
funny; ridiculous;comic;absurd

śmieszyć (shmye-shich) v. make
laugh; cause laughter;amuse

śmietana (shmye-tá-na) f. sour-
cream; clotted cream

śmietanka (shmye-tan-ka) f.
cream; flower(of society etc.)

śmietnik (shmyet-ńeek) m. garbage can; garbage dump

śmiga (shmee-ga) f. (wind mill)
sail

śmigło (shmeeg-wo) n. propeller

śmigłowiec (shmeeg-wóv-yets)
m. helicopter

śniadanie (shńa-da-ńe) n. breakfast ; luncheon

śniady (shńa-di) adj.swarthy;
sun-tanned;dusky;tawny

śnić (shńeech) v. dream (about
something);have a dream

śniedź (shńedzh) f. verdigris

śnieg (shńeg) m. snow;snowscape

śniegowce (shńe-góv-tse) pl.
snowboots;overshoes; galishes

śnieg pada (shńeg pa-da) exp.:
it snows

śnieżka (shńezh-ka)f. snowball

śnieżnobiały (shńezh-no-bya-
wi) adj. m. snow-white

śnieżny (shńezh-ni) adh. m.
snowy;snow white; snow-

śnieżyca (shńe-zhi-tsa) f.
snow-storm; blizzard

śpiący (shpyówn-tsi) adj. m.
sleepy;drowsy;slumberous

śpiączka (shpyównch-ka) f.
sleeping sickness

śpieszyć się (shpye-shich shań)
v. hurry;hasten;be in a hurry

śpiew (shpyev) m. song;singing

śpiewaczka (shpye-vach-ka) f.
singer, (girl or woman)

śpiewać (shpye-vach) v. sing

śpiewak (shpye-vak) m. singer

śpiewnik (shpyev-ńeek) m.
songbook; hymn-book

śpiewny (shpyev-ni) adj. m.
melodious; singsong-(accent)

śpioch (shpyokh) m. sleepy
head; lie-abed; slug-abed

śpiwór (shpee-voor) m. sleeping
bag

średni(shred-ńee) adj. m. average; medium; mean(temperature)

średnica (shred-ńee-tsa) f. diameter; bore; middle register

średnik (shred-ńeek) m. semicolon

średnio (shred-ńo) adv. average ; medium- ;fairly well

średniowiecze (shred-ńo-vye-
che) n. Middle Ages

średniowieczny (shred-ńo-vyech-
ni) adj. m. medieval

środa (śhro-da) f. Wednesday
środek (śhro-dek) m. center;
middle; measures; means; remedy;midst;inside;agent;medium
środkowy (śhrod-ko-vi) adj. m.
central; center-(line);middle
środowisko (śhro-do-vees-ko) n.
surroundings; environment;circle
śródmieście (śhrood-myesh-che)
n.city center; center of town
Śródziemne morze (śhrood-zhem-ne mo-zhe) n. Mediterranean
sea; Mediterranean
śruba(śhroo-ba) f. screw
śrubokręt (śhroo-bo-krant) m.
screwdriver; turn-screw
śrut (śhroot) m. (lead) shot
świadczenie (śhvyad-che-ne) n.
benefit; charge; testimony
świadczyć (śhvyad-chich) v.
witness;attest;bear witness
świadectwo (śhvya-dets-tvo) n.
certificate; bill of health
świadek naoczny (śhvya-dek na-och-ni) exp.: eyewitness
świadomość (śhvya-do-moshch) f.
consciousness; awareness
świadomy (śhvya-do-mi) adj.m.
conscious; aware; wilful
świat (śhvyat) m. world
światło (śhvyat-wo) n. light
światłomierz (śhvyat-wo-myezh)
m. lightmeter ; photometer
światopogląd (śhvya-to-pog-lownd)
m. ideology ;outlook on life
światowy (śhvya-to-vi) adj. m.
world; worldly;global;society-
świąteczny (śhvyown-tech-ni)
adj. m. festive;holiday(mood...)
świątynia (śhvyown-ti-na) f.
temple;place of worship
świder (śhvee-der) m. drill;
auger; bore; borer;perforator
świdrować (śhvid-ro-vach) v.
drill;bore;perforate;pierce
świeca (śhvye-tsa) f. candle
świecić (śhvye-cheech) v. light
up; shine; glitter; sparkle
świecki (śhvyets-kee) adj. m.
secular;mundane;laic;lay
świecki ksiądz (śhvyets-kee
kshownts) m. secular priest

świeczka (śhvyech-ka) f. (small)
candle
świecznik (śhvyech-neek) m.
chandelier; candlestick
świergot (śhvyer-got) m. twitter;
chirp ; warble; chirrup; tweet
świergotać (śhvyer-go-tach) v.
chirp;chirrup;warble; tweet
świerk (śhvyerk) m. fir tree
świerkowy (śhvyer-ko-vi) adj.
m. fir;spruce; of spruce
świerszcz (śhvyershch) m. cricket; grasshopper
świerzb (śhvyezhb) m. scabies
świerzbieć (śhvyezh-byech) v.
itch; be itching
świetlica(śhvyet-lee-tsa) f.
reading hall;community center
świetlik (śhvyet-leek) m. firebug ;glow worm; skylight;fire fly
świetlny(śhvyetl-ni)adj.m.
lighting (gas etc.)
świetność (śhvyet-noshch) f.
splendor; magnificence;glamor
świetny (śhvyet-ni) adj. m.
splendid ;excellent;first rate
świeżo (śhvye-zho) adv. fresh
świeży (śhvye-zhi) adj. m. fresh;
new; recent; fresh;raw;ruddy
święcenie (śhvyan-tse-ne) n. celebration; blessing ;observance
święcić (śhvyan-cheech) v. celebrate ;keep a holiday; bless
święcone (śhvyan-tso-ne) n. Easter blessed food (Polish style)
święta (śhvyan-ta) pl. holidays
święto (śhvyan-to) n. holiday
świętokradztwo (śhvyan-to-krads-tvo) n. sacrilege
świętoszek (śhvyan-to-shek) m.
bigot;sanctimonious hypocrite
świętość (śhvyan-toshch) f. sanctity; holiness; sainthood
święty (śhvyan-ti) adj. m. saint;
holy; saintly; pious;sacred
świnia (śhvee-na) f. swine;hog;pig
świnić (śhvee-neech) v. make
a mess; litter up; play dirty
świnka morska (śhveen-ka mor-ska)
f. guinea-pig ;cavy
świństwo (śhveen-stvo) n. dirty
deed ;meanness;nasty stuff;dross

świsnąć (śhvees-nównch) v.
whistle; pilfer; bolt
świst (śhveest) m. whistle
sound; bullet sound
świstak (śhvees-tak) m. marmot
świstawka (śhvees-tav-ka) f.
whistle
świstek (śhvees-tek) m. scrap
of paper; slip of paper
świt (śhveet) m. daybreak; dawn
świtać (śhvee-tach) v. dawn
(upon) ; rise (of sun or moon)
świtezianka (śhvee-te-żhán-ka)
f. water-nymph
tabaka (ta-bá-ka) f. snuff
tabakierka (ta-ba-kér-ka) f.
snuffbox
tabela (ta-bé-la) f. table;
index; list
tabletka (tab-lét-ka) f. tablet;
pill;blackboard;switchboard;slab
tablica (tab-lee-tsa) f. board;
tablica rozdzielcza (tab-lee-
tsa roz-dzhél-cha) switchboard
tabliczka mnożenia (tab-leéch-ka
mno-zhé-ña) f. multiplication
table
tabor kolejowy (tá-bor ko-le-
yó-vi) m. rolling stock (r.r.)
taboret (ta-bo-ret) m. taboret
tabu (tá-boo) n. taboo
tabun (ta-boon) m. horse herd
taca (tá-tsa) f. tray; salver
taczki (tách-kee) m. wheelbarrow
tafla (taf-la) f. plate; slab
taić (tá-eech) v. hide; conceal
tajać (ta-yach) v. thaw; melt
tajemnica (ta-yem-neé-tsa) f.
secret; mystery;secrecy
tajemniczy (ta-yem-ñee-chi) adj.
m. mysterious;inscrutable'weird
tajny (táy-ni) adj. m. secret
tak (tak) part. yes; adv. thus;
as;indecl.:like this;so
tak czy tak (tak chi tak) exp.
anyhow ; either way;in any case
taki (tá-kee) adj. m. such
taki sam (ta-kee sam) adj. m.
identical ; similar
takielunek (ta-ke-loo-nek) m.
rig; rigging; tackle

taksa (ták-sa) f. tariff; rate
taksacja (tak-sáts-ya) f. tax-
appraisal
taksowac (tak-so-vach) v. estimate; rate; appraise;value
taksówka (tak-soóv-ka) f. taxi
takt (takt) m. tact
taktowny (tak-tóv-ni) adj. m.
tactful;cosiderate
taktyczny (tak-tích-ni) adj.m.
tactical; political
taktyka (tak-ti-ka) f. tactics
także (ták-zhe) adv. also; too;
as well; likewise; alike
talent (tá-lent) m. talent
talerz (tá-lesh) m. (food)plate;
plateful; disk ;planting scalp
talerzyk (ta-le-zhik) m. small
plate ; ski-stick disk; scale
talia (tál-ya) f. waist; card
deck; tackle; middle
talk (tá-lk) m. talcum ;talc
talon (ta-lon) m. coupon
tam (tam) adv. there; yonder
tama (tá-ma) f. dam; dike
tamowac (ta-mó-vach) v. dam up;
block ; check; stem; clog
tamtejszy (tam-téy-shi) adj. m.
from there; living there
tamten (tam-ten) pron. that
tamtędy (tam-tán-di) adv. that
way; the other way
tamże (tam-zhe) adv. there in;
in the same place;ay which place
tancerka (tan-tsér-ka) f. dancer ; ballet-dancer; partner
tancerz (tán-tsesh) m. dancer
tandeta (tan-dé-ta) f. trashy
products; shoddy goods
taneczny (ta-néch-ni) adj. m.
dancing ;dance-(step;music etc.)
tangens (tán-gens) m. tangent
tani (tá-ñee) adj. m. cheap
taniec (tá-ñets) m. dance
taniec (tá-ñech) v. get cheaper; cheapen grow cheaper
taniość (tá-ñoshch) f. cheap-
ness; low prices
tańczyc (tań-chich) v. dance
tankowiec (tan-ko-vyets) m.
tanker
tapczan (táp-chan) m. couch;
convertible bed

tapeta (ta-pe-ta) f. wallpaper
tapicer (ta-pee-tser) m. upholsterer ;upholsterer's shop
taran (ta-ran) m. battering ram
tarapaty (ta-ra-pa-ti) pl.
trouble; predicament;sad fix
taras (ta-ras) m. terrace
tarasować (ta-ra-so-vach) v.
block;stand in the way plank
tarcica (tar-chee-tsa) f. deal;
tarcie (tar-che) n. friction;
frictional resistance
tarcza (tar-cha) f. shield;disk
tarczowa piła (tar-cho-va pee-
wa) circular saw
tarczyca (tar-chi-tsa) f. thy-
roid gland
targ (targ) m. country market
targać (tar-gach) v. tear;jerk
targować (tar-go-vach) v. sell;
bargain; trade; haggle ;deal
tarka (tar-ka) f. rasp; grater
tartak (tar-tak) m. sawmill
taryfa (ta-ri-fa) f. tariff
tarzać się (ta-zhach shan) v.
wallow; welter; roll(in mud)
tasak (ta-sak) m. chopper;
cleaver
tasiemiec (ta-she-myets) m.
tapeworm; cestoid; taenia
tasiemka (ta-shem-ka) f. ribbon;
tape
tasować (ta-so-vach) v. shuffle
taśma (tash-ma) f. band; tape
taśma ruchoma (tash-ma roo-kho-
ma) f. belt conveyor
tatarka (ta-tar-ka) f. buckwheat
taternik (ta-ter-neek) m. mountain climber ;alpinist
tatuować (ta-too-o-vach) v. tattoo; make a tattoo mark
tatuś (ta-toosh) m. daddy;dad
tchawica (tkha-vee-tsa) f. tra-
chea ; windpipe
tchnąć (tkhnownch) v. inspire
tchnienie (tkhne-ne) n. breath
tchórz (tkhoosh) m. skunk; coward;craven;poltroon; funk
tchórzliwy (tkhoo-zhlee-vi)
adj. m. cowardly;chicken-hearted
tchórzostwo (tkhoo-zhoost-vo)
n. cowardice

teatr (te-atr) m. theatre;the stage
teatralny (te-a-tral-ni) adj.
m. theatrical; scenic; stage-
techniczny (tekh-neech-ni) adj.
m. technical(terms,school,staff...)
technik (tekh-neek) m. technician; engineer; mechanic
technika (tekh-nee-ka) f. technique; engineering;technology
technologia (tekh-no-log-ya) f.
technology;production engineering
teczka (tech-ka) f. briefcase;
folder;portfolio;jacket;binder
tegoroczny (te-go-roch-ni)adj.m.
this year's
teka (te-ka) f. (large) briefcase; portfolio;file;folder
tekst (te-kst) m. text;wording
tekstylny (teks-til-ni) adj.m.
textile;textile-;draper-;clothier-
tektura (tek-too-ra) f. cardboard; pasteboard(corrugated)
telefon (te-le-fon) m. telephone;phone;phone receiver
telefonistka (te-le-fo-neest-
ka) f. telephone operator
telefonować (te-le-fo-no-vach)
v. ring up; telephone;call up
telegraf (te-le-graph) m. telegraph;telegraph office
telegraficzny (te-le-gra-feech-
ni) adj. m. telegraphic
telegrafować (te-le-gra-fo-
vach) v. cable; wire; telegraph
telegram (te-le-gram) m. telegram; cable; wire;cablegram
telepatia (te-le-pat-ya) f. te-
lepathy;thought transference
teleskop (te-les-kop)m. telescope; telescopic spring
teleskopowy (te-les-ko-po-vi)
adj. m. telescopic
telewizja (te-le-veez-ya) f.
television; TV
telewizor (te-le-vee-zor) m.
television set;TV set
temat (te-mat) m. subject
temblak (tem-blak) m. sling
temperament (tem-pe-ra-ment)
m. temper;nature;mettle
temperatura (tem-pe-ra-too-ra)
f. temperature; fever

temperować (tem-pe-ro-vach) v.
 temper; sharpen; mitigate
temperówka (tem-pe-roov-ka) f.
 pencil sharpener
tempo (tém-po) n. rate; tempo
temu (té-mu) adv. ago
ten; ta, to (ten, ta, to) m.f.n.
 pron. this
ten sam (ten sam) pron. the
 same (man, pencil, etc.)
tendencja (ten-den-tsya) f. tendency; inclination; proclivity
tendencyjny (ten-den-tsiy-ni)
 adj. m. biased; tedentious
tenis (té-nees) m. tennis
tenor (té-nor) m. tenor(voice)
tenuta (te-noo-ta) f. land holding; rent; tenure; lease
tenże (tén-zhe) m. pron. the
 same (individual etc.)
teolog (te-o-lok) m. theologian
teologia (the-o-lóg-ya) f. theology; Faculty of Theology
teoretyczny (te-o-re-tich-ni)
 adj. m. theoretical; speculative
teoretyk (te-o-ré-tik) m. theo-
 retician; theorist
teoria (te-ór-ya) f. theory
terapia (te-ráp-ya) f. therapeut-
 ics; therapy
teraz (té-ras) adv. now; nowadays
teraźniejszość (te-rażh-ney-
 shoshch) f. present (time)
teraźniejszy kurs (te-rażh-ney-
 shi koors) m. present rate
teren (té-ren) m. terrain
terenowy samochód (te-re-no-vi
 sa-mo-khood) m. cross-country
 car (four wheel drive)
terkotać (ter-ko-tach) v. rattle; clatter; chatter(away)
termin (tér-meen) m. term; apprenticeship; time limit(fixed)
termin ostateczny (tér-meen os-
 ta-tech-ni) m. deadline
terminator (ter-mee-ná-tor) m.
 apprentice; terminator
terminarz (ter-mee-nash) m. appointment calendar; agenda
terminologia (ter-mee-no-log-
 ya) f. terminology; nomenclature
terminowo (ter-mee-nó-vo) adv.
 on time; in due time; punctually

termit (tér-meet) m. termite
termometr (ter-mo-metr) m.
 thermometer
termos (tér-mos) m. thermos-
 bottle; vacuum bottle(flask)
terpentyna (ter-penti-na) f.
 turpentine(oil)
terror (tér-ror) m. terror
terroryzować (ter-ro-ri-zo-
 vach) v. terrorize; bully
terytorialny (te-ri-tor-yal-
 ni) adj. m. territorial
terytorium (te-ri-tor-yoom) n.
 territory
testament (tes-ta-ment) m.
 testament; (last) will
teściowa (tesh-chó-va) f.
 mother-in-law
teść (téshch) m. father-in-law
teza (té-za) f. thesis; argument
też (tesh) adv. also; too; likewise
tęchnąć (tánkh-nownch) v. get
 musty; grow mouldy; reduce swelling
tęcza (tán-cha) f. rainbow
tęczówka (tán-choov-ka) f. iris
tędy (tán-di) adv. this way
tęgi (tán-gee) adj. m. stout;
 strong; solid; fat; big; portly
tego (tán-go) adv. stoutly; ably;
 amply; mightly; powerfully
tepak (tán-pak) m. dullard
tepić (tán-peech) v. dull;
 blunt; destroy; combat; exterminate; oppose; persecute
tepota (tan-pó-ta) f. dullness;
 stupidity; obtuseness; stolidity
tępy (tán-pi) adj. m. dull;
 point less; slow-witted
tesknić (tánsk-neech) v. long
 (for); yearn; be nostalgic
tesknota (tánsk-no-ta) f. longing; hankering; nostalgia
teskny (tánsk-ni) adj. m. melancholy; wietful; longing; yearning
tetent (tán-tent) m. hoof beat
tetnica (tán-tnee-tsa) f. artery
tetnic (tánt-neech) v. pulsate
tetno (tant-no) n. pulse; vibrations
tężec (tán-zhets) m. tetanus
tężec (tán-zhech) v. stiffen;
 solidify; set; clot; curdle; coagulate;
 grow stronger; acquire vigor

tężyzna (tan-zhiz-na) f. vigor
tkacki (tkáts-kee) adj. m. textile; weaver's;of textiles
tkactwo (tkáts-tvo) n. weaving
tkacz (tkách) m. weaver (man)
tkać (tkách) v. weave; poke
tkanina (tka-ñee-na) f. fabric
tkanka (tkan-ka) f. tissue
tkliwość (tklee-voshch) f. tenderness;love;affection
tkliwy (tklee-vi) adj. m. tender;loving;affectionate;sensitive
tknąć (tknownch) v. touch;size
tkwić (tkveech) v. stick;stay
tleć (tlech) v. smoulder
tlen (tlen) m. oxygen
tlenek (tle-nek) m. oxide
tlić się (tleech shañ) v.
smoulder; glow; burn lightly
tło (two) n. background
tłocznia (twóch-ña) f. press
tłoczyć (two-chich) v. press;
crowd; print; stamp; crush
tłok (twók) m. piston; crowd
tłuc (twoóts) v. pound; hammer;
batter; smash; shatter
tłuczek (twoo-chek) m. pestle
tłuczeń (twoo-cheñ) m. macadam;
broken stone; road gravel
tłum (twoóm) m. crowd;mob;host
tłumacz (twoo-mach)m. interpreter ; translator
tłumaczenie (twoo-ma-che-ñe) n.
translation;explanation;excuse
tłumaczyć (twoo-ma-chich) v.
translate; interpret;justify
tłumić (twoo-meech) v. muffle;
put down; dampen;suppress;stifle
tłumik (twoo-meek) m. muffler
tłumny (twoom-ni) adj. m. crowded ; numerous ;populous
tłumok (twoo-mok) m. bundle
tłusty (twoos-ti) adj. m. obese;
fat(meat,pig etc.);podgy; oily
tłuszcz (twooshch) m. fat ;
grease
tłuszcza (twoosh-cha) f. mob
tłuścić (twoosh-cheech) v.
grease; smear with grease
to (to) pron. it; this; that;so
toaleta (to-a-le-ta) f. toilet
toaletowe przybory (to-a-le-tó-
ve pzhi-bo-ri) pl. toilet-
articles; cosmetics

toast (to-ast) m. toast
tobół (to-boow) m. pack; bundle
toczony (to-cho-ni) adj. m.
turned; shaped;rounded
toczyć (to-chich) v. roll; machine; wage (war);wheel;carry on
toga (to-ga) f. gown;Roman toga
tok (tok) m. course; progress
tokarka (to-kár-ka) f. lathe
tokarnia (to-kár-ña) f. lathe
tokarz (to-kash) m. machinist;
turner; lathe operator
tokować (to-ko-vach) v. toot
tolerancja (to-le-ran-tsya) f.
tolerance;broad-mindedness
tolerować (to-le-ro-vach) v.
tolerate;suffer;stand for
tom (tom) m. volume
ton (ton) m. sound; tone;note
tona (to-na) f. ton(metric etc.)
tonacja (to-nats-ya) f. pitch ;
key ; mode; tone
tonaż (to-nash) m. tonnage
tonąć (to-nownch) v. drown
toń (toń) f. deep (water);
flood;deep sea;depth of water
topaz (to-pas) m. topaz
topić (to-peech) v. drown;thaw;
melt down; smelt (metals);sink
topiel (to-pyel) f. abyss;gulf
topliwy (top-lee-vi) adj. m.
meltable;fusible;liquescent
topnieć (top-ñech) v. melt
topografia (to-po-gráf-ya) f.
topography;lay of the land
topola (to-po-la) f. poplar
toporek (to-pó-rek) m. hatchet
topór (to-poor) m. (big) hatchet; axe; battle axe
tor (tor) m. track;lane;path
tor kolejowy (tor ko-le-yó-vi)
m. rail-track;railroad track
torba (tor-ba) f. bag; bagful
torcik (tor-cheek) m. small
layer cake
torebka (to-reb-ka) f. (hand)
bag; purse; small bag(or pouch)
torf (torf) m. peat
torfowisko (tor-fo-vees-ko) n.
peat bog; turbary
torować (to-ro-vach) v. clear;
pave; clear a path;show the way
torpeda (tor-pe-da) f. torpedo;motor driven rail car

torpedować (tor-pe-do-vach) v.
torpedo; scuttle;obstruct
torpedowiec (tor-pe-do-vyets)
m. torpedo boat
tors (tors) m. torso
tort (tort) m. tort (multi-lay-
er) fancy cake
tortura (tor-too-ra) f. torture
torturować (tor-too-ro-vach) v.
torture;torment;put to torture
totalny (to-tal-ni) adj. m. totalitarian; total;entire
towar (to-var) m. merchandise
towarowy dom (to-va-ro-vi dom)
m. department store
towarzystki (to-va-zhis-kee)
adj- m. sociable; social
towarzystwo (to-va-zhist-vo) n.
company;society;companionship
towarzysz (to-va-zhish) m. companion;pal;associate;camerade
towarzyszka (to-va-zhish-ka) f.
companion (female);associate
towarzyszyć (to-va-zhi-shich) v.
accompany;escort;keep company
tożsamość (tozh-sa-moshch) f.
identity; sameness
tracić (tra-cheech) v. lose;
waste;shed(leaves); execute
tradycja (tra-dits-ya) f. tradition;handing down customs etc.
tradycyjny (tra-di-tsiy-ni) adj.
m. traditional
traf (traf) m. happenstance;
chance,luck; coincidence
trafem (tra-fem) adv. by chance
trafiac (traf-yach) v. hit
(target);guess right; home
trafnosc (traf-noshch) f. accuracy; rightness; soundness
trafny (traf-ni) adj. m. exact;
correct; right; fit; apt
tragarz (tra-gash) m. porter
tragedia (tra-ged-ya) f. trag-
edy:very sad or tragic event
tragiczny (tra-geech-ni) adj. m.
tragic; disastrous;very sad
tragikomedia (tra-gee-ko-med-
ya) f. tragicomedy
trajkotać (tray-ko-tach) v.
chatter; jabber;rattle;gabble
trak (trak) m. square saw;frame
saw

trakcja (trak-tsya) f. traction
trakt (trakt) m. highway; course
traktat (trak-tat) m. treaty
traktor (trak-tor) m. tractor
traktować (trak-to-vach) v.deal;
treat; negotiate ; discuss
trampolina (tram-po-lee-na) f.
spring board; diving board
tramwaj (tram-vay) m. tramway
tramwajarz (tram-va-yash) m.
tramway worker
tran (tran) m. (cod or whale)
oil; cod liver oil
trans (trans) m. trance ;ectasy
transakcja (trans-akts-ya) f.
transaction; deal
transatlantycki (trans-at-lan-
tits-kee) adj. m. transatlantic
transformator (trans-for-ma-tor)
m. transformer;converter
transfuzja (trans-fooz-ya) f.
transfusion(of blood etc.)
transmisja (trans-mees-ya) f.
transmission; broadcast
transmitować (trans-mee-to-vach)
v. transmit; broadcast
transparent (trans-pa-rent) m.
(marching) slogans; banner
transport (trans-port) m. transport; haulage; consignment
tranzyt (tran-zit) m. transit
tranzytowy (tran-zi-to-vi) adj.
m. transit-;through(traffic etc.)
trapez (tra-pes) m. trapeze
trapic (tra-peech) v. molest;
pester; worry; annoy; bother
trasa (tra-sa) f. route;(bus)line
trasa podróży (tra-sa pod-roo-
zhi) f. itinerary
tratować (tra-to-vach) v. trample; tred down
tratwa (trat-va) f. raft;float
trawa (tra-va) f. grass
trawić (tra-veech) v. digest
trawienie (tra-vye-ne) n. digestion;consumption
trawnik (trav-neek) m. lawn
trąba (trown-ba) f. trumpet;
trunk (elephant); tornado;
twister;horn;whirlwind; ninny
trąba wodna (trown-ba vod-na) f.
waterspout; wind spout

trąbić (trown-beech) v. bugle; toot;hoot; roar; proclaim

trąbka (trownb-ka) f. horn;bugle

trącać (trown-tsach) v. jostle; elbow; tip; knock; nudge;strike

trącić (trown-cheech) v. jostle; smell;be fusty;be out of date

trąd (trownd) m. leprosy

trel (trel) m. trill

trelować (tre-lo-vach) v. trill

trema (tre-ma) f. stage fright

trener (tre-ner) m. coach;trainer

trening (tre-neeng) m. training

trenować (tre-no-vach) v. train; coach; practise(shooting)

trepanacja (tre-pa-nats-ya) f. trepanation

trepki (trep-kee) pl. sandals

tresować (tre-so-vach) v. train; tame; drill; break in(horses)

tresura (tre-soo-ra) f. taming; training(of animals)

tresciwy (tresh-chee-vi) adj.m. concise ; substantial;meaty;pithy

tresc (treshch) f. content;jist; substance; essence;pith;marrow

trębacz (tran-bach) m. trumpeter

trędowaty (tran-do-va-ti) adj.m. leprous ; leper

triumfować (tree-oom-fo-vach) v. triumph;achieve triumphs;prevail

troche (tro-khan) adv. a little bit; a few ;some;awhile;a spell

trociny (tro-chee-ni) pl. saw- dust; scraps (of writings etc.)

trofea (tro-fe-a) pl. trophies

trojaki (tro-ya-kee) adj. m. threefold; triple;treble;triplex

troje (tro-ye) num. three

troki (tro-kee) pl. straps

trolejbus (tro-ley-boos) m. trolleybus

tron (tron) m. throne;the throne

trop (trop) m. track; trace

tropic (tro-peech) v. track

tropikalny (tro-pee-kal-ni) adj. m. tropical;of the tropics

troska (tros-ka) f. care; anx- iety; worry; concern;solicitude

troskac sie (tros-kach shan) v. care and worry about;be cocerned

troskliwosc (tros-klee-voshch) f. thoughtfulness; care; heed

troskliwy (tros-klee-vi) adj.m. careful; attentive;thoughtful

troszczyc sie (trosh-chich shan) v. care; be anxious about ; take care;look after

trotuar (tro-too-ar) m. side- walk; pavement(for pedestrians)

trojbarwny (trooy-barv-ni) adj. m. tricolor ;three-colored

trojca (trooy-tsa) f. trinity

trojka (trooy-ka) f. three

trojkąt (trooy-kownt) m. triangle; set square

trojnasob (trooy-na-soob) three times as much

trojnik (trooy-neek) m. three- way (pipe) connection;"T"(-tee) joint; "Y" joint; wye ; tee

truchtem (trookh-tem) adv. by jogging ; by trot;at a trot

trucizna (troo-cheez-na) f. poison; venom

truc (trooch) v. poison; bother (slang); molest; worry

trud (troot) m. pains; toil

trudnic sie (trood-neech shan) v. occupy oneself;be engaged

trudno (trood-no) adv.with difficulty; too bad;hard

trudnosc (trood-noshch) f. difficulty; hardshiphandicap

trudny (trood-ni) adj. m. difficult;hard;tough;laborious

trudzic (troo-dzheech)v. trou- ble; disturb; cause trouble

trujący (troo-yown-tsi) adj. m. poisonous; toxic; poison-

trumna (troom-na) f. coffin

trunek (troo-nek) m. drink

trup (troop) m. corpse;cadaver

trupiarnia (troop-yar-na) f. mortuary; morgue

truskawka (troos-kav-ka) f. strawberry

truten (troo-ten) m. drone

trwać (trvach) v. last; per- sist; stay; remain;linger on

trwaly (trva-wi) adj. m. durable

trwanie (trva-ne) n. duration

trwoga (trvo-ga) f. awe; fright

trwonic (trvo-neech) v. waste; squander; trifle away; fritter away (money,time, energy etc.)

trwoźliwy (trvozh-leé-vi) adj.
m. timid; fearful; shy
trwożny (trvozh-ni) adj. m.
anxious; fearful; timid ;shy
trwożyć (trvo-zhích) v. startle;
frighten; scare ;be frightening
tryb (trib) m. manner; mode;
mood; gear; procedure ;course
trybuna (tri-boo-na) f. tribune;
stand; speaker's platform
trybunał(tri-boo-naw) m.tribunal
trychina (tri-khee-na) f. trichina; trichinosis
trygonometria (tri-go-no-metr-ya)
f. trigonometry(spherical etc.)
tryk (trik) m. 1.ram(ing);2.trik
trykot (tri-kot) m. tricot
trykotowy (tri-ko-tó-vi) adj.m.
tricot; made of tricot
trykotaże (tri-ko-tá-zhe) pl.
hosiery; knittings
trykotowy (tri-ko-tó-vi) adj.m.
knitted(goods,fabric,wear etc.)
trylion (tril-yon) num. trillion
tryskać (tris-kach) v. spurt;
spout; gush ;jet;squirt ;flow
trywialny (tri-vyal-ni) adj.m.
trivial; vulgar; coarse; trite
trzask (tzhask) m. crack ; bang
trzaska (tzhás-ka) f. chip(wood)
trzaskać (tzhás-kach) v. crack;
bang ; smash; shatter ;knock;hit
trząść (tzhównshch) v. shake
trzcina (tzhchee-na) f. cane;
reed(of bamboo etc.)
trzcina cukrowa (tzhchee-na
coo-kró-va) f. sugar cane
trzcinowy (tzhchee-nó-vi) adj.
m. cane(chair);made out of cane
trzeba (tzhe-ba) v. imp. ought
to;one should ⌐gut;geld
trzebić (tzhe-beech) v. clear;
trzeci (tzhe-chee) num. third
trzeć (tzhech) v. rub; grate
trzepaczka (tzhe-pach-ka) f.
whisk; beater;carpet beater
trzepać (tzhe-pach) v. hit
dust out ; beat(carpet); slap
trzepnąć (tzhep-nównch) v. hit;
crump; strike;spank;slap;wag
trzepotać (tzhe-pó-tach) v.
flap; flutter;flicker; toss

trzeszczeć (tzhesh-chech) v.crack;
crackle;creak;crunch;rustle
trzewia (tzhev-ya) pl. bowels;guts
trzewik (tzhe-veek) m. shoe;slipper
trzeźwić (tzhézh-veech) v. sober up;bring back to consciousness
trzeźwość (tzhézh-voshch) f.
sobriety;level-headedness
trzeźwy (tzhézh-vi) adj. m.
sober;clear headed;wide awake
trzęsawisko (tzhán-sa-vees-ko)
n. bog;swamp;quagmire;slough
trzęsienie ziemi (tzhán-she-ne
zhe-mee) n. earthquake
trzmiel (tzhmyel) m. bumblebee
trznadel (tzhna-del) m. yellow
bunting;yellow hammer;bunting
trzoda (tzho-da) f. herd;
flock; heard(of swine,pigs etc.)
trzon (tzhon) m. handle; hilt;core
trzonek (tzho-nek) m. shaft;shank;
handle(of a hammer, axe etc.)
trzonowy ząb (tzho-no-vi zównb)
m. molar; grinder
trzpień (tzhpyeń) m. pin
trzpiot (tzhpyot) m. giddy; gay
trzustka (tzhoost-ka) f. pan-
creas; sweetbread
trzy (tzhi) num. three
trzydziestokrotny (tzhi-dzhes-
to-krót-ni) adj. m. thirtyfold
trzydziestoletni (tzhi-dzhes-to-
lét-nee) adj. m. thirty year
old(man,oak,house,horse etc.)
trzydziesty (tzhi-dzhes-ti) num.
thirtieth
trzydzieści (tzhi-dzhesh-chee)
num. thirty
trzykrotny (tzhi-krót-ni) adj.
m. threefold
trzylampowy (tzhi-lam-pó-vi)
adj. m. three-lamp
trzyletni (tzhi-lét-nee) adj.
m. three year old(boy,car etc.)
trzymać (tzhi-mach) v. hold;
keep;cling;clutch;hold on to
trzynasty (tzhi-nás-ti) num.
thirteenth
trzynaście (tzhi-nash-che) num.
thirteen
trzypiętrowy (tzhi-pyán-tro-vi)
adj. m. three-story high(house)

trzysta (tzhís-ta) num.
three hundred
tu (too) adv. here;in here
tuba (too-ba) f. tube;horn
tubka (toob-ka) f. small tube
tuberkuliczny (too-ber-koo-leech-ni) adj. m. tuberculous
tubylczy (too-bil-chi) adj. m.
native;indigenous; local
tubylec (too-bi-lets) m. native;
aboriginal; local inhabitant
tucznik (tooch-ñeek) m. porker
tuczyc (too-chich) v. fatten
tulejka (too-ley-ka) f. socket
tulic (too-leech) v. hug; fondle
tulipan (too-lee-pan) m. tulip
tułacz (too-wach) m. wanderer;
vagrant ;exile ;homeless wander-er
tułaczka (too-wach-ka) f. home-less wandering;wandering life
tułac się (too-wach shañ) v.
wander;be homeless;be in exile
tułów (too-woov) m. torso
tum (toom) m. cathedral;minster
tuman (too-man) m. 1. dust-cloud;
2. dummie;nitwit;duffer
tunel (too-nel) m. tunnel
tupac (too-pach) v. stamp;tramp
tupet (too-pet) m. nerve;chutz-pah; self-assurance;impudence
tur (toor) m. bison; aurochs
turbina (toor-bee-na) f. turbine
turecki (too-réts-kee) adj. m.
Turkish(saddle,fashion etc.)
turkawka (toor-kav-ka) f. tur-tledove;wild dove
turkot (toor-kot) m. rumble;rattle
turkotac (toor-ko-tach) v.
rumble ;bump along; rattle
turkus (toor-koos) m. turquoise
turniej (toor-ñey) m. tournament
turysta (too-ris-ta) m. tourist
turystyczny (too-ris-tich-ni)
adj. m. tourist; touring-
tusz (toosh) m. 1. shower; hit;
2. India ink;mascara
tusza (too-sha) f. corpulence
tuszowac (too-sho-vach) v.
1. draw with ink; 2. cover up;
hush up; stifle (a scandal etc.)
tutaj (too-tay) adv. here
tutejszy (too-téy-shi) adj. m.
local;of this place;of our place

tuzin (too-zheen) m. dozen
tuż (toosh) adv. near by;
close by; just before;just after
tuż obok (toosh o-bok) adv.
next too; near by: close by
twardniec (tvárd-ñech) v. hard-en; stiffen; fix; bind
twardosc (tvar-doshch) f. hard-ness ; stiffness; severity
twardy (tvar-di) adj. m. hard
twarozek (tva-ró-zhek) m. cot-tage cheese;small cottage cheese
twarog (tva-roog) m. cottage
cheese curds; cottage cheese
twarz (tvash) f. face;physionomy
twarzowy (tva-zhó-vi) adj. m.
becoming; facial(bone etc.)
twierdza (tvyér-dza) f. for-tress ; stronghold;citadel
twierdzący (tvyer-dzown-tsi)
adj. m. affirmative(answer etc.)
twierdzenie (tvyer-dze-ñe) n.
affirmation; theorem;assertion
twierdzic (tvyér-dzheech) v.
assert; maintain;affirm; say
twornik (tvór-ñeek) m. armature
tworzyc (tvo-zhich) v. create;
form; compose; produce; make
tworzywo sztuczne (tvo-zhi-vo
shtooch-ne) n. plastic
twoj (tvooy) pron. yours; your
twor (tvoor) m. creation; piece
of work; origination;outgrowth
tworca (tvoor-tsa) m. creator;
author; maker;originator
tworczosc (tvoor-choshch) f.
creation;output ;production
tworczy (tvoor-chi) adj. m.
creative; originative:formative
ty (ti) pron. you(familiar form)
tyczka (tich-ka) f. pole; perch
tyczyc się (ti-chich shañ) v.
concern; regard;refer to
tyc (tich) v. grow fat
tydzień (ti-dzheñ) m. week
tyfus (ti-foos) typhus
tygiel (ti-gel) m. crucible
tygodnik (ti-god-ñeek) m.
weekly (magazine etc.)
tygodniowy (ti-god-ño-vi) adj.
m. weekly (pay etc.)
tygrys (tig-ris) m. tiger ;type
of German tank in World War II

tygrysica (tig-ri-shee-tsa) f.
tigeress

tyka (ti-ka) f. perch; pole

tyka miernicza (ti-ka myer-nee-cha) f. surveyor's rod; affect;

tykać (ti-kach) v. touch; tick; strike

tykwa (tik-va) f. pumpkin

tyle (ti-le) adv. so much; as many; as much; so many; that much

tylekroc (ti-le-kroch) adv. so many times; that many times

tylko (til-ko) adv. only; but; just

tylko co (til-ko tso) adv. just now; a moment ago; this instant

tylna straż (til-na strash) f. rear guard

tylny (til-ni) adj. m. back; hind(leg etc.); rear (light etc.)

tył (tiw) m. back; rear; stern

tym lepiej (tim le-pyey) adv. so much better

tymczasem (tim-cha-sem) adv. meantime; during; at the time

tymczasowo (tim-cha-so-vo) adv. provisionally; temporarily

tymczasowy (tim-cha-so-vi) adj. m. temporary; provisional

tynk (tink) m. plaster(work)

tynkować (tin-ko-vach) v. plaster; rough cast (a wall)

tynktura (tink-too-ra) f. tincture; tinge; light color

typ (tip) m. type; model; guy

typowy (ti-po-vi) adj. m. typical; standard(article etc.)

tyrada (ti-ra-da) f. tirade

tyran (ti-ran) m. tyrant; bully

tyrania (ti-ran-ya) f. tyranny

tyranski (ti-ran-skee) adj.m. tyrannical; tyrannous; bullying

tysiąc (ti-shownts) num. thousand

tysiąclecie (ti-shownts-le-che) n. millennium

tysiącletni (ti-shownts-let-ni) adj. m. millenary

tysięczny (ti-shanch-ni) num. thousandth

tytan (ti-tan) m. titan; titanium; demon(of work etc.)

tytaniczny (ti-ta-neech-ni) adj. m. titanic; huge

tytoniowy (ti-to-no-vi) adj.m. tobacco; of tobacco leaves

tyton (ti-ton) m. tobacco

tytularny (ti-too-lar-ni) adj. m. titular; nominal

tytuł (ti-toow) m. title

tytułowa strona (ti-too-wo-va stro-na) f. title page

tytułować (ti-too-wo-vach) v. entitle; address; style as a...

u (oo) prep. beside; at; with; by; on; from; in; (idiomatic)

u boku (oo bo-koo) exp.; at one's side (to have a helper, a sabre...)

ubarwić (oo-bar-veech) v. color

ubawić się (oo-ba-veech shan) v. have fun; have a good laugh

ubezpieczac (oo-bez-pye-chach) v. insure; secure; protect

ubezpieczalnia (oo-bez-pye-chal-na) f. health insurance center; insurence company

ubezpieczenie (oo-bez-pye-che-ne) n. insurance; protection

ubezpieczenie życia (oo-bez-pye-che-ne zhi-cha) n. life insurance; life assurance

ubezpieczenie społeczne (oo-bez-pye-che-ne spo-wech-ne) n. social security insurance

ubiec (oo-byets) v. run; pass

ubiegać się (oo-bye-gach shan) v. solicit; compete for

ubiegły (oo-byeg-wi) adj. m. past; last (year, week etc.)

ubierać (oo-bye-rach) v. dress

ubijaczka (oo-bee-yach-ka) f. stamper; compactor; kitchen whisk

ubijac (oo-bee-yach) v. stamp; churn; chip; kill; pack; ram

ubijac interes (oo-bee-yach een-te-res) v. strike a bargain; strike a deal

ubikacja (oo-bee-kats-ya) f. toilet; rest room; powder room; W.C.

ubiór (oob-yoor) m. attire; grab

ubliżać (oo-blee-zhach) v. insult; offend; affront

ubliżający (oo-blee-zha-yown-tsi) adj. m. offensive; insulting; disparaging

uboczny produkt (oo-boch-ni pro-dookt) m. byproduct

ubogi (oo-bo-gee) adj. m. poor
ubolewać (oo-bo-lé-vach) v,
deplore; feel sympathy for...
ubolewanie (oo-bo-le-va-ñe) n,
regret; lamentation;sympathy
ubożeć (oo-bó-zhech) v. become
poor; become impoverished
ubój (oo-booy) m. slaughter
ubóstwiać (oo-boóst-vyach) v.
idolize; love;be crazy about
ubóstwo (oo-boóst-vo) n. poverty;destitution;meagerness
ubosc (oó-boóshch) v. gore
ubrać (oób-rach) v. dress
ubranie (oob-rá-ñe) n. clothes;
decoration:putting in a fix
ubytek (oo-bi-tek) m. decrease
ubytek krwi (oo-bí-tek krvee)
blood loss
ubywać (oo-bi-vach) v. retire;
go; lessen; reduce; decrease
ucałować (oo-tsa-wó-vach) v.
kiss (good night,good bye etc.)
ucho (oo-kho) n. ear; handle;
(needle) eye;ring(of anchors)
uchodzić (oo-khó-dzheech)v. go
away; flee; pass (for)
uchodźca (oo-khódzh-tsa) m.
refugee;displaced person
uchować (oo-khó-vach) v. save;
preserve;save;retain;keep;rear
uchronić (oo-khro-ñeech) v.
guard; preserve;protect;keep
uchwalać (oo-khva-lach) v.
pass a law ; resolve; decide
uchwała (oo-khvá-wa) f. resolution; vote; law
uchwycić (oo-khvi-chich) v.
grasp; catch; seize; see ;get
uchwyt (oókh-vit) m. handle
uchwytny (oo-khvit-ni) adj.m.
graspable; palpable;audible
uchybiać (oo-khib-yach) v.
fail; offend ; transgress
uchybienie (oo-khi-byé-ñe) n.
offense ; transgression;insult
uchylać (oo-khi-lach) v. put
aside ; half-open; set ajar
uciążliwy (oo-chown-zhlee-vi)
adj. m. burdensome ; heavy
ucichać (oo-chee-khach) v.
calm down ; be hushed;abate
uciecha (oo-che-kha) f. joy

ucieczka (oo-chech-ka) f. escape ; flight; desertion;recourse
ucieleśnić (oo-che-lésh-ñeech)
v. embody ; personify
uciekać (oo-che-kach) v. flee
uciemiężać (oo-che-myañ-zhach)
v. oppress ; burden;tread down
ucierać (oo-che-rach) v. wipe
off; grind ; grate; level;pound
ucierpieć (oo-cher-pyech) v.
suffer ; be hard hit;sustain a loss
ucieszny (oo-chesh-ni) adj. m.
funny ; comical; droll;amusing
ucieszyć (oo-che-shich) v. gladden ; please; gratify ; delight
ucinać (oo-chee-nach) v. cut off
ucisk (oó-cheesk) m. oppression
uciskać (oo-cheés-kach) v. press;
pinch; opress ; hurt ;compress
uciszyć (oo-chee-shich) v. silence ; quiet; still; soothe;lull
uciułać (oo-choo-wach) v. scrape
together ; save ;put aside
uczcić (oóch-cheech) v. honor;
dignify ; celebrate ;commemorate
uczciwy (ooch-chee-vi) adj. m.
honest ; upright; straight
uczelnia (oo-chel-ña) f. school;
college ; academy ;university
uczenie (oo-che-ñe) adv. learned-
ly ; n. learning ; teaching
uczennica (oo-chen-ñee-tsa) f.
schoolgirl;(girl) pupil
uczeń (oó-cheñ) m. schoolboy
uczepić (oo-che-peech) v. hang
on ; hitch; hook; attach;fasten
uczesać (oo-che-sach) v. comb
(hair);brush hair;dress hair
uczesanie (oo-che-sa-ñe) n.
hairdo ; hairstyle; coiffure
uczestniczyć (oo-chest-ñee-chich)
v. take part ; share in;participate
uczestnik (oo-chest-ñeek) m.
participant ;(sport)competitor
uczęszczać (oo-chañsh-chach) v.
frequent; attend(concerts,school...)
uczony (oo-cho-ni) m. scientist;
learned; erudite; scholarly man
uczta (ooch-ta) f. feast;banquet
uczucie (oo-choo-che) n. feeling
uczuciowy (oo-choo-cho-vi)adj.
m. sensitive ; emotional;sentimental
uczuć (oó-chooch) v. feel ;realize

uczyć (oo-chich) v. teach; train
uczyć się (oo-chich shan) v.
learn; study; take lessons
uczynek (oo-chi-nek) m. deed
uczynić (oo-chi-neech) v. make
uczynność (oo-chin-noshch) f.
kindness ; helpfulness
uczynny (oo-chin-ni) adj. m.
obliging ; helpful ;cooperative
udany (oo-da-ni) adj. m. successful; put on; sham
udar słoneczny (oo-dar swo-
nech-ni) m. sunstroke
udaremnić (oo-da-rem-neech) v.
frustrate; foil; upset; defeat
udawać (oo-da-vach) v. pretend
udawać się(oo-da-vach shan)v.go;
succeed;manage;pan out;make for
udeptać (oo-dep-tach) v. tread
down; beat a path ;tread on
uderzać (oo-de-zhach) v. hit
uderzenie (oo-de-zhe-ne) n.
blow; stroke; hit; bump ;impact
udo (oo-do) n. thigh
udobruchać (oo-do-broo-khach)
v. appease; win over; coax
udogodnić (oo-do-god-neech) v.
facilitate; improve
udoskonalenie (oo-dos-ko-na-le-
ne) n. perfection;improvement
udoskonalić (oo-dos-ko-na-leech)
v. perfect; improve
udostępnić (oo-dos-tanp-neech)
v. give access;put within reach
udowodnić (oo-do-vod-neech) v.
prove; demonstrate;substantiate
udowodnienie (oo-do-vod-ne-ne)
n. evidence; proof;demonstration
udręka (ood-ran-ka) f. anguish;
torment; distress; worry
udusić (oo-doo-sheech) v. strangle; smother; stifle; throttle
udział (oo-dzhaw) m. share;
part; quota;participation
udziałowiec (oo-dzha-wo-vyets)
m. shareholder; partner
udzielać (oo-dzhe-lach) v.
give; grant; furnish; apply
udzielenie (oo-dzhe-le-ne) n.
giving; granting;dispensing
ufać (oo-fach) v. trust;confide
ufność (oof-noshch) f. confidence; trust; reliance

ufny (oof-ni) adj. confident;
trustful;hopeful;reliant;sanguine
ufundować (oo-foon-do-vach) v.
found; set up ;endow;establish
uganiać się (oo-ga-nach shan)
v. chase after;seek(graces,job...)
ugaszczać (oo-gash-chach) v.
entertain ; treat; feast;treat to
uginać (oo-gee-nach) v. bend-
down ; deflect; inflect;bow before
ugłaskać(oog-was-kach) v. tame
ugniatać (oog-na-tach) v. press-
down ; exert pressure; pinch
ugoda (oo-go-da) f. agreement
ugodowiec (oo-go-do-vyets) m.
compromiser;advocate of conciliation
ugodowy (oo-go-do-vi) adj.m.
conciliatory ; amicable
ugodzić (oo-go-dzheech)v.hit;hire
ugór (oo-goor) m. fallow
ugryźć (oog-rishch) v. bite off
ugrzęznąć (oo-gzhanz-nownch)
v. stick; be stuck; get bogged
uiszczenie (oo-eesh-che-ne) n.
payment(of a bill,rent etc.)
uiścić (oo-eesh-cheech) v. pay
up ; remit (a sum); acquit(a debt)
ujadać (oo-ya-dach) v. yelp;quarrel
ujarzmić (oo-yazh-meech) v.
subdue ; enslave; subjugate ; enthrall;
ujawniać (oo-yav-nach) v. reveal ; disclose ;expose;unmask;show
ująć (oo-yownch) v. conceive;
deduct ; seize; grasp; lessen ;win
ujednolicić (oo-yed-no-lee-
cheech) v. standardize ;unify
ujemny (oo-yem-ni) adj. m.
negative(value,etc.);unfavorable
ujeżdżać (oo-yezh-dzhach) v.
break in (a horse);smooth(a road)
ujeżdżalnia (oo-yezh-dzhal-na)
f. riding school ;manege
ujęcie (oo-yan-che) n. grasp
ujma (ooy-ma) f. detraction
ujmować (ooy-mo-vach) v. seize
restrain;embrace;apprehend;express
ujmujący (ooy-moo-yown-tsi) adj.
m. winsome ;egaging;prepossessing
ujrzeć (ooy-zhech) v. see;glimpse
ujście (ooysh-che) n. escape;
(river) mouth;withdrawal;retreat;
outlet;issue;vent (to indignation)

ukamienˀwaá (oo-ka-mye-no-vach)
v. stone to death; lapidate
ukazac (oo-ka-zach) v. show
(appear) ; exhibit; reveal
ukasic (oo-kown-sheech) v. bite
ukąszenie (oo-kown-she-ne) n.
bite ; sting
uklęknąc (oo-klank-nownch) v.
genuflect; kneel down
układ (ook-wat) m. scheme; agreement; disposition;system
układac się (ook-wa-dach shán)
v. lay down; negotiate;pan out
układanka (oo-kwa-dan-ka) f.
jigsaw puzzle;building blocks
układny (ook-wad-ni) adj. m. polite ; urbane; affable;mannerly
ukłon (ook-won) m. bow (greeting)
ukłonic się (oo-kwo-neech shán)
v. bow; tip one's hat ; greet
ukłucie (oo-kwoo-che) n. prick;
sting; sharp pain; prod;twinge
ukochac (oo-ko-khach) v. take
a fancy ; grow fond; hug
ukochana (oo-ko-kha-na) adj. f.
beloved ; darling; pet (female)
ukochany (oo-ko-kha-ni) adj. m.
beloved ; darling; pet (male)
ukoic (oo-ko-eech) v. soothe
ukojenie (oo-ko-ye-ne) n. relief ; consolation;allevivtion
ukonczyc (oo-kon-chich) v. complete; finish ; end (school etc.)
ukos (oo-kos) m. slant ; incline
ukosny (oo-kosh-ni) adj. m. oblique ; sloping; skew; diagonal
ukracac (oo-kra-tsach) v. curb;
subdue ; reform; check;put an end
ukradkiem (oo-krad-kem) adv.
stealthily ; by stealth;furtively
ukraiński (ook-ra-een-skee) adj.
m. Ukrainian; of Ukraine
ukrajac (oo-kra-yach) v. cut off
ukręcic (ook-ran-cheech) v.
twist off ; roll up; wrench off
ukrop (ook-rop) m. boiling water ; feverish bustle
ukrocic (ook-roo-cheech) v. repress; curb; reform;put an end to
ukrycie (ook-ri-che) n. hiding
place ; hideaway; hideout;cover
ukrywac (oo-kri-vach) v. hide;
cover up ; conceal; hold back

ukryty (ook-ri-ti) adj. m. hidden; concealed;put out of sight
ukrywac (ook-ri-vach) v. hide
ukształtowac (ook-shtaw-to-
vach) v. shape; fashion; cast
ukształtowanie (oo-kshtaw-to-
va-ne) n. configuration; for-
mulation; form; shape
ukuc (oo-kooch) v. hammer out
ul (ool) m. beehive ; hive
ulac (oo-lach) v. pour off;
cast(metal);pour off water
ulatac (oo-la-tach) v. fly off
ulatniac się (oo-lat-nach shán)
v. evaporate; volatize; vanish; melt away; leak; escape
ulatywac (oo-la-ti-vach) v.
fly away; leak (vapors; odors,
smells) ; rise in the air
uleczalny (oo-le-chal-ni) adj.
m. curable; remediable; medicable
uleczenie (oo-le-che-ne) n.
cure; successful recovery
uleczyc (oo-le-chich) v. heal
ulegac (oo-le-gach) v. yield
ulegly (oo-leg wi) adj. m.
submissive; docile; compliant
ulepszac (oo-lep-shach) v.
improve; better; ameliorate
ulepszenie (oo-lep-she-ne) n.
improvement; amelioration
ulewa (oo-le-va) f. rainstorm
ulewac (oo-le-vach) v. pour
off; cast (metals);pour(water)
ulga (ool-ga) f. relief;solace
uleżec się (oo-le-zhech shán)
v. mellow; settle;lie quiet
ulica (oo-lee-tsa) f. street
uliczka (oo-leech-ka) f. lane
ulicznica (oo-leech-nee-tsa)
f. prostitute; streetwalker
ulicznik (oo-leech-neek) m.
gamin; guttersnipe ;nipper
ulitowac się (oo-lee-to-vach
shán) v. have pity;take pity
ulotka (oo-lot-ka) f. hand -
bill ; leaflet;throwaway
ultimatum (ool-tee-ma-toom) n.
ultimatum;final offer(demand)
ultrafioletowy (ool-tra-fyo-le-
to-vi) adj. m. ultraviolet
ulubieniec (oo-loo-bye-nets) n.
favorite ; darling; pet

ulubiony (oo-loo-byó-ni) adj.
m. beloyed;favorite; pet
ulżyc (ool-zhich) v. relieve
ułamać (oo-wa-mać) v. break
off ; be broken off;come off
ułamek (oo-wa-mek) m. fraction;
fragment;mathematical fraction
ułamkowy (oo-wam-ko-vi) adj.m.
fractional(number,report etc.)
ułan (oo-wan) m. uhlan (Polish
light cavalryman (lancer)
ułaskawic (oo-was-ka-veech) v.
pardon(a condemned person)
ułaskawienie (oo-was-ka-vye-ne)
n. pardon; reprieve
ułatwić (oo-wat-veech) v. facilitate; simplify make easier
ułatwienie (oo-wat-vye-ne) n.
facilitation; simplification
ułomność (oo-wóm-noshch) f. de-
formity; defect ; frailty
ułomny (oo-wóm-ni) adj. m. disabled; defective; lame;faulty
ułożony (oo-wo-zhó-ni) adj.m.
arranged; well-mannered; set
umacniać (oo-máts-nach) v.
strengthen; fortify; secure
umaczać (oo-ma-chach) v. dip;
wet; soak; sop;have hand in;
umarły (oo-már-wi) adj. m. deceased; dead
umartwiać (oo-márt-vyach) v.
mortify(a person)
umarzać (oo-ma-zhach) v. amortize; discontinue ; remit
umawiać się (oo-máv-yach shań)
v. make a date (or plan)
umeblowac (oo-meb-ló-vach) v.
furnish; fit out; fit up
umeblowanie (oo-meb-lo-va-ne)
n. furniture ;furnishings
umiar (oóm-yar) m. moderation
umiarkowany (oo-myar-ko-vá-ni)
adj.,m. moderate; temperate
umiec (oó-myech) v. know how
umiejętnosc (oo-mye-yáńt-noshch)
f. science; skill; know how
umiejscowic (oo-myey-stsó-veech)
v. locate; assign a place;place
umierac (oo-myé-rach) v. die
umieszczać (oo-myésh-chach) v.
place; put; set;insert;seat

umilać (oo-mée-lach) v. make
pleasant; add charm:give charm
umilknąć (oo-meelk-nóWńch) v.
fall silent ; cease talking
umiłowany (oo-mee-wó-va-ni) adj.
m. beloved ; favorite; dear
umizgać się (oo-meéz-gach śhań)
v. flirt; woo; court; ogle
umizgi (oo-meez-gee) pl. flirt-
ing ; courtship; love making
umniejszać (oo-mnéy-shach) v.
diminish; lessen belittle;abate
umocnic (oo-móts-neech) v.
strengthen; fortify; beef up
umocnienie (oo-mots-ne-ne) n .
consolidation; fortification
umocowac (oo-mo-tsó-vach) v.
fasten; hitch; fix; secure
umorzyć (oo-mó-zhich) v. absolve;
amortize; extinguish
umowa (oo-mó-va) f. contract
umowny (oo-móv-ni) adj. m.
contractual; conventional
umożliwic (oo-mozh-leé-veech)
v. make possible; enable
umowic ≈ umawiac
umundurowanie (oo-moon-doo-ro-
va-ne) n. uniforms; uniform
umyc (oó-mich) v. wash up
umykac (oo-mi-kach) v. run away
umysł (oó-misw) m. mind; intellect
umysłowy (oo-mis-wo-vi) adj.m.
mental; intellectual; brain-
umyslnie (oo-mishl-ne) adv. on
purpose ; specially; purposely
umyslny (oo-mishl-ni) adj. m.
intentional; deliberate;special
umywac się (oo-mi-vach shań) v.
wash up; be fit for comparison
umywalnia (oo-mi-wal-ňa) f.
washbasin ; washroom;washstand
unaocznić (oo-na-óch-ňeech) v.
make evident; visualize
unarodowic (oo-na-ro-dó-veech)
v. nationalize;put to state control
unarodowienie (oo-na-ro-do-vye-
ňe) nationalization
uncja (oón-tsya) f. ounce
unia (oón-ya) f. union
unicestwic (oo-ňee-tsés-tveech)
v. annihilate ; frustrate

unicestwienie (oo-ñee-tses-tvye-ñe) n. annihilation;frustration

uniemożliwić (oo-ñe-mozh-lee-veech) v. make impossible

unieruchomić (oo-ñe-roo-khó-meech) v. immobilize ; tie up

unieszkodliwić (oo-ñe-shkod-lee-veech) v. render harmless

unieść (oó-ñeshch) v. lift up

unieważnić (oo-ñe-vazh-ñeech) v. annul ; void; cancel; repeal

unieważnienie (oo-ñe-vazh-ñe-ñe) n. annulment; invalidation

uniewinnić (oo-ñe-veen-ñeech) v. acquit;exculpate; excuse

uniewinnienie (oo-ñe-veen-ñe-ñe) n. acquittal

uniezależnić (oo-ñe-za-lezh-ñeech) v. make independent

uniform (oo-ñee-form) m. uniform

unikać (oo-ñee-kach) v. avoid; shun; steer clear;abstain from

unikat (oo-ñee-kat) m. unique item ; rare specimen;curiosity

uniwersalny (oo-ñee-ver-sal-ni) adj. m. universal ;versatile

uniwersytet (oo-ñee-ver-si-tet) m. university

unizać się (oo-ñee-zhach shañ) v. humble oneself;be servile

uniżony (oo-ñee-zho-ni) adj.m. humble ; servile; cringing

unormować (oo-nor-mo-vach) v. normalize; regulate:regularize

unosić (oo-nó-sheech) v. carry up; lift off;bear (a weight)

unowocześnić (oo-no-vo-chesh-ñeech) v. modernize

uodpornić (oo-od-pór-ñeech) v. immunize; harden; inure

uogólnić (oo-o-gool-ñeech) v. generalize (rules,observations)

uogólnienie (oo-o-gool-ñe-ñe) n. generalization

uosabiać (oo-o-sa-byach) v. personify;embody;typify

uosobienie (oo-o-so-bye-ñe) n. personification;embodiment

upadać (oo-pa-dach) v. fall down; collapse; topple over

upadek (oo-pa-dek) m. fall;drop

upadłość (oo-pad-woshch) f. bankruptcy ; insolvency

upadły (oo-pad-wi) adj. m. fallen; bankrupt; insolvent

upajać (oo-pá-yach) v. intoxi-cate; elate; fuddle ; make drunk

upalny dzień (oo-pál-ni dzheñ) m. hot day ;very hot day

upał (oó-paw) m. (intense) heat

upanstwowić (oo-pañ-stvó-veech) v. nationalize; socialize

upanstwowienie (oo-pañ-stvo-vye-ñe) n. nationalization

uparty (oo-pár-ti) adj. m. stubborn; obstinate;pigheaded

upatrywać (oo-pa-tri-vach) v. look for; suspect; perceive

upełnomocnić (oo-pew-no-mots-ñeech) v. give powers (of at-torney); empower; commission

upewnić (oo-pév-ñeech) v. as-sure ; reassure ; make sure

upić się (oo-peech shañ) v. get drunk; be intoxicated

upierać się (oo-pye-rach shañ) v. persist; insist; stick to

upinać (oo-pee-nach) v. fasten on; pin up; tie(one's hair)

upiór (oóp-yoor) m. ghost

upiorny (oo-pyór-ni) adj. m. ghostly;weird;nightmarish;ghastly

upłynnienie (oo-pwin-ñe-ñe) n. make fluid;flux; liquefaction

upływ (oóp-wiv) m. run off; (blood) loss; lapse; expiration

upływać (oo-pwi-vach) v. flow away; pass; lapse; go by;flow

upłynąć (oo-pwi-nównch) v. elapse; pass; expire ;sail away

upodobać (oo-po-dó-bach) v. take a liking ; take to; fancy

upodobanie (oo-po-do-ba-ñe) n. liking; fancy; predilection for

upodobnić się (oo-po-dób-ñeech shañ) v. assimilate; conform to

upoić (oo-pó-eech) v. intoxi-cate; make drunk; elate

upojenie (oo-po-ye-ñe) n. ine-briation; rapture ;intoxication

upokorzenie (oo-po-kozhe-ñe) n. humiliation; abasement

upokorzyć (oo-po-kó-zhich) v. humiliate ;make eat crow;abase

upominać (oo-po-mee-nach) v. admonish; warn; scold;rebuke

upominek (oo-po-mee-nek) m.
gift; souvenir;present;token
uporać się (oo-po-rach shań)
v. get over;cope with;negotiate
uporczywy (oo-por-chi-vi) adj.
m. stubborn;obstinate;severe
uporządkować (oo-po-zhownd-ko-
vach) v. put in order;tidy up
uposazenie (oo-po-sa-zhe-ńe)
n. pay; allowance;salary;wages
uposazyć (oo-po-sa-zhich) v.
endow; give allowance
uposledzenie (oo-poshle-dze-ńe)
n. handicap(mental,physical etc.)
uposledzony (oo-po-shle-dzo-ni)
adj. m. feebleminded;deprived
upowaznić (oo-po-vazh-ńeech) v.
authorize;commission;entitle
upowaznienie (oo-po-vazh-ńe-ńe)
n. authorization;full powers
upowszechniać (oo-pov-shekh-
ńach) v. put into general use
upór (oo-poor) m. obstinacy
upragniony (oo-prag-ńo-ni) adj.
m. desired; longed for
upraszać (oo-pra-shach) v. request; beg; beseech
uprawa (oo-pra-va) f. culture;
cultivation;agriculture;tillage
uprawiać (oo-prav-yach) v.
cultivate;till(the soil)
uprawnić (oo-prav-ńeech) v. entitle; qualify; legalize
uprawniony (oo-prav-ńo-ni)
adj. m. entitled
uprosić (oo-pro-sheech) v. get
by begging; persuade;ask to do
uproscic (oo-prosh-cheech) v.
simplify; reduce; cancel
uprowadzić (oo-pro-va-dzheech)
v. abduct; kidnap;lead away
uprzątać (oo-pzhown-tach) v.
clean up; tidy up;put away;kill
uprząż (oop-zhownsh) f. harness;
(horse);gear of draught animals
uprzedni (oo-pzhed-ńee) adj.
m. previous;prior;foregoing
uprzedzać (oo-pzhe-dzach) v.
anticipate; warn; have bias
uprzedzenie (oo-pzhe-dze-ńe) n.
anticipation; prejudice;notice
uprzedzony (oo-pzhe-dzo-ni) adj.
m. prejudiced; forewarned

uprzejmosc (oo-pzhey-moshch) f.
polite kindness;courtesy
uprzejmy (oo-pzhey-mi) adj.m.
kind ; polite; nice; suave;affable
uprzemysłowic (oo-pzhe-mi-swo-
veech) v. industrialize
uprzemysłowienie (oo-pzhe-mi-
swo-vye-ńe) n. industrializa-
tion ;development of industry
uprzykrzyc się (oo-pzhik-zhich
shań) v. get fed up with
uprzystepnic (oo-pzhis-- tanp-
ńeech) v. facilitate; make
available; make accessible
uprzytomnic (oo-pzhi-tom-ńeech)
v. realize; impress upon (sb)
uprzywilejowany (oo-pzhi-vee-le-
yo-ya-ni) adj. m. privileged
upuscic (oo-poosh-cheech) v.
let fall;let drop; bleed
upychac (oo-pi-khach) v. staff;
pack tight;cram;ram; fill
urabiac (oo-rab-yach) v. fashion
uraczyc (oo-ra-chich) v. treat
uradowac (oo-ra-do-vach) v.
gladden ; delight; rejoice
uradzic (oo-ra-dzheech)v. agree
decide; resolve; contrive
uran (oo-ran) m. uranium
urastac (oo-ras-tach) v. grow
uratowac (oo-ra-to-vach) v.
save ; salvage; rescue
uraz (oo-ras) m. injury; complex; resentment; grudge
uraza (oo-ra-za) f. grudge;
rancor; soreness; ill feeling
urazic (oo-ra-zheech) v. hurt;
offend ; wound sb's feelings
uragac (oo-rown-gach) v. insult
uregulowac (oo-re-goo-lo-vach)
v. stettle; put in order; pay
urlop (oor-lop) m. leave; fur-
lough ; vacation; holiday
urna (oor-na) f. urn;ballot box
uroczy (oo-ro-chi) adj. m.
charming;enchanting ;delightful
uroczystosc (oo-ro-chis-toshch)
f. celebration; festivity
uroczysty (oo-ro-chis-ti) adj.
m. solemn ; ceremonial;festive
uroda (oo-ro-da) f. beauty;
loveliness; attraction; charm

urodzaj (oo-ró-dzay) m. good
harvest;abundance; harvest;crop
urodzajny (oo-ro-dzáy-ni) adj.
m. fertile; fecund
urodzenie (oo-ro-dze-ńe) n.
birth
urodzić (oo-ró-dźheech) v. give
birth; breed; bear; yield
urodziny (oo-ro-dźhee-ni) n.
birthday; birth
urodzony (oo-ro-dzó-ni) adj.
m. born; born and bred
uroić (oo-ró-eech) v. imagine
urojenie (oo-ro-ye-ńe) n.
fiction; fancy; illusion
urojony (oo-ro-yo-ni) adj.m.
imaginary; abstract; fictitious
urok (oó-rok) m. charm; spell
uronić (oo-ró-ńeech) v. shed;
drop; let fall; lose;shed;miss
urozmaicenie (oo-roz-ma-ee-tse-
ńe) n. variety; diversity;change
urozmaicić (oo-roz-ma-eé-cheech)
v. diversify; vary ;while away
uruchomić (oo-roo-khó-meech) v.
start; put in motion;set going
urwać (oór-vach) v. tear off;
pull off; wrench away; deduct
urwis (oór-vees) m. urchin
urwisko (oor-vees-ko) n. precipice; crag; cliff ; steep rock
urwisty (oor-vees-ti) adj. m.
steep; precipitous; abrupt
urywek (oo-ri-vek) m. fragment
urząd (oózh-ownt) m. office
urzadzać (oozh-own-dzach) v.
arrange; settle; set up
urządzenie (oo-zhówn-dze-ńe) n.
furniture; installation;gear
urzec (oó-zhets) v. enchant;
bewitch; fascinate;cast a spell
urzeczywistnić (oo-zhe-chi-
veést-ńeech) v. make real;fulfil
urzeczywistnienie (oo-zhe-chi-
veest-ńe-ńe) n. realization
urzędnik (oo-zhánd-ńeek) m.
official; white-collar worker
urzędowanie (oo-zhań-do-vá-ńe)
n. office hours;clerical duties
urzędowy (oo-zhań-do-vi) adj.
m. official(document,capacity...)
urzynać (oo-zhi-nach) v. cut off

usadowić się (oo-sa-dó-veech
śhań) v. sit or settle down
uschły (oós-khwi) adj. m.
dried up; withered;wasted away
usiąść (oo-śhównshch) v. sit
down; take a seat;perch;alight
usidłać (oo-śheed-wach) v.
entrap; ensnare ;enmesh;inveigle
usilny (oo-śheel-ni) adj.m.
strenuous; intense; pressing
usiłować (oo-śhee-wó-vach) v.
strive; try hard; attempt
usiłowanie (oo-śhee-wo-vá-ńe)
n. attempt; efford; endeavor
uskarżać się(oos-kár-zhach śhań)
v.complain; grumble (about...)
uskutecznić (oo-skoo-tech-
ńeech) v. bring about;effect
usłuchać (oo-swoó-khach) v.
follow order (advice);obey
usługa (oo-swoó-ga) f. service;
favor; good turn; help
usługiwać (oo-swoo-geé-vach)
v. wait on; serve;attend
usłużyć (oo-swoó-zhich) v.
do a service; do a good turn
usnąć (oó-snównch) v. fall
asleep; go to sleep
uspokoić(oo-spo-kó-eech) v.
calm down; soothe; set at ease
uspołecznić (oos-po-wéch-ńeech)
v. socialize; civilize;collectivize
usposobić (oos-po-só-beech) v.
dispose; predispose; incline
usposobienie (oos-po-so-bye-
ńe) n. disposition;temper;mood
usprawiedliwić (oos-pra-vyed-
leé-veech) v. justify;explain
usprawiedliwienie (oos-pra-
vyed-lee-vye-ńe) n. excuse;
apology; plea; reason;justification
usprawnić (oos-práv-ńeech) v.
rationalize; make efficient
usta (oós-ta) n. mouth; lips
ustalenie (oo-sta-lé-ńe) n.
determination; settlement
ustalić (oo-stá-leech) v. determine; settle; fix; set
ustały (oo-sta-wi) adj. m.
settled (fluid)
ustanawiać (oo-sta-ná-vyach)
v. constitute; enact; set up

ustanowienie (oo-sta-no-vye-ñe)
n. instituting; establishing
ustatkować się (oo-stat-ko-
vach shañ) v. settle down
ustawa (oo-sta-ya) f. law; rule
ustawać (oo-sta-vach) v. cease;
be weary ; hardly stand
ustawiać (oo-stav-yach) v. arrange ; place; put; set up
ustawiczny (oo-sta-veech-ni)
adj. m. constant; continual
ustawienie (oo-sta-vye-ñe) n.
dispositon; installation
ustawodawca (oo-sta-vo-dav-tsa)
m. legislator
ustawodawstwo (oo-sta-vo-dav-
stvo) n. legislation
usterka (oo-ster-ka) f. defect
ustęp (oos-tañp) m. restroom;
paragraph ; passage
ustępliwy (oos-tañp-lee-vi) adj.
m. yielding ; compliant
ustępować (oos-tañp-po-vach) v.
yield ;withdraw; recede;cease
ustepstwo (oos-tañp-stvo) n.
concession;meeting half way
ustnik (oost-neek) m. mouthpiece
ustny (oost-ni) adj. m. oral;
verbal; spoken
ustosunkowany (oo-sto-soon-ko-
va-ni) adj. m. influential
ustrój (oos-trooy) m. structure;
government system; organism
ustrzec (oos-tzhets) v. guard;
avoid; safeguard .protect from
usunięcie (oo-soo-ñañ-che) n.
removal; withdrawal
usuwać (oo-soo-vach) v. remove
usychać (oo-si-khach) v. wither
usypać (oo-si-pach) v. pile up;
pour out; pour off (sand etc.)
usypiać (oo-sip-yach) v. put to
sleep;lull to sleep;send to sleep
uszanować (oo-sha-no-vach) v.
respect; spare(life etc)
uszanowanie (oo-sha-no-va-ñe)
n. respect; respects
uszczelka (oosh-chel-ka) f.
gasket;seal; packing
uszczelniać (oosh-chel-ñach) v.
pack; caulk; stop(a leak etc.)
uszczęśliwić (oosh-chañ-shlee-
veech) v. make happy ;delight

uszczerbek (oosh-cher-bek) m.
harm ; damage; loss
uszczuplić(oosh-choop-leech)
v. curtail; reduce ;lessen
uszczypliwy (oosh-chip-lee-vi)
adj. m. sarcastic; biting
uszko (oosh-ko) m. (small) ear;
(needle) eye ; ravioli
uszkodzenie (oosh-ko-dze-ñe)
n. damage; injury ;imperment
uszkodzić (oosh-ko-dzheech) v.
damage ;injure; impair; spoil
uszny (oosh-ni) adj. m. ear
uścisk dłoni (oosh-cheesk dwo-
ñee)m.handshake
uścisnąć (oosh-chees-nownch) v.
embrace; grasp;hug;squeeze(hand)
uśmiac sie (oosh-myach shañ) v.
laugh heartily;have a good lough
uśmiech (oosh-myekh) m. smile
uśmiechać sie (oosh-mye-khach
shañ) v. smile; give a smile
uśmiercić (oosh-myer-cheech)
v. kill; put to death
uśmierzyc (oosh-mye- zhich)
v. calm down;mitigate;alleviate
uśpić (oosh-peech) v. put to
sleep; anesthetize ;etherize
uświadomic (oosh-vya-do-meech)
v. instruct; initiate;realize
uświadomienie (oosh-vya-do-mye-
ñe) n. consciousness;information
uświetnić (oosh-vyet-ñeech) v.
give prestige; add splendor
utaić (oo-ta-eech) v. conceal
utajony (oo-ta-yo-ni) adj.m.
secret ; latent; potential
utalentowany (oo-ta-len-to-va-
ni) adj. m. talented ; gifted
utarczka (oo-tarch-ka) f. skirmish; encounter; squabble
utarg (oo-tark) m. receipts ;
take ; takings
utargować (oo-tar-go-vach) v.
make a bargain; realize
utarty (oo-tar-ti) adj. m.
usual; well-worn;wide spread
utęsknienie (oo-tañs-khe-ñe-ñe) n.
longing; earnest desire
utknąć (oot-knownch) v. get stuck
stall; stick fast; get to a stop
utlenić (oo-tle-ñeech) v. oxi-
dize(metals);peroxidize(hair)

utłuc (oót-woots) v. pound;
bruise;crush; pestle;mash;grind
utonąć (oo-to-nównch) v. be
drowned ; sink;be lost
utopia (oo-top-ya) f. Utopia
utopic (oo-to-peech) v. sink;
drown(an animal etc.)
utorować (oo-to-ro-vach) v.
clear a path; show the way
utożsamić (oo-tozh-sa-meech) v.
identify with
utracić (oo-tra-cheech) v.loose;
waste ; forfeit a right(etc)
utracjusz (oo-trats-yoosh) m.
spendthrift; squanderer
utrapienie (oo-trap-ye-ne) n.
worry; torment; nuisance
utrata (oo-tra-ta) f. loss
utrącać (oo-trówn-tsach) v.
chip; knock of; blackball
utrudniać (oo-trood-nach) v.
make difficult; hinder
utrudnienie (oo-trood-ne-ne) n.
difficulty; hindrance
utrwalić (oo-trva-leech) v.
make permanent; fix; record
utrzymanie (oo-tzhi-ma-ne) n.
living ; upkeep; board;support
utuczyć (oo-too-chich) v.
fatten; grow fat;fatten up
utulić (oo-too-leech) v. comfort; console;nestle (face...)
utwierdzić (oo-tvyer-dzheech)v.
confirm ; fix; set; consolidate
utworzenie (oo-tvo-zhe-ne) n.
formation; initiation;creation
utworzyć (oo-tvo-zhich) v.
create; form; compose;initiate
utwor (oot-voor)m. work; composition; production;creation
utyć (oo-tich) v. become fat
utykać (oo-ti-kach) v. limp
utylitarny (oo-ti-lee-tar-ni)
adj. m. utilitarian; useful
utyskiwać (oo-tis-kee-vach) v.
complain ; grumble (at,about)
uwaga (oo-va-ga) f. attention;
remark ; notice;exp.: Caution!
uwalniać (oo-val-nach) v. set
free ; rid; let off; dismiss
uważać (oo-va-zhach) v. pay
attention ; be careful; mind;
take care; look after;
watch out;consider;reckon

uważny (oo-vazh-ni) adj. m.
careful; attentive; watchful
uwiąd (oov-yównt) m. atrophy
uwiązać (oo-vyówn-zach) v.
attach; bind; tie; fasten
uwidocznić (oo-vee-doch-neech)
v. make evident; show; expose
uwiecznić (oo-vyech-neech) v.
perpetuate; immortalize
uwielbiać (oo-vyel-byach) v.
adore; worship; admire
uwielbienie (oo-vyel-bye-ne) n.
adoration;admiration;worship
uwierać (oo-vye-rach) v. (shoe)
pinch; rub; hurt
uwierzytelnić (oo-vye-zhi-tel-
neech) v. legalize;certify;attest
uwierzytelnienie (oo-vye-zhi-
tel-ne-ne) n. certification;
accreditation; authentication
uwięzić (oo-vyán-zheech) v.
imprison;throw into prison
uwijać się (oo-vee-yach shán)
v. be busy; bustle about
uwikłać (oo-veek-wach) v. entangle;involve;get entangled
uwłaczać (oov-wa-chach) v. belittle ; insult; outrage;affront
uwłosiony (oo-vwo-sho-ni) adj.
m. hairy; hirsute; pilose
uwodziciel (oo-vo-dzhee-chel)
m. seducer (of women);inveigler
uwodzić (oo-vo-dzheech) v. seduce (men or women)
uwolnić (oo-vol-neech) v. free
uwolnienie (oo-vol-ne-ne) n.
liberation;rescue; acquittal
uwydatnić (oo-vi-dat-neech) v.
accentuate; set off; bring out
uwypuklić (oo-vi-pook-leech) v.
accentuate; set off;protrude
uwzglednić (oovz-gland-neech)
v. consider; comply; acquiesce
uwzglednienie (oovz-gland-ne-ne)
n. allowance for;compliance
uzależnić (oo-za-lezh-neech) v.
make dependent; subordinate
uzasadnić (oo-za-sad-neech) v.
substantiate; justify;motivate
uzasadnienie (oo-za-sad-ne-ne)
n. justification; motive
uzbrajać się (ooz-bra-yach shán)
v. arm oneself; equip oneself

uzbrojenie (ooz-bro-ye-ńe) n.
arming; armament ; weapons
uzda (ooz-da) f. bridle
uzdolnić (ooz-dol-ńeeć) v.
enable ; qualify;capacitate
uzdolnienie (ooz-dol-ńe-ńe) n.
talent ; gift; aptitude
uzdolniony (ooz-dol-ńo-ni) adj.
m. gifted; talented;capable;apt
uzdrawiać (ooz-dra-vyać) v.
heal; cure;bring back to health
uzdrowisko (ooz-dro-vees-ko)
n. health resort
uzębienie (oo-zań-bye-ńe) n.
dentition;toothing(of gears...)
uzgadniać (ooz-gad-ńać) v.
reconcile;coordinate;adjust
uziemienie (oo-źhe-mye-ńe) n.
grounding ; earth
uzmysłowić (ooz-mi-swo-veeć)
v. visualize; convey (meaning)
uznawać (ooz-na-vać) v. acknowledge; do justice;confess
uznanie (ooz-na-ńe) n. recognition ; admission; approval
uzupełniać (oo-zoo-pew-ńać) v.
complete ; fill up;make up
uzurpator (oo-zoor-pa-tor) m.
usurper(who takes without right)
uzyskać (oo-zis-kać) v. obtain;
gain; win ;get; acquire;secure
użerać się (oo-zhe-rać śhań)
v. fight over; quarrel;wrangle
użyczać (oo-zhi-chać) v.
grant; give; lend; spare;impart
użyć (oo-zhić) v. use; exert;
take (medicine); profit;employ
użyteczny (oo-zhi-teć-ni) adj.
m. useful ; serviceable;helpful
użytek (oo-zhi-tek) m. use
użytkownik (oo-zhit-kov-ńeek)
m. user (of appartment etc.)
używać (oo-zhi-vać) v. use;
enjoy; exercise right;make use
używalność (oo-zhi-val-noshćh)
f. use;enjoyment;utilization
używalny (oo-zhi-val-ni) adj.m.
usable; in working order
używany (oo-zhi-va-ni) adj.m.
used; second-hand ;worn
użyźniać (oo-zhiźh-nać) v.
fertilize; enrich(the soil)

w (v) prep. in ; into; at
we (ve) prep. in; into; at
wabić (va-beech) v. lure
wabik (va-beek) m. decoy; lure
wachlarz (vakh-lash) m. fan;
range(of questions, subjects..)
wada (va-da) f. fault; defect;flaw
wadliwy (wad-lee-vi) adj. m.
faulty;defective;;imperfect
wafel (va-fel) m. wafer; cornet
waga (va-ga) f. weight; balance;
pair of scales; importance
wagary (va-ga-ri) pl. skipping
school; playing truant; the wag
wagon (va-gon) m. car; wagon
wagon restauracyjny (va-gon res-
taw-ra-tsiy-ni) dining car
wahac się (va-khać śhań) v.
hesitate ;sway; rock; swing
wahadło (va-kha-dwo) n. pendu-
lum(swinging backwards and forwards)
wahadłowy (va-khad-wo-vi) adj.
m. rocking; swinging; oscilatory
wakacje (va-kats-ye) pl. vacation; holidays;taking a holiday
walać (va-lać) v. soil; stain;dirty
walc (valts) m. waltz
walcować (val-tso-vać) v. roll;
flatten; mill; laminate
walczyć (val-chić) v. fight; vie;
straggle;be in conflict;contend
walec (va-lets) m. cylinder; roller
waleczność (va-leć-noshćh) f.
bravery ; valor;gallantry;courage
waleczny (va-leć-ni) adj. m.
valiant; brave; gallant;courageous
walić (va-leećh) v. demolish;hit;pile
walijski (va-leey-skee) adj.m.
Welsh; of Wales
walizka (va-leez-ka) f. suitcase; valise; portmanteau
walka (val-ka) f. struggle;
fight; war; battle; wrestling
walny (val-ni) adj. m. general;
complete; decisive;outstanding
walor (va-lor) m. value;quality
waluta (va-loo-ta) f. currency
wał (vaw) m. 1. rampart; dike;bank;
2. shaft;arbor; billow
wałach (va-wakh) m. gelding
wałek (va-wek) m. roller; shaft;
cylinder ; rolling pin ;wad; roll

wałęsać się (va-wän-sach shän) v. rove; loaf; idle about

wałkoń (vaw-koń) m. loafer; do-nothing; idler

wałkować (vaw-kó-vach) v. roll; mangle ; debate; thresh out

wampir (vam-peer) m. vampire

wandal (van-dal) m. vandal

wanienka (va-nen-ka) f. little tub ; bathtub; laboratory dish

wanna (van-na) f. bath tub

wapienny (va-pyen-ni) adj.m. limy; limestone;calcareus

wapień (va-pyeń) m. limestone

wapno (vap-no) n. lime

wapn (vapn) m. calcium

warcaby (var-tsá-bi) pl. checkers; draughts (game)

warchlak (várkh-lak) m. boar-cub;young wilde boar; piglet

warchoł (var-khow) m. brawler ; discord sower; squabbler

warczec (var-chech) v. growl

warga (vár-ga) f. lip; labium

wariant (vár-yant) m. variant

wariactwo (var-yáts-tvo) n. madness;piece of folly; folly

wariat (var-yat) m. lunatic; insane ; madman; fool;crazy man

wariować (var-yó-vach) v. go insane ; rave ;go mad; be mad

warkocz (var-koch) m. braid

warkot (vár-kot) m. growl; whirr; throb; rattle; drone

warowny (va-róv-ni) adj. m. fortified;made into fortress

warować (va-ró-vach) v. fortify

warstwa (várs-tva) f. layer; stratum; coat;coating; class

warstwowy (var-stvo-vi) adj. m. laminar; stratal;foliated

warsztat (vársh-tat) m. workshop; workbench;(weaver's)loom

warsztatowy (var-shta-tó-vi) adj. m. workshop-(equipment etc.)

warta (vár-ta) f. watch; guard

wartki (várt-kee) adj. m. rapid ; fast(current);animated

wartko(várt-ko) adv. fast; rapidly ; impetuously

warto (vár-to) adv. it's worth (while); it's proper; it's worth one's while; it pays

wartosciowy (var-tosh-cho-vi) adj. m. valuable; precious

wartosc (var-toshch) f. value; worth ;quality;power;magnitude

wartownik (var-tov-neek) m. guard; sentry;sentinel

warunek (va-roo-nek) m. condition; requirement; term;stipulation

warunkowy (va-roon-kó-vi) adj. m. conditional;contingent;provisory

warząchew (va-zhówn-khev) v. ladle

warzyć (va-zhich) v. cook; brew

warzywa (va-zhi-va) pl. vegetables: pot herbs;truk garden produce

warzywny (va-zhiv-ni) adj. m. vegetable ; vegetable-

wasz (vash) pron. your; yours

waśnić (vash-neech) v. saw discord (among men or women)

waśn (vashn) f. quarrel

wata (va-ta) f. cotton wool

watować (va-tó-vach) v. pad; quilt ;wad (a jacket etc.)

wawrzyn (vav-zhin) m. laurel

waza (vá-za) f. vase;soup tureen

wazelina (va-ze-lee-na) f. vaseline

wazon (va-zon) m. flower pot

ważki (vazh-kee) adj. m. grave; weighty ; ponderable

ważny (vazh-ni) adj. m. important;valid; significant

ważyć (va-zhich) v. weigh

ważyć się (va-zhich shän) v. dare; weigh oneself;poise;venture

wąchać (vown-khach) v. smell

wągr (vowngr) m. blackhead; scolex; comedo;tapeworm larva

wąs (vowns) m. moustache;whisker

wąski (vown-skee) adj. m. narrow; tight(fitting);narrow-(gage)

wąskotorowa kolej (vówns-ko-to-ro-va ko-ley) f. narrow gauge railroad

wątek (vown-tek) m. weft; plot

wątły (vównt-wi) adj. m. frail

wątpić (vównt-peech) v. doubt

wątpliwy (vownt-plee-vi) adj. m. doubtful;open to doubt;toss-up

wątroba (vown-tro-ba) f. liver

wątróbka (vown-troob-ka) f. liver (dish);(calf's) liver

wąwóz (vown-voos) m. ravine;
 gorge; gully ; canyon ; defile
wąż (vownsh) m. snake; hose
wbiec (vbyets) v. run in;run up
wbijać (vbee-yach)v.hammer in
wbrew (vbrev) prep. in spite
 of ; in defiance; against
wbudować (vboo-do-vach) v.
 build in; incorporate
w bród (v broot) adv. 1. in
 abundance; 2. fording (river)
wcale (vtsa-le) adv. quite
wcale nie (vtsa-le ñe) not at
 all (exp); not in the least
wchłaniać (vkhwa-ñach) v. absorb; soak up; take in;soak in
wchodzić (wkho-dżheech) v. enter; get in; set in; climb
w ciągu (v chown-goo) adv.
 during ;while; in time of
wciągać (vchown-gach) v. pull
 in; drag in; inhale;implicate
wciąż (vchownsh) adv. continual-
 ly; constantly;persistently
wcielać (vche-lach) v. incorporate; embody; merge; realize
wcielenie (vche-le-ñe) n. in-
 carnation; embodiment;merger
wcierać (vche-rach) v. rub in
wcięcie (vchañ-che) n. incision
 notch .narrow waist;low cut neck
wciskać (vchees-kach) v. press
 in; squeeze in;wedge; cram
w czas (v chas) on time
wczasy (vcha-si) pl. vacations
wczesny (vches-ni) adj. m.
 early;in the small hours
wcześnie (vchesh-ñe) adv. early
wczoraj (vcho-ray) adv. yesterday; during yesterday
wczoraj wieczorem (vcho-ray vye-
 cho-rem) adv. last night
wczuwać się (vchoo-vach shañ)
 v. sympathize; get in spirit
wdarcie (vdar-che) n. invasion
wdawać się (vda-vach shañ) v.
 1. intervene; 2. associate
wdech (vdekh) m. aspiration
wdowa (vdo-va) f. widow
wdowiec (vdo-vyets) m. widower
w dół (v doow) adv. down; downwards ; downstairs; (go)lower

wdrapać się (vdra-pach shañ) v.
 climb up ; shin up(a tree)
wdrażać (vdra-zhach) v. train;
 implant ; accustom to;enter upon
wdychać (vdi-khach) v. breathe;
 inhale ; breathe in; imbibe
wdzierać się (vdżhe-rach shañ)
 v. break in; struggle up hill
wdziewać (vdżhe-vach) v. put
 on (clothes); slip on;take(the veil)
wdzięcznosć (vdżhanch-noshch)
 f. gratitude ; thankfulness
wdzięczny (vdżhanch-ni) adj.
 m. grateful; thankful;graceful;cute
wdzięk (vdżhañk) m. grace;charm
według (ved-wook) prep. according to; after; along;near;next
wegetacja (ve-ge-tats-ya) f.
 vegetation; bare existence
wegetarianin (ve-ge-tar-ya-neen)
 m. vegetarian(on meatless diet)
wegetować (ve-ge-to-vach) v.
 exist barely; vegetate
wejrzeć (vey-zhech) v. glance
 in;look in;get an insight;inspect
wejrzenie (vey-zhe-ñe) n.glance
 in; (eye)expression; insight
wejscie (veysh-che) n . entrance; way in; admission;entry
wejsciowy (veysh-cho-vi) adj.
 m. entrance-(door;gate,etc.)
wejsc (veyshch) v. enter;get in
weksel (vek-sel) m. loan note
welon (ve-lon) m. veil
wełna (vew-na) f. wool
wełniany (vew-ña-ni) adj. m.
 woolen; worsted; wool-(fabric...)
wełnisty (vew-nees-ti) adj.m.
 wooly; fleecy;wool bearing
weneryczna choroba (ve-ne-rich-
 na kho-ro-ba) f. venereal
 disease
wenezuelski (ve-ne-zoo-el-skee)
 adj. m. Venezuelan;of Venezuela
wentyl (ven-til) m. vent;valve
wentylacja (ven-ti-lats-ya) f.
 ventilation;ventilation system
wentylator (ven-ti-la-tor) m.
 ventilator; ventilating-fan
weranda (ve-ran-da) f. porch
werbel (ver-bel) m. ruffle;
 drum-call; drumbeat ;drum

werbować (ver-bo-vach) v. enlist; recruit; canvas
werbunek (ver-boo-nek) m. draft;
recrutment;enlisting;recruting
wersja (vee-sya) f. version
werwa (ver-ya) f. verve;zip;pep
weryfikować (ve-ri-fee-ko-vach)
v. verify;confirm
wesele (ve-se-le) n. wedding
wesołość (ve-so-woshch) f.joy
gaiety; glee; hilarity
wesoły (ve-so-wi) adj. merry;
gay; jolly; gleeful; funny
wespoł (ves-poow) adv. together;
jointly; all together
westchnienie (vest-khne-ńe) n.
sigh(of relief etc.)
wesz (vesh) f. louse
wet za wet (vet za vet) exp.:
tit for tat; retaliate
weteran (ve-te-ran) m. veteran
weterynarz (ve-te-ri-nash) m.
vet; veterinary; farrier
wetknąć (vet-knownch) v. stick
in;slip in;tuck away; stuff
wewnątrz (vev-nowntsh) prep.,
adv. inside; within; intra-
wewnętrzny (vev-nańtzh-ni) adj.
m. inner;internal; inward
wezbrać (vez-brach) v. swell
wezbrany (vez-bra-ni) adj. m.
flush; overflowing; swollen
wezwać (vez-vach) v. call in
wezwanie (vez-va-ńe) n. call
węch (vańkh) m. smell; nose
wędka (vańd-ka) f. fishing rod
wędkarz (vańd-kash) m. angler
wędlina (vańd-lee-na) f. meat
products; pork products
wędliniarnia (vand-lee-ńar-na)
f. pork-butcher's shop
wędrować (vań-dro-vach) v.
wander; roam; rove; hike
wędrowiec (vań-dro-vyets) m.
wanderer; tramp; rover
wędrówka (vań-droov-ka) f. mi-
gration; roam; tramp;wandering
wędzic (vań-dzeech) v. smoke;
cure; meat; bloat fish
wędzidło (vań-dzheed-wo) n.
(horse) bit;bridle;curb
wędzonka (vań-dzon-ka) f. bacon

węgiel (vań-gel) m. coal;crayon
węgielny kamień (vań-gel-ni ka-
myeń) m. corner stone;corner stone
węgieł (vań-gew) m. corner; quoin
węgierski (vań-ger-skee) adj.
m. Hungarian; of Hungary
węglan (vań-glan) m. carbonate
węglowodan (vań-glo-vo-dan) m.
carbohydrate (chemical compound)
węglowodór (vań-glo-vo-door) m.
hydrocarbon ;rock oil etc.
węglowy (vań-glo-vi) adj. m.
carbonic; coal; carboniferous;
carbon-
węgorz (vań-gosh) m. eel
węzeł (vań-zew) m. knot; junction; noose; loop; snarl;hitch
węższy (vańzh-shi) adj. m. nar-
rower(than)
wgląd (vglownt) m. insight; view
wglądać (vglown-dach) v. look
into; get an insight;inquire
wgłębic się (vgwań-beech shań)
v. sink; study;go into (matter)
wgryzć się (vgrizhch shań) v.
penetrate; get teeth into...
wiać (vyach) v. blow; beat it
wiadomo (vya-do-mo) v. (imp.)
it is known;everybody knows
wiadomość (vya-do-moshch) f.
news; information; message
wiadomy (vya-do-mi) adj. m.
known; a certain;well known
wiadro (vya-dro) n. bucket;pail
wiadukt (vya-dookt) m. viaduct
wianek (vya-nek) m. flower
crown; wreath; maidenhead
wiara (vya-ra) f. faith;belief
wiarogodny (vya-ro-god-ni) adj.
m. reliable; credible;veracious
wiarołomny (vya-ro-wom-ni) adj.
m. unfaithful; treacherous
wiarus (vya-roos) m. veteran
(old guard) breeze
wiatr (vyatr) m. wind;gale;
wiatrak (vyat-rak) m. windmill
wiatrówka (vya-troov-ka) f.
air gun; wind breaker (jacket)
wiąz (vyowns) m. elm (Ulmus)
wiązać (vyown-zach) v. tie; bind
wiązanie (vyown-za-ńe) n. tie;
truss; bond; link;fixation;weave

wiązanka (vyówn-zán-ka) f. garland; bunch ; banquet;cluster
wiązka (vyównz-ka) f. bundle;
bunch ; cluster; beam(of rays)
wibracja (vee-brá-tsya) f.
vibration ; jarring ; jar
wichrować się (vee-khró-vach
shán) v. warp; curl
wicher (vee-kher) m. windstorm ;
gale;strong wind
wichrzyciel (veekh-zhi-chel) m.
warmonger; firebrand;instigator
wichrzyć (veékh-zhich) v. make
trouble; create discord;tousle
wichura (vee-khoo-ra) f. windstorm; gale; strong wind
wichura śnieżna (vi-khoo-ra-
shńezh-na) snowstorm ;blizzard
wić (veéch) v. wind; meander;
build nest; curl ;m.twig;osier
widelec (vee-de-lets) m. fork
widełki (vee-déw-kee) pl.
fork (small) ;forked branch
widełkowaty (vee-dew-ko-vá-ti)
adj. m. forked;fork shaped
widły (veéd-wi) pl. pitch fork
widmo (veéd-mo) n . ghost;
phantom ;spectrum;specter
widno (véd-no) adv. 1. evidently; 2. in daylight ;in light
widnokrąg (veed-no-krównk) m.
horizon ; sea-line ;true horizon
widocznie (vee-dóch-ńe) adv.
evidently ;apparently; clearly
widocznosc (vee-doch-noshch)
f. visibility ;field of vision
widoczny (vee-dóch-ni) adj. m.
visible; evident; noticeable
widok (vee-dok) m. view; sight
widokówka (vee-do-koóv-ka) f.
picture postcard
widowisko (vee-do-veés-ko) n.
show; spectacle ; pageant
widownia (vee-dóv-ńa) f. audience; theatre house ;scene
widz (veets) m. spectator
widzenie (vee-dzé-ńe) n. sight;
vision ; visit; hallucination
widzialny (vee-dźhál-ni) adj.
m. visible (to the naked eye...)
widziec (veé-dźhech) v. see
wiec (vyets) m. meeting ;rally

wieczerza (vye-zhé-zha) f. supper ;Lord's Supper
wiecznosc (vyech-noshch) f.
eternity; ages ;eternal life
wieczny (vyéch-ni) adj. m.
eternal; perpetual; endless
wieczorek (vye-cho-rek) m. evening (party); nice evening
wieczorem (vye-cho-rem) exp.; in
the evening ;during the evening
wieczorny (vye-chór-ni) adj. m.
evening -(dress,newspaper,etc.)
wieczorowy (vye-cho-ró-vi) adj.
m. nightly; evening (performance)
wieczór(vye-choor) m. evening
wieczysty (vye-chis-ti) adj. m.
eternal; perpetual;imperishable
wiedza (vyé-dza) f. knowledge;
learning;erudition; science
wiedzieć (vyé-dźhech) v. know
wiedzma (vyedżh-ma) f. witch
wiejska droga (vyey-ska dró-ga)
f. village road; country road
wiejski (vyéy-skee) adj. m.
village; rural; rustic;country
wiek (vyek) m. age; century
wiekowy (vye-kó-vi) adj. m.
secular; ancient; aged;very old
wiekuistosc (vye-koo-eés-toshch)
f. eternity ; all time
wiekuisty (vye-koo-eés-ti) adj.
m. eternal; everlasting
wielbiciel (vyel-beé-chel) m.
devotee; admirer; idolator (man)
wielbicielka (vyel-bee-chél-ka)
f. devotee; idolatress (woman)
wielbłąd (vyél-bwównd) m. camel
wielce (vyél-tse) adv. very;
greatly; extremely ;very much
wiele (vyé-le) adj. m. many;
a lot;much; far out;a great deal
wielebny (vye-léb-ni) adj. m.
reverend (Father etc.)
Wielkanoc (vyel-ká-nots) f.
Easter
wielkanocny (vyel-ka-nóts-ni)
adj. m. Easter; of Easter
wielki (vyél-kee) adj. m. big;
large; great ; vast; keen;mighty
wielkoduszny (vyel-ko-doósh-ni)
adj. m. magnanimous ;generous
wielkolud (vyel-kó-lood) m.giant

wielkomiejski (vyel-ko-myey-skee) adj. m. metropolitan; urban ; of a large city

wielkosc (vyel-koshch) f. greatness; size; dimension

wielobarwny (vye-lo-barv-ni) adj. m. multicolor (ed)

wieloboczny (vye-lo-boch-ni) adj. m. multilateral ;polygonal

wielokrążek (vye-lo-krown-zhek) m. set of pulleys ; pulley-block

wielokrotny (vye-lo-krot-ni) adj. m. repeated ; multiple

wieloletni (vye-lo-let-ni) adj. m. long; years long;many years'

wielopiętrowy (vye-lo-pyan-tro-vi) adj. m. multistory

wieloraki (vye-lo-ra-kee) adj. m. manifold ; varied ;multiple

wieloryb (vye-lo-rib) m. whale

wielorybnik (vye-lo-rib-neek) m. whaler;whaleman;whaling ship

wielostronny (vye-lo-stron-ni) adj. m. multilateral ;many-sided ; versatile; various

wielozgłoskowy (vye-lo-zgwos-ko-vi) adj. m. polysyllabic

wieloznaczny (vye-lo-znach-ni) adj. m. multivocal; ambiguous

wielożeństwo (vye-lo-zhen-stvo) n. polygamy

wieniec (vye-nets) m. wreath; garland; crown ; chaplet

wieńczyc (vyen-chich) v. crown

wieprz (vyepsh) m. hog; pig

wieprzownina (vyep-zho-vee-na) f. pork (meat)

wieprzowy (vyep-zho-vi) adj.m. pork ;pork's;pig's;hog's;porcine

wiercenie (vyer-tse-ne) n. drilling ; perforation.boring

wiercić (vyer-chich) v. bore; drill ; pester ; bother

wiernosc (vyer-noshch) f. fidelity; loyalty ; faith; truth

wierny (vyer-ni) adj. m. faithful ; true;loyal;exact

wiersz (vyersh) m. verse; poem

wiertarka (vyer-tar-ka) f. drill

wiertnictwo (vyert-neets-tvo) n. drilling (activity)

wierutny (vye-root-ni) adj.m. stark(liar); notorious; through-and-through ; rank; arrant;born

wierzacy (vye-zhown-tsi) adj. m. believer; believing Christian

wierzba (vyezh-ba) f. willow

wierzch (vyezhkh) m. top; brim head; surface; cover; lid

wierzchni (vyezh-khnee) adj. m. upper ; top; outer;outside

wierzchołek (vyezh-kho-wek) m. top; peak; summit; apex;vertex

wierzyciel (vye-zhi-chel) m. creditor; mortgagee; obligee

wierzycielka (vye-zhi-chel-ka) f. creditor (woman)

wierzyc (vye-zhich) v. believe; trust;rely; believe in God

wierzytelnosc (vye-shi-tel-noshch) f. debt; claim

wieszac (vye-shach) v. hang

wieszadło (vye-shad-wo) v. hanger; peg; ;coat-stand

wieszak (vye-shak) v. rack

wieszcz (vyeshch) m. bard; seer; poet (leading,national)

wieszczy (vyesh-chi) adj. m. prophetic ;visionary

wieś (vyesh) f. village; coun-tryside; hamlet;the villagers

wieśc (vyeshch) 1. f. news 2. v. lead; conduct; draw; succeed ;stand at the head

wieśniaczka (vyesh-nach-ka) f. countrywoman ;peasant woman

wieśniak (vyesh-nak) m. country-man; villager; yokel ;rustic

wietrzec (vyet-zhech) v. decay

wietrzyc (vyet-zhich) v. ven-tilate; smell; nose;aerate

wietrzenie (vyet-zhe-ne) n. ventilation; decay (of rocks)

wiewiórka (vye-vyoor-ka) f. squirrel; squirrel fur

wieźć (vyezhch) v. carry (on wheels) ;transport;convey;drive

wieża (vye-zha) f. tower; rook

wieżowiec (vye-zho-vyets) m. skyscraper;high-rise(building)

wieżyczka (vye-zhich-ka) f. turret; pinnacle;small tower

więc (vyants) conj. now; well; therefore ; so;consequently

więcej (vyan-tsey) adv. more

więdnąc (vyand-nownch) v. wither; fade ; wilt

więcierz (vyań-chezh) m. fishing net (set taut on hoops)
większość (vyank-shoshch) f.
majority; the bulk; most
większy (vyank-shi) adj. m.
bigger; larger; greater
więzić (vyań-zheech) v. imprison ;confine; detain;restrain
więzienie (vyań-zhe-ńe) n. prison; confinement; jail;restraint
więzień (vyań-zheń) m. prisoner
więzy (vyań-zi) pl. fetters;
restrains; chains; bonds
wigilia (vee-geel-ya) f. Xmas
Eve; eve
wiklina (vee-klee-na) f. osier
wikłać (veek-wach) v. entangle
wikt (veekt) m. board; keep
wilczur (veel-choor) m.wolf dog
wilgoć (veel-goch) f. humidity
wilgotny (veel-got-ni) adj. m.
moist; humid ; damp; wet
wilia (veel-ya) f. eve
wilk (veelk) m. wolf;wolfskin
wilżyć (veel-zhich) v. moisten
wina (vee-na) f. guilt; fault
winda (veen-da) f. elevator
winiarnia (vee-ńar-ńa) f. wine-
shop ;vine vault; winery
winić (vee-ńeech) v. accuse;
blame for ;fix the blame on
winien (vee-ńen) adj. m. indebted; owing; guilty; at fault
winnica (veen-ńee-tsa) f. vine
yard; vine growing plantation
winny (veen-ni) adj. m. guilty
winny (veen-ni) adj. m. of wine;
vineous ; vine-; winy
wino (vee-no) n. wine ;grapevine
winogrono (vee-no-gró-no) n.
grape
winorośl (vee-no-roshl) f. vine
winowajca (vee-no-váy-tsa) m.
culprit; evildoer;the guilty one
winszować (veen-sho-vach) v.
congratulate (on having success)
wiosenny (vyo-sen-ni) adj. m.
spring -(flowers,month etc.)
wioska (vyos-ka) f. hamlet
wiosło (vyos-wo) n. oar;paddle
wiosłować (vyos-wó-vach) v. row
wiosna (vyos-na) f. Spring (time)

wioślarz (vyosh-lash) m. oarsman ; rower
wiotki (vyot-kee) adj. m. limp
wiór (vyoor) m. shaving ; chip
wir (veer) m. whirl; eddy ;vortex
wiraż (vee-rash) m. curve; bend
wirować (vee-ro-vach) v. whirl
wirówka (vee-roóv-ka) f. centrifuge ;hydro-extractor
wirtuoz (veer-too-os) m. virtuoso ;maestro; great musician etc.
wirus (vee-roos) m. virus
wisieć (vee-shech) v.hang; sag
wisiorek (vee-shó-rek) m. pendant
wiśnia (veesh-ńa) f. cherry (tree)
wiśniak (veesh-ńak) m. cherry-
brandy; cherry liqueur
witać (vee-tach) v. greet; welcome; meet to welcome;bid welcome
witamina (vee-ta-mée-na) f. vitamin (A,B,C,D,E etc.)
witryna (vee-tri-na) f. shop-
window ; glass case
wiza (vee-za) f. visa
wizerunek (vee-ze-roo-nek) m.
likeness; image;picture; effigy
wizja (veez-ya) f. vision ;view
wizyta (vee-zi-ta) f. call;
visit; be on a visit
wizytówka (vee-zi-toóv-ka) f.
calling card; visiting card
wjazd (vyazt) m. (car) entrance
wjeżdżać (vyézh-dzhach) v.
drive in ;ride to the top
wkleić (vkle-eech) v. stick in
wklęsłodruk (vklań-swo-drook)
m. copper plate print
wklęsły (vklańs-wi) adj. m.
concave; hollow; sunken
wkład (vkwat) m. input; deposit;
investment; outlay; inset
wkładać (vkwa-dach) v. put in
w koło (vkó-wo) adv. round;in
circles; over and over again
wkoło (vkó-wo)prep. round; about;
in circles   appear;
wkraczać (vkra-chach) v. step in;
invade; intervene; enter; stalk
wkradać się (vkra-dach shań) v.
steal in; slip in; creep in
wkrapiać (vkráp-yach) v. put
drops in; beat up

wkręcać (vkrań-tsach) v. screw
in ; drive in; push into a job
wkroczyć (vkro-chich)v. enter
(formally) ; appear ; invade
wkrótce (vkroot-tse) adv. soon
wkupić się (vkoo-peech shań) v.
buy way in;pay one's footing
wlać (vlach) v. pour in
wlatywać (vla-ti-vach) v. fly
in ; rush in; dart in;run in
wlec (vlets) v, drag ; tow
wlepić (vle-peech) v. l. paste
in; 2, glare at; stare at
wlewać (vle-vach) v. pour in
wleźć (vleżhch) v. crawl in ;
climb up; barge in; step in
wliczenie (vlee-che-ne) n. inclusion; counting in
wliczyć (vlee-chich) v. count
in ; reckon in ;include
w lot (v lot) adv. in a flash;
quickly; in a hurry
wlot (vlot) m. inlet ; intake
wlot kuli (vlot koo-lee) m.
bullet entry
władać (vwa-dach) v. rule ;wield
władca (vwad-tsa) m. ruler
władny (vwad-ni) adj. m. sovereign ; having the authority
władza (vwa-dza) f. authority
włamać się (vwa-mach shań) v.
break in; burglarize
włamanie (vwa-ma-ne) n. burglary ; house breaking
włamywacz (vwa-mi-vach) m. burglar; housebreaker; picklock
własnoręcznie (vwa-sno-rańch-ne)
adv. personally; with one's
hand ; with one's own hand
własność (vwas-noshch) f. property ; characteristic feature
własnowolny (vwas-no-vol-ni)
adj. m. spontaneous ;voluntary
własny (vwas-ni) adj. m. own;very
właściciel (vwash-chee-chel) m.
proprietor ; holder ;owner
właściwy (vwash-chee-vi) adj.m.
proper ; right; suitable; due
właściwość (vwash-chee-voshch) f.
propriety; characteristic
właśnie (vwash-ne) adv. exactly;
just so; precisely; very;just
as;just now;just then;only just

wraz (vwas) m. manhole ;hatch
włazić (vwa-żheech) v. crawl
in ; barge in; step in;go deep
włączać (vwown-chach) v. include; switch on; plug in
włącznie (vwownch-ne) adv. in-
clusively; inclusive;including
włączenie (vwown-che-ne) n.
inclusion ; merger ;incorporation
włochaty (vwo-kha-ti) adj. m.
hairy ; shaggy; hirsute;nappy
włos (vwos) m. hair ; fur
włosień (vwo-sheń) m. trichina
włoski (vwos-kee) adj.m. Italian; of Italy
włoskowaty (vwos-ko-va-ti) adj.
m. capillary ; hairlike (tubes)
włoszczyzna (vwozh-chiz-na) pl.
vegetables ; Italian studies
włościanin (vwosh-cha-neen) m.
farmer ; peasant ; country man
włożyć (vwo-zhich) v. put in
włóczęga (vwoo-chań-ga) m.
tramp ;rover; vagrant;roam
włóczka (vwooch-ka) f. yarn
włócznia (vwooch-na) f. spear
włóczyć (vwoo-chich) v. drag
włókienniczy (vwo-kyen-nee-chi)
adj. m. textile(trade,fiber etc.)
włókniarz (vwook-nash) m.
weaver; textile worker
włóknisty (vwook-nees-ti) adj.
m. fibrous; stringy;thready
włókno (vwook-no) n. fibre
wmawiać (vmav-yach) v. talk
into; persuade; make believe
wmieszać się (vmye-shach shań)
v. interfere; join; mix;mingle
wmuszać (vmoo-shach) v. force
(upon) ; press upon directly
wnet (vnet) adv. soon; shortly;
wnęka (vnań-ka) f. niche ;recess
wnętrze (vnań-tzhe) n. interior
wnętrzności (vnantzh-nosh-chee)
pl. bowels ; intestines;entrails
Wniebowzięcie (vne-bo-vzhań-che)
n. Assumption put in; infer;
wnieść (vneshch) v. carry in ;
gather;conclude
wnikać (vnee-kach) v. penetrate
wnikliwy (vnee-klee-vi) adj. m.
penetrating;discerning;piercing
wniosek (vno-sek) m. conclusion;
proposition; suggestion;motion

wnioskodawca (vnos-ko-dav-tsa)
m. mover; giver of a motion
wnioskować (vnos-ko-vaćh) v.
conclude; deduct;infer; gather
wnioskowanie (vnos-ko-va-ńe)
n. conclusion; inference
wnosić (vno-sheećh) v. carry in;
conclude; infer; gather
wnuczka (vnooch-ka) f. granddaughter
wnuk (vnook) m. grandson
wnyk (vnik) m. snare
woalka (vo-al-ka) f. veil(hat)
wobec (vo-bets) prep. in the
face of; before; towards
woda (vo-da) f. water;froth; bull
wodnisty (vod-nees-ti) adj. m.
watery; wishy-washy;aqueous
wodno-płatowiec (vod-no-pwa-to-
vyets) m. hydroplane;water plane
wodny (vod-ni) adj. m. water-
wodociąg (vo-do-chownk) m. waterworks ; water tap
wodolecznictwo (vo-do-lech-neets-
tvo); n. hydrotherapy;water cure
wodopój (vo-do-pooy) m. watering spot ; cow-pond;water hole
wodorost (vo-do-rost) m. seaweed; alga
wodorowa bomba (vo-do-ro-va
bom-ba) f. H-bomb
wodospad (vo-do-spat) m. waterfall; cascade
wodotrysk (vo-do-trisk) m. fountain; waterspout
wodować (vo-do-vaćh) v. launch
on water ; splash down(on water)
wodowstręt (vo-do-vstrańt) m.
hydrophobia; rabies
wodor (vo-door)m. hydrogen
wodza (vo-dza) f. rein;hold;sway
wodzić (vo-dzheećh) v. lead;run
wodzirej (vo-dzhee-rey) m. dance
leader; ringleader;bell wether
w ogóle (vo-goo-le) adv. generally; on the whole; in the main
wojak (vo-yak) m. warrior;soldier
wojenny (vo-yen-ni) adj. m. military; war;wartime; of war
wojewodztwo (vo-ye-voodz-tvo) n.
province; voivodeship
wojłok (voy-wok) m. felt (thick)

wojna (voy-na) f. war ;warfare
wojna domowa (voy-na do-mo-va)
f. civil war
wojować (vo-yo-vaćh) v. wage
war ; combat; contend
wojowniczy (vo-yov-nee-chi)
adj. m. warlike; aggresive
wojownik (vo-yov-neek) m.
(tribal) warrior
wojsko (voy-sko) n. army;troops
wojskowosc (voy-sko-voshćh) f.
military science;the army
wojskowy (voy-sko-vi) adj.m.
military ; army(post etc.)
wokalny (vo-kal-ni) adj. m.
vocal _[all around
wokoło (vo-ko-wo) adv. round;
wola (vo-la) f. will;volition
wolec (vo-lech) v. prefer
wolno (vol-no) adv. slowly
wolnomysliciel (vol-no-mi-
shlee-chel) m.freethinker
wolnosć (vol-noshćh) f. liberty; freedom ; independence
wolnosciowy (vol-nosh-cho-vi)
adj. m. for liberation
wolny (vol-ni) adj. m. free
wolt (volt) m. volt
woltomierz (vol-to-myesh) m.
voltmeter
wołać (vo-waćh) v. call;cry
wołanie (vo-wa-ńe) n. call;cry
wołowina (vo-wo-vee-na) f.
beef
wonny (von-ni) adj. m. fragrant;aromatic; sweet-smelling
woniec (vo-ńech) v. scent;
smell ; be fragrant
won (von) f. fragrance
woreczek (vo-re-chek) m. small
bag ; pouch; cyst
worek(vo-rek) m. bag ; sack
wosk (vosk) m. wax
woskować (vos-ko-vaćh) v. wax
wozic (vo-zheećh) v. carry (on
wheels); transport;drive;cart
wozownia (vo-zov-na) f. coach
house
woznica (vozh-nee-tsa) m. coach-
man ;driver; waggoner
wożenie (vo-zhe-ńe) n. transport; transportation;carriage

wódka (voód-ka) f. vodka

wódz (voots) m. commander;chief

wójt (vooyt) m. village mayor

wół (voow) m. ox ;steer;bullock

wór (voor) m. (big) sack(ful)

wówczas (voóv-chas) adv. then;
that time; at the time

wóz (voos) m. car; cart;wagon

wózek (voó-zek) m. (small) car

wpadać (vpa-dać) v. fall in;
rush in; drop in;run into

wpajać (vpa-yach) v. put in
(head); implant; instill

wpatrywać się (vpa-trí-vach
shań) v. stare;look intently

wpełzać (vpéw-zach) v.crawl in;
creep in(into a cave etc.)

wpędzać (vpań-dzach) v. drive
sb in;bring on sb...(death etc)

wpić się (vpeech shań) v. sink
into; penetrate; bury(teeth)

wpierw (vpyerv) adv. first

wpis (vpees) m. enrollment

wpisać (vpeé-sach) v. write in

wpisowe (vpee-só-ve) n. registration fee;inscription fee

wplatać (vplá-tach) v. twine
in; weave; braid ;intersperse

wplątać (vplówn-tach) v. entangle; implicate;involve

wpłacać (vpwa-tsach) v. pay in

wpłata (vpwá-ta) f. payment

wpław (vpwaf) adv. (swim)across

wpływ (vpwif) m. influence; income ; effect; impact of

wpływać (vpwi-vach) v. flow in;
influence ; have effect

wpływowy (vpwi-vó-vi) adj. m.
influential

w pobliżu (v po-blee-zhoo) adv.
near ;in the vicinity;close by

w poprzek (v pó-pzhek) prep.
adv. across; crosswise

wpół (vpoow) adv. in half; halfway ; half past;half-;semi-

w pośród (v pósh-rood) adv.
among ;in the midst of

wprawa (vprá-va) f. skill;
practice ; proficiency

wprawdzie (vpráv-dzhe) adv. in
truth ; to be sure; indeed

wprawić (vprá-veech) v. set in;
train in ; insert; put in

wprawny (vpráv-ni) adj. m.
skillful ;trained; experienced

wprost (vprost) adv. directly;
straight ahead; outright;simply

wprowadzenie (vpro-va-dzé-ńe) n.
introduction; initiation

wprowadzać (vpro-vá-dzach) v.
usher; introduce; lead in;put in

wprzęgać (vpzhań-gach) v. harness, (horse, river etc)

wprzód (vpshoot) adv. ahead; before; first; in the first place

wpuszczać (vpoósh-chach) v. let
in; admit; insert;allow to enter

wpychać (vpí-khach) v. push in

wracać (vrá-tsach) v. return

wrastać (vrás-tach) v grow in

wraz (vras) prep., together

wrażenie (vra-zhé-ńe) n. impression;sensation;feeling;thrill

wrażliwosc (vrazh-lee-voshch) f.
sensitivity ; susceptibility

wrażliwy (vrazh-leé-vi) adj. m.
sensitive ; thin-skinned;tender

wreszcie (vrésh-che) adv. at
last;finally; after all;eventually

wręcz (yránch) adv. down right

wręczac (vrań-chach) v. hand in

wrodzony (vro-dzó-ni) adj. m.
innate; inborn; inbred;congenital

wrogi (vro-gee) adj. m. hostile

wrogosć (vró-goshch) f. hostility; ill-will; enmity;malevolence

wrona (vró-na) f. crow

wrota (vró-ta) n. gate

wrotki (vrót-kee) pl. roller
skates

wróbel (vroó-bel) m. sparrow

wrócic (vroó-cheech) v. return

wróg (vrook) m. foe; enemy

wróżba (vroózh-ba) f. omen

wróżbiarz (vroózh-byash) m.
fortune-teller ; soothsayer

wróżka (vroózh-ka) f. fortune-
teller ;palmist; fairy

wrożyć (vroo-zhich) v. tell
fortunes; foretell ;predict

wryć się (vrich shań) v. dig in;
sink in ; imbed

wrzask (vzhask) m. scream;yell

wrzaskliwy (vzhas-kleé-vi) adj.
m. shrill;piercing; clamorous

wrzawa (vzha-va) f. noise
wrzący (vzhown-tsi) adj. m.
boiling ; scalding (hot)
wrzątek (vzhown-tek) m. boiling
water
wrzeciono (vzhe-cho-no) n.
spindle ; verge
wrzec (vzhech) v. boil ; rage
wrzesien (vzhe-shen) m. September
wrzeszczec (vzhesh-chech) v.
shriek ; yell; scream; cry
wrzos (vzhos) m. heather
wrzosowisko (vzho-so-vees-ko)
n. heath; moor
wrzod (vzhoot) m. abscess
wrzucac (vzhoo-tsach) v. throw
in; drop in; put in; cast
wsadzac (vsa-dzach) v. put in;
plant ; stick; lock sb up
wschodni (vskhod-nee) adj. m.
east; easterly; eastern
wschodzic (vskho-dzheech) v.
shoot up; rise; sprout
wschod słonca (vskhood swon-
tsa) m. sunrise
wsiadac (vsha-dach) v. get in;
mount; get on board; take seat
wsiąkac (vshown-kach) v. sink
in; infiltrate ;percolate
wskazany (vska-za-ni) adj. m.
advisable;indicated;desirable
wskazowka (vska-zoov-ka) f.
hint; direction; (clock) hand
wskazujący palec (vska-zoo-yown-
tsi pa-lets) m. forefinger
wskazywac (vska-zi-vach) v.
point out;show; indicate
wskaznik (vskazh-neek) m. index; pointer; indicator;signal
w skos (v skos) adv. slant
wskros (vskrosh) prep. through
wskutek (vskoo-tek) prep. as
a result; due to; thanks to
wskrzesic (vskzhe-sheech) v.
resuscitate; revive;wake;recall
wspaniałomyslny (vspa-na-wo-
mishl-ni) adj. m. magnanimous
wspaniałosc (vspa-na-woshch) f.
splendor; grandeur;lordliness
wspaniały (vspa-na-wi) adj. m.
superb; glorious; grand;great;
smashing; magnificient;splendid

wsparcie (vspar-che) n. support
wspierac (vspye-rach) v. support ; prop up; assist; help
wspinac się (vspee-nach shan)
v. climb up;toil up hill;rear
wspomagac (vspo-ma-gach) v. help
wspominac (vspo-mee-nach) v.
remember ; recall; mention
wspornik (vspor-neek) m. cantilever (beam);bracket; support
wspolnik (vspool-neek) m. partner; accomplice ; associate
wspolny (vspool-ni) adj. m. common ; joint; combined ;collective
wspołczesnosc (vspoow-ches-noshch)
f. the present time (day,age)
wspołczesny (vspoow-ches-ni) adj.
m. contemporary ; modern ;present
wspołczucie (vspoow-choo-che) n.
sympathy ; compassion ;pity
wspołczynnik (vspoow-chin-neek)
m. coefficient ; factor
wspołdziałac (vspoow-dzha-wach)
v. cooperate ; act jointly
wspołistniec (vspoow-eest-nech)
v. coexist
wspołistnienie (vspoow-eest-ne-
ne) n. coexistence
wspołpraca (vspoow-pra-tsa) f.
cooperation ; team-work
wspołrzędna (vspoow-zhand-na) f.
coordinate axis
wspołudział (vspoow-oo-dzhaw) m.
participation; share
wspołwłasciciel (vspoow-vwash-
chee-chel) m. joint owner
wspołzawodnictwo (vspoow-za-vod-
neets-tvo) m. competition
wspołzawodnik (vspoow-za-vod-
neek) m. competitor; rival
wspołzyc (vspoow-zhich) v. get
along; live together; coexist
wstawac (vsta-vach) v. get up
wstawiac (vsta-vyach) v. set in
wstawiac się (vsta-vyach shan) v.
get tipsy; plead for sb
wstąpic (vstown-peech) v. step
in; drop in; step up; enter
wstążka (vstownzh-ka) f. ribbon
wstecz (vstech) adv. backwards
wsteczny (vstech-ni) adj. m.
reactionary; reverse;backward

wstęga (vstán-ga) f. (large) ribbon ; band;sash;wreath;wisp

wstęp (vstánp) m. entrance; admission ; preface; opening

wstępny (vstánp-ni) adj. m.introductory ; initial;preliminary

wstręt (vstránt) m. aversion

wstrętny (vstránt-ni) adj. m. hideous ; foul;vile; nasty

wstrząs (vstzhówns) m. shock

wstrząsający (vstzhówn-sa-yówn-tsi) adj. m. shocking; thrilling

wstrzemięźliwość (vstzhe-myán-żhleé-vośhch) f. moderation

wstrzemięźliwy (vstzhe-myán-żhleé-vi) adj. m. moderate

wstrzykiwać (vstzhi-keé-vach) v. inject; give a shot

wstrzymać (vstzhi-mach) v. stop; abstain; put off; hold back

wstyd (vstid) m. shame; dis - grace;dishonor;indecency

wstydliwy (vstid-leé-vi) adj.m. shy; bashful; timid;embarassing

wstydzić się (vsti-dźheech śhán) v. be ashamed; blush for sb

wsunąć (vsoo-nównch) v. slip in; put in; insert into;tuck in

wsypa (vsí-pa) f.a bad break; gaffe; give-away of a plot

wsypać (vsí-pach) v. pour in; tell on somebody; pour (grain)

wszakże (vshák-zhe) conj. adv. yet; however; nevertheless

wszcząć (vshównch) v. start; be-gin; institute; enter (talks)

wszechmocny (vshekh-móts-ni) adj. m. omnipotent; almighty

wszechnica (vshekh-neé-tsa) f. university

wszechstronny (vshekh-strón-ni) adj. m. universal; versatile

wszechświat (vshekh-śhvyat) m. universe; cosmos ; macrocosm

wszelki (vshél-kee) adj. m. every; all; any; whatever

wszerz (vshesh) adv. broadside

wszędzie (vshán-dźhe) adv. every-where; on all sides ;all over

wszystek (vshís-tek) adj. m. whole; all; ever; the whole

wszywać (vshí-vach) v. sew in

wścibski (vśhcheéb-skee) m. busybody; meddler; snooper

wściekać się (vśhché-kach śhán) v. rage; rave; be furious

wścieklizna (vśhche-kleéz-na) f. rabies ; madness;hydrophobia

wściekłość (vśhchek-wośhch) f. fury; rage; tantrums;madness

w ślad (vśhlad) adv. following in tracks; following closely

wśliznąć się (vśhleéz-nównch śhán) v. sneak in; slip in

wśród (yśhroot) prep. among

wtaczać (vta-chach) v. roll in

wtajemniczyć (vta-yem-neé-chich) v. initiate; acquaint;instruct

wtargnąć (vtarg-nównch) v. in-vade; break into; interrupt

wtedy (vte-di) adv. then

wtem (vtem) adv. suddenly

wtenczas (vtén-chas) adv. then; at that time; at this junction

wtoczyć (vtó-chich) v. roll in

wtorek (vto-rek) m. Tuesday

wtórny (vtoór-ni) adj. m. sec-ondary ; incidental;repeated

wtrącać się (vtrówn-tsach śhán) v. meddle; cut into; butt in

wtyczka (vtích-ka) f. plug

wtykać (vti-kach) v. insert

w tył (vtiw) adv. back

wuj (vooy) m. uncle

wujenka (voo-yén-ka) f. aunt

wulgarny (vool-gár-ni) adj. m. vulgar; coarse; low

wulkan (vool-kan) m. volcano

wulkanizować (vool-ka-neé-zó-vach) v. vulcanize ;cure(rubber)

wwozić (v-vó-żheech) v. import

wwóz (v-voos) m. import;importation

wy (vi) pron. you; you people

wybaczać (vi-ba-chach) v. for-give; pardon; buckle out of line

wybawca (vi-báv-tsa) m. savior; rescuer; liberator ;redeemer

wybawić (vi-bá-veech) v. save; deliver ; free;rescue; rid

wybebeszyć (vi-be-bé-shich) v. gut (chicken etc.)

wybić (vi-beéch) v. knock out (something); strike; cover;kill

wybiec (vi-byets) v. run out

wybieg (vi-byek) m. evasion;
runway; playground; fowl run
wybielic (vi-bye-leech) v. whitewash; bleach; coat with tin
wybierac (vi-bye-rach) v. choose
elect; select; pick out ; mine
wybierak (vi-bye-rak) m. selec-
tor (technical term)
wybieralny (vi-bye-rál-ni) adj.
m. elective; eligible ; electable
wybitny (vi-beet-ni) adj. m.
prominent; eminent ; marked
wybladły (vi-blád-wi) adj. m.
pale; dim; faded; colorless
wybłagac (vi-bwa-gach) v. get by
entreaty; impetrate
wyblakły (vi-blák-wi) adj. m.
faded; dim; dilute; weathered
wyboisty (vi-bo-ees-ti) adj.m.
rough; full of holes; bumpy
wyborca (vi-bor-tsa) m. voter
wyborczy (vi-bor-chi) adj. m.
electoral; election-(precinct...)
wyborny (vi-bor-ni) adj. m. excellent; prime; choice; splendid
wyborowy (vi-bo-ro-vi) adj. m.
choice; select; first rate
wybory (vi-bo-ri) pl. election
wybor (vi-boor) m. choice; option
wybrany (vi-bra-ni) adj. m.
elected; chosen; selected
wybredny (vi-bréd-ni) adj. m.
fastidious; particular; exacting
wybrnąc (vibr-nownch) v. get out;
pull through; wade; clear out of
wybrukowac (vi-broo-kó-vach) v.
pave (the road, the street etc.)
wybryk (vi-brik) m. prank; freak;
antic; whim; frolic; caprice
wybrzeże (vi-bzhe-zhe) n. coast;
beach; sea-shore; sea-coast
wybrzuszenie (vi-bzhoo-she-ñe)
n. bulge; swelling; knob; belly
wybuch (vi-bookh) m. explosion;
eruption; outbreak; outburst
wybudowac (vi-boo-do-vach) v.
build ; erect; raise; construct
wycelowac (vi-tse-lo-vach) v.
take aim; level a gun at
wychodek (vi-khó-dek) m. privy
wychodzic (vi-kho-dzheech) v.
get out; walk out; climb out

wychodzca (vi-khodzh-tsa) m.
emigrant; émigré
wychowac (vi-khó-vach) v. bring
up; rear; rise; train; educate
wychowanek (vi-kho-vá-nek) m.
pupil; alumnus; ward; foster child
wychowanie (vi-kho-vá-ñe) n.
upbringing; manners; education
wychowawca (vi-kho-váv-tsa) m.
tutor; educator; foster father
wychudły (vi-khóod-wi) adj. m.
gaunt; skinny; haggard; emaciated
wychwalac (vi-khvá-lach) v.
praise; exalt; extol; speak highly
wychylac (vi-khí-lach) v. stick
out; empty (glass); bend; incline
wychylac się (vi-khi-lach shañ)
v. lean out; stick one's neck
out; hang out; appear; be visible
wyciąg (vi-chownk) m. extract;
elevator; hoist; winch; excerpt
wyciągac (vi-chown-gach) v.
pull out; stretch out; derive;
wycie (vi-che) n. howl; scream
wycieczka (vi-chéch-ka) f. trip;
excursion; outing; ramble; hike
wyciekac (vi-ché-kach) v. leak
out; flow out; ooze out; scamper
wycieńczac (vi-cheñ-chach) exhaust
wycieńczenie (vi-cheñ-che-ñe) n.
exhaustion; weakness; debility
wycieraczka (vi-che-rach-ka) f.
wiper; doormat
wycierac (vi-che-rach) v. wipe;
erase; efface; dust; wear out
wycięcie (vi-chán-che) n. opening; cut; décolleté; notch; jag
wycinac (vi-chee-nach) v. cut
out ; carve out; fell; cut down
wycisk (vi-cheesk) m. press;
squeeze; beating (slang)
wyciskac (vi-chees-kach) v.
squeeze out; impress; wring
wycofac (vi-tsó-fach) v. withdraw; remove; retract; call off
wycofanie (vi-tso-fa-ñe) n .
withdrawal; recall; retirement
wyczerpac (vi-chér-pach) v.
exhaust; drain; deplete; scoop
wyczerpanie (vi-cher-pa-ñe) n.
exhaustion; depletion; prostration
wyczesywac (vi-che-si-vach) v.
comb out; dress hair (beard etc.)

wyczuwać (vi-choo-vach) v. sense;
feel; scent; ascertain; perceive
wyczyn (vi-chin) m. feat; stunt
wyczyszczać (vi-chish-chach) v.
clean; brush; clean out; polish
wyć (vich) v. howl; roar; shriek
wyćwiczony (vich-vee-cho-ni)
adj. m. trained; skilled
wydajność (vi-day-noshch) f.
yield; productivity; output
wydajny (vi-day-ni) adj. m.
productive ; effective
wydalać (vi-da-lach) v. dismiss;
sack ; expel; eliminate; excrete
wydalenie (vi-da-le-ne) n. expulsion ; dismissal; excretion
wydanie (vi-da-ne) n. edition
wydarty (vi-dar-ti) adj. m.
torn out; plucked out; snached out
wydarzać się (vi-da-zhach shañ)
v. happen; turn out well; occur
wydarzenie (vi-da-zhe-ne) n.
event ; happening; circumstance
wydatek (vi-da-tek) m. expense
wydatkować (vi-dat-ko-vach) v.
spend ; lay out funds; expend
wydatny (vi-dat-ni) adj. m.
prominent; salient; distinct
wydawać (vi-da-vach) v. spend;
give the change; publish
wydawca (vi-dav-tsa) m. publisher; editor; publishing house
wydawnictwo (vi-dav-neets-tvo)
n. publication; publishing
house; publishing firm
wydąć (vi-downch) v. expand;
puff up; inflate ; blow up
wydech (vi-dekh) m. exhalation
wydeptać ścieżkę (vi-dep-tach
shchezh-kañ) beat a path (exp.)
wydłubywać (vi-dwoo-bi-vach) v.
scrape out; poke; hollow out
wydłużać (vi-dwoo-zhach) v. prolong; lengthen; elongate
wydma (vid-ma) f. dune; snowdrift
wydobrzeć (vi-dob-zhech) v. recover; get better ; improve
wydobycie (vi-do-bi-che) n, output; yield; production
wydobywać (vi-do-bi-vach) v. extract; mine; wring; get; obtain
wydostać (vi-dos-tach) v. bring
out; extricate; obtain; pull out

wydra (vi-dra) f. otter; vulg.:
bitch; hussy; minx; vixen
wydrapać (vi-dra-pach) v.
scratch out; erase a stain
wydrapać się (vi-dra-pach shañ)
v. climp up; scramble up (out)
wydrążać (vi-drown-zhach) v.
hollow out ; drill; excavate
wydrwić (vi-drveech) v. jeer;
mock; cheat; gibe; deride
wydrwigrosz (vi-drvee-grosh)
m. swindler; fraud; take-in
wydusić (vi-doo-sheech) v.
squeeze out; extort; strangle
wydychać (vi-di-khach) v.
breathe out; exhale; emit
wydymać (vi-di-mach) v. puff out;
inflate ; belly out; blow up; bulge
wydział (vi-dzhaw) m. department
wydziedziczać (vi-dzhe-dzhee-
chach) v. disinherit
wydzielać (vi-dzhe-lach) v. emit;
detach; distribute; secrete
wydzielenie (vi-dzhe-le-ne) n.
secretion; assignment; elimination ; emanation; issue
wydzieliny (vi-dzhe-lee-ni) pl.
sercreta; excretions; discharge
wydzielony (vi-dzhe-lo-ni) adj.
m. emited; segregated; alloted
wydzierać (vi-dzhe-rach) v. tear
out; roar out ; blare out; scramble
wydzierżawić (vi-dzher-zha-veech)
v. lease; farm out ; rent; let out
wydzierżawienie (vi-dzher-zha-
vye-ne) n. leasing; renting
wyegzekwować (vi-eg-zek-vo-vach)
v. exact; enforce ; carry out
wyekwipowanie (vi-ek-vee-po-va-
ne) n. outfit; equipment
wyeleganciec (vi-e-le-gan-chech)
v. acquire elegance; become elegant
wyeliminowanie (vi-e-lee-mee-no-
va-ne) n. elimination; exclusion
wyga (vi-ga) m. old experienced
hand; sly fox; old stager
wygadać (vi-ga-dach) v. blab out
wygadany (vi-ga-da-ni) adj. m.
glib; eloquent; wordy; talkative
wyganiać (vi-ga-ñach) v. expel;
chase out ; turn out (cattle)
wygarniać (vi-gar-ñach) v. rake
out; tell off ; say openly; shoot

wygasać (vi-ga-sach) v. extinguish; expire; go out; die out

wyginać (vi-gee-nach) v. bend

wygląd (vig-lownd) m. appearance;aspect; air; looks; semblance

wyglądać (vig-lown-dach) v. look out; appear;appear; look

wygładzać (vi-gwa-dzach) v. smooth;level;even; sleek

wygłodzić (vi-gwo-dżheech) v. starve out; underfeed; famish

wygłosić (vi-gwo-sheech) v. pronounce; utter;deliver(speech)

wygnać (vig-nach) v.expel;banish

wygnanie (vig-na-ne) n. exile

wygniatać (vi-gna-tach) v. press out; squeeze out; extort; kill

wygoda (vi-go-da) f. comfort

wygodny (vi-god-ni) adj. m. comfortable; cozy; handy

wygolony (vi-go-lo-ni) adj. m. clean-shaven; well shaven

wygotować (vi-go-to-vach) v. boil away; distill; prepare

wygórowany (vi-goo-ro-va-ni) adj. m. excessive; stiff(price)

wygrać (vi-grach) v. win; score

wygramolić się (vi-gra-mo-leech shan) v. scramble up (out)

wygrana (vi-gra-na) f. winning; victory; prize; a win

wygryzać (vi-gri-zach) v. 1.bite out; corrode; 2. drive out by harassment;oust;bore a hole

wygrzebywać (vi-gzhe-bi-vach) v. dig out; unearth; rake out

wygrzewać się (vi-gzhe-vach shan) v. bask; warm oneself

wygwizdać (vi-gveez-dach) v. hiss off (stage); whistle away

wyjałowic (vi-ya-wo-veech) v. sterilize; exhaust(brain,soil...)

wyjaśnić (vi-yash-neech) v. explain; clear up; elucidate

wyjaśnienie (vi-yash-ne-ne) n. explanation; interpretation

wyjawić (vi-ya-veech) v. disclose;reveal; bring to light

wyjazd (vi-yazt) m. departure

wyjąkać (vi-yown-kach) v. stammer out;stutter out; falter out

wyjątek (vi-yown-tek) m. exception; excerpt; extract

wyjątkowy (vi-yown-ko-vi) adj. m. exceptional;unusual;unique

wyjechać (vi-ye-khach) v. drive away; leave ;come out with

wyjeżdżać (vi-yezh-dzhach) v. leave; drive away ; set out

wyjmować (viy-mo-vach) v. take out; remove; extract; excerpt

wyjście (viysh-che) n. exit; way out; departure;egress

wyka (vi-ka) f. vetch ; tare

wykadzić (vi-ka-dżheech) v. smoke out; fumigate; perfume

wykałaczka (vi-ka-wach-ka) f. toothpick

wykarczować (vi-kar-cho-vach) v. grub out; clear;dig up(trees)

wykaz (vi-kas) m. list; register; roll; schedule;docket

wykąpać (vi-kown-pach) v. bathe

wykipieć (vi-keep-yech) v. boil over (milk,water,soup etc.)

wyklęty (vi-klan-ti) adj. m. cursed; excommunicated

wykluczyć (vi-kloo-chich) v. exclude; expel; shut out ;except

wykład (yik-wat) m. lecture

wykładać (vi-kwa-dach) v. lecture; lay out ; display; cover

wykładnik (vi-kwad-neek) m. exponent; expression; ratio

wykładowca (vi-kwa-dov-tsa) m. lecturer ; instructor

wykłuwać (vi-kwoo-vach) v. stab out; put out; tattoo;prick out

wykoleic (vi-ko-le-eech) v. derail; lead astray;ditch(a train)

wykombinować (vi-kom-bee-no-vach) v. contrive; think out

wykonać (vi-ko-nach) v. execute; do; fulfil ; carry out; perform

wykonalny (vi-ko-nal-ni) adj.m. feasible ; workable;realizable

wykonanie (vi-ko-na-ne) n. execution;realization;fulfilment

wykonawczy (vi-ko-nav-chi) adj. m. executive ;executory(details...)

wykończenie (vi-kon-che-ne) n. finish ; trimming;last touch

wykończyć (vi-kon-chich) v. finish off ; dress; do sb in

wykop (vi-kop) m. excavation ; potato lifting; flying kick

wykopać (vi-ko-pach) v. dig out
wykopalisko (vi-ko-pa-lees-ko)
n. find (archaeological)
wykorzenić (vi-ko-zhe-ñeech) v.
  root out ; uproot; eradicate
wykorzystać (vi-ko-zhis-tach) v.
  take advantage ; exploit;use up
wykpić (vik-peech) v. deride
wykraczać (vi-kra-chach) v. step
  over; break law; transgress
wykradać (vi-kra-dach) v. steal;
  kidnap ;purloin;pilfer;abduct
wykrajać (vi-kra-yach) v. cut
  out ; carve out;make a low cut
wykres (vi-kres) m. graph; chart
wykreslić (vi-kresh-leech) v.
  trace; cross out ; draw ;erase
wykręcać (vi-kran-tsach) v. screw
  out; distort; elude ; twist
wykręt (vi-krant) m. shift;
  excuse ; dodge ;guibble
wykrętny (vi-krant-ni) adj. m.
  shifty ;evasive; sophistical
wykroczenie (vi-kro-che-ñe) n.of-
  fense ; misdemeanor;delinquency
wykroić (vi-kro-eech) v. cut out
wykruszyć (vi-kroo-shich) v.
  crumble out ; shell(corn etc.)
wykryć (vi-krich) v. discover;
  detect ; reveal(the truth etc.)
wykrztusić (vi-kzhtoo-sheech) v.
  cough up; choke out ;hawk up
wykrzyknąć (vi-kzhik-nownch) v.
  call out ; shout; cry out
wykształcić (vi-kzhtaw-cheech) v.
  educate ; train; shape; form
wykup (vi-koop) m. ransom
wykupić (vi-koo-peech) v. buy up
wykurzać (vi-koo-zhach) v. smoke
  out (foxes,bees, etc.)
wykwintny (vi-kveent-ni) adj.m.
  elegant; exquisite ; urbane
wyleczalny (vi-le-chal-ni) adj.
  m. curable;possible to cure
wyleczyć (vi-le-chich) v. cure
wylew krwi (vi-lev krvee)
  hemorrhage; blood effusion
wylewać (vi-le-vach) v. pour out;
  overflow;spill;bail out water
wylęgać (vi-lan-gach) v. hatch
wylękły (vi-lank-wi) adj. m.
  frightened ; scared ;terrified

wyliczać (vi-lee-chach) v.
  count up; count out; recite
wylosować (vi-lo-so-vach) adj.
  m. draw out by lots ;toss for
wylot (vi-lot) m.flight departure; nozzle; exhaust; exit
wyludniać (vi-lood-nach) v.
  depopulate;desolate;devastate
wyładowac (vi-wa-do-vach) v.
  unload; discharge; cram;pack
wyładowanie (vi-wa-do-va-ñe)
  n. unloading; discharge
wyłamać (vi-wa-mach) v. break
  out;break loose;break away
wyławiać (vi-wav-yach) v. fish
  out; spot out; catch (a sound)
wyłaniać (vi-wa-ñach) v. evolve;
  emerge; show; appoint;form
wyłączać (vi-wown-chach) v.
  exclude; switch off;disconnect
wyłącznik (vi-wownch-ñeek) m.
  switch; circuit-breaker;cut off
wyłączny (vi-wownch-ni) adj.
  m. exclusive; sole; only;entire
wyłudzić (vi-woo-dzheech) v.
  coax; beguile; trick; fool
wyłom (vi-wom) m. breach; gap
wyłuskać (vi-woos-kach) v. husk;
  scale; fleece; shell; hull; pod
wymaczać (vi-ma-chach) v. soak
wymagać (vi-ma-gach) v. require;
  expect; demand; need; exact
wymaganie (vi-ma-ga-ñe) n. requirement; demand;requisite;need;
                              want
wymawiać (vi-mav-yach) v. pronounce; reproach; cancel;express
wymazać (vi-ma-zach) v. erase;
  efface; blot out; smear; use up
wymiana (vi-mya-na) f. exchange
wymiar (vi-myar) m. dimension
wymiatac (vi-mya-tach) v.
  sweep out; clean out; sweep
wymieniac (vi-mye-ñach) v.
  exchange; convert; replace
wymierać (vi-mye-rach) v. die
  out; become extinct(gradually)
wymierzać (vi-mye-zhach) v. aim;
  measure; assess; survey;mete out
wymię (vi-myań) n. udder evade
wymijać (vi-mee-yach) v. pass by;
wymiotować (vi-myo-to-vach) v.
  vomit; be sick;spew up(one's food)

wymogi (vi-mó-gee) pl. require-
ments; exigencies;needs
wymowa (vi-mó-va) f. pronunciation; significance(of facts...)
wymowny (vi-móv-ni) adj. m.
eloquent; telltale; telling
wymoc (vi-moots) v. extort;
compel; wring; force;prevail
wymówienie (vi-moov-ye-ńe) n.
notice (to quit or dismiss)
wymówka (vi-moóv-ka) f. reproach;
pretext; excuse; put-off;evasion
wymusić (vi-moó-shich) v. extort
wymuszenie (vi-moo-she-ńe) n.
extortion;blackmail;shakedown
wymykać się (vi-mi-kach śhań)
v. escape;slip away;sneak out
wymysł (vi-misw) m. fiction;
invention ;fiction; abuse
wymyślać (vi-miśh-lach) v. think
up; call names; invent; abuse
wymyślny (vi-miśhl-ni) adj. m.
clever ; ingenious;sophisticated
wymywać (vi-mi-vach) v. wash out
wynagradzać (vi-na-grá-dzach) v.
reward; pay; indemnify;make up
wynagrodzenie (vi-na-gro-dze-ńe)
n. reward; pay; fee; reparation
wynajdywać (vi-nay-dí-vach) v.
find (out); invent; devise
wynajmować (vi-nay-mo-vach) v.
hire ; rent   ʃrent; hire
wynajem (vi-ná-yem) m. lease ;
wynalazca (vi-na-láz-tsa) m.
inventor; contriver
wynalazek (vi-na-lá-zek) m. invention ; device;contrivance
wynaleźć (vi-ná-leżhch) v. invent
wynaradawiać (vi-na-ra-dáv-yach)
v. denationalize ; divest
wynik (vi-ńeek) m. result; score
wyniosłość (vi-ńos-woshch) f.
eminence; haughtiness ; prance
wyniosły (vi-ńos-wi) adj. m.
lofty; high-handed ;insolent
wyniszczać (vi-ńeesh-chach) v.
ruin ; exhaust; weaken;devastate
wynosić (vi-nó-sheech) v. carry
out; elevate; amount ;wear out
wynudzać (vi-noó-dzach) v. get
by bothering; bore stiff
wynurzenie (vi-noo-zhe-ńe) n.
emergence; (personal) outpouring

wyobraźnia (vi-o-bráżh-ńa) f.
imagination ; fancy;empty fancy
wyobrażać (vi-o-brá-zhach) v.
imagine; picture; fancy;suppose
wyobrażenie(vi-o-bra-zhé-ńe) n.
notion; idea ; image;representation
wyodrębniać (vi-od-ránb-ńach)
v. single out; separate; isolate
wyodrębnienie (vi-od-ranb-ńe-
ńe) n. separation; isolation
wyolbrzymiać (vi-ol-bzhí-myach)
v. magnify; exaggerate(very much)
wypaczyć (vi-pá-chich) v. warp
wypad (ví-pat) m. sally; attack
wypadać (vi-pá-dach) v. fall
out; rash out; become; turn
out; happen; occur; work out
wypadek (vi-pa-dek) m. accident;
case ;event; chance;instance
wypadkowa (vi-pad-kó-va) f. resultant (force, effect etc.)
wypakować (vi-pa-kó-vach) v.
unpack; cram ; pack tight
wypalać (vi-pá-lach) v. burn out
wypaplać (vi-páp-lach) v. babble
out ; blurt out(the truth,secret)
wyparcie się (vi-par-che śhań)
n. disclaimer ; repudiation
wyparować (vi-pa-ro-vach) v.
evaporate ; vanish into thin air
wypatrywać (vi-pa-trí-vach) v.
watch (for) ; look out;espy;descry
wypełniać (vi-pew-ńach) v. fulfil; fill up ; while away;fill in
wypełnienie (vi-pew-ńe-ńe) n.
fulfilment ; order execution;filler
wypędzać (vi-pán-dzach) v. drive
out; expel ; discharge;dislodge
wypiekać (vi-pyé-kach) v. bake;
wypierać (vipyé-rach) v. oust;
push out;force out;supplant
wypierać się (vi-pye-rach śhań)
v. deny ; repudiate;disown;abjure
wypijać (vi-pee-yach) v. drink
(empty); drink to; drink off
wypinać (vi-pee-nach) v. extend;
strech out ; show one's back side
wypis (vi-pees) m. extract;passage
wypisywać (vi-pee-sí-vach) v.
(write) extract;make out(a check)
wyplątać (vi-plown-tach) v.
extricate ; disentangle;disengage;
free from tangles

wyplątany (vi-plown-tá-ni) adj.
m. disembroiled;extricated
wyplenić (vi-ple-ñeech) v. weed
out; root out; eradicate
wypluć (vi-plooch) v. spit out
wypłacać (vi-pwa-tsach) v. pay
out; pay up; pay off; repay
wypłacalny (vi-pwa-tsal-ni) adj.
m. solvent; sound(financially)
wypłata (vi-pwa-ta) f. pay (day)
wypłoszyć (vi-pwo-shich) v.
scare away; drive away (cats...)
wypłowieć (vi-pwo-vyech) v. fade
wypłukać (vi-pwoo-kach) v. rinse;
wash out; swill out ;give a rinse
wypływ (vi-pwiv) m. outflow;
discharge; efflux; leakage
wypływać (vi-pwi-vach) v. flow
out; sail out; swim out; rise
wypocić (vi-po-cheech) v. sweat
out; perspire ;be soaked in sweat
wypoczynek (vi-po-chí-nek) m.
rest; repose
wypoczywać (vi-po-chí-vach) v.
rest;have a rest;take a rest
wypogadzać się (vi-po-ga-dzach
shań) v. clear up; cheer up
wypomnieć (vi-pom-ñech) v. reproach; remind ;keep reminding
wyporność (vi-por-noshch) f.
displacement; draught ;buoyancy
wyposażać (vi-po-sa-zhach) v.
equip; endow; fit out; stock
wyposażenie (vi-po-sa-zhe-ñe) n.
equipment; outfit; wages ;dowry
wyposażyć (vi-po-sa-zhich) v.
endow; equip; fit out ;stock
wypowiadać (vi-po-vya-dach) v.
pronounce; declare ; express
wypowiedzenie (vi-po-vye-dze-ñe)
n.(discharge) notice; (war) declaration; renunciation;utterance
wypożyczać (vi-po-zhi-chach) v.
lend out ;borrow from;hire to
wypożyczalnia (vi-po-zhi-chal-ña)
f. rental business ;rental agency
wypracowanie (vi-pra-tso-va-ñe)
n. (school) composition; elaboration ;essay; exercice
wyprać (vi-prach) v. wash out
wypraszać (vi-pra-shach) v.
1. plead; 2. show (the door) ;
give somebody the gate;turn out

wyprawa (vi-prá-va) f. expedition; outfit; tanning;dowry
wyprawiac (vi-pra-vyach) v.
send; tan;plaster;give(a party)
wyprężać (vi-pran-zhach) v.
stretch out; tense(a muscle etc.)
wyprostowac (vi-pros-to-vach)
v. straighten;set streight
wyprowadzać (vi-pro-va-dzach)
v. lead out; move out; trace
wypróbować (vi-proo-bó-vach)
v. test; try out;put to test
wypróżniac (vi-proozh-ñach) v.
empty; clear out; evacuate
wyprzedawać (vi-pzhe-dá-vach)
v. sell out; clear out(stock)
wyprzedaż (vi-pzhe-dash) v.
(clearance) sale
wyprzedzać (vi-pzhe-dzach) v.
pull ahead;outpace;overtake
wyprzęgać (vi-pzhan-gach) v.
unharness; unhitch (a horse)
wypukły (vi-pook-wi) adj. m.
convex; bulging; cambered
wypuścić (vi-poosh-cheech) v.
let out; set free; let go;
omit;release;launch;lease out
wypychac (vi-pi-khach) v. oust;
push out; stuff;pack; fill;cram
wypytywac (vi-pi-ti-vach) v.
question;ask questions;inquire
wyrabiac (vi-rá-byach) v.
1. make; form; 2. play pranks
wyrachowany (vi-ra-kho-vá-ni)
adj. m. scheming; thrifty
wyratować (vi-ra-to-vach) v.
rescue; save (a life etc.)
wyraz (vi-ras) m. word; expression; look; term (in vocabulary)
wyraźny (vi-rázh-ni) adj. m.
explicit; clear; distinct
wyrażać (vi-ra-zhach) v. express
wyrażenie (vi-ra-zhe-ñe) n.
expression; utterance; phrase ;
statement
wyrąb (vi-rownp) m. clearing;
felling; cutting ; slash;fell
wyrąbać (vi-rown-bach) v. cut
out (with axe); clear; hack out
wyręczać (vi-ran-chach) v. help
out; replace; relieve of tasks
wyrobnik (vi-rob-ñeek) m. laborer; day-laborer ; navvy

wyrocznia (vi-róch-ña) f. oracle

wyrodny (vi-ród-ni) adj. m. degenerate;unnatural (son);base

wyrodzić się (vi-ró-dźheećh śháñ)
v. degenerate;deteriorate

wyrok (ví-rok) m. sentence; verdict; judgment,; pronouncement

wyrostek (vi-rós-tek) m. out-
growth; stripling; teenager

wyrośnięty (vi-rosh-nán-ti)adj.
m. grown up ; overgrown

wyrozumiały (vi-ro-zoo-myá-wi)
adj. m. indulgent; lenient

wyrozumienie (vi-ro-zoo-myé-ñe)
n. sympathetic understanding

wyrób (vi-roob), m. manufacture

wyrównać (vi-roóv-nach) v.
equalize; pay up; smooth

wyrównanie (vi-roov-ná-ñe) m.
leveling;balancing(accounts)offset

wyróżniać (vi-roózh-ñach) v.
distinguish ; favor; single out

wyruszyć (vi-roó-shićh) v. start
out;set out;march out;sail away

wyrwać (vir-vach) v. extract;
tear out; pull out; run away

wyrywki (vi-riv-kee) pl. random

wyryć (vi-rićh) v. engrave; root
up; dig out;gully;furrow;incise

wyrzec się (vi-zhets śháñ) v.
renounce;give up; forgo;repudiate

wyrzucać (vi-zhoo-tsach) v. expel; throw out; dump; reproach

wyrzut (vi-zhoot) m. reproach

wyrzutnia (vi-zhoot-ña) f. launch
(ing)pad; chute; launcher

wyrzutek (vi-zhoo-tek) m. outcast

wyrzynać (vi-zhi-nach) v. cut out;
carve; slaughter; bang; slap

wysadzić (vi-sá-dźheećh) v. set
out;land; blow up ; eject;plant

wyschnąć (vís-khnówñćh) v. dry up

wysepka (vi-sép-ka) f. islet

wysiadać (vi-śha-dach) v. get out
(from car etc.); go bust;get off

wysiadywać (vi-śha-di-vach) v.
sit out; hatch out; sit late

wysiedlać (vi-śhed-lach) v. expel (from home). resettle;eject

wysilać (vi-śhee-lach) v. exert

wysiłek (yi-śhee-wek) m. effort

wyskoczyć (vi-skó-chićh) v. jump
out; pop up;run out;bale out

wyskok (vís-kok) m. 1. fling;
freak; 2. cam ;ledge;run out

wyskokowy (vis-ko-kó-vi) adj.
m. alcoholic; intoxicating

wyskrobać (vi-skro-bach) v.
scratch out; erase ;scratch

wyskubać (vi-skoó-bach) v.
pluck out; pull out(hair etc.)

wysłać (vi-swach) v. send off;
dispatch ;emit; let fly

wysłaniec (vi-swa-ñets) m.
messenger; envoy ; deputy

wysłowić (vi-swó-veećh) v. express ;say; utter; speak

wysłuchać (vi-swoo-khach) v.
hear out ;give a hearing

wysługiwać się (vi-swoo-gee-
vach śháñ) v. lackey; use s.o.

wysmarować (vi-sma-ro-vach) v.
smear ;lubricate; soil;stain

wysmażony (vi-sma-zhó-ni) adj.
m. well done (meat);cooked

wysmukły (vi-smoók-wi) adj.m.
slender ; slim and tall

wysoce (vi-só-tse) adv. highly

wysoki (vi-só-kee) m. tall;
high ; soaring; lofty;towering

wysokość (vi-só-koshćh) f.
height; altitude;level;extent

wysokościomierz (vi-so-kosh-cho-
myesh) m. altimeter

wyspa (vís-pa) f. island; isle

wyspać się (vís-pach śháñ) v.
sleep enough; sleep off

wyspowiadać się (vis-po-vya-
dach śháñ) v. confess

wyssać (vís-sach) v. suck out ;
suck dry

wystarać się (vi-stá-rach śháñ)
v. procure ;obtain; secure

wystarczyć (vi-stár-chićh) v.
suffice ; do enough;be enough

wystawa (vi-stá-va) f. exhibition; display (window dressing)

wystawać (vi-stá-vach) v. stand
out; stand long time ;stick out

wystawca (vi-stáv-tsa) m. exhibitor; signer (of check)

wystawiac (vi-stáv-yach) v.
put out; stick out; sign
(check) ; exhibit ;expose

wystawienie (vi-sta-vyé-ñe) n.
exposition; exposure ;display

wystąpić (vi-stówn-peech) v.
step forward;perform;resign
wystąpienie (vi-stówn-pye-ñe)
n. withdrawal; appearance
występ (vi-stånp) m. protrusion;
(stage) appearance; utteramce
występek (vi-stáñ-pek) m. felony; crime; vice,; offenße
występny (vi-stañp-ni) adj. m.
criminal; immoral; illicit
wystraszyć (vi-strá-shich) v.
frighten away; terrify; scare
wystroić (vi-stró-eech) v. dress
up ; trig out; deck out; adorn
wystrzał (vi-stzhaw) ṃ. shot
wystrzegać się (vi-stzhé-gach
sháñ) v. avoid ; beware; shun
wystrzelić (vi-stzhe-leech) v.
fire a gun ;shoot out; go off
wystrzępić (vi-stzháñ-peech) v.
ravel out ; fray,; unravel
wystygać (vi-sti-gach) v. cool
off ; grow cold,;get cold
wysuszyć (vi-soo-shich) v. dry
up ; wither;parch; shrivel
wysuwać (vi-soo-vach) v. shove
forward ; protrude; put out
wyswobodzic (vi-svo-bo-dźheech)
v. liberate; deliver ; free
wysychać (vi-si-khach) v. dry out
wysypać (vi-si-pach) v. pour out
wysypka (vi-sip-ka) f. (skin)
rash ; eruption ;exanthema
wysysać (vi-si-sach) v. suck
wyszczególnić (vi-shche-gool-
ñeech) v, specify;detail out
wyszeptać (vi-sheptach) v. whis-
per(not vibrating the vocal chords)
wyszkolić (vi-shko-leech) v.
train ;school; educate ;instruct
wyszpiegować (vi-shpye-gó-vach)
v. spy out; spy out that...
wyszukać (vi-shoo-kach) v. find
out ; hunt up; search out
wyszukany (vi-shoo-ká-ni) adj.m.
choice; unusual ; elaborate
wyszydzać (vi-shi-dzach) v.
scoff at ; jeer; deride
wyszynk (vi-shink) m. liquor
store; liquor retail on licence
wyszywać (vi-shi-vach) v. embroider;desing with needlework

wyścielać (vi-śhćhé-lach) v.
pad; line; strew;cushion
wyścig (vish-cheek) m. race;
contest ; rivalry ;(horse)race
wyśledzic (vi-śhle-dźheech) v.
spy out; track out ;detect
wyśliznąć się (vi-śhleez-nównch
shañ) y. slip out;slide out
wyśmiac (vish-myach) v. laugh
at; deride ;mock;ridicule
wyśmienity (vish-mye-ñee-ti)
adj. m. choice; excellent
wyśpiewać (vi-śhpye-vach) v.
squeal; sing; say ;sound praises
wyświadczyć (vish-vyád-chich)
v. do (favor); do (good);do (wrong)
wyświechtany (vi-śhvyekh-tá-ni)
adj. m. well worn; beat up
wyświetlać (vish-vyét-lach) v.
clear up; project (film)
wytaczać (vi-tá-chach) v. roll
out ; set forth; draw ;turn
wytargować (vi-tar-gó-vach) v.
buy by haggling; haggle a lot
wytarty (vi-tár-ti) adj.m.
worn out; thread bare;shabby
wytchnąć (vi-tkhnównch) v. rest
up ; relax ;take a rest;breathe
wytchnienie (vi-tkhñe-ñe) n.
rest; break; relax; truce
wytępić (vi-táñ-peech) v.extermi-
nate ; eradicate; wipe out
wytężać (vi-tañ-zhach) v. strain
wytknąć (vit-knównch) v. put out;
point out; reproach; trace
wytłuc (vi-twoots) v. kill off;
break up ; ruin; beat up
wytłumaczenie (vi-two-ma-che-
ñe) n. explanation; excuse
wytłumaczyć (vi-twoo-má-chich)
v. explain; excuse; justify
wytrawny (vi-tráv-ni) adj. m.
experienced; dry (wine);seasoned
wytrącać (vi-trówn-tsach) v.
knock of; deduct; snatch
wytrwały (vi-trvá-wi) adj. m.
enduring; persevering; dogged
wytrwanie (vi-trvá-ñe) n. endurance; persistence ;lasting
wytrwać (vi-trvach) v. persevere
wytrych (vi-trikh) m. pick-a-
-lock; pass-key; skeleton-key

wytrząsć (vi-tzhōwnshch) v.
shake out ; empty ; jolt
wytrzebić (vi-tzhe-beech) v.
devastate; exterminate ; clear
wytrzeźwieć (vi-tzhezh-vyech) v.
sober up ;get sober; sober down
wytrzymać (vi-tzhi-mach) v. endure; stand ;hold out; keep
wytrzymałosć (vi-tzhi-ma-woshch)
f. endurance ; stamina ;strength
wytrzymały (vi-tzhi-ma-wi) adj.
m. enduring ; tough; durable
wytworny (vi-tvor-ni) adj. m.
exquisite ;elegant; stylish
wytwórca (vi-tvoor-tsa) m. producer; manufacturer ; maker
wytwórczosć (vi-tvoor-choshch)
v. productivity ; output ;product
wytwornia (vi-tvoor-ña) f. manufacture; factory; plant ;works
wytyczna (vi-tich-na) f. direc-
tive; guideline: guiding rule
wyuzdanie (vi-ooz-da-ñe) n. unbridled license ;adv.dissolutely
wywiad (vi-vyat) m. interview;
reconnaissance ; espionage
wywiazać się (vi-wyōwn-zach shañ)
v. develop; arise; discharge
(duty); result; set in; evolve
wywierać (vi-vye-rach) v. exert
wywiercać (vi-vyer-tsach) v. bore
out; sink a well;drill a hole
wywlekać(vi-vle-kach) v. drag
out ; tug; bring out ;pull out
wywietrzać (vi-vyet-zhach) v.
ventilate ; air; nose out
wywłaszczać (vi-vwash-chach) v.
expropriate ;dispossess
wywłaszczenie (vi-vwash-che-ñe)
n. expropriation;dispossession
wywnioskować (vi-vnos-ko-vach)
v. infer; draw a conclusion
wywodzić (vi-vo-dzheech) v. lead
out; derive ; deduce ;lead nowhere
wywojować (vi-vo-yo-vach) v.
fight out ; gain by force
wywołać (vi-vo-wach) v. call;
cause; develop (film); recall
wywozić (vi-vo-zheech) v. export
wywód (vi-voot) m. deduction
wywoz (vi-voos) m. export ;removal
wywracać (vi-vra-tsach) v. overturn; overthrow; reverse ;upset

wywyzszać (vi-vizh-shach) v.
exalt; elevate;extol;rise
wyzbyć się (viz-bich shañ) v.
get rid;sell out;get over
wyzdrowieć (vi-zdro-vyech) v.
recover; get well;recuperate
wyziębić (vi-zhañ-beech) v.
chill ;let get cold ;cool
wyzionąc (vi-zho-nownch) v.
expire; give up(the ghost)
wyznaczać (vi-zna-chach) v.
mark out; appoint; point out
wyznanie (vi-zna-ñe) n. denomination; declaration ;creed
wyznawać (vi-zna-vach) v. profess;
declare; hold a belief;confess
wyznawca (vi-znav-tsa) m. believer; follower; advocate
wyzuć (vi-zooch) v. deprive;
take off (shoe); strip;divest;
bereave
wyzywać (vi-zi-vach) v. challenge ; call names;abuse;revile
wyzwalać (vi-zva-lach) v. liberate; free;let loose; exempt
wyzwolenie (vi-zvo-le-ñe) n .
liberation; release; exemtion
wyzwolić (vi-zvo-leech) v. liberate; free; release; set free
wyzysk (vi-zisk) m. exploita-
tion; sweating(of labor)
wyzyskiwacz (vi-zis-kee-vach) m.
exploiter; slave driver
wyż (vizh) m. hight; highland;
high pressure; peak; atm.high
wyżarty (vi-zhar-ti) adj. m.
over-fed; corroded; bloated
wyżej (vi-zhey) adv. higher;
above ; mentioned above;higher up
wyżeł (vi-zhew) m. pointer
wyżerać (vi-zhe-rach) v. eat
away; corrode; erode; eat up
wyżłobić (vi-zhwo-beech) v.
hollow out ;gully; erode;groove
wyżłobienie (vi-zhwo-bye-ñe) n.
groove; gully; erosion;channel
wyższosć (vizh-shoshch) f. superiority; excellence;predominance
wyższy (vizh-shi) adj. m. higher
(up); taller; superior;top(floor)
wyżyć (vi-zhich) v. use up;
hardly live ; make ends meet;
pull through;survive;pull through;
find an outlet for...

wyżyć się (vi-zhich shan) v.
live up; fulfill oneself
wyżymaczka (vi-zhi-mach-ka) f.
wringer (also machine)
wyżymać (vi-zhi-mach) v. wring
wyżyna (vi-zhi-na) f. high
ground; upland;summit(of glory)
wyżywić (vi-zhi-veech) v. feed
wyżywienie (vi-zhi-vye-ne) m.
food; board; subsistance;diet
wzajemny (vza-yem-ni) adj. m.
mutual; reciprocal; inter-
w zamian (vza-myan) adv. in
exchange; instead; in return
wzbić się (vzbeech shan) v.
soar (up); shoot up; rise
wzbogacić (vzbo-ga-cheech) v.
enrich; add to; dress;make rich
wzbraniać (vzbra-nach) v. forbid; prohibit
wzbroniony (vzbro-no-ni) adj.m.
forbidden; prohibited
wzbudzać (vzboo-dzach) v. excite; inspire;arouse; stir
wzburzenie (vzboo-zhe-ne) n.
agitation; unrest; tumult
wzburzyć (vzboo-zhich) v. stir
up; agitate;dishevel;covulse
wzdąć (vzdownch) v. puff up;fan
wzdłuż (vzdwoosh) prep. along
wzdrygać się (vzdri-gach shan)
v. flinch; object; shudder
wzdychać (vzdi-khach) v. sigh
wzgarda (vzgar-da) f. contempt
wzgardliwy (vzgard-lee-vi) adj.
m. disdainful; scornful
względność (vzgland-noshch) f.
relativity (of understanding...)
względny (vzgland-ni) adj. m.
relative; indulgent; kind of
względy (vzglan-di) pl. favors
wzgórze (vzgoo-zhe) n. hill
wziąć (vzhownch) v. take;possess
wziernik (vzher-neek) m. peep-
hole; scope;view-finder;spy-hole
wzięty (vzhan-ti) adj. m. popular;in demand; in vogue
wzlot (vzlot) m. ascend; rise
wzmacniać (vzmats-nach) v. reinforce; brace up; fortify
wzmagać (vzma-gach) v. intensify
wzmianka (vzmyan-ka) v. mention

wzniesienie (vzne-she-ne) n.
elevation; height;erection
wznieść (vzneshch) v. raise;
elevate; erect; lift; rear
wzniosły (vznos-wi) adj. m.
lofty; noble; elevated;sublime
wznowić (vzno-veech) v. renew
wznowienie (vzno-vye-ne) n.
resumption; come back;reissue
wzorowy (vzo-ro-vi) adj. m.
exemplary ;model; perfect
wzór (vzoor) m. pattern; model;
formula; fashion; standard
wzrok (vzrok) m. sight; vision
wzrost (vzrost) m. growth;size;
height; increase; rise;stature
wzruszać (vzroo-shach) v. move;
touch; affect; thrill; stir
wzruszający (vzroo-sha-yown-tsi)
adj. m. touching; moving;pathetic
wzuć (vzooch) v. put on (shoe)
wzuwacz (vzoo-vach) m. shoe
horn(for pulling boots,shoes on)
wzwyż (vzvizh) adv. up; upwards
skok wzwyż (skok vzvizh) m.
high jump
wzywać (vzi-vach) v. call; call
in; summon; cite; ask in
z (z) prep. with; off; together
ze (ze) prep. with; off; together;from(the ceiling etc.)
za (za) prep. behind; for; at;
by; beyond; over(a wall)
zabarwić (za-bar-veech) v. stain;
dye ; tint; color;tinge;tincture
zabarwienie (za-bar-vye-ne) n.
color(ing); pigmentation; tinge
zabawa (za-ba-va) f. play; fun;
party; game; recreation;amusement
zabawiać (za-bav-yach) v. entertain ;amuse;dwell;stay; last
zabawka (za-bav-ka) f. toy;trife
zabawny (za-bav-ni) adj. m.
funny; comical; ridiculous
zabezpieczenie (za-bez-pye-che-
ne) n. protection ; safety
zabezpieczyć (za-bez-pye-chich)
v. safeguard; secure ;protect
zabić (za-beech) v. kill; slay;
plug up; nail down;beat(a card)
zabieg (za-byek) m. measure;
procedure; exertions; fuss

zabiegać (za-bye-gach) v. strive;
try hard; court; woo; fuss over
zabierać (za-bye-rach) v. take
away; take along;take on (up)
zabierać się (za-bye-rach shan)
v. clear out; get ready for
zabijać (za-bee-yach) v. kill;
deaden ; wear out; exhaust
zabijaka (za-bee-ya-ka) m. bully;
blusterer ; swaggerer; hector
zabity (za-bee-ti) adj. m. killed; dead; out-and-out;thorough
zabliźniać (za-bleezh-nach) v.
form cicatrize ; scar up
zabłądzić (za-bwown-dzheech) v.
go astray; get lost ; stray
zabłąkany (za-bwown-ka-ni)adj.
m. stray (bullet, man,steer,etc)
zabłocić (za-bwo-cheech) v. get
muddy ; muddy (shoes etc)
zabobon (za-bó-bon) m. superstition;belief in omens,stars etc.
zaboleć (za-bó-lech) v. ache
zaborca (za-bór-tsa) m. invader
zabójca (za-booy-tsa) m. killer
zabójczy (za-booy-chi) adj. m.
murderous ; seductive ;lethal
zabójstwo (za-booy-stvo) n. killing; murder ; homicide
zabór (za-boor) m. annexed territory ; annexation;rape(of Peru..)
zabraniać (za-bra-nach) v. forbid
zabrudzać (za-broo-dzach) v. dirty;
soil; make a mess (of something)
zabudować (za-boo-dó-vach) v.
build over; build upon; close
zabudowania (za-boo-do-va-na) pl.
buildings (on farm,factory etc.)
zaburzenie (za-boo-zhe-ne) n.
disorder; rout; agitation
zabytek (za-bi-tek) m. relic;
monument(of art,nature etc.)
zachcianka (zakh-chan-ka) f. fad;
fancy; caprice ; whim ;megrim
zachęta (za-khan-ta) f. encouragement; stimulus ;incentive;spur
zachłanność (za-khwan-noshch) f.
greed ; rapacity ;cupidity
zachłysnąć się (za-khwis-nównch
shan) v. choke;swallow a bad way
zachmurzyć (za-khmoo-zhich) v.
cloud; become gloomy;overcloud

zachmurzenie (za-khmoo-zhe-ne)
n. cloudiness; gloom;gloominess
zachodzić (za-kho-dzheech) v.
call on; occur; arise; become;
set; creep from behind;drop in
zachodni (za-khód-nee) adj. m.
western; westerly
zachorować (za-kho-ró-vach) v.
get sick; fall ill;be taken ill
zachowanie (za-kho-va-ne) n.
behavior; maintainance;manners
zachowawczy (za-kho-váv-chi)
adj. m. conservative
zachowywać (za-kho-vi-vach) v.
preserve; maintain;keep(calm)
zachowywać się (za-kho-vi-vach
shan) v. behave; survive;go on
zachód (za-khoot) m. west;sunset;
pains; trouble; endeavor
zachód słońca (za-khoot swon-
tsa) m. sunset
zachrypnięty (za-khrip-nan-ti)
adj. m. hoarse;of a hoarse voice
zachwalać (za-khva-lach) v.
praise; crack up;boost;cry up
zachwiać (zakh-vyach) v. rock;
shake; unsettle (balance etc.)
zachwycać (za-khvi-tsach) v.
fascinate; charm ;delight;enchant
zachwyt (zakh-vit) m. fascination; rapture ;enchantment
zaciąg (za-chowng) m. recruit-
ment; levy; draft ;conscription
zaciągać (za-chown-gach) v.
recruit; drag to; run in debt
zaciekać (za-che-kach) v. leak;
stain; run down ; fill(up)
zaciekawić (za-che-ka-veech) v.
interest; puzzle; intrigue
zaciekawienie (za-che-ka-vye-ne)
n. interest; curiosity
zaciekły (za-chek-wi) adj. m.
stubborn; bitter; rabid;stiff
zaciemnić (za-chem-neech) v.
obscure; dim; darken ;black out
zacieniać (za-che-nach) v.
shade; darken ;throw shade
zacierać (za-che-rach) v. efface; erase; hush up ;cover up
zaciesniać (za-chesh-nach) v.
tighten up ; narrow; limit
zacięty (za-chan-ti) adj. m.
obstinate ; stubborn ;dogged

zacinać (za-chee-nach) v. notch;
cut; lash; hack; taper;set(teeth)
zaciskać (za-chees-kach) v.
tighten; clench; squeeze;clasp
zacisze (za-chee-she) n. retreat
zacny (zats-ni) adj. m. worthy;
good; upright;respectable
zacofany (za-tso-fa-ni) adj.m.
backward;old fashioned
zaczaić się (za-cha-eech shan)
v. lie in ambush; lurk; hide
zaczarować (za-cha-ro-vach) v.
enchant; bewitch; cast a spell
zacząć (za-chownch) v. start;
begin; fire away; go ahead
zaczepiać (za-chep-yach) v.
hook on; accost; touch upon
zaczepny (za-chep-ni) adj. m.
aggressive; offensive;provocative
zaczerpać (za-cher-pach) v.
scoop up; dip up; draw; lade
zaczerwienić (za-cher-vye-neech)
v. redden; blush; flush;paint red
zaczynać (za-chi-nach) v. start;
begin; cut (into a new loaf)
zaćmienie (zach-mye-ne) n. e-
clipse ; obfuscation
zad (zad) m. posterior; rump
zadać (za-dach) v. give; put;
deal; associate; treat with
zadanie (za-da-ne) n. task; charge; assignment; problem;job;stint
zadatek (za-da-tek) m. earnest
money; down payment;installment
zadławić (za-dwa-veech) v. choke
zadłużyć się (za-dwoo-zhich shan)v.
get in debt;debit; take mortgage
zadłużenie (za-dwoo-zhe-ne) n.
debts; indebtedness; liabilities
zadowalający (za-do-va-la-yown-
tsi) adj. m. satisfactory; fair
zadowolić (za-do-vo-leech) v.
satisfy; gratify; please;suffice
zadowolony (za-do-vo-lo-ni) adj.
m. satisfied ; content;pleased
zadra (za-dra) f. sliver; splinter (in one's finger etc.)
zadrapać (za-dra-pach) v. scratch
open; make a scratch; scratch
zadrasnąć (za-dras-nownch) v.
scratch ; wound (pride etc)
zadrażnić (za-drazh-neech) v.
irritate; embitter; inflame

zadrgać (zadr-gach) v. twitch;
vibrate ; tremble; flicker
zadrwić (za-drveech) v. sneer
zaduch (za-dookh) m. bad air;
stuffy air; stink;fustiness;fug
zaduma (za-doo-ma) f. meditation; reverie;musing;wistfulness
zadusić(za-doo-sheech) v.throttle;
smother; choke ;strangle;suffocate
Zaduszki (za-doosh-kee) n.
All Souls Day
zadymka (za-dim-ka) f. snow-
storm; blizzard
zadyszany (za-di-sha-ni) adj.
m. breathless; panting
zadzierać (za-dzhe-rach) v.
tear open; turn up; quarrel
zadzierżysty (za-dzher-zhis-
ti) adj. m. defiant; perky
zadziwiać (za-dzheev-yach) v.
astonish; amaze; astound
zadzwonić (za-dzvo-neech) v.
ring; ring up ; ring for
zagadka (za-gad-ka) f. puzzle;
riddle ; crux; problem;quizz
zagadnienie (za-gad-ne-ne) n.
problem ; question; issue
zagajnik (za-gay-neek) m. grove
shubbery ; scrub ;coppice;copse
zagiąć (za-gyownch) v. bend
zaginiony (za-gee-no-ni) adj.
m. lost ; missing (person)
zaglądać (za-glown-dach) v.
peep; look up; look into
zagłada (za-gwa-da) f. extinc-
tion ; extermination;annihilation
zagłębić (za-gwan-beech) v.
plunge; sink; dip;immerse
zagłodzic (za-gwo-dzheech) v.
starve to death; starve out
zagłuszać (za-gwoo-shach) v.
silence; jam; drown out; stifle
zagmatwać (za-gmat-vach) v.
entangle; confuse; embroil
zagniewany (za-gne-va-ni) adj.
m. angry; cross; sore;in a huff
zagospodarowywać (za-gos-po-da-
ro-vi-vach) v. make property
productive ; manage (an estate)
zagotować (za-go-to-vach) v.
boil; start boiling; flare up
zagrabić (za-gra-beech) v. rake
over; grab; seize;carve out

zagradzac (za-gra-dzach) v. bar;
fence; obstruct; intercept
zagranica (za-gra-nee-tsa) f.
foreign countries;ouside world
zagraniczny (za-gra-neech-ni)
adj. m. foreign;external(trde...)
zagrazac (za-gra-zhach) v.
threaten; impend;be imminent
zagroda (za-gro-da) f. farm
house with yard; enclosure
zagrodzic (za-gro-dzeech) v.
fence in; bar; enclose;obstruct
zagrozony (za-gro-zho-ni) adj.
m. threatened; endangered
zagrzebac (za-gzhe-bach) v.
bury (in the grave,in the past...)
zagrzewac (za-gzhe-vach) v.heat;
warm up; animate;inspire;spur
zahaczac (za-kha-chach) v. hook;
question; accost;find fault
zahamowac (za-kha-mo-vach) v.
restrain; put brakes on; stop
zaimek (za-ee-mek) m. pronoun
zainteresowanie (za-een-te-re-
so-va-ne) n. interest;concern
zaiste (za-ees-te) adv. truly;
indeed; very true; verily; yea
zajadac (za-ya-dach) v. enjoy
eating ; gorge;eat heartily
zajadly (za-yad-wi) adj. m.
fierce; rabid;bitter driveway
zajazd (za-yazt) m. motel; inn;
zajac (za-yownts) m. hare
zajac (za-yownch) v. occupy
zajechac (za-ye-khach) v. drive
up; block; stump; pull in ;stink
zajecie (za-yan-che) v. occupation ; work;trade; interest
zajmowac(zay-mo-vach) v. occupy
zajmujacy (zay-moo-yown-tsi) adj.
m. interesting; absorbing
zajscie (zaysh-che) n. incident
zakalec (za-ka-lets) m. slack
baked bread (or cake)
zakatarzony (za-ka-ta-zho-ni)
adj. m. having a cold
zakatowac (za-ka-to-vach) v.
flog to death;torture to death
zakaz (za-kas) m. prohibition
zakazic (za-ka-zheech) v. infect
zakazywac (za-ka-zi-vach) v.
forbid; ban; suppress;prohibit;
forbid to do;suppress(activity..)

zakazny (za-kazh-ni) adj. m.
infectious ; contagious
zakaska (za-kowns-ka) f. snack
zaklecie (za-klan-che) n. spell;
curse; incantation;charm;entreaty
zaklad pogrzebowy (za-kwat po-
gzhe-bo-vi) m. funeral parlor
zaklad (za-kwat) m. plant;shop;
institute; bet; wager; fold
zakladac (za-kwa-dach) v.
found; initiate; put on; lay
zakladka (za-kwad-ka) f. fold;
book- mark;tuck;pleat;splice
zakladnik (za-kwad-neek) m.
hostage (for ransom etc.)
zaklamanie (za-kwa-ma-ne) n.
hypocrisy ;mendacity;distortion
zaklopotanie (za-kwo-po-ta-ne)
n. embarrassment;confusion
zaklocac (za-kwoo-tsach) v.
disturb; unsettle;ruffle
zakluwac (za-kwoo-vach) v. stab
to death ; prick ;stick (a pig)
zakochac sie (za-ko-khach shan)
v.fall in love ;become infatuated
zakochany (za-ko-kha-ni) adj.m.
in love ; infatuated;enamorated
zakomunikowac (za-ko-moo-nee-ko-
vach) v. communicate; let
know; convey a message; notify
zakon (za-kon) m. monastic
order ;convent; sisterhood
zakonnica (za-kon-nee-tsa) f.
nun ;religious (woman)
zakonnik (za-kon-neek) m. monk
zakonczenie (za-kon-che-ne) n.
end; ending; termination;tip
zakopac (za-ko-pach) v. bury
zakorkowac (za-kor-ko-vach) v.
plug up;cork up;jam(the traffic)
zakorzenic sie (za-ko-zhe-neech
shan) v. get roots in;take roots
zakorzeniony (za-ko-zhe-no-ni)
adj. m. rooted; deep rooted
zakradac sie (za-kra-dach shan)
v. creep; steal; sneak(into)
zakrapiac (za-krap-yach) v.
put drops in; sprinkle; have
a drink;instil(in one's eyes)
zakres (za-kres) m. range;field;
scope; domain; sphere;realm
zakreslic (za-kresh-leech) v.
outline; mark off; encircle

zakręcić (za-kran-cheech) v.
turn; twist; turn off; curl
zakręt (za-krant) m. curve;bend
turn ⌐ turnbuckle ; cap; nut;
zakrętka (za-krant-ka) f. latch;
zakrwawić (za-krva-veech) v.
stain with blood;draw blood
zakryć (za-krich) v. cover; hide
zakrzatnąc sie (za-kzhownt-
nownch shan) v.get busy;bustle
zakrztusić (za-kzhtoo-sheech)v.
choke (on food,fish bone etc.)
zakrzywić (za-kzhi-veech) v.
bend; bend down; bend back
zaksięgować (za-kzhan-go-vach)
v. post; enter in the books
zakup (za-koop) m. purchase
zakurzony (za-koo-zho-ni) adj.
m. dusty ;covered with dust
zakuty (za-koo-ti) adj. m.
shackled; chained; dull (witted)
zakwitnąc (za-kveet-nownch) v.
blossom out; go moldy
zalażek (za-lown-zhek) m. germ;
ovule;seed; origin;embryo
zalecać (za-letsach) v. recommend ; advise; enjoin; court; woo
zaledwie (za-led-vye) adv. barely;
scarcely ; merely; but; only just
zalegać (za-le-gach) v. be behind (in paying);lie useless;fill
zaległy (za-leg-wi) adj. m. unpaid; overdue;unaccomplished
zalepić (za-le-peech) v. glue(up)
over; gum up; paste over;seal up
zalesienie (za-le-she-ne) n.
forestation ; afforestation
zaleta (za-le-ta) f. virtue;
advantage ; quality; good point
zalew (za-lev) m. flood; bay;
invasion ; deluge;lagoon
zalewać (za-le-vach) v. pour
over; flood;submerge;swarm;spill
zależeć (za-le-zhech) v. depend
zależny (za-lezh-ni) adj.m.
dependent; contingent;subordinate
zaliczać (za-lee-chach) v. in-
dude; count in; credit rate;accept
zaliczka (za-leech-ka) f. earnest
money; down payment;installment
zalotnica (za-lot-nee-tsa) f.
flirt; coquette; kitten(slang)

zalotnik (za-lot-neek) m. suit-
or ; wooer; wheedler
zaloty (za-lo-ti) adj. m.
courtship;wooing;love making
zaludniac (za-lood-nach) v.
populate ;bring in population
zaludnienie (za-lood-ne-ne) n.
population;population density
załadować (za-wa-do-vach) v.
load up; embark;ship(goods)
załagodzic (za-wa-go-dzheech)
v. mitigate; alleviate; soothe
załamać (za-wa-mach) v. break
down; collapse; crash; slump
załamanie (za-wa-ma-ne) n.
break down; (light) refraction
załatwiać (za-wat-vyach) v.
settle; transact; deal;dispose
załączac (za-wown-chach) v.
enclose ; connect;annex;plug in
załącznik (za-wownch-neek) m.
enclosure; attachment; annex
załoga (za-wo-ga) f. crew;
garrison; staff; personnel
założenie (za-wo-zhe-ne) n.
layout; foundation; assumption
założyciel (za-wo-zhi-chel) m.
founder; initiator;promotor
zamach (za-makh) m. attempt;
swing; sweep; coupd'état;spar
zamaczać (za-ma-chach) v. steep;
dip; wet; soak; drench
zamarzły (za-mar-zwi) adj.m.
frozen; frezen over;frozen stiff
zamarznąc (za-mar-znownch) v.
freeze up;freeze over;congeal
zamaskować (za-mas-ko-vach) v.
mask; conceal; hide; disguise
zamaszysty (za-ma-shis-ti) adj.
m. brisk; vigorous;dashing;heavy
zamawiać (za-ma-vyach) v. reserve; order ;book; engage(workers)
zamazać (za-ma-zach) v. smear
over; soil up; daub;blur(a picture)
zamącić (za-mown-cheech) v.ruffle;
disturb; make turbid; stir a liquid
zamąpojście (za-mownzh-pooy-
shche) n. marriage
zamek (za-mek) m. lock; castle
zamek błyskawiczny (za-mek
bwis-ka-veech-ni) m. zipper
zamęt (za-mant) m. confusion;welter

zamężna (za-mánzh-na) adj. f.
married(woman in married state)
zamiana (za-mya-na) f. exchange
zamianowac (za-mya-no-vach) v.
nominate ; appoint;design
zamiar (za-myar) m. purpose ;
zamiast (za-myast) prep. instead of;in place;in lieu
zamiatac (za-mya-tach) v. sweep
zamieć (za-myech) f. snowstorm;
blizzard;snow in a windstorm
zamiejscowy (za-myeys-tso-vi)
adj. m. out of town;long distance
zamienic (za-mye-neech)v. change;
convert; replace;swap;turn into
zamienny (za-myen-ni) adj. m.
exchangeable;interchangeable
zamierac (za-mye-rach) v. die
out; fade out ; wither;die away
zamierzac (za-mye-zhach) v. intend; mean;propose;plan;think
zamierzenie (za-mye-zhe-ne) n.
aim; purpose ; plan; project
zamieszac (za-mye-shach) v. stir
up; blend; mix up ; involve
zamieszanie (za-mye-sha-ne) n.
confusion ; disarray;turmoil;stir
zamieszkac (za-myesh-kach) v.
take up residence ;put up;live
zamieszkiwac (za-myesh-kee-vach)
v. inhabit ; reside ;occupy;live
zamilknać (za-meel-kownch) v.
became silent ; be hushed
zamiłowanie (za-mee-wo-va-ne) n.
predilection ; fondness ;liking
zamknać (zám-known'ch) v. close;
shut; lock ;wind up; fence in
zamoczyc (za-mo-chich) v. wet;
soak; steep; drench ;submerge
zamorski (za-mor-skee) adj. m.
overseas; from overseas
zamożny (za-mozh-ni) adj. m.rich;
wealthy ; affluent ;well to do
zamowic (za-moo-veech) v. order;
reserve ; commission ;book;engage
zamówienie (za-moo-vye-ne) n.
order ; commission ;custom order
zamrażac (za-mra-zhach) v. freeze
zamroczyc (za-mro-chich) v. dim;
gloom; confuse; darken ;bewilder
zamsz (zamsh) m. chamois; suede
zamulic (za-moo-leech) v. fill
with slime ; silt up (a harbor)

zamurowac (za-moo-ro-vach) v.
brick over ; brick up ;wall up
zamydlic (za-mid-leech) v.
soap over ;pull wool over eyes
zamykac (za-mi-kach) v. shut;
conclude ; close (the view etc.)
zamysł (za-misw) m. design
zamyślac sie (za-mish-lach shán)
v. contemplate; muse; ponder
zamyślenie (za-mi-shle-ne) n.
reverie; pondering; meditation
zanadto (za-nad-to) adv. too
much ; excess ;beyond measure
zaniechac (za-ne-khach) v.
give up ; wave; desist from
zanieczyscic (za-ne-chish-cheech)
v. soil ; dirty; litter;grime
zaniedbanie (za-ned-ba-ne) n.
neglect; negligence ;sloppiness
zaniemoc (za-ne-moots) v. become ill ; fall ill ;get sick
zaniemówic (za-ne-moo-veech)
v. become speechless (dumb)
zaniepokoic (za-ne-po-ko-eech)
v. alarm ; up set; disturb
zaniepokojenie (za-ne-po-ko-ye-
ne) n. anxiety ; alarm; concern
zaniesc (za-neshch) v. carry
zanik (za-neek) m. disappearance
zanikac (za-nee-kach) v. disappear ;vanish; decay; wither
zanim (za-neem) conj. before ;
zanocowac (za-no-tso-vach) v.
stay over night ; put up at
zanotowac (za-no-to-vach) v.
note; write down ;take down
zanurzyc (za-noo-zhich) v. dip
zaocznie (za-och-ne) adv. in
absence;(judgement)by default
zaognic (za-og-neech) v. inflame ; irritate ;excite;kindle
zaokraglic (za-o-krowng-leech)
v. round off ; make even
zaopatrzenie (za-o-pa-tzhe-ne)
n. supplies;equipment;provision
zaopatrzyc (za-o-pa-tzhich) v.
provide ; equip; supply ;fit out;
furnish;stock
zaorac (za-o-rach) v. plough
over(a field etc.);plough up
zaostrzyc(za-os-tzhich) v. sharp-
en; whet; tighten (restrictions);
stimulate(the appetite);intensify

zaoszczędzić (za-osh-chąn-
dzheech) v. save ; spare(trouble)
zapach (za-pakh) m. smell;aroma
zapadać (za-pa-dach) v. fall in;
sink ; set in; drop; settle
zapakować (za-pa-kó-vach) v.
pack up ; stow away; pack off
zapalczywy (za-pal-chi-vi) adj.
m. hotheaded; impetuous
zapalenie (za-pa-lé-ńe) n. ignition ; inflammation(of the skin...)
zapaleniec (za-pa-le-ńets) m.
fanatic ; enthusiastic;hot head
zapalić (za-pa-leech) v. switch
on light; set fire ; animate
zapalniczka (za-pal-ńeech-ka)
f. (cigarette) lighter
zapalnik (za-pál-ńeek) m. fuse
zapalny (za-pál-ni) adj. m.
inflammable ; ardent;impetuous
zapał (za-paw) m. enthusiasm
zapałka (za-paw-ka) f. match
zapamiętać (za-pa-myąn-tach) v.
remember ; memorize;keep in mind
zaparcie (za-pár-che) n. constipation; denial
zaparzać (za-pá-zhach) v. draw
(tea);brew; gall;make(tea);heat
zapas (za-pas) m. stock; store;
reserve ; supply ;fund;refill
zapasowy (za-pa-só-vi) adj. m.
spare ; emergency(door,part,etc)
zapaść (za-pashch) v. collapse
zapaśnik (za-pásh-ńeek) m.
wrestler
zapatrywać się (za-pa-tri-vach
śhąn) v. have opinion; consider; stare ; take example
zapatrywanie (za-pa-tri-va-ńe)
n. opinion; view ;slant
zapełnić (za-pew-ńeech) v. fill
up ; stop a gap ;fill(a space etc.)
zaperzyć się (za-pe-zhich śhąn)
v. flare up ; be testy ;get mad
zapewne (za-pev-ne) adv. certainly ; surely; doubtless ;I daresay
zapewnić (za-pev-ńeech) v. assure
zapewnienie (za-pev-ńe-ńe) n. assurance ; protestation ;assertion
zapieczętować (za-pye-chąn-to-
vach) v. seal up;seal with wax
zapierać się (za-pye-rach śhąn)
deny; disavow ;resist;repudiate

zapinać (za-pee-nach) v. button up; fasten;buckle up
zapis (za-pees) m. registration;
bequest; record; notation
zapisać (za-pee-sach) v. note
down; prescribe; enroll; bequeath; record; write down
zapisek (za-pee-sek) m. note
zaplątać (za-plown-tach) v.
entangle ;snarl;involve
zaplecze (za-ple-che) n. hinterland; base(of supplies etc.)
zapłacić (za-pwa-cheech) v. pay
zapłakany (za-pwa-ka-ni) adj.
m. in tears; tearful;tear stained
zapłata (za-pwa-ta) f. payment
zapłodnić (za-pwód-ńeech) v.
fertilize ; inseminate;fecundate
zapłon (za-pwon) m. ignition
zapobiegać (za-po-byé-gach) v.
prevent;avert; ward off;stave off
zapobiegliwy (za-po-bye-glee-
vi) adj. m. anticipating;thrifty
industrious;thrifty;provident
zapodziać (za-pó-dźhach) v.
misplace;mislay; get lost
zapominać (za-po-mee-nach) v.
forget;neglect; unlearn
zapomnienie (za-pom-ńe-ńe) n.
oblivion; forgetfulness
za pomocą (za-po-mó-tsówn) adv.
by means; with help(of a tool...)
zapomoga (za-po-mó-ga) f. hand
out; relief; benefit; grant
zapora (za-pó-ra) f. dam; obstacle ; barrier;check;barrage
zapotrzebowanie (za-po-tzhe-bo-
va-ńe)n. (demand) requisition
zapowiadać (za-po-vya-dach) v.
announce ; forecast; pretend
zapoznać (za-póz-nach) v. acquaint ;introduce;instruct
zapożyczać (za-po-zhi-chach) v.
borrow; adopt from ;take from
zapracować (za-pra-tsó-vach) v.
earn; get by hard work
zapracowany (za-pra-tso-va-ni)
adj. m. earned; overworked
zapraszać (za-pra-shach) v.
invite(to dinner etc.);offer
zaprawa (za-pra-va) f. mortar;v.
seasoning; training ;work out

zaprawdę (za-praw-dán) adv. in deed ; to tell you the truth...

zaprawić (za-pra-veech) v. season ;train; learn;dress;spice

zaproszenie (za-pro-she-ne) n. invitation (to dinner etc.)

zaprowadzić (za-pro-va-dżheech) v. lead in; establish ;initiate

zaprząg (za-zhowng) m. team

zaprzeczać (za-pzhe-chach) v. deny ; contest ; dispute

zaprzeczenie (za-pzhe-che-ne) n. denial ; negation;contradiction

zaprzepaścić (za-pzhe-páshćheech) v. loose; waste ; miss

zaprzestać (za-pzhes-tach) v. discontinue; stop ; cease;quit

zaprzęg (za-pzhang) m. team; cart; harness ; yoke; carriage;turn out

zaprzyjaznić się (za-pżhi-yażhńeech śhán) v. make friends

zaprzysiąc (za-pzhi-shownts) v. swear by oath ;vow; pledge

zaprzysiężony (za-pzhi-shán-zhoni) adj. m. sworn in ;pledged

zapusty (za-poós-ti) pl.carnival; Shrovetide

zapuszczać (za-poósh-chach) v. let in (dye) ; grow (hair); neglect ; let down;sink into

zapychać (za-pi-khach) v. stuff; cram ;fill;block ;choke;crowd

zapytanie (za-pi-tá-ne) n. question; inquiry ; query; asking

zapytywać (za-pi-ti-vach) v. ask

zarabiać (za-ráb-yach) v. earn

zaradczy (za-rád-chi) adj. m. preventive ; remedial(measure)

zaradny (za-rád-ni) adj. m. resourceful (man, boy etc.)

zaranie (za-rá-ne) n. downing

zarastać (za-rás-tach) v. overgrow; cicatrize (a wound)

zaraz (zá-ras) adv. at once; directly;right away; soon

zaraza (za-rá-za) f. infection; plague ; epidemic ;pestilence

zarazek (za-rá-zek) m. virus; germ ; microbe ;(disease)bacteria

zarazem (za-rá-zem) adv. at the same time ; as well; also

zarazić (za-rá-żheech) v. infect

zarażenie (za-ra-żhé-ne) n. infection (with a disease etc.)

zardzewieć (zar-dze-vyech) v. rust ; get rusty;corrode

zaręczyny (za-rán-chi-ni) n. betrothal; engagement ;engagement-

zarobek (za-ró-bek) m. gain;bread; earnings; wages;livelihood;living

zarobkować (za-rob-kó-vach) v. earn working ; earn a living

zarodek (za-ró-dek) m. embryo

zarosły (za-rós-wi) adj. m. overgrown (with vegetation etc.)

zarost (zá-rost) m. beard; hair

zarosla (za-rósh-la) n. thicket

zarozumiały (za-ro-zoo-myá-wi) adj. m. conceited ; uppish

zarówno (za-roóv-no) adv. equally; as well ; alike ; both

zarumienić się (za-roo-mye-neech śhán) v. blush ;flush; brown

zaryglować (za-rig-lo-vach) v. bolt a door; bar an entrance

zarys (zá-ris) m. sketch; outline ; broad lines;design;draft

zarząd (zá-zhownd) m. management ; administration; board

zarządca (za-zhównd-tsa) m. administrator ; manager

zarządzenie (za-zhówn-dze-ne) n. administrative order

zarzucać (za-zhoó-tsach) v. fill; give up; reproach ; fling ;cast

zarzut (zá-zhoot) m. reproach; objection ; accusation; blame

zasada (za-sá-da) f. principle; alkali; base ; law ;rule;tenet

zasadniczy (za-sad-nee-chi) adj. m. fundamental;essential; basic

zasadzka (za-sádz-ka) f. ambush

zasądzić (za-sówn-dżheech) v. sentence ; adjudge to (somebody)

zasępiony (za-sán-pyo-ni) adj. m. gloomy; despondent;dejected

zasiadać (za-śhá-dach) v. take a seat ; sit down; settle down

zasięg (zá-śhánk) m. reach ;scope

zasięgać rady (za-śhán-gach rádi) v. consult; seek advice

zasiłek (za-śhee-wek) m. handout; grant ;relief;subvention

zaskarżyć (za-skár-zhich) v. sue

zasklepić się (za-skle-peech
śhäń) v. scab; shut oneself
up (in); seal up; vault;wall up
zaskoczyć (za-sko-chich) v. sur-
prise; attack unawares;click;lock
zaskórny(za-skoor-ni) adj. m.
subcutaneous;underground(water)
zasłabnąć (za-swab-nownch) v.
faint; get sick;grow faint;swoon
zasłać (za-swach) v. cover (bed)
zasłona (za-swo-na) f. blind;
veil; screen; curtain;shield
zasłonić (za-swo-neech) v.
curtain; shade ; shield;cover up
zasługa (za-swoo-ga) f. merit
zasługiwać (za-swoo-gee-vach)
v. deserve ; be worthy;merit
zasłużony (za-swoo-zho-ni) adj.
m. man of merit ;just; fair
zasmucić (za-smoo-cheech) v.
sadden ; pain; distress;grieve
zasmucony(za-smoo-tso-ni) adj.
m. sad; grieved;distressed
zasnąć (za-snownch) v. fall a-
sleep; sleep;drop off to sleep
zasobnik(za-sob-neek) m. con-
tainer; tank;storage tank
zasób (za-soop) m. store; re-
source ; stock; supply
zaspa (zas-pa) f. snowdrift;
dune; drifted sand;drifted snow
zaspać (zas-pach) v. oversleep
zaspokoić (za-spo-ko-eech) v.
satisfy; quench; appease;provide
zastanowić się (za-sta-no-veech
śhäń) v. reflect; puzzle;ponder
zastaw (za-stav) m. pawn; depos-
it; security;pledge;forfeit;lien
zastawić (za-sta-veech) v.
1. bar; 2. pledge; 3. set a
table ; cram a room; lay(snares)
zastąpić (za-stown-peech) v. re-
place; bar passage;do duty for
zastępca (za-stánp-tsa) adj.m.
proxy; substitute ; deputy
zastępczo (za-stánp-cho) adv.
replacing; temporary ; in lieu
zastępstwo (za-stánp-stvo) n.
replacement ;proxy; agency
zastosować (za-sto-so-vach) v.
adopt; apply ; employ;make use
zastosować się (za-sto-so-vach
śhäń) v. comply ; toe the line

zastosowanie (za-sto-so-va-ñe)
n. application; use compliance
zastój (za-stooy) m. stagnation
zastraszyć (za-stra-shich) v.
intimidate ;cow;bully;bulldoze
zastrzał (za-stzhaw) m. (knee)
brace; strut; boom; cramp
zastrzec (za-stzhets) v. re-
serve ; stipulate;condition
zastrzeżenie (za-stzhe-zhe-ñe)
n. reservation; proviso
zastrzyk (za-stzhik) m. in-
jection ; shot(in the arm)
zastygnąć (za-stig-nownch) v.
congeal ; set; harden;petrify
zasuszyć (za-soo-shich) v. dry
up ; wither ; shrivel(the skin)
zasuwa (za-soo-va) f. bar;
(door) bolt;valve ;shutter
zasuwka (za-soov-ka) f. small
bolt ;damper; valve
zasypać (za-si-pach) v. bury;
cover; add (to soup);fill up
zasypiać (za-sip-yach) v. cat
nap; doze off; fall asleep
zaszczepiać (za-shche-pyach)
v. inoculate; graft;instill
zaszczycać (za-shchi-tsach) v.
honor; dignify; favor; grace
zaszczyt (zash-chit) m. honor;
distinction; privilege;dignity
zaszkodzić (za-shko-dzheech) v.
harm; hurt; damage; injure
zasznurować (za-shnoo-ro-vach)
v. tie up; lace(shoes);tighten
zaszyć (za-shich) v. sew up
zaszyć się (za-shich śhäń) v.
hide; burrow ; conceal oneself
zaś (zaśh) conj. but; whereas;
and ; while; specially
zaślepić (za-śhle-peech) v.
blind; infatuate;blind to facts
zaślepiony (za-śhle-pyo-ni) adj.
m. infatuated; fanatic ;blind
zaślubić (za-śhloo-beech)v.
marry ; get married
zaślubiny (za-śhloo-bee-ni) pl.
wedding ; marriage ;nuptials
zaśmiecić (za-śhmye-cheech) v.
litter ; clutter up (a room etc.)
zaśniedziały (za-śhñe-dźhá-wi)
adj. m. rusty; stagnant

zasrubować (za-shroo-bó-vach) v. screw tight ; screw on (a lid) zaświadczenie (za-shvyad-che-ñe) n. certificate ;affidavit zaświadczyć (za-shvyad-chich)v. certify; attest; witness zaświecić (za-żhvye-cheech) v. put light on ; light up ;turn on zataczać (za-tá-chach) v. roll in; describe(a circle); stagger;wheel zataic (za-tá-eech) v. conceal; suppress; keep secret ;hold back zatamować (za-ta-mó-vach) v. dam up; stop ; block ;impede zatańczyc (za-tań-chich) v. dance; perform a dance zatapiać (sa-tap-yach) v.flood; sink ; penetrate ;inundate;scuttle zatarasować (za-ta-ra-só-vach) v. obstruct; block up; bolt zatarg (zá-tark) m. conflict zatem (zá-tem) adv. then; consequently; therefore ; and so zatemperować (za-tem-pe-ró-vach) v. sharpen a pencil etc. zatkać (zá-tkąch) v. stop up zatlic się (zá-tleech shań) v. catch fire ; smoulder zatłoczony (za-two-cho-ni) adj. m. crowded ; crammed; cluttered zatoka (za-tó-ka) f. bay; gulf zatonąć (za-tó-nownch) v. sink zator (zá-tor) m. (traffic) jam zatracic (za-trá-cheech) v. lose; waste ; lose all sense of zatroskać(za-trós-kach) v. grieve zatrucie (za-troó-che) n. poisoning ; intoxication; toxaemia zatruc (zá-trooch) v. poison zatrudniac (za-trood-nach) v. employ ; engage ;take on(workers) zatrzask (zá-tzhask) m. (door) latch; (snap) fastener lock zatrzymać (za-tzhi-mach) v. stop; retain; detain ;arrest; hold zatwardzenie (za-tvar-dzé-ñe) n. constipation; costiveness zatwierdzać (za-tvyér-dzach) v. approve ;confirm; ratify ;affirm zatwierdzenie (za-tvyer-dzé-ñe) n. ratification; approval;assent zatwierdzic (za-tvyér-dzheech) v. ratify; approve ;confirm;validate

zatyczka (za-tich-ka) f. plug zatykac (za-ti-kach) v. stop up ; plug up; insert a plug zaufac (za-oó-fach) v. confide zaufanie (za-oo-fá-ñe) n. confidence ; trust ;faith; reliance zaufany (za-oo-fá-ni) adj. m. reliable; confidential;trusted zaułek (za-oó-wek) m. alley; back street ; lane ;recess; nook zauważyc (za-oo-vá-zhich) v. notice; catch sight;remark zawada (za-vá-da) f. obstruction; nuisance; hindrance zawadiaka (za-vad-ya-ka) m. bully; blusterer;swashbuckler zawadzac (za-vá-dzach) v. hinder; scrape; touch ;be a drag zawalac (za-vá-lach) v. soil zawalic (za-vá-leech) v. collapse; obstruct; bury;bungle zawartosc (za-vár-toshch) f. contents ; subject (of a book) zawczasu (za-vcha-soo) adv. in good time ;in advance zawczoraj (za-vchó-ray) adv. the day before yesterday zawdzięczac (za-vdźhań-chach) v. owe (gratitude) ; be indebted zawezwac (za-véz-vach) v. call; summon ; call in (a doctor etc) zawiadomic (za-vya-do-meech) v. inform; give notice ;let know zawiadomienie (za-vya-do-mye-ñe) n. notification ;information zawiadowca stacji (za-vya-dóv-tsa státs-yee) m. stationmaster ;superintendent zawiasa (za-vyá-sa) f. hinge zawiązac (za-vyówn-zach) v. tie up ; bind; set up (a club) zawieja (za-vyé-ya) f. blizzard za wiele (za-vye-le) adv. too much ; too many (expenses etc.) za widna (za veed-na) adv. in day light; in light;before dark zawierac (za-vyé-rach) v. contain; conclude; shut ;strike up zawierucha (za-vye-roó-kha) f. wind storm ; gale ;(war)clouds zawieszenie broni (za-vye-shé-ñe bró-ñee) n. armistice ;truce ; cessation of hostilities

zawietrzna (za-vyetzh-na) f.
lee side(sheltered from the wind)
zawijać (za-vee-yach) v. wrap
up; tuck in; put in at a port
zawikłać (za-veek-wach) v. complicate; entangle;embroil;tangle
zawiły (za-vee-wi) adj. m. intricate; baffling;knotty(problem)
zawinąc (za-vee-nownch) v. wrap
zawinic (za-vee-neech) v. be
guilty;commit an offense
zawisły (za-vees-wi) adj. m.
dependent(on somebody etc.)
zawistny (za-veest-ni) adj. m.
envious;jealous (of something...)
zawiść (za-veeshch) f. envy
zawitac (za-vee-tach) v. call
on; come and see   ⌐wrap
zawlec (za-vlets) v. drag;tug;
zawodnik (za-vod-neek) m. competitor (in sport);contestant
zawodowiec (za-vo-do-vyets) m.
professional; specialist
zawody (za-vo-di) pl. (sport)
competition;match;race;game;event
zawodzic (za-vo-dzheech) v.
1. lead; 2. disillusion;lament
zawołać (za-vo-wach) v. call out;
exclaim; shout; cry out; summon
zawołany (za-vo-wa-ni) adj. m.
excellent; perfect;born(poet etc.)
zawozic (za-vo-zheech) v. convey;
take to; cart; deliver;give rides
zawod (za-vood) m. 1. profession;
2. disappointment; deception
zawor (za-voor) m. valve; vent
zawrot głowy (za-vroot gwo-vi) m.
dizziness; vertigo;giddiness
zawstydzic (za-vsti-dzheech) v.
shame; embarrass;overwhelm
zawsze (zav-she) adv. always;
evermore;(for)ever;at all times
zawszyc (zav-shich) v. louse up
zawziąc się (zav-zhownch shan) v.
be obstinate; persist ; set on
zawziętosc (zav-zhan-toshch) f.
persistence; obstinacy; keenness
zazdrosny (zaz-dros-ni) adj. m.
jealous; envious;resentful
zazdrosc (zaz-droshch) f. envy
zaziębic się (za-zhan-beech shan)
v. catch a cold

zaznaczyc (za-zna-chich) v.
mark ; make a note; state;
zaznac (zaz-nach) v. experience;
taste ; enjoy; undergo
zaznajomic (za-zna-yo-meech)
v. acquaint ; introduce to
zazwyczaj (za-zvi-chay) adv.
usually ; generally; ordinarily
zazalenie (za-zha-le-ne) n.
complaint; grievance
zazarty (za-zhar-ti) adj. m.
fierce; bitter;vehement
zaządac (za-zhown-dach) v.
demand ; require; order
zazenowac (za-zhe-no-vach) v.
shame ;embarrass;confuse;abash
zazyły (za-zhi-wi) adj. m. familiar; intimate ;close;chummy
zazywac pigułki (za-zhi-vach
pee-goow-kee) v. take pills
ząb (zownp) m. tooth; fang;
prong; cog;otch;indentation
ząb mleczny (zownp mlech-ni)
m. milk tooth (of a child etc.)
ząb trzonowy (zownp tzho-no-vi)
adj. m. molar
ząbkowac (zownb-ko-vach) v.
teethe ; jag;cut one's teeth
zbaczac (zba-chach) v. deviate
zbankrutowany (zban-kroo-to-va-
ni) adj. m. bankrupt; insolvent
zbawca (zbav-tsa) m. savior
zbawiciel (zba-vee-chel) m.
savior; redeemer; Saviour
zbawicielka (zba-vee-chel-ka)
f. savior ; redeemer
zbawic (zba-veech) v. save;
redeem ; rescue;take(time)
zbawienie (zba-vye-ne) n. salvation;deliverance;rescue;redemption
zbesztac (zbesh-tach) v. scold
zbezcescic (zbez-chesh-cheech)
v. desecrate; defile;profane
zbędny (zband-ni) m. superfluous ; redundant; needless;useless
zbieg(zbyek) m. fugitive ;runaway
zbieg okolicznosci (zbyek o-ko-
leech-nosh-chee) m. coincidence ;occurrence at the same time
zbiegac (zbye-gach) v. run down
zbiegowisko (zbye-go-vees-ko)
n. concourse; throng; crowd

zbieracz (zbye-rach) m. collector; gatherer ; picker
zbierać (zbye-rach) v. gather;
pick; summon; clear; take in
zbieżny (zbyezh-ni) adj. m.
convergent; tapering;concurrent
zbijać (zbee-yach) v. knock
together; refute;beat down
zbiornik (zbyor-ñeek) m. tank;
reservoir; container;receptacle
zbiór (zbyoor) m. harvest; collection; set; crop;class;series
zbiórka (zbyoor-ka) f. rally;
assembly ;meeting;gathering
zbir (zbeer) m. thug; ruffian
zbity (zbee-ti) adj. m.close;
l beaten up; 2. compact;dense
zblednąc (zbled-nownch) v.pale;
grow pale ; fade;turn pale
z bliska (zblees-ka) adv. from
near ; close up ;from near
zbliżać (zblee-zhach) v. nearby
zbliżyć się (zblee-zhich shan)
v. become close; approach;be near
zbliżenie (zblee-zhe-ñe) n. rap-
prochement; close-up
zbliżony (zblee-zho-ni) adj. m.
approximate ; nearing;congenial
zbłądzic (zbwown-dzheech) v.
go astray; make mistake; lose
trail;err; wander off;err;blunder
zbocze (zbo-che) n. (hill) slope
zboczenie (zbo-che-ñe) n. deviation; aberration;drift;sag
zbolały (zbo-la-wi) adj. m. aching ; sore; woeful; wretched
zboże (zbo-zhe) n. corn; grain
zbój (zbooy) m. bandit; robber
zbór ewangielicki (zboor e-van-
ge-leets-kee)m. Protestant
Church; Evangelical Church
zbratać się (zbra-tach shan) v.
fraternize; chum up (with)
zbroczony krwią (zbro-cho-ni
krvyown) adj. m. blood-stained
zbrodnia (zbrod-ña) f. crime
zbrodniarz (zbrod-ñash) m. criminal; felon; malefactor
zbroic (zbro-eech) v. arm
zbroja (zbro-ya) f. armor
zbrojony beton (zbro-yo-ni beton) m. reinforced concrete

zbrojownia (zbro-yov-ña) f.
arsenal; armory ; gunroom
zbryzgac (zbriz-gach) v. spatter ; bespatter; splash
zbrzydnąc (zbzhid-nownch) v.
grow ugly; lose good looks
zbudować (zboo-do-vach) v. build
zbudzic się (zbob-dzheech shan)
v. wake up ; awake; be roused
zbujać (zbob-yach) v. fool;
hoax : pull one's leg
zburzyc (zbob-zhich) v. demolish
zbutwiec (zbob-tvyech) v. mold-
er. ; rot;decompose;decay;spoil
zbydlęcic (zbi-dlan-cheech) v.
imbrute;turn into a brute
zbyt (zbit) adv. too, (much)
zbyt wiele (zbit vye-le) adv.
too much ; excessively;over-
zbyt (zbit) m. sale; market
zbyteczny (zbi-tech-ni) adj. m.
superfluous ;needless;redundant
zbytek (zbi-tek) m. frills;
luxury ;pl :pranks;follies
zbytni (zbit-ñee) adj. m. excessive; undue;more than needed
zbytnik (zbit-ñeek) m. rogue
zbywać (zbi-vach) v. dispose;
dismiss; put off;sell;lack;want
z czasem (z cha-sem) adv.
with time ;eventually;later
z dala (z da-la) adv. from far
z daleka (z da-le-ka) adv. from
far; from afar; away from
zdalnie (zdal-ñe) adv. remote;
from afar; by remote control
zdanie (zda-ñe) n. opinion;
judgment; sentence; proposition
zdanie sprawy (zda-ñe spra-vi)
n. report; account;giving account
zdarzac się (zda-zhach shan) v.
happen; take place;occur
zdarzenie (zda-zhe-ñe) n. happening; event; incident
zdatnosc (zdat-noshch) f. fitness; capability;suitability
zdatny (zdat-ni) adj. m. able;
fit; apt;suitable (for the purpose)
zdawać (zda-vach) v. entrust;
submit;turn over;give up;pass(tests)
zdawać się (zda-vach shan)
l. seem; 2. surrender; 3.rely

z dawien dawna (zda-vyen dav-na) adv. from way back

z dawna (zdav-na) adv. since a long time; from way back

zdążyć (zhown-zhich) v. come on time; keep pace; tend

zdechlak (zdekh-lak) m. weakling

zdechły (zdekh-wi) adj. m. peaky; dead (animal); weakly; sickly

zdecydować się (zde-tsi-do-vach śhan) v. decide ; determine

zdejmować (zdey-mo-vach) v. take off ; strip(clothes); snap(photo)

zdenerwowany (zde-ner-vo-va-ni) adj. m. nervous ; excited

zderzak (zde-zhak) m. bumper

zderzenie (zde-zhe-ne) n. collision; clash; crash; smash-up

zderzyć się (zde-zhich śhan) v. collide ; clash; run into

zdjęcie (zdyan-che) n. snapshot

zdjęcie rentgenowskie (zdyan-che rent-ge-nov-skye) n. X-ray picture; X-ray phtograph

zdmuchiwać (zdmoo-khee-vach) v. blow off ; blow out; blow away

zdobić (zdo-beech) v. decorate

zdobycz (zdo-bich) f. booty; spoils; prey; prize; trophy

zdobyć (zdo-bich) v. conquer

zdolność (zdol-noshch) f. ability; capacity ; talent; aptitude

zdolny (zdol-ni) adj. m. clever; able ; capable; fit ; competent

zdołać (zdo-wach) v. be able

zdrada (zdra-da) f. treason

zdradliwy (zdrad-lee-vi) adj.m. treacherous; tricky; unsafe

zdradzać (zdra-dzach) v. betray

zdrajca (zdray-tsa) adj. m. traitor ; informer; turncoat

zdrapać (zdra-pach) v. scratch off ; scrape off; loosen up

zdrętwieć (zdrant-vyech) v. grow numb ; stiffen ; grow torpid

zdrętwienie (zdrant-vye-ne) n. numbness; stiffnes; torpidity

zdrobniały (zdrob-na-wi) adj.m. diminutive; grown smaller

zdrojowisko (zdro-yo-vees-ko) n. spa ; health resort ; baths

zdrowie (zdrov-ye) n. health ; good constitution; being well

zdrowotne jedzenie (zdro-vot-ne ye-dze-ne) n. health food

zdrowy (zdro-vi) adj. m. healthy; sound ; mighty ; in good health

zdrożny (zdrozh-ni) adj. m. vicious ; wicked; wrong ; fatigued

zdrój (zdrooy) m. spring ; spa

zdrów i cały (zdroov ee tsa-wi) m. safe and sound

zdrzemnąc się (zdzhem-nownch śhan) v. doze off; sleep light ; catnap; take a nap

zdumienie (zdoo-mye-ne) n. astonishment ; amazement

zdumiony (zdoo-myo-ni) adj.m. astonished ; flabbergasted

zdun (zdoon) m. stove fitter

zdwajać (zdva-yach) v. double

zdychać (zdi-khach) v. die

zdyszany (zdi-sha-ni) adj.m. breathless ; panting; out of breath

zdziałać (zdzha-wach) v. accomplish ; achieve ; manage to do

zdziczec (zdzhee-chech) v. grow wild; become savage; turn wild

zdziecinnieć (zdzhe-cheen-nech) v. grow childish(in the old age)

zdzierać (zdzhe-rach) v. strip off; fleece; tear down; peel

zdzierstwo (zdzher-stvo) n. extortion; exorbitance

zdziwaczeć (zdzhee-va-chech) v. become odd; grow whimsical

zdziwić (zdzhee-veech) v. surprise; astonish; make wonder

zdziewienie (zdzhee-vye-ne) n. surprise; wonderment; astonishment

zebra (ze-bra) f. zebra

zebrać (ze-brach) v. gather; clear

zebranie (ze-bra-ne) n. meeting

zecer (ze-tser) m. type setter

zechcieć (zekh-chech) v. be willing; feel inclined; choose

zegar (ze-gar) m. clock ; meter

zegar słoneczny (ze-gar swo-nech-ni) sundial

zegarek (ze-ga-rek) m. watch

zegarmistrz (ze-gar-mees tsh) m. watchmaker; watchmaker's shop

zejście (zeysh-che) n. descent

zejść (zeyshch) v. descend

zejść się (zeyshch śhan) v. meet; rendez vous; have a date

zelówka (ze-loov-ka) f.(shoe)sole
zelżec (zél-zhech) v. lighten
up ;ease; let up ;diminish;abate
zemdlec (zem-dlech) v. faint;
pan out ; swoon ;feel weak
zemsta (zem-sta) f. revenge
zepchnąc (zép-khnownch) v. push
down; drive out ;shove down
zepsuc (zép-sooch) v. damage;
spoil; worsen; pervert,harm;injure
zepsuty (zep-soo-ti) adj. m.
damaged; spoiled ; corrupt ;bad
zerkac (zér-kach) v. squint;peep
zero (zé-ro) n. zero; nought; nil
zerwac (zér-vach) v. pick off;
snap loose; break off; sprain
zerwanie (zer-vá-ne) n. rupture
zeskakiwac (ze-ska-keé-vach) v.
jump down ; dismount ;jump off
zeskrobywac (se-skro-bi-vach) v.
scrape off ; erase;srcape clean
zesłac (ze-swach) v. deport;
send down ; send into exile
zesłanie (ze-swa-ne) n. deportation ; exile; penal colony
zespolic (ze-spo-leech) v. unite
zespół (ze-spoow) m. team; group;
gang ; crew; set; troupe;complex
zestarzec sie (ze-sta-zhech shan)
v. grow old ; age; stale;get old
zestawienie (ze-sta-vye-ne) n.
comparison; balance sheet; list
zestrzelenie (ze-stzhe-le-ne) n.
shotting down; downing(a plane)
zeszłoroczny (ze-shwo-rocz-ni)
adj. m. last year's (crop etc.)
zeszpecic (ze-shpe-cheech) v.
disfigure ; make look ugly;deface
zeszyt (ze-shit) m. notebook
zeslizgiwac sie (ze-shleez-gee-
vach shan) v. glide down; slip
zetknąc sie (zét-knownch shan)
v. meet face-to-face; get in
touch; contact; meet;put in touch
zew (zef) n. call ; appeal;slogan
zewnątrz (zév-nowntsh) adv.& prep.
out; outside; outwards;outdoors
zewnętrzny (zev-nantzh-ni) adj.
m. exterior;external; outward
zewsząd (ze-vshownt) adv. from
everywhere; from all points
zez (zez) m. squint; crosseye

zeznawac (zez-na-vach) v. declare; testify ;give evidence
zezowac (ze-zo-vach) v. squint
zezwalac (zez-va-lach) v. allow ; give permission;permit
zezwolenie (zez-vo-le-ne) n.
permission ; leave;license
zębaty (zan-ba-ti) adj. m.
toothed ; cogged; indented
zębate koło (zan-ba-te ko-wo)
n. cog wheel; gear (wheel)
zęby (zan-bi) pl. teeth; cogs
zgadywac (zga-di-vach) v.
guess . anticipate ;give a guess
zgadzac sie (zga-dzach shan)
v. agree ;fit in;see eye-to-eye
zgaga (zga-ga) f. heartburn
zganic (zga-neech) v. blame
zgarnąc (zgar-nownch) v. rake
together ;gather; brush aside
zgasic (zga-sheech) v. put out;
extinguish; switch off; dim
zgęszczenie (zgan-shche-ne) n.
condensation ; compression
zgiełk (zgyewk) m. uproar;
clamor ; turmoil; tumult
zgięcie (zgyan-che) n. bend;
fold ; inflection ;inflexion
zginac (zgee-nach) v. bend
(over); fold; stoop ; bow
zgliszcza (zgleesh-cha) pl.
cinders ; ashes ;site of fire
zgłaszac (zgwa-shach) v. notify; call for ; tender ;submit
zgłębic (zgwan-beech) v. probe;
sound out ; deepen ;go deeply
zgłodniały (zgwod-ná-wi) adj.
m. hungry ; starving ;hungering
zgłosic (zgwó-sheech) v. notify
zgłoska (zgwos-ka) f. syllable
zgłupiec (zgwoo-pyech) v. grow
silly ; grow stupid ;be astounded
zgnębic (zgnan-beech) v. depress ; deject; oppress ;dishearten
zgnic (zgneech) v. rot ;decay;ret
zgniesc (zgneshch) v. crush;stub;
squash ; suppress; quell ;squeeze
zgnilizna (zgnee-leez-na) f.
rot; corruption; foul smell
zgniły (zgnee-wi) adj. rotten;foul
zgoda (zgo-da) f. concord; assent;
consent ;unity; approval;harmony

zgodnie (zgód-ne) adv. according;
in concert ; peaceably ;in unison
zgodnosc (zgód-noshch) f. accord
agreement ; unanimity ;consistence;
zgodny (zgód-ni) adj. m. compatible ; good-natured ;unanimous
zgoic sie (zgó-eech shán) v.
heal up; heal over ;heal a wound
zgon (zgon) m. death; decease
zgorszyc (zgór-shich) v. horrify;
scandalize ; shock; arouse
zgorzkniały (zgozh-kná-wi) adj.
m. sour; embittered;acrimonious
zgotowac (zgo-tó-vach) v. prepare;cook; give (an ovation)
z góry (zgoó-ri) adv. in advance
zgrabny (zgráb-ni) adj. m.skill -
ful; clever; deft; smart;neat;
shapely ; slick; deft;well-built
zgraja (zgrá-ya) f. gang; mob
zgromadzenie (zgro-ma-dzé-ne) n.
assembly ; congress; meeting
zgromadzac sie (zgro-má-dzach
shán) v. assemble ; gather
zgroza (zgró-za) f. horror
z grubsza (zgroób-sha) adv.
roughly; approximatively
zgryzota (zgri-zó-ta) f. grief
zgryźliwy (zgriżh-lee-vi) adj.
m. sarcastic; peevish; harsh
zgrzac sie (zgzhach shán) v.
get hot; sweat; become hot
zgrzebło (zgzhéb-wo) n. horse-
comb ; harrow ;curry comb;comb
zgrzyt (zgzhit) m. screech;jar
zguba (zgoó-ba) f. loss; doom;
undoing ; ruin; destruction
zgubic (zgoó-beech) v. lose;
undo;drop;bring to ruin;destroy
zgubic sie (zgoo-beech shán) v.
get lost; get mixed up ;be mislaid
zgubny (zgoób-ni) adj. m. disastrous; fatal; ruinous ;calamitous
zgwałcic (zgvaw-cheech) v. rape
ziarnisty (żhar-neés-ti) adj.m.
granular ; grainy ;whole grain-
ziarno (żhár-no) n. grain; corn
ziele (żhé-le) n. weed; herb
zieleń (żhe-leń) f. greenery
zielonawy (żhe-lo-ná-vi) adj. m.
greenish;of greenish color
zielony (żhe-ló-ni) adj. m.green;
young and inexperienced (man)

ziemia (żhém-ya) f. earth; land
ground; soil ;native land;district
ziemianin (żhe-mya-neen) m.
squire; landowner ; mortal
ziemianka (żhe-myán-ka) f.
1. dugout; 2. landowner's wife
ziemniak (żhém-nak) m. potato
ziemski (żhém-skee) adj. m.
earthly ; worldly; landed ;land-
ziewac (żhe-vach) v. yawn; gape
zięba (żhan-ba) f. finch;chaffinch
ziębic (żhan-beech) v. cool;
chill;expose to the cold
zięc (żhánch) m. son-in-law
zima (żhee-ma) f. winter
zimno (żheém-no) n. cold ;chill
zimno (żheém-no) adv. coldly
zimny (żheém-ni) adj. m. cold
zimowac (żhee-mó-vach) v.
hibernate; winter;pass the winter
zioło (żhó-wo) n. herb(mint,sage...)
ziszczac (zeésh-chach) v. realize; fulfill ; carry out (a plan)
zjadac (zya-dach) v. eat; eat
up ; have food; ruin ; drain
zjadliwy (zya-dlee-vi) adj.m.
biting; caustic ; spiteful ;vicious
zjawa (zyá-va) f. apparition;
ghost ; vision ;specter; phantom
zjawisko (zya-veés-ko) n. fact;
event; phenomenon ;vision ;occurence
zjazd (zyazt) m. meeting; coming; descent ; downhill drive ;slide
zjednoczenie (zyed-no-che-ne) n.
union ; unification ;association
zjesc (zjeshch) v. eat up ;outdo
zjeżdżac (zyézh-dzhach) v. ride
down; slide down ;make way;slate
zlecac (zle-tsach) v. commission;
order ;entrust; instruct;charge with
zlecenie (zle-tse-ne) n. commission; order ; errand; message
z ledwoscią (zled-vósh-chown)
adv. hardly; with difficulty
z lekka (zlék-ka) adv. lightly;
softly ; slightly; gently
zlepek (zle-pek) m. agglomerate
zlew (zlef) m. sink;kitchen sink
zlewac (zle-vach) v. pour off;
pour together ; mix ;flunk;whip
zliczyc (zlee-chich) v. count
up; total; add up ; reckon ;tot up

zlikwidować (zlee-kvee-do-vach)
v. liquidate; wind up ;destroy
zlodowacenie (zlo-do-va-tse-ñe)
n. freezing; glaciation
zlot (zlot) m. rally ;flocking in
złagodzenie (zwa-go-dze-ñe) n.
mitigation; softening
złagodzić (zwa-go-dżheech) v.
mitigate ;soothe;lessen;soften
złamać (zwa-mach) v. break ;smash
złamanie (zwa-ma-ñe) n. fracture
złazic (zwa-żheech) v. climb
down ; get off; come off;peel off
złączenie (zwown-che-ñe) n. connection;junction ;weld link;fuse
złączyc (zwown-chich) v. join;
złe (zwe) n. evil; wrong; ill
zło (zwo) n. evil; devil ;harm
złocenie (zyo-tse-ñe) n. gilding
złocic (zwo-cheech) v. gild
złoczyńca (zwo-chiñ-tsa) m.
evildoer; criminal;malefactor
złodziej (zwo-dżhey) m. thief
złodziejka (zwo-dżhey-ka) f.
thief ; electrical adapter
złom (zwom) m. scrap; waste
złość (zwoshch) f. anger; malice;
spite ; soreness; resentment
złośliwy (zwosh-lee-vi) adj.m.
malignant; spiteful ;malicious
złotnik (zwot-ñeek) m. goldsmith
złoto (zwo-to) n . gold;gold work
złoty (zwo-ti) adj. m. 1, golden
m. 2. Polish money unit
złowic (zwo-veech) v. catch;net;
hook (a fish,a husband etc)
złowrogi (zwo-vro-gee) adj.m.
ominous ; sinister;protentous
złoże (zwo-zhe) n. stratum; bed
złożony (zwo-zho-ni) adj. m.
complex; multiple; intricate
złuda (zwoo-da) f. illusion
złudny (zwood-ni) adj. m. illusory; deceptive; illusive
zły (zwi) adj. m. bad; evil;ill;
vicious ; cross; poor;rotten
zmagać się (zma-gach shañ) v.
struggle with; grapple with
zmaganie (zma-ga-ñe) n. struggle
zmarły (zmar-wi) adj. m. deceased; dead; defunct; the late
zmarszczka (zmarshch-ka) f.
wrinkle; crease; fold; pucker

zmartwienie (zmar-tvye-ñe) n.
worry; sorrow; grief;trouble
zmartwychwstać (zmar-tvikh-
vstać) v. rise form the dead
zmartwychwstanie (zmar-tvikh-
vsta-ñe) n. resurrection
zmarznąc (zmar-znownch) v.
freeze ; freeze over; be cold
zmawiać się (zma-vyach shañ) v.
conspire ; plot; arrange;collude
zmaza (zma-za) f. stain; blemish; blot; wet dream; slur
zmazywac (zma-zi-vach) v. wipe
out; efface ; erase; expiate
zmęczenie (zmañ-che-ñe) n. fatigue ; weariness;lassitude
zmiana (zmya-na) f. change ;
variation; shift; relay;exchange
zmiatac (zmya-tach) v. sweep up
zmiażdżyc (zmyazh-dzhich) v.
crush ; overwhelm(the enemy etc.)
zmienic (zmye-ñeech) v. change
zmierzac (zmye-zhach) v. aim;
tend; make one's way;drive at
zmierzch (zmyezhkh) m. dusk;
twilight; decline; fall; dark;
at dark
zmierzyc (zmye-zhich) v. measure; gauge ; take aim;make for
zmieszanie (zmye-sha-ñe) n.
mix up; confusion, embarrassment
zmiłowanie (zmee-wo-va-ñe) n.
mercy; pity;disposition to forgive
zmniejszenie (zmñey-she-ñe) n.
reduction; decrease; relief
zmniejszyc (zmñey-shich) v.
diminish; lessen; abate; reduce
zmoczyc (zmo-chich) v. wet; soak
zmora (zmo-ra) f. nightmare;bane
zmorzyc (zmo-zhich) v. overpower
zmordowac (zmor-do-vach) v.tire
wear; do in; tire out; exhaust
zmowa (zmo-va) f. conspiracy;
collusion; plot;secret deal
zmrok (zmrok) m. dusk; twilight
zmurszały (zmoor-sha-wi) adj.m.
mouldy, decaying; rotten;musty
zmuszac (zmoo-shach) v. coerce;
compel; force; oblige;constrain
zmykac (zmi-kach) v. cut and run;
bolt; scoot off; scurry away
zmylic(zmi-leech) v. fool; mislead; deceive; lose way;outwit

zmysł (zmisw) m. sense; instinct;knack;aptitude;reason
zmysłowy (zmis-wo-wi) adj. m.
sensual ;sensory;sense-; lewd
zmyślać (zmish-lach) v. invent;
trump up ; fake up; bluff;cook up
zmyślony (zmish-lo-ni) adj.m.
fictitious; invented ; unreal
znaczący (zna-chown-tsi) adj.
m. significant ; emphatic;telling
znaczek (zna-chek) m. sign;stamp
znaczny (znach-ni)adj.m. notable;
znać (znach) v. know;know how
goodly
znajdować (znay-do-vach) v.
find ; see; meet; experience
znajomość (zna-yo-moshch) f.
acquaintance ; knowledge
znajomy (zna-yo-mi) adj. m.well
acquainted·well known;familiar
znak (znak) m. mark; sign; stamp
znakomity (zna-ko-mee-ti) adj.
m. excellent ; illustrious
znalazca (zna-laz-tsa) m. finder
znaleźne (zna-lezh-ne) n.find-
er's reward;finder's share
znamienny (zna-myen-ni) adj.m.
significant ; characteristic
znamię (zna-myan) n. stigma;
mole ; trait; birthmark
znany (zna-ni) adj. m. noted;
known ; famed; familiar;well known
znawca (znav-tsa) m. expert
znecać się (znan-tsach shan) v.
torment; harass ; ill-treat
znekany (znan-ka-ni) adj. m.
dejected; harassed ; wasted
znicz (zneech) m. (holy) fire;
fireside ; pilot-light
zniechęcać (zne-khan-tsach) v.
discourage ; sicken; indispose
zniecierpliwić się (zne-cher-
plee-veech shan) v. grow impatient ; get vexed;lose patience
znieczulić (zne-choo-leech) v.
anesthetize ; deaden; harden
zniedołężniały (zne-do-wan-zhna-
wi) adj. m. impotent; decrepit;
infirm ; disable; feeble(old man)
zniekształcać (zne-ksztaw-tsach)
v. deform; disfigure ;distort
zniemczać (znem-chach) v.German-
ize; make into a German;force
to accept German identity

znienacka (zne-nats-ka) adv.
all of a sudden;unawares
znienawidzieć (zne-na-vee-
dżheech) v. grow to hate;loathe
znieprawić (zne-pra-veech) v.
deprave; demoralize; debauch
zniesienie (zne-she-ne) n.
abrogation; abolition;repeal
zniesławienie (zne-swa-vye-ne)
n. defamation; slander
zniewaga (zne-va-ga) f. insult
zniewalać (zne-va-lach) v.
coerce; rape; captivate; win
znikać (znee-kach) v. vanish
zniewieściały (zne-vyesh-cha-
wi) adj. m. effeminate;sissy
znikąd (znee-kownt) adv. from
nowhere; out of nowhere
znikomy (znee-ko-mi) adj. m.
perishable;negligible;minute
zniszczeć (zneesh-chech) v. decay; go to ruin; be worn out
zniszczenie (zneesh-che-ne) n.
destruction ; ravage;ruin;havoc
zniszczyć (zneesh-chich) v. destroy; ruin; ware out;ravage
zniweczyć (znee-ve-chich) v.
annihilate; wreck; lay waste
zniżać (znee-zhach) v. lower
zniżka (zneezh-ka) f. reduction;
decline; slump; drop; fall
znosić (zno-sheech) v. annul;
endure; carry down;ware out
znośny (znosh-ni) adj. m. tolerable; bearable; so-so; fair
znowu (zno-voo) adv. again;anew
znój (znooy) m. toil; sweat
znów (znoof) adv. again; anew
znudzenie (znoo-dze-ne) n.bore-
dom; till one is sick and tired
znużenie (znoo-zhe-ne) n. weariness; fatigue (people,metals etc.)
zobaczyć (zo-ba-chich) v. see
zobojętnić (zo-bo-yant-neech)
v. neutralize;make indifferent
zobojętnieć (zo-bo-yant-nech)
v. grow indifferent;grow listless
zobowiązać (zo-bo-vyown-zach)
v. oblige ;obligate to do
zobowiązanie (zo-bov-yown-za-
ne) n. obligation;commitment
zobrazować (zob-ra-zo-vach) v.
illustrate; describe ;depict

zogniskować (zog-ńees-kó-vach)
v. focus ; concentrate
zohydzać (zo-khi-dzach) v. defame; make loathsome;sicken of
zoolog(zo-ó-log) m. zoologist
zorza północna (zó-zha poow-
nóts-na) f. aurora borealis
zostać (zós-tach) v. remain;stay;
become ; get to be; be left
zostawiać (zos-táv-yach) v.
leave;abandon; put aside
z powodu (zpo-vó-doo) prep.
because of; owing to;due to
z powrotem (zpov-ró-tem) adv.
back; backwards;on the way back
zrabować (zra-bo-vach) v. rob
z rana (zrá-na) adv. in the
morning;during the morning
zranić (zra-ńeech) v. wound;
injure; hurt(feelings);mangle
zrastać (zras-tach) v. grow
into one; fuse; heal up;blend
zrazu (zrá-zu) adv. at first
zrażać (zra-zhach) v. discourage; set against; alienate
zrąb (zrownp) m. frame (work);
clearing ; trunk; shell
zrąbać (zrown-bach) v. hew; cut
down; hack; chop; pick to pieces
zrealizować (zre-a-lee-zó-vach)
v. realize; actualize; execute
zredagować (zre-da-gó-vach) v.
draw up; compose; edit; draft
zresztą (zrésh-town) adv.
1. moreover; besides; 2.after
all; though; any way;in the end
zręczność (zrańch-noshćh) f.
cleverness; dexterity; skill
zrobić (zro-beech) v. make; do;
turn; execute; perform
zrodzić (zro-dźheech) v. give
birth; beget; originate
zrosnąć się (zros-nównch śhań)
v. grow into one; fuse;blend
zrozpaczony (zros-pa-chó-ni) adj.
m. desperate; brokenhearted
zrozumiały (zro-zoo-myá-wi) adj.
m. intelligible; understandable
zrozumieć (zro-zoo-myech) v.
understand;grasp;see;make out
zrozumienie (zro-zoo-myé-ńe) n.
understanding;sympathy; sense;
grasp; comprehension; spirit

zrównać (zroóv-nach) v. level;
make even; align;equalize
zrównoważyć (zroov-no-vá-zhich)
v. balance; equalize;equilibrate
zróżniczkować (zroozh-ńeech-kó-
vach) v. differentiate
zryć (zrich) v. dig up; furrow
zrywać (zri-vach) v. rip; tear
off; tear down; pick; quarrel
z rzadka (zzhád-ka) adv. rarely
zrządzenie losu (zzhown-dzé-ńe
ló-soo) n. fate ;decree of fate
zrzeczenie się (zzhe-ché-ńe
śhań) n. resignation; renunciation ; renouncement;abdication
zrzeszenie (zzhe-shé-ńe) n.
association; union
zrzęda (zzhań-da) m. grumbler
zrzucać (zzhoo-tsach) v. throw
(down); buck off; drop; shed
zrzut lotniczy (zzhoot lot-ńee-
chi) m. drop (from plane)
zsiadać (zsha-dach) v. dismount
zstąpić (zstown-peech) v. descend;step down(one time)
zstępować (zstań-pó-vach) v.
descent; step down
zsyłać (zsi-wach) v. deport;exile
zsyłka (zsiw-ka) f. deportation
zsypywać (zsi-pí-vach) v. heap
up; pour off;shoot into
zszyć (zshich) v. sew together
zubożeć (zoo-bó-zhech) v. im-
poverish; grow poor;pauperize
zuch (zookh) m. brave fellow
zuchwalstwo (zookh-vál-stvo) n.
insolence; audacity; impudence
zuchwały (zookh-va-wi) adj. m.
insolent; impudent; bold
zupa (zoó-pa) f. soup
zupełny (zoo-péw-ni) adj. m.
entire;whole;total;out and out
zużycie (zoo-zhi-che) n. consumption; wear and tear; waste
zużytkować (zoo-zhit-ko-vach) v.
utilize ; use up; exploit
zużyty (zoo-zhi-ti) adj.m. worn
out; used up; wasted; trite
zwać (zvach) v. call; name
zwalczyć (zval-chich) v. overpow
er; overcome; cope; strive
zwalić (zva-leech) v. demolish;
fell; collapse; pile up;knock down

zwalniac (zval-nach) v. release;
loosen; let go; slow dawn;vacate
zwal (zvaw) m. heap; bank ; pile
zwapnienie (zvap-ne-ne) m. cal-
cification adv.densely;closely
zwarcie (zvar-che) n. short
(cirquit); contraction;infighting
zwariowac (zvar-yo-vach) v. go
mad ; go crazy; alter (a score...)
zwarzyc (zva-zhich) v. boil; nip;
frost damage ; turn sour ;blight
zwazac (zva-zhach) v. pay attention ; weigh (words);consider
zwazyc (zva-zhich) v. weigh;
consider ; give heed ;regard
zwachac (zvown-khach) v. smell
out; get wind; sniff ;scent
zwatpic (zvownt-peech) v. despair of ; lose hope ;give up
zwedzic (zvan-dzheech) v. swipe
zweglic (zvang-leech) v. carbon-
ize ; char; get charred
zwezic (zvan-zheech)v. narrow
down ; contract; restrict ;confine
zwiady (zvya-di) pl. reconnaissance ; scouting ;reconnoitring
zwiastowac (zvyas-to-vach) v.
announce ; herald ;foreshadow
zwiastowanie (zvyas-to-va-ne) n.
Annunciation
zwiastun (zvyas-toon) m. harbinger ; herald; omen ;forerunner
zwiazac (zvyown-zach) v. bind;
fasten; join; tie up;strap;frame
zwiazek (zvyown-zek) m. alliance;
connection; bond· compound ;tie
zwichnac (zveekh-nownch)v. strain;
dislocate; disjoin; luxate ;warp
zwichniecie (zveekh-nan-che) n.
dislocation ; luxation; sprain
zwiedzac (zvye-dzach) v. visit;
see the sights ; tour; see ;inspect
zwiedzanie (zvye-dza-ne) n.
sightseeing ;touring
zwierciadlo (zvyer-chad-wo) n.
mirror ; reflection ;looking glass
zwierz (zvyesh) n. beast of prey
zwierzac sie (zvyc-zhach shan) v.
disclose a secret; confide in...
zwierzchnik (zvyezh-khneek) m.
boss; superior ; chief; lord ;
master; suzerain;feudal lord

zwierzchnictwo (svyezh-khneets-
tvo) n. sovereignty; superior
authority; supremacy; control
zwierze (zvye-zhan) n. animal
zwierzyna (zvye-zhi-na) f.
game (animals); game
zwierzyniec (zvye-zhi-nets) m.
zoo; zoological garden ;zodiac
zwieszac (zvye-shach) v. hang
low ;droop; dangle ; hang down
zwietrzec (zvye-tzhech) v. de-
compose ; go stale; spoil
zwiewac (zvye-vach) v. cut and
run; blow away ; run away
zwiedly (zvyand-wi) adj. m.
withered ; wilted ;faded
zwiednac (zvyand-nownch) v.
wither; wilt; fade
zwiekszyc (zvyank-zhich) v. increase; magnify; heighten
zwiezly (zvyanz-wi) adj. m.
concise; brief; terse;compact
zwijac (zvee-yach) v. roll up;
wind up ;coil; twist up ;furl
zwilzac (zveel-zhach) v. moist-
en; wet; dampen(often)
zwilzyc (zveel-zhich) v. moist-
en ; wet; dampen(one time)
zwinac (zvee-nownch) v. roll
up; wind up; coil up; twist up
zwinny (zveen-ni) adj. m. agile;
nimble; deft; dexterous ;lissome
zwisac (zvee-sach) v. hang
down; droop; dangle ;sag;beetle
zwlekac (zvle-kach) v. delay
zwlaszcza (zvwash-cha) adv.
particularly; chiefly; especially; most of all;specially
zwloka (zvwo-ka) f. delay;respite
zwloki (zvwo-kee) n. corpse
zwodzic (zvo-dzheech) v. delude;
deceive; let down; lower
zwolenniczka (zvo-len-neech-ka)
f. adherent; follower;advocate
zwolennik (zvo-len-neek) m. adherent; follower; advocate
zwolna (zvol-na) adv. slowly
zwolniec (zvol-nech) v. slow
down; slack off; relax ;slacken
zwolnienie (zvol-ne-ne) n.
1. dismissal; release; acquittal; sack;exemption;2.slowing

zwoływać (zvo-wi-vach) v. call together: assemble; convene zwój (zvooy) m. roll;reel;coil zwracać (zvra-tsach) v. return; give back; pay(attention) zwrot (zvrot) m. 1; turn; 2. restitution 3.revulsion;4.phrase zwrotka (zvrot-ka) f. stanza zwrotnica (zvrot-nee-tsa) f. switch (large); steering zwrotnik (zvrot-neek) m. tropic zwrotny (zvrot-ni) adj. m. flexible; returnable;repayable zwrócić się (zvroo-cheech shan) v. turn (to); give back zwycięski (zvi-chans-kee) adj. m. victorious;triumphant;winning zwycięstwo (zvi-chans-tvo) n. victory; triumph; win zwyciężać (zvi-chan-zhach) v. conquer ; win; prevail;overcome zwyczaj (zvi-chay) m. custom; habit; fashion; usage;practice zwyczajny (zvi-chay-ni) adj. m. usual; ordinary; common;simple zwyczajowy (zvi-cha-yo-vi) adj. m. customary; regular; usual zwykły (zvik-wi) adj. m. common zwyrodniały (zvi-rod-na-wi) adj. m. degenerate; degenerated zwyrodnienie (zvi-rod-ne-ne) n. degeneration ; degradation zwyżka (zvizh-ka) f. rise;advance zwyżka cen (zvizh-ka tsen) f. price rise ;price increase zygzak (zig-zak) m. zigzag zysk (zisk) m. gain; profit zyskać (zis-kach) v. gain ;earn zyskownosc (zis-kov-noshch) f. profitability;remunerativeness zyskowny (zis-kow-ni) adj. m. profitable ; lucrative zza (z-za) prep. from behind zziajać się (zzha-yach shan) v. get out of breath;tire oneself zzieleniec (zzhe-le-nech) v. turn green ; become green zziębnąć (zzhanb-nownch) v. feel cold;be chilled to the bone zziębnięty (zzhanb-nan-ti) adj. m. chilled(to the bone) zżyć się(zzhich shan) v. grow familiar ;grow accustomed

zżymac (zzhi-mach) v. wring zżynac (zzhi-nach) v. cut down; reap; mow (the grass etc.) zżywac się (zzhi-vach shan) v. grow familiar ; reconcile zdzbło (zhdzhbwo) n. stalk; blade ;trifle; a bit; a little zle (zhle) adj. n,& adv. ill; wrong; badly; falsely;mistakenly zrebak (zhre-bak) m. colt zrebię (zhre-byan) n. foal;colt zrenica (zhre-nee-tsa) f. pupil zródlany (zhrood-la-ni) adj.m. spring (water); of spring zródło (zhrood-wo) n. spring; source ; well;fountain head zródłosłów (zhrood-wo-swoof) m. root word; etymology; radical zródłowy (zhrood-wo-vi) adj.m. original; spring (water) żaba (zha-ba) f. frog żaden (zha-den) pron. none; neither; not any; no one ; no- żagiel (zha-gel) m. sail żakiet (zha-ket) m. jacket żal (zhal) m. regret; grief; sorrow; remorse;grudge; rancor żalić się (zha-leech shan) v. complain ; lament;find fault żaluzja (zha-looz-ya) f. blind żałoba (zha-wo-ba) f. mourning żałobny marsz (zha-wob-ni marsh) m. funeral march żałosny (zha-wos-ni) adj. m. lamentable; wretched;plaintive żałosc (zha-woshch) f. grief; desolation; sorrow ;deep sorrow żałowac (zha-wo-vach) v. regret żar (zhar) m. heat; glow; ardor żarcie (zhar-che) n. swill;dub żargon (zhar-gon) m. jargon żarliwosc (zhar-lee-voshch) f. ardor; zeal; earnestness żarliwy (zhar-lee-vi) adj. m. ardent; zealous;fervent żarłoczny (zhar-woch-ni) adj.m. greedy;voracious ; gluttonous żarłok (zhar-wok) m. glutton żarówka (zha-roov-ka) f. light bulb; electric bulb; bulb żart (zhart) m. joke; jest;quip; żartowac (zhar-to-vach) v. joke make fun; poke fun; trifle ;jest

żarzyć (zha-zhich) v. glow;anneal
żąć (zhownch) v. mow; cut; reap
żądać (zhown-dach) v. demand;
require; exact; stipulate
żądanie (zhown-da-ne) n. demand;
claim;requirement;stipulation
żądło (zhownd-wo) n . sting;fang
żądny (zhownd-ni) adj. m. eager;
anxious; greedy;avid (of fame etc.)
żądny przygód (zhownd-ni pzhi-
goot) adventurous (man)
że (zhe) conj. that; then; as
żebrać (zhe-brach) v. beg
żebraczka (zhe-brach-ka) f. beggar; pauper (girl, woman)
żebrak (zhe-brak) m. beggar (man)
żebranina (zhe-bra-nee-na) f.
beggary; begging; alms
żebro (zhe-bro) n. rib;fin
żeby (zhe-bi) conj. so as; in
order that;if;may;if only
żeglarski (zhe-glar-skee) adj.m.
nautical; seaman's (life etc.)
żeglarstwo (zhe-glar-stvo) n.
sailing;navigation;seamanship
żeglarz (zhe-glash) m. seaman;
sailor; mariner; seafarer
żeglować (zhe-glo-vach) v. sail;
navigate (the seas,the ocean)
żeglowny (zhe-glow-ni) adj. m.
navigable (river, canal etc.)
żegluga (zhe-gloo-ga) f. navigation ; shipping; sailing
żegnać (zheg-nach) v. bid farewell; bless;bid good-bye;see off
żelatyna (zhe-la-ti-na) f.jelly
żelazko (zhe-laz-ko) n. press-
iron ; cutting iron; edger
żelazny (zhe-laz-ni) adj. m. iron
żelazo (zhe-la-zo) n. iron ;armor
żelazobeton (zhe-la-zo-be-ton)
m. reinforced concrete
żelaztwo (zhe-laz-tvo) n. scrap
iron; hardware;iron junk
żelbet (zhel-bet) m. reinforced
concrete
żeliwo (zhe-lee-vo) n. cast iron
żenić (zhe-neech) v. marry
żenować (zhe-no-vach) v. embarrass
żeński (zhen-skee) adj. m. female
żer (zher) m. food; prey; feeding
żerdka (zherd-ka) f. (small)perch

żerdź (zherdzh) f. perch
żłobek (zhwo-bek) m. crib
żłobić (zhwo-beech) v. channel; erode; furrow; groove
żłób (zhwoop) m. trough; crib
żmija (zhmee-ya) f. viper;
adder; poisonous snake
żmudny (zhmood-ni) adj. m.
uphill; toilsome; strenuous
żniwiarka (zhnee-vyar-ka) f.
harvester; reaper
żniwo (zhnee-vo) n. harvest
żołądek (zho-wown-dek) m.
stomach
żołądź (zho-wowndzh) f. acorn
żołd (zhowd) m. (soldier's)
pay
żołdactwo (zhow-dats-tvo) n.
soldiery ;the soldiery
żołnierz (zhow-nesh) m. soldier
żona (zho-na) f. wife
żonaty (zho-na-ti) adj. m.
married; family man
żółć (zhoowch) f. bile
żółciowy (zhoow-cho-vi) adj.m.
gall; peevish; harsh; biting
żółknąć (zhoow-knownch) v. turn
yellow; become yellow
żółtaczka (zhow-tach-ka) f.
jaundice; the yellows
żółtawy (zhow-ta-vi) adj. m.
yellowish;nankeen; sallow
żółtko (zhoowt-ko) n. yolk
żółty (zhoow-ti) adj. m. yellow
żółto-blady (zhoow-to-bla-di)
adj. yellow-pale; sallow
żółw (zhoowf) m. turtle;tortoise
żółwi krok (zhoow-vee krok) m.
snail's pace; turtle's gait
żrący (zhrown-tsi) adj. m.
corrosive; caustic; biting
żubr (zhoobr) m. (European-Po-
lish) bison; aurochs
żuchwa (zhookh-va) f. jawbone
żuć (zhooch) v. chew;masticate
żucie (zhoo-che) n. chewing;
mastication; chew;munducation
żuk (zhook) m. beetle;dung beetle
żulik (zhoo-leek) m. swindler;
rogue; cheat; street urchin
żuławy (zhoo-wa-vi) pl. marsh-
land ; lowlands;fertile lowlands

żupa (zhoo-pa) f. saltworks
żupan (zhoo-pan) m. old Polish
costume; (hist.) district chief
żur (zhoor) m. soup of ferment-
ed meal; sour soup
żuraw (zhoo-rav) m. crane;gantry
żurawina (zhoo-ra-vee-na) f.
cranberry
żurnal (zhoor-nal) m. fashion
magazine
żużel (zhoo-zhel) m. slag; cinder; scoria;clinker;cinder track
żużlobeton (zhoo-zhlo-be-ton) m.
slag concrete
żwawo (zhva-vo) adj. m. briskly;
alertly; apace ; jauntily
żwawy (zhva-vi) adj. m. brisk;
quick; lively; spry ;sprightly
żwir (zhveer) m. gravel upkeep
życie (zhi-che) n. life ;pep;
życiodajny (zhi-cho-day-ni) adj.
m. life-giving ; vivifying
życiorys (zhi-cho-ris) m. biography; life history
życzenie (zhi-che-ne) n. wish;
desire ; request ; greeting
życzliwy (zhich-lee-vi) adj.m.
favorable; friendly; kindly
żyć (zhich) v. be alive; live;
exist; subsist; get along
Żyd (zhid) m. Jew
żydowski (zhi-dov-skee) adj.m.
Jewish; Judaic; Yiddish
żydostwo (zhi-dos-tvo) n. Jewry
Żydówka (zhi-doov-ka) f. Jewess
żyjący (zhi-yown-tsi) adj.m.
living ; pl. the living
żyjatko (zhi-yownt-ko) n. ani-
malcule ; tiny animal
żylak (zhi-lak) m. varix
żylakowy (zhi-la-ko-vi) adj.m.
varicose; of varicose vein
żylasty (zhi-las-ti) adj. m.
venous; stringy; sinewy
żyletka (zhi-let-ka) f. (razor)
blade; safety razor blade
żyla (zhi-wa) f. vein; seam;
core; strand; streak; string
żylka (zhi-w-ka) f. veinlet; thread
żyrafa (zhi-ra-fa) f. giraffe
żyrant (zhi-rant) m. endorser
żyrować (zhi-ro-vach) v. endorse

żytni (zhit-nee) adj. m. rye
żytniówka (zhit-noov-ka) f.
corn vodka ; gin; rye vodka
żyto (zhi-to) n. rye
żywcem (zhiv-tsem) adv. alive
żywe srebro (zhi-ve sreb-ro)
n. mercury; restless person
żywica (zhi-vee-tsa) f. resin
żywiec (zhi-vyets) m. cattle
for slaughter; live bait
żywić (zhi-veech) v. feed;
nourish; cherish ; feel
żywioł (zhi-vyow) m. element
żywiołowy (zhi-vyo-wo-vi) adj.
m. elemental; spontaneous;
impulsive; impetuous
żywność (zhiv-noshch) f. food;
provisions; eatables; fodder
żywo (zhi-vo) adv. quickly;
briskly ;exp.: make it snappy!
żywopłot (zhi-vo-pwot) m. hedge
żywość (zhi-voshch) f. animation; liveliness; vivacity;
vitality; vigor; esprit
żywot (zhi-vot) m. life; womb;
belly ;life (of a saint)
żywotnie (zhi-vot-ne) adv. vi-
tally; exuberantly;luxuriantly
żywotność (zhi-vot-noshch) f.
vitality ; liveliness;vivacity
żywotny (zhi-vot-ni) m. vital
żywy (zhi-vi) adj. m. alive;
lively; vivid; intense; gay;
brisk; live;acute; keen; bright
żyzność (zhiz-noshch) f. fertility ; fruitfulness;richness
żyzny (zhiz-ni) adj. m. fertile;
generous (soil): fruitful; fat;
fecund; rich

ENGLISH-POLISH

a (ej) art.jeden; pewien;
pierwsza litera angielskiego
alfabetu; pierwszej kategorii
A-0'k (ej okej) zupełnie gotów
aback (e'baek) adv. wstecz;
w tył: do tyłu; nazad
abandon (e'baendon) v. opuszczać ; porzucić ; zarzucić
abandonment (e'baendonment) s.
opuszczenie;brak pohamowania
abashed (e'baeszt) adj. speszony; zmieszany (czymś)
abate ('ebejt) v. osłabiać;
zmniejszać; mitygować;uciszyć
abbey ('aebi) s. opactwo
abbreviate (e'bry:wjejt) v.
skrócić; skracać
abbreviation (e'bry:wjejszyn)
s. skrót: skrócenie; skracanie
ABC ('ej'bi:'si) alfabet
abdicate ('aebdykejt) v. zrzekać się ; abdykować
abdomen ('aebdemen) s. brzuch
abduct (aeb'dakt) v. uprowadzić: porwać; porywać
abhor (eb'ho:r) v. mieć odrazę
abide, abode, abode (e'bajd,
e'boud, e'boud)
abide (e'bajd) v. znosić; obstawać; dotrzymywać; trwać
ability (e'bylyty) s. zdolność
abject ('aebdżekt) adj. podły;
nędzny; nikczemny: skrajny
abjure (eb'dżuer) v. poprzysiąc
able ('ejbl) adj. zdolny; zdatny; utalentowany; poczytalny
abnormal (aeb'no:rmel) adj.
anormalny; nieprawidłowy
aboard (e'bo:rd) adv. na pokła-
dzie; na statku; w pociągu
abode (e'boud) v. był posłuszny
abode (e'boud) s. mieszkanie;
v. zob. abide
abolish (e'bolysz) v. obalić;
znieść: znosić; obalać
abolition (aebe'lyszyn) n. obalenie; zniesienie(zwyczaju etc)
A-bomb ('ejbom) s. bomba atomowa; bomba jądrowa
abominable (e'bomynebl) adj.
ohydny; wstrętny; obrzydliwy

abortion (e'bo:rszyn) s.przerwa-
nie ciąży; poronienie
abound (e'baund) v. obfitować
about (e'baut) adv. naokoło;
około:dookoła; po; o; wobec;przy
about (e'baut) prep. o; przy;
odnośnie; naokoło; wokoło
about to (e'baut tu) gotów do
above (e'baw) adv. powyżej;
w górze; wyżej; na górze
above (e'baw) prep. nad; ponad
above (e'baw) adj. powyższy
abreast (e'brest) adv. obok;
rzędem; ramię przy ramieniu
abridge (e'brydż) v. skrócić
abroad (e'bro:d) adv. zewnątrz;
za granicą: za granicę; w dal
abrogate ('aebrogejt) v. obalić:
unicestwić; odwoływać; znosić
abrupt (e'brapt) adj. nagły;
szorstki; urwany; ostry; oschły
abscess ('aebses) s. wrzód:ropień
absence ('aebsens) s. brak;
nieobecność; niestawiennictwo
absent ('aebsent) adj. nieobecny;v. być nieobecnym
absent-minded ('aebsent'majndyd)
adj. roztargniony
absolute ('aebselu:t) adj. abso-
lutny; zupełny: nieodwołalny
absolutely ('aebselu:tly) adv.
absolutnie; oczywiście
absolve (eb'zolw) v. rozgrzeszyć;
darować; uwolnić; oczyścić
absorb (eb'zo:rb) v. chłonąć;
tłumić; absorbować; łagodzić
abstain (eb'stejn) v. powstrzymywać się; być abstynentem
abstention (eb'stenszyn) s.
wstrzymanie się(od jedzenia...)
abstinence ('aebstynens) s.
wstrzemięźliwość: abstynencja
abstract ('aebstraekt) adj.
oderwany; abstrakcyjny;
s. abstrakcja; streszczenie;
v. streszczać; abstrahować;
odrywać: ukrasć: sprzątnąć
absurd (eb'se:rd) adj. absurdalny; bezsensowny: niedorzeczny
abundance (e'bandens) s. obfitość: znaczna ilość: dostatek

abundant (e'bandent) adj. obfity;liczny;bogaty; zasobny;płodny
abuse (e'bju:s) s. nadużycie;
obelga; (e'bju:z) v. obrażać;
nadużywać;lżyć;obrzucać obelgami
abyss (e'bys) n. otchłań; przepaść; głębia;pierwotny chaos
acacia (e'kejsze) s. akacja
academic (,aeke'demyk) adj.
akademicki;jałowy; s.uczony
academy (e'kaedemy) s. akademia
accelerate (aek'selerejt) v.
przyspieszać; przyspieszyć
accelerator (aek'selerejter) s.
przyśpieszacz; gaźnik; akcele-
rator; katalizator
accent ('aeksent) s. wymowa;
akcent; (aek'sent) v. akcento-
wać; uwydatniać; znakować
accept (ek'sept) v. akceptować;
zgadzać się na;zechcieć wziąść
acceptable (ek'septebl) adj.
do przyjęcia; znośny; zadawalający; mile widziany
access ('aekses) s. dostęp
accessible (aek'sesybl) adj.
dostępny; przystępny
accession (aek'seszyn) s.
wstąpienie; dostęp; dojście;
przystąpienie;objęcie(urzędu)
accessory (aek'sesery) s. dodatek; adj. dodatkowy; pomocniczy
access road ('aekses roud)
droga dojazdowa
accident ('aeksydent) s. traf;
wypadek; katastrofa;awaria
accidental (,aeksy'dentl) adj.
przypadkowy; nieważny;uboczny
acclimatize (e,klajmetajz) v.
aklimatyzować
accommodate (e'komedejt) v. przystosować; zakwaterować; wyświadczyć; załagodzić(spór)
accommodation (e,kome'dejszyn)
s. wygoda; dostosowanie; kwatera; pogodzenie się; ugoda
accompaniment (e'kampenyment) s.
towarzyszenie; akompaniament
accompany (e'kampeny) v. towarzyszyć;odprowadzać;akompaniować
accomplice (e'komplys) s. współ-
sprawca; współwinny

accomplish (e'kamplysz) v. do-
ty;liczny; spełnić; zrealizować
accomplished (e'kamplyszt) adj.
utalentowany; znakomity; wy-
kończony; z ogładą;skończony
accomplishment (e'kamplyszment)
s. osiągnięcie; realizacja;
dokonanie;wykonanie: ogłada
accord (e'ko:rd) s. zgoda;
v. uzgadniać; dać; licować
according (e'ko:rdyng) prep.
według; zależnie od
accordingly (e'ko:rdyngly) adv.
odpowiednio; więc; zatem
accost (e'kost) v. zaczepić
(kogoś);zagadnąć;przystąpić do
account (e'kaunt) s. rachunek;
sprawozdanie; v. wyliczać;
wytłumaczyć; uważać; oceniać
account for (e'kaunt fo:r) v.
dać powód; wytłumaczyć
accountant (e'kauntent) s.
księgowy
accounting (e'kauntyng)s. księ-
gowość
accumulate (e'kju:mju,lejt) v.
gromadzić;zbierać;piętrzyć
accuracy ('aekjuresy) s. scisłość; dokładność; celność
accusation (aekju:zejszyn) s.
oskarżenie;winienie;posądzenie
accuse (e'kju:z) v. oskarżać
accused (e'kju:zd) adj. oskarżony; oskarżony
accustom (e'kastem) v. przyzwyczajać; przyzwyczaić
accustomed (e'kastemd) adj.
przyzwyczajony; zwykły;zwyczajny
ace (ejs) s. as; oczko(in cards)
ache (ejk) s. ból; v.boleć
achieve (e'czi:w) v. dokonać;
osiągnąć(cel);zdobywać(sławę)
achievement(e'czi:wment) s.
osiągnięcie; wyczyn;zdobycz
aching ('ejkyng) adj. bolący
acid ('aesyd) adj. kwaśny;
s. kwas; kwaśna substancja
acid trip ('aesyd tryp) halu-
cynacje po narkotyku
acknowledge (ek'nolydż) v.
uznać; potwierdzić; przyznać

acknowledgement (ek'nołlydżment)
s. przyznanie; potwierdzenie;
uznanie; dowód uznania
acoustics (e'ku:styks) pl. akus-
tyka
acquaint (e'kłejnt) v. zaznajo-
mić; zapoznać; zapoznawac(kogoś)
acquaintance (e'kłejntens) s.
znajomość; znajomy
acquiesce (,aekły'es), v. zgadzać się; przyzwalać (bez oporu); przychylić się(do prośby)
acquire (e'kłajer) v. nabywać
acquisition (,aekły'zyszyn) s.
nabytek; nabycie; zdobycz
acquit (e'kłyt) v. zwolnic; wy-
wiązać się;spłacić;uniewinnić
acquittal (e'kłytl) s. zwolnienie;uiszczenie;wywiązanie się
acre (ejker) s. akr; morga;
4047 m²
acrid ('aekryd) adj. żrący;
ostry; cierpki;kwaskowaty
acrimonious (,aekry'mounjes)
adj. szorstki; zjadliwy;
cierpki; zgorzkniały
acrobat ('aekrebaet) s. akrobata
across (e'kros) adv. w poprzek;
na krzyż; prep. przez; na przełaj; po drugiej stronie (czegoś)
act (aekt) v. czynić; działać;
postępować; s. czyn; akt; uczynek;akt sztuki;uchwła;ustawa
action ('aekszyn) s. działanie;
czyn; akcja; ruch;poces
active ('aektyw) adj. czynny;
obrotny; rzutki; ożywiony;żywy
activity (aek'tywyty) s..dzia-
łalność; czynność;ożywienie;ruch
actor ('aekter) s. aktor
actress ('aektrys) s. aktorka
actual ('aekczuel) adj. istotny;
faktyczny; bieżący; obecny
actually ('aekczuely) adv. rzeczywiście; obecnie;istotnie;nawet
acute (e'kju:t) adj. ostry;
przenikliwy; bystry;przenikliwy
ad (aed) s. ogłoszenie (reklama)
(slang)
adapt (e'daept) v. dostosować;
przerobić;przystosować;dostrajać

adaptation (,aedaep'tejszyn)
s. przystosowanie;dostrojenie
add (aed) v. dodać; doliczyć
addict (aedykt), s. nałogowiec;
v. oddawać; poświęcać się
addicted (e'dyktyd) adj. nałogowy; nałogowo poswięcający się
addition (e'dyszyn) s. dodawanie; dodatek; (ponadto)
additional (e'dyszynl) adj.
dodatkowy; dalszy
address (e'dres) s. adres; mowa; odezwa; v. zwracać się;
adresować; skierować(prośbę)
addressee (,aedre'si:) s. ad-
resat; adresatka
adequate ('aedykłyt) s. stosowny; dostateczny;właściwy
adhere (ed'hjer) v. lgnąć; należeć; trzymać; przylegać
adhesion (ed'hi:żyn) s. lep-
kość; zrost;przynależność
adhesive (ed'hi:syw) adj. lepki; przylegający; s. plaster
adjacent (e' dżejsent) adj.
przyległy; sąsiedni
adjective ('aeddżyktyw) s.
przymiotnik;adj.dodatkowy
adjoin (e'ddżoyn) v. stykać się;
sąsiadować; dołączać
adjourn (e'ddże:rn) v. odraczać;
przerywać; zakończyć (obrady)
adjust (e'ddżast) v. dostosowywać; uregulować ; nastawić
administer (ed'mynyster) v. dawać; sprawować; administrować
administration (ed,myny'strejszyn) s. zarząd; rząd; administracja; ministerstwo; wymiar
administrative (ed'mynystrej-
tyw) adj. administracyjny
administrator (ed'mynystrejtor)
s. zarządca; administrator
admirable ('aedmerebl) adj.
godny podziwu;zachwycający
admiral ('aedmyrel) s. admirał
admiration (aedmy'rejszyn) s.
podziw;zachwyt;przedmiot podziwu
admire (ed'majer) v. podziwiać
admirer (ed'majrer) s. wielbiciel; wielbicielka

admissible (ed'mysybl) adj. dopuszczalny; do przyjęcia
admission (ed'myszyn) s. wstęp: dostęp; przyznanie; uznanie; (dopływ); bilet wstępu
admission ticket (ed'myszyn'tykyt) bilet wstępu
admit (ed'myt) v. wpuszczać; uznać; przyjmować; przyznać
admittance (ed'mytens) s. dostęp; przyjęcie;przyznanie się
admonish (ed'monysz) v. upominać; ostrzegać; pouczać
ado (e'du) s. wrzawa; kłopot; trudności; grymasy; narzekania
adolescence (,aede'lesns) s. młodość(pokwitanie-dojrzałość)
adolescent (,aede'lesnt) adj. młodociany; dorastający
adopt (e'dopt) adoptować; przyjmować; akceptować; wybierać
adoption (e'dopszyn) s. adopcja; adaptacja; przyjęcie; przysposobienie;akceptacja; wybór
adorable (e'do:rebl) adj. godny uwielbienia; bardzo miły
adoration (,aede:rejszyn) s. uwielbienie; wielka miłość
adore (e'do:r) v. czcić; uwielbiać; bardzo lubieć; kochać
adorn (e'do:rn) v. zdobić; upiększać; być ozdobą
adrift (e'dryft) adv. na fali; na wodzie bez steru zdany na los
adult ('aedalt) adj. dorosły; dojrzały; s. osoba dorosła
adulterate (e'dalterejt) v. fałszować; podrabiać;zatruwać
adultery (e'daltery) s. cudzołóstwo
advance (ed'waens) v. iść naprzód; pospieszać; awansować; przedkładać; popierać; pożyczać; adj. wysunięty; wczesniejszy; w przodzie
advanced (ed'waenst) adj. postępowy; światły; wysunięty naprzód; stary; przedwczesny
advanced reservation (ed'waenst, rezełwejszyn) rezerwacja z góry zamówiona

advantage (ed'waentydż) s. korzyść; pożytek; przewaga
advantageous (,aedwacn'tejdżes) adj. korzystny; zyskowny
adverb ('aedwe:rb) s. przysłówek(oznaczający czas,sposób...)
adversary ('aedwersery) s. przeciwnik; wróg; oponent
adverse ('aedwe:rs) adj. wrogi; przeciwny; szkodliwy;niekorzystny
advertise ('aedwertajz) v. ogłaszać; reklamować
advertisement ('edwertysment) s. ogłoszenie; reklama
advertising ('aedwertajzyng)s. reklama; ogłoszenia handlowe
advice (ed'wajs) s. rada; informacje;porada;pouczenie
advisable (ed'wajzebl) adj. wskazany; rozsądny;ostrożny
advise (ed'wajz) v. radzić; powiadamiać; pouczać
adviser (ed'wajzer) s. doradca; radca(prawny etc.)
advocate ('aedwekejt) v. zalecać; bronić;s.rzecznik;orędownik
aerial ('eerjel) adj. powietrzny; s. antena (radiowa etc.)
aeronautics (eere'no:tyks) s. aeronautyka; lotnictwo
aeroplane ('eereplejn) s. samolot
aesthetic (i:stetyk) adj. estetyczny;wrażliwy na piękno
afar (e'fa:r) adv. daleko;z daleka
affair (e'feer) s. sprawa; interes; romans; przedsięwzięcie
affect (e'fekt) v. wpływać; oddziaływać;wzruszać;dotyczyć;udawać
affected (e'fektyd) adj. dotknięty;przejęty; sztuczny
affection (e'fekszyn) s. uczucie; przywiązanie; choroba; miłość
affectionate (e'fekszynyt) adj. czuły; kochający;tkliwy;przwiązany
affidavit (aef'ydejwyt) s. poręczenie pod przysięgą
affinity (e'fynyty) s. pokrewieństwo;przyciąganie;powinowactwo
affirm (e'fe:rm) v. potwierdzać; zapewniać;zaręczać

affirmation (,aefe:r'mejszyn) s. twierdzenie; oświadczenie; zapewnienie; zatwierdzenie(wyroku)

affirmative (e'fe:rmetyw) adj. pozytywny; twierdzący

afflict (e'flykt) v. gnębić

affliction (e'flykszyn) s. przygnębienie; choroba; ból; cierpienie

affluence ('aefluens) s. dostatek; bogactwo; obfitosc; natłok

affluent ('aefluent) adj. zamożny; s. dopływ (rzeki)

afford (e'fo:rd) v. zdobyć się; dostarczyć ; stać na coś

affront (e'frant) v. znieważać

afficionado (éfisienado) s. entuzjasta (walki byków etc.)

aflame (e'flejm) adv. w ogniu; w podnieceniu

afraid (e'frejd) adj. przestraszony; wyrażający rezerwę

African ('aefryken) adj. afrykański

Afro ('aefro) s. (niby) styl afrykański (uczesania, ubioru)

after ('a:fte:r) prep. po; za; odnośnie; według; poniekąd

after all ('a:fte: o:l) prep. jednak; przecież; mimo wszystko

after that ('a:fte: daet) następnie ; potem

afternoon ('a:fte:rnu:n) s. popołudnie; adj. popołudniowy

afterwards ('aftełerdz) adv. później; potem; następnie

again (e'gen) adv. ponownie; znowu; na nowo; więcej; ponadto

again and again (e'gen end e'gen) wciąż; ciągle

against (e'genst) prep. przeciw; wbrew; na; pod; na wypadek

age (ejdż) s. wiek; stulecie; czas

aged ('ejdżyd) adj. stary; sędziwy; wiekowy; w podeszłym wieku

age ten (ejdż ten) w wieku lat dziesięciu

agency ('ejdżensy) s. ajencja; działanie; pośrednictwo

agenda (e'dżende) s. agenda; lista; porządek dzienny

agent ('ejdżent) s. pośrednik; ajent; czynnik; przedstawiciel

aggravate ('aegrewejt) v. pogarszać; rozjątrzać; denerwować

aggression (e'greszyn) s. napaść; agresja; napastliwość

aggressive (e'gresyw) adj. napastliwy; zaczepny; napastniczy

aggressor (e'grese:r) s. napastnik; agresor

aghast (e'gaest) adj. przerażony; osłupiały; skonsternowany

agile ('aedżyl) adj. zwinny; obrotny; zręczny; ruchliwy

agitate ('aedżytejt) v. poruszać; miotać; agitować

agitation (,aedżytejszyn) s. poruszenie; agitacja; podniecenie

agitator ('aedżytejter) s. agitator; mieszadło; trzęsarka

agnostic (áegnostyk) s. agnostyk; adj. agnostyczny

ago (e'gou) adv. przed; ...temu

agonize ('aegenajz) v. męczyć się; dręczyć się

agony ('aegeny) s. śmiertelna męka; agonia; katusze; spazm

agree (e'gri:) v. godzić się; zgadzać się; uzgadniać

agree about (e'gri: e'baut) v. zgadzać się co do...

agree to (e'gri: tu) v. zgadzać się na...

agreeable (e'gri:ebl) adj. zgodny; miły; chętny; sympatyczny

agreement (e'gri:ment) s. zgoda; umowa; porozumienie; układ

agricultural(,aegry'kalczerel) adj. rolniczy; rolny

agriculture (,aegry'kalczer) s, rolnictwo; uprawa ziemi

agriculturist (,aegry'kalczeryst) s. rolnik

ague ('ejgju:) s. febra; dreszcze; malaria; zimnica

ahead (e'hed) adv. naprzód; dalej; na przedzie; z przodu

aid (ejd) s. pomoc; pomocnik; v. pomagać; subwencjonować

aide (ejd) s. asystent; pomocnik

ailing ('ejlyng)s. choroba

aim (ejm) s. zamiar; cel; v. celować; mierzyć; zamierzać; skierować; dążyć

aimless (éjmlys) adj. bezcelowy
air (eer) s. 1. powietrze;
2. mina; postawa;wygląd;nastrój
air ('eer) v. 1. wietrzyć;
2. obnosić się; nadawać
air base ('eerbejs) s. baza lotnicza (wojskowa)
air brake ('eer,brejk) s. hamulec na sprężone powietrze
air-conditioning (,eer-ken'dy-
szynyn) s. klimatyzacja
air compressor (,eer-kem'presor)
s. sprężarka
aircraft ('eer-kra:ft) s. samolot;lotnictwo(wiedza,flota etc.)
aircraft carrier ('eer-kra:ft'
kaerje:r) s. lotniskowiec
airfield ('eer-fi:ld) s. lotnisko (do startowania i lądowania)
air force ('eer fo:rs) s. lotnictwo (wojskowe)
airline ('eerlajn) s. linia lotnicza (system transportu)
airmail ('eermejl) s. poczta
lotnicza
airplane ('eerplejn) s. samolot
airport ('eerpo:rt) s. lotnisko
air raid ('eerejd) atak lotniczy
air show ('eerszou) pokaz lotniczy
airsickness ('eersyknys) s.cho-
roba powietrzna
airtight ('eertajt) adj. hermetyczny
air traffic ('eer-traefyk) ruch
lotniczy(samolotów, pasażerów)
airway ('eerłej) linia lotnicza
airy ('eery) adj. przewiewny
aisle (ajl) s. przejście; nawa
boczna(kościoła)
ajar (e'dża:r) adv. uchylony;
pół otwarty;nieco otwarty
akin (e'kyn) adj. pokrewny
alacrity (e'laekryty) s. ochota;
gotowość; żwawość; skwapliwość
alarm (e'la:rm) s. popłoch;
strach; sygnał alarmowy;trwoga;
v. alarmować; trwożyć;płoszyć
alarm clock (e'la:rm,klok) s.
budzik
alas ! (e'laes)excl. niestety
alcohol ('aelkehol) s. alkohol;
spirytus

alcoholic (,aelke'holyk) s.
alkoholik; adj.alkoholowy
alcove ('aelkouw) s. altanka;
alkowa; nisza
alder ('o:lder) s. olcha; ol-
sza
ale (ejl) s, piwo (gorzkie,
angielskie)
alert (e'le:t) adj. czujny;
raźny; żwawy; s.alarm
algae ('aeldżi:) pl. glony;
algi
alias ('ejliaes) adv. inaczej;
alias; vel; s. pseudonim
alibi ('aelybaj) s. alibi; wymówka; v.usprawiedliwiać się
alien ('ejljen) adj. obcy
alienate ('ejljenejt) v. od-
stręczać; odrywać; zrażać
alike (e'lajk) adj. jednakowy;
podobny; adv. tak samo; jedna-
ko; podobnie; zarówno; także
alimony ('aelimeny) s. alimenty
alive (e'lajw) adj. żywy; żyjący; ożywiony;pełen życia
all (o:l) adj.& pron. cały;
wszystek; każdy; adv. całkowicie; w pełni; s. wszystko
all of us (o:l ow as) my
wszyscy; my wszyscy razem
all at once (o:l et łans)wszys-
cy na raz; wszyscy jednocześnie
all the better (o:l dy bete:r)
tym lepiej
all told (o:l told) wszystkiego
razem ; razem wziąwszy
alleged(e'ledźd) adj. rzekomy
alleviate (e'li:wjejt) v. łagodzić; zmniejszac
alley ('aely)s. aleja; przejście; zaułek; boczna ulica ;tor
alliance (e'lajens) s. związek;
sojusz; powinowactwo;skoligacenie
allot (e'lot) v. przydzielać;
losować; wyznaczać;wyasygnować
allotment (e'lotment) s. przydział; działka; asygnata
allow (e'lau) v. pozwalać; użyczać; uznawać; uwzględniać
allow for (e'lau fo:r) v.
uwzględniać; dawać (czas)
allowance (e'lauens) s. przydział; pozwolenie; kieszonkowe

alloy ('aeloj) s. stop; próba;
domieszka;stop kilku metali
all—round (o:l-raund) adj.
wszechstronny; universalny
allude (e'lu:d) v. robić aluzje
allure (e'lju:) v. wabić; kusić;
oczarować;nęcić;znęcić;zwabić
allusion (e'lu:żyn) s. aluzja;
przymówka;przytyk;napomknienie
ally (e'laj) v. sprzymierzać
się; łączyć;połączyć;skoligacić
ally ('aelaj) s. sprzymierze-
niec; sojusznik
almighty (o:l'majty) adj.
wszechmogący;ogromny;straszliwy
almond (am 'end) s. migdał
almost ('o:lmoust) adv. prawie;
niemal;jak gdyby;o mało;ledwo
almost never ('o:lmoust'newer)
prawie nigdy; rzadko kiedy
alms (a:mz) s, jałmużna
aloft (e'loft) adv. wysoko;hen;
w górze; w górę; do góry
alone (e'loun) adj. sam; samotny;w pojedynkę;sam jeden;jedyny
along (e'lo:ng) adv. naprzód;
wzdłuż; z sobą
alongside (e'lo:ngsajd) adv.
obok; wzdłuż ;przy(molu,burcie...)
aloof (e'lu:f) adv. z dala; na
uboczu; z daleka
aloud (e'laud) adv. głosno
alphabet ('aelfebyt) s. alfabet
already (o:l'redy) adv. już;
wcześniej;poprzednio;uprzednio
also (o:lsou) adv. także;również
altar ('o:lter) s, ołtarz
alter ('o:lter) v. zmieniać;
poprawiać;odmienić;przemienić
alteration (o:lte'rejszyn) s.
zmiana; poprawka;przemiana
alternate ('o:lternejt) v. zmieniać się (kolejno);brać kolejno
alternate ('o:lternyt) adj. co
drugi; na zmianę;kolejny
alternating current (o:lternej-
tyngkarent) prąd zmienny
alternative (ol-ter'netyw) s.
alternatywa; adj.alternatywny
although (o:lzou) conj. chociaż
altitude ('aeltytju:d) s. wy-
sokość(nad poziomem morza)

altogether (o:lte'gedze:r) adv.
zupełnie; całkowicie
aluminum (e'lumynem) s.
aluminium
alumnus (e'lamnes) s. były
student uczelni
always ('o:lłejz) adv. stale;
zawsze;ciągle;wciąż
am (aem) v. jestem
amass (e'maes) v. gromadzić
amateur ('aemecze:r)s, miłosnik; amator;dyletant
amaze (e'mejz) v. zdumiewać;
zadziwiać;wprawić w zdumienie
amazement (e'mejzment) s. zdumienie; osłupienie
amazing (e'mejzyng)adj. zdumiewający; zadziwiający
ambassador (aem'baesede:r)s.
ambasador; poseł
amber ('aembe:r)s. bursztyn
ambient ('aembient) adj. ota-
czający
ambiguous (aem'bygjues) adj.
dwuznaczny;mętny;zagadkowy
ambition (aem'byszyn) s. ambicja;chęć wybicia się
ambitious (aem'byszes) adj.
ambitny; żądny
ambulance ('aembjulens) s.
ambulans
ambush ('aembusz) s. zasadzka
amen (ej'men) amen
amend (e'mend) v. poprawiać
amendment (e'mendment) s. poprawa; ulepszenie; uzupełnienie
amends (e'mendz) s. odszkodowanie; zadośćuczynienie
American (e'meryken) s. Amerykanin; adj. amerykański
amiable ('ejmjebel) adj. miły;
uprzejmy; sympatyczny
amicable ('aemykebl) adj. po-
lubowny; przyjacielski
amid (e'myd) prep. wśród; pośród; między; pomiędzy
amidst (e'mydst) prep. wśród;
pośród; między; pomiędzy
amiss (e'mys) adv. na opak;
błędnie ; źle;niefortunnie
ammo ('aemou) s. amunicja
ammunition (,aemju'nyszyn) s.
amunicja

amnesty (aemnysty) s. ułaskawienie; amnestia

among (e'mang) prep. wśród; pomiędzy; między; pośród

amongst (e'mangst) prep. wśród; pomiędzy; między; pośród

amount (e'maunt) v. wynosic; s. suma; kwota; wynik

amount to (e'maunt tu) v. wynosic (w sumie)

ample ('aempl) adj. rozległy; dostatni;hojny;suty;obfity

amplifier ('aemplyfajer) v. wzmacniacz; amplifikator

amplify ('aemplyfy) v. rozszerzać; wzmacniac; przesadzać

amplitude ('aemplytju:d) s. amplituda; wielkość; obfitość

amply ('aemply) adv. obszernie; szeroko;zupełnie wystarczająco

amulet ('aemjulyt) s. amulet

amuse (e'mju:z) v. bawic;ubawić; śmieszyc; zabawić;rozśmieszać

amusement (e'mju:zment) s. rozrywka; zabawa

amusing (e'mju:zyng)adj. zabawny: śmieszny

an (aen; en) art. jeden ;jakiś

anemia (e'ni:mja) s. anemia

anesthetic (e'nystetyk) s. środek znieczulający

analogous (e'naeleges) adj. analogiczny; zbieżny

analogy (e'naeledży) s. podobieństwo; analogia

analysis (e'naelysys) s. analiza

analyze (e'naelajz) v. analizować; rozpatrywac; zanalizować

anathema (e'naetyma) s, klątwa

anatomize (e'naetemajz) v. rozbierac; anatomizować

anatomy (e'naetemy) s. anatomia

ancestor ('aensester) s. przodek

ancestry ('aensestry) s. przodkowie; starożytnosc rodu

anchor ('aenker) s. kotwica

anchovy ('aenchewy) s. sardela

ancient ('ejnszent) adj. starodawny; stary;sędziwy;wiekowy

and (aend; end) conj. i; coraz

anecdote ('aenyk,dout)s. dykteryjka ; anegdota

anew (e'nju:) adv. na nowo

angel ('ejndżl) s. anioł

anger ('eanger) s. gniew; złość;v.gniewac;irytować

angina (aendżajna) s. angina

angle ('aengl) s. kąt; narożnik; kątówka v. kluczyc

Anglican ('aenglyken) adj. anglikański

Anglo-Saxon (aenglou'saeksen) adj. anglo-saski

angry (aengry) adj. zagniewany

anguish (aengłysz) s. udręka; męka;udręczenie;boleść;ból

angular ('aengjuler) adj. kanciasty; narożny; kątowy; graniasty

animal ('aenyml) s. zwierzę; stworzenie;adj.zwierzęcy

animate ('aenymejt) v. ożywiać; adj. ożywiony; żywy

animated cartoon ('aenymejtyd 'ka:rtu:n) film rysunkowy;kreskówka

animation (,aeny'mejszyn) s. ożywianie; ożywienie; żywosc

animosity (,aeny'mosyty) s. uraza; niechęc; animozja

ankle ('aenkl) s. kostka u stopy;staw między stopą i łydką

annex ('aeneks) v. przyłączac; wcielac;s.przybudówka;załącznik

annihilate (e'najelejt) v. unicestwić; niszczyć;niweczyć

anniversary (,aeny've:rsery) s. rocznica adj. doroczny(obchód)

annotation (,aene'tejszyn) s. uwaga; komentarz;przypis

announce (e'nauns) v. zapowiadac; ogłaszać;oznajmiać

announcement (e'naunsment) s. zapowiedź; zawiadomienie

announcer (e'naunser) s. 1. zapowiadacz; 2. (radio) speaker; konferansjer

annoy (e'noj) v. dokuczać; drażnic; nękać;trapić;martwić

annoyance (e'nojens) s. udręka; przykrość;irytacja ; kłopot

annoyed (e'nojd) adj. rozgniewany; rozdrażniony;strapiony

annual ('aenjuel) adj. coroczny; s. rocznik;jednorocznik

annuity (e'njuyty) s. renta
roczna; renta dożywotnia
annul (e'nal) v. unieważniac;
anulować; skasować; kasować
anodyne ('aenedajn) s. anodyna;
środek od bólu ,łagodzący
anomalous (e'nomeles) adj. nienormalny; nietypowy
anonym ('aenenym) s. anonim
anonymous (e'nonymes) adj. bez-
imienny; anonimowy
another (e'nadzer) adj.& pron.
drugi;inny; jeszcze jeden
another time (e'nadzer,tajm)
kiedy indziej;innym razem
answer ('aenser) s. odpowiedź;
v. odpowiadać; spełnić(prośbę)
answer for ('aenser fo:r) v.
odpowiadać za(przed kimś)
ant (aent) s. mrówka
antagonist (aen'taegenyst) s.
przeciwnik; przeciwniczka
antagonize (aen'taege'najz) v.
zrażać; narażać; zwalczac
antelope ('aentyloup) s. anty-
lopa
anterior (aen'tierjer) adj. poprzedni;uprzedni;wcześniejszy
anthem ('aentem) s. hymn narodowy
anti ('aenty) pre . przeciw-
anti-aircraft ('aentaj'e:r-
kra:ft) adj. przeciwlotniczy
antibiotic ('aentybajotyk) s.
antybiotyk
antic ('aentyk) adj. dziwaczny;
groteskowy; s. figiel; dzi-
wactwa; błazeństwo
anticipate (aen'tysypejt) v.
przewidywać; uprzedzać
anticipation (aen'tysypejszyn)
s. uprzedzenie; przewidywanie;
przyśpieszenie;oczekiwanie
anticlimax ('aenty'klajmaeks)
s. rozczarowanie; zawod
anticyclone (,aenty'sajkloun)
s. antycyklon; wyż(atmosf.)
antidote ('aentydout) s. odtrutka ; antidotum
antifreeze('aentyfri:z) s. mieszanka niemarznąca
antiknock ('aentynok) s. mieszanka przeciwstukowa

antipathy (aen'typety) s. odraza; niechęć (do kogoś)
antiquated ('aentykłejtyd) adj.
przestarzały; staroświecki
antique (aen'ti:k)adj.stary;
starożytny; staromodny
antiquity (aen'tykłyty) s. sta-
rożytnosć; zabytki
antiseptic (aenty'septyk) adj.
antyseptyk; przeciwgnilny
antlers ('aentlerz) pl. rogi
(np. jelenia)
anvil ('aenvyl) s. kowadło
anxiety (aeng'zajety) s. niepokój; troska; pożądanie
anxious ('aeŋkszes) adj. zaniepokojony; zabiegający;pragnący
anxious about ('aeŋkszes e'baut)
troskliwy o...;niepokojący się o...
anxious for ('aeŋkszes fo:r)
pragnący bardzo czegoś
anxious to ('aeŋkszes tu) pragnący żeby;mający ochotę na
any ('eny) pron. jakikolwiek;
któryś; jakiś;żaden;lada;byle
any farther ('eny fa:rdzer) trochę dalej;nieco dalej
any more ('eny mo:r) trochę
więcej; teraz; obecnie
anybody ('eny'body) pron. ktoś;
ktokolwiek; każdy; nikt
anyhow ('enyhau) adv. jakkolwiek
anyone ('enyłan) pron. ktokolwiek; każdy; ktos; nikt
anything ('enytyŋg)pron. coś;
cokolwiek; wszystko(oprócz);nic
anything else ('enytyŋgels)
jeszcze coś; coś więcej
anyway ('enyłej) adv. w każdym
razie; jakkolwiek;byle jak
anywhere ('enyhłeer) adv.gdzie-
kolwiek;byle gdzie; nigdzie
apart (e'pa:rt) adv. osobno;
niezależnie;na boku;od siebie
apart from (e'pa:rt, from) niezależnie od...;poza;oprócz;prócz
apartment (e'pa:rtment) s.
mieszkanie; izba; pokój
apartment house (e'pa:rtment,
haus) blok mieszkalny;kamienica
apathetic (aepe'tetyk) adj.
apatyczny;obojętny;bez uczuć

ape (ejp) s. małpa (bezogonowa)
v. małpować;naśladować;błaznować
apex ('ejpeks) s. szczyt; czubek; wierzchołek
apiary ('ejpjery) s. pasieka
apiece (e'pi:s) adv. na osobę; od sztuki;za sztukę; każdy
aplomb (e'plom) s. pewność siebie; opanowanie; zimna krew
apologize (e'poledżajz) v. usprawiedliwiać; przepraszać
apology (e'poledży) s. usprawiedliwienie; obrona;przeprosiny
apoplexy ('aepepleksy) s. apopleksja ; udar
apostle (e'posl) s. apostoł
apostolic (,aepe'stolyk) adj. apostolski
apostrophe (e'postrefy) s. apostrof; apostrofa
appal (e'po:l) v. przerażać
apparatus (aepe'rejtes) s. aparat; urządzenie;przyrząd;organ
apparent (e'paerent) adj. jawny; pozorny; oczywisty;widoczny
appeal (e'pi:l) v. apelować; odwoływać się;uciekać się do
appeal to (e'pi:l tu) v. zwracać się do...;zwracać się z apelem
appear (e'pier) v. ukazywać się; zjawiać się;pokazywać się
appearance (e'pierens) s. wygląd; pozór; wystąpienie;zjawienie się
appease (e'pi:z) v. łagodzić; uśmierzać; zaspakajać;ugłaskać
append (e'pend) v. dołączać; doczepiać;dodawać;zawieszać
appendicitis (ependy'sajtys) s. zapalenie wyrostka robaczkowego
appendix (e'pendyks) s. dodatek; uzupełnienie;ślepa kiszka
appetite ('aepitajt) s. apetyt
appetizing ('aepitajzing) adj. apetyczny; smakowity
applaud (e'plo:d) v. oklaskiwać; klaskać;bic brawo;przyklasnąć
applause (e'plo:z) s. aplauz; oklaski;poklask;pochwała;aprobata
apple ('aepl) s. jabłko
apple-pie('aeplpaj) s. placek jabłkowy ; szarlotka

applesauce ('aepl so:s) s. purée z jabłek
apple tree ('aepltri:) s. jabłoń
appliance (e'plajens) s. przyrząd; urządzenie;akcesoria
applicant ('aeplykent) s. petent; zgłaszający się;kandydat
application (,aeply'kejszyn) s. podanie; użycie; zastosowanie;przykładanie;pilność
apply (e'plaj) v. używać; stosować; odnosić się;naciskać
apply for (e'plaj fo:r) v. starać się o...;wnosić podanie o
apply to (e'plaj tu) v. zwracać się do..;zgłaszać się do(o coś)
appoint (e'point) v. mianować; wyznaczać; ustanawiać;ustalić
appointment (e'pointment) s. nominacja; oznaczenie czasu i miejsca; umówione spotkanie
apportion (e'po:rszyn) v. wyznaczać; wydzielać;przydzielać
appreciate (e'pri:szjejt) v. cenić wysoko; zyskiwać na wartości;ocenić; oszacować;docenić
appreciation (e'pri:szjejszyn) s. ocena; uznanie; wzrost wartości;zrozumienie czegoś
apprehend (,aepry'hend) v. ująć; pojmać; rozumieć
apprehension (,aepry'henszyn) s. obawa; pojęcie; aresztowanie;lęk
apprehensive (,aepry'hensyw) adj.obawiający się; pojętny
apprentice (e'prentys) s. czeladnik; uczeń; terminator
apprenticeship (e'prentysszyp) s. termin;nauka rzemiosła
approach (e'proucz) v. zbliżać się; podchodzić;s. dostęp
approach road (e'proucz,roud) droga dojazdowa
appropriate (e'prouprjejt) adj. właściwy; odpowiedni;stosowny
appropriation (e'prouprejszyn) s. asygnowanie; przywłaszczenie;przeznaczenie; kredyty
approval (e'pru:wel) s. aprobata; uznanie; zatwierdzenie

approximate (e'proksymyt) adj.
zbliżony; przybliżony; mniej
więcej;v.zbliżać(się);być około
apricot ('ejprykot) s. morela
April ('ejprel) s. kwiecień
apron ('ejpren) s. fartuch;
płyta przednia;przedpole
apropos (aepre'pou) adv. do tego celu; w związku z tym ,,
apt (aept) v. mieć skłonność
apt to (aept tu) v. być skłon-
nym do...;często coś robić
aquarium (e'kłerjem) s. akwarium
aquatic (e'kłaetyk) adj. wodny
aquatic sports (e'kłaetyk
spo:rts) sport wodny
aqueduct ('aekłydakt) s. wodociąg; akwedukty rzymskie
aquiline ('aekłylajn) adj. orli
Arabic (ae'rebyk) adj. arabski
arable ('aerebl) adj. orny
arbitrary ('a:rbytrery) adj. dowolny; samowolny
arbor ('a:rber) s. altanka; wał
napędowy; oś maszyny; drzewo
arc (a:rk) s. łuk
arc lamp (a:rk lemp) lampa łu-
kowa
arcade (a:r'kejd) s. arkada;
podcienie
arch (a:rcz) s. łuk; sklepienie;
podbicie;v. tworzyć łuk
arch (a:rcz) adj.chytry; wierutny;
arcy...;figlarny
archaeologist (a:rky'oledżyst)
s. archeolog
archeology (a:rky'oledży) s.
archeologia
archaic (a:rkejyk) adj. archai-
czny; przestarzały; staroświecki
archangel ('a:rkejndżel) s.
archanioł
archbishop ('a:rczbyszep) s.
arcybiskup
archer ('a:rczer) s. łucznik
archery ('a:rczery) s. łucznic-
two; łuki i strzały
architect ('a:rkytekt) s. architekt;twórca;budowniczy
architecture ('a:rkytekczer) s.
architektura;styl budowy

archives ('a:rkajwz) pl. archi-
wa ; archiwum
archway ('a:rczłej) s. skle-
pione przejście ; brama
arctic ('a:rktyk) adj. arktycz-
ny ; polarny
ardent ('a:rdent) adj. rozpalo-
ny; prażący ;płonący;gorliwy
ardor ('a:rder) s. żar; żarli-
wość; gorliwość; zapał
arduous ('a:rdżues) adj. mozolny; wytrwały; stromy;żmudny
are (a:r) v. są ;jesteś;jesteście
area ('e:rje) s. obszar; zakres;
powierzchnia;teren;okolica;strefa
Argentine ('a:rdżentajn) adj.
argentyński
argot ('a:rgou) s. żargon
(złodziejski)
argue ('a:rgju:) v. wykazywać;
rozumować; spierać się; rozpatrywać; dowodzić;udowadniać
argument ('a:rgjument) s. argument; dowód; sprzeczka ;spór
argumentation (,a:rgjumen'tejszyn) s. roztrząsanie; argu-
mentacja; rozumowanie
arid ('aeryd) adj. suchy; jałowy; oschły;wypalony;spieczony
arise, arose, arisen (e'rajz;
e'rouz; e'r,:zn)
arise (e'rajz) v. powstawać;
wstawać; wynikać;nadarzyć się
arithmetic (,aeryt'metyk) s.
rachunki; adj. arytmetyczny;
rachunkowy
ark (a:rk) s. arka; skrzynia
arm (a:rm) s. ramię; odnoga;
konar; rękaw; poręcz
arm (a:rm) s. broń (rodzaj);
uzbrojenie; v. uzbroić; opan-
cerzyć; nastawiać (zapłon)
armament ('a:rmement) s. uzbrojenie; zbrojenia; siły zbrojne
armament race ('a:rmement, rejs)
wyścig zbrojeń
armchair (,a:rm'cze:r) s. fotel
armistice ('a:rmystys) s. zawieszenie broni;rozejm
armor ('a:rmer) s. zbroja;
opancerzenie;v.zbroić w płyty
pancerne;opancerzać

armored car ('a:rmerd,ca:r)
samochód pancerny
arm-twisting ('a:rm,tłystyŋ)
napór na (kogoś); (wykręcanie
ręki);nagabywanie kogoś
arms ('a:rmz) pl. broń; uzbrojenie; herby; herb
army ('a:rmy) s. wojsko; armia
aroma (e'roume) s. aromat
arose (e'rouz) v. powstał;
wstał; wynikł; zob. arise
around (e'raund) prep. dokoła;
naokoło; wokoło; adv. wokół;
tu i tam; około; wszędzie
arousal (e'rauzel) s. pobudze-
nie do czynu (działania)
arouse (e'rauz) v. pobudzić;
budzić; wzniecać(uczucia)
arraign(e'rejn) v. pozwać;
oskarżyć;atakować pogląd
arrange (e'rejndż) v. układać;
szykować; porządkować;ustalać
arrangement (e'rejndżment) s.
układ; ułożenie się; urządzenie; zaaranżowanie;porządek;szyk
array (e'rej) v. szykować; przybrać; rozmieszczać; s. szyk;
szereg; uszeregowanie;wystawa
arrears (e'rierz) pl. zaległości;
długi;zaległe prace(płatności)
arrest (e'rest) s. areszt;
aresztowanie; zatrzymanie;
v. aresztować; zatrzymywać;
wstrzymywać;przyciągać(uwagę)
arrival (e'rajwel) s. przyjazd;
przybysz; rzecz nadeszła
arrive (e'rajw) v. przybyć;
dojść; osiągnąć;wspólnie ustalać
arrive at (e'rajw,aet) v. dojść
do...;wspólnie ustalać
arrogance ('aeregens) s. zarozumiałość; buta; arogancja
arrogant ('aeregent) adj. butny; arogancki; wyniosły
arrow ('aerou) s. strzała;
strzałka (kierunkowa)
arrow head ('aerou hed) s. grot
arse (a:rs) s. vulg. rzyć; zadek; dupa ; dupsko
arsenal ('a:rsynl) s. arsenał
arsenic ('a:rsnyk) s. arszenik;
arsen; ('a:rsenyk) adj. arse-
nowy

arson ('a:rsen)s. podpalenie
(zbrodnia); podpalanie
art (a:rt) s. sztuka; chytrość;
zręczność; rzemiosło;fortel
arterial (a:r'tyerjal) adj.
tętniczy; magistralny
arterial road(a:r'tyerjal,roud)
magistrala;główna szosa
artery (a:rtery) s. arteria;
tętnica; arteria ruchu
artful ('a:rtful) adj. chytry;
zręczny; pomysłowy;dowcipny
article ('a:rtykl) s. rodzajnik;
artykuł; warunek;paragraf;temat
articulate (a:rtykjulejt) v.
wyrażać jasno; adj. artykuło-
wany; wyraźny;stawowy
artifact (,a:rty'faekt) s. wytwór ludzkiej ręki
artificial(,a:rty'fyszel) adj.
sztuczny;udany;symulowany
artillery (a:r'tylery) s. artyleria
artisan ('a:rtyzaen) s. rzemieślnik
artist ('a:rtist) s. artysta;
artystka
artiste (a:r'ty:st) s. artysta;
odtwórca; artysta estradowy
artless ('artlys) adj. niewinny; niedołężny;szczery;otwarty
as (aez; ez) adv. pron. conj;
jak; tak; co; jako; jaki; skoro; żeby; choć; z (dniem)
as... as (ez...ez) tak jak
as far as (ez fa:r ez) co do
as many (ez meny) tak wiele
as well (ez łel) również
as well as (ez łel ez) jak także ; tak jak; jak również
as for (ez fo:r) co się tyczy
asbestos (aez'bestes) s. azbest
ascend (e'send) v. piąć się;
iść w górę; wznosić się; wracać w przeszłość; wstępować
ascension (e'senszyn) s. wznoszenie się; Wniebowstąpienie
ascent (e'sent) s. wzlot;
wzrost;stok; postęp;wchodzenie
ascertain (aeser'tejn) v.
stwierdzać; ustalać;konstatować
ascetic (e'setyk) s. asceta;
adj. ascetyczny;odmawiający sobie

ascribe (e'skrajb) v. przypisywać; przypisać(coś komuś)
aseptic ('eseptyk) adj. jałowy; wyjałowiony; aseptyczny
ash (aesz) s. popiół ;jesion
ashamed (e'szejmd) adj. zawstydzony ;zażenowany
ashamed of (e'szejmd ow)adj. wstydzący się czegoś
ash can (aesz kaen) wiadro na śmieci; wiadro na popiół
ashen ('aeszen) adj. popielaty
ashes ('aeszyz) s. popioły
ashore (e'szo:r) adv. na brzeg; na brzegu ; na ląd; na lądzie
ashtray ('aesztrej) s. popielniczka
Ash Wednesday (,aesz'łenzdy) - Środa Popielcowa
Asiatic (,ej ży'atyk) adj. azjatycki
aside (e'sajd) adv. na stronę; na stronie; na boku;na uboczu
aside from (e'sajd,from) adv. oprócz; z wyjątkiem; poza;prócz
asinine ('aesynajn) adj. ośli; głupi; idiotyczny
ask (aesk) v. pytać ;zapytywać
ask a question ('a:sk ej'kłeszczyn) stawiać pytanie; pytać
ask to dinner ('a:sk tu'dyner) zapraszać na obiad
ask for ('aesk fo:r) prosić o...
askance (es'kaens) adv. z ukosa; zezem ; niepewnie; podejrzliwie
askew (es'kju:) adv. krzywo; skośnie ; z ukosa
aslant (e'sla:nt) adv. ukośnie; skośnie ; na ukos; w poprzek
asleep (e'sli:p) adv. we śnie; adj. śpiący;zdrętwiały;ścierpły
asparagus (es'paereges) s. szparag
aspect ('aespekt) s. aspekt; wygląd; wyraz; faza; postać; strona;mina;przejaw;wystawa domu
aspen ('aespen) s. osika; osina
asphalt ('aesfo,lt) s. asfalt
aspire (es'pajer) v. dążyć; marzyć; wzdychać do...
aspire after (es'pajer'a:fter) aspirować; dążyć do (czegoś); mieć aspiracje żeby...

ass (aes) s. osioł;wulg.: dupa
assail (e'sejl) v. napadać; przystępować;atakować;uderzać
assailant (e'sejlent) s. napastnik
assassin (e'saesyn) s. morderca (najęty); zamachowiec
assassinate (e'saesynejt) v. zamordować; dokonać zamachu
assassination (e,saesy'nejszyn) s. morderstwo;zabójstwo;zamach
assault (e'sa:lt) s. napad; atak; zgwałcenie;v.atakować;bić
assemblage (e'semblydż) s. zebranie; zbiór; zmontowanie
assemble (e'sembl) v. zbierać; montować;nagromadzać;złożyć
assembly (e'sembly) s. zebranie; zbiórka; montaż
assembly line (e'sembly,lajn) taśma montażowa;linia montażowa
assent (e'sent) s. zgoda; pogodzenie się;v.zgadzać się;uznawać
assent to (e'sent tu) v. zgadzać się na coś;zatwierdzać coś
assert (e'se:rt) v. twierdzić; upominać się;dowieść;stawiać się
assess (e'ses) v. szacować; oceniać; wymierzać; opodatkować;nałożyć podatek
assets ('aesets) pl. własność; aktywa; wartościowi pracownicy
assign (e'sajn) v. przydzielać; ustalać; odnosić; przekazywać
assignment (e'sajnment) s. przydzielenie; przypisanie; przekazanie;przydział;podział
assimilate (e'symylejt) v. upodabniać; wcielać; wchłaniać; asymilować;przyswajać sobie
assist (e'syst) v. pomagać; brać udział; być przy
assistance (e'systens) s. pomoc; asysta; wsparcie
assistant (e'systent) s. asystent; pomocnik;adj.pomocniczy
assizes (e'sajzyz) pl. okresowe sesje sądu (wyjazdowe)w Anglii
associate (e'souszjejt) s. towarzysz; wspólnik-sprzymierzeniec; rzecz związana z czymś, v. łączyć;obcować ; kojarzyć; brać do spółki;adj.towarzyszący

association (e,souszy'ejszyn) s.
łączenie; współpraca; kojarzenie; przyłączanie się ;związek
assort (e'so:rt) v. sortowac;
dobierać; obcować; klasyfikować
assorted (e'so:rtyd) adj. dobrany; posortowany; mieszany
assortment (e'so:rtment) s.
asortyment; wybór; sortowanie
assume (e'sju:m) v. zakładać;
obejmować; przybierać; przypuszczać ;wdziewać;udawać
assurance (e'szu:rens) s. zapewnienie; pewność; ubezpieczenie
assure (e'szu:r) v. zapewniać;
ubezpieczać zabezpieczać
assured (e'szu:rd) adj. pewny
(siebie); s. ubezpieczony
asthma (aesma) s. dusznica;
astma ; dychawica
astigmatic (,aestyg'maetyk) adj.
astygmatyczny
astir (e'ste:r) adv. poruszony;
w ruchu; na nogach ;ożywiony
astonish (es'tonysz) v. zadziwiać; zdumiewać ;zdziwić
astonished (es'tonyszt) adj.
zdumiony ; bardzo zdziwiony
astonishment (es'tonyszment) s.
zdumienie ; zdziwienie
astray (es'trej) adv. na błędną
drogę; na bezdrożu ;na manowce
astride (es'trajd) adv. okrakiem;
rozstawionymi nogami
astringent (es'tr.ndżent) adj.
ściągający; surowy ;wstrzymujący
astrodome('aestre,doum)s. astro-
kopuła (nad stadionem sportowym)
astrologer (es'troledżer) s.
astrolog
astronaut ('aestreno:t) s. astro-
nauta
astute (es'tu:t) adj. bystry;
przebiegły ;wnikliwy
asunder (e'sander) adv. oddziel-
nie; na boki; na strony
asylum (e'sajlem) s. azyl; schronisko ; przytułek; schronienie
at (aet; et) prep. w; na; u;
przy; pod; z ;za; do; o; po
ate (ejt) v. jadłem; jadłes; jadł
etc; zob. eat

athlete ('aetli:t) s. atleta;
siłacz; sportowiec
athletic ('aet'letyk) adj.
atletyczny; sportowy
athletics (aet'letyks) pl.atle-
tyka; sport;wychowanie fizyczne
Atlantic (et'laentyk) adj.
atlantycki
atlas ('aetles) s. atlas
atmosphere('aetmesfier) s.
atmosfera ;otoczenie;nastrój
atoll ('aetol) s, atol
atom ('aetem) s. atom
atom bomb ('aetem bom) s. bomba atomowa
atomic (e'tomyk) adj. atomowy
atomic age (e'tomyk ejdż)
epoka atomowa
atomic pile (e'tomyk pajl)
stos atomowy
atomic weight (e'tomyk łejt)
ciężar atomowy
atomize ('aetemajz) v. rozbijać
na atomy ; rozpylać
atomizer ('aetemajzer) s. rozpylacz (cieczy)
atone (e'toun) v. odpokutować;
okupić; załagodzić
atrocious (e'trouszes) adj.
potworny; okropny ;skandaliczny
atrocity (e'trosyty) s. okrucieństwo ;okrutny czyn;ohyda
attach (e'taecz) v. przywiązy-
wac; przyczepiać; przydzielać;
łączyc ;przymocowywać;nalepiać
attachment (e'taeczment) s. załącznik; przymocowanie ;więź
attack (e'taek) v. napadać;
atakować; s. atak; uderzenie
attempt (e'tempt) v. usiłować;
czynić zamach; próbować
s. próba; usiłowanie; zamach
attend (e'tend) v. uczęszczać;
leczyć; obsługiwać ;towarzyszyć
attendance (e'tendens) s. obsługa; opieka; uczęszczanie
attendant (e'tendent) s. obecny; służący ;adj.towarzyszący
attention (e'tenszyn) s. uwaga;
uprzejmość ;troska;opieka
attentive (e'tentyw) adj. uważny; gorliwy; uprzejmy ;pilny

attest (e'test) v. poświadczyć;
stwierdzać;zalegalizować
attic ('aetyk) s. poddasze;
attyka; strych
attitude ('aetitu:d) s. postawa; ustosunkowanie się;poza
attorney (e'te:rny) s. pełnomocnik; adwokat;prawnik
attract (e'traekt) v. przyciągać;zwabić; być pociągającym
attraction (e'traekszyn) s.
przyciąganie;powab;urok;atrakcja
attractive (e'traektyw) adj. pociągający;przyciagajacy; miły
attribute ('aetrybju:t) s, przymiot; cecha;właściwość
attribute (e'trybju:t) v. przypisywać komuś; odnosić do czegoś
attrition (e'tryszyn) s. wy-
niszczenie; ścieranie; skrucha
auburn ('o:bern) adj. (barwa)
kasztanowa; złotobrązowa
auction ('o:kszyn) s. licytacja;
aukcja
auction off ('o:kszyn of) v.
licytować; sprzedawać na licytacji;wystawiać na licytację
audacious (o:'dejszes) adj. odważny; śmiały; zuchwały
audacity (o:'daesyty) s. śmiałość; odwaga; zuchwałość
audible ('o:dybel) adj. słyszalny;odbierany słuchem
audience ('o:djens) s. publiczność; audiencja
audit ('o:dyt) s. sprawdzenie
rachunków; rozliczenie;
v. kontrolować rachunki
aught (a:t) s. coś; nic; zero
August ('o:gest) s, sierpień
august ('o:gast) adj. wyniosły;
dostojny;majestatyczny
aunt (aent) s. ciotka; wujenka;
stryjenka
aurora (o:'ro:re) s. brzask;
jutrznia; jutrzenka; zorza po-
larna
austere (o:s'tier) adj. surowy;
poważny; prosty;czysto użytkowy
austerity (o:s'teryty) s. surowość; powaga; prostota;srogość;
charakter czysto użytkowy

Australian (o:s'trejljen) adj.
australijski
Austrian ('o:strjen) adj.
austriacki;s. Austryjak
authentic (o:'tentyk) adj.
autentyczny; prawdziwy
author ('o:ter) s. autor; pisarz; sprawca
authoritative (o:'torytejtyw)
adj. stanowczy; miarodajny
authority (o:'toryty) s. władza; autorytet; znaczenie;
powaga;moc rozkazywania
authorize ('o:terajz) v. upoważniać; zatwierdzać;aprobować
authorship ('o:terszyp) s.
autorstwo;zawod pisarza
autobiography ('o:tebaj'ogrefy)
s. autobiografia
autograph ('o:tegraef) s. podpis; autograf
automat ('o:temaet) n . restauracja z automatem na monety
automatic (,o:te'maetyk) adj.
automatyczny; machinalny
automation (,o:te'mejszyn) s.
automatyzacja
automobile ('o:temeby:l) s. samochód; auto
autumn ('o:tem) s. jesień
auxiliary (o:g'zyljery) adj.
pomocniczy
avail (e'wejl) v. pomagać;
znaczyć; być przydatny
available (e'wejlebl) adj.
dostępny; osiągalny
avalanche ('aewelaencz) s. lawina; v. spadać lawiną
avarice ('aewerys) s. chciwość;
skąpstwo
avaricious (,aewe'ryszes) adj.
chciwy; skąpy
avenue ('aewynju:)s. bulwar;
aleja;ulica;dojazd;dojście
average ('aewerydż) adj. przeciętny; średni; s. średnia;
przeciętna; v. osiągać średnio; obliczać średnią; wy-
posrodkowywać;pracować średnio..
averse (e'we:rs) adj. niechętny; czujący odrazę;przeciwny
aversion (e'werżyn) s. odraza;
niechęć

avert (e'we:rt) v. odwracać
(np. myśli; oczy); oddalić(cios)
aviation (,ejwy'ejszyn) s. lotnictwo
aviator ('ejwyejter) s.lotnik
avid ('ewyd) adj. chciwy; zachłanny
avoid (e'woyd) v. unikać; uchylać się; stronić
avow (e'wau) v. wyznawać
avowal (e'wauel) s. wyznanie;
przyznanie się; zeznanie
await (e'łejt) v. czekać; oczekiwać;być a oczekiwaniu
awake; awoke; awoke (e'łejk;
e'łouk; e'łouk)
awake (e'łejk) v. budzić się;
otwierać oczy na...; adj. czujny; przebudzony; na jawie
awaken (e'łejkn) v. budzić;
uświadamiać komuś (kogoś)
award (e'ło:rd) v. przysądzać;
wyznaczać; s. nagroda; zapłata; grzywna sądowa
aware (e'łeer) adj. świadomy
away (e'łej) adv. precz; z dala
awe (o:) s. lęk; nabożna część
awful ('o:ful) adj. straszny;
budzący lęk i szacunek
awhile ('ehłajl) adv. na krótko;
przez chwilę;chwilę; króciutko
awkward ('o:kłerd) adj. niezgrabny; niezdarny; kłopotliwy;
nieporęczny;zaklopotany;trudny
awning ('o:nyŋg)s. dach z płot-
na; markiza; zasłona; stora
awoke (e'łouk) v. zbudzony;
zob. awake
awry (e'raj) adv. skośnie; krzywo; na opak; adj. krzywy; błędny; opaczny; wypaczony
ax (aeks) s. siekiera; topor;
v. obcinać siekierą;redukować
axe (aeks) = ax
axes (aeksyz) pl. osie;siekiery
axis ('aeksys) s. oś ;ośka
axle ('aeksel) s. oś (koła);
ośka(łącząca tylnie koła wozu)
azimuth ('aezymet) s. azymut
azure ('aeżer) s. błękit; lazur;
adj. błękitny; lazurowy

b (bi) b; druga litera alfabetu angielskiego
babble ('baebl) v. paplać; gadać; s. paplanina; gadanina
babe (bejb) s. niemowlę
baboon (be'bu:n) s. pawian
baby ('bejby) s. niemowlę
baby carriage ('bejby kaerydż)
s. wózek dziecinny
babyhood ('bejbyhud) s. nie-
mowlęctwo
bachelor ('baecheler) s. niezamężna; nieżonaty; stopień
uniwersytecki (najniższy)
back (baek) s. tył; grzbiet;
v. cofać się; wycofać się
backbone ('baekboun) s. kręgosłup; stos pacierzowy
backdoor ('baek'do:r) s. tylne
drzwi;adj.zakulisowy;potajemny
backfire ('baek'fajer) s. wybuch odwrotny;   zawiść; v.
spalić na panewce
background ('baekgraund) s. tło;
dalszy plan; przeszłość czyjaś
back number('baeknamber)s. zaległy numer;stare wydanie pisma
backseat ('baek'si:t) s. tylne
siedzenie;wycofanie się z akcji
backstairs ('baeksteerz) s.
tylne schody;adj.zakulisowy
backstroke ('baek'strouk) s.
pływanie na plecach; rzut
odbity od lewa w tenisie
back tire ('baek'tajer) s. tylna
opona samochodowa (slang)
backward ('baekłerd) adj. tylny; zacofany;zapóźniony
backwards ('baekłerds) adv.
w tyle; odwrotnie; do tyłu
back wheel('baekhłil) s. tylne
koło (samochodu,ciężarówki)
bacon ('bejkn) s. słonina; bo-
czek; bekon
bacon and eggs ('bejkn end egz)
jajka z boczkiem
bacterium (baek'tierjem) s.
bakteria
bacteria (baek'tierje) pl.
bakterie
bad (baed) adj. zły; niedobry;
przykry;sfałszowany;słaby;zdrożny

bade (baed) v. proponował; oferował cenę; kazał; zob.: bid
badge (baedź) s. odznaka; oznaka (członkostwa, rangi etc.)
badger ('baedżer) s. borsuk; v. zadręczać (narzekaniem)
badly ('baedly) adv. źle; bardzo
badly wounded ('baedl 'Xu:ndyd) ciężko ranny ;ciężko zraniony
badminton ('baedmynten) s. rodzaj tenisa (piłka z piórkiem)
bad mouth('baedmaus) v. oczerniać; obgadywać; obmawiać
baffle ('baefl) v. udaremniać; łudzić ;niveczyć;s.przegroda
bag (baeg) s. torba; worek; babsztyl; v. pakować; zwędzić
baggage ('baegydź) s. bagaż
baggage check ('baegydź,czek) kwit bagażowy
baggy ('baegy) adj. workowaty
bag-pipe ('baegpajp) s. kobza
bail (bejl) s. kaucja; poręka
bail out (bejl'ałt) v. zwolnić za kaucją;wywinąć się z opresji
bailiff ('bejlyf) s. woźny sądowy; komornik ;rządca majątku
bait (bejt) s. przynęta; pokusa
bake (bejk) v. piec; wypalać
baker ('bejker) s. piekarz
bakery (bejkery) s. piekarnia
baking powder ('bejkyŋ,pałder) proszek do pieczenia
balance ('baelens) s. waga; bilans; równowaga; v. równoważyć; bilansować ; wahać się
bald (bo:ld) adj. łysy ;jawny
bale (bejl) s. zwój płótna; bela; v. zob. bail
balk (bo:k) v. opierać się; przeszkadzać; zniechęcać; s. belka ;miedza; zawada .
ball (bo:l) s. l. piłka; pocisk; kłębek; 2. bal;zabawa taneczna
ballad ('baeled) s. ballada; pieśń (sentymentalna opisowa)
ballast ('baelest) s. balast; v. obciążać balastem
ball bearing ('bo:l'bearyŋ) łożysko kulkowe
ballet ('baelej) s. balet ; zespół baletowy(tancerzy)

ball game('bo:lgejm) s. rozgrywka; gra w piłkę
ballistic (be'lystyk)adj.balistyczny
balloon (be'lu:n) s. balon
ballot ('bealet) s. (tajne) głosowanie; kartka; v. tajnie głosować
ballot box ('baeletboks) s. urna wyborcza
ball-point pen ('bo:l-point-pen) s. kulkowy pisak;długopis
balm (ba:m) s. balsam
balmy ('ba:my) adj. błogi; balsamiczny
balustrade (,baeles'trejd) s. poręcz; balustrada
bamboo (baem'bu:) s. bambus
ban (baen) s. zakaz; klątwa; v. zabraniać;wyjąć spod prawa
banana (be'na:ne) s. banan
band (baend) s. szajka; kapela; taśma; v. wiązać się; przepasywać opaską ;zrzeszać
bandage ('baendydź) s. bandaż; v. bandażować ; obandażować
bandmaster ('baend,ma:ster) s. kapelmistrz
bandstand ('baendstaend) s. estrada
bang (baeŋg) s. huk; zryw; uciecha; bęc; v. trzaskać ;walnąć
banish ('baenysz) v. wygnac; usunąć; wykluczać ;wypędzać
banishment ('baenyszment) s. wygnanie ; banicja
banisters ('baenystez) pl. banistry (schodów); poręcze
banjo ('baendżou) s. rodzaj gitary okrągłej pokrytej skórą
bank ('baeŋk) s.l.brzeg;łacha;nasyp; szkarpa; 2. bank; 3. stoł roboczy; 4. rząd;5.nachylenie toru v. 1. prowadzić bank; 2. składać w banku; 3. piętrzyć; pochylać; 4. polegać 5.obwałować
bank bill ('baeŋk,byl) s. banknot
banker ('baeŋker) s. bankier
banking ('baeŋkyŋg)s. bankowość
bank note('baeŋknout) s. banknot ; papierowy pieniądz

bankrate ('baeŋkrejt) s. stopa dyskontowa;stopa procentowa

bankrupt ('baeŋkrept) s. bankrut

banner ('baener) s. chorągiew; transparent; tytuł (czołowy)

banns (baenz) pl. zapowiedzi

banquet ('baenkłyt) s. bankiet

baptism ('baeptyzem) s. chrzest

baptize ('baeptajz) s. chrzcić

bar (ba:r) s. belka; drąg; rogatka; krata; v. zagradzać; hamować; prep.: oprócz

bar (ba:r) s. 1. izba adwokacka, sądowa; 2. bar; bufet z wyszynkiem ;szynkwas

barb (ba:rb) s. haczyk; docinek; kolec; skaza (na odlewie);szew

barbarian (ba:r'bearjen) s. barbarzyńca; adj. barbarzyński

barbed wire ('ba:rbd,łajer) drut kolczasty

barber ('ba:rber) s. fryzjer (męski); golibroda

barbiturate (ba:r'byczeret) s. lek uspakajający ;nasenny lek

bare (beer) adj. nagi; goły; łysy; v. obnażać ;odkrywać

barefoot ('beerfut) adj.& adv. boso; bosy

bareheaded ('beerhedyd) adj. z gołą głową

barely ('beerly) adv. ledwie; otwarcie; ubogo; zaledwie

bargain ('ba:rgyn) s. ubicie targu; dobre kupno; v. targować się; spodziewać się

barge (ba:rdż) s. barka; v. pakować się; trynić się

bark (ba:rk) s. 1. kora; 2. szczeknięcie; v. zdzierać korę; garbować korę; szczekać; pyskować; kaszleć;warkliwie mówić; wyszczekać; zakaszleć

barley ('ba:rly) s. jęczmień

barmaid ('ba:rmejd) f. bufetowa; kelnerka; szynkarka

barn (ba:rn) s. stodoła; stajnia; obora; wozownia ;remiza

barometer(be'romyter) s. barometr

barracks ('baereks) pl. koszary; baraki; budynki koszarowe etc.; wygwizdywanie (zawodników,graczy)

barrel ('baerel) s. beczka; lufa; rura;cylinder;walec;bęben

barren ('baeren) adj. jałowy; wyczerpany;nieurodzajny

barricade (,baery'kejd) s. barykada; v. barykadować się

barrier ('baerjer) s. zapora; zastawa; rogatka;ogrodzenie

barrister ('baeryster) s. adwokat;adwokatka;obrońca;obrończyni

barrow ('baerou) s. taczki

bartender ('ba:rtender) s. barman; bufetowy;bufetowa;barmanka

barter ('ba:rter) v. wymieniać; handlować; s. handel wymienny

base (bejs) n. podstawa; nasada; adj. podły; nędzny; niski

baseball ('bejsbo:l) s. palant amerykański(grany piłką i maczugą)

baseless ('bejslys) adj. bezpodstawny;nieuzasadniony

basement ('bejsment) s. suterena; piwnica ;podziemie

bashful ('baeszful) a. wstydliwy;nieśmiały;trwożliwy;lękliwy

basic ('bejsyk) a. podstawowy; zasadniczy ;zasadowy

basin ('bejsn) s. miednica; zbiornik; dorzecze; zagłębie

basis ('bejsys) pl. fundamenty; podstawy;podłoże;grunt;zasada

bask (baesk) v. wygrzewać się na słońcu;wylegiwać się;pławić się

basket ('ba:skyt) s. kosz; koszyk;v. wrzucać do kosza

basketball ('ba:skytbo:l) s. koszykówka; piłka do koszykówki

bass (bejs) s. bas (głos,śpiewak)

bass (baes) s. okoń; łyko lipowe ; okoń morski lub rzeczny

bastard ('baesterd) s. bękart; bastard;adj. nieślubny;nędzny

baste (bejst) v. fastrygować; polewać tłuszczem pieczeń

bat (baet) s. nietoperz; maczuga; kij;v. mrugać; hulać(slang)

bath (ba:s) s. kąpiel; łazienka

bathe (bejz) v. kąpać; moczyć; rosić; przemywać; wykąpać

bathing (bejzyŋg)s. kąpanie

bathing cap ('bejzyŋgkaep) czapka kąpielowa

bathing suit ('bejzyŋg sju:t)
strój kąpielowy; kostjum kąpielowy
bathing trunks ('bejzyŋg traŋks)
spodenki kąpielowe
bathrobe ('ba:zroub) s. płaszcz
kąpielowy
bathroom ('ba:zru:m) s. łazienka; ubikacja; ustęp; klozet
bath towel ('ba:z tałel) ręcznik kąpielowy
bathtub ('ba:ztab) s. wanna
baton ('baeton) s. buława; pałka; batuta; pałeczka dyrygenta
battalion (be'taeljen) s. batalion ; pododdział pułku
batter ('baeter) v. tłuc; walić
battered ('baeterd) adj. pobity
battery ('baetery) s. bateria;
komplet; pobicie; zestaw armat
battle ('baetl) s. bitwa ; walka
battleship ('baetlszyp) s. okręt
wojenny
baulk (bo:k) s. przeszkoda;
rozczarowanie; v. przeszkadzać
bawl (bo:l) v. wrzeszczec; drzec
się; krzyczec; zwymyslać
bay (bej) adj. czerwono-brązowy;
gniady (koń); wawrzyn; laur
bay (bej) s. zatoka; wnęka;
przęsło; v. ujadac ; wyć
bay window ('bej'łyndoł) okno
we wnęce
bazaar (be'za:r) s. bazar
be; was; been (bi:; łoz; bi:n)
be (bi:) v. być; żyć; trwać;
dziac się ; istniec; stawać się
beatnik (bi:tnyk) s. nonkonfor-
mista; (-tka)
be reading (bi:'ry:dyŋ) czytać
własnie; być w trakcie czytania
beach (bi:cz) s. brzeg; plaża
beachhead ('bi:czhed) s. przyczółek (nad wodą)
beachwear ('bi:człe:r) s. odzież
plażowa ; kostiumy, płaszcze etc.
beacon ('bi:ken) s. sygnał (og-
niowy); latarnia morska
bead (bi:d) s. paciorek; kora-
lik; v. nawlekać korale; per-
lić się ; ozdabiac paciorkami
beak (bi:k) s. dziób ; belfer

beam (bi:m) s. belka; dźwigar;
promień; radosny usmiech
v. promieniowac; nadawać sygnał; rozpromieniać się
bean (bi:n) s. fasola; bób;
ziarnko; łeb; animusz
bear; bore; borne (beer; bo:r;
bo:rn)
bear (beer) s. niedźwiedź;
v. dźwigać; ponosić; znosić;
trzymać się ; rodzić; miec (podpis)
beard (bierd) s. broda (zarost)
bearer ('beerer) s. nosiciel;
okaziciel; zwiastun; karawaniarz
bearing ('beeryŋg) s. zachowanie;
wzgląd; wspornik; rodzenie; łożysko
beast (bi:st) s. bestia; bydle
beastly ('bistly) adj. bydlęcy;
potworny; adv. straszliwie; okrutnie
beast of prey ('bi:st ow prej)
s. drapieżnik
beat; beat; beaten (bi:t; bi:t;
bi:tn)
beat (bi:t) v. bić; bic się;
ubijac ; tłuc; trzepotać; zbić; kuć
beat it ! ('bi:t, yt) excl.:
precz ! wynoś się! wynoscie się !
beaten ('bi:tn) adj. ubity; wy-
deptany; wyczerpany; znany
beautiful ('bju:teful) adj.
piękny; cudny; wspaniały; swietny
beautify ('bju:tyfaj) v. upiększać; upiększyć
beauty ('bju:ty) s. piękność;
piękno ; uroda; piekna kobieta
beauty parlor ('bju:ty'pa:rler)
salon kosmetyczny
beaver ('bi:wer) s. bóbr;
przedsiębiorczy człowiek
because (bi'ko:z) conj. dlatego; że; gdyż; adv. z powodu
beckon ('beken) v. skinąć; nęcić; s. skinienie
become; became; become (bi'kam;
bi'kejm; bi'kam)
become (bi'kam) v. stawać się;
nadawać się ; zostawać kims (czyms)
becoming ('bikamyŋg) adj. stosowny; odpowiedni; twarzowy
bed (bed) s. łoże; łożysko; klomb;
grządka ; ławica ; podkład; nocleg

bedclothes ('bedklouz) s. pos- ciel; przescieradła,kołdry etc.
bedding ('bedyng)s. posciel
bed linen ('bed,lynyn) s. pos- ciel ;bielizna pościelowa
bedridden ('bed,rydn) adj. ob- łożnie chory ;złożony chorobą
bedroom ('bedrum) s. sypialnia
bedside ('bedsajd) przy łożu
bedsore ('bedso:r) s. odleżyna
bedtime ('bedtajm) s. pora do spania ;pora snu
bee (bi:) s. pszczoła
beech (bi:cz) s. buk ;adj.bukowy
beef (bi:f) s. wołowina; siła; narzekanie ;wyrzekanie(slang)
beefsteak ('be:f'stejk) s. bef- sztyk (do smażenia lub pieczenia)
beefy ('bi:fy) adj. krzepki; flegmatyczny ;muskulary
beehive ('bi:hajw) s. ul
beekeeper ('bi:kiper) s. pszcze- larz
beeline ('bi:lajn) s. najkrótsza droga ;linia powietrzna
been (bi:n) v. były, zob. be
beer (bier) s. piwo
beet (bi:t) s. burak
beetle ('bi:tl) s. tłuczek; ubi- jak;v.ubijać;wystawać;zwisać
beetroot ('bi:tru:t) s. burak
befall (by'fo:l) v. zdarzać się; przydarzać się; przytrafiać się
before (by'fo:r) adv. przedtem; dawniej; z przodu;na przedzie
beforehand (by'fo:rhend) adv. uprzednio; przedtem; z góry
befriend (by'frend) v. zaprzy- jaźniac się; wspomagać
beg (beg) v. prosic; żebrać
began (b 'gaen) v. zaczęty; zob. begin
beget; begot; begotten (by'get; by'got; by'gotn)
beget (by'get) v. płodzic; ro- dzić; powodować ;wywoływać
beggar ('beger) s. żebrak
begin; began; begun (by'gyn; by'gaen; by'gan)
begin (by'gyn) v. zaczynać
beginner (by'gyner) s. początku- jący ;nowy(człowiek)

beginning (by'gynyng)s. począ- tek ;rozpoczęcie
begun (by'gan) v. p.p. zob. begin
behalf (by'hae:f) s. w imie- niu kogos ; poparcie
behave (by'hejw) v. zachowy- wać się; prowadzic się
behavior (by'hejwjer) v. po- stępowanie; zachowanie się
behind (by'hajnd) adv. w tyle; z tyłu; do tyłu; prep. za; poza; being ('by:yng)s. byt; s.tyłek istnienie; istota
belated (by'lejtyd) adj. spóź- niony ;zapóźniony;późny
belch (belcz) v. zionąc; od- bijać się; s. bekanie; bucha- nie; huk ;odbijanie się
belfry ('belfry) s. dzwonnica
Belgian ('beldżen) adj. bel- gijski
belief (by'li:f) s. wiara; wierzenie, zaufanie;przekonanie
believe (by'li:w) v. wierzyc; sądzic;miec przekonanie;zakładać
believer (by'li:wer) s. wyznaw- ca; wierzący ;zwolennik
bell (bel) s. dzwon; dzwonek
belligerent (by'lydżerent) adj. wojujący; wojowniczy;wojenny
bellow ('belou) v. ryczec; s. ryk ;ryczenie;porykiwanie
bellows ('belouz) s. miech; płuca;przedmiot podobny do miecha
belly ('bely) s. brzuch;żołądek
belong (bylong) v. należec
belongings (bylongynz) pl. rzeczy; bagaż; przynależności
beloved (by'lawd) adj. ukocha- ny; drogi;s.kochana osoba
below (by'lou) adv. niżej; w dole; na dół; pod spodem; prep. poniżej; pod ;w piekle
belt (belt) s. pas; pasek; strefa; v. bić pasem ;opasywać
bench (bencz) s. ława; ławka; stół; terasa;miejsce sędziego
bend; bent; bent (bend; bent; bent)
bend (bend) s. zgięcie; krzywa; v. giąc;wyginać;przeginać;zginać

beneath (by'ni:s) prep. pod; po→
niżej; pod spodem; na dół
benediction (,beny'dykszyn) s.
błogosławieństwo
benefactor (,beny'faekter) s.
dobroczyńca; dobrodziej
beneficient(bi'nefyszent)adj.
dobroczynny
beneficial (,beny'fyszel) adj.
pożywny;korzystny;dobroczynny
benefit ('benyfyt) s. korzyść;
dobrodziejstwo;pożytek;zasiłek
benevolent (by'newelent) adj.
dobroczynny;życzliwy;łaskawy
bent (bent) s. sitowie; skłonność; zgięcie; adj. skłonny;
zgięty; zdecydowany;uparty
benzene ('benzi:n) s. benzen
benzine ('benzi:n) s. (lekka)
benzyna (do czyszczenia)
bequeath (by'kłys) v. zostawiac
w spadku;przekazać potomności
bequest (by'kłest) s. zapis;
spadek;spuścizna; legat
bereave; bereft; bereaved
(by'ri:w, by'reft; by'ri:wd)
bereave (by'ri:w) v. pozbawiac;
odzierac;wyzuwać; osierocić
bereft (by'reft) adj. osierocony; pozbawiony;wyzuty
beret ('berej) s. beret
berry ('bery) s. jagoda;ikra
berth (be:rs) s. koja; łóżko;
stoisko;miejsce postoju statku
beseech; besought; besought
(by'si:cz; by'so:t; by'so:t)
beseech (by'si:cz) v. błagać;
upraszać; zaklinać
beside (by'sajd) adv. poza tym;
ponadto; inaczej; prep. obok;
przy; w pobliżu; w porównaniu
besides (by'sajdz) adv. prócz
tego; poza tym; prep.: oprócz;
poza;ponadto w dodatku
besiege (by'si:dż) v. oblegać
best (best) adj.& adv. najlepszy; najlepiej;v.okpiwać
best wishes (best łyszys) naj-
lepsze życzenia
best of all (best,ow o:l) najlepszy: najlepiej ;a najlepiej...

bestow (by'stou) v. podarować;
składać ;nadawać;użyczać;darzyć
bet (bet) s. zakład; v. zakładać się ;iść o zakład
betray (by'trej) v. zdradzić;
mylić; zawodzić dawać dowód
betrayal (by'trejel) s. zdrada
betrayer (by'trejer) s. zdrajca
better ('beter) adv. lepiej;
lepszy; v. poprawić; przewyż-
szyć ;prześcignąć;prześcigać
better than ('beter dzaen) exp.
więcej (slang); ponad ; lepiej
between (by'tłi:n) prep. między
adv. w pośrodku; tymczasem
beverage ('bewerydż) s. napój
beware (by'łe:r) v. strzec się
beware of the dog (by'łe:r ow
dy dog) strzec się psa; zły
pies
bewilder (by'łylder) v. zmie-
szać (kogoś);oszołamiać
bewilderment (by'łylderment) s.
zaczarowanie ;oszołomienie;chaos
bewitch (by'łycz) v. zaczarować oczarować;ując(kogoś czymś)
beyond (by'jond) adv.& prep.
za; poza; dalej niż; nad; ponad ;dalej(położony etc.)
bias ('bajes) s. uprzedzenie;
fałsz; kierunek; v. skłonić;
nachylić; uprzedzić ;usposabiać
biased ('bajest) adj. stronniczy; uprzedzony ;nastawiony
bib (byb) s. śliniak;v.popijać
Bible ('bajbl) s. Biblia
bicycle ('bajsykl) s. rower
bid (byd) v. oferować cenę; licytować; kazać; s. oferta na
licytacji ;stawka; zaproszenie
bid farewell (byd fa:rłel)
żegnać się ;pożegnać kogoś
bier (bjer) s. mary (pod trumną)
big (byg) adj. & adv. duży;
wielki; ważny ;głośny;godny
big business (byg'byznys) wielkie interesy;wielkie korporacje
big wig (byg łyg) s. wielka
szyszka ; ważniak;gruba ryba
bike (bajk) s. rower
bilateral (baj'laeterel) adj.
dwustronny; obustronny

bile (bajl) s. żółć;zgorzkniałość
bilious ('byljes) adj. żółciowy;zrzedny;popędliwy;tetryczny
bill (byl) s. dziób;pika;cypel
bill (byl) s. rachunek; kwit;
afisz; plakat; v. ogłaszać;
afiszować;oblepiać afiszami
billboard ('byl,bo:rd) s. tablica ogłoszeniowa
billfold ('byl,fould) s. port-
fel(na dokumenty i pieniądze)
billiards ('byljerdz) s. bilard
billion ('byljen) s. tysiąc
milionów (USA); miliard
bill of exchange ('byl,ow'
eksczendż) weksel
billow ('bylou) s. bałwan; kłąb;
v. piętrzyć; falować;balwanić się
bin (byn) s. skrzynia; paka;
v. pakować; chować do skrzyni
bind (bajnd) v. wiązać; zobowiązywać; opatrywać; oprawiać
binding ('bajndyng)adj. wiążący;
s. połączenie; oprawa;wiązanie
binoculars (bajnokjulez) pl.
lornetka(polowa,teatralna etc.)
biography (baj'ogrefy) s. bio-
grafia;opis życia i dziłalności
biology (baj'oledży) s. biologia
birch (be:rcz) s. brzoza
bird (be:rd) s. ptak ;dziwak
bird of passage ('be:rd ow
paesydż) przelotny ptak
bird of prey ('de:rd ow prej)
drapieżny ptak
bird's eye view ('be:rds aj,wju)
widok z lotu ptaka
birth (be:rt) s. urodzenie
birth control ('be:rt kon,troul)
kontrola urodzin
birthday ('be:rtdej) s. urodziny; początek czegoś
birthday party ('be:rtdej'
pa:rty) przyjęcie urodzinowe
birthplace ('be:rt-plejs)
miejsce urodzenia
biscuit ('byskyt) s. bułka;
sucharek lekko strawny
bishop ('byszep) s. biskup
bison ('bajsn) s. bizon
bit (byt) s. wędzidło; ostrze;
wiertło; ząb; szczypta;odrobina;
12½centów;moment;krótki czas

bitch (bycz) s. suka;wulg.kurwa
bite; bit; bitten (bajt; byt;
bitn)
bite (bajt) v. gryźć; kąsać;
docinać; s. pokarm; przynęta;
ukąszenie;ciętość;lekki posiłek
bitter ('byter) adj. gorzki;
ostry; zły;zgorzkniały;przykry
blab (blaeb) v. paplać; gadać;
s. plotkarz; gaduła;plotkarka
black (blaek) adj. czarny; ponury; s, murzyn;v.czernić
blackberry ('blaekbery) s. jeżyna
blackbird ('blackbe:rd) s. kos
blackboard ('blackbo:d) s. tablica
blacken ('blaekn) v. czernić
black eye ('blaekaj)   s. pod-
bite oko
blackhead ('blaekhed) s. wągier
blackmail ('blaemejl) s. szantaż; wymuszenie
black-market ('black ma:rkyt)
. s. czarny rynek
blackout   ('blaekaut) s. za-
ciemnienie (miasta, okien)
black pudding ('blaek'pudyng)
s. kaszanka; kiszka
blacksmith ('blaeksmys) s. ko-
wal(wiejski)
bladder ('blaeder) s. pęcherz
blade (blejd) s. zdźbło; liść;
ostrze;płetwa;klinga;wesołek
blame (blejm) s. wina; nagana;
v. tajać; ganić ;winić
blame for ('blejm fo:r) v. winić za (coś)
blameless ('blejmlys) adj. bez
winy; niewinny
blank (blaenk) adj. biały;
pusty; s. puste miejsce; nie-
wypełniony formularz;ślepak
blanket ('blaenkyt) s. koc wełniany ;ciepły koc
blasphemy ('blaesfymy) s. bluź-
nierstwo;pogarda dla Boga
blast (bla:st) s. wybuch; podmuch; odgłos eksplozji;
v. wysadzić w powietrze; de-
tonować; niszczyć
blast furnace ('bla:st,fe:rnys)
s. wielki piec hutniczy

blatant ('blejtent) adj. krzykliwy; ryczący; przesądny
blaze (blejz) s. błysk; płomień; wybuch; v. płonąć
bleach (bli:cz) v. wybielać
bleak (bli:k) adj. ponury;
smutny;wystawiony do wiatru
blear (blier) adj. mętny; zamglony ; niewyraźny
bleat (bli:t) v. beczeć
bleed; bled; bled (bli:d; bled;
bled)
bleed (bli:d) v. krwawić
blemish ('blemysz) s. plama;
wada; v. zniekształcić; splamić;poplamić;pobrudzić
blend; blent; blent (blend;
blent; blent)
blend (blend) v. mieszać się;
łączyć się; s, mieszanina
bless (bles) v. błogosławić
bless my soul ('bles,maj'so:l)
excl.: o Boże !
blessed ('blesyd) adj. błogosła-
wiony;święty; kojący
blessing ('blesyŋg)s. błogosławieństwo ;aprobata;dobra rzecz
blew (blu:) v. zob.: blow
blight (blajt) s. zniszczenie;
zaraza ;v.niszczyć
blind (blajnd) adj. ślepy;
v. oślepić; s. zasłona
blind alley ('blajnd,alej)
ślepa ulica
blindfold ('blajnd,fould)
adj.& adv. na ślepo; z zawiąza-
nymi oczami; v. zawiązywać
oczy ;s. zasłona oczu
blink (blyŋk) v. mrugać;
s. błysk oka ;mignięcie
bliss (blys) s. radość; błogość
blithe ('blajz) adj. wesoły;
blizzard ('blyzerd) s. śnieżyca;
zawieja ;zadymka;zamieć
bloat (blout) v. nadymać; nabrzmiewać ;uwędzić;wędzić
bloater ('blouter) s. śledź wędzony ; pikling
block (blok) s. blok; kloc; zeszyt; przeszkoda; v. tamować;
wstrzymywać;tarasować;zatykać;
zablokować;blokować;zatamować

block up ('blokap) v. zablokować ;zablokowywać;zamurować
blockade (blo'kejd) s. blokada;
v. blokować ;robić zator
blonde (blond) s. blondynka
blood (blad) s. krew ;pokrewieństwo
bloodshed ('bladszed) s. krwi
rozlew ; rozlew krwi
bloodshot ('bladszot) adj. nabrzmiały krwią ;zaszły krwią
blood vessel ('blad,wesl) s.
naczynie krwionośne
bloody ('blady) adj. krwawy
bloom (blu:m) s. kwiecie;
v. kwitnąć ;rozkwitać
blooming (blu:myŋg) adj. kwitnący; przeklęty (slang)
blossom ('blosem) v. kwitnąć;
s. kwiecie ; kwiat
blot (blot) s. plama; v. plamić
blot out ('blot aut)v.wymazać;
usunąć ;wykreślać;zamazywać
blotter (bloter) s. bibularz;
rejestr aresztowań;suszka
blotting paper ('blotyŋg‚pejper)
bibuła ;suszka
blouse (blauz) s. bluza
blow; blew; blown (blou; blu;
blołn)
blow (blou) s. cios; rzut; rozkwit; v. zakwitać; rozkwitać
blue (blu:) adj. niebieski;
smutny; v. farbować na niebiesko ;pomalować na niebiesko
bluebell ('blu:bell) s. dzwonek
(kwiat)
blues (blu:s) pl. smutek; przygnębienie ;smutne piosenki
bluff (blaf) s. oszustwo; nabieranie; adj. szorstki; stromy; v. wprowadzać w błąd
bluish ('blu:ysh) adj. niebieskawy
blunder ('blander) s. ciężki
błąd ;v.popełniać błąd (gafę)
blunt (blant) adj. tępy; nieczuły; v. stępić ;przytępić
blur (ble:r) s. plama v. za-
trzeć; splamić; zamazać
boar (bo:r) s. dzik; odyniec
board (bo:rd) s. deska; władza
naczelna ;tablica;rada;pokład

boarder ('bo:rder) s. pensjo-
nariusz; pasażer;stołownik
boardinghouse ('bo:rdynghaus)
s. pensjonat
boarding school ('bo:rdyng,sku:l)
s. szkoła z internatem
boardwalk ('bo:rd łok) chodnik z desek
boast (boust) v. chwalić się;
s. samochwalstwo;przechwałki
boat (bout) s. łódź; statek
boat race('bout ,rejs) s. regaty; wyścigi łodzi
bob (bob) v. kiwać się; krótko
strzyc; szturchnąć; s. wisiorek; kłęb włosów; szturchnięcie
bobby ('boby) s. angielski policjant
bobsled ('bob sled) s. bob-
slej; sanki z kierownicą etc.
bodice ('bodys) s. stanik
bodily ('bodyly) adj.& adv.
osobiście; fizycznie; całkowicie;gremialnie; cieleśnie
body ('body) s. ciało; karoser-
ja; korpus;grupa;gromada;ogół
bodyguard ('bodyga:rd) s. straż
przyboczna;ochrona osobista
bog (bog) s. bagno
boil (bojl) v. wrzeć; kipieć;
gotować; s. wrzenie; czyrak
boil over ('bojl,ouwer) v. wygotować; wygotować się
boiled eggs ('bojld egs) gotowane jajka
boiler ('bojler) s. kocioł
boisterous ('bojsteres) adj.
hałaśliwy;niesforny;burzliwy
bold (bould) adj. śmiały; zuchwały; zauważalny;wyraźny
bolster ('boulster) s. miękka
podkładka; v. miękko podeprzeć
bolt (boult) s. zasuwa; bolec;
piorun; wypad; v. zasuwać;
rzucić się; wypaść;czmychać
bomb (bom) s. bomba; v. bombar-
dować;atakować bombami
bombard (bom'ba:rd) v. bombardo-
wać(artylerią lub bombami)
bond (bond) s. więz; obligacja
bone (boun) s. kość;osc
bonfire ('bonfajer) s. płonący
stos ;ognisko (obozowe etc.)

bonnet ('bonyt) s. czapka
(damska) ; czepek
bonny ('bony) adj. piękny; ładny
bonus ('bounes) s. premia
bony ('bouny) adj. kościsty
book (buk) s. książka; v. księgować; rezerwować; aresztować
booked up ('bukt ap) adj. wy-
przedany; pełny
bookcase ('bukkejs) s. półka
na książki
booking clerk ('bukyn,klerk)
s. kasjer kolejowy
booking office ('bukyn,ofys)
biuro biletowe-rezerwacyjne
bookkeeper ('buk,ki:per) s.
księgowy; księgowa
bookkeeping ('buk,ki:pyng)s.
księgowosc
booklet ('buklyt) s. książeczka
bookseller ('buk,seler) s. księgarz
book shop('bukszop) s. księgarnia
bookstore ('buksto:r) s. księgarnia
boom (bu:m) s. huk; nagła zwyżka; v. zwyżkować; podbijać ceny
boomerang ('bu:meraeng) s. bumerang;v.działać jak bumerang
boor (bu:r) s. prostak; gbur;
chłop; prostaczka
boost (bu:st) v. forsować; podnosić znaczenie; zachwalać;
wzmacniać;rozreklamować
boot (bu:t) s. but; cholewa
booth (bu:s) s. budka; stragan
booty ('bu:ty)s.łup. zdobycz
booze('bu:z)s. alkohol pitny
border ('bo:rder) s. granica;
brzeg; rąbek; v. obrębiać;
graniczyć;oblamować;obszyć
bore (bo:r) v. wiercić; drążyć;
nudzić; s. otwor; nudy; nudziarz;natręt;rzecz nieznośna
bore (bo:r) v. zob. bear
born (bo:rn) adj. urodzony
borough ('be:rou) s. miasteczko
borrow ('borou) v.(za)pożyczać
bosom ('busem) s.(łono) piers
boss (bo:s) s. szef; v. rządzić
botany ('boteny) s. botanika
botch (bocz) s. fuszerka; lata-
nina; v. partaczyć; fuszerować

both (bous) pron.& adj. obaj;
obydwaj ;obie;obydwie;oboje
bother (bodzer) s. kłopot;
v. niepokoić; dokuczać;dręczyć
bother about (,bodzer e'baut)
v. kłopotać się czyms
bottle ('botl) s. butelka
bottom ('botem) s. dno; spód;
dolina; głąb; adj. dolny;
spodni; podstawowy; v. sięgac
dna; wstawiać dno ;osiągać dno
bough (bau) s. konar ;gałąź
bought (bo:t) v. kupiony; zob.:
buy (zakupiony,przekupiony...)
boulder ('boulder) s. głaz
bounce (bauns) v. odbijać się;
podskakiwać; s. gwałtowne odbicie ;odskok;samochwalstwo
bound (baund) s. granica; adj.,
będący w drodze; v. graniczyc
boundary (baundry) s. linia
graniczna ;adj. graniczny
boundless (baundlys) adj. bezgraniczny ; niezmierzony
bouquet, (bu:'kej) s. bukiet
kwiatów; zapach (wina)
bout (baut) s. okres; runda;
próba sił ;atak(choroby)
bow (bau) s. łuk; kabłąk; smyczek; ukłon; v. zginać się;
kłaniać się ;wygiąc w kabłąk
bowels ('bauelz) pl. trzewia;
wnętrznosci
bower ('bauer) s. altana; chatka; kotwica przednia
bowl (boul) s. miska; czerpak;
stadion; szala; v. grać kulami (w kręgle); toczyc koło
box (boks) s. skrzynka; pudełko;
loża; boks; v. pakować; oddzielać; uderzać pięścią
boxer ('bokser) s. pięściarz;
bokser
boxing ('boksyŋg)s. pięściarst-
wo; boks
box office('boks,ofys) s. kasa
w teatrze ;kasa biletów wstepu
boy (boj) s. chłopak; służący
boycott ('bojkot) s. bojkot;
v. bojkotować
boyfriend ('boy-frend) przyjaciel (dziewczyny);kochanek

boyhood('bojhud) s. wiek chłopięcy ;dzieciństwo chłopca
boyish ('bojysz) adj. chłopięcy
boy-scout ('boj-skaut) harcerz
bra (bra:) s. biustnik; stanik;
biustonosz
brace (brejs) s. klamra; korba;
podpora; v. wzmacniać; krzepic;
podpierać :spiać klamrą;związać
brace up (brejs ap) v. wytężyc
się; zebrać siły; orzeźwić
bracelet ('brejslyt) s. bransoletka; kajdanek
bracket ('braekyt) s. wspornik;
ramię; nawias; grupa; klamra;
v. brać w nawiasy; grupować
brag (braeg) v. chełpić się
braggart('braegert) s. samochwał; pyszałek ;bufon;fanfaron
braid (brejd) s. warkocz; plecionka; v. pleść; opasywać
brain (brejn) s. mózg; rozum
brain wave(brejnłejw) s. swietny pomysł ;swietna mysl
brake (brejk) s. hamulec
bramble ('braembel) s. krzak ja-
gody ;krzak jeżyny; jeżyna
branch (bra:ncz) s. gałąź; odnoga; filja; v. odgałęziać się;
zbaczać ;rozwidlać się
brand-new (,braen'nju) adj. nowiutki;nowiusieńki;jak z igły
brass (braes) s. mosiądz; spiż;
ranga; starszyzna; instrumenty
dęte :forsa;pieniadze;czelność;
śmiałość;przedmioty z mosiądzu
brass band(,braes'baend) s. kapela dęta ;orkiestra dęta
brassiere (bre'zier) s. biustnik;
stanik; biustonosz
brat (braet) s. brzdąc; bachor
brave (brejw) adj. dzielny zuch;
v. stawiać czoło ;odważyć się
Brazilian (Bre'zyljen) a. bra-
zylijski ;s.Brazylijczyk
breach (bry:cz) s.naruszenie;
wyłom; zerwanie; v. przełamać
(się); zrobic wyłom ;przerwać się
bread (bred) s. chleb; forsa
(slang);środki utrzymania
bread and butter (bred-en-bater)
chleb z masłem ;srodki utrzymania

breadth (breds) s. szerokość;
rozmach; szerokość pogladów
break; broke; broken (brejk;
brouk)
break (brejk) v. łamać; rujnować; przerywać; s. załamanie;
wyłom; nagła zmiana; wada
break away ('brejk ełej) v.
oderwać (się);uciekać
break down ('brejk dałn) v. za-
łamać(się); s. zepsucie się;
upadek; rozbiór;awaria
break in ('brejkyn) v. włamać
(się);wtargnąć;wtrącić się
break off ('brejkof) v. urwać;
odłamać;zerwać stosunki
break out ('brejkaut) v. wyrwać
(się);pokryć się pryszczami
break up ('brejkap) v. połamać
(się);rozpadać się;rozejść się
breakable('brejkebel) adj. kruchy; łamliwy;łatwy do zbicia
breakfast ('brekfest) b. śniadanie; v. jeść śniadanie
breast (brest) s. piers
breaststroke ('brest,strouk)
pływanie żabką
breath (bres) s. oddech; tchnienie;dech;oddychanie;powiew
breathe (bri:z) v. oddychać;
tchnąć; żyć; dać wytchnąc; powiewać;natchnąć;wionąć;szepnąć
breathing ('bri:zyng) s. oddech; wytchnienie;adj.żywy
breathless (breslys) adj. bez
tchu;zasapany;zadyszany;zziajany
bred (bred) zob.: breed;wychowany
breeches ('bry:czyz) pl. spodnie do konnej jazdy; bryczesy
breed; bred; bred; (bri:d; bred;
bred)
breed (bri:d) v. rodzić; rozmnażać; hodować; s. chów; rasa;
ród;plemię; ród ludzki
breeder ('bri:der) s. hodowca;
rozsadnik (choroby);rozpłodnik
breeding (bri:dyng) s. hodowla;
obejście; dobre wychowanie
breeze (bri:z) s. wietrzyk;zwada;
v. wiać; śmigać;odejść;oszukać
brevity ('brewyty) s. zwięzłość;
krótkość ; krótkotrwałość

brew (bru:) v. warzyć (piwo);
knuć; s. napój uwarzony; preparat;warzenie;parzenie;odwar
brewery (bru:ery) s. browar
bribe (brajb) v. dawać łapówkę;
przekupywać; s. łapówka
bribery ('brajbery) s. przekupstwo; łapownictwo;korupcja
brick (bryk) s. cegła; kostka;
adj. ceglany; v. obmurować;
zamurować(okno;drzwi,etc.)
bricklayer ('bryk,lejer) s.
murarz
brickwork ('brykłork) s. muro-
wanie;wykonana robota murarska
brickyard ('brykja:rd) s. cegielnia
bridal ('brajdel) adj. ślubny;
weselny;s.ślub;wesele
bride (brajd) s. panna młoda
bridegroom ('brajdgru:m) s, pan
młody; nowożeniec
bridesmaid ('brajdzmejd) s.
druhna;drużka
bridge (brydż) s. most; mostek;
v. łączyć mostem;zapełnić lukę
bridgehead ('brydżhed) s. przyczółek mostowy;przyczółek
bridle ('brajdl) s. uzdzienica;
uzda; cuma; v. kiełzać; pow-
ściągać;opanowywać;okiełzać
bridle path ('brajdl,pas) s.
ścieżka do konnej jazdy
brief (bri:f) s. streszczenie;
odprawa; krótkie majtki;
v. zwięźle streścić; pouczyć;
informować; adj. krótkotrwały;
treściwy; zwięzły;krótki
briefcase ('bri:f,kejs) s.
teczka
brigade (bry'gejd) s. brygada
bright (brajt) adj. jasny;
świetny; bystry; adv. jasno,
brighten ('brajtn) v. rozjasnić; błyszczeć; promieniować
brightness (brajtnys) s. jasność;światło;blask;żywość
brilliance ('bryljens) s.blask;
wielkie zdolności;świetność
brilliancy ('bryljensy) s.
świetność ; blichtr; połysk
jasne swiatło;blask;jasność

brilliant ('bryljent) adj. błyszczący; świetny; wybitny
brim (brym) s. brzeg (naczynia); rondo (kapelusza);v.napełniać
brimful ('brym'ful) adj. pełen po brzegi;przepełniony
bring; brought; brought (bryng; bro:t; bro:t)
bring (bryng)v. przynosić; przyprowadzać;powodować;zmusić (się)
bring an action ('bryngen'aekszyn) v. wszczynać działanie, akcje
bring about ('brynge'baut) v. uskutecznić;wywoływać;dokonać
bring forth ('bryng,fo:rs) v. ujawniac; wywoływać;urodzić
bring in (bryngyn)v. wprowadzać; przynosić;wydawać(wyrok etc.)
bring up ,(bryngap) v. poruszyć; przynieść na górę; przysunąć
brink (brynk) s. skraj; brzeg
brisk (brysk) adj. żywy; raźny; rześki;trzaskający;wesoły
bristle ('brysl) s. szczecina
British ('brytysz) adj. brytyjski; Anglik
brittle ('brytl) a. kruchy
broach (broucz) v. żłobić; zaczynac; poruszać;s.szydło;rożen
broad (bro:d) adj. szeroki; z rozmachem; wyraźny; obszerny s. szeroka płaszczyzna; wulg.: kobieta; adv. szeroko;z akcentem
broadcast ('bro:dka:st) v. transmitować; rozsiewać; szerzyć
broadminded ('bro:d'majndyt) adj. pobłażliwy; z otwartą głową
brochure ('brouszjuer) s. broszura
broke (brouk) adj. złamany; bez grosza; zob. break
broken (brouken) adj. połamany; zepsuty; zob. break
broker (brouker) s. pośrednik; ajent;makler;handlarz narkotyków
bronchia ('bronkje) pl. oskrzela
bronze (bronz) s. brąz; adj.brązowy; v. brązować; brązowieć
brooch (broucz) s. brosza; spinka
brood (bru:d) s. wyląg; potomstwo; v. wysiadywać; tkwić; rozmyślac ponuro;być pogrążonym w myślach

brook (bruk) s. potok;v.ścierpieć
broom (bru:m) s. miotła; v. zamiatac;wymiatać;obmiatać
broth (brosz) s. rosół;bulion
brothel ('brodżel) s. burdel
brother ('bradżer)s. brat
brothers and sisters ('bradzers, en'systers) rodzeństwo
brotherly ('bradzerly) adj. braterski
brought (bro:t) adj. przyniesiony; zob. bring
brow (brau) s. brew; czoło; nawias;szczyt;pomost;kładka
brown (braun) adj. brunatny; brązowy; opalony; v. brązowieć; opalać się;przyrumieniać (mięso)
brown paper ('braun,pejpe:r)s. papier pakunkowy
bruise (bru:z) s. siniak; stłuczenie; v. tłuc; otłuc; połamać kości; ranić;zgnieść;wyklepać
brush (brasz) s. szczotka; pędzel; draśnięcie; v. szczotkować; otrzepać; pędzlować
brush up ('brasz ap) v. wygładzić; odświeżyć;zgarnąć szczotką
brutal ('bru:tl) a. brutalny; zmysłowy;zwierzęcy
brutality (bru:'taelyty) s. brutalstwo ; brutalność
brute (bru:t) s. bydlę; zwierzę ludzkie; adj. tępy; brutalny; bezduszny; bydlęcy;nieokrzesany
bubble ('babl) s. bąbel; bańka; kipienie; v. kipieć; burzyć się; wydzielać bańki;musować
buck (bak) s. kozioł; fircyk; dolar adj. rogowy; męski; zwykły (szeregowy); v. skakać narowiście; opierać się;ługować
bucket ('bakyt) s. wiadro; czerpak (koparki);tłok;miska
buckle ('bakl) v. spinać; łączyć; wichrować; s. spinka; sprzączka
buckle on ('bakl on) v. pozapinać się ; zapiąć pas;przypiąć
buckskin ('bakskyn) s. wyprawiona koźla skóra (też sarnia)
bud ,(bad) s. pączek; v. pączkować; wyrastać;byc w zarodku;rozwijać się;dobrze zapowiadać się

buddy ('bady) s. bliski kolega

budget ('badżyt) s. budżet;
v. budżetować;asygnować

buffalo ('bafelou) s. bawół

buffer ('bafer) s. bufor;
zderzak ;odbój

buffet ('bafyt) s. bufet; kułak; cios ;raz;uderzenie

buffet ('befej) s. niski kredens ;dania barowe

bug (bag) s. owad; pluskwa;
defekt; amator ;insekt;robak

bugle ('bju:gl) s. róg (do
trąbienia) ;v.trąbić;zatrąbić

build; built; built (byld;bylt;
bylt)

build (byld) v. budować; rozbu-
dowywać ;stworzyć;wznosić

builder ('bylder) s. budowniczy

building ('byldyŋg)s. budowla

built (bylt) adj. zbudowany;
zob. build

bulb (balb) s. cebula; żarówka

bulge (baldż) v. wzdymać; wybrzu-
szać; wydymać; wytrzeszczać;
s. wypukłość; wzdęcie; wzdyma-
nie się;wybrzuszenie;przewaga

bulk (balk) s. masa; kolos;
większość;v.gromadzić;komasować

bulky ('balky) adj. wielki;otyły;
ciężki; masywny;nieporęczny

bull (bul) s. byk; duży samiec;
głupstwo;nonsens=bull-shit(bul-
szyt)

bullet ('bulyt) s. kula (nabój)

bulletin ('buletyn) s. komunikat; biuletyn

bulletin board ('buletyn,bo:rd)
s. tablica na ogłoszenia

bullion ('buljen) s. złoto i
srebro w sztabach

bully ('buly) v. dręczyć; tyranizować; s. awanturnik; kłotnik; najęty drab; adj. byczy;
żywy; wesoły;świetny;kapitalny

bum (bam) s. włóczęga; nierób;
popijawa; zadek; v. włóczyć
się; cyganić; pić; adj. marny

bumblebee ('bambl-bi:) s.
trzmiel

bump (bamp) v. zderzyć się; łup-
nąć; odbić się z łomotem; nabić guza: s. zderzenie; grzmotnięcie; guz;wybój;wstrząs; uderzenie; wypukłość; zdolności

bumper ('bamper) s. zderzak;
pełny kielich ;rekord

bun (ban) s. ciastko drożdżowe;
kok(włosów)

bunch (bancz) s. pęk; banda;
zgraja; guz; v. składać w pęki; skupiać się; kulić się

bunch of grapes ('bancz,ow
grejps) kiść (gałązka) winogron ; pęk winogron

bundle ('bandl) s. tłumok;
wiązka ;v.pakować(w tobół)

bundle up ('bandl,ap) v. zawinąć się ;zebrać;zbierać

bungalow ('baŋgelou) s. domek
letni parterowy

bungle ('baŋgl) s. partactwo;
v. partaczyć; bałaganić

bunion ('banjen) s. zapalenie
stawu w stopie(bolesny guz)

bunk (baŋk) s. koja ;baniąluki

bunk bed ('baŋk,bed) s. łóżko
piętrowe ; łóżko do podnoszenia

bunny ('bani) s. królik; truś

buoy (boj) s. boja; znak pływający ;pława;v.znaczyć bojami

burden ('be:rdn) s. brzemię;
ciężar; obowiązek; v. obciążać;
przygniatać; obładowywać

bureau ('bjurou) s. komoda;
biuro ;sekretarzyk; urząd

bureaucracy (bju'rokresy) s.
biurokacja

burglar (be:rgler) s. włamywacz

burglary ('be:rlery) s. włama-
nie(zwłaszcza w nocy)

burial ('berjel) s. pogrzeb

burly ('be:rly) adj. krzepki;
tęgi;duży i silny

burn; burnt; burnt (be:rn;
be:rnt; be:rnt)

burn (be:rn) v. palić; płonąc;
zapalić; s, oparzelizna;
dziura wypalona;oparzenie

burner ('be:rner) s. palnik

burning ('be:rnyŋg) s. palenie

burnt (be:rnt) v. spalony;
zob. burn(przypalony,opalony...)

burst; burst; burst (be:rst;
be:rst; be:rst)

burst (be:rst) v. rozsądzać;
rozrywać; s. wybuch;pęknięcie;
salwa; zryw;szał;grzmot;hulanka

burst of laughter ('be:rst,ow
'lafter) wybuch śmiechu
burst into flames ('be:rst,
yntu'flejms) buchać ogniem
burst into tears ('be:rst,
yntu'tiers) wybuchnąć płaczem ;zalać się łzami
bury ('bery) v. pochowac; za-
grzebać; chować ;zakopywać
bus (bas) s. autobus
bush (busz) s. krzak; gąszcz
bushel ('buszel) s. korzec
(8 galonów);v.przerabiać
bushy ('buszy) adj. nastroszony;
krzaczasty ;gęsty
business ('byznys) s. interes;
zajęcie ;sprawa;przedsiębiorstwo
business hours ('byznys,aurs)
godziny urzędowe
business letter ('byznys,leter)
oficjalny list
businesslike ('byznys,lajk)
adj. rzeczowy ;solidny;powazny
businessman ('byznysman) s.
przedsiębiorca; człowiek inte-
resów ;handlowiec
business trip ('byznys,tryp)
podróż służbowa
bus stop ('bas-stop)s.przysta-
nek autobusowy
bust (bast) s. popiersie; biust;
v. rujnować; psuć; rozwalić;
niszczyc ;bankrutować;wybuchnąć
bustle ('basl) v. krzątac się;
zapędzac do pracy; s. rozgardiasz; krzątanina ;bieganina
busy ('byzy) adj. zajęty;
skrzętny; wścibski; ruchliwy
busybody ('byzy,body) wścibski;
złośliwy ;plotkarz;intrygant
but (bat) adv. conj.prep. lecz;
ale; jednak; natomiast; tylko;
inaczej niż; z wyjątkiem
but for ('bat fo:r) exp. oprócz;
bez ; gdyby nie
but now ('bat nau) exp. dopiero
teraz ;dopiero w tej chwili
but once ('bat łans) exp. tylko
raz ;chociaż tylko raz
butcher ('buczer) s. rzeźnik ;kat;
v.zarzynac; mordować; masakrować;brutalnie zabijać;partaczyć

butt (bat) 1. s. drzewce; kol-
ba; nasada; niedopałek papierosa; pośladki; cel; przedmiot
kpin; ofiara; tarcza; v. bóść;
trącać; przytykać; 2. s. styk;
zetknięcie; uderzenie głową
butt in ('bat yn) v. wtrącac
się;przerywać rozmowę
butter ('bater) s. masło; v.
smarować masłem ;przychlebiać
buttercup ('baterkap) s. jas-
kier
butterfly ('baterflaj) s. motyl;
adj. motyli
buttocks ('bateks) pl. pośladki
button ('batn) s. guzik;v.zapinąc
button up ('batn ap) v. zapinać
się ; zapinać na guziki
buttonhole ('batnhoul) s. dziurka od guzika;v.zmuszać do słuchania
buttress ('batrus) s. podpora
buxom ('baksem) adj. dorodny;
okazały;pełny(biust);ładna(babka)
buy; bought; bought (baj; bo:t;
bo:t)
buy (baj) v. kupować ;przekupić
buyer (bajer) s. nabywca
buzz (baz) s. brzęczenie;
v. brzęczec ;przelotywać nisko
buzzard ('bazed) s. myszołów
by (baj) prep. przy; koło; co(dzień);
przez; z; po;w(nocy);o;według
by myself ('baj majself) ja sam
by and large ('baj end'la:rdż)adv.
ogólnie mowiąc; ogólnie biorąc
by twos ('baj,tuz) dwojkami
by the dozen('baj dy 'dazn) tu-
zinami
by the end ('baj dy,end) przy
końcu ;ku końcowi;z końcem
by land ('baj,laend) lądem
by bus ('baj,bas) autobusem
by day ('baj,dej) za dnia
by-and-by ('baj-end-baj) s.
przyszłosc; adv. wnet ;po chwili
bye-bye ! ('baj'baj) excl.: pa !
by-election (,baj-e'lekszyn) s.
wybory uzupełniające
bygone ('bajgon) adj. miniony;
przestarzały ;s.zdarzenia minione
bygones ('bajgonz) pl. przeszłosc; dawne urazy ;dawne zatargi

bylaw ('bajlo:) s. przepis; zarządzenie (miejscowe etc.)

byname ('bajnejm) s. przydomek

bypass ('baj-pas) s. droga dojazdowa; objazd ;v.objeżdżać

by-product (,baj-'prodakt) s. produkt uboczny

byroad (,baj-'roud) s. boczna droga ;droga drugorzędna

bystander (,baj-'stander) s. przygodny widz

bystreet (,baj-'stri:t) s. boczna ulica (drugorzędna)

byway ('baj-łej) s. boczna droga ;boczne przejście

byword ('baj-,łe:rd) s. przysłowie; przydomek (pogardliwy)

by work ('baj,-łe:rk) s. praca uboczna poza zajęciem głównym

c (si:) litera "c"; trzecia litera alfabetu angielskiego

cab (kaeb) s. taksówka; dorożkaszoferka ;budka maszynisty

cabaret (,kaebe'rej) s. lokal taneczny ; kabaret;serwis na tacy

cabbage ('kaebydż) s. kapusta

cabin ('kaebyn) s. kabina; chatka ;prymitywnie zbudowany domek

cabinet ('kaebynyt) s. szafka; rada ministrów adj.tajny

cabinetmaker ('kaebynyt,mejke:r) s. stolarz meblowy

cable ('kejbl) s. przewód; lina; depesza; v. depeszować; umocowywać liną ;przesyłać kablem

cable-car ('kejbl,ka:r) s. wóz linowy ; kolejka; linowa

cabman ('kaebmen) s. taksówkarz

cabstand ('kaeb staend) s. postój taksówek

cackle ('kaekl) v. gdakać; gęgać; chichotać; s. gdakanie; gęganie; chichot

cacti ('kaektaj) pl. kaktusy

cactus ('kaektes) s. kaktus

cad (kaed) s. ordynus; cham

café ('kaefej) s. kawiarnia; kawa ;restauracja; bar

cafeteria (,kaefy'tierja) s. restauracja samoobsługowa

cage (kejdż) s. klatka; kosz; v. zamykać w klatce

cake (kejk) s. ciastko; kostka (mydła); smażony placek (z ryby)

cake tin ('kejk,tyn) s. forma na ciastko

calamity (ke'laemyty) s. nieszczęście; klęska ;niedola

calculate ('kaelkjulejt) v. rachować; sądzić; oceniać

calculation (,kaelju'lejszyn) s. liczenie ;ostrozność

calendar ('kaelynder) s, kalendarz ;terminarz

calf (kaef) s. cielak; łydka

caliber ('kaelyber) s. średnica wewnętrzna; kaliber; wzorzec; sprawdzian

call (ko:l) v. wołać; wzywać; telefonować; odwiedzać; zawijać do portu; wyzywać;

s. krzyk; wezwanie; apel; powołanie; wizyta ;nazwanie;rządanie

call for help ('ko:l,fo:r help) wołanie o pomoc ;wzywanie pomocy

call names ('ko:l,nejmz) przezywać; wyzywać ;ubliżać

call back ('ko:l,baek) odtelefonować; odwołać z powrotem

call at ('ko:l,aet) odwiedzać

call for ('ko:l,fo:r) żądać; chodzić po coś (żeby otrzymać)

call on ('ko:l,on) odwiedzać (kogoś);prosić o wypowiedz

call up ('ko:l,ap) telefonować

caller ('ko:ler) s. gość; odwiedzający ;adj.rześki;świerzy

calling ('ko:lyng) s. zawód; powołanie ;zatrudnienie;fach

callous ('kaeles) adj. stwardniały; nieczuły ;zrogowaciały

calm (ka:m) adj. spokojny; cichy; s. spokój ; cisza ;opanowanie; v. uspokajać; uciszać ;uciszyć się

calm down ('ka:m,dałn) v. uciszyć się ;uspokoić się

calorie ('kaelery) s. kaloria

calves (ka:wz) pl. cielaki; łydki

camber ('kaember) v. wyginać; s. wygięcie ;wypukłość (jezdni)

came (kejm) v. przyszedł; zob. come

camel ('kaemel) s. wielbłąd

camera ('kaemere) s. aparat fotograficzny; prywatna izba

camomile ('kaemoumajl) s. rumianek

camouflage ('kaemufla:ż) s. maskowanie; v. maskować (wojsk.)

camp, (kaemp) s. obóz; v. obozować; rozlokowywać w namiotach

camp out (kaemp aut) v. obozować w namiocie

campaign (kaem'pejn) s, kampania; akcja; v, odbywać kampanię; agitować

camp bed ('kaemp,bed) s. łóżko polowe;łóżko składane

camper ('kaemper) adj.obozujący;s. wóz lub przyczepa do obozowania; mieszkalny wóz (turystyczny)

camping ('kaempyŋg) s. obozowanie; życie obozowe

camping ground ('kaempyŋg,graund) obozowisko; miejsce do obozowania

campus ('kaempes) s. teren uniwersytecki lub szkolny

can (kaen) s., puszka blaszana; ustęp; v. móc; konserwować; wyrzucać:umieć;zdołać;potrafić

Canadian (ke'nejdjen) adj. kanadyjski

canal (ke'nael) s. kanał ;kanalik

canard (kae'na:rd) s. kaczka dziennikarska; plotka

canary (ke'nery) s. kanarek,

cancel ('kaensel) v. znosić; kasować;odwoływać;skreślać

cancer ('kaenser) s. rak (choroba); nowotwór

candid ('kaendyd) adj. szczery; bezstronny;otwarty

candidate ('kaendydyt) s. kandydat;kandydatka

candied ('kaendyd) adj. pocukrzony; lukrowany

candle ('kaendl) s. świeca

candlestick ('kaendlstyk) s. świecznik; lichtarz

candy ('kaendy) s. cukierki; lukier;cukier lodowaty

cane (kejn) s. trzcina; laska; pałka; v. chłostać ;wyplatać trzciną; ukarać trzciną

canned (kaend) adj. zakonserwowany w puszce

cannery (kaenery) s. fabryka konserw

cannibal ('kaenybel) s. ludożerca; adj. ludożerczy

cannon ('kaenen) s. działo,

cannot ('kaenot) v. nie móc (od cannot);nie potrafić

canoe (ke'nu:) s. czółno; kajak; v. jeździć kajakiem; wiosłować

canopy ('kaenepy) s. baldachim; okap;firmament; sklepienie

cant ('kaent) s. żargon; frazes

can't (ka:nt) v. nie móc(od can);nie potrafić

canteen (kaen'ti:n) s. manierka; menażka; kantyna

canvas ('kaenves) s. płótno impregnowane

canvass ('kaenves) s. badanie; zabieganie; v.zabiegać; badać; starać się o głosy

cap (kaep) s. czapka; pokrywa; wieko; kapiszon;beret

cap (kaep) v. wkładać czapkę lub nakrywkę; wieńczyć; zakładać spłonkę; zakasować

capability (,kaepe'bylyty) s. zdolność;zdatność; możliwość

capable (,kejpebl) adj. zdolny

capacity (ke'paesyty) s. zdolność; kompetencja; pojemność; właściwość;nośność;objętość

cape (kejp) s. 1. peleryna; 2. przylądek

caper (kejper) v. wywijać kozły; s. hołubiec; sus; skok

capital ('kaepytl), s. stolica; kapitał; adj. główny; zasadniczy; stołeczny; fatalny

capital crime ('kaepytl,krajm) s. morderstwo

capitalism ('kaepytlyzem)s. kapitalizm

capital letter ('kaepytl,leter) duża litera

capital punishment ('kaepytl 'panyszment) kara śmierci

capricious (ke'pryszes) adj. kapryśny

capsize (kaep'sajz) v. wywracać (statek) dnem do góry

capsule ('kaepsju:l) s. kapsułka;torebka;pochewka;kabinka

captain ('kaeptyn) s. kapitan; naczelnik;v.dowodzić

caption ('kaepszyn) s. nagłówek; napis ;poświadczenie;aresztowanie

captivate ('kaeptywejt) v. ująć; czarować; urzekać;zniewalać

captive ('kaeptyw) adj. jeniec

captivity ('kaeptyvyty) s. niewola

capture ('kaepczer) s. owładniecie; łup; v. pojmać; owładnąć

car (ka:r) s, samochód; wóz

caravan('kaerevaen) s. karawana; wóz kryty;przyczepka mieszkalna

carbohydrate ('ka:rbe'hajdrejt) s. węglowodan

carbon ('ka:rben) s. węgiel; kopia (kalka)

carbon dioxide ('ka:rben daj'oksajd) s. CO_2 dwutlenek węgla

carbon paper ('ka:rben,pejper) s. kalka

carburetor ('ka:rbjureter) s. gaźnik

car carrier (ka:r-'kaerjer) s. woz do przewozu aut

carcass ('ka:r-kes) s. ścierwo; padlina; szkielet

card ('ka:rd) s. karta; bilet; pocztówka;legitymacja; atut

cardboard ('ka:rdbo:rd) s. tektura;adj.tekturowy

card box('ka:rdboks) s. karton

cardigan ('ka:rdygen) s. wełniana kurta (kamizelka)

cardinal ('ka:rdynl) adj. główny; kardynał

card index ('ka:rd yndeks) s. kartoteka

car papers (ka:r pejpers) s. dokumenty samochodowe

care (keer) s. opieka; troska; ostrożność;zgryzota;dozór;uwaga

care of (keer ow) c/o: adres (u kogoś)

care for (keer fo:r) v. dbać o kogoś;lubić;kochać;mieć ochotę

career (ke'rier) s. kariera; zawód;tok;pęd;bieg;v. cwałować

carefree (keerfri:) adj. beztroski

careful (keerful) adj. ostrożny; troskliwy;dbały;pieczołowity

careless (keerles) adj. niedbały; nieuważny;nieostrożny

caress (ke'res) s. pieszczota; v. pieścić; popieścić

caretaker ('keertejker) s. dozorca; stróż

careworn ('keerło:rn) s.zgnębiony kłopotami

carfare ('ka:rfeer) s. opłata za jazdę

cargo ('ka:rgou) s. ładunek

caricature (,kaeryke'czjuer) s. karykatura;v.karykaturować

car mechanic (ka:r-my'kaenyk) s. mechanik samochodowy

carnation ('ka:r'nejszyn) 1. s.& adj. ciemno-czerwony;cielisty;2. goździk ogrodowy

carnival ('ka:rnywel) s. karnawał;zapusty

carnivorous (ka:r'nyweres) adj. mięsożerny

carol ('kaerel) s. kolenda; v. kolendować

carp (ka:rp) s. karp; v. czepiać się;ganić;przycinać

car parking ('ka:r-pa:rkyŋg) s. parking samochodowy

carpenter ('ka:rpynter) s. cieśla; stolarz

carpet ('ka:rpyt) s. dywan; v. wyścielać dywanem

carriage ('kaerydż) s. wagon; powóz; postawa;kareta;chód

carrier ('kaerjer) s. firma przewozowa; nośnik; tragarz; rozsadnik (zakażenia); lotniskowiec;okaziciel

carrion ('kaerjen) s. padlina

carrot ('kaeret) s. marchewka

carry ('kaery) v. nosić; wozić; zanieść; unosić

carry off ('kaery,of) v. uprowadzić; zabrać;zdobywać(nagrodę)

carry on ('kaery,on) v. kontynuować;wytrwać;awanturować się

carry out ('kaery,aut) v. wykonać; przeprowadzic;spełnić
cart ('ka:rt) s. woz
cartel ('ka:rtel) s. kartel
carter ('ka:rter) s. woźnica
cart horse ('ka:rt͜hors) s. koń pociągowy
carton ('ka:rten) s. karton
cartoon (ka:r'tun) s. karykatura;v. rysować karykatury
cartoonist (ka:r'tunyst) s. karykaturzysta
cartridge ('ka:rtrydź) s. nabój
cartwheel ('ka:rt-hłi:l) s. kołodziej
carve ('ka:rw) v. rzezbic'; krajać;cyzelować;pociać an części
carver ('ka:rwer) s. snycerz
carving ('ka:rwyŋg) s. rzeźba
cascade (kaes'kejd) s. wodospad;v.spadać jak wodospad
case (kejs) s. 1. wypadek; sprawa; dowód; 2. skrzynia; pochwa; torba; 3. sprawa sądowa; v. zamykać w pochwie; otaczać czyms ;oszalować; oprawić
casement ('kejsment) s. rama okienna; okno z kwaterami
cash (kaesz) s. gotówka; pieniądze; v. spieniężać; inkasować; płacić (gotówką)
cash on delivery (kaesz on dy'lywery) zapłata przy odbiorze; C.O.D.
cashier (kae'szjer) s. kasjer
cash register(kaesz'redżyster) s. kasa (zmechanizowana)
casing ('kejsyŋg)s. 1. powłoka; pochwa; 2. obudowa; oprawa; 3. łuska; 4. opancerzenie
cask (kaesk) s. beczułka
casket (kaeskyt) s. trumna ; urna; szkatuła
cassock ('kaesek) s. sutanna
cast; cast; cast (ka:st; ka:st; ka:st)
cast (ka:st) s. rzut; odlew; gips; odcień: v, rzucać; łowić; odlewać; powalic; dzielic role teatralne
castaway ('ka:st,e'łej) s. wyrzutek ;rozbitek

cast down (ka:st dałn) adj. przygnębiony; v.deprymować
caste (ka:st) s. kasta
cast iron(ka:stajren) s. żeliwo
castle ('ka:sl) s. zamek
castor oil ('ka:ster,ojl) s. olej rycynowy
cast steel ('ka:st,sti:l) s. lana stal
casual ('kaeżuel) adj. przypadkowy; niedbały;dorywczy
casualty ('kaeżuelty) s. wypadek; ofiara wypadku; lista strat;nieszczęście
cat (kaet) s. kot;jędza
catalog ('kaetelog) s. katalog
catamaran (,kaeteme'raen) s. dwu-czółnowa łódź
cataract ('kaeteraekt) s. katarakta; ulewa;wodospad
catarrh (ke'ta:r) s. katar
catastrophe (ke'taestrefy) s. katastrofa
catch; caught; caught (kaecz; ko:t; ko:t)
catch (kaecz) v. łapac'; łowic'; ujmować; słyszec'; wybuchać; nabawić się; s. łup; połów
catch cold (kaecz kold) v. zaziębiac się
catch fire (kaecz fajer) v. zapalać się
catch up (kaecz ap) v. dogonić
catching (kaeczyŋg)adj. zaraźliwy;s.tryby;uchwyt;zazębienie
category ('kaetygery) s. kategoria
cater ('kejter) v. dostarczać żywności; obsługiwać
caterpillar ('kaetepyler) s. gąsie nica (traktora.czołgu etc.)
cathedral (ke'ti:drel) s. katedra
Catholic ('kaetelyk) adj. katolicki; s. katolik
cattle (kaetl) s. bydło rogate
caucus ('ko:kes) s. tajne narady partyjne; klika
caught (ko:t) złapany; zob. catch
cauldron ('ko:ldren) s,kocioł

cauliflower ('kalyflauer) s. kalafior

cause (ko:z) s. przyczyna; sprawa;racja;motywacja;proces

causeless(ko:zles) adj. przypadkowy ; bezpodstawny

caution ('ko:szyn) s. ostrożność; uwaga;v.ostrzegać

cautious ('ko:szes) adj. ostrożny;rozważny;roztropny;uważny

cavalry ('kaevelry) s. kawaleria

cave (kejw) s. pieczara; jaskinia; v. zapadać się; drążyć

cavern ('kaewen) s. jama; jaskinia; grota; pieczara

cavity ('kaewyty) s. wklęsłość; dziura(w zębie);dół;wydrążenie

cease (sy:s) v. ustawać; przestawać; położyć kres

ceaseless (sy:slys) adj. bezustanny;ciągły; nieprzerwany

cede (si:d) v. ustąpić; cedować

ceiling ('sy:lyng)s. sufit; pułap; górna granica

celebrate ('selybrejt) v. święcić ;uczcić;sławić;obchodzić

celebrated ('selybrejtyd) adj. sławny; słynny; głośny

celebration ('selybrejszyn) s. obchód; odprawianie; święcenie

celebrity ('sylebryty) s. sławna osoba;sława;znakomita osobowość

celery ('selery) s. seler (jarzyna)

celibacy ('selybesy) s. bezżeństwo; celibat

cell (sel) s. cela; komórka

cellar ('seler) s. piwnica

Celtic (keltyk) adj. celtycki

cement (sy'ment) s. cement; v. cementować; kleić; utwierdzać ;spoić; złączyć

cemetery ('semytry) s. cmentarz

censor ('sensor) s. cenzor

censorship ('senserszyp) s. cenzura

censure ('senszer) s. nagana; krytyka; v. krytykować

cent (sent) s. cent

centenary (sentynery) adj. stuletni; s. stulecie; setna rocznica

centennial ('sen'tenjel) s. stulecie; adj. stuletni

center ('senter) s. ośrodek; v. ześrodkowywać

centigrade ('sentygrejd) adj. stustopniowy(termometr)

centimeter ('sentymi:ter) s. centymetr

central ('sentral) adj. środkowy; czołowy ; s. centrala

Central Europe ('sentral juerop) Europa Środkowa

central heating ('sentrel hi:tyng)centralne ogrzewanie

centralize ('sentrelajz) v. centralizować;ześrodkowywać

center ('senter) s. ośrodek centrum; v. ześrodkowywać; centrować ;skupiać się

century ('senczury) s.stulecie

cereals ('syerjelz) pl, zboża

cerebral ('serybrel) adj. mózgowy

ceremonial (,sery'mounjel) adj. ceremonialny; s. rytuał; ceremonial; ceremonialność

ceremonious (,sery'mounjes) adj. drobiazgowy; ceremonialny

ceremony ('serymeny) s. ceremonia;v.sztywno się zachowywać

certain ('se:rtyn) adj. niejaki; pewien;pewny;ustalony;jakiś

certainly ('se:rtnly) adv. napewno; oczywiście;bezwzględnie

certainty ('se:rtynty) s. pewność; pewnik; rzecz pewna

certificate (se'rtyfykyt) s. świadectwo; poświadczenie; v. zaświadczać ;dyplomować

certify ('se:rtyfaj) v. zaświadczać; zapewniać; uznawać za

certitude ('se:rtytju:d) s. pewność; przeświadczenie

chafe (czejf) v. trzeć; otrzeć; irytować; s. tarcie; otarcie; irytacja; rozdrażnienie; złość

chaff(cza:f) s. 1. sieczka; 2. żart; naciąganie; wyśmiewać żartobliwie; naciągać

chagrin ('szaegryn) s. smutek; rozczarowanie; v.upokarzać;rozczarowywać boleśnie

chain (czejn) s. łańcuch; syndykat; trust; v, wiązać na łań-
cuchu; mierzyc;uwiązać; zakuć
chair (czeer) s. krzesło; stołek; fotel; katedra; v. prze-
wodniczyc; sadzac na krzesle
chair lift ('czeerlyft)s. wyciąg linowy
chairman ('czeermen) s. przewodniczący; prezes
chalk (czo:k) s. kreda;v.pisać [kredą
challenge ('czaelyndż) s. wyzwanie; zadanie; v. wyzywać; zarzucac; wzywać;korcić;prowokować
chamber ('czejmber) s. izba; komora;sala;pokój;v.wydrążyć
chambermaid ('czejmbermejd) s.
pokojowa
chamois ('szaemła:) s. giemza;
ircha; zamsz
champagne ('szaem'pejn) s. szampan
champion ('czaempjen) s. mistrz;
obronca; v. bronic; walczyc o...
championship ('czaempjenszyp)
s. mistrzostwo
chance (cza:ns) s. okazja; przypadek; szczęscie; szansa;ryzyko;
adj. przypadkowy; przygodny;
v. zdarzac się; ryzykowac; próbowac;przytrafić się;natknąć się
chancellor (cza:seler) s. kanclerz; pierwszy sekretarz (amba-
sady);najwyższy sędzia
chandelier (szaendy'lyer) s.
żyrandol; świecznik
change (czejndż) s, zmiana; wymiana; drobne; v. zmienić;
przebierać (się); wymieniac
change one's mind ('czejndż,
łans'majnd) zmienic czyjes
zdanie (przekonania etc.)
change trains ('czejndż,trejns)
v. przesiąsc się (na kolei)
changeable('czejndżebl) adj.
zmienny;podlegajacy zmianom
channel ('czaenl) s. kanał; koryto; łożysko; v, żłobić;
przesyłac drogą (urzędową)
chaos ('kejos) s. chaos
chap (czaep) s. chłop; chłopiec;
człek; v.pękac; powodować
pęknięcia (warg);zarysowywać

chapel ('czaepel) s. kaplica
chaplain ('czaeplyn) s. kapelan
chaps (cza:ps)pl. skórzane no-
gawice (kowboja);ochraniacze
chapter ('czaepter) s. rozdział;
oddział; v. dzielic na rozdzia-
ły
character ('kaerykter) s. charakter; typ; cecha; reputacja;
moralnosć; facet; znak
characteristic ('kaerykterystyk)
adj. charakterystyczny; typowy; s. cecha; własnosć; własci-
wosć
characterize ('kaerykterajz) v.
charakteryzować (opisywać)
charge (cza:rdż) s. ciężar; ładunek; obowiązek; piecza; podopieczny; zarzut; opłata; należność; szarża; godło; v. ładować; nasycać; obciążać; zadać;
liczyc sobie; oskarżać; atakować; szarżować
charge account (cza:rdż e'kaunt)
s. otwarty kredyt (w banku)
charge card (cza:rdż'ka:rd) s.
karta kredytowa do zakupów
chariot ('czaerjet) s. wóz; rydwan
charitable ('czaerytebl) adj.
litosciwy; dobroczynny
charity ('czaeryty) s. miłosierdzie; dobroczynnosć
charm (cza:rm) s, czar; urok;
amulet; v. czarowac; oczarować
charming (cza:rmyng)adj. czarujący
chart (cza:rt) s. wykres; mapa
morska; v. robic wykres; wyty-
czac; pokazywać (jak)
charmless (cza:rmlys) adj. bez
wdzięku
charter (cza:rter)s. statut;
przywilej; dyplom; akt nadania
prawa do... v. nadawać; zakładac na statutach; wynajmowac
statek lub samolot
charter plane (cza:rter plejn)
s. wynajęty grupowo samolot
charwoman ('cza:rłumen) s.
sprzątaczka; dochodząca sprza-
taczka;posługaczka

chase 1. (czejs) s. pościg; pogoń; polowanie; v. gonić; ścigać; polować; wyganiać
chase 2. (czejs) s. łożysko; wgłębienie; wykop; v. żłobić
chasm ('kaezem) s. otchłań
chaste (czejst) adj. czysty; niewinny;nieskażony;cnotliwy
chastity ('czaestyty) s. niewinność; prostota;dziewictwo
chat (czaet) s. pogawędka; v. gawędzić; gadać;rozmawiać
chatter (czaeter) v. szczebiotać; klapać; s.szczebiot; klapanie; klekot;paplanie;terkot
chatterbox (czaeterboks) s. trajkotka;gaduła;pleciuga
chauffer ('szoufer) s. zawodowy kierowca; przenośny piecyk
cheap (czi:p) adj. tani; marny
cheapen (czi:pen) v. taniec; obniżać wartość;spadać w cenie
cheat (czi:t) s. oszust; oszustwo; v. oszukiwać; zdradzać (w małżeństwie);okpiwać
check (czek) s. wstrzymanie ; przerwa; sprawdzenie; czek; kwit; szach; a. szachownicowy; kontrolny; pokreślony; v. hamować; sprawdzać; zakreślać; nadawać; zgadzać się; szachować;ganić;krytykować;opanowywać
check in (czek yn) v. wmeldowywać się (w pracy,w wojsku etc.)
check out (czek aut) v. wymeldowywać się;zapłacić za hotel
checked (czekt) adj, w kratkę
checkroom (czekrum) s. przechowalnia (bagażu);szatnia
cheek (czi:k) s. policzek; bezczelne gadanie; v. mówić bezczelnie do kogoś; stawiać się
cheeky ('czi:ky) adj. bezczelny; zuchwały;pełen tupetu;z tupetem
cheer (czier) s. brawo; hurra; radość; jadło; v. krzyczeć; rozweselać;dodawać otuchy
cheer on ('czier on) v. zachęcać ;zagrzewać;dodawać otuchy
cheer up ('czier ap) v. pocieszać; nabrać otuchy;rozpogodzić
cheerful ('czierful) adj. pogodny; wesoły; ochoczy;rozweselający

cheerless ('czierlys) adj. ponury; smutny; przybity
cheery ('cziery) adj. wesoły; radosny; pogodny
cheese ('czi:z) s. ser
chef (czef) s. kuchmistrz
chemical ('kemykel) adj. chemiczny;s.substancja chemiczna
chemicals ('kemykels) pl. chemikalia;leki;lekarstwa
chemise (sze'mi:z) s. damska koszula luźna i długa
chemist ('kemyst) s. chemik; aptekarz
chemistry ('kemystry) s. chemia
cheque (czek) s. czek (poza USA)
chequered ('czekerd) adj. kratkowany; urozmaicony; burzliwy
cherish ('czerysz) v. lubić; tulić; żywić (uczucie);miłować
cherry ('czery) s. czereśnia; wiśniowy kolor; vulg.:prawiczka; adj. wiśniowy; vulg.: prawiczy; czerwony
chess (czes) s. szachy
chess-board (czes-bo:rd) s. szachownica
chess man(czesmen) s. figurka szachowa
chest (czest) s. skrzynia; komoda; piers ;płuca;kufer;skrzynka
chestnut ('czesnat) s. kasztan
chest of drawers (czest ow dro:ers) komoda
chew (czu:) v. żuć; przeżuwać; besztać; gderać; s. żucie; tytoń do żucia; prymka
chewing gum('czu:yng gam) s. guma do żucia
chicken ('czykyn) s. kurcze; adj.tchórzliwy; bojący się
chicken out ('czykyn aut) v. stchórzyć;ustąpić ze strachu
chide (czajd; chidden (czajd; czyd; czydn)
chide (czajd) v. łajać; droczyć się; skarżyć;besztać; łajać
chicken pox('czykyn poks) s. ospa wietrzna
chief (czy:f) s. wódz; szef; adj. główny; naczelny
chilblain ('czylblejn) s, odmrożenie

child (czajld) s. dziecko
childish ('czajldysz) adj.
dziecinny
childless ('czajldlys) adj. bezdzietny
childlike ('czajldlajk) adj.
dziecięcy; jak dziecko
children('czyldren) pl. dzieci
chill (czyl) s. chłód; dreszcz;
v. studzić; mrozić ;oziębiać
chilly (czyly) adj. chłodny;
adv. chłodno; zimno
chime ('czajm) s. dzwony grające;
rytm; kurant; v. bić w dzwony;
wydzwaniać; rymować;zabrzmieć
chimney ('czymny) s. komin; wylot; szkło lampy naftowej
chimney sweeper ('czymny,sli:per)
s. kominiarz;adj. kominiarski
chin (czyn) s. broda; v. podciągać brodę do drążka;s.podbródek
china ('czajna) s. porcelana
chinese ('czaj'ni:z) adj. chiński;Chinese s. chińczyk
chink('czypk) 1. s. brzęk; v.po-
brzękiwać; brzęczeć; 2. szpara;
szczelina; v. zapychać szpary
chip (czyp) s. drzazga; odłamek;
skrawek; v. otłuc; obijać; dokuczać; nabierać; ciosać;
ćwierkać; piszczeć; nogę pod-
stawiać; złuszczać się;odłupać
chirp (czy:rp) s. świergot;
v. ćwierkać; szczebiotać
chisel ('czyzl) s. dłuto; przecinek; v. ciąć; rzeźbić;oszukać
chivalrous ('czywelres) adj.
rycerski
chivalry ('czywelry) s. rycer-
stwo; rycerskość
chive (czajw) s. szczypiorek
chlorine ('klo:ry:n) s. chlor
chloroform ('klo:refo:rm) s.
chloroform; v. maczać w chlo-
roformie;usypiać chloroformem
chock (czok) s. klin; v. osadzać na klinach; adv. szczelnie; ciasno; mocno ; w pełni
chocolate ('czoklyt) s. czekolada;adj. czokoladowy(kolor etc.)
choice (czoys) s. wybór; wybran-
ka; adj.wyborowy;doborowy

choir ('kłajer) s. chór
choke (czouk) v. dusić; zadusić; tłumić; dławić; s. durze-
nie; dławik; gardziel; prze-
wężenie;odgłosy duszenia;zawór
choke down (czouk dałn) v. dławić;zmniejszać gardziel
choke up (czouk ap) v. zatykać
(rurę); zadławić(motor etc.)
choose; chose; chosen (czu:z;
czouz; czouzn)
choose (czu:z) v. wybierać; woleć; postanowić;zadecydować
chop (czop) v. rąbać; obcinać;
s. rąbnięcie; kotlet;krótka fala
chop down (czop dałn) v. powalić (drzewo etc.); ściać;zrąbać
chord (ko:rd) s. struna; cięciwa;struna głosowa
chorus ('ko:res) s. chór;
v. mówić chórem;śpiewać chórem
chose (czouz) v. wybrał; zob.
choose
chow (czau) s. jadło (slang)
Christ (krajst) Chrystus
christen ('krisn) v. ochrzcić
Christian ('krystjen) adj.
chrześcijański; s. chrześci-
janin(slang:cywilizowany)
Christianity (krys'czaenyty) v.
chrześcijaństwo
Christian name ('krystjen,nejm)
s. imię(inne niż nazwisko)
Christmas ('krysmas) s. Boże
Narodzenie
Christmas Day ('krysmas dej)
Dzień Bożego Narodzenia
Christmas Eve ('krysmas i:w)
wilia, wigilia Bożego Narodzenia
chromium ('kroumjem) s. chrom
chronic ('kronyk) adj. chroniczny;strawszliwy (ból)
chronicle ('kronykl) s. kronika
chronological (krone'lodżykel)
adj. chronologiczny
chubby ('czaby) adj. pucołowaty; pyzaty;mały i gruby
chuck (czak) v. rzucać; gdakać;
cmokać; s. kurczątko; dzieci-
na; kochanie;gdakanie;cmokanie

chuckle (czakl) v. chichotać;
s. chichot; zduszony śmiech
chum (czam) v. przyjaźnić się
blisko; s. serdeczny kolega;
współlokator;v.przyjaźnić sie
church (cze:rcz) s. kościół
churchyard (čze:rczja:rd) ,s.
cmentarz; dziedziniec kościelny; adj. cmentarny
churn (cze:rn) v. robić masło;
kłócić się; burzyć się; kotłować się; pienić się; s. maślni-
ca; maślniczka;bańka na mleko
chute (szu:t) s. koryto zrzuto-
we; spadek; wodospad; spadochron; tor zjażdżalni dla dzięci
chutzpah (hucpa) s. nachalność;
śmiałość;tupet(po nowohebrajsku)
cider ('sajder) s. wino z jabłek
cigar (sy'ga:r) s. cygaro
cigaret(te) (sige'ret) s. papieros
cinder ('synder) s. popiół; żużel; v. spalać na żużel
cinderella (,synde'rele) s. kopciuszek; Kopciuszek
cinder track ('synder-traek) s.
bieżnia żużlowa;tor żużlowy
cine camera ('syni-'kaemere) s.
aparat filmowy
cinema ('syneme) s. kino
cinema projector ('syneme-
prodżekter) s. rzutnik filmowy
cipher ('sajfer) s.,cyfra; szyfr;
zero; v. szyfrować; rachować
circle ('se:rkl) s. koło; krąg;
obwód; v. otaczać; kręcić się
w koło; opasywć; krążyć;okrążać
circuit ('se:rkyt) s. obwód;
okrężna; okólna (podróż)
circular ('se:rkjuler) s. okólnik; adj. okrągły; kolisty
circulate ('se:rkjulejt) v.
krążyć; cyrkulować; puszczać
w obieg; być w obiegu
circulation ('se:rkjulejszyn)
s. krążenie; obrót; nakład
circumference (se'rkamfyrens)
s. obwód (koła etc.)
circumcision (se:rkem'syžyn)s.
obrzezanie;obcięcie napletka

circumscribe (,se:rkem'skrajb)
v. opisywać; zakreślać
circumstance ('se:rkemstaens)
s. okoliczności; szczegóły
circus ('se:rkes) s. cyrk;
okrągły plac;rondo; desant(sl.)
cistern ('systern) s. zbiornik
na wodę; cysterna
cite (sajt) v. cytować; przy-
taczać; pozywać; wymieniać
w komunikacie;wzywać do sądu
citizen ('sytyzn) s. obywatel
citizenship ('sytyzenszyp) s.
obywatelstwo;cnoty obywatelskie
city ('syty) s. (wielkie) miasto; centrum finansowe;ośrodek
city center ('syty,senter) s.
centrum miasta
city guide ('syty'gajd) s. plan
miasta;przewodnik po mieście
city hall('syty,ho:l) s. zarząd
miasta; magistrat
civics ('sywyks) s. nauka praw
i obowiązków obywatela[uprzejmy;
civil ('sywl) adj. społeczny;
obywatelski;cywilny(kodeks);
civilian (sy'wyljen) adj. cywilny; s. cywil; obywatel
civility (sy'wylyty) s. uprzejmość; grzeczność
civilization (,sywylaj'sejszyn)
s. cywilizacja;całość kultury
civilize ('sywylajz) v. cywili-
zować; ucywilizować
civil marriage ('sywl'maerydż)
s. ślub cywilny
civil rights ('sywl,rajts) s.
prawa obywatelskie
civil service ('sywl'se:rwys)
s. służba państwowa
civil war ('sywl,ło:r) s. wojna domowa
clack (klaek) v. klekotać; gdakać; s. klekot; wieko
clad (klaed) adj. odziany; zob.
clothe
claim (klejm) v. żądać; twierdzić; s. żądanie; twierdzenie;
działka;skarga;zażalenie;dług
claimant (klejment) s. rości-
ciel; pretendent;adj.pilny;rażący

clammy ('klaemy) adj. mokro-
lepki;wilgotny i zimny
clamor ('klaemer) s. zgiełk;
krzyk; v. krzyczeć; robić
wrzawę; wymuszać krzykiem
clamorous ('klaemeres) adj.
zgiełkliwy; krzykliwy
clamp (klaemp) s. klamra; zacisk v.zaciskać (jak)klamrą
clan (klaen) s. klan; szczep
szkocki;v.tworzyć klikę
clandestine (klaen'destyn) adj.
potajemny; skryty; tajny
clang (klaeng) s.dźwięk: szczęk;
klekot; v. dzwięczeć; szczękać;
klekotać;rozbrzmiewać;dzwonić
clank (klaenk) s. chrzęst;
brzęk; v. brzękać; chrzęścić
clap (klaep) s. huk; klaskanie;
v. łopotać; oklaskiwać; klepać
claret ('klaeret) s. czerwone
wino; bordo; slang:krew
clarify ('klaeryfaj) v. wyjas-
niać; rozjaśniać; oczyszczać
clarity ('klaeryty) s. czystość;
jasność; przejżystość;klarowność
clash (klaesz) s. brzęk; starcie;
v. brzęczeć; ścierać się; kolidować; uderzać w coś
clasp (klaesp) s. klamra; uchwyt; okucie; v. spinać; ściskać
clasp knife ('klaesp-najf) s.
scyzoryk;kozik; nóż składany
class (klaes) s. klasa; lekcja;
rocznik; grupa; v. klasyfikować ;segregować; sortować
classmate ('kla:s,mejt) s. kolega szkolny
classroom ('kla:s,rum) s. klasa
(w szkole); sala szkolna
class struggle (,kla:s'stragl)
s. walka klas w społeczeństwie
classic ('klaesyk) s. klasyk;
studia klasyczne; adj. klasyczny; uznany autotytet;klasyk
classical ('klaesykel) adj. typowy; klasyczny;humanistyczny
classification (klaesyfy'kejszyn)
s. klasyfikacja;klasyfikowanie
classify ('klaesyfaj) v. klasyfikować; sortować; zaklasyfikować
clatter ('klaeter) v. brzęczeć;
klapać; s. brzęk;łoskot;gwar

clause (klo:z) s. klauzula;
zdanie; punkt umowy
claw (klo:) s. pazur; szpon;
łapa; kleszcze; v. drapać; wydrapać; łapać w szpony
clay (klej) s. glina; sl.trup
clean (kli:n) adj. czysty; wyraźny; zgrabny; adv. całkiem;
zupełnie; poprostu; v, oczyścić; opróżniać; ogołocić; wygrać; uprzątnąć;dużo zyskać(sl,)
clean out ('kli:n aut) v. oczyścić; opróżniać;wyczyścić
clean up ('kli:n ap) v. po-
sprzątać; wygrać; zrobić na
czysto;robić porządek
cleaner ('kli:ner) s. czyści-
ciel; oczyszczalnik; właściciel pralni;pralnia chemiczna
cleaning ('kli:nyng) s. czyszczenie; sprzątanie;porządki
cleanliness ('klenlynys) s.
czystość;zamiłowanie do czystości
cleanly ('klenly) adj. czysty;
adv. czysto; schludnie
cleanness ('kli:nnys) s. czystość;zamiłowanie do czystości
cleanse (klenz) v. czyścić;
zmywać (grzechy);oczyszczać
clear (klier) adj. jasny; czysty; bystry; adv. jasno; wyraź-
nie; z dala; zupełnie; dokładnie; s. wolna przestrzeń
clear away('klier,ełej) v. usunąć (przeszkodę etc.)
clear up('klier,ap) v. wyjaśnić
clear-cut ('klier,kat) adj. wyraźny; czysty ; poprawny
clearing ('klieryng) s. karczo-
wisko; rozrachunek;obrachunek
clearly ('klierly) adv. wyraź-
nie; jasno; oczywiście
cleave; cleft; cleft (kli:w;
kleft; kleft)
cleave (kli:w) v. 1. łupać; pękać; rozdwajać; 2. trzymać się
wiernie ; nie odstępować
clef (klef) s. klucz (muzyczny)
cleft (kleft) s. szczelina;
pęknięcie; zob. cleave
clemency ('klemensy) s. miłosierdzie;łagodność (klimatu etc.)

clench (klencz) v. ściskać; zaciskać; zewrzeć się; s. uścisk; zaciśnięcie; zagięcie;ubić(targu)
clergy ('kle:rdży) s. duchowieństwo ;kler
clergyman ('kle:rdżymen) s. duchowny; ksiądz; pastor
clerical ('klerykel) adj. urzędniczy; duchowny; biurowy
clerk (kla:rk) s. subjekt; urzędnik; pisarz; ekspedient
clever ('klewer) adj. zdolny; sprytny; zręczny;pomysłowy;uprzejmy
click (klyk) v. szczękać; cmokać; trzaskać; dopiąć swego; wygrać; s. trzask; zatrzask; klamka;mlaśnięcie;klekot;brzęk
client ('klajent) s. klient
cliff (klyf) s. urwisko; stroma ściana; ściana skalna
climate ('klajmyt) s. klimat
climax ('klajmaeks) s. szczyt; zakończenie; v. stopniować; szczytować; kuliminować
climb (klajm) s.wspinaczka; miejsce wspinania; v. piąć się; wspinać; wzbijać się;wdrapać się
climb up (klajm ap) v. wspinać się w górę; wdrapywać się
climber (klajmer) s.taternik; karierowicz; pnącz (roślina)
clinch (klyncz) v. zaciskać; zaginać; zanitować;zakończyć
cling: clung; clung (klyng;klang; klang)
cling (klyng)v. trzymać się; chwytać się; czepiać się;trwać
clinic ('klynyk) s. klinika; poradnia; adj. kliniczny
clink (klynk) s. dzwonienie; ciupa ; v. dzwonić (kluczami etc.)
clip 1. (klyp) s. sprzączka v. spinać; 2. s strzyżenie; nożyce; v. strzyc; orżnąć
clippings ('klypyns) pl. wycinki (z gazet);okrawki;obrzynki
cloak (klouk) s. płaszcz;maska; v. okryć płaszczem;wdziewać
clock (klok) s. zegar ścienny
clockwise ('klokłajz) adj. (obrót) w prawo wg zegarka

clod (klod) s. gruda; ziemia; gamoń;v.obrzucać grudkami ziemi
clog (klog) s. kłoda; chodak; v. zatykać; zapychać;zawadzać
cloister ('klojster) s. krużganek; klasztor
close (klouz) v. zamykać; zatykać; zakończyć; zwierać; zgodzić się; s. zakończenie; koniec; miejsce ogrodzone; adv. szczelnie; blisko; prawie adj. zamknięty; skąpy; gęsty; bliski; ścisły;eksluzywny;skąpy
close to ('klous tu) przy;tuż obok
close by ('klous baj) obok
close down ('klouz dałn) v. zamykać;kończyć (działalność etc.)
close in (klouz yn) v. nadchodzić; ogarniać; okrążyć;otoczyć
closet ('klozyt) s. pokoik; klozet; kredens
close-up ('klousap) s. zdjęcie zbliżone; zbliżenie
closing time ('klouzyng,tajm) s. koniec pracy; zamknięcie (sklepu);koniec urzędowania
clot (klot) s. skrzep; v. ścinać się; skrzepnąć;zsiadać się
cloth (klos) s. materiał; szmata; szafa; obrus;sukno;żagiel
cloth-bound (klos baumd) s. oprawny w płótno
clothe (klouz) s. materiał; sukno;v.przywdziewać; zamaskować
clothes (klouz) pl. ubranie; pościel; pranie; odzierz;ubiór
clothes brush ('klouz,brasz) s. szczotka do ubrań
clothes hanger ('klouz,hanger) s. wieszak do ubrań
clothesline ('klous,lajn) s. sznur na bieliznę do suszenia
clothespin ('klouz,pyn) s. spinacz do bielizny
clothing (klouzyng) s. odzież; osłona; bielizna;odzienie
cloud (klaud) s. chmura; obłok; zasępienie; v. chmurzyć; sępić; rzucać cień ;ufarbować
cloudy ('klaudy) adj. chmurny; posępny; zamglony; mętny

clove (klouw) s. goździk; ząbek czosnku: zob. cleave

clover (klouwer) s. koniczyna

clown (klaun) s. błazen; prostak; v. błaznować; wygłupiać się

club (klab) s. klub; pałka; kij; v, bić pałką; zbijać; łączyć; zrzeszać;stowarzyszać się

clue (klu:)· s. klucz; ślad; wątek; v. informować(o wątku)

clumsy ('klamzy) adj. niezgrabny; nietaktowny;niekształtny

clung (klang)vprzywarty; zob. cling

cluster ('klaster) s. grono; kiść; pęk; kupka; v. tworzyć pęki; skupiać się; zbierać się

clutch (klacz) s. chwyt; szpon; sprzęgło;v.trzymać się kurczowo

clutch pedal ('klacz,pedl) s. pedał sprzęgła

coach (koucz) s. wóz pasażerski; trener; v. jechać wozem; trenować; uświadamiać;pouczać

coagulate (kou'aegjulejt) v. stężać; skrzepnąć;koagulować

coal (koul) s. węgiel

coalfield ('koul'fi:ld) s. zagłębie węglowe

coalition (,koue'lyszyn) s. związek; koalicja;przymierze

coal mine(koul-majn) s. kopalnia węgla

coal pit ('koul-pyt) s. kopalnia węgla ;szyb kopalniany

coarse (ko:rs) adj. pospolity; gruboziarnisty ; szorstki

coast (koust) s. brzeg; v. jechać bez napędu;płynąć brzegiem

coastguard ('koustga:rd) s. straż przybrzeżna

coat (kout) s. marynarka; surdut; powłoka; v. okrywać; pokrywać warstwą ;powlekać(farbą)

coat hanger('kouthaenger) s. wieszak (do ubrania)

coating (koutyng) s. powłoka; warstwa ;pokrycie

coat of arms('kout ow,a:rms) s. herb; godło

coax (kouks) v. namówić pochlebstwem; udobruchać;przymilać się; wycyganiać; wyczrowywać(z butelki)

cob (kob) s. głąb; kucyk; łabędź samiec;kaczan;kutwa;bochenek

cobra ('koubre) s. kobra

cobweb ('kobłeb) s. pajęczyna

cock (kok) s. kogut; kurek; kran; kutas (vulg.) v. postawić; nastroszyć; napiąć; odwodzic; podnieść; zadzierać;wznieść

cock-and-bull ('koken'bul) exp.: o żelaznym wilku

cockchafer ('kok,chejfer) s. chrząszcz

cockle ('kokl) s. kąkol;piecyk

cockpit ('kokpyt) s. kokpit; kabina;arena do walki kogutów

cockroach('kokroucz) s. karaluch

cocksure ('kokszuer) adj. pewny siebie; zarozumiały

cocktail ('koktejl) s. cocktail

coco ('koukou) s. palma kokosowa; kokos

cocoa ('koukou) s. kakao

coconut ('koukenat) s. orzech kokosowy

cocoon (ke'ku:n) s. kokon oprzęd

cod(kod)s.dorsz;sztokfisz;wątłusz;v.wystrychnąć na dudka

coddle ('kodl) v. podgotować; pieścić; tuczyć; zepsuć

code (koud) s. kodeks; szyfr; v. szyfrować ;pisać szyfrem

cod-liver oil ('kod,lywer ojl) s. tran (lekarski)

coexist ('kouyg'zyst) v. współistnieć;koegzystować

coexistence ('kouyg'zystens) s. współistnienie;współżycie

coffee('kofy) s. kawa

coffee bean ('kofy-bi:n) s. ziarno kawy

coffee mill ('kofy-myl) s. młynek do kawy

coffeepot ('kofy-pot) s. maszynka do kawy

coffin ('kofyn) s. trumna

cogwheel ('kog-hłil) s. koło zębate; tryb

coherence ('kou'hierens) s. sens; spoistość ;związek logiczny

coherency (kou'hierensy) s. sens; zwartość ;spójność

coherent (kou'hierent) adj. logiczny; zwarty; spoisty

cohesive (kou'hi:syw) adj. spoisty; zwarty ; kleisty

coiffure (kƚa:'fjuer) s. fryzura; styl uczesania

coil (kojl) s. zwój; cewka; lok; v. zwijać; skręcać; wić się

coin (koyn) s. moneta; v. bić monety; spieniężać; ukuć (nowe pojęcie) ;tłoczyć

coinage (koynydź) s. bicie monety; monety; system monetarny; wymysł; nowe słowo

coincide (kouyn'sajd) v. zbiegać się; pokrywać się; przystawać do siebie; pasować

coincidence (kou'ynsydens) s. zbieg okoliczności; zgodność; przystawanie; zgodność faktów

coke (kouk) s. koks; kokaina; Coca-Cola; v. koksować

cold (kould) s. zimno; przeziębienie; adj.zimny;chłodny;mroźny

cold storage room(kouldstoredźru:m) chłodnia

colic ('kolyk) s. kolka (w brzuchu);ostry ból w brzuchu

collaborate (ke'laeberejt) v. współpracować;kolaborować

collaboration (ke'laeberejszyn) s. współpraca; kolaboracja

collapse (ke'laeps) s. załamanie się; v. załamać się; upaść; opaść; zawalić się;zalamywać

collapsible (ke'laepsebl) adj. składany (mebel,,stół,łóżko etc.)

collar ('koler) s. kołnierz; szyjka; pierścień; obroża; chomąto; piana (na piwie) v.wkładać obrożę; pojmac; ująć

collarbone ('koler-boun) s. obojczyk

colleague ('koli:g) s. kolega (po fachu);współpracownik

collect ('ke'lekt) v. zbierać; odbierać; inkasować

collected ('ke'lektyd) adj. skupiony; opanowany ;spokojny

collection ('ke'lekszyn) s. zbiór; kolekcja; inkaso ;zainkasowane pieniądze

collective ('ke'lektyw) adj. zbiorowy; wspólny;s. kolektyw

collector ('ke'lektor) s. inkasent; poborca; zbieracz

college ('kolydż) s. uczelnia; kolegium;zrzeszenie;akademia

collide (ke'lajd) v. zderzyć się; kolidować;wejść w kolizję

colliery ('koljery) s. kopalnia węgla

collision (ke'lyżen) s. zderzenie; kolizja

colloquial (ke'loukƚjel) adj. potoczny (język);familiarny

colon ('koulen) s. grube jelito; dwukropek

colonel('ke:nl) s. pułkownik

colonial (ke'lounjel) a. kolonialny;s. mieszkaniec kolonii

colonialism (ke'lounjelyzem)s. kolonializm

colonist ('kolenyst) s. osadnik ;mieszkaniec kolonii

colonize ('kolenajz) v. osiedlać; kolonizować

colony ('koleny) s. kolonia

color ('kaler) s. barwa; farba; koloryt; v. barwić; farbować; koloryzować; rumienić się

color bar ('kaler ba:r) s. oddzielenie ras

colored ('kaleret) s. murzyn; kolorowy;adj.przekręcony

colored man ('kaleret men) s. murzyn

colored people ('kaleret'pi:pl)s. murzyni

colorful ('kalerful) adj. pstry; barwny ;żywy;kolorowy

coloring ('kaleryŋg) s. koloryt; kolorowanie; rumieńce

colorless ('kalerlys) adj. bezbarwny; nudny;monotonny

colorline ('kalerlajn) s. przedział rasowy

color print ('kaler,prynt) s. chromodruk

colt (koult) s. źrebak

column ('kolem) s. kolumna; stos; trzon; szpalta;formacja

coma ('koume) s. omdlenie; koma; śpiączka;ogon(komety)

comb (koum) s. grzębień; grzbiet
(fali); v. czesać; kłębić sie
combat ('kombet) s. walka;
v. zwalczać; walczyć
combatant ('kombetent) adj.
walczący; s. kombatant;bojownik
combination (komby'nejszyn)s.
kombinacja; zespół;związek
combine-harvester (kembajn-
ha:rwyster) s. kombajn
combustible (kem'bastebl) adj.
palny; s. paliwo; materiały
palne;opał;adj.popędliwy
combustion (kem'bastszyn) s.
spalanie; zapłon
come; came; come (kam; kejm;
kam)
come (kam) v. przybyć; pochodzić; wynosić;dziać się;być
come about ('kam,e'baut) v. zdarzyć się;stać się;odwracać się
come across ('kam,e'cros) v.
natknąć się;dać się przekonać
come along ('kam,e'long) v.
pospieszyć się; nadejść
come around ('kam,e'raund) v.
zmienic zdanie; odwiedzić
come at ('kam,et) v. podejść;
dotrzeć; przyjść o (czwartej...)
come by ('kam,baj) v. dojść do
czegoś; minąć; nabyć
come for ('kam,for) v. przyjsć
po coś
come loose ('kam,luz) v. ob-
luźniac się
come off ('kam,of) v. odpasć;
odleciec;puszczać;mieć miejsce
come on ('kam,on) v. chodź-że;
przestań; daj spokój!
come round ('kam,raund) v. zmienic zdanie; przechytrzyc;obejść
come to see ('kam tu si:) v. od-
wiedzic;przyjść z wizytą
come up to ('kam ap tu) v. podejść do..;wejść na sam(szczyt)
come-and-go ('kam-en'-go) s.
bieganina;ruch tam i z powrotem
comeback ('kam-'baek) s. powrót ; bystra odpowiedz;poprawa
comedian (ke'mi:djen) s. komik;

comedy ('komydy) s.komedia

comer ('kamer) s. przybysz
comet ('komyt) s. kometa
comfort ('kamfert) s. wygoda;
pociecha; v. pocieszać; czynic wygodnym;dodawać otuchy
comfortable ('kamfertebl) adj.
wygodny; zadowolony;spokojny
comforter ('kamferter) s. po-
cieszyciel; kołdra;smoczek
comical ('komykel) adj. zabawny; śmieszny;komiczny
comic strips ('komyk,stryps) s.
seryjne obrazkówki;kreskówki
comma ('kome) s. przecinek
command (ke'maend) v. rozkazy-
wać; kazać; rozporządzać; panować nad; dowodzić; s. rozkaz;
nakaz; komenda;dowództwo
commander (ke'maender) s. dowódca; komendant;kapitan(fregaty)
commander-in-chief (ke'maender
yn'czi:f) głównodowodzący
commandment (ke'maendment) s.
przykazanie (boskie)
commend (ke'mend) v. chwalić;
zalecac; polecać opiece
comment ('koment) s. objasnie-
nie; v. robić uwagi krytyczne
lub złośliwe;wypowiadać zdanie
comment on('koment on) v. ko-
mentować; oceniać (utwór etc.)
commentary('komentery) s. komentarz;uwaga; notatka
commentator('komentejter) s.
komentator; sprawozdawca
commerce ('kome:rs) s. handel
commercial (ke'ke:rszel) adj.
handlowy;s.ogołoszenie(w radiu...)
commissar (,komy'sa:r) s. komisarz w ZSRR
commission (ke'myszyn) s. zlecenie; misja; urząd; v. delegować; powierzać; objąć; zlecać;zamianować;upoważniać
commissioner (ke'myszener) s.
delegat; pełnomocnik; komisarz
rządowy;członek komisji rządowej
commit (ke'myt) v. powierzać;
przekazywać; odsyłać; popełniać; wciągać; zobowiazywać
się;oddawać w opiekę;zamykć w
(domu wariatów);obiecywać

commitment (ke'mytment) s. zobowiązanie; dopuszczenie się;
przekazanie;zaangażowanie się
committee (ke'myti:) s. komitet;
komisja;opiekun(umysłowo chrego)
commodity (ke'modyty) s. towar;
rzecz przydatna;artykuł handlu
common ('komen) adj. wspólny;
publiczny; ogólny; pospolity;
zwyczajny;prosty;publiczny
commoner ('komener) s. człowiek
z gminu; nie szlachcic
common law marriage ('komen,lo:
'maerydż) pożycie na wiarę
common market ('komen'ma:rkyt)
wspólny rynek (Zach.Eur.)
commonplace ('komen-plejs) s.
banał; adj. banalny;oklepany
common sense ('komen,sens)
zdrowy rozsądek
commonwealth ('komen,łels) s.
wspólnota; rzeczpospolita
commotion (ke'mouszyn) s. zamieszki; tumult; poruszenie
commune ('komju:n) s. gmina;
komuna; v. obcować; rozmawiac
communicate (ke'mju:ny,kejt) v.
dzielić się; komunikować; łączyć się;przenosic (ciepło etc.)
communication (ke,mju:ny'kejszyn)
s. łączność; komunikacja; po-
rozumiewanie się zakomunikowanie
communicative (ke'mju:nykejtyw)
adj. otwarty; rozmowny; towarzyski; przystępny
communion (ke'mju:njen) s. obcowanie; uczestnictwo; wspólnota; komunia;wyznanie wiary
communism ('komju,nyzem) s. komunizm;ruch komunistyczny
communist ('komjunyst) s. komunista;adj. komunistyczny
community (ke'mju:nyty) s. środowisko; społeczność; gmina;
kolektyw; wspólnota;koło;zakon
commute (ke'mju:t) v. zamieniać;
zastępować; łagodzić; dojeżdżac
do pracy;brać bilet okresowy
comose ('koumous) adj. włochaty;
puszysty;włóknisty
compact (kem'paekt) adj. gęsty;
zbity; zwarty; v. ubijać; zbijać; zagęszczać;s.puderniczka

compact ('kempaekt) s. 1. ugoda;
porozumienie; 2. puderniczka
samochód średniej wielkości(USA)
companion (kem'paenjen) s. towarzysz; (coś) do pary
companionship (kem'paenjenszyp)
s. koleżeństwo; towarzystwo
company ('kampeny) s. towarzystwo; załoga; goście; partnerzy;
spółka; kompania;trupa teatralna
comparable ('komperebl) adj.
porównywalny;wytrzymujacy porównanie
comparative (kem'paeretyw) adj.
porównawczy; względny; stosunkowy;s, stopień wyższy(przymiot-
nika
compare (kem'peer) v. porówny-
wać; dawać się porównać; stopniować (gram)
comparison (kem'paeryson) s. porównanie;zestawienie
compartment (kem'pa:rtment) s.
przedział; przegroda; komora
wodoszczelna
compass ('kampes) s. kompas;
busola; obwód; obręb;cyrkiel
zasięg v. obchodzić; otaczać;
ogarniać;osiągać;dopiąć
compassion (kem'paeszyn) s;
litość; współczucie
compassionate (kem'paeszynyt)
adj. litościwy;v.litować się
compatible (kem'paetebl) adj.
zgodny;licujący; do pogodzenia
compatriot (kem'paetryet) s.
rodak; ziomek;rodaczka
compel (kem'pel) v. zmuszać;
wymuszać (coś);wzbudzać
compensate ('kompen,sejt) v.
wyrównywać; nagradzać; wypłacić
odszkodowanie; kompensować
compensation (,kompen'sejszyn)
s. rekompensata; wynagrodzenie;
odszkodowanie;wyrównanie
compete (kem'pi:t) v. konkuro-
wać; rywalizować; ubiegać się
compete for (kem'pi:t,fo:r) v.
(o coś) współzawodniczyć;
współubiegać się;prześcigać się
competence ('kompytens) s. fa-
chowość; kwalifikacja; uzdolnienie; zasobność; dobrobyt
competent ('kompytent) adj. właściwy;kwalifikowany;odpowiedni;
kompetentny

competition (,kompy'tyszyn) s. konkurencja; konkurs; zawody; współzawodnictwo;tuniej

competitor (kem'petyter) s. rywal; konkurent; współzawodnik;współzawodniczka;rywalka

compile (kem'pajl) v. zbierać; zestawiać; kompilować

complacent (kem'plejsnt) adj. zadowolony (z siebie; ze świata);błogi

complain (kem'plejn) v. żalić się; narzekać; skarżyć; wnosić zażalenie;wnosić skargę

complaint (kem'plejnt) s. skarga; zażalenie; dolegliwość

complete (kem'pli:t) adj. całkowity; zupełny; kompletny; v. uzupełniać; udoskonalić; ukończyć;wypełniać (formularz)

completion (kem'pli:szyn) s. ukończenie; uzupełnienie; udoskonalenie;spełnienie(woli)

complexion (kem'plekszyn) s.cera; płeć; postać; aspekt (charakter);wygląd

complicate ('komply,kejt) v. wikłać; splątać; komplikować

compliment ('komplyment) s. komplement; gratulacje; ukłony; uszanowanie; v. mówić komplementy; gratulować

comply (kem'plaj) v. zastosować się; spełnić; podporządkować się;uczynić zadość;przestrzegać

comply with (kem'plaj,łys) v. spełniać;przestrzegać czegoś

component (kem'pounent) s. składnik; część składowa; siła składowa;adj.składowy

compose ('kem'pouz) v. składać; układać; tworzyć; komponować; skupiać (myśli); uspokoić; załagodzić;uspokajać się

composed (kem'pouzd) adj. opanowany; spokojny;stateczny

composer (kem'pouzer) s. kompozytor;kompozytorka

composition (,kempe'zyszyn) s. skład; układ; ugoda; wypracowanie; budowa;usposobienie

composure (kem'poużer) s. spokój; opanowanie;zimna krew

compote ('kompout) s. kompot (z puszki);kompotiera

compound (kom'paund) adj. złożony; sprężony; s. związek(chem.) mieszanka; złożenie; v. mieszać; składać; powiększać; łączyć;zawrzeć;załatwić

comprehend (,kompry'hend) v. pojmować; rozumieć; zawierać

comprehensible (,kompry'hensebl) adj. zrozumiały;pojętny

comprehensive (,kompry'hensyw) adj. obszerny; szeroki;rozumowy; wyczerpujący;ogólny;wszechstronny

compress (kem'pres) v. ściskać; s. kompres; okład;v.streszczać

comprise (kem'prajz) v. włączać; obejmować;składać się

compromise ('kompre,majz) s. kompromis; ugoda; kompromitacja; narażenie; v. załatwiać ugodowo; kompromitować

compulsion (kem'palszyn) s. przymus; siła przymusu

compulsory (kem'palsery) adj. przymusowy;przymuszający

compunction (kem'pankszyn) s. skrucha;żal za grzechy

computation (,kompju'tejszyn) s, obliczenie; kalkulcja

computer (kem'pju:ter) s. kalkulator; komputer; przelicznik

comrade ('komread) s. kolega; druh; współpracownik

comradeship ('komraedszyp) s. koleżeństwo; braterstwo

conceal (ken'si:l) v. taić; ukrywać;przemilczać;zataić

concede (ken'si:d) v. przyznawać; ustępować; poddawać się

conceit (ken'si:t) s. próżność; zarozumiałość;mniemanie;koncept

conceited (ken'si:tyd) adj. próżny; zarozumiały

conceivable (ken'si:webl) adj. wyobrażalny; zrozumiały

conceive (ken'si:w) v. wymyślić; wyobrażać; rozumieć; ujmować; zajść w ciążę;pojąć;redagować

concentrate ('konsentrejt) v. skupiać się; stężać;s.roztwór

conception (ken'sepszyn) s. pomysł; poczęcie (dziecka);początek

concern (ken'se:rn) s. interes;
troska; związek; v. tyczyć się;
dotyczyć; obchodzić; niepokoić
się o...;wchodzić w grę
concerned (ken'se:rnd) adj. zainteresowany; zaaferowany;
strapiony; niespokojny
concert ('konsert) s. koncert;
porozumienie; v. ułożyć; ukar-
towac;porozumieć się
concession (ken'se szyn) s.
koncesja; ustępstwo;przyzwolenie
conciliate (ken'syly,ejt) v.
zjednywać; jednać; godzić; łagodzić; pogodzić;udobruchać
conciliatory (ken'syljeto:ry)
adj. pojednawczy
concise (ken'sajs) adj. zwięzły;
treściwy ;krotki i węzłowaty
conclude (ken'klu:d) v. zakończyć; zawierać; wnioskować;
postanawiać ;kończyć się
conclusion (ken'klu:żyn) s. zakończenie; wynik; postanowienie; wniosek; konkluzja; zawar-
cie układu ;wynik ostateczny
conclusive (ken'klu:syw) adj.
rozstrzygający; dowodny
concord ('konko:rd) s. zgoda;
jedność; harmonia;v. zgadzać się
concrete ('konkri:t) s. beton;
konkret; adj. rzeczywisty;
realny; zwarty; stały; konkretny; specyficzny; betonowy
concur (ken'ke:r) v. zgadzać
się; schodzić się;współdziałać
concurrence (ken'ke:rens) s.
zgodność; zbieżność ; zgoda
concussion (ken'kaszyn) s.
wstrząs (mozgu); uderzenie
condemn (ken'dem) v. potępiać;
skazywać ;krytykować;wybrakować
condemnation (,kendem'nejszyn)
s. potępienie; skazanie
condense (ken'dens) v. kondenso-
wać; zgęszczać;streszczać
condenser (ken'denser) s. kondensator; skraplacz
condescend (,kondy'send) v.
zniżać się; raczyć; zezwalać;
zachowywać się z wyższością

condition (ken'dyszyn) s. stan;
warunek; zastrzeżenie; poprawka; v.uwarunkowywać; zastrze-
gać; naprawiać; przygotowywać; przyzwyczajać;klimatyzować
conditional (ken'dyszynl) adj.
warunkowy;uzależniony;zależny
condole (ken'doul) v. składać
kondolencje;współczuć;ubolewać
condolence (ken'doulens) s.
wyrazy współczucia;kondolencje
conduct (kon'dakt) s. prowadzenie; sprawowanie; prowadzenie
się; sprawowanie się; kierownictwo; v. prowadzić; wieść;
przewodzić;dyrygować;dowodzić
conduction (kon'dakszyn) s.
przewodzenie (fiz.)
conductor (kon'dakter) s. kierownik; przewodnik; dyrygent;
przewód;odgromnik;piorunochron
cone (koun) s. stożek; szyszka;
v. nadawać kształt stożka
confection (ken'fekszyn) s.
sporządzanie; konfitura; słodycze; konfekcja (damska)
confectioner (ken'fekszyner) s.
cukiernik;właściciel cukierni
confectionery (ken'fekszynery)
s. cukiernia; wyroby cukier-
nicze
confederacy (ken'federesy) s.
konfederacja; sojusz; związek; spisek; sprzysiężenie
confederate (ken'federyt) adj.
sprzysiężony; v. jednoczyć;
spiskować; knuć;sprzymierzać
confederation (ken,fede'rejszyn)
s. sprzymierzenie; skonfedero-
wanie; konfederacja
confer (ken'fe:r) v. naradzać
się; nadawać ;przyznawać
conferee (,konfe'ri:) s. uczestnik konferencji; nagrodzony
conference ('konferens) s. narada; liga;zebranie;zjazd
confess (ken'fes) v. wyznać;
przyznać się; spowiadać się
confession (ken'feszen) s. wyznanie; spowiedź; przyznanie
się ; religia

confessor (ken'feser) s. spowiednik; ksiądz spowiednik
confide (ken'fajd) s. ufac (komuś); zwierzac sie; powierzac
confidence ('konfydens) s. zaufanie; bezczelnosc; pewnosc; ufnosc; zwierzenie;śmiałosc
confident ('konfydent) adj. dufny; bezczelny ;przekonany
confidential (,konfy'denczel) adj. tajny; poufny; zaufany; poufały;intymny
confine ('konfajn) v. ograniczac; odosabniac;s,kres;granica
confinement (kon'fajnment) s. uwięzienie; ograniczenie; odosobnienie; połog; poród
confirm (ken'fe:rm) v. potwierdzac; zatwierdzac; umacniac; bierzmowac;utwierdzac;pokrzepic
confirmation (,konfer'mejszyn) s. potwierdzenie; zatwierdzenie; bierzmowanie;pokrzepienie
confiscate ('konfyskejt) v. konfiskowac; skonfiskowac
conflagration (,konfle'grejszyn) s. pozar; pozoga
conflict ('konflykt) s. zatarg; starcie; konflikt; kolizja
conform (kon'fo:rm) v. dostosowac; upodabniac;dostrajac
conformity (kon'fo:rmyty) s. zgodnosc; dostosowanie się
confound (kon'faund) v. mieszac; zawiesc; pokrzyzowac;poplątac
confound it ! (kon'faund,yt) exp. do licha ! niech to diabli wezmą!
confront (ken'frant) v. stawiac czoło; konfrontowac;unaocznic
confuse (ken'fju:z) v. zmieszac (kogos; siebie);wikłac;gmatwac
confusion (ken'fju:żyn) s. nieład; zamieszanie;bałagan;chaos
congeal (ken'dżi:l) v. mrozic; scinac; marznąc;zakrzepnąc
congestion (ken'dżestczyn)s. przeludnienie; przeciążenie (ruchu); przekrwienie
conglomerate (ken'glomerejt) v. skupiac; zlewac w jedną masę
congratulate (ken'graetju,lejt) v. gratulowac ;składac(komus) gratulacje;pogratulowac

congratulation (ken,graetju'lejszyn) s. gratulacje; gratulowanie; gratulacja
congregate ('kongry,gejt) adj. zbiorowy; v. skupiac; zbierac (się); gromadzic (się)
congregation (,kongry'gejszyn) s. zbieranie; zgromadzenie
congress ('kongres) s. zjazd; zebranie; parlament USA
conjecture (ken'dżekczer) s. domysł; przypuszczenie; v. przypuszczac; mniemac
conjugal ('kondżugel) adj. małżeński
conjugate ('kondżu,gejt) v. odmieniac się; kopulowac; parzyc się;adj.połączony
conjugation (,kondżu'gejszyn) s. koniugacja; zespalanie się; kopulacja;odmiana czasownika
conjunction (ken'dżankszyn) s. zbieg; związek; skojarzenie; spójnik; połączenie
conjunctive mood (ken'dżanktyw, mu:d) s. tryb łączący
conjure (kan'dżuer) v. zaklinac; błagac;robic sztuczki
conjure ('kandżer) v. czarowac
conjurer ('kandżerer) s. czarownik; magik;kuglarz
connect (ke'nekt) v. łączyc; wiązac;miec połączenie
connected (ke'nektyd) a. zwarty (logiczny); ustosunkowany
connection(xion) (ke'nekszyn) s. połączenie; pokrewieństwo
conquer ('konker) v. zdobyc; zwyciężyc; pokonac
conqueror ('konkerer) s. zdobywca; zwyciezca
conquest ('konkłest) s. podbój; zdobycie;zawojowanie
conscience ('konszyns) s. sumienie;świadomosc zła i dobra
conscientious (,konszy'enszes) adj. sumienny;skrupulatny
conscious ('konszes) adj. przytomny; świadomy;naumyślny
consciousness ('konszesnys) s. świadomosc;całosc mysli i uczuc
conscript ('konskrypt) s.& adj. poborowy ;s. rekrut;v. rekwirowac; brac do wojska

consecrate ('konsy,krejt) v.
poświęcać;adj.poświęcony
consecutive (ken'sekjutyw)
adj. kolejny;nieprzerwany;skut-
consent (ken'sent) s. zgoda;^{kowy}
v. zgadzać się;przyzwalać
consequence ('konsykłens) s.wy-
nik; znaczenie; konsekwencja
consequently ('konsykłently)
adv. a zatem; przeto; tym samym;w skutek tego; więc
conservative (ken'se:rwatyw)
adj. ostrożny; zachowawczy;
konserwatywny; s. konserwatys-
ta; środek konserwujący
conserve (ken'se:rw) v. konserwować; zachowywać; zabezpieczać; s. konserwa owocowa
consider (ken'syder) v. rozważać; rozpatrywać; uważać; szanować; mieć wzgląd;sądzić
considerable (ken'syderebl)
adj. znaczny;adv.znacznie
considerate (ken'syderyt) adj.
myślacy; uważający; troskliwy
consideration (ken,syde'rejszyn)
s. wzgląd; rozważanie; warunek;
uprzejmość; rekompensata
consign (ken'sajn) v. przekazać;
powierzać;złożyć do(banku,grobu..)
consignment(ken'sajnment) s.
przesyłka ; powierzenie
consist (ken'syst) v. składać
się; polegać;zgadzać się
consistency (ken'systensy) s.
konsystencja; solidność; stałość; zgodność;logiczność
consistent (ken'systent) adj.
zgodny; stały; konsekwentny
consolation (,konse'lejszyn) s.
pocieszenie; pociecha;ukojenie
console (ken'soul) v. pocieszać;
s. konsola; wspornik;podpora
consolidate (ken'solydejt) v.
utwierdzać; scalać; jednoczyć
consonant ('konsenent) s. spółgłoska; adj. spółgłoskowy;
zgodny; harmonijny
conspicuous ('ken'spykjues) adj.
widoczny; zwracający uwagę
conspiracy (ken'spyresy) s. spisek; konspiracja; zmowa; umowa

conspirator (ken'spyreter) s.
spiskowiec; konspirator
conspire (ken'spajer) v. konspirować;spiskować;uknuć
constable ('kanstebl) s. policjant; posterunkowy
constant ('konstent) adj. stały; trwały;s. liczba stała
consternation (,konste:rnejszyn)
s. przerażenie;osłupienie
constipation (,konsty'pejszyn)
s. zatwardzenie; zaparcie
constituency (ken'stytjuensy)
s. okręg wyborczy; wyborcy
constituent (ken'stytjuent)
adj. składowy; s. wyborca;
część składowa; element
constitute ('konsty,tju:t) v.
stanowić; ustanawiać; wyznaczać
constitution (,konsty'tju:szyn)
s. statut; konstytucja; struktura; założenie;układ psychiczny
constitutional (,konsty'tu:szenl)
adj. zasadniczy; istotny; zdrowotny;s.przechadzka dla zdrowia
constrain (ken'strejn) v. wymuszać; zmuszać; ograniczać;
więzić; zniewalać;przymuszać
constraint (ken'strejnt) s.
przymus; skrępowanie; ograniczenie swobody(ruchów etc.)
construct (ken'strakt) v. budować; tworzyć; rysować(figury geom.)
construction (ken'strakszyn)
s. budowa; konstrukcja;układ:
konstruowanie;ujęcie;interpretacja
constructive (ken'straktyw)
adj. twórczy; konstruktywny
consul ('konsel) s. konsul
consular ('konsjuler) adj.
konsularny
consulate ('konsjulyt) s. konsulat;uprawnienia konsula
consulate general ('konsjulyt'
'dżenerel) s. konsulat generalny
consult (ken'salt) v. radzić
się; informować się
consultation (,konsel'tejszyn)
s. porada; konsultacja
consultative (ken'saltetyw) a.
doradczy; konsultatywny

consume (ken'sju:m) v. spożywać; zużywać; trawić; niszczeć; marnieć;uschnąć
consumer (ken'sju:mer) s. konsumer; spożywca;odbiorca
consummate(ken'samyt) a. doskonały;wielkiej miary;skończony
consummate('kensemejt) v. spełniać małżeństwo
consumption (ken'sampszyn) s. zużycie; suchoty; pylica
contact ('kontaekt) s. styczność; stosunki; znajomości
v. kontaktować; porozumiewać się;stykać się;zetknąć się
contact lenses ('kontaekt,lenzys) pl. szkła kontaktowe
contagious (ken'tejdżes) a. zaraźliwy ; zakaźny;udzielający się
contain (ken'tejn) v. zawierać; opanowywać się; wiązać;hamować
container (ken'tejner) s. zasobnik; zbiornik; naczynie
contaminate (ken'taemynejt) v. zakazić;skalać;deprawować
contamination (ken'taemynejszyn) s. kontaminacja; zakażenie; skażenie; ujemny wpływ
contemplate ('kontemplejt) v. oglądać; rozważać; liczyć się z (czyms) ; medytować;planować
contemplation ('kontemplejszyn) s. oglądanie; kontemplacja; rozważanie;planowanie;medytacja
contemplative ('kontemplejtyw) adj. kontemplacyjny; zamyślony
contemporary (ken'temperery) adj.& s. współczesny (rówieśnik)
contempt (ken'temt) s. pogarda; lekceważenie;obraza (sądu· etc.)
contemptible (ken'temtebl) adj. godny pogardy, lekceważenia
contemptuous (ken'temtjues) adj. pogardliwy;nadęty;lekceważący
contend (ken'tend) v. spierać się; walczyć;rywalizować;upierać się
content 1. (ken'tent) adj. zadowolony; s. zadowolenie; v. zadowalać
content 2. ('kontent) s. zawartość; tresc; objętość; pojemność ;powierzchnia;kubatura;istota

contented (ken'tentyd) adj. zadowolony; zaspokojony
contents ('kontents) s. zawartość(pojemnika,treści
contest ('kontest) s. rywalizacja; spór; v. walczyć; spierać się; ubiegać; kwestionować
context ('kontekst) s. kontekst
continent ('kontynent) s. kontynent; część świata
continental ('kontynentl) adj. kontynentalny; s. mieszkaniec kontynentu
continual (ken'tynjuel) adj. ciągły; powtarzający się;stały
continuance (ken'tynjuens) s. ciągłość; trwanie; przebieg; ciąg dalszy;odroczenie;pobyt
continuation (ken,tynju'ejszyn) s. kontynuacja; ciąg dalszy
continue (ken'tynju:) v. kontynuować; ciągnąc dalej; trwać; ciągnąc się ;odroczyć;upierać
continuous (ken'tynjues) adj. nieprzerwany ;stały;ciągły
contort (ken'to:rt) v. skręcać; wykrzywiać ;zwichnąć;przekrzywić
contour ('kontuer) s. zarys; kontur;warstwica;v.konturować
contraceptive (,kontre'septyw) s. środek zapobiegający zapłodnieniu ;adj.antykoncepcyjny
contract ('kontraekt) s. umowa; układ; kontrakt ;obietnicą
contract (ken'traekt) v. ściągać; kurczyć; zobowiązywać
contractor (ken'traekter) s. przedsiębiorca (budowlany etc.)
contradict (,kontre'dykt) v. zaprzeczać ;posprzeczać się
contradiction (,kontre'dykszyn) s. sprzeczność ;zaprzeczenie
contradictory (,kontre'dyktery) adj. sprzeczny;przekorny;kłótliwy
contrary ('kontrery) adj. przeciwny; s. przeciwieństwo; adv. w przeciwieństwie
contrariwise ('kontrery,łajz) adv. odwrotnie; natomiast
contrast (ken'traest) v.przeciwstawiać; kontrastować; s.kontrast; przeciwieństwo

contribute (ken'trybjut) v.;
przyczynić się; dostarczyć;
współdziałać;zasłużyć się
contribution (,kontry'bju:szyn)
s. przyczynek; wkład; ofiara;
kontrybucja;datek;wsparcie
contributor (ken'trybjuter) s.
ofiarodawca; współpracownik
(pisarz);współpracowniczka
contrite (ken'trajt) adj. skruszony ;pełen skruchy
contrivance (ken'trajwens) s.
pomysł; sztuczka; fortel; wynalazek;wynalazczość;pomysłowość
contrive (ken'trajw) v. wymyślić; wynaleźć; doprowadzić do
czegoś; zaplanować;wykombinować
control (ken'troul) v. sprawdzać; rządzić; kontrolować;
opanować; s. kontrola; sterowanie; regulowanie; ster;władza
controller (ken'trouler) s.
kontroler;regulator;zarządca
controversial (,kentre'we:rżel)
adj. sporny; sprzeczający się
controversy ('kontre,we:rsy)
s. spór;kłótnia;polemika;dysputa
contuse (ken'tju:z) v. stłuc;
kontuzjować
convalesce (,konwe'les) v. wyzdrowieć i odzyskać siły
convalescence (,konwe'lesens)
s. wyzdrowienie
convalescent (,konwe'lesnt) s.
rekonwalescent; ozdrowieniec
convenience (ken'wi:njens) s.
wygoda; korzyść;dogoność
convenient (ken'wi:njent) adj.
wygodny;łatwy do osiągnięcia
convent ('konwent) s. zakon
convention (ken'wenszyn) s.·
zjazd; zgromadzenie; układ;
umowa; konwent;zebranie
conventional (ken'wenszynl)
adj. zwyczajowy; konwencjonal-
ny; umowny;powszechnie stosowany
conversation (,konwer'sejszyn)
s. rozmowa; konwersacja
converse (ken'we:rs) v. rozmawiać;obcować;prowadzić rozmowę
converse ('konwe:rs) s. rozmowa;
adj. odwrotny; s.rzecz odwrotna

conversion (ken'we:rżyn) s.od-
wrócenie; przemiana; nawrócenie;przeistoczenie
convert (ken'we:rt) v. zmieniać; nawracać; przekształcać;
odwracać;przemieniać;przystosować
convert ('konwert) s. neofita
convertible (ken'we:rtybl) adj.
wymienialny; s. otwarty samochód z podnoszonym dachem
convey (ken'wej) v. przewozić;
przenosić; przesyłać; przekazywać; komunikować;zapisywać
conveyance (ken'wejens) s. przewóz; przenoszenie; uzmysławia-
nie; pojazd; przekazanie
conveyor belt (ken'wejer,belt)
s. przenośnik taśmowy
convict ('konwykt) s. skazaniec;
więzień; v. udowadniać; przekonywać; uznać winnym
conviction (ken'wykszyn) s.
przeświadczenie; przekonanie;
zasądzenie;skazanie
convince (ken'wyns) v. przekonać;przekonywać
convoy ('konwoj) s. konwój;
eskorta; straż
convoy (kon'woj) v. konwojować
convulsion (ken'valszyn) s.
drgawki; wstrząs; konwulsje
convulsive (ken'walsyw) adj.
konwulsyjny;niepohamowany
cook (kuk) s. kucharz; kucharka; v. gotować; preparować
cooking (kukyng) s. gotowanie
cool (ku:l) adj. chłodny;
oziębły; spokojny; v. chłodzić;
studzić; ochłonąć; s. chłód
cooler ('ku:ler) s. chłodnica;
element chłodzący;więzienie
coolness ('ku:lnys) s. chłód;
zimna krew;opanowanie;spokój
co-op (kou'op) s. spółdzielnia
cooperate (kou'operejt) v.
współpracować; współdziałać
cooperation (kou,ope'rejszyn)
s. współpraca; współdziałanie
kooperacja; spółdzielczość
cooperative (kou,ope'rejtyw)
adj. spółdzielczy; uspołecznio-
ny; uczynny; współpracujący

cooperator (kou'ope,rejter) s.
współpracownik; współdzielca
coordinate (kou'o:rdynejt) adj.
współrzędny; współrzędna
cop (kop) s. policjant (slang)
v. złapać; wygrać; buchnąć;
nakryć ;porwać; ukraść(slang)
coPartner (kou'pa:rtner) s.
uczestnik; wspólnik; udziało-
wiec(we wspólnym interesie)
cope ('koup) v. uporać; dawać
sobie radę; pokrywać; zwień-
czać; s. kapa;peleryna(duża)
copilot ('kou'pajlot) s. ko-
pilot;zastępca pilota
copious ('koupjes) adj. obfity;
suty; bogaty;płodny;obfitujący
copper ('koper) s. miedź; v.mie-
dziować; slang: glina; policjant;miedziak;kocioł z miedzi
copy ('kopv) v. kopiować; przepisywać; naśladować; s. kopia;
odpis; odbitka; egzemplarz;
wzór; model;rękopis do druku
copybook ('kopy,buk) s. zeszyt
copyright ('kopy,rajt) s. prawo
autorskie.v.chronić prawem auŧor-
skim
coral ('korel) s. koral
cord (ko:rd) s. sznur; lina;
v. wiązać; ustawiać w sągi
cordial ('ko:rdźel) adj. serdeczny; nasercowy;s.lek nasercowy
cordiality (,ko:rdy'aelyty) s.
serdeczność; kordialność
corduroys ('ko:rde,rojz) pl.
sztruksowe spodnie
core (ko:r) s. rdzeń v. usuwać
rdzeń; wycinać rdzeń
cork (ko:rk) s, korek;v.korkować
corkscrew ('ko:rk,skru:) s. korkociąg;adj.w kształcie korkociąga
corn (ko:rn) s. 1. ziarno; zboże; kukurydza; 2. nagniotek
corner ('ko:rner) s. róg; narożnik; kąt; zakręt; zapędzać do
kąta; zmuszać; monopolizować
cornered ('ko:rnerd) adj. rogaty;
schwytany;zapędzony w ślepą uli-
cę
cornet ('ko:rnyt) s. kornet;
trąbka (mosiężna)
cornflakes ('ko:rn,flejks) pl.
płatki z kukurydzy

coronary disease('korenery dy
'zi:z)s.choroba wieńcowa nacja
coronation(,kore'nejszyn)s.koro-
coroner('korener)s. sędzia śledczy,lekarz sądowy(oględziny zwłok)
corporal ('ko:rperel) adj. cielesny; osobisty; s. kapral
corporation (,ko:rpe'rejszyn)
s. korporacja; zrzeszenie;
osoba prawna zbiorowa
corpse (ko:rps) s. trup;zwłoki
corpulent ('ko:rpjulent) adj.
tęgi; otyły; gruby;tłusty
corral (ke'rael) s. ogrodzenie
dla bydła; tabór; v. zamykać
w ogrodzeniu; łapać; ustawiać
tabor;wpędzać do ogrodzenia
correct (ke'rekt) adj, poprawny;
v. korygować; karcić; prostować;leczyć;naprawiać
correction (ke'rekszyn) s. poprawka; korektura ;kara
correspond (,korys'pond) v.
odpowiadać; korespondować
correspondence (,korys'pondens)
s. zgodność; korespondencja
correspondent (,korys'pondent)
s. korespondent; adj. odpowiedni; zgodny z; odpowiadający
corridor ('korydo:r) s. korytarz
corrigible ('korydźybl) adj.
dający się poprawić;uległy
corroborate (ke'robe,rejt) v.
potwierdzić ;potwierdzać
corrode (ke'roud) v. zżerać;
rdzewieć; niszczeć; niszczyć
corrosion (ke'rouźyn) s. koroz-
ja; zżeranie; niszczenie
corrugate ('korugejt) v.
marszczyć; fałdować;karbować
corrugated iron('korugejtyd'
'ajron) s. pofałdowana blacha
corrupt (ke'rapt) adj. zepsuty;
sprzedajny;v.korumpować;psuć się
corruption (ke'rapszyn) s. zepsucie; korupcja;rozkład;fałszowanie
corset ('ko:rsyt) s. gorset;
sznurówka;v.wkładać gorset
cosmetic (koz'metyk) s. kosmetyk; adj. kosmetyczny
cosmetician (koz'metyszyn) s.
kosmetyczka

cosmonaut ('kozme,no:t) s. kosmonauta ;astronauta (w USA)

cost; cost; cost (kost; kost; kost)

cost (kost) v. kosztować; s. koszt; strata; cena

costly ('kostly) adj. kosztowny; wspaniały;drogi;cenny

costume ('kostju:m) s. kostium; strój; v. przystroić w kostium

cosy ('kouzy) adj. przytulny; v. przytulić się

cot (kot) s. łóżko składane; szałas; schronienie

cottage ('kotydż) s. chata; dworek;domek letniskowy

cottage cheese ('kotydż, czi:z) s. biały ser krowi z kwaśnego mleka

cotton ('kotn) s. bawełna; v.polubić; kapować;adj.bawełniany

cotton wool ('kotn,łul) s. wata

couch (kaucz) s. tapczan; posłanie; łóżko;v.rozsiadać się;mówić

cougar ('ku:ger) s. puma; kuguar

cough (kof) s. kaszel; v. kaszleć ; wykaszleć; zakaszleć

could (kud) v. mogłby; zob.:cań; mogł

council ('kaunsyl) s. rada; konsylium; sobor;zarząd (miejski etc.)

councilor ('kaunsyler) s. radny; radca; członek zarządu)

counsel ('kaunsel) s. rada; zamysł; radca prawny; v. radzić; doradzać; przyjmować radę

count (kaunt) v. liczyć; sądzić; liczyć się; znaczyć; s. rachuba; liczenie; suma; zarzut; hrabia

countdown (kaunt-dałn) s. liczenie do startu (rakiety)

count in (kaunt yn) v. brać w rachubę; wliczać; włączyć

count out (kaunt aut) v. wyliczyć; nie brać w rachubę

countenance ('kauntynens) s. mina; wyraz twarzy; śmiałość; pewność siebie; animusz; fantazja; v. zachęcać; popierać; zatwierdzać;usankcjonować

counter ('kaunter) s. 1. kantor; lada; licznik; żeton; 2. przeciwieństwo; cios odbijający; napiętek; adj. przeciwny; prze-

ciwległy; podwójny; v. sprzeciwiać się; reagować; uderzać; adv. przeciwnie; na przekór; wbrew (instrukcjom,poleceniom..)

counteract (,kaunter'aekt) v. przeciwdziałać;neutralizować

counterbalance ('kaunter,-,baelens) s. przeciwwaga

counterespionage ('kaunter'-'espje,na:ż) s. kontrwywiad

counterfeit ('kaunterfyt) adj. fałszywy; podrobiony:v.udawać;

counterintelligence ('kaunteryn'tylydżens) s. kontrwywiad fałszować

counterpart ('kaunter,pa:rt) s. odpowiednik; duplikat

countess ('kauntys) s. hrabina; hrabianka

countless ('kauntlys) adj. niezliczony; nie do zliczenia

country ('kantry) s. kraj; ojczyzna; wieś; prowincja

country house ('kantry-'haus) s. dom wiejski;dom na wsi

countryman ('kantrymen) s. rodak; wieśniak;człowiek ze wsi

countryside ('kantry,sajd) s. okolica; krajobraz;ludzie ze wsi

country town ('kantry,tałn) s, miasteczko: duża wieś

county ('kaunty) s. powiat; hrabstwo ;adj.powiatowy

couple ('kapl) s. para; v. łączyć; parzyć się; żenić

coupling ('kaplyng) s. złącze; skojarzenie; sprzęgło

coupon ('ku:pon) s. odcinek; kupon wymienny(w sklepie,banku...)

courage ('karydż) s. odwaga

courageous (ke'rejdżes) adj. odważny; śmiały;dzielny;waleczny

courier ('kurjer) s, posłaniec; goniec;kurier; agent turystyczny

course (ko:rs) s. bieg; kierunek; ruch naprzód; droga; danie; kolejność; bieżnia; warstwa; kurs; ciąg; v. gnać; pędzić; ścigać; uganiać się

court (ko:rt) s. podwórze; hala; dwór; hotel; sąd; v.zalecać się; wabić; zabiegać;

courteous ('ke:rcjes) adj.
grzeczny; uprzejmy i miły
courtesy ('ke:rtysy) s. grzeczność; uprzejmość; kurtuazja;
(darmowa) usługa; gest przez
grzeczność; adj.grzecznościowy
courtly ('ko:rtly) adj. układny;wytworny; dworski;dostojny
courtmartial ('ko:rt'ma:rszel) s.
sąd wojenny;v.sądzic sadem wojsko-
court of justice ('ko:rt,ow
'dżastys) s. sad
courtroom ('ko:rt.ru:m) s. sala sądowa (rozpraw)
courtship ('ko:rtszyp) s. zaloty; umizgi do kobiety
courtyard ('ko:rt,ja:rd) s. podwórze; dziedziniec
cousin ('kazyn) s. kuzyn; kuzynka; krewny;cioteczny brat(siostra)
cover ('kawer) s. koc; wieko;
oprawa; osłona; koperta; nakrycie (stołu); pokrycie; v. kryc;
pokryc (klacz);ubezpieczac; dac
opis;nakrywac;rozlac;chowac;przejechac
coverage ('kawerydż) s. pokrycie ubezpieczeniem; zasięg radiowy; omówienie w prasie
covering ('kaweryng) s. osłona;
pokrycie (dachu);przykrycie
covert ('kawert) s. schronienie;
adj. ukryty; potajemny;przebrany
covet ('kawyt) v. pożadac (cu-
dzego);patrzyc z zawiścią
covetous (kawytes) adj. chciwy;
pożądliwy; łapczywy;zawistny
cow (kał) s. krowa; v. zastra-
szyc się; przestraszyc się
coward ('kauerd) s. tchórz;
adj. tchórzliwy; bojaźliwy
cowardice ('kauerdys) s.
tchórzostwo ;tchorzliwość
cowardly ('kauerdly) adj.
tchórzliwy; adv. tchórzliwie
cowboy ('kałboj) s. konny pastuch;pastuch bydła;krowiarz
cower ('kauer) v. skulic się;
kucnąc; przykucac do ziemi
cowherd ('kał,he:rd) s. pasterz
bydła; pastuszka
cowhide ('kał,hajd) s. krowia
skóra; skóra wołowa

cowshed ('kał,szed) s. krowia
szopa; obora
cowslip ('kał,slyp) s. pier-
wiosnek(kwiat bagienny)
coxcomb ('koks,koum) s. błazen;
fircyk; pajac;głupi zarozumialec
coxswain ('kok,słejn) s. sternik na regatach
coy (koj) adj. skromny; nieśmiały; ostrożny; cichy;udający
wym
cozy (kouzy) adj. wygodny;
przytulny;s.okrycie czajnika
crab (kraeb) s. krab; rak;
(wulg.) menda; v. łowic kraby;
krytykowac; rujnowac;narzekac
crab louse ('kraeb,laus) s.
wesz łonowa
crack (kraek) s. trzask; rysa;
szpara; próba; dowcip;
v. trzaskac; żartowac; łupac;
uderzyc; rujnowac; adj. wyso-
kiej jakości; doskonały
crack a joke (kraek e dżok) v.
palnąc żart;palnąc kawał
crack a smile('kraek,e smajl)
v. (slang) uśmiechnąc się
cracker ('kraeker) s. sucharek; petarda; łupacz;kłamstwo
crackpot ('kraekpot) s. wariat;
bez piątej klepki (slang)
crackle ('kraekl) v. trzeszczeć; s. trzeszczenie; pajęczyna; porcelana zdobiona
cradle ('krejdl) s. kołyska;
kolebka; wywrotka; v. kraśc
w kołysce; kołysac; kosic
(kosa z ramą);płukac złoto
craft (kraeft) s. rzemiosło;
branża; sztuka; cech; podstęp;
chytrosc; biegłość; pojazd
craftsman ('kraftsmen) s. rzemieślnik;mistrz w swoim zawodzie
crafty ('kra-fty) adj. sprytny;
zręczny; podstępny;przebiegły
crag (kraeg) s. skała (stroma);
turnia;nawis skalny
cram (kraem) v. tłoczyc; napychac; opychac; wytłaczac; wkuwac (się); s. tłok; cizba;
wkuwanie się do egzaminu;ścisk;
kłamstwo; uczenie się do egzaminu
intensywnie i w pośpiechu

cramp (kraemp) s.skurcz; klamra; zwornik; v. ściskać; krępować; ograniczać; adj. ściśnięty; stłoczony; nieczytelny; sztuczny ;uchwycony w imadło

cranberry ('kraenbery) s. żurawina; brusznica błotna

crane (krejn) s. żuraw; dźwig; v. podnosic; wyciągać szyję

crank (kraenk) s. korba; dziwak; bzik; v. puszczać w ruch (korba); kręcic; wydębic

crank up ('kraenk,ap) v. zapuszczać (motor);uruchomić(motor)

crape (kraep) s. gra w kości; brednie; bzdury,nonsens

crape (krejp) s. krepa

crash (kraesz) s. huk; łomot; upadek; katastrofa; ruina; krach; samodział; v. trzaskać; huczeć; roztrzaskiwać; wpaść na...; adv. z hukiem;z trzaskiem ;z łomotem;z hałasem

crash helmet ('kraesz,helmyt) s. kask ochronny (motocyklisty)

crash landing ('kraesz;laendyng) s. rozbicie się przy lądowaniu

crate (krejt) s. stare pudło; skrzynia; paka; v. pakować w skrzynie;wkładac do pak

crater ('krejter) s. krater

crave (krejw) v. pożądac; pragnąć; prosic usilnie; błagać

crawfish ('kro:fysz) s. rak; v. wycofywać się(rakiem)

crawl (kro:l) v. pełzac; czołgac się; wlec; roic się; s. czołganie; pływanie kraulem; ciarki;basen do hodowli raków

crayfish ('krejfysz) s. rak (rzeczny);rak morski bez kleszcz

crayon ('krejen) s. kredka; rysunek kredką; v. rysować kredką; szkicowac;narysować węglem

crazy ('krejzy) adj. zwariowany; pomylony; walący się (np.dom)

crazy about ('krejzy,e'baut) zwariowany na punkcie czegos

creak (kri:k) v. skrzypieć; trzeszczeć; s. skrzypienie; pisk; zgrzyt; trzask; trzeszczenie;pisknięcie; zgrzytnięcie

cream (kri:m) s. śmietana; śmietanka; krem; v. ustac się; zbierać śmietankę; zabielac

cream cheese(kri:m,czi:z) s. ser śmietankowy(biały i miękki)

creamy ('kri:my) adj. śmietankowy ; jak śmietana

crease ('kri:s) s. fałda; kant (spodni); v. fałdować; plisować; prasować; zmiąc ;pomiąc

create (kry:'ejt) v. tworzyc; wywoływać ;zapoczątkować ;powodować

creation (kry'ejszyn) s. stworzenie; kreacja; świat ;wszechświat

creative (kry'ejtyw) adj. twórczy ;wynalazczy;tworzący

creator (kry'ejter) s. twórca

creature ('kry:czer) s. stwór; istota; kreatura (dominowana)

credentials (kry'denszelz) pl. dokumenty; listy uwierzytelniające (tożsamość posła etc.)

credibility gap (,kredy'bylyty gaep) s. niedowierzanie; luka w zaufaniu ;brak zaufania

credible ('kredybl) adj. wiarogodny ; wiarygodny

credit ('kredyt) s. kredyt; wiara; autorytet; powaga; uznanie; chluba; v. dawać wiarę; zapisywac na rachunek; zaliczac ;przypisywać(coś komuś)

creditable ('kredytebl) adj. zaszczytny; chlubny;godny pochwały

credit card ('kredyt ka:rd) karta kredytowa do zakupow

creditor ('kredyter) s. wierzyciel(handlowy,prywatny etc.)

credulous ('kredjules) adj. łatwowierny;zbyt łatwowierny

creed (kri:d) s. wiara; wierzenia; głębokie przekonania

creek (kri:k) s. potok; zatoka

creep; crept; crept (kri:p; krept; krept)

creep (kri:p) v. pełzać; wkradać się; miec ciarki; s. pełzanie; ciarki; obsuwanie; poślizg; nędzny typ;pełzanie się

creeper ('kri:per) s. pnącz

cremate (krymejt) v. spalac zwłoki na popiół

crept (krept)v.podpełzał; zob.:
creep
crescent ('kresnt) s. półksiężyc; adj. półksiężycowy; rosnący; przybywający;&rogalik
cress (kres) s. rzeżucha
crest (krest) s. czub; grzebień; grzywa; pióropusz; kita;
hełm; klejnot; grzbiet; v.for-
mować grzbiet; osiągnąć szczyt
crestfallen (krest-folen) adj.
z opadnietym czubem; speszony;
zawstydzony; przygnębiony
crevasse (kry'waes) s. szczelina; pęknięcie (w lodowcu etc.)
crevice ('krewys) s. szczelina; rysa; pęknięcie; szpara
crew (kru:)s. załoga; drużyna;
zgraja; zob. crow
crib (kryb) s. żłob z pętami;
stajnia; obora; ciupka; pokoik;
domek; kojec; plagiat; v. stła-
czać; wyposażac w żłoby; ocemb-
rować; zwędzic;używać ściągaczki
cricket ('krykyt) s. świerszcz;
krykiet; v. grać w krykieta
crime (krajm) s. zbrodnia
criminal ('krymynl) s. zbrodniarz; kryminalista; adj. :
zbrodniczy; kryminalny
crimson ('krymzn) s. & adj. kar-
mazyn(owy); v. zabarwiać na
karmazynowo; zaczerwieniać się
cringe (kryndż) s. uniżonosc;
v. kulic; kurczyć sie; kłaniać
się; płaszczyć sie (usłużnie)
cripple ('krypl) kulawy; kaleka
v. okulawic; osłabiac; kulec;
utykać; okaleczyć;przeszkadzać
crisis ('krajsys) s. przesilenie; kryzys;krytyczna sytuacja
crises ('krajsi:z) pl. prze-
silenia; kryzysy; opały
crisp (krysp) adj. rześki;
chrupki; energiczny; v.robic
kruchym;marszczyć; kędzierza-
wic;fryzować; ufryzowac
critic ('krytyk) s. krytyk
critical ('krytykel) adj. kryty-
kujący; krytyczny; trudny do
nabycia; ważny(moment etc.)

criticism ('krytysyzem) s. krytyka; krytycyzm;znajdowanie błędów
criticize ('krytysajz) s. krytykować; ganic; znajdywać błędy
croak (krouk) v. rechotac; kra-
kac;s. rechot;rechotanie;krąkanie
crochet ('krouszej) v. robic
na szydełku ; szydełkować
crockery ('krokery) s. naczynia gliniane(dzbany, słoje etc.)
crocodile ('krokedajl) s. krokodyl; adj.krokodylowy
crocus ('kroukes) s. krokus;
szafran(z rodziny irysów)
crook (kruk) s. hak; zagięcie;
krzywizna; kanciarz; krzywic;
wyginac; krasć; kantowac
crooked (krukyd) adj. zakrzy-
wiony; krzywy; wypaczony;
zgarbiony; cygański; szachraj-
ski; oszukańczy;zgięty;wygięty
crop (krop) s. plon; biczysko:
bacik; całość; przycinanie;
krótko strzyżone włosy; ucinek;
v. strzyc; skubać; zbierać;
zasiewać; obrodzic; wyłaniac
się; uprawiac ziemię; obradzać
crop up (krop ap) v. nagle
zjawiac się; wyskoczyć nagle
cross (kros) s. krzyż; skrzyżowanie; mieszaniec; kant;
cygaństwo; v. żegnac się;
krzyżować; przecinać coś; isc
w poprzek; przekreślac;
udaremnic; adj. poprzeczny;
skosny; krzyżujący; przeciwny; gniewny; opryskliwy
cross out ('kros,aut) v. wy-
kreślac;skreślac;przekreślać
cross-examination ('kros -
ig'zaemynejszyn) s. przesłuchanie; badanie (w sledztwie)
crossing ('krosyng) s. skrzyżowanie; przejście lub przejazd na drugą stronę (rzeki...)
crossroads ('krosroudz) pl.
rozstaje; skrzyżowanie dróg
crossword puzzle ('krosłord-
'pazl) s. krzyżówka
crouch (kraucz) v. kulic się;
kurczyć; przysiąsc;gotować się
do skoku

crow (krou) s. kruk; wrona;
pianie; wesoły pisk; v. piac;
piszczec wesoło;krzyczec z rados-
crowbar ('krouba:r) s. drąg;
lewar; łom(do podważania etc.)
crowd (kraud) s. tłum; tłok;
banda; mnóstwo; v. tłoczyc;
natłoczyć; napierac; wpychac;
śpieszyc; przepełniac
crowded ('kraudyd) adj. zatłoczony; zapchany;przeludniony
crown (kraun) s. korona; wieniec; v. wieńczyc; koronowac
crucial ('kru:szel) adj. decydujący; przełomowy; krytyczny
crucifixion (,kru:sy'fykszyn)
s. ukrzyżowanie; krucyfiks
crucify (kru:syfaj) v. ukrzyżo-
wac;torturowac;znęcac się
crude (kru:d) adj. surowy;
szorstki; niepożyty;obskórny
cruel (kruel) adj. okrutny
cruelty ('kuelty) s. okrucieństwo; znęcanie się(nad kims)
cruet ('kru:yt) v. flaszeczka;
ampułka;buteleczka(na ocet etc.)
cruise (kru:z) v. krążyc; leciec; podrożowac; s. wycieczka
morska; przejaźdźka; rejs
crumb (kram) s. okruch; (slang)
dran; v. kruszyc; drobic; dodawac okruszyn;obtoczyć(w bułce)
crumble ('kramb) v. kruszyc (się)
crumple ('krampl) v. zmiąc;
zmarszczyc;załamywac się
crumple up ('krampl,ap) v. po-
miąc; zawalic się;załamac się
crunch (krancz) v. miażdżyc;
chrupac; s, chrupanie; chrzęst
crusade (kru:'sejd) s. wyprawa
krzyżowa;v.isc z krucjatą
crusader (kru:'sejder) s. krzy-
żowiec;aktywny działacz
crush (krasz) v. kruszyc; miażdżyc; miąc; s, miażdżenie;
tłok; cizba; zadurzenie się
crusher (kraszer) s. łamacz;
miażdżarka;druzgocący cios
crust (krast) s. skorupa; skóra;
v. zaskorupiac (się)
crutch (kracz) s. kula; podpórka ;laska;v.podpierac się

cry (kraj) s. krzyk; płacz;
wrzask; okrzyk; hasło; v.krzy-
czec; płakac; urągac; ujadac
cry-baby ('kraj,bejby) s. mazgaj; beksa; płaksa(dziecinna)
crying ('krajyŋg) s. wołanie;
płacz adj. płaczący;skandalicz-
cry of rage ('kraj,ow'rejdż) ny
s. krzyk szału (wściekłości)
crypt (krypt) s. krypta
crystal ('krystl) s. kryształ;
szkiełko od zegarka;adj.kryszta-
crystalline ('krystelajn) adj. łowy
krystaliczny;kryształowy
crystallize ('krystelajz) v.
krystalizować się
cub (kab) s. szczenie (dzikie-
go zwierza); zuch;młodzik
cube (kju:b) s. sześcian; kostka; (slang) facet; v. podnosić do sześcianu; obliczac
kubaturę;formowac w sześciany
cube root ('kju:b,ru:t) s.
pierwiastek sześcienny
cubicle ('kju:bykl) s. pokoik;
mała sypialnia;małe mieszkanie
cuckoo ('kuku) s. kukułka;
głuptas;kukanie;dureń
cucumber ('kju:kamber) s. ogórek
cuddle ('kadl) s. tulic;
pieścic; kulic się;gnieździc
się
cudgel ('kadżel) s. pałka;
v. bic pałką
cue (kju:) s. wskazówka; nastrój; ogonek (do sklepu); kij
bilardowy; warkocz;v.dać wska-
zówkę
cuff (kaf) s. mankiet; kajdan-
ki; v. bic pięscią; uderzac;
kułakowac;potarmosic;szturchac
cuff links ('kaf,lyŋks) pl.
spinki do mankietów
culminate ('kalmynejt) v.
szczytowac; kulminowac
culmination (,kalmy'nejszyn) s.
kulminacja; punkt szczytowy
culprit ('kalpryt) s. oskarżony; winowajca;winowajczyni
cultivate ('kaltywejt) s. uprawiac; rozwijac; kultywowac;
pielęgnowac; spulchniac

cultivation (,kaltu'wejszyn)
s. uprawa; kultura; kultywo-
wanie;kultura duchowa
cultivator ('kaltyvejter) s.
plantator; kultywator;rolnik
cultural ('kalczerel) adj.
kulturalny;kulturowy
culture ('kalczer) s. kultura;
uprawa; v. uprawiac; hodowac;
kształcic;hodować bakterie
cultured ('kalczerd) adj.
kulturalny;oczytany;wykształcony
cumulative ('kju:mjulejtyw)
adj. łączny; kumulacyjny;
skumulowany; kumulujący się
cunning ('kanyng) s. chytrosc;
przebiegłosc; adj. chytry;
przebiegły; miły; ładny
cup (kap) s. kubek; kielich;
czasza; filiżanka; v. wgłę-
biac; stawiac banki
cupboard ('kaberd) s. kredens;
szafka;półka na kubki
cupola ('kju:pele) s. kopuła;
piec kopułowy; żeliwiak
cur (ke:r) s. kundel; szelma
curable ('kjuerebl) adj. uleczalny; wyleczalny
curate ('kjueryt) s. wikary
curb (ke:rb) s. krawężnik;
łancuszek; wędzidło; oszczep;
twarda spuchlizna; v. okieł-
zac; hamowac; ograniczac
curd (ke:rd) s. twaróg; tłuszcz
curdle (ke:rdl) v. scinac;
zsiadac się;formować w gródki
cure (kjuer) s. kuracja; lek;
lekarstwo; v. uleczyć; wyle-
czyc; zaradzic; wykurowac
cure-all ('kjuero:l) s. pana-
ceum;lek na wszystkie dolegliwosci
curfew ('ke:rfju:) s. godzina
policyjna: capstrzyk
curio ('kjuerjou) s. okaz;
osobliwosc;unikat; rzadkość
curiosity (,kjurj'osyty) n.
ciekawosc; osobliwość
curl (ke:rl) s. kędzior; lok;
pukiel; skręt; spirala; wir
v. kręcic; skręcac; zwijac;
marszczyc; złoscic;skulic się
curl up ('ke:rl ap) v.zwinac (się)

curly ('ke:rly) adj. kędzierzawy; kręty ;falujący;kręcony
currant ('karent) s. porzeczka;
rodzynek bez pestki
currency ('karensy) s. waluta;
obieg; potocznosc; popularnosc
current ('karent) adj. bieżący; obiegowy; obiegający; powszechnie znany; panujący (pogląd);.s. prąd; bieg; nurt;
tok ;strumień;natężenie pradu
curriculum (ke'rykjulem) s.
plan studiów ;program nauki
curriculum vitae (ke'rykjulem,
wajti:) s. życiorys
curse (ke:rs) s. przeklenstwo;
klątwa; v. przeklinac; wykli-
nac; kląc; bluznic;złorzeczyć
cursed (ke:rsyd) adj. przeklęty; cholerny; adv. paskudnie;
cholernie ;po diable
curt (ke:rt) adj. krotki; zwięzły; lakoniczny;szorstki;suchy
curtail (ke:r'tejl) v. obcinac;
skracac; zmniejszac ;uczszuplac
curtain ('ke:rtn) s. zasłona;
firanka; kurtuna; v. zasłaniac
curtsy ('ke:rtsy) s. dyg; v. dy-
gac ;złożyć głęboki ukłon
curve (ke:rw) s. krzywa; krzywizna; krzywka; v. wyginac
(się); wykrzywiac (się);zakręcać
cushion ('kuszyn) s. poduszka
custody ('kastedy) s. opieka;
nadzor; areszt ;przetrzymanie
custom ('kastem) s. zwyczaj;
klientela; zrobiony na zamówienie ;nawyk;stałe zaopatrywanie się
customary ('kastemery) adj. zwyczajny; zwyczajowy,s.zbior praw
customer ('kastemer) s. klient
customhouse ('kastem-haus) s.
komora celna ;urząd celny
custom-made ('kastem-mejd) adj.
zrobiony na zamówienie
customs ('kastemz) pl. cło
customs clearance ('kastemz;
klierens) s. odprawa celna
customs declaration ('kastemz,
decle'rejszyn) s. deklaracja
celna (przy przekraczaniu gra-
nicy etc.)

customs examination ('kastemz
ig,zamy'nejszyn) s. rewizja
celna (bagażu,towarów etc.)
cut; cut; cut; (kat; kat; kat)
cut (kat) s. cięcie; przecięcie; wycięcie; ścięcie; odrzy-
nek; krój; styl (krawiecki);
wykop; drzeworyt; v. ciąć;
zaciąć; skaleczyć; ranić; krajać; kroić; przycinać; kosić;
rznać; rzeźbić; szlifować; wycinać; obcinać; uciać; ścinać
cut down ('kat,dałn) v. obniżać;
redukować;wyciąć w pień(wroga)
cut in ('kat,yn) v. wtrącać się
cut off ('kat,of) v. odcinać;
przerwać(dopływ);wydziedziczać
cut out ('kat,aut) v. wykroić;
przestać;zaprzestać (palić etc.)
cut up ('kat,ap) v. posiekać;
skrytykować;wypatroszyć;siec
cute (kju:t) adj. miły; ładny;
chytry; sprytny;ciekawy;bystry
cuticle ('kju:tykl) s. naskórek
cuticle scissers ('kju:tykl'-
syez) s. nożyczki od naskórka
cutlery ('katlery) s. wyroby
nożownicze; sztućce
cutlet ('katlyt) s. kotlet (bity);kotlet mielony(mięsny,rybi)
cut-off ('katof) s. odcięcie;
skrót; wyłącznik; wycinek; za-
wór(wodny,parowy,gazowy etc.)
cutout ('kat aut) = cut-off
cutpurse ('kat pe:rs) s. rzezimieszek; kieszonkowiec;opryszek
cutter ('kater) s. kuter; przecinek; przykrawacz; odcinacz
cutting ('katyng) adj. bolesny;
przenikliwy; cięty;s.sadzonka
cycle (sajkl) s. cykl; rower;
v. jechać na rowerze; obiegać
cyklicznie(tam i nazad,w koło...)
cyclist ('sajklyst) s. rowerzysta;
rowerzystka ; cyklista;cykilstka
cyclone ('sajkloun) s. cyklon
cylinder ('sylynder) s. walec;
cylinder;bęben(rewolweru etc.)
cynic ('synyk) s. cynik
cynical ('synykel) adj. cynicz-
ny(pomysł,programczłowiek etc.)
cynicism('syny,syzem)s.cynizm

cypress ('sajprys) s. cyprys
cyst (syst) s. cysta; torbiel
czar (za:r) s. car; (od nafty;
sportu;komisarz generalny USA)
Czech (czek) adj. czeski
Czechoslovak ('czekou,slouwaek)
adj. czechosłowacki
d (di) czwarta litera alfabetu
angielskiego; oznaczenie centa
dab (daeb) v. musnąć; klepać;
dotknąć; dziobnać; s. muśnie-
cie; klaps; stuknięcie; dziobnięcie;plama;bryzg;odrobina
dachshund ('daekshund) s. jamnik ;a.jamniczy;jamnika
dad (daed) s. tato; tatuś
daddy ('daedy) s. tatuś
daffodil ('daefedyl) s. żółty
narcyz ;żonkil;adj.bladożółty
daffy ('daefy) adj. zwariowany
daft ('daeft) adj. pomylony;
głupkowaty; zwariowany
dagger ('daeger) s. sztylet;
v. sztyletować ;s. odsyłacz
daily ('dejly) adj. codzienny;
adv. codziennie; s. dziennik
dainty ('dejnty) adj. wyszukany; wyborowy; delikatny;
gustowny; miły; wybredny
daiquiri ('daikery) s. rum z
sokiem cytrynowym, cukrem
i lodem (po amerykańsku)
dairy ('deery) s, mleczarnia
dairyman ('deerymen) s. mleczarz;właściciel mleczarni
daisy (dejzy) s. stokrotka;
ładny okaz(człowieka)
dale (dejl) s. dolina
dally ('daely) v. marudzic;
igrać; flirtować;tracić czas
dam (daem) s. tama; zapora
damage ('daemydż) s. szkoda;
uszkodzenie; odszkodowanie;
(slang) koszt; v. uszkodzić;
ponieść szkody; uwłaczać
dame (dejm) s. dziewczyna;
kobieta; pani(starsza)
damn (daem) v. potępiać; prze-
klinać; adj. przeklęty
damnation (daem'nejszyn) s. potępienie; excl.: psiakrew; cholera;a niech to piorun trzaśnie!

damp (daemp) v. zwilżyć; skropić; tłumić; ostudzić; amortyzować; butwieć; s. wilgoć; przygnębienie; zwątpienie
dampen ('daempen) v. wilgotnieć ; zwilgotnieć;zwilżyć
dance (da:ns) s. taniec; zabawa taneczna; v. tańczyć; skakać; kazać tańczyć; huśtać
dancer ('da:nser) s. tancerz; tancerka; baletnica
dancing ('da:nsyng) s. taniec; adj. tańczący;do tańca
dandelion ('daendylajon) s. mniszek lekarski; mlecz
dandruff ('daendref) s. łupież
danger ('dejndżer) s. niebezpieczeństwo; groźba
dangerous ('dejndżeres) adj. niebezpieczny;niepewny(grunt...)
dangle ('daengl) v. dyndać; bujać; kręcić się;nadskakiwać
Danish (dejnysz) adj. duński
dapper ('daeper) adj. wytworny; elegancki;dobrze ubrany;zwinny
dare (deer) v. śmieć; ważyć się; wyzywać; s. wyzwanie
daring ('deeryng) adj. śmiały; s. śmiałość; odwaga
dark (da:rk) adj. ciemny; ponury; s. ciemnosć; mrok; cień; murzyn;tajemniczość;niewiedza
dark-brown ('da:rk brałn) adj. ciemno-brazowy
darken (da:rkn) v. zaciemniać
darkness ('da:rknys) s. ciemnosć; ciemnota; śniadosć
darling ('da:rlyng) s. kochanie; ulubieniec; adj. kochany; ulubiony; ukochany
darn (da:rn) v. cerować; s.cera; adj. (slang) przeklęty
dart (da:rt) s. żądło; szybki ruch; oszczep; zryw; v. pędzic; rzucać; wybuchać;strzelać
dash (daesz) v. roztrzaskać; rzucać się; pędzić; popisywać się; zakropić; opryskać; niweczyć; mieszać; onieśmielać; odbić; naszkicować; s. uderzenie; zderzenie; plusk; barwna plama; szczypta; przy-

mieszka;myślnik; kreska; pęd; skok; rozmach; rozpęd; popis
dash-board ('daeszbo:rd) tablica rozdzielcza; zestaw zegarów (lotniczych, samochodowych, etc,) ; błotnik
dashing (daeszyng) adj. dziarski; z werwą; z rozmachem
data ('dejte) pl. dane; podstawa odniesienia ;dane liczbowe
data processing ('dejte'prousesyng) s. przetwarzanie danych
date (dejt) v. datować; nosić datę; chodzic z kims; s. data; spotkanie; randka; umówienie się; palma daktylowa; daktyl
date from ('dejt,from) data z... (dnia, miejsce)
dative case('dejtyw,kejs) trzeci przypadek ;celownik
datum ('dejtem) s, dana (fakt; szczegół);punkt wyjściowy
daub (do:b) v. babrać; mazać; oblepiać; s. tynk; polepa; plama; kicz sknocony ;gips
daughter ('do:ter) s. córka
daughter-in-law ('do:ter,yn lo:) s. synowa
dawdle ('do:dl) v. próżniaczyc; mitrężyć ;wałkonić się
dawdle away ('do:dl,a'łej)v. marnować czas;trcić czas
dawn (do:n) v. świtać; zaświtać; dnieć; jaśnieć; s. świt; brzask; zaranie;zdanie sobie sprawy
day (dej) s. dzień; doba
daybreak('dejbrejk)s.świt;brzask
day by day('dej,baj dej)exp.: dzień w dzień ;dzień po dniu
daydream('dejdri:m)s. marzenie;v. marzyć;budować zamki na lodzie
day in day out('dej,yn'dej aut)exp. codziennie; dzień w dzień
daylight('dejlajt)s.swiatło dzienne: biały dzień (dzienny)
day nursery('dej,ne:rsery)s.żłobek
day off('dej of)s.dzień wolny
days to come('dejs,tu kam) exp.: przyszłość
day's work('dejz,łe:rk)s. dniówka
daytime ('dejtajm)s. dzień od świtu do zmroku

daze (dejz) v. oszałamiac;
otumaniac; oślepiac; s. oszołomienie; otumanienje
dazzle (daezl) v. oślepiac;
olśniewac; zamaskowac;
s. oślepiający blask
dead (ded) adj.& s. zmarły;
martwy; wymarły; matowy
dead body (ded'body) s. zwłoki
dead center ('ded'senter) s.
punkt martwy, zwrotny
deaden ('deden) v. zabijac siłY, uczucia etc.: tłumic;
osłabiac; stępiac; zmartwiec;
obumrzec; pozbawiac blasku,
połysku, zapachu;znieczulac
dead end('dedend)s.ślepa(ulica)
deadline('dedlajn)s.nieprzekra-
czalny termin;ostateczna granica
deadlock ('dedlok) s. impas;
martwy punkt;v. powoдować impas
deadly (dedly) adj. śmiertelny;
adv. śmiertelnie;nieludzko
deadweight ('dedłejt) s. ciężar własny (urządzenia); kula
u nogi;kamień u szyi
deaf (def) adj. głuchy
deafen (defn) v. ogłuszac
deafening (defnyng) adj. ogłu-
szający
deal; dealt; dealt (di:1; delt;
delt)
deal (di:1) v. zajmowac się;
traktowac o: załatwiac; prze-
stawac z; postępowac; handlowac; rozdzielac (karty)
s. ilość; sprawa;sporo;wiele
deal with ('di:1 łyt) v. postępowac z ···;miec do czynienia
dealer ('di:ler) s. kupiec;
handlarz;rozdający karty
dealing ('di:lyng)s. postępowanie z; stosunki; transakcje
dealt (delt) zob. deal
dean (di:n) s. dziekan
dear (kier) adj. kochany; drogi
dear Sir ('dier,se:r) exp.: szanowny panie;Drogi Panie
dear me ! (kier mi) exp.: ojej !
moj Boże ! czyżby! ależ nie!
death (des) s. smierc; zgon
deathly (desly) adj. śmiertelny;
adv. śmiertelnie;grobowo;trupio

debar ('dyba:r) v. wykluczac;
zabraniac (komuś);zakazywac
debase (dy'bejs) v. obniżac;
poniżac; fałszowac;upadlac
debate (dy'bejt) v. roztrząsac;
rozważac; debatowac;s.debata
debauchery ('dy'bo:czery) s.
rozpusta;wyuzdanie;rozwiązłość
debit ('debyt) s. debet; obciążenie rachunku
debrief (dy'bri:f) s. przesłu-
chania po (akcji); v. przesłuchiwac po (akcji)
debris ('dejbri:) pl. gruzy
debt (det) s. dług
debtor ('deter) s. dłużnik;
dłużniczka
decade ('dekejd) s. dziesięcio-
letni okres
decadence ('dekejdens) s. de-
kadencja; chylenie się ku
upadkowi; schyłek; upadek
decapitate (dy'kaepytejt) v.
ścinac głowę;pozbawic wodza
decay (dy'kej) v. gnic; rozpa-
dac się; psuc się; s. upadek;
ruina; zanik; rozkład; gnicie
decease (dy'si:s) v. umierac;
s. zgon ; śmierć
deceased (dy'si:st) adj. zmarły; s. nieboszczyk
deceit (dy'si:t) s. oszukanst-
wo; podstęp; złuda ; fałsz
deceitful (dy'si:tfel) adj.
kłamliwy; zwodniczy;podstępny,
deceive (dy'si:w) v. okłamywac;
zwodzic; łudzic; zawodzic
deceiver (dy'si:wer) s. oszu-
kaniec; zwodziciel; kłamca
decelerate (dy:'selerejt) v.
zwalniac;zmniejszac szybkość
December (dy'sember) s. gru-
dzien
decency ('di:snsy) s. przyzwoitość; obyczajnosc;dobre obyczaje
decent ('di:sent) adj. przyzwoity; porządny; znosny
deception (dy'sepszyn) s. łu-
dzenie; okłamywanie; podstęp;
zawod; szachrajstwo;oszukanie
decide (dy'sajd) v. rozstrzygac;
postanawiac; decydowac sie;
zadecydowac; skłaniac sie

decided (dy'sajdyd) adj. zdecydowany; stanowczy;definitywny
decimal ('desymel) adj. dzie-
siętny;s. ułamek dzisiętny
decipher (dy'sajfer) v. odcyfrować; rozszyfrować;rozwiazać
decision (dy'syżyn) s. rozstrzygnięcie; postanowienie;
decyzja; zdecydowanie; stanowczosc; wygrana na punkty
(sport);ustalenie;rezolutność
decisive (dy'sajsyw) adj. decydujący; rozstrzygający;
zdecydowany; stanowczy
deck (dek) s. pokład; pomost;
podłoga; talia; v. pokrywac
pokładem; przystrajać
deck chair (dek,czeer) s. leżak (do opalania się na statku)
declaration (dekle'rejszyn) s.
deklaracja; zapowiedz; oswiadczenie (oficjalne)
declare, (dy'kle:r) v. deklaro-
wać; oświadczać; zeznawać;
ogłaszać; uznawać za; stwier-
dzac;wykazać;dawać do oclenia
declension (dy'klenszyn) s. de-
klinacja (gram.); przypadkowa-
nie; odchylenie; upadek
decline (dy'klajn) v. uchylac
(się); pochylac (się);skłaniac
(się); isć ku schyłkowi; opadać; obnizać; podupadać; marnieć; słabnąć; zanikać; przy-
padkowac;s.schyłek;utrata;spadek
declivity (dy'klywyty) s. pochyłość; spadzistosc;stok;skłon
decode (, dy'koud)v.rozszyfrować
decorate('dekerejt)v.ozdabiac;od-
znaczać; udekorować; upiększać
decompose(,dy:kem'pouz)v.rozkła-
dać się; rozłożyć się;gnić
decoration (,deke'rejszyn) s.
ozdoba; odznaczenie;medal etc.
decorative (,deke'rejtyw) adj.
ozdobny; dekoracyjny
decorator ('dekerejter) s. dekorator; architekt wnętrz
decoy ('dy:koj),s. wabik; przynęta; v. wabić; usidlać; zwa-
biać; wciągać w pułapkę;zacia-
gać sidła;wabić w pułapkę

decrease ('dy:kri:s) v. zmniejszac; słabnąć; obnizać;
s. zmniejszenie; spadek(cen)
decree (dy'kri:) s. dekret;
rozporządzenie; wyrok rozwodowy; postanowienie o separa-
cji; v. zarządzac; dekretować;
rozporządzać;nakazywac dekretem
decrepit (dy'krepyt) adj.
zgrzybiały; wyniszczony
decry (dy'kraj) v. potępic;
okrzyczeć;zohydzic;obgadać
dedicate ('dedykejt) v. dedyko-
wać; poswięcac; inaugurować
dedication ('dedykejszyn) s.
dedykacja; poswięcenie;otwarcie
deduce (dy'du:s) v. wnioskować;
dedukować; wywodzić (rodowód)
deduct (dy'dakt) v. potrącać;
odciągać;odejmować;odtrącać
deduction (dy'dakszyn) s. potrącenie; odciągnięcie; wnioskowanie; wniosek;wywód
deed (di:d) s. czyn; wyczyn;
akt; v. przekazywać aktem
(własność);przelewać pieniadze
deep (di:p) adj. głęboki;
s. głębia; adv. głęboko
deepen('di:pn) v. pogłębiać
deep-freeze ('di:p,fri:z) s.
(głębokie) zamrozenie
deeply ('di:ply) adv. głęboko
deep-rooted ('di:p'ru:tyd)
adj. głęboko zakorzeniony
deer, (dier) s. jeleń; sarna;
łos; łania ;daniel;renifer
deface (dy'fejs) v. szpecic -
zniekształcać; zacierać
defame (dy'fejm) v. zniesławić
defeat, (dy'fi:t) v. pokonać;
pobić; unicestwić; udaremnić;
uniemozliwić; uniewaznić
prawnie;s.klęska;udaremnienie
defect (dy'fekt) s. brak; wada; błąd; defekt; v. odpaśc;
skłonić do odstępstwa;odstąpić
defective (dy'fektyw) adj. wadliwy; wybrakowany; niepełny
defence (dy'fens) = defense
defend (dy'fend) v. bronic
defendant (dy'fendent) s. pozwany;oskarżony; obrońca

defender (dy'fender) s. obrońca (prawo i sport)

defensive (dy'fensyw) adj. obronny; defensywny; s. defensywa; być w defensywie

defense (dy'fens) s. obrona

defenseless (dy'fenslys) adj. bezbronny

defer (dy'fe:r) v. odraczać; ustępować; ulegać;mieć wzgląd

defiant (dy'fajent) adj. zbuntowany; nieufny;buntowniczy

deficiency (dy'fyszynsy) s. brak; niedobór; należność niezapłacona ; niedostatek;słabość

deficit ('defysyt) s. deficyt; niedobór ; nadwyżka rozchodu

defile ('dy:fail) v. kalać; plugawić; brukać; bezcześcić; iść szeregami;defilować

define (dy'fajn) v. określać; definiować; zakreślać (granice); zarysować;określać

definite ('defynyt) adj. określony; wyraźny; pewny; prostolinijny;określający(rodzajnik)

definition (,drfy'nyszyn) s. określenie; definicja; ostrość; czystość;oznaczenie

definitive (dy'fynytyw) adj. ostateczny; definitywny; stanowczy;konkluzywny;definiujący

deflate (dy'flejt) v. wypuszczać powietrze (z dętki); zmniejszać(obieg ,znaczenie etc.)

deform (dy'fo,rm) v. szpecić; zniekształcać;oszpecać

deformed (dy'fo:rmd) adj. ułomny; szpetny;zniekształcony

defrost ('dy:frost) v. odmrozić

defunct ('dy'fankt) adj. zmarły; zlikwidowany;już nie istniejący

defy (dy'faj) v. stawiać czoło; rzucać wyzwania (by zrobić,wykazać)

degenerate (dy'dżeneryt) adj. zwyrodniały; s. degenerat

degrade (dy'grejd) v. poniżać; obniżać; wyrodnieć;znieważać

degree (dy'gri:) s. stopien (np. naukowy, ciepła etc.)

dejected (dy'dżektyd) adj. przygnębiony ;zgaszony(człowiek) zdeprymowany;strapiony

dejectedly (dy'dżektydly) adv. z przygnębieniem;z niechęcią

delay (dy'lej) v. odraczać; opóźniać; zwlekać; s. odroczenie; zwłoka; opóźnienie

delegate ('delegejt) s. zastępca; wysłannik; v. delegować; udzielać delegacji; zlecać (władzę);udzielać(władzy)

delegation (,dely'gejszyn) s. delegacja;grupa delegatów

deliberate (dy'lyberejt) adj. rozmyślny; spokojny; v. rozmyślać; rozważać; obradować; naradzać się (dy,ly'berejt)v.

delicacy ('delykesy) s. delikatność; smakołyk;takt

delicate ('delykyt) adj. delikatny; wyśmienity;taktowny

delicatessen (,delyka'tesn) s. sklep z delikatesami

delicious (dy'lyszes) adj. rozkoszny;bardzo smaczny etc.

delight (dy'lajt) s. rozkosz; v. zachwycać się; rozkoszować się; lubować się

delightful (dy'lajtful) adj. zachwycający; czarujący

delinquency (dy'lynkłensy) s. zaniedbanie; wina; przestępstwo;nie płacenie należności

delinquent (dy'lynkłent) a. winny; zaniedbany; zalegający z zapłatą (podatkiem); s. winowajca; przestępca (nieletni);osoba zalegająca etc.

deliver (dy'lywer) v. doręczać; zdawać; wydawać; wygłaszać; zadawać; uwalniać;podawać

deliverance (dy'lywerens) s. uwolnienie;wygłoszenie(opinii)

deliverer (dy'lywerer) s. zbawca;oswobodziciel;wybawca

delivery (dy'lywery) s. dostawa; wydawanie; wygłaszanie; podanie; poród; przekazanie

deluge ('delju:dż) s. potop

delusion (dy'lu:żyn) s. urojenie; zwodzenie;ułuda;iluzja

delusive (dy'lu:syw) adj. złudny;oszukańczy;bałamutny;zwodniczy

demand (dy'ma:nd)s. zadanie;popyt; v.zadać; dopytywać się

demeanor (dy'mi:ner) s. zachowanie się;postepowanie: postawa
demented (dy'mentyd) adj. obłąkany;oszalały;umysłowo chory
demi-('demy) pref. pół-
demilitarized ('dy:mylyterajzd)
adj. zdemilitaryzowany
demise (dy'majz) s. zgon; przekazanie spadku; v. przekazywać
testamentem lub zgonem
demobilize (dy:,moubylajz) v.
demobilizować;zdemobilizować
democracy (dy'mokresy) s. demokracja
democrat ('demokreat) s. demo-
krata; demokratka
democratic (,deme'kraetyk) adj.
demokratyczny
demolish (dy'molysz) v. burzyć;
niszczyć; obalać; demolować
demon ('di:men) s. diabeł; demon;doskonały zawodnik sportowy
demonstrate ('demenstrejt) v.
wykazywać; udowadniać; demon-
strować;urządzać manifestację
demonstration (,demen'strejszyn)
s. wykazywanie; okazywanie;
demonstracja;adj.wzorcowy;pogla-
demonstrative (dy'menstrejtyw)
adj. wylewny; dowodowy; wskazujący;dowodzący;ekspansywny
demurrage (dy'me:rydż) s. prze-
stój; opłata za postojowe
den (den) s. nora; jaskinia;
ustronie; cicha pracownia
denial (dy'najel) s. zaprzeczenie; odmowa;wyparcie się
denomination (dynomy'nejszyn)
s. nazwa; miano; określenie;
wyznanie (rel.);kategoria
denounce (dy'nauns) v. oskarżać;
donosić; wypowiadać;denuncjować
dense (dens) adj. gęsty; zwarty;
tępy (człowiek);niepojętny
density ('densyty) s. gęstość;
zwartość; głupota;spoistość
dent (dent) s. wgłębienie; wrąb;
znaczenie;v.szczerbić;wyginać
dental ('dentl) adj. zębowy;
dentystyczny;stomatologiczny
dentist ('dentyst) s. dentysta;
dentystka; stomatolog

denture (denczer) s. (sztuczne) uzębienie; szczęka
deny (dy'naj) v. zaprzeczyć;
odrzucić; odmawiać; wypierać
się;zdementować; przeczyć
depart (dy'pa:rt) v. odjeżdżać;
odbiegać;robić dygresje;odejść
department (dy'pa:rtment) s.
wydział; ministerstwo; dział
department store (dy'pa:rtment,
sto:r) s. dom towarowy
departure (dy'pa:rczer) s. odjazd; rozstanie; odchylenie
depend on (dy'pend on) v. polegać na...;zależeć od
depend upon (dy'pend,apon) v.
być zależnym od..;być na utrzymaniu..
depends (dy'pends)v. zależy
deplorable (dy'plo:rebl) adj.
godny pożałowania;opłakany
deplore (dy'plo:r) v. ubolewać;
boleć nad...;wyrażać ubolewanie
depolarize (dy'poulerajz) v.
depolaryzować;rozwiać złudzenia
depopulate (dy'popjulejt) v.
wyludniać;pustoszyć;opustoszyć
deport (dy'po:rt) v. zsyłać;
deportować; zachowywać się
depose (dy'pouz) s. składać;
zeznawać;usunąć(z tronu etc.)
deposit (dy'pozyt) s. osad;
warstwa; kaucja; depozyt;
v. składać; osadzać; depono-
wać; nawarstwiać;złożyć (jaja...)
depositor (dy'pozyter) s. de-
ponent; osadnik
depot (depou) s. stacja kole-
jowa; skład;remiza; kadra
depraved (dy'prejwd) adj. zde-
prawowany;zepsuty moralnie
depress (dy'pres) v. przygnębiać; deprymować; spychać
w dół(ceny);deprymować;martwić
depression (dy'preszyn) s.
przygnębienie; depresja
deprive (dy'prajw) v. odzierać;
wykluczać; umartwiać się; pozbawiać;odwołać (z urzędu etc.)
depth (deps) s. głębokość;
głębia; głębina;dno(nędzy etc.)
deputy ('depjuty) s. zastępca;
deputowany; poseł; wice-

derail (dy'rejl) v. wykoleic
(się)(czyjś plan,zamiar etc.)
derange (dy'rejndż) v. pomieszac; rozstrajac; psuc; zakło-
cac; powodowac obłęd
deride (dy'rajd) v. wysmiewac
derision (dy'ryżyn) s. szyderstwo; posmiewisko; drwina
derisive (dy'rajsyw) adj.kpią-
cy; ironiczny;wart smiechu
derive (dy'rajw) v. uzyskiwac;
czerpac; wywodzic; pochodzic
derogatory (dy'rogeto:ry) v.
pomniejszający; uszczuplający;
uwłaczający ; szkodliwy
descend (dy'send) v. zejsc;spasc
zniżac się;pochodzic; opadac
descendant (dy'sendent) s. po-
tomek(przedka;rodziny;grupy etc.)
descent (dy'sent) s. zejscie;
spadek; pochodzenie;nagły atak
describe (dys'krajb) v. opisywac; okreslac;przerysowywac
description (dy'skrypszyn)
s. opis;sposob opisywania
desegregate (dy'segrygejt) v.
(Am.) zniesc podział rasowy
desert ('desert) adj. pustynny;
pusty; s. pustynia;pustkowie
desert (dy'ze:rt) v. porzucac;
opuszczac; dezerterowac; s.za-
służenie; zasługa;nagroda;kara
deserted (dy'ze:rted) adj.
opuszczony;bezludny
deserter (dy'ze;rter) s. dezer-
ter;dezerterka;zbieg;zbiegła
desertion (dy'ze:rszyn) s.
opuszczenie; dezercja;porzucenie
deserve (dy'ze:rw) v. zasługiwac na...;miec zasługi wobec...
design (dy'zajn) s. zamiar;
plan; szkic; v. pomyslec; zamierzac; przeznaczac; projekto-
wac;zamyslac;uplanowac;kreslic
designate ('dezygnejt) v. wyznaczac; okreslac; desygnowac
designer (dy'zajner) s. projek-
tant; konstruktor; rysownik;
intrygant;projektodawca;autor
desirable (dy'zajerebl) adj. pożądany;pociągający;atrakcyjny
celowy;mile widziany;wskazany

desire (dy'zajer) v. pożądac;
pragnąc; życzyc sobie
desirous (dy'zajeres) adj. żądny;pragnący;spragniony
desk (desk) s. biuro; referat;
pulpit; ambona ;ławka szkolna
desk set ('desk set) s. zestaw
przyborów do pisania
desolate ('deselyt) adj.
opuszczony; posępny;wyludniony
desolate (deselejt) v. pustoszyc; wyludniac; opuszczac
desolation (,dese'lejszyn) s.
wyludnienie; spustoszenie;
pustka; żałosc; strapienie
despair (dys'peer) s. rozpacz
despairingly (dys'peeryngly)
adv. rozpaczliwie;beznadziejnie
desperate ('desperyt) adj.
rozpaczliwy;beznadziejny;zacie-
desperation (,despe'rejszyn)kły
s. rozpacz; desperacja
despise (dys'pajz) v. pogar-
dzac;gardzic;lekceważyc
despite (dys'pajt) s. przekora; złosc; prep. pomimo;
wbrew;na przekór(komus,czemus)
despond (dys'pond) v. przygnę-
biac się;s.przygnębienie
despondent (dys'pondent) adj.
przygnębiony; zniechęcony
dessert (dy'ze:rt) s. deser;
legumina; ciastka
destination (desty'nejszyn) s.
miejsce przeznaczenia
destine ('destyn) v. przezna-
czac(z góry);przeznaczyc
destiny ('destyny) s. przezna-
czenie(wypadków,ludzi...);los
destitute ('destytju:t) adj.
bez srodków;pozbawiony;w nędzy
destroy (dy'stroj) v. burzyc;
niweczyc;zabijac;zagładzac
destroyer (dy'strojer) s.kontr-
torpedowiec; niszczyciel
destruction (dys'trakszyn) s.
zniszczenie;ruina;zguba;zagłada
destructive (dy'straktyw) adj.
niszczycielski;s.niszczyciel
detach (dy'taecz) v. odczepic;
odłączyc; odpiąc; odwiazac;
odkomenderowac;odlepiac;urwac

detached (dy'taeczt) adj. odosobniony; obojętny;niezależny

detail ('di:tejl) s. szczegół;
wyszczególnienie; v. wyłuszczać; przydzielać do zadań

detain (dy'tejn) v. wstrzymywać; więzić; przeszkadzać

detect (dy'tekt) v. wykrywać;
wysledzić;wypatrzyć;przychwycić

detection (dy'tekszyn) s. wy-
krywanie; wysledzenie

detective (dy'tektyw) s. detektyw; adj. detektywistyczny

detention (dy'tenszyn) s. więzienie; zatrzymanie;przetrzymanie

deter (dy'te:r) v. odstraszać
od...;pohamować;oniesmielać

detergent (dy'te:rdżent) s.&
adj. czyszczący (środek)

deteriorate (dy'tierjerejt) s.
psuć; marnieć;tracić na wartosci

determination (dyte:rmy'nejszyn)
s. okreslenie; postanowienie;
ustalenie; orzeczenie;wygasnięcie

determine (dy'te:rmyn) v. rozstrzygać; okreslać; postanawiać; ustalać;zdefiniować

deterrent (dy'terent) adj. od-
straszający; s.(czynnik) od-
straszający;srodek zaradczy

detest (dy'test) v. nienawidzić;
czuć wstręt;nie cierpieć

detestable (dy'testebl) adj.
wstrętny; nienawistny;obmierzły

detonate ('detounejt) v. wybuchać; powodować wybuch

detour ('dy:tuer) s. objazd

devaluation (,dy:vaelju'ejszyn)
s. dewaluacja;zdewaluowanie

devaluate(dy:waelju:ejt)v.dewalu-
ować;obniżać wartość;zdewaluować

devastate ('devestejt) v. pustoszyć;niweczyć;dewastować

develop (dy'velop) v. rozwijać
(się); wywoływać (zdjęcia)

development (dy'velepment) s.
rozwój; rozbudowa; osiedle;
wywoływanie(filmu);ewolucja

deviate ('di:wejt) v. zbaczać;
odchylać;schodzić z drogi

device (dy'wajs) s. plan; pomysł;
urządzenie; dewiza; hasło;srodek

devil ('dewl) s. chart; diabeł

devilish ('dewlysh) adj. szatański; diabelski;adv.diabelsko

devise (dy'wajz) v. zapisać
(komuś); wymyslać; obmyslać

devoid (dy'woyd) adj. pozbawiony;próżny;czczy;wolny od.,.

devote (dy'wout) v. poswięcać;
ofiarować;oddawać się

devoted (dy'vouted) adj. oddany;przywiązany (do kogoś,.)

dew (dju:) s. rosa; swieżość;
powiew; v. rosić; zraszać

dew point ('dju:point)
temperatura powstawania rosy

dexter ('dekster) a. prawy

dexterity (deks'teryty) s.
zręczność; bystrość;sprawność

diabetes (,daje'by:ty:z) s.
cukrzyca;choroba cukrowa

diagram ('dajegraem) s. wykres;
schemat; diagram

dial ('dajel) s. tarcza nume-
rowa (zwł. zegarowa);
v. mierzyć; nakręcać (numer)

dial tone ('dajel,toun) s.
sygnał połączenia (tel.)

dialect ('dajelekt) s. gwara;
narzecze; dialekt

dialog(ue) ('dajelog) s. rozmowa; dialog(na scenie etc.)

diameter (dai'aemyter) s. sred-
nica; długość srednicy

diamond('dajemend) s. diament;
romb; a. diamentowy; romboidalny;s.boisko do gry w palanta

diaper ('dajeper) s. pielusz-
ka; wzór romboidalny;
v. przewijać; ozdabiać w romby

diaphragm ('dajefraem) s. przepona; membrana;przesłona

diarrhea (daje'rye) s. biegunka

diary ('daiery) s. dziennik

dice (dajs) v. grać w kości;
kratkować; pl. od die=kostka do
gry

dictate (dyk'tejt) s. nakaz;
v. dyktować;narzucać(wolę etc.)

dictation (dyk'tejszyn) s.
dyktat; dyktowanie ;nakaz

dictator (dyk'tejter) s. dyktator;dyktujący dyktando;dyk-
tujący na głos (tekst;list etc.)

dictatorship (dyk'tejterszyp)
s. dyktatura;władza nieograniczo-
na/
dictionary ('dykszeneeryj.słow-
nik;mała encyklopedia
did (dyd) v. zrobić; zob.: do
die (daj) v. umierać; zdech-
nąć; zginąć; s. matryca;
sztanca; pl. zob,: dice
die-hard ('daj-ha:rd) adj.
twardy; nieustępliwy; s. zagorzały bojownik(szermierz etc.)
diet ('dajet) s. dieta; zjazd;
sejm; v. trzymać na diecie
differ ('dyfer) v. różnić się;
nie zgadzać się(z opinią etc.)
difference ('dyferens) s. różnica; sprzeczka; nieporozumienie
different ('dyferent) adj. różny; odmienny; niezwykły
difficult ('dyfykelt) adj.
trudny;ciężki; niełatwy
difficulty ('dyfykelty) s.
trudność; przeszkoda
diffident ('dyfydent) adj. nieśmiały; bez wiary we własne
siły;bez zaufania do siebie
diffuse (dy'fju:z) adj. rozwlekły; rozproszony; v. rozlewać; szerzyć; rozpraszać
dig; dug; dug (dyg; dag; dag)
dig (dyg) v. kopać; ryć; rozumieć; ocenić; bawić się; kuć
się; s. szarpnięcie; przytyk;
kujon;szturchnięcie;docinek
digest (dy'dżest) v. trawić;
przetrawiać; s. streszczenie;
skrót; przegląd;zbiór praw
digestible (dy'dżestebl) adj.
strawny;łatwy do przyswojenia
digestion (dy'dżestszyn) s.
trawienie; wygotowanie
diggings ('dygynz) s. kopalnia
(złota); mieszkanie
dignified ('dygnyfajd) adj. dostojny;godny;pełen godności
dignity ('dygnyty) s. godność;
dostojeństwo;powaga;zaszczyt
digress ('daj'gres) v. zbaczać;
odbiegać od rzeczy (tematu etc.)
digs (dygz) s, mieszkanie; pokój; buda; melina
dihedral (daj'hi:drel)adj.(kąt)
między dwoma ścianami

dike (dajk) s. tama; grobla;
row; v. osuszać rowem; otamować
dilapidated (dy'laepydejtyd)
adj. zniszczony;walący się
dilate (daj'lejt) v. rozszerzać; rozwodzić się;rozciągać
diligence ('dylydżens) n. pilność;przykładanie się do pracy
diligent ('dylydżent) adj. pilny;przykładający się do pracy
dill (dyl) s. koper ogrodowy
dill-pickle ('dyl,pykl) s. kiszony ogorek
dilute (daj'lju:t) v. rozpuszczać; rozcieńczać; rozrzedzać;
adj. rozpuszczony; rozcieńczo-
ny; rozrzedzony; rozwodniony;
wypłukany; wybladły;spłowiały
dim (dym) v. przyćmić; zaciemnić; zamglić; adj. przyćmiony;
blady zamazany; niewyrazny
dime (dajm) s. dziesięcio-
centowa moneta U.SA.
dimension (dy'menszyn) s. wymiar; rozmiar; wielkość
diminish (dy'mynysz) v. zmniejszać; zwężać;uszczuplać;niknąć
diminutive (dy'mynjutyw) adj.&
s. drobniutki; zdrobniały;
zdrobnienie:malutka kobieta
dimple ('dympl) s. dołek (w
twarzy) ; v. robić dołki; mieć
dołki (w twarzy etc.)
dine (dajn) v. jeść obiad;
jeść; mieć na obiedzie
diner (dajner) s. stołówka
wagon restauracyjny; osoba
jedząca;restauracja
dining car ('dajnyŋg,ka:r) s.
wagon restauracyjny
dining room ('dajnyŋg,ru:m)
s. jadalnia;pokój jadalny
dinner ('dyner) s. obiad
dinner-jacket ('dyner,dżaekyt)
s. smoking
dinner-party ('dyner,pa:rty)
s. przyjęcie; obiad proszony
dip (dyp) v. zanurzać; czerpać;
farbować; pogrążać; płukać;
nachylać sie; opadać; s. zanurzenie; zamoczenie; rozczyn;
nachylenie; obniżenie; łojówka;
sos do macznia;skok do wody

diphtheria (dyfteria) s. dyfteryt; błonica
diploma (dy'plouma) s. dyplom
diplomacy (dy'ploumesy) s. dyplomacja;takt
diplomat ('dyplemaet) s. dyplomata;człowiek taktowny
diplomatic(,dyple'maetyk) adj. dyplomatyczny; taktowny
direct, (dy'rekt) v. kierowac; kazac; zarządzic; dowodzic; zaadresowac;nakierowywac; wymierzac polecic; dyrygowac;adj.
prosty; bezposredni; otwarty; szczery; wyrazny; adv. wprost; prosto; bezposrednio
direct current (dy'rekt'karent) s. prąd stały
direction (dy'rekszyn) s. kierunek; kierowanie; kierownictwo; zarząd; wskazówka; adres
directions (dy'rekszyns) pl. instrukcje; przepisy; przepis
directly (dy'rektly) adv. bezposrednio; wprost; od razu; zaraz;natychmiast;dokładnie
director (dy'rektor) s. dyrektor; reżyser; celownik; kierownik;zarządzający
directory (dy'rektery) s. książka adresowa; telefoniczna(lub przepisów);skorowidz
dirigible ('dyrydżebl) adj.& s. sterowy; sterowiec
dirt (de:rt) s. brud; błoto; swinstwo; ziemia; język plugawy; mówienie oszczrstw;plotki
dirt-cheap (de:rt'czi:p) adv. za bezcen; adj, bardzo tani; tani jak barszcz;śmiesznie tani
dirty (de:rty) adj. brudny; sprosny; podły; wstrętny
disability (,dyse'dylyty) s. inwalidztwo; niemoc;niemożność
disabled (dyżejbld) s. kaleka; inwalida wojenny
disadvantage (dysed'wa:ntydż) s. niekorzysc; wada; strata; szkoda; niekorzystne położenie;v.szkodzic;zaszkodzic(komu)
disadvantageous (dysaedwa:ntejdżes) adj. niekorzystny; szkodliwy;ujemny

disagree (dyse'gri:) v. nie zgadzac się; roznic się; nie służyc (jedzenie; klimat)
disagreeable (,dyse'gri:ebl) adj. nieprzyjemny; niemiły
disagreement (,dyse'gri:ment) s. niezgoda; różnica
disallow (,dyse'lau) v. niepozwalac; nie dopuszczac
disappear (,dyse'pier) v. znikac;zapodziewac się; przepasc
disappearance (,dyse'pierens) s. zniknięcie;zanik;zginięcie
disappoint (dyse'point) v. zawiesc;rozczarowac;nie spełnic
disappointment (dyse'pointment) s. zawod; rozczarowanie
disapproval (dyse'pru:wel) s. potępienie; niechęc;desaprobata
disapprove (dyse'pru:w) v. potępiac; ganic;zle widziec(kogos)
disarm (dys'a:rm) v. rozbroic; unieszkodliwic;odebrac bron
disarmament (dys'a:rmement) s. rozbrojenie;a.rozbrojeniowy
disarrange (,'dyse'rejndż) v. rozstrajac; dezorganizowac
disarray (,dyse'rej) v. wprowadzac nieład; rozstrajac; s. nieład; zamieszanie; bałagan;niekompletny strój
disaster (dy'za:ster) s. nieszczęscie; klęska(żywiołowa etc.)
disastrous (dy'za:stres) adj. katastrofalny; zgubny;fatalny
disbelief ('dysby'li:f) s. niewiara; niedowierzanie;nieufnośc
disbelieve ('dysby'li:w) v. niewierzyc; niedowierzac
disc (dysk) s. krążek; tarcza; płyta; dysk;płyta gramofonowa
discard (dys'ka:rd) v. wyrzucac; odrzucac;zaniechac
discard ('dyska:rd) s. odrzucenie; odrzucona (rzecz lub osoba);odpadek;rzecz wybrakowana
discern (dy'se:rn) v. rozrozniac;odrożniac;rozpoznawac
discharge (dys'cza:rdż) v. rozładowac; odciążac; zwalniac; wypuscic; wystrzelic; s. rozładowaniewystrzał; zwolnienie; wydzielina;odpływ;odchody;ropa

disciple (dy'sajpl) s. uczeń;
wyznawca;jeden z apostołów
discipline ('dyscyplyn) s.
dyscyplina; karność; v. karać; ćwiczyć; musztrować
disc-jockey (dysk'dżoki) s.
nadający muzykę z płyt ;
(disk jockey)
disclaim (dys'klejm) v. wypierać się;rezygnować';zrzekać się
disclcse (dys'k-ouz) v. odsłaniać; ujawniać;wyjawiać;odkryć
discolor (dys'kaler) v. odbarwiać
discomfort (dys'kamfert) s. niewygoda; niepokój; v. sprawiać
niewygody lub złe samopoczucie;krępować;żenować;dolegać
discompose (,dyskem'pouz) v.
niepokoić; mieszać;zmieszać
disconcert (,dysken'ser:t) v.
żenować; krzyżować plany
disconnect ('dyske'nekt) v. odłączyć; oderwać; odhaczyć
disconnected ('dyske'nektyd)
adj. bez związku; bezładny;
rozłączony; chaotyczny
disconsolate (dys'konselyt) adj.
niepocieszony; posępny
dicontent. ('dysken'tent) s. niezadowolenie; adj. niezadowolony; v. wywoływać niezadowolenie ;wywoływać rozgoryczenie
discontented ('dysken'tentyd)
adj. niezadowolony; rozgory-
czony; zniecierpliwiony
discontinue ('dysken'tynju:) v.
zaprzestawać; przerywać; ustawać;zakończyć; zaniechać
discord ('dysko:rd) s. niezgoda; różnica; dysonans;niesnaski
discordance,('dysko:rdens) s.
niezgodność ;dysonans
discotheque ('dyskoutek) s.
dyskoteka; nocny lokal z muzy-
ką z płyt do tańca
discount ('dyskaunt) s. dyskont;
rabat; odjęcie; v. potrącać;
odliczać; nie dawać wiary
discourage (dys'karydż) v. zniechęcać; odstraszać;być przeciwnym
discover (dys'kawer) v. wynaleźć; odkryć; odsłaniać;zobaczyć

discoverer (dys'kawerer) s.
odkrywca; wynalazca
discredit (dys'kredyt) v. dys-
kredytować; przynosić ujmę;
pozbawiać zaufania; s. utrata zaufania i dobrego imienia;
niewiara;zła opinia(kogo ,czego)
discreet (dys'kri:t) a. rozsądny; dyskretny; z rezerwą
discrepancy (dys'krepensy) s.
sprzeczność ;rozbieżność
discretion (dys'kreszyn) s.
swoboda decyzji; rozwaga;
powściągliwość; dyskrecja
discriminate (dys'krymynejt)
v. odróżniać; dyskryminować;
robić różnice;wyróżniać
discriminate against (dys'krymynejt e'genst) wprowadzać
dyskryminację w stosunku do..
discuss (dys'kas) v. dyskutować; roztrząsać ;debatować
discussion (dys'kaszyn) s.
dyskusja; debata ;debaty
disdain (dy'dejn) s. pogarda;
wzgarda;v.gardzić;lekceważyć
disease (dy'zi:z) s. choroba
diseased (dy'zi:zd) adj. chory; schorzały;cierpiący na...
disembark ('dysym'ba:rk) v.wy-
ładować; wysiadać; lądować
disengage ('dysen'gejdż) v.
odczepiać; wyłączać;odwikłać
disengaged ('dysyn'gejdżd) adj.
wolny; nie zajęty;zwolniony
disentangle ('dysyntaengl) v.
wyplątać; rozplątać;wywikłać
disfavor ('dys'fejwer) s. niełaska; dezaprobata; v. odnosić się nieprzychylnie; z niechęcią traktować;dezaprobować
disfigure ('dys'fyger) v. zniekształcić ;zeszpecić
disgrace (dys'grejs) s. hańba;
niełaska; v. hańbić; zniesławić; pozbawiać łaski;narobić wsty-
disgraceful (dys'grejsfel) adj. du
haniebny; hańbiący;sromotny;niecny
disguise (dys'gajz) v. przebierać; ukrywać; maskować; z_taić;
s. charakteryzacja; udawanie;
pozory ;zamaskowanie; maska

disgust (dys'gast) s. odraza;
wstręt; obrzydzenie; v. budzić odrazę, wstręt, obrzydzenie, rozgoryczenie,oburzenie
disgusting (dvs'gastyng)adj.
wstrętny; obrzydliwy;oburzający
dish (dysz) s. półmisek; naczynie;potrawa; danie; v. nakładać; podawać; drążyć;okpiwać
dishes ('dyszyz) pl. statki;
naczynia;smaczne potrawy
dish-cloth ('dysz,klos) s.
ścierka do wycierania talerzy
disheveled (dy'szeweld) adj.
rozczochrany; zaniedbany
dishonest (dys'onyst) adj. nieuczciwy; nie godny zaufania
dishonesty (dys'onysty) s. nie-
uczciwość;nieuczciwy postępek
dishonor (dys'oner) s. hańba;
dyshonor; niehonorowanie;v.lżyć
dishonorable (dys'onerebl) adj.
haniebny; podły;bez czci i wiary
dishwasher ('dysh,łoszer) s.
pomywacz(ka)
dish-water (dysz,ło:ter) s. pomyje
disillusion (,dysy'lu:żyn) s.
rozczarowanie;otrzeźwienie
disincline (,dysyn'klajn) v.
zniechęcać; mieć niechęc
disinclined (,dysyn'klajnd) adj.
zniechęcony;źle usposobiony
disinfect (,dysyn'fekt) v. odkażać ;zdyzenfekować
disinfectant (,dysyn'fektent)
s. środek odkażający
disinherit ('dysyn'heryt) v.
wydziedziczyć; wydziedziczać
disintegrate (dys'yntegrejt) v.
rozpadać (się); rozkładać (się)
disinterested (dys'yntrystyd)
adj. bezinteresowny; nie zainteresowany;obiektywny
disjoint(dys'dżoint)v. rozłączać;
rozdzielać;zwichnać;rozerwać
disk (dysk) s. krążek; tarcza;
płyta gramofonowa; dysk
dislike (dys'lajk) v. nie lubić;
mieć odrazę; s. odraza; niechęc;awersja; wstręt

dislocate ('dyslekejt) v.
zwichnąć; przesunąć;zatrącić
disloyal (,dys'lojel) adj. niewierny; nielojalny; zdradziecki
dismal ('dyzmel) adj. nieszczęsny; ponury; posępny
dismantle (dys'maentl) v. roz-
montowywac; ogołacać; odzierać;rozbroić;pozbawiać
dismay (dys'mej) s. trwoga;
przestrach; v. przerażać;
konsternować;skonsternować
dismember (dys'member) v. roz-
członować; rozebrać na części
dismiss (dys'mys) v. odprawiać;
zwalniać; odsuwać od siebie
dismissal (dys'mysel) s. zwolnienie; dymisja;rozejście się
dismount ('dys'maunt) v. zsiadać z konia; wyjmować z opra-
wy; wysadzać z siodła
disobedience (dyse'bi:djens)
s. nieposłuszeństwo; opór
disobedient (dyse'bi:djent)
adj. nieposłuszny; oporny
disobey (,dyse'bej) v. nie-
słuchać; byc nieposłusznym
disoblige (,dyse'blajdż) v.
lekceważyć; bagatelizować
disorder (dys'o:rder) s. nieporządek; zamieszki;zaburzenie
disorderly (dys'o:rderly)adj.
nieporządny; niesforny; gorszący; burzliwy;bezładny
disown (dys'oun) v. wypierać
się; zaprzeczac; nie uznawać
disparage (dys'paerydż) v.
poniżać; ubliżać; dyskredyto-
wać;uwłaszczać;lekceważyć
dispassion (dys'paeszyn) s.
beznamiętność; odiektywizm
dispassionate (dys'paeszynyt)
adj. beznamiętny;obiektywny
dispatch (dys'paecz) s. wysył-
ka; wysłanie; sprawnosć; szyb-
kosć; szybkie załatwienie;
v. wysyłać; załatwiać
dispel (dys'pel) v. rozwiewać
(obawy);rozpędzać (chmury)
dispensable (dys'pensebl) adj.
zbędny; niekonieczny;do uchyle-
nia

dispense (dys'pens) v. wydzielac; wymierzac; wydawac;
udzielac;sporządzać(lekarstwo)
dispense with (dys pens łys)
v. pomijac; obyc się
disperse (dys'pe:rs) v. roz-
praszac; rozpędzac; rozjeż-
dżac się; rozsiewac;płoszyc
displace (dys'plejs) v. prze-
mieszczac; wypierac; usuwac
display (dys'plej) v. wystawiac; popisywac się; s. wystawa; popis; pokaz;parada
displease (dys'pli:z) v. ura-
żac; draznic; gniewac; dotykac; oburzac; irytowac
displeased (dys'pli:zd) adj.
urażony; zirytowany; niezadowolony;obrażony;poirytowany
displeasure (dys'pleżer) s.
niezadowolenie; gniew;irytacja
disposal (dys'pouzel) s. rozkład; zbyt; sprzedaż; przekazanie; rozporządzenie;niszczenie
dispose (dys'pouz) v. rozmieszczac; rozporządzic; pozbyc
się; sprzedac;usunac;niszczyc
disposed (dys'pouzd) adj. skłonny; usposobiony(dobrze,źle etc.)
disposition (dys'pouzyszyn) s.
skłonnosc; pociąg; zarządzenie; dyspozycje;rozporządzanie
disproportionate (,dyspre'po:r-
sznyt) adj. nieproporcjonalny
dispute (dys'pju:t) s. spór;
kłotnia; v. sprzeczac się;
kłocic się; kwestionowac
disqualify (dys'kłolyfaj) v.
dyskwalifikowac
disquiet (dys'kłajet) v. niepokoic; s. niepokój; adj. niespokojny;zaniepokojony
disregard (,dysry'ga:rd) v. pomijac; lekceważyc;s.lekceważe-
disrepute (,dysry'pju:t) s. nie
niesława;hańba; zła reputacja
disrespectful (,dysry'spektfel)
adj. niegrzeczny; niedelikatny
disrupt (dys'rapt) v. rozrywac;
rozdzierac;przerwac; obalic
dissatisfaction ('dysseatys'-
faekszyn) s. niezadowolenie

dissatisfied (dys,satys'fajd)
adj. niezadowolony
dissension (dy'senszyn) s. wasn;
niezgoda; swary
dissent (dy,sent) s. różnica;
rozbieżnosc zdan; v. różnic
się w zapatrywaniach;odstępstwo
dissimilar ('dy'symyler) adj.
niepodobny; różny
dissipate (dy'sypejt) v. roz-
praszac; marnowac; trwonic;
marnotrawic;rozgonic;hulac
dissociate (dy'souszjejt) v.
rozłączac; zrywac(z kims,czyms)
dissolute ('dyselu:t) adj. rozwiązły; rozpustny
dissolution (,dys'elu:szyn) s.
rozkład; zanik; rozpuszczenie;
rozwiązanie;smierc;zgon;rozpad
dissolve (dy'zolw) v. rozpuszczac; rozkładac; niszczyc;
rozwiązywac; zanikac;skasowac
dissuade (dy'słejd) v. odradzac;
odwodzic (kogos);wyperswadowac
distance ('dystens) s. odległosc;
odstęp; oddalenie;v.zdystansowac
distant ('dystent) adj. daleki;
odległy; powsciągliwy;z rezerwą
distaste (,dys'tejst) s. niesmak;
niechęc; odraza; awersja
distasteful (,dys'tejstful) adj.
odstręczający;wstrętny;przykry
distend (dys'tend) v. rozdymac;
rozszerzac;nabrzmiewac;nadąc
distill (dy'styl) v. przekrap-
lac; destylowac;przesączac;kapac
distinct (dys'tynkt) adj. odmienny; odrębny; wyrazny; dobitny
distinction (dys'tynkszyn) s.
rozróżnienie; wyróżnienie;
wytwornosc; podział;wyrazistosc
distinctive (dys'tynktyw) adj.
odrożniający się;charakterystyczny
distinguish (dys'tyngłysz) v.
rozrożniac; klasyfikowac;odznaczyc
distinguished (dystyngłyszt)
adj. wybitny; znakomity;
dystyngowany;odznaczający się
distort (dys'to:rt) v. wykrzywiac; wykręcac; przekręcac
distract (dys'traekt) v. odry-
wac; rozproszyc; oszołomic

distracted (dys'traektyd) adj.
oszalały; w rozterce; skłopo-
tany;roztargniony;rozproszony
distraction (dys'traekszyn) s.
dystrakcja; roztargnienie;
rozrywka; rozterka; szaleństwo;zamieszanie;odwrócenie uwagi
distress (dys'tres) s. męka;
strapienie; niedostatek; potrzeba; niebezpieczeństwo
distressed (dys'trest) adj.
umęczony; udręczony;w niedoli
distribute (dys'trybju:t) v.
udzielać; rozmieszczać;rozdać
distribution (dys'tryju;szyn)
s. rozdział; podział; dystry-
bucja;roznoszenie;a.rozdzielczy
district ('dystrykt) s. okręg;
powiat; dystrykt;dzielnica;rejon
distrust (dys'trast) s. nie-
ufność; niedowierzanie; v.nie-
ufać; niedowierzać;podejrzewać
disturb (dys'te:rb) v. przeszkadzać; niepokoić; zakłócać;
mącić; zaburzyć;denerwować
disturbance (dys'te:rbens) s.
zakłócenie; zaburzenie; naruszenie;burda;awantura;rozruchy
disuse (dys'ju:z) v. zarzucenie; nieużywanie;s.nieużywanie
ditch (dycz),s. rów; v. kopać;
drenować; utknąć w rowie; rzucać do rowu(samolot w morze)
dive (dajw) v. nurkować; zanurzać się; skakać z trampoliny;
s. nurkowanie; zanurzenie; melina;lot nurkowy;pikowanie;knajpa
diver ('dajwer) s. nurek;skoczek
z trampoliny;ptak nurkujący
diverge (daj'we:rdż) v. rozchodzić się; odchylać się; zbaczać;
odbiegać;rozbiegać się
diverse (daj'we:rs) adj. odmienny; rozmaity;inny;zmienny
diversion (daj'we:rżyn) s.odchy-
lenie;objazd;rozrywka;dywersja
diversion (dy'we:rżyn) s. zboczenie; dywersja; rozrywka;odwróce-
nie uwagi;oderwanie uwagi
diversity (daj'we:rsyty) s. roz-
maitość;różnorodność;urozmaicenie

diversity (dy'we:rsyty) s. od-
mienność;roznorodność;rozmaitość
divert (daj'we:rt) v. odwracać (uwagę); odrywać; rozerwać; rozbawić;bawić(kogoś)
divide (dy'wajd) v. dzielić;
rozdzielać; oddzielać; różnić
divide by (dy'wajd,baj) v.
dzielić przez...(liczbę)
divine (dy'wajn) adj. boski;
boży; v. wróżyć; przepowiadać
diving ('dajwyŋg) s. skakanie
z trampoliny;pikować samolotem
divinity (dy'wynyty) s. bóstwo;
boskość; teologia
divisible (dy'wyzebl) adj. podzielny (przez,na etc.)
division (dy'wyżyn) s. podział;
rozdział; dzielenie; dział;
wydział; oddział; dywizja
divorce (dy'wo:rs) s. rozwód;
rozdzielenie; v. rozwodzić
się; oddzielać;a.rozwodowy
dizzy ('dyzy) adj. wirujący;
oszołomiony;v.oszałamiać
do (du:) v. czynić; robić; wykonać; zwiedzać;przyrządzać
do away ('du,ełej) v. znieść;
pozbyć się; zabić;skasować
do not ('du not) = don't (dont)
nie(rób);nie(idź);nie(stój,etc.)
do in ('du,yn) v.uwięzić; zlikwidować; zabić;wsadzić do paki
do up ('du,ap) v. przerobić;
odnowić; zmęczyć;upudrować etc.
do well (,du'łel) v. mieć się
dobrze; powodzić się
do without (,du'łygout) v.oby-
wać się bez (kogoś,czegoś)
do you know? (du: ju nou) expr.
czy pan wie (zna) ? czy pan sły-
szał?
docile ('dousajl) adj. uległy;
posłuszny;pojętny;giętki;łagodny
dock (dok) s. dok; basen; molo;
miejsce oskarżonego; v. umieścić w doku; cumować przy molu
dockyard (dokja:rd) s. stocznia
doctor ('dakter) s. lekarz;
doktor (medycyny;filozofii etc.)
doctrine ('daktryn) s. doktryna

document ('dokjument) s. dokument;v. udokumentować
documentary (,dokju'mentery)s.
adj. dokumentarny (film etc.)
dodge (dodż) v. uchylić; uniknąć; zwodzić; s, unik; kruczek; sztuczka;odskok;kiwanie
doe (dou) s. łania ;pl.:does (douz)
does (daz) v. on czyni; robi;
zob.: do
dog (dog) s. pies;uchwyt;klamra
dog-catcher (dog'kaeczer) s.
rakarz; oprawca; hycel
dogged ('dogyd) adj. uparty;
zawzięty;wytrwały
doggie ('dogi) s. psina
dogma ('dogme) s. dogmat
dog-tired ('dog'tajerd) adj.
skonany; ledwo żywy;zmęczony
doings ('du:yngs) pl. sprawki;
uczynki; wyprawiania;psoty
dole (doul) s. zasiłek; zapomoga; smutek;v.mało dawać
doll (dol) s. lalka; (slang)
dziewczyna;v.wystroić się
dollar ('doler) s. dolar
dollish ('dolysz) adj. lalko-
waty(a);lalusiowaty
dolorous ('douleres) adj.
smętny; żałosny; zbolały
dolphin ('dolfyn) s. delfin
dome (doum) s. kopuła; sklepienie;v.nakrywać kopułą
domestic (de'mestyk) adj. domowy; krajowy; domatorski;
s. służący; służąca
domesticate (de'mestykejt) v.
oswajać; zadomowić
domicile ('domysajl) s, miejsce zamieszkania; v. osiedlać;
zamieszkać na stałe
dominate ('domynejt) v. domi-
nować; gorować; przeważać;
panować;mieć zwierzchnictwo
domination ('domynejszyn) s.
władza; panowanie; przewaga
domineer (,domy'nier) v. domi-
nować; rządzić się; rozkazy-
wać;tyranizować;panoszyć się
domineering (,domy'nieryng)
adj. tyranizujący; apodyktyczny; despotyczny; władczy

donate (dou'nejt) v. podarować
donation (dou'nejszyn) s. daro-
wizna, donacja; dar
done (dan) adj. zrobiony; uczy-
niony; zob.: do
donkey ('donky) s. osioł
donor ('douner) s. donator;
dawca (krwi etc.);darujący
doom (du:m) s. zguba; zły los;
śmierć; potępienie; v. potępiać; skazać na zgubę;przesądzać
Doomsday ('du:mzdej) s. dzień
sądu ostatecznego
door (do:r) s. drzwi;brama
door handle ('do:r,haendl) s.
klamka
doorkeeper ('do:r,ki:per) s.
dozorca;portier; oddźwierny
doorknob ('do:r,nob) s. klamka
doormat ('do:r,maet) s, wycieraczka (przy drzwiach)
doorway ('do:r,łej) s. wejście
dope (doup) s. maź; lakier; narkotyk; informacja (poufna);
głupiec (slang). v. narkotyzo-
wać; zaprawiać;fałszować
dormitory ('do:rmytry) s. dom
studencki; sypialnia
dose (dous) s. dawka; dodatek;
dawkowanie; v. dawkować (lekarstwo); mieszać; fałszować
(wino);leczyć;dozować
dot (dot) s. kropka; punkt;
v. kropkować; rozsiewać
dote (dout) v. wariować; kochać
przesadnie; dziecinnieć
double ('dabl) adj. podwójny;
dwukrotny; fałszywy; v. pod-
wajać; adv. podwójnie;w dwójnasób
double up ('dabl,ap) v. składać
się we dwoje; zsuwać się (razem);przybiegać;dzielić pokój
double bed ('dabl,bed) podwójne
łóżko
double-breasted ('dabl,brestyd)
adj. dwurzędowy(płaszcz,marynarka)
double-decker ('dabl-'deker) s.
dwupokładowiec; dwupiętrowiec
double-park ('dabl-pa:rk) v.
parkować podwójnie (na jezdni)
double-room ('dabl,ru:m) s.
pokój dwuosobowy(w hotelu etc.)

doubt (daut) s. wątpliwość; niedowierzanie; v. wątpić; powąt-
piewać; niedowierzać
doubtful ('dautful) adj. wątpliwy; niepewny;niezdecydowany
doubtless ('dautlys) adv. nie-
wątpliwie; bez wątpienia
douche (du'sz) s. natrysk
dough (dou) s. ciasto; (slang)
forsa; pieniądze
doughnut ('dounat) s. pączek
(z dziurą)
dove (daw) s. gołąb(ica)
down (dałn) s. wydma; puch;
meszek ;puszek;piórka
down (dałn) adv. na dół; niżej;
nisko; v. obniżać; poniżać;
przewrócić; strącić; przełknąć
downcast ('dałnka:st) adj.
przybity; przygnębiony; ze
spuszczonymi oczyma
downfall ('dałnfo:l) s. upadek;
klęska; ruina ; zguba
downhill ('dałn'hyl) adj. opa-
dający; s. spadek ;adv.na dół
downpour ('dałnpo:r) s. ulewa
downright ('dałnrajt) adv. zupełnie; wprost; adj. zupełny;
szczery; otwarty; uczciwy
downstairs ('dałn'steerz) adv.
na dół; w dole ;na dole;pod nami
downtown ('dałntałn) s. centrum
miasta; adv. w śródmieściu;
adj. śródmiejski
downwards ('dałnłodz) adv.
w dół; ku dołowi ;na dół;z góry
downy ('dałhy) adj. puszysty;
(slang):chytry ;falisty;puchaty
dowry ('dałry) s. posag; wiano;
dar wrodzony ; talent
doze (douz) s. drzemka; v. drzemać; zdrzemnąć się; zasnąć
dozen ('dazn) s. tuzin
drab (draeb) s.& adj. brudno-
brunatny; nudny; szary; brudas;
prostytutka; v. puszczać się
draft (dra:ft) s. szkic; brulion
zarys; przekaz; pobór; rysunek;
v. szkicować; projektować; rysować; odkomenderować;wyżłobić
draftsman ('dra:ftsmen) s. kreślarz; rysownik; projektodawca

drag (draeg) v. wlec; ciągnąć;
s. pogłębiarka; pojazd; wleczenie; opór czołowy
dragon ('draegen) s. smok
dragonfly ('draegenflaj) s.
ważka
drain (drejn) v. odwadniać;
wysączać; ociekać; s. dren;
spust; ściek;rów odwadniający
drainage ('drejnydż) s. odwad-
nianie; wody ściekowe; obszar odpływowy (rzeki)
drainpipe ('drejnpajp) s.dren
drake (drejk) s. kaczor
drama ('dra:ma) s. dramat
dramatic (dre'maetyk) adj.
dramatyczny;jak w sztuce;żywy
drank (draenk) s. pijak; pijany; zob.: drink
drape (drejp) v. upinać; spadać fałdami; drapowaćs.kotara
drastic ('draestyk) adj. drastyczny ;gwałtowny; surowy
draught (draeft) s. przeciąg;
ciąg; łyk; dawka; zanurzenie
statku ;wyporność;a.pociągowy
draw; drew; drawn (dro:; dru:;
dro:n)
draw (dro:) v. ciągnąć; wyciągać; przyciągać; czerpać; wdychać; sciągać (wodze); spuszczać (wodę); napinać (łuk);
wlec ;rysować; kreślić
draw near(dro:nier) v. zbliżać
się;przybliżać się
drawback (dro:baek) s. strona
ujemna; v. cofać się(draw back)
draw up (dro:,sp) v. podciągać
(się); redagować; zbliżać się;
zrównać się; ustawiać(wojsko)
drawer ('dro:er) s. szuflada;
kreślarz; rysownik;bufetowy
drawers ('dro:ers) pl. kalesony; majtki(damskie,dziecięce...)
drawing ('dro:yng) s. rysunek
drawing pen ('dro:yng,pen) s.
grafion ;piórko kreślarskie
drawing room ('dro:yng,ru:m)
s. salon ;wagon salonowy
drawn (dro:n) adj. nierozstrzygnięty; ciągniony; wychudzony;
zob.: draw(wyciągnięta:szabla)

drawn-out (dro:n aut) adj.
przewlekły ;wyciągniety(z pochwy)
dread (dred) s. strach; postrach; lęk; v. bać się bardzo; lękać się; adj. straszny
dreadful (dredful) adj. przeraźliwy; okropny ;straszny
dream; dreamt; dreamt (dri:m;
dremt; dremt)
dream (dri:m) v. śnić; marzyć;
s. sen; marzenie;mrzonka;uroje-
dreamt (dremt) v. miec sen,
marzenie; zob.: dream
dreamy ('dri:my) adj. marzycielski; mglisty;niewyraźny
dreary ('dryery) adj. posępny;
ponury;smętny;melancholijny
dregs (dregz) pl. osady; męty
drench (drencz) v. zmoczyć;
przemoczyć ;s. ulewa
dress (dres) s. ubiór; strój;
szata; suknia; v. ubierać;
stroic; opatrywać; czyścić;
czesać; przyrządzać; wykańczać; wyprawiać ;wygarbowac
dress down ('dres dałn) v.
besztac ; czyscic (konia)
dress up ('dres,ap) v. stroic
dressing ('dresyng) s. przyprawa; opatrunek; nawoz ;ubiór
dressing-case ('dresyng,kejs)
s. neseser
dressing-gown('dresyn,gołn) s.
podomka; szlafrok
dressing-room (?dresyng,ru:m) s.
garderoba ;ubieralnia;umywalnia
dressing-table ('dresyng,tejbl)
s. toaleta (mebel)
dressmaker ('dresmejker) s.
krawiec damski; krawcowa
drew (dru:) zob.: draw
drift (dryft) s. dryf; znoszenie; biernosc; prąd; dążnosc;
tresc; zamieć; zaspa; nanos
v. dryfowac; znosić; plątac
się; nanosic;płynąc z prądem
drill 1. (dryl) s. świder; wiertarka; dryl; musztra; v. wier-
cic; swidrowac; cwiczyc; musztrowac;drążyc;sortowac(wagony)
drill 2. (dryl) s. rowek do sia-
nia; siewnik rzędowy; v. siać;
obsadzać w rowkach

drink; drank; drunk ('drynk;
draenk; drank)
drink ('drynk) v. pic; przepi-
jac; s, napój; woda (morze)
drip (dryp) v. kapac; ociekać;
ciec; s. kapanie; okap; piła(sl);
nudziara ;kapka;kropla(wody etc.)
drip-dry ('dryp,draj) s. bielizna niewymagająca prasowa-
nia (schnąca na wieszaku etc.)
dripping ('drypyng) s. tłuszcz
spod pieczeni; adj. kapiący;
ociekający ; przemoczony
drive; drove; driven (drajw;
drouw; drywn)
drive (drajw) v. pędzic; gnac;
wiezc; powozic; prowadzic; na-
pędzac; jechac; wbijać ;drążyc
s. przejażdżka; obława; napęd;
droga; dojazd ;energia;pościg
drive at (drajw et) v. kierowac (rozmowę ku...)
drive out (drajw,aut) v. wy-
jeżdzac (z garażu;wypędzać
drive-in (drajw,yn) s. obsługa
w samochodzie :bank; jadłodajnia; kino; sklep;poczta
drive-in movies (drajw,yn
mu:wiz) kino do oglądania
z samochodu
driven (drywn) v. napędzany;
zob.: drive
driver (drajwer) s. kierowca
driving license ('drajwyng-
lajsens) s. prawo jazdy
drizzle ('dryzl) s. mżący
deszcz; v. mżyc; adj. mżący;
drobny (deszcz)
drone (droun) s. truten; bucze-
nie; dudniący mowca; v. zbijac
bąki; buczec; dudnic(monotonnie)
droop (dru:p) v. opadac; zwisac;
zwieszac (głowę); s. zwis;
spadek (tonu); utrata (otuchy)
drop (drop) v. kapac; ciec;
upuszczac; spadac; opadac;
s. kropla; cukierek; spadek
(temperatury);łyk;kieliszek;zniż-
ka;kotara;upadek;obniżenie
drop in ('drop,yn) v. wpasc (do
kogos);wejsc na chwilę
dropout (dropaut) s. osoba prze-
rywająca (studia lub szkołę)

drove (drouw) zob.: drive

drown (draun) v. tonąc; topic;
tłumic; głuszyc; zagłuszać

drowsy ('drauzy) adj. senny;
śpiący; ospały;na pół spiący

drudge (dradż) s. niewolnik;
popychadło; v. harowac

drug (drag) s. lek; lekarstwo;
v. narkotyzowac; przesycac

drug-addict ('drag,aedykt) s.
narkoman

drugstore ('drag,stor) s. apteka; drogeria

drum (dram) s. bęben; v. bębnic;zwoływac bębnieniem;zjedny-
drummer ('dramer) s. dobosz wac

drunk (drank) adj. pijany;
zob.: drink

drunken driving (dranken
drajwyng) s. kierowanie po
pijanemu (samochodem etc.)

dry (draj) adj. suchy;wytrawny
(wino) v. osuszac; suszyc;(łzy)
zeschnąc ;wyjaławiac;wycierąc
dry up (draj,ap) v. wycierac;
wysychac;zapomniec;zaniemowić

dry-clean ('draj kli:n) v.
oczyscic chemicznie (sucho)

dry goods('drajgudz) pl. materiały do szycia;konfekcja

dual ('dju:el) adj. podwójny;
dwoisty ;dwudzielny;wspólny

duchess ('daczys) s. księżna

duck (dak) s. kaczka; unik; v.
zanurzyc; zrobic unik;nurkować

duct (dakt) s. przewód; kanał

dud (dad) s. poroniony pomysł;
safanduła; nieuk; niewypał;
strach na wróble;adj.niezdolny

dude (d(j)u:d) s. elegancik;
laluś; turysta;goguś;wycieczko-
dude ranch ('du:d,ra:nch) ran-
czo wakacyjne(dla mieszczuchów)

due (dju:) adj. należny; płatny;
należyty; adv. w kierunku na
(wschód); s. to co się należy;
naleznośći ; opłata;składka

due to ('dju:,tu) exp. z powodu

duel ('dju(;)el) s. pojedynek

dug (dag) s. cycek; wymię; zob.:
dig

dug2.(dag)s. dójka

dugout ('dagaut) s. ziemianka;
łódz drążona; okop; schron

duke (dju:k) s. książe

dull (dal) adj. tępy; głuchy;
ospały; niemrawy; nudny; ponury; ciemny;v.tępic;tłumic

duly ('dju:ly) adv. właściwie;
należycie; punktualnie;słusznie

dumb (dam) adj. niemy; milczący; głupi;v.odbierać mowę

dumbfounded (dam'faundyd) adj.
osłupiony;osłupiały;oniemiały

dummy ('damy) s, imitacja; bałwan; manekin; (wulg.) niemowa;
adj. udany; podstawiony; imito-
wany ; na niby; niby to

dump (damp) s. śmietnisko; hałda;
magazyn; v. zwalac; rzucac; zarzucac (towarem obcym)

dun (dan) s. wierzyciel; inkasent długów; v. napastowac
o zapłatę długu;a.ciemnobrązowy

dune (dju:n) s. wydma ;diuna

dung (dang)s. nawóz; gnój; bagno moralne; v. nawozic; użyzniac
ziemię ; gnoic

dungeon ('dandżen) s. loch;baszta
v. więzic w lochu lub baszcie

dupe (du:p) s. ofiara; wystrych-
nięty na dudka ;v. okpic;nabrac

duplicate ('dju:plykyt) adj.
podwójny; s. duplikat; w dwu
egzemplarzach; v. podwajac;
duplikować (niepotrzebnie)

duplicity (dju:'plysyty) s. dwu-
licowosc; podstęp;fałsz;obłuda

durable ('djuerebl) adj. trwały

duration (dju'rejszyn) s. trwanie; czas trwania

duress (dju'res) s. przymus

during ('djueryng) prep. podczas; w czasie ;w ciągu;przez;za

dusk (dask) s. zmierzch; mrok;
cień; adj. ciemny; mroczny;
v. zacmic; zamroczyc

dust (dast) s. pył; kurz; pro-
chy; pyłek; v. odkurzac; trze-
pac; kurzyc się; posypywac

dust bowl (dast,boul) s. kraj
suszy i burz(zamieci)piaskowych

dustcover ('dast, kawer) s.
obwoluta; pokrowiec od kurzu

duster ('daster) s. odkurzacz; wiatr z kurzem;zmoitka

dust-pan ('dast,paen) s. śmietniczka;łopatka na śmieci

dust-storm ('dast,sto:rm) s. wicher z tumanami kurzu

dusty ('dasty) adj. zakurzony; pokryty kurzem; suchy; nudny

Dutch (dacz) adj. holenderski; w niełasce; lichy

duty ('dju:ty) s. powinność; obowiązek; szacunek; służba; uległość; cło; podatek od sprzedaży;funkcja;obowiązki

dwarf (dło:rf) s. karzeł; krasnoludek; adj. karłowaty; v. pomniejszać; karleć; skarleć;skarłowacieć;zmniejszać

dwell; dwelt; dwelt (dłel; dłelt; dłelt)

dwell (dłel) v. mieszkać; zatrzymywać się; rozwodzić się (o czyms); zwlekać;przystanąć

dwelling (dłelyŋg) s. mieszkanie;pomieszczenie mieszkalne

dwelt (dłelt) v. mieszkał... zob,: dwell

dwindle (dłyndl) v. maleć; topnieć; marnieć; kurczyc się; tracić znaczenie;zwyrodnieć

dye (daj) v. barwić; farbować; s. barwa; barwik;farba

dying (dajyŋg) v. umierający; zanikający; zob.: die

dyke (dajk) s. grobla; rów; tama;v.ogroblić;ochronić tamą

dynamic (daj'naemyk) adj. dynamiczny;energiczny;z wigorem

dynamics (daj'naemyks) s. dynamika (sił działających razem)

dynamite ('dajne,majt) s. dynamit;v.wysadzać dynamitem

dynamo ('dajne,mou) s. dynamo

dynasty ('dajnesty) s. dynastia

dysentery ('dysnetry) s. czerwonka; dyzenteria(krwawa)

e (i:) piąta litera angielskiego alfabetu

each (i:cz) pron. każdy;za(sztukę)

each other ('i:cz, odzer)siebie; nawzajem (dwie osoby);sobie

eager ('i:ger) adj. gorliwy;ostry; żądny;ożywiony pragnieniem;żywy

eagerness('i:gernyss) s. gorliwość;skwapliwość;pochopnosć

eagle ('i:gl) s. orzeł;a.orli

ear (ier) s. ucho; słuch; kłos (zboża);a.uszny;dotyczący uszu

eardrum ('ierdram) s. bębenek ucha; błona bębenkowa(ucha)

early ('e:rly) adj. wczesny; adv. wcześnie;przedwcześnie

earn (e:rn) v. zarabiać; zasługiwać;zapracować;zdobywać(sławę)

earnest ('e:rnyst) adj. poważny; gorliwy; s. powaga;zadatek;dowód

earnings ('e:rnynz) pl. zarobki

earphone ('ierfoun) s. słuchawka;loki ułożone na uszach

earring ('ieryŋg) s. kolczyk

earshot ('ier,szot) w zasięgu głosu ;w zasięgu słuchu

earth (e:rs) s. ziemia;świat;gleba

earthen ('e:rsen) adj. ziemisty; gliniany;wypiekany z gliny

earthenware ('e:rsen,łe:r) s. wyroby garncarskie(wypiekane)

earthly ('e:rsly) adj. ziemski

earthquake('e:rs,kłejk) s. trzęsienie ziemi

earthworm ('e:rs,łe:rm) s. (glista);dżdżownica

ease (i:z) v. łagodzić; uspokoić; odciążyć; s. spokój; wygoda; beztroska;ulga;łatwość;bezczynność

easel ('i:zl) s. sztaluga

easily ('i:zyly) adv. łatwo; lekko; swobodnie;bez trudności

east (i:st) s. wschód; adj. wschodni; adv. na wschód

Easter ('i:ster) s. Wielkanoc

eastern ('i:stern) adj. wschodni;człowiek wschodu;prawosławny

eastwards ('i:stłerdz) adv. ku wschodowi;na wschód;adj.wschodni

easy (i:zy) adj. łatwy; beztroski; wygodny; adv. łatwo; swobodnie; lekko;s.odpoczynek

easy chair ('i:zy,czeer) s. fotel (klubowy) miękki

eat; ate; eaten (i:t; ejt: i:tn)

eat (i:t) v. jeść (posiłek)

eat up ('i:t,ap) v. wyjeść
eaten (i:tn) adj. zjedzony;
zob. eat
eaves (i:wz) pl. okap(dachu)
eavesdropping ('i:wzdropyŋg)
s. podsłuchiwanie(rozmowy)
ebbtide ('ebtajd) s. odpływ
w morze;v.odpływać(jak morze)
ebony ('ebeny) s. heban
eccentric (ik:sentryk) adj.
dziwaczny; s., ekscentryk;
dziwak; mimośród;dziwaczka
ecclesiastic (ik,ly:zi'eastyk)
adj. kościelny; s. duchowny
echo ('ekou) s. echo; v. odbijać się echem; powtarzać za
kims; odbijać głos
eclipse (i'klyps) s. zaćmienie;
v. zaciemniac;zaćmiewać
ecology (i'koledży) s. ekologia;
związek między środowiskiem
a organizmem(część biologii)
economic (,i:ke'nomyk) adj;
ekonomiczny;gospodarczy
economical (,i:ke:nomykel) adj.
oszczędny; ekonomiczny
economics (,i:ke'nomyks) pl.
nauka o ekonomii (gospodarce)
economist (i'konemyst) s. ekono-
mista;specjalista od gospodarki
economize (i:kone,majz) v.
oszczędzac;zmniejszać wydatki
economy (i,konemy) s. ekonomia;
gospodarka;oszczędność
economy class (i'konemy,kla:s)
s. druga klasa (w pociągu;
samolocie);klasa turystyczna
ecstasy ('ekstesy) s. zachwyt;
ekstaza; uniesienie;siódme niebo
eddy ('edy) s. wir; v. wirować
edelweiss ('ejdl,wajs) s. szarotka (kwiat górski)
edge (edż) s. ostrze; krawędź;
kraj; v. ostrzyc; obszywać;
wyślizgać się;przysuwać po trochu
edging ('edżyŋg) s. brzeg; ob-
szywka; lamówka;skraj
edgy ('edży) adj. nerwowy;
podniecony;o ostrych kantach
edible('edybl) adj. jadalny
edict ('i:dykt) s. edykt; dekret

edifice ('dyfys) s. budowla;
gmach (duży i imponujący)
edifying ('edyfajyŋg) adj. po-
uczający(zwłaszcza moralnie)
edit ('edyt) v. redagować; wydawać;zarządzać gazetą etc.
edition (i'dyszyn) s. wydanie;
nakład (ksiażki,gazety etc.)
editor (e'dyter) s. redaktor;
wydawca;pisarz"od redakcji"
editorial (,edy'to:rjel) s.
artykuł od redakcji; adj.
redakcyjny; redaktorski
educate ('edju:kejt) v. kształcić; wychowywać;płacić za szko-
education (,edju'kejszyn) s. łę
wykształcenie; nauka; oświata;
wychowanie; tresura;wiedza
educational (,edju'kejszenl)
adj. kształcący; wychowawczy
educator ('edju,kejter) s.
wychowawca; wychowawczyni
eel (i:l) s. węgorz
effect (i'fekt) s. skutek; wrażenie; v. wykonywać; dokonywać
effects (i'fekts) pl. ruchomości; dobytek;manatki
effective (i'fektyw) adj. skuteczny; wydajny; rzeczywisty;
efektowny;wchodzący w życie
effeminate (i'femynyt) adj.
zniewieściały;nie męski;słaby
effervescent (,efer'wesnt) adj.
musujący; kipiący;tryskający ży-
efficacy ('efykesy) s. skutecz- ciem
ność;dawanie porządanych wyników
efficiency (i'fyszensy) s. wydajność; skuteczność; spraw-
ność(przy minimum nakładów)
efficient(i'fyszent) adj. skuteczny; wydajny; sprawny
effigy ('efydży) s. wizerunek;
podobizna; czyjaś kukła
effort ('efert) s. wysiłek;
usiłowanie;wyczyn;próba;popis
effusive (i'fju:syw) adj. wylewny;wylany;ekspansywny;wulka-
egg (eg) s. jajko; v. zachęcać; niczny
namawiać;podbechtać;podniecać
eggcup ('eg,kap) s. kieliszek
na jajko;kieliszek do jaj

egghead ('eg,hed) s. intelektualista (nieżyciowy)

egoism ('egou,zyem) s. egoizm

egress ('i:gres) s. wyjście; wyjazd; uchodzenie;wypływ

Egyptian (i'dżypszen) adj. egipski

eiderdown ('ajder,dałn) s. kaczy puch; kołdra;pierzyna

eight (ejt) num.osiem; s. ósemka; ośmioro;ośmiu wioślarzy

eighteen('ejt'i:n) num. osiemnaście; osiemnaścioro;osiemnastka

eightfold ('ejt,fould) num. ośmiokrotny; adv. ośmiokrotnie ;osiem razy

eighty ('ejty) num. osiemdziesiąt; s. osiemdziesiątka

either ('ajdzer) pron. każdy (z dwu); obaj; obie; oboje; jeden lub drugi;adv.także;też

either... or ('ajdzer..o:r) albo... albo

ejaculate (i'dżaekju,lejt) v. zawołać; krzyknąć;wytrysnąć

eject (i'dżekt) v. wyrzucać (się); eksmitować;usuwać

elaborate (i'laebe,rejt) v. opracować; adj. wypracowany; staranny;skomplikowany

elapse (i'laeps) v. minąć; przeminąć ;przemijać

elastic (i'laestyk) adj. sprężysty; rozciągliwy; elastyczny; s. guma; gumka(do majtek...)

elated (i'lejtyd) adj. podniecony; uniesiony; dumny

elbow ('elboł) s. łokieć; zakręt; kolanko; v. szturchać; przepychać się; zakręcać

elbow grease ('elboł,gri:s) s. ciężka praca; wysiłek

elder ('elder) s. człowiek starszy; adj. starszy (z dwóch);należący do starszyzny

elderly ('elderly) adj. podstarzały; starszy;starszawy

eldest ('eldyst) adj. najstarszy (syn)(w rodzinie)

elect (i'lekt) v. wybrać; postanawiać; decydować; adj.wybrany; wyborny; wyborowy

election (i'lekszyn) s. wybór; wybory (głosowaniem)

elector (i'lekter) s. wyborca; elektor;członek kolegium wyborczego

electric (i'lektryk) adj. elektryczny;bursztynowy;electryzujący

electrical engineer (e'lektrykel,endży'nier) s. inżynier elektryk

electric chair (i'lektryk,cze:r) s. krzesło elektryczne (do egzekucji) (w USA)

electrician (ilek'tryszen) s. elektryk (monter) (instalator)

electricity (ilek'trysyty) s. elektryczność;prąd elektryczny

electrify (i'lektryfaj) v. elektryfikować; elektryzować

electrocute (i'lektrekju:t) v. uśmiercić prądem elektrycznym

electron (i'lektron) s. elektron

elegance ('elygens) s. elegancja

elegant ('elygent) adj. elegancki;dostojny;doskonały

element('elyment) s. żywioł; pierwiastek; część składowa; ogniwo; część podstawowa

elemental (,ely'mentl) adj. żywiołowy; zasadniczy; elementarny; podstawowy;konieczny

elementary (,ely'mentery) adj. elementarny; zasadniczy; niepodzielny; pierwiastkowy

elementary school (,ely'mentery sku:l) s. szkoła powszechna

elephant ('elyfent) s. słoń

elevate ('ely,wejt) v. podnosić; unosić; wynosić (wzwyż)

elevation (ely'wejszyn) s. wysokość; godność; fasada; podwyższenie

elevator ('ely,wejter) s. winda; dźwig; wyciąg; spichlerz

eleven (i'lewn) num. jedenaście; s. jedenastka; jedenaścioro

eleventh (i'lewnt) num. jedenasty; jedenastka

eligible ('elydżebl) adj. nadający się; odpowiedni na wybór

eliminate (i'lymy,nejt) v. usuwać; wydzielać;pozbywać się;nie brać pod uwagę;opuszczać

elimination (i,lymy'nejszyn)
s. eliminacja ;pozbycie się
elk (elk) s. łoś
ell (ell) s. łokiec (miara)
ellipse (i'lyps) s. elipsa
elm (elm) s. wiąz
elongate (i'longejt) v. wydłużać się;adj.wydłużony
elope (i'loup) v. uciekac
z ukochanym (potajemnie)
eloquence ('eloukłens) s. elo-
kwencja; krasomówstwo
eloquent ('elokłent) adj. elo-
kwentny; wymowny(też w piśmie)
else (els) adv.inaczej; bo
inaczej; w przeciwnym razie;
poza tym; jeszcze;adj.różny in-
elsewhere (els'hłer) adv. gdzie
indziej;w innym miejscu
elude (i'lu:d) v. ujść; wymknąc
się;obejść prawo;uchylić się
elusive (ilu:syw) adj. nieuchwytny; wymykający się
emanate ('eme,nejt) v. wydobywać; pochodzić;wydzielać się
emancipate (i'maens,ypejt) v.
wyzwolić; wyemancypować
embalm (im'ba:lm) v. zabalsamo-
wać; napełnić aromatem
embankment (im'baeŋkment) s.
nasyp; grobla; nabrzeże
embargo (em'ba:rgou) s. zakaz
handlowania, wjazdu, wyjazdu
embark (im'ba:rk) v. ładowac
(się); wsiadać (na statek);
rozpoczynać (przedsięwzięcie)
embark upon (im'ba:rk e'pon) v.
rozpoczynać ;przedsięwziąć
embarrass (im'baeres) v. zakłopotanie; wikłać; przeszkadzać;powodować zadłużenie
embarrassing (im'baeresyŋg)
adj. żenujący; kłopotliwy;
krępujący;zawstydzający
embarrassment (im'baeresment)s.
zakłopotanie; powikłanie;
skrępowanie;zaaferowanie
embassy ('embesy) s. ambasada
embed (im'bed) v. osadzić; sadzić;wmurowac;wryć;wkopać
embedded (im'bedyd) adj. osadzo-
ny; wsadzony;wryty;wmurowany
embellish (im'belysz) v. upiększać;ozdabiać;podkolorowywać

embers ('emberz) pl. niewygas-
łe węgle; żar;palące się polana
embezzle (ym'bezl) v. sprzeniewierzać (pieniądze,własność etc.)
embitter (im'byter) v. rozgory-
czać; zatruwać; pogarszać
emblem ('emblem) s. godło; wzor
embody (im'body) v. wcielać;
uosabiać; zawierać;włączać
embolden (im'boulden) v. ośmielać; rozzuchwalać ;dodać śmiałości
embolism (embelyzem) s. zator
embrace (im'brejs) v. uścisnąc
się; obejmować; przystępować:
imać się; korzystać; s. uścisk;
objęcie ;włączenie(do kategorii)
embroider (im'brojder) v. hafto-
wać;wyszywać;upiększać opowiadanie
embroidery (im'brojdery) s. haft;
hafciarstwo;upiększanie opowiadania
emerald ('emereld) s. szmaragd
emerge (y'me:rdż) v. wynurzac
się; wyłaniać;wyniknąć;nasunąć się
emergency (y'me:rdżensy) s.
nagła potrzeba; stan wyjątkowy
emergency brake (y'me:rdżensy,
,brejk) s. ręczny hamulec
w samochodzie;hamulec zapasowy
emergency call (y'me:rdżensy,kol)
s. wzywanie pogotowia (nagłe)
emergency exit (y'me:rdżensy,
,eksyt) s. wyjście zapasowe
emergency landing (y'merdżensy,
, laendyŋg)s. przymusowe lądowanie (samolotu)
emigrant ('emygrent) s. wychodzca; emigrant;adj.wychodzczy
emigrate ('emygrejt) v. emigro-
wać; wywędrować;przeprowadzać się
emigration (,emy'grejszyn) s.
emigracja; wychodżstwo
emigré ('emygrej) s. emigrant
(polityczny);a.emigracyjny(rząd)
eminent ('emynent) adj. dostojny; wybitny; wyniosły; wysoki
eminently ('emynently) adv.
szczególnie; wybitnie;wysoce
emit (y'myt) v. wydawać; wysyłać (swiatło; fale radiowe;
ciepło; opinie); wypuszczać
(banknoty);nadawać(audycje)
emotion (y'mouszyn) s. wzruszenie; emocja; uczucie(miłości,stra-
chu,gniewu,oburzenia,współczucia)

emotional (y'mouszynel) adj.
emocjonalny;poruszający uczucia
emperor ('emperer) s. cesarz
emphasis ('emfesys) s. nacisk;
emfaza;uwypuklenie;uwydatnienie
emphasize ('emfesajz) v. podkreślać; kłaść nacisk;uwypuklać
emphatic (ym'faetyk) adj. dobitny; wyraźny; stanowczy;
emfatyczny;mówiący z naciskiem
empire ('empajer) s. cesarstwo;
imperium ;adj.empirowy
emplacement (yn'plejsment) s.
umiejscowienie; stanowisko
employ (ym'ploj) v. zatrudniać;
używać; zajmować się; poświęcać (czas);posługiwać się
employee (,emploj'i:) s. pracownik;siła (robocza,biurowa...)
employer (em'plojer) s. pracodawca;pracodawczyni;szef
employment (ym'plojment) s. za-
trudnienie; używanie; zajęcie
employment agency (ym'plojment
'ejdżensy) agencja pośrednict-
wa pracy;biuro zatrudnienia
empower (ym'pałer) v. upełnomocnić; upoważniać;umożliwiać
empress ('emprys) s. cesarzowa
emptiness ('emptynys) s. pustka
empty ('empty) adj. pusty; próżny; v. wypróżniać; wysypywać;
wylewać;wpływać(do morza)
emulate ('emjulejt) v. rywalizować; współzawodniczyć
enable (y'nejbl) v. umożliwiać;
upoważniać;dawać możność
enact (y'naekt) v. postanawiać;
uchwalać; grać (rolę); odgrywać (sztukę); uprawomocnić
enamel (y'naemel) s. emalia;
szkliwo(na zębach etc.)
encase (yn'kejs) v. wsadzać do
pochwy; oprawiać;wpakowywać
enchant (yn'czaent) v. zaczarować; oczarować; zachwycać
encircle (yn'se:rkl) v. otaczać;
okalać;okrążać;okrążyć;otoczyć
enclose (yn'klouz) v. ogradzając;
zamykać; dołączać; załączać;
zawierać;okrążyć(wroga)

enclosure (yn'kloużer) s. ogrodzenie; załącznik;ogradzanie
encounter (yn'kaunter) s. spotkanie; potyczka; pojedynek;
v. natknąć się; spotykać się;
potykać się; mieć utarczkę
encourage (yn'ka:rydż) v. zachęcać; ośmielać; popierać;
dodawać odwagi;pomagać
encouragement (yn'ka:rydżment)
s. zachęta; ośmielenie; po-
pieranie;dodanie odwagi
encroach (yn'kroucz) v. wdzierać się; naruszać; wkraczać
na cudze;targnąć się na cudze
encumber (yn'kamber) v. krępować; tarasować; obarczać; za-
wadzać;obciążać(długami etc.)
end (end) s. koniec; cel;
skrzydłowy w nożnej piłce;
v. kończyć (się); skończyć;
dokończyć;położyć kres
endanger (yn'dejndżer) v. narażać na niebezpieczeństwo
endear (yn'dier) v. czynić
drogim; lubianym;przymilać się
endeavor (yn'dewer) v. starać
się; usiłować; s. usiłowanie;
wysiłek; dążenie;zabiegi;próba
ending ('endyng) s. zakończenie; końcówka (wyrazu etc.)
endless ('endlys) adj. niekończący się; nieskończony;
ustawiczny;wieczny;ciągły
endorse (yn'do:rs) v. potwierdzać; popierać; podżyrować;
notować na odwrocie
endow (yn'dał) v. uposażyć;
wyposażyć;ufundować;zapisywać
endurance (yn'djuerens) s. wytrzymałość; cierpliwość
endure (yn'djuer) v. znosić
(ból); cierpieć; wytrzymać;
przetrwać; ostać się
enema ('enyme) s. lewatywa
enemy ('enymy) s. wróg; przeciwnik; adj. wrogi; nieprzyjacielski;przeciwny
energetic (,ene:r'dżetyk) adj.
energiczny; z wigorem
energy ('enerdży) s. energia

enervate ('ene:rwejt) v. osłabiać (nerwowo,na zdrowiu)wyczer-
pywać
enervate (y'ne:rwyt) adj. słaby; bez energii;wyczerpany
enfold (yn'fould) v. zawijac;
obejmować;zapakowywać
enfranchise (un'fraenczajz) v.
wyzwalać; nadawać prawo wyborcze; uwalniać;uwłaszczać
engage (yn'gejdż) v. zajmować;
angażować; skłaniać; ścierać
się;zaręczyć;zobowiązywać się
engaged (yn'gejdżd) adj. zajęty; zaręczony; włączony
engagement (yn'gejdżment) s.
zobowiazanie; zaręczyny
engine ('endżyn) s. silnik;
parowóz; maszyna; motor
engine-driver ('endżyn,drajwer)
s. maszynista (kolejowy)
engineer (,endży'nier) s. inżynier;v.planować;zręcznie prowadzić
engineering (,endży'nieryng)s.
technika; mechanika; inżynieria;zarząd dróg,maszyn etc.
engine trouble ('endżyn'trabl)
s. zepsucie silnika (samocho-
dowego);kłopot z silnikiem
English ('yŋglysz) adj. angielski (język)
english ('yŋglysz) v. uderzyć
piłkę fałszem; s. fałsz; pod-
kręcona piłka; v. zangielszczyć
engorge (yn'go:rdż) v. pożerać
engrave (yn'grejw) v. rytować;
ryć; grawerować;wyryć;wyrytować
engraving (yn'grejwyŋg) s.
sztych;rytownictwo;grawiura
engross (yn'grous) v. pochłaniać; monopolizować (rozmowę)
enigma (y'nygme) s. zagadka
enjoin (yn'dżoyn) v. nakazywać;
zarządzać; zakazywać;zalecać
enjoy (yn'dżoj) v. cieszyć się;
rozkoszować;mieć;posiadać
enjoyment (yn'dżojment) s. uciecha; korzystanie z uprawnie-
nia; rozkosz; przyjemność
enlarge (yn'la:rdż) v. powiększać; poszerzać;zwalniać z ciupy
enlargement (yn'la: rdżment) s.
powiększenie; poszerzenie

enlighten (yn'lajtn) v. oświecać; oswietlać;objaśniać
enlist (yn'lyst) v. zaciągać
(się); werbować;wstępować
enliven (yn'lajwn) v. ożywiać
enmesh (yn'mesz) v. wplatać
(w sieć); usidlać;usidlić
enmity ('enmyty) s. wrogość;
nieprzyjazń;nienawiść
enormous (y'no:rmes) adj. olbrzymi; ogromny; kolosalny
enough (y'naf) adj.,s.& adv.
dosyć; dość;na tyle;nie więcej
enounce (y'nauns) v. ogłaszać;
wymawiać;wypowiadać;wymówić
enquire (yn'kłajer) v. pytać;
dowiadywać się;rozpytywać się
enquiry (yn'kłajry) s, pytanie;
śledztwo;badania;pytanie
enrage (yn'rejdż) v. rozwścieczać;doprowadzać do wściekłości
enraged (yn'rejdżd) adj. rozwścieczony; rozwścieczona
enrapt (yn'raept) adj. zachwycony;pogrążony w zachwycie
enrapture (yn'reapczer) v. zachwycać;oczarowywać;porywać
enrich (yn'rycz) v. wzbogacać;
użyźniać;ozdobić;ozdabiać
enrol(l) (yn'roul) v. zaciągać
(się); zapisywać (się)
ensue (yn'su:) v. wynikać; następować;wypływać (z czegoś)
ensure (yn'szuer) v. zabezpieczać; zapewniać ;asekurować
entangle (yn'taengel) v. gmatwać; wplątać;zmieszać;komplíko-
wać
enter ('enter) v. wchodzić; wpi-
sywać;penetrować;wkładać;wpisywać
enter into ('enter,yntu) v. wdawać się; brać udział;zawierać
enter upon ('enter,apon) v.
wchodzić w posiadanie; przystępować do tematu; zaczynać
enterprise ('enterprajz) s.
przedsięwzięcie; przedsiębiorstwo; przedsiębiorczość
enterprising ('enterprajzyŋg)
adj. przedsiębiorczy;ryzykujący
entertain (,enter'tejn) v. zabawiać; przyjmować; żywić;
nosić się;brać pod uwagę

entertainer (,enter'tejner) s.
artysta (kabaretowy)
entertainment (,enter'tejnment)
s. rozrywka; zabawa; uciecha
enthusiasm (yn'tju:zjaezem)
s. zapał; entuzjazm
enthusiast (yn'tju:zaest) s.
entuzjasta;zapaleniec
enthusiastic (yn'tu:zy'aestyk)
adj. entuzjastyczny;zapalony
entice (yn'tajs) v. znęcic;
zwabić(nagrodą,przyjemnością)
entire (yn'tajer) adj. cały;
całkowity;nietknięty
entirely (yn'tajerly) adv.
całkowicie; jedynie; wyłącz-
nie;kompletnie;niepodzielnie
entitle (yn'tajtl) v. uprawniac;
tytułować; zatytułować;nadawać
entity ('entyty) s. byt; istnienie; jednostka;istota
entraiis ('entrejlz) pl.jelita
wnętrznosci;wnętrze ziemi
entrance ('entrens) s. wejscie;
wstęp(za opłatą);dostęp;wjazd
entrance (,entraens) v. przejmować; wprawiac w trans
entrance fee ('entrens,fi:)
opłata za wstęp;bilet wstępu
entreat (yn'tri:t) v. błagać
entreaty (yn'tri:ty) s. błaganie; usilna prozba
entrust(yn'trast) v. powierzać
entry ('entry) s. wejscie; wpis;
hasło (słownika);uczestnik wys-
entry permit ('entry,per'myt)
pozwolenie wejscia; wjazdu
enumerate (y'nju:merejt) v.
wliczać; sporządzać wykaz
envelop (yn'welep) v. owijac;
otaczac; ogarniac;okryć(cał-
envelope ('enweloup) s. koperta; otoczka;teczka(papierowa)
envenom (yn'wenem) v. zatruwać
enviable ('enwjebl) adj. godzien zazdrosci;godny pażądania
envious (enwjes) adj. zazdrosny; zawistny;pełen zazdrosci
environment (yn'wajerenment)
s. otoczenie; srodowisko
environmental pollution (yn'wa-
jerenmentel pel'u:szyn) za-
nieczyszczanie srodowiska

environs (yn'wajerenz) s. okolice podmiejskie;przedmiescia
envoy ('enwoj) s. wysłannik
envy ('enwy) s. zawisc; zazdrosc; przedmiot zazdrosci
epic ('epyk) adj. epicki;
s. epos(o bohaterstwie)
epidemic (,epy'demyk) s. epi-
demia; adj. epidemiczny
epidermis (,epy'de:rmys) s. na-
skorek; skora(powierzchnia)
epilepsy ('epylepsy) s. epileps-
ja; padaczka
epilog(ue) ('epylog) s. epilog
episode ('epysoud) s. epizod
epitaph ('epytaef) s. napis
na grobie(ku pamięci zmarłego)
epoch (i:'pok) s. epoka
equal ('i:kłel) adj. rowny;
jednaki; jednakowy; jednostajny; zrownoważony; s. rowny
(stanem); v. rownać się; do-
równywać; wyrównywać;wyrównywać
equality (i'kłolyty) s. rownosc
equalize (i'kłelajz) v. wyrównywać; rownać;zrownywać(się)
equanimity (,i:kłe'nymyty) s.
opanowanie; spokój; rownowaga
equate (i'kłejt) v. rownać;
przyrównywać;stawiać na równi
equation (i'kłejżyn) s. rowna-
nie; równoważenie;bilansowanie
equator (i'kłejter) s. rownik
equilibrium (,i:kły'lybrjem) s.
rownowaga
equip (i'kłyp) v. wyposażać;
zaopatrywać;uzbrajać;ekwipować
equipment (i'kłypment) s. wyposażenie; ekwipunek;sprzęt
equitable ('ekłytebl) adj.
słuszny; sprawiedliwy
equivalent (i'kływelent) adj.
równowartosciowy; równoznaczny; równej wielkości;s.rowno-
era ('yere) s. era ważnik
erase (y'rejz) v. wycierać;
wymazywać;zatrzeć;zacierać
erect (y'rekt) adj. prosty; wy-
prężony; najeżony;v.budować;sta-
wiac
erection (y'rekszyn) s. podniesienie; wyprostowanie; najeże-
nie; erekcja; budowla; montaż

erosion (y'rouźyn) s. wyźera-
nie; źłobienie; erozja
ermine ('e:rmyn) s. gronostaj
erotic (y'rotyk) adj. erotyczny; miłosny; s. erotyk; ero-
toman; wiersz erotyczny
err (e:r) v. błądzić; być
w błędzie;grzeszyc; zgrzeszyć
errand ('erand) s. posyłka;
zlecenie; cel;sprawunek
erratic (y'raetyk) adj. błędny;
nieobliczalny;dziwny;s.dziwak
erroneous (y'rounjes) adj.
błędny;mylny;fałszywy
error ('erer) s. błąd
erudite ('erudajt) adj. uczony; s. erudyta (b.oczytany etc.)
erupt (y'rapt) v. wybuchać;
wyrzucać;przerzynać (się);
wysypywać się;wybuchać lawa,
eruption (y'rapszyn) s. wybuch;
przerzynanie się; wysypka
escalation (,eske'lejszyn) s.
wzmożenie;rozszerzenie się
escalator ('eskelejter) s. ru-
chome schody; ruchoma skala
płac(wg. kosztów utrzymania etc.)
escape (ys'kejp) s. ucieczka;
wyciekanie; wchodzenie;ocalenie;
v. wymknąć się; zbiec; wyjść
cało; uchodzić;ratować się uciec-
ką
escort, ('esko:rt) s. eskorta;
konwój; mężczyzna towarzyszą-
cy kobiecie; kawaler;v.eskorto-
wać
escort (i'sko:rt) v. eskortować
especial, (ys'peszel) adj.
szczególny; wyjątkowy; specjalny; szczególny; główny
especially (ys'peszely) adv.
szczególnie; zwłaszcza
espionage (,espje'na:dż) s. wywiad; szpiegostwo;szpiegowanie
esprit (es'pri:) s. żywość; życie; dowcip;silne poczucie humoru
espy (ys'paj) v. spostrzegać;
wyśledzić;wykombinować
essay ('esej) s. esej; szkic
literacki; próba; v. próbować;
wypróbować;poddać próbie
essence ('esens) s. esencja;
istota czegoś; wyciąg; treść
istotna treść;sedno sprawy;olej

essential (y'senszel) adj. niezbędny; istotny; zasadniczy;
zupełny; eteryczny; s. cecha
istotna, nieodzowna, zasadni-
cza;rzecz podstawowa,konieczna
establish (ys'taeblysz) v. zakładać; osadzać; ustalać;
wprowadzać;udowodnić;ufundować
establishment (yz'taeblyszment)
s. założenie; osadzenie; ustalenie; ustanowienie; zakład;
gospodarstwo;koła rządzące;
organizacja państwowa lub wojskowa;firma;przedsiębiorstwo
estate (ys'tejt) s. majątek;
stan majątkowy;położenie w życiu
estate tax (ys'tejt,taeks) s.
podatek spadkowy (majątkowy)
esteem (ys'ti:m) v. cenić;
szanować; poważać; s. poważanie; szacunek;dobra opinia
estimate ('estymejt) v. oceniać;
szacować; s. szacunek; kosztorys; ocena;opinia;oszacowanie
estimation (,esty'mejszyn) s.
szacowanie; poważanie; szacunek;zdanie;mniemanie;sąd
estrange (ys'trejndż) v. od-
stręczać; zrażać;zniechęcać
estray (ys'trej) s. stworzenie
bezpańskie; zgubione
estuary ('estjuery) s. ujście
(rzeki) do morza (oceanu)
eternal (y'ternl) adj. wieczny;
odwieczny;bez początku i końca
eternity (y'ternyty) s. wiecz-
ność;trwnie bez końca i odpoczyn-
ku
ether ('i:ter) s. eter
ethics ('etyks) pl. etyka
ethnic ('etnyk) adj. etniczny;
pogański;odrębny zwyczajami i je-
etymology (,ety'moledży) s. ety-
mologia;pochodzenie i rozwój słów
eulogy ('ju:ledży) s, mowa
pochwała (pogrzebowa)
eunuch ('ju:nek) n. eunuch;
rzezaniec;człowiek wykastrowany
European (,ju:re'pi:en) adj.
europejski; s. Europejczyk
evacuate (y'waekjuejt) v. ewa-
kuować; opróżniać; wypróżniać;
wydalać;usuwać; wycofywać się

evacuation (y,waejku'ejszyn) s.
ewakuacja; wypróżnienie (się)
evade (y'wejd) v. ujść; uniknąć; obchodzic; wymykac się;
wykręcać się; pomijać
evaluate (y'waeljuejt) v. obliczać; oceniać; analizować
evaporate (y'waeperejt) v. parować; ulatniac się; poddawać
parowaniu;wyparowywac;umrzec
evasion (y'wejżyn) v. uniknięcie; wymknięcie się; obejście;
wykręt;oszustwo(podatkowe);wykręt
evasive (y'wejsyw) adj. wykrętny; wymijający; nieuchwytny
eve (i:w) s. wilia; wigilia
even ('i:wen) adj. równy;
jednolity; parzysty; adv. nawet; v. równać; wyrównać;
zemscic się;wygładzać;ujednostaj
even-handed ('i:wen,haendyd) adj.
sprawiedliwy; bezstronny
evening ('i:wnyng) s. wieczór
evening dress ('i:wnyn, dres)s.
strój wieczorowy
evening paper ('i:wnyn'pejper)
gazeta wieczorna
evensong ('i:wensong) s. nieszpory; pieśń wieczorna
event (y'went) s. wydarzenie;
możliwość; wynik; rezultat; zawody (sportowe);konkurencja
eventful(y'wentful) adj. burzliwy; pamiętny; pełen wydarzeń
eventual (y'wenczuel) adj.
w końcu pewny
eventually (y'wenczuely) adv.
w końcu napewno
ever ('ewer) adv. w ogóle; niegdyś;kiedyś; jak tylko; ile tylko; kiedykolwiek;jeszcze wciąż
ever after (,ewer'after) do tego czasu;już od tego czasu
ever since (,ewer'syns) od tego
czasu ; od kiedy (był etc.)
everlasting (,ewer'lastyng)adj.
wieczny; ciągły; nieustanny
evermore ('ewer'mi:re) adv.
zawsze; na zawsze; na wieki
every ('ewry) adj. każdy; wszelki; co(dzień, noc, rano etc.)
every other day ('ewry,odzer'dej)
co drugi dzień

everybody ('ewrybody) pron.
każdy; wszyscy(ludzie)
everyday ('ewrydej) adj. codzienny; powszedni; zwykły
everyone ('ewryłan) pron.
każdy; wszyscy;każda rzecz
everything ('ewrytyng) pron.
wszystko (co jest, etc.)
everywhere ('ewryhłer) adv.
wszędzie; gdziekolwiek
evidence ('ewydens) s. znak;
dowód; świadectwo; oczywistość;
jasność; v. świadczyć; dowodzic (czegoś);manifestować
evident ('ewydent) adj. oczywisty; widoczny;jawny;jasny
evil ('i:wl) adj. zły;fatalny
evildoer ('i:wl-duer) s.
złoczyńca
evince (y'wyns) v, wykazywać;
okazywać (życzenie);przejawiac
evoke (y'wouk) v. wywoływać;
wydobywac; zdobywać (odpowiedź)
evolution (,ewe'lu:szyn) s.
rozwój; ewolucja; rozwinięcie
(się); pierwiastkowanie
evolve (y'wolw) v. rozwijać;
wypracowywać; wytwarzać (ciepło etc.);rozwijać się stopniowo
ewe (ju:) s. owca
ex-(eks) pref. były; była;
prep. bez; ze; s. (litera)"x"
exacerbate (eks'aeserbejt) v.
draznic; pogorszyc; irytowac
exact (yg'zaekt) adj. dokładny;
scisły; v. wymagać; sciągać;
egzekwować ;wymuszać
exactitude (yg'zaektytju:d)s.
scisłość; dokładność;punktualność
exactly (yg'zaektly) adv. dokładnie; scisle; własnie;
zgadza się ;punktualnie; ostro
exactness (yg'zaektnys) s. dokładność; precyzja
exaggerate (yg'zaedżerejt) v.
przesadzać; wyolbrzymiac
exaggeration (yg'zaedże'rejszyn)
s. przesada; wyolbrzymienie
exalt (yg'zo:lt) v. wywyższac;
podnosic ;wychwalać;chwalić
exam (yg'zaem) s. egzamin
(slang); klasówka; egzamin w
szkole lub na universitecie

examination (yg,zaemy'nejszyn)
s. egzamin; badanie;rewizja
examine (yg'zaemyn) v. badac;
sprawdzac; egzaminowac; rozpatrywac; rewidowac; przesłuchiwac;przeprowadzac śledztwo
example (yg'za:mpl) s. przykład; wzór; precedens
exasperate (yg'za:sperejt) v.
rozjątrzac; rozgoryczac; pogarszac; powodowac rozpacz
excavate ('ekskewejt) v. kopac; odkopac; wykopac; drą-
życ;pogłębiac;wybierac(ziemię)
exceed (yk'si:d) v. przewyższac; celowac; przekraczac
exceedingly (ek'si:dynly) adv.
niezmiernie; nadzwyczajnie
excel (yk'sel) v. przewyższac;
wybijac się; celowac(w czyms)
excellence (yk'selens) s. wyż-
szosc; doskonałosc; zaleta
excellent (yk'selent) adj. doskonały; wyborny;świetny;celuja-
except (yk'sept) conj. chyba
że...; żeby;oprucz;poza;wyjąwszy
except (yk'sept) v. wykluczac;
wyłączac; prep. z wyjątkiem;
pomínawszy; wyjąwszy;chyba że
exception (yk'sepszyn) s. wyjątek; wyłączenie; zarzut;obiekcja
exceptional(yk'sepszenl) adj.
nadzwyczajny; wyjątkowy
excess (yk'ses) s. nadmiar;
nadwyżka;a.nadmierny;nad-
excess fare(yk'ses,fe:r) s. dopłata do biletu
excessive (yk'sesyw) adj. nadmierny;zbytni;nieumiarkowany
excess luggage (yk'ses,lagydż)
nadwyżka bagażu
exchange (yks'czendż) s. wymiana; zamiana; giełda; centrala
telefoniczna; v. wymienic;_łtowy
zamienic (się);a.wymienny;walu-
excitable (yk'sajtebl) adj. pobudliwy;pobudzajacy;podniecaja-
excite (yk'sajt) v. pobudzac;
podniecac;prowokowac
excited (yk'sajtyd) adj. podniecony; zdenerwowany

excitement (yk'sajtment)
podniecenie; zdenerwowanie
exciting (yk'sajtyng) adj.
emocjonujący; pasjonujący
exclaim (yks'klejm) v. zawołac;
wykrzyknąc; zaprotestowac
exclamation (,ekskla'mejszyn)
s. okrzyk; krzyk; wykrzyknik
exclamation mark (,ekskla'mejszyn,ma:rk) wykrzyknik
exclude (yks'klu:d) v. wykluczac; wydalac; usuwac
exclusion (yks'klu:żyn) n.
wykluczenie; wydalenie; usunięcie; wyłączenie
exclusive (yks'klu:syw) adj.
modny; wykluczający; wyłączny;
jedyny ; ekskluzywny
excursion (yks'ker:żyn) s. wycieczka;dygresje;a.wycieczkowy
excuse (yks'kju:z) v. usprawiedliwiac; przepraszac; darowac; zwalniac; s. usprawiedliwienie; wymówka ;pretekst
excuse me (yks'kju:z,mi)
przepraszam; przepraszam pana
excusable (iks'kju:zebl) adj.
usprawiedliwiony;wybaczalny
execute ('eksykju:t) v. wykonac (wyrok, plan); stracic
execution (,eksy'kju:szyn) s.
wykonanie; egzekucja;stracenie
executive (yg'zekjutyw) adj.
wykonawczy; s. władza wykonaw-
cza; stanowisko kierownicze
exemplary (yg'zemplery) adj.
wzorowy; przykładny; przykła-
dowy;wymierzony dla odstraszenia
exempt (yg'zempt) v. zwalniac;
adj. wolny; zwolniony; s. osoba zwolniona;człowiek zwolniony
exercise ('eksersajz) s. ćwiczenie; wykonywanie (zawodu);
korzystanie; v, ćwiczyc; używac;
wykonywac;spełniac;pełnic
exercise book ('eksersajs,buk)
s. zeszyt (szkolny)
exert (yg'ze:rt) v. wytężac
(się); wysilac (się); wywierac
(nacisk, wpływ, etc);zabiegac

exertion (yg'ze:rszyn) s. wytężenie; wysiłek; wywieranie
exhale (eks'hejl) v. wyziewać; wydychać; zionąć; parować
exhaust (yg'zo:st) v. wydychać; wyczerpywać; wyciągać; wypróżniać; odgazować; s. wydech; wydmuch; rura wydechowa; opróżnianie (z powietrza); aspirator;rura wydechowa(auta)
exhaust fumes (yg'zo:st,fjums) gazy wydechowe(z motoru)
exhaustion (yg'zo:stszyn) s. wyczerpanie; opróżnienie; zużycie; pochłonięcie;zmęczenie
exhaust-pipe (yg'zo:st,pajp) s. rura wydechowa (w aucie)
exhibit(yg'zybyt) s. wystawa; pokaz; eksponaty; v. wystawiać; okazywać; pokazywać; wykazywać; popisywać się czyms;przedkładać;mieć wystawę
exhibition(,eksy'byszyn) s. wystawa; wystawianie; pokazywanie;pokaz; widowisko;popis
exhibitor(yg'zybyter) s. wystawca; wystawczyni
exile ('eksajl) s. wygnanie; tułaczka; emigracja; wygnaniec; v. wygnać na banicję
exist (yg'zyst) v. istniec;być; żyć; egzystować ;zdarzać się
existence (yg'zystens) s. istnienie; byt; egzystencja
existent (yg'zystent) a. istniejący;będący;znajdujący się
exit ('eksyt) s. wyjscie; odejscie; ujscie; wylot; swobodne wyjscie; v, wychodzic; kończyć (slang);schodzić ze sceny
exit visa ('eksyt,wyza) s. wiza wyjazdowa
expand (yks'paend) v. rozszerzac; powiększac; wzrastać; rozprężac; rozwijać; rozruszac;rozpościerać;powiększać
expanse (yks'paens) s. bezmiar; rozległa przestrzeń; ekspansja
expansion (yks'paenszyn) s. rozszerzanie; rozprężanie się; ekspansja; rozpościeranie; rozwijanie (się);ilość ekspansji

expansive (yks'paensyw) adj. rozszerzalny; rozległy; rozprężalny; obszerny; wylewny
expect (yks'pekt) v. spodziewać się; przypuszczać;zgadywać
expectation (,ekspek'tejszyn) s. oczekiwanie; nadzieja; widoki;prospekt;przewidywanie
expedient (yks'pi:djent) adj. celowy; wygodny; oportunistyczny; korzystny; s. środek; zabieg; sposób;wybieg;fortel
expedition (,ekspy'dyszyn) s. wyprawa; ekspedycja; sprawność; szybkość;pośpiech;marsz do akcji
expel (yks'pel) v. wypędzać; wydalać; usuwać; wyrzucać
expend (yks'pend) v. wydawać; zużywać;poświęcać czas etc.
expense (yks'pens) s. koszt; wydatek;rachunek;strata;ofiara
expensive (yks'pensyw) adj. drogi; kosztowny;wysoko wyceniony
experience (yks'pierjens) s. doświadczenie; przeżycie; v. doświadczać; doznawać; dzić poznać (coś);przeżywać;przecho-
experienced (yks'pierjenst) adj. doswiadczony;doznany
experiment (yks'peryment) s. próba; eksperyment; doświadczenie; v. eksperymentować; robić doświadczenia
expert ('ekspe:rt) s. biegły; ekspert; znawca; adj. biegły; światły;mistrzowski;wykonany przez eksperta
expiration (,ekspi'rejszyn) s. wygaśnięcie: upłynięcie; wydech; wyzionięcie ducha;smierć
expire (yks'pajer) v. wygasać; upływać; wydychać; wyzionąć ducha;umierać;kończyć się
explain (yks'plejn) v. wyjasnic; objasnić; wytłumaczyć
explanation (,eks'plaenejszyn) s. wyjasnienie; wytłumaczenie
explicable ('eksplykebl) adj. dający się wyjasnić
explicit (yks'plysyt) adj. jasny; wyrazny; szczery; otwarty;definitywny;wygadany

explode (yks'ploud) v. wybuchać; explodować; demaskować (fałsz) ;obalić(teorię etc.)
exploit (yks'ploit) v. użytkować; exploatować; wyzyskiwać
exploit ('eksploit) s. wyczyn
exploration (,eksplo:'rejszyn) s. poszukiwanie; badanie
explore (yks'plo:r) v. badać; sondować;wybadać;przebadać
explorer (yks'plo:rer) s. badacz; sonda ;odkrywca;odkrywczyni
explosion (yks'ploużyn) s. explozja; wybuch (kłótni etc.)
explosive (yks'plousyw) s, materiał wybuchowy; adj. wybuchowy;mogący wybuchnąć
exponent (yks'pounent) adj. interpretujący; s. eksponent; wyraziciel; interpretator; wykładnik (potęgi);przedstawiciel
export (yks'po:rt) v. wywozić; eksportować; s. wywóz; eksport; towar wywozowy;wywożenie
expose (yks'pouz) v. wystawiać (na wpływ); poddawać (czemuś); odsłaniać; demaskować; eksponować; naświetlać; porzucać (dziecko);zrobić zdjęcie
exposé (,ekspou'zej) s. zdemaskowanie; odsłonięcie skandalu
exposition (,ekspe'zyszyn) s. wystawa; wykład; przedstawienie; wyjaśnienie; opis; naświetlenie; ekspozycja; po—rzucenie (dziecka)
exposure (yks'poużer) s. wystawienie (na zimę. etc); ujawnienie; zdemaskowanie; naświetlenie;jedno zdjęcie na filmie
exposuremeter (yks'poużer'mi:ter) s. swiatłomierz
expound (yks'paund) v. wykładać; wyjaśnić szczegółowo;przedstawić
express (yks'pres) s. ekspres; przesyłka pospieszna; adj. wyraźny; umysłny; dokładny; adv. pospiesznie;expresem
expression (yks'preszyn) s. wyrażenie; wyraz; ekspresja; ton; wydawanie; wytłoczenie;zwrot wyciśnięcie;wyżymanie

expressive (yks'presyw) adj. wyrażający; wyrazisty: ekspresyjny;pełen wyrazu
expressly (yks'presly) adv.wyraźnie; kategorycznie; naumyślnie;specjalnie;formalnie
express way (yks'pres,łej) s. drogą przelotcwa (bez skrzyżowań jednopoziomowych)
expulsion (yks'palszyn) s. wydalenie; wyrzucenie; wypędzenie;wygnanie;wyparcie
exquisite ('ekskłyzyt) adj. wyborowy; wyborny; wysmienity; nadzwyczajny; ostry; przeszywający;s.laluś;goguś;pięknis
extent ('ekstent) adj. pozostały; jeszcze istniejący
extemporaneous (eks,tempe'rejnjes) adj. zaimprowizowany
extend (yks'tend),v wyciągać (się); rozciągać (się);przeciągać (się); rozszerzac (się); dawać i udzielać; przedłużać; powiększać;rozpościerać się
extendible (yks'tendybl) adj. rozszerzalny; rozciągalny
extension (yks'tenszyn) s. rozciąganie; wyciąganie; rozwinięcie; przedłużenie; zasięg; rozmiar; zakres ;skrzydło(domu)
extensive (yks'tensyw) adj. obszerny; rozległy ;ekstensywny
extent (yks'tent) s. obszar; rozmiar; zasięg; miara; stopień; wysokość ;oszacowanie
extenuate (yks'tenjnejt) v. zmniejszać; łagodzić
exterior (eks'tierjer) s. powierzchowność; wygląd zewnętrzny; strona zewnętrzna ;fasada
exterminate (yks'te:rmynejt) v. tępić (np; pogląd);wyniszczyć
external (eks'te:rnal) adj. zewnętrzny; zagraniczny
extinct (yks'tyŋkt) adj. wygasły; zgasły ;zanikły;wymarły
extinguish (yks'tyŋgłysz) v. zgasić; zagasić; niszczyć; unicestwić; umierać ;tępić
extirpate ('ekster,pejt)v. wykorzeniać;plewić; tępić

extol (yks'tol) v. wysławiac; wynosic pod niebiosa

extort (yks'tort) v. wymuszac; zdzierac(pieniadze);wydrzec

extra ('ekstre) adj. specjalny; dodatkowy; luksusowy; nadzwyczajny; ponad normę; adv. nadzwyczajnie; dodatkowo; s. dodatek; dopłata; rzecz szczególnie dobra;statysta

extra charge ('ekstre,cha:rdż) s. dopłata;nadpłata

extract ('ekstraekt) s. wyciąg; ekstrat;wyjątek;wypis

extract (yks'traekt) v. wyciągac; wydobywac; wypisywac

extraction (eks'traekszyn) s. wyciągnięcie; wydobycie; wyrwanie (zęba); pochodzenie;ród

extradite ('ekstredajt) v. wydawac (przestępcę przez granicę)do miejsca zbrodni

extraordinary (yks'tro:rdnery) adj. niezwykły; nadzwyczajny

extravagance (yks'traewygens) s. przesada; rozrzutnosc; nieumiarkowanie; głupstwo; niedorzecznosc; ekstrawagancja

extravagant (yks'traewegent) adj. rozrzutny; przesądny; zwariowany;wygórowany;szalony

extravaganza (yks,traeve'gaenze) s. ekstrawagancja;fantazja

extreme (yks'tri:m) adj. skrajny; krancowy; najdalszy; ostatni; s. kraniec; ostateczna granica; ostatecznosc;skrajnosc

extremity (yks'tremyty) s. koniec; kraniec; skrajnosc; krancowosc; kończyna; krytyczne położenie;potrzeba;ostatecznosc

extrude (yks'tru:d) v. wypierac; wyrzucac; przeciągac lub ciągnąc odlew;wytłoczyc

exuberant (yg'zju:berent) adj. wybujały; pełen życia; kwitnący; wylewny; płodny; obfity

exult (yg'zalt) v. triumfowac; unosic się radoscią

eye (aj) s. oko;wzrok;v.patrzec

eyeball ('ajbo:l) s. gałka oczna w oczodołach za powiekami

eyeball to eyeball ('ajbo:l,tu 'ajbo:l) oko w oko

eyebrow ('ajbrau) s. brew

eyeglasses ('ajgla:sys) pl. okulary;lupy;monokle

eyelash ('ajlaesz) s. rzęsa

eyelid ('ajlyd) s. powieka

eyesight ('aj-sajt) s. wzrok

eyewash ('ajłosz) s. woda do oczu; mydlenie oczu (slang)

eyewitness ('aj'łytnes) s. swiadek naoczny

f (ef) szósta litera angielskiego alfabetu; stopien "f" failure = niedostatecznie

fable (fejbl) s. bajka

fabric ('faebryk) s. tkanina; materiał; osnowa; szkielet; budowa; wytwór;a.sukienny

fabricate ('faebrykejt) v. tworzyc; wymyslac; zmyslac; montowac;wyssac z palca;sfałszowac

fabulous ('faebjules) adj. bajeczny;legendarny;fantastyczny

facade (fe'sa:d) s. fasada

face (fejs) s. twarz; oblicze; mina; grymas; czelnosc; smiałosc; powierzchnia lica; prawa strona; obuch; v. stawiac czoła; stanąc wobec; napotykac; stac frontem do..; wykładac powierzchnię;oblicowac

face-lifting ('fejs-lyftyng) v. operacyjnie usuwac zmarszczki

facetious (fe'si:szes) adj. żartobliwy;krotochwilny

facilitate (fe'sylytejt) v. ułatwiac ; udogadniac;uprzystępniac

facility (fe'sylyty) s. łatwosc; zręcznosc; udogodnienia; układnosc; swada;zgodnosc

fact (faekt) s. fakt; stan rzeczywisty;podstawa twierdzenia

factor ('faekter) s. czynnik; współczynnik; częsc;okolicznosc

faculty ('faekelty) s. zdolnosc; władza; wydział; fakultet; grono profesorskie;dar; zmysł

fad (faed) s. moda; kaprys;konik; bzik;chwilowa moda;dziwactwo

fade (fejd) v. więdnąc; blednąc; zanikac;płowiec;pełznąc fail (feil) v. chybić; zawodzić; nie udać się; brakować; bankrutować; omieszkać; słabnąć; załamać się; zamierać;zepsuć się; failure ('fejljer) s. niepowodzenie; brak; upadek; zawał (serca); niezdara; stopień niedostateczny; pechowiec

faint (fejnt) adj. słaby; omdlały; bojaźliwy; s. omdlenie; v. mdleć; słabnąć;zasłabnąć

fair (feer) adj. piękny; jasny; uczciwy; honorowy; czysty; pomyślny; niezły; adv. prosto; honorowo; pomyślnie; pięknie; v. wypogadzać się; wygładzać; przepisywać na czysto; s. targ; targi; jarmark;targowisko

fairly ('feerly) adv. słusznie; uczciwie; całkowicie; zupełnie; dość;rzetelnie;wręcz;poprostu

fairplay ('feer'plej) szlachetne postępowanie;czysta gra

fairness ('feernys) s. piękność; jasność; sprawiedliwość; bezstronność; uczciwość;uroda

fairy ('feery) s. czarodziejka; adj. zaczarowany;czarodziejski

fairy-tale ('ferrytejl) s. bajka

faith (fejs) s. wiara; zaufanie; wierność; wyznanie;słowność

faithful ('fejsful) adj. wierny; uczciwy;sumienny;skrupulatny

faithless ('fejslys) adj. niewierny; wiarołomny;zdradziecki

fake (fejk) v. fałszować; oszukiwać; podrabiać; s. fałszerstwo; oszustwo;kant;lipa;szwindel

falcon ('fo:lken) s. sokół

fall; fell; fallen (fo:l; fel: fo:len)

fall (fo:l) v. padać; opadać; wpadać; marnieć; zdarzać się; przypadać; s. upadek; spadek; jesień;opad;schyłek;obniżka

fall back ('fo:l, baek) v. cofać się

fall ill ('fo:l,yl) v. zachorować ;rozchorować się

fall in love ('fo:l,yn'law) v. zakochać się

fallout ('fo:laft) s. skutek uboczny; pył radioaktywny; wrażenie na publiczności i prasie(z wypowiedzi,planów)

fall out ('fo:l,aft) v. poroznić się; rozejść się! (komenda)

fall short ('fo:l,szo:rt) v. nieosiągnąć; niewywiązać się

fallen ('fo:len) upadły; zob. fall

false (fo:ls) adj. fałszywy; kłamliwy;adv.zdradliwie;fałszywie

falsehood ('fo:lshud) s. fałsz; kłamstwo;nieprawda;kłamliwość

falsify ('fo:lsyfaj) v. fałszować; przekręcać; kłamać; zawodzić;podrabiać;oszukać

falter ('fo:lter) v. chwiać się; wahać się; potykać się; jąkać się; s. chwiejność; jąkanie

fame (fejm) s. sława; wieść;fama

famed (fejmd) adj. sławny; znany; głośny; słynący z

familiar (fe'myljer) adj. zażyły; poufały; znany; obeznany

familiarity (fe,myly'aeryty) s. zażyłość; poufałość; obeznanie;znajomość;zażyłość

familiarize (fe'myljerajz) v. obeznać; obznajomić; oswoić; spoufalić;spopularyzować

family ('faemyly) s. rodzina; adj. rodzinny

family name ('faemyly,nejm) s. nazwisko

family tree ('faemyly,tri:) s. drzewo genealogiczne

famine ('faemyn) s. głód; klęska głodu; ogólne braki wszystkiego

famish ('faemysz) v. głodzić; wygłodnieć; głodować;morzyć głodem

famous ('fejmes) adj. znany; jaki sławny;znakomity; świetny;nie byle

fan (faen) v. wachlować; rozdmuchiwać; wiać; rozpościerać; wywiewać; s. wachlarz; wentylator; wialnia; żagiel i śmigło (wiatraka); entuzjasta; miłośnik;kibic;a.wachlarzowaty

fanatic (fe'naetyk) adj. zagorzały; fanatyczny; s, fanatyk

fanciful ('faensyful) adj. dziwaczny; kaprysny; fantastyczny;zmyslony;wyszukany;fantazyjny
fancy ('faensy) s. urojenie;
zludzenie; fantazja; kaprys;
humor; pomysl; chetka;a.pstry...
fancy dress ball('faensy'fres,
,bo:l) s. bal kostiumowy
fancy-free ('faensy,fri:) adj.
wolny od trosk; niezakochany
fancywork ('faensy,le:rk) s.
robotki reczne
fang (faeng) s. zab jadowity;
kiel;sztyft;korzen;v.dlawic pom-
fantastic (faen'taestyk) adj. pe
fantastyczny;s.fantastyk
far (fa:r) adv. daleko
far away ('fa:r,elej) adv.
hen; daleko;adj.daleki;odlegly
far from ('fa:r,from) adv. bynajmniej; daleko od
fare (feer) s. pasazer; bilet
pasazerski; pozywienie; potrawa; v, byc w polozeniu. miec
sie; wiesc sie; czuc sie; od-
zywiac sie; jadac; podrozowac
farewell (,feer'lel) s. pozeg-
nanie; adj. pozegnalny;
v. zegnaj; do widzenia
farfetched (,fa:r'feczt) adj.
przesadny; naciagany; wyszukany;nierozsadny
far-flung (,fa:r'flang) adj.
szeroko rozrzucony; rozgale-
ziony;zakrojony na szeroka skale
farm (fa:rm) s. ferma; gospodarstwo rolne; kolonia hodowlana;
v. uprawiac; dzierzawic; wy-
dzierzawiac; wynajmowac; pod-stwo
dzierzawiac;prowadzic gospodar-
farmer ('fa:rmer) s. rolnik;
farmer; dzierzawca;hodowca
farmhand ('fa:rm,haend) s. parobek;robotnik rolny
farmhouse ('fa:rm,haus) s. dworek; gospodarski dom mieszkalny
farming ('fa:rmyng)s. rolnictwo;
gospodarka rolna; dzierzawa
farm worker (,fa:rm'le:rker) s.
robotnik rolny; parobek
farmyard ('fa:rm,ja:rd) s. pod-
worze fermy;podworze gospodar-
skie na fermie

farsighted ('fa:r'sajtyd) adj.
przewidujacy; dalekowidz;
dalekowzroczny;dalekowidz
farther('fa:rdzer) adj. dalszy;
adv. dalej;ponadto;poza tym; procz-tego
farthest ('fa:rdzest) adj. najdalszy; adv. najdalej;najpozniej
fascinate ('faesynejt) v. urze-
kac; czarowac; fascynowac;
hipnotyzowac;zachwycic
fascination (,faesy'nejszyn) s.
urok; czar;oczarowanie;olsnienie
fascist ('faeszyst) s. faszysta;
adj. faszystowski;faszystowska
fashion ('faeszyn) s. moda; fason; ksztalt; wzor; sposob;
v. ksztaltowac; fasonowac;
modelowac; urabiac
fashionable ('faesznebl) adj.
modny; s. czlowiek wytworny
fast (faest) adj. szybki; przy-
twierdzony; mocny; twardy;
zwodniczy; adv. mocno; pewnie;
trwale; v. poscic; s. post
fasten ('faesn) v. umocowac;
zamykac;przymocowac
fastener ('faesner) s. przymocowanie (np. gwozdz); spinacz
zatrzask; zasuwka
fastidious (fes'tydjes) adj.
wybredny; grymasny; wymagajacy
fat (faet) s. tluszcz ; tusza;
adj. tlusty; tuczny; glupi;
tepy;urodzajny;zyskowny
fatal ('fejtl) adj. fatalny;
smiertelny; nieuchronny
fate ('fejt) s. los; przeznaczenie; zguba;fatum;v.los rzadzi...
father ('fa:dzer) s. ojciec
fatherhood ('fa:dzerhud) s.
ojcostwo;starszenstwo(w sluzbie)
father-in-law ('fa:dzerynlo:) s.
tesc;ojciec meza lub zony
fatherland ('fa:dzerlaend) s.
ojczyzna; ojczysty kraj
fatherly ('fa:dzerly) adj. oj-
cowski;jak ojciec;dobrotliwy
fathom ('faedzem) s. sazen
fathomless ('faedzemlys) s. bez-
denny; niezglebiony
fatigue (fe'ti:g) s. zmeczenie
(czlowieka lub materialu);sluz-
ba porzadkowa;v.trudzic;meczyc

fatten ('faetn) v. tuczyć; tyć;
urzyźniać ziemie: utyć;utuczyc
faucet ('fo:syt) s. kurek (od
wody); czop; tuleja
fault ('fo:lt) s. błąd; wada;
wina; uskok; usterka;brak;defekt
faultless ('fo:ltlys) adj. bezbłędny; nienaganny;doskonały
faulty ('fo:lty) adj. wadliwy;
nieprawidłowy;niescisły;błędny
favor ('fejwer) s. łuska;uprzej-
mość; upominek; v. sprzyjać;
zaszczycać; faworyzować
favorable ('fejwerebl) adj. życzliwy; łaskawy; sprzyjający;
korzystny(dla kagoś,czegoś)
favorite ('fejweryt) s. ulubieniec; faworyt; adj. ulubiony
fawn (fo:n) v. ocielić; łasić
się; przymilać (się); s. je-
lonek; sarenka; adj. brunatny;
płowy;płaszczyć się(przed kimś)
fear (fier) s. strach; obawa;
v. bać się; obawiać się
fearful ('fierful) adj. okropny;
straszny; wystraszony; bojaźliwy; bojący się;pełen strachu
fearless ('fierlys) adj. nieustraszony;bardzo odważny
feast (fi:st) s. święto; odpust;
biesiada; v. ucztować; sycić
się; ugaszczać pragnienie
feat (fi:t) s. wyczyn; czyn
(bohaterski);(dokazana)sztuka
feather ('fedzer) s. pioro;
v. zdobić piorami
featherbed ('fedzerbed) s. piernat;pierzyna;lekka praca
feathered ('fedzerd) adj. upie-
rzony; pokryty piorami
feathery ('fedzery) adj. pucho-
waty; miękki jak puch:leciutki
feature ('fi:czer) s. cecha;
rys; atrakcja; film długo-
metrażowy;v.cechować;odgrywac
February ('februery) s. luty
fed (fed) adj. karmiony; zob.
feed
federal ('federel) adj. związkowy; federalny
federation (,fede'rejszyn) s.
federacja; konferencja

fee (fi:) s. opłata; wpisowe;
należność; honorarium; v. płacić honorarium;płacić wpisowe
feeble ('fi:bl) adj. słaby
feed: fed; fed (fi:d; fed; fed)
feed (fi:d) v. karmić; paść;
zasilać; s. pasza; obrok; za-
silacz; posuw
feeder (fi:der) s. boczna (droga); dopływ; przewod zasila-
jący
feel; felt; felt (fi:l; felt;
felt)
feel (fi:l) v. czuć (się); odczuwać; macać; dotykać
feel well ('fi:l,łel) v. czuć
się dobrze; być zdrowym
feel bed('fi:l,baed) v. czuć
się źle
feeler ('fi:ler) s. macka; sonda; próbny balon; szperacz
feeling ('fi:lyng) s. dotyk;
uczucie; odczucie; poczucie;
takt; wrażliwość; adj. wrażliwy; czuły; współczujący; szczery; wzruszony; szczery
feet (fi:t) pl. stopy; nogi
fell (fel) v. ścinać (drzewo);
zob. fall
felloe ('felou) s. dzwono(koła)
fellow ('felou) s. towarzysz;
człowiek; chłop; gość; facet;
odpowiednik;wykładowca;adjunkt
fellow being ('felou bi:yng) s.
bliźni
fellow citizen ('felou'sytyzen)
s. współobywatel
fellowship ('felouszyp) s.
udział; wspólnota; związek;
towarzystwo; przyjazn; cech
felon ('felen) s. przestępca;
adj. okrutny; zły;zbrodniczy
felony ('feleny) s. przestępstwo;
zbrodnia
felt (felt) czuły; zob.; feel
felt (felt) s. wojłok; filc
female ('fi:mejl) s. kobieta;
niewiasta; samica; adj. żeński;
kobiecy; wewnętrzny (gwint)
feminine ('femynyn) adj. żeński;
kobiecy; zniewieściały; s. rodzaj żeński;a,rodzaju żeńskiego

fen (fen) s. bagno; trzęsawisko;nizina bagienna
fence (fens) s. płot; ogrodzenie; szermierka; v. ogrodzić;
fechtować się;odpowiadać wykręt-
fencing ('fencyng) s. szermierka;płot;ogrodzenie;paserstwo
fend for ('fend,fo:r) v. zaspo-
kajać potrzeby;utrzymywać
fend off ('fend,of) v. odbijać;
odparowywać;chronić;ochraniać
fender ('fender) s. błotnik;
(zderzak);zasłona;zderzak
fennel ('fenel) s. koper
ferment ('fe:rment) s. ferment;
fermentacja; v. wywoływać ferment; podniecać; fermentować
fermentation (,fe:rmen'tejszyn)
s. fermentacja; ferment
fern (fe:rn) s. paproć
ferocity (fe'rosyty) s. dzikość;
okrucieństwo; srogość
ferry ('fery) v. przeprawiać
promem; kursować; s. prom
ferryboat ('ferybout) s. prom
fertile ('fe:rtajl) adj. żyzny;
płodny;zapłodniony;obfitujący
fertility (fer'tylyty) z. żyzność; płodność;urodzjność
fertilize ('fe:rtylajz) v. użyźniać;nawozić;zapładniać;zapylać
fertilizer ('fe:rtylajzer) s.
nawóz sztuczny
fervent ('fe:rwent) adj. żarliwy; gorący;płomienny;gorliwy
fester ('fester) v. jątrzyć (się)
ropieć; gnić; s. ropiejąca rana; mały wrzód;ropniak;zajad
festival ('festewel) adj. świąteczny;odświętny;s.święto
festive ('festyw) adj. uroczysty;
wesoły; radosny;biesiadny
festivity (fes'tywyty) s. wesołość; zabawa; uroczystość
fetch (fecz) v. iść po coś;
przynieść; przywieźć;s.odległość
fetter ('feter) v. skuć; spętać
feud (fju:d) s. lenno; waśń ro-
dowa;wojna między klanami
feudal ('fju:dl) adj. feudalny
fever ('fy:wer) s. gorączka
feverish ('fy:werysz) adj. go-
rączkowy;rozgorączkowany

few (fju:) adj.& pron. mało;kilka;
niewielu ; nieliczni;kilku;kilko-
fiance (fi'a:nsej) s. narzeczo-
ny(a)
fib (fyb) s. kłamstwo; v. cyganić;okładać;s. cios;uderzenie
fiber ('fajber) s. włókno; siła ducha;charakter;łyko;budowa
fibrous ('fajberes) adj.
włóknisty; łykowaty
fickle ('fykl) adj. zmienny;
niestały;płochy; wietrzny
fiction ('fykszyn) s. fikcja;
urojenie; beltrystyka;wymysł
fictitious (fyk'tyszes) a.
fikcyjny; urojony; fałszywy
fiddle ('fydl) v. grać na
skrzypcach; baraszkować;
s. skrzypce
fiddler ('fydler) s. skrzypek;
skrzypaczka
fidelity (fy'delyty) s. wierność; dokładność; ścisłosc
fidget ('fydżyt) v. wiercić
się; niepokoić się; s. niepokój; człowiek niespokojny
fidgety ('fydżyty) adj. wiercą-
cy sie; niespokojny;niecirpliwy
field (fi:ld) s. pole; boisko;
drużyna; dziedzina; v. ustawiać na boisku; zatrzymać
(piłkę);poprowadzić do akcji
field-events('fi:ld,y wents) pl.
lekkoatletyka
field-glasses('fi:ld,glasys) pl.
lornetka polowa
field-gun('fi:ld,gan) s. działo
polowe
fiend ('fy:nd) s. zły duch;
szatan; demon; nałogowiec;
zagorzalec
fierce (fiers) adj. dziki; srogi; zażarty; wściekły; zaw-
ziety;nieopanowany;gwałtowny
fiery ('fajery) adj. ognisty;
płomienny; palący; zapalny;
burzliwy;popedliwy;choleryczny
fife (fajf) s. piszczałka; v.
grać na piszczałce (na fujarce)
fifteen ('fyf'ti:n) num. piet-
naście;piętnaścioro;piętnastka
fifteenth ('fyf'ti:nt) num.
piętnasty;jedna piętnasta czesc

fiftieth ('fyftjet) num. pięćdziesiąty;jedna piędziesiąta

fifty ('fyfty) num. pięćdziesiąt

fig (fyg) s. figa; strój

fight; fought; fought (fajt; fo:t; fo:t)

fight (fajt) s. walka; bitwa; zapasy; bój; duch do walki; mecz bokserski; v. walczyć (przeciw lub o coś);bić się

fighter ('fajter) s. bojownik; zapaśnik; samolot myśliwski

figurative ('fygjurejtyw) adj. obrazowy; przenośny;symboliczny

figure ('fyg'er) s. kształt; postać; wizerunek; cyfra; wzór; v. figurować; liczyć; rachować; oznaczać cenami; wyobrażać; przedstawiać

figure out ('fyger,aut) v.obliczać; wynosić;składać się na

figure skating ('fyger, skejtyng) s, jazda figurowa na łyżwach

file (fajl) s. rejestr; archiwum; seria; pilnik; v. archiwować; defilować; piłować pilnikiem; wnosić (podanie; skargę);iść rzędem(rzędami);maszerować

fill (fyl) v. napełniać; plombować ząb; obsadzać; s. wypełnienie; napicie i najedzenie do syta; nasyp ;ładunek;porcja

fill in ('ful,yn) v. zapełniać; wypełniać (formularze,blankiety)

fill up ('fyl,ap) v. wypełniać; zapełniać ;nabierać benzyny

fillet ('fylyt) s. wstążki; zraz zawijany; dzwonko; v.przepasywać ;wycinać filety

fillet ('fylej) v. dzielić na dzwonka ;wycinać dzwonka

filling ('fylyng) s. nadziewka; plomba; wątek ;zapas benzyny

filling station ('fylyng,st'ejszyn) s. stacja benzynowa

filly ('fyly) s. źrebica; koza; młoda dziewczyna ;dzierlatka

film (fylm) s. powłoka; błona; warstwa; film; mgiełka; bielmo; v. pokrywać błoną; filmować

filter ('fylter) s. filter; sączek; v. filtrować; przeciekać

filth (fyls) s. brud; plugastwo

filthy (fylsy) adj. brudny; plugawy;niegodziwy;sprośny

fin (fyn) s. płetwa; v. obcinać płetwy; ruszać płetwami

finagle ('fy'nejgl) v. oszukiwać; wyłudzać;nabierać

final ('fajnl) adj. końcowy; ostateczny; s. finał (sport; egzamin etc)coś ostatecznego

finally ('fajnly) adv. w końcu; wreszcie; na końcu;ostatecznie

finance (faj'naens) s. finanse; skarbowość; v. finansować; udzielać pożyczki

financial (faj'naenszel) adj. pieniężny; finansowy

financier (,fynaen'sjer) s. finansista; v. spekulować; sprzeniewierzać pieniądze

finch (fynch) s. łuszczak;ptak z krótkim dziobem

find; found; found (fajnd; faund; faund)

find (fajnd) v. znajdować; konstatować;dowiedzieć się

find out ('fajnd, aut) v. wykryć; wynaleźć; dowiedzieć się

finder ('fajnder) s. znalazca; odkrywca;wizier;dalekomierz

finding ('fajndyng) s. odkrycie; stwierdzenie;dane;wniosek

fine (fajn) adj. piękny; misterny; czysty; przedni; wyszukany; swietny; dokładny; adv. swietnie; wspaniale; s. grzywna; kara; v. ukarać grzywną

finery ('fajnry) s. szyk; elegancja; strojny ubiór

finger ('fynger) s. palec; kciuk; v. przebierać w palcach; wskazywać palcem;brać palcami

finger nail ('fynger,nejl) s. paznokieć

finger print ('fynger,prynt) odcisk palca

finish ('fynysz) s. koniec; wykończenie; v. kończyć; skończyć; wykończyć ;dokończyć

finite ('fajnajt) adj. skończony; ograniczony;końcowy

Finnish ('fynusz) adj. fiński

fir (fe:r) s. jodła ;jedlina

fire ('fajer) s. ogień; pożar

fire alarm ('fajer,e'la:rm) s. sygnał pożarowy ;alarm pożaro-wy

firearm ('fajera:rm) s. broń palna (armaty.strzelby etc.)

firebug ('fajer,bag) s. świetlik ;robaczek swietojanski

fire brigade ('fajerbry,gejd) s. straż pożarna

fire department ('fajer,dy'-pa:rtment) s. miejska straż pożarna;straż ogniowa

fire engine ('fajer'endżyn) s. wóz straży ogniowej(pompa)

fire escape ('fajerys,kejp) s, wyjście zapasowe;schody zapaso-we

fire extinguisher ('fajeryks,-,tyngłyszer) s. gaśnica

fireman ('fajermen) s. strażak

fireplace ('fajer-plejs) s. kominek; palenisko

fireproof ('fajerpru:f) adj. ogniotrwały: ognioodporny

fireside ('fajersajd) s. przy kominku;kominek;ognisko domowe

firewood ('fajerłud) s. drzewo opałowe; drewno opalowe

fireworks ('fajerłe:rks) pl. ognie sztucznie;hałasliwe sceny

firm (fe:rm) s. firma; adv. mocno; adj. pewny; stanowczy; trwały; v. ubijać; osadzać (mocno);umacniac sie

firmness ('fe:rmnys) s. stałość; trwałość; stanowczosć; jedrnosć;moc;energia

first ('fe:rst) adj. pierwszy; adv. najpierw; po raz pierwszy; poczatkowo; na poczatku

first of all ('fe:rst,ow'o:l) przede wszystkim;najpierw

first aid ('fe:rst,ejd) pierwsza pomoc;dorazna pomoc;opatru-nek

first aid kit ('fe:rst,ejd kyt) podreczna apteczka; zestaw pierwszej pomocy(opatrunkow etc.

firstborn ('fe:rstbo:rn) adj. pierworodny(syn, dziecko etc.)

first class ('fe:rst'klas) s. pierwsza klasa;a.najlepszej ja-kości

first-class ('fe:rst'klas) adj. pierwszorzedny; wspanialy

first floor ('fe:rst flo:r) s. parter(w Anglii pierwsze piętro)

first hand ('fe:rst,haend) adj. bezpośredni; z pierwszej ręki

firstly ('fe:rstly) adv. po pierwsze; najpierw

first name ('fe:rst,nejm) s. imię (chrzestne)

first-rate ('fe:rst,rejt) adj. pierwszorzędny; adv. pierwszorzędnie ;bardzo dobrze

firth (fe:rs) n. odnoga morska; zatoka (zwłaszcza w Szkocji)

fish (fysz) s. ryba;v.łowić ryby

fishbone ('fyszboun) s. ość

fisherman ('fyszemen) s. rybak

fishery ('fyszery) s. rybołóstwo; teren połowu lub hodowli

fishing ('fyszyng) s. wędkarstwo; rybołóstwo; połow

fishing line ('fyszyng,lajn) s. linka; żyłka (od wedki)

fishing rod ('fyszyng,rod)s. wędka

fishing tackle ('fyszyng,taekl) s. sprzęt rybacki

fishmonger ('fyszmanger) s. handlarz ryb;sklep z rybami

fission ('fyszyn) s. dzielenie; rozbicie (atomu);rozszczepienie; rozerwanie

fissure ('fyszer) s. szczelina; pęknięcie; v. rozszczepiać; pękać; łupać (sie)

fist (fyst) s. pięsć ;v.uderzac

fit (fyt) s. atak (choroby; gniewu etc.); krój; dopasowanie; adj. dostosowany; odpowiedni; nadajacy się; gotow; zdatny; dobrze lezący; v. sprostać; dobrze leżeć;przygotować sie

fit on (fyt on) v. przymierzac

fit out (fyt aut) v. zaopatrywać; s. wyposażenie; umeblowanie

fitness ('fytnys) s. stosownosc; kondycja;trafnosc(uwagi);przyzwo-itosc

fitter ('fyter) s,. monter; krawiec dokonywujacy przymiarek;slu-sarz

fitting ('fytyng) s. okucie; oprawa; przymiarka; adj. odpowiedni; wlasciwy;trafny;stosowny

five (fajw) num. pieć ;piecioro; piata(godzina);piatka (numer opu-wia)

fix (fyks) v. umocować; przyczepiać; ustalać; utkwić;,
ustalać; zgęszczać; tężeć;
krzepnąć; urządzić kogoś(źle);
usytuować; zaaranżować wynik (zapasów); s. kłopot;
dylemat; położenie nawigacyj-
ne (statku,samolotu etc.)
fix up (fyks,ap) v. naprawić;
uporządkować;ulokować(kogoś)
fixed (fykst) adj. trwały;
stały;nieruchomy;niezmienny
fixedly ('fyksydly) adv. stale; trwale; uporczywie
fixture ('fyksczer) s. urządzenie przymocowane
fizz (fyz) s. syk; napój musujący; v. syczeć; musować
flabbergast ('flaebergaest) v.
zdumieć; odebrać mowę (ze
zdumienia);osołamiać
flabby ('flaeby) adj. zwiotcza-
ły; obwisły; miękki; słaby;
niedbały;bez charakteru
flag (flaeg) s. flaga; chorągiew; lotka; v. wywieszać
flagę; sygnalizować
flagstone ('flaeg,stoun) s. płyta brukowa; płyta chodnikowa
flak (flaek) s. artyleria prze-
ciwlotnicza (niemiecka)
flake (flejk) s. płatek; łuska;
iskra; v. prószyć; odpryskiwać;
łuszczyć;padać płatkami
flake oft ('flejk;of) v. złuszczać (się);odpadać płatkami
flame (flejm) s. płomień;miłość;
v. zionąć; błyszczeć; płonąć;
opalać; migotać;być podnieconym
flank (flaenk) s. bok; flanka;
v. flankować; strzec flanki
flannel ('flaenl) s. flanela;
v. wycierać flanelą; ubierać
we flanelę (lekką wełnę)
flap (flaep) s. trzepot; klap-
nięcie; klapa; poła; płat; pokrywa; v. trzepotać; zwisać;
klapnąć;uderzyć czyms płaskim
flare (fleer) v. błyszczeć;
sygnalizować; popisywać się;
rozszerzać się;s.jasny płomień
flare up (fleer ap) s. wybuch;
błysk; v.wybuchnąć (gniewem;
płomieniem);reagować gwałtownie

flash (flaesz) s. błysk; blask;
adj. błyskotliwy; fałszywy;
gwarowy; v. zabłysnąć; sygnalizować; pędzić; mknąć; wysyłać
(natychmiastowo wiadomości etc.)
flashbulb ('flaeszbalb) s. żarówka (do zdjęć);flesz
flashlight ('flaeszlajt) s.
latarka (elektryczna)
flashy ('flaeszy) adj. błyskot-
liwy(chwilowo);jaskrawy;krzykliwy
flask (flaesk) s. flaszka; fla-
kon; kolba;opleciona flaszka wina
flat (flaet) adj. płaski; płytki;
nudny; równy; stanowczy; oczywisty; matowy; bezbarwny;
adv. płasko; stanowczo; dokładnie; s. płaszczyzna; równina;
mieszkanie; przedziurawiona
dętka ;v.rozpłaszczyć;matować
flatten ('flaetn) v. spłaszczyć
(się);matowieć;wietrzeć;równać
flatter ('flaeter) v. pochlebiać
flattery ('flaetery) s. pochleb-
stwo; schlebianie komuś
flavor ('flejwer) s. smak; zapach; v. dawać smak;mieć posmak
flaw (flo:) s. skaza; rysa; pęknięcie; v. psuć; pękać
flawless ('flo:les) adj. bez
skazy;(przedstawienie)bez usterek
flax (flaeks) s. len
flaxen(fkak'sn)adj.płowy;lniany
flea (fli:) s. pchła
fled (fled) zob. flee
fledgling ('fledżlyng) s. świeżo opierzony ptak;żółtodziób
flee; fled; fled (fli:; fled;
fled)
flee (fli:) v. uciekać;pierzchać
fleece (fli:s) s. runo; wełna;
czupryna; puch; v. strzyc;
skubać; pokrywać puchem
fleet (fli:t) s. flota; park,po-
jazdów; v, mknąć; przemknąć;
mijać; adv. płytko; adj. płytki
flesh (flesz) s. ciało; miąższ
fleshy ('fleszy) adj. mięsisty;
tłusty;cielesny;zmysłowy
flew (flu:) zob. fly
flexible (fl'eksybl) adj. giętki; gibki; układny; obrotny;
elastyczny;łatwo przystosowywu-
jący się; ustępliwy;poddający się

flick (flyk) s. przytyk; śmignięcie; smuga; v. śmignąć;
trzepnąć; rzucać się; trzepotać się;zapalać zapalniczkę
flicker ('flyker) s. mig; mi-
ganie; drganie; trzepot;
v. migać; drgać; trzepotać;
machać;lekko się poruszać
flier ('flajer) s. lotnik;
ulotka;pośpieszny pociąg etc.
flight (flajt) s. lot; przelot; ucieczka;kondygnacja schodów
flight engineer ('flajt,endży'-
nier) s. mechanik pokładowy
flimsy ('flymzy) adj. cienki;
wątły; słaby(papier,wymówka...)
flinch (flyncz) v. uchylać się;
cofać się; drgać;s.unik
fling; flung; flung (flyng;
flang; flang)
fling (flyng) v. rzucać (się);
powalić; wypaść; wierzgać
fling open('flyn,oupen) v.
rozewrzeć (gwałtownie)
flint (flynt) s. krzemień;
krzesiwo;kamyk do zapalniczki
flip (flyp) v. przytykać ; rzucać;wyprztykiwać;s.prztyk
flippant ('flypent) adj. nie-
poważny; impertynencki
flipper ('flyper) s. płetwa
nożna; graba;łapa;błona pławna
flirt (fle:rt) v. flirtować;
machać; s. flirciarz; flir-
ciarka; machnięcie (raptowne)
flirtation (,fle:r'tejszyn) s.
flirt;powierzchowny romans
flit (flyt) v. biegać; fruwać;
wyjechać;poruszać się zwinnie
float (flout) v. unosić się;
pływać na powierzchni; spławiać; puszczać w obieg; lan-
sować; s. pływak; tratwa;
platforma na kołach; gładzik
do tynku;niezdecydowany ruch
flock (flok) s. trzoda; stado;
tłum; v. tłoczyć się; iść
tłumem; gromadzić się
floe (flou) s. kra (lodowa)
flog (flog) v. chłostać; smagać; bić;biczować się
flood (flad) s. powódź; wylew;
potok; v. zalewać; nawadniać

floodlights ('flad,lajts) pl.
reflektory (szeroko-stożkowe)
flood tide ('fladtajd) s. przypływ (morza) ;fala powodziowa
floor (flo:r) s. podłoga;dno
floor cloth ('flo:rklo:s) s.
szmata do podłogi;linoleum
floor lamp ('flo:r,laemp) s.
lampa stojąca na podłodze
floor show ('flo:r,szou) s.
przedstawienie kabaretowe
flop (flop) s. klapanie; klapa;
fiasco; v. klapnąć; załamać
się; zrobić klapę;a.dziadowski
florist ('floryst) s. kwiaciarz;
kwiaciarka;hodowca kwiatów
flounder ('flaunder) s. flądra;
brnięcie; v. brnąć; brodzić;
błądzić; wystękać (mowę)
flour (flauer) s. mąka; v. mleć
na mąkę;dodawać mąki(posypywać)
flourish ('flarysz) s. fanfara;
wymachiwanie; v. kwitnąć; zdobić kwiatami; wymachiwać
flow (flou) s. strumień; prąd;
przepływ; dopływ; v. płynąć;
lać się; zalewać;ruszać się płyn-
nie
flower (flauer) s. kwiat;
v. kwitnąć;być w rozkwicie
flown (floun) zob. fly
fluctuate ('flaktjuejt) v.
falować; wahać się;być niezdecydowanym
flu (flu:) s. grypa;influenza
fluent ('fluent) adj. płynny;
biegły i wymowny(mówca;pisarz...)
fluff (flaf) s. puch;v.trzepać;kno-
fluffy ('flafy) adj. puszysty;lekki
cić
fluid ('flu:yd) s. płyn; adj.
płynny;płynnie poruszający się
flung (flang) zob. fling
flunk (flank) v. oblać (egzamin)
spalić (ucznia); nie zdać;zawalić
flurry ('fle:ry) s. wichura;
ulewa; śnieżyca; podniecenie;
rozgardiasz; v. oszałamiać;
denerwować;wprowadzać zamieszanie
flush (flasz) v. rumienić się;
napełniać; spłukiwać; s. rumieniec; rozkwit; blask; adj.
wylewający się; krzepki; rumiany; równy; etc.; adv. równo;
prosto ;gładko;pełno;poziomo;sowi-
cie(wyposażać w pieniądze)

fluster ('flaster) s. podniecenie; niepokój; v. podniecać; oszałamiać; kręcić się
flute (flu:t) s. flet;rowkowanie
flutter ('flater) s. trzepotanie; dygotanie; niepokój; v. trzepotać; drzeć; dygotać; płoszyć;powodowac trzepotanie
flux (flaks) s. prąd; przepływ; potok; płynnosć; krwotok; przypływ;pasta do lutowania
fly (flaj) s, mucha;klapka
fly; flew; flown(flaj; flu; floun) v. latać; lecieć; powiewać; uciekać; przewozic samolotem; puszczać (latawca)
fly across (,flaj e'kros) v. przelatywać (przez)
flyblown ('flaj-bloun) adj. popstrzony przez muchy
fly into a rage ('flaj,yntu ej'rejdż) v. wpasć w pasję
flyer ('flajer) s. lotnik
flying ('flajyng)adj. latający; lotny; lotniczy; krótkotrwały;samolotowy;pospieszny
flying boat ('flajynbout) s. hydroplan (do wodowania)
flying buttress ('flajyn,batrys) s. łuk przyporowy
flying machine ('flajyng ,meszi:n) s. samolot
flying time ('flajyng,tajm) s. czas przelotu;czas lotu
fly weight ('flaj,łejt) s. waga musza (112 funtów lub mniej)
flywheel ('flajhłi:l) s. koło zamachowe (do regulowania szybkości)
foal (foul) s. źrebię
foam (foum) s, piana; v. pienić się ;a.piąnowy;piankowy
foamy ('foumy) adj. pieniący się ;pienisty;spieniony
focus ('foukes) s. ognisko; ogniskowa; v. skupiać; ogniskować; koncentrować;zesrodkowywać
fodder ('foder) s. pasza
foe (fou) s. wróg ;przeciwnik
fog (fog) s. mgła;v.otumaniać
foggy ('fogy) adj. mglisty
foible (fojbl) s. słabostka;lekka słabosć charakteru; słabosć; wątłosć

foil (fojl) s. folia; tło; floret; trop; slad; v. udaremnic; zacierać (slad) ;niweczyc
fold (fould) s. fałda; zagięcie; zagroda (owiec) v. składac; zaginać (się); splatać; zamykać owce (w owczarni);faldować
folder ('foulder) s. składana teczka; broszura;falcownik
folding ('fouldyng) adj. składany; rozsuwany;s.fałd;fałda
folding boat ('fouldyng bout) składana łodź(turystyczna etc.)
folding chair ('fouldyng, czeer) składane krzesło(kampingowe etc.)
foliage ('fouljydż) s. listowie; liscie (rosnące);ulistnienie
folk (fouk) s. ludzie; krewni; lud; rasa; adj. ludowy;folklorystyczny
folklore ('fouklo:r) s. folklor
folksy ('fouksy) adj. towarzyski; prosty;ludzki
folk song ('fouksong) s. piesń ludowa (regionalna etc.)
follow ('folou) v. isc za; następować za; sledzić; rozumieć (kogoś) wnikać;gonić;wynikać
follower ('folouer) s. stronnik; zwolennik; uczen; pomocnik
following ('folouyng) s. zwolennicy; adj. następujący; następny;s.orszak;swita;posłuch;autorytet
folly ('foly) s. szaleństwo
foment (fou'ment) s. podżegać; podsycać;nagrzewać;pobudzać
fond (fond) adj. kochający; czuły; łatwowierny;głupio czuły
fondle ('fondl) v. piescić
fondness ('fondnys) s. czułosc; miłosc; zamiłowanie;pociag
food (fu:d) s. żywnosć; strawa; pokarm; jedzenie;a.żywnosciowy;
fool (fu:l) s. głupiec; głuptas; błazen; v. błaznować; wysmiewac; oszukiwać ;okpiwać;partaczyć
foolhardy ('fu:l,ha:rdy) adj. szaleńczy; wariacki; lekkomyslny ;nieroztropny;gwałtowny
foolish ('fu:lysz) adj. głupi
foolishness ('fu:-lysznys) s. głupota ; głupstwo;bzdura;nonsens
foolproof ('fu:l,pru:f) adj. niezawodny ;nie do zepsucia

foot (fut) s. stopa; dół; spód; miara (30,5 cm);piechota;v.pła-
foot the bill ('fut,ty'byl) v. zapłacić rachunek
football ('fut,bo:l) s. piłka nożna; futbol;piłka do nożnej
foot brake ('fut,brejk) s. hamulec nożny(w samochodzie)
foothills ('futhylz) pl. podgórze(przy łancuchu górskim)
foothold ('futhould) s. oparcie (dla nóg); miejsce gdzie można stanąć;pewna pozycja
footing ('futyŋg) s. fundament; ostoja; podstawa; położenie
footpath ('futpas) s. ścieżka dla pieszych; chodnik
footprint ('futprynt) s. ślad stopy
footstep ('fut,step) s. odgłos kroku; ślad;długość kroku
for (fo:r) prep. dla; zamiast; z; do; na; żeby; że; za; po; co do; co się tyczy; jak na; mimo; wbrew; po coś; z powodu; conj. ponieważ; bowiem; gdyż; albowiem; dlatego że
for two vears ('fo:-tu-je:rs) przez dwa lata
forbade (fe:r'bejd) zob. forbid
forbear ; forbore; forborne (fo:'beer; fe'bo:r; fe'bo:rn), forbear ('fo:r'beer) v. znosić cierpliwie; powstrzymywać(się) s. wyrozumiałość; przodek
forbid; forbade; forbidden (fer'byd; fe:r'bejd; fer'bydn) forbid (fe'rbyd) s. zakazywać; zabraniać; niedopuszczać; uniemożliwiać;nie pozwalać
forbidding (fe'rbydyŋg) adj. odpychający; posępny; ponury
forbore (fer'bo:r) zob. forbear
forborne (fer'bo:rn) zob. forbear
force (fo:rs) s. siła; moc; potęga; sens; v, zmuszać; pędzić; wpychać; forsować
forced landing ('fo:rst,laendyŋg) przymusowe lądowanie
forceps ('fo:rsyps) pl. kleszcze; szczypce;szczypczyki

forcible ('fo:rsybl) adj. gwałtowny; przymusowy; przekonywujący ;mocny;dosadny;bezprawny
ford (fo:rd) v.przeprawiać się brodem; s. bród (płytkie miejsce)
fore (fo:r) adj. przedni; adv. na przedzie; s, przednia część
foreboding (fo:r'boudyŋg) s. przeczucie (złego) ;złe przeczucie
forecast ('fo:r-ka:st) v. przewidywać; s. przewidywanie
forefather ('fo:r,fa:dzer) s. przodek ; antenat
forefinger ('fo:rfyŋger) s. palec wskazujący
forefoot ('fo:r-fut) s. przednia noga (zwierzęcia)
foregone (fo:r'gon) adj. przesądzony ;miniony
foreground ('fo:rgraund) s. pierwszy plan (obrazu)
forehead ('fo:ryd) s. czoło
foreign('foryn) adj. obcy; obcokrajowy ;cudzozieski
foreign currency (,foryn'karensy) s. obca waluta
foreigner ('foryner) s. cudzoziemiec; cudzoziemka;obcokrajowiec
foreign policy ('foryn,polysy) polityka zagraniczna
foreign trade ('foryn,trejd) handel zagraniczny
foreleg ('fo:rleg) s. przednia noga (zwierzęcia)
foreman ('fo:rmen) s. majster; sztygar; starszy przysięgły
foremost ('fo:r,maust) adj. główny; przedni; adv. przede wszystkim ;w pierwszym rzędzie
forenoon ('fo:rnu:n) s. przedpołudnie ;s.przedpołudniowy
foresee ('fo:rsi:) v. przewidywać ;przewidzieć;wiedzieć z góry
foresight ('fo:rsajt) s. przezorność; przewidywanie; muszka celownika (przy strzelbie etc.)
forest ('foryst) s. las; v. zalesiać ;a. leśny; w lesie
forester ('foryster) s. leśniczy; leśnik;ptak leśny;ćma leśna
forestry ('forystry) s. leśnictwo; lasy ;wiedza o lesie

foretaste ('fo:rtejst) s. przed-smak;zapowiedź tego co ma nastą-pić

foretell; foretold; foretold (fo:rtel; fo:'rtould; fo:'rtould)

foretell (fo:r'tel) v. przepo-wiadać; zapowiadać ;wrózyć

forever (fe'rewer) adv. wiecz-nie; na zawsze; ustawicznie

foreword ('fo:rℓe-rd) v. przed-mowa; przedsłowie;słowo wstępne

forfeit ('fo:rfyt) s. grzywna; fant; zastaw; utrata; v. stra-cić(w skutek konfiskaty);utracić

forge ('fo:rdż) s. kuźnia; huta: v. kuć; fałszować; posuwać się z trudem;wykuwać sobie przysz-łość

forgery ('fo:rdżery) s. fałszer-stwo;podrobiony dokument

forget; forgot; forgotten (fer'get; fer'got; fer'gotn)

forget (fer'get) v. zapominac; pomijac; przeoczyc;zaniedbac

forgetful (fer'getful) adj. za-pominający;zapominalski;niepomny

forget-me-not (fer'getmyna:t) s. niezapominajka

forgive; forgave; forgiven (fer'gyw; fer'gejw; fer'gywn)

forgive (fer'gyw) v. przeba-czać; darowac ;odpuszczać

forgiveness (fer'gywnys) s. prze-baczenie; darowanie; wybaczenie

forgiving (fer'gywyng)adj. wyro-zumiały; pobłażliwy

forgo (fo:r'gou) v. powstrzymy-wać się; obchodzic się bez czegoś ;zrzekać się czegoś

forgot (fer'got) zob. forget

fork (fo:rk) s. widły; widelec; widełki; v. rozwidlać (się); brać na widły;spulchniac(ziemię)

forlorn (fer'lo:rn) adj. zapusz-czony; opuszczony; beznadziej-ny; rozpaczliwy;niepocięszony

form (fo:rm) v. formowac (się); kształtowac (się); utworzyć (się); organizować (się); wy-tworzyc; s, forma; kształt; postac; formuła; formułka; for-mularz;.blankiet;styl;układ

formal ('fo:rmel) adj. formalny; urzędowy; oficjalny;s.strój wie-czorowy

formation ('fo:rmejszyn) s. for-macja; szyk; układ; tworzenie (się); kształtowanie; formowa-nie (się); powstawanie;budowa

formative ('fo:rmetyw) adj. for-mujący; kształtujący; tworzą-cy (się);słowotwórczy

former ('fo:rmer) adj. & pron. poprzedni; byłly; miniony; daw-ny;s. formierz;giser;wzornik

formerly ('fo:rmerly) adv. daw-niej; przedtem; poprzednio

formidable ('fo:rmydebl) adj. straszny;strszny;potężny;ogromny

formulate ('fo:rmjulejt) v. formułować;wyrażać;redagować

fornicate ('fo:rnykejt) v. cudzołożyć ;spółkować bez ślubu

forsake; forsook; forsaken (fer'sejk; fer'suk; fer'sejken)

forsake (fer'sejk) v. opuszczać; porzucać;poniechać;zaprzeć się.

fort (fo:rt) s. fort

forth (fo:rs) adv. naprzód; da-lej;wobec;na zewnątrz etc.

forthcoming (fo:rs'kamyng) adj. zbliżający się;nadchodzący

forthwith ('fo:rs'łys) adv. bezzwłocznie;natychmiast

fortieth ('fo:rtyjes) num. czterdziesty;czterdziesta(część)

fortify ('fo:rtyfaj) s. wzmac-niac; fortyfikować;umacniać

fortnight ('fo:rtnajt) s. dwa tygodnie (czternaście nocy)

fortran ('fo:rtraen) = formula translation, język dla progra-mów na komputery

fortress ('fo:rtrys) s. twier-dza; forteca ;warownia

fortunate ('fo:rcznyt) adj. szczęśliwy;pomyślny;udany

fortunately ('fo:rcznytly) adv. na szczęście; szczęśliwie

fortune ('fo:rczen) s. szczęś-cie; los; majątek;traf;ślepy los

forty ('fo:rty) num. czterdzies-ci;czterdziestka;czterdziescioro

forward ('fo:rℓerd) adj. przed-ni; naprzód; postępowy; wczes-ny; chętny; gotowy; v. przyspie-szac; ekspediowac; s. napast-nik (w sporcie);gracz w ataku

forwards ('fo:rłerds) adv. naprzód; dalej;adj.frontowy;śmiały
foster-child ('foster.czajld)
s. wychowanek; wychowanka
fought (fo:t) zob, fight
foul (faul) adj. zgniły;plugawy;
wstrętny; adv. nieuczciwie;
wbrew regułom; s, nieuczci-
wosc; v. zawalać (się); za-
brudzić (się);plugawić się;kalać
found (faund) v. 1. uzasadniać;
zakładać; odlewać; 2. zob.
find
foundation (faun'dejszyn) s.
podstawa; założenie; fundament; fundacja;podwalina
founder ('faunder) s. odlew-
nik; założyciel; v. zatonąć;
przepaść;okulawic;zatopic
foundling ('faundlyng) s.
podrzutek ; znajda
fountain ('fauntyn) s. fontanna; zródło;wodotrysk;poijalnia
fountainpen ('fauntyn,pen) s.
wieczne pióro
four (fo:r) num; cztery;czwórka; czworo;
fourscore ('fo:rskor) num.
osiemdziesiąt
four-stroke engine ('fo:r,strok-
'endżyn) motor cztero-taktowy
fourteen ('fo:rti:n) num. czternaście;czternaścioro;czternastka
fourth ('fo:rs) num. czwarty
fourthly (fo:rsly) adv. po
czwarte;na czwartym miejscu
fowl (faul) s. drób; ptaki
fox (foks) s. lis; v.przechytrzyć
fraction ('fraekszyn) s. ułamek;część;odłam;frakcja
fracture ('fraekczer) s. złamanie; v. złamac;łamac się
fragile ('fraedżajl) adj. kruchy; łamliwy;słabowity;wątły
fragment ('fraegment) s. fragment;urywek;odłamek;okruch
fragrance ('frejgrens) s. zapach; woń; aromat
fragrant ('frejgrent) adj. pachnący;aromatyczny;wonny
frail (frejl) adj. kruchy; wątły;lekkomyslny;s.kosz;plecionka
frailty ('frejlty) s. słabosc;
wątłość ;chwila słabosci

frame ('frejm) s. oprawa; rama;
struktura; szkielet; v. oprawiać; kształtować; wrabiać
frame of mind ('frejm,ow'majnd)
s. nastrój; nastawienie psychiczne;usposobienie do czegos
frame-house ('frejm,haus) s.
drewniany dom (typowy w USA)
framework ('frejm,łe:rk) s.
struktura; zrąb;szkielet;wiąza-
nie
franchise ('fraenczajz) s.
przywilej; prawo do prowadzenia filii lub firmy,do głosowania
frank (fraenk) adj. szczery;
otwarty;v.wysyłać bez opłaty
frankness ('fraenknys) s.
szczerość; otwartość
frantic ('fraentyk) adj.
wariacki; szalony;zapamiętały
fraternal (fre'te:rnl) adj.
braterski;bratni;bracki
fraternity (fre'te:rnyty) s.
braterstwo;korporacja studencka
fraud (fro:d) s. oszustwo;oszust
fray (frej) v. strzępic; wycierac; s. bójka; burda
freak (fri:k) s. kaprys; wybryk; potwor;a.fantazyjny
freckle ('frekl) s. pieg; v.po-
krywać piegami;powodowac piegi
free (fri:) adj. wolny; bezpłatny; nie zajęty; v. uwolnic;
wyzwolic; oswobodzic; adv.wol-
no; swobodnie; bezpłatnie
free and easy ('fri:,end'i:zy)
adj. beztroski;bez ceremonii
freedom ('fri:dem) s. wolnosć;
swoboda;nieskrępowanie;prawo do
freemason ('fri:,mejsn) s.
mason; wolnomularz
free port ('fri:, port) s.
wolnocłowy port
freethinker ('fri:tynker) s.
wolnomysliciel;wolnomyslicielka
freeway ('fri:łej) s. szosa
przelotowa wieloliniowa
freewheel ('fri:hłi:l) s. wolne koło (np, od roweru)
freeze; froze; frozen (fri:z;
frouz; frouzn)
freeze (fri:z) v. marznąc; za-
marzac;krzepnąć;przymarznąc;
mrozic;wyrugować(konkurenta)

freezing point ('fri:zyn,point) s. punkt zamarzania

freight (frejt) s. przewóz; fracht; v. przewozić; frachtować statek;a.towarowy(pociąg etc.)

freighter ('frejter) s. frachtowiec; statek towarowy

French (frencz) adj. francuski

frenzy ('frenzy) s. szał; szaleństwo;v.doprowadzać do szału

frequency ('fri:kłensy) s. częstość; częstotliwość

frequent ('fri:kłent) adj. częsty; rozpowszechniony; v. uczęszczać; odwiedzać; bywać

fresh (fresz) adj. świeży; nowy; zuchwały; niedoświadczony; adv. świeżo; niedawno;dopiero co

freshman ('freszmen) s. student pierwszego roku

freshness ('fresznys) s. świeżość; zuchwałość;zuchwalstwo

freshwater ('fresz;ło:ter) adj. słodkowodny; s. woda słodka

fret (fret) v. gryźć się: niepokoić się; s. rozdrażnienie; niepokój;zdenerwowanie;irytacja

fretful ('fretful) adj. rozdrażniony; drażliwy;nerwowy;wzburzony

friar ('frajer) s. mnich; zakonnik ; biała plamka

friction ('frykszyn) s. tarcie; ścieranie się; ucieranie

Friday ('frajdy) s. piątek

fridge (frydż) s. lodówka (slang)

fried (frajd) adj. smażony

friend (frend) s. znajomy; znajoma; przyjaciel;kolega;klient

friendly ('frendly) adj. przyjazny; przychylny ;życzliwy

friendship ('frendszyp) s. przyjaźń osobista; dobra znajomość; znajomość powierzchowna; stosunki koleżeńskie lub handlowe

fright (frajt) s. strach;przerażenie;strach na wróble

frighten ('frajtn) v. straszyć

frightened ('frajtnd) adj.przestraszony ;zastraszony;wylękniony

frightful ('frajtful) adj. straszny; przerażający;strzeliwy; alarmujący;nieprzyjemny;wstrętny

frigid ('frydżyd) adj. zimny; lodowaty; oziębły;zimna(kobieta)

frill (fryl) v. plisować; s. falbanka; pl. fochy; fanaberie;niepotrzebne ozdóbki

fringe (fryndż) s. frędzla; obrębek; v. obrębiać; obramowywać; ograniczać;wystrzępić

frisk (frysk) v. brykać; s.sus; podskok; skok;v.rewidować

frisky ('frysky) adj. rozbrykany; ożywiony; swawolny

fro (frou) exp.: to and fro; tu i tam; tam i z powrotem

frock (frok) s. sukienka; habit;mundur;surdut;anglez

frog (frog) s. żaba; strzałka (w kopycie konia);vulg.Francuz

frolic ('frolyk) s. wybryk;figiel swawola; v. dokazywać; swawolić; figlować; adj. rozbawiony; swawolny; figlarny

frolicsome ('frolyksem) adj. figlarny; swawolny;rozbawiony

from (from) prep. od; z; przed (zimnem); ze;(ponieważ; żeby)

from under (from ander) prep; spod (czegos)

from... to (from... tu) exp. stąd... dotąd ;od ..,do

front (frant) s. przód; front; czoło; adj, przedni; frontowy; czołowy; v. stawiać czoło; stać frontem; konfrontować

front-door ('frant,do:r) s. główne drzwi wejściowe

frontier ('frantjer) s. granica ; a. pograniczny

front-page ('frant,pejdż) s. strona tytułowa;a.sensacyjny

front tire ('frant,tajer) s. przednia opona (samochodu)

front-wheel ('frant,hłi:l) s. przednie koło (wozu)

front wheel drive ('frant, hłi:l'drajw) s. napęd na przednie koła (auta,etc.)

frost (frost) s. mróz; przymrozek; oziębłość;v.zmrozić;oszronić

frostbite ('frost,bajt) s. odmrożenie(nosa,reki,stopy etc.)

frosted ('frostyd) adj. matowy; oszroniony; matowy odcień

frosty ('frosty) adj. mroźny;
oszroniony; lodowaty
froth (froś) s. piana; szumowiny; v. pienić się;ubijać białko
frothy (frośy) adj. spieniony
frown (fraun) v. marszczyć brwi;
s. zachmurzone czoło; wyraz
dezaprobaty;niezadowolona mina
froze (frouz) zob. freeze
frozen food ('frouzn, fu:d) s.
mrożonki;mrożona żywność
frugal ('fru:gel) adj. oszczędny;tani; skromny(posiłek etc.)
fruit (fru:t) s. owoc; v. owo-
cować;a. owocowy
fruitcake ('fru:t,kejk) s.
świąteczne ciasto z kandyzowa-
nymi owocami i orzechami
fruitful ('fru:tful) adj.
owocny;owocujący;zyskowny;wydaj-
fruitless ('fru:tlys) adj. bezowocny; bezpłodny;nieudany
frustrate (fra'strejt) v. udaremnić; zniechęcić; zawieść
fry (fraj) v. smażyć;s.narybek
frying pan (frajyn,paen) s.
patelnia
fuel (fjuel) s. paliwo; opał
fugitive ('fju:dżytyw) s. zbieg;
adj. zbiegły; przelotny
fulfill (ful'fyl) v. spełnić;
wykonać; dokonać; skończyć
fulfilment (ful'fylment) s.
spełnienie; wykonanie; dokonanie;wypełnienie;wysłuchanie
full(ful) adj. pełny; pełen; za-
pełniony; całkowity; kompletny;
cały; adv. w pełni; całkowicie
full board ('ful'bo:rd) s. pełne
utrzymanie;wikt i opierunek
full moon ('ful'mu:n) s. pełnia
księżyca
fullness (ful'nys) s. pełność;
dokładność;drobiazgowość
full-time ('ful'tajm) adj. pełno-
etatowy; całkowicie zajęty
fumble ('fambl) v. szperać; partaczyć; s. gmeranie; partactwo;
niezdarność;niezdarne zagranie
fume (fju:m) v. dymić; kopcić;
s. dym (ostry); wyziew(przykry)
gazy spalinowe;zapach;woń;na-
pad gniewu;wybuch gniewu

fun (fan) s. uciecha; zabawa;
wesołość; śmiech;powód do wesołoś-
in fun (yn,fan) adv. żartem;
make fun (mejk fan) v. dokuczać; kpić;wyśmiewać się
function ('fankszyn) v. działać; funkcjonować; s. działanie; funkcja; praca; obowiązek;
impreza; uroczystość;czynność
functionary ('fanksznery) s.
urzędnik; funkcjonariusz
fund (fand) s. fundusz
fundamental (,fande'mentel) adj.
podstawowy; s. zasada; podstawa zasada;nakaz;podstawa
funeral ('fju:nerel) s. pogrzeb;
adj. pogrzebowy;żałosny
funereal (fju'njerjel) adj. żałobny;pogrzegowy
funicular railway (fju'nykju-
ler'rejlłej) kolejka linowa
funnel ('fanl) s. lej; lejek;
komin (maszyny parowej etc.)
funny ('fany) adj. zabawny;
śmieszny; dziwny;humorystyczny
fur (fe:r) s. futro :v.okładać
furious ('fjuerjes) adj. wściekły; rozjuszony;gwałtowny;zaciek-
furl (fe:r) v. składać (się);
złożyć (się);s.zwitek;zawinięcie
furnace ('fe:rnys) s. piec
(centralny);palenisko;piekło
furnish ('fe:rnysz) v. zaopatrzyć; dostarczyć; umeblować;
wyposażyć;uzbrajać;meblować
furniture ('fe:rnyczer) s.
umeblowanie; urządzenie
furrier ('farjer) s. kuśnierz
furrow ('farou) s. bruzda;
zmarszczka; koleina; v. orać;
przeorać; zryć;ryć;pruć;żłobić
further ('fe:rdzer) adv. dalej;
dodatkowy; adj. dalszy; dodatkowy; v. pomagać; ułatwiać;
posuwać naprzód;sprzyjać;popierać
further more ('fe:rdzermo:r) adv.
ponadto; oprócz tego; w dodatky
furtive ('fe:rtyw) adj. skryty;
potajemny;ukradkowy;skradający się
furuncle ('fjuerankl) s. czyrak
fury ('fjuery) s. szał; furja;
pasja; gwałtowna siła; jędza;
megiera;siła burzy;siła wiatru

fuse (fju:z) v. stopić; s. zapalnik; bezpiecznik; korek
fuselage ('fju:zyla:ż) s. kadłub (samolotu)bez skrzydeł i o-
gona
fusion ('fju:żen) s. stopienie;
spawanie; zlewanie się
fuss (fas) v. niepokoić; denerwować; krzątac się; s. wrzawa;
zamieszanie; krzątanina
fussy ('fasy) adj. grymasny;
hałasliwy; nieznosny; zrzędny
futile ('fju:tajl) adj. daremny; bezskuteczny; prozny
future ('fju:tczer) s. przyszłosc; adj. przyszły(czas...)
fuzzy ('fazy) adj. kędzierzawy;
kręty; puszysty; niewyrazny;
zamazany(obraz,pojęcie etc.)
g (dżi:) siodma litera angielskiego alfabetu
gab (gaeb) s. gadanie (slang)
gable ('gejbl) s. szczyt (dachu)trójkąt płaszczyzn dachu
gad-fly ('gaedflaj) s. giez;
bąk;osoba zaczepna jak giez
gag (gaeg) s. knebel; v. kneb-
lowac; nałożyc kaganiec;
zamknąc debatę;oszukiwac
gage (gejdż) s. wskaznik; miara; rękojmia; v, mierzyc;
oceniac; zastawiac;sadzic
gaiety ('gejety) s. wesołosc
gaily ('gejly) adv. wesoło
gain (gejn) s. zysk; zarobek;
korzysc; v. zyskiwac; zdobywac; pozyskiwac; wygrywac;
osiągac;miec korzysc;wyprzedzac
gait (gejt) s. chod;bieg(konia)
gaiter ('gejter) s. kamasz;
getr
gale (gejl) s. poryw wiatru;
sztorm;wybuch smiechu;zefir
gall (go:l) s. zołc; złosc; gorycz;tupet;otarcie;v.urazic...
gallant ('gaelent) s. bawidamek; galant; adj. piękny;
dzielny; waleczny; szarmancki
gallery ('gaelery) s. arkady;
galeria; kruzganek;balkon;chor
galley ('gaely) s. galera;
kuchnia na statku;szufelka
galley proof ('gaely,pru:f) s.
odbitka na korektę(szczotkowa)

gallon ('gaelen) s. miara płynu
(ok. 4,5 litra)(am.gal.=3,78,1.)
gallop ('gaelep) v. galopowac;
s. galop; cwał;galopada
gallows ('gaelouz) s. szubienica;kobylica;szelki;a.szbieniczny
galore (gr'lo:r) s. mnostwo;
adv. w brod;bardzo wiele
gamble ('gaembl) s. hazard; ryzyko; v, uprawiac hazard; ryzykowac;igrac;spekulowac
gambler ('gaembler) s. gracz-
hazardzista; ryzykant
gambol (gaembel) v. podskakiwac; s. podskok; skok
game (gejm) s. gra; zabawa; zawody; sztuczki; machinacje;
adj. dzielny; odwazny; kulawy;
v. uprawiac hazard
gamekeeper ('gejm,ki:per) s.
gajowy; lesnik
gander ('gaender) s. gąsior
gang (gaeng) s. banda; szajka;
grupa;v.łaczyc się w bandę
gangster ('gaengster) s. gans-
ster; bandyta
gangway ('gangłej) s. przejscie;
kładka;chodnik w kopalni
gaol-jail (dżejl) s. więzienie;
ciupa;v.uwiezic;wsadzac do więzienia
gaoler=jailer ('dżejler) s. dozorca więzienny;strażnik więzienny
gap (gaep) s. szpara; luka;otwór;
przerwa;odstęp;wyrwa;przełęcz;wyłom
gape (gejp) v. gapic się; ziewac; s. ziewanie; gapienie się
garage (gaera:dż) s. garaż;
v. garazowac; zagarażowac
garbage ('ga:rbydż) s. odpadki;
smieci;bezwartosciowe publikacje
garden ('ga:rdn) s. ogrod;uprawiac o-
gród
gardener ('ga:rdner) s. ogrodnik
gardening ('ga:rdenyng) s. og-
rodnictwo(warzywa,kwiatowe etc.)
gargle ('ga:rgl) v. płukac
gardło;v.płyn do płukania gardła
garland ('ga:rlend) s. girlanda
garlic ('ga:rlik) s. czosnek
garment ('ga:rment) s. częsc
ubrania;szaty;v.odziewac
garnish ('ga:rnusz) v. ozdabiac;
s. ozdoba; przybranie (potraw)
upiększenia literackie

garret ('gaeret) s. poddasze; strych; mansarda;sl.:łeb
garrison ('gaerysn) s. załoga; garnizon; v. garnizonować
garter ('ga:rter) s. podwiązka
gas (gaes) s. gaz; benzyna
gaseous ('gejzjes) adj. gazowy
gash (gaesz) s. skaleczyć się; s. szrama; skaleczenie;blizna
gasket ('gaeskyt) s. uszczelka
gas-meter ('gaes,mi:ter) s. gazomierz;zegar gazowy
gasoline ('gaesely:n) s. gazolina; benzyna
gasp (ga:sp) v. ciężko dyszeć; sapać; s. ciężki oddech
gas station ('gaes,stejszyn) s. stacja benzynowa
gas-stove ('gaes'stouw) s. kuchenka gazowa;kuchnia gazowa
gate (gejt) s. brama; furtka; wrota; szlaban; ilość publiczności;wpływy kasowe ze wstępu
gateway ('gejtłej) s. przejscie; wjazd; brama wjazdowa,
gather ('gaedzer) v. zbierać; wnioskować;wzbierać;narastać
gather speed ('gaedzer spi:d) nabierać szybkości;rozpędzać się
gathering ('gaedzeryng) s. zebranie;nagromadzenie; ropień
gaudy (go:dy) adj. jaskrawy; krzykliwy; s. obchód(uroczysty)
gauge (gejdż) s. wskaźnik; miara; skala; v. kalibrować; oceniać;szacować; oszacować
gaunt (go:nt) adj. chudy; nędzny;wycienczony;ponury;posępny
gauze ('go:z) s. gaza; siateczka;mgiełka;gaza metalowa
gave (gejw) zob. give
gay (gej) adj. wesoły; jaskrawy; pstry; rozpustny; s. pederasta;pedzio;pedał
gaze (gejz) s. spojrzenie; v. przyglądać się;przypatrywać się,
gaze at (gejz aet) v. wpatrywać (się)w kogoś, w coś
gear (gier) v. włączyć (napęd) s. przybory; bieg; układ
gear change ('gier,czeindż) zmiana biegów

gearbox ('gier,boks) s. skrzynka biegów;skrzynia biegów
gearing ('gieryng) s. przekładnia;mechanizm napędowy
gear wheel ('gier-hłi:l) s. tryb; koło zębate
geese (gi:s) pl. gęsi
gem (dżem) s. klejnot;perła
gender ('dżender) s. rodzaj; płeć; wytwór; potomstwo
general ('dżenerel) adj. ogólny; powszechny; generalny; naczelny; główny; nieścisły; ogólnikowy; s. generał; wódz
generalize ('dżenerelajz) v. uogólniać; mówić ogólnikami
generally ('dżenerely) adv. ogólnie; zazwyczaj; powszechnie; najczęściej; w ogóle,
generate ('dżenerejt) v. rodzić; wytwarzać;płodzić; wywoływać
generation ('dżenerejszyn) s. powstawanie; pokolenie
generator ('dżenerejter) s. prądnica; sprawca;generator
generosity (,dżene'rosyty) s. szczodrość; wspaniałomyślność
generous ('dżeneres) adj. hojny; wielkoduszny; suty; obfity; bogaty; żyzny;mocny; krzepiący
genial ('dżi:njel) adj. wesoły; łagodny; miły;jowialny;ożywczy
genitive (dżenytyw) s. (gram.) dopełniacz;adj.wesoły;łagodny
genius (dżi:njes) s. geniusz; duch; talent;duch epoki etc.
genocide ('dżenousajd) s. ludobójstwo(stematyczne mordowanie)
gentle ('dżentl) adj. łagodny; delikatny; subtelny.stopniowy
gentleman ('dżentlmen) s. pan; człowiek honorowy; dżentelmen
gentlemanly ('dżentlmenly) adj. dżentelmeński; honorowy
gentleness ('dżentlnys) s. łagodność; delikatność
gentlewomen ('dżentl,łumen) s. szlachcianka; dama;dama dworu
gentry ('dżentry) s. ziemiaństwo; szlachta; światek
genuine ('dżenjuyn) adj. prawdziwy; autentyczny; szczery

geography (dży'ogrefy) s. geografia; fizyczne cechy rejonu
geologist (dży'oledżyst) s.
geolog
geology (dży'oledży) s. geologia
geometry (dży'omytry) s. geometria
germ (dże:rm) s. zarodek; zarazek; nasienie; pączek
German ('dże:rmen) adj. niemiec-
ki(jezyk,człowiek)s.Niemiec
germinate ('dże:rmynejt) v.
kiełkować; rozwijać się
gerund (dżerend) s. rzeczownik
odsłowny(z końcówką:"ing")
gestation ('dżes'tejszyn) s.
ciąża
gesticulate ('dżes'tykjulejt)
v. gestykylować; mówić na migi
gesture ('dżesczer) s. gest
get; got; got (get; got; got)
get (get) v. dostac; otrzymać;
nabyć; zawołać; łupać; przynieść; zmusic; musić; miec; dostac się; wpływać;wsiadać
get about (,get e'baut) v. poruszac się;rozchodzić się
get along (,get e'long) v. dawać sobie radę; współpracować
get away (,get e'łej) v. uciec;
odejsć;wyjeżdżać;oderwać się
get in (,get'yn) v. wejsc; wsiasc
get off (,get'of) v. wysiasc;
get on (,get'on) v. wdziewać;
posuwać się; robić dalej
get out (,get'aut) v. wysiasc;
wyjmować; wyciągać;wynosic się
get to (,get'tu) v. dotrzec;
przyjsc; musiec;być zamuszonym
get together (,get te'gedzer) v.
zebrać się; s. zebranie
get up (,get'ap) v. wstac;zbudzic się
get-up ('getap) s.wygląd;ubiór
get ready (,get'redy) v. przygo-
towac(się);przygotowywać się
get to know ('get,tu'nou) v. za-
poznac się (bliżej)
geyser ('gajzer) s. gejzer
ghastly ('ga:stly) adj. ohydny;
upiorny; blady;adv.okropnie
gherkin ('ge:rkyn) s, korniszon
ghost (goust) s. duch; cień;widmo

ghostly ('goustly) adj. upiorny
giant ('dżajent) s. olbrzym
gibbet ('dżybyt) s. szubienica
gibe ('dżajb) s. kpina; drwina;
v. kpić; szydzic; wysmiewac
giblets ('dżyblyts) pl. pod-
robki (np. kurze);podroby
giddy ('gydy) adj. zawrotny; mający zawrót głowy; roztrzepany;
v. przyprawiac o zawrót głowy
gift (gyft) s. dar; upominek;
talent; uzdolnienie;a.darowany
gifted ('gyftyd) adj. utalentowany;mający naturalne zdolności
gigantic (dżaj'gantyk) adj.
olbrzymi; gigantyczny;kolosalny
giggle ('gygl) s. chichot;
v. chichotac;głupio śmiać się
gild (gyld) v. złocic; pozło-
cic;nadać lepszego wyglądu
gill (gyl) s. skrzela; wąwóz; potok;jedna czwarta galona
gilt (gylt) adj. pozłacany;
s. złocenie; pozłocenie
gin (dżyn) s. jałowcówka
ginger ('dżyndżer) s. imbir
ginger bread ('dżyndżer,bred)
s. piernik;przesadne dekoracje
gingerly ('dżyndżerly) adj.
ostrożny; delikatny; adv.
ostrożnie; delikatnie; niesmia-
gipsy ('dżypsy)s. cygan
giraffe (dży'ra:f) s. żyrafa
gird; girt; girt (ge:rd; ge:rt;
ge:rt)
gird (ge:rd) v. opasac;kpić.s.kpi-
girder ('ge:rder) s. dzwigar;
belka; wzdłużnik
girdle ('ge:rdl) s. pas; v.
opasac; okrążyć;opasywać
girl (ge:rl) s. dziewczyna;ukocha-
girlhood ('ge:rlhud) s. wiek
dziewczęcy; dziewczeta (kraju etc.)
girl scout ('ge:rl skaut) s.
harcerka
girl's name ('ge:rls,nejm) s.
panieńskie nazwisko
girt (ge:rt) zob. gird
girth (ge:rt) s. popręg; obwod
gist (dżyst) s. tresc; istota;
sedno; esencja; osnowa;sens;
główna tresc

give; gave; given (gyw; gejw;
gywn)
give (gyw) v. dac; dawac; byc
elastycznym; zawalic się;
ustąpic; s. elastycznosc;
ustępstwo pod naciskiem
give away (,gyw e'łej) v. wydawac; zdradzac;wydawac córkę,
give in (,gyw'yn) v. ustępowac;
podawac(nazwisko);uznawac w końcu
give up (,gyw'ap) v. poddac się;
ustąpic; zaniechac;dac za wygraną
give way (,gyw'łej) v. zrobic
miejsce; ustąpic;obsunąc się
glacier ('glaesjer) s. lodowiec
glad (glaed) adj. rad; wesoły;
radosny;dający radosc;ochoczy
gladly ('glaedly) adv. z przy-
jemnoscią; chętnie;własciwie
gladness ('glaednys) s. wesołosc; pogoda ducha; przyjemnosc
glamorous ('glaemeres) adj. czarujący; wspaniały; fascynujący
glance (gla:ns) v. spojrzec;
zesliznąc się; błyszczec; połyskiwac; s. rzut oka; błysk;
połysk;rekoszet;odbicie się
glance at ('gla:ns et) v. spojrzec na (cos);rzucic spojrzenie
gland (glaend) s. gruczoł
glare (gleer) v. błyskac; razic;
wlepiac wzrok; s.błysk; blask
glass (gla:s) s. szkło; szklanka;lampka;kieliszek;szyba etc.
glasses ('gla:sys) pl. okulary;
szkła
glassy ('gla:sy) adj. szklisty;
szklany;przezroczysty;bez wyrazu
glaze (glejz) v. szklic; oszklic
glazier ('glejzjer) s. szklarz
gleam (gli:m) s. połysk; v. połyskiwac;zjawic się nagle
glee (gli:) s. wesele; radosc
glen (glen) s. dolina(zaciszna)
glib (glyb) adj. gładki; zwawy;
płynny; wygadany(zanadto)
glide ('glajd) s. poslizg; szy-
bowanie; v. slizgac się; szybowac; powodowac poslizg
glider ('glajder) s. szybowiec
glimmer ('glymer) v. migotac;
słabo swiecic; s. słabe swiatło;
migotanie;słabe postrzeganie

glimpse (glymps) s. mignięcie;
przelotne spojrzenie; v. ujrzec w przelocie;zerknąc
glint (glynt) s. błysk; odblask; v. błysnąc; zamigotac
glisten ('glysn) s. połysk;
v. połyskiwac;lsnic;iskrzyc się
glitter ('glyter) v. swiecic
się; błyszczec; s. połysk;
blask; pretensjonalnosc
gloat ('glout) v. napawac się;
zle patrzec;pożerac oczami
gloat over ('glout,ower) v.
napawac się (cudzym nie-
szczęsciem);unosic się
globe (gloub) s. globus; kula
ziemska;jabłko krolewskie;gałka
gloom (glu:m) s. smutek; mrok;
przygnębienie; v. zasmucac
(się); zaciemniac (się);posęp-
niec
gloomy ('glu:my) adj. ponury;
mroczny;posępny;przygnębiony
glorify ('glo:ryfaj) v. chwalic; wychwalac; gloryfikowac
glorious ('glo:rjes) adj. sławny; wspaniały;przepiękny;chlubny
glory ('glo:ry) s. chwała; sława; v. szczycic się; chlubic
się;chwalic się;chełpic się
gloss (glos) s. połysk; v. polerowac;interpretowac(błędnie)
glossary ('glosery) s. słownik
(przy tekscie);glosarjusz
glossy ('glosy) adj. lsniący
glove (glaw) s. rękawiczka
glow (glou) v. żarzyc się; pałac; s. jarzenie; zapał; żarliwosc;łuna;rumieniec;jasnosc
glowworm ('glou,łe:rm) s. ro-
baczek swiętojański
glue (glu:) s. klej; v. kleic;
zalepiac;wlepiac(oczy);zlepic
glutton ('glatn) s. żarłok
gluttonous ('glatnes) adj.
żarłoczny;jedzący zbyt dużo
gluttony ('glatny) s. żarłocz-
nosc;zwyczaj jedzenia za dużo
glycerine (,glyse'ry:n) s.
gliceryna
gnarled ('na:rld) adj. sękaty;
wykrzywiony; węzłowaty
gnash (naesz) v. zgrzytac zębami
jak w złosci

gnat (naet) s. komar;owad
gnaw (no:) v. gryźć; wgryzać;
ogryzać; nękać(stałym bólem)
go; went; gone (gou; lent; gon)
go (gou) v. iść; chodzić; jechać; stać się;być na chodzie
go about (,gou e'baut) v. za-
jąć się (czymś);afiszować się
go along (,gou e'loŋg) v. towarzyszyć; zgadzać się;iść sobie
go away (,go e'łej) v. iść
precz; odchodzić;wyjeżdżać
go back (,gou'bek) v. wracać;
cofać się;sięgać wstecz
go by (,gou'baj) v. mijać
go on (,gou'on) v. iść naprzód;
ciągnąć dalej; kontynuować
go out (,gou'aut) v. wychodzić
(z kimś); gasnąć;bywać(u ludzi)
go through (,gou'tru) v. przechodzić; brnąć przez ;przebrnąć
go under (,gou'ander) v. tonąć; ulegać; zniknąć;umrzeć
goad (goud) s. kolec; bodziec;
v. popędzać; drażnić; prowokować;doprowadzać do zrobienia
goal (goul) s. cel; meta; bramka
goalie (gouli) s. bramkarz
go-between (,gouby'tły:n) s.
pośrednik; stręczyciel
goblet ('goblyt) s. kieliszek;
czara;puchar;kielich na nóżce
goblin ('goblyn) s. chochlik
god (god) s. Bóg; bożek;bóstwo
godchild ('godczajld) s. chrześ-
niak; chrześniaczka
goddess ('godys) s. bogini
godfather ('god,fa:dzer) s.
ojciec chrzestny;v.trzymać do chrztu
godless ('godlys) adj. bezboż-
ny;grzeszny;niegodziwy;nikczemny
godmother ('god,madzer) s.
matka chrzestna
goggles ('goglz) pl. okulary
ochronne; gogle; okrągłe okulary
going ('gouyŋg)s. chodzenie;
jazda ;tempo;adj.ruchliwy;istnie-
going rate ('gouyŋ,rejt) bieżący kurs (dolara,oprocentowania)
gold (gould) s. złoto;adj.złoty
gold digger ('gould,dyger)
poszukiwacz złota ; naciągaczka

golden ('gouldn) adj. złoty
gold-plated ('gould,plejtyd)
s. plater złoty ;platerowany
goldsmith ('gould,smys) s.
złotnik golfa
golf (golf) s. golf ;v.grać w
golf course ('golf,ko:rs) s.
pole golfowe
gondola ('gondele) s. gondola
(np. balonu);otwarty,niski wagon towarowy
gone (gon) v. zob. go
good (gud) adj. dobry; s. dobro; pożytek; zaleta;wartość
better ('beter) lepszy;
best (best) najlepszy
good at it ('gud,et'yt) dobry
w tym; dobrze to robi
good-bye (,gud'baj) s. do widzenia; pożegnanie
good-for-nothing ('gudfe:r,na-
syŋg) s. nicpoń ;hultaj;łobuziak
good-looking ('gud'lukyŋg)adj.
przystojny; ładny
good-natured ('gud'nejczerd)
adj. dobroduszny;poczciwy
goodness ('gudnys) s. dobroć
good will ('gud'ływl) s. dobra
wola;wartość reputacji firmy
goose(gu:s) s. gęś; pl. geese
(gi:s) gęsi;gęsie mięso;duren
gooseberry ('gusbery) s. agrest
gooseflesh ('gu:sflesz) s. gę-
sia skórka (z zimna,strachu etc.)
gopher ('goufer) s. suseł;
v. grzebać;ryć;plądrować gospo-darke
gore (go:r) v. bóść; klinować;
s, klin w krawiectwie;posoka
gorge ('go:rdż) s. wąwóz; żarłoczność; treść żołądka; prze-
jedzenie; gardziel; v, obżerać
się; pożerać; połykać;opychać się
gorgeous ('go:rdżes) adj. wspaniały; okazały; suty; ozdobny;
wystawny;wspaniały;cudowny
gospel ('gospel) s. ewangielia
gossip ('gosyp) s. plotka;
plotkarz; plotkarka; v. plotkować;pisać popularne artykuły
got (got) zob. get
Gothic ('gotyk) adj. gotycki
gotten ('gotn) = got; zob. get
gourd (go:rd) s. bania; tykwa

gourmet ('guermej), n. smakosz

gout (gaut) s. gościec;podagra

govern ('gawern) v. rządzić;
kierować; dowodzić;trzymać w ryzach

governess ('gawernys) s. guwer-
nantka;nauczycielka;instruktor-
ka

government ('gawernment) s.
rząd; ustrój;okręg;a.rządowy

governor ('gawerner) s. gubernator; zarządca;naczelnik;szef

gown (gaun) s. suknia; toga;
v. układać togę;ubierać suknię

grab (graeb) v. łapać; zagar-
niać; grabić; s. łapanie;
chwyt; zagarnięcie;porwanie

grace (grejs) s. łaska; wdzięk;
przyzwoitość; v. czcić; ozdabiać; dodawać wdzięku;zaszczy-
cić

graceful ('grejsful) adj. pełen
wdzięku; wdzięczny;łaskawy

gracious ('grejszes) adj. łaskawy; miłosierny;exp. goodness gracious('gudnys'grejszes) Boże miłosierny!

grade (grejd) s. stopień; klasa; nachylenie; v. stopniować;
dzielić na stopnie; cieniować;
równać teren;niwelować;profilo-
wać

grade crossing ('grejd'krosyng)
s. skrzyżowanie dróg; przejazd
przez tory(jedno poziomowe)

grade school('grejd'sku:l) s.
szkoła podstawowa

gradient ('grejdjent) s. nachylenie; stopień nachylenia

gradual ('graedżuel) adj. stopniowy;po trochu

graduate ('graedżuejt) s. absol-
went; v. stopniować; ukończyć
studia;adj. podyplomowy(kurs)

graduation (,graedżu'ejszyn) s.
ukończenie wyższych studiów;
stopniowanie;cechowanie;podział
ka

graft (gra:ft) v. szczepić; dawać łapówkę; przeszczepiać;
s. szczepienie; łapówka; przeszczep;szufla(pełna ziemi)

grain (grejn) s. ziarno; zboże;
odrobina; grań; włókno; słój;
v. granulować; ziarnować

gram (graem) s. gram;1/28uncji

grammar ('graemer) s. gramatyka

grammar school ('graemer-sku:l)
s. szkoła podstawowa

grammatical (gre'maetykel) adj.
gramatyczny(poprawny)

gramme (graem) s. gram (ang.)

gramophone ('graemefoun) s.
patefon; gramofon

grand (graend) adj. wielki; główny; wspaniały; świetny; okazały;
(slang):1000 dolarów;całkowity

grandchild ('graen,chajld) s.
wnuk

granddaughter ('graen,do:ter) s.
wnuczka

grandeur ('graendżer) s. wielkość; dostojność; okazałość;
wspaniałość;majestat;blask;pompa

grandfather ('graend,fa:dzer)s.
dziadek

grandma ('graenma:) s. babcia

grandmother ('graen,madzer) s.
babka

grandpa ('graenpa:) s. dziadzio

grandparents ('graen,pearents)
pl. dziadkowie

grandson ('graensan) s. wnuk

grandstand ('graenstaend) s.
główna trybuna;popisywać się

granny ('graeny) s. babunia

grant (gra:nt) v. nadawać; udzielać; uznawać; zgadzać się na;
przekazywać; s,pomoc; przekazanie tytułu własności;darowizna

granulated ('graenjulejtyd) adj.
ziarnisty;rozdrobniony;granulowa-
ny

grape (grejp) s. winogrona

grapefruit ('grejp-fru:t) s.
greipfrut(owoc lub drzewo)

grape-sugar ('grejp,szuger) s.
cukier gronowy

grapevine ('grejp-wajn) s. winorosl; poczta pantoflowa; szep-
tanka;źródło kaczek prasowych

graph (fraef) s. wykres; krzywa

graphic ('graefyk) adj. graficz-
ny; plastyczny; obrazowy(dosadny)

grasp (gra:sp) v. łapać; chwytać; pojmać; pojmować; dzierżyć; s. chwyt; uchwyt; pojęcie;
panowanie;zrozumienie;kontrola

grass (gra:s) s. trawa; (slang):
marijuana; "pot";haszysz

grasshopper ('gra:s,hoper) s.
konik polny (z czterema skrzydłami) ży; świetny; znakomity; wspa-
grass widower ('gra:s,łydouer)
s. słomiany wdowiec
grate (grejt) s. krata; ruszt;
v. trzeć; ucierać; zgrzytać;
skrzypieć;irytować;być irytującym
grateful ('grejtful) adj.
wdzięczny;dobrze widziany
grater ('grejter) s. tarko;
tarło;raszpla;tarnik do drzewa
gratification (,graetyfy'kejszyn)
s. zaspokojenie; wynagrodzenie; gratyfikacja;łapówka
gratify ('graetyfaj) v. dogadzać; uprzyjemniac; zadawalać;
przekupywać·wynagradzać
grating ('grejtyŋg) s. krata;
adj. zgrzytliwy; ochrypły
gratis ('grejtys) adv. gratis;
bezpłatnie; adj. bezpłatny;
gratisowy ;darmowy
gratitude ('graetytju:d) s.
wdzięcznosć(za pomoc etc.)
gratuitous (gre'tjuites) adj.
bezpłatny; niepotrzebny
gratuity (gre'tjuity) s. napiwek; zasiłek przy zwolnieniu
grave ('grejw) s. grób; adj.
poważny; v. wyryć; wryć;wykopać
gravel ('grawel) s. żwir; piasek;v.psypywać żwirem; kłopotać
graveyard ('grejwja:rd) s. cmentarz; nocna zmiana w pracy
gravitation (,graewy'tejszyn)
s. ciążenie(ciał);grawitacja
gravity ('graewyty) s. siła
ciężkości; ciężkość; powaga
(np. sytuacji);ciężar (gatunkowy)
gravy ('grejwy) s. sos mięsny;
sok;dodatkowy zysk;osobista ko-
gray (grej) adj. szary; zob. rzyść
grey ;v.szarzeć;s.szary kolor
graze (grejz) v. pasc; drasnąć;
s. drasnięcie; muśnięcie;odarcie
grazing land ('grejzyŋg,laend)
s. pastwisko; pastwiska
grease (gri:s) s. tłuszcz; smar;
v. brudzić; smarować; nasmarować smarem(samochod etc.)
grease gun ('gri:s,gan) s. sma-
rownica wyciskowa ;towotnica
greasy('gri:sy)adj.tłusty;śliski

great (grjet) adj. wielki; duży; świetny; znakomity; wspaniały ;zamiłowany;doniosły;pra-
greatcoat ('grejt'kout) s.
palto; płaszcz;opończa
great grandchild ('grejt'graend-
czajld) s. prawnuk
great grandfather ('grejt'-
graendfa:dzer) s. pradziadek
great grandmother ('grejt'-
grand,madzer) s. prababka
greatness ('grejtnys) s. wielkość; ogrom;wielkoduszność;powa-ga
greed (gri:d) s. chciwosc; zachłanność;żądza(władzy etc)
greedy (gri:dy) adj. chciwy;
zachłanny; łakomy; łapczywy;
żądny;zarłoczny;spragniony
Greek adj. grecki; (niezrozumiały);s.język grecki;Grek
green (gri:n) adj. zielony;
naiwny; młody; niedoświadczony; świeży; s. zieleń; zieleni-
na; trawnik;v.zielenić;naciągać
greenback ('gri:nbaek) s.
(slang) dolar(banknot)
greenhorn ('gri:nhorn) s. nowicjusz ;żółtodziub
greenhouse ('gri:nhaus) s.
cieplarnia
greenish ('gri:nysh) adj. zie-
lonkawy
greet ('gri:t) v. kłaniac się;
pozdrawiac; ukazac się; dojść
do (uszu);zaprezentować się
greeting ('gri:tyŋg)s. pozdrowienie; powitanie;pozdrowienia
grew (gru:) zob. grow
grey (grej) adj. szary; siwy;
s. szarość; v. szarzeć; siwiec (ortografia brytyjska)
greyhound ('grejhaund) s.
chart(wysoki;chudy,szybki,pies)
grid (gryd) s. krata; sieć;
siatka ;sieć wysokiego napięcia
grief (gri:f) s. zmartwienie;
zgryzota ;smutek;żal
grievance ('gri:wens) s. uraza;
krzywda; skarga; zażalenie
grieve (gri:w) v. martwic;
krzywdzić; smucić ;zasmucić
grievious ('gri:wes) adj. dre-
czący; przykry ;ciężki;smutny

grill (gryl) s. rożen; krata;
potrawa z rusztu; v. smażyć
na rożnie; przesłuchiwać
grim (grym) adj. srogi; ponury;
okrutny;groźny;odrażający
grimace (gri'mejs) s. grymas;
v. grymasić
grime (grajm) s. brud; v. bru-
dzić(sadzą, smarem etc.)
grimy ('grajmy) adj. brudny;
wysmarowany; zatłuszczony
grin (gryn) v. szczerzyć zęby;
uśmiechać się; s. uśmiech
grind; ground; ground (grajnd;
graund; graund)
grind (grajnd) v. ostrzyc; toczyć; mleć; zgrzytać; trzeć;
harować; s. mlenie; harówka;
kujon;ciężka rutyna;kucie się
grindstone ('grajnd,stoun) s.
kamień szlifierski:harówka
grip (gryp) s. uchwyt; trzonek;
rękojeść; ucisk dłoni;walizka;
v. chwycić; złapać; trzymać
gripes (grajps) pl. kolka
gristle ('grysl) s. chrząstka
grit (gryt) s. żwir; piasek;
odwaga; wytrzymałość;charakter;
v. zgrzytać; skrzypieć;posypy-
wać;
groan (groun) s. jęk; v. jęczeć
grocer ('grouser) s. właściciel
sklepu spożywczego
groceries ('grouserys) pl. towary spożywcze
grocery ('grousery) s. sklep
spożywczy;artykuł spożywczy
groin (grain) s. pachwina
groom (grum) s, parobek; pan
młody; v. obrządzać; przygotowywać do objęcia stanowiska
groove (gru:w) s. bruzda; rowek; rutyna; v. żłobić; rowkować;nacinać zwojnik;gwintować
grope (group) v. szukać po omacku; iść po omacku;iść na slepo
gross (grous) adj. gruby; ordynarny; prostacki; całkowity;
hurtowy; tłusty; niesmaczny;
spasły; wybujały; s. 12 tuzi-
nów; v. uzyskać brutto...
ground (graund) s. grunt;zie-
mia; podstawa; podłoże; teren;
dno(morza);osad;powód;przyczyna

dno; v. l. osiąść na mieliźnie;
uziemiać; gruntować; zagrunto-
wać; v. 2. zob. grind
ground control ('graund,ken'troul)
kontrolna stacja (lotów)
ground crew ('graund.kru:) s.
załoga, ekipa na ziemi
ground floor ('graund,flo:r) s.
parter(bliski poziomu gruntu)
ground glass ('graund,glas) s.
tłuczone szkło
groundhog ('graundhog) s. świstak (amerykański)
groundless ('graundlys) adj.
bezpodstawny;gołosłowny
groundnut ('graundnat) s. orzeszek ziemny
ground staff ('graund,staf) s.
personel naziemny(lotnictwa etc.)
groundwork ('graundłerk) s. podstawa; podłoże; zasada; fundament;tło;osnowa;kanwa(utworu)
group (gru:p) s. grupa; v. grupować;rozsegregowywać na grupy
grove (grouw) s. gaj
grow; grew; grown(grou; gru:
groun)
grow (grou) v. rosnąć; stawać
się; dojrzewać; hodować; sadzić
growl (graul) s. ryk; pomruk;
warczenie; v. mruknąć; warknąć;
burczeć; warczeć; odburknąć;
gderać;mrukliwie odpowiadać
grown (groun) v. zob. grow
grown-up ('groun,ap) adj. dorosły; s. dorosły człowiek
growth (grous) s. rozwój; wzrost;
uprawa; narosl;porost;przyrost
grub (grab) .v karczować; dłubac: harować; wcinać (jedzenie)
grubby (graby) adj. brudny;
niechlujny;robaczywy
grudge (gradż) v. żałować; ską-
pić; zazdroscić; mieć niechęć;
s. żal; uraza; niechęć
gruel (gruel) s. kaszka; kleik;
v. wymęczyć ;zadawać bobu(komuś)
gruesome ('gru:sem) adj. okropny
gruff (graf) adj. burkliwy;
gburowaty; ochrypły;gruby(głos)
grumble ('grambl) v. narzekać;
utyskiwać;gderać;skarżyć się;
s.narzekanie; pomruk;szemranie

grumbler (grambler) s. zrzęda
grunt (grant) s. kwik; v. kwiczeć;chrząkać;wymruczeć
guarantee (,gaeren'ti:) v.
gwarantować; poręczać; s. poręczyciel;poręka;rękojmia
guarantor (,gaeren'to:r) s.
poręczyciel; poręczycielka
guaranty (,gaerenty) s. gwarancja; poręka;rękojmia;poręczenie
guard (ga:rd) v. pilnować;chronić; s. strażnik; opiekun;
obrońca; bezpiecznik
guard against ('ga:rd.e'genst)
v. zabezpieczać się przed...
guardhouse ('ga:rdhaus) s.
wartownia;tymczasowy areszt
guardian ('ga:rdjen) s. opiekun; kustosz;adj.opiekuńczy
guardianship ('ga:rdjenshyp)s.
opieka; opiekuństwo; kuratela
guess (ges) v. zgadywać; przypuszczać; myśleć; s. zgadywanie; przypuszczenie;zgadnięcie
guest (gest) s. gość
guest house ('gesthaus) s. pensjonat; osobny domek dla gości
guest room ('gestru:m) s. pokój gościnny;gościnna sypialnia
guidance ('gajdens) s. kierownictwo; poradnictwo;kierowanie
guide (gajd) s. przewodnik;
doradca;v.wskazywać drogę;prowadzić
guidebook ('gajdbuk) s. przewodnik (książka)dla turystów
guild (gyld) s. cech; związek
guildhall('gyld'ho:1) s. dom
cechowy; ratusz;dom związkowy
guile (gajl) s. oszustwo
guileless ('gajllys) adj.
szczery; otwarty(w postępowaniu)
guilt (gylt) s. wina;przestępstwo
guiltless ('gyltlys) adj. niewinny;wolny od zarzutu
guilty ('gylty) adj. winny
guinea pig ('gynypyg) s. świnka morska;przedmiot experymentów
guitar (gy'ta:r) s. gitara
gulf (galf) s. zatoka; przepaść; wir; v. pochłaniać
gull (gal) s. mewa;v.oszukiwać
gullet (galyt) s. przełyk; gardło; gardziel

gully ('galy) s. wąwóz; ściek;
kanał; v. żłobić;wyżłobić;poryć
gulp (galp) s. łyk; duży kęs
gulp down (galpdałn) v. łykać;
dławić się; hamować łzy
gum (gam) s. dziąsło; guma;
v. kleić;wydzielać żywicę
gun (gan) s. strzelba; armata;
pistolet;działo;wystrzał armatni
gunpowder ('gan,pałder) s. proch
strzelniczy;proch armatni
gurgle ('ge:rgle) v. bulgotać;
bełkotać;s.bulgotanie;szemranie
gush (gasz) s. ulewa; wylew;
v. tryskać; lać się;wytrysnąć
gust (gast) s. podmuch; wybuch
gut (gat) s. kiszka; v. patroszyć;wypalić wnętrze (domu)
guts (gats) pl. wnętrzności
gutter ('gater) v. wyżłobić;
okapywać; s. rynna; rynsztok;
rów; wyżłobienie; adj. rynsztokowy; brukowy(dziennik)
guy (gaj) s. facet; człek; cuma; v. cumować; uwiązać
gym (dżym) s. sala gimnastyczna;
gimnastyka(przedmiot w szkole)
gymnasium (dżym'nejzjem) s. sala gimnastyczna;hala sportowa
gymnastics (dżym'naestyks) s.
gimnastyka;ćwiczenia fizyczne
gynecologist (,gajny'koledżyst)
s. ginekolog
gypsy ('dżypsy) s. cygan; cyganka;cyganeria;język cygański
gyrate (,dżaje'rejt) v. wirować;
kręcić się(wg.koła lub spirali)
h (ejcz) ósma litera angielskiego alfabetu (prawie niema)
haberdasher ('haeberdaeszer) s.
kupiec galanteryjny;szmuklerz
habit ('haebyt) s. zwyczaj; nałóg; usposobienie; przyzwyczajenie; habit; v. odziewać się
habitation (,haeby'tejszyn) s.
miejsce zamieszkania;zamieszkiwanie
habitual (he'bytjual) adj.
zwykły; nałogowy; zwyczajny
hack (haek) v. siekać; rąbać;
kopać; kaszleć; s. szrama; motyka; szkapa; najemnik; taksówka; adj. wynajęty; spowszedniały; banalny;oklepany;szablonowy

hacksaw ('haekso:) s. piła do
metalu (z drobnymi zębami)
had (haed) zob. have
haddock ('haedek) s. łupacz
h(a)emorrhage ('hemerydż) s.
krwotok;v. mieć krwotok
hag (haeg) s. wiedźma; czarownica;brzydka zła kobieta
haggard ('haegerd) adj. wynędz-
niały; strapiony; wychudły
hail (hejl) s. grad; powitanie;
v. grad pada; witac; pozdrawiac; zawołac;walic jak gradem
hair (heer) s. włos; włosy
hairbrush ('heerbrasz) s.
szczotka do włosów
haircut ('heerkat) s. ostrzyże-
nie;styl strzyżenia włosów
hairdo ('heerdu:) s. uczesanie;
fryzura;styl uczesania
hairdresser ('heer,dreser) s.
fryzjer damski
hairdryer ('heer,drajer) s. suszarka do włosów(elektryczna)
hairless ('h-erlys) adj. bez-
włosy; łysy;wyłysiały
hairpin ('heerpyn) s. szpilka
do włosów
hairy (heery) adj. włochaty
half (ha:f) s. połowa; adj.pół;
adv. na pół; po połowie
half an hour ('ha:f,en'aur) s.
pół godziny
half brother ('ha:f,bradżer)
s. przyrodni brat
half-breed ('ha:f,bri:d) s.
mieszaniec
halftime ('ha:f'tajm) s. przerwa; pół etatu;a.pół-etatowy
halfway ('ha:f'łej) adv. w pół
drogi; w połowie drogi
hall (ho:l) s. sień; sala; hala;
dwor; gmach publiczny;westybul
hallo ! (he'lou) excl.;czesc !
halo ! czolem! dzień dobry!
halo ('hejlou) s. nimb; aureola
halt (ho:lt) v. zatrzymać; utykać; kulec; wahać się; s.po-
stoj; przystanek;utykanie
halter ('ho:lter) s. kantar pa-
stewny; stryczek;v.nakładać kan
halve (ha:w) v. przepołowic;po-
dzielic się po połowie

ham (haem) s. szynka
hamburger ('haembe:rger) s. sie-
kany kotlet wołowy; bułka z
siekanym kotletem wołowym
hamlet ('haemlyt) s. wioska;
sioło; malutka wies
hammer ('haemer) s. młotek;
v. bic młotkiem; walic
hammock ('haemok) s. hamak
hamper ('haemper) v. zawadzac;
krępowac; s. kosz z wiekiem
hamster ('haemster) s. chomik
hand (haend) s. ręka; dłon;
pismo; v. podac; zwijac; pomagac;a.podręczny;przenosny
hand back ('haend,baek) v. oddac; podac do tyłu
hand down ('haend,dałn) v. przekazac; dac w spadku;podac w dół
hand in ('haend,yn) v. wręczyc
hand over ('haend,ouwer) v.,
wręczyc; podac; dostarczyc
handbag ('haendbaeg) s. damska
torebka
handbill ('haendbyl) s. ulotka
handbook ('haend-buk) s. podręcznik; poradnik
hand brake ('haend,brejk) s.
hamulec ręczny
handcuff ('haendka:f) s. kajdany; v. zakuwac w kajdany
handful ('haendful) s. garsc;
garstka; kłopotliwa osoba
handicap ('haendykaep) s. przeszkoda; uposledzenie; trudnosc
handicraft ('haendykra:ft) s.
rzemiosło; rękodzieło (tkactwo
etc.)
handkerchief ('henkerczy:f) s.
apaszka; chustka do nosa
handle ('haendl) s. trzonek;
rękojesc; uchwyt; sposob;
v. dotykac; manipulowac; traktowac; załatwiac; dac radę;
handlowac;zarządzać;kontrolować
handlebar ('haendlba:r) s. kie-
rownica(od roweru)
hand luggage ('haend,lagydż) s.
bagaż ręczny
handmade ('haend'mejd) adj.
ręcznie zrobiony
handrail ('haend,rejl) s. poręcz; bariera;balustrada

handshake ('haend,shejk) s. uścisk dłoni(w pozdrowieniu,tar-gu) s.

handsome ('haensem) s. przystojny; szczodry;znaczny(datek)

handwork ('haend,łe:rk) s. robota ręczna;praca fizyczna

handwriting ('haend,rajtyŋg) s. pismo; charakter pisma

handy ('haendy) adj. zręczny; wygodny; bliski;pod ręką

hang; hung; hung (haeŋg; haŋg; haŋg)

hang (haeŋg) s. wieszac; powiesic; rozwiesic; wywiesic; zwisac; s. nachylenie; pochyłosc;powiązanie;orientacja

hang around ('haeŋg e'raund) v. wałęsac się;obijać się

hang out ('haeŋg'aut) v. wywieszac; wychylac się

hang up ('haeŋg,ap) v. zaczepic się; powiesic słuchawkę; opoźniac (pracę);wstrzymywac

hangar ('haeŋger) s. hangar

hang-glider ('haeŋg'glajder) s. lotnia; skrzydło Rogali

hangings ('haeŋyŋz) s. kotary; portiery;draperie;obicia;firanki

hang loose ('haeŋ,lu:z) v. byc rozluźniony w akcji (sportowej); zwisac swobodnie

hangover ('haeŋg,ouwer) s. (slang) kac; przeżytek

hanky-panky ('haeŋky-paenky) s. hokus-pokus;też rozwiązłosc

haphazard ('haep'haezerd) s. los szczęścia; przypadek; adj. przypadkowy; dorywczy; adv. przypadkowo;na chybił trafił

happen ('haepen) v. zdarzac się; trafic się; przypadkowo byc (gdzieś);miec(nie)szczęście

happen on ('haepen,on) v. przypadkiem spotkac;natknąc się na

happening ('haepenyŋg) s. wydarzenie; wypadek;zdarzenie

happily ('haepyly) adv. szczęsliwie;na szczęście;trafnie

happiness ('haepynys) s. szczęscie; zadowolenie; radość

happy ('haepy) adj. szczęsliwy; zadowolony;właściwy (wybór); mądra (rada); radosny

happy-go-lucky ('haepy,gou-laky) adj. beztroski

harass ('haeres) v. niepokoic; trapic; dręczyc; nękac

harbor ('ha:rber) s. przystań; port; v. goscic; dawać schronienie; zawijac do portu

hard (ha:rd) adj. twardy; surowy; trudny; ciężki; ostry; adv. usilnie; wytrwale; ciężko; z trudem; siarczyście

hard by ('ha:rd,baj) adv. blisko;tuż obok; w pobliżu

hard up ('ha:rd,ap) byc w kłopotach pieniężnych

hard of hearing (ha:rd,ow'-hieryŋg) adj. głuchawy

harden ('ha:rdn) v. twardniec; uodpornic; stabilizowac

hardheaded ('ha:rd'hedyd) adj. trzezwy; praktyczny;twardy człowiek

hardhearted ('ha:rd'ha:rtyd) adj. nieczuły; niemiłosierny

hardly ('ha:rdly) adv. ledwie; zaledwie; prawie; z trudem; surowo;chyba nie; rzadko

hardness ('ha:rdnys) s. twardosc; wytrzymałosc;odpornosc

hardship ('ha:rdszyp) s. trudnosc; trudy; męka; znój

hardware ('ha:rdłeer) s. wyroby żelazne;towary żelazne

hare (heer) s. zając;królik

harebell ('heer-bel) s. dzwonek okrągłolistny

hark (ha:rk) v. słuchaj; uważaj; odejdz;słuchaj uważnie

harm (ha:rm) s. szkoda; krzywda; v. szkodzic; krzywdzic

harmful ('ha:rmful) adj. szkodliwy;szkodzący;zadający ból

harmless ('ha:rmlys) adj. nieszkodliwy; niewinny

harmonious (ha:rmounjes) adj. harmonijny;melodyjny;zgodny

harmonize ('ha:rmenajz) s. uzgadniac; harmonizowac

harmony ('ha:rmeny) s. harmonia (dzwięków,ludzi);zgoda

harness ('ha:rnys) s. uprząż; v. zaprzęgac:zużytkowac(wiatr...)

harp (ha:rp) s. harfa; v. gadac w kółko; grac na harfie

harpoon (ha:'rpu:n) s. harpun;
v. ugodzić harpunem

harrow ('haerou) s. brona; v.
bronować; dręczyć; szarpać;
ranić; pustoszyć; niszczyć

harsh (ha:rsz) adj. szorstki;
zrący; ostry; cierpki; przykry; surowy;nieprzyjemny

hart (ha:rt) s. rogacz (dorosły)(powyżej pięcioletni)

harvest('ha:rwyst) s. żniwa;
zbiory; zbiór; urodzaj; plony; v. zbierać (zboże); zbierać (plony);sprzątać z pól

harvester ('ha:rwyter) s. żniwiarz; żniwiarka (mechaniczna)

has (haez) (on,ona.ono) ma;
zob. have

hash (haesz) s. siekane mięso;
v. siekać;knocić;przemieszać

haste (hejst) s. pospiech
hasten (hejstn) v. przyspieszać;
spieszyć;być szybkim

hasty ('hejsty) adj. pospieszny; prędki; porywczy;niecier-
hat (haet) s. kapelusz   pliwy

hatch (haecz) v. wysiadywać;
wylęgać; wykluwać; knuć; za-
kreskować; s. wyląg; łuk;
drzwiczki; sluza; kreska

hatchet ('haeczyt) s. toporek

hatchet man('haeczyt,men) s.
człowiek przeprowadzający
czystkę(odrabiający brudną robotę)

hate (hejt) s. nienawiść;
v. nienawidzieć;nieznosić

hateful ('hejtful) adj. nienawistny;zasługujący na nienawiść

hatred ('hejtryd) s. nienawiść

haughtiness ('ho:tynys) s.pysz-
ność; hardość;zarozumialstwo

haughty ('ho:ty) adj. hardy;
pyszny;zarozumiały;wzgardliwy

haul (ho:l) s. wleczenie; holowanie; ładunek; połów; zysk;
v. wlec; ciągnąć; holować;
wozić; transportować;taszczyć

haunch (ho:ncz) s. biodro z udem

haunt (ho:nt) v. nawiedzać;
s, miejsce często odwiedzane;
melina; spelunka;legowisko

have; had; had (haew; haed;
haed)

have (haew) v. mieć; otrzymać;
zawierać; nabyć; musieć

have-not ('haev,nat) adj. nie-
posiadający; biedny

have on ('haew on) v. mieć na
sobie;być ubranym w

have to do ('haew,tu'du) v. musieć (coś) robić

haven ('hejwn) s. przystań; port;
v. dawać schronienie; wprowadzać do portu

havoc ('haewek) s. spustoszenie

hawk (ho:k) s. jastrząb; packa;
chrząknięcie; v. polować
z jastrzębiem; sprzedawać na
ulicy; chrząkać głosno

hawthorn ('ho:torn) s. głog

hay (hej) s. siano

haycock ('hejkok) s. stóg siana

hayfever ('hej'fi:ver) s. uczu-
lenie; katar sienny

hayloft ('hej-loft) s. strych
na siano (w stodole etc.)

hayrick ('hejryk) s. stóg siana

haystack ('hejsta:k) s. stóg
siana (w polu, na łące etc.)

hazard ('haezerd) s. przypadek;
traf; ryzyko; v. ryzykować

hazardous ('haezerdes) adj. ryzykowny; hazardowny; niebezpieczny

haze (hejz) s. lekka mgła

hazel ('hejzl) s. leszczyna;
kolor orzechowy

hazel-nut ('hejzl-nat) s. orzech
laskowy

hazy ('hejzy) adj. mglisty;
zamglony; nieco podchmielony

H-bomb ('ejcz bom) s. bomba wodorowa

he (hi:) pron. on

head (hed) s. głowa: łeb; szef;
naczelnik; nagłówek; szczyt;
v. prowadzić; kierować (się)

head over heels ('hed,ouwer'-
hi:ls) do góry nogami; na łeb
na szyję; panicznie;w panice

head or tail ('hed,o:r'tejl)
orzeł czy reszka

headache ('hedejk) s. ból głowy

headgear ('hedgi:r) s. nakrycie głowy;ubiór głowy

heading ('hedyŋ) s. nagłówek

headland ('hedlend) s. przylądek (daleko wysunięty w morze)

headlights ('hedlajts) pl. główne światła samochodu

headline ('hedlajn) s. nagłówek (w gazecie);wiadomość w skrócie

headlong ('hedloŋg) adv. na łeb na szyję; na złamanie karku; na oślep;głową na przód

headmaster ('hedma:ster) s. dyrektor (szkoły)

headphones ('hedfouns) pl. słuchawki(radiowe,gramofonowe)

headquarters ('hed'kło:terz) pl. kwatera główna;główne biuro

headstrong ('hedstroŋg) adj. zawzięty; uparty;bezwzgledny

headway ('hedłej) s. postęp

heal (hi:l) v. leczyć; łagodzić; uspakajać;wyleczać się

heal up ('hi:l,ap) v. zagoić

health (hels) s. zdrowie

health resort (hels ry'zo:rt) s. uzdrowisko

healthy (helsy) adj. zdrowy; potężny;spowodowany zdrowiem

heap (hi:p) s. kupa; gromada; v. gromadzić; ładować na stos; obsypywać dużą ilością

hear; heard; heard (hier; he:rd; he:rd)

hear (hier) v. słyszeć; usłyszec; sluchac; dowiedziec się

heard (he:rd) zob. hear

hearing ('hieryŋg)s. słuch; posluch; przesłuchanie; rozprawa;zasięg głosu;słyszenie

hearsay ('hiersej) s. pogłoska

hearse (he:rs) s. karawan

heart (ha:rt) s. serce; odwaga; otucha; sedno;symbol serca

heartbreaking ('ha:rtbrejkyŋg) adj. rozdzierający serce

heartburn ('ha:rtbe:rn) s. zgaga; pieczenie w żołądku

hearth (ha:rs) s. palenisko

heartless ('ha:rtlys) adj. nieczuły; bez serca

heart transplant ('ha:rt,traens- pla:nt) przeszczepienie serca

hearty ('ha:rty) adj. serdeczny; szczery; otwarty;pożywny;obfity; solidny;dobry;krzepki;rzeski

heat (hi:t) s. gorąco; upał; żar; ciepło; uniesienie; pasja; popęd płciowy (zwierząt)

heater ('hi:ter) s. grzejnik; piec

heath (hi:s) s. wrzos; wrzosiec; wrzosowisko

heathen (hi:zen) adj. pogański; s. poganin. ciemniak

heather ('hedzer) s. wrzos

heating ('hi:tyŋg)s. ogrzewanie

heave; hove; hove (hi:w; houw; houw)

heave (hi:w) v. unosić; dźwigać; podważać; nabrzmiewać; wyciągać; sapać; s. dźwignięcie; przesunięcie

heaven ('hewn) s. niebo; raj; niebiosa

heavenly ('hewnly) adj. niebieski; niebiański; boski

heaviness ('hewynys) s. ciężkość; ociezałość

heavy ('hewy) adj. ciężki; duży; ponury; zrozpaczony

heavy-handed ('hewy'haendyd) adj. niezgrabny; nietaktowny; bezwzględny

heavy traffic ('hewy'traefyk) ciężki ruch (np. kołowy)

heavyweight ('hewyłejt) s. waga ciężka

hectic ('hektyk) adj. gorący; dziki; niszczący; rozgorączkowany

hedge (hedź) s. płot; żywopłot; ogrodzenie; zapora; ubezpieczenie; v. ogradzac; wykręcać się; ubezpieczac się w spekulacji

hedgehog ('hedżhog) s. jeż; świnka morska

heed (hi:d) s. troska; dbałość; uwaga; wzgląd; ostrożność; v. uważać; baczyć

heedful ('hi:dful) adj. uważny; ostrożny

heedless ('hi:dlys) adj. niedbały; nieostrożny; nieuważny

heel (hi:l) s. pięta; obcas; przechył; łajdak; v.dotykać piętą; podbijać obcas;zaopatrywać; przechylać się;tupać obcasem

he goat ('hi:gout) s. kozioł
heifer ('hefer) s. jałówka
height (hajt) s. wysokosć;
wzniesienie; wyniosłosć;
szczyt;najwyższa granica
heighten (hajtn) v. podnosic,
podwyższać;powiększać etc.
heinous ('hejnes) adj. potworny; ohydny;nienawistny;haniebny
heir (eer) s. spadkobierca;
dziedzic; nastepca
heiress ('eerys) s. spadkobierczyni; następczyni; dziedziczka (majątku, tytułu etc.)
held (held) zob. hold
helicopter ('helykopter) s.
śmigłowiec; helikopter
hell (hel) s. piekło; psiakrew ! miejsce nędzy i okrucieństwa
hello ('he'lou) excl.: hallo !
helm (helm) s. ster;v.sterować
helmet ('helmyt) s. hełm; kask
help (help) v. pomagać; usługiwac; nakładać (jedzenie)
s. pomoc; pomocnik; robotnik
helper ('helper) s. pomocnik
helpful ('helpful) adj. pomocny; przydatny; użyteczny
helping ('helpyng) s. porcja
(jedzenia);udzielanie pomocy
helpless ('helplys) adj. bezradny; bez pomocy ;słaby
helplessness ('helplysnys) s.
bezradność ;słabość
helter-skelter ('helter'skelter)
adv. na łapu-capu; na łeb na
szyję; s. popłoch; bezładny
pospiech(w bałaganie)
hem (hem) s. brzeg; obrąbek;
chrząkanie; v. obrębiać; otoczyć; pochrząkiwać; wahać się
hem in ('hem,yn) v. okrążyć;
zamknąc; obrębić
hemisphere ('hemysfier) s. półkula (zachodnia,wschodnia etc.)
hemline ('hemlajn) s. obrąbek
(spódnicy)
hemlock ('hemlek) s. szalej;
cykuta jadowita; drzewo tsuga
hemp (hemp) s. konopie; adj.
konopny (sznur etc.)
hemstitch ('hemstycz) s. mereżka; v. mereżkować(ozdobnie)

hen (hen) s. kura; kwoka; baba
hence (hens) adv. stąd; odtąd;
a więc; przeto; dlatego
henceforth (hens'fo:rs) adv.
odtąd; na przyszłosć;od teraz
hen coop ('henku:p) s. kurnik
hen house ('henhaus) s, kurnik
henpecked ('henpekt) s. pantoflarz;adj.będący pod pantoflen
her (he:r) pron. ją; jej; adj.
jej (należący)do niej
herald ('hereld) s. zwiastun;
v. zwiastować; wprowadzać
heraldry ('hereldry) s. heraldyka;pompa; ceremonia
herb (he:rb) s. zioło (jednoroczne)
herd (he:rd) s. trzoda; stado;
pastuch; v. isc stadem;zganiac
w stado; pasć;popędzać stadem
herdsman ('he:rdzmen) s. pasterz; pastuch
here (hier) adv. tu; tutaj; oto
here you are (,hier'ju:,a:r)
exp.:tu pan ma ! proszę bardzo !
hereafter ('hier'a:fter) adv.
odtąd; poniżej; potem; w życiu pozagrobowym; s, przyszłosć; przyszłe życie
hereby ('hier'bay) adv. przez
to; w ten sposób; skutkiem
tego; w pobliżu
hereditary (hy'redytery) adj.
dziedziczny; odziedziczony;
tradycyjny;przekazany dziedzicznie
herein ('hie'ryn) adv. tutaj;
tam że; wobec tego; w tych
warunkach,w tym(rozdziale etc.)
hereof ('hier'ow) adv. tego;
o tym ;w odniesieniu do tego
heresy ('herysy) s. herezja
hereupon ('hiere'pon) adv.
potem; skutkiem tego; o tym
herewith ('hier'łys) adv. niniejszym ;w ten sposób
heritage ('herytydż) s. spuścizna; spadek; dziedzictwo
hermit ('he:rmyt) s. pustelnik;
odludek;eremita;pustelnica
hero ('hierou) s. bohater
heroic ('hierouyk) adj. bohaterski ;heroiczny;epiczny; bardzo wymowny; podniosły

heroine ('hierouyn) s.bohaterka
heroism ('hierouyzem) s.
bohaterstwo (w czynach i ce-
chach)
heron ('heren) s. czapla
herring ('heryŋg)s. śledz
hers (he:rz) pron. jej
herself (he:r'self) pron. ona
sama; ona sobie; ja sama
hesitate ('hezytejt) v. wahać
się ;byc niepewnym;zatrzymać się
hesitation (,hezytejszyn) s.
wahanie;byc niezdecydowanym
hew; hewed; hewn (hju:; hju:d;
hju:n)
hew (hju:) v. rąbać; ciosac;
kuc; wyrąbywać(ścieżkę etc.)
hewn (hju:n) zob: hew
hey (hej) excl.: hej ! ej że!
heyday ('hejdej) s. pełnia;
rozkwit; świetny nastrój
hi (haj) excl.: hej ! (pozdrowienie) ; cześć! czołem!
hiccup; hiccough ('hykap) s.
czkawka; v. miec czkawkę
hid (hyd) zob, hide
hidden (hydn) zob. hide
hide; hid; hidden (hajd; hyd;
hydn)
hide (hajd) v. chować; ukrywać;
s. kryjówka; skóra (zwierzęca)
hide-and-seek ('hajd,en si:k)
exp.: zabawa w chowanego
hideous ('hydjes) adj. ochydny;
wstrętny ;paskudny;odrażający
hiding ('hajdyng)s. kryjówka;
skórobicie ; lanie;manto
hiding place ('hajdyŋg'plejs)
s. kryjówka; melina
hi-fi ('haj'faj) = high-fideli-
ty ('haj fy'delyty) wiernie
odtwarzający dźwięk (aparat)
high (haj) adj. wysoki; wyniosły; silny;cienki(głos)
highbrow ('hajbrau) s. intelektualista;a. intelektualny
high diving('hajdajwyŋg) s.
skakanie z wieży do wody
high jump('hajdżamp) s. skok
wzwyż (w sporcie)
highlands ('hajlend) s. pod-
górze; góry;górzysty kraj
highlights ('hajlajts) pl. głow-
ne punkty (np. programu)

highly ('hajly) adv. wysoko; wysoce; wielce; zaszczytnie
highness ('hajnys) s. wysokość
(tytuł); wyniosłość
high-pitched ('haj'pyczt) adj.
wysoki; ostry; cienki (głos)
spadzisty; stromy (dach)
high-powered ('haj'pałerd) adj.
potężny
high-pressure ('haj'preszer)
adj. wysokiego ciśnienia; na-
chalny
highroad ('haj'roud) s. szosa;
główna droga
high-school ('haj'sku:l) s.
gimnazjum; szkoła srednia
high-strung ('haj'straŋg)adj.
nerwowy; napięty; wrażliwy
high-tide ('haj'tajd) s. przypływ
highway ('haj'łej) s. szosa
highwayman ('haj,łejmen) s.
rozbójnik
hijack ('hajdżaek) v. rabować;
grabić
hike (hajk) v. włoczyc się;
wędrować; wyciągać do góry;
s. wycieczka; podwyżka
hilarious (hy'leerjes)adj.wesoły;
hałasliwie wesoły
hill (hyl) s. górka; pagórek;
kopiec; v. sypać kopiec
hillbilly ('hylbyly) s. pro-
wincjał
hillside ('hyl'sajd) s. stok
hilly ('hyly) adj. pagórkowaty;
górzysty
hilt (hylt) s. rękojesć; garda
him (hym) pron. jego; go; jemu;
mu
himself (hym'self) pron. się;
siebie; sobie; sam; osobiście;
we własnej osobie
hind (hajnd) s. parobek; łania;
adj. tylny; zadni
hinder ('hynder) v. przeszkadzać; powstrzymywać
hind leg ('hajnd,leg) s. tylna
noga
hindrance ('hyndrens) s. przeszkoda ; zawada;zawadzanie
hindsight('hajnd,sajt)s.zrozu-
mienie co trzeba było zrobić

hinge (hyndż) s. zawiasa; v.ob-
racać; zależeć; zawiesić na
zawiasach;wisieć na zawiasach
hinny (hyny) s. muł (z oślicy
i ogiera)
hint (hynt) s. aluzja; przytyk;
wskazówka; v. napomknąć; dać
do zrozumienia;zrobić aluzję
hinterland ('hynter,laend) s.
zaplecze; daleki teren
hip (hyp) s. biodro; naroże
dachu; chandra;adj.biodrowy
hippie (hypi:) s. niekonformista; adj. zbuntowany przeciw
tradycji (wyobcowany)
hippopotamus (hype'potemes) s.
hipopotam
hire (hajer) s. najem; opłata
za najem; v. najmować; wynajmować; dzierżawić;odnajmować
hire out ('hajer aut) v. wynaj-
mować(się do pracy,na służbę...)
hire purchase ('hajer'pe:rczys)
wynajem - zakup na raty
his (hyz) pron. jego
hiss (hys) v. syczec; gwizdać;
s. syk; gwizd;głoska sycząca
historian (hys'to:rjen) s.
historyk;historyczka
historic (hys'toryk) adj. histo-
ryczny;sławny w historii
history ('hystory) s. historia;
dzieje; przeszłość (znana)
hit (hyt) s. uderzenie; przytyk; sukces; sensacja; v. uderzyć; utrafić; natrafić; zabić
hit and run ('hyt,en'ran) adj.
uciekający od wypadku (drogowego); walczący podjazdowo;
dorywczy i niepewny
hitman ('hytmen) s. najemny
zabójca;najemny morderca
hit or miss (hyt o:r mys) adv.
na chybił trafił;przypadkiem
hit upon ('hyte'pon) v. natrafić (na coś,na kogoś)
hitch (hycz) s. zacisnięcie;
węzeł; przeszkoda; szarpnięcie;
uchwyt; służba (wojskowa)
v. doczepić; uczepić; pociągnąć; szarpnąć; przywiązać; za
czepić się;ciagnąć szarpiąc

hitchhike ('hycz,hajk) v. jechać autostopem
hitchhiker ('hycz,hajker) s.
jadący autostopem
hither ('hydzer) adv. dotąd;
tutaj;adj. bliżej
hitherto ('hydzer'tu:) adv.
dotychczas; do tej pory
hive (hajw) s. ul; rojowisko;
v. umieszczać w ulu; wchodzić
do ula;zbierać do ula
hoard (ho:rd),v. gromadzić;
zbierać; s. zapas. zbiór; skarb
hoarfrost ('ho: r'frost) s.
szron(na trawie,włosach etc.)
hoarse (ho:rs) adj. zachrypnięty; v. zachrypnąć;mieć chrapliwy
hoax (houks) v. bujać; nabie- głos
rać; s. bujda; kaczka;kawał
hobble ('hobl) s. pętą; utyka-
nie; v. utykać; kuleć; pętać
hobby ('hoby) s. hobby; pasja
(np. filatelistyka)
hobbyhorse ('hobyho:rs) s.
konik na kiju do zabawy(na biegu- nach)
hobgoblin ('hob,goblyn) s.
skrzat; chochlik
hobnob ('hobnob) v. być za pan
brat;blisko się zadawać
hobo('haubou) s. włóczęga
hock (hok) s. pęcina; v. zastawić (się) w lombardzie
hockey ('hoky) s. hokej
hoe (hou) s. motyka; graca;
v. gracować;okopywać motyką
hog (hog) s. wieprz; człowiek
zachłanny; v. łapać dla siebie; jechać środkiem; wyginąć
łukowato w środku;zagarniać so- bie
hoist (hojst) s. dźwig; wyciąg;
v. wyciągać ładunek w górę;
wywieszać(flagę);podciągać do góry
hold; held; held (hould; held;
held)
hold (hould) v. trzymać; posiadać; zawierać; powstrzymywać;
uważać; obchodzić; wytrzymywać; trwać; s. chwyt; pauza;
pomieszczenie; więzienie;
twierdza;silny wpływ;uchwyt
hold back ('hould,baek) v.
powstrzymać; zataić;wahać się

hold on ('hould,on) v. trzymać
się; wytrzymywać;powstrzymać
holdup ('hould'ap) s. zatrzymanie; zator; napad rabunkowy
holder ('houlder) s. właściciel; posiadacz; uchwyt
holding ('houldyng) s. posiadłość; portfel akcji; dzierżawa;uchwyt;ujęcie;trzymanie
hole (houl) s. dziura; nora;
dołek; v. dziurawić; przedziurawić;przekopywać(tunel)
holiday ('holedy) s. święto;
wakacje; urlop;adj.wesoły;ra-/
holidaymaker ('holedy,mejker)
s. wczasowicz; letnik; turysta;wycieczkowicz;letniczka
holler ('holer) v. wrzeszczeć;
krzyczeć(po prostacku)
hollow ('holou) s. dziupla;
dziura; kotlina; dolina;
adj. wklęsły; dziurawy; fałszywy; głuchy; pusty; czczy;
głodny;nieszczery;adv.pusto
hollow out ('holou,aut) v.
drążyć;wydrążyć;żłobić
holly ('holy) s. ostrokrzew
holy ('holy) adj. święty
homage ('homydż) s. hołd
home (houm) s. dom; ojczyzna;
kraj; schronisko; bramka;
adj. domowy; rodzinny; krajowy; wewnętrzny; ojczysty
homeless ('houmlys) adj. bezdomny;bez dachu nad głowa
homely ('houmly) adj, swojski;
pospolity; nieładny; prosty;
skromny;niewybredny;niewyszu-/
homemade ('houm'mejd) adj.
domowego wyrobu; krajowy
homesick ('houm-syk) adj.
stęskniony za domem rodzinnym;
stęskniony za (czymś swoim)
homesickness ('houm,syknys)
s. nostalgia;tęsknota za domem
home team ('houm-ti:m) s. drużyna miejscowa (sportowa)
home trade ('houm-trejd) s.
handel wewnętrzny
homewards ('houm-łedz) adv. ku
domowi (ojczyźnie);do domu

homework ('houmłerk) s. zadanie
domowe;odrabianie lekcji
homicide ('homy,sajd) s. zabójca; zabójstwo
honest ('onyst) adj. uczciwy;
prawy; przyzwoity; szczery;
adv. naprawdę
honesty ('onesty) s. zacność;
prawość; rzetelność; uczciwość
honey ('hany) s. miód;słodycz
honeycomb ('hany,koum) s. (woskowy) plaster pszczeli;
v. dziurawić; przenikać
honeymoon ('hany,mu:n) s. miodowy miesiąc;v.spędzić miodowy mie-
honk (honk) s. krzyk gęsi; głos
trąbki, klaksonu; v. trąbić;
(slang; wymyślać)
honorary ('onerery) adj. honorowy (np. urząd);bezpłatny
honor ('oner) s. cześć; uczciwość; cnota; tytuł sędziego;
v. czcić; zaszczycać; honorować
honorable ('onerebl) adj. czcigodny; uczciwy; szanowny; honorowy; zaszczytny;poważany
hood (hud) s. kaptur; kapturek;
maska; buda; v. zaopatrywać
w kaptur; przykrywać
hoodlum ('hu:dlem) s. opryszek;
chuligan;łobuz
hoodwink ('hudłynk) v. oczy mydlić; zmylić;zawiązywać oczy
hoof ('hu:f) s. kopyto; v. kopać; iść; tańczyć;iść pieszo
hook (huk) s. hak; v. zahaczyć;
zakrzywić (się);złapać (męża)
hoop ('hu:p) s. obręcz; v. otaczać obręczą;wykrzyknąć
hooping cough ('hu:pyng-kof) s.
koklusz; krztusiec,zob.whooping-
                                cough
hoot (hu:t) s. hukanie; odgłosy
niezadowolenia; v. hukać; gwizdać; wyć; trąbić:wygwizdać
hooves (hu:wz) pl. kopyta
hop (hop) s. chmiel; skok; po-
tańcówka; v. podskakiwać; poderwać (się); przeskakiwać
hope (houp) s. nadzieja; v.
mieć nadzieję;spodziewać sie;ufać;
żywić nadzieję

hopeful ('houpful) adj, pełen nadziei; ufny; obiecujący; rokujący nadzieje

hopeless ('houplys) adj. beznadziejny; rozpaczliwy; zrozpaczony;zdesperowany

horde (ho:rd) s. horda; gromada

horizon (he'rajzen) s. horyzont widnokrąg; warstwa oznaczona

horizontal (,hory'zontel) adj. poziomy; horyzontalny; widnokręgowy; s. płaszczyzna pozioma;poziom równy i płaski

horn (ho:rn) s. róg; trąbka; syrena; kula (siodła) v. bóśc; przebóść;wmieszac się

hornet ('ho:rnyt) s. szerszeń

horny ('ho:rny) adj. rogowy; zrogowaciały;rogaty;jak róg

horrible ('horebl) adj. straszny; okropny;szokujący;paskudny

horrid ('horyd) adj. straszny; ohydny; odrażajacy;paskudny

horrify ('horyfaj) v. przerażac; oburzac;ciężko szokowac

horror ('horer) s. groza; wstręt; odraza; przerażenie;dreszcz

horse (ho:rs) s. koń; konnica; jazda; kozioł z drzewa

horseback ('ho:rs,baek) s. grzbiet koński;adv. konno

horsefly ('ho:rs,flaj) s.giez

horsehair ('ho:rs,heer) s. włosie końskie;sztywna tkanina

horseman ('ho:rsmen) s. jeździec

horse opera ('ho:rs'opere) s. film kowbojski (nie-realistyczny)

horseplay ('ho:rs,plej) s. ordynarna zabawa (brutalna)

horsepower ('ho:rs,pałer) s. koń mechaniczny= 746 watów

horse race ('ho:rs,rejs) s. wyścigi konne

horseradish ('ho:rs,raedysh) s. chrzan; a. chrzanowy

horseshoe ('ho:rs,szu) s. podkowa;a.w kształcie podkowy

horticulture('ho:rty,kaltczer) s. ogrodnictwo

hose (houz) s. pończochy; wąż do podlewania(wiedza i praktyka)

hosiery ('haouzery) s. trykotaże; pończochy

hospitable ('hospytebl) adj. gościnny; szczodry dla gości

hospital ('hospytl) s. szpital; lecznica;a. szpitalny

hospitality (, hospy'taelyty) s. gościnność

host (houst) s. gospodarz; żywiciel; chmara;czereda;tłum

hostage ('hostydż) s. zakładnik; zastaw;zakładniczka

hostel ('hostel) s. dom studencki; bursa ;zajazd

hostess ('houstys) s. gospodyni; stewardesa; fordanserka

hostile ('hostajl) adj. wrogi; nieprzyjemny; antagonistyczny

hostility (hos'tylyty) s. wrogość; stan wojny;ostra opozycja

hot (hot) adj. gorący; palący; pieprzny; ostry; nielegalny; swieży; pobudliwy; adv. gorąco

hotbed ('hot,bed) s. inspecty; wylęgarnia;siedlisko;rozsadnik

hot dog ('hot,dog) s. kiełbaska w bułce;kiełbaska smażona

hotel (hou'tel) s. hotel

hothead ('hot,hed) s. człowiek zapalczywy; raptus;a.porywczy

hothouse ('hot,haus) s. cieplarnia; oranżeria

hot-pants (,hot'paents) exp. obcisłe damskie szorty; vulg.: panna puszczalska

hot water bottle (hot'ło:ter' botl) s. gorąca butelka

hound (haund) s. ogar; łajdak; v. tropic; szczuć; podjudzać

hour ('auer) s. godzina; pora

hourly ('auerly) adj. cogodzinny; adv. co godzinę; ustawicznie;z godziny na godzinę

house (haus) s. dom; zajazd; teatr; widzowie; v. gościć; dawać pomieszczenie; mieszkać

housekeeper ('haus,ki:per) s. najęta gosposia ;pomoc domowa

housekeeping ('haus,ki:pyng) s. gospodarka domowa

housemaid ('haus,mejd) s. pokojówka; pomoc domowa

housewife ('haus,łajf) s. gospodyni (niepracująca poza domem)

housework ('haus‚ℓe:rk) s. pra-
ce domowe;sprzątanie i gotowanie
housing ('hauzyŋg) s. pomieszczenie; kolonia; osłona; pokrywa; czaprak;obudowa
hove (houw) zob. heave
hover ('hower) v. unosic się;
kręcic się; byc w niepewności;
s. stan niepewności; unosze-
nie się;wahanie się;przywieranie
how (hau) adv. jak; jak ?sposób
how do you do ('hau‚du'ju:du)
exp.:dzień dobry !; dobry
wieczór ! (jak sie pan(i) ma ?)
how are you ('hau‚a:r'ju) exp.:
jak sie pan(i) ma ?
how about ('hau‚e'baut) exp.:
może ?; pozwolisz ? etc.
how much ('hau‚macz) exp.: ile ?
how many ('hau‚meny) exp.: ile?
ilu ? jak wielu?
how much is it ? ('hau‚macz'yz‚
yt) ile to kosztuje ?
however (hau'ewer) adv. jakkolwiek; jednak; niemniej
howl (haul) s. wycie; ryk;
v. wyc; wyganiac (gonic)wrzas-
kiem
howler ('hauler) s. gruby błąd
hub (hab) s. piasta; osrodek;
slang: maż;środek(rozgrywki)
hubbub ('habbab) s. zgiełk;gwar;
awantura; wrzawa;tumult
hubby ('haby) s. mężulek (slang)
huckleberry ('hakelbery) s.
borówka amerykańska(krzak i jagoda)
huddle together ('hadl‚tu'gedzer)
v. przytulac sie; tulic sie
huddle up ('hadl‚ap) v.skulic się
zwinac sie w kłębek
hue (hju:) s. barwa; odcień
hug (hag) s. uścisk; chwyt za-
paśniczy; v. ściskac; przycis-
kac; tulic (sie);uściskać
huge (hju:dż) adj. ogromny
hull (hal) s. łuska; kadłub;
v. łuszczyc; godzic w kadłub
hullabaloo ('halebelu:) s.
harmider;zgiełk;wrzawa;gwar
hullo (he'lou) excl.: hola!‚halo!
hum (ham) v. nucic; buczec; mruczec; chrząkac; s. pomruk;
chrząkanie; wahanie się; blaga

human ('hju:men) adj. ludzki;
s. istota ludzka
humane ('hju:mejn) adj. ludzki; humanitarny ;litosciwy
humanitarian (hju‚maeny'teerjen) adj. humanitarystyczny;
s. humanitarysta;filantrop
humanity (hju'maenyty) s.
ludzkosc; rasa ludzka; cechy
ludzkie; dobre uczynki
humble ('hambl) adj. pokorny;
uniżony; skromny; v. upoka-
żac; poniżac; poniżyc
humbleness ('hamblnys) s. pokora; bezpretensjonalnosc
humbug ('hambag) s. oszustwo;
blaga; bujda; oszust; blagier;
v. blagowac; oszukiwac; nabierac;wyłudzac opowiadaniem bred-
ni
humdrum ('hamdram) adj. nudny;
banalny; monotonny; s. szarzyzna; banalnosc; nudziarz
humidity (hju'mydyty) s. wilgoc; wilgotnosc(powietrza etc.)
humiliate (hju'myly‚ejt) v.
upokarzac; poniżac;martwic
humiliation (hju‚:myly'ejszyn)
s. upokorzenie; poniżenie
humility (hju'mylyty) s. skromnosc; pokora ducha etc.
humming-bird ('hamyŋg‚byrd) s.
koliber
humor ('hju:mer) s.humor; nastroj; kaprys; wesołosc;
v. dogadzac; zaspakajac; zadowalac; ustępowac; dostosowac się do zachcianek etc.
humorous ('hju:meres) adj.
śmieszny; pocieszny; pełen
humoru; zabawny;komiczny
hump (hamp) s. garb; v. garbic się; wyginac w łuk
humpback ('hampbaek) s. garbus
hunchback ('hancz‚baek) s. garbus;garb na plecach
hundred ('handred) num. sto;
s. setka;niezliczona ilosc
hundredth ('handredt) num.
setny; jedna setna
hundredweight ('handred‚łejt)
s. cetnar angielski
hung (haŋg) zob. hang

Hungarian (han'geerjen) adj.
węgierski ;s. Węgier
hunger ('hanger) s. głód;
v. głodować; łaknąc; głodzić
hunger strike ('hanger-strajk)
s. strajk głodowy
hungry ('hangry) adj. głodny;
zgłodniały; pożądliwy; ubogi;
jałowy ; nieurodzajny;łaknący
hunt (hant) s. polowanie;
teren łowiecki; v. polować;
gonic; przeszukiwać; szukac
hunter ('hanter) s. myśliwy
hunting ('hantyng) s. polowanie; adj. myśliwski
hunting ground ('huntyng,graund)
s. teren myśliwski
huntsman ('hantsmen) s. myśliwy; łowca
hurdle ('he:rdl) s. opłotki;
v. porać się; skakać przez
płotki; grodzic;przebijac się
hurdler ('he:rdler) s. zawodnik
wyścigów (z płotkami)
hurdle race ('he:rdl,rejs) s.
wyścigi (z płotkami;przez płotki
hurl (he:rl) s. rzut; v. rzucać
hurrah (he'ra:) excl.; hura !
hurray (he'rej) excl.: hura !;
v. krzyczeć hura (z radości etc.)
hurricane ('haryken) n. huragan; orkan tropikalny
hurried ('haryd) adj. pospieszny
hurry ('hary) s. pospiech
hurry up ! ('hary,ap) v. śpiesz
się ! ruszaj się!
hurt; hurt; hurt; (he:rt;
he:rt; he:rt)
hurt (he:rt) v. ranić; kaleczyc;
urazic; uszkodzić; bolec; dokuczać; s. skaleczenie; rana;
szkoda; krzywda; uraz; uszkodzenie ;ból;ujma;ranka
husband ('hazbend) s. mąż;
v. gospodarować oszczednie;
wydawać za mąż
husbandry ('hazbendry) s. rolnictwo; uprawa; hodowla
hush (hasz) s. cisza; spokój;
milczenie; v. cicho ! sza !;
uciszyć się; milczec; tuszować (coś);ululać; załagodzić

hush up ('hasz,ap) v. siedzieć
cicho; zatuszować (coś)
husk (hask) s. łuska; v. łuszczyc; wyłuszczać;złuszczac
husky ('hasky) adj. krzepki;
suchy; zachrypniety; łuszczas-
ty; s. pies eskimoski; język
eskimoski
hustle ('hasl) s. pospiech;
krzątanina; bieganina; popy-
chanie; v. spieszyć się; krzątać się; popychać; pchać się;
szturchac; popędzać; wypchnąc
hut (hat) s. chata; barak; chałupa; v. mieszkać w chałupie
hutch (hacz) s. skrzynia; klatka; domek; v. wkładać cos do
skrzyni;s.kurnik;chlewik;chatka
hybrid ('hajbryd) s. mieszaniec;
adj. mieszany;mieszanego pochodze-nia
hydrant ('hajdrent) s. hydrant
hydraulic ('haj'dro:lyk) adj.
hydrauliczny
hydro ('hajdrou) adj. wodo- ;
wodoro-; wodny
hydrocarbon ('hajdrou'ka:rben)
s. węglowodór
hydrochloric acid (,hajdrou'-
klo:ryk,asyd) s. kwas solny
hydrogen ('hajdrydżen) s. wo-
dór
hydrogen bomb ('hajdydżen,bom)
s. bomba wodorowa
hydroplane ('hajdrou,plejn) s.
wodnopłatowiec; ślizgacz
hyena (haj'y:ne) s. hiena
hygiene ('hajdżi:n) s. higiena
hymn (hym) s. hymn; v. śpiewać
hymn ;chwalic hymnem
hyphen ('hajfen) s. łącznik;
v. używać łącznika
hypnotize ('hypne,tajz) v.
hipnotyzować
hypocrisy (hy'pokresy) s. hipo-
kryzja ;udawanie cnoty etc.
hypocrite ('hypekryt) s. hipokryta ;obłudnik;obłudnica
hypocritical (,hypou'krytykel)
adj. obłudny; hipokryzyjny;
dwulicowy ;udający cnotę etc.
hypodermic (,hajpe'de:rmyk)
adj. podskórny (zastrzyk)

hypothesis (haj'po̱tysys) s.
hipoteza;niesprawdzona teoria
hysterectomy (,histe'rektemy)
s. wycięcie macicy
hysteria (hys'tyerje) s. histeria;wybuch podniecenia
hysterical (hys'terykel) adj.
histeryczny;podlegający histerii
hysterics (hys'teryks) pl.
atak histerii
hysterotomy (,histe'rotemy)
s. operacja macicy
I (aj) pron. ja; dziewiąta litera angielskiego alfabetu
I-beam ('aj,bi:m) s. belka
dwuteowka (stalowa)
ice (ajs) s. lód; lody; v. zamrażac; mrozic; lukrować
Ice Age('ajsejdż) s. epoka lodowa;epoka lodowcowa
iceberg ('ajsbe:rg) s. góra lodowa (na morzu)
ice-cream ('ajskri:m) s. lody
icicle ('ajsykl) s. sopel
ice floe ('ajs-flou) s. kra
icing ('ajsyŋ) s. lukier
icy ('ajsy) adj. lodowaty
idea (aj'die) s. idea; pojęcie;
pomysł;wyobrażenie; myśl;plan
ideal (aj'diel) adj. idealny;
s. ideał; model doskonały
idealize (aj'dielajz) v. ideali-
zowac;wyidealizować
identical (aj'dentykel) adj.
taki sam; identyczny; tożsamoś-
ciowy;zupełnie podobny
identification (ajdentyfy'kejszyn) s. utożsamienie; identy-
fikacja;stwierdzenie tożsamości
identification papers (aj,denty-
fy'kejszyn'pejpers) s. dowód
tożsamości; dowód osobisty
identify (aj'dentyfaj) v. utoż-
samic; identifikować
identity (aj'dentyty) s. tożsa-
mosc; identyczność
identity card (aj'dentyty ka:rd)
s. dowód osobisty
ideological (,ajdye'lodżykel)
adj. ideologiczny
idiom ('ydjem) s. wyrażenie
zwyczajowe; wyrażenie idioma-
tyczne; dialekt;typowy styl

idiot ('ydjet) s. idiota;dureń
idiotic (,ydy'otyk) adj. idiotyczny;bardzo głupi
idle ('ajdl) adj. niezajęty;
bezczynny; leniwy; pusty;
czczy; jałowy; zbyteczny;
v. próżnowac; byc na wolnym
biegu;byc bez pracy;obijać się
idle away ('ajdle'łej) v. marnowac (czas);roztrwonić czas
idleness ('ajdlnys) s. bezczynnosc; lenistwo; próżniactwo;
daremnosc;bezpodstawność
idol ('ajdl) s. bożyszcze; bałwan;posąg bożka
idolize ('ajdelajz) v. ubóst-
wiac; uwielbiac; bałwochwalic
idyl ('ydyl) s. sielanka; idyl-
la;opis raju na wsi(w poezji)
if (yf) conj. jeżeli; jeśli;
gdyby; o ile; czy; żeby(tylko)
iffy (yffy) adj. wątpliwy
(slang) gdybowany
igloo ('iglu:) s. eskimoska
chata kopulasta ze śniegu
ignite (yg'najt) v. zapalic
ignition (yg'nyszyn) s. zapłon;
zapalenie; elektryczny zapłon
ignition key (yg'nyszyn,ki:)
s. klucz do zapłonu (w aucie)
ignoble (yg'noubl) adj. nędzny;
podły; haniebny; niecny; marny;
niegodziwy;niskiego pochodzenia
ignorance ('ygnerens) s. nie-
świadomosc; ignorancja; nieuctwo; ciemnota;obskurantyzm
ignorant ('ygnerent) adj. nieświadomy; ciemny; bez wykształcenia;zdradzający ignorancję
ignore (yg'no:r) v. pomijac;
lekceważyc; odrzucac;nie zważać
ill (yl) adj. zły; chory; słaby; lichy; s. zło; adv. zle;
nie bardzo;kiepsko;niepomyślnie
ill-advised ('yled'wajzd) adj.
nierozsądny; nierozważny
ill-affected ('yle'fektyd) adj.
źle usposobiony;nieżyczliwy
ill-bred ('yl'bred) adj. źle
wychowany;grubiański
illegal (y'li:gel) adj. bezprawny; nielegalny;samowolny;
przeciw prawu i ustawom

illegible (y'ledźybl) adj. nieczytelny;źle napisany(wydrukowany)
illegitimate (,yly'dźytymejt)
adj. bezprawny; nieprawny;
nieprawowity; nieślubny
ill-fated ('yl-fejdyd) adj.
fatalny; nieszczęśliwy;niesczęsny
ill-humored ('yl'hju:merd)
adj. w złym humorze
illicit (y'lysyt) adj. bezprawny; niedozwolony;niewłaściwy
illiterate (y'lyteryt) s. analfabeta; adj. niepiśmienny
ill-judged ('yl'dżadżd) adj.
nierozważny; nierozsądny
ill-mannered ('yl'maenerd) adj.
źle wychowany;grubiański
ill-natured ('yl'nejczerd) adj.
zły; złośliwy; opryskliwy
illness ('ylnys) s. choroba
illogical (y'lodżykel) adj.
nielogiczny;nierozsądny
ill-tempered ('yl'temperd) adj.
w złym humorze;zły;kłótliwy
ill-timed ('yl'tajmd) adj. nie
na czasie;niefortunny
ill-treat ('yl'tri:t) v. maltretować; znęcać się(nad kimś)
illuminate (y'lju:mynejt) v.
oświetlać; oswiecać; uświetniać
illumination (y,lju:my'nejszyn)
s. oświecenie; oświecanie;
uświetnianie;rozjaśnienie
illusion (y'lu:źyn) s. złudzenie; iluzja; złuda
illusive (y'lu:syw) adj. złudny; iluzyjny;iluzoryczny;zwodni-
illusory (y'lu:sery) adj. złud- czy
ny; iluzoryczny;zwodniczy
illustrate ('yles,trejt) v.
wyjaśniać; ilustrować
illustration (,yles'trejszyn)
s. ilustracja; ilustrowanie
illustrative ('yles,trejtyw)
adj. objaśniający; ilustru-
jący(przykład,zdarzenie etc.)
illustrious (y'lastrjes) adj.
znakomity; wybitny; sławny
ill will ('yl'łyl) s. niechęć
image ('ymydż) s. wizerunek;
obraz; wcielenie; v. wyobrażać; odzwierciadlać; ucieles-
niać; dawać obraz(wyobrażenie)

imagery ('ymydżery) s. wizerun-
ki; podobizny; gra wyobraźni;
porównanie przez przykłady
imaginable (y'maedżynebl) adj.
wyobrażalny; możliwy;do pomyśle-
imaginary (y'maedżynery) a. nia
urojony; zmyślony;nierzeczywisty
imagination (y,maedży'nejszyn)
s. wyobraźnia; fantazja; urojenie;tworzenie nowych pomysłów
imagine (y'maedżyn) v. wyobrażać sobie;przypuszczać;myśleć
imbecile ('ymby,syl) adj. upośledzony; głupi; niedorozwinięty; cherlawy; s. człowiek
uposledzony; imbecyl(niedorozwi-niety)
imitate ('ymytejt) v. naśladować; małpować;imitować;wzorować sie
imitation (,ymy'tejszyn) s. naśladowanie; naśladownictwo;
imitacja;falsyfikat;podróbka
immaterial (,yme'tierjel) adj.
nieistotny; bezcielesny;błachy
immature (,yme'tjuer) adj. niedojrzały;niewyrobiony;niedorosły
immeasurable (y,meżerebl) adj.
niezmierzony; ogromny;bezmierny
immediate (y'mi:djet) adj.
bezpośredni; natychmiastowy;pil-ny;nagły
immediately (y'mi:djetly) adv.
natychmiast; bezpośrednio
immense (y'mens) adj. olbrzymi;ogromny;świetny;kpitalny
immerse (y'me:rs) v. zanurzać;
pogrążać;ochrzcić przez zanużenie
immigrant ('ymygrent) s. imigrant; adj. imigrujący;osadniczy
immigrate ('ymygrejt) v. imigrować;przywędrować;sprowadzać osad-nikow
immigration (,ymy'grejszyn) s.
imigracja;urząd imigracyjny
imminent ('ymynent) adj. nadchodzący; grozny;nadciągający;blis-ki
immobile (y'moubajl) adj. nieruchomy;przytwierdzony na stałe
immoderate (y'moderyt) adj.
nieumiarkowany;niepohamowany;nad-mierny
immodest (y'modyst) adj. nieskromny; bezczelny; zuchwały
immoral (y'morel) adj. niemoralny;nieetyczny;rozpustny
immorality(ym'e-ral'ety)s.rozpus-
ta; niemoralność

immorality (,yme'raelyty) s.
niemoralność;rozpusta
immortal (y'mo:rtl) adj. nieśmiertelny; wiekopomny
immortality (,ymo:r'taelyty) s.
nieśmiertelność
immovable (y'mu:webl) adj.nie-
ruchomy; niezmienny; nieczuły; nieugięty;niewzruszony
immune (y'mju:n) adj. odporny;
uodporniony;wolny(od przepisów)
imp (ymp) s. skrzat; diablik
impact ('ympaekt) v. wgnia-
tać; s. zderzenie; uderzenie;
wpływ;wstrząs;kolizja;działanie
impair (ym'peer) v. uszkadzac;
osłabiac; nadwyrężać;umniejszać
impart (ym'pa:rt) v. dawac;
udzielac;zakomunikować
impartial (ym'pa:rszel) adj.
bezstronny; sprawiedliwy
impartiality ('ym,pa:rszy'aelyty) s. bezstronność;sprawiedli-
impassable (ym'pa:sebl) adj.¬wosc
nieprzebyty; nie do przebycia
impassive (ym'paesyw) adj.
niewzruszony; obojętny;nieczuły
impatience (ym'pejszens) s.
zniecierpliwienie; niecierpli-
wosc;irytacja(z powodu czegoś)
impatient (ym'pejszent) adj.
niecierpliwy; zniecierpliwiony;palący się do:podrażniony
impediment (ym'pedyment) s.
przeszkoda; utrudnienie
impend (ym'pend) v. grozic;
zbliżać się;zagrażać(z bliska)
impenetrable (ym'penytrebl)
adj. nieprzenikniony; niedostępny;niezglebiony;nie do prze-
imperative (ym'peretyw) adjblici
stanowczy; rozkazujący; konieczny;naglący;niezbędny
imperceptible (,ym-pe'rseptebl)
adj. niedostrzegalny;nieuchwytny
imperfect (ym'pe:rfykt) adj.
niedoskonały; niedokończony;
wadliwy; niezupełny;niedokonany
imperial (ym'pierjel) adj.
cesarski; imperialny; do-
stojny;rozkazujący;majestatycz-ny
imperialism (ym'pierjelyzem)s.
imperializm(budowanie imperium)

imperil (ym'peryl) v. zagrażać;
narazić na niebezpieczeństwo
imperious (ym'pierjes) adj.
władczy; naglący;nakazujący
imperishable (ym'peryszebl) adj.
niezniszczalny; nieprzemijają-
cy;trwały;wieczysty
impermeable (ym'pe:rmiebl) adj.
nieprzemakalny; nieprzenikniony;nieprzepuszczający
impersonal (ym'pe:rsenl) adj.
nieosobowy; nieosobisty
impersonate(ym'pe:rsenejt) v.
wcielac; uosabiac; odgrywać
kogos;personifikować
impertinence (ym'pe:rtynens) s.
niestosowność; impertynencja;
niewłasciwość; natręctwo;nietakt
impertinent (ym'pe:rtynnent) adj.
niestosowny; impertynencki;
bezczelny; natrętny;bez związku
imperturbable (,ympe:r'te:rbebl)
adj. niewzruszony; spokojny
impervious (ym'pe:rwjes) adj.
nieprzepuszczalny; niedostępny
impetuous (ym'petjues) adj.
popędliwy; porywczy; gwałtowny
implacable (ym'plekebl) adj.
nieubłagalny;nieprzejednany
implement ('ymplyment) s. narzędzie; srodek; sprzęt;
v. uzupełniac; urzeczywistniac;
wykonac;uprawomocniac;spełniac
implicate ('ymplykejt) v. uwikłać; owijac; włączac;wplątać;wmie-szać
implication (,ymply'kejszyn) s.
uwikłanie; włączenie; sugestia
implicit (ym'plysyt) adj. rozu-
miejący się sam przez się;
niezaprzeczalny;domniemany;ślepy
implore (ym'plo:r) v. błagac
imply (ym'plaj) v. zawierać
w sobie; miescic; sugerowac;
zakładać;nasuwac wniosek
impolite (,ympo'lajt) adj. nieuprzejmy; niegrzeczny
import (ym'po:rt) s. import;treść
v. oznaczac; importowac; przywozic z zagranicy;a.importowy
import ('ympo:rt) s. tresc;
znaczenie;ważność;doniosłość
importance (ym'po:rtens) s.
znaczenie; ważność;doniosłość

important (ym'po:rtent) adj.
ważny; znaczący; doniosły
importation (,ympo:r'tejszyn)
s. przywóz; importowanie
importune (ym'po:rtju:n) v.
dokuczać; żądać natarczywie;
narzucać się;naprzykrzać się
impose (ym'pouz) v. nadawać;
narzucać; oszukiwać; imponować;narzucać;nakładać obowiązek
impose upon (,ym'pouz e'pon)
v. narzucać się komus;okpiwać
imposing (ym'pouzyŋg) adj.
imponujący;wspaniały;okazały
impossibility (ym,posy'bylyty)
s. niemożliwość
impossible (ym'posybl) adj.
niemożliwy(do zrobienia,zniesienia)
impostor (ym'poster) s. oszust
(podszywający się);szarlatan
impotence ('ympotens) s. niemoc; zniedołężnienie (płciowe);nieudolność;niesprawność
impotent ('ympotent) s. bezsilny; impotent; nieudolny
impracticable (ym'praektykebl)
adj. niewykonalny;krnąbrny
impregnate ('ympregnejt) v. za-
pł1adniać; impregnować; nasycać;wpoić;zaszczepić;nasiąkać
impress (ym'pres) v. odcisnąć;
wycisnąć; robić wrażenie;
s. odcisk; odbicie; piętno
impression (ym'preszyn) s. wrażenie; druk; odbicie; nakład
impressive (ym'presyw) adj. robiący wrażenie; uderzający;
podniosły;wstrząsający;frapujący
imprint (ym'prynt) v. odbijać;
wpajać; wydrukować; wbijać
w pamięć;wyryć w pamięci
imprint ('ymprynt) s. odbicie;
nadruk; odcisk;piętno;znak firmowy
imprison (ym'pryzn) v. uwięzić
imprisonment (ym'pryznment) s.
uwięzienie(kara więzienia)
improbable (ym'probebl) adj.
nieprawdopodobny
improper (ym'proper) adj. niewłaściwy; nieprzyzwoity;zdrożny
improve (ym'pru:w) v. poprawić;
udoskonalić; ulepszać (jakość)

improvement (ym'pru;wment) s.
poprawa; udoskonalenie; wy-
korzystanie(sposobności);poprawa
improvise ('ymprowajz) v. improwizować;sklecić na poczekaniu
imprudent (ym'pru:dent) adj. nierozsądny; nieopatrzny; nierozważny;nieoględny;niebaczny
impudence ('ympjudens) s. bez-
wstyd; bezczelność; tupet
impudent ('ympjudent) adj. bezwstydny; bezczelny;zuchwały;z tupetem
impulse ('ympals) s. impuls;poryw;
poped;pęd;siła napędowa;bodziec
impulsive ('ympalsyw) adj. im-
pulsywny; porywczy; pobudliwy
impunity (ym'pju:nyty) s. bez-
karność;swoboda od skutków(kary)
impure (ym'pjur) adj. nieczysty; zanieczyszczony
impute (ym'pju:t) v. oskarżać;
przypisywać(zbrodnię;błąd etc.)
in (yn) prep. w; we; na; za; po;
do; u; nie-
in and out ('yn,end'aut) exp.:
na wylot; wchodzić i wychodzić
in a week ('yn,ej'łi:k) exp.: za
tydzień;w ciągu tygodnia
in my opinion ('yn,maj e'pynjen)
exp.: według mnie;moim zdaniem
in order that ('yn.o:rder'daet)
exp.: ażeby;w celu;poto żeby
in pairs ('yn,peers) exp.: parami
in Shakespeare ('yn,Szekspir)
u Szekspira;w sztukach Szekspira
inability (,yne'bylyty) s. niezdolność;niemożność
inaccessible (ynaek'sesybl) adj.
niedostępny; nieprzystępny
inaccurate (yn'aekjuryt) adj.
nieścisły; niedokładny
inactive (yn'aektyw) adj. bezczynny;bierny;obojetny;inertny
inadequate (yn'aedykłyt) adj.
nieodpowiedni; niewystarczalny
inadmissible (,yned'mysebl)
adj. niedopuszczalny;nie do przyjęcia
inadvertent (,yned'we:rtent)
adj. nieuważny; niedbały; nie-
rozmyślny;mimowolny;nieumyślny
inalterable (yn'o:lterebl) adj.
niezmienny

inanimate (yn'aenymyt) adj.
martwy; nieożywiony; bezduszny; nieorganiczny
inappropriate (,yne'prouprjyt) adj. niewłaściwy;niestosowny
inapt (yn'aept) adj. niezdatny
inarticulate (,yna:r'tykjulyt) adj. nieartykułowany; niewyraźny; niemy;słabo mówiący
inasmuch (,ynez'macz) adv.
o tyle; ponieważ; wobec tego; że; skoro;zważywszy;jako że
inasmuch as (,ynez'macz,aez) adv. gdyż ;o tyle że;o tyle o ile
inattentive (,yne'tentyw) adj. nieuważny; nie uważający
inaudible (yn'o:debl) adj. niesłyszalny;nie uchwytny dla ucha
inaugural (y'no:gjurel) adj. inauguracyjny
inaugurate (y'no:gjurejt) v. otwierać uroczyście; inaugurować;uroczyście zapoczątkowywać
inborn ('yn'bo:rn) adj. wrodzony ;przyrodzony;z natury
incalculable (yn'kaelkjulebl) adj. nieobliczalny;nieprzewidziałny
incapable (yn'kejpebl) adj. niezdolny; nie będący w stanie
incapacitate ('ynke'paesytejt) v. czynić niezdatnym; dyskwalifikować;uznać za niezdatnego
incapacity (,ynke'paesyty) s. niezdolność; nieudolność
incarnate (yn,ka:rnejt) adj. wcielony; v. wcielać; ucieleśniać (się);być wcieleniem
incautious (yn'ko:szes) adj. nierozważny; niebaczny
incendiary (yn'sendjery) adj. zapalający; podżegający; s. podpalacz; podżegacz
incense ('ynsens) s. kadzidło
incense (yn'sens) v. rozwścieczać; doprowadzać do szału
incertitude (un'se:rtytju:d) s. niepewność; niepokój
incessant (yn'sesnt) adj. ustawiczny; bezustanny; stały
incest ('ynsest) s.kazirodztwo a.kazirodczy
inch (yncz) s. cal (2.54 cm) v. posuwać cal po calu

incident ('ynsydent) s. zajście; wydarzenie; incydent; adj. padający; związany;prawdopodobny
incidental (,ynsy'dentl) adj. przypadkowy; uboczny;drugorzędny
incidentally (,ynsy'dently) adv. przypadkowo; ubocznie; nawiasem mówiąc;mimochodem;przy spobności
incinerate (yn'synerejt) v. spalić; spopielić;palić na popiół
incise (yn'sajz) v. naciąć; wyryć;wyrzeźbić;wygrawerować
incision (yn'syżyn) s. nacięcie; cięcie; ciętość; bystrość;ostrość
incisive (yn'sajsyw) adj. przenikliwy; ostry; tnący; bystry; sieczny; zjadliwy;wcinający się
incisor (yn'sajzer) s. siekacz; (ząb)każdy z przednich zębów między kłami
incite (yn'sajt) v. zachęcać; podburzać;podżegać;namawiać
inclement (yn'klement) adj. surowy;ostry (klimat etc.)
inclination (ynkly'nejszyn) s. skłonność; nachylenie;pociąg
incline (yn'klajn) v. miec skłonność; pochylać się
inclose (yn'klous) v. ogrodzić; załączyć; włączyć;zamknąć
include (yn'klu:d) v. zawierać; włączać; wliczać(w cenę);obejmować
inclusive (yn'klu:syw) adj. włączony;obejmujący;adv.włacznie
incoherent (,ynkou'hierent) adj. bez związku; nieskoordynowany
income ('ynkam) s. dochód
income tax ('ynkam,taeks) s. podatek dochodowy
incoming ('yn,kamyng) adj. nadchodzący;następujący; przyrastający; s. przybycie; dochod
incomparable (yn'komperebl) adj. niezrównany; nie do porownania; nieporównywalny
incompatible (,ynkem'paetebl) adj. niezgodny; sprzeczny
incompetent (yn'kompytent) adj. niekompetentny; nieudolny
incomplete (,ynkem'pli:t) adj. niezupełny; nieukończony
incomprehensible (yn,kompry'hensebl) adj. niepojęty; niezrozumiały

inconceivable (,ynken'si:webl)
adj. niepojęty; nieprawdopodobny; nieprawdopodobny
inconclusive (,ynken'klu;syw)
adj. nieprzekonywujący; nie-
rozstrzygający;nie decydujący
inconsequent (yn'konsykłent)
adj. bez związku; niekonsekwentny; nielogiczny
inconsiderable (,ynken'syderebl)
adj. nieznaczny; niepokaźny
inconsiderate (,ynken'syderyt)
adj. bezwzględny; nierozważny
inconsistent (,ynken'systent)
adj. niejednolity; niekonsekwentny; niezgodny;bez związku
inconsolable (,ynken'soulebl)
adj. niepocieszony;nieutulony
inconstant (yn'konstent) adj.
zmienny; niestały; nieregularny
inconvenience (,ynken'wi:n jens)
s. niewygoda; kłopot; v. niepokoic; przeszkadzac; sprawiac
kłopot;deranżować
inconvenient (,ynken'wi:njent)
adj. niewygodny; niedogodny;
kłopotliwy; uciażliwy
incorporate (yn'ko:rperejt) v.
jednoczyc; wcielac; zrzeszac
(yn'ko:rperyt) adj. zrzeszony
incorporated (yn'ko:rperejtyd)
adj. zarejestrowany; zalegali-
zowany;wcielony; złączony
incorrect (,ynke'rekt) adj. niepoprawny; nieścisły: błędny
incorrigible (yn'korydżybl) adj.
niepoprawny;nie do poprawienia
increase (yn'kri:s) v. wzrastac;
zwiększac się; pomnażac się;
wzmagac się;rozmnażac się ; s.
('ynkri:s) wzrost; przyrost;
podwyżka;rozrost;mnożenie się
increasingly (yn'kri:syngly)
adv. coraz więcej; coraz bardziej; coraz to; wciąż
incredible (yn'kredebl) adj.
nie do wiary; niewiarygodny;
nieprawdopodobny;nie do pomyśle-
incredulous (yn'kredjules) adj.
nie
incriminate (yn'krymynejt) v.
obwiniac; oskarżac;pomawiac;
objąc (kogoś) oskarżeniem

incubator ('ynkjubejter) s. wy-
lęgarka; inkubator
incur (yn'ke:r) v. narażac się;
poniesc; zaciągac;natknąc się na
incurable (yn'kjuerebl) adj.
nieuleczalny;s.człowiek nieuleczal
indebted (yn'detyd) adj. dłużny;
zobowiązany; wdzięczny;zawdzięcza-
indecency (yn'di:sensy) s. nie-
skromnosc; nieprzyzwoitosc
indecent (yn'di:sent) adj. nieprzyzwoity;obrażający moralnosc
indecision (,yndy'syżyn) s.
chwiejnosc; niezdecydowanie
indecisiveness(,yndy'sajsywnys)s.
chwiejnosc; niezdecydowanie
indecisive (,yndy'sajsyw) adj.
nie rozstrzygnięty; niezdecydowany;chwiejny;nie rozstrzygający
indeed (yn'di:d) adv. naprawdę;
istotnie; rzeczywiscie; faktycznie;wprawdzie; co prawda;własciwi
indefatigable (,yndy'faetygebl)
adj. niestrudzony; niezmordowany
indefinite (yn'defynyt) adj.
nieokreslony;niewyrazny;nie sprecy
indelible (yn'delybl) adj. nie-
zatarty; trwały;nie do zmazania
indelicate (yn'delykyt) adj. niedelikatny; nietaktowny;niestosowny
indemnify (yn'demnyfaj) v. dawac odszkodowanie; zabezpieczac
przed(np. szkodą);powetowac
indemnity (yn'demnyty) s. odszkodowanie; zabezpieczenie
przed...;wynagrodzenie
indent (yn'dent) v. naciąc; wy-
ciąc; wyrznąc; zamówic; zawierac umowę; tłoczyc; s. wgłębienie;nacięcie;karbowanie
indent ('yndent) s. wcięcie; nacięcie; karbowanie; zamówienie
independence (,yndy'pendens) s.
niezależnosc; niepodłegłosc;
niezależnosc materialna
independent (,yndy'pendent) adj.
niepodległy; niezależny (ma-
terialnie);osobny;oddzielny
indescribable (,yndys'krajbebl)
adj. nieopisany; nie do opisania (poza możliwosciami opisania)
indeterminate (,yndy'te:rmynyt)
adj.nieokreslony;niewyrazny

index ('yndeks) s. wskaźnik;
indeks; v. umieszczać ~ spi-
sie (indeksie);robić indeks
Indian ('yndjen) adj. indiański;
hinduski ⌐babie lato
Indian Summer ('yndjen'samer)
exp.: słoneczne dni w jesieni;
India-rubber ('yndje'raber) s.
guma (naturalna,elastyczna)
indicate ('yndykejt) v. wskazywać; stwierdzać; wymagać
indication (,yndy'kejszyn) s.
wskazówka; wskazanie; znak
indicative (yn'dyketyw) adj.
oznajmiający; dowodzący
indicator ('yndykejter) s.
wskaźnik; indykator; licznik
indict (yn'dajt) v. oskarżyć
indictment (yn'dajtment) s.
oskarżenie; akt oskarżenia
indifference (yn'dyferens) s.
obojętność ;nieistotność;błahość
indifferent (yn'dyfrent) adj.
obojętny;mierny;błachy;neutralny
indigent ('yndydżent) adj.
ubogi; biedny;s.biedak;biedaczka
indigestible (,yndy'dżestebl)
adj. niestrawny ;źle strawny
indigestion (,yndy'dżestczyn) s.
niestrawność
indignant (yn'dygnent) adj.
oburzony (na niesprawiedliwość...)
indignation (,yndyg'nejszyn) s.
oburzenie
indirect (,yndy'rekt) adj; pośredni; okrężny; nieuczciwy
indiscreet (,yndys'kri:t) adj.
nierozważny; niedyskretny
indiscretion (,yndys'kreszyn)
s. nierozwaga; niedyskrecja;
uchybienie(słowem,czynem etc.)
indiscriminate (,yndys'krymynyt)
adj. bezkrytyczny; pomieszany
indispensable (,yndys'pensebl)
adj. nieodzowny; niezbędny;
konieczny;niezastąpiony
indisposed (,yndys'pouzd) adj.
niezdrów; niedysponowany; niechętny;bez zapału;niedomagający
indisposition (,yndyspe'zyszyn)
s. niedyspozycja; niechęć; odraza;dolegliwość;niedomaganie

indisputable (,yndys'pju:tebl)
adj. bezsporny;niezaprzeczalny
indistinct (,yndys'tynkt) adj;
niewyraźny;niejasny;mętny
individual (,yndy'wydjuel) adj.
pojedyńczy; odrębny; s. jednostka; osobnik;okaz;chłowiek
individualist (,yndy'wydjuelyst)
s. indiwidualista;individualistka
indivisible (,yndy'wyzebl) adj.
niepodzielny;nieskończenie mały
indolence ('yndelens) s. lenistwo; opieszałość;próżniactwo
indolent ('yndelent) adj. leniwy;opieszały;obojętny;niebolesny
indomitable (yn'domytebl) adj.
nieposkromiony; nieugięty
indoor ('yndo:r) adj. domowy;
wewnętrzny; pokojowy;zakładowy
indoors ('yndo:rz) adv. w domu;
pod dachem ;do domu;do mieszkania
indorse(yn'do:rs) v. potwierdzić (podpisem)
induce (yn'dju:s) v. skłonić;
namówić; powodować; wnioskować;pobudzić;nakłonić;powodować
induct (yn'dakt) v. wprowadzać;
tworzyć; brać do wojska
indulge (yn'daldż) v. pobłażać;
znosić; ulegać; dogadzać; używać sobie ;dawać upust;zaspokajać
indulgence (yn'daldżens) s. do-
gadzanie; nałog; oddawanie się;
pobłażanie; odpust;uleganie
indulgent (yn'daldżent) adj. pobłażliwy ;ulegający;folgujący
industrial (yn'dastrjel) adj.
przemysłowy (towar,robotnik etc.)
industrial area (yn'dastrjel'
eerje) s. teren przemysłowy
industrial city (yn'dastrjel'
syty) s. miasto przemysłowe
industrialist (yn'dastrjelyst)
s. przemysłowiec
industrialize (yn'dastrjelajz)
v. uprzemysławiać
industrious (yn'dastrjes) adj.
skrzętny; pilny; pracownity
industry ('yndastry) s. przemysł; pilność; pracowitość;
skrzętność;gałąź przemysłu;włas-
ciciele i zarządcy przemysłu

ineffective (,yny'fektyw) adj.
bezskuteczny; niesprawny
inefficient (,yny'fyszent)
adj. niewydajny; niesprawny
inequality (,yny'kłolyty) s.
nierówność; niewystarczalność;
zmienność(krajobrazu);niestałość
inert (y'ne:rt) adj. bezwładny;
ociężały; obojętny; opieszały
inertia (y'ne:rszja) s. inercja; bezwład; ociężałość
inestimable (yn'estymebl) adj.
nieoceniony;bezcenny
inevitable (yn'ewytebl) adj.
nieunikniony; nieuchronny
inexact (,ynyg'zaekt) adj. nieścisły; niedokładny
inexcusable (,ynyks'kju:zebl)
adj. niewybaczalny; nie-
usprawiedliwiony;nie do darowa-nia
inexhaustible (,ynyg'zo:stebl)
adj. niewyczerpany; nieprzebrany; niestrudzony;bez dna
inexpensive (,ynyks'pensyw) adj.
niedrogi; niekosztowny; tani
inexperience (,ynyks'pierjens)
s. niedoświadczenie;brak wprawy
inexplicable (yn'eksplykebl)
adj. niewytłumaczalny; nie-
wyjaśniony;zagadkowy
inexpressible (,yneks'presebl)
adj. niewysławiony; niewyra-
żalny;niewymowny
inexpressive (,ynyks'presyw)
adj. bez wyrazu
infallible (yn'faelebl) adj.
nieomylny; niezawodny; niechybny;bezbłędny;zawsze słuszny
infamous ('ynfemes) adj. haniebny; niesławny; hańbiący;podły
infamy ('ynfemy) s. hańba; niesława; podłość;utrata praw obywa-telskich
infancy ('ynfensy) s. nie-
mowlectwo; dziecinstwo
infant ('ynfent) s. niemowlę;
dziecko;noworodek;a.dziecinny
infantile ('ynfentajl) adj.
dziecięcy;infantylny;niemowlęcy
infantry ('ynfentry) s. piechota (wojsko)
infatuated with (yn'faetjuejtyd
łys) adj. szalejący za...;rozko-
chany w;nierozsądnie zakochany

infect (yn'fekt) v. zakazic;
zarazić; zatruwać
infection (yn'fekszyn) s. zakażenie; zarażenie; zaraza
infectious (yn'fekszes) adj. zakaźny; zaraźliwy;infekcyjny
infer (yn'fe:r) v. wnioskować;
zawierać w sobie pojęcie
inference ('ynferens) s. wniosek; konkluzja;domniemanie
inferior (yn'fierjer) adj.
niższy; podrzędny; pośledni
inferior to (yn'fierjer,tu)
adj. ustępujący; gorszy
inferiority (yn,fiery'oryty) s.
niższość;poczucie niższości
infernal (yn'fe:rnel) adj. piekielny; diabelski; szatański
infest (yn'fest) v. nawiedzać;
trapić;być utrapieniem
infidelity (,ynfy'delyty) s.
niewiara; niewierność
infiltrate ('ynfyltrejt) v.
wsiąkać; przesiąkać; przenikać
infinite ('ynfynyt) adj. nieskończony; bezgraniczny; niezliczony; ogromny;bezkresny
infinitive (yn'fynytyw) s. bezokolicznik;adj.nieokreślony
infinity (yn'fynyty) s. nie-
skończoność
infirm (yn'fe:rm) adj. słaby;
niedołężny;dotknięty niemocą
infirmary (yn'fe:rmery) s.
szpital; lecznica; izba chorych
infirmity (yn'fe:rmyty) s. niemoc; słabość; zniedołężnienie
inflame (yn'flejm) v, zapalić;
rozognić; pobudzać;zagrzewać
inflammable (yn'flaemebl) adj.
zapalny; pobudliwy; palny
inflammation (,ynfle'mejszyn)
s. zapalenie; zaognienie
inflammatory(yn'flaemeto:ry)
adj. podżegający; zapalny
inflate (yn'flejt) v. nadąć;
rozdąć; powodować inflacje
inflation (yn'flejszyn) s.
inflacja; nadymanie; nadmu-
chanie;zwyżka cen
inflect (yn'flekt) v. zginąc;
skrzywić; odmieniać ;naginać

inflexible (yn'fleksebl) adj.
sztywny; nieugięty;nieelastycz-
ny
inflection(yn'flekszyn) s.
fleksja; modulacja; końcówka;
wygięcie ;nadgięcie;odchylenie
inflict (yn'flykt) v. zadać;
narzucać; zsyłać(na kogoś)
infliction (yn'flykszyn) s.
zadanie (ciosu) narzucanie;
przykrość;nieszczęście;strapie-
nie
influence ('ynfluens) s. wpływ
v. wywierać wpływ;oddziaływać
influential (,ynflu'enszel)
adj. wpływowy(polityk etc.)
influenza (,ynflu'enza) s.
grypa; influenca
inform (yn'fo:rm) v. powiado-
mić; nadawać; donosić;ożywić
inform against(yn'fo:rme'genst)
v. donosić na (kogoś)
information (,ynfer'mejszyn)
s. wiadomość; wiedza; objas-
nienie;informacja;doniesienie
information desk (,ynfer'mejszyn,desk) punkt informacyjny (w banku,hotelu,na wystawie)
information officer (,ynfer'-
mejszyn 'ofyser) oficer in-
formacyjny(w banku etc.)
informative (yn'fo:rmetyw)
adj. objaśniający; pouczający
informer (yn'fo:rmer) s. donosiciel; konfident;konfidentka
infuriate (,yn'fjuerjejt) v.
rozwścieczać; rozjuszać
infuse (yn'fju:z) v. wlewać;
zalewać; zaparzać;dodać(odwagi)
ingenious (yn'dżi:njes) adj.
pomysłowy; dowcipny(pomysł)
ingenuity (,yndży'njuyty) s.
pomysłowość;oryginalność;dowcip
ingot ('yngot) s. sztaba
ingratiate (yn'grejszjejt) v.
wkradać się w łaski czyjeś
ingratitude(yn'graetytju:d) s.
niewdzięczność
ingredient (yn'gri:djent) s.
składnik (mieszanki etc.)
ingress ('yngres) s. wejście
inhabit (yn'haebyt) v. za-
mieszkiwać; mieszkać
inhabitable (yn'haebytebl)adj.
mieszkalny(godny zamieszkania)

inhabitant (yn'haebytent) s.
mieszkaniec; mieszkanka
inhale (yn'hejl) v. wdychać; zaciągać się (dymem);wziewać
inherent (yn'hierent) adj. nieodłączny; właściwy;wrodzony
inherit (yn'heryt) v. dziedziczyć; być spadkobiercą
inheritance (yn'herytens) s.
spadek; spuścizna; dziedzictwo
inhibit (yn'hybyt) v. wstrzymywać; wzbraniać; zakazywać
inhibition (,ynhy'byszyn) s.
zakaz; zahamowanie; wstrzymanie
inhospitable (yn'hospytebl) adj.
niegościnny
inhuman (yn'hju:men) adj. nieludzki; okrutny;brutalny etc.
initial (y'nyszel) adj. początkowy;v.znaczyć własnymi inicjała-
mi
initiate (y'nyszjejt) v. zapoczątkować; wprowadzać; zainicjo-
wać; wtajemniczać;s.nowicjusz
initiation (y,nyszy'ejszyn) s.
wprowadzenie;zapoczątkowanie
initiative (y'nyszjetyw) s.
inicjatywa; adj. początkowy
inject (yn'dżekt) v. wstrzyknąć
injection (yn'dżekszyn) s.
zastrzyk;wstrzyknięcie;a.wytrysko-
wy
injudicious (,yndżu'dyszes) adj.
nierozważny; nieroztropny
injure ('yndżer) v. zranić;
uszkodzić; krzywdzić; zepsuć
injurious (yn'dżuerjes) adj.
szkodliwy; krzywdzący; obel-
żywy;przynoszący ujmę;obraźliwy
injury ('yndżery) s. szkoda;
krzywda; rana; uszkodzenie
injustice (yn'dżastys) s. niesprawiedliwość; krzywda
ink (ynk) s. atrament; tusz
inkling ('ynklyng)s. wzmianka;
podejrzenie; przypuszczenie
ink-pot ('ynk,pot) s. kałamarz
inland ('ynlend) s. wnętrze
kraju; adj. z głębi kraju;
wewnętrzny; adv. w głębi;
w głąb kraju;w głębi kraju
inlet ('ynlet) s. wstawka; zatoka; wlot; wejście;a.wlotowy
inmate ('ynmejt) s. mieszkaniec;
lokator; współ-(więzień etc.)

inmost ('ynmoust) adj. głęboko
utajony; skryty;najtajniejszy
inn (yn) s. gospoda; oberża
innate ('y'nejt) adj. wrodzony
inner ('yner) adj. wewnętrzny
innermost ('ynermoust) adj.
głęboko ukryty; najskrytszy
inner tube ('yner,tju:b) s.
dętka(samochodowa,rowerowa)
innkeeper ('yn,ki:per) s.
oberżysta;właściciel zajazdu
innocence ('ynesns) s. niewinność; naiwność;prostoduszność
innocent ('ynesynt) adj. niewinny; naiwny; nieszkodliwy;
niemądry; s. prostaczek;
niewiniątko; głuptas
innovation (,ynou'wejszyn) s.
innowacja;wprowadzanie zmian
innumerable (y'nju:merebl) adj.
niezliczony; bez liku
inoculate (y'nokjulejt) s.
szczepić;wpajać;oczkować roślin
inoffensive (,yne'fensyw) adj.
nieszkodliwy; spokojny;obojętny
inpatient ('ynpejszent) s.
pacjent leżący w szpitalu
inquest ('ynkłest) s. śledztwo
inquire (yn'kłajer) s. pytać
się; dowiadywać się; dociekać
inquiry (yn'kłajry) s. badanie;
zasięganie informacji; śledztwo; poszukiwanie;ankieta;wywiad
inquisitive (yn'kłyzytyw) adj.
badawczy; ciekawy;wścipski
insane (yn'sejn) adj. chory
umysłowo;zwarjowany;bez sensu
insanity (yn'saenyty) s. obłęd
insatiable (yn'sejszjebl) adj.
nienasycony;niezaspokojony;chci-
insatiate (yn'sej'szjyt) adj.
nienasycony;niezaspokojony
inscribe (yn'skrajb) v, wpisać;
napisać;umieszczać na liście
inscription (yn'skrypszyn) s.
napis; dedykacja
insect ('ynsekt) s. owad
insecure (,ynsy'kjuer) adj. niepewny; niezabezpieczony
insensible (yn'sensybl) adj.
nieświadomy; bez zmysłów;w stanie omdlenia;niedostrzegalny

insensitive (yn'sensytyw) adj.
nieczuły; niewrażliwy
inseparable (yn'seperebl) adj.
nierozłączny;nieodstępny
insert (yn'se:rt) v. wstawiać;
wkładać; s. wkładka; wstawka
insertion (yn'se:rszyn) s. wkładka; wstawka; włożenie; wsta-
wienie;przyczep;przyczepienie
inshore (yn'szo:r) adv. blisko
brzegu; przy brzegu; adj. przybrzeżny; bliski brzegu
inside 'ynsajd) s. wnętrze;
adj. wewnętrzny;adv.wewnatrz
inside (yn'sajd) adv. wewnątrz
inside out ('ynsajd'aut) exp.:
na lewą stronę (np. marynarki)
insight ('ynsajt) s. wgląd;
intuicja;wnikliwość
insignificant (,ynsyg'nyfykent)
adj. mało znaczący;błachy
insincere (,ynsyn'sier) adj.
nieszczery;zwodny;dwulicowy
insinuate (yn'synjuejt) v. in-
synuować; podsuwać;sugerować
insipid (yn'sypyd) adj. mdły;
tępy; bez sensu;głupi;ckliwy
insist (yn'syst) v. nalegać;
nastawać;utrzymywać;obstawać
insist on (yn'syst,on) v. domagać się;upierać się;nastawać
insolent ('ynselent) adj. bezczelny;zuchwały;butny;wyniosły
insoluble (yn'soljubl) adj. nierozpuszczalny;nie do rozwiązania
insolvent (yn'solwent) adj. niewypłacalny; s. bankrut;bankrutka
insomnia (yn'somnja) s. bezsen-
ność (nie normalna)
insomuch (,ynsou'macz) adv.
o tyle; do tego stopnia;tak dale-ce
inspect (yn'spekt) v. oglądać;
doglądać; mieć nadzór;badać
inspection (yn'spekszyn) s.
przegląd; oglądanie; inspekcja;
doglądanie;sprawdzanie;kontrola
inspector (yn'spekter) s. inspektor;nadzorca;kontroler
inspiration (,ynspe'rejszyn) s.
natchnienie ;wdech;wdychanie
inspire (yn'spajer) v. natchnąć;
podsunąć; zainspirować;wdychać

install(yn'sto:1) v. instalowac;
wprowadzac na stanowisko
installation (,ynsto:'lejszyn)
s. instalacja; wprowadzenie
na stanowisko;zamontowanie
instal(1)ment (yn'sto:lment)
s. część całości; rata
instance ('ynstens) s. wypadek;
przykład ;v.przytaczac przykład
instant ('ynstent) adj. nagły;
natychmiastowy; bieżący;
s. moment; chwila (szczególna)
instantaneous (,ynsten'tejnjes)
adj. natychmiastowy; momentalny ;zdarzający się w momencie
instantly (yn'stently) adv.
natychmiast; momentalnie
instead (yn'sted) adv. zamiast
tego; natomiast; w miejsce
instead of (yn'sted,ow) adv.
zamiast (kogoś, czegoś)
instigate ('ynstygejt) v. pod-
żegac;podjudzac;prowokowac
instigator ('ynstygejter) s.
podżegacz;prowokator;poduszczyciel
instil(1) (yn'styl) v. wsączac;
wpajac (uczucia etc.);wkraplac
instinct ('ynstynkt) s. instynkt;adj.tchnący(czymś);pełen
instinctive (yn'stynktyw) adj.
instynktowny; odruchowy
institute ('ynstytju:t) s. instytut; v. zakładac; ustanawiac; zarządzac(śledztwo etc.)
institution (,ynty'tju:szyn) s.
instytucja; ustanowienie
instruct (yn'strakt) v. uczyc
instruction (yn'strakszyn) s.
pouczenie; nauka; instrukcja
instructive (yn'straktyw) adj.
pouczający; kształcący
instructor (yn'strakter) s.
nauczyciel;wykładowca;instruktor
instructress (yn'straktrys) s.
nauczycielka ;instruktorka
instrument ('ynstrument) s.
instrument; przyrząd;dokument
insubordinate (,ynseb'o:rdnyt)
adj. niesforny; nieposłuszny
insufferable (yn'saferebl) adj.
nieznośny; nie do zniesienia
insufficient (,ynse'fyszent)
adj. niedostateczny;nieodpowiedni

insulate ('ynsjulejt) v. izolowac;oddzielac;odosabniac
insult ('ynsalt) s. zniewaga;
insult (yn'salt) v. lżyc; znie-
ważac;uchybiac;zelżyc
insupportable (,ynse'po:rtebl)
adj. nie do zniesienia; nieznośny;nieuzasadniony
insurance (yn'szuerens) s.
ubezpieczenie;a.ubezpieczeniowy
insurance policy (yn'szuerens'-
polysy) s. polisa ubezpieczeniowa;polisa asekuracyjna
insure (yn'szuer) v. ubezpieczac
(się);asekurowac;zabezpieczac
insurmountable (,ynse:r'maun-
tebl) adj. niepokonany
insurrection (,ynse'rekszyn) s.
powstanie; insurekcja
intact (yn'taekt) adj. nietknięty ;nie uszkodzony
integrate ('yntygrejt) v. scala-
lic; uzupełnic; całkowac
integrity (yn'tegryty) s. uczci-
wosc; rzetelnosc; czystosc;
prawosc ;niepodzielnosc
intellect ('yntylekt) s. rozum;
umysł;rozsądek;wybitne umysły
intellectual (,ynty'lekczuel)
adj. intelektualny; umysłowy;
s. intelektualista;inteligent
intelligence (yn'telydżens) s.
inteligencja; informacja; wywiad;wiadomości;nowiny;informacja
intelligent (yn'telydżent) adj.
inteligentny;łatwo uczący się
intelligentsia (yn'tely'dżencja)
s. inteligencja (warstwa kraju)
intelligible (yn'telydżybl) adj.
zrozumiały; jasny;wyraźny
intemperate (yn'temperyt) adj.
nieumiarkowany; bez umiaru
intend (yn'tend) v. zamierzac;
przeznaczac; miec na myśli
intense (yn'tens) adj. napięty;
usilny; gorliwy;wytężony;uczucio-
wy
intensify (yn'tensyfaj) v.
wzmoc; wzmocnic; napiąc;wzmagac
intensity (yn'tensyty) s. inten-
sywnosc; wzmożenie;natężenie
intensive (yn'tensyw) adj. intensywny; wzmożony ;silny; wzmacniający

intent (yn'tent) s. plan; zamiar; adj. uważny; zamierza-
jący; zajęty;pochłonięty;zdecy-
dowany
intent on (yn'tent on) adj.
pochłonięty; zajęty czymś
intention (yn'tenszyn) s. zamiar; cel;zamierzenie(czynu)
intentional (yn'tenszenel)
adj. umyślny; celowy;zamierzony
inter (yn'te:r) v. grzebać
intercede (,ynte:r'si:d) v.
wstawiać się; orędować
intercept ('ynte:rsept) v.
przechwycić; przejąć; przerwać; udaremnić; podsłuchać
intercession (,ynter'seszyn)
s. wstawiennictwo;orędownictwo
interchange (,ynte:r'czejndż)
s. wzajemna wymiana; v. wymieniać się; zmieniać się
intercourse ('ynterko:rs) s.
stosunek; obcowanie;spółkowanie
interdict (,ynter'dykt) s. zakaz; v. zakazywać;zabraniać
interest('yntryst) s. zainteresowanie; ciekawość; odsetki;
interes;procent;v.zainteresować
interested ('yntrystyd) adj.
zaciekawiony; zainteresowany
interesting ('yntrystyŋg) adj.
ciekawy; interesujący
interfere (,ynter'fier) v.
wtrącać się; wdawać się; kolidować; zakłócać;dokuczać
interfere with (,ynter'fier,łys)
v. mieszać się do kogoś
interference (,ynter'fierens)
s. wtrącanie się; zakłócenie
interior (yn'tierjer) adj. wewnętrzny; środkowy; s. wnętrze
głąb kraju;głąb duszy(serca)
interior decorator (yn'tierjer
'dekerejter) s. architekt
wnętrz; sprzedawca mebli
interjection (,ynter'dżekszyn)
s. okrzyk; wykrzyknik
interlude (ynter'lu:d) s.
przerwa; antrakt
intermediary (,ynter'mi:diery)
adj. pośredni; pośredniczący;
s. pośrednik;pośredniczka;po-
średnie stadium;pośrednia forma
pośredni produkt; agent

intermediate (,ynter'mi:djet)
adj. pośredni; środkowy; średni;s.pośrednik;v.pośredniczyć
intermingle (,ynter'myŋgl) v.
mieszać (się); pomieszać (się)
intermission (,ynter'myszyn) s.
przerwa;pauza; antrakt
intermittent (,ynter'mytent)
adj. przerywany; niemiarowy
intern (yn'te:rn) v. internować;
odbywać praktykę lekarską;
intern ('ynte:rn) s. praktykant
lekarski w szpitalu
internal ('ynte:rnl) adj. wewnętrzny; krajowy; domowy
international (,ynter'naeszenl)
adj. międzynarodowy; s. mię-
dzynarodówka; zawody między-
narodowe;zawodnik międzynarodowy
interpose (,ynter'pouz) v. wstawać; wtrącać (się); przerywać
interpret (yn'ter:pryt) v. tłumaczyć i objaśniać; interpretować;rozumieć(opatrznie etc.)
interpretation (yn,te:rpry'tejszyn) s. interpretacja; tłumaczenie;sposób zrozumienia
interpreter (yn'te:rpryter) s.
tłumacz (ustny)
interrogate (yn'teregejt) v.
wypytywać; przesłuchiwać
interrogation (yn,tere'gejszyn)
s. przesłuchanie; pytanie
interrogative (,ynte'rogetyw)
adj. pytający (np. ton)
interrupt (,ynte'rapt) v. przerywać; zasłaniać (widok)
interruption (,ynte'rapszyn) s.
przerwa (w czynności etc.)
intersect (,ynte:r'skt) v.
przecinać (się);pokrzyżować)się)
intersection (,ynter'sekszyn) s.
przecinanie się; skrzyżowanie
interval ('ynterwel) s. odstęp;
przerwa;antrakt;okres(pogody)
intervene (,ynter'wi:n) s. wdawać się; interweniować; zdarzyć
sie; zajść;być między(dwoma etc.)
intervention (,ynter'wenszyn)
s. interwencja; wdanie się
interview ('ynterwju:) s. wywiad;
rozmowa; v. mieć wywiad; wi-
dzieć się z kimś (dla wywiadu)

interviewer ('ynterwju:er) s.
przeprowadzający wywiad
intestines, (yn'testynz) pl.
wnętrzności ; jelita
intimacy ('yntymesy) s. zażyłość; intymność; poufałe sto-
sunki(płciowe);poufałość
intimate ('yntymyt),adj. zażyły; wewnętrzny; intymny;
v. zawiadamiać; dawać do zrozumienia;s.serdeczny przyjaciel
intimation (,ynty'mejszyn) s.
zawiadomienie; danie do zrozumienia;napomknięcie;znak(czegoś)
intimidate (yn'tymydejt) v.
zastraszyć; onieśmielić
into ('yntu:) prep. do; w; na
intolerable· (yn'tolerebl) adj.
nieznośny;nie do zniesienia
intolerant (yn'telerent) adj.
nietolerancyjny; nie znoszący
czegoś (cudzych przekonań etc.)
intoxicate (yn'toksykejt) v.
upić; upajać; odurzać się
intransitive (yn'traensytyw)
adj. & s. nieprzechodni
intrepid (yn'trepyd) adj. nieustraszony ;śmiały;odważny
intricate ('yntrykyt) adj. zawiły ;trudny do zrozumienia
intrigue (yn'tri:g) s. intryga;
potajemna miłość; v. intrygować; potajemnie utrzymywać
stosunek miłosny; zaciekawiać
introduce (,yntre'dju:s) v.
wprowadzać (coś lub kogoś);
przedstawiać; rozpoczynać; wsuwać; wysuwać; wkładać;zapoznawać
introduction (,yntre'dakszyn) s.
wstęp; wprowadzenie; włożenie;
wsunięcie; przedstawienie
(kogoś);przedmowa;innowacja etc.
introductory (,yntre'daktery)
adj. wstępny; wprowadzający
intrude (,yn'tru:d) v. wpychać
(sie); wciskać (sie); wedrzec
(sie); narzucać (sie) (komuś)
intruder (yn'tru:der) s. natręt;
intruz; nieproszony gość
intrusion (yn'tr:żyn) s. wcis-
nięcie (się); wepchnięcie (się);
narzucanie (sie); wdarcie (się)
w cudze prawa

intuition (,yntju'yszyn) s.
intuicja;przeczucie;wyczucie
inutile (yn'ju:tyl) adj. niepotrzebny; bezcelowy;bezużytecz-ny
invade (yn'wejd) v. najeżdżać;
wdzierać się; zalewać; owła-
dać; ogarniać; wtargnąć
invader (yn'wejder) s. najeźdźca ;okupant
invalid (yn'weli:d) s. chory;
inwalida ;kaleka;człowiek słaby
invalid (yn'waelyd) adj. nieważny ;nieprawomocny
invalidate (yn'daelydejt) v.
unieważniać (prawnie etc.)
invaluable (yn'waeljuebl) adj.
bezcenny; nieoceniony
invariable (yn'weeryebl) adj.
niezmienny;stały;równomierny
invariably (yn'v-eryebly) adv.
niezmiennie;stale;równomiernie
invasion (yn'wejżyn) s. inwazja; najazd; wdarcie (się)
invective (yn'wektyw) s. ,in-
wektywa; obelga; napaść (słow-
na);obelżywe słowa
invent (yn'went) v. wynaleźć;
wymyślić ;zmyślić(coś na kogoś)
invention (yn'wenszyn) s. wynalazek; wymysł; zmyślenie
inventive (yn'wentyw) adj. pomysłowy; wynalazczy
inventor (yn'wentor) s. wynalazca (w nauce,mechanice etc.)
inverse (yn'we:rs) adj. odwrotny; s. odwrotność (czegoś)
inversion (yn'we:rżyn) s. odwrócenie; inwersja; homo-
seksualizm ;wynicowanie
invert (yn'we:rt) v. odwrócić;
przestawić; s. homoseksualista
inverted commas (yn'we:rtyd -
'komes) cudzysłów
invest (yn'west) v. inwestować;
wyposażać; oblegać; obdarzać
investigate (yn'westygejt) v.
badać; prowadzić dochodzenie
investigation (yn,westy'gejszyn) s. badanie; dochodzenie; śledztwo;rozpatrzenie;do-
ciekanie
investigator (yn'westygejtor)
s. badacz ;agent(prokuratury)

investment (yn'westment) s.
inwestycja; lokata; oblężenie;osaczenie;obleczenie
invincible (yn'wynsebl) adj.
niepokonany; niezwyciężony
inviolable (yn'wajelebl) adj.
nienaruszalny; nietykalny;
niepogwałcony ;niezniszczalny
invisible (yn'wyzybl) adj.
niewidoczny; niewidzialny
invitation (,ynwy'tejszyn) s.
zaproszenie (pisemne,słowne)
invite (yn'wajt) v. zapraszać;
wywoływać; ściągać; nęcić;
zachęcać; prosić o (radę)
invoice ('ynwois) s. faktura;
v. fakturować
invoke (yn'wouk) v. wzywać;
odwoływać się; wywoływać
involuntary (yn'wolentery) adj.
mimowolny; nieumyślny; bez-
wiedny (czyn,ruch etc.)
involve (yn'wolw) v. gmatwać;
wikłać; wmieszać; komplikować; obejmować; wymagać
invulnerable (yn'walnerebl)
adj. nie do zranienia; nienaruszalny; nie do zdobycia
inward ('ynłerd) adj. wewnętrzny; adv. wewnątrz;w sercu etc.
inwards ('ynłerds) adv. wewnątrz ;w duchu ; w myśli
iodine ('ajoudi:n) s. jod
IOU. =I owe you ('ajou'ju:) s.
kwit; skrypt dłużny
irascible (y'raesybl) adj.
gniewliwy; popędliwy; wybuchowy;skory do gniewu
iridescent (,yry'desnt) adj.
mieniący się; tęczowy
iris ('ajerys) s. tęczówka
Irish ('ajerysz) adj. irlandz-
ki;s. Irlandczyk
iron ('ajern) s. żelazo; żelazko;(pistolet; rewolwer;)adj.
żelazny; v. zakuwać; prasować
ironic(al) (aj'ronyk(el)) adj.
ironiczny; drwiący;uczczypliwy.
ironing ('ajernyng) s. prasowa-
nie (bielizna etc.)
ironmonger ('ajern,manger) s.
handlarz wyrobów żelaznych;właś-
ciciel sklepu żelaznego

iron mo.ld ('ajernmould) s.
plama od rdzy
ironworks ('ajernłe:rks) s. huta żelaza ;przetwórnia żelaza
irony ('ajereny) s. ironia
irradiate (y'rejdjejt) v. oświetlać; naświetlać; oświecać;
rozjaśniać; rozpromienić
irrational (y'raesznel) adj.
nieracjonalny; nierozumny;
niewymierny;s.liczba niewymierna
irreconcilable (y'rekesajlebl)
adj. nieprzejednany; nie dający się pogodzić(z wiarą etc.)
irrecoverable (,yry'kawerebl)
adj. niepowetowany; nie do
odzyskania;stracony bezpowrotnie
irredeemable (,yry'di:mebl)
adj. niewymienny; beznadziej-
ny;nieodwracalny;nieodkupny
irregular (y'regjuler) adj. nieregularny; nierówny; nieporządny; nielegalny;nieprawidłowy
irrelevant (y'relywent) adj.
nieistotny; niestosowny; oderwany; od rzeczy;nie do rzeczy
irremovable (,yry'mu:webl) adj.
nieusuwalny;nie do pokonania
irreparable (y'reperebl) adj.
niepowetowany;nie do naprawie-
irreplaceble (,yry'plejsebl) adj.
niezastąpiony;nie do zastąpienia
irrepressible (,yry'presybl)
adj. niepohamowany;nieodparty
irreproachable (,yry'prouczebl)
adj. nienaganny; bez zarzutu
irresistible (,yry'zystybl) adj.
nieodparty;porywający;gwałtowny
irresolute (y'rezelu:t) adj.
niezdecydowany; chwiejny
irrespective (.yrys'pektyw) adj.
niezależny; adv. niezależnie;
bez względu na...;bez szacunku
irresponsible (,yrys'ponsybl)
adj. nieodpowiedzialny;nieobli-
czalny
irretrievable (,yry'tri:webl)
adj. bezpowrotnie stracony
irreverent (y'rewerent) adj.
lekceważący; uchybiający
irrevocable (y'rewekebl) adj.
nieodwołalny;nie do odwołania
irrigate ('yrygejt) v. nawadniać; przepłukiwać; oświeżać

irritable ('yrýtebl) adj.
draźliwy; wraźliwy; nerwowy;
przewraźliwiony;skory do gniewu
irritate ('yrytejt) v. denerwowac; irytowac; draźnic;
rozdraźniac;uniewaźnic prawnie
irritation (,yry'tejszyn) s.
irytacja; rozdraźnienie
is (yz) v. jest; zob. be
island ('ajlend) s. wyspa;
wysepka (na bruku)
isle (ajl) s. wyspa; v. źyc
na wyspie ;zrobic (jak)wyspę
isn't ('yznt) = is not; exp.:
nie jest (w domu etc.)
isn't it ? ('yznt yt) nieprawda ? czy nie prawda?
isolate ('ajselejt) v. odosabniac; izolowac;osamotnic
isolated ('ajselejtyd) adj.
odosobniony;osamotniony
isolation (,ajse'lejszyn) s.
odosobnienie; izolacja; wyodrębnienie;osamotnienie
issue ('yszu:) s. wydanie;
przydział; zeszyt; spor; problem; argument; wynik; koniec;
ujscie; wyjscie; wypływ; potomstwo; upuszczenie; dochod;
v. wysyłac; wypuszczac; wydawac; dawac w wyniku; wychodzic; pochodzic ;emitowac
isthmus ('ysmes) s. przesmyk;
międzymorze ;ciesn; węzina
it (yt) pron. to; ono
Italian (y'taeljen) adj. włoski
itch ('ycz) s. swędzenie;
świerzb;chętka; v. czuc swędzenie; swędzic;miec ochotę
item ('ajtem) s. pozycja; punkt
programu; artykuł; wiadomosc;
adv. podobnie; takźe;teź dóty-
itemize ('ajte,majz) v. wy-
szczególniac(rachunek,spis)
itinerary (aj'tynerery) s. marszruta; szlak; przewodnik;
adj. podróźny; drogowy
its (yts) pron. jego; jej; swoj
itself (yt'self) pron. się; siebie; sobie; sam; sama; samo
ivory ('ajwery) s. kosc słoniowa;klawisz fortepianu;biel kre-
mowa;adj.z kości słoniowej;biały

ivy ('ajwy) s. bluszcz
j (dźej) dziewiąta litera
angielskiego alfabetu
jab (dźaeb) s. szturchaniec;
dźgnięcie; v. szturchac; dźgac
jack (dźaek) s. lewarek; dźwignia; przyrząd; walet; flaga;
gniazdko elektr.; złącze
jack up ('dźaek,ap) v. podniesc
lewarkiem;wysrubowanie(cen)
jackal ('dźaeko:l) s. szakal;
sługus;harowac za kogos
jackass ('dźaekaes) s. osioł;
duren; bałwan;menda;niedojda
jackdaw ('dźaekdo:) s. kawka
jacket ('dźaekyt) s. marynarka;
źakiet; kurtka; okładzina; obwoluta; osłona; v. okrywac; nakładac okładzinę;wkładac do teki
jack-in-the-box ('dźaek-yn-dy-
boks) s. figurka wyskakująca
z pudełka;typ ognia sztucznego
jackknife ('dźaeknajf) s.
scyzoryk; nóź składany
jack-of-all-trades ('dźaek,ow-
'o:l,trejds) majster do
wszystkiego;majster klepka
jackpot ('dźaek,pot) s. główna
wygrana; pula
jackscrew ('dźaekskru:) s. lewar srubowy (podnosnik)
jag (dźaeg) s. ostry występ;
zadarcie; nacięcie; podniecenie; popijawa; zabawa; v. poszarpac; postrzepic; ząbkowac
jagged ('dźaegyd) adj. po-
strzępiony;wyszczerbiony;szczerba-
jaguar ('dźaegjuer) s. jaguar
jail (dźejl) s. ciupa; więzienie;v. więzic; uwięzic(kogos)
jam (dźaem) s. tłok; zator; korek; zła sytuacja; v. stłoczyc;
zablokowac; zaciąc; zagłuszyc
janitor ('dźaenitor) s. portier;
dozorca;sprzątacz biurowy etc.
January ('dźaenjuery) s. styczeń ; a.styczniowy (dzień etc.)
Japanese (,dźaepe'ni:z) adj.
japoński; s.Japończyk
jar (dźa:r) s. słój; słoik;
zgrzyt; kłótnia; drganie;
v. zgrzytac; draźnic; wstrząsac; kłócic się ;trzasc;razic

jaundice ('dźo:ndys) s. żół- taczka ;v.powodować żazdrość (żółtaczkę)
javelin ('dżaewlyn) s. oszczep
jaw (dżo:) s. szczęka; v. glę- dzić; gadać;wstawiać mowę
jaw-bone ('dżo:boun) s. kość szczękowa; v. nakłaniać słowami (pod presją)
jazz (dżaz) s. muzyka jazzowa; v. kłamać;adj.zgrzytliwy;krzyk- liwy
jazz it up ('dżaz,yt'ap) v. ożywiać; ulepszać (coś)
jay (dżej) s. sójka; dudek; pleciuga; gaduła (arogancki)
jay-walker ('dżej,ło:ker) s. nieprawidłowo przechodzący jezdnię ;roztrzepaniec
jealous ('dżeles) adj. zazdrosny; baczny (nadzór);zawistny
jealousy ('dżelesy) s. zazdrość; zawiść ;wybuch zazdrości
jeep (dżi:p) s. łazik; samochód terenowy (silnie zbudowany)
jeer (dżier) s. kpina; szyderstwo; drwina; v. drwić; kpić; wykpiwać (ordynarnie i złośliwie)
jelly ('dżely) s. galareta; kisiel;v.zgalarecieć;robić galaretę
jellyfish ('dżelyfysz) s. meduza;człowiek słabej woli
jeopardize ('dżepe,dajz) v. narazić na niebezpieczeństwo
jerk (dże:rk) s. szarpnięcie; skręt; skurcz; pchnięcie; bzik; frajer; v. szarpać; targać; pchnąć; rzucać się;wzdrygać się
jerky ('dże:rky) adj. urwany; trzesący; bzikowaty;spazmatyczny
jersey ('dże:rzy) s. sweter
jest (dżest) s. żart; dowcip; zabawa; pośmiewisko; v. żartować; dowcipkować;przekomarzać się
jester ('dżester) s. błazen; trefnis; błazen nadworny
jet (dżet) s. strumien; wytrysk; płomień; dysza; rozpylacz; odrzutowiec; v. tryskać;a.czarny jak smoła
jet engine (,dżet'endżyn) s. motor odrzutowy
jet lag ('dżet,laeg) s.ujemny efekt zmiany sfer czasu na pasażera samolotu ódrzutowego

jet plane ('dżet,plejn) s. samolot odrzutowy;odrzutowiec
jet-propelled ('dżet-pre,peld) adj. odrzutowy
jet set ('dżet,set) s. złota młodzież; prominenci
jetty (dżety) s. grobla; molo; adj. czarny jak smoła
jewel ('dżu:el) s. klejnot; drogi kamień; v. ozdabiać klejnotami; osadzać na kamieniach(zamontować)
jeweler ('dżu:eler) s. jubiler;wlaściciel sklepu jubilerskiego
jewelry ('dżu:elry) s, klejnoty; biżuteria;kosztowności
Jewish ('dżu:ysz) adj. żydowski
jibe (dżajb) v. zgadzać się; pasować (do czegoś);harmonizować
jiffy ('dżyfy) s. mig; chwileczka;momencik;skundka
jiggle ('dżygl) v. kołysać; lekko hustać;wstrząsać zrywnie
jingle ('dżyngl) v. brzękać; szczękać; dzwonić; s. brzęk; szczek; wierszyk(rymy);dzwonek
job (dżob) s. robota; zajęcie; zadanie; posada; v. pracować; robić; handlować; wynajmować
job (dżob) v. ukłuć; dżgnąć; dziobnąć; s. dżgnięcie;praca; dziobnięcie;zadanie;robota;fach
jobless ('dżoblys) adj. bezrobotny ;bez pracy
job-work ('dżobłerk) s. praca na akord (zob. piece-work)
jockey ('dżoky) s. dżokej; v. oszukać; nabrać;pchać się na pozycje
jocular ('dżokjuler) adj. wesoły; żartobliwy;krotochwilny
jocularity (,dżokju'laeryty) s. wesołość; żartobliwość; żarty;ktotochwilność;figlarność
jocund ('dżoukend) adj. wesoły
jog (dżog) s. potrącenie; poruszenie; trucht; róg;występ; v. potrącać; poruszać; przebiedować; biec truchtem;telepać się
jog-trot ('dżog'trot) s. trucht;a.monotonny;jednostajny

join (dżoyn) v. łączyć; przyłączac (się); przytykac do;
spotykac się;brać udział
joiner ('dżojner) s. stolarz
joint (dżoynt) v. spajac;łą-
czyc; ćwiartowac; kantowac;
s. spojenie; fuga; złącze;
zestawienie; zawiasa francuska;
część; lokal; melina; a. wspólny; połączony;dzielący się z kimś
joint stock ('dżoynt,stok) adj.
akcyjny (bank);udziałowy
joke (dżouk) s. żart; dowcip;
figiel; v. żartowac z kogos;
dowcipkowac;wysmiac;zadrwic
joker ('dżouker) s. żartownis;
dowcipnis; gosc; facet; dżo-
ker; pułapka; trudnosc
jolly ('dżoly) adj. wesoły; miły; podochocony; adv. szalenie;
bardzo; v. przychlebiac; nabierac; zachęcac;mitygowac;uglas-
jolt (dżoult) v. wstrząsac;
podrzucac; s. wstrząs; podrzu-
cenie; szarpnięcie;podskok
jostle ('dżosl) v. rozpychac
(się); roztrącac; szarpac się;
walczyc (z kimś); s. pchnięcie;
starcie;szturchnięcie;tłok;scisk
jot down ('dżot,dałn) v. zapisac napredce;zanotować pospiesz- nie
journal ('dże:rnl) s. dziennik;
czasopismo; czop;os w łożysku
journalism ('dże:rnlyzem) s.
dziennikarstwo
journey ('dże:rny) v. podrożowac;
s. podróż;jazda;wycieczka
journeyman ('dże:rnymen) s. cze-
ladnik(nauczony rzemiosła)
jovial ('dżouwjel) adj. wesoły;
jowialny;pełen dobrego humoru
joy (dżoj) s. radosc; uciecha
joyful ('dżoyful) adj. radosny;
wesoły;zadowolony(bardzo)
joyous ('dżojes) adj.=joyful
jubilant ('dżu:bylent) adj.
triumfujący; rozradowany
jubilee ('dżu:byli:) s. jubileusz; wielka radosc;a.jubileuszowy
judge (dżądż) v. sądzic; osądzac;
rozsądzac; s. sędzia; znawca; nach
znawczyni;człowiek biegły w oce-

judgment ('dżadżment) s.
sąd; sądzenie; wyrok; rozsądek;opinia; ocena; decyzja
judicial (dżu'dyszel) adj. sądowy; sędziowski; bezstronny;
krytyczny;sądownie zastrzeżony
judicious (dżu'dyszes) a. rozsądny;rozumny;wykazujący rozum
jug (dżag) s. dzbanek; koza;
ciupa; v. gotowac; wsadzac do
kozy, ciupy;dusic (potrawkę)
juggle ('dżagl) v. żonglowac;
cyganic; robic sztuczki;
s. kuglarstwo;żonglerka
juggler ('dżagler) s. kuglarz;
żongler;oszust;kanciarz
jugglery ('dżaglery) s. kuglarstwo;podstęp;oszukaństwo;żon-glerka
Jugoslav ('ju:gou'sla:v) adj.
jugosłowiański;Jugosłowianin
juice (dżu:s) s. sok; tresc;
benzyna; elektrycznosc;
v. wyciskac sok; doic
juicy ('dżu:sy) adj. soczysty;
jędrny;barwny;deszczowy etc.
juke box ('dżuk,boks) s. auto-
mat-gramofon(na monety)
July (dżu:laj) s. lipiec
jumble ('dżambl) s. pomieszac;
kotłowac; mieszanina; galimatias; bigos;trzęsąca jazda
jumble-sale ('dżambl,sejl) s.
wyprzedaż wysortowanych to-
warów(często dobroczynna)
jump (dżamp) s. skok; sus; podskok; wyskok; v. skakac; pod-
skoczyc; wskoczyc; wyskoczyc;
wyprzedzac; podnosic cenę;się
wykoleic;poderwac się;rzucac
jumper ('dżamper) s. skoczek;
typ sukni (bez rękawów)
jumpy ('dżampy) adj. nerwowy;
zmienny;nierówny;kapryśny
junction ('dżankszyn) s. połączenie; złącze; stacja węzło-
wa; węzeł;skrzyżowanie(dróg)
juncture('dżankczer) s. połączenie; stan rzeczy; krytycz-
na chwila; chwila;przesilenie
June (dżu:n) s. czerwiec
jungle ('dżangl) s. dżungla;
gąszcz zarosli,lian etc.

junior ('dżu:njer) s. junior;
młodszy; student trzeciego
roku (USA);a.młodszy;z młodszych
junk ('dżąk) s.złom; szmelc;
narkotyki; v. wyrzucać
junkie ('dżanki) s. narkoman
jurisdiction (,dżurys'dykszyn)
s. wymiar sprawiedliwości;
sądownictwo;zasięg władzy
jurisprudence (,dżurys'pru:-
dens) s. prawoznawstwo
juror ('dżuerer) s. sędzia
przysięgły; ławnik; zaprzysiężony;juror
jury ('dżuery) s. sąd przysięgłych; sąd konkursowy
just (dżast) s. sprawiedliwy;
słuszny; dokładny; adv. własnie; poprostu; zaledwie; przecież; dokładnie; moment wczes-
niej;ściśle;równie;tak samo
just now ('dżast,nał) exp.:
właśnie teraz;przed chwilą
justice ('dżastys) s. sprawiedliwość; słuszność; sę-
dzia(pokoju,sądu najwyższego)
justification (,dżastyfy'kejszyn) s. uzasadnienie;
usprawiedliwienie;wykazanie
justify ('dżastyfaj) v. usprawiedliwić; wytłumaczyć; umoty-
wować; uzasadnić;dać dowody
justly ('dżastly) adv. słusznie;
poprawnie;właściwie;sprawiedli-
jut (dżat) s. występ;v.wystawać
jut out ('dżat,aut) v. wystawać;
sterczeć(na zewnątrz);występować
juvenile ('dżu:wynajl) adj.
małoletni; nieletni; s. wyrostek; młodzik;podrostek
juvenile court ('dżu:wynajl,-
,ko:rt) s. sąd dla nieletnich
juvenile delinquent ('dżu:wy-
najl,dy'lynkłent) s. młodociany przestępca
juxtaposition (,dżakstepe'zyszyn) s. zestawienie; bezpoś-
rednie sąsiedztwo(tuż obok)
k (kej)jedenasta litera angielskiego alfabetu
kangaroo (,kaenge'ru:) s. kangur;a.samosądny;nielegalny
kayak ('kajaek)s.kajak;s.kajakowy

keel (ki:l) s. stępka; kil;
v. wywracać do góry stępką
keen (ki:n) adj. ostry; dotkliwy; żywy; cięty; serdeczny;
gorliwy; zapalony; bystry;
przenikliwy; wrażliwy; czuły
keen on ('ki:n.on) adj. palący się do..;czujący miętę
keep; kept; kept (ki:p; kept;
kept)
keep (ki:p) v. dotrzymywać;
przestrzegać; dochować; obchodzić; strzec; pilnować; utrzymywać; prowadzić; trzymać(się)
powstrzymywać się; mieszkać;
kontynuować; s. utrzymanie;
jedzenie; wikt;umocnienie
keep away ('ki:p,ełej) v. trzymać się z daleka;odstraszać
keep back ('ki:p,baek) v. powstrzymać; nie zbliżać się
keep down ('ki:p,dałn) v. trzymać w ryzach; tłumić; kulić
się;utrzymywać na niskim pozio-mie
keep in('ki:p,yn) v. zatrzymywać; nie wychodzić; pozostawać;nie pokazywć się
keep off ('ki:p,of) v. nie dopuszczać; trzymać się z dala
keep on ('ki:p,on) v. kontynuować; iść dalej;nudzić;męczyć
keep on doing ('ki:p,on'du:yng)
v. robić dalej; nie przestawać;nie dawać spokoju;nudzić
keep out ('ki:p, ałt) v. nie
wchodzić; trzymać się na uboczu;nie pozwolić wejść;odpędzać
keep talking ('ki:p'to:kyng)v.
mówić dalej;kontynuować rozmowę
keep time ('ki:p'tajm) v. być
punktualnym;zapisywać czas pracy
keep to oneself ('ki:p,tu'łan-
self) v. trzymać się na uboczu; żyć w odosobnieniu
keep up ('ki:p,ap) v. dotrzymywać; utrzymywać w porządku;
nie dawać iść spać; trzymać
się w dobrym stanie;czuwać
keep up with ('ki:p,ap'łys) v.
śledzić; dotrzymywać (kroku)
keeper ('ki:per) s. opiekun;
dozorca; strażnik; konserwator;
klamra; kotwica magnesu;skobel

keeping ('ki:pyŋg) s. opieka; zgoda; harmonia;a.do przechowywania

keepsake ('ki:psejk) s. upominek; pamiątka od kogoś

keg (keg) s. beczułka;100 funtów

kennel ('kenl) s. psiarnia; psia buda; ściek; v. trzymać w budzie; mieszkać w norze

kept (kept) v. zob. keep

kerb stone ('ke:rb,stoun) s. krawężnik (ang.) zob. curb

kerchief ('ke:rczyf) s. chustka (na głowę);chustka do nosa

kernel ('ke:rnl) s. jądro; ziarno;sedno sprawy;istotna rzecz

ketchup ('keczap) s. sos pomidorowy (gotowy) do mięsa

kettle ('ketl) s. kocioł; czajnik; imbryk na herbatę

kettledrum ('ketl,dram) s.bęben-kocioł(półkulisty)miedziany

key (ki:) s. klucz; klawisz; klin; ton; rafa; wysepka; v. stroić; zamykać kluczem lub zwornikiem;adj.ważny;kontrolujacy

keyboard ('ki:bo:rd) s. klawiatura (maszyny do pisania etc.)

keyhole ('ki:houl) s. dziurka od klucza (w drzwiach etc.)

keynote ('ki:nout) s. nuta kluczowa ;myśl przewodnia

keystone ('ki:stoun) s. zwornik;zasada;główna część

kick (kɪk) s. kopniak; kopnięcie; wierzgnięcie; wykop; strzał; odrzut; skarga; narzekanie; przyjemność; uciecha; krzepa; miłe podniecenie; opór; v. kopać; wierzgać; skrzywić się; protestować; opierać się

kickback ('kykbaek) s. łapówka za kontrakt;dawanie łapówki

kick downstairs ('kykdałn'steerz) v. degradować; zrzucać ze schodów (kopniakiem)

kick-off ('kykof) s. rozpoczęcie meczu; pierwszy strzał

kick out ('kʌk aut) v. wyrzucić; wykopać ; pozbyć się

kick the bucket ('kɪk,dy'bakyt) v. umrzeć; odwalić kitę; wyciagnać nogi;wykitować

kid (ky.d) s. koźlę; dzieciak; smyk; młodzik; blaga; bujda; v. urodzić koźlę; bujać; nabierać; żartować;dowcipkować

kid glove ('kydglaw) s. rękawiczka;adj.galowy;delikatny

kidnap ('kydnaep) v. porywać; uprowadzać;ukraść dziecko etc.

kidnapper ('kydnaeper) s. porywacz (dziecka;zakładnika etc.)

kidney ('kydny) s. nerka; rodzaj;a.w kształcie nerki

kidney bean ('kydny,bi:n) s. fasola szparagowa; piesza

kill (kyl) v. zabijać; uśmiercać; wybić; zatrzymać (piłkę, motor) ścinać (piłkę); s.upolowane zwierzę; zabicie; mord

kill time (,kyl'tajm) v. zabijać czas; marnować czas

killer ('kyler) s. zabójca; morderca; narzędzie śmierci

kiln (kyln) s. piec do wypalania lub wysuszania cegieł etc.

kilogram(me) ('kylougraem) s. kilogram;a. kilogramowy

kilometer ('kyle,mi:ter) s. kilometr; a. kilometrowy

kilt (kylt) s. spódniczka męska (szkocka); v. podkasać;szkocka plisować pionowo;s.spódnica

kin (kyn) s. rodzina; krewni; ród; adj. spokrewniony;pokrewny

kind (kajnd) s. rodzaj; jakość; gatunek; charakter; natura; adj. grzeczny; uprzejmy; życzliwy;łagodny;wyrozumiały

kindergarten ('kynder,ga:rtn) s. przedszkole (do sześciu lat wieku)

kindhearted ('kajnd'ha:rtyd) adj. dobrotliwy;współczujacy

kindle ('kyndle) v. rozpalić; rozżarzyć; rozniecać; podniecać;zapalać się

kindly ('kajndly) adj. uprzejmie; życzliwie; adj. dobry; dobrotliwy; życzliwy;adv.uprzej-mie

kindness ('kajndnys) s. dobroć; uprzejmość; łaskawość; życzliwość ;życzliwy postępek

kindred ('kyndryd) s. krewni; pokrewieństwo; adj.pokrewny

king (kyŋg) s. król
kingdom ('kyŋgdom) s. królestwo;monarchia;świat(roslin etc.)
kingsize ('kyŋgsajz) adj. wielki; duży;królewskich wymiarów
kingly ('kyŋgly) adj. królewski
kinsman ('kynzmen) s. krewny;
powinowaty (męszczyzna)
kipper ('kyper) s. śledź wędzony; ryba suszona; v. suszyć;
wędzić i solić; zasuszać(ryby)
kiss (kys) s. całus; v. całować; pocałowac;lekko dotknąć
kit (kyt) s. przybory; narzę-
dzia; wyposażenie; zestaw;
komplet; torba; bagaż; ceb-
rzyk; kubeł;komplet(narzędzi)
kitchen ('kyczn) s. kuchnia
kitchenette ('kyczynet) s.
kuchenka(mała w kawalerce etc.)
kite (kajt) s. latawiec;v.szybo-
kitten ('kytn) s. kotek
knack (naek) s. spryt; sztuczka; chwyt; dryg; talent
knapsack ('naepsaek) s. plecak
knave (nejw) s. łajdak; łotr;
szelma; walet;naciągacz;kanalia
knavery ('nejwery) s. łajdactwo; szelmostwo;niegodziwość
knead ('ni:d) v. miesić; gniesć;
masować;kształcić(charakter)
knee ('ni:) s. kolano;v.klękać
knee breeches ('ni:bryczyz) pl.
spodnie do kolan
kneel; knelt; knelt (ni:l; nelt;
nelt)
kneel ('ni:l) v. klękać
knelt(nelt) zob. kneel
knew (nju:) zob . know
knickerbockers ('nikerbockers)
s. pumpy; krótkie spodnie
spięte pod kolanami
knickknack ('niknaek) s. cacko;
fatałaszek; przysmaczek
knife (najf) s. nóż; v. krajac;
kłuć nożem; zakłuc;zadżgać nożem
knight (najt) s. rycerz; v. nadawać szlachectwo;nobilitować
knit; knit; knit (nyt; nyt; nyt)
knit (nyt) v. robić na drutach;
dziać; marszczyć (brwi); łączyć; ściągać;powodować zrośnię-
cie(kości);spajać(cementem)

knitting (nytyŋg) s. dzianie;
trykotarstwo;dziewiarstwo
knives (najwz) pl. noże; pl.od
knife
knob (nob) s. guzik; guz; gałka; sęk;uchwyt;pokrętło;rączka
knock (nok) s. stuk; uderzenie;
pukanie; stukać; pukać; zapu-
kać; uderzyc; zderzyc; szturchać;zderzyć się
knock down ('nok,dałn) v. powalic; obniżać cenę;rozkręcać
knock out ('nok,aut) v. nokau-
tować; wybijać; wymęczyć
knock over ('nok,ower) v. przewracać; przewrócić
knocker ('noker) s. kołatka na
drzwiach;malkontent;opukiwacz
knot (not) s. węzeł; kokarda;
sęk; zgrubienie; dystans morski 1853 m; v. wiązac; zawiązywać; komplikować; motać
knotty ('noty) adj. węzłowaty;
sękaty; zawiły; zagadkowy
know; knew; known (nou; nju:;
noun)
know (nou) v. wiedzieć; umieć;
znać; móc odróżniac; poznac
know-how ('nouhau) s. umiejęt-
nosć; znajomość rzeczy
knowingly ('nouyŋgly) adj. świadomie; naumyślnie; chytrze
knowledge ('noulydż) s. wiedza;
nauka; znajomość;zasięg wiedzy
knowledgeable ('nolydżebl) adj.
dobrze poinformowany; mądry
knuckle ('nakl) s. staw palca;
kastet; uderzac kośćmi palców
kotow ('kou,tał) = kowtow
kowtow ('koł,tał) v. bić czołem; płaszczyć się; s. ukłon
starochiński czołem do ziemi
Kraut (kraut) adj. szkopski
(niemiecki) ; kapuściany
kudos ('kju:dos) s. nagroda
lub uznanie za znaczne osiągnięcie; sława (slang)
Ku Klux Klan ('kju:,kluks'klaen)
s. rasistowska tajna organizacja w USA przeciw murzynom,
żydom i katolikom
kulak (ku:'la:k) s. zamożny
chłop; kułak

l (el) dwunasta litera alfabetu
angielskiego; klauzura; kolanko (rury); kątownik
lab (laeb) s. (slang):labora-
torium; a. laboratoryjny
label ('lejbl) s. nalepka; etykieta; naklejka; przezwisko;
v. przylepiać etykiety (na
coś; komuś);przezywać
labor ('lejber) s. praca; robota; trud; mozół; wysiłek;
klasa robotnicza; poród;
v. ciężko pracować; mozolić
się; borykać się; łudzić się;
brnać; opracować; rozwodzić
się; rodzić;szczegółowo opracować
laboratory (lae'boretery) s.
laboratorium; pracownia
laborious (le'bo:rjes) adj.
pracowity; mozolny; wypracowany;ciężko pracujący
labor union('lejber'ju:njen)
s. związek zawodowy
laborer ('lejberer) s. robotnik płatny na godzinę(fizyczny)
laborite ('lejberajt) s. członek partii pracy (w Anglii)
lace (lejs) s. sznurówka; sznurowadło; koronka; v. sznurować; przetykać; koronkować;
urozmaicać; chłostać; zakra-
piać (wódkę);młocić;bić;walić
lack (laek) s. brak; niedostatek; v. brakować; nie mieć
czegoś;być bez czegoś
laconic (le'konyk) adj. lakoniczny; zwięzły; treściwy
lacquer ('laeker) s. lakier;
v. lakierować;emaliować
lad (laed) s. chłopak; chłopiec
ladder ('laeder) s. drabina;
v. pruć; rozpruć;puszczać oczka
ladder proof ('laeder,pru:f)
adj. nie prujące się (np. pończochy);nie puszczający oczek
laden ('lejdn) adj. obciążony;
obarczony;pogrążony(w smutku)
lading ('lejdyng)s. fracht; za-
ładowanie; ładunek (statku etc.)
ladle ('lejdl) s. warząchew;
czerpak; chochla; v. czerpać;
nalewać warząchwią (czerpakiem)

lady ('lejdy) s. pani; dama
lady killer ('lejdy,kyler) s.
pożeracz serc niewieścich
ladylike ('lejdylajk) adj. wytworny; zniewieściały
lag (laeg) s. zaleganie; opóź-
nianie; zwłoka;v. zalegać;
wlec się z tyłu; nie nadążać
lag behind ('laeg,by'hajnd) v.
pozostawać w tyle;zalegać
lager ('la:ger) s. wystałe piwo
lagoon (le'gu:n) s. laguna
laid (lejd) zob. lay
lain (lejn) zob. lie
lair (leer) s. barłóg; legowisko; szałas; v.iść na legowisko
lake (lejk) s. jezioro;a.jeziorny
lamb (laem) s. jagnię; baranina
lame (lejm) adj. kulawy; ułomny; v. okulawić; okaleczyć
lament (le'ment) s. lament;
biadanie; v. lamentować; biadać; opłakiwać; narzekać; ubolewać;zawodzić;być w żałobie
lamentable ('laementebl) adj.
opłakany; godny ubolewania;
żałosny;wyrażający ubolewanie
lamentation (,laemen'tejszyn) s.
lament; biadanie;lamentacja
lamp (laemp) s. lampa; latarka;
kaganek; v. świecić; oświetlać;
gapić się;zobaczyć;widzieć
lamppost ('laemppoust) s. słup
latarniany ;latarnia uliczna
lamp shade ('laempszejd) s.
abażur
lance (la:ns) s. lanca; lansjer;
lancet; v.kłuć; przebijać lan-
cą lub lancetem; rozcinać
land (laend) s. ląd; ziemia;
grunt; kraj; v. wyciągać na ląd;
wyładować; zdobyć (np. nagrodę)
landholder ('laend,houlder) s.
właściciel ziemski; dzierżawca
landing ('laendyng) s. lądowanie;
pomost; przystań; półpiętrze
landing field ('laendyng,fi:ld)
s. lotnisko polowe ;lądowisko
landing gear ('leandyng,gier)
s. podwozie (z kołami-samolotu)
landing stage ('laendyng,stejdż)
s. pomost pływający ; wyładunek

landlady ('laend,lejdy) s.
właścicielka domu; hotelu
etc.;gospodyni (pensjonatu)
landlord ('laend,lo:rd) s.
właściciel domu czynszowego;
gospodarz odnajmujący pokój
landmark ('laendma:rk) s. punkt
orientacyjny; słup graniczny
landowner ('laend,oŕner) s.
właściciel ziemski
landscape ('laendskejp) s.
krajobraz; v. kształtować
teren i ogród (upiększać)
landslide ('laendslajd) s.
osuwisko; lawina głosów
landslip ('laendslyp) s. osuwisko; obsunięcie się ziemi
lane (lejn) s. tor; uliczka;
szlak; przejście; linia ruchu kołowego ;trasa(samolotu)
language ('laengłydź) s. mowa;
język mowiony i pisany
languid ('laengłyd) s. ospały;
omdlały; słaby; ociężały; powolny; rozmarzony; tęskny
languish ('laengłysz) v. omdle-
wać; marnieć; ginąć z tęsknoty ;mieć wyraz zadumy
languor ('laenger) s. omdlenie;
osłabienie;ociężałość; ospa-
łość; tęsknota; rozmarzenie;
powolność;brak wigoru;słabość
lank (laenk) adj. mizerny; wysoki; chudy; wychudzony;
prosty; gładki ;długi i płaski
lanky ('laenky) adj. wychudzony; wysoki i chudy
lanolin ('laenolyn) s. lanolina
lantern ('laentern) s. latarnia
lap (laep) s. łono; podołek;
poła; okrążenie; zanadrze;
dolinka; chlupotanie; lura;
v. spowijać; otulać; zakładać
(jak dachówki); wystawać;
chłeptać; chlupotać;chlupać
lapel (le'pel) s. klapa
(płaszcza) dochodząca kołnierza
lapse (laeps) s. lapsus; upływ;
okres; omyłka; v. potknąć się;
odstąpić; omylić sie; upłynąć;
stracić ważność; minąć; przechodzić;pogrążyć się w stan...

larceny ('la:rseny) s. kradzież
larch (la:rcz) s. modrzew
lard (la:rd) s. smalec; v. szpikować; naszpikowywać;ozdabiać
larder ('la:rder) s. spiżarnia
large (la:rdż) adj. wielki;
rozległy; obfity; hojny
largely ('la:rdżly)adv. znacz-
nie; hojnie; suto; w dużym
stopniu; w dużej ilości;głównie
lark (la:rk) s. skowronek; zabawa; uciecha; v. figlować;
żartować; przeskakiwać
larva ('la:rwa) s. larwa
larynx ('laerynks) s. krtań
lascivious (le'syvjes) adj.
lubieżny;wzbudzający lubieżność
lash (laesz) s. bicz; uderzenie;
nagana; rzęsa; v. chłostać; machać; walić; pędzić; uwiązać
lass (laes) s. dziewczyna;
dziewczę; młoda kobieta
lasso (lae'su:) s. lasso;
v. chwytać na lasso
last (laest) adj. ostatni; ubiegły; ostateczny; adv. po raz
ostatni; ostatnio; wreszcie;
w końcu; v. trwać; wytrzymać;
wystarczyć; długo służyć;
s. koniec; kres; wytrzymałość;
kopyto szewskie ;ostatnie dziecko
last but one ('laest,bat'łan)
exp.: przedostatni
lasting ('la:styng) adj. stały;
trwały ;długo trwały
lastly ('la:stly) adv. w końcu;
na końcu;w konkluzji;ostatecznie
last night ('laest,najt) exp.
wczoraj wieczór
last name ('laest,nejm) s. nazwisko
latch (laecz) s. zasuwka; rygiel; zatrzask; v. zamykać na
zasuwkę, rygiel lub zatrzask
latch onto ('laecz,ontu) v.
uczepić się kogoś
late (lejt) adj. & s. późny;
spóźniony; były; zmarły; adv.
późno; poniewczasie; niegdyś
lately ('lejtly) adv. ostatnio
later on ('lejter,on) adv.
później; potem; dalej

lath (laes) s. łata; deseczka;
v. pokrywać łatami(do tynkowa-nia)
lathe (lejz) s. tokarnia; koło
garncarskie; v. toczyć (na
tokarni); obrabiać(na obrabiarce)
lather ('laedzer) s. piana;
mydliny; v. mydlić (brodę);
zapienić (się); prać; łoić
Latin ('laetyn) adj. łaciński;
s. łacina; łacinnik
latitude ('laetytju:d) s. szerokość (geograficzna); szerokość poglądów; zakres; roz-
miary; wolność; swoboda (np.
działania); tolerancja
latter ('laeter) adj, drugi;
końcowy; schyłkowy;ostatni
latterly ('laeterly) adv. ostatnio; niedawno; pożniej
lattice ('laetys) s. kratownica; v. kratować;ułożyć w kratę
laudable ('lo:debl) adj. chwalebny ;godny pochwały
laugh (laef) v. smiać się; za-
śmiać się;roześmiać się
laugh at ('laef,et) v. wysmie-
wać;uśmiać sie(z czegoś)
laugh away ('laef,e'łej) v. zbyć
śmiechem
laugh off ('laef,of) v. obrócić
w żart;pokryć zmieszanie śmie-chem
laughter ('laefter) s. smiech
launch (lo:ncz) v. puszczać
w ruch; spuszczać na wodę;
miotać; rzucać; zadawać; wydawać; s. szalupa; spuszczenie
na wodę (statku,okrętu,etc.)
launching pad ('lo:nczyng,paed)
s. wyrzutnia (rakiet)
launderette (lo:n'dret) s. pralnia samoobsługowa
laundry ('lo:ndry) s. pralnia;
bielizna do prania
laurel ('lorel) s. wawrzyn;
laur; v. wieńczyć wawrzynem
lavatory ('laewetery) s. umywalnia; ustęp; umywalka
lavender ('laewynder) s. lawenda; v. wkładać lawendę w bieliznę ;a. lawendowy
lavish ('laewysz) adj. hojny;su-
ty; rozrzutny; v. nie szczedzić
pieniędzy, miłości etc.)

law (lo:) s. prawo; ustawa; reguła; sądy;posłuszeństwo prawu
lawful ('lo:ful) adj, legalny;
słuszny; prawowity; z prawego
łoża; prawnie uznany
lawless ('lo:lys) adj. bezprawny; łamiący prawo; rozpustny
lawn (lo:n) s. trawnik; murawa
lawsuit ('lo:sju:t) s. proces
(sądowy) ;sprawa sądowa
lawyer ('lo:jer) s. prawnik;
adwokat ;radca prawny
lax (laeks) adj. luźny; nieszczelny; niedbały; nieścisły;
mający rozwolnienie ;wolny
laxative ('laeksetyw) adj.& s.
przeczyszczający (środek)
laxity ('laeksyty) s. luźność;
nieścisłość; niedokładność;
niedbalstwo;rozwiązłość
lay; laid; laid(lej; lejd;
lejd)
lay (lej) v. kłaść; uspokajać;
układać; skręcać (się); zaczaić
się; spać z kims; s. położenie; układ; spanie (z kims);
adj. świecki; laicki; niefachowy; lay- zob. lie
layout ('lejout) s. rozkład;
plan ;założenie; układ
lay out ('lej.aut) v. układać;
projektować; powalić; (slang):
zabić; wydatkować; wyłożyć
lay up ('lejap) v. zbierać;
gromadzić; przechowywać
layer ('lejer) s. warstwa; od-
kład; kura niosąca; zakładają-
cy się;pokład
layman ('lejmen) s. człowiek
świecki; laik
lazy ('lejzy) adj. leniwy;
prożniaczy;ociężały
lead (led) s. ołow; v. pokrywać
ołowiem; obciążać ołowiem
lead; led; led (li:d; led;led)
lead (li:d) v. prowadzić; kierować; dowodzić; naprowadzać;
nasunąć; namówić; dyrygować;
przewodzić; s. kierownictwo;
przewodnictwo; przewaga; prym;
wskazówka ;przykład;powodzenie
leaden ('ledn) adj. ołowiany;
ciężki;ociężały;ponury;szary

leader ('li:der) s. przywódca;
lider; przewodnik; prowadzący
leading ('li:dyŋg) adj. kierow-
niczy; naczelny; główny;
s. kierownictwo; prowadzenie;
przewodnictwo;przywództwo
leaf (li:f) s. liść; kartka;
pl. leaves (li:wz)
leaflet (li:flyt) s. listek;
ulotka (często złożona)
league (li:g) s. liga; związek;
mila; v. łączyć (się) w ligę
leak (li:k) s. dziura; otwór;
przeciekanie; v. cieknąć;
przeciekać; wyciekać (sekrety);wysączać; zaciekać
leakage (li:kydż) s. przeciekanie (sekretów); wyciekanie
(pieniędzy); rozproszenie
leaky ('li:ky) adj. dziurawy;
nieszczelny; cieknący; niedyskretny;nie dochowujący sekre-
lean; leant; leant (li:n; lent;
lent)
lean (li:n) v. nachylać (się);
pochylać (się); opierać(się)
(o coś); adj. chudy; s. chu-
de mięso;nachylenie;skłonność
leant (lent) v. zob. lean
leap; leapt; leapt (li:p; lept;
lept)
leap (li:p) v. skakać; przeskoczyć; s. skok; podskok
leapt (lept) zob . leap
leap-year ('li:pye:r) s. rok
przestępny
learn; learnt; learnt (le:rn;
le:rnt; le:rnt)
learn (le:rn) v. uczyć się;
dowiadywać się;zapamiętać
learned ('le:rnyd) adj. uczony
learner ('le:rner) s. uczący
się; uczeń; uczennica
learning ('le:rnyŋg) s. nauka;
wiedza; erudycja;umiejętności
learnt (le:rnt) v. zob. learn
lease (li:s) s. dzierżawa;
v. dzierżawić;wydzierżawić
leash (li:sh) s. smycz
least (li:st) adj. najmniejszy
adv. najmniej; w najmniejszym
stopniu; s. najmniejsza rzecz;
drobnostka najmniej ważna

leather ('ledżer)s. skóra; adj.
skórzany; v. pokrywać skórą;
oprawiać w skórę ;sprać(rzemie-
niem)
leave; left; left (li:w; left;
left)
leave (li:w) v. zostawiać;
opuszczać; odchodzić; odjeżdżać;
pozostawiać; s. pożegnanie;
urlop; pozwolenie
leaven (lewn) s. drożdże
leaves (li:wz) pl. liście;
zob. leaf
lecture ('lekczer) s. wykład;
nagana; v. wykładać; udzielać
nagany;przemawiać do sumienia
lecturer ('lekczerer) s. wykła-
dowca(w uczelni,klasie etc.)
led (led) zob. lead
ledge (ledż) s. występ; stopień;
półka; gzyms; listwa; rafa
lee (li:) s. strona zawietrzna;
osłona;adj.zawietrzny;osłonięty
leech (li:cz) s. pijawka
leek (li:k) s. por
leer (lier) s. spojrzenie z ukosa; v. łypać okiem znacząco
(chytrze,złośliwie,pożądliwie)
left (left) adj. lewy; adv. na
lewo; s. lewa strona; zob. leave
left-hand ('left,haend) s. lewa
ręka;adj.lewoskrętny;lewostronny
left-handed ('left'haendyd) s.
mańkut; adj. leworęki; niezgrabny;wątpliwy;nieszczery
left side ('left,sajd) s. lewa
strona (drogi,samochodu etc.)
leg (leg) s. noga; nóżka; podpórka; odcinek;kończyna;udziec
legacy (legesy) s. spadek;
spuścizna;dziedzictwo;zapis
legal ('li:gel) adj. prawny;
prawniczy ;ustawowy;legalny
legation (li'gejszyn) s. poselstwo (włącznie z posłem)
legend ('ledżend) s. legenda
legendary ('ledżendery) adj.
legendarny ;tradycyjny
legible ('ledżebl) adj. czytelny ;łatwo czytelny
legion ('li:dżen) s. legion;
legia ;wojsko;wielka ilość;
mnóstwo;tłumy;mnogość

legislation (,ledžys'lejszyn)
s. prawodawstwo; ustawodawstwo
legislative ('ledžysletyw) adj.
prawodawczy; ustawodawczy
legislator ('ledžyslator) s.
prawodawca; poseł do parlamen-
tu (sejmu,senatu etc.)
legitimate (ly'džytymyt) adj.
ślubny; prawowity; słuszny;
uzasadniony;logiczny;rozsadny
leg-pull ('legpu:l) s. kawał;
żart; sztuczka;naciąganie
leisure ('li:żer) s. wolny czas;
swoboda od zajęć;wolne chwile
leisurely ('li:żerly) adv. swobodnie; bez pospiechu; adj.
mający czas; spokójny; robiony
w wolnym czasie
lemon ('lemen) s. cytryna;
tandeta;adj.cytrynowy;z cytryn
lemonade ('lemenejd) s. lemo-
niada(z soku cytrynowego etc.)
lend; lent; lent (lend; lent;
lent)
lend (lend) v. pożyczać; użyczać; udzielać
length (lenks) s. długość
lengthen ('lenksen) v. przedłużać; wydłużać(się);podłużać
lengthwise ('lensłajz) adv. adj.
wzdłuż; na długość
lenient ('li:njent) adj. wyro-
zumiały; łagodny
lens (lenz) s. soczewka; objektyw ;lupa
lent (lent) s. post; zob. lend
leopard ('leperd) s. lampart
leper ('leper) s. trędowaty;
trędowata
leprosy ('lepresy) s. trąd
less (les) adj. mniejszy; adv.
mniej; s. coś mniejszego;
prep. bez;nie tak dużo(więcej)
lessen (lesn) v, zmniejszać(się);
maleć; pomniejszać
lesser ('leser) adj. mniejszy
lesson (lesn) s. lekcja; nauczka;urywek z Biblji;wykład
lest (lest) conj. ażeby nie; że
let; let; let (let;let;let)
let (let) v. zostawić; wynajmować; dawać; puszczać ; pozwalać

let alone ('let,e'loun) s. zostawić w spokoju; dać spokój
let down ('let,dałn) v. robić
zawód; spuszczać; opuszczać;
upokorzyć;odmawiać pomocy
let go ('let,gou) v. wypuszczać;
zwalniać; pozwolić odejść
let know ('let,nou) v. zawiadomić; donieść;powiadomić
let up ('let,ap) v. zelżeć;
złagodnieć; s. zelżenie
lethal ('li:gel) adj. śmiertelny; zgubny;smiercionośny
letter ('leter) s. litera; list;
czcionka; v. drukować; oznaczać literami;kaligrafować
letter-box ('leter,boks) s.
skrzynka pocztowa
letter-carrier ('leter'kaerjer)
s. listonosz
lettuce ('letys) s. sałata (gło-
wiasta);liście sałaty
leukemia (lju'ki:mje) s. białaczka;leukemia
level ('lewl) s. poziom; płaszczyzna; równina; poziomnica;
adj. poziomy; adv. poziomo;
równo; v. zrównywać; celować
level crossing('lewl'krosyng)
s. skrzyżowanie dróg (koli-
zyjne)w jednej płaszczyźnie
lever ('li:wer) s. dźwignia;
lewar; v. podważać; podnosić
dźwigiem(lewarem)
levity ('lewyty) s. lekkomyśl-
ność
levy ('lewy) v. pobierać; nakładać (podatek); s. pobór
lewd (lu:d) adj. zmysłowy; lubieżny;pożądliwy;sprosny
liability (,laje'bylyty) s.
odpowiedzialność; obowiązek;
obciążenie; zadłużenie;ryzyko
liable ('lajebl) adj. odpowiedzialny; podlegający; podatny;
skłonny;narażony;mający widoki
liable to ('lajebl,tu) adj.
skłonny do... ;adv. łatwo(zgnije)
liaison (ly'ejzo:n) s. łączność;
związek; romans (nielegalny)
liar ('lajer) s. kłamca; łgarz
libation(laj-bej'szyn)s.libacja

libel ('lajbel) s. paszkwil;
oszczerstwo; zniesławienie
(publiczne w piśmie; filmie
etc.);v.zniesławiac
liberal ('lyberel) s. liberał;a.
liberalny; hojny;tolerancyjny
liberate ('lyberejt) v. uwal-
niac; zwalniac;wyzwalac
liberation ('lyberejszyn) s.
uwolnienie; oswobodzenie
liberator ('lyberejter) s.
oswobodziciel;wyzwoliciel
liberty ('lyberty) s. wolnosc;
swoboda;nadużywanie wolnosci
librarian (laj'breerjen) s.
bibliotekarz
library ('lajbrery) s. biblioteka; księgozbiór
lice (lajs) pl. wszy; zob.
louse
license(ce) ('lajsens) s. licencja; pozwolenie; upoważnienie; swoboda; rozpusta;
v. upoważniac; udzielac poz-
wolenia; nadużywac wolnosci
licensee (,lajsen'si:) s. posiadacz zezwolenia; koncesjo-
nariusz;własciciel licencji
lichen ('lajken) s. liszaj
lick (lyk) s. liznięcie; odrobina; cios; raz; wybuch;
energia; v. lizac; polizac;
wylizac; bic; smarowac
licking ('lykyŋg)s. (slang):
bicie; pobicie; młocka
lid (lyd) s. wieko; powieka;
pokrywa ;nakrywka;przykrywka
lie !. lay ; lain (laj; lej;
lejn)
lie (laj) v. leżec; s. układ;
położenie;konfiguracja;legowisko
lie 2. lied; lied (laj; lajd;
lajd)
lie (laj) v. kłamac; s. kłamstwo;łgarstwo;fałsz
lie down('laj,dałn) v. kłasc
się;położyc się;nie reagowac
lie in ('laj,yn) v. byc w poło-
gu; leżec w (łóżku)
lie over ('laj,ouwer) v. byc
odroczonym; zostac przez noc
lieutenant (lef'tenant; lu:te-
nant) s. porucznik

life (lajf) s. życie; życiorys;
zob. pl. lives
life assurance ('lajfe'szuerens)
s. ubezpieczenie na życie
life belt ('lajfbelt) s. pas
ratunkowy
lifeboat ('lajfbout) s. łódz
ratunkowa
lifeguard ('lajfga:rd) s. ratownik
life insurance ('lajf,yn'szuerens) s. ubezpieczenie na życie
life jacket ('lajfdżaekyt) s. kowa
kurta ratownicza;kamizelka ratun-
lifeless ('lajflys) adj. bez
życia; martwy;zamarły;wymarły
lifelike ('lajflajk) adj. jak
żywy(człowiek,osoba,stworzenie)
life sentence ('lajf,sentens)
s. kara dożywocia(wyrok)
life-style ('lajfstajl) s. styl
życia; modła życia;sposób życia
lifetime ('lajf,tajm) s. życie; całe życie
lift (lyft) s. dźwig; winda;
przewóz; podniesienie; wzniesienie; v. podnieśc; dźwignąc;
podnosic się; krasc; spłacic
(np. dom); kopnąc;buchnąc;awanso-
lift-off ('lyft,of) s. start
lotu (np. rakiety)
ligament ('lygement) s. scięgno
ligature ('lygeczuer) s. przywiązanie; ligatura; podwiąza-
nie;bandaż;nic chirurgiczna
light; lit; lit (lajt; lyt;lyt)
light (lajt) s. swiatło; oswietlenie; ogień; adj. swietny; jasny; łatwy; lekki; błahy; słaby; beztroski; niefrasobliwy; lekkomyslny; v.swie-
cic; oswiecac; zapalac; ujaw-
nic; poswięcic; rozjasnic;
przyswiecic; zsiadac; wsiadac;
wpasc; wyjechac; adv. lekko
light up ('lajtap) v. zaswie-
cic; rozjasnic; oswiecic
lighten ('lajtn) v. ulżyc; zel-
życ; oswiecac; rozjasnic się;
błysnąc; błyskac się
lighter ('lajter) s. zapalniczka; latarnik ;lampiarz

lighthouse ('lajthaus) s. latarnia morska
lighting ('lajtyng) s. oswietlenie; oswietlanie
light-minded ('lajt'majndyd)
adj. lekkomyslny;roztargniony
lightness ('lajtnys) s. jas-
nosc; lekkosc; łagodnosc;
łatwosc; lekkomyslnosc
lightning ('lajtnyng)s. błyska-
wica; piorun;a.błyskawiczny
lightning rod ('lajtnyng,rod)
s. piorunochron;odgromnik
lightweight ('lajt-łejt) s.
waga lekka; adj. lekkiej wagi;
błachy(127 do 135 funtowy boks-
light-year ('lajt,je:r) s. rok
swietlny(ok.6x10¹²mil=10x10¹²km.)
lignite ('lygnajt) s. węgiel
brunatny; lignit
like (lajk) v. lubiec; upodobac
sobie; (chciec); miec zamiłowanie, ochotę; adj. podobny;
analogiczny; typowy; adv. podobnie; w ten sam sposob;
s. drugi taki sam; rzecz podobna; conj. jak; tak jak;po;
w ten sposob; niby to;niczym
like that ('lajk'dzaet) adv.
tak; w ten sposob;własnie tak
likelihood ('lajklyhud) s.
prawdopodobienstwo
likely ('lajkly) adj. możliwy;
prawdopodobny; odpowiedni;
nadający się; obiecujący;
adv. pewnie; prawdopodobnie
likeness ('lajknys) s. podo-
bienstwo; podobizna; pozory
likewise ('lajkłajz) adv. także; rowniez; podobno; podobnie;w ten sam sposob;też
liking ('lajkyng) s. sympatia;
upodobanie; zamiłowanie
lilac ('lajlek) s. bez; adj.
lila; liljowy;blado siny
lily ('lyly) s. lilja;a.jak lilia
lily of the valley ('lyly,ow'
'dy,waely) s. konwalia
limb (lym) s. konczyna; konar;
brzeg; krawędz;ramię;noga;skrzy-
lime 1. (lajm) s. wapno; v.
wapnic; adj. wapienny

lime 2. (lajm) s. lipa; cytrus
(dzika cytryna) ;a.cytrusowy
limelight ('lajmlajt) s. swiatło wapienne; swiatło reflekto-
row; widok publiczny
limestone ('lajmstoun) s. wa-
pien; a. z wapienia
limey ('lajmy) s. (slang): Bry-
tyjczyk (wulg.) zwłaszcza marynarz
limit ('lymyt) s. granica; kres;
v. ograniczac; ustalac granic
limitation (,lymy'tejszyn) s.
ograniczenie; zastrzeżenie;
prekluzja;przedawnienie
limited liability ('lymytyd,la-
je'bylyty)s. ograniczona odpowiedzialnosc
limp (lymp) adj. wiotki; bez sił;
osłabiony; v. kulec; chromac
line (lajn) s. linia; kreska;
bruzda; lina; sznur; przewod;
granica; zajęcie; zainteresowa-
nia; szereg; rząd; linka;
v. liniowac; wyscielac; pod-
bic podszewką;służyc za podszew-
lineup ('lajnap) s. uszeregowanie; rząd; ustawianie w rząd
line up ('lajnap) v. ustawic
w rząd; uszeregowac
lineaments ('lynjements) pl.
rysy twarzy;cechy szczegolne
linear ('lynjer) adj. liniowy;
linijny; wąski i długi
linen ('lynyn) s. płotno; bielizna; adj. lniany; płocienny
linen closet('lynen'klozyt) s.
schowek na bieliznę
liner ('lajner) s. samolot pasazerski; statek pasazerski
linger ('lynger) v. ociągac
się; zwlekac; pozostawac w tyle ; marudzic; tkwic; wlec życie
lingerie ('le:nżeri) s. damska
bielizna ;damskie artykuły bieliz-
lining ('lajnyng) s. podszewka;
podkład; okładzina; zawartosc
link (lynk) s. ogniwo; więz;
spinka; 20,1 cm; v. połączyc;
zczepiac; związac; sprzęgac
links (lynks) pl. wydmy; boisko golfowe ;wydmy piaszczyste
lion (lajon) s. lew ;a.lwi;lwie

lioness (lajonys) s. lwica
lip (lyp) s. warga; brzeg;
ostrze; bezczelne gadanie;
v. dotykać wargami; mruczeć
lipstick ('lypstyk) s. kredka
do warg; pomadka do ust
liquid ('lykłyd) s. płyn;
adj. płynny;niestały;nie ustalo-
liquor ('lyker) s. napój alko-
holowy; sok; odwar;bulion
liquorice ('lykorys) s. lu-
krecja
lisp (lysp) v. seplenić; seplenić jak niemowle;s.seplenienie
list (lyst) s. lista; spis;
listwa; krawędz; v. wciągaćna
listę; obramowywać; przechylać (się); pochylać (się);
s. pochylenie; przechył
listen ('lysen) v. słuchać;
usłuchać;przysłuchiwać się
listen in ('lysen,yn) v. pod-
słuchiwać;posłuchać(radia etc)
listen to ('lysen,tu) v. usłuchać kogoś (czyjejś rady)
listener ('lysener) s. słuchacz
listless ('lystlys) adj. apatyczny; obojętny; zobojętnia-
ły;bierny(z powodu choroby)
lit (lyt) zob. light
liter ('li:ter) s. litr
literal ('lyterel) adj. literal-
ny; dosłowny; prozaiczny; li-
terowy;rzeczowy(umysł etc.)
literary ('lyterery) adj. literacki;obeznany w literaturze
literature ('lytereczer) s. literatura; piśmiennictwo
lithe (lajs) adj. giętki; gibki; łatwo gnący się
litter ('lyter) s. śmieci; pod-
ściołka ; barłóg; v. śmiecić;
podścielać; urodzić szczenia-
ki;porozrzucać niechlujnie
litter bin ('lyter,byn) s.
śmietnik ;kosz na śmiecie
little ('lytl) adj. mały; niski;
nieduży; adv. mało; niewiele
little bit ('lytl,byt) adv.
trochę ;bardzo mało;troszeczkę
little one ('lytl,łan) s.
dziecko ;dziecina;dzieciatko

little by little ('lytl,bay'
'lytl) exp. po trochu; stopniowo;po mału;po malutku
live (lyw) v. żyć; mieszkać;
przeżywać; przetrwać; ocalić
live (lajw) adj. żywy; żyjący;
ruchliwy;energiczny;niewyeksplo-
live on ('lyw,on) v. żyć
z czegoś; żyć czymś
live wire ('lajw'łajer) s.
przewód pod napięciem
livelihood ('lajwly,hud) s.
utrzymanie;środki do życia
lively ('lajwly) adj. żywy;
wesoły; ożywiony; żwawy; gorący;rześki;pełen życia;jaskrawy
liver ('lywer) s. wątroba;
wątróbka ;a.wątroby
livery ('lywery) adj. wątrobia-
ny; chory na wątrobę; opryskliwy; s. liberia; utrzymanie
konia; wynajem (wozów)
lives (lajws) pl. żywotny;
zob. life
livestock ('lajwstok) s. żywy
inwentarz ;zwierzęta domowe
livid ('lywyd) adj. siny;
wściekły ;posiniaczony
living ('lywyng) s. życie;
utrzymanie; tryb życia
living room('lywyn,ru:m) s.
salon; bawialnia; pokój
lizard ('lyzerd) s. jaszczurka
load (loud) s. ładunek; waga;
ciężar; obciążenie; v. ładować; załadować; naładować;
obciążać; nasycać; fałszować
load up ('loud,ap) v. brać ładunek; opychać się
loader ('louder) s. ładowniczy;
maszyna do ładowania
loading ('loudyng) s. ładunek;
ładowanie ;a.ładunkowy(pomost)
loaded words ('loudyd,łe:rds)
s. słowa tendencyjne (nie-
sprawiedliwe)(uwłaszczające)
loaf (louf) s. bochenek; głowa
(cukru); pl. loaves (louvz)
v. wałęsać się;marnować czas
loafer ('loufer) s. włóczęga;
łazik; próżniak ;nierób;wałkoń;
wygodny bucik sportowy

loam (loum) s. gleba ilasta;
ił ;zaprawa gliniana(murarska)
loan (loun) s. pożyczka;
v. pożyczać ; pożyczać
loath (louß) adj. niechętny
loathe (louß) v. nienawidzieć;
czuć wstręt
loathsome ('loußsem) adj.
wstrętny; obrzydliwy; ohydny
loaves (louwz) zob. loaf
lobby ('loby) s. przedpokój;
kuluar; v. urabiać senatora
lub posła na czyjąś korzyść
(przekupywać)
lobbyist('lobyst) s. inter-
wencjonalista kuluarowy (często oficjalnie rejestrowany
w USA); lobbyista
lobe (loub) s. płat (np. płucny)
lobster ('lobster) s. homar
local ('loukel) adj. lokalny;
miejscowy;s.oddział związku zawodowego
locality (lou'kaelyty) s.okolica;
miejscowość; strefa;rejon
localize ('loukelajz) v. umiejs-
cowić; lokalizować
locate ('loukejt) v. umieścić;
znaleźć; osiedlić się
located ('loukejtyd) adj. zamieszkały; umieszczony;znaleziony
location ('loukejszyn) s. położenie; ulokowanie; miejsce
zamieszkania;miejsce zaznaczone
loch (lok) s. jezioro; wąska
zatoka (zwłaszcza w Szkocji)
lock (lok) s. zamek; zamknięcie;
śluza; lok; v. zamykać (na
klucz);przechodzić śluzę
lock in ('lokyn) v. zamykać
(wewnątrz); otaczać (górami etc.)
locker ('loker) s. szafka; kabina; skrzynia; schowek
lock out ('lokaut) v. wykluczać;
s. lokaut (lockout)
locksmith ('loksmyß) s. ślusarz
locomotive ('louke,moutyw) s.
lokomotywa; adj. ruchomy
locust ('loukest) s. szarańcza;
akacja
lodge (lodż) s. chata; loża;
kryjówka; domek myśliwski; nora
v. przenocować; zdeponować;
umieszczać; wnosić (skargę)etc.

lodger ('lodżer) s. lokator
lodging ('lodżyng) s. mieszkanie (tymczasowe,wynajęte etc.)
loft (loft) s. strych; poddasze;chór;v.podbić pilkę golfową
lofty ('lofty) adj. wzniosły;
wyniosły; wysoki;dumny;hardy
log (log) s. kłoda; kloc; log;
dziennik operacyjny (statku;
szybu) v. wycinać drzewa;
ciąć na kłody; wciągać do
dziennika okrętowego etc.
logbook ('logbuk) s. dziennik
pokładowy;książka raportowa
log cabin ('log,kaebyn) s. chata (z belek) (z okrąglaków)
logic ('lodżyk) s. logika
logical ('lodżykel) adj. logiczny;rozumujący poprawnie
loin (loin) s. lędźwie; polędwica; comber;krzyże;biodra
loiter (lojter) v. marudzić;
wałęsać się; guzdrać; mitrężyć;kręcić się podejrzanie
lol (lol) v. rozwalać się;
opierać się niedbale; wywieszać
(język psa); zwisać
loneliness ('lounlynys) s. samotność;osamotnienie;odludność
lonely ('lounly) adj. samotny
lonesome ('lounsom) adj.
osamotniony; odludny
long (long) adj. długi; długo-
trwały; v. tęsknić; pragnąć
(czegoś); adv. długo; dawno
long ago (,long'egou) adv.
dawno temu;adj.dawno miniony
long before ('long,befor) adv.
dużo wcześniej;znacznie wcześniej
long since ('long,syns) adv.
dawno temu ; od dawna
long distance call ('long'dystans,kol) s. telefon między-
miastowy;rozmowa międzymiastowa
longing (longyng) s. pragnienie;
tęsknota;ochota;adj.tęskny
long jump ('long,dżamp) s.
skok w dal
longshoreman ('long,szo:rmen)
s. doker; robotnik portowy
long-sighted ('lon'sajtyd) adj.
dalekowzroczny; przewidujący
long spun ('lon'span)a.rozwlekły

long-term ('lon'term) adj.
długoterminowy;długofalowy
long-winded ('lon'łyndyd)
adj. gadatliwy; długo mówiący;(koń) ze zdrowymi płucami
look (luk) s. spojrzenie; wygląd; v. patrzeć; wyglądać
look after ('luk,a:fter) v. doglądać; opiekować się(kimś)
look at ('luk,et) v. patrzec
na (kogoś, na coś)
look for ('luk,fo:r)v. szukac
look forwards ('luk fo:rłerds)
v. oczekiwać; cieszyć się
look into ('luk,yntu) v. badać; wglądać
look on ('luk,on) v. przypatrywać się;przyglądać się;kibicować
look out ('luk,aut) v. byc
na baczności;wyjrzec;wyszukac
look over ('luk,ouwer) v.
przeglądać;przejrzeć
look around ('luk,e'raund) v.
rozglądać się;poszukiwać wzro-
look up ('luk,ap) v. szukac;
odwiedzać; patrzec w górę
looker-on('luker'on) s. widz;
przyglądający się ;kibic
looking-glass ('lukynglass) s.
lustro; zwierciadło
lookout ('luk,aut) s. widok;
uwaga; czaty;czujność
look out ('luk,aut) v. wyjrzec;
uważac; wyszukac;byc w pogotowiu
loom (lu:m) s. krosna; warsztat
tkacki; v. wynurzać się; zagrażać;grozic;zamajaczyc
loop (lu:p) s. pętla; węzeł;
supeł; v. robic pętlę, kokardę;
podwiązywac;splatać (się)
loophole ('lu:p,houl)s. strzelnica; droga ucieczki (od podatków);wykręt; luka;furtka
loose (lu:s) adj. luźny; roz-
luzniony; obluzniony; wolny;
na wolności; rzadki; sypki;
rozwiązły; s. upust; v. luzo-
wac; obluzniac; zwalniac
loosen ('lu:sn) v. rozluzniac
(się); obluzniac (się); roz-
walniac;leczyc zatwardzenie
loot (lu:t) s. łupy; (nadużycia
urzędnika);v.pladrowac;szabrowac

lop (lop) v. obcinac; ciąć; zwisac; plątać się; wałęsac się;
s. ścięcie; obcięte (gałęzie)
lop off ('lop,of) v. obciąc
lope (loup) v. biec susami;
pędzic krotkim galopem; s.
krotki galop; sus
lord (lo:rd) s. pan; władca;
magnat; Bog; v. grac pana;
nadawac tytuł lorda
lorry ('lory) s. ciężarówka;
platforma; lora;przyczepa
lose; lost; lost (lu:z; lost;
lost)
lose (lu:z) v. stracic; schud-
nąc; zgubic; zabłądzic; nie-
dosłyszec; spóznic się; prze-
grac; byc pokonanym,pozbawionym
loss (los) s. strata; utrata;
zguba; ubytek;szkoda;kłopot
lost (lost) adj. stracony; zgu-
biony; zob. lose
lot (lot) s. doba; las; losowanie; udział; działka; par-
cela; grupa; zespół; partia;
sporo; wiele; v. parcelowac;
dzielic; losowac;adv.bardzo duzo
loth (louθ) adj. niechętny;
wstrętny;z ciężkim sercem
lotion ('louszyn) s. płyn
(leczniczy)
lottery ('lotery) s. loteria
lotto ('lotou) s. loteryjka
loud (laud) adj. głosny; smrodliwy; krzykliwy; adv. na cały
głos; głos; głosno;w głosny sposób
loudspeaker ('laud'spi:ker) s.
głosnik; megafon
lounge (laundż) v. prożnowac;
wylegiwac; łazic; s. lokal;
salonik; hall; włoczęga;
wolny krok;wygodna kanapa
louse (laus) s. wesz; pl. lice
lousy ('lauzy) adj. zawszony;
wstrętny;dobrze zaopatrzony (sl.)
lout (laut) s. gbur; prostak
love (law) s. kochanie; miłosc;
lubienie; ukochana; ukochanie;
gra na zero; v. kochac; lubic;
byc przywiązanym ;piescic;umizgac się
love-affair ('lawefeer) s. romans; przygoda miłosna;osobiste
troski w sprawach miłosnych

loveless ('lawlys) adj. niekochany; nie kochający; bez miłości;nie kochany przez nikogo

lovely ('lawly) adj. śliczny; uroczy; rozkoszny;przyjemny(bardzo)

lovemaking ('law,mejkyŋg) s. zaloty; umizgi; spółkowanie

lover ('lawer) s. kochanek; miłośnik; amator czegoś

loving ('lavyŋg) adj. kochający; s. kochanie; miłość

low (lou) s. ryk (bydła); ryczeć; adj. niski; niewysoki; słaby; przygnębiony; cichy; podły; mały; adv. nisko; niewysoko; słabo; skromnie; cicho; szeptem; marnie; podle

lower ('louer) adj. niższy; dolny; młodszy; adv. niżej; v. obniżac; zniżac; spuszczac; poniżyc; sciszyc; zmniejszyc; osłabiac; opadac; spadac;ryczec(jak bydło)

low-grade ('lougrejd) adj. niskoprocentowy; niskiej jakosci;kiepski;tandetny

lowland ('loulend) pl. nizina; adj. nizinny

lowly ('louly) adj. skromny; adv. skromnie;bez pretensji

low-necked('lou'nekyd) adj. dekoltowany (głęboko)

low-pressure ('lou'preszer) s. niskie cisnienie; adj. niskoprężny;pod niskim cisnieniem

low tide ('lou'tajd) s. odpływ (morza)

loyal(lojel) adj. lojalny; wierny(krajowi,ideałom etc.)

loyalty ('lojelty) s. lojalnosc; wiernosc

lozenge ('lozyndż) s. romb; tabletka; pastylka

lubber ('laber) s. niezdara; niedołęga;niezdarny marynarz

lubricant ('lu:brykent) s. smar; adj. smarujący; smarowniczy

lubricate ('lu:brykejt) v. smarowac; oliwic;robic sliskim

lubrication ('lu:brykejszyn) s. smarowanie; oliwienie

ubricity(lu:'brysyty)s. smarownosc;

lucid ('lu:syd) adj. swiecacy; jasny; błyszczacy; klarowny; przezroczysty; czysty;oczywisty

luck (lak) s. los; traf; szczescie; szczęsliwy traf;powodzenie

luckily ('lakyly) adv. na szczęscie; szczęsliwie

luckless ('laklys) adj. niefortunny; nieszczęsliwy

lucky ('laky) adj. szczęsliwy

lucky fellow ('laky'felou) s. szczęsciarz

ludicrous ('lu:dykres) adj. smieszny; nonsensowny; absurdalny;komicznie głupi

lug (lag) v. wlec; pociągac; przytłaczac; s. wleczenie; szarpanie; ucho; uchwyt

luggage ('lagydż) s. bagaż; walizki

luggage carrier ('lagydż'kaerjer) s. bagażowy

luggage rack ('lagydż'raek) s. półka na walizki

luggage slip ('lagydż'slyp) s. kwit bagażowy

luggage van ('lagydż'waen) s. woz bagażowy

lukewarm ('lu:kło:rm) adj. ciepławy; letni; obojętny; oziębły; niezainteresowany

lull(lal) v. ukołysac; uciszyc; usmierzyc; s. cisza; zastoj

lullaby ('lalebaj) s. kołysanka

lumbago (lam'bejgou) s. lumbago; ischias

lumbar ('lamber) adj. lędzwiowy

lumber ('lamber) s. budulec (drewniany); rupiecie; graty; v. zwalac; wycinac; ciężko stąpac; poruszac się ociężale

lumberjack ('lamber'dżaek) s. drwal(przygotowujący do tartaku)

lumber mill ('lambermyl) s. tartak

luminous ('lu:mynes) adj. swietlny; jasny; adj. swiecący; wyjasniający;zrozumiały

lump (lamp) s. bryła; gruda; masa; hurt; guz; niezdara; niedołęga; v. zwalac; gromadzic; dojsc do ładu;zcierpiec;znosic

lump of('lamp,ow) s. kawałek
lump sugar ('lamp,szu:ger) s.
gruda cukru
lump sum ('lamp,sam) s. suma
całościowa
lunar ('lu:nar) adj. księżyco-
wy;mierzony ruchem księżyca
lunar module ('lu:nar,modjul)
s. kapsula do lądowania na
Księżycu
lunatic ('lu:netyk) s. wariat
(chory umysłowo); adj. obłąkany; zwariowany; lunatyk
lunch (lancz) s. obiad (popołudniowy); v. jeść obiad;
gościc obiadem
lunch-hour ('lancz'auer) s.
przerwa obiadowa (w południe)
lung (lang) s. płuco
lunge (landż) s. wypad;
pchnięcie; v. pchnąc; zrobic
wypad;spowodowac wypad
lurch (le:rcz) v. opuszczac
w potrzebie; słaniac się na
nogach; przechylac się; s.
nagłe przechylenie się (na
bok);trudna sytuacja
lure (ljuer) s. przynęta; wabik; urok; powab; v. kusic;
nęcic; wabic;przywabiac
lurk (le:rk) v. czaic się;
s. czaty ; ukrycie
luscious ('laszes) adj. sło-
dziutki; ckliwy ;soczysty
lush (lasz) adj. bujny; soczysty;miękki i pełen soku
lust (last) s. żądza; lubież-
nośc; namiętnośc; pożądli-
wosc; v. pożądac(namiętnie)
luster ('laster) s. blask; połysk; świecznik; świetnośc;
v. glansowac; wyswiecac
lusty ('lasty) adj. krzepki;
pełen wigoru (młodzieńczego)
lute (lu:t) s. lutnia; glina;
v. lepic gliną;kitowac
luxate ('laksejt) v. zwichnąc
(np. nogę)(staw)
luxation (lak'sejszyn) s.
zwichnięcie (nogi w kostce;
stawu biodrowego etc.)

luxurious (lag'żjuerjes) adj.
zbytkowny; luksusowy;zmysłowy
luxury ('lakszery) s. zbytek;
luksus;rozkosz;a.od zbytku
lying ('lajyng) adj. kłamliwy;
zob. lie; s. kłamstwo; adj.le-
żący; zob. lie; s. leżenie;
posłanie;pozycja leżąca
lying-in (,lajyng'yn) adj. po-
łozniczy; połogowy; s. połog
lymph (lymf) s, limfa; szczepionka; wysięk; serum, (czy-
sta woda)
lynch (lyncz) v. zlinczowac;s.
linczowanie;zabijanie bez wyro-
lynx (lynks) s. rys   ku
lyre ('lajer) s. lira
lyric ('lirik) adj. liryczny;
s. słowa piesni; poemat liryczny;tekst piosenki
lysol ('lajsol) s. lizol
m (em) trzynasta litera alfabetu
angielskiego;cyfra rzymska:1000
ma'am (maem) s. pani (madam)
mac (maek) s.nieprzemakalny materiał (płaszcz) mackintosh
machine (me'szi:n) s. maszyna;
machina (polityczna) v. obrabiac maszynowo;adj.maszynowy
machine-made (me'szi:nmejd) adj.
maszynowy; maszynowo robiony
machine-gun (me'szi:ngan) s.
karabin maszynowy
machinery (me'szi:nery) s, maszyneria;maszyneria;aparat
machinist (me'szi:nyst) s, maszynista (np. tokarz)(szwaczka)
macho (ma:czou) s. bardzo męski
mężczyzna (slang)
mack (maek) s. zob. mac
mackintosh ('maekyntosz) s.
zob. mac
mad (maed) adj. obłąkany; szalony; zły; wsciekły; v. doprowadzac do obłędu; byc obłąkanym
madam ('maedem) s. pani; (panienka)(w zwrocie:proszę pani)
madcap ('maedkaep) s. narwaniec
madden ('maedn) v. rozwscieczac;
szalec; wsciekac sie;wariowac
made (mejd) v. zrobiony; zob.
make (wykombinowany;fabryczny...)

madman ('maedmen) s. wariat;
szaleniec;furiat;obłąkaniec
madness ('maednys) s. obłęd;
obłąkanie; furia; wściekłosc;
wścieklizna;szał;szaleństwo
magazine (maege'zi:n) s. czasopismo; magazynek (na kule);
skład broni dla wojska
maggot ('maeget) s. dziwactwo;
chimera; larwa
magic ('maedżyk) s. magia; adj.
magiczny; działający jak magia
magician (me'dżyszyn) s. czarodziej; magik
magistrate ('maedżystrejt) s.
sądownik; stroż prawa
magnanimous (maeg'neanymes)
adj. wielkoduszny
magnet ('maegnyt) s. magnes
magnetic (maeg'netyk) adj.
magnetyczny; przyciągający
magnificence (maeg'nyfysns) s.
wspaniałosć; swietnosć;
okazałosć
magnificent (maeg'nyfysnt)adj.
wspaniały; okazały
magnify ('maegnyfaj) v. powiększać; potęgowac; wyolbrzymiac
magpie ('maegpaj) s. sroka;
gaduła
maid (mejd) s. dziewczyna;
dziewka; panna ;służaca
maiden ('mejden) s. dziewczyna;
panna; adj. panieński; dzie-
wiczy; swieży; nowy
maidenly ('mejdenly) adj.
dziewczecy; panieński
maiden name ('mejden,nejm) s.
nazwisko panieńskie
mail (mejl) s. poczta; kolczu-
ga; v. wysyłac poczta
mailbag ('mejl,baeg) s. worek
pocztowy
mailbox ('mejl,boks) s, skrzynka pocztowa
mailman (mejlmen) s. listonosz
mail-order house ('mejlorder,
,haus) s. firma sprzedająca
przez pocztę (z katalogu)
maim (mejm) v. okaleczyc
main (mejn) s. głowny (przewod)
adj. glowny; najważniejszy

mainland ('mejnlaend) s. konty-
nent(w odroznieniu od bliskich
wysp)
mainly('mejnly) adv. głownie;
przeważnie;po większej częsci
main road('mejnroud) s. głowna
droga;głowna szosa
main street('mejn.stri:t) s.
głowna ulica
maintain (men'tejn) v. utrzymywac (w dobrym stanie); trzymac (pozycję); podtrzymywac;
zachowywac; twierdzic; miec
na utrzymaniu;bronic;pomgac
maintenance ('mejntenens) s.
utrzymanie; utrzymywanie; poparcie; wyżywienie
maize (mejz) s. kukurydza
majestic (medżestyk) adj. majestatyczny
majesty ('maedżysty) s. majestat;godnosc;wielkosc
major ('mejdżer) s. major; pełnoletni; przedmiot kierunkowy
specjalizacji; adj. większy;
głowny; ważniejszy; pełnoletni;
starszy;v.specjalizowac się w stu-
diach
majorette ('mejdżeret) s. tancerka na defiladach i w przer-
wach meczow w USA
majority ('me'dżoryty) s.
większosć;a. wiekszosciowy
major road ('mejdżer,roud) s.
droga głowna;ważniejsza droga
make; made; made (mejk; mejd;
mejd)
make (mejk) v. robic; tworzyc;
sporządzac;powodowac; wynosic;
doprowadzac; ustanawiac; stac
się; postanowic etc.
make-believe ('mejk,by'li:w) s.
udawanie; pozory
make off ('mejkof) v. uciec;
uciekac .gwiznąc cos komus
make up ('mejkap) v. uzupełnic;
wynagrodzic; sporządzic; zmonto-
wac; ucharakteryzowac
makeup ('mejkap) s. makijaż;
charakteryzacja; układ (gra-
ficzny); stan (kogos,czegos)
make up your mind ('mejk,ap'-
'jo:r,majnd) exp.: zdecyduj się
(czego chcesz,co wolisz, na co
masz ochote,gdzie jedziesz etc.)

maker ('mejker) s. wytwórca; sprawca; producent; fabrykant; konstruktor(Maker= Bóg)

makeshift ('mejkszyft) s. namiastka; urządzenie prowizoryczne;adj.prowizoryczny

malady ('maeledy) s. choroba

male (mejl) s. mężczyzna; samiec; adj. męski; samczy; wewnętrzny; obejmowany

malediction (,maely'dikszyn) s. przekleństwo; złorzeczenie

malefactor ('maelyfaekter) s. złoczyńca; zbrodniarz

malevolent (me'lewelent) adj. niechętny; wrogi

malice ('maelys) s. złośliwość; zła wola; zły zamiar

malicious (me'lyszys) adj. złośliwy; zły;powodowany złością

malignant (me'lygnent) adj. złośliwy; zjadliwy

malnutrition ('maelnju'tryszyn) s. niedożywienie

malt (mo:lt) s. słod; v. słodować ;adj. słodowy;zcukrzony

maltreat (mael'tri:t) v. poniewierać; maltretować

mamma (me'ma:) s. mama;gruczoł mlekowy

mammal (me'ma:l) s. ssak;a.ssakowy

man (maen) s. człowiek; mężczyzna; mąż; v. obsadzać (np. załogą); pl. men (men)

manacle('maenekl) s. kajdany; v. zakuwać w kajdany

manage ('maenydż) v. kierować; zarządzać; posługiwać się; obchodzić się; opanowywać; poskramiać; radzić sobie

manageable ('maenydżebl) adj.do pokierowania (możliwy,łatwy)

management ('maenydżment) s. zarząd; kierownictwo; dyrekcja; posługiwanie się; obchodzenie się ;sprawne zarządzanie

manager('maenydżer) s. kierownik zarządzający; gospodarz

manageress ('maenydżeres) s. kierowniczka

mane (mejn) s. grzywa

maneuver (me'nu:wer) s. manewr; v. manewrować;manipulować

manger ('mejndżer) s. żłob; koryto

mangle ('maengl) s. magiel; v. maglować; poszarpać; pokaleczyć; poprzekręcać

manhood ('maenhud) s. męskość; ludność męska ;wiek męski

mania ('mejnje) s. bzik; obłęd; mania;zbytni entuzjazm;szał

maniac ('mejnjaek) s. maniak; szaleniec;adj.umysłowo chory

manifest ('maenyfest) adj. jawny; oczywisty; v. manifestować; ujawniać; s. manifest okrętowy (szczegółowa lista ładunku)

manifold ('maenyfould) adj. różnorodny; wieloraki; wielokrotny; v. powielać (tekst)

manipulate (me'nypjulejt) v. manipulować; umiejętnie; zręcznie pokierować (niesprawiedliwie)

mankind (,maen'kajnd) s. ludzkość; rodzaj ludzki

mankind ('maenkajnd) pl. mężczyzni ;cały rodzaj męski

manly('maenly) adj. dzielny; mężny; męski;adv.po męsku

manner ('maener) s. sposob; zwyczaj; zachowanie (się); wychowanie; maniera;procedura;rodzaj

manoeuvre (me'nu:wer) s. manewr; v. namewrować(pisownia brytyjska)

man-of-war ('maenew'ło:r) s. okręt wojenny;uzbrojony statek

manor ('maener) s. dwor; rezydencja (w Anglii:duży majatek)

man power('maen,pałer) s. siła robocza; rezerwy ludzkie

mansion ('maenszyn) s. rezydencja; pałac;duży dwor

manslaughter ('maen,slo:ter) s. zabojstwo (bez premedytacji)

mantelpiece ('maentlpi:s) s. gzyms kominka (obramowanie)

manual ('maenjuel) s. podręcznik; manuał; adj. ręczny;ręcznie zrobiony

manufacture (,maenju'faekczer) v. wyrabiać; s. wyrob; produkcja; produkt (zwłaszcza masowy)

manufacturer (,maenju'faekczerer) s. wytwórca; producent; fabrykant;przedsiębiorstwo wytwor-

manure (me'njuer) s. nawóz;
v. nawozic (gnój)
manuscript ('maenjuskrypt) s.
rękopis; adj. ręcznie pisany
many ('meny) adj. dużo; wiele
many-sided ('meny'sajdyd) adj.
wielostronny; wieloboczny;
wszechstronny
map (maep) s. mapa; plan;
v. planować; robić mapę
maple ('mejpl) s. klon
marble ('ma:rbl) s. marmur; kul-
ka do zabawy; adj, marmurowy;
v. marmurkować (np. papier)
March (ma:rcz) s. marzec
march (ma:rcz) s. marsz; v.ma-
szerować
mare (meer) s. klacz; kobyła
margarine ('ma:rdże,ri:n) s.
margaryna
margin ('ma:rdżyn) s. margines;
brzeg; krawędź; nadwyżka;
rezerwa
marine (me'ri:n) adj. morski;
s. marynarka; żołnierz piechо-
ty desantowej (USA)
mariner ('maeryner) s. marynarz;
żeglarz
maritime ('maerytajm) adj. morski
mark (ma:rk) s. marka (pieniądz)
ślad; znak; oznaczenie; nota;
cenzura; cel; uwaga; v. oznaczać; określać; notować; zwracać uwagę
marked (ma:rkt) adj. wybitny;
wyraźny; znaczny
mark out ('ma:rk,aut) v. wyznaczać; wytyczać (np. granicę)
market ('ma:rkyt) s. rynek;
zbyt; targ; v. robić zakupy;
sprzedawać na targu
marketing ('ma:rkytyŋg) s. orga-
nizowanie rynku;handlowanie
market-place ('ma:rkytplejs) s.
rynek; plac targowy
marksman ('ma:rksmen) s. strzelec (doborowy)
marmalade ('ma:rmelejd) s.
marmolada (pomarańczowa)
marmot ('ma:rmet) s. świstak
marriage ('maerydż) s. małżen-
stwo (skojarzenie);a.ślubny

marriageable ('maerydżebl) adj.
na wydaniu;odpowiedni do małżeń-
stwa
marriage certificate ('maerydż,
ser'tyfykyt) s. świadectwo
ślubu
married ('maeryd) adj. żonaty;
zamężna; małżeński; ślubny
married couple ('maeryd,kapl)s.&
adj. para małżeńska
marrow ('mearou) s. szpik
(kostny); dynia
marry ('maery) v. poślubić;
udzielać ślubu; ożenić (się)
brać ślub; pobierać się;
wychodzić za mąż
marsh (ma:rsz) s. moczary; bagno;błota;a.bagienny
marshal ('ma:rszel) s. marszałek; mistrz ceremonii; komisarz policji; v. uszykować
(uroczyście); przetaczać wagony;uporządkować;uszykować
marshy ('ma:rszy) adj. bagnisty; bagienny;błotnisty
marten ('ma:rtyn) s.kuna
martial ('ma:rszel) adj. wojenny; wojowniczy; wojskowy
martyr ('ma:rter) s. męczennik; v. zamęczać;zadręczać
marvel ('ma:rwel) s. cudo; cud;
v. podziwiać; dziwić się
marvelous ('ma:rwyles) adj.
cudowny; zdumiewający
mascot ('maesket) s. maskotka
masculine ('maeskjulyn) adj.
męski;płci męskiej
mash (maesz) s. zacier; papka;
mieszanka; v. warzyć; tłuc na
papkę; umizgać się
mashed potatoes ('maeszt,pe'tej-
tous) s. gniecione ziemniaki
mask (ma:sk) s. maska; v. zamaskować; maskować
mason ('mejsn) s. murarz; ka-
mieniarz;v.wymurować;murować
masonry ('mejsnry) s. murarstwo;
obmurowanie;kamieniarstwo
masque (ma:sk) s. maskarada;
pantomima (amatorska)
mass (maes) s. mszą; masa; rzesza; v. gromadzić; zrzeszać
massacre ('maeseker) s. masakra; v. masakrować;urządzić rzeź

massage ('maesa:ż) s. masaż;
v. masować ;zrobić masaż
massif ('maesyw) s, masyw
górski
massive ('maesyw) adj. masywny;
ciężki;zwarty;bryłowaty;ciężki
mast (ma:st) s. maszt
master ('ma:ster) s. mistrz;
nauczyciel; pan; gospodarz;
szef; kapitan statku; panicz;
v. panować; kierować; nabywać (np.wprawy);owładnąć
master key ('ma:sterki:) s.
wytrych
masterly ('ma:sterly) adj.
mistrzowski
master of ceremony ('ma:ster,ow-
sere'mouny) s. mistrz ceremonii
masterpiece ('ma:sterpi:s) s.
arcydzieło
mastership ('ma:sterszyp) s.
mistrzostwo; władza; panowanie; zwierzchnictwo
mastery ('ma:stery) s. władza;
panowanie; mistrzostwo
mat (maet) s. mata; v. plątać;
adj. matowy(bez połysku)
match (maecz) s. zapałka; lont;
mecz; dobór; małżeństwo;
v. swatać; współzawodniczyc;
dobierac;dorównywać
matchless ('maeczlys) adj. niezrównany;nie mający równego
matchmaker ('maecz,mejker) s.
swat; swatka;aranżujący mecze
mate (mejt) s. kolega; małżonek;
samiec; pomocnik; łączyc ślu-
bem; parzyć (się); pobierac
się;zadawać mata(w szachach)
material (me'tierjal) s. materiał; tworzywo; tkanka; adj.
materialny; cielesny
maternal (me'te:rnl) adj. macierzyński; matczyny
maternity (me'te:rnyty) s. ma-
cierzynstwo;adj.położniczy
maternity hospital (me'te:rnyty'
'hospytl) s. szpital położniczy
mathematician (,maetyme'tyszyn)
s. matematyk
mathematics (,maety'maetyks) s.
matematyka

math (maes) s. matematyka
(slang)
matriculate (me'trykjulejt) v.
immatrykulować; zdawać wstępny
egzamin (uniw.);zapisać się na.,.
matrimony ('maetrymeny) s. małżeństwo;akt ślubu
matron ('mejtren) s. matrona;
kobieta zamężna; (gospodyni)
matter ('maeter) s. rzecz;
tresć; materiał; substancja;
sprawa; kwestia; v. znaczyć;
mieć znaczenie;odgrywać rolę
matter-of-fact ('maeter,ow'faekt)
adj. rzeczowy; praktyczny
mattress ('maetrys) s. materac
mature (me'tjuer) adj. dojrzały;
płatny; v. dojrzewać; stawać
się płatnym (np.pożyczka)
maturity (me'tjueryty) s. doj-
rzałosć; termin płatności
mauve (mouw) s. kolor różowo-
liliowy ;adj.różowo-liliowy
maw (mo:) s. żołądek; wole
maxim ('maeksym) s. maksyma
maximum ('maeksymem) s. maksi-
mum
May (mej) s. maj
may (mej) v. byc może; might
(majt) mógłby
maybe ('mejbi:) adv. byc może;
może byc;możliwe że
may I ? ('mej aj) czy mogę ?
may-bug ('mejbag) s. chrabąszcz
mayor (meer) s. burmistrz
maypole ('mejpoul) s. słup do
tańca "gaik", 1-go maja
maze (mejz) s. labirynt; gmatwa-
nina; v. w błąd wprowadzić;
oszołomic;dezorientować;mieszać
mazurka (me'ze:rke) s. mazur;
mazurek
me (mi:) pron. mi; mnie; mną;
(slang): ja
meadow ('medou) s. łąka
meager ('mi:ger) adj. chudy;
cienki; skromny;nie obradzający
meal (mi:l) s. posiłek; grubo
mielona maka;czas posiłku
mealtime ('mi:l-tajm) s. pora
posiłku(ustalona zwyczajem)
mealy('mi:ly)adj.mączysty;nie--
szczery;słodziutki; oblesny

mean; meant; meant (mi:n;
ment; ment)
mean (mi:ņ) v. myśleć; przypuszczać; znaczyć; s. przeciętna; średnia; środek;
adj. ubogi; nędzny; podły;
marny; skąpy;tandetny;skąpy
meaning ('mi:nyņg) s. znaczenie; sens; treść; adj. znaczący;mający zamiar
meaningless ('mi:nyņglys) adj.
bez sensu; bez znaczenia
meant (ment) przeznaczony;
zob. mean
meantime ('mi:n'tajm) adv.
tymczasem;w tym samym czasie
meanwhile ('mi:n,hłajl) adv.
tymczasem
measles ('mi:zlz) s. odra
measure ('meżer) s. miara;
miarka; środek; zabieg; sposób; v. mierzyc; mieć rozmiar; oszacować;być...wzrostu
measureless ('meżerlys) adj.
bezmierny; nieskończony
measurement ('meżerment) s.
wymiar; miara; mierzenie
meat (mi:t) s. mięso; danie
mięsne;treść (książki etc.)
mechanic (my'kaemyk) s. mechanik ;rzemieślnik;technik
mechanical (my'kaenykel) adj.
mechaniczny
mechanics (my'kaenyks) s. mechanika
mechanism ('mekenyzem) s. mechanizm;maszyneria
mechanize ('mekenajz) v. zme-
chanizować
medal ('medl) s. medal
meddle ('medl) v. wmieszać się;
wtrącać się w cudze sprawy
mediaeval (,medy'i:wel) adj.
średniowieczny
mediate ('my:djejt) adj. pośredni; v. pośredniczyć
mediator ('my:djejt) s. rozjemca; mediator
medical ('medykel) adj. lekarski; medyczny
medical certificate ('medykel,
,sertyfykyt) s. świadectwo lekarskie

medicated ('medykejtyd) adj.
leczony; zaprawiony substancją
leczniczą
medicinal (me'dysynl) adj. leczniczy; lekarski; medyczny
medicine ('medysyn) s. medycyna;
lek; lekarstwo; v. leczyć lekarstwami
medieval (,medy'i:wel) adj.
średniowieczny
mediocre ('my:djouker) adj. mierny; średni; przeciętny
meditate ('medytejt) v. obmyślac;
rozmyślać; medytować
meditation (,medy'tejszyn) s.
rozmyślanie ;planowanie
meditative ('medytejtyw) adj.
zadumany; zamyślony; medyta-
cyjny ;kontemplacyjny
Mediterranean (,medyter'rejnjen)
adj. śródziemnomorski
medium ('mi:djem) s. środek;
średnia; przewodnik; środek
obiegowy; środowisko; rozpuszczalnik; sposób; środkowa droga; adj. średni;adv.średnio
medley ('medly) s. mieszanina;
pstrokacizna; rozmaitości
meek (mi:k) s. potulny; łagodny; skromny ;bez wigoru
meet; met; met (mi:t; met;met)
meet (mi:t) v. spotykać; zbierać
się; gromadzić; iść na kompromis; zgadzać się; zaspokajac;
s. spotkanie; zbiórka; miejsce
spotkania; spotkanie sportowe;
zawody(na bieżni etc.)
meet with ('mi:t,łys) v. spotkać się z (kimś);doświadczyc
meeting ('mi:tyņg) s. spotkanie;
połączenie się; posiedzenie;
zgromadzenie; wiec; zawody;
konferencja; pojedynek
melancholy ('melenkely) s. melancholia; adj. smutny; melan-
cholijny;zasmucający;ponury
mellow ('melou) adj. słodki;
miękki; soczysty; uleżały; zła-
godzony (wiekiem); łagodny; wesoły; pogodny; podchmielony;
dojrzały; miły; świętny; przyjemny; v. dojrzewać; zmiękczac;
uleżeć się;łagodnieć; łagodzić

melodious (my'loudjes) adj.
melodyjny ;harmonijny
melody ('meledy) s. melodia;
piosenka
melon ('melen) s. melon
melt (melt) s. stop; stopienie;
topnienie; wytop; v. topic;
topniec; roztapiac (się);
rozpuszczac; przetapiac; od-
lewac; wzruszyc;roztkliwiac
melting point ('meltyŋg'point)
s. temperatura topnienia
member ('member) s. członek;
człon(odrożniajacy się)
membership ('memberszyp) s.
członkowstwo; przynależnosc;
skład członkowski
membrane ('membrejn) s. błona;
przepona; membrana
memoir ('memła:r) s. pamiętnik;
życiorys;autobiogrfia
memorable ('memerebl) adj. pamiętny;znaczny
memorial (my'no:riel) s. pomnik; memorial; petycja; posąg (na pamiatkę)
memorize ('memerajz) v. za-
pamietywac; uczyc się na pamięc
memory ('memery) s. pamięc;
wspomnienie
men (men) pl. mężczyźni; robot-
nicy; zob.: man
menace ('menes) s. grozba; za-
grożenie; v. grozic; zagrażac
mend (mend) s. naprawa; na-
prawka; reperowac; zaszyc
menial ('mi:njel) s. sługa;
służalec; adj. czarno-robo-
czy; służalczy; służebny
mental ('mentl) adj. umysłowy;
pamięciowy; psychiatryczny;
s. (slang) umysłowo chory
mental hospital ('mentl'hospytl)
s. szpital psychiatryczny
mentality (men'taelyty) s.
umyslowosc; mentalnosc
mention ('menszyn) v. wspominac; wymieniac; nadmieniac;
wzmiankowac; s. wzmianka
menu ('menju:) s. jadłospis
meow (mi:'au) v. miauczec jak kot

mercantile ('me:rkentajl) adj.
handlowy; kupiecki
mercenary ('me:rsynery) adj.
najemny; wyrachowany; s. najemnik; żołnierz najemny
merchandise('me:rczendajz) s.
towar(y); v. handlowac
merchant('me:rczent) s. kupiec;
handlowiec; adj. handlowy;
kupiecki
merciful ('me:rsyfůl) adj. miłosierny; litosciwy
merciless ('me:rsylys) adj. bezlitosny; niemiłosierny
mercurial (me:r'kjuerjel) adj.
rtęciowy; żywy; bystry; rozgarnięty; zmienny
mercy ('me:rsy) s. miłosierdzie;
litosc; łaska;rzecz pomyslna
mercy killing ('me:rsy'kylyŋg)
s. eutanazja; zabójstwo z li-
tosci
mere (mjer) adj. zwykły; zwyczajny;nie więcj niż
merely ('mjerly) adv. tylko; jedynie; zaledwie; po prostu
merge (me:rdż) v. roztapiac
(się); zlewac; łączyc (się)
merger ('me:rdżer) s. połączenie; zlanie się; fuzja
meridian (me'rydjen) s. południk; zenit; szczyt; adj. południowy; szczytowy
merit ('meryt) s. zasługa; zaleta; odznaczenie; v. zasługiwac
meritorious (,mery'to:rjes) adj.
chwalebny; zasłużony
mermaid ('me:rmejd) s. rusałka;
syrena
merriment ('meryment) s. uciecha; radosc; wesołosc
merry ('mery) adj. wesoły; radosny; podochocony;odswiętny;
podchmielony
merryandrew ('mery'aendru:) s.
błazen; trefnis ;wesołek
merry-go-round ('merygou,raund)
s, karuzela
merry-making ('mery,mejkyŋ) s.
zabawa;uciecha;weselenie się
mesh (mesz) s. siatka; siec;
układ siatkowy; v. łapac w
siec; zazebiac;wplatac

mess (mes) s. nieporządek; bałagan; bród; świnstwo; paskudztwo; paćka; papka; zupa;
bigos; posiłek wspólny; stołówka; wspólny stół; v. za-
babrać; zapaskudzić; zabru-
dzić; zabałaganic; pokpic;
sfuszerować; obijać się; bawić; dawać jeść (posiłek);
stołowac się (wspólnie)
mess up (,mes'ap) v. zepsuc;
zaprzepaścić; sknocić;zagmat-
wać;pobrudzic;zabałaganic
message ('mesydż) s. wiadomosc;
orędzie; morał; wypowiedz;
v. komunikować;podawać;posłac
messenger ('mesyndżer) s. posłaniec; zwiastun
messy ('mesy) adj. kłopotliwy;
zapaskudzony; sfuszerowany;
brudny etc. upaćkany;niechlujny
met (met) v. zob. meet
metal ('metl) s. metal; v. pokrywać metalem;a.metalowy
metallic (my'taelyk) adj. meta-
liczny; metalowy;metalurgiczny
meteor ('mi:tjer) s. meteor
meteorology (,mi:tjero'ledży)
s. meteorologia
meter ('mi:ter) s. metr; licznik; v. mierzyć;a.metrowy
method ('meted) s. metoda; me-
todyka; metodycznosc; sposób
methodical (me'todykel) adj.
metodyczny;systematyczny
meticulous (my'tykjules) adj.
drobiazgowy; szczegółowy;
drobnostkowy; pedantyczny
metric system ('metryk'system)
s. system metryczny
metropolitan (,metre'polyten)
adj. wielkomiejski; metropoli-
talny; s. mieszkaniec metro-
polii; metropolita (duchowny)
mew (mju:) v. miauczeć;pierzyć się
Mexican ('meksyken) adj. meksy-
kanski;Meksykanin;Meksykanka
miaow (mi:'au) v. miauczec
mica ('maike) s. mika; łuszczyk
mice (majs) pl. myszy; zob.:
mouse
micron('majkron)s. mikron

microphone ('majkrefoun) s. mikrofon
microscope ('majkreskoup) s. mikroskop podczas;posród;między-
mid (myd) adj. srodkowy;prep. w;
midday ('myddej) adj. południowy;
s. południe
mid summer (,myd'samer) exp.
w srodku lata
middle ('mydl) s. srodek; kibić;
stan; adj. srodkowy; v. składać w srodku; kopać na srodek
middle aged ('mydl'ejdżd) adj.
w srednim wieku
Middle Ages ('mydle'ejdżys) s.
sredniowiecze
middle class ('mydl,kla:s) s.
klasa srednia; klasa srednioza-
można;a.ze sredniozamożnej klasy
middle name ('mydl,nejm) s. drugie imię
middle sized ('mydl,sajzd) adj.
sredniej wielkosci; sredni
middleweight ('mydl,łejt) s.
waga srednia; adj. sredniej
wagi (148 do 160 funtów)
middling ('mydlyng) adj. sredni;
przeciętny; adv. srednio
midge ('mydż) s. muszka
midget ('mydżyt) s. karzełek;
maleństwo; adj. miniaturowy
midland ('mydlend) s. srodek
kraju; adj. leżący w srodku
kraju; w głębi kraju
midmost ('mydmoust) adj. leżący
w samym srodku;prep.posród
midnight ('mydnajt) s. północ;
adj. północny; o północy
midway ('myd'łej) s. połowa drogi; adv. w połowie drogi
midwife ('mydłájf) s. położna;
okuszerka
might (majt) s. moc; potęga;
v. mógłby; zob.: may
mighty ('majty) adj. potężny;
adv. bardzo; wielce
migrate ('maj,grejt)v. wędrować;
przesiedlać się
migratory ('maj,gretery) adj.
wędrowny(ptak etc.)
mild (majld) adj. łagodny; powolny; potulny; słaby;delikatny

mildew (,myldju:) s. plesń;
v. plesniec;rdzewiec (o zbożu)
mildly ('majldly) adv. łagod-
nie; umiarkowanie;oględnie
mildness ('majldnys) s. łagodnosc; nieostrosc
mile (majl) s. mila; 1,609 km
mil(e)age ('majlydż) s. milaż;
odległosc w milach
milestone ('majlstoun) s. kamień milowy
military ('mylytery) adj. wojskowy; pl. wojskowy; wojsko
milk (mylk) s. mleko; v. doic
(krowy); wykorzystac; exploatowac;podsłuchiwac (telefon)
milking machine ('mylkyng,ma'-
'szi:n) s. maszyna do dojenia
milkman ('mylkmen) s. mleczarz
milk shake ('mylkszejk) s. mieszany napoj mleczny
milksop ('mylksop) s. mamin-
synek;fajtlapa;oferma;niedołęga
milky ('mylky) adj. mleczny;
zniewiesciały; koloru mleka
mill (myl) s. młyn; huta; fabryka; (1/1000); walcownia;
krawędz ząbkowana; v. mleć;
frezowac; pilsnic; kręcic się
miller ('myler) s. młynarz
millet ('mylyt) s. proso
milliner ('mylyner) s, modniarka; modystka
million ('myljen) num. milion
millionaire('myljeneer) s. milioner
millionth ('myljent) num.
milionowy; jedna milionowa
(częsc)
milt (mylt) s. mlecz rybi ;
v. zapładniac ikrą
mimic ('mymyk) s. nasladowca;
imitator; v. nasladowac; mał-
powac; adj. nasladowniczy;udany;
mimiczny;zmyslony;fikcyjny
mince (myns) v. siekac; mowic
bez ogrodek; cedzic (słowa);
drobic nogami; s. siekane
mięso; nadzienie mięsne
mincing (mynsyng) adj. mizdrzą-
cy sie; afektowany;sztucznie
zachowujący się(wykwintny)

mind (majnd) s. umysł; pamięc;
zdanie; opinia; postanowienie;
zamierzenie; v. pamietac; zważac; przejmowac się; baczyc;
miec cos przeciwko;byc posłusznym
mind your own business ('majnd;-
jo:'ołn'byznys) pilnuj swego
nosa; nie wtrącaj się
minded ('majndyd) adj. nastawiony na; skłonny do; gotow; gotowy
mindful ('majndful) adj. pomny;
dbały; uważający; troskliwy
mindless ('majndlys) adj. nierozumny; niedbały; nieuważający
mine (majn) pron. moj; moje; mo-
ja; s. kopalnia; podkop; mina;
bomba; v. kopac;.podkopywac;
exploatowac; minowac
miner ('majner) s. gornik
mineral ('mynerel) s. minerał;
adj. mineralny;zawierający mine-
mingle ('myngl) v. mieszac się;
przyłączac się (do innych)
miniature ('mynjeczer) s. miniatura; adj. miniaturowy
minimum ('mynymem) s. minimum;
adj. minimalny;najmniejszy
mining ('majnyng) s. gornictwo;
adj. gorniczy; kopalniany
miniskirt ('myny,ske:rt) s. spod-
nica (mini) (b. krotka)
minister ('mynyster) s. duchowny;
minister; v. stosowac; przyczy-
niac się; udzielac; pomagac
ministry ('mynystry) s. dusz-
pasterstwo; kler; duchowienstwo;
ministerstwo; gabinet ministrow;
służba; pomoc;posługa
mink (mynk) s. norka; adj. z norek; z futer norek
minor ('majner) adj. mniejszy;
mało ważny; młodszy; nieletni;
s. człowiek niepełnoletni
minority (maj'noryty) s. mniej-
szosc; niepełnoletnosc
minster ('mynster) s. katedra;
kosciół klasztorny
minstrel ('mynstrel) s. bard;
spiewak przebrany za murzyna
mint (mynt) s. mięta; mennica;
majątek; żrodło; v. bic pieniądze; wymyslac; tworzyc; kuc

minute ('mynyt) s. minuta;
chwilka; notatka; v. szkicować;
protokołować; (maj'nju:t) adj.
szczegółowy; bardzo mały; znikomy
miracle ('myrekl) s. cud; a.cudowny
miraculous (my'raekjules) adj.
cudowny ; nadprzyrodzony
mirage ('myra:dż) s. miraż;
fata morgana ; złudzenie wzroko-
mire ('majer) s. muł; błoto;
bagno; v. grzęznąć (w trudnościach); zabłocić się
mirror ('myrer) s. zwierciadło;
v. odzwierciedlać
mirth (me:rs) s. wesołość; radość ; uciecha(pełna śmiechu)
miry ('majry) adj. błotnisty;
mulisty ; bagnisty
mis-(mys) przedrostek: nie; źle;
(błędnie) nie-; źle-
misadventure ('mesed'wenczer)
s. niepowodzenie; zła przygoda
misanthrope ('myzentroup) s.
mizantrop ; wróg ludzkości
misapply ('myse'plaj) v. nadu-
żyć; źle zastosować
misapprehend ('mys,aepry'hend)
v. nie pojąć; źle zrozumieć
misbehave ('mysby'hejw) v. nie-
odpowiednio zachowywać się
miscalculate ('mys'kaelkjulejt)
v. przeliczyć się; przerachować
miscarriage (mys'kaerydż) v.
poronienie; omyłka; niepowodzenie
mischief ('mysczyf) s. szkoda;
krzywda; psota; utrapienie;
złośliwość; figiel; figlarność;
licho; szkodnik; bieda; niezgoda
mischievous ('mysczywes) adj.
szkodliwy; niegodziwy; niesforny; niegrzeczny; psotny
misdeed ('mys'di:d) s. przestępstwo; zły czyn(karygodny)
misdemeano(u)r ('mysdy'mi:ner)
s. wykroczenie; złe sprawowanie
miser ('majzer) s. sknera; chciwiec; skąpiec; kutwa
miserable ('myzerebl) adj. nędzny; chory; marny; żałosny
miserably ('myzerebly) adv.
nędznie; marnie; żałośnie
misfortune ('mys'fo:rczen) s.
nieszczęście; pech; zły los

misgiving (mysgywyng) s. złe
przeczucie; obawa; powątpiewanie
misguide (,mys'gajd) v. wprowadzać w błąd; sprowadzać na manowce
mishap ('myshaep) s. (mały; nie-
poważny) wypadek(niepowodzenie)
misinform ('mysyn'form) v. źle
informować; zwieść z drogi
mislay (mys'lej) v. zatracić;
zob. lay; zagubić; zapodziać
mislead (mys'li:d) v. wprowadzić
w błąd; zob. lead; zbałamucić
mismanage (,mys'maenydż) v. źle
prowadzić; źle pokierować
misplace (,mys'plejs) v. zatracić; położyć; nie na miejscu
misprint (,mys'prynt) v. błędnie wydrukować; s. omyłka druku; błąd drukarski
mispronounce ('myspre'nauns) v.
błędnie wymawiać; źle wymawiać
misrepresent ('mysrepry'zent)
v. przekręcić; błędnie przedstawić ; fałszywie przedstawić
Miss (mys) s. panna; panienka
miss (mys) v. chybić; nie trafić; nie znaleźć; nie dostać;
brakować; tęsknić; zacinać się;
s. pudło; niepowodzenie;
opuszczenie; chybienie
miss out ('mys,aut) v. wypuścić
(słowo); chybić; nie dostać
missile ('mysajl) s. pocisk; rakieta; adj. nadający się do
rzucania (oszczep; rakieta etc.)
missing ('mysyng) adj. nieobecny; brakujący; zaginiony
mission ('myszyn) s. misja; delegacja; v. wysyłać z misją;
zakładać misje ; a.misyjny
missionary ('myszynery) s.
misjonarz ; adj.misjonarski
misspelling ('mys'spelyng) s.
błąd ortograficzny
mist (myst) s. lekka mgła;
v. zachodzić parą (mgiełką)
mistake (mys'tejk) s. omyłka;
nieporozumienie; v. pomylić
(się) (co do faktu lub człowieka); źle zrozumieć; mylić się
mistaken (mys'tejken) adj. mylny; błędny ; pomylony; nie mający
zrozumienia sytuacji etc.

mistakenly (mys'tejknly) adv.
blędnie;pomyłkowo;nierozsądnie
Mister ('myster) s. pan (używane z nazwiskiem); skrót Mr.
(bez nazwiska niegrzecznie !)
mistletoe (mysltou) s. jemioł-
ka, jemioła;liście jemioły
mistress ('mystrys) s. kochan-
ka; nauczycielka; (myzys) s.
pani; (skrót Mrs); zob.Mister
mistrust (mys'trast) v. podejrzewac; nie ufac; s. niedowierzanie; nieufnosc
misty ('mysty) adj. mglisty;
zamglony;niejasny;nieokreslony
misunderstanding ('mysande r-
staendyng) s. nieporozumienie
misuse ('mys'ju:z) v. naduzywac; zle uzywac; ('mys'ju:s)
s. naduzycie; złe uzycie
mite (majt) s. molik; kruszyna;
drobiazg; grosz (wdowi); berbec;mała sumka pieniędzy
mitigate ('mytygejt) v. koic;
usmierzac; łagodzic; łagodniec; ukoic;złagodzic
mitten ('mytn) s. rękawiczka
bez palcow; (slang):rękawica
bokserska(zimowa etc.)
mix (myks) v. mieszac; obcowac;
wspołżyc; s. mieszanka; mieszanina; zamieszanie
mix-up ('myks'ap) s. gmatwani-
na; platanina;zamieszanie;bójka
mixed up with ('mykst'ap,łys)
adj. zamieszany (w cos)
mixture ('myksczer) s. mieszanka; mieszanina;mikstura
moan (moun) s. jęk; v. jęczec;
lamentowac;mowic jęczac
moat (mout) s. fosa; row;
v. opasywac fosą
mob (mob) s. tłum; motłoch;
banda; v. napastowac; atako-
wac tłumnie;stłoczyc się
mobile ('moubajl) adj. ruchomy;
ruchliwy; zmienne; s. rzezba-
kompozycja wiszaca(abstrakcyj-
mock (mok) v. wykpic; przedrzez-
niac; zmylic; stawiac czoło;
zartowac z kogos; s. kpiny;
przedrzeznianie;nasladownictwo;
adj.fałszywy; udany; pozorny

mockery ('mokery) s. kpiny; się
smiech; posmiewisko;pokrzywianie
mode (moud) s. sposob; tryb; moda;rzecz modna(lub zwyczajowa)
model ('modl) s. model; wzor; mo-
delka; manekin; v. modelowac
moderate ('moderyt) adj. umiarkowany; sredni; s. człowiek umiarkowany (w pogladach etc.)
moderate ('moderejt) v.powsciagac;
uspokoic (się);prowadzic(zebranie)
moderation (,mode'rejszyn) s.
umiarkowanie; umiar;spokoj
modern ('modern) adj. wspołczesny;
nowoczesny; nowozytny
modernize ('modernajz) v. unowo-
czesnic (się);modernizowac
modest ('modyst) adj. skromny
modesty ('modysty) s. skromnosc
modification (,modyfy'kejszyn) s.
modyfikacja; łagodzenie z lekka
modify ('modyfaj) v. modyfikowac;
zmieniac częsciowo; łagodzic
modulate ('modjulejt) v. modulo-
wac; regulowac; dostosowywac
module ('modju:l) s. moduł; kabina (astronauty)
moist (mojst) adj. wilgotny
moisten(mojsen) v. wilgnąc; zwil-
żac (sobie usta etc.);wilgotniec
moisture ('mojsczer) s. wilgoc;
wilgotnosc;lekkie zamoczenie
molar (mouler) s. trzonowy (ząb);
adj. trzonowy
mole (moul) s. kret; grobla; molo; znamię;brodawka etc.
molecule ('molykju:l) s. molekuła; cząsteczka
molest (mou'lest) v. napastowac;
dokuczac; molestowac;naprzykrzac się
mollify ('molyfaj) v. łagodzic;
miękczyc; mięknąc;usmierzać
moment ('moument) s. chwila; moment; waga; znaczenie; motyw;
powod;doniosłość;ważność
momentary ('moumentery) adj.
chwilowy; mijajacy;lada chwila
monarch ('monerk) s. monarcha;
krol;duży motyl tropikalny
monarchy ('monerky) s. monarchia
monastery ('monestery) s. klasztor (głównie męski);miejsce za
mieszkania mnichow (zakonnic)

Monday ('mandy) s. poniedziałek; a. poniedziałkowy
monetary ('manytry) adj. monetarny;pieniężny;walutowy
money ('many) s. pieniądze
money-order ('many,o:rder) s.
przekaz pieniężny
monger ('manger) s. handlarz;
przekupień;kupiec
monk (mank) s. mnich
monkey ('manky) s, małpa; v. do- (ogoniasta)
kazywać; małpować;wygłupiać sie
monkey business ('manky'byznys)
s. małpie figle (dokuczliwe)
monkey wrench ('manky'rencz) s.
francuski klucz (dostosowywalny)
monolog(ue) ('monelog) s. monolog ;a.monologowy
monopolize (me'nopelajz) v.
monopolizować; skupiac na sobie uwagę wszystkich etc.
monopoly (me'nopely) s. monopol
monotonous (me'notnes) adj.
monotonny; jednolity
monotony (me'notny) s. monotonia
monster ('monster) s. potwór;
adj. olbrzymi;potworny;okrutny
monstrous ('monstres) adj. potworny; ogromny;okrutnie zły
month (man_) s. miesiąc
monthly ('mantly) adj. miesięcz-
ny; adv. miesięcznie; s. mie-
siecznik;adv.co miesiac;na mie- ⌐siac
monument ('monjument) s. pomnik
moo (mu:) v. ryczeć; s. ryk
(krowy)
mood (mu:d) s. humor; nastrój;
(gram.) tryb;usposobienie
moody (mu:dy) adj. ponury; majacy humory;markotny
moon (mu:n) s. księżyc;a.księżyco- ⌐wy
moonlight ('mu:nlajt) s. światło
księżyca; v. miec kilka posad
równoczesnie
moonlit ('mu:nlyt) adj. oświe-
cony księżycem
moonshine ('mu:nszajn) s. światło księżyca; alkohol pędzony
nielegalnie lub przemycony
Moor (muer) adj. mauretański;
s. Maur

moor (muer) s. otwarty teren łowiecki; wrzosowisko; bagno;
trzęsawisko; v. cumować; umocować;przybijać do brzegu
moorings ('mueryns) pl. kotwica
martwa; miejsca przycumowania
moose (mu:s) s. łoś amerykański
mop (mop) s. szmata do podłog;
grymas; v. wycierać; zgarniać;
robić miny;spuscić manto
moral ('morel) s. morał; pl.
moralność;adj.moralny;obyczajny
morale (me'rael) s. nastrój;
duch (w wojsku,w narodzie)
morality (me'raelyty) s. moralność; moralizowanie; etyka
moralize ('morelajz) v. umoral-
niać; moralizować
morass (me'raes) s. moczar; bagno;mokradła;grzęzawiska
morbid ('mo:rbyd) adj. chorobliwy; chorobowy;niezdrowy;schorzały
more (mo:r) adv. bardziej; wiecej; adj. liczniejszy;dalszy
morel (mo'rel) s. (grzyb)
smardz;psianka;a.psiankowaty
more or less ('mo:r,or'les) adv.
mniej więcej;w przybliżeniu
moreover (mo:'rouwer) adv. co
więcej; prócz tego;nadto;pozá⌐tym
morgue (mo:rg) s. morga (na
zwłoki) ; kostnica;a.kostnicy
morning ('mo:rnyng) s. rano;
poranek; przedpołudnie
morose (mo'rous) adj. ponury;
zasępiony;przygnębiony;markotny
morphine ('mo:rfi:n) s. morfina ;a.morfinowy
morsel ('mo:rsel) s. kęs; kąsek;
kawałek; smakołyk; v. dzielić
na kawałki;rozdrabniąc;rozparce- ⌐łowywać
mortal ('mo:rtl) s. śmiertelnik;
adj. śmiertelny; straszny
mortality (mo;'rtaelyty) s.
śmiertelność;liczba ofiar
mortar ('mo:ter) s. moździerz;
zaprawa murarska; v. tynkować;
kłaść zaprawę; strzelać z
moździerza;zwiazać zaprawą
mortgage ('mo:rgydż) s. hipoteka; v. hipotekować

mortician (mo:r'tyszen) s.
przedsiębiorca pogrzebowy
mortification (mo:rtyfy'kejszyn) s. upokorzenie; umartwia-
nie się;wstyd;gangrena
mortify ('mo:rtyfaj) v. zamierać; ranić (uczucia); upo-
karzać; umartwiać (się);
powsciągać;zgangrenować
mortuary ('mo:rtjuery) s. trupiarnia; kostnica;a.pogrzebowy
mosaic (mou'zejyk) s. mozaika;
adj. mozaikowy;mojżeszowy
mosque (mosk) n. meczet
mosquito (mes'ki:tou) s. komar;
moskit;a.moskitowy
moss (mos) s, mech; v. pokrywać
mchem (torfowiskiem)
most (moust) adj. największy;
najliczniejszy; adv. najbardziej; najwięcej; s. najwięk-
sza ilosc;maksimum
mostly ('moustly) adv. przeważnie; głównie;po największej częś-ci
moth (mos) s. cma; mól
moth-eaten ('mos,i:tn)adj.zje-
dzony przez mole;przestarzały
mother ('madzer) s. matka;v.mat-kować
mother country ('madzer'kantry)
s. ojczyzna;kraj rodzinny
motherhood ('madzer,hud) s. macierzyństwo
mother-in-law ('madzer,yn'lo:)
s. tesciowa
motherly ('madzerly) adj. macierzyński
mother tongue ('madzer,tang) s.
język ojczysty
motif (mou'ti:f) s. motyw
(artystyczny);główny temat
motion ('mouszyn) s. ruch; wniosek; stolec; v. kierować skinieniem, znakiem; skinąć na
kogos znaczącym gestem
motionless ('mouszenlys) adj.
bez ruchu; unieruchomiony
motion picture ('mouszyn'pykczer) s. film ruchomy
motivate ('moutywejt) v. uzasad-
niac; pobudzać kogos;zachęcać
motive ('moutyw) s. motyw; podnieta; adj. napędowy;poruszający

motor ('mouter) s. motor; adj.
ruchowy; mechaniczny; samochodowy; v. jezdzic; przewozic
samochodem;prowadzic wóz
motorbike ('mouter,bajk) s.
motocykl;rower z motorkiem
motorboat ('mouter,bout) s.
motorówka;łódź motorowa
motorcycle ('mouter,sajkl) s.
motocykl
motorcyclist ('mouter,sajklyst)
s. motocyklista
motoring ('mouteryng) s. jazda
samochodem;automobilizm
motorist ('mouteryst) s. auto-
mobilista; kierowca
motorize ('mouterajz) v. motory-
zować;zmotoryzować
mottle ('motl) s. cętka; plamka;
v. cętkować;nakrapiac;upstrzyć
motto (motou) s. motto;dewiza
mo(u)ld (mould) s. plesn; ziemia;
modła; forma; v. plesniec; od-
lewac; kształtowac;urabiać
moulder ('moulder) v. gnic;
pruchniec; niszczyc się; kruszyc się;zgłupiec;s.odlewacz
mouldy ('mouldy) adj. splesniały;
zgniły;stęchły;przeżyty;nudny
moult (moult) v. liniec;s.linienie
mound (maund) s. hałda; kopiec
mount (maunt) s. oprawa; podstawa; wierzchowiec; v. stanąć (na);
wsiąsć (na konia); podniesc;
wchodzic; oprawic; osadzić; wy-
posazyc;zmontowac;wyrezyserować
mountain ('mauntyn) s. góra; sterta; adj. gorski; górzysty
mountaineer (,maunty'nier) s.
góral; alpinista
mountainous ('mauntynes) adj.
górzysty;olbrzymi;zawrotny
mourn (mo:rn) v. byc w żałobie;
opłakiwać;pogrążać się w smutku
mournful ('mo:rnful) adj. żałobny;ponury;przygnębiony
mourning ('mo:rnyng) s. żałoba
mouse (maus) s. mysz; pl. mice
(majs);podbite oko;v.myszkować
moustache (mos'ta:sz) s. wąsy
mouth (maus) s. usta; ujście; wylot;v.mówic przesadnie (patosem)

mouth (mouŋ) v. deklamować;
brać w usta; robić złą minę
mouthful ('mauŋful) s. pełne
usta; kęs; dzwięk trudny do
wymówienia; powiedzieć do
rzeczy;ważne słowa;dużo czegoś
mouthpiece ('mauspi:s) s. ustnik; rzecznik;kiełzno
mouthwash ('mausłosz) s. woda
do ust;płukanka do ust
move (mu:w) s. ruch; pociągnięcie; krok; zmiana mieszkania;
przeprowadzka; v. ruszać się;
posuwać; przesuwać; postępować; przeprowadzać się; wzruszać; nakłonić; zwracać się;
wnosić;zrobić ruch;działać
move in ('mu:wyn) v. wprowadzać się;wtargnąć ;wejść
move on ('mu:w,on) v. jechać
dalej; iść dalej;ruszyć(w drŏ-ge)
move out ('mu:w,aut) v. wyprowadzać się;wynieść się
movement (mu:wment) s. ruch;
poruszenie; przemieszczenie;
mechanizm; wypróżnienie
movies ('mu:wyz) s. (slang)
kino;film niemy;film
moving ('mu:wyŋg) adj. ruchomy;
wzruszający; s. przeprowadzka
moving violation ('mu:wyŋ,wa-
je'lejszyn) przestępstwo drogowe w czasie jazdy (autem)
mow; mowed; mown (mol; mołd;
moln)
mow (mol) v. kosić(trawę)
mower ('moler) s. kosiarz
mown (molh) v. zob. mow
Mr. (myster) s. pan (używane
z nazwiskiem)
Mrs. (mysyz) s. zamężna pani
(używane z nazwiskiem)
much (macz) adj.& adv. wiele;
bardzo; dużą sporo;niemało
much too much (,macz'tu,macz)
exp. dużo za dużo; zbyt dużo
mucus ('mju:kes) s. śluz
mud (mad) s. błoto; brud
muddle ('madl) v. nurzać się;
mącić; bełtać; mieszać; brnąć;
wikłać się; s. powikłanie;
trudne położenie;nieład;zamęt

muddle through ('madl,tru:) v.
przebrnąć;wybrnąć z kłopotów
muddy ('mady) adj. zabłocony;
błotnisty; mętny;v.błocić;mącić
muff (maf) s. zarękawek; fuszerka; fuszer; v. fuszerować
muffle (mafl) v. tłumić; owinąć;
otulić;s.pysk(przeżuwaczy,gryzoni)
muffler ('mafler) s. tłumik;
szal; rękawica bokserska;szalik
mug (mag) s. dzban; kubek; gęba
mulberry ('malbery) s. morwa
mule (mju:l) s. muł (zwierzę)
mull (mal) v. rozmyślać; pokpic;
sfuszerować; zagrzać i zaprawić (np. piwo); s. bałagan;
muślin; przylądek; tabakiera
mullion ('malion) s. pret; drążek okienny;słupek okienny
multiple ('maltypl) s. wielokrot-
na; adj. wielokrotny;złożony
multiplication (,maltyply'kejszyn) s. mnożenie;rozmnażanie się
multiplication table (,malty-
ply'kejszyn tejbl) s. tabliczka mnożenia
multiply ('malyplaj) v. mnożyć
(się) rozmnażać się;pomnożyć
multitude ('maltytju:d) s. mnóstwo; tłum;pospólstwo;mnogość
mumble ('mambl) s.mruknięcie;
bąknięcie; v. mruknąć; bąknąć;
żuć bezzębnymi dziąsłami;mamrotać
mummy ('mamy) s. mumia; miazga;
brunatny barwik; mamusia
mumps ('mamps) s. (choroba);
świnka; zapalenie ślinianki
munch (mancz) v. chrupać;schrupać
municipal (mju:'nysypel) adj.
miejski; samorządowy; komunalny
municipality (mju:,nysy'paelyty)
s. zarząd miasta;miasteczko
mural ('mjuerel) s. malowidło
ścienne; fresk;adj.ścienny
murder ('me:rder) s. mord; mor-
destwo;v.mordować;paskudzić(rolę)
murderer ('me:rderer) s. morderca
murderess ('me:rderys) s. morder-
czyni
murderous ('me:rderes) adj. morderczy; śmiercionośny

murmur ('me:rmer) s. mrucze-
nie; pomruk; pomrukiwanie;
szmer; szmeranie; sarkanie;
v. mruczec; szmerac
muscle ('masl) s. mięsień;
muskuł ;v. pchac się na siłę
muscle bound ('masl,baund) adj.
z zerwanymi mięśniami
muscular ('maskjuler) adj.
mięśniowy; krzepki; muskularny;wykonany muskułami etc.
muse (mju:z) v. dumac ;s.zaduma
museum (mju:'ziem) s. muzeum
mush (masz) s. papka; kulesza
(z kukurydzy);v.isc po śniegu
mushroom ('maszrum) s. grzyb;
pieczarka polna; dorobkiewicz;
v. zbierac grzyby; rozszerzac
się (jak grzyby po deszczu)
music ('mju:zyk) s. muzyka;
nuty ;konsekwencje postępku(sl)
musical ('mju:zykel) adj. muzyczny; muzykalny; s. komedia
lub film muzyczny
music hall ('mju: zykho:l) s.
teatr rewiowy
musician ('mju:zyszen) s. muzyk (zawodowy)
music stand('mju:zyk,staend) s.
pulpit (na nuty)
musk (mask) s. piżmo
musket ('maskyt) s.muszkiet
muskrat ('mask,raet) s.
piżmoszczur; futro piżmoszczura
Muslim ('muslym) adj. muzułman-
ski; s. muzułmanin
muslin ('mazlyn) s. muslin
musquash ('maskłosz) s. piżmo-
wiec;piżmoszczyr
mussel('masl) s. małz
must (mast) s. moszcz winny;
stęchlizna; szał; v. musiec;
adj. konieczny;nieodzowny
mustache ('mastasz) s. wąsy
mustard ('masterd) s. musztarda
muster ('master) v. musztrowac;
zbierac (się); s. przegląd;
zebranie; zbiór; apel;zebrani
muster in ('master,yn) v. zaciągac do wojska (powołac)
muster out ('master,aut) v. zwalniac z wojska

musty ('masty) adj. stęchły; za-
pleśniały;zbutwiały;przestarzały
mute (mju:t) adj. niemy;v.tłumic
mutilate ('mju:tylejt) v. okaleczyc; psuc;okroic(tekst książki)
mutineer (,mju:ty'nier) s.
buntownik; winny buntu
mutinous ('mju:tynes) s. buntowniczy ; zbuntowany
mutiny ('mju:tyny) s. bunt;v.bun-
towac
mutter ('mater) v. mamrotac; mruczec; szemrac (przeciw); szeptac; pomrukiwac; s. mamrot; pomruk; szemranie; narzekanie
mutton ('matn) s. baranina;a.bara-
ni
mutton chop ('matn,czop) s.
kotlet barani
mutual ('mju:tjuel) adj. wzajemny; wspólny; obustronny;wspólny
muzzle ('mazl) s. wylot lufy;
pysk; kaganiec; v. nakładac
kaganiec (psu;dziennikarzowi etc.)
my (maj) pron. mój;moja;moje;moi
myelitis (,maje'lajtys) s. zapalenie rdzenia pacierzowego
myriad ('myryed) s. krocie; ro-
je; 10.000; miriada; adj. niezliczony; wielostronny
myrrh (me:r) s. mirra
myrtle ('me:rtl) s. mirt
myself (maj'self) pron. ja sam;
sam osobiscie; siebie; sobie
mysterious (mys'tierjes) adj.
tajemniczy;niezgłębiony
mystery ('mystery) s. tajemnica;
tajemniczosc ;misterium
mystify ('mystyfaj) v. wprowadzac w błąd; okrywac tajemnicą
myth (mys) s. mit; postac mi-
tyczna; bajka;mistyfikacja
mystic ('mystyk) s. mistyk;
adj. mistyczny; tajemniczy
n (en) czternasta litera
angielskiego alfabetu
nab (naeb) v. capnąc; złapac;
przydybac;aresztowac;przyłapac
nag (naeg).v. gderac; dokuczac;
dręczyc; s. szkapa;kucyk;konik
nail (nejl) s. gwozdz; pazno-
kiec; pazur; v. przybijac;
utkwic(wzrok); ujawnic(kłam-
przygwozdzic; chwytac   stwo)

naive (na:'i:w) adj. naiwny
naked ('nejkyd) adj. nagi; goły; goła(prawda etc.);obnażony
name (nejm) s. imię; nazwa;
nazwisko; v. nazywac; mianowac; wymieniac;naznaczyc(datę)
nameless ('nejmlys) adj. bez-
imienny; nieznany; niesłychany; nieopisany;anonimowy
namely ('nejmly) adv. mianowicie; właśnie;żeby(wyjaśnić)
nanny ('naeny) s. niańka; koza
nanny -goat ('naeny,gout) s.
koza (żywicielka,mlekodajna)
nap (naep) v. drzemac; zdrzemnąc się;s.drzemka; meszek;puch;
włos;stroszenie meszku
nape(nejp) s. kark
nappy ('naepy) adj. mocny;
podchmielony; puszysty; v. napój; piwo; półmisek; serwetka
narcosis (na:r'kousys) s. narkoza;uśpienie narkotykami
narcotic(na:r'kotyk) adj.narko-
tyczny; s. narkotyk; narkoman
narrate (nae'rejt) v. opowiadac (coś);opowiedziec
narration (nae'rejszyn) s. opowiadanie;opowieść
narrative ('naeretyw) adj. nar-
racyjny; s. opowiadanie
narrator (nae'rejter) n, narrator,opowiadający;opowiadacz
narrow ('naerou) adj. wąski;
ciasny; ograniczony; s. przesmyk; cieśnina; v. zwężac;
ścieśniac; kurczyc się; zmniejszac się; redukowac do...
narrow -minded ('naerou'majndyd)
s. ciasny; ograniczony
nasty ('na:sty) adj. obrzydliwy; wstrętny; nieznośny; grozny: brudny; nieprzyzwoity
nation ('nejszyn) s. naród;
kraj; państwo
national ('naeszenl) adj. narodowy; państwowy; s. członek
narodu; obywatel; ziomek
nationality (,naesze'naelyty)
s. narodowość; obywatelstwo
nationalize ('naesznelajz) v.
upaństwowic; nadawac obywatelstwo (imigrantom etc.)

native ('nejtyw) adj. rodzinny;
krajowy; miejscowy; wrodzony;
naturalny; prosty; s. tubylec;
autochton; człowiek miejscowy
native language ('nejtyw'laeng-
łydż) s. ojczysty język
nativity (ne'tywyty) s. narodzenie
natural ('naeczrel) adj. naturalny; przyrodniczy; przyrodzony; doczesny; fizyczny; przyrodni; pierwotny; nieślubny;
dziki; s. biały klawisz (pia-
nina); kasownik (muzyczny)
naturalize ('naeczerelajz) v.
naturalizowac (się); aklimaty-
zowac (się); robic naturalnym;
przyswajac sobie; pozbawiac
cech nadprzyrodzonych
naturally ('naeczrely) adv. na-
turalnie ;z przrodzenia;oczywiś-
cie
natural-science ('naeczerel'sajens) s. przyroda; nauka przy-
rody; przyrodoznawstwo
nature ('nejczer) s. natura;
przyroda; usposobienie; rodzaj
naught (no:t) s. nic; zero
naughty ('no:ty) adj. niegrzeczny; nieposłuszny; nieprzyzwoity
nausea ('no:sje) s. nudnosc;
mdłość; choroba morska; obrzydzenie; wstręt;chęc wymiotowania
nauseating ('no:sjejtyng)adj.
obrzydliwy; przyprawiający
o mdłosci ,wymioty etc.
nautical ('no:tykel) adj. ma-
rynarski; morski
nautical mile ('no:tykel,majl)
s. mila morska; 1853 m.
naval (nejwel) adj. morski
naval base ('nejwel,bejz) s.
baza morska (wojskowa)
nave (nejw) s. 1. nawa; 2. piasta (u koła)
navel ('nejwel) s. pępek (ośrodek)
navigable ('naewygebl) adj.
spławny; żeglowny; sterowny;
podatny do żeglugi
navigate ('naewygejt) v. żeglo-
wac; kierowac; (np.balonem)
navigation (,naewy'gejszyn) s.
żegluga;podróż morska;nawigacja

navigator ('naewygejter) s.
żeglarz; nawigator
navy (nejwy) s. marynarka
wojenna;granatowy kolor
nay (nej) adv. nie; nawet; co
więcej; s. sprzeciw
near (nier) adj. bliski; dokładny; v. zbliżac się; adv. blisko; prawie; oszczędnie
nearby ('nier'baj) adj. pobliski; sąsiedni; adv. w pobliżu
nearly ('nierly) adv. prawie;
blisko; oszczędnie;nie całkiem
nearness ('niernys) s. bliskosc
nearsighted ('nier-sajtyd) s.
krótkowzroczny
neat (ni:t) adj. schludny;
zgrabny;proporcjonalny
neatness ('ni:tnys) s. schlud-
nosc;prostota; porządek; gus-
townosc;dobre proporcje
necessary ('nesysery) adj. konieczny; potrzebny;wynikający
necessitate (ny'sesytejt) v.
wymagac; czynic koniecznym
necessity (ny'sesyty) s. potrzeba; koniecznosc; artykuł
pierwszej potrzeby; niedostatek;los;zrządzenie los
neck (nek) s. szyja; kark;
szyjka; przesmyk;v.pieścic się
necklace ('neklys) s. naszyjnik
neck-tie ('nektaj) s. krawat
nee (nej) z domu (nazwisko
panieńskie)
need (ni:d) s. potrzeba; trud-
nosci; bieda; v. potrzebowac;
musiec; cierpiec biedę
needful (ni:dful) adj. potrze-
bujący; potrzebny;konieczny
needle ('ni:dl) s. igła;v.kłuc
needless ('ni:dlys) adj. niepotrzebny; zbyteczny;zbędny
needy ('ni:dy) adj. będący
w potrzebie, w biedzie etc.
negate (ny'gejt) s. zaprzeczac;
negowac ; anulowac
negation (ny'gejszyn) s. zaprzeczenie; odmowa; niebyt
negative ('negetyw) adj. przeczący; negatywny; odmowny;
ujemny; s. zaprzeczenie;odmowa;
forma przecząca;wartosc ujemna;

negatyw; v. sprzeciwic się;
odrzucac(np. plan)
neglect (ny'glekt) v. zaniedby-
wac; nie zrobic; s. zaniedbanie; pominięcie; lekceważenie
negligent ('neglydżent) adj.
niedbały; opieszały;nieuważny
negotiate (ny'gouszjejt) v. pertraktowac; omawiac; załatwiac;
przezwyciężac;przebic się przez
negotiation (ny,gouszy'ejszyn)
s. pertraktacje; omawianie
Negress ('ni:grys) s. murzynka
Negro ('ni:grou) s. murzyn; adj.
murzyński
neigh (nej) s. rżenie; v. rżec
neighborhood ('nejberhud) s.
sąsiedztwo; sąsiedzi; okolica
neighboring ('nejberyng) adj.
sąsiedni; sąsiadujący
neither ('ni:dzer) pron. & adj.
żaden (z dwóch); ani jeden
ani drugi; ani ten ani tamten;
conj. też nie;jeszcze nie
neither... nor ('ni:dzer...no:r)
exp. ani,.. ani
neon ('ni:en) s. neon;a.neonowy
neon sign('ni:en,sajn) s. reklama neonowa
nephew ('nefju:) s. siostrzeniec; bratanek
nerve (ne:rw) s. nerw; siła;
energia; odwaga; opanowanie;
zuchwalstwo; tupet; czelnosc;
v. dodawac sił, odwagi
nervous (ne:rwes) adj. nerwowy
nervousness ('ne:rwesnys) s.
nerwowosc; zdenerwowanie
nest (nest) s. gniazdo; wyląg
v. budowac; gnieździc się
nestle ('nesl) v. skulic; stu-
lic się; przytulic się;urządzic
nestle down ('nesl,dałn) v. się
usadawiac się (wygodnie)
nestle up to ('nesl,ap'tu) v.
przytulic się (do kogoś)
net (net) adj. czysty; netto;
s. siatka; siec; v. łowic sie-
cią; trafic w siatkę; zarobic
na czysto (na sprzedarzy etc.)
nettle ('netl) s. pokrzywa;
v. parzyc pokrzywą; drażnic;
irytowac;docinac(komus)dopiekac

network ('net,łe:rk) s. sieć
(np. elektryczna)
neurosis (njue:rousys) s. nerwica;zaburzenia psychiczne
neuter ('nju:ter) adj. nijaki;
neutralny; bezstronny; bezpłciowy; s. człowiek bezstronny; rodzaj nijaki
neutral ('nju:trel) adj. bezstronny; neutralny; obojętny;
pośredni; nieokreślony; bezpłciowy; s. państwo neutralne
neutrality (nu'traelyty) s.
neutralnosć;obojetnosc
neutralize ('ny:trelajz)v.neutra-
lizować;unieszkodliwiac;zobo-
jętniać
neutron ('nu:tron).s. neutron
never ('never) adv. nigdy;
chyba nie; wcale; ani nawet
nevermore ('newer'mo:r) adv.
nigdy wiecej(przenigdy)
nevertheless (,newerty'les) adj.
niemniej; jednak; pomimo tego
new (nju:) adj. nowy; świeży;
nowoczesny;adv.znowu;na nowo
newborn ('nju:,bo:rn) adj. nowo urodzony; s. noworodek
newcomer (nju:'kemer) adj. no-
woprzybyły; s. przybysz
news (nju:z) s. nowiny; wiadomości; aktualności;zadrzenia
newscast ('nju:z,ka:st) s. na-
dawanie wiadomości
newspaper ('nju:s,pejper) s.
dziennik (gazeta);tygodnik etc.
newsreel ('nju:sri:l) s. kronika filmowa
newsstand ('nju:staend) s.kiosk
z gazetami
new year ('nju:je:r) s. nowy
rok; pierwszego stycznia
New Year's Eve ('nju:,je:rs'i:w)
s. Sylwester(31go grudnia)
next (nekst) adj. następny;
najbliższy; sąsiedni; adv. następnie; potem; z kolei; tuż
obok;prep.obok;najbliżej
next but one ('nekst,bat'łan)
adj. przedostatni
next day ('nekst,dej) exp. na-
stępnego dnia
next door ('nekst,do:r) adj.
(dom) obok; sąsiedni(budynek)

next to ('nekst,tu) prep. obok
nibble at ('nybl,et) v. obgryzać; nadgryzać; brać (przynętę); s. ogryzanie; dziobanie
nice (najs) adj. miły; sympatyczny; przyjemny; uprzejmy;
ładny; wybredny; dokładny
nicely ('najsly) adv. przyjem-
nie; miło; grzecznie; ściśle;
dokładnie; skrupulatnie
nicety ('najsyty) s. delikat-
nosć; subtelnosć; zawiłosć;
drobiazgowosć; dokładnosć;
drobny szczegół; małe rozróz-
nienie;precyzja;akuratność
niche (nycz) s. nisza; v. chować (się)w niszy
nick (nyk) s. karb; otłuczenie;
moment; v. karbować; podcinać;
przecinać; trafić; natrafić;
odgadnąc; oszukać; złapać
otłuc
nickel ('nykl) s. nikiel; 5 centów USA: v. niklować
nick-nack ('nyk,naek) = knickknack; ozdóbka;świecidełko
nickname ('nyknejm) s. zdrobnia-
łe imię; przezwisko; v. nazywać
zdrobniale; przezywać
niece (ni:s) s. siostrzenica;
bratanica
niggard ('nyged) s. sknera; adj.
żałujący (czegoś); skąpiący
night (najt) s. noc; wieczór
night cap ('najtkaep) s. kieliszek przed snem; czepek do spania;szklanka wina przed snem
nightclub ('najtklab) s. nocny
lokal (rozrywkowy)
nightgown ('najtgałn) s. damska
koszula nocna;nocny ubiór
nightingale ('najtyŋgejl) s.
słówik; a. słowikowy; słowika
nightly ('najtly) adv. co noc;
w nocy;adj. nocny; jak noc
nightmare ('najtmeer) s. koszmar; przerażające doświadczenie
night school ('najtsku:l) s.
szkoła wieczorowa
nightshirt ('najtsze:rt) s.
koszula nocna
nighty ('najty) s. koszulka
nocna (dziecinna,kobieca)

nil (nyl) s. nic; zero
nimble ('nymbl) adj. zwinny;
zgrabny;bystry;żywy;żwawy
nine (najn) num. dziewięć;
s. dziewiątka;dziewiecioro
ninepins ('najnpynz) pl. kręgle
nineteen ('najn'ti:n) num.
dziewiętnaście;dziewiętnastka
nineteenth ('najn't:ng) num.
dziewiętnasty;dziewiętnasta część
ninetieth ('najntyyg) num.
dziewiędziesiąty
ninety ('najty) num. dziewięc-
dziesiąt;dziewiędziesiątka
ninth ('najng) num. dziewiąty
ninthly ('najnsly) adv. po
dziewiąty (raz)
nip (nyp) v. uszczypnąc; przy-
chwycic; odszczepic; stłumic;
zmrozic; buchnąc; ukrasc; po-
pędzic; poleciec; ucinac; cie
niszczyc;s.ukąszenie;uszczypnię dyskontent; niekonformista
nipoff ('nypof) v. zemknąc
nipple ('nypl) s. brodawka
sutkowa; smoczek; złącze
gwintowane rury; wzniesienie;
pagórek;bańka;złączka;nasówka
niter ('najter) s. saletra
nitrogen ('najtrydżen) s. azot
no (nou) adj. nie; żaden;
odmowa; adv. nie; bynajmniej;
nic;wcale nie;s.odmowa;sprzeciw
no one ('nou,łan) adj. żaden;
ani jeden; nikt (w ogóle)
nobility (nou'bylyty) s. szla-
chetnosc; szlachta
noble (noubl) adj. szlachetny;
szlachecki; wspaniały; wielkoduszny; s. szlachcic
nobleman (noublmen) s. szlachcic
nobody ('noubedy) s. nikt;
człowiek bez znaczenia
nod (nod) v. skinąc głową;
ukłonic się; drzemac; przyzwa-
lac skinieniem;byc nachylonym
noise ('nojz) s. hałas; zgiełk;
wrzawa; szum; odgłos; szmer;
v. rozgłaszac cos;rozgłosic
noiseless ('nojzlys) adj. cichy;
bezszelestny;nie hałaśliwy
noisy ('nojzy) adj. hałaśliwy;
krzykliwy; wrzaskliwy

nomadic ('noumaedyk) adj. wędrowny; koczowniczy ;wędrujący
nominal ('nomynl) adj. nominalny;
imienny; symboliczny ;tylko z nazwy
nominate ('nomynejt) v. mianowac; wyznaczac; obierac
nomination (,nomy'nejszyn) s.
nominacja
nominative ('nomynetyw) s. mianownik (gram.); ta sprawa(sądowa)
non- (non) prefix nie-; bez-;
nonalcoholic ('non,aelke'holic)
adj. bezalkoholowy
noncommissioned ('nonke'myszend)
adj. bez rangi oficerskiej
(podoficer)
noncommital ('nonke'mytl) adj.
wymijający;nie zobowiazujący(się)
nonconducting ('nonken'daktyng)
adj. nieprzewodzący
nonconformist ('nonken'fo:rmyst)
nondescript ('nondyskrypt) adj.
nieokreslony; s. człowiek nieokreślony (trudny do opisania)
none (non) pron. nikt; żaden;
nic; adv. wcale nie; bynajmniej
nie
nonexistence (,nony'ksystens)
s. niebyt;nie istnienie
nonfiction (,non-'fykszyn) s.
reportaże; opowiesc prawdziwa;
opisy faktow (w dziennikach etc.)
nonsense ('nonsens) s. niedorzecznosc; nonsens; głupstwo
nonskid ('nonskyd) adj. prze-
ciwslizgowy; nie slizgający
się (samochód, opona etc.)
nonsmoker ('non'smouker) s.
osoba niepaląca; przedział dla
niepalących(w pociągu etc.)
nonstop ('non'stop) adj. bezpośredni;bez lądowania; bez
postoju; nieprzerwany (lot etc.)
nonunion ('non'ju:njen) adj.
nie należący do związku zawodowego;nie uznający związku zawodowego
nonviolence ('non'wajelens) s.
(polityka) bez gwałtów
noodle ('nu:dl) s. makaron; kluska; cymbał; pała; głupek;łeb
nook (nuk) s. kącik; zakątek

noon (nu:n) s. południe
noose (nu:s) s. pętla; stryczek; sidła; lasso; v. usid-
lić; zrobić pętlę
nor (no:r) conj. też nie
norm (no:rm) s. norma;wzorzec;
standard
normal ('no:rmel) adj. normalny; prostopadły; prawidłowy;
s. stan normalny; prostopadła
normalize ('no:rmelajz) v. normalizować; unormować
Norman ('no:rmen) adj. normań-
ski ;Normandczyk;Normandka
north (no:rs) adv. na północ;
s. północ; adj. północny
northeast (no:rs'i:st) adj.
północno-wschodni
northerly ('no:rdzerly) adj.
północny; adv. na północ
northerner ('no:rdzerner) s.,
człowiek z północnych stanów
northward ('no:rsłerd) adj.
północny; adv. na północ
northwest ('no:rs'łest) adj.
północno-zachodni; adv. na
północny-zachód; s. północny-
zachód
Norwegian (no:rłi:dżen) adj.
norweski ;s.Norweg
nose (nouz) s. nos; węch; wylot; dziób; v. węszyć; pocierać nosem; wtykać nos
nosegay ('nouzgej).s. wiązanka;
bukiet
nostril ('noustryl) s. nozdrze;
chrapy; dziura w nosie
nosy ('nouzy) adj. wścibski;
śmierdzący; aromatyczny; no-
sacz wielki;stęchły;cuchnący
not (not) adv. nie ;ani(jeden)
not a (not ej) adv. żaden
notable ('noutebl) adj. znakomity; sławny; wybitny; s. dostojnik ;wybitny człowiek
notary public ('noutery'pablyk)
s. notariusz
notation (nou'tejszyn) s. znako-
wanie; notacja; symbol
notch (nocz) s. nacięcie; karb;
przełęcz; v. nacinać; karbować; rowkować ;s.krok(dalej)

note (nout) s. nuta; znak; zna-
mie; uwaga; notatka; banknot;
v. zapisywać; zauważać
note down ('nout'dałn) v. zano-
tować;zapisywać
notebook ('noutbuk) s. zeszyt;
notatnik ;notes; notesik
noted ('noutyd) adj. znany;
znakomity; wybitny
notepaper ('nout,pejper) s.
papier listowy;blok
noteworthy ('nout,łe:rsy) adj.
godny uwagi; wybitny;osobliwy
nothing ('nasyng) s. nic; drobiazg; adv. nic; nie; w żaden
sposób ;bynajmniej nie;wcale nie
nothing but ('nasyng'bat) s.
nic tylko.. (coś najlepszego)
notice ('noutys) v. zauważyć;
spostrzec; traktować grzecznie;
powiadamiać; s. zawiadomienie;
uwaga; recenzja ;spostrzeżenie
noticeable ('noutysebl) adj.
godny uwagi; widoczny
notification (,noutyfy'kejszyn)
s. zawiadomienie ;zgłoszenie
notify (noutyfaj) v. zawiadomić
notion ('nouszyn) s. pojęcie;
wyobrażenie; zamiar ;wrażenie
notorious ('nou'to:rjes) adj.
notoryczny; osławiony ;jawny
notwithstanding (,noutłys'staendyng) adv. jednakże; niemniej;
mimo; prep. pomimo(tego);mimo
nought (no:t) s. nic; zero
noun (naun) s. rzeczownik
nourish ('narysz) v. żywić;
karmić ;utrzymywać
nourishing ('naryszyng) adj.
pożywny ;pokrzepiający
nourishment ('naryszment) s.
pokarm; pożywienie; żywienie;
karmienie ;żywność; jedzenie
novel ('nowel) s. powieść; opowieść; nowela; adj. nowy; nowa-
torski; osobliwy ;oryginalny
novelist ('nowelyst) s. po-
wieściopisarz
novelty ('nowelty) s. nowość;
innowacja ;oryginalność
November (nou'wember) s. listopad; adj. listopadowy

novice ('nowys) s. nowicjusz;
neofita; początkujący
now (nał) adv. teraz; obecnie;
dopiero co; otóż; a więc;
s. teraźniejszość; chwila
obecna; chwila dzisiejsza
now and again ('nał,endə gejn)
exp. od czasu do czasu
now and then ('nał,end'dzen)
exp.: nieraz; od czasu do czasu; czasem;co jakiś czas
nowadays ('nałe,dejz) adv.
obecnie; dzisiaj; s. obecne
czasy;dzisiejsze czasy
nowhere ('nouhłer) adv. nigdzie; s. niepowodzenie etc.
noways ('noułejz) adv. bynajmniej ; wcale nie
noxious ('nokszes) adj. szkodliwy; niezdrowy (moralnie etc.)
nozzle ('nozl) s. dysza; rozpylacz; dziób; wylot (rury etc.)
nuclear ('nu:kli:er) adj. jądrowy; o napędzie nuklearnym
nuclear fission('nu:kli:er'fyszyn) v. rozszczepienie jądra
nuclear power plant ('nu:kli:-
er'pałer'pla:nt) s. elektrownia atomowa
nuclear reactor ('nu:kli:er,ri:-
'aekter) s. reaktor nuklearny
nucleus ('nu:kljes) s. jądro
nude (nju:d) adj. nagi; goły:
nie ważny (prawnie); s. człowiek nagi; nagość; akt
nudge (nadż) v. trącać lekko;
s. trącenie łokciem
nugget ('nagyt) s. bryłka; złoty samorodek
nuisance ('nju:sns) s. zawada;
naruszenie porządku publiczne-
go; osoba sprawiająca zawadę
null and void ('nal,end'woid)
exp. nieważny; bez znaczenia;
unieważniony;nic, nie zanczący
numb (nam) adj. ścierpły; zdręt-
wiały; odrętwiały; v. drętwieć;
odurzać;paraliżować;zdrętwieć
number ('namber) s. liczba; numer; ilość; v. liczyć; numerować; wyliczać; zaliczać
numberless ('namberlys) adj.
niezliczony; bez numeru

number plate ('namber'plejt) s.
płyta z numerem rejestracji
samochodu;motoru etc.
numeral ('nju:merel) adj. liczbowy; cyfrowy; s. liczebnik;
cyfra(pisana,mówiona etc.)
numerous ('nju:meres) adj. liczny; obfity;liczebny;rytmiczny
nun (nan) s. zakonnica:mniszka
nunnery('nanery) s. zakon żeński
nuptials ('napszels) pl. zaślubiny;gody;wesele;ślub
nurse (ne:rs) s. pielęgniarka;
pielęgniarz; mamka; osłona;
v. pielęgnować; leczyć; opiekować się; żywić; podsycać;
szanować; obejmować; karmić;
pić powoli;(piersią) niańczyć
nursery ('ne:rsery) s. pokój
dziecinny; żłobek; przedszkole; ochronka; wylęgarnia;
szkółka (roślin)(drzewek)
nursery school ('ne:rsery'sku:l)
s. przedszkole
nursing bottle ('ne:rsyng'botl)
s. flaszka do karmienia
nursing home ('ne:rsyn'houm)
s. przytułek - lecznica dla
starych i kalekich;dom zdrowia
nut (nat) s. orzech; bzik; dziwak; nakrętka; zakrętka;
v. szukać i zbierać orzechy
nutcracker ('natkraeker) s.
dziadek do orzechów
nutmeg ('natmeg) s. gałka
muszkatołowa
nutria ('nju:trje) s. nutria
(futro);nutrie
nutrient ('nju:trjent) adj.
pożywny; odżywczy ;s.odżywka
nutriment ('nju:tryment) s.
środek odżywczy
nutrition (nju'tryszyn) s. odżywienie; pokarm
nutritious (nju'trysxes) adj.
pożywny; odżywczy
nutshell ('natszel) s. łupka
od orzecha; istota rzeczy;
sama treść(w paru słowach)
nutty ('naty) adj. orzechowy;
pomylony; zbzikowany;dziwaczny;
zwariowany;pikantny;zakochany

nuzzle ('nazl) v. wsadzać nos
(w coś); ryć; węszyć; wtulać
się(twarzą w czyjeś ramię)
nylon ('najlon) s. nylon; pończochy nylonowe
nymph (nymf) s. nimfa
nymphomania (,nymfe'mejnia) s.
nimfomania(kobieca żądza miłos)
o (ou) piętnasta litera
angielskiego alfabetu;zero
oak (ouk) s. dąb;a.dębowy
oar (o;r) s. wiosło; v. wiosłować
oarsman ('o:rzmen) s. wioślarz
oasis (ou'ejsys) s. oaza ;
zieloneiżyżne miejsce wsród
pustynnej okolicy
oat (out) s. owies
oatmeal ('outmi:l) s. owsianka [stwo;świętokradztwo etc.
oath (ouŝ) s. przysięga;przekleń-
obedience (e'bi:djens) s. posłuszeństwo
obedient (e'bi:djent) adj. posłuszny
obey (e'bej) v. słuchać; być
posłusznym (rozsądkowi etc.)
obituary (e'bytjuery) s. nekrolog; adj. pośmiertny; żałobny
object ('obdżykt) s. przedmiot;
rzecz; cel; śmieszny człowiek;
dopełnienie; v. zarzucać coś;
być przeciwnym ;sprzeciwiać się
objection (eb'dżeksjyn) s. zarzut; sprzeciw; przeszkoda;
trudność; wada; niechęć
objective (eb'dżektyw) s. cel;
objektyw; adj. przedmiotowy;
obiektywny;rzeczywisty
obligation (obly'gejszyn) s.
zobowiązanie; obowiązek; obligacja;dług(wdzięczności etc.)
oblige (e'blajdż) v. zobowiązywać; spełniać prośbę
obliging (e'blajdżyng) adj.
uprzejmy; uczynny ;usłużny
oblique (e'bli:k) adj.posredni;
ukośny; skosny; kręty; nieszczery; potajemny;v.iść na ukoś
obliterate (e'blyterejt) s. zacierać; zamazywać; wykreślić;
zniszczyć;skasować (zanczek etc.)

oblivion (e'blywjen) s.
zapomnienie; niepamięć
oblivious (o'blywjes) adj. zapominający; niepomny; nieswiadomy; dający zapomnienie
oblong('oblong)adj. podłużny;
s. podłużny przedmiot
obscene (ob'si:n) adj. sprośny;
nieprzyzwoity; niemoralny
obscure (eb'skjuer) adj. ciemny;
skromny; niejasny; ukryty; nieznany; v. zaciemniać; przyciemniać; zaćmiewać
obsequies ('obsykłyz) pl. pogrzeb
observance (eb'ze:rwens) s. obrzęd; zwyczaj; przestrzeganie;
szacunek;poszanowanie;rytuał
observant (eb'ze:rwent) adj.
uważny; przestrzegający; spostrzegawczy;bystry; czujny
observation (,obzer'wejszyn) s.
obserwacja; spostrzeżenie;
uwaga;spostrzegawczość
observatory (eb'ze:rweto:ry) s.
obserwatorium;punkt obserwacyjny
observe (eb'ze:rw) v. obserwować;
przestrzegać; obchodzić; zauważać;wypowiedzieć uwagę;zbadać
observer (eb'ze:rwer) s. obserwator;człowiek przestrzegający
obsess (eb'ses) v. opętać; prześladować;nie dawać spokoju;nawiedzać
obsession (eb'seszyn) s. obsesja;
opętanie;natręctwo (myślowe)
obsolete ('obseli:t) adj. przestarzały; szczątkowy;zarzucony
obstacle ('obstekl) s. przeszkoda; zawada
obstetrics (ob'stetryks) s. położnictwo
obstinacy ('obstynesy) s. upior
obstinate ('obstynyt) adj. uparty; uporczywy;zawzięty;wytrwały
obstruct (eb'strakt) v. tamować;
zagradzac; zasłaniać; wstrzymywać;wywoływać zator;zawadzać
obtain (eb'tejn) v. uzyskać;
trwać; panować;obowiązywać
obtainable (eb'tejnebl) adj.
osiągalny (do nabycia etc.);
możliwy do nabycia

obtrusive (eb'tru:syw) adj.
natarczywy; natrętny
obvious ('obwjes) adj. oczywisty; rzucający się w oczy
occasion (e'kejżyn) s. sposobność; okazja; powód
occasional (e'kejżenl) adj.
przypadkowy; okazyjny;
okolicznościowy; rzadki
Occident ('oksydent) s. Zachód (jako kultura, ekonomia
etc.)-całość geogaficzna
occult (o'kalt) adj. tajemny
occupant ('okjupent) s. mieszkaniec; posiadacz (faktyczny)
occupation (,okju'pejszyn) s.
okupacja; zawód; zajęcie;
zajmowanie;zamieszkiwanie
occupy ('okjupaj) v. okupować;
zajmować (się czyms);zatrudniać
occur (e'ke:r) v. zdarzać się;
przychodzić na myśl; poja-
wiać się;dziac sie;trafić sie
occurrence(e'karens) s. wydarzenie; przypadek;występowanie
ocean ('ouszen) s. ocean;a.ocea-
o'clock (e'klok) adv. na zegarze;według zegara
October (ok'touber) s. październik ;a,październikowy
ocular ('okjuler) adj. oczny;na-
oczny;na oko;okiem;s.okular
oculist ('okjulyst) s. okulista
odd (od) adj. nieparzysty;
dziwny; dziwaczny; zbywający;
pozostały; dodatkowy;od pary
odds (ods) pl. szanse; fory;
nadwyżka; różnica; drobne
szczegóły; spór; nierówność
(w grze);sprzeczność;różnica
odds-and-ends ('ods,end'ends)
exp.: resztki; rupiecie
oddity ('odyty) s. osobliwość;
dziwak;dziwactwo;dziwna rzecz
odor ('ouder) s. odor; won;
slad; reputacja;sława;posmak
of (ow) prep. od; z; o; w
of Cracow (ow'Krakau) exp.:
z Krakowa(pochodzeniem etc.)
of charity (ow'chaeryry) exp.
z miłosierdzia
off (of) adv. od; z; na boku;
precz; zdala; przy;prep.z dala

offshore (of'szo:r) adv. przy
wybrzeżu ;adj.od lądu(na morze)
offense (e'fens) s. obraza; za-
czepka; przekroczenie;ofenzywa
offend (e'fend) v. obrażać; razić; występować przeciw (np.
prawu);zawinić;wykroczyć
offender (e'fender) s. winowajca ;przestępca;strona winna
offensive (e'fensyw) adj. obraźliwy; drażniący; przykry; cuchnący; zaczepny; s. ofensywa;
postawa zaczepna
offer ('ofer) s. oferta; propozycja (np. ślubu); v. ofiarować (się); oświadczyć (się);
oferować; nastręczyć się; nada-
rzyc się;występować z propozycją
offering ('oferyng) s. ofiara
office ('ofys) s. biuro; urząd;
obowiązek; służba urzędowania;
posada;funkcja;stanowisko;gabi-
net
officer ('ofyser) s. urzędnik;
oficer; policjant; v. obsądzać
kadra; dowodzic; kierować
official (e'fyszel) s. urzędnik;
adj. urzędowy; oficjalny
officious (e'fyszes) adj. narzucający się; natrętny; gorliwy;
nieurzędowy;nieoficjalny
offish ('ofysz) adj. chłodny;
sztywny; z rezerwą;nieprzystępny
offset (o':fset) s. offsetowy
druk; gałąź; odgałęzienie;
odrośl; potomek; wyrownanie;
kompensata;v.wynagradzać;rozras-
tać się
offspring ('o:fspryng)s. potomek;
wynik; potomstwo
often ('o:fn) adv. często
oh ! (ou) excl.:och !; ach !
oil (ojl) s. oliwa; olej; ropa;
nafta; farba olejna; v. oliwić;
smarować; przetapiac;pochlebiać
oilcloth ('ojlklos) s. cerata
oily ('ojly) adj. oleisty;
olejny; tłusty; oblesny;służalczy
ointment ('oyntment) s. masc
O.K., okay ('ou'kej) adv. w porządku; tak; adj. b. dobry;
s. zgoda; v. zaaprobować (coś)
old (ould) adj. stary; staroświecki; doświadczony; były
s.dawne czasy;dawno temu

old age ('ould,ejdż) s. starość
old-age ('ould ejdż) adj. daw-
ny; stary; starczy
old-fashioned ('ould'faeszend)
adj. staromodny; staroświecki
old-time ('ould,tajm) adj.
dawny
old town ('ould,tałn) s. starów-
ka; stare miasto
olive ('olyw) s. oliwka; drzewo oliwne; (kolor) oliwkowy;
oliwa stołowa
olive-branch ('olywbra:ncz) s.
gałązka oliwna
Olympic Games (ou'lympyk,gejms)
pl. igrzyska olimpijskie
ombudsman (om'bu:dz,men) s.
rzecznik ludu - załatwia skar-
gi na biurokratów
omelet(te) ('omlyt) s. omlet
omen ('oumen), s. omen; wróżba;
znak ;v. być wróżbą;być znakiem
ominous ('omynes) adj. złowieszczy ; źle wróżący
omission (e'myszyn) s. opuszczenie; zaniedbanie
omit (ou'myt) v. opuszczać;
pomijać; zaniedbywać
omnipotent (om'nypetent) adj.
wszechmocny,wszechmogący
omniscient (om'nysjent) adj.
wszechwiedzący
on (on) prep. na; ku; przy; nad;
u; po; adv. dalej; przed siebie; naprzód ;przy sobie
on and on ('on,end'on) exp.; coraz dalej;bez końca;wciąż
on demand ((,on dy'ma:nd) exp.:
na żądanie
on the street ('on,dy'stri:t)
exp.:na ulicy
on to ('ontu) exp. na; do
once (łans) adv. raz; nagle;
naraz; zaraz; kiedyś; niegdyś;
dawniej; s. raz; conj. raz;
gdy; skoro ;od razy;zarazem etc.
one (łan) num. jeden; adj. pierwszy; pojedynczy; jedyny; pewien;
s. dowcip; kieliszek; pron. ten;
który;ktoś; niejaki;s.jedynka
one Adams ('łan,aedems) exp.:pe-
wien Adams ;niejaki Adams

one day ('łan,dej) exp.pewnego
dnia; kiedyś;niegdyś
one by one ('łan,baj'łan) adv.
pojedyńczo;jeden za drugim
one antoher (,łan e'nadzer) adv.
jeden drugiego; wzajemnie
oneself (łan'self) pron. się;
siebie; sobie; sam; osobiście;
samodzielnie; samotnie.
one-sided ('łan'sajdyd) adj.
jednostronny
one-up-manship, ('łan,ap'-men-
szyp) s. "wyscig" nerwów
(w zatargu etc.)
one-way ('łan,łej) adj. jedno-
kierunkowy(ruch)
onion ('anjen) s. cebula
onlooker ('onluker) s. widz
only ('ounly) adj. jedyny; jedynak; adv. tylko; jedynie;
ledwo; dopiero; conj. tylko
że;cóż z tego ,kiedy...
onward ('onłerd) adj. naprzód;
ku przodowi; adv. naprzód;
dalej;dalej naprzód
ooze (u:z) v. sączyć się; wydzielać się; ciec; s. szlam;
muł; wyciek; rzadkie błoto
opaque, (ou'pejk) adj. nieprzezroczysty; matowy; mętny;
niejasny; s. rzecz matowa;
nieprzezroczysta
open ('oupen) adj. otwarty; rozwarty; dostępny; wystawiony;
jawny; odsłonięty; wakujący;
otwarty; wolny; v. otworzyć;
zwierzyć się; umożliwić; rozpoczynać; rozchylić;udostępnić
open air ('oupen,eer) s. świeże
powietrze; wolna przestrzeń
opener ('oupener) s. otwieracz
(np. puszek);przyrząd do otwie-
rania
open-handed ('oupn'haendyd) adj.
szczodry; hojny
open-hearted ('oupn,ha:rtyd) adj.
szczery; serdeczny
opening ('oupnyŋg) s. otwor; wylot; otwarcie; początek; zbyt
adj. początkowy; wstępny
openly ('oupnly) adv. otwarcie;
szczerze; publicznie ; bez ogrodek;po prostu; wprost(powiedzieć)

open-minded ('oupn'majndyd) adj. z otwartą głową; bez przesądów; bez stronny

opera ('opere) s. opera

opera glasses ('operegla:sys) s. lornetka (teatralna)

operate ('operejt) v. działać; zadziałać; oddziaływać; pracować; operować (kims; kogoś); wywoływać; prowadzić; kierować; obsługiwać;spekulować

operation (,ope'rejszyn) s. działanie; czynności; operacja; obsługiwanie; akcja

operative ('oprejtyw) adj. skuteczny; działający; praktyczny; operacyjny;s.pracownik;agent mechanik; robotnik; detektyw; agent wywiadu

operator ('operejter) s. operator; pracownik; obsługujący maszynę; telefonista; kierownik; przemysłowiec; finansista; spekulant

opinion (e'pynjen) s. pogląd; opinia; zdanie;zapatrywnie;sąd

opponent (e'pounent) s. przeciwnik; oponent; adj. przeciwny; przeciwległy

opportunity (,oper'tju:nyty) s. sposobność; okazja

oppose (e'pouz) v. przeciwstawiać; sprzeciwiać się

opposed (e'pouzd) adj. przeciwny;przeciwdziałający

opposite ('epezyt) adj. przeciwny; przeciwległy; odmienny; adv. na przeciwko;na przeciw s. przeciwieństwo;odwrotność

opposition (,ope'zyszyn) s. sprzeciw; opór; opozycja; przeciwstawienie (się); przeciwieństwo;a.opozycyjny

oppress (e'pres) v. przygniatac; uciskać; ciemiężyć; gnębić; nużyć; męczyć

oppression (e'preszyn) s. ucisk

oppressive (e'presyw) adj. uciążliwy; dręczący; gnębicielski; ciężki; duszny;deprymujący

opt (opt) v. wybierać z dwu alternatyw;optować na rzecz cze- ~gos

optical ('optykel) adj. optyczny; wzrokowy;pomocny w widzeniu

optician (op'tyszen) s. optyk

optimism ('optymysem) s. optymizm;pogodny pogląd na życie

optimize ('optymajz) v. używac najwydajniej,najsprawniej

option ('opszyn) s. możnosc wyboru; opcja; wybor; v. wybrac alternatywę

or (o:r) conj. lub; albo; czy; ani; inaczej; czyli; s. złoto; adj. złoty

or else ('o:rels) exp. bo jak nie..; w przeciwnym razie

oral ('o:rel) adj. ustny; doustny; s. egzamin ustny

orange ('oryndż) s. pomarańcza; adj. pomaranczowy

orangeade ('oryn'dżejd) s. oranżada(z pomarańcz ,cukru)

orator ('oreter) s. mówca

orbit ('o:rbyt) s. orbita; oczodół; v. latac w orbicie (ziemi)(słońca etc.)

orchard ('o:rczerd) s. sad

orchestra ('o:rkystra) s. orkiestra

ordain (o:r'dejn) v. wyświęcac; mianowac; nakazywac; przeznaczac;zarządzac;nakazać

ordeal (o:r'di:l) s. ciężka próba; ciężkie doswiadczenie

order ('o:rder) s. rozkaz; zlecenie; zarządzenie; przekaz; porządek; szyk; układ; stan; zakon; order; obrzęd; zamówienie; zadanie; v. rozkazac; zamawiac; komenderowac; zarządzac; wyswiecac; porzadkowac

orderly ('o:rderly) s. posługacz; ordynans; adj. adv. porządny; czysty; dokładny; skromny; spokojny; dyżurny

ordinal ('o:rdynl) s. liczebnik porządkowy; adj. porządkowy

ordinary ('o:rdnry) adj. zwyczajny; zwykły; przeciętny; pospolity; typowy; s. rzecz zwykła,codzienna,przecietna

ore (o:r).s. ruda; kruszec; a. kruszcowy;rudowy

organ ('o:rgen) s. narząd;
organ; organy;czasopismo
organic ('o:rgaenyk) adj. organiczny;usystematyzowany
organization (,o:rgenaj'zejszyn) s. organizacja; organi-
zowanie;struktura;zrzeszenie
organize ('o:genajz) v. organizować;zrzeszyć;nadawać ustrój
organizer('o:genajzer) s. organizator
orgy ('o:rdży) s. orgia
Orient ('o:rjent) adj. orien-
talny; wschodni;s.Wschód(bliski)
orient ('o:rjent) v. oriento-
wać;ukierunkowywać;ustawiać
origin('orydżyn) s. pochodzenie;
poczatek;źrodło;geneza
original (e'rydżynel) adj.
oryginalny; początkowy;
s. oryginał; dziwak
originality (e,rydży'naelyty)
s. oryginalność
originate (e'rydżynejt) v. zapoczątkować; powstawać
ornament ('o:rnament) s. ozdoba; v. ozdabiac;upiększać
ornamental (,o:rne'mentl) adj.
ozdobny; dekoracyjny; zdobni-
czy;upiększający
orphan ('o:rfen) s. sierota;
adj. sierocy; osierocony
orphanage ('o:rfenydż) s. sie-
rociniec; sieroctwo
orthodox ('o:tedoks) adj. pra-
wowierny; prawosławny
oscillate ('osylejt) v. drgać;
wahać się; oscylować
ostrich ('ostrycz) s. struś
other ('adzer) pron. inny; drugi; adv. inaczej;odmiennie
otherwise ('adzerłajz) adv.
inaczej; poza tym; skądinąd
ought (o:t) v, powinien; trzeba;
żeby; należy; zobowiazany etc.
ounce (auns) s. uncja; odrobina; lampart;1/16 funta
our ('aur) adj. nasz
ours ('auerz) pron. nasz
ourselves (auer'selwz) pl.pron.
my; my sami;(dla)nas,etc.
oust (aust) v. usuwać; wypierać; wyrzucać;wywłaszczać

out (aut) adv. na zewnątrz;
precz; poza; na dworze; poza
domem;nieobecnym(być) etc.
out-and-out (auten'aut) adj.
całkowity; adv. całkowicie
out of ('autow) adv. z; bez;
poza ;nie (modne,rozsądne)
outbalance (aut'baelens) v.
przeważyć;przewyższać
outbid (aut'byd) v. przelicy-
towac;dac więcej (niż inny)
outbreak ('autbrejk) s. wybuch
(np. wojny)(epidemii etc.)
outburst ('autbe:rst) s. wybuch (np. gniewu)(vulkanu)
outcast ('autka:st) s. wyrzutek; wygnaniec; adj. wygnany
outcome ('autkam) s. wynik;
rezultat;konsekwencje
outcry ('autkraj) s. okrzyk;
wrzawa;silny protest
outdoors ('aut'do:rz) adj. na
wolnym powietrzu; s. wolna
przestrzeń;adv.zewnatrz(domu)
outer ('auter) adj. zewnętrzny
outermost ('auter'moust) adj.
najbardziej zewnętrzny
outfit ('autfyt) s. wyposażenie; drużyna; zespół; towarzystwo; zestaw narzędzi; v. wyposażyć; zaopatrywać;wyekwipować
outgoing ('aut,gouyng)adj. od-
chodzacy; odjeżdżający; przyjazny;komunikatywny;towarzyski
outgrow (aut'grou) v. przerastać; wyrastać z..; wyrosc(z ro-
outing ('autyng) s. wycieczka(na
otwarte morze,do lasu etc.);wy-
outlast (aut'la:st) v. przetrwać (coś,kogoś);wytrwać dłużej
outlaw ('aut-lo:) v. zakazywać;
wyjmowac spod prawa; s. przestępca; banita;notoryczny krymi-
outlet ('autlet) s. wylot; rynek zbytu; wyjście; ujscie
outline ('autlajn) s. zarys;
szkic; v. konturować; szkicować; przedstawiać(plany etc,)
outlive (aut'lyw) v. przeżyć;
przetrwać;wytrwać dłużej
outlook ('autluk) s. widok; pogląd; obserwacja; widoki
(na przyszłość);czaty

outnumber (aut'namber) v. przewyższać liczebnie;być liczniej-
szym
out-of-date (autew'dejt) adj.
przestarzały; niemodny
outpatient ('aut,pejszent) s.
pacjent dochodzący (z domu),
output ('autput) s. wydajność;
wydobycie; moc; produkcja
outrage ('autrejdż) s, gwałt;
zniewaga; v. gwałcić; znieważać;urągać(zdrowemu rozsądkowi)
outrageous (aut'rejdżes) adj.
wołający o pomstę; bezecny;
gwałtowny;skandaliczny;obrażają-
cy
outright (aut'rajt) adj. całkowity; zupełny; stanowczy; bezpośredni; adv. odrazu; całkowicie; zupełnie; otwarcie
outrun (aut'ran) v. przegonić;
wyścignąć
outside ('aut'sajd) s. okładka;
fasada; strona zewnętrzna; adj.
zewnętrzny; adv. zewnątrz;
oprócz; z wyjątkiem
outside right ('aut'sajd'rajt)
exp. na zewnątrz po prawej
outsider ('aut'sajder) s. człowiek obcy; niewtajemniczony;
laik; obcy zawodnik
outsize ('autsajz) s. wielkość
nietypowa, za duża
outskirts ('aut,ske:rts) s.
krańce; kraj; peryferie
outspoken (aut'spouken) adj.
szczery; otwarcie wypowiedzia-
ny, bez ogródek,prosto w oczy
outspread (aut'spred) adj. rozpostarty; rozpowszechniony
outstanding ('autstaendyng)
adj. wybitny; wyróżniający się;
otwarty; niezałatwiony; zaległy; wystający; sterczący
outstretched (aut'streczt) adj.
rozpostarty; wyciągnięty
outward ('autłerd) adj. zewnetrz-
ny; powierzchowny; pozorny;
cielesny; s. strona zewnętrzna;
wygląd zewnętrzny;adv.na zewnątrz
outweigh (aut'łej) v. przeważyć
outwit (aut'łyt) v. przechytrzyć
oval ('ouwel) s. owal; adj.
owalny;owalnego kształtu

oven ('own) s. piekarnik; piec
over ('ouwer) prep. na; po;
w; przez; ponad; nad; powyżej;
adv. na drugą stronę; po powierzchni; całkowicie; od początku; zbytnio; znowu; raz
jeszcze(odrabiać zadanie etc.)
over again ('ouwer,e'gejn) adv.
na nowo; jeszcze raz
over-and-over ('ouwer,end'ouwer) adv. w kółko
overall ('ouwero:l) adj. ogólny; wszystko obejmujący;
pl. s. kombinezon roboczy
overboard ('ouwerbo:rd) adv.
(zaniechać) za burtę (wyrzucić)
overburden (,ouwe'rbe:rden) v.
przeładowywać; s. ciężar po-
kładów (np. nad kopalnią);
nadmiar ciężaru;ciężar warstw
overcast ('ouwerka:st) adj. za-
chmurzony; mroczny; ponury;
obrębiony; v. mroczyć; chmurzyć (się); obrębiać
overcharge (,ouwer'cza:rdż) v.
przeciążać; zdzierać (pieniądze); stawiać za wysokie ceny
overcoat ('ouwerkout) s. płaszcz
overcome (,ouwer'kam) v. pokonać
overcrowd (,ouwer'kraud) s. za-
tłoczyć;przepełniać
overdo (,ouwerdu:) v. przeciążać; przesadzać; przegotowywać;
niszczyć przesadą;robić za dużo
overdraw (,ouwer'dro:) v. wyczerpać (konto); przesadzać;
pisać czeki bez pokrycia
overdue (,ouwer'dju:) adj. zaległy;zapóźniony(pociąg etc.)
overestimate (,ouwer'esty,mejt)
v. przecenić; s. za wysoka
ocena;zbyt duże oczekiwania
overflow (,ouwer'flou) v. przepełniać; przelewać; s. wylew;
przelew;kanał przelewowy etc.
overgrow (,ouwer'grou) v. obrastać; przerastać; rosnąć
nadmiernie;rość zbyt szybko
overhang ('ouwer'haeng) v. zwisać; sterczeć; zagrażać;
s. występ; zwis; nawis (dachu);
występ(skały);zwis(skalny etc.)

overhaul (.ouwer'ho:l) v.gruntownie naprawic; gruntownie zbadac; s. gruntowny remont

overhead ('ouwer'hed) s. wydatki administracyjne; adv., powyzej; na gorze; adj. gorny

overhear (,ouwer'hier) v. uslyszec przypadkiem; podsluchac

overheat ('ouwerhi:t) v. przegrzac; s. nadmiernie goraco; przegrzanie

overjoyed (,ouwer'dzojd) adj. nieposiadajacy sie z radosci

overlap (,ouwer'laep) v. zachodzic na siebie; s. zachodzenie (na siebie)

overload (,ouwer'loud) v.przeladowac,s.nadmierny ciezar; przeciazenie(dachu etc.)

overlook (,ouwer'luk) v. przeoczyc; puszczac plazem; miec widok z gory; nadzorowac; wybaczyc; widok z gory; nadzor

overlord ('ouwerlo:rd) s. suzeren; samodzierzca

over-night ('ouwer'najt) adv. przez noc; poprzedniego wieczoru; adj. nocny; na noc

overpass (,ouwer'oa:s) s.skrzyzowanie wiaduktem; przejazd wiaduktem; v. przecinac; przekraczac; przewyzszac; przezwyciezac; pomijac(w kolejce etc.)

overrate ('ouwer'rejt) v. przeceniac;spodziewac sie zbyt duzo

overrule (,ouwer'ru:l) v. opanowac; uchylac; odrzucac; uniewazniac;zmieniac czyjes postanowienie

overrun (,ouwer'ran) v. najechac; zalewac; przelewac; s. przekraczanie ceny umowionej

overseas ('ouwer'si:z) adv. za morzem; do krajow zamorskich; adj. zamorski

oversee ('ouwer'si:) v. dozorowac; dogladac

overseer ('ouwer'si:er) s. nadzorca

overshadow ('ouwer'szaedou) v. przycmiewac; zacmiewac

oversight ('ouwersajt) s. przeoczenie

oversleep ('ouwer'sli:p) v. zaspac; przespac

overstrain ('ouwer'strain) v. przemeczac; s. przeciazenie; przemeczenie

overtake ('ouwer'tejk) v. doganiac; przeganiac; zaskoczyc

overthrow ('ouwer'grou) v., przewrocic; obalic; pobic; s. obalenie

overtime ('ouwertajm) s. godziny nadliczbowe; adv. nadprogramowa; adj. nadprogramowy; v. przeswietlic; przeeksponowac

overtone ('ouwertoun) s. niedomowienie; sugestia; akcent; glowna nuta

overture ('ouwer,tjuer) s. rozpoczecie rokowan; propozycja; uwertura; v. proponowac

overturn (,ouwer'te:rn) v. wywracac; obalac; s. przewracanie; przewrot;podboj

overweight ('ouwer'lejt) s. nadwaga; dodatkowa waga; otylosc; adj. ponad normalna wage

overwhelm (,ouwer'hlelm) v. przygniatac; przywalac; zalewac; rujnowac; ogarniac

overwork ('ouwer'le:rk) v. przepracowywac sie; przeciazac praca; zmuszac do za ciezkiej pracy; przemeczac sie; s. nadmierna praca

ovulate ('ouwjulejt) v. jajeczkowac; wytwarzac jaja

owe (ol) v.byc winnym; zawdzieczac

owing ('olyng) adj. dluzny; nalezny; prep. z powodu; skutkiem

owing to ('olyng,tu) prep. poniewaz

owl (aul) s. sowa

own (oln) v. miec; posiadac; przyznawac (sie); adj. wlasny; rodzony

owner ('olner) s. wlasciciel

ownership ('olnerszyp) s. wlasnosc; posiadanie

ox (oks) s. wol; pl. oxen

oxen ('oksen) pl. woły; zob.ox
oxide ('oksajd) s. tlenek
oxidation (oksy'dejszyn) s.
utlenienie; oksydacja
oxidize (oksydajz) v. utleniac
oxygen (oksydżen) s. tlen
oyster ('ojster) s. ostryga
ozone ('ouzoun) s. ozon
p (pi:) szesnasta litera
angielskiego alfabetu
pa (pa:) s. tato
pace (pejs) s. krok; chód;
v. kroczyc; mierzyc krokami;
ustalac rytm kroku; cwiczyc
krok (np. konia); przebywac
(drogę);chodzić(tam i na zad)
pacer ('pejser) s. regulator
rytmu (serca; kroku etc)
pacific (pe'syfyk) adj. spokojny; pokojowy
pacify ('paesyfaj) v. uspakajac; zaspokajac
pack (paek) s. pakunek; tłumok;
toboł; stek; sfora; okład;
kupa; v. pakowac; opakowac;
owijac; stłoczyc; napychac;
objuczyc; zbierac w stado
pack up ('paek,ap) v. spakowac
package ('paekydż) s. pakunek;
paczka
package deal ('paekydż'di:l)
s. przyjęcie złożonej propo-
zycji bez zmian
packer ('paeker) s. pakier;
przedsiębiorca od pakowania
artykułow żywnościowych; maszyna do pakowania
packet ('kaekyt) s. pakiet;
v. zawijac
packing ('paekyng) s. pakowa-
nie; opakowanie; uszczelka;
okładzina; tampon
packthread ('paektred) s. szpagat
pact (paekt) s. pakt; układ
pad (paed) s. wyściółka; notes;
blok (papieru); bibularz; łapa;
pa; podkładka; v. wysciełac;
wywoływac; rozdymac
padding ('paedyng) s. obicie;
wyściółka; podbicie; podszy-
cie; rozwadnianie tekstu

paddle ('paedl) s. wiosełko
kajakowe; v. wiosłowac
paddock ('paedek) s. wybieg
(koński)
padlock ('paedlok) s. kłodka
v. zamykac na kłodkę
pagan ('pejgen) s. poganin;
adj. pogański
page (pejdż) s. stronnica;
karta; paz; goniec
pagent ('paedżent) s. widowisko
(np. historyczne)
paid (pejd) adj. zapłacony; płatny; zob. pay
pail (pejl) s. wiadro
pain (pejn) s. ból; cierpienie;
trud; starania; v. zadawac ból;
bolec; dolegac
painful ('pejnful) adj. bolesny;
przykry
painless (pajnlys) adj. bezbolesny
paint (pejnt) s. farba; szminka;
v. malowac
paintbrush ('pejntbrasz) s. pędzel
painter ('pejnter) s. malarz
painting ('pejntyng) s. malarstwo; obraz
pair (peer) s. para; parka; stadło; y. dobierac do pary; stanowic parę
pajamas (pe'dża;mez) pl. piżama
pal (pael) s. kumpel; druh; przyjaciel
palace ('paelys) s. pałac
palate ('paelyt) s. podniebienie
pale (pejl) s. pal; granica; adj.
blady; v. otaczac palami; blednąc; spowodowac bledniecie
pallor ('paeler) s. bladosc
palm (pa:m) s. palma; dłoń;
piędz; v. ukrywac w dłoni; dotykac dłonią
palpitation (,paelpy'tejszyn)
s. palpitacja; mocne bicie serca;kołatanie serca;drżenie;dygota-
nie
pamper ('paemper) v. rozpiesz-
czac;przekarmiac;zbyt pobłażac
pamphlet ('paemflyt) s. broszura natury polemicznej na tematy
bieżące, kontrowersyjne etc.

pan (paen) s. patelnia; rondel;
rynka; szalka; panewka; gęba;
kra; v. gotować na patelni;
udawać się; krytykować
pancake ('paen,kejk) s. naleśnik; adj. płaski
pane (paen) s. szyba; krata;
ścianka; płaszczyzna
panel ('paenl) s. tafla; oto-
czyna; płyta; wstawka; tablica (rozdzielcza); komitet;
lista (przysięgłych; lekarzy
etc); czaprak
pang (paeng)s. ostry ból; męka;
wyrzuty (sumienia etc.)
panhandler (,paen'haendler) s.
kwestarz; ksiądz z tacą
panic ('paenyk) s. panika; popłoch; v.wpaść w panikę; wywoływać panikę ;poddać się panice
pan-Slavism ('paen'sla:wyzem)
s. panslawizm
pansy ('paensy) s. bratek
pant (paent) s. zadyszka;
v. sapać; dyszeć
panther ('paenţer) s. pantera
panties ('paentyz) pl. majtki
(damskie)
pantry ('paentry) s. spiżarnia
pants (paents) pl. spodnie; kalesony
panty hose ('paenty'houz) s.
rajstopy; pończochy z majtkami
pap (paep) s. papka; bzdury;
sutka; brodawka piersiowa
papa ('pa:pe) s. papa; tata
paper ('pejper) s. papier; gazeta; tapeta; rozprawa nauko-
wa; papierowe pieniądze; adj.
papierowy; rzekomy; v. zawiną
w papier; tapetować
paper-backed ('pejper.baekt)
adj. w papierowej okładce;
kieszonkowe wydanie książki
paper-bag ('pejper,baeg) s.
torba papierowa
paper-hanger ('pejper,haenger)
s. tapeciarz
paper-hangings ('pejperhaengyngs)
pl. tapety
paper-money ('pejper'many) s.
pieniądze papierowe

paper-weight ('pejper,łejt) s.
przycisk
par (pa:r) s. stan równości;
norma
parable ('paerebl) s. przypowieść
parachute ('paere,szu:t) s.
spadochron
parachutist ('paere,szu:tyst)
s. spadochroniarz
parade (pe'rejd) s. parada; pochód; rewia; defilada; popisywać się; obnosić się (z
czyms)
paradise ('paere,dajs) s. raj;
adj. rajski
paragraph ('paere,gra:f) s.
ustęp; odnośnik; notatka;
v. dzielić na ustępy; pisać
notatkę
parallel ('paere,lel) adj.
równoległy; odpowiedni (czemuś)
s. równoległa; równoleżnik; porównanie; v. być równoległym;
kłaść równolegle; zestawiać;
znaleźć odpowiednik
paralyze ('paere,lajz) v. pa-
raliżować; porażać
paralysis (pe'raelysys) s. paraliż
paramount ('paere,maunt) adj.
główny; najważniejszy; kapi-
talny; najwyższy
parasite ('paere.sajt) s. pasożyt
parcel ('pa:rsl) s. paczka;
działka; v. dzielić; pakować
w paczki
parch ('pa:rcz) v. wysuszać
(się); prażyć; cierpieć z
pragnienia
parchment ('pa:rczment) s. pergamin
pardon('pa:rdn) s. ułaskawienie;
przebaczenie; v. przebaczać;
darować ;ułaskawiać
pardon me ('pa:rdn,mi:) exp.:
przepraszam
pardonable ('pa:rdnebl) adj.
wybaczalny
pare (peer) v. obcinać; obie-
rać; obskrobać

parent ('peerent) s. ojciec; matka; rodziciel;rodzicielka

parental (pe'rentl) adj. rodzicielski

parenthesis (pe'rentysys) s. nawias

parentheses (pe'renty,si:z) pl. nawiasy

parings ('peerynz) pl. łupiny; obrzynki

parish ('paerysz) s. parafia

parishioner (pe'ryszener) s. parafianin

park (pa:rk) s. park; postój samochodów; v. parkować

parking ('pa:rkyng) s. postój samochodów; parkowanie

parking garage ('pa:rkyng'gaera:ż) s. garaż parkingowy

parking lot ('pa:rkyn,lot) s. plac parkingowy

parking meter ('pa:rkyn'mi:ter) s. licznik do płacenia za parking(na ograniczony czas)

parking ticket ('pa:rkyn'tykyt) s. mandat karny za złe parkowanie lub za niezapłacenie

parkway ('pa:rkłej) s. czteroliniowa szosa, przedzielona roślinnością

parliament ('pa:rlyment) s. parlament

parliamentary (,pa:rly'mentery) adj. parlamentarny

parlo(u)r ('pa:rler) s. salon; sala; pokój (przyjęć)

parquet ('pa:rkej) s. parkiet; v. wyłożyć parkietem

parrot ('paeret) s. papuga; v. powtarzać jak papuga

parsley ('pa:rsly) s. pietruszka; a. pietruszkowy

parry ('paery) v. parować; odpierać; s. odparcie

parson ('pa:rsn) s. proboszcz

parsonage ('pa:rsnydż) s. plebania

part (pa:rt) s. część; ustęp; udział; rola; strona; przedział (włosów); v; rozchodzić (się); rozdzielać; dzielić; pękać; robić (przedział); wyjeżdżać;adj.mniejszy niż całość

partake (pa:r'tejk) y. brak, udział; dzielić coś z kims; zob. take

partaken (pa:r'tejkn) v. zob. partake

partial ('pa;rszel) adj. stronniczy; częściowy; mający słabość do...;nie pełny

partiality (,pa:rszy'aelyty) s. stronniczość; upodobanie

participant (pa:r'tysypent) s. uczestnik;adj.uczestniczący

participate (pa:r'tysypejt) v. brać udział

particle ('pa:rtykl) s. cząstka; odrobina; partykuła

particular ('per'tykjuler) adj. szczególny; szczegółowy; specjalny; prywatny; grymaśny dokładny; uważny; dziwny; niezwyczajny; ostrożny; s. szczegół; fakt

particularity (per,tykju'laeryty) s. osobliwość; szczegółowość; drobiazgowość; wybredność

particularly (per,tykju'laerly) adv. osobliwie; szczególnie

particulars (per'tykjulers) s. dane osobiste

parting ('pa:rtyng) s. przedziałek (włosów); rozstanie; rozdział; pożegnanie; rozdroże; zgon

partition (pa:r'tyszyn) s. podział; rozbiór; rozdział; v. dzielić; przegradzać

partition off (pa:rtyszyn,of) v. oddzielać

partly ('pa:rtly) adv. częściowo;po części; poniekąd

partner ('pa:rtner) s. wspólnik

partnership ('pa:rtnerszyp) s. spółka

partook (pa:r'tuk) v. zob. partake

partridge('pa:trydż) s. kuropatwa

part-time ('pa:rt,tajm) adv. na niepełnym etacie; na niepełnym czasie;adj.niepełnoetatowy

party ('pa:rty) s. partia; przyjęcie towarzyskie; towarzystwo; grupa;strona; uczestnik;osobnik

pass (pa:s) s. przełęcz; odnoga
rzeki; przepustka; wypad; bilet; umizg; sztuczka; v, przechodzic; mijac; pomijac; zdac;
przekazac; wymijac; wyprzedzac;
przeprowadzic; przewyższac;
spędzac; puszczać w obieg; podawac; odchodzic; umierac;
dziac się; krążyc
pass away ('pa:se,łej) v. odchodzic;umierac
pass by ('pa:s,baj) v. mijac;
pomijac
pass for ('pa:s,fo:r) v. uda-
wac (kogos)
pass out ('pa:s,aut) v. zemdlec;
umrzec; wyjsc
pass round ('pa:s,raund) v.
podawac wkoło (np. gosciom)
pass through ('pa:s,tru) v.
przechodzic (przez, na wskros)
passable ('paesebl) adj. nadający się do przebycia;
(stopien) dostateczny; znosny
passage ('paesydż) s. przejscie;
przejazd; przeprawa; przelot;
upływ; korytarz; urywek tekstu
passenger ('paesyndżer) s. pasażer; pasażerka
passer-by ('pa:ser'baj) s. prze-
chodzien
passion ('paeszyn) s. namiętnosc;
pasja; Męka Panska; stan bierny
passionate ('paeszenyt) adj. namiętny; porywczy; zapalczywy;
żarliwy ;ognisty
passive ('paesyw) adj. bierny;
s. strona bierna
passport ('pa:s,po:rt) s. paszport
password('pa:s,łó:rd) s. hasło
past (pa:st) adj. przeszły;
miniony; ubiegły; prep. za;
obok; po; przed; adv. obok;
s. przeszłosc; czas przeszły
paste (pejst) s. pasta; ciasto;
klej maczny; klajster; masa;
makaron; uderzenie (slang);
v. przylepiac; oblepiac;
obic (kogos)
pasteboard ('pejst,bo:rd) s.
karton; tektura; adj.tekturo-
wy; kartonowy; lichy

pastime ('pa:s,tajm) s. roz-
rywka(po pracy etc.)
pastry('pejstry) s. wyroby cu-
kiernicze; ciastka
past tense ('pa:st tens) s.
czas przeszły (gram.)
pasture ('pa:sczer) s. pastwisko
pat (paet) s. głaskanie; kle-
panie; krążek (np. masła);
v. pogłaskac; poklepac; po-
chwalic (kogos) adv. trafnie;
w sam raz; adj. trafny; biegły ;na czasie;zupełnie własciwy
patch (paecz) s. łata; plama;
skrawek; pólko; zagon; grządka; klapka (na oko); przepaska; v. łatac; załatac; szyc
z łat; sztukowac; naprawic;
skleic; załagodzic
patch pocket ('paecz,pokyt) s.
naszywana kieszen
patchwork ('paecz,łe:rk) s.
łatanina; szachownica
pate (pejt) s. slang: głowa;
łeb; pała;szczyt głowy
patent ('paetnt) s. patent;
v. opatentowac; a. patentowa-
ny; opatentowany ;oczywisty
patent ('pejtnt) adj. jasny;
otwarty; oczywisty ;chroniony
patentem
patent-leather ('paetnt'ledzer)
s. skóra lakierowana
paternal (pe'te:rnl) adj. oj-
cowski; po ojcu
paternity (pe'te:rnyty) s.
ojcostwo; pochodzenie po ojcu;
autorstwo (książki,planu etc.)
path (pa:s) s. sciezka; tor;
droga ruchu; zob. paths
pathetic (pe'tetyk) adj. żałosny: smutny; uczuciowy;
wzruszający; rozrzewniający
paths (pa:sz) pl. sciezki; tory;
drogi ruchu
patience ('pejszens) s. cierpliwosc; pasjans
patient ('pejszent) adj. cierpliwy; wytrwały; s. pacjent;
pacjentka; chory; chora
patio ('pa:ti:o) s. ogródek
wewnętrzny ; taras

patriot ('pejtryet) s. patry-
jota
patriotic(,paetry'otyk) adj.
patriotyczny
patriotism ('paetrye,tyzem) s.
patriotyzm
patrol (pe'troul) v. patrolo-
wac; s. patrolowanie; patrol
patrolman (pe'troulmen) s. policjant (drogowy USA)
patron ('pejtren) s. klient;
opiekun; patron
patronage ('paetrenydż) s.
opieka; poparcie; klientela;
US rozdawanie posad etc.;
protekcjonalnosc; przywileje;
posady
patronize ('paetre,najz) v. popierac; protegowac; traktowac
protekcjonalnie
patsy ('paecy) s. oferma przez
wszystkich zawsze naduzywana
patter ('paeta) s. stukot; traj-
kot; trajkotanie; gwara; kle-
panie; szybka recytacja; żargon; v. stukac; bębnic; traj-
kotac; klepac (np. pacierze);
odklepywac; klapac; gadac
pattern ('paetern) s. próbka;
wzór; układ; materiał na suknię lub ubranie (USA); zespół;
cechy charakterystyczne; slady
dy kul (na tarczy) v. wzoro-
wac; modelowac; ozdabiac wzo-
rami
paunch ('pa:ncz) s. (duży)
brzuch; żołądek krowy
paunchy ('pa:nczy) adj. brzu-
chaty ;z wydatnym brzuchem
pause (po:z) s. przerwa; pauza;
v. robic przerwę; wahac się
pave (pejw) v. brukowac; torowac drogę
pavement ('pejwment) s. bruk;
posadzka; materiał do bruko-
wania
pavement-café ('pejwment'kaefej)
s. kawiarnia ze stolikami na
chodniku
paw (po:) s. łapa; (slang):
tatuś; v. uderzac łapą lub
kopytem; miętosic w łapach;
macac (poufale)

pawn (po:n) s. zastaw; fant;
pionek; v. zastawiac; dawac
w zastaw
pawnbroker ('po:n,brouker) s.
lichwiarz pożyczający pod zastaw; właściciel lombardu
pawnshop ('po:n-szop) s. lom-
bard; sklep zastawniczy
pay; paid; paid (pej; peid;
peid)
pay (pej) v. płacic; zapłacic;
wynagradzac; udzielac (uwagi);
dawac (dochód); opłacac (się)
s. płaca; zapłata; pobory;
wynagrodzenie; adj. płatny
(np. automat telefoniczny);
opłacalny
pay back ('pej baek) v. zwrócic
dług; odpłacac
payday ('pej dej) s. dzień wy-
płaty
pay down ('pej dałn) v. dawac
zadatek; płacic pierwszą ratę
gotówka
pay for ('pej,fo:r) v. płacic
(za cos)
pay in ('pej,yn) v. wpłacac
pay off ('pej,of) v. spłacac
pay out ('pej,aut) v. wydatko-
wac; wypuszczac linę (na statku); wypłacac; płacic
pay up ('pej,ap) v. wyrównywac
(dług); zapłacic
payable ('pejebl) adj. płatny;
dochodowy; opłacający się
payee ('pej'i:) s. odbiorca
płatności
payer ('pejer) s. płatnik
payment ('pejment) s. płatność;
wypłata; zapłata
pea (pi:) s. groch; ziarnko
grochu
peace (pi:s) s. pokój; pojednanie; spokój
peaceful ('pi:sful) adj. spokojny; pokojowy
peach (pi:cz) s. brzoskwinia;
wspaniała rzecz, dziewczyna,
człowiek; v. (slang):sypac;
donosic (na kogos)
peacock ('pi:,kok) s. paw;
v. pysznic się jak paw; chodzic
jak paw; paradowac

peak (pi:k) s. (ostry) szczyt;
wierzchołek; daszek (u czapki);
szpic; garb (krzywej)
peak hour ('pi:k'auer) s. godzina szczytu ruchu
peal (pi:l) s. huk; łoskot; bicie w dzwony; huczny śmiech;
zespoł dzwonów; v. huczec;
bic w dzwony; grac (cos) hucz-
nie
peanut ('pi:nat) s. orzeszek
ziemny; drobnostka; a; drobny;
prowincjonalny
pear (peer).s. gruszka
pearl (pe:rl) s. perła
peasant ('pezent) s. chłop;
wiesniak; adj. chłopski
peat (pi:t) s. torf
peat bog ('pi:t'bog) s. torfowisko
pebble ('pebl) s. kamyk; oto-
czak; v. granulowac; obrzucac
kamykami
peck (pek) v. dziobac; wcinac
(jedzenie); dziobnąc; cmoknąc
(mężda); stukac; wydziobac;
dłubac; odziobac; v. dziobnięcie; cmok; slad dziobania
peculiar (py'kju:ljer) adj.
szczegolny; dziwny; osobliwy;
charakterystyczny;dziwaczny
peculiarity (py'kju:li'aeryty)
s. własciwosc; cecha; osobliwosc; dziwacznosc
pedal ('pedl) s. pedał; nuta
pedałowa; v. pedałowac; naciskac pedał; ('pi:dl) adj. pe-
dałowy; nożny
peddle ('pedl) v. sprzedawac po
domach; byc domokrążcą; wydzielac po trochu
peddler ('pedler) s. domokrążca
pedestal ('pedystl) s. piedestał;
podstawa;Ɂstawiac na piedestał
pedestrian (py'destrjen) adj.
pieszy; przyziemny; prozaiczny;
s. piechur;pieszy człowiek
pedestrian crossing (pu'destrjen'krosyng) v. przejscie dla
pieszych; zebra; pasy
pedigree ('pedygri:) s. rodowód;
drzewo genealogiczne
pedlar('peler)s.przekupien;hand-

peek ('pi:k) v. podglądac
peel (pi:l) s. skóra; skórką;
łupa; v. obierac; zdzierac;
łuszczyc się; (slang):rozbierac
(się)
peep (pi:p) v. zerkac; podglądac;
wynurzac (się); wychodzic nie-
postrzeżenie
peeping Tom ('pi:pyng,tom) s.
podglądający natręt
peer (pier) s. rowny (komus)
stanem, pochodzeniem etc.
peerless ('pierlys) adj. nie-
zrownany
peevish ('pi:wysh) adj. drazliwy; zły; gniewny;zirytowany
peg (peg) s. czop; kołek; zatyczka; szpunt; v. zakołkowac;
przymocowac kołkami
pelican ('pelyken) s. pelikan
pelt (pelt) s. futro; kanonada;
grzmocenie; pospiech; v. ostrze-
liwac; obrzucac; obsypywac gradem; rzucac zniewagi; obsypywac
zniewagami; walic
pelvis ('pelwys) s. miednica;
a. miedniczny
pen (pen) s. pioro; kojec; ogrodzenie; schron; (slang):więzie-
nie; v. pisac; układac list;
zamykac w ogrodzeniu
penal ('pi:nl) adj. karny; karalny
penalty ('penlty) s. kara
penalty kick ('penlty,kik) s.
karny strzał (do bramki)
penance ('penens) s. pokuta
pence (pens) pl. grosze; zob.
penny
pencil ('pensl) s. ołowek; ry-
sowac; pisac
pencil sharpner ('pensl'sza:rp-
ner) s. strugaczka do ołowka
pendant ('pendent) s. wisiorek;
proporzec; adj. wiszący; zwi-
sający; nierozstrzygnięty; to-
czący się; do rozstrzygnięcia
pending ('pendyng) adj. niezałatwiony; będący w toku; wiszący; prep.: aż do; podczas
penetrate ('peny,trejt) v. przenikac; przepajac; przedostawac
się przez ;wtargnąc;zanurzyc

penetration („peny'trejszyn)
s. penetracja; przenikanie;
przenikliwość
pen friend („penfrend) s. znajomy z listów
penguin ('pengłyn) s. pingwin
penholder ('pen,houlder) s.
piórnik; obsadka; stojak na
pióro
penicillin („peny'sylyn) s.
penicylina
peninsula(py'nynsjule) s. półwysep
penitent ('penytent) s. żałujący grzesznik; pokutnik; adj.
żałujący; skruszony
penitentiary („peny'tenszery)
s. więzienie; adj. karany
więzieniem; poprawczy
penknife ('pen.najf) s. scyzoryk
penniless ('penylys) adj. w nędzy; bez grosza
penny ('peny) s. cent; grosz;
pl. pennies ('penyz); Br.pl.
pence (pens)
pennyworth ('penyłe:rs) s. wartość centa; exp. za centa
pension ('penszyn) s. renta;
emerytura; pensjonat; v. wyznaczać pensje; pensjonować
pension off ('penszyn,of) v.
przenosić na emeryturę
pensive ('pensyw) adj. zamyslo-
ny
penthouse ('penthaus) s. mieszkanie z ogrodem na szczycie
budynku; przybudówka na dachu
people („pi:pl) s. ludzie;
ludność; lud; v. zaludniać
pep (pep) s. animusz; werwa;
wigor; adj. ożywiony; wesoły;
dowcipny; dodający animuszu
pep pills ('pep,pyls) pl. pigułki podniecające
pep up ('pep,ap) v. ożywić; dodać animuszu
pepper ('peper) s. pieprz; papryka; v. pieprzyć; kropić;
zasypywać kulami; dać lanie
per (pe:r) prep. przez; za; na;
według; co do;za pośrednictwem

perceive (per'si:w) v. uświadamiać sobie; odczuć; dostrzegać;
spostrzegać
percent (per'sent) s. odsetek;
od sta
percentage (per'sentydż) s. odsetek; procent; od sta
perceptible (per'septebl) adj.
dostrzegalny
perception (per'sepszyn) s.
spostrzeganie;percepcja
perch (pe:rcz) s. okoń; grzęda;
żerdź; pręt; v. siedzieć na
grzędzie; sadzać na grzędzie
percussion (per'kaszyn) s. uderzenie; zderzenie;bicie(bębna)
peremptory (per'emptery) adj.
stanowczy; apodyktyczny; ostateczny; nieodwołalny
perfect ('pe:rfykt) adj. doskonały; zupełny; v. udoskonalić;
wykończyć
perfect tense ('perfykt'tens)
s. gram. czas przeszły dokona-
ny
perfection (per'fekszyn) s.
doskonałość; szczyt; wykończenie; udoskonalenie
perforate ('pe:rferejt) v.
przedziurawiać; dziurkować;
przenikać; przebijać się
perform (per'fo:rm) v. wykonywać; odgrywać; spełniać; występować
performance (per'fo:rmens) s.
przedstawienie; wyczyn; wykonanie; spełnienie
performer (per'former) s. wy-
konawca
perfume ('pe:rfju:m) s. perfuma;
zapach ; (pe'rfju:m) v. perfu-
mować
perhaps (per'haeps, praeps) adv.
może; przypadkiem
peril ('peryl) s. niebezpieczeństwo; ryzyko; v. narazić
na niebezpieczeństwo
perilous ('peryles) adj. niebezpieczny; ryzykowny
period ('pieried) s. okres;
period; menstruacja; kropka;
kres; pauza;miesiączka;a.stylo-
wy

periodic (,piery'odyk) adj.
okresowy; periodyczny
periodical (,piery'odykel) s.
czasopismo; periodyk; adj.
okresowy; periodyczny
perish ('perysz) v. zgiąć;
niszczyć; nękać; trapić; gnębić;ginąc (przedwczesną śmiercią)
perishable ('peryszebl) adj.
zniszczalny; s; łatwo psujący się towar
perjury ('pe:rdżery) s. krzy-
woprzysięstwo; złamanie
obietnicy
perm (pe:rm) s. trwała ondulacja
permanent ('pe:rmenent) adj.
trwały; permanentny
permanent wave ('pe:rmenent,
,łejw) s. trwała ondulacja
permeable ('pe:rmjebl) adj.
przepuszczalny; przenikalny
permission (per'myszyn) s. pozwolenie; zezwolenie
permit (per'myt) s. pisemne
zezwolenie; pozwolenie; v.po-
zwalać; zezwalać; dopuszczać
perpendicular (,pe:rpen'dykju-
ler) adj. prostopadły; s, prostopadła; pion
perpetual (per'petjuel) adj.
wieczny; wieczysty; trwały;
dożywotni
persecute ('pe:rsy,kju:t) v.
prześladować
persecution (,pe:rsy'kju:szyn)
s. prześladowanie
persecutor ('pe:rsy,kju:ter) s.
prześladowca
persevere (,pe:rsy'wier) v.
wytrwać
persist (pe'rsyst) v. obstawać;
wytrwać; upierać się
persistence (per'systens); per-
sistency (per'systensy) s. wy-
trwałość; uporczywość; trwałość
persistent (per'systent) adj. wytrwały; uporczywy; trwały
person ('pe:rson) s. osoba;
człowiek
personage ('pe:rsonydż) s.
osobistość;ważny człowiek

personal ('pe:rsenel) adj. osobisty; robiący osobiste uwagi;
s. wiadomość osobista
personality (,pe:se'naelyty) s.
osobowość; powierzchowność;
postawa; indywidualność; pl.
wycieczki (uwagi) osobiste
personify (pe:r'sony,faj), v.
uosabiać; personifikować
personnel (,pe:rse'n el) s.
personel
personnel manager (,pe:rse'-
'nel'maenydżer) s. kierownik
oddziału personalnego; personalny
perspiration (,pe:rspy'rejszyn)
s. pocenie się; pot
perspire (,pe:r'spajer) v. pocić się; wypacać się
persuade (pe:r'słejd) v. przekonywać; namawiać
persuasion (pe:r'słejżyn) s.
perswazja; przekonywanie;
namawianie; przekonanie; wyznanie; wierzenie
persuasive (pe:r'słejsyw) adj.
przekonywujący; s. motyw; pobudka (do czegoś)
pert (pe:rt) adj. śmiały; arogancki; (slang) żwawy
pertain (per'tejn) v. należeć
do czegos; być właściwym czemuś; odnosić się; wchodzić
w zakres
perusal (pe'ru:zal) s. przestu-
diowanie; dokładne przeczyta-
nie
peruse (pe'ru:z) v. czytać
uważnie; studiować (np. twarz)
pervade (per'wejd) v. przenikać;
owładnąć; ogarniać; szerzyć się
perverse (per'we:rs) adj. przewrotny; przekorny; wyuzdany
pesky ('pesky) adj. (slang): dokuczliwy; natrętny;cholerny
pessimism ('pesy,myzem) s. pe-
symizm ;spodziewanie się najgorszego
pest (pest) s. plaga; zaraza
pet (pet) s. faworyt; ulubieniec (np. pies); adj; ulubiony; v. (slang):pieścić; być
w złym nastroju; gniewać się;
migdalić się; wypieścić

petal ('petl) s. płatek

petition (py'tyszyn) s. petycja; prośba; podanie; v, prosic; wnosic podanie

petrify ('petry,faj) v. zamieniac (się) w kamien; powodowac kostnienie

petroleum (py'trouljem) s. ropa naftowa; olej skalny

pet shop ('petszop) s. sklep zwierzątek pokojowych

petticoat ('petykout) s. halka; spodniczka; kobieta; adj. kobiecy

petty ('pety) adj. drobny

petty cash (,pety'kaesz) s. gotówka podręczna

pew (pju:) s. ławka (kościelna)

pharmacy ('fa:rmesy) s. apteka; farmacja

phase (fejz) s. faza (np. rozwojowa); aspekt

pheasant ('feznt) s. bażant

philanthropist (fy'laentrepyst) s. filantrop

philologist (fy'loledżyst) s. filolog ;lingwista;językoznawca

philology (fy'loledży) s. filologia; językoznawstwo;ligwistyka

philosopher (fy'losefer) s. filozof

philosophize (fy'lose,fajz) v. filozofowac

philosophy (fy'losefy) s. filozofia

phone (foun) s. telefon (slang)

phonetic (fou'netyk) adj. fonetyczny

phon(e)y (founy) adj. fałszywy; udawany; s. rzecz fałszywa; podrabiana;ktos udający

photo ('foutou) s. fotka; fotografia; v. fotografowac

photograph ('foute,gra:f) s. fotografia; zdjęcie; v. fotografowac

photographer (fe'togrefer) s. fotograf; fotografik

photography (fe'tegrefy) s. fotografia; fotografika

phrase (frejz) s. wyrażenie; zwrot; v. wyrażac; wypowiadac wyrażeniami lub słowami

physical ('fyzykel) adj. fizyczny; cielesny

physician ('fyzyszyn) s. lekarz

physicist('fyzysyt) s. fizyk

physics ('fyzyks) s. fizyka

physique (fy'zi:k) s. budowa ciała; rozwój; wygląd fizyczny;kondycja;siła muskularna

piano (py'aenou) s. fortepian; pianino

pick (pyk) v. wybierac; dorabiac; kopac; krytykowac; dłubac; obierac; zbierac; usuwac; oskubac; wydziobac; krasc; okrasc; s, kilof; dłuto; wybór; czołenko; nitka wątka

pick-off('pyk,of) v. zedrzec; wystrzelac pojedyńczo(wrogów)

pick out('pyk,aut) v. wybrac; dobrac; doszukiwac się

pick over ('pyk,ouwer) v. przebierac;wybierac co lepsze

pick up ('pyk,ap) v. podnosic; brac; nauczyc się; zarabiac; odnalezc; odzyskac; przyjsc do siebie; poznac się; s. adapter; lekka ciężarówka

picket ('pykyt) s. palik; koł; pikieta; posterunek; v. rozstawiac pikiety strajkowe; słuzyc jako pikieta; zabezpieczac pikietami

pickle ('pykel) s. kiszony ogórek; marynata; kłopot; łobuz; v. marynować; kisic; wytrawiac

pickpocket ('pyk,pokyt) s. złodziej kieszonkowy; kieszonkowiec

picnic ('pyknyk) s. piknik; majówka; v. brac udział w pikniku, majówce,posiłku na dworze

pictorial (pyk'to:rjel) adj. obrazowy; ilustrowany; malowniczy; malarski; s.(czaso)pismo ilustrowane; ilustracja (trzywymiarowa)techniczna

picture ('pykczer) s. obraz; film; rysunek; rycina; portret; widok; v. odmalowywac; przedstawiac; opisywac; wyobrażac sobie; dawac obraz czegos

picturesque (,pykcze'resk) adj. malowniczy;żywy i przyjemny

pie (paj) s. placek; szarlotka; pasztet; pasztecik;(ptak) sroka

piece(pi:s) s. kawałek; częsc; sztuka; moneta; utwor; v. łączyc; zeszyc; łatac; naprawiac

piecework ('pi:s,łe:rk) s. robota na akord

pier (pier) s. pomost ładunkowy; molo; falochron; filar (np. mostu)

pierce (piers) v. przewiercac; wnikac; przedziurawiac; przebijac; przedostawac się

piercing (piersyŋg) adj. przeszywający; ostry; rozdzierający ;przenikający

piety ('pajety) s. pobożnosc

pig (pyg) s. wieprz; świnia; prosię; v. prosic się

pigeon ('pydżyn) s. gołąb; v. oszukiwac

pigeon-hole ('pydżyn,houl) s. przegrodka; v. umieszczac w przegrodkach

pigheaded ('pyg'hedyd) adj. uparty ; głupi

pigskin ('pyg,skyn) s. świnska skora; (slang):piłka; siodło

pigtail ('pyg,tejl) s. warkocz

pike(pajk) s. rogatka; dzida; pika; szpic; ostrze; szczupak

pile (pail) s. stos; sterta; kupa; pal; słup; puszek; meszek; włos; v. układac w stos; gromadzic na kupę;stawiac w kozły

pile up ('pail,ap) v. walic na kupę; s. zwalenie na kupę

piles (pailz) pl. hemoroidy

pilfer ('pylfer) v. ukrasc; zwędzic; buchnąc

pilgrim ('pylgrym) s. pielgrzym

pilgrimage ('pylgrymydż) s. pielgrzymka

pill (pyl) s. pigułka; tabletka

pillar ('pyler) s. filar; słup; podpora

pillbox('pylboks)s. bunkier; pudełeczko na pigułki;kapelusz

pillion ('pyljen) s. tylne siodełko (np. na motocyklu)

pillory ('pylery) s. pręgierz; v. stawiac pod pręgierzem

pillow ('pylou) s. zagłowek; jasiek; poduszka; podkładka; v. spoczywac; opierac (np. głowę)

pillowcase ('pylou,kejs) s. poszewka

pillow slip ('pylou,slyp) s. poszewka

pilot ('pajlet) s. pilot; sternik; v. pilotowac; sterowac; przeprowadzic

pimp (pymp) s. stręczycielka; alfons; v. stręczyc

pimple ('pympl) s. pryszcz; wągier

pin (pyn) s. szpilka; sztyft; sworzen; kołek; kręgiel v. przyszpilic; przymocowac

pincers ('pynserz) pl. kleszcze; obcęgi

pinch (pyncz) v. szczypac; gniesc; cisnąc; przycisnąc; przyskrzynic; krępowac; dokuczac;doskwierac; podważac łomem; s. uszczypnięcie; szczypta; łom; (slang) aresztowanie; obława; kradzież

pinch bar ('pyncz ba:r) s. łom (ze stopką)

pine (pajn) s. sosna; ananas; v. usychac

pineapple ('pajnaepl) s. ananas

pinion ('pynjen) s. kołko zębate; wrzeciono zębate; wał przekładni; koniec piora; lotka v. podcinac (skrzydła); pętac; przywiazywac

pink (pynk) s. rożowy kolor; radykał (komunizujacy); goździk; v. urazic do żywego; przekłuwac

pinnacle ('pynekl) s. szczyt; wieżyczka; v. zwieńczac; postawic na szczycie; stanowic szczyt

pint (pajnt) s. połkwarcie; 0.47 litra ; 1/8 galona

pioneer (,paje'nier) s. pionier; saper; v. torowac drogę

pious (pajes) adj. pobożny
pip (pyp) s. pestka; oczko;
gwiazdka; ziarnko; punkcik;
pypeć; dźwięk gwizdka; v. piszczeć; wykluwać się; pobić;
trafić; postrzelić
pipe (pajp) s. rura; rurka;
przewód; piszczałka; (slang)
łatwizna; drobiazg; v. doprowadzać rurami; włączyć;
połączyć; prowadzić dźwiękiem
fujarki; grać na fujarce;
grać na kobzie; gwizdać; piszczeć
pipeline ('pajp,lajn) s. rurociąg;(slang);informator;
v. przesyłać rurociągiem
piper (pajper) s. kobziarz
pipes (pajps) s. kobza
pirate (pajeryt) s. korsarz;
pirat; statek piracki; maruder; v. grabić; uprawiać kor-
sarstwo; wydawać bezprawnie
(książki)
pistol ('pystl) s. pistolet
piston ('pysten) s. tłok
pit(pyt) s. dół; jama; kopalnia; pestka; v. puszczać do
walki; robić dołki; wkładać
do dołu; wyjmować pestki
piston-stroke ('pysten,strouk)
s. suw tłoka
pitch (pycz) v. rozbijać (obóz);
umieszczać; rzucać; ustawiać;
chwiać się; upaść ciężko; kołysać (na fali); przechylać;
wybierać; ostro pracować;
rzucać się na...; smołować;
s. stopień; najwyższy punkt;
wzniesienie; wzdłużne kołysanie statku: spadek dachu; odstęp między (falami; zębami
kół etc.);skok (uzwojenia,
śruby); smoła
pitcher ('pyczer) s. dzban;
rzucający piłką
piteous ('pytjes) adj. żałosny;
nędzny
pitfall ('pytfo:l) s. pułapka;
wilczy dół
pith (pys) s. miękisz; rdzeń;
tężyzna; moc; v. wyjmować
rdzeń; przecinać rdzeń w celu
zabijania bydła (w rzeźni etc.)

pitiable ('pytjebl) s. żałosny;
godny pożałowania
pitiful ('pytyful) adj. litościwy;
żałosny; nędzny
pitiless ('pytylys) adj. bezlitosny
pity ('pyty) s. litość; współczucie; szkoda; v. litować się;
współczuć; żałować kogoś
pivot ('pywet) s. czop; oś;
ośrodek ;v.obracać jak na osi
pivotal ('pywetel) s. adj. centralny ;kardynalny;kluczowy;decydu-
jący
placard ('plaeka:rd) s. afisz;
plakat; (ple'ka:rd) v. rozle-
piać plakaty
place (plejs).s. miejsce; miejscowość; plac; ulica; dom; mieszkanie; zakład; krzesło; posada;
v. umieszczać; położyć; ulokować; dać stanowisko; pokładać;
powierzyć; określać
placid ('plaesyd) adj. łagodny;
spokojny
plague (plejg) s. plaga; dżuma;
zaraza; v. dręczyć
plaice (plejs) s. płastuga pospo-
lita
plaid (plaed) s. sukno; pled
w kratę ;rysunek w kratę
plain (plejn) adj. wyraźny; prosty; gładki; szczery; płaski;
równy; adv. jasno; szczerze;
s. równina
plain clothesman ('plejn,klozmen)
s. tajny policjant
plaintiff ('plejntyf) s. powód
(zaskarżający); powódka
plaintive ('plejntyw) adj. żałosny; płaczliwy
plait (plejt) s. plecionka; warkocz; fałda; zakładka; v. pleść;
splatać; fałdować
plan (plaen) s. plan; v. planować; zamierzać
plane (plejn) s. płaszczyzna;
równina; poziom; samolot; płat
(skrzydła); strug; wiórnik; gładzik; platan (owoc); v. ślizgać;
ześlizgiwać się; heblować
planet ('plaenyt) s. planeta
plank ('plaeŋk) s. deska; tarcica; punkt programu (polityczne-
go w USA); v.pokrywać deskami

plank down ('plaeŋk,daɪn) v. wybulić gotówkę

plant ('pla:nt) s. roślina; fabryka; zakład; wtyczka; (slang) oszustwo; włamanie; kant; v. zasadzać; zakładać; umieszczać; pozorować; ukrywać; wtykać; sadzić(rośliny)

plantation (plaen'tejszyn) s. plantacja

planter ('pla:nter) s. plantator; maszyna do sadzenia; skrzynka na kwiaty

plaque (plaek) s. tablica (pamiątkowa); odznaka

plaster ('pla:ster) s. tynk; wyprawa wapienna; przylepiec v. tynkować; wyprawiać; powlekać; zalepiać; oblepiać

plaster cast ('pla;ster,ka:st) s. odlew gipsowy; opatrunek gipsowy

plaster of Paris ('pla:ster of 'paerys) s. gips

plastic ('plaestyk) s. plastyk; sztuczne tworzywo; adj. plastyczny; giętki

plastics ('plaestyks) s. tworzywa sztuczne

plate (plejt) s. talerz; danie; płyta; taca; tafla; v. platerować; opancerzać

platform ('plaet,fo:rm) s. platforma; podium; trybuna; rampa; program polityczny

platinum ('plaetynem) s. platyna

platter ('plaeter) s. półmisek

plausible ('plo:zebl) adj. pozornie słuszny, prawdziwy, uczciwy; obłudnie przymilny

play (plej) s. gra; zabawa; sztuka; v. grać; bawić się; zagrać; udawać

play back('plej,baek) v. reprodukować; przegrywać

playboy ('plej,boj) s. lekkoduch

player('plejer) s. gracz; muzyk; aktor; zawodnik

playful ('plejful) adj. wesoły; żartobliwy;figlarny; filuterny; swawolny;rozbawiony;zabawny; rozbrykany;ożywiony

playground ('plej,graund) s. boisko; park

playhouse ('plej,haus) s. teatr

playmate ('plej,mejt) s. towarzysz zabaw(dziecinnych,intymnych)

play-off ('plejof) s. rozgrywka poremisowa

play off ('plej.of) v. rozgrywać partię poremisową

plaything ('plejtyŋg) s. zabawka

playwright ('plej,rajt) s. dramaturg

plea (pli:) s. usprawiedliwienie; wywód; apel; prośba

plead (pli:d) v. bronić; błagać; powoływać się

plead guilty ('pli:d'gylty) v. przyznawać się do winy

pleasant ('plesnt) s. przyjemny; miły; wesoły

please (pli:z) v. podobać się; zadowalać

please ! (pli:z) v. proszę

pleased (plizd) adj. zadowolony

pleasing ('pli:zyŋg) adj. przyjemny; miły

pleasure ('pleżer) s. przyjemność; adj. rozrywkowy

pleat (pli:t) s. fałda; v. plisować

pledge (pledż) v. zobowiązywać (się); zastawiać; s. zastaw; gwarancja; przyrzeczenie

plenipotentiary (,plenype'tenszery) s. pełnomocnik; adj. pełnomocny

plentiful ('plentyful) adj. obfity; liczny

plenty ('plenty) s. obfitość; mnóstwo; adv. zupełnie; aż nadto;adj.obfity;liczny;obszerny

pliable ('plajebl) adj. giętki

pliers ('plajerz) pl. szczypce

plight (plajt) s. trudności; stan; położenie; przyrzeczenie; v. ręczyć; dawać słowo

plod (plod) v. mozolić się; ślęczeć; s. harowanie; kucie

plod along ('plod,e'loŋg) v. wlec się;mozolić się;trudzić się

plot (plot)s. osnowa; fabuła; spisek;działka; wykres; mapa; v.knuć; spiskować;nanosić na mapę; planować; dzielić

plough (plau) s. pług; v. orać
plow (plau) s. pług; v. orać
plowshare ('plau-szeer) s.le-
miesz
pluck (plak) v. wyrwać; zerwać;
szarpnąć
pluck up courage ('plak,ap'karydż) exp.: zdobyć się na odwagę
plucky ('plaky) adj. śmiały;
odważny
plug (plag) s. czop; zatyczka;
kurek; reklama; świeca (silnika); v. zatykać
plug up ('plag,ap) v. zatkać
plum (plam) s. śliwka; rodzyn-
ka; gratka; adv. pionowo
plumage ('plu:mydż) s. upierze-
nie
plumb (plam) adj. pionowy; zupełny; adv. pionowo; prosto;
dokładnie; zupełnie; s. pion
murarski; sonda; v. pionować;
sondować
plumber ('plamer) s. hydraulik
plumbing ('plambyng) s.instalac-
ja wodociągowo-ściekowa budynku
plume (plu:m) s. pióro; pióropusz; v. ozdabiać piórami;
czyścić pióra
plummet ('plamyt) s. pion murarski; v. spadać pionowo
plump (plamp) adj. pulchny;
tęgi; stanowczy; otwarty;
v. tuczyć; tyć; wypełniać
(się); ciężko upaść; upuścić;
rzucić; popierać w wyborach
masowym głosowaniem; adv. prosto; nagle; ciężko; s. upadek
plum pudding('plam'pudyng)s.
budyń świąteczny
plunder ('plander) s. grabierz;
rabunek; łup; v. plądrować;
łupić; grabić
plunge (plandż) v. pogrążać
(się) ; zanurzać (się); wpadać;
spadać; s. skok do wody; pływalnia
plunk (plank) v. brząkać; wybulić; s. brzęk; adv. z brzę-
kiem; prościutko;v.ciskać;rzucać
upaść ciężko;szarpać(struny);
strzelić do kogoś;s.sl.:dolar

pluperfect ('plu:'pe:rfykt)
adj. zaprzeszły; s. czas zaprzeszły; plusquamperfectum
plural ('pluerel) s. liczba
mnoga; adj. pluralny; mnogi
plus (plas) prep. plus; więcej;
adj. dodatni; dodatkowy;
s. znak plus; dodatek
plush (plasz) s. plusz; adj.
pluszowy; okazały
ply (plaj) v. uprawiać gorliwie;
używać czegoś; zasypywać (np.
pytaniami) ; kursować po...;
s. warstwa; grubość; skłonność;
pasmo
plywood ('plaj,łud) s. sklejka;
dykta
pneumatic (nju'maetyk) adj.
pneumatyczny
pneumonia (nju'mounje) s. zapalenie płuc
poach (poucz) v. uprawiać kłu-
sownictwo; grzęznąć; rozrabiać;
udeptywać; rozmiękać; gotować
jajko na miękko bez skorupki
poached egg ('pauczt,eg) s.
jajko gotowane na miękko bez
skorupki
poacher ('poucher) s. kłusownik
pocket ('pokyt) s. kieszeń;
dziura (powietrzna) v. wkładać do kieszeni
pocketbook ('pokyt,buk) s.
portfel
pocketknife ('pokyt,najf) s.
scyzoryk
pocket money ('pokyt,many) s.
kieszonkowe
pod (pod) s. strączek; kokon;
stadko; obsada; v. rodzić
strączki; łuszczyć; spędzać
razem
poem (pouim) s. wiersz ; poemat
poet (pouyt) s. poeta
poetess ('pouytys) s. poetka
poetic (pou'etyk) adj. poetycz-
ny ; poetycki;poetycznie piękny
poetry ('pouytry) s. poezja
pogrom ('pougrem, pe'grom) s.
pogrom
poignant ('pojnent) adj.przej-
mujący; uszczypliwy; cięty;
ostry; dotkliwy;wzruszający

point (point) s. punkt; ostry
koniec; szpiczaste narzędzie;
przylądek; kropka; pointa; cecha; sedno; sens; v. zaostrzać;
celować; wskazywać; punktować;
kropkować;dowodzić;dążyć;pokazywać
point at ('point,aet) v, wycelowac; wskazac
point of view ('point,ow'wju:)
s. punkt widzenia
point out ('point,aut) v. wskazywac; uwydatnic
point to ('point,tu) v. wskazac
kierunek (kogos, cos)
pointed ('pointyd) adj. spiczasty; ostry; cięty; zjadliwy
point-blank ('point'blaenk) adj.
(strzelac) na wprost, bezposredni; bezceremonialny; bez
ogrodek; adv. bezpośrednio;
z bliska; wprost; bez ogrodek;
w prostej linii; bez zastano-
wienia się
pointer ('pointer) s. wskaznik;
wskazowka
poise (pojz) s. rownowaga; postawa; swoboda; stan zawiesze-
nia; stan niepewności; v. row-
noważyc; ważyc w rękach; za-
wisnąc w powietrzu; byc przy-
gotowanym do ataku
poison ('pojzn) s. trucizna;
v. truc; zatruc; zakazic
poisonous ('pojznes) adj. trujący; jadowity; szkodliwy
poke (pouk) v. wtykac; wpychac;
szturchac; dłubac; sterczec;
wtrącac się; plątac
poker ('pouker) s. pogrzebacz;
poker
polar ('pouler) adj. polarny
polar bear ('pouler beer) s.
biały niedzwiedz
Pole (poul) s. Polka; Polak
pole (poul) s. biegun; słup;
żerdz; dyszel; maszt
pole jump ('poul dżamp) s. skok
o tyczce
police (pe'li:s) s. policja;
v. rządzic; pilnowac; utrzymywac porządek
policeman (pe'li:smen) s. policjant

police officer (pe'li:s,ofyser)
s. policjant
police station (pe'li:s,stejszyn)
s. komisariat
policewoman (pe'li:s,łumen) s.
policjantka
policy ('polysy) s. polityka
rządzenia; polityka postępowa-
nia; mądrosc polityczna; polisa ubezpieczeniowa
polio ('pouljou) s. poliomyeli-
tis (,poliou,maje'lajtis) s.
paraliż dziecięcy; choroba
Haine-Medina
Polish ('poulysz) adj. polski
(język) (obywatel etc.)
polish ('polysz) v. polerowac;
gładzic; pochlebiac; nabierac
połysku; s. pasta (do butow);
połysk; politura; polor
polite (pe'lajt) adj. grzeczny;
uprzejmy; kulturalny
politeness (pe'lajtnys) s.
grzecznosc; ogłada; kultura;
uprzejmosc
political (pe'lytykel) adj.
polityczny
politician (,poly'tyszyn) s.
polityk; politykier
politics ('polytyks) s. polityka
poll (poul) s. głosowanie; reje-
strowanie głosow; wyniki głosowania; lista; wykaz; lokal
wyborczy; urny wyborcze; ankieta; głowa; tył głowy; obuch
v. oddawac głosy; obliczac
głosy; rejestrowac; dostawac
głosy; strzyc włosy; obcinac
rogi
pollen ('polyn) s. pył kwiato-
wy
pollute (pe'lju:t) v. zanie-
czyszczac; skazic
pollution (pe'lju:szyn) s. skażenie; zanieczyszczenie
pomp (pomp) s. pompa
pompous ('pompes) adj. napuszony; nadęty; pompatyczny
pond (pond) s. staw
ponder ('ponder) v. rozważac;
rozmyslac;przemysliwac;dumac;
zastanawiac się;zadumac się

ponderous ('ponderes) adj.
ciężki; niezgrabny

pontoon (pon'tu:n) s. ponton

pony ('pouny) s. kuc; bryk;
v. odpisywać; ściągać;zrzynać

poodle ('pu:dl) s. pudel(pies)

pool (pu:l) s. kałuża; sadzawka; pływalnia; v. składać się
razem; zbierać się w grupę

poor (puer) adj. biedny; ubogi; lichy; marny; słaby;
kiepski; nędzny; skromny

poorhouse ('puer,haus) s.
przytułek

poorly ('puerly) adv. licho;
kiepsko; skąpo; skromnie;
biednie; ubogo; adj. nie-
zdrów

pop (pop) s. trzask; puknię-
cie; strzał; napój musujący;
lombard; tatuś (slang);
v. strzelać; pukać; nagle wyrzucać; nagle wsadzać; skakać;
wściekać się

popcorn ('pop,ke:rn) s. su-
cha prażona kukurydza

pop in ('pop,yn) v. wskoczyć

pop out ('pop,aut) v. wyskoczyć

pope (poup) s. papież

poplar ('popler) s. topola

poppy ('popy) s. mak

popular ('popjuler) adj, ludowy; rozpowszechniony; popularny (tani)

popularity (,popju'laeryty) s.
popularność

populate ('popjulejt) s. zaludniać

population ('popjulejszyn) s.
ludność

populous ('popjules) adj. ludny; gęsto zaludniony

porch (po:rch) s. weranda; ga-
nek; portyk

porcupine ('po:rkjupajn) s.
jeż; jeżozwierz; kolczątka

pore (po:r) v. rozmyslać; slę-
czeć; wpatrywać się; s. por
(skóry)

pore over ('po:r,ouwer) v. rozmyslać nad czyms;slęczeć (nad
książką);zagłebiać się

pork (po:rk) s. wieprzowina

porous ('po:res) adj. porowaty

porpoise ('po:rpes) s. morswin;
ssak morski

porridge ('porydż) s. owsianka

port (po:rt) s. port; przystań;
otwór; otwór ładunkowy; postawa; trzymanie się; prezentowa-
nie (broni); wino porto; lewa
burta; sterowanie w lewo

portable ('po:rtebl) adj. przenosny; polowy

porter ('po:rter) s. tragarz;
kolejarz od sypialnego wagonu

portion ('po:rszyn) s. część;
porcja; udział; posag; los;
v. dzielić; przydzielać

portion out ('po:rszyn,aut) v.
wydzielać; wyposażać

portly ('po:rtly) adj. dostojny; godny; tęgi; postawny;
okazały

portrait ('po:rtryt) s. portret

pose (pouz) v. pozować; upozo-
wać; stawiać (np. problem);
kłopotać (za pytaniem); s. poza

posh (posz) adj. elegancki; szykowny; v. wyelegantować się

position (pe'zyszyn) s. położenie; stanowisko; postawa;
twierdzenie; umieszczenie;
v. umieszczać; ulokować

positive ('pozetyw) adj. pozytywny; stanowczy; ustanowiony;
zupełny; dodatni; pozytywistycz-
ny; s. znak dodatni; wartość
dodatnia; pozytyw

possess (pe'zes) v. posiadać;
opanować; opętać; przepajać

possessed (pe'zest) adj. opęta-
ny

possession (pe'zeszyn) s. posiadanie; posiadłość; własność;
dobytek;opanowanie

possessor (pe'zeser) s. posiadacz; własciciel

possibility (pose'bylyty) s.
możliwość; możność;ewentualność

possible ('posebl) adj. możliwy; ewentualny

possibly ('posebly) adv. może;
wogóle możliwe; możliwie

post (poust) s. słup; posada; posterunek; poczta; v. ogłaszać; wywieszać; zalepiać plakatami

postage ('poustydż) s. opłata pocztowa

postage stamp ('poustydż,staemp) s. znaczek pocztowy

postal ('poustel) adj. pocztowy

postal order ('poustel'o:rder) s. przekaz pocztowy

postcard ('poust,ka:rd) s. pocztówka

post code ('poust,koud) = zipcode ('zyp,koud) pocztowy numer kierunkowy

poster ('pouster) s. plakat

poste restante ('poust'resta:nt) s. list lub przesyłka do odebrania na poczcie

posterity (po'teryty) s. potomność

post-free ('poust'fri:) adj. wolny od opłaty pocztowej

posthumous ('postjumes) adj. pośmiertny

postman ('poustmen) s. listonosz

postmark ('poust,ma:rk) s. stempel pocztowy

postmaster ('poust,ma:ster) s. naczelnik poczty

post office ('poust,ofys) s. poczta

post office box ('poust,ofys'-'boks) s. skrytka pocztowa

postpaid ('poust,pejd) s. opłata pocztowa z góry uiszczona

postpone (poust'poun) v. odłożyć; odroczyć; odwlekać

postscript ('pous,skrypt) s. dopisek; postscriptum

posture('poszczer) s. postawa; stan; położenie; v. przybrać postawę; pozować

postwar ('poust'ło:r) adj. powojenny

posy ('pouzy) s. bukiet

pot (pot) s. garnek; imbryk; czajnik; nocnik; doniczka; wazonik;rondel;dzban;kocioł; kufel;słój;puchar;więcierz;łuza

szklanka; haszysz; v. wsadzać do garnka; polować; strzelać

potato (po'tejtou) s. ziemniak

potent ('potent) adj. potężny; skuteczny; jurny

potion ('pouszyn) s. dawka; napój

potter ('poter) s. garncarz; v. grzebać się; włoczyć się; łazić

potter about ('poter,e'baut) v. włóczyć się

potty ('poty) adj. marny; lichy; błachy; łatwy; stuknięty; pomylony; zbzikowany

pouch (paucz) s. worek; torba; brzuszysko; ładownica; sakiewka; v. nadawać formę worka; łykać

poulterer ('poulterer) s. handlarz drobiu

poultice ('poultys) s. okład; v. kłaść okład

poultry ('poultry) s. drób

pounce (pauns) s. szpon; nagły atak z góry; v. rzucać się na coś; trybować; pumeksować; posypywać (rysunek) proszkiem (kolorowym)

pound (paund) s. funt (pieniądz; waga); stuk; tupot; uderzenie; tłuczenie; walnięcie; ogrodzenie; magazyn; areszt; v.tłuc; walić; tupać;biegać; więzić; zamykać

pour (po:r) v. wysypać; posypać; lać; polać; wylać; rozlać; nalać

pour out ('po:r,aut) v. wysypać; wylać

pout (paut) v. dąsać się; wydymać; s. wydęcie warg; kwaśna mina

poverty('powerty) s. bieda; ubóstwo

powder ('pałder) s. proch; pył; puder; proszek; v. posypywać; pudrować; proszkować

powder room ('pałder,ru:m) s. toaleta damska

power ('pałer) s. potęga; moc; energia; siła; własność; władza; mocarstwo; v. napędzać; wspomagać;dostarczać energii

power brake ('pałer,brejk) s.
serwohamulec; wspomagany hamulec

powerful ('pałerful) adj, potężny; mocny

powerless ('pałerlys) adj.
bezsilny

power plant ('pałer,plaent)
s. siłownia

power station ('pałer,stejszyn)
s. elektrownia

powwow ('pał,łał) v. naradzać
się co do taktyki; leczyć;
s. sejmik Indian; odprawa ofi-
cerska; czarownik indiański

practicable ('praektykebl) adj.
wykonalny; możliwy do przeprowadzenia

practical ('praektykel) adj.
praktyczny

practice ('praektys) s. praktyka; ćwiczenie; v. praktykować;
uprawiać; ćwiczyć

practise ('praektys) v. = practice

practitioner(praek'tyszener) s.
zawodowiec; praktykujący·le-
karz

prairie('preery) s. preria

praise (prejz) s. pochwała;
v. chwalić; sławić

praiseworthy ('prejz,łe:rsy)
adj. chwalebny; godny pochwały

pram (praem) s. ręczny wózek

prance (praens) v. stawać dęba;
tańczyć; paradować; hasać;
kazać koniowi·stawać dęba

prank (praenk) s. psota; figiel; v. wystroić; popisywać
się

prattle ('praetl) v. paplać;
s. paplanina

prawn (pro:n) s. krewetka;
v. łowić krewetki

pray (prej) v. modlić się; prosić; błagać

prayer ('prejer) s. modlitwa;
prośba

prayer book ('prejer,buk) s.
modlitewnik; książka do
nabożeństwa

pre-(pri:-)prefix,przed-;z góry

preach (pri:cz) v. głosić; kazać;
wygłaszać

preacher (pri:czer) s. kaznodzieja; pastor

precarious (pry'keeries) s. niepewny; niebezpieczny; dowolny

precaution (pry'ko:szyn) s. przezorność; środek ostrożności

precede (pry:'si:d) v. poprzedzać;
mieć pierwszeństwo

precedence (pry'si:dens) s. pierwszeństwo;nadrzędność

precedent (pry'si:dent) adj.
uprzedni; poprzedzający

precedent ('presydent) s. precedens

precept('pry:sept) s. nakaz;
przykazanie; nauka moralna; reguła

precinct ('pry:synkt) s. okręg
(wyborczy); obręb; granice

precious ('preszes) adj. drogi;
cenny; afektowany; wyszukany;
wspaniały; adv. bardzo; niezwykle

precipice ('presypys) s. przepaść

precipitate (pry'sypytejt) s.
opad; osad; przyspieszać (zdarzenia);skraplać (się); rzucać;
spadać

precipitation (pry,sypy'tejszyn)
s. opady; przyspieszanie; po-
chopność; upadek; strącanie

precipitous (pry'sypytes) adj.
przepaścisty; spadzisty

precis ('prejsi:) s. skrót; v.
robić skrót

precise (pry'sajs) adj. dokładny; wyraźny; v. precyzować;
wyszczególniać

precision (pry'syżyn) s. precyzja;
dokładność

precocious (pry'kouszes) adj.
przedwczesny; przedwcześnie roz-
winięty; kwitnący

preconceived ('pry:ken'si:wd)
adj. uprzedzony do; powzięty
z góry

predatory ('predetery) adj. łu-
pieżczy; grabieżczy; drapieżny

predecessor ('pry:dyseser) s.
poprzednik; przodek

predetermine ('pry:dy'te:rmyn)
v. z góry ustanowić; z góry
okreslić; z góry zadecydować
predicament (pry'dykement) s,
kłopot; kłopotliwe położenie
predicate ('predy,kejt) v.
opierać się na czyms; łączyć
się z czyms; przypisywać cze-
mus; orzekać o czyms; mieścić
pojęcie czegos; ('predykyt) s.
cecha; orzecznik; adj. orzecze-
niowy; dopełnienie orzeczenia
predict (pry'dykt) v. przepo-
wiadać
prediction (pry'dykszyn) s.
przepowiednia
predisposition ('pri:dyspe'zyszyn) s. skłonność; predyspo-
zycja
predominant(pry'domynent) adj.
przeważający; panujący; góru-
jący
predominate (pry'domynejt) v.
górować; przeważać
preface ('prefys) s. przedmowa;
wstęp
prefect ('pry:fekt) s. prefekt
prefer (pry'fe:r) v. woleć;
przekładać; dawać awans
preferable ('preferebl) adj.
lepszy
preferably ('preferebly) adv.
raczej
preference ('preferens) s.
pierwszeństwo; uprzywilejowa-
nie; możność wyboru; rzecz bardziej ulubiona, upodobana
preferment (pry'fe:rment) s.
wybór; awans
prefix ('pry:fyks) s. przedrostek; prefiks; tytuł przed
nazwiskiem; v. umieszczać
przedrostek; umieszczać na
wstępie
pregnancy ('pregnensy) s. ciąża
pregnant ('pregnent) adj. brze-
mienny; doniosły; sugestywny;
płodny ;ciężarna (kobieta)
prejudice ('predżudys) s. uprzedzenie; szkoda; v. uprzedzać się
do kogos; szkodzić (komuś);
rozpowszechniać uprzedzenie

prejudiced ('predżudyst) adj.
uprzedzony ;mający uprzedzenie
preliminary (pry'lymynery) adj.
wstępny; przygotowawczy;
s. wstęp
prelude ('prelju:d) s. wstęp;
preludium; v. grać preludium;
dawać wstęp do czegos
premature (,preme'tjuer) adj.
przedwczesny; przedwcześnie
dojrzały
premeditate (pry'medy,tejt) v.
obmyslać; rozważać
premier ('premjer) adj. pierwszy; najważniejszy; premier;
prezes rady ministrów
premises ('premysys) pl. lokal;
obejście
premium ('pri:mjem) s. nagroda;
premia
preoccupied (pry:'okju,pajd)
adj. pochłonięty; zaabsorbowany
preparation (,prepe'rejszyn) s.
przygotowywanie; przyrządzanie
prepare (pry'peer) v. przygotowywać (się); szykować (się);
przyrządzać
prepay ('pry'pej) v. opłacać
z góry
preposition (,prepe'zyszyn) s.
przyimek
prepossess (,pry:po'zes) v.
wpoić; usposobić; natchnąć
prepossessing (prype'zesyng)
adj. miły; sympatyczny
preposterous (pry'posteres) adj.
niedorzeczny; absurdalny
prerequisite (pry'rekłyzyt) adj.
& s. (warunek) wstępny; podstawowy
prescribe (prys'krajb) v. prze-
pisać; nakazać; zaordynować
prescribtion (prys'krypszyn) s.
nakaz; przepis; recepta
presence ('presens) v. obecność
presence of mind ('prezens,ow'
'majnd) v. przytomność umysłu
present ('preznt) s. upominek;
prezent; teraźniejszość; adj.
obecny; niniejszy; teraźniejszy;v.stawiać się;nadarzyć się

present tense ('presnt,tens) s.
czas teraźniejszy
presentation (,prezen'tejszyn)
s. przedstawienie; ofiarowa-
nie; podarek; darowanie; prze-
dłożenie
presentiment (pry'zentyment) s.
przeczucie
presently ('prezently) adv.
wkrótce; niebawem; zaraz
preservation (,preze:r'wejszyn)
s. zachowanie; ochrona; zabezpieczenie
preserve (pry'ze:rw) v. zachowywać; chronić; przechowywać;
konserwować; ochraniać;
s. konserwa; rezerwat
preside (pry'zajd) v. przewod-
niczyć
president ('prezydent) s. prezydent
press (pres) s. prasa; dzienni-
ki; tłocznia; druk; drukania;
nacisk; tłok; ścisk; pospiech;
v. cisnąć; ściskać; przyciskać;
ciążyć; pracować; naglić; narzucać; wciskać; tłoczyć
press in ('pres-yn) v. wciskać
pressing ('presyng) adj. naglący; natarczywy
pressure ('preszer) s. ciśnienie; napór; parcie
prestige (pres'ty:dż) s. prestiż (szacunek i uznanie)
presumable(pry'zju:mebl) adj.
przypuszczalny
presume (pry'zju:m) v. przypuszczać; wykorzystywać (kogoś);
ośmielać się
presumedly (pry'zju:mydly) adv.
przypuszczalnie
presuming (pry'zju:myng) adj.
zarozumiały
presumption (pry'zampszen) s.
przypuszczenie; założenie;
zarozumiałość
presumptuous (pry'zamptjues)
adj. zarozumiały
presuppose (pry:se'pouz) v.
przypuszczać; zakładać z góry;
stawiać warunek
pretend (pry'tend) v. udawać;
pretendować

pretender (pry'tender) s. pretendent
pretense (pry'tens) s. udawanie;
pozór; pretensja; pretensjonalnosc
pretension (pry'tenszyn) s.
aspiracje; roszczenie; preten-
sjonalność; pretensja
preterite ('preteryt) adj.
przeszły; s. czas przeszły
pretext ('pry:tekst) s. pretekst;
pozór;
pretext (pry'tekst) v. wymawiać
się; powoływać się
pretty ('pryty) adj. ładny;
adv. dość; dosyć
prevail (pry'wejl) v. przeważać;
brać górę; przekonać; panować
(np. zwyczaj)
prevalent ('prewelent) adj. panujący; przeważający
prevent (pry'went) v. zapobiec;
powstrzymywać
prevention (pry'wenszyn) s. za-
pobieganie; środek zapobiegający
preventive (pry'wentyw) adj.
zapobiegawczy; prewencyjny
previous ('pry:wjes) adj. poprzedni; wcześniejszy od...;
przedwczesny; nagły; pochopny
previous to ('pry:wjes,tu) adv.
przed czyms
previously ('pry:wjesly) adv.
wcześniej
prewar ('pri:'ło:r) adj.
przedwojenny
prey (prej) s. zdobycz; łup;
ofiara; v. grabić; trawić
price (prajs) s. cena; koszt;
v. wyceniać
priceless ('prajslys) adv.
bezcenny; nieoceniony
prick (pryk) s. ukłucie;
(wulg.) penis; v. kłuć; przekłuwać
prick up one's ears ('pryk,ap-
'łans,eerz) s. nadstawiać
uszu; postawić uszy
prickle ('prykl) s. kolec;
ciern; v. ukłuć; jeżyć się
prickly ('prykly) adj. kolczasty

pride (prajd) s. duma; pycha;
ambicja; chluba; v. być dum-
nym z czegoś;chełpic' się;pysznić
priest (pri:st) s. kapłan; duchowny
primarily ('prajmeryly) adv.
głownie; przede wszystkim
primary ('prajmery) adj. głowny; zasadniczy; pierwotny;
s. wybór kandydatów (U.S.A.)
primary school ('prajmery,sku:l)
s. szkoła podstawowa
prime ('prajm) adj. pierwszy;
najważniejszy; głowny;v.przygoto-
prime minister ('prajm-'mynyster) wać
s. premier
primer ('prajmer) s. elementarz;
podręcznik (elementarny)
primitive ('prymytyw) adj. prymitywny; pierwotny
primrose ('prymrous) s. pier-
wiosnek
prince ('pryns) s. książę
princess (pryn'ses) s. księżna;
księżniczka
principal ('prynsepel) adj.
głowny; s. kierownik; zlecenio-
dawca; kapitał; sprawca
principality (prynsy'paelyty)
s. księstwo
principle ('prynsepl) s. zasada;
reguła;podstawa;źrodło;składnik
prink (prynk) v. stroic' się;
muskac' się
print (prynt) s. ślad; odcisk;
druk; pismo; fotka; v. wy-
cisnąc'; wytłoczyć; wydrukować;
byc' w druku;drukować się;odbic'
printed matter ('prynted'maeter)
v. druki;materiały drukowane
printer ('prynter) s. drukarz
printing ('pryntyng) s. druk;
drukowanie; nakład;a.drukarski
printing ink ('pryntyng,ynk) s.
farba drukarska
printing office ('pryntyn,ofys)
s. drukarnia
prior ('prajer) adj. wcześniejszy; ważniejszy; s. przeor
prior to ('prajer,tu) adv.
przed czyms;wcześniej od czegos'
priority ('praj'oryty) s.
pierwszeństwo;starszeństwo

prison ('pryzn) s. więzienie
prisoner ('pryzner) s. więzień
privacy ('prajwesy) s. odosobnienie; samotnosc'; utrzymanie
w dyskrecji (tajemnicy); życie
prywatne, intymne, osobiste
private ('prajwyt) adj. prywatny; tajny; ukryty; s. szerego-
wiec;(private parts=genitalia)
private hotel ('prajwyt,hou'tel)
s. pensjonat
privation (praj'wejszyn) s.
prywacja; niedostatek
privilege ('prywylydż) s. przywilej;prawdziwa satysfakcja
privileged ('prywylydżd) adj.
uprzywilejowany;zaszczycony
prize (prajz) v. podważyć; zajmowac'; cenic'; nagroda; premia;
wygrana; łup;a.kapitalny.v.cenić
prizefighter ('prajz,fajter)
s. zawodowy bokser
prizewinner ('prajz,łyner) s.
laureat; zdobywca nagrody
pro (prou) s. zawodowiec (slang)
adv. za; dla;prep. pro(forma etc.)
probability (proba'bylyty) s.
prawdopodobieństwo;widoki;szanse
probable ('probebl) adj. prawdopodobny;wiarogodny;mający szanse
probation (pro'bejszyn) s. okres próbny; próba;zawieszenie kary
probe (proub) s. sonda; v. son-
dowac'; zagłębiac' się;badac' w śledz-
problem ('problem) s. problem; twie
zadanie; zagadnienie;a.problemowy
procedure (pre'si:dżer) s. postępowanie; procedura(sądowa)
proceed (pre'si:d) v. isc' dalej;
postępowac';kontynuowac';zaskarżać
proceed from (pre'si:d,from) v.
wychodzic' z...;isc' dalej z...
proceedings (pre'si:dyngs) pl.
sprawozdanie (z sesji etc.)
proceeds ('prousi:dz) pl. zysk;
dochody;przychód (ze sprzedaży)
process ('prouses) s. przebieg;
proces; postęp; v. obrabiac';
przerabiac'; załatwiac'; proce-
sowac';poddawać procesowi;mleć
procession (pre'seszyn) s. pochód; procesja;kontynuowanie;
prowadzenie dalej;dalszy rozwoj

proclaim (pre'klejm) v. proklamować; ogłaszać; zakazywać; wskazywać;wprowadzać ograniczenia

proclamation (,prokle'mejszyn) s. proklamacja; obwieszczenie

procrastinate (pre'kraesty,nejt) v. zwlekać; odkładać na później

procure (pre'kjuer) v. postarać się; stręczyć do nierządu

prodigal ('prodygel) adj. marnotrawny; s. marnotrawca;utracjusz

prodigious (pre'dydżes) adj. niezwykły; cudowny; olbrzymi

prod (prod) v. szturchać; kłuć; drażnić; popędzać; s. dźgnięcie; bodziec; szpikulec

prodigy ('prodydży) s. dziwo; cud;genialne dziecko etc.

produce ('produ:s) s. produkty; plony; wynik; produkcja; wydajność; wydobycie;produkty rolne

produce (pre'dju:s) v. wytwarzać; produkować; dostarczać; wydobywać; wystawiać; okazywać

producer ('produ:ser) s. wytwórca (filmowy); producent

product ('predakt) s. produkt; wynik; iloczyn;wytwór(natury etc.)

production (pre'dakszyn) s. wytwórczość; wydobycie; produkcja; utwór;produkty;a.produkcyjny

productive (pre'daktyw) adj. wydajny; produktywny; produkcyjny; urodzajny; żyzny

profess (pre'fes) v. twierdzić; zapewniać; udawać; wyznawać; uprawiać (zawód);być profesorem

professed (pre'fest) adj. jawny; rzekomy; zawodowy

profession (pre'feszyn) s. zawód; wyznanie; zapewnienie; oświadczenie;śluby zakonne

professional (pre'feszenl) s. zawodowiec; adj. zawodowy; fachowy;należący do wolnego zawodu

professor (pre'feser) s. profesor; wyznawca;nauczyciel(tańca)

proficiency (pre'fyszensy) s. biegłość; sprawność

proficient (pre'fyszent) adj. biegły; sprawny; s. mistrz;biegły;znający(obcy język);fachowiec

profile ('proufajl) s. profil; szkic biograficzny; v. przedstawiać z profilu; profilować

profit ('profyt) s. zysk; dochód; korzyść; pożytek; v. korzystać; być korzystnym; przydawać się;mieć zyski

profitable ('profytebl) adj. korzystny;intratny;zyskowny

profiteer (,profy'tier) v.paskować; spekulować; s. paskarz; spekulant(na czarnym rynku etc.)

profound (pro'faund) adj. głęboki;gruntowny;s.otchłań

profusion (pro'fju:żyn) s. obfitość; rozrzutność;nadmiar

prognoses (prog'nousi:z) pl. prognozy; rokowania

prognosis (prog'nousys) s. prognoza; rokowanie

program ('prougraem) s. program; plan; audycja; przedstawienie; v. planować

progress ('prougres) s. postęp; bieg; rozwój;kolejne etapy etc.

progress (pro'gres) v. robić postępy; iść naprzód;być w toku

progressive (pro'gresyw) adj. postępowy;stopniowy;s.postępowiec

prohibit (pro'hybyt) v. zakazywać; zabraniać

prohibition (,prouy'byszyn) s. zakaz; prohibicja

project ('prodżekt) s. projekt; plan;przedsięwzięcie;schemat

project (pro'dżekt) v. projektować; miotać; rzutować; sterczeć; wystawać;wyświetlać(na ekranie)

projection (pro'dżekszyn) s. rzut; planowanie; projektowanie; rzutowanie; wystawanie; projekcja; wyświetlanie

projector (pro'dżekter) s. rzutnik;aparat projekcyjny

proletariat (,proule'teerjet) s. proletariat;robotnicy przemysłowi

prolog ('proulog) s.prolog

prolong (prou'long) v. przedłużać; wydłużać;prolongować(spłaty)

promenade (,promy'nejd) s. przechadzka;przejażdżka; deptak; promenada; v.przechadzać się

prominent ('promynent) adj. wydatny; wybitny; sterczący; wystający; wyróżniający się;sławny
promise ('promys) s. obietnica;
przyrzeczenie; v. obiecywać;
przyrzekać; zaręczać; zapewniać;robić obietnice;zapowiadać się
promising('promysyng) adj. obiecujący; rokujący nadzieje
promontory ('promento:ry) s.
przylądek; wyrostek
promote (pre'mout) v. popierać;
promować; awansować; (slang)
oszukiwać; kombinować
promoter (pre'mouter) s. organizator;krzewiciel; inspirator
promotion (pre'mouszyn) s. po-
pieranie; ułatwienie; awans;
promowanie; lansowanie
prompt (prompt) adj. szybki;
natychmiastowy; v. nakłaniać;
pobudzać; podpowiadać; sufle-
rować;adv.punktualnie;co do mi-
nuty
prompter ('prompter) s. sufler
(w teatrze);podżegacz
promptly ('promptly) adv. natychmiast; z miejsca; bezzwłocznie; punktualnie
prone (proun) adj. leżący twarzą na dół; stromy; skłonny
prong (prong) s. ząb (wideł);
róg; v. kłuć; przebijać;
zaopatrywać w zęby
pronoun ('prounaun) s. zaimek
pronounce (pre'nauns) v. oświadczać; wymawiać; mieć wymowę;
wypowiadać się
pronto ('prontou) adv. (slang):
prędko; już;natychmiast;zaraz
pronunciation (pra,nansy'ejszyn)
s. wymowa ;zapis fonetyczny
proof (pru:f) s. dowód; próba
(np. złota); sprawdzian; wy-
próbowanie; korekta; próbna
odbitka; adj. odporny; wypró-
bowany ;sprawdzony;nieprzemakalny
prop(up) ('prop,ap) v. podpierać; s. podpórka ;ostoja;oparcie
propagate ('prope,gejt) v. rozmnażać (się); rozszerzać; propagować; przekazywać
propagation (,prope'gejszyn) s.
rozmnażanie się; propagowanie

propel (pre'pel) v. napędzać;
poruszać; pędzić
propeller (pre'peler) s. śmigło;
śruba (okrętowa)
proper ('proper) adj. właściwy;
własny; przyzwoity
properly ('properly) adv. właściwie; słusznie; przyzwoicie
property ('property) s. własność;właściwość;cecha;nierucho-
mość
prophecy ('profysy) s. proroctwo
prophet ('profyt) s. prorok;
apostoł
proportion (pre'po:rszyn) s.
proporcja; stosunek; rozmiar;
część; v. dostosowywać; rozdzielać;dawkować;dozować
proportional (pre'po:rsznl) adj.
proporcjonalny (do czegoś)
proposal (pre'pouzel) s. propozycja; projekt; oświadczyny
propose (pre'pouz) v. proponować; przedkładać; zamierzać
proposition (,prope'zyszyn) s.
propozycja; sąd; zagadnienie;
twierdzenie; v. robić nie-
przyzwoite propozycje
proprietary (pre'prajetery) adj.
należący; będący prywatną
własnością; s. właściciel;
własność
proprietor (pre'prajeter) s.
właściciel;posiadacz;gospodarz
propulsion (pre'palszyn) s. napęd; bodziec; popędzanie
prose (prouz) s. proza;v.nudzić
prosecute ('prosy,kju:t) s. ścigać prawnie; prowadzić (np.
studia) ;nie zaniedbywać;pilno-
wać
prosecution (,prosy'kju:szyn)
s. oskarżenie
prosecutor ('prosy,kju:ter) s.
prokurator; oskarżyciel
prospect ('prospekt) s. widok;
perspektywa; ewentualny klient;
potencjalne złoża; v. przeszukiwać (okolice); próbnie
exploatować kopalnie; szukać
złota etc.;badać(teren etc.)
prospective (pres'pektyw) adj.
przyszły; ewentualny
prospectus (pres'pektes) s.
prospekt (nowego przedsiębiors-
twa)

prosper ('prosper) v. prosperować; sprzyjać powodzeniu
prosperity (pros'peryty) s. dobrobyt; powodzenie; koniunktura; pomyślność
prosperous ('prosperes) adj. mający powodzenie; kwitnący; pomyślny; zamożny
prostate (pros'tejt) s. prostata; gruczoł krokowy
prostitute ('prosty,tu:t) s. prostytutka; v. prostytuować (się);adj.wszeteczny;rozpustny
prostrate ('prostrejt) v. powalić (np. ze zmęczenia); adj. leżący twarzą w dół; powalony; wyczerpany; bezsilny; kłaniający się ;leżący plackiem
protect (pre'tekt) v. chronić; bronić; ochraniać;zabezpieczać
protection (pre'tekszyn) s. ochrona; opieka; protekcja; list żelazny; wymuszanie pieniędzy przez grożenie gwałtem
protective (pre'tektyw) adj. ochronny;zapobiegawczy
protector (pre'tekter) s. opiekun; protektor; ochraniacz
protest (pro'test) v. protestować; zapewniać;oponować
protest ('proutest) s. protest
protestant ('protystent) s. ewangielik; protestant
protestation (proutes'tejszyn) s. uroczyste zapewnienie; protest;zaprotestowanie
protract(pre'traekt) v. przeciągać; przedłużać; wystawiać; przedstawiać w skali
protrude (pre'tru:d) v. wystawać; wysuwać ;sterczeć
proud (praud) adj. dumny; napawający dumą;piękny;szczęśliwy
prove (pru:w) v. udowadniać; wykazać (się); uprawomocnić; poddawać próbie; okazywać się
proverb ('prowe:rb) s. przysłowie ;przypowieść
proverbial (pre'we:rbjel) adj. przysłowiowy
provide (pre'wajd) v. zaopatrywać; przygotowywać; postarać się; sprzyjać; postanawiać; zaplanować

provide for (pre'wajd,fo:r) v. zaopatrywać (dla kogoś)
provided that (pre'wajdyd,daet) exp.: pod warunkiem że...; o ile
providence ('prowydens) s. opatrzność; oszczędność; przezorność; skrzętność
province ('prowyns) s. prowincja; zakres; dziedzina
provincial (pre'wynszel) adj. zaściankowy; prowincjonalny; s. człowiek z prowincji
provision (pro'wyżyn) s. klauzula; dostawa; przygotowanie się; (pl.) prowianty; v. prowiantować; zaopatrywać w żywność;zaprowiantować
provisional (pro'wyżenl) adj. prowizoryczny; tymczasowy
provocation (,prowe'kejszyn) s. prowokacja; rozdrażnienie; podniecenie;spowodowanie
provocative (pro'woketyw) adj. prowokujący; zaciekawiający; drażniący;wyzywający
provoke (pre'wouk) v. prowokować; podniecać; pobudzać; wywoływać; podżegać;jątrzyć
prowl (praul) v. grasować; s. grasowanie (po łup)
proxy ('proksy) s. zastępstwo; pełnomocnik
prude (pru:d) s. świętoszka
prudence ('pru:dens) s. rozwaga; roztropność ;ostrożność
prudent ('pru:dent) s. rozważny; roztropny;ostrożny
prudish ('pru:dysz) adj. pruderyjny;przesadnie skromny
prune (pru:n) s. śliwka (suszona) v. obcinać (np. gałązki); oczyszczać (z czegoś)
psalm (sa:m) s. psalm
pseudonym ('sju:de,nym) s. pseudonim;fikcyjne nazwisko
psyche ('sajki:) s. dusza; duch; umysł (zwierciadło odchylone)
psychiatrist (saj'kajetryst) s. psychiatra
psychiatry (saj'kajetry) s. psychiatria
psychological (,sajke'lodżykel) adj. psychologiczny

psychologist (saj'koledżyst) s. psycholog

psychology (saj'koledży) s. psychologia

pub (pab) s. Br., knajpa

puberty ('pju:berty) s. dojrzałość płciowa

public ('pablyk) s. publiczność; adj. publiczny; obywatelski

publication (,pably'kejszyn) s. opublikowanie; ogłoszenie; publikacja;wydanie książki

public house ('pablyk,haus) s. szynk; oberża

publicity (pab'lysyty) s. rozgłos; reklama;a.reklamowy

publish ('pablysz) v. publikować; wydawać; ogłaszać; rozgłaszać;wydać drukiem

publisher ('pablyszer) s. wydawca; nakładca

publishing house ('pablyszyng,-haus) s. firma wydawnicza

pudding ('pudyng) s. budyń

puddle ('padl) s. kałuża

puff (paf) v. pykać; sapać; dmuchać; reklamować; pudrować; s. puszek; pyknięcie; dmuchnięcie; blaga reklamowa; pierzyna;kłąb dymu;zwoj włosów

puff paste ('paf,pejst) s. francuskie ciasto

puffy ('pafy) adj. dychawiczny; nadęty; pękaty; napuszony; otyły; porywisty;dychawiczny

pull (pul) v. pociągnąć; szarpnać; wyrwać; wyciągać; przeciągać; wiosłować;zciągnać

pull down ('pul,dałn) v. spuścić; rozbierać (np. budynek); osłabiać;sciągac(store etc.)

pull for ('pul,fo:r) v. popierać

pull in ('pul,yn) v. wciągac

pull off ('pul,of) v. ściągać; zdobywać;potrafic;zdołac;stanac

pull out ('pul,aut) v. wyrwać; wycofać; s. wycofanie się

pulley ('puli) s. bloczek; blok krążkowy; v. podnosic bloczkiem

pullover ('pul,ouwer) s. pulower

pulp (palp) s, miazga; miąższ; papka; v.rozcierac na miazgę

pulpit ('pulpyt) s. ambona; kazalnica;kaznodzieje; kazanie

pulpy ('palpy) adj. papkowaty; miąższowy

pulsate (pal'sejt) v. tętnic; pulsowac;drgac;trząść się

pulse (pals) s. tętno; puls; v. tętnic; pulsować

pulverize ('palwerajz) v. proszkowac (się); rozpylać; scierać w proch;zemleć na proch

pump (pamp) s. pompa; lakierek; v. pompowac;pytac uporczywie

pump gun ('pamp,gan) s. strzelba (do repetowania)

pumpkin ('pampkyn) s. dynia

pun (pan) s. gra słów (dwuznacznych); v. robic kalambury

punch (pancz) s. uderzenie (pięścią); poncz; przebijak; krzepa; siła; sztanca; kułak; rozmach; v. dziurkowac; tłoczyc; walic; szturchać

punctual ('panktjuel) adj. punktualny; punktowy

punctuate ('panktju,ejt) v. przestankować; przerywać

punctuation (,panktju'ejszyn) s. interpunkcja

punctuation mark (,panktju'ejszyn ma:rk) s. kropka; znak przestankowy

puncture ('pankczer) s. przebicie; punkcja; v. przekłuwać; przedziurawiac;przebic

pungent ('pandżent) adj. kłujący; ostry; cierpki; zjadliwy; gryzący;sarkastyczny;pikantny

punish ('panysz) v. karac;dac bobu

punishment ('panyszment) s. kara;sromotna klęzka (na boisku)

pupil ('pju:pl) s. zrenica; uczen; wychowanek;małoletni;niepełnoletni

puppet ('papyt) s. kukiełka; marionetka;a.kukiełkowy;marionetkowy

puppet show ('papyt,szou) s. występy marionetek

puppet state ('papyt,stejt) s. państwo marionetkowe

puppy ('papy) s. szczenie; szczeniak; piesek;zarozumialec

purchase ('pe:rczes) s. zakup;
kupno; dźwignią; v. kupić;
okupić;nabywać; podnosić (np.
kotwicę);sprawiać sobie
purchaser (pe:rczeser) s. nabywca; kupujący
pure (pjuer) adj. czysty; zupełny; szczery; niewinny; nie
zepsuty,zwykły;czystej krwi
purgative ('pe:rgetyw) adj. przeczyszczający; s. środek na
przeczyszczenie
purgatory ('pe:rgetery) s. czyś-
ciec; adj. oczyszczający
purge (pe:rdż) v. przeczyszczać;
oczyścić; usuwać; dawać na
przeczyszczenie; s. oczyszczenie; czystka; środek przeczyszczający;rafinowanie;klarowanie
purify ('pjuery,faj) v. oczyszczać (się);klarować;rafinować
purity ('pjueryty) s. czystość
purloin (pe:rloyn) v. ukraść;
ściągać;porwać
purple ('pe:rpl) s. purpura;
adj. purpurowy; v. robić purpu-
rowym;robić szkarłatnym
purpose ('pe:rpes) s. cel. zamiar; skutek; decyzja; wola;
v. zamierzać;mieć na celu;plano-
wać) umieszczać; wsadzać; pouczać;
purposeful ('pe:rpesful) adj.
celowy; znaczący; rozmyślny;
zdecydowany; stanowczy
purposeless ('pe:rpeslys) adj.
bezcelowy; bezsensowny; daremny; próżny(wysiłek etc.)
purposely ('pe:rpesly) adv. naumyślnie; celowo; rozmyślnie
purr (pe:r) v. mruczeć; mrucze-
nie; pomrukiwać;s.pomruk
purse (pe:rs) s. sakiewka; torebka damska; kiesa; nagroda;
v. ściągać (się);marszczyć(czoło)
pursue (per'sju:) v. ścigać; tropić; iść dalej; uprawiać (np.
zawód); działać wg.planu; prześladować; kontynuować; towarzyszyć;spełniać(obowiązek)
pursuer(per'sju:er) s. ścigający;
prześladowca ;dążący do czegoś
pursuit (per'sju:t) s. pościg; po-
goń; zawód; zajęcie; rozrywka

pursy (pe:rsy) adj. dychawiczny; wydęty; otyły;sciągnięty
purvey (pe:r'wej) v. dostarczyć;
zaopatrywać; być dostawcą
purveyor (pe:rwejer) s. dostawca
pus (pas) s. ropa
push (pusz) s. pchnięcie; suw;
nacisk; wypad; wysiłek; energia; dryg; bieda; kryzys; zdecydowanie; v. pchać; posunąć;
szturchnąć; nakłonić; dopingo-
wać; odpychać; spychać; pomiatać; robić karierę ;ponaglać
push along ('pusz,e'long) v. iść
dalej; ciągnąć się dalej; jechać dalej; spieszyć się
push around ('pusz,a'round) v.
pomiatać kims
pusher ('puszer) s. popychacz;
(uliczny): sprzedawca narkotyków
puss (pus) s. kociak; dziewczyna; (slang):gęba;kot(tygrys)
pussycat ('pusy,kaet) s. kociak;
pliszka; (wulg) narząd płciowy
żeński; ('pasy) adj. ropny
put; put; put (put; put; put)
put (put) v. kłaść; stawiać;
umieszczać; wsadzać; pouczać;
przedkładać; ujmować; wystawiać; dodawać; wlewać; szacować; nakładać; opierać; składać;
narażać; wypychać (np. kule);
zanosić (np. prośby); s. rzut;
adj. nieruchomy(pozostający na)
_w miejscu
put back ('put,baek) v. przestawić do tyłu;odłożyć z powrotem
put down ('put,dałn) v. położyć;
stłumić;spuścić w dół;zapisywać
put forth ('put,fo:rþ) v. wydobyć; wytężyć(siły);wydawać(pismo)
put off ('put,of) v. odłożyć;
odroczyć ;zbywać;odwieść ;pozbyć_sie
put on ('put,on) v. wdziewać;
przybierać; tyć;udawać;dodawać
put out ('put,aut) v. zwichnąć;
zgasić; wytężyć (się); produkować; wydawać;wysunąć(rękę etc.)
put together (,put'tugedzer) v.
łączyć; montować; powiązać;
zbierać(myśli);kojarzyć;zliczyć

put up('put,ap) v. ustawiać;
wywieszać; cierpieć; wetknąć;
schować;dzwigać do góry;ustawić
putrefy ('pju:try,faj) v.gnić;
ropieć;ulegać zepsuciu
putrid ('pju:tryd) adj. zgniły;
zepsuty; cuchnący; śmierdzący;
wstrętny; obrzydliwy
putty ('paty) s. kit; szpachlów-
ka; v. szpachlować; zakitować
putty knife ('paty,najf) s.
szpachla
puzzle ('pazl) s. zagadka; łamigłówka; zakłopotanie;
v. intrygować; wprawiać w zakłopotanie; odgadnąć; wymyślić
puzzler ('pazler) s. łamigłówka
pyjamas (pe'dża:mez) pl. piżama
pyramid ('pyremyd) s. piramida;
ostrosłup; v. zarabiać na
spekulacji; wznosić (się)
piramidalnie;budować jak piramide
python ('pajsen) s. pyton
q (kju:) siedemnasta litera
angielskiego alfabetu (q.=kwarta)
quack (kłaek) s. znachor; szarlatan; kwakanie; v. uprawiać
znachorstwo; gadać jak szarlatan; kwakać
quad (kłod) (skrót): s. kwadrat;
czworokąt
quadrangle (kło'draengl) s.
czworokąt
quadruped ('kładru,ped) adj.
czworonożny
quadruple (kło'drupl) adj.
czterokrotny; cztery razy
większy;czterokrotnie większy
quadruplets (kło'dru:plets) s.
czworaczki
quail (kłejl) s. przepiórka;
v. drżeć przed czyms
quaint (kłejnt) adj, malowniczy; trochę dziwaczny
quake (kłejk) s. trzęsienie
(ziemi); v. trząść się (np.
z zimna)(ze strachu etc.)
quaky (kłejky) adj. trzesący
się; grząski
qualification (,kłolyfy'kejszyn)
s. warunek; określenie; kwalifikacja; uzdolnienie(do pracy)

qualified ('kłolyfajd) adj. wy-
kwalifikowany; uwarunkowany;
kwalifikujący się
quality ('kłolyty) s. jakość;
gatunek; własciwość; zaleta
qualm (kło:m) s. mdłości; nudności; obawa; wyrzuty; skrupuły
quandary ('kłondery) s. zakłopotanie; kłopot;dylemat
quantity ('kłontyty) s. ilość;
wielkość; hurt; obfitość
quarantine ('kłorenti:n) s.
kwarantanna; v. izolować
quarrel ('kło:rel) s. kłótnia;
zerwanie; spór; sprzeczka;
v. kłócić się; sprzeczać się;
zerwać z sobą;robić wyrzuty
quarrelsome ('kłorelsem) adj.
kłótliwy; swarliwy
quarry ('kłory) s. kamieniołom;
kopalnia odkrywkowa; łup; zdobycz; płytka; szybka; v. łamać;
wygrzebywać; wydobywać; exploatować;szperać(za wiadomosciami)
quarter ('kło:ter) v. ćwiarto-
wać; kwaterować; rozpłatać;
stacjonować; s. ćwierć; ćwiart-
ka; kwadrans; kwatera; 25 centów (moneta); kwadra; dzielnica;
strona świata; czynniki wpływo-
we (pl.) sfery(rządzące);kwartał
quarterly ('kło:terly) adj. kwartalny; adv. kwartalnie; s. kwar-
talnik;pismo kwartalne
quartet(te) (kło:r'tet) s. kwar-
tet; czworka
quarto ('kło:rtou) s. format
ćwiartkowy
quaver ('kłejwer) s. drżenie
głosu; tryl; v. drżeć; drgać;
wibrować; trelować
quay (ki:) s. molo;nadbrzeże
queasy ('kłi:zy) adj. przeczulony; mdlejący; grymaśny;wrażliwy
queen (kłi:n) s. królowa;królówka
queen bee ('kłi:n.bi:) s. królowa pszczoła
queer (kłir) adj. dziwny; dziwaczny; nieswój; podejrzany; fałszywy; pederasta; v. zepsuć;
wpakować w złą sytuację; mdlić

quench ('kłencz) v. gasić;
tłumic; nagle oziębiać (metal)
querulous ('kłerules) adj. na-
rzekający; zrzędny;płaczliwy
query ('kłiery) s. zapytanie;
pytajnik; znak zapytania;
v. pytać; kwestionować
quest (kłest) s. poszukiwanie;
śledztwo; v. szukać
question ('kłesczyn) s. pytanie;
zagadnienie; kwestia; wątpli-
wości; v. wypytywać; przesłuchiwać; badać; kwestionować;
pytać się;przeegzaminować
questionable ('kłesczenebl) adj.
wątpliwy (moralnie); sporny;
niepewny; niejasny
question mark ('kłesczyn,ma:rk)
s. znak zapytania
questionnaire (,kłejstje'neer)
s. kwestionariusz
queue (kju:) s. warkocz; ogonek; kolejka; v. czekać
w kolejce;czekać w ogonku
queue up ('kju:,ap) v. ustawiać się w kolejce
quibble ('kłybl) s. kruczek;
v. szukać wykrętów
quick (kłyk) adj. prędki; szybki; bystry; pomysłowy; żywy;
lotny; rudonośny; adv. szybko;
chyżo; v. przyspieszać; ożywiać (się);zwiększać szybkość
quicken ('kłyken) v. przyspieszać; pobudzać; ożywiać się;
wrócić do życia
quickly ('kłykly) adv. szybko;
prędko; z pośpiechem
quickness ('kłyknys) s. prędkość; ostrość
quicksand ('kłyk,saend) s.
grząski piasek
quicksilver ('kłyk,sylwer) s.
rtęć; żywe srebro
quick-tempered ('kłyk'temperd)
adj. porywczy
quick-witted ('kłyk'żytyd)
adj. bystry; rozgarnięty
quid (kłyd) s. funt szterling;
prymka;kawałek do żucia
quiet ('kłajet) adj. spokojny;
cichy; s. spokój; cisza;

v. uspokoić (się); uciszyć
(się);uspokajać;zciszyć;ucichnąć
quiet down ('kłajet dałn) v.
uspakajać;przyciszyć;ucichnąć
quietness ('kłajetnys) s. spokój; cisza;łagodność;skromność
quietude ('kłajetju:d) s. spokój (ducha)
quill (kłyl) s. lotka; dutka;
kolec; szpulka; pióro
quilt (kłylt) s. pikowana
kołdra; pikowana narzuta;
v. pikować; watować; robić
kołdry; zszywać;sprawić lanie
quince (kłyns) s. pigwa
quinine ('kłajnajn) s. chinina
quintal ('kłyntl) s. cetnar;
kwintal
quintuple ('kłyntjupl) adj.
pięciokrotny
quintuplets ('kłyntjuplyts) pl.
pięcioraczki
quit (kłyt) v. przestać; odejść;
odjechać; zabrać się; wyprowa-
dzić się; opuszczać; porzucać;
rezygnować; adj. wolny;uwolniony
quite (kłajt) adv. całkowicie;
zupełnie; raczej; wcale
quiver ('kływer) s. kołczan;
drżenie; drganie; v. drzeć;
drgać; trzepotać skrzydłami
quixotic ('kłyks,otyk) s. marzyciel w stylu Don Kichota
quiz (kłyz) s. klasówka; egzamin; badanie; przesłuchanie;
kawał; v. egzaminować; badać;
przesłuchiwać'przeglądać;kpić
quota ('kłouta) s. udział;
kontyngent;norma
quotation (kłou'tejszyn) s. cytata: cytowanie; notowanie;
przytaczanie(bieżącej ceny)
quotation marks (kłou'tejszyn
,ma:rks) pl. cudzysłów
quote (kłout) v. cytować; przy-
taczać; umieszczać w cudzysło-
wie; notować; podawać kurs;
powoływać się na kogoś
quotient ('kłouszent) s. iloraz
r (a:r) osiemnasta litera
angielskiego alfabetu
rabbi ('raebaj) s. rabin

rabbit ('raebyt) s. królik

rabble ('raebl) s. motłoch

rabid ('raebyd) adj. wściekły; szalony;rozjuszony;rozzłoszczony

rabies ('raebi:z) s. wścieklizna; wodowstręt

raccoon (ra'ku:n) s. pracz pospolity

race (rejs) s. rasa; plemię; szczep; ród; rodzaj; bieg; gonitwa; wyścigi; prąd; kanał; v. ścigać (się); gonić (się); pędzić; iść w zawody

racer ('rejser) s. wyścigowiec

racial ('rejszel) adj. rasowy

racing ('rejsyng) adj. wyścigowy; s. wyścigi; biegi

racist ('rejsyst) s. rasista

rack (raek) s. ruina; zagłada; zniszczenie; koło tortur; wieszak; drabina stajenna; półka; stojak; zębatka; szybki kłus; v. niszczęc; łamać kołem; torturować; cedzić; szarpać; męczyć; dręczyć

racket ('raekyt) s. rakieta; rak; zabawa; hulanka; awantura hałas; afera; granda; nieuczciwe interesy; kant; v. hałasować; hulać; bumblować; zabawiać się; awanturować się

racketeer (,raeky'tier) s. szantażysta; opryszek; v. szantażować; robić grandę

racoon (re'ku:n) s. szop

racy ('rejsy) adj. typowy; cięty; żywy; dosadny; aromatyczny; pikantny; nieprzyzwoity

radar ('rejder) s. radar

radiance ('rejdjens) s. promieniowanie; blask; promienność

radiant ('rejdjent) adj. promieniujący; promienny; rozpromieniony;rzucający promienie

radiate ('rejdyejt) v. promieniować (ciepłem, swiatłem etc.)

radiation (,redy'ejszyn) s. promieniowanie;zrodło promieniowania

radiator ('rejdy'ejter) s. grzejnik; kaloryfer; chłodnica (samochodowa);radiowa antena nadawcza;radioaktywna substancja wydzielająca promienie

radical ('raedykel) s. pierwiastek; radykał; adj. zasadniczy; radykalny; podstawowy; pierwiastkowy; korzeniowy

radio ('rejdjou) s. radio; adj. radiowy; v. nadawać przez radio ;wysyłać drogą radiową

radioactive ('rejdjou'aektyw) adj. radioaktywny; promieniotwórczy

radio set ('rejdjou,set) s. aparat radiowy; odbiornik radiowy

radiotherapy ('rejdjou-'terepy) s. radioterapia

radish ('raedysz) s. rzodkiewka

radius ('rejdjes) s. promień

raffle ('raefl) s. loteria fantowa; rupiecie; v. sprzedawać na loterii; kupować los

raft (raeft) s. tratwa; (slang): mnóstwo; v. spławiać na tratwie; robić tratwę

rafter (raefter) s. krokiew

rag (raeg) s. szmata; łachman; łupek; dachówka; v. (slang): besztać; dokuczać

rage (rejdż) s. szaleć; wściekac się; s. szał; wściekłość; namiętność

ragged (raegyd) adj. szmatławy; obdarty; podarty; poszarpany; kosmaty; zapuszczony; zaniedbany; wadliwy; chropowaty

raid (rejd) s. obława; nalot; najazd; v. urządzać obławę; najeżdżać ;dokonywać napadu

rail (rejl) s. poręcz; szyna; kolej; listwa; erekcja (slang); v. ogradzać poręczami; kłaść szyny; przewozić koleją; drwić; gorzko narzekać ;pomstować

rail in ('rejl,yn) v. przywozić koleją (materiały,towar)

rail off ('rejl,of) v. wywozić koleją (ludzi;towary etc.)

railing ('rejlyng)s. sztachety; ogrodzenie; poręcz;balusrada

railroad ('rejlroud) s. kolej; v. przewozić koleją; przepychać pospiesznie (np.ustawę); (slang) wpakowywać niesłusznie do więzienia

railway ('rejlžej) s. kolej;
tor kolejowy;tor na szynach
railway man('rejlžej,men) s.
kolejarz
rain (rejn) s. deszcz; v. pada
deszcz; spadać deszczem
rainbow ('rejn,bož) s. tęcza
raincoat ('rejnkout) s. płaszcz
nieprzemakalny
rainfall ('rejn,fo:l) s. opad;
ilość opadów
rainproof ('rejn,pru:f) adj.
nieprzemakalny
rainy ('rejny) adj. deszczowy;
dżdżysty; mokry od deszczu
rainy day ('rejny,dej) exp.
czarna godzina
raise (rejz) v. podnosić;
wskrzeszać; wznosić; wynosić;
hodować; wychowywać; wysuwać;
wytaczać; wzniecać; zrywać;
wywoływać; budzić; zbierać
(np. fundusze); wydobywać;
przerywać (np. oblężenie);
znosić (zakaz); s. podwyżka
(płac); podwyższenie
raisin ('rejzyn) s. rodzynek
rake (rejk) v. grabić; przegrze-
bać; grzebać; ostrzeliwać
(wzdłuż); obrzucać wzrokiem;
nachylać do tyłu; uganiać się
za zwierzyną; s. grabie; grab-
ki; rozpustnik
rake-off ('rejk,of) s. niele-
galna prowizja;łapówka
rake out ('rejk,aut) v. wygrzebywać; wygarniać (popiół etc.)
rakish ('rejkisz) adj. zgrabny;
rozpustny; hulaszczy;(pozornie)
szybki (okręt)(z wygladu)
rally ('raely) s. zbierać (się);
skupiać (się); przyjść do siebie; ochłonąć; okrzepnąć; ulegać poprawie (giełda); żartować
z kogoś; s. zbiórka; wiec;
okrzepnięcie; ożywienie walki
bokserskiej; wymiana ciosów;
poprawa (konjunktury)
ram (raem) s. tryk; baran; ta-
ran; tłok; dźwig hydrauliczny;
bijak; v. uderzyć; zderzyć się;
ubijać; wtłaczać; bić taranem;
upychać;ugniatać;najechać;zanu-
rzać

ramble ('raemb) v. włóczyć się;
przechadzać się; pnąc się (np.
o bluszczu); mówić bez związku;
odbiegać od tematu;s.wędrówka
ramify ('raemyfaj) v. rozgałę-
ziać (się); odgałęzienie (się)
ramp (raemp) s. rampa; v. rzucać się; stawać na tylnych
łapach;opadać pochyło;szaleć
rampart (raempa:rt) s. wał;
szaniec; v. umacniać (szańcem)
ran (raen) v. zob. run
ranch (raencz) s. rancho (gospodarstwo hodowlane) v. prowadzić rancho(farmę etc.)
rancher ('raenczer) s. właściciel rancha
rancid ('raensyd) adj. zjełczały (tłuszcz, oliwa etc.)
rancor('raenker) s. uraza; za-
jadłość; zawziętość; złość
random ('raendem) s. na chybił
trafił; adj. przypadkowy;
pierwszy lepszy;nie planowany
rang (raeng)v. zob. ring
range (rejndż) s. skala; zasięg;
rozpiętość; nośność; strzelnica; pasmo; obszar; wędrówka;
pastwisko; piec kuchenny;
s. ustawiać; układać; klasyfikować; wędrować; nastawiać teleskop; mieć zasięg; wstrzeli-
wać się; ciągnąć się; zaliczać
się;rozciągać się;sięgać;nieść
range finder ('rejndż,fajnder) s.
dalekomierz ; odległościomierz
ranger (rejndżer) s. strażnik
leśny; policjant; komandos;
wędrowiec;desantowiec etc.
rank (raenk) s. ranga; stan;
stanowisko; v. ustawiać rzędem;
układać; klasyfikować; zaszere-
gować; przewyższać rangą; miec
rangę; adj. wybujały; zjełczały;
śmierdzący; zupełny; jaskrawy;
obrzydliwy; sprosny;wierutny
ransack ('raensaek) v. przetrząsać; plądrować;grzebać
ransom ('raensem) s. okup; zwolnienie za okupem; v. wykupić;
zwalniać za okupem
rant (raent)v.deklamować z patosem;s.tyrada;bombastyczna mowa

rap (raep) v. dać klapsa; stukać; krytykować; s. klaps; ko-
łatanie; nagana; zarzut; skazanie na więzienie; odrobina
rapacious (re'pejszes) adj.
drapieżny;chciwy
rape (rejp) s. zgwałcenie (kobiety); zniewolenie; splądro-
wanie; uprowadzenie; v. gwałcić (kobietę); uprowadzać;
plądrować;pogwałcić neutralność
rapid ('raepyd) adj. prędki;
szybki; bystry; stromy
rapidity('raepydyty) s. szybkość; bystrość;rwący nurt(rzeki)
rapids ('raepyds) pl. progi
(na rzece); wodospad
rapt (raept) adj. zaabsorbowany;
zachwycony;urzeczony;oczarowany
rapture ('raepczer) s. zachwyt;
uniesienie;wzięcie żywcem do nieba
rare (reer) adj. rzadki; niedo-
pieczony (np. kotlet); na pół
surowy;nie dosmażony;adv.rzadko
rarity ('reeryty) s. rzadkość
rascal ('raeskel) s. hultaj;
łobuz; adj. hultajski
rascally ('raeskely) adj. hultajski; łobuzerski
rash (raesz) s. wysypka skórna;
ulewa; powódź; adj. pochopny;
popędliwy; nieprzemyślany
rasher ('raeszer) s. płatek
(np. szynki)
rasp (raesp) s. raszpla; pilnik;
zgrzytanie; v. drapać; skrobać;
drażnić; chrapliwie mówić
raspberry (ra:zbery) s. malina
rat (raet) s. szczur; łamistrajk;
donosiciel; v. polować na szczury; zdradzać; donosić;zaprzeda-
wać
rats (raets) pl. szczury; bzdura
rate (rejt) s. stopa; stosunek;
proporcja; wysokość; poziom;
szybkość; cena; stawka; opłata;
podatek; stopień; klasa; v. szacować; oceniać; ustalać; zaliczać; opodatkować; zasługiwać;
besztać; wymyślać
rate of exchange ('rejt of
yks'czejndż) s. kurs wymiany
rate of interest (,rejt of
'yntryst) s. stopa procentowa

rather ('raedzer) adv. raczej;
chętniej; dość; nieco; do pewnego stopnia;poniekąd;zamiast
ratify ('raetyfaj) v. zatwierdzać; ratyfikować
ration ('raeszyn) s. przydział;
porcja; racja; v. racjonować;
sprzedawać na kartki
rational ('raeszynl) adj. rozumny; rozsądny; racjonalny; wy-
mierny;sensowny
rationalize ('raeszyne,lajz) v.
racjonalizować; usprawiedliwiać
rattle ('raetl) v. grzechotać;
szczekać; brzęczeć; stukać;
trzaskać; terkotać; paplać
wiersze; s. grzechotanie; ter-
kot; stuk; paplanina; gaduła
rattler ('raetler) s. grzechotnik
rattlesnake ('raetl,snejk) s.
grzechotnik
ravage ('raewydż) s. spustoszenie; zniszczenie; v. pustoszyć; niszczyć;plądrować
rave (rejw) v. bredzić; maja-
czyć; szaleć; wściekać się;
wyć; zachwycać się; v. wrzask;
wycie; zaślepienie; przesadna
pochwała (entzjastyczna)
raven (rejwn) s. kruk; adj. kruczy; ('raewen) s. grabież; łup;
v. pożerać; szukać łupu; mieć
szalony apetyt
ravenous ('raewynes) adj. wy-
głodniały; zgłodniały; żarłoczny; drapieżny
ravine (re'wi:n) s. parów;jar;
wąwóz
raving ('rejwyng) adj. bredzący;
szalony; porywający (np. pięk-
nością); s. atak furii; bre-
dzenie; majaczenie
ravish ('raewysh) v. porywać
(kobietę); gwałcić (kobietę)
raw (ro:) adj. surowy; otwarty
(np. rana); wrażliwy; nieokrzesany; brutalny; nieprzyzwoity;
s. gołe ciało; surówka;
v. ocierać (skórę)
ray (rej) s. promień; promyk;
(ryba) płaszczka; v. promieniować; naświetlać; prześwietlać
wysyłać promienie(swiatła etc.)

rayon ('rejon) s. sztuczny jedwab
razor ('rejzer) z. brzytwa
razor blade ('rejzer'blejd) s.
żyletka; ostrze brzytwy
re (ri:) prep. w sprawie; tyczy; dotyczy; przedrostek :
znowu; od nowa
reach (ri:cz) v. osiągać; wy-
ciągnąć (np. rękę) dosięgnąć;
dotrzec; docierać; sięgnąć;
s. sięgnięcie; zasięg; połać;
przestrzeń ;pobliże;granice
reach out ('ri:cz,aut) v. wy-
ciągnąć (rękę etc.)
react (ri:'aekt) v. reagować;
oddziaływać; przeciwdziałać
reactor (ri:'aekter) s. reaktor (np. jądrowy)
read; read; read (ri:d; red;
red)
read (ri:d) v. czytać; tłumaczyć; interpretować
read out ('ri:d,aut) v. wydalać kogoś ;wyczytywać
readout ('ri:daut) s. odczyt
wyników komputera
read to ('ri:d tu) v. czytać
komuś
reader ('ri:der) s. czytelnik;
korektor; lektor; czytanka;
wypisy;recenzent(wydawnictwa)
readily ('redyly) adv. łatwo;
chętnie;ochoczo;bez tudu
readiness ('redynys) s. gotowość; pogotowie; obrotność;
ciętość; przytomność umysłu
reading ('ri:dyng)s. czytanie;
oczytanie; interpretacja;
lektura; czytelnictwo; adj.
czytający
readjust ('ri:e'dżast) v. dopasować na nowo
ready ('redy) adj. gotów; gotowy; przygotowany; adv.
w przygotowaniu; gotowy;
v. przygotowywać
ready-made ('redy'mejd) s.
konfekcja; adj. gotowy
ready-to-wear ('redy,tu'łeer)
s. odzież fabrycznej pro-
dukcji

real (ryel) adj. prawdziwy;
rzeczywisty; realny; istotny;
prawdziwy;autentyczny;faktyczny
real estate ('ryel,ys'tejt) s.
nieruchomość; realność
realism ('ryelyzem) s. realizm
realistic ('ryelyst) s. adj.
realistyczny
reality ('ty'aelyty) s. rzeczywistość; realizm; prawdziwość
realization (,ryelaj'zejszyn)
s. realizacja; spełnienie;
wykonanie; spieniężenie; uświadomienie sobie
realize ('ry:e,lajz) v. urzeczywistnić; realizować; uprzytam-
niać; zdawać sobie sprawę;
uzyskiwać; zdobywać (majątek)
really ('ryely) adv. rzeczywiście; naprawdę; doprawdy; faktycznie; istotnie
realm (relm) s. królestwo; dziedzina; sfera; zakres
realpolitik (rej'a:lpouly'tyk)
s. polityka egoistyczna
realtor ('ryelter) s. pośrednik
sprzedaży nieruchomości
realty ('ryelty) s. nieruchomość
reap (ry:p) v. żąć; zbierać
plony, owoce pracy etc.
reaper ('ry:per) s. żniwiarz:
żniwiarka
reappear ('ry:e'pier) v. zjawić
się ponownie;znowu ukazać się
rear (rier) s. tył; tyły; ustęp;
v. stawać dęba; hodować; wychowywać; wznosić (się); wybudować;
wystawiać
rear guard('rier,ga:rd) s. tylna
straż
rear-light ('rier,lajt) s. tylne
światło samochodu
rearm ('ry:'a:rm) v. ponownie
uzbrajać
rearmament ('ry:'a:rmement) s.
remilitaryzacja
rearmost (rie:r,moust) adj.
końcowy ;ostatni
rearview mirror ('rier,wju:'-
'myrer) s. (tylne) lusterko
w samochodzie (do sprawdzania
ruchu za samochodem)

rearrange ('ry:erejndż) v.
przestawiać; zmieniać (porządek);poprawic(fryzurę etc.)
rearwards ('rierłedz) adv.
wstecz;ku tyłowi; na tył
reason ('ri:zn) s. rozum; powód; uzasadnienie; motyw; przesłanka; rozsądek; v. rozumowac;
rozważać; wnioskować; rozpra-
wiac; przekonywać; dowodzic
reason out ('ri:zn,aut) v.
przemyślać;wrozumowac;dociekać
reason with ('ri:zn,łys) v.
przekonywac kogoś
reasonable ('ri:znebl) adj.
rozumny; rozsądny; umiarkowany; słuszny; racjonalny
reassure (,ry:a'szuer) v. zapewniac; upewniac; ubezpieczac
na nowo; uspakajac; przywracac
zaufanie;upewniac na nowo
reassuring (,ry:a'szueryng)
adj. uspokajający
rebate (ry'bejt) s. rabat;
zwrot (części kwoty); v. udzielac rabatu; potrącać (z rachunku);zamortyzować;przytępiać
rebel ('rebel) s. buntownik;
v. buntowac się; adj. zbuntowany; buntowniczy
rebellion (ry'beljen) s. bunt;
powstanie
rebellious (ry'beljes) adj.
zbuntowany; buntowniczy; niesforny;oporny;zbuntowany
rebirth (ry'be:rs) s. odrodzenie;odżywanie
re-book ('ry:buk) v. zamawiac
na nowo (program teatralny;
bilety lotnicze etc.)
rebound (ry'baund) s. odbicie;
odskok; rykoszet; v. odskakiwac; odbijac (się) (sobie na
kims)
rebuff (ry'baf) s. ofuknięcie;
odrzucenie; v. ofuknąc; dać
odprawę;odesłac z kwitkiem
rebuild('ry:byld) v. odbudowy-
wac; przebudowywac
rebuke (ry'bju:k) s. nagana;
v. upominac; łajac
recall (ry'ko:1) v. odwoływać;
przypominać (sobie);wycofywac;
cofać (obietnicę);s.nakaz powrotu

recap ('ry:kaep) s. opona ponownie gumowana; v. ponownie
wulkanizować opony; powtarzac
dla podsumowania
recapture ('ri:'kaepczer) v.
odzyskac; s. odzyskanie
recede (ry'si:d) v. cofać się;
oddalac sie; malec; słabnąc
receipt (ry'si:t) s. pokwitowanie; odbiór; recepta
receive (ry'si:w) v. otrzymy-
wac; dostawac; odbierac; przyjmowac (np. gości)
receiver (ry'si:wer) s. odbiornik (radiowy); słuchawka (telefoniczna); odbiorca; syndyk;
zarządca upadłości
recent ('ri:snt) adj. niedawny;
świeży; nowy
recently ('ri:sntly) adv. niedawno; swieżo; ostatnio;wspol-
reception (ry'sepszyn) s. przyjęcie; odbiór; recepcja
reception desk (ry'sepszyn,desk)
s. biuro do przyjmowania inte-
resantow;portiernia;biuro przyjęc
receptionist (ry'sepszynyst) s.
recepcjonistka; sekretarka
przyjmująca klientów;portier
recess (ry'ses) s. przerwa
(między lekcjami); ferie;
wgłębienie; nisza; wnęka;
v. odraczac; wkładać do wnęki;
robic wnękę;rozjeżdżać się na
recession (ry'seszyn) s. cof-
nięcie; recesja (gospodarcza);
wgłębienie; wnęka;kryzys;zastdj
recipe ('rysypy) s. przepis;
recepta
recipient (ry'sypjent) adj. od-
biorczy; s. odbiorca; zdobywca
nagrody; osoba obdarowana
reciprocal (ry'syprekel) adj.
wzajemny; odwrotny; s. odwrot-
nosć (w matematyce)
recital (ry'sajtl) s. przedstawienie; opowiadanie; recytacja;
koncert;deklamowanie utworu
recite (ry'sajt) s. recytowac
(wiersz); wyliczać
reckless ('reklys) adj. (nie-
bezpiecznie) lekkomyślny;
nieuważający;na oslep;wariacki
brawurowy;szaleńczy;zuchowaty

reckon ('reken) v. liczyć; sądzić; myśleć że;polegać na
reckon up ('reken,ap) v. zliczać;zsumować; podsumowywać
reckon with ('reken,łys) v. liczyć się (z kimś)
reckoning ('rekenyng) s. obliczanie (położenia); rachuba; obrachunek;kalkulacja;rozliczenie
reclaim (ry'klejm) v. odzyskiwać (pod uprawę); użyźniac; przerabiać odpadki; wyprowadzać z (zaniedbania; błędu etc.);zażądać zwrotu;dochodzić
recline (ry'klajn) v. kłaść się; wyciągać się; złożyć (np. głowę);spoczywać pół leżąc
recognition (,rekeg'nyszyn) v. rozpoznanie; uznanie; pozdrowienie; dowód uznania
recognize ('rekeg,najz) v. rozpoznawać; pozdrowić; uznawać; przyznawać; udzielać (głosu)
recoil (ry'kojl) v. wzdrygać się; cofać się; kopać (np. kolbą); odskoczyć; odbijać; s. odskok; odrzut; odbicie; wzdrygnięcie się
recollect (reke'lekt) v. wspominać; przypominać sobie; zbierać na nowo;przypominać sobie z trudem
recollection (,reke'lekszyn) s. wspomnienie; pamięć
recommend (reke'mend) v. polecać; zalecać;dobrze świadczyć
recommendation(,rekemen'dejszyn) s. polecenie; zlecenie
recompense ('rekem,pens) v. odpłacać; dawać odszkodowanie; s. wynagrodzenie; zadosćuczynienie;odszkodowanie;rekompensata
reconcile ('rekensajl) v. godzić (sprzeczności); zażegnać (spór); pojednać;pogodzić się
reconciliation (,reken,syly'ejszyn) s. pojednanie; pogodzenie
reconsider (,ri:ken'syder) v. ponownie rozważyć; reasumować
reconstruct (,ri:ken'strakt) v. odbudowywać; odtwarzać
reconstruction ('ri:ken'strakszyn) s. rekonstrukcja; odbudowa

record ('reko:rd) v. zapisywać; notować; rejestrować; zaznaczać; nagrywać; s. zapiska; archiwum; rejestracja; dokument; przeszłość (czyjaś); pamięć o kimś; nagranie; rekord
recorder (ry'ko:rder) s. registrator; aparat zapisujący; pisak;pisarz archiwista
record holder ('reko:rd,houlder) s. rekordzista; mistrz
recording ('reko:rdyng) s. nagranie (płyta)
record player ('reko:rd,plejer) s. adapter
recourse (ry'ko:rs) s. uciekanie się (ratunek)
recover (ry'kawer) v. odzyskać; nadrabiać; powetować sobie; uzyskać; przywracać; wyzdrowieć; ochłonąć; przyjść do siebie
recovery (ry'kawery) s. odzyskanie (pozycji); wyzdrowienie; poprawa (gospodarcza)
recreation (,rekry'ejszyn) s. rozrywka; zabawa; odtworzenie
recruit (ry'kru:t) s. rekrut; poborowy; v. werbować; uzupełniać (stan zatrudnienia)
rectangle ('rektaengl) s. prostokąt; a.prostokątny
rectify ('rektyfy) v. prostować (np. błąd); poprawiać (np. plan); usuwać (np. nadużycia)
rector ('rekter) s. proboszcz; rektor
rectory ('rektery) s. probostwo
recur (ry'ke:r) v. powtarzać się; przypominać się; nawiązywać do czegoś (wielokrotnie)
recurrent (ry'karent) adj. powracający; nawracający
red (red). adj. czerwony; s. czerwień; lewicowiec; komunista ;radykał(skrajny);forsa(sl.)
red-bait('redbejt) v. oskarżać o komunizm (USA)
red-blooded('red,bladyd) adj. męski; krzepki ;jurny
redden ('reden) v. zaczerwienić się ;zarumienić się
reddish ('redysz) adj. czerwonawy

redeem (ry'di:m) v. wykupywac;
okupywac; wybawiac; zbawiac;
odkupic; zamienic;kompensowac
redemption (ry'dempszyn) s.
wykup; okupienie; odkupienie;
wybawienie;umorzenie;zbawienie
red-handed ('red'haendyd) adj.
splamiony krwią; exp. na gorącym uczynku
red letter day ('red'leter, dej)
s. dzień specjalny; dzień
swiąteczny
redouble (ry'dabl) v. podwoic
(się); zwijac się
reduce (ry'dju:s) v. zmniejszac (się); chudnąc; redukowac; ograniczac; obniżac; dostosowac; sprowadzac; doprowadzac; rozcienczac; osłabiac;
odtleniac; wytapiac
reduction (ry'dakszyn) s.
zmniejszenie; redukcja; obniżka; sprowadzenie; dostosowanie; odtlenianie; wytapianie
reed (ri:d) s. trzcina; słoma;
fujarka; strzała; płocha
tkacka; stroik (muzyczny)
reeducation ('ry:edju'kejszyn)
s. przeszkolenie ponowne
reef (ri:f) s. rafa; skała podwodna; ref; v. refowac
reek (ri:k) s. odor; para; dym;
v. śmierdziec; parowac; dymic;
wędzic; ociekac (krwią)
reel (ri:l) s. szpula; cewka;
rolka; chwianie się; kręcenie
się; v. nawijac; odwijac; rozwijac; recytowac; chwiac się;
zataczac się; kręcic się; dostawac zawrotu głowy; dawac zawrót
głowy;zachwiac sie na nogach
reel off ('ri:l,of) v. odwijac
reel up ('ri:l,ap) v. nawijac
reelect ('ri:y'lekt) v. ponownie wybierac
reenter ('ri:'enter) v. ponownie wchodzic (w posiadanie etc.)
reentry ('ri:'entry) s. ponowne wejscie;rewindykacja
re-establish (,ry:ys'taeblysz)
v. ponownie: zakładac; ustanawiac; ustalac; wprowadzac

refer (ry'fe:r) v. odsyłac; po-
wiązywac; skierowac; odwoływac;
cytowac; odnosic się; dotyczyc;
powoływac się
referee (refe'ri:) s. sędzia
sportowy; rozjemca; v. sędzio-
wac
reference ('refrens) s. odsyłacz; odnosnik; odwoływanie
się; aluzja; informacja; referencja; stosunek; związek;
wzgląd;przelotna wzmianka
reference book ('referens,bu:k)
s. tekst podręczny;podręcznik
reference library ('referens
laj'brery) s. biblioteka podręczna naukowo-informacyjna
refill (ry:'fyl) s. ponowne;
napełnienie; wypełnienie; nowy
zapas; v. ponownie napełniac,
wkładac,zapełniac etc.
refine (ry'fajn) v. oczyszczac;
rafinowac; wysubtelniac; roz-
prawiac subtelnie
refinement (ry'fajnment) s.
rafinowanie; wyrafinowanie;
subtelnosc; wytwornosc
refinery (ry'fajnery) s. rafineria
reflect (ry'flekt) v. odbijac;
odzwierciadlac; rozmyslac; zastanawiac się; krytykowac;
przynosic (zaszczyt; ujmę)
reflection (ry'flekszyn) s. odbicie; odzwierciedlenie; odbicie swiatła; zarzut; rozwaga;
namysł;wzmianka;pomysl;wstyd
reflex ('ry:fleks) s. odruch;
refleks; odbicie; odzwierciedlenie; adj. refleksyjny; odbity; wygięty; v. poddawac
refleksom; wyginac wstecz
reflexive (ry'fleksyw) adj.
odbijający; pełen zadumy;
refleksyjny
reform (ry'fo:rm) v. reformowac;
poprawic; usuwac; ulegac refor-
mie; s. reforma; poprawa
reformation (,refer'mejszyn) s.
reformacja; poprawa
reformer (ry'fo:rmer) s. refor-
mator(moralnosci,warunków etc.)

refract (ry'fraekt) v. załamywać światło;wyginać promień swiatła

refractory (ry'fraektery) adj. oporny; uporczywy; krnąbrny; odporny; ogniotrwały

refrain (ry'frejn) v. powstrzymywać się; s. refren

refresh (ry'fresh) v. odświeżyć; wzmacniać; pokrzepiac

refreshment (ry'freszment) s. odpoczynek; wytchnienie; odświeżenie; zakąska

refrigerator (ry'frydże,rejter) s. lodówka; chłodnia

refuel ('ry:'fjuel) v. zaopatrzyc w paliwo; dodac paliwa

refuge ('refju:dż) s. schronienie; azyl;przytułek;v.schronic się

refugee (,refju'dżi:) s. zbieg; uchodźca; uciekinier

refund (ry'fand) s. zwrot; spłata; v. zwracac pieniądze

refusal (ry'fju:zel) s. odmowa; prawo opcji; wbijanie do oporu

refuse (ry'fju:z) v. odmawiac; odrzucac; adj. odpadowy; s. odpadki; rupiecie

refute (ry'fju:t) v. zbijac (np. twierdzenie)

regain (ry'gejn) v. odzyskać; wrocić (do zdrowia)

regard (ry'ga:rd) v. spoglądac; zważac; uważac; dotyczyc; s. wzgląd; spojrzenie; szacunek; uwaga;pozdrowienia;ukłony

regarding (ry'ga:rdyng) prep. odnosnie;co się tyczy;w sprawie

regardless (ry'ga:rdlys) adv. w każdym razie; adj. nie zważający; bez względu (na kłopoty etc.);nie liczac się(z wydatkami)

regard of (ry'ga:rd,ow) exp. co się tyczy; w sprawie etc.

regent ('ri:dżent) s. regent; opiekun; członek zarządu,

regime (ry'żi:m) s. ustroj; reżym; tryb życia; system; rządy

regiment ('redżyment) s. pułk; zastęp; v. organizowac; koszarowac; wcielac do pułku

region ('ri:dżen) s. okolica; sfera; rejon; obszar; dzielnica

register ('redżyster) v. rejestrowac; zapamiętywac; wysyłac polecony list; prowadzic rejestr; wstrzeliwac się; wyrażac minami

registered letter ('redżysterd, ,leter) s. list polecony

registration (,redzys'trejszyn) s. rejestracja; meldunek; ilość zarejestrowana

regret (ry'gret) s. ubolewanie; żal; v. żałowac czegos

regrettable (ry'gretebl) adj. godny ubolewania

regular ('regjuler) adj. regularny; stały; zawodowy; poprawny; przepisowy; s. regularny (żołnierz; ksiądz etc.); stały gość; wierny partyjnik

regularity (,regju'laeryty) s. regularnosc; systematycznosc

regulate ('regjulejt) v. regulowac;przystosowywac do wymogów

regulation (,regju'lejszyn) s. przepis; regulowanie; adj. przepisowy; zwykły

rehearsal (ry'he:rsel) s. próba; powtarzanie

rehearse (ry'he:rs) v. odbywac próbę; powtarzac

reign (rejn) v. panowac; władac; s. władza; panowanie

rein (rejn) v. kierowac wodzami; trzymac na wodzach

reins (rejns) pl. wodze

reindeer ('rejn.dier) s. renifer

reinforce (,ri:yn'force) v. wzmocnic;popierac;dodac sił

reject (ry'dżekt) v. odrzucic; odpalic; zwracac; ('rydżekt) s. wybrakowany towar; niezdatny do wojska;cos odrzuconego

rejection (ry'dżekszyn) s. odrzucenie; odmowa; wybrakowany towar;oblanie studenta;odkosz

rejoice (ry'dżojs) v. radowac; cieszyc się; weselic się

rejoicing (ry'dżojsyng) s. radość;uradowanie;adj.uradowany

rejoin ('ri:dżoyn) v. ponownie łączyc (się); zestawiac połamane częsci; odpowiadac na zarzut

relapse (ry'laeps) s. nawrót;
pogorszenie; v. ponownie popadać; zapadać z powrotem
relate (ry'lejt) v. opowiadać;
referować; łączyć się
related (ry'lejtyd) adj. bliski;
spokrewniony; spowinowacony;
związany;pokrewny;powinowaty
relation (ry'lejszyn) s. sprawozdanie; opowiadanie; stosunek; związek; pokrewieństwo;
powinowactwo; krewny
relationship (ry'lejszynszyp)
s. stosunek; pokrewieństwo;
powinowactwo;zależność
relative ('reletyw) adj.
względny; stosunkowy; podrzędny; zależny; dotyczący;
adv. odnośnie; w sprawie;
s. krewny; zaimek względny
relax (ry'laeks) v. odprężać
(się); osłabnąć; rozluźniać
się; łagodnieć; odpoczywać
relaxation (,ry:laek'sejszyn)
n. odprężenie; odpoczynek;
rozrywka; złagodzenie
relay(ry'lej) s. bieg rozstawny; wzmacniacz;v.przekazywać;
zmieniać (tor);kłaść na nowo
relay race (re'lej,rejs) s.
bieg rozstawny; bieg sztafetowy
release (ry'li:z) v. wypuszczać; uwalniać; zwalniać;
s. zwolnienie; uwolnienie;
puszczenie (do druku); spust;
wyzwalacz;wypuszczenie(filmu)
relent (ry'lent) v. łagodnieć;
mięknąć;dać się wzruszyć
relentless (ry'lentlys) adj.
nieugięty; bezlitosny; nieprzejednany;nieustępliwy;srogi
relevant ('relewent) adj.
istotny; trafny; na miejscu;
należący do rzeczy
reliability (ry,laje'bylyty) s.
rzetelność; solidność; pewność
reliable (ry'lajebl) adj. pewny; solidny; rzetelny
reliance (ry'lajens) s. zaufanie; otucha
reliant (ry'lajent) adj. ufny
w siebie;liczący na kogoś;zależny od czegoś

relic ('relyk) n. zabytek; relikwia;pozostałość;resztka
relief (ry'li:f) n. odprężenie;
ulga; urozmaicenie; zapomoga;
pomoc; zmiana (np. warty);
płaskorzeźba;uwypuklenie
relieve (ry'li:w) v. nieść pomoc, ulgę; ulżyć (sobie);
oddać mocz; ożywić; zmieniać
wartę; zluzować; uwypuklić
(na tle czegoś);uwydatnić
religion (ry'lydżyn) s. religia;
obrządek; wyznanie; zakon
religious (ry'lydżes) adj. pobożny; religijny; zakonny;
s. zakonnik; zakonnica
relinquish (ry'lynkłysz) v. porzucać; wyrzekać się czegoś;
zaniechać; zrzekać się; rezygnować;wypuścić coś z rąk
relish ('relysz) s. smak; posmak;
przyprawa; przysmak; urok; zamiłowanie; v. smakować w czyms;
czynić smaczniejszym; przyprawiać; mieć dobry smak; być
przyjemnym;dodawać smaku
reluctance (ry'laktens) s. niechęć; opór(magnetyczny);wstręt
reluctant (ry'laktent) adj. niechętny; oporny
rely on (ry'laj,on) v. polegać
na czymś lub kimś ;liczyc na
remain (ry'mejn) v. pozostawać
remains (ry'mejns) pl. pozostałości; resztki; przeżytki;
zwłoki; szczątki
remainder (ry'mejnder) s. reszta; pozostałość; remanent
remand (ry'maend) v. odsyłać
(do niższej instancji lub więzienia); s. odesłanie do
więzienia; człowiek odesłany
z powrotem
remark (ry'ma:rk) v. zauważyć;
zrobić uwagę; s. uwaga
remarkable (ry'ma:rkebl) adj.
wybitny; godny uwagi
remedy ('remydy) s. lekarstwo;
środek; rada; v. leczyć; zaradzać ;naprawiać
remember (ry'member) v. pamiętać;
przypominać; pozdrawiać; modlić
się za kogoś;mieć w pamięci

remembrance (ry'membrens) s.
wspomnienie; pamiątka; pamięć; pozdrowienie;ukłony
remind (ry'majnd) v. przypominac'coś komus;przypomnieć
reminder (ry'majnder) s. przypomnienie; upomnienie; ponaglenie;ktoś przypominający
reminiscent (,remy'nysnt) adj.
przypominający; wspominający; pełen wspomnień
remiss (ry'mys) adj. niedbały;
ospały; niechlujny
remit (ry'myt) s. przekazywać
(pieniądze); darowac'(dług);
odpuszczac'(grzechy); odsyłac'; przywracac'; łagodzic';
łagodniec'; słabnąc'
remitance (ry'mytens) s. przesyłka pieniężna; wypłata
remnant ('remnent) s. resztka;
pozostałość; ślad czegoś
remodel (ry'modl) v. przerabiac'; odnowic'; przemodelowac'
remonstrate ('remenstrejt) v.
protestować
remorse (ri'mo:rs) s. wyrzuty
sumienia; skrupuły
remorseless (ri'mo:rslys) adj.
bezlitosny ;nie skruszony
removal (ry'mu:wl) v. usunięcie; przeprowadzka
remove (ry'mu:w) v. usuwac';
przewozic'; zdejmowac'; przeprowadzac'się; opuszczac';
s. przeprowadzka; odległość;
stopień;oddalenie
remover (ry'mu:wer) s. usuwacz
(plam); środek do usuwania
renaissance (ry'nesens) s. odrodzenie;renesans;a.renesansowy
rend; rent; rent (rend; rent;
rent)
rend (rend) v. drzec'; targac';
wydzierac'; urągac'; rozdzierac'
render ('render) v. uczynic';
zrobic'; oddawac'; okazywac';
składac'; wydawac'; płacic'; odpłacac'; oczyszczac'; wytapiac';
tynkowac'; s. odpłata (np.
w naturze); pierwsza warstwa
tynku

rendezvous ('ra:ndy,wu:) s.
randka; umowione spotkanie;
miejsce spotkań
renew (ry'nu:) v. odnawiac'; ponawiac'; wznawiac'; odswiezac';
prolongowac'
renewal (ry'nu:el) s. odnowienie (np. kontraktu)
renounce (ry'nauns) v. zrzekac'
się; zrezygnowac'; wyrzekac'się;
wypowiadac'; odstępowac'; nieuznawac'
renovate (ry'nowejt) v. odnowic';
naprawic'
renown (ry'naun) s. sława; rozgłos; pogłoska
renowned (ry'naund) adj. sławny
rent 1. (rent) v. zob. rend
rent 2. (rent) s. komorne;
czynsz; renta; najem; rozdarcie; szczelina; rozłam; parow;
v. wynajmowac'; dzierzawic'; pobierac'czynsz; byc'wynajmowanym
rental ('rentl) s. czynsz; komorne; wypozyczanie; adj. czynszowy
rental agency ('rentl'ejdzensy)
s. biuro wynajmu (narzędzi;
mieszkań etc)
rent free ('rent'fri:) adj.
wolny od opłaty czynszowej
repair (ry'peer) v. pójsc';
uczęszczac'; naprawiac'; reperowac'; remontowac'; powetowac';
wynagrodzic'; s. naprawa; remont; stan
repair shop (ry'peer,shop) s.
warsztat naprawy
reparation (repa'rejszyn) s.
naprawa; remont; odszkodowanie
repartee (repa:r'ti:) s. ripos-
ta; cięta odpowiedz; odcinanie się
repay (ry:'pej) v. spłacic';
zwrócic'; wynagrodzic'; odwzajemnic'się; oddac'
repeat (ry:'pi:t) v. powtarzac'
(się); repetowac'; odbijac'się;
robic'powtorkę; robic'ponownie;
odtwarzac'; s. powtórka; powtórzenie; powtórne zamówienie
a.powtórny;wielokrotny

repel (ry'pel) v. odpierać;
odrzucać; odtrącać; budzić
odrazę ,niechęć, wstręt etc.

repent (ry'pent) v. żałować

repentance (ry'pentens) s.
skrucha; żal

repentent (ry'pentent) adj.
żałujący; pełen skruchy

repetition (,repy'tyszyn) s.
powtórzenie; powtórka

replace (ry'plejs) v. zastępować; zwracać; oddawać; umieszczać z powrotem; przywrócić;
wymienić

replacement (ry'plejsment) s.
zastępstwo; zastępca; zastąpienie; wymiana (części)

replenish (ry'plenysz) v. ponownie napełniać; wypełniać;
uzupełniać

replay (ry'plej) v. ponownie
rozgrywać; ('ry:plej) s. ponowna rozgrywka

reply (ry'plaj) v. odpowiadać;
s. odpowiedź

report (ry'po:rt) v. opowiadać;
meldować; dawać sprawozdanie;
zdawać sprawę; pisać sprawozdanie; referować; s. raport;
sprawozdanie; komunikat;
opinia; huk; wybuch; pogłoska

reporter (ry'po:rter) s. dziennikarz; sprawozdawca; reporter

repose (ry'pouz) s. odpoczynek;
spokój; v. odpoczywać; spoczywać; polegać; opierać; pokładać

represent (,repry'zent) v.
przedstawiać; reprezentować;
wyobrażać; grać (kogoś)

representation (,repryzen'tejszyn) s. przedstawicielstwo;
reprezentacja; przedstawienie;
wyobrażenie

representative (,repry'zentetyw) adj. przedstawiający;
reprezentujący; wyobrażający;
s. przedstawiciel; reprezentant (poseł na sejm)

repress (ry'pres) v. tłumić;
hamować; powstrzymywać; poskromić

reprieve (ry'pri:w) v. zawieszać; odraczać; dawać odroczenie; s. odroczenie; darowanie,
zmiana kary (śmierci)

reprimand ('reprymaend) v. karcić; udzielać nagany; s. nagana

reproach (ry'proucz) v. robić
wyrzuty; wymawiać; s. wyrzut;
zarzut; wymówka

reproachful (ry'prouczful) adj.
pełen wyrzutu

reproduce (,rypre'du:s) v. odtwarzać;reprodukować; rozmnażać; wznawiać

reproduction (,ri:pre'dakszyn)
s. reprodukcja; rozmnażanie
się; płodzenie

reproof (ry'pru:f) s. nagana

reprove (ry'pru:w) v. ganić

reptant ('reptent) adj. pełzający

reptile ('reptajl) s. gad; płaz;
gadzina; adj. pełzający; gadzinowy

republic (ry'pablyk) s. republika; rzeczpospolita

republican (ry'pablyken) adj.
republikański; s. republikanin

repugnance (ry'pagnens) s. odraza; niechęć; niezgodność;
sprzeczność

repugnant (ry'pagnent) adj.
odrażający; oporny; sprzeczny;
niezgodny

repulse (ry'pals) v. odpierać;
odrzucać; odtrącać; s. odparcie; odrzucenie; odmowa

repulsive (ry'palsyw) adj. odrażający; wstrętny; odpychający;budzący odrazę

reputable ('repjutebl) adj.
szanowany; zaszczytny

reputation (,repju'tejszyn) s.
reputacja; sława; dobre imię

repute (ry'pju:t) s. reputacja;
sława; v. uważać za coś

request (ry'kłest) s. prośba;
życzenie; żadanie; zapotrzebowanie; v. prosić o pozwolenie;
upraszać ;poprosić o przysięgę

require (ry'kłajer) v. żądać;
nakazywać;wymagać;być wymaganym

required (ry'kłajerd) adj.
obowiązkowy;wymagany;żądany
requirement (ry'kłajerment) s.
wymaganie; zadanie; potrzeba
requisite ('rekłyzyt) adj. wy-
magany; s. rzecz konieczna,
potrzebna; rekwizyt
requisition (,rekły'zyszyn) s.
zadanie; nakaz; zapotrzebowanie; v. wydawać zapotrzebowanie; zapotrzebowywać; rekwiro-
wać;zarzadać dostaw
requite (ry'kłajt) v. odwzajemniać się;wynagradzać;zemścić
rescue ('reskju:) v. ratować;
wybawiać; odbijać z więzienia;
s. ratunek; odbicie z więzienia; odebranie przemocą
research (ry'se:rcz) s. poszukiwanie; badanie
researcher (ry'se:rczer) s. badacz (naukowy etc.);badaczka
resemblance (ry'zemblens) s.
podobieństwo
resemble (ry'zembl) v. byc po-
dobnym (z wyglądu)
resent (ry'zent) v. czuc urazę
resentful (ry'zentful) adj.
urażony;obrażony;zawziety
resentment (ry'zentment) s.
uraza;złosc;oburzenie;obraza
reservation (,rezer'wejszyn) s.
zastrzeżenie; zarezerwowanie;
miejsce zarezerwowane; rezerwat (np. indiański); rezerwa;
zapas;ograniczenie
reserve (ry'ze:rw) v. odkładać;
zastrzegac; zarezerwowac;
s. rezerwa; zapas; rezerwat;
zastrzeżenie; warunek
reserved (ry'ze:rwd) adj.zare-
zerwowany; powsciągliwy; pełen rezerwy;z rezerwą;zastrzeżo-
reservoir ('reserwła:r) s.
zbiornik; zbiór; pokład kopalniany; v. składać w zbiorniku
reside (ry'zajd) v. mieszkać;
tkwic;spoczywać w;osadzac się
residence ('rezydens) s. miejsce zamieszkania; pobyt (stały)
residence permit ('rezydens,-
per'myt) s. prawo pobytu

resident ('rezydent) s. stały
mieszkaniec; adj. zamieszkały;
umiejscowiony;zamieszkujący
residue ('rezydju:) s. reszta;
pozostałosc;reszta spadkowa
resign (ry'zajn) v. zrzekać się;
wyrzekac się; godzić się z losem
resignation (,rezyg'nejszyn) s.
dymisja; zrzeczenie się; wyrzeczenie się;pogodzenie sie(z losem)
resigned (ry'zajnd) adj. zrezyg-
nowany;w stanie spoczynku
resin ('rezyn) s. żywica; v. zaprawiać żywicą
resist (ry'zyst) v. opierac się;
stawiac opór; byc odpornym;
powstrzymywac się
resistance (ry'zystens) s. opór;
sprzeciw; wytrzymałosc; odpor-
nosc; opornica;a.oporowy
resistant (ry'zystent) adj. odporny; opierający się; s. cos
lub ktos odporny,opierajacy się
resolute ('rezelu:t)adj. rezolutny; śmiały; zdecydowany
resolution (,rese'lu:szyn) s.
uchwała; postanowienie; rezo-
lucja; śmiałosc; rozłożenie;
rozwiązanie;rozkład(sił)
resolve (ry'zolw) s. postanowienie; decyzja; stanowczosc;
v. rozkładac; rozwiązywac;
uchwalac; decydowac; postanawiac; usuwac;przemieniac;skłaniac
resolved (ry'solwd) adj. zdecydowany; śmiały
resonance ('resnens) s. oddźwięk;
odgłos ; rezonans
resonant ('reznent) adj. rezonu-
jący; rozbrzmiewający
resort (ry'zo:rt) v. uciekać się;
uczęszczać; s. uzdrowisko;
uczęszczanie; ucieczka; uciekanie się; ratunek; wyjscie
resort to (ry'zo:rt,tu) v. uciekać się do...
resound (ry'zaund) v. rozbrzmie-
wac; odbijąc; opiewac; obiegac;
wypowiadac się;odbijąc się echem
resource (ry'so:rs) s. zasoby;
środki; bogactwa; zaradnosc;
pomysłowosc;zasoby naturalne

resourceful (ry'so:rsful) adj.
zaradny; pomysłowy
respect (rys'pękt) v. szanować; dotyczyc; zważać;
s. wzgląd; szacunek; poważanie;związek;łacznosć;pozdrowienia)
respectable (rys'pektebl) adj.
chwalebny; godny szacunku;
poważny; pokaźny
respectful (rys'pektful) adj.
pełen szacunku
respectfully (rys'pektfuly)
adv. z poważaniem; z uszanowa-
niem
respecting (rys'pektyŋg) prep.
odnosnie do...
respective (rys'pektyw) adj.
odpowiedni ;poszczególny
respectively (rys'pektywly)
adv. odpowiednio; każdemu
z osobna ;kolejno
respiration (,respy'rejszyn)
s. oddech; oddychanie
respite ('respajt) s. wytchnienie (krótkie); odroczenie;
v. odraczac (stracenie); przynosic (krótką) ulgę
resplendent (rys'plendent) adj.
błyszczący silnie;jasny
respond (rys'pond) v. odpowiadac; reagować; byc czułym
respondent (rys'pondent) adj.
odpowiadający; wrażliwy;
s. pozwany; obrońca
response (rys'pons) s. odpowiedz; odzew; reakcja; oddźwięk ;odezwanie się
responsibility (rys,ponse'bylyty) s. odpowiedzialnosc
responsible (rys'ponsebl) adj.
odpowiedzialny (wobec; przed)
rest (rest) s. odpoczynek;
spokój; przerwa; przestanek;
podpórka; pomieszczenie;
schronienie; reszta; v. spoczywac; odpoczywac; dawac odpoczynek; uspokoic; byc spo-
kojnym; podpierac się; polegac
restaurant ('resterent) s. restauracja ;jadłodajnia
restful ('restful) adj. spokojny; uspokajający;wypoczęty

restless ('restlys) adj. niespokojny; bezsenny ;niesforny
restlessness ('restlysnys) s.
niepokój ;zniecierpliwienie
restoration (,reste'rejszyn) s.
odnowienie; rekonstrukcja; restytucja; odtworzenie
restore (rys'to:r) v. przywracac; uleczyc; odnawiac; restau-
rowac; restytuowac; zwracac;
rekonstruowac; odtwarzac
restrain (rys'trejn) v. powstrzymywac; powsciągac; krępowac;
ograniczac ;trzymac w ryzach
restraint (rys'trejnt) s. skre-
powanie; uwięzienie; zamknięcie w szpitalu psychiatrycznym;
wstrzemięzliwosc; umiar
restrict (rys'trykt) v. ograniczac do; zamykac w (granicach)
restriction (rys'trykszyn) s.
ograniczenie
rest room('rest,rum) s. ustęp;
toaleta
result (ry'zalt) s. rezultat;
wynik; v. wynikac; dawac w wyniku ;wypływac;pochodzic
result in (ry'zalt,yn) v. konczyc się na
resultant (ry'zaltent) adj. wy-
nikający;(np. siła) wypadkowa
resume (ry'zju:m) v. wznawiac;
ponownie podejmowac; obejmowac;
zajmowac; odzyskiwac; ciagnąc
dalej; streszczac ;odzyskac
resumption (ry'zampszyn) s.
wznowienie; odzyskanie; podjęcie
na nowo ;powrót do czegos
resurrection (,reze'rekszyn) s.
odżycie; zmartwychwstanie;
wskrzeszenie ;wznowienie(zwyczaju)
retail ('ri:tejl) s. detal; adj.
detaliczny; v. sprzedawac de-
talicznie; szczegółowo opowiadac ;adv.detalicznie;a.detaliczny
retailer (ri:'tejler) s. sklepikarz; detalista; plotkarz
retain (ry'tejn) v. zatrzymywac;
zapamiętywac; zgodzic (do pracy);zachowywac(tradycje)
retaliate (ry'taeliejt) v. od-
wzajemniac się; brac odwet

retaliation (ry,taely'ejszyn)
s. odwet;zemsta;odpłata

retell ('ri:'tel) y. ponownie
opowiedziec;powtórzyc

retention (ry'tenszyn) s. zatrzymanie (np. moczu); zdoj-
nosc zatrzymywania; pamięc

retinue ('retynu:) s. orszak;
swita;czeladz;poczet(dostojnika)

retire (ry'tajer) v. wycofywac
(się); isc na spoczynek;
pensjonowac;s.sygnał odwrotu

retired (ry'tajerd) adj. emery-
towany; ustronny;odosobniony

retirement (ry'tajerment) s.
przejscie w stan spoczynku;
ustronie; odosobnienie; wy-
cofanie(weksla);odwrót

retort (ry'to:rt) v. odpłacac
się; odcinac się; odparowac;
ripostowac; s. retorta; ri-
posta; odwet; odwrócenie
(oskarzenia) ; cięta odpowiedź

retrace (ry'trejs) v. odtwo-
rzyc; przypomniec sobie; badac początek   (1)

retrace (ry:'trejs) v. ponownie liniowac; kopiowac (2)

retract (ry'traekt) v. cofnąc
się; odwołac; chowac się;
wciągac(się)(pazury)

retreat (ry'tri:t) v. cofac
się; s. odwrót; wycofanie się
w zacisze; kryjówka; odosobnienie; przytułek;ustronie

retribution (,retry'bju:szyn)
s. odpłata; kara; nagroda

retrieve (ry'tri:w) v. odzyskac; powetowac; odszukac; uratowac; uprzytommic sobie;
aportowac; s. odzyskanie; od-
szukanie; powetowanie; urato-
wanie ;ruch wsteczny(powrotny)

retrospect ('retrespekt) s.
spojrzenie wstecz; rozwazanie
przeszłosci; v. rzucac okiem
wstecz; nawiązywac do (przeszłosci);patrzyc w przeszłosc

retrospective('retrespektyw)
adj. retrospektywny; działający wstecz;z mocą retroaktywną

return (ry'te:rn) v. wracac;
przynosic dochód;złozyc(zezna-nie)

obracac w..; oddawac; odwzajemnic; odpowiedziec; wybrac;
s. powrót; nawrót; dochód;
zysk; zwrot; rewanz; sprawozdanie (np podatkowe)

return flight (ry'te:rn,flajt)
s. lot powrotny

return ticket (ry'te:rn,tykyt)
s. powrotny bilet

reunification ('ri:ju:nyfy'kejszyn) s. ponowne zjednoczenie

reunion ('ri:'ju:njen) s. zjazd;
ponowne połączenie; zebranie

revaluation (ri:'waelju'ejszyn)
s. ponowna ocena; przewartoscio-
wanie(po ponownej ocenie)

revaluate (ri:'waelju':ejt)v.
ponownie ocenic; przewartoscio-
wac(dom w celach podatkowych)

revamp (ry:'waemp) v. przerabiac; reorganizowac; rewidowac;
okapowac (buty);odnowic

reveal (ry'wi:l) v. ujawniac;
objawiac; odsłaniac; s. rama
okna w karoserii

revel ('rewl) s. zabawa; hulanka; v. hulac; uzywac sobie

revelation (,rewy'lejszyn) s.
ujawnienie; objawienie; odsłonięcie; rewelacja;odkrycie

revenge (ry'wendz) s. zemsta;
msciwosc; v. pomscic; zemscic
się(za zniewagę,krzywdę etc.)

revengeful (ry'wendzful) adj.
msciwy

revenue ('rewy,nu:) s. dochód
(z podatków)

revenue office ('rewy,nu:'ofys)
s. urząd podatkowy (finansowy)

revere (ry'wier) v. czcic;
odnosic się z czcią

reverence ('rewerens) s. czesc;
szacunek; wielebnosc

reverend ('rewerend) adj. czcigodny; wielebny; s. duchowny

reverse (ry'we:rs) s. odwrot-
nosc; rewers; tył; niepowodzenie; wsteczny bieg; adj. odwrotny; przeciwny; wsteczny;
v. odwracac; zmieniac kierunek; obalac (np. przepis)

reverse gear (ry'we:rs,gier) s.
wsteczny bieg(w samochodzie)

reverse side (ry'we:rs,sajd)
s. odwrotna strona
review (ry'wju:) v. przeglądać; pisać recenzje; przeglądać w myśli; dokonywać przeglądu; s. recenzja; przegląd; rewia;ponowny przeglad
reviewer (ry'wju:er) s. recenzent; krytyk
revile (ry'wajl) v. wyzywać; wymyślać; przezywać
revise (ry'wajz) v. przejrzeć; zrewidować; przerabiać
revision (ry'wyżyn) s. rewizja; przejrzane wydanie; przeróbka
revival (ry'wajwel) s. ożywienie; odżywanie; powrot do życia;powrót do stanu użyteczności
revive (ry'wajw) v. wskrzeszać; przywracać do życia; wznawiać; ożywiać; odżywać; wracać do przytomności
revolt (ry'woult) s. bunt; powstanie; v. buntować się; wzdrygać się; mieć odrazę; budzić odrazę
revolution (,rewe'lu:szyn) s. obrót; rewolucja
revolutionary (,rewe'lu:sznry) adj. rewolucyjny; s. rewolucjonista
revolutionist (,rewe'lu:szynyst) s. rewolucjonista
revolutionize (,rewe'lu:szn,ajz) v. zrewolucjonizować; wywoływać rewolucje
revolve (ry'wolw) v. obracać; krążyć; obracać się; obmyślać
revolving (ry'wolwyng) adj. obrotowy
reward (ry'ło:rd) s. nagroda; wynagrodzenie; v. wynagradzać
rheumatism ('ru:metyzem) s. reumatyzm; gościec stawowy
rhubarb ('ru:ba:rb) s. rabarbar; (slang):kłótnia
rhyme (rajm) s. rym; rymować się
rhythm ('rytm) s. rytm
rhythmic ('rytmyk) adj. rytmiczny; miarowy
rib (ryb) s. żebro; żeberko; wręga; v. żeberkować; nabierać; wyśmiewać;droczyć się;płytko ora-
ribbed(rybd)adj.żebrowany

ribbon ('ryben) s. tasma; pasek; strzęp; wstążka; v. drzeć na strzępy, paski; ozdabiać wstążką;wić się wstęgą
rice (rajs) s. ryż
rich (rycz) adj. bogaty; kosztowny; suty; obfity; tuczący; pożywny; soczysty; mocny (zapach); pełny; tłusty (np. pokarm); pocieszny (zdarzenie)
riches ('ryczyz) pl. bogactwo; bogactwa
richness ('rycznys) s. bogactwo; pełnia
rick (ryk) s. stóg; v. ustawiać w stogi; stawiać stóg
rickets ('rykyts) s. choroba angielska; krzywica; rachityzm
rickety,('rykyty) adj. chwiejny; koslawy; rachityczny
rid; rid; ridded (ryd; ryd; 'rydyd)
rid (ryd) v. uwalniać się od...; oczyszczac się; pozbywać się
ridden ('rydn) zob. v. ride
riddle ('rydl) s. zagadka; v. zadawać zagadki; mówić zagadkami; rozwiazywać zagadki
ride; rode; ridden (rajd; roud; 'rydn)
ride (rajd) v. pojechać; jechać (też statkiem); jeździć; tyranizować; wozić; nosić; dokuczać; s. przejażdżka; jazda; nabieranie (kogoś); droga
rider ('rajder) s. jeździec; dżokej; dodatek; poprawka; klauzula; ciężarek przesuwany; nasadka;poprawka na dokumencie
ridge (rydż) s. grzbiet (też góry); krawędź; kalenica; pasmo górskie; wał; skiba; grobla; v. pokrywać skibami; robić krawędzie; marszczyć
ridicule,('rydy,kju:l) v. wyśmiewać się; s. kpiny
ridiculous (ry'dykju:les) adj. śmieszny; bezsensowny
riding ('rajdyng) s. konna jazda; adj. jadący;do konnej jazdy
rifle (rajfl) s. karabin; gwintówka; gwint;strzelec; v.gwintować (lufę); strzelać;ograbić; okraść; pokrzyżować

rift (ryft) s. szczelina; różnica zdań; v. rozszczepiać
się ;pęknąć;popękać

rig (ryg) v. zaopatrywać; klecić; montować; stroić; robić
kanty; manipulować ceny;
s. sprzęt (wiertniczy); wóz
z koniem; kostium; machlojka

right (rajt) adj. prawa; prawy; poprawny; prawoskrętny;
prosty (też kąt); właściwy;
słuszny; dobry; odpowiedni;
prawidłowy; w porządku; zdrowy; adv. w prawo; na prawo;
prosto; bezpośrednio; bezzwłocznie: dokładnie; słusznie; dobrze; s. prawa strona;
prawo; dobro; słuszność;
sprawiedliwość; pierwszeństwo;
v. naprostować; naprawić;
sprostować; odpłacać; mścić;
usprawiedliwiać

right ahead ('rajt,e'hed) exp.
wprost ;na wprost;przed siebie

right away ('rajt,e'łej) exp.
zaraz ;natychmiast;już teraz

righteous ('rajtszes) adj.
sprawiedliwy; prawy ;słuszny

rightful ('rajtful) adj. słuszny; sprawiedliwy; prawowity;
należny z prawa;prawy

right-hand ('rajt,haend) adj.
praworęki; położony na prawo

right-handed ('rajt-'haendyd)
adj. praworęczny; dostosowany
do prawej ręki; idący wg.ru-
chu zegara; obracający się
w prawo (gwint etc.)

right of way ('rajt,ow'łej)
exp.; prawo pierwszeństwa na
drodze; prawo przejazdu; grunt
pod drogą (kolej)(pod szosą etc.)

rightist ('rajtyst) s. prawico-
wiec; adj. prawicowy

rightly ('rajtly) adv. spra-
wiedliwie; słusznie; poprawnie; właściwie;na miejscu

rigid ('rydżyd) adj. sztywny;
nieugięty; surowy;nieustępliwy

rigor ('ryger) s. rygor; surowość; zesztywnienie

rigorous ('rygeres) adj. surowy; rygorystyczny

rim (rym) s. brzeg; krawędź;
obręcz; powierzchnia wody
(przy żeglowaniu); v. robić
krawędź; posuwać wzdłuż kra-
wędzi;dawać oprawę(do okularów)

rimple ('rympl) v. marszczyć

rind (rajnd) s. kora; łupina;
skórka; v. zdzierać korę

ring (ryng) s. pierścień; obrączka; kółko; koło; zmowa;
szajka; słój; arena; ring
(bokserski); v. otaczać; kołować; krajać w kółko

ring; rang; rung (ryng; raeng;
rang)

ring (ryng) v. dzwonić; dźwięczeć; brzmieć; rozbrzmiewać;
wydzwaniać; telefonować; wybijać czas na zegarze kontrolnym;
sprawdzać monetę dźwiękiem;
s. dzwonek; dzwony; dźwięk;
brzęk; telefonowanie

ring off ('ryng,of) v. skończyć
rozmowę telefoniczną

ring the bell ('ryng,dy'bel) v.
dzwonić (do drzwi etc.)

ring up ('ryng,ap) v. wybijać
kwotę (na kasie rejestracyj-
nej);zatelefonować(do kogoś)

ringleader ('ryng,li:der) s.
prowodyr; herszt

rink (rynk) s. ślizgawka; tor
jazdy na wrotkach; boisko do
gry w kule

rinse (ryns) v. płukać; s. wy-
płukanie

rinse out ('ryns,aut) v. wypłukać;przepłukiwać

riot ('rajot) s. zgiełk; zamęt; rozruchy; bunty; rozpusta; hulanka; rozprężenie;
orgia; v. buntować się; robić
rozruchy, zamieszki; hulać;
używać sobie;uprawiać rozpustę

riotous ('rajetes) adj. buntowniczy; rozpustny; hulaszczy;
hałaśliwy; bujny;oporny;niesfor-
ny

rip (ryp) v. odrywać; zrywać;
łupać; rozpruwać; piłować
wzdłuż; pękać; pędzić; s. roz-
prucie; rozpustnik; hulaka;
szkapa; rzecz nie warta nic;
wir;wzburzona powierzchnia wody

ripe (rajp) adj. dojrzały
ripen ('rajpn) v. dojrzewac;
przyspieszac dojrzewanie
ripeness ('rajpnys) s. dojrzałość
ripple ('rypl) s. zmarszczki
(na wodzie); fale (na włosach);
falowanie; grzebien do lnu;
v. marszczyc; falowac; roz-
czesywac; rozwodzic się
rise; rose; risen (rajz; rouz;
'ryzn)
rise (rajz) v. podniesc się;
stanąc; wstawac; powstawac;
buntowac się; wzbierac; wzbijac się; wzmagac się; spros-
tac; s. wschod; wznoszenie
się; podwyżka; wzrost; powodzenie; początek; stopien
risen ('ryzn) v. zob. rise
riser (rajzer) s. osoba wstają-
ca; pionowy przewod (też rura);
podstawka stopnia (na schodach)
rising ('rajzyng) s. wzniesienie; powstanie; zmartwychwstanie; bąbel; pryszcz; zaczyna-
nie ciasta; adj. podnoszący
się; wzrastający; wschodzący
risk (rysk) s. ryzyko ; niebezpieczenstwo; v. narażac się;
ryzykowac; ponosic ryzyko
risky ('rysky) adj. niebezpieczny; ryzykowny; pikantny; drastyczny
rite (rajt) s. obrządek; obrzęd
(slubny); rytuał
rival ('rajwel) s. rywal; wspołzawodnik; v. rywalizowac
rivalry ('rajwelry) s. rywalizacja; wspołzawodnictwo
river ('rywer) s. rzeka
riverboat ('rywer,bout) s. statek rzeczny; łodz rzeczna
riverside ('rywer,sajd) s.
brzeg rzeki
rivet ('rywyt) s. nit; v. nitowac; utkwic; przykuc
rivulet ('rywjulyt) s. rzeczuł-
ka. mały strumien; mały potok
road (roud) s. droga; kolej;
reda; v. topic
road hog ('roud,hog) s. pirat
drogowy (lekceważący przepisy)

road map ('roud,maep) s. mapa
drogowa; mapa samochodowa
roadside ('roud,sajd) s. bok
drogi; adj. przydrozny
roadsign ('roud,sajn) s. znak
drogowy
roam (roum) v. włoczyc się;
s. włoczęga; wędrowka
roar (ro:r) v. ryczec; huczec;
s. ryk; huk(armat); ryk(smiechu)
roars of laughter ('ro:rs,ow-
'lafter) exp. wybuchy smiechu
roast (roust) v. piec; opiekac;
przypiekac; wypalac; osmieszac;
krytykowac ostro; s. pieczen;
pieczenie; kpiny; krytyka
ostra; adj. pieczony
roast beef ('roust,bi:f) s.
pieczen wołowa
roast meat ('roust,mi:t) s.
pieczone mięso
rob (rob) v. grabic; rabowac;
ograbic; pozbawiac (czegos)
robber ('rober) s. rabus
robbery ('robery) s. rabunek
robe (roub) s. podomka; suknia;
szata; płaszcz kąpielowy; toga; v. przyodziewac; przyoblekac
robin ('robyn) s. drozd; rudzik
robot ('roubot) s. robot
robust ('roubast) adj. krzepki;
trzezwy; szorstki; hałasliwy;
ciężki; silny; mocny
rock (rok) s. kamien; skała;
forsa; kołysanie; taniec
(rock and roll); pl. kostki
lodu w napoju; v. kołysac się;
bujac się; hustac się; wstrząsac; wypłukiwac piasek; płukac (się); a.kamienny; skalisty
rocker ('roker) s. biegun; łyz-
wa holenderka
rocket ('rokyt) s. rakieta;
v. wznosic się
rocket power ('rokyt'pafer) s.
napęd rakietowy
rocketry ('rokytry) s. bron
rakietowa; technika rakietowa
rocking chair ('rokyng,czeer)
s. krzesło na biegunach
rocky ('roky) adj. skalisty;
chwiejny; kamienisty; skalny

rod (rod) s. pręt; drąg; rózga;
wędka; (pręt = 5.029 m)
rode (roud) v. zob. ride
rodent ('roudent) s. gryzoń
roe (rou) s. sarna; łania;
ikra we wnętrzu ryby;sperma ry^{by}
rogue (roug) s. łobuz; łajdak;
psotnik; słoń samotnik
roguish ('rougysz) adj. psotny;
figlarny; łobuzerski
role (roul) s. rola
roll (roul) s. rólka; zwój;
zwitek; rulon; bułka; rożek;
spis; wykaz; rejestr; lista;
wokanda; wałek; walec; wałek;
kołysanie (się); werbel; huk;
toczyć; wałkować; tarzać;
grzmieć; dudnic; rozlegac się;
zataczać beczkę; toczyć koło;
kręcić; obracać; wymawiać "r";
rozwałkowywać ;wałkować
roll up ('roul,ap) v. zawinąć
(rękawy); kłębic się; pod-
jeżdżać; skumulować (się)
roller ('rouler) s. wałek; rolka; kółko; długa tocząca się
fala ;narzędzie do wałkowania
roller coaster ('rouler'kou-
ster) s. kolejka wysokogórska;
wesołe miasteczko
roller-skate ('rouler'skejt) s.
wrotka
rolling mill ('roulyn,myl) s.
walcownia
Roman ('roumen) adj. rzymski
romance (rou'maens) s. romans
średniowieczny; powieść miłosna; sprawa miłosna; adj. romański; v. romansować; koloryzować; przesadzać;pisac romanse
romantic (rou'maentyk) adj. romantyczny; s. romantyk
romp (romp) s. urwis; zbytki;
swawole; figle; igraszki;
v. figlować; dokazywać; uga-
niac; łatwo wygrać (wyścigi)
rompers ('rompers) pl. kombinezon do zabawy dla dziecka
roof (ru:f) s. dach; v. pokrywac dachem
roof over ('ru:f,ouwer) v. pokrywac dachem

rook (ruk) s. gawron; szuler;
wieża (w szachach); v. ograc;
oszukać; zdzierac skórę
room (rum) s. pokój. miejsce;
mieszkanie; izba; wolna przestrzeń; sposobność; powód;
v. dzielic pokój lub mieszkanie;mieszkać lub odnajmować pokój
room-mate ('rum,mejt) s. współ-
mieszkaniec; współlokator
roomy ('rumy) adj. przestronny;
obszerny
roost (ru:st) s. grzęda; v. siedzieć na grzędzie
rooster (ru:ster) s. kogut
root (ru:t) s. korzeń; nasada;
podstawa; istota; źródło; sedno;
pierwiastek; v. posadzić; zakorzenic; ryc; szperac; wygrze-
bywac; popierac; dopingowac
root out ('ru:t,aut) v. wykorzeniać; wyrywać z korzeniami
rope (roup) s. sznur; powróz;
lina; stryczek; v. związac;
przywiązac; łapac na lasso;
ogradzac sznurami; ciagnąc na
linie; przyciągac; zdobywac;
obsliznąc
rope off ('roup,of) v. ogradzac
linami
rose (rous) s. róża; kolor różowy; rozetka; v. zarożowic;
zob. rise
rosy ('rouzy) adj. różowy
rot (rot) s. zgnilizna; rozkład;
zepsucie; głupstwa; brednie;
motylica; v. gnic; butwiec;
rozkładac się
rotary ('routery) adj. rotacyjny;
obrotowy
rotate ('routejt) v. obracać
(się); kolejno zmieniac (się);
wirowac ;adj.kółkowy
rotation (rou'tejszyn) s. ro-
tacja; ruch obrotowy; obracanie
(się); płodozmian; ciągła wymiana; kolejne następstwo
rotor ('router) s. wirnik
rotten ('rotn) adj. zgniły; zepsuty; zdemoralizowany; lichy;
kiepski; marny;chory na moty-
licę ;do niczego;do chrzanu

rotund (rou'tand) adj. okrągły; zaokrąglony; szumny;
przysadkowaty

rough (raf) adj. szorstki; chropowaty; ostry; nierówny; wyboisty; nieokrzesany; brutalny;
drastyczny; cierpki; nieprzyjemny; nieociosany; surowy;
gruby; burzliwy; gwałtowny;
hałaśliwy; ciężki; pobieżny;
przybliżony; prymitywny;
wstępny; szkicowy; adv. ostro;
szostko; grubiańsko; z grubsza; s. nierówny teren; stan
naturalny - nieobrobiony;
hacel;huligan; v. być szorst-
kim; szorstko postępować;
hartować (się); jeżyć (się);
burzyć (się); szlifować z grubsza; pasować z grubsza; obrabiac z grubsza; szkicować;
przebiedować; ujeżdżać (konia);
robić coś z grubsza; podkuwać
hacelami

roughness ('rafnys) s. szorstkość; grubiaństwo; chamstwo

rough-neck ('rafnek) s. członek
obsługi szybu; łobuz; brutal;
chuligan

round (raund) adj. okrągły; zaokrąglony; kolisty; okrężny;
tam i nazad; kulisty; sferyczny; adv. wkoło; kołem; dookoła; prep. dookoła; s. koło;
obwód; kula; obrót; krąg; bieg
cykl; ciąg; zasięg; seria;
objazd; obchód; runda; za-
okrąglenie; pasmo (np. trudności); przechadzka; v. zaokrą-
glac; wygładzać; okrążyć; obchodzić; opływać

round off ('raund,of) v. za-
okrąglac

round out ('raund,out) v. za-
okrąglac się; tyć

round up ('round,ap) v. spędzac
(bydło)

round-up ('round'ap) s. spędza-
nie bydła

roundabout ('raundebaut) adj.
okrężny; s. rondo; karuzela

round trip ('raund,tryp) s. podróż tam i nazad

rouse (rauz) v. pobudzić;
wzniecać; ruszyć; ożywiać;
podsycać; wyrywać; wypłoszyc;
obudzić się; otrząsnąć się

roustabout ('rauste,baut) s.
robotnik portowy; robotnik
przemysłu naftowego

route (ru:t) s. droga; trasa;
marsz; szlak

routine (ry:'ti:n) s. rutyna;
tok zajęc

rove (rouw) v. wałęsac się;
błądzic wzrokiem; łowic; skręcac włókno; s. niedoprzęd

rover ('rouwer) s. wędrowiec;
włóczęga; korsarz; pirat

row (roł) s. szereg; rząd;
jazda łodzią; v. wiosłować

row (rał) s. zgiełk; hałas;
kłótnia; bójka; burda; nagana;
bura; v. besztac; pokłócic się

row-boat ('roł,bout) s. łódź
wiosłowa

rower ('rołer) s. wioślarz

rowing boat ('rołyngbout) s.
łódź wiosłowa

royal ('rojel) adj. królewski

royalty ('rojelty) s. królew-
skość; honorarium autorskie

rub (rab) v. trzec; potrzec;
wytrzec; wycierać; głaskać;
nacierac; s. tarcie; nacie-
ranie

rub down ('rab,dałn) v. nacierac;wcierac

rub in ('rab,yn) v. wcierać;
wytykac

rub off ('rab,of) v. zetrzec

rub out ('rab,aut) v. wymazac

rubber('raber) s. guma; masażysta; pl. kalosze; v. pokrywac gumą; odwracac (głowę)

rubberneck ('raber,nek) s.
ciekawski; turysta; gapa

rubber plant ('raber,plaent)
s. kauczukowa roślina

rubbish ('rabysz) s. śmiec;
gruz; tandeta; nonsens; brednie; głupstwa; bzdury

rubble ('rabl) s. gruz; rumowisko skalne; kamień łamany

ruby ('ru:by) s. rubin

rucksack ('ruksaek)s. plecak

rudder ('rader) s. ster

ruddy ('rady) adj. rumiany; czerstwy; czerwony; v. rumienić się

rude (ru:d) adj. szorstki; niegrzeczny; ostry; surowy; prosty; pierwotny; nagły; gwałtowny; krzepki

ruff (raf) s. kołnierz; kreza; batalion; bojownik; bicie atutem; v. przebić atutem

ruffian ('rafjen) s. zbój; łotr

ruffle ('rafl) s. kreza; żabot; mankiet koronkowy; kłopot; zamieszanie; marszczenie; v. marszczyć (powierzchnię); rozwiewać; rozczochrać; nastroszyć; wzburzyć (się)

rug (rag) s. pled; kilim; dywan

rugby ('ragby) s. (sport) rugby

ruin ('ruyn) s. ruina; v. rujnować (się); zniszczyć (się)

rule (ru:l) s. przepis; prawo; reguła; zasada; rządy; panowanie; postanowienie; miarka; linijka; v. rządzić; panować; kierować; orzekać; postanawiać; liniować

rule out ('ru:l,aut) v. wykluczać

ruler ('ru:ler) s. władca; liniał; linijka

rum (ram) s. rum; adj. dziwny

rumble ('rambl) v. dudnić; grzmieć; turkotać; s. huk; grzmot; dudnienie; tylne miejsce w pojeździe na bagaż lub służącego

ruminant ('ru:mynent) adj. przeżuwajacy; s. przeżuwacz

rummage ('ramydż) s. szperanie; przetrząsanie; wyprzedaż resztek; v. grzebać; przetrząsać

rumor ('ru:mer) s. pogłoska; słuchy; v. puszczać pogłoski

rump (ramp) s. zad; kuper; comber; kadłub

rumple ('rampl) v. zmiąć; zmiętosić; mierzwić; czochrać

run; ran; ran (ran; raen; raen) **run** (ran) v. biec; biegać; pędzić; spieszyć się; jechać; płynąć; kursować; obracać się; działać; funkcjonować; pracować; uciekać; zbiec; prowadzić; toczyć się; wynosić (sumę); rozpływać się; łzawić; głosić; spotykać; narzucać się; molestować; zderzyć się; sprzeciwiać się; wpaść etc.; s. bieg; przebieg; bieganie; rozbieg; rozpęd; przebieg; passa; sekwens; okres; seria; ciąg; dostęp; wybieg; pastwisko; zjazd; tor

run about ('ran,e'baut) v. biegać tu i tam; s. wędrowiec; adj. wędrowny

run across ('ran,e'kros) v. spotkać przypadkowo

run after ('ran,aefter) v. gonić

run away ('ran,e'łej) v. uciekać; ponieść

run down ('ran,dałn) v. przejechać; wyczerpać; wytropić

run in ('ran,yn) v. wpaść na...; dotrzeć

run off ('ran,of) v. uciekać; recytować; drukować

run out ('ran,aut) v. skończyć się; wygasnąć; wydrukować

run over ('ran,ouwer) v. przejechać; przepełniać

run up ('ran,ap) v. dobiec; dojść do..; dodać; wyśrubować; s. dochodzenie do celu

rung (rang) s. poprzeczka; szczebel; szprycha; v. zob. ring

runner ('raner) s. goniec; biegacz; posłaniec; woźny; akwizytor; łopatka; obsługujący maszynę; chodnik; przemytnik; płoza; łożysko ślizgowe; wałek

running ('ranyng) adj. bieżący; biegający; będacy w biegu; cieknący; ropiejący; w ruchu; ruchomy; ciągły; nieustanny; pochyły; nieprzerwany; s. bieg; wyścig; kandydowanie; funkcjonowanie; ropienie; kierownictwo

running board ('ranyŋg,bo:rd)
s. stopien; pomost
runway ('ran,łej) s. bieznia
(do ładowania); tor (jezdny)
rupture ('rapczer) s. złamanie;
zerwanie; przepuklina; v.
przerywac; zrywac; poderwac
się (miec przepuklinę)
rural ('ruerel) adj. wiejski
ruse (ru:z) s. podstęp
rush (rasz) v. pędzic; poganiac; ponaglac; rzucac się na
cos; przeskakiwac; wysyłac
pospiesznie; zdobywac szturmem; zdzierac (pieniądze);
słac sitowiem; s. pęd; ruch;
pospiech; napływ; atak; intensywny popyt; sitowie
rush hour ('rasz,auer) s. godzina szczytu; chwila uderze-
nia
Russian ('raszyn) adj. rosyjski ;s.Rosjanin
rust (rast) s. rdza (zbożowa)
v. rdzewiec;niszczyc się
rust-eaten ('rast.i:tn) adj.
zardzewiały
rustic ('rastik) adj. wiejski;
prostacki; s. wiesniak; prostak
rustle ('rasl) v. szelescic;
krasc bydło; krzątac się;
s. szelest
rusty ('rasty) adj. zardzewiały; zaniedbany; wyszły z wprawy ;podniszczony
rut (rat) s. koleina; bruzda;
utarty szlak; rutyna; nawyk;
rowek; wyżłobienie; ruja;
bełkowisko; rykowisko
ruthless ('ru:tlys) adj. bezlitosny; bezwzględny; niemiłosierny
rutted ('ratyd) adj. rozjezdżo-
ny; wyjeżdżony
rutty ('raty) adj. wyjeżdżony
rye (raj) s. żyto; żytniówka
rye whisky (raj, hłysky)
szkocka żytnia wódka
s (es) dziewiętnasta litera
alfabetu angielskiego
's skrót: is, has, us

saber ('seiber) s. szabla; pałasz; v. ciąc; ranic; scinac
sable ('sejbl) s. soból; czern;
adj. czarny;sobolowy(z futer)
sabotage ('saebeta:z) s. sabo-
taż; v. sabotowac
sabre ('sejber) s. szabla; zob.
saber
saccharin ('saekeryn) s. sacharyna
sack (saek) s. worek; torebka;
sak; luzny płaszcz; plądrowa-
nie; v. pakowac do workow;
zwalniac z pracy; plądrowac
sacrament ('saekrement) s. sakrament
sacred ('sejkryd) adj. poswięco-
ny; nienaruszalny
sacrifice ('saekryfajs) s. ofiara; wyrzeczenie (się); v. ofia-
rowywac; poswięcac; wyrzekac
się w zamian za cos innego
sacrilegious (,saekry'lydzes)
adj. swiętokradzki
sad (saed) adj. smutny; bolesny;
posępny; ponury; okropny
sadden ('saedn) v. zasmucac (się);
posmutniec
saddle ('saedl) s. siodło;
v. siodłac; obarczac; wkładac
ciężar (komus)(na kogos)
sadness ('saednys) s. smutek
safe (sejf) adj. pewny; bezpieczny; s. schowek bankowy;
kasa pancerna; spizarnia
wietrzona; (slang):kondon
safeguard ('seifga:rd) v. ochra-
niac; zabezpieczac; gwarantowac;
s. zabezpieczenie; gwarancja
safety ('sejfty) s. bezpieczenstwo; zabezpieczenie; bezpiecznik ; adj.dający bezpieczenstwo
safety belt ('sejfty,belt) s.
pas bezpieczenstwa (np. w samochodzie)
safety lock ('sejfty,lok) s. zamek bezpieczenstwa
safety pin ('sejfty,pyn) s.
agrafka
safety razor ('sejfty,rejzer) s.
maszynka do golenia się żyletka-
mi (które się wymienia po zużyciu)

safety-valve ('sejfty,waelw)
s. klapa bezpieczeństwa; zawór bezpieczeństwa
sag (saeg) v. obwisać; zwisać;
wyginać (się); przechylać się;
spadać w cenie; s. zwis; wygięcie; spadek(ceny)
sagacity (se'gaesyty) s. rozwaga; mądrość; roztropność;
bystrość
said (sed) v. zob. say
sail (sejl) s. żagiel; podróż
morska; żaglować; kroczyć okazale; sterować okrętem; bawić się modelem statku
sail-boat ('sejl,bout) s. żag-
lówka
sailing-ship('sejlyng,szyp) s.
statek żaglowy
sailor ('sejlor) s. żeglarz;
marynarz
saint (sejnt) s. & adj. święty
sake (sejk) s. czyjeś dobro;
wzgląd
salad ('saeled) s. sałata
salary ('saelery) s. pensja;
pobory; wynagrodzenie
sale (sejl) s. sprzedaż; wyprzedaż
saleslady ('sejls'lejdy) s.
sprzedawczyni
salesman ('sejlsmen) s. sprzedawca
salesmanager (,sejls'maenydżer)
s. kierownik działu sprzedaży
saliva (se'lajwa) s. ślina
sallow ('saelou) adj. ziemisty;
blady; żółtawy; v. dawać żółtawy odcień; s. iwa (wierzba)
sally ('saely) s. wypad; wycieczka z oblężenia; docinek
(cięty)
sally out ('saely,aut) v. wy-
ruszać w podróż
salmon ('saemen) s. łosoś; adj.
łososiowy; łososiowego koloru
saloon (se'lu:n) s. bar; szynk;
sala (zabaw); salon (na okrę-
cie)
salt (so:lt) s. sól; adj; słony; v. solić
saltcellar ('so:lt,seler) s.
solniczka

salt-free ('so:lt,fri:) adj.
bezsolny;pozbawiony soli
salty ('so:lty) adj. słony
salutation (,saelju:'tejszyn)
s. pozdrowienie; przywitanie
salute (se'lu:t) s. pozdrowienie; salutowanie; honory wojskowe; salwa (powitalna);
v. pozdrowić; powitać; salutować; odbierać defiladę; przejść
przed kompanią honorową
salvation (sael'wejszyn) s.
zbawienie; ratunek; wybawienie
salve (sa:w) v. natrzeć; złagodzić; uspokoić; s. maść; balsam
same (sejm) adj. ten sam; taki
sam; jednostajny; monotonny;
adv. tak samo; identycznie;
bez zmiany; pron. to samo
sample ('sa:mpl) s. próbka;
wzór; v. próbować; dawać próbki
sanatorium (,saene'to:rjem) s.
sanatorium
sanctify ('saenkty,faj) v.
uświęcać; poświęcać
sanction ('saenkszyn) v.
usankcjonować; s. sankcja
sanctuary ('saenkczuery) s.
przybytek; azyl
sand (saend) s. piasek; v. posypywać piaskiem; obrabiać papie-
rem ściernym
sandal ('saendl) s. sandał; rzemyk; v. wkładać sandały; przywiązywać rzemykiem
sandwich ('saendłycz) s. kanapka;
sandwicz; v. wkładać (między)
sandy ('saendy) adj. piaskowy;
piaskowego koloru
sandy beach ('saendy,bi:ch) s.
plaża
sane (sejn) adj. zdrowy na umyśle; rozsądny; normalny
sang (saeng) v. zob. sing
sanitarium (,saeny'teerjem) s.
sanatorium
sanitary ('saenytery) adj. hi-
gieniczny; zdrowy
sanitary napkin ('saenytery
'naepkyn) s. podpaska higie-
niczna

sanitation (,saeny'tejszyn) s.
higiena; kanalizacja; urządzenia sanitarne
sank (saenk) v. zob. sink
Santa Claus (,saenta'klo:z)
s. Dziadek Mróz; Święty Mikołaj
sap (saep) s. żywica; sok; głupiec; kujon; nudziarstwo; sapa; podkopywanie; v. wyciągać
soki; usuwać biel z drzewa;
podkopywać; podmywać; kopać
sapę
sappy('saepy) s. soczysty; pełen wigoru; energiczny
sarcasm ('sa:rkaezem) s. sarkazm
sardine (sa:r'di:n) s. sardynka
sash (saesz) s. szarfa; rama
okienna do pionowego suwania
okien; v. instalować ramy
okienne
sash window('saesh'żyndou) s.
suwane okno
sat (saet) v. zob. sit
Satan ('sejtn) s. szatan
satchel ('saeczel) s. torba
z rzemieniami na plecy
satellite ('saete,lajt) s. satelita
satin ('saetyn) s. atlas; adj.
atlasowy; v. satynować (papier)
satire ('saetajer) s. satyra
satirize ('saety,rajz) v. wykpiwać; wyśmiewać; satyryzować
satisfaction (,saetys'faekszyn)
s. zadowolenie; satysfakcja;
spłacenie długu ;zaspokojenie
satisfactory (,saetys'faektery)
adj. zadawalający; odpowiedni
satisfy ('saetys,faj) v. zaspokoić; uiścić; spełnić; zadowalać; odpowiadać; przekonywać
Saturday ('saeterdy) s. sobota
sauce (so:s) s. sos; kompot;
v. przyprawiać jedzenie; nagadać komuś ;stawiać się
saucebox ('so:s,boks) s. impertynent ;zuchwalec
saucepan ('so:spen) s. patelnia; rondel

saucer ('so:ser) s. spodek
saunter ('so: nter) s. przechadzka; przechadzać się; chodzić
powolnym krokiem
sausage ('sosydż) s. kiełbasa
save (sejw) v. ratować; oszczędzać; zachowywać pozory; zbawiać;
uniknąć; zyskiwać (czas); prep.
oprócz; wyjąwszy; poza; pominąwszy; conj. że; poza tym;
chyba że; z wyjątkiem
save for a car ('sejw,fo:r'ej-
,ca:r) exp.: oszczędzać na samochód
saver ('sejwer) s. osoba oszczędzająca; przedmiot oszczędzający
(np, czas)
saving ('sejwyng) adj. zbawienny;
oszczędny; prep. wyjąwszy
savings-bank ('sejwynz'baenk) s.
kasa oszczędności
savior ('sejwjer) s. zbawca;
zbawiciel
savor ('sejwer) s. smak; aromat;
powab; v. mieć smak; pachnieć;
smakować; nadawać smak
savory ('sejwery) adj. smaczny;
apetyczny; smakowity; pikantny;
aromatyczny
saw; sawed; sawn (so:; so:d;
so:n)
saw (so:) v. zob. see; piłować;
s. piła
sawdust ('so:,dast) s. trociny
sawmill ('so:,myl) s. tartak
Saxon ('saeksn) adj. saksoński;
saski ; s. Sas
say; said; said (sej; sed; sed)
v. mówić; powiedzieć; odprawiać; twierdzić
sayso ('sejso) s. rozkaz; powiedzenie; ostatnie słowo
saying ('sejyng) s. powiedzonko;
powiedzenie
scab (skaeb) s. strup; parch;
świerzb; łamistrajk
scaffold ('skaefeld) s. rusztowanie; platforma; estrada; szafot; v. stawiać rusztowanie
scaffolding ('skaefeldyng) s.
rusztowanie
scald (sko:ld) v. oparzyć; wyparzyć; pasteryzować; s. oparzenie

scale (skejl) s. skala; podziałka; układ; drabina;
szalka; łuska; kamień nazębny;
v. wyłazić; wdzierać się;
mierzyć (podziałką); ważyć;
łuszczyć; łuskać; złuszczac
się
scale down ('skejl,dałn) v.
zmniejszac (proporcjonalnie)
scale up ('skejl,ap) v. powiększac (proporcjonalnie)
scales ('skejls) pl. waga
scalp ('skaelp) s. skalp; skóra na głowie; v. oskalpowac;
złośliwie krytykowac
scan (skaen) v. badawczo przeglądac; skandowac; miec rytm
scandal ('skaendl) s. skandal;
zgorszenie; oszczerstwo;
plotki
scandalous ('skaendeles) adj.
skandaliczny; gorszący;
oszczerczy
Scandinavian (,skaendy'nejw-
jan) adj. skandynawski
scant (skaent) adj. skąpy;
ograniczony; ledwo wystarczający; niedostateczny
scapegoat ('skejp,gout) s. kozioł ofiarny
scar (ska:r) s. blizna; szrama;
wyrwa; urwisko; v. pokieraszo-
wac (się); zabliźniac się
scar over ('ska:r,ouwer) v.
zabliźnic
scarce (skeers) adj. rzadki;
niewystarczający
scarcely ('skeersly) adv. zaledwie; ledwo; z trudem;
z trudnością
scarcity ('skeersyty) s. niedostatek; niedobór; brak
scare (skeer) s. popłoch; panika; strach; v. nastraszyc;
przestraszyc; siac popłoch
scare away ('skeere,łej) v.
odstraszac
scarecrow ('skeer,krou)s.
straszydło; strach na wróble
scarf (ska:rf) s. szalik;
chustka na szyję; szarfa
scarfs (ska:rfs) pl. styk;
złącza

scarlet ('ska:rlyt) s. szkarłat;
adj. szkarłatny
scarlet fever ('ska:rlyt,fi:wer)
s. szkarlatyna ; płonica
scarp (ska:rp) s. skarpa; urwisko
scarred (ska:rd) adj. poznaczo-
ny bliznami; poszarpany
scarves (ska:rwz) pl. zob.scarf;
chusty na szyję; szarfy etc.
scathing ('skejzyng) adj. kostyczny; zjadliwy; niszczący
scatter ('skaeter) v. rozpra-
szac (się); rozsypywać; rozrzucac; rozwiewac; posypywac;
rozpierzchnąc (się)
scavenge ('skaewyndż) v. czyscic; oczyszczac; wyrzucac spa-
liny; byc zamiataczem ulic
scene (si:n) s. scena; miejsce
zdarzen; widowisko; widok; obraz; awantura publiczna
scenery (si:nery) s. widok;
krajobraz; dekoracje sceniczne
scent (sent) v. węszyc; wietrzyc; wydawac zapach; s. zapach; nos (węch); perfumy
sceptic ('skeptyk) s. sceptyk;
adj. sceptyczny ;powątpiewajacy
sceptical ('skeptykel) adj.
sceptyczny;powątpiewający we
wszystko
schedule ('skedżul) s. rozkład
jazdy; wykaz; zestawienie; tabela; taryfa; harmonogram; lista; plan; v. planowac; wciagac
na listę ;naznaczac wg. planu
scheme (ski:m) s. intryga; podstęp; plan
scholar ('skoler) s. uczony;
stypendysta; uczen ;student
scholarship ('skolerszyp) s.
poziom naukowy; stypendium;
erudycja ;systematyczna wiedza
school (sku:l) s. szkoła; katedra; nauka; ławica; adj. szkolny; v. szkolic; kształcic; nauczac; wycwiczyc; tworzyc ła-
wicę;karcic; sprawdzac naukę
schoolboy ('sku:l,boj) s.
uczen
schoolgirl ('sku:l,ge:rl) s.
uczennica

schooling ('sku:lyŋg) s. nauka;
szkolenie; wykształcenie
schoolmaster ('sku:l,ma:ster)
s. kierownik szkoły
schoolmate ('sku:l,mejt) s. kolega szkolny
school of driving ('sku:l,ow-
'drajwyŋg) s. nauka jazdy
(samochodem)
schooner ('sku:ner) s. skuner;
szklanka na piwo
science ('sajens) s. wiedza;
nauka; umiejętność
scientific ('sajentyfyk) adj.
naukowy; umiejętny
scientist ('sajentyst) s. uczony; przyrodnik; naukowiec
scissors ('syzez) s. nożyce;
nożyczki
scoff (skof) v. szydzić; kpić;
drwić; s. pośmiewisko; szyderstwo; kpiny; drwiny
scold (skould) v. besztać;
skrzyczec; obrugac; łajac;
złorzeczyc; s. jędza; sekutnica; megiera
scone (skon) s. placek trójkątny z jęczmiennej mąki
scoop (sku:p) v. zaczerpnąć;
wygarnąc; wybrac; s. czerpak;
szufelka; chochla; kubeł; sensacyjna wiadomość
scooter ('sku:ter) s. skuter;
hulajnoga
scope (skoup) s. zasięg; zakres;
dziedzina; meta; sposobność;
możliwość
scorch (sko:rcz) v. spalić;
przypiekac; przypalac; dopie-
kac; wypłowiec; pędzić samochodem jak szalony; s. poparzenie
score (sko:r) v. zdobyć (punkt);
podkreslic; zanotowac; zapisac;
wygrac; osiągnąc; strzelic
bramkę; s. ilość (zdobytych
punktów lub bramek); zacięcie;
rysa; znak; dwadzieścia
scorn (sko:rn) s. lekceważenie;
wzgarda; v. lekceważyc; gardzić;odrzucac z pogardą
scornful('sko:rnful) adj. pogardliwy (i zagniewany);odrzuca-
jący z gniewem i pogardą

Scot (skot) adj. szkocki
Scotch (skocz) adj. szkocki
scot-free ('skot'fri:) adj.
cały; nietknięty; niezraniony;
gratis; bezpłatny
scoundrel ('skaundrel) s. kanalia; łotr
scour ('skauer) v. podmyc; szo-
rowąc; przepłukiwac; poszukiwac; grasowac; przetrząsac;
s. podmycie; przemywanie;
przepłukiwanie
scout (skaut) s. harcerz; zwia-
dowca; v. isc na zwiady; robic
rekonesans
scoutmaster ('skaut,ma:ster)
s. harcmistrz
scowl (skaul) v. chmurzyć się;
patrzec spode łba; grożnie,
patrzec; s. zła mina; grozne
spojrzenie; krzywa mina
scramble ('skraembl) s. ubija-
nie się; gramolenie się; do-
bijanie się; robienie jajeczni-
cy; v. ubijac się; gramolic się;
dobijac się; robic jajecznicę
scrambled eggs ('skraembld,egs)
s. jajecznica
scrap (skraep) s. szmelc; odpadki; skrawki; wycinki; bójka; v. wyrzucac na szmelc; odrzucac; wycofac; bic się
scrape (skrejp) s. skrobanie;
tarapaty; szurnięcie; ciułanie;
drasnięcie; v. skrobać; drasnąc;
ciułać; szurnąc
scrape off ('skrejp,of) v. ze-
skrobac
scrape out ('skrejp,aut) v. wy-
skrobac
scrape together (skrejp,tu'gedzer) v. uciułac
scrap iron('skraep,ajern) s.
złom żelazny
scrappy ('skraepy) adj. niejednolity; bez związku; frag-
mentaryczny
scratch (skraecz) s. drasnięcie;
zadrapanie; rozdarcie; skrobanie; linia startu; adj. do pisania (np. brulion; brulionowy);
v. drapac (się); zadrasnąc;
gryzmolic; wydrapac; wykreślic

scream (skri:m) s. krzyk; pisk; gwizd; kawał; v. krzyczec przenikliwie; śmiac się hałasliwie i histerycznie

screech(skri:cz) s. zgrzyt; pisk; skrzypienie; v. zgrzytac; piszczec; skrzypiec

screen (skri:n) s. zasłona; osłona; siatka na komary; ekran; sito; siewnik; filtr (światła) v. zasłaniac; osłaniac; zabezpieczac; wyswietlac; przesiewac; sortowac; badac; przesłuchiwac; filmowac; izolowac

screw (skru:) s. sruba; propeler; smigło; zwitek; wyzyskiwacz; dusigrosz; (slang):stosunek płciowy; v. przysrubowac; wyduszac; naciskac; wykrzywiac; zabałaganic; obracac się; (slang):spółkowac; wkopac (kogos);oszukac

screwdriver ('skru:,drajwer) s. srubokręt; wodka z sokiem pomarańczowym

scribble ('skrybl) s. gryzmoły; bazgranina; v. gryzmolic; bazgrac; pisac naprędce

script (skrypt) s. rękopis; scenariusz

scripture ('skrypczer) s. Pismo Swięte

scroll (skroul) s. zwitek; krzywa; spirala

scrub (skrab) s. zarosla; zagajnik; karłowate drzewo; pętak; niepozorny człowiek; szorowanie; v. szorowac; oczyszczac;adj.lichy;marny;maławy

scruple ('skrupl) s. skrupuł; v. wahac się; miec skrupuły

scrupulous ('skru;pjules) adj. sumienny; dokładny; skrupulatny; pedantyczny

scrutinize ('skru:tynajz) v. badac szczegółowo

scrutiny ('skru:tyny) s. dokładne badanie

scuff (skaf) s. włóczenie nogami; wytarte miejsca; v. powłóczyc nogami; wycierac; rozrzucac; porysowac ;musnąc;zedrzec;zdzierac;szurac

scuffle (skafl) s. włóczenie nogami; szamotanie się; utarczka; bójka; v. szamotac się; bic się; powłóczyc nogami;szurac;zaszurac

sculptor ('skalpter) s. rzezbiarz

sculpture ('skalpczer) s. rzezba; v. rzezbic

scum (skam) s. szumowiny; v. zbierac szumowiny; wytarzac

scurf (ske:rf) s. łupiez;strup;parchy

scurvy ('ske:rwy) s. szkorbut; adj. podły; nędzny

scuttle ('skatl) s. wiaderko; szybka ucieczka; właz; v. pędzic; uciekac; robic dziury w dnie; zatapiac

scuttlebutt ('skatelbat) s. kadz; pogłoska

scythe (sajz) s. kosa; v. kosic

sea (si:) s. morze; fala

sea breeze ('si:'bri:z) s. wiatr od morza

seafarer ('si:,feerer) s. zeglarz; podróznik morski

seafood ('si:fu:d) s. potrawy morskie (ryby; skorupiaki)

sea gull ('si:gal) s. mewa

seal (si:l) s. foka; futro foki; uszczelka; zagadka; plomba; pieczątka; piętno; znak; v.polowac na foki; uszczelniac; plombowac; pieczętowac; zalakowac

seal up ('si:l,ap) v. zaplombowac; uszczelnic; zamknąc; zalakowac; zapieczętowac

sea level('si:,lewl) s. poziom morza

sealskin ('si:lski:n) s. futro z fok

seam (si:m) s.szew; rąbek; pokład; blizna; szpara; szczelina; v. łączyc szwami; pękac; pokierezowac

seaman ('si:men) s. marynarz; zeglarz

seamstress ('semstrys) s. szwaczka

seaplane ('si:,plejn) s. hydroplan

seaport ('si:,po:rt) s. port morski

sea-power ('si:,paŕer) s. potęga morska

search (se:rcz) s. poszukiwa-
nie; badanie; szperanie; rewizja; v. badać; dociekać;
szukać; przetrząsać; rewidowac

searching ('se:rczyŋg) adj.
badawczy; przenikliwy

seashore ('si:,szo:r) s. wybrzeże; brzeg morski

seasick ('si:,syk) adj. chory
na morską chorobę

seaside ('si:'sajd) s. wybrzeże morskie

season ('si:zn) s. pora roku;
pora; sezon; v. zaprawiac;
przyprawiac; okrasic

seasonable (si:znebl) adj. stosowny; odpowiedni; właściwy na
porę roku; w porę

seasonal ('si:zenl) adj. sezo-
nowy

seasoned ('si:znd) adj. zaprawiony; wdrożony; przyprawiony;
pikantny; wystały

seasoning ('si:znyŋg) s. przyprawa

season ticket ('si:sn'tykyt) s.
abonament; karta wstępu; bilet (np. na serię przedstawień)

seat (si:t) s. siedzenie; ławka; krzesło; miejsce siedzące;
siedlisko; siedziba; gniazdo;
v. posadzic; usadowic; wybierac (do sejmu); siąsc; osa-
dzic

seat belt ('si:t,belt) s. pas
ochronny w samolocie lub samochodzie ; pas beapieczeństwa

seaward ('si:łerd) adv. ku
(otwartemu) morzu; adj. skiero-
wany ku morzu

seaweed ('si:łi:d) s. wodorost

seaworthy ('si:,łe:rsy) adj.
zdatny do podróży morskiej
(m.in. wodoszczelny)

secession (sy'seszyn) s. secesja; oddzielenie się

seclude (sy'klu:d) v. odosabniac (się)

secluded (sy'klu:dyd) adj. odosobniony

seclusion (sy'klu:żyn) s. odosobnienie; ustronie; zacisze

second ('sekend) adj. drugi;
wtórny; powtórny; ponowny; za-
stępczy; zapasowy; drugorzędny;
v. poprzec; sekundowac; s. sekunda; moment; chwila; drugi;
sekundant; delegat; zastępca

secondary ('sekendery) adj.
drugorzędny; wtórny; pochodny

secondary school ('sekendery-
,sku:l) s. szkoła średnia

second floor ('sekend,flo:r) s.
pierwsze piętro

secondhand ('sekend,haend)
adj. z drugiej ręki; używany

secondly ('sekendly) adv. po
drugie

second-rate ('sekend'-rejt)
adj. drugorzędny; lichy; kiepski

secrecy ('si;krysy) s. tajemnica; skrytość; dyskrecja

secret ('si:kryt) adj. tajny;
tajemny; sekretny; skryty;
ustronny; dyskretny; s. tajemnica; sekret; pl. wstydliwe
części ciała

secretary ('sekretry) s. sekretarz; sekretarka; sekretarzyk

secretary of state ('sekretry-
,ow'stejt) minister spraw
zagranicznych USA

secrete (sy'kri:t) v. wydzielac;
ukrywac

secretion (sy'kri:szyn) s. wydzielina; wydzielanie; ukrycie

section ('sekszyn) s. część;
wycinek; etap; oddział; grupa;
dział; ustep; paragraf; sekcja;
przekrój; żelazo profilowe;
przedział; drużyną robocza;
v. dzielic na części; robic
przekrój

sector ('sekrer) s. wycinek;
odcinek

secular ('sekjuler) adj. świecki; wiekowy; stuletni; s.
ksiądz świecki

secularize (,sekjulerajz) s.
sekularyzować

secure (sy'kjuer) v. zabezpieczać (się); umacniać; uzyskiwać; zapewniac sobie; adj;
spokojny; bezpieczny; pewny
security (sy'kjueryty) s. bezpieczeństwo; zabezpieczenie;
pewność; zastaw; papier wartościowy; zbytnia ufność
sedan (sy'daen) s. samochód
4-osobowy
sedate (sy'dejt) v. uspokajac
(lekarstwami); adj. spokojny;
opanowany; zrównoważony
sedative ('sedetyw) adj. & s.
(środek) uspakajający, nasen-
ny
sediment ('sydyment) s. osad;
nanos; (skała osadowa)
seduce (sy'du:s) v. uwodzic
seduction (sy'dakszyn) s. uwo-
dzenie; pokusa; poneta; powab
seductive (sy'daktyw) adj. kuszący; necący
sedulous ('sedjules) adj. pilny; skrzętny; staranny; skwapliwy
see; saw; seen (si:, so:,si:n)
see (si:) v. zobaczyc; widziec;
ujrzec; zauważyc; spostrze-
gac; doprowadzic; odprowadzic;
zwiedzac; zrozumiec; odwie-
dzac; przeżywac; dożyc; uważac; zastanawiać się; dopil-
nowac
see off ('si:,of) v. odprowa-
dzac
see out ('si:,aut) v. odprowadzic do drzwi
see through ('si:,tru:) v.prze-
prowadzic do końca; doczekac
się końca
see to ('si:,tu) v. troszczyc
się o...
seed (si:d) v. obsiewac; obsypywac się; zasiewac; wybierac;
s. nasienie; zarodek; plemię
seek; sought; sought (si:k;
so:t; so:t)
seek (si:k) v. szukac; starac
się; chciec; zadac; nastawac;
usiłowac; próbowac; przetrząsac; dążyc

seek out ('si:k,aut) v. odszuki-
wac; wykrywac
seem (si:m) v. zdawać się; robic
wrażenie; okazywac się; miec
wrażenie
seeming (si:myng) adj. pozorny;
widoczny
seemingly ('si:myngly) adv. na
pozór; widocznie
seemly ('si:mly) adj. właściwy;
przyzwoity
seen (si:n) v. zob. see
seep (si:p) v. sączyc się; wyciekac
seesaw ('si:so:) s. hustawka
(na desce); adj. wahadłowy;
hustawkowy; s. hustac się; wahac się; adv. (poruszac czyms)
do góry i na doł
segment ('segment) s. odcinek;
segment; v. podzielic na częsci
segregate('segry'gejt) v. oddzielac; segregowac
segregation ('segry'gejszyn) s.
oddzielenie; segregacja
seize (si:z) v. uchwycic; złapac; zrozumiec; owładnąc; sko-
rzystac; zaciąc się; zatrzec
się; zablokowac się
seizure ('si:zer) s. zagarnięcie;
zawładnięcie; zajęcie; napad;
atak apopleksji; zatarcie; za-
blokowanie ;atak drgawek
seldom ('seldem) adv. rzadko;
z rzadka
select (sy'lekt) v. wybierac;
wyselekcjonowac; adj. wybrany;
doborowy; ekskluzywny
selection (sy'lekszyn) s. wybór;
dobór; selekcja
self (self) prefix, samo; auto-
matycznie; s. jazn; osobowosc;
własne dobro; pl.selves (selwz)
self-acting ('self'aektyng) adj.
samoczynny
self-command ('self,ke'ma:nd) s.
spokój; panowanie nad sobą;
opanowanie
self-confidence ('self,konfydens)
s. pewnosć siebie; tupet
self-conscious ('self'konszes)
adj.niesmiały; zażenowany

self-control ('self,ken'troul)
s. zimna krew; opanowanie
self-defense ('self,dy'fens) s.
samoobrona
self-employment ('self,ym'plojment) samozatrudnienie
self-government ('self'gawen-
ment) s. samorząd; autonomia
self-interest ('self'yntryst)
s. interesowność; własne dobro
selfish ('selfysz) adj. samolubny; egoistyczny
self-made ('self'mejd) adj.
przez samego siebie osiągnięty
self-possessed ('self,pe'zest)
adj. opanowany; spokojny
self-reliant ('self,ry'lajent)
adj. na sobie polegający
self-respect ('self,rys'pekt) s.
poczucie własnej godności
self-righteous ('self'rajczes)
adj. nadmiernie pewny siebie
self-service ('self'se:rwys) s.
samo-obsługa
sell; sold; sold (sel; sould;
sould)
sell (sel) v. sprzedawać; za-
przedawać; sprzyniewierzyć;
wykiwać; mieć zbyt; być na
sprzedaż; wyprzedawać
sell out ('selaut) v. wyprzedawać
seller ('seler) s. sprzedawca
selves (selwz) pl. zob. self
semblance ('semblens) s. pozór;
podobieństwo
semen ('si:men) s. nasienie
semicolon ('semy'koulen) s.
średnik
semifinal ('semy'fajnl) s. pół-
finał
senate ('senyt) s. senat
senator ('seneter) s. senator
send; sent; sent (send; sent;
sent)
send (send) v. posyłać; wysyłać;
nadawać; transmitować; wystrze-
liwać; sprawiać; wywoływać
send away ('send,e'łej) v. odprawiać; wypędzać
send for ('send,fo:r) v. zawołać; zamawiać; kazać przynieść

send in ('send,yn) v. posłać;
nadesłać
send off ('send'o:f) v. wysyłać;
odprowadzać (np. na lotnisko);
pożegnać kogoś (na stacji)
sender ('sender) s. nadawca;
nadajnik (np. radiowy)
send-off ('send'o:f) s. pożegnanie
senior ('si:njer) adj. starszy
(np. rangą); s. starszy człowiek; senior; student ostat-
niego roku
sensation (sen'sejszyn) s. wrażenie; doznanie; uczucie; sensacja
sensational (sen'sejszenl) adj.
sensacyjny; wrażeniowy
sense (sens) s. zmysł; poczucie; uczucie (np. zimna); świadomość (czegoś); rozsądek;
znaczenie; sens; v. wyczuwać;
czuć; rozumieć
senseless ('senslys) adj. bez
sensu; nierozumny; nieprzytomny
sensibility (,sensy'bylyty) s.
wrażliwość
sensible ('sensybl) adj. rozsądny; świadomy; przytomny;
wrażliwy; odczuwalny; pozna-
walny; sensowny
sensitive ('sensytyw) adj.
wrażliwy; delikatny
sensual ('senszuel) adj. zmysłowy (też seksualnie)
sensuous ('senszues) adj. zmysłowy (nie seksualnie)
sent (sent) v. zob. send
sentence ('sentens) s. zdanie;
powiedzenie; wyrok; sentencja;
v. wydawać wyrok; skazywać
sentiment ('sentyment) s. sentyment; uczucie; opinia; zdanie;
życzenie; sentymentalność
sentimental (,senty'mentl) adj.
uczuciowy; sentymentalny
sentimentality (,senty'ment'aelyty) s. uczuciowość; czułost-
kowość; sentymentalność
sentry ('sentry) s. posterunek;
wartownik

separable ('seperebl) adj. roz-
łączny
separate ('seperejt) v. rozłączyć; rozdzielic; oddzielic;
oderwać; odseparować (się);
odgrodzic; rozszczepić;
separate ('sepryt) adj. odrębny;
oddzielny; osobny; indywidualny; poszczególny
separation (,sepe'rejszyn) s.
separacja; rozdzielenie; oddzielenie; rozłączenie
September (sep'tember) s.
wrzesien
septic ('septyk) adj. septyczny;
zakazny
sepulcher ('sepelker) s. grób;
v. składac do grobu
sequel ('si:kłel) s. ciąg dalszy; wynik; następstwo
sequence ('si:kłens) s. następstwo; kolejnosc; porządek;
progresja
serene (sy'ri:n) adj. pogodny;
spokojny; s. spokojne morze;
pogodne niebo etc. v. rozpogo-
dzic
sergeant ('sa:rdżent) s. sierżant
serial('sierjel) a. seryjny;
periodyczny; kolejny; odcin-
kowy
series ('sieri:z) pl. seria;
szereg; rząd
serious ('sierjes) adj. poważny
sermon ('se:rmen) s. kazanie;
nagana
serpent ('se:rpent) s. wąż
serum ('sierem) s. surowica
servant ('se:rwent) s. służący;
sługa; służąca; urzędnik
(państwowy)
serve (se:rw) s. służyc; odbywac służbę (też kadencję;
praktykę etc.); nadawać się;
obsłużyć; podawac; sprzedawac;
dostarczyc; wręczyć; potrakto-
wac; postępowac; spełniac
fukcje; sprawowac urząd; odbywac karę (więzienia); zaserwo-
wac

service ('se:rwys) s. służba;
obsługa; praca; urząd; zaopatrzenie; instalacja;
uprzejmość; grzecznosc; przysługa; pomoc; użytecznosc;
nabożenstwo; serw; serwis
(stołowy); wręczenie; v. doglądac; naprawic; kryc (sami-
ce)
serviceable ('se:rwysebl) adj.
pożyteczny; użyteczny; praktyczny; wygodny; mocny; trwały
service-station('se:rwys-'stejszyn) s. stacja obsługi
i sprzedaży benzyny
session ('seszyn) s. posiedzenie; siedzenie; półrocze
set; set; set (set; set; set)
set (set) v. stawiac; ustawiac;
wstawic; urządzic; umieszczac;
przykładac; nastawiac; osadzac;
wbijac; wyznaczac; ustalac;
sądzic; nakrywac; składac;
wysadzac (czyms); scinac się;
okrzepnąc; adj. zastygły; nieruchomy; zdecydowany; stały;
ustalony; s. seria; garnitur;
skład; komplet;zespół; grupa;
szczepek; zachod: ustawienie;
układ; twardnienie; gęstosc;
rozstęp; oszalowanie
set at ease ('set,et'i:z) v.
uspokoic
set-back ('setbaek) s. pogorszenie; nawrot; zahamowanie
set free ('set,fri:) v. uwolnic
set off ('set,of) v. uwydatnic;
wyodrębnic; wystrzelic; wysa-
dzic; wywołac; wyruszyc; wy-
jeżdżac
set out ('set,aut) v. wystawiac;
ozdabiac; wykładac; wyruszac;
zacząc się
set to ('set,tu) v. zabierac
się (do czegos)
set up ('set,ap) v. ustawiac;
zakładac; zaczynac; zaopatrywac; roscic; wysuwac; przywracac; podnosic; założyc; podawac
się (za kogos)

settee (se'ti:) s. kanapa; sofa
setting ('setyŋg) s. otoczenie;
oprawa; ułożenie; układ; inscenizacja
settle (setl) v. osiedlić (się);
umieścić (się); uregulować;
osadzić (się); ustalić; roz-
strzygnąć; zapłacić (dług);
zamieszkać; usadowić (się);
uspokoić (się); zawierać (umowę); układać (się)
settle down ('setl,dałn) v.
ustatkować się; osiedlić się;
zabrać się do czegoś
settlement ('setlment) s. osiedle; osada; kolonia; osiadanie;
sedymentacja; załatwienie; rozstrzygnięcie; ustalenie
settler ('setler) s. osadnik;
kolonista
set-up ('set,ap) s. postawa;
układ; drużyna; dodatki do
alkoholu; (slang):ukartowane
zawody; łatwa sprawa
seven ('sewn) num. siedem;
s. siódemka
seventeen ('sewn'ti:n) num.
siedemnaście; s. siedemnastka
seventh ('sewent) adj. siódmy
seventy ('sewnty) num. siedemdziesiąt; s. siedemdziesiątka
sever ('sever) v. odrywać; odłączyć; zrywać; urywać; rozchodzić się
several ('sewrel) adj. kilku;
kilka; kilkoro
severe (sy'wier) adj. surowy;
srogi; ostry; dotkliwy; bolesny; zacięty
severity (sy'weryty) s. surowość; srogość; ostrość; za-
ciętość; ciężki stan
sew; sewed; sewn (sou; soud;
soun)
sew (sou) v. szyć; uszyć
sewage ('sju:ydż) s. ścieki
sewer ('suer) s. kanał ścieko-
wy; v. kanalizować
sewer ('souer) s. osoba szyjąca
sewerage ('su:erydż) s. kanalizacja; system kanalizacyjny
sewing ('souyŋg) s. szycie

sewing-machine ('souyŋgme,szi:n)
s. maszyna do szycia
sewn (soun) v. zob. sew
sex (seks) s. płeć
sex appeal ('sekse'pi:l) s.
atrakcyjność płciowa; seksapil
sexton ('seksten) s. grabarz
sexual ('sekszjuel) adj. seksualny; płciowy
Sejm (sejm) s. sejm
shabby ('szaeby) adj. brudny;
skąpy; odrapany; wytarty;
nędzny; podły
shack (szaek) s. buda; szałas;
dom
shack up ('szaek,ap) v. spędzać
noc z kims (slang)
shackle ('szaekl) s. kajdany;
klamra; pęta; v. zakuwać;
szczepiać
shade (szejd) s. cień; odcień;
abażur; stora; pl. ustronie;
piwnica na wino; v. zasłaniać;
zamroczyć; cieniować
shadow ('szaedou) s. cień
(czyjś); v. pokrywać cieniem;
śledzić kogoś
shady ('szejdy) adj. cienisty;
nieczysty; mętny
shaft (szaeft) s. drzewce; trzon;
strzała; promień; wał; trzonek;
dyszel; szyb
shaggy ('szaegy) a. włochaty;
krzaczasty
shake; shook; shaken (szejk;
szuk; szejken)
shake (szejk) v. potrząsać;
uścisnąć dłoń; grozić (palcem);
wstrząsać; drżeć; dygotać;
s. dygotanie; dreszcze; drżenie; potrząsanie
shake-up ('szejkap) s. otrząsnię-
cie (się); czystka (slang)
shaky ('szejky) adj. drżący;
rozklekotany; słaby; zachwiany;
chwiejący się
shale (szejl) s. łupek
shall (szael) v. będę; będziemy;
musisz; musi; muszą (zrobić)
shallow ('szaelou) s. mielizna;
adj. płytki; powierzchniowy;
v. spłycać; płycieć; obniżać
poziom (wody)

sham (szaem) adj. fałszywy;
oszukańczy; sztuczny; udawany; symulowany; upozorowany;
s. poza; symulowanie; symu-
lant; pozór; udawanie; v.uda-
wac, symulować
shambles ('szaemblz) pl. jatki; rzeź
shame (szejm) s. wstyd; v.wsty-
dzic się
shame on you ! ('szejm,on'ju:)
exp.: wstydź się !
shameful ('szejmful) adj. sromotny; haniebny
shameless ('szejmlys) adj. bezwstydny; bezczelny
shampoo (szaem'pu:) s. szampon;
mycie głowy szamponem; v. myć
szamponem
shank (szaenk) s. golen; trzonek; uchwyt
shape (szejp) v. kształtowac;
rzeźbic; modelować; formuło-
wac; wyobrazić; s. kształt;
kondycja; postac; zjawa; widmo; model
shaped ('szejpt)adj. ukształto-
wany
shapeless('szejplys) adj. bezkształtny; nieforemny; niezgrabny
shapely ('szejply) adj. kształtny; foremny; zgrabny
share (szeer) s. udział; należ-
na część; lemiesz; v. rozdzielic; dzielic (się); podzielac;
brac udział
share-holder ('szeer,houlder)
s. akcjonarjusz
shark (sza:rk) s. rekin
sharp (sza:rp) adj. ostry; bystry; pilny; wyraźny; chytry; do-
minujacy; inteligentny; adv.
punktualnie; szybko; biegiem
sharpen ('sza:rpen) v. ostrzyc;
temperowac; obostrzyc; za-
ostrzyc
sharpener ('sza:rpner) s. tem-
perowka; narzędzie do ostrze-
nia
sharpness ('sza:rpnys) s. ost-
rosc; bystrosc; chytrosc; pil-
nosc

sharp-witted ('sza:rp'łytyd)
adj. bystry; dowcipny; rozgarnięty
shatter ('szaeter) v. grucho-
tac; roztrzaskac; niweczyc;
szarpac
shave; shaved; shaven (szejw;
szejwd; szejwn)
shave (szejw) v. golic (się);
oskrobac; strugac; s. golenie;
musnięcie
shaven (szejwn) v. zob. shave
shaving ('szejwyng) v. golenie;
skrobanie; wiórkowanie; s.
wiór
shawl(szo:l) s. szal
she (szi:) pron. ona
sheaf (szi:f) s. snop; wiązka;
wiązanka; plik; pl. sheaves
(szi:wz)
shear; sheared; shorn (szier;
szierd; szo:rn)
shear (szier) v. scinac; ucinac; ostrzyc; s. scinanie; pl.
nożyce (shears)
sheath (szi:s) s. pochwa; futerał; powłoka; prezerwatywa
sheaves (szi:wz) pl. od sheath
shed (shed) s. szopa; buda;
v. zrzucac; strącac; pozbywac
(się); pogubic; ronic; przelewac (krew); wydzielac; promieniowac
sheep (szi:p) pl. owce
sheep dog ('szi:p,dog) s. owczarek
sheepish ('szi:pysz) adj. bojaźliwy; niesmiały; zakłopota-
ny; zbaraniały; ogłupiały
sheer (szier) v. schodzic z kur-
su; skręcac nagle; adj. zwykły;
jawny; czysty; zwyczajny; stromy; prostopadły; pionowy;
przejrzysty; przewiewny; lekki;
adv. zupełnie; pionowo; stromo
sheet (szi:t) s. arkusz; prze-
scieradło; gazeta; tafla; obszar; warstwa; v. pokrywac
przescieradłem; okrywac brezen-
tem
sheet iron ('szi:t,ajren) s.
blacha stalowa

shelf (szelf) s. półka; rafa;
mielizna; pl. shelves (szelwz)
shell (szel) s. łupina; skorupa; powłoka; osłona; łupina;
pancerz; muszla; szkielet;
łuska; pocisk; granat; gilza;
v. ostrzeliwać z armat; wyłus-
kiwać
shellfish ('szel,fysz) s. sko-
rupiak; mięczak
shelter ('szelter) s. schronienie; ochrona; osłona; v. chronić; osłaniać; udzielać schro-
nienia; zabezpieczać
shelve (szelv) v. odkładać (na
półkę); wkładać do szuflady;
opadać (wzdłuż stoku)
shelves (szelwz) pl. zob.shelf
shepherd ('szeperd) s. pastuch;
pasterz; v. paść; (pilotować)
prowadzić
shield (szi:ld) s. tarcza;
osłona; v. osłaniać; ochraniać
shift (szyft) v. zmieniać (np.
biegi); przesuwać; przełączyć;
zwalić; s. przesunięcie; zmiana; szychta; wykręt; wybieg
shiftless ('szyftlys) adj. niezaradny
shifty ('szyfty) adj. zmienny;
fałszywy; chytry
shilling ('szylyng) s. szyling
shin (szyn) s. goleń; v. kopać
w goleń
shine; shone; shone (szajn;
szon; szon)
shine (szajn) v. zabłyszczeć;
zajaśnieć; oczyścić na połysk;
s. jasność; blask; (slang):
granda; awantura; sympatia
shingle ('szyngl) s. gont; szyld;
wywieszka; kamyk; v. pokryć
gontami; krótko ostrzyc
shingles ('szynglz) pl. półpa-
siec
shiny ('szajny) adj. błyszczący;
wypolerowany
ship (szyp) s. okręt; statek;
samolot; v. załadować; zaokre-
tować; posyłać
shipment ('szypment) s. załadunek; przesyłka; fracht

shipowner ('szyp,ołner) s. armator
shipping ('szypyng) s. flota
handlowa; żegluga; załadunek;
usługi żeglugowe; przesyłka;
adj. spedycyjny; okrętowy
shipping company ('szypyng'kampeny) s. firma okrętowa; armator
shipwreck ('szyp,rek) s. rozbicie statku; v. ulec rozbiciu;
spowodować rozbicie statku;
rozbić się
ship-wrecked('szyp,rekt) s. rozbitek
shipyard('szyp,ja:rd) s. stocznia
shire ('szajer) s. hrabstwo
(powiat)
shirk (sze:rk) v. uchylać się;
wymigiwać się; s. nierób; wy-
migiwacz
shirt (sze:rt) s. koszula
shirt sleeves ('sze:rt,sli:wz)
pl. rękawy od koszuli; bez
marynarki; adj. prosty; domowy
shit (szyt) v. wulg.: srać;s.gów-
no
shitty ('szyty) adj. wulg.: za-
srany
shiv (szyw) s. majcher (slang)
shiver ('szywer) v. drżeć;
trząść się; rozbijać się w kawałki; s. dreszcz; kawałek
shock (szok) s. wstrząs; cios;
uderzenie; starcie; porażenie;
czupryna; kopka; v. wstrząsać;
gorszyć; oburzać; porazić
shock absorber ('szok-eb,so:r-
ber) s. tłumik drgań; amorty-
zator
shocking('szokyng) adj. okropny; wstrętny; skandaliczny;
oburzający; niestosowny
shoddy ('szody) adj. tandetny
shoe; shod; shod (szu:, szod,
szod)
shoe (szu:) s. but; półbucik;
trzewik; okucie; podkowa;
nakładka (hamulca); obręcz;
nasada; v. obuwać; podkuwać

shoehorn ('szu:,ho:rn) s. łyżka do butów; wzuwacz
shoelace ('szu:,lejs) s. sznurowadło
shoemaker ('szu:,mejker) s.
szewc
shoestring ('szu:,stryŋ) s.
sznurowadło; bardzo mały kapitał
shoeshine ('szu:,szajn) s.
czyszczenie butów (na połysk)
shone (szon) v. zob. shine
shook (szuk) v. zob. shake
shoot; shot; shot (szu:t; szot;
szot)
shoot (szu:t) v. strzelić; wystrzelić; zastrzelić; rozstrzelać; zrobić zdjęcie; na-
kręcić film; mknąć; przemknąć;
spłynąć; rwać; kiełkować;
s. pęd; kiełek; polowanie;
progi; plac zwozu śmieci
shooter ('shu:ter) s. strzelec;
rewolwer
shooting ('shu:tyŋ) adj. mkną-
cy; pędzący; strzelający
shooting gallery ('shu:tyŋ,gae-
lery) s. strzelnica
shooting-star ('shu:tyŋ,sta:r)
s. spadająca gwiazda
shooting-party ('shu:tyŋ,pa:r-
ty) s. wyprawa łowiecka; polowanie
shop (szop) s. sklep; pracownia;
warsztat; zakład; v. robić zakupy
shopkeeper ('szop,ki:per) s.
kupiec; sklepikarz
shoplifter ('szop,lyfter) s.
złodziej sklepowy
shopping center ('szopyŋ,sen-
ter) s. skupisko sklepów;
ośrodek zakupów
shopping mall ('szopyŋ,mol) s.
skupisko sklepów wzdłuż krytej
hali ;pasaż handlowy
shop·window('szop'łyndoł) s.
wystawa
shore (szo:r) s. brzeg; wybrzeże; podpora; v. podpierać;
podstęplować
shorn (szo:rn) v. zob. shear

short (szo:rt) adj. krótki;
niski; zwięzły; oschły; niecały; niewystarczający; adv.
krótko; nagle; za krótko;
s. skrót; zwarcie; pl. szorty
shortage ('szo:rtydż) s. brak;
niedobór; deficyt
short circuit ('sho:rt'se:rkyt)
s. krótkie spięcie; zwarcie
shortcoming ('sho:rt'kamyŋ)
s. wada; niedociągnięcie; brak;
niedobór
shorten ('szo:rtn) v. skracać
shorthand ('szo:rthaend) s.
stenografia
shortly ('szo:rtly) adv. wkrótce; niebawem
shortness ('szo:rtnys) s. krótkość; niedobór
shorts ('szo:rts) pl. szorty;
kalesony (krótkie)
shortstory ('szo:rt,sto:ry) s.
nowela
short-sighted ('szo:rt'sajtyd)
adj. krótkowzroczny; nieprze-
widujący
short-term ('szo:rt'term) adj..
krótkoterminowy; krótko-
trwały
short-winded ('szo:rt'łyndyd)
adj. zasapany; krótko mówiący
shot (szot) v. zob. shoot; ładować broń; s. strzał; pocisk;
śrut; zastrzyk; docinek; adj.
mieniący się
shotgun ('szotgan) s. dubeltówka; śrutówka; strzelba
should (szud) v. tryb warunkowy
od shall
shoulder ('szoulder) s. ramię;
plecy; łopatka; pobocze; v.
brać na ramię; rozpychać się
shout (szałt) s. krzyk; okrzyk;
wrzask; v. krzyczeć; wykrzy-
kiwać
shove (szaw) v. popychać; posuwać (coś); s. pchnięcie
shovel ('szawl) s. łopata;
szufla; v. przerzucać łopatą
lub szuflą
show; showed; shown (szou;
szoud; szoun)

show (szou) v. pokazywać; wskazywać; s. wystawa; przedstawienie; pokaz

show around ('szou,e'raund) v. oprowadzać

show off ('szou,o:f) v. popisywać się; paradować; starać się imponować

show up ('szou,ap) v. demaskować; zjawiać się; ukazywać się

show business ('szou'byznyz) s. przemysł widowiskowy

shower ('szałer) s. tusz; prysznic; przelotny deszcz; grad; stek; przelotnie kropić; obsypywać; oblewać

shower bath ('szałer,ba:t) s. tusz; prysznic

shown (szołn) v. zob. show

showy ('szoły) adj. ostentacyjny; okazały

shrank (szraenk) s. zob. shrink

shred (szred) s. strzęp; v. ciąć na strzępy

shrew (szru:) s. złośnica; sekutnica; sorek

shrewd (szru:d) a. przenikliwy (np. obserwator)

shriek (szri:k) v. wrzeszczeć; piszczeć; rechotać; s. wrzask; pisk; gwizd (ostry)

shrill (szryl) adj. ostry; przenikliwy; przeraźliwy; v. rozlegać się przenikliwie; adv. przenikliwie

shrimp (szrymp) s. krewetka; karzełek; v. łowić krewetki

shrine (szrajn) s. przybytek; relikwiarz; v. umieszczać w przybytku

shrink; shrank; shrunk (szrynk; szraenk; szrank)

shrink (szrynk) v. kurczyć (się) wzbraniać (się) wzdrygać się; s. kurczenie się; (slang):psychiatra

shrinkage ('szrynkydż) s. kurczenie się; ubytek na wadze

shrivel ('szrywl) v. kurczyć (się)

Shrovetide ('szrouwtajd) s. ostatki; zapusty

Shrovetide Tuesday ('szrouwtajd'tju:zdy) s. tłusty wtorek

shrub (szrab) s. krzew; krzak

shrubbery ('szrabery) s. krzaki

shrubby ('szraby) adj. krzaczasty

shrug (szrag) s. wzruszenie ramion; v. wzruszyć ramionami

shrunken ('szrankn) v. zob. shrink

shudder ('szader) s. dreszcz; (slang):nudziarz; v. zadrzeć; wzdrygać się

shuffle ('szafl) v. wlec się; powłóczyć; kręcić; tasować; mieszać; s. krok suwany; krętactwo; tasowanie (kart); wleczenie się; szuranie

shun (szan) v. unikać; wystrzegać się; s, baczność; uwaga

shut; shut; shut (szat; szat; szat)

shut (szat) v. zamykać (się); przytrzasnąć; adj. zamknięty

shut down ('szat,dałn) s. zamknięcie; wstrzymanie pracy; v. zamykać; kłaść koniec; zasłaniać; (o zakładzie) stanąć

shut up ('szat,ap) v. pozamykać; zamknąć gębę; zamilknąć; bądź cicho; wulg.:stul pysk!

shutter ('szater) s. okiennica; zasłona; migawka; regulator organów; v. zamykać okiennice

shy (szaj) adj. płochliwy; wstydliwy; nieśmiały; nieufny; ostrożny; skąpy; szczupły; v. płoszyć się; stronić; rzucać; s. rzut (w coś)

shyness ('szajnys) s. skromność; nieśmiałość

shyster ('szajster) s. chytry (polityk) bez zasad; adwokat-krętacz

sick (syk) adj. chory; znudzony; chorowity; skażony zarazkami; chorobowy

sickbed ('sykbed) s. łóżko chorego; łoże boleści

sick benefit ('syk'benefyt) s. zasiłek chorobowy

sicken ('sykn) v. zaczynać chorować; wywoływać obrzydzenie; brzydzić (się)

sickle ('sykl) s. sierp

sick leave ('sykli:w) s. zwolnienie lekarskie; urlop chorobowy

sickly ('sykly) adj. chorowity; słabowity; niezdrowy; chorobliwy; ckliwy

sickness ('syknys) s. choroba; wymioty; nudności

sick room ('syk-ru:m) s. izba chorych; pokój chorego

side (sajd) s. strona; adj. uboczny; v. stać po czyjejś stronie

side by side ('sajd,baj'sajd) exp.: obok siebie; jeden przy drugim

side arms ('sajda:rmz) pl. broń boczna (np. szable)

sideboard ('sajdbo:rd) s. kredens

sidecar ('sajd,ka:r) s. przyczepa do motocykla

sided ('sajdyd) adj. stronny; mający strony

side dish ('sajd,dysz) s. przystawka

side-kick ('sajdkyk) s. (slang): kompan; pomagier

sideroad ('sajd,roud) s. boczna droga

side line ('sajd,lajn) v. odsuwać na bok; zapobiegać

sidewalk ('sajd-łо:k) s. chodnik; trotuar

sidewalk café ('sajdłо:kaefej) s. kawiarnia na chodniku

sidewards ('sajdłedz) adv. bokiem; w bok

sideways ('sajdłejz) adv. bokiem; na poprzek; adj. boczny

side with ('sajd,łys) v. brać czyjąś stronę

siege (si:dż) s. oblężenie

sieve (syw) s. sito; rzeszoto; przetak; v. przesiewać

sift (syft) v. przesiewać; przebierać; oddzielać; proszyć; posypywać

sigh (saj) s. westchnienie; v. wzdychać

sight (sajt) s. wzrok; widok; celownik; przeziernik

sighted ('sajtyd) adj. spostrzeżony

sightly ('sajtly) adj. dający dobry widok; miły; przyjemny

sight seeing ('sajtsi:yng) s. zwiedzanie; adj. turystyczny

sightseeing tour ('sajtsi:yng,tu:r) s. zwiedzanie z wycieczką; wycieczka krajoznawcza

sightseer ('sajtsi:er) s. turysta; zwiedzający

sign (sajn) s. znak; omen; godło; napis; wywieszka; szyld; skinienie; oznaka; objaw; ślad; znak drogowy; hasło; odzew; v. znaczyć; naznaczyć; podpisać; skinąc

sign up ('sajn,ap) v. zapisywać się

sign out ('sajn,aut) v. wypisywać się

signal ('sygnl) s. sygnał; znak; v. sygnalizować; zapowiadać; dawać znak

signature ('sygnyczer) s. podpis; sygnatura; klucz

signature-tune('sygnyczer,tju:n) s. oznaczenie tonacji

signboard ('sajnbo:rd) s. wywieszka; szyld; godło

signet ('sygnyt) s. sygnet; pieczątka; v. pieczętować

significance (syg'nyfykens) s. wyraz; ważność; znaczenie

significant (syg'nyfykent) adj. istotny; znaczący; doniosły; znamienny; ważny

signification (syg'nyfykejszyn) s. znaczenie

signify ('sygnyfaj) v. znaczyć; mieć znaczenie; oznaczać; zaznaczać

signpost ('sajn,poust) s. drogowskaz

silence ('sajlens) s. milczenie; cisza; v. nakazywać milczenie; cicho !

silencer ('sajlenser) s. tłumik

silent ('sajlent) adj. milczący;
cichy; małomówny

silk (sylk) s. jedwab; adj.
jedwabny

silken ('sylkn) adj. jedwabny;
jedwabniczy

silky ('sylky) adj. jedwabisty

sill (syl) s. próg; podkład;
parapet

silly ('syly) s. głupiec; adj.
głupi; ogłupiały

silver ('sylwer) s. srebro;
v. posrebrzać; adj. srebrny;
srebrzysty

silvery ('sylwry) adj. srebrzysty

similar ('symyler) adj. podobny; rzecz podobna

similarity (,symy'laeryty) s.
podobieństwo

simmer ('symer) v. wolno gotować (się); burzyc się wewnątrz;
s. gotowanie na wolnym ogniu

simple ('sympl) adj. prosty;
zwykły; naturalny; szczery; naiwny; głupkowaty; zwyczajny

simplicity(sym'plysyty) s.
prostota

simplification (,symplyfy'kejszyn) s. uproszczenie

simplistic ('symplystyk) adj.
zbyt upraszczający

simplify ('symplyfaj) v.upros-
cić; ułatwić

simply ('symply) adv. po prostu

simulate ('symjulejt) v. udawać; naśladować

simultaneous (symel'tejnjes)
adj. równoczesny; jednoczesny

sin (syn) s. grzech; v. grze-
szyć

since (syns) adv. odtąd; potem;
conj; skoro; ponieważ; od czasu jak

sincere (syn'sier) adj. szczery

sincerely (syn'sierly) adv.
szczerze

sincerity (syn'seryty) s. szczerość

sinew ('synu:) s. ścięgno

sinews ('synu:s) pl. muskulatu-
ra; siła; moc

sinewy ('synuy) adj. muskularny; mocny

sing; sang; sung (syng; saeng;
sang)

sing (syng) v. śpiewać; wyć;
zawodzić; bzykać; świstać;
opiewać; s. śpiew; świst

singe (syndź) v. opalać; osma-
lać

singer (synger) s. śpiewak

single ('syngl) adj. pojedynczy; jeden; samotny; szczery;
uczciwy; s. bilet w jedną
stronę; gra pojedyncza; v. wybierać; wyróżniać

single out ('syngl,aut) v. wybierać

single-handed ('syngl'haendyd)
adj. adv. w pojedynkę; na
własną rękę; samodzielny; samodzielnie

single room ('syngl'ru:m) s.
pojedynczy pokój

single ticket ('syngl'tykyt) s.
bilet w jedną stronę

singles bar ('syngls,ba:r) s.
bar dla samotnych

singular ('syngjuler) adj.
osobliwy; niezwykły; pojedynczy; liczba pojedyncza

singularity (,syngju'laeryty)
s. osobliwość; niezwykłość;
niezwykły człowiek

sinister ('synyster) adj.
zbrodniczy; złowieszczy; lewy

sink; sank; sunk (synk; saenk;
sank)

sink (synk) v. zatonąć; zato-
pić; zagłębić (się); opuścić;
obniżyć; pogrążyć; zanikać;
zmaleć; wykopywać; ukrywać;
wyryć; zainwestować; amortyzować; s. zlew; ściek; bagno
zepsucia

sinking ('synkyng)s. uczucie
mdłości (np. z przerażenia)

sinner ('syner) s. grzesznik

sip (syp) s; łyk; popijanie;
v. popijać

sir (se:r) s. pan; v. nazywać
panem; exp.: proszę pana !

sirloin (se:rloyn) s. polędwica

sister (syster) s. siostra

sister in law ('syster yn,lo:)
s. szwagierka

sit; sat; sat (syt; saet; saet)

sit (syt) v. siedziec; przesia-
dywac; usiąsc; zasiadac; obra-
dowac; leżec; pozowac

sit down ('syt,dałn) v. usiąsc

sit up ('syt,ap) v. wyprostowac się siedząc; czuwac;
usiąsc prosto

site (sajt) s. miejsce; plac
(np. budowy); położenie;
v. umieszczac

sitting ('sytyŋg) s. posiedzenie; sesja

sitting-room ('sytyŋg,ru:m) s.
bawialnia; salon

situated ('sytjuejtyd) adj.
umieszczony; stojący; usytuo-
wany

situation (,sytu'ejszyn) s. położenie; posada; sytuacja

six (syks) num. szesc; s. szost-
ka

sixteen ('syks'ti:n) num. szes-
nascie; s. szesnastka

sixth (sykst) num. adj. szosty;
s. jedna szosta

sixthly ('sykstly) adv. po
szoste

size (sajz) s. wielkosc; numer;
format; klajster; krochmal;
rzadki klej; v. sortowac wg
wielkosci; oceniac wielkosc;
nadawac się; krochmalic; usz-
tywnic klejem

sized-up ('sajzd,ap) adj. oce-
niony (co do wielkosci, siły
lub ważnosci)

sizzle ('syzl) v. skwierczec;
s. skwierczenie

skate (skejt) s. łyżwa; wrotka;
płaszczka; szkapa; pętak; pa-
tałach; v. slizgac się; jeżdzic na wrotkach

skater ('skejter) s. łyżwiarz;
wrotkarz

skeleton ('skelytn) s.szkielet

skeptic ('skeptyk) adj. sceptyczny; s. sceptyk

sketch ('skecz) s. szkic; skecz;
zarys; v. szkicowac ;przedstawic
w ogolnych zarysach(w krotkich
słowach);robic wstępny rysunek

sketch block ('skecz,blok) s.
szkicownik

sketchbook ('skecz,bu:k) s.
szkicownik

ski (ski:) s. narta; wyrzutnik
bomb; v. jeżdzic na nartach

skid (skid) s. deska; płoza;
podporka; klin hamowniczy;
poslizg; zarzucenie; v. slizgac się; zarzucac; umieszczac
na płozach; hamowac

skier ('ski:er) s. narciarz

skiing ('skiyŋg) s. narciarstwo; jazda na nartach

ski lift ('ski lyft) s. wyciąg narciarski

skill ('skyl) s. zręcznosc;
wprawa

skilled ('skyld) adj. wykwali-
fikowany; wykonany fachowo

skillful ('skylful) adj. zręczny; wprawny

skillet (skylyt) s. patelnia;
(slang): draka

skim (skym) v. zbierac (smie-
tankę); szumowac; przebiegac
wzrokiem; puszczac po powierzchni; szybowac; s. zbieranie;
mleko zbierane; adj. zbierany

skimmer ('skymer) s. warzęchwa;
cedzidło

skimp (skymp) v. skąpic

skimpy (skympy) adj. skąpy; za
mały; niewystarczający

skin (skyn) s. skora; skorka;
cera; szawłok; (slang):oszust;
v. zdzierac skorę; pokrywac
naskorkiem; sciągac z siebie

skin-deep('skyn'di:p) adj.
powierzchowny

skindiver ('skyn'dajwer) s.
płetwonurek

skindiving ('skyn'dajwyŋg) s.
sportowe nurkowanie (z płetwami)   skora i kosci

skinny ('skyny) adj. chudy ;

skip (skyp) v. skakac; przeskakiwac; odskakiwac; pomijac;
(slang):uciekac; s. skok;
przeskok; kapitan sportowy

skipper ('skyper) s. szyper;
kapitan statku; skoczek; kapitan drużyny

skirt ('ske:rt) s. spódnica; poła; wulg.:kobietka; przepona; brzeg; v. jechać brzegiem; obchodzić; leżeć na skraju skit ('skyt) s. skecz; satyra; mnóstwo

skoal (skoul) excl.:na zdrowie!

skull (skal) s. czaszka

sky (skaj) s. niebo; klimat

skyjack ('skaj,dżaek) s. porwanie samolotu w locie; v. porwać samolot w locie (uprowadzać)

skyjacker ('skaj,dżaeker) s. pirat powietrzny

skylark ('skajla:rk) s. skowronek; v. dokazywać; swawolić

skylight ('skajlajt) s. okno dające górne światło; okno w suficie

skyscraper ('skaj.skrejper) s. drapacz chmur

skywards ('skajłerdz) adv. ku niebu

slab (slaeb) s. płytka; v. krajać na płytki (kromki)

slack (slaek) adj. luźny; wolny; rozlazły; opieszały; ospały; leniwy; niedbały; v. zluźniać; zwalniać; popuszczać; zaniedbywać; gasić (np. ogień); s. luźna część; lenistwo; zastój; bezczelność; miał węglowy ;zwis;impertynencja

slacken (slaeken) v. rozluźniać (się); zwalniać; poluźniać (się); popuszczać; zaniedbywać; gasić (np. wapno)

slacks (slaeks) pl. (luźne) spodnie

slain (slejn) zabity; zob.slay

slake (slejk) v. gasić (np. wapno); wywierać (np.zemstę)

slam (slaem) v. zatrzasnąć (się); (slang) krytykować ostro; pobić; s. trzaśnięcie; ostra krytyka; ciupa

slang (slaeng) s. gwara; żargon; slang; adj. gwarowy; żargonowy; v. nawymyślać komuś

slangy (slaengy) adj. gwarowy

slant (sla:nt).s. pochyłość; skos; tendencja; punkt widze-

nia; spojrzenie; adj. ukośny; v. iść skośnie; pochylać (się); odchylać (się); być nachylonym

slap (slaep) s. klaps; plaśnięcie; v. plasnąć; dać klapsa; uderzyc; narzucić; adv. nagle; prościutko; regularnie

slapstick ('slaep,styk) s. laska arlekina; błazeńska komedia

slash ('slaesz) v. pokiereszować; przeciąć; hłostać; smagać; walić; ciąć; s. cięcie; szrama; przecięcie; wyrąb; odpadki drzewne; porosłe (krzakami) moczary

slate(slejt) s. łupek; dachówka łupkowa; tabliczka do pisania; lista (kandydatów w USA); v.pokrywać dachówkami; umieszczać na liście kandydatów; łajać; wymyślać; krytykować

slate pencil ('slejt'pensl) s. rysik

slattern ('slaete:rn) s. brudas; flejtuch; kocmołuch

slaughter ('slo:ter) v. rżnąć; zabijać; wymordować; s. ubój; rzeź; masakra

Slav (sla:w) adj. słowiański

slave (slejw) adj. niewolniczy; s. niewolnik; v. harować

slavery ('slejwery) s. niewolnictwo

slay; slew; slain (slej; slu:, slejn) v. zabić; uśmiercać

sled (sled) s. sanie; v. wozić saniami

sledge hammer ('sledż-haemer) s. oburęczny młot

sleek (sli:k) adj. gładki; ulizany; v. gładzić; wygładzać

sleep; slept; slept (sli:p; slept; slept)

sleep (sli:p) v. spać; spoczywać; dawać nocleg; s. sen; spanie; drzemka

sleep off ('sli:p,of) v. odespać wtyczka (szpiegowska etc)

sleeper ('sli:per) s. człowiek śpiący; dźwigar; potencjalny przedmiot rozgłosu;truteń;leń

sleeping-bag ('sli:pyng,baeg) s. śpiwór

sleeping car ('sli:pyng,ca:r)
s. wagon sypialny

sleeping partner ('sli:pyng-
'pa:rtner) s. cichy wspólnik

sleeping pill ('sli:pyng,pyl)
s. pigułka nasenna

sleepless ('sli:plys) adj. bezsenny

sleepwalker ('sli:p,ło:ker) s.
lunatyk

sleepy ('sli:py) adj. śpiący

sleet (sli:t) s. słota; deszcz
ze śniegiem; gołoledź

sleeve (sli:w) s. rękaw; tuleja; łuska; nasadka; tuba;
zanadrze

sleeved ('sli:wd) adj. z ręka-
wami

sleigh (slej) v. saneczkować
(się); jechać saniami

slender ('slender) adj. wysmukły;szczupły; wiotki; nikły;
skromny; niewielki; słaby

slept (slept) v. zob. sleep

slew (slu:) v. zob. slay

slice (slajs) s. kromka; płatek;
plasterek; kawałek; łopatka
kuchenna; v. krajać na kromki;
kawałki etc. przecinać; wios-
słować; wyjmować łopatką

slick (slyk) adj. gładki; tłusty; oślizgły; miły; pociągający; pierwszorzędny; adv. gładko; prościutko; s. tłusta plama (na morzu); szerokie dłuto

slicker ('slyker) s. gładki
płaszcz od deszczu; oszust

slid (slyd) v. zob. slide

slide; slid; slid (slajd; slyd;
slyd)

slide (slajd).v, suwać (się);
sunąć (się); ślizgać (się);
s. ślizganie się; suwak; pro-
wadnica ślizgowa; poślizg;
przeźrocze; zrzutnia

slide rule('slajd,ru:l) s. suwak logarytmiczny

slight (slajt) adj. wątły; niewielki; drobny; skromny; nieznaczny; v. lekceważyć;
s. lekceważenie

slim (slym) adj.szczupły; wysmukły; słaby; (slang):chytry;
v. wyszczuplać; odchudzać (się)

slime (slajm) s. szlam; muł;
śluz; płynna smoła ziemna;
v. zamulać; odmulać; zwilżać
(np. śliną)

slimy (slajmy) adj. mulisty;
zamulony; oblesny; oślizgły

sling; slung; slung (slyng;
sląng; sląng)

sling (slyng) s. proca; rzut;
pętla (np. do ładowania dzwi-
giem); temblak; rzemień do
strzelby itp. v. rzucać;
strzelać z procy; podnosić na
pętli; zawieszać na (np. rze-
mieniu)

slinger ('slynger) s. procarz

slinky ('slynky) adj. ukradko-
wy; (slang):mający ruchy węża

slip; slipped; slipped (slyp;
slypd; slypd)

slip (slyp) v. pośliznąć (się);
wyśliznąć (się); ześliznąć
(się); popełnić nietakt; zrobić błąd; przepuścić (np.okaz-
je); wymknąć się; zerwać się;
zapomnieć; spuszczać (np. ze
smyczy); s. poślizg; potknięcie; pomyłka; błąd; przemówienie się; zsuw; halka; świstek
(papieru); pochylnia

slip off ('slyp,of) v. zdejmować; rozbierać się; ześlizgiwać się; spadać

slip on ('slyp,on) v. wdziewać

slip out ('slyp,aut) v. wymknąć się

slip up ('slyp,ap) s. błąd; za-
chwianie się; przemówienie się;
zsuw; ślizg; v. zrobić błąd;
pomylić się; potknąć się

slipper ('slyper) s. pantofel

slippery ('slypery) adj. śliski;
niebezpieczny; ryzykowny;
nieuczciwy; nieczysty; drażliwy; delikatny; wykrętny;
chytry

slit; slit; slit (slyt; slyt;
slyt)

slit (slyt) v. rozszczepić;
rozedrzeć wzdłuż; s. szpara;
szczelina; rozcięcie
slobber ('slober) s. ślina; roz-
czulenie; v. oślinic się; roz-
czulic się
slogan ('slougen) s. slogan;
hasło; powiedzonko (np. rekla-
mowe)
sloop (slu:p) s. slup (łódź)
slop (slop) v. rozlewać; przepełniać płynem; rozpryskiwać;
s. kałuża; brudna woda; pomyje; lura
slop over ('slop,ouwer) v.
przelewać się przez wierzch
slope (sloup) s. pochyłość;
spadek; nachylenie; spadzis-
tość; stok; skarpa; zbocze;
pochylnia; v. byc pochylonym;
miec nachylenie; nachylać;
pochylac; wałęsac się; łazi-
kowac
sloping (sloupyng) adj. pochyły; skośny
sloppy ('slopy) adj. błotnisty;
pochlapany; zaniedbany; rozlazły; ckliwy
slot (slot) s. szczelina; rozcięcie; trop; ślad; v. roz-
ciąć; naciąć; wyżłobic
sloth (slous) s. lenistwo; le-
niwiec
slot-machine ('slotme,szi:n)
s. (grający lub sprzedający)
automat na monety
slouch (slaucz) s. przygarbie-
nie; niedbała postawa; wałkoń;
v. garbic się; iśc ociężale;
opuszczac rondo kapelusza
slough (slau) s. bagno; trzęsawisko
slaugh (slaw) v. leniec; zrzucac skórę
sloven ('slawn) s. niechlujny;
brudas; flejtuch; fuszer;
partacz
slovenly ('slawnly) adj. niechlujny; partacki
slow (sloł) adj. powolny; nie-
gorliwy; nieskory; opieszały;
leniwy; tępy; nudny; adv. wolno; powoli

slow down ('sloł,dałn) v. zwalniac; przyhamowac
slow-motion ('sloł'mouszyn) s.
zwolnione tempo; w zwolnionym
tempie
slowworm ('sloł,łe:rm) s. padalec
sluggish ('slagysz) adj. ospały; leniwy; powolny
sluice ('slu:s) s. śluza; ściek;
rynna; v. puszczac wodę (ze
stawu etc). spłukiwac; zalewac; chlusnąc; spływac ze
śluzy
slums (slamz) s. dzielnica nędzy
slumber ('slamber) v. spac lekko; drzemac; s. sen; drzemka;
spokój; bezczynnosc
slung (slang) v. zob . sling
slush (slasz) s. chlapa; odpadki tłuszczowe; smar; fundusz
z odpadków; tajny fundusz na
przekupstwo; v. opryskac; wy-
smarowac; pokrywac zaprawą
slut (slat) s. flejtuch; kocmołuch; plucha; pinda; szmata;
flądra; suka
sly (slaj) ad. szczwany; chytry;
filuterny
slyboots ('slajbu:ts) s. urwis;
spryciarz; chytrus (udający
głupiego)
smack (smaek) s. posmak; odrobina; trzask; mlaśnięcie;
cmoknięcie; klaps; jednomasz-
towiec; v. cmokac; strzelac
z bata; dac w pysk; obliziwac
(wargi)
smacking ('smaekyng) adj.
zgrabny; raźny; mocny (wiatr)
small (smo:l) adj. mały; drobny; niewielki; skromny; ciasny;
nieliczny; nieznaczny; małostkowy; adv. drobno; na małą ska-
lę; cicho; s. drobna rzecz;
mała częsć
small change ('smo:l,czejndż)
s. drobne (pieniądze)
small hours ('smo:l,auers) pl.
bardzo wczesne ranne godziny
smallish ('smo:lysz) adj. ma-
ławy

small of the back ('smo:l,ow-
'dy,baek) s. krzyże
smallpox ('smo:l,poks) s. ospa
smart (sma:rt) adj. dotkliwy;
cięty; zręczny; żwawy; dowcipny; szykowny; zgrabny; elegancki; v. piec; palić (np.
w oczy); cierpieć; szczypać;
parzyć; odczuwać boleśnie;
pokutować
smart aleck('sma:rt,alek) s.
Jędrek-medrek
smash (smaesz) v. rozbić; rozwalić; roztrząskać; zmiażdżyc;
potłuc; palnąc; rozgromić;
upadać; zbankrutować; ścinać
piłkę
smashing('smaeszyng) adj. nadzwyczajny; niezwykły
smattering('smaeteryn) s. znajomości po łebkach; wiedza
powierzchowna
smear (smier) v. osmarować;
zasmarować; wlepić komuś sma-
ry; s. plama; smar
smell; smelt; smelled (smel;
smelt; smeld)
smell (smel) s. węch; won; zapach; odor; smród; v. pachnieć; tracić; mieć zapach;
śmierdzieć; mieć powonienie;
obwachiwać; czuć zapach;
zwietrzyć; zwąchać; poczuć
smelt (smelt) v. sob. smell;
stapiać; wytapiać (metal);
s. stynka (ryba)
smile (smajl) v. uśmiechać się;
s. uśmiech
smite; smote; smitten (smajt;
smout; 'smytn)
smite (smajt) v. uderzać; porazić; powalić; zabić; nękać;
karać; oczarować; s. cios;
uderzenie;sprobo
smith (smyß) s. kowal
smithy (smyßy) s. kuźnia
smitten ('smytn) v. zob.smite
smock (smok) s. chałat; kitel;
v. ubierać chałat; ozdabiać
rysunkiem szachownicy
smog (smog) s. mgła zanieczysz-
czona dymem (Londyn,Los Angeles)

smoke (smouk) s. dym; palenie;
papieros; v. dymić; kopcić; wykurzać; wyjawiać; wykadzać; oka-
dzać; okopcić; uwędzić; przypa-
lać; palić (tytoń)
smoke-dried ('smouk,drajd) adj.
wędzony
smoker ('smouker) s. palący; pa-
lacz
smoking ('smoukyng) s. palenie
(tytoniu)
smoking·car ('smoukyng,ka:r) s.
wagon dla palących
smoking·compartment ('smoukyng-
kaem,pa:rtment) s. przedział
dla palących
smoky ('smouky) adj. dymiący;
przydymiony; zadymiony; okopcony
smolder ('smoulder) v. tlić się;
s. tlenie się; dym
smooch (smu:cz) v. brudzić; walać; całować się; ściskać się;
migdalić się
smooth (smu:ß) adj. gładki; spokojny; łagodny; v. gładzić; łagodzić; adv. gładko; s. wygła-
dzenie
smooth down ('smu:ß,dałn) v.
wygładzić; uspakajać (się)
smother ('smadżer) v. stłumic;
stłamsić; obcałowywać; zatuszować; okrywać
smudge (smadż) v. poplamić; za-
brudzić; s. plama; kleks; brud
smuggle ('smagl) v. przemycać
smuggler ('smagler) s. przemytnik
smut (smat) v. poplamić; s. brud
z sadzy; sprośności; tłuste
kawały; śnieć
smutty ('smaty) adj. sprośny;
brudny od sadzy
snack (snaek) s. zakąska
snack bar ('snaek,ba:r) s. bufet; bar
snafu (snae'fu:) v. zabałaganic;
s. bałagan (slang)
snail (snejl) s. ślimak
snake (snejk) s. wąż; v. wić
się; wlec (za sobą);pełzać jak
wąż;przybierać kształt węża

snap (snaep) v. łapać zębami;
warczeć; błysnąć; urwać; złamać; chwytać; zapalić się do;
przerwać szorstko; poprawić
się; mieć się na baczności;
zatrzasnąć (się); strzelać
z bicza; pstryknąć; sfotografować; śpiesznie załatwiać;
machnąć ręką lekceważąco;
s. ugryzienie; warknięcie;
trzask; zatrzask; dociskacz;
zdjęcie; rzecz łatwa; adj.
prosty; łatwy; doraźny; nagły

snap bolt ('snaep,boult) s.
zatrzask u drzwi

snap fastener('snaep,fa:sner)
s. zatrzask

snappish ('snaepysz) adj.
zgryźliwy; kostyczny

snappy ('snaepy) adj. zgryźliwy; kostyczny; żwawy; prędki

snapshot ('snaepszot) s. zdjęcie migawkowe; strzał na chybił trafił

snare (sneer) v. usidlać; łapać w sidła; s. sidła; pułapka

snarl (sna:rl) s. warknięcie;
plątanina; v. warczeć; plątać (się); zaplątać; robić
zator

snatch (snaecz) v. złapać;
wyrwać; s. złapanie; urywek;
strzęp; mig

sneak (sni:k) v. chyłkiem zakradać się; przemykać się;
zerkać; zwiać; s. podły
tchórz

sneakers ('sni:kers) pl. trzewiki; trampki

sneer (snier) v. uśmiechać się
szyderczo; kpić; drwić; s.
szyderstwo; szydercze spojrzenie

sneeze (sni:z) v. kichać;
s. kichnięcie

sniff (snyf) v. prychać; pociągać nosem; krzywić się na
coś; powąchać; obwąchać; zwąchać; wyczuć; s. prychnięcie;
pociągnięcie nosem

sniffle ('snyfl) s. katar; pociąganie nosem; v. pociągać
nosem

snipe (snajp) s. bekas; strzał
z ukrycia; v. z ukrycia: strzelać; trafić, zabić

sniper ('snajper) s. strzelec
wyborowy; strzelec z ukrycia

snivel ('snywel) s. śluz z nosa;
biadolenie; udawanie; v. smarkać się; skamleć; biadolić;
płakać; rozczulać się

snob (snob) s. człowiek wywyższający się

snoop (snu:p) v. myszkować;
wścibiać nos; s. szpicel

snoop around ('snu:p,e'raund)
v. przemyszkowywać; szpiegować

snooze (snu:z) s. drzemka;
v. drzemać; zdrzemnąć się

snore (sno:r) v. chrapać; s.
chrapanie

snort (sno:rt) v. parskać;
s. parsknięcie

snout (snaut) s. ryj; pysk; morda; wylot

snow (snou) s. śnieg; (slang):
kokaina; heroina; v. ośnieżyć;
śnieg pada; zasypać śniegiem;
pobić na głowę; omamiać

snowball ('snoubo:l) s. kula
śnieżna; v. bić się śniegiem;
rosnąc jak lawina

snow blindness ('snou'blajndnys)
s. śnieżna ślepota

snowdrift ('snou'dryft) s. zaspa śnieżna

snowdrop ('snoudrop) s. śnieżyczka

snow job ('snou,dżob) s. naciąganie pochlebstwami

snow-white ('snou'hłajt) adj.
śnieżnobiały

snowy ('snoły) adj. śnieżny;
śniegowy

snub (snab) v. ofuknąć; dać po
nosie; traktować lekceważąco;
nagle zatrzymać; adj. perkaty;
zadarty nos; s. bura; ofuknięcie;ostra odprawa;afront;ucieranie nosa komuś;przywodzenie
kogoś do porządku

snuff(snaf) s. tabaka; proszek
do zażywania przez nos; zapach;
opalony koniec knota; v. zażywać tabakę; pociągać nosem;
czyścić koniec knota
snug (snag) adj. przytulny;
wygodny; ukryty; v. tulić się;
zrobić przytulnym
snuggle ('snagl) v. przytulić
się
so(sou) adv. tak; a więc; w ta-
kim razie; a zatem; też; tak
samo; bardzo to; także; excl.:
to tak ! no, no !
so far ('sou fa:r) adv. jak
dotąd ; jak do tej pory
soak (souk) v. moczyć (się);
nasycać (się); przenikać; namoknąć; (slang):wyciągać (od
kogoś) pieniądze; mocno uderzyć; s. moczenie (się); woda
do moczenia; popijawa; zastaw
soap (soup) s. mydło; pochleb-
stwo; wazelinowanie się (komuś); v. mydlić (się); pochlebiać; adj. mydlany; myd-
larski
soap box ('soup,boks) s. skrzynia od mydła; mównica (np.
uliczna). v. przemawiać na
ulicy, w parku etc.
soap opera ('soup'opere) s.
(popołudniowe) przedstawienie
radiowe lub telewizyjne pełne
małżeńskich kryzysów, tragedii,
cierpień, płaskiej czułostko-
wości i melodramatycznych za-
kończeń
soar (so:r) v. wznosić się;
osiągać wyżyny; iść w górę
(np. ceny)
sob (sob) v. łkać; szlochać;
s. łkanie; szloch
sober ('souber) adj. trzeźwy;
wstrzemięźliwy; stateczny;
zrównoważony; rzeczowy; poważny; spokojny; v. trzeźwieć;
wytrzeźwieć; wytrzeźwiać ;
otrzeźwieć; opanować się
sober up ('souber,ap) v. wytrzeźwieć
sober-minded ('souber,majndyd)
adj.stateczny; zrównoważony

so-called ('sou-ko:ld) adj.
tak zwany
soccer ('soker) s. piłka nożna
sociable ('souzebl) adj. towarzyski; przyjacielski; gro-
madny; stadny
social ('souzel) adj. społeczny; socjalny; s. zebranie
towarzyskie
social democrat ('souzel'de-
mekraet) s. socjaldemokrata
socializm ('souszelyzem) s.
socjalizm
social security ('souszel-
sy'kjueryty) s. ubezpiecze-
nia społeczne
socialist ('souszelyst) s.
socjalista; adj. socjalistycz-
ny
social worker ('souszel'łerker) s. pracownik społeczny;
pracownik urzędu opieki spo-
łecznej
socialize ('souszelajz) v.
upaństwowić; uspołecznić
social welfare ('souszel,łel-
feer) s. opieka społeczna
society (so'sajety) s. towarzystwo; społeczeństwo; społeczność; spółka (np. akcyj-
na)
sock (sok) s. skarpetka; cios;
szturchaniec; v. cisnąć w kogoś; uderzyć; walnąć; adv.
prosto (np. w nos)
socket ('sokyt) s. oprawka;
oczodół; zębodół; gniazdko;
wydrążenie
sod (sod) s. darń; darnina;
wulg.; skurwysyn; sodomita
sofa ('soufe) s. kanapa; sofa
soft (soft) adj. miękki; delikatny; przyciszony; łagodny;
słaby; głupi; wygodny
soft drink ('soft,drynk) s.
napój bezalkoholowy
soft goods ('soft,gu:ds) pl.
tekstylia
soften ('softn) v. zmiękczyć;
osłabić; złagodzić; złagodnieć; zmięknąć
soil (sojl) s.gleba; rola; ziemia; brud;plama; v.zabrudzić;
powalać; poplamić;wysmarować

sojourn ('sedʒe:rn) s. pobyt;
v. przebywać; zatrzymywać (się)
sold (sould) v. sprzedany; zob.
sell
soldier ('souldʒer) s. żołnierz
najemnik; adj. żołnierski;
v. służyć w wojsku
sole (soul) s. podeszwa; podwa-
lina; zelówka; stopa; spodek;
sola; adj. jedyny; wyłączny
solemn ('solem) adj. solenny;
uroczysty; poważny
solicit (se'lysyt) y. prosić;
zwracać się (o coś); nagabywać; ubiegać się; zwracać (np.
uwagę)
solicitor (se'lysyter) s. radca prawny; akwizytor; agent
firmowy
solicitous (se'lysytes) adj.
pragnący; troszczący się o...;
niepokojący się
solicitude (se'lysytju:d) s.
troska; pieczołowitość;
troskliwość
solid ('solyd) adj. stały; masywny; lity; trwały; mocny;
rzetelny; solidny; ciało stałe; bryła
solidarity (,soly'daeryty) s.
solidarność
solidity (so'lydyty) s. masyw-
ność; trwałość; rzetelność
soliloquy (se'lylekły) s. monolog; mówienie do siebie
solitary ('solytery) adj. samotny; odosobniony; odludny;
pojedynczy; wyjątkowy; adj.
pustelnik; odludek; samotnik
solitude ('solytju:d) s. samotność; osamotnienie; odludne
miejsce
solo ('soulou) adj. adv. w pojedynkę; adj. jednoosobowy;
s. solo
soloist ('soulyst) s. solista
soluble ('soljubl) adj. rozpuszczalny; możliwy do rozwiązania
solution (so'ljuszyn) s. rozczyn; roztwór; rozwiązanie
(problemu)

solve (solw) v. rozwiązywać
(np. problemy)
solvent ('solwent) adj. wypłacalny; rozpuszczający; s.
rozpuszczalnik
somber ('somber) adj. mroczny;
ciemny; posępny; ponury
some (sam) adj. jakiś; pewien;
niejaki; nieco; trochę; kilku;
kilka; kilkoro; niektórzy;
niektóre; sporo; niemało; nie
byle jaki; adv. niemało; mniej
więcej; jakieś; pron.: niektórzy; niektóre; kilku; kilka
some more ('sam,mor) exp.: nieco
więcej
somebody ('sambedy) pron. ktoś;
s. ktoś ważny
someday ('samdej) adv. kiedyś
somehow ('samhał) adv. jakoś;
w jakiś sposób
someone ('samłan) pron. ktoś;
s. ktoś
somersault ('samerso:lt) s.
salto; koziołek
something ('samsyng) s. coś;
coś niecoś; ważna osoba; adv.
trochę; nieco; (slang):co się
zowie
sometime ('samtajm) adj. były;
adv. kiedyś; swego czasu
sometimes ('samtajmz) adv. niekiedy; czasem; czasami
someway ('sam,łej) adv. jakoś
somewhat ('samhłot) adv. nieco;
do pewnego stopnia; niejaki
somewhere ('samhłe:r) adv.
gdzieś
son (san) s. syn
song (song)s. pieśń; śpiew
song-bird ('songbe:rd) s. ptak
śpiewający
song-book ('songbuk) s. śpiewnik
sonic ('sonyk) adj. dźwiękowy
sonic boom ('sonyk,bu:m) s.
grzmot samolotu przekraczają-
cego szybkość dźwięku
son-in-law ('san,ynlo:) s. zięć
sonnet ('sonyt) s. sonet
soon (su:n) adv.wnet; niebawem;
wkrótce; zaraz; niedługo

sooner ('su:ner) adv. wczes-
niej; adj. chętnie
soot (sut) s. sadza; kopeć;
v. brudzić sadzą; użyźniać
sadzą
soothe (su:z) v. uspakajać;
uciszać
sooty ('suty) adj. okopcony;
zakopcony; czarny jak sadza
sophisticated (se'fystykejtyd)
adj. wyszukany; wyrafinowany;
wymyślny; doświadczony
sophomore ('sofemo:r) s. student drugiego roku
sorcerer ('so:rserer) s. czarownik; czarodziej
sorceress ('so:rserys) s. czarodziejka
sorcery ('so:rsery) s. czary
sordid ('so:rdyd) adj. brudny
(np. zysk); nikczemny; podły;
skąpy
sore (so:r) adj. bolesny; drażliwy; wrażliwy; dotkliwy; dotknięty; złoszczący się; zmartwiony; adv. srodze; bardzo;
akrutnie
sore throat ('so:r,trout) s.
zapalenie gardła; angina
sorrow ('sorou) s. zmartwienie;
żal; smutek ; narzekanie;
v. martwić się; boleć za...
sorrowful ('sorouful) adj.
smutny; zmartwiony; przykry
sorry ('so:ry) adj. żałujący;
zmartwiony; przygnębiony;
nędzny; marny
sorority (se'ro:ryty) s. korporacja studentek (w USA)
sort (so:rt) s. rodzaj; gatunek; sorta; v. sortować
sortie ('so:rty) s. wypad wojskowy; lot bojowy
so-so ('sou-sou) adj. taki sobie; adv. tak sobie
sought (so:t) v. zob. seek
soul (soul) s. dusza
soulless (soulys) adj. bezduszny
sound (saund) s. dźwięk; ton;
szmer; cieśnina wodna; pęcherz
pławny; sonda; v. dźwięczeć;

brzmieć; grać (na trąbce); bić
na alarm; głosić; opukiwać;
wymawiać; zabierać głos; chwalić się; sondować; zanurzać
się do dna
soundless ('saundlys) adj. bezdźwięczny
soundproof ('saundpru:f) adj.
dźwiękoszczelny
soundwave ('saundłejw) s. fala
dźwiękowa
soup (su:p) s. zupa
sour ('sauer) adj. kwaśny;
skwaszony; cierpki; v. kisnąć;
kwasić się; zniechęcać się
source (so:rs) z. źrodło
south (saus) adj. południowy;
z. południe; adv. na południe
southeast ('saus'i:st) s. południowy wschód; adj. południowo-
wschodni; adv. na południowy
wschód
southern ('sadzern) adj. południowy; s. południowiec
southernmost (,sadzern'moust)
adj. najbardziej na południe
southwards ('sausłerdz) adv.
ku południowi; na południe
southwest ('saus'łest) s. południowy zachód; adj. południowo-zachodni; adv. na południowy zachód
southwesterly ('saus'łesterly)
adj. południowo zachodni
souvenir ('su:venier) s. pamiątka
sovereign ('sawryn) s. suweren;
władca; adj. suwerenny; wyniosły; najwyższy
sovereignty('sawrenty) s. su-
werenność; zwierzchnictwo;
najwyższa władza
Soviet ('souwjet) adj. sowiecki;
radziecki
sow; sowed; sown(sou; soud;
soun)
sow (sou) v. siać; zasiewać; posiać
sow (sau) s. maciora; koryto
odlewnicze
sown (soun) v. zob. sow
spa (spa:) s. zdrojowisko; zdrój
mineralny; (USA) sport zdrowotny za opłatą

space (spejs) s. przestrzeń;
miejsce; obszar; odstęp; okres;
przeciąg (czasu); chwila;
v. robić odstępy; rozstawiać
spacecraft ('spejs,kra:ft) s.
pojazd międzyplanetarny
spaceship ('spejs,szyp) s. statek międzyplanetarny(kosmiczny)
space suit ('spejs;sju:t) s.
kombinezon międzyplanetarny
spacious ('spejszes) adj. przestronny; obszerny
spadę (spejd) s. łopata; v. kopać łopatą
spades (spejdz) pl. piki (w kar-
tach)
spadework ('spejd-łe:rk) s.
praca przygotowawcza
span; spanned; spanned (spaen;
spaend; spaend)
span (spaen) v. zob. spin; sięgać (np. przez rzekę); rozciąg-
gać się (np. nad rzeką); obejmować (pamięcia); mierzyc pię-
dzia; posuwać się stopniowo;
łączyć brzegi; s. piędź; rozpiętość; prześwit; przęsło;
przeciąg (czasu) zasięg; roz-
ciągłość; para; zaprzęg
spangle ('spaengl) s. świecideł-
ko; błyskotka; v. pokrywać
świecidełkami; błyszczeć świecidełkami
spangled ('spaengld) adj. pokryty (świecidełkami)
Spanish ('spaenysz) adj. hiszpański
spank ('spaenk) s. klaps; v. dawać klapsa; popędzać klapsami;
isc kłusem
spanking (spaenkyng) s. skoro-
bicie; lanie; adj. chyży; zamaszysty; silny; solidny; świetny; adv. bardzo (slang)
spanner ('spaener) s. ścięgno
(mostu); klucz do nakrętek
gasienica miernikowa
spare (speer) v. oszczędzać; zaoszczędzić; odstępować; obywać
sie; zachować; przeznaczać;
szanować (uczucia); szczędzić;
a. zapasowy; oszczędny; skromny;

drobny; szczupły; wolny (np.
czas) s. część zapasowa; koło
zapasowe
spare time ('speer,tajm) s.
wolny czas
spare tire ('speer,tajer) s.
koło zapasowe
sparing ('speeryng) adj. oszczędny; wstrzemięźliwy
spark (spa:rk) s. iskra; zapłon;
wesołek; zalotnik; v. iskrzyć
się; sypać iskrami; zapalać się;
dawać początek; zalecać się
grać galanta
spark plug ('spa:rk,plag) s.
świeca samochodowa (zapłonowa)
sparrow ('spaerou) s. wróbel
sparse (spa:rs) adj. rzadki;
z rzadka; rozsiany; szczupły
spasm ('spaezem) s. skurcz;
spazm; napad (kaszlu)
spastic ('spaestyk) adj. skur-
czowy; spazmatyczny; chory na
paraliż kurczowy
spat (spaet) v. zob . spit;
kłócić się; dawać klapsy; składać jaja (przez ostrygi); s.
jaja mięczaków; kłótnia;
klaps; lekki cios
spatial ('spejszel) adj. przestrzenny
spawn (spo:n) s. ikra; skrzek;
nasienie; v. składać (ikrę;
skrzek); wylęgać się; płodzić;
zasiewac grzybnię
spayed (spejd) adj.(samica)
z usuniętymi jajnikami; bez-
płodna: wytrzebiona
speak; spoke; spoken (spi:k;
spo:k; 'spoken)
speak (spi:k) v. mówić; przema-
wiac; szczekać na rozkaz; grać;
sygnalizowac do statku
speak out ('spi:k,aut) v. wypowiadać (się); mówić otwarcie;
mowic głośno
speak up ('spi:k,ap) v. wypowie-
dzieć się bez osłonek
speaker ('spi:ker) s. mówca;
głosnik; marszałek sejmu; przewodniczący

spear (spier) s. dzida; włócznia; oszczep; kopia; oścień;
źdźbło; v. przebijać dzidą;
kłuć; wystrzelić w górę
spearhead ('spierhed) s. ostrze dzidy; czołówka; v. prowadzić; być na czele
special ('speszel) adj. specjalny; wyjątkowy; osobliwy;
dodatkowy; nadzwyczajny;
s. dodatkowy autobus; nadzwy-
czajne wydanie; reklamowa
dzienna zniżka ceny w sklepie
specialist ('speszelyst) s.
specjalista
speciality (,speszy'aelyty)
s. specjalność; specjalna
cecha
specialize ('speszelajz) v.
wyspecjalizować (się); wyszczególniać; precyzować;
różniczkować(się); ograniczać
(się)
specially ('speszely) adv.
specjalnie; szczególnie
specialty ('speszelty) s.spec-
jalność; specjalizacja
species ('spi:szi:z) s. gatunek; rodzaj; postać czegoś
specific (spy'syfyk) adj.
określony; wyraźny; gatunkowy;
charakterystyczny; specyficzny
specify ('spesyfaj) v. wyszczególniać; precyzować; konkrety-
zować; sporządzić specyfika-
cję
specimen ('spesymyn) s. okaz;
przykład; wzór; typ; próba;
numer okazowy
spectacle ('spektekl) s. widowisko
spectacles ('spektekls) pl. okulary
spectacular (spek'taekjuler)
adj. widowiskowy; efektowny;
sensacyjny; okazały; s. film
widowiskowy "wielki"
spectator ('spektejter) s.
widz
speculate ('spekjulejt) v.
spekulować; rozmyślać nad..;
rozważać

speculation (,spekju'lejszyn)
s. spekulacja; domysł; rozmyślanie
sped (sped) v. zob. speed
speech (spi:cz) s. mowa; przemówienie; język; wymowa; przemowa
speechless ('spi:czlys) adj.
(chwilowo) niemy; oniemiały;
(slang): pijany (kompletnie)
speed; sped; sped (spi:d; sped;
sped)
speed (spi:d) v. pospieszyć;
popędzić; pędzić; odprawić;
kierować spiesznie; popierać
(np. sprawę); s. szybkość;
prędkość; bieg
speedboat ('spi:dbout) s.
ślizgacz
speed limit ('spi:d,lymyt) s.
ograniczenie szybkości
speedometer (spi'domyter) s.
szybkościomierz
speed up ('spi:d,ap) v. przyspieszyć; s. przyspieszenie
speedy ('spi:dy) adj. szybki
spell; spelled; spelt (spel;
speld; spelt)
spell (spel) v. przeliterować
(poprawnie); napisać ortogra-
ficznie; znaczyć; mozolnie
odczytywać; sylabizować; zaczarować; urzec; dać (wytchnienie); odpoczywać; zaczarować;
pracować na zmiany; s. chwila
pracy; chwila; okres; pewien
czas; zaklęcie; czar
spellbound ('spel baund) adj.
zaczarowany; urzeczony;
oczarowany
spelling ('spelyŋg) s. pisownia
spelt (spelt) v. zob. spell
spend; spent; spent (spend;
spent; spent)
spend (spend) v. wydawać (np.
pieniądze); spędzać (czas);
zużywać (się); wyczerpywać;
tracić (np. siły); składać
ikrę
spent (spent) v. wyczerpany;
wydany; zob. spend

sperm (spe:rm) s. sperma; nasienie męskie

spew (spju:) v. wypluwac; wymiotowac; wyrzucac z siebie

sphere (sfier) s. kula; globus; ciało niebieskie; sfera (np. działalności)

spice (spajs) s. wonne korzenie; pikanteria; v. przyprawiac korzeniami; dodawac pikanterii

spicy ('spajsy) adj. korzenny; zaprawiony korzeniami; aromatyczny; pikantny; nieco nieprzyzwoity; elegancki; żywy; ostry

spider (spajder) s. pająk

spike (spajk) s. cwiek; bretnal; kolec; gwozdz do szyn; szpic; ostrze; fanatyk religijny; kłos; v. przymocowywac gwozdziami; zaostrzac konce; ranic kolcami; zagważdżac armatę; zaprzeczac pogłoskom; odpierac; zakrapiac alkoholem; wspinac się na słup ostrymi okuciami(na butach)

spiky ('spajky) adj. kolczasty; wydłużony; ostro zakonczony; fanatyczny religijnie

spill; spilled; spilt (spyl; spyld; spylt)

spill (spyl) v. rozlewac (się): rozsypywac (się); uchylac żagiel z wiatru; wyspiewac; wygadac (się); powiedziec wszystko; popsuc sprawę; s.rozlanie; rozsypanie; ilosc rozlana; ilosc rozsypana; odłamek; zatyczka; upadek; fidybus do zapalania swiec

spilt (spylt) v. zob. spill

spin; spun; span (spyn; span; spaen)

spin (spyn) v. snuc; prząsc; kręcic (się); puszczac bąka; toczyc na tokarni; łowic ryby na błyszczkę; zawirowac; s. kręcenie (się); zawirowanie; ruch wirowy; przejażdżka; korkociąg (w locie)

spinach ('spynycz) s. szpinak

spinal column ('spajnel'kolem) s. stos pacierzowy ;kręgosłup

spinal cord ('spajnel'ko:rd) s. rdzeń kręgowy

spindle ('spyndl) s. wrzeciono; oś; wał; 14400 jardow lnu; 15120 jardow bawełny; v. miec kształt wrzecionowaty

spine ('spajn) s. kręgosłup; grzbiet; ciern

spinning mill ('spynyŋg,myl) s. przędzarnia

spinster ('spynster) s. stara panna

spiny ('spajny) adj. ciernisty; kolczasty; trudny

spiral ('spajerel) s. spirala; adj. spiralny; v. poruszac się spiralnie; szybko isc w gorę (np. ceny); nadawac kształt spirali

spire ('spajer) s. iglica; hełm wieży; zwoj; spirala; ostry szczyt; szpic; pęd; v. strzelac w gorę; nakładac hełm na wieżę

spirit ('spyryt) s. duch; intelekt; umysł; zjawa; odwaga; nastawienie; nastrój; v. zachęcac; ożywiac; rozweselac; zabierac (potajemnie)

spirits ('spyryts) s. spirytus; alkohol

spirited ('spyrytyd) adj. ożywiony; z werwą; napisany z zacięciem

spiritual ('spyryczuel) adj. duchowy; duchowny; natchniony; s. murzynska piesn religijna

spit; spat; spat (spyt; spaet; spaet)

spit (spyt) v. pluc; zionac; splunąc; wypluc; lekceważyc; fuknąc; parsknąc; mżyc; kropic; pryskac; nadziewac na rożen; s. plucie; slina; parskanie; mżenie; jaja owadow; rożen; językowaty połwysep; głebokosc łopaty

spite (spajt) s. złosc; uraz; złosliwosc; v. zrobic na złosc; in spite of= wbrew; pomimo

spiteful ('spajtful) adj. złosliwy; msciwy

spittle ('spytl) s. plwocina;
slina
splash (splaesz) v. chlapac;
pryskac; plusnac; rozpryskac;
upstrzyc; s. rozprysk; plusk;
zakropienie; plamka; sensacja
splash down ('splaesz,dałn) v.
wodowac; s. wodowanie
spleen (spli:n) s. sledziona;
przygnębienie; splin; złosc
splendid ('splendyd) adj.
wspaniały; swietny; doskonały
splendor ('splender) s. wspaniałosc; przepych, blask
splint (splynt) s. łupek; szyna; patyk; kosc piszczelowa;
v. wstawiac w szyny złamaną
kosc
splinter ('splynter) s. drzazga;
odłamek
split; split; split (splyt;
splyt; splyt)
split (splyt) v. łupac; pękac;
rozszczepiac (się); dzielic;
oddzielac (się) odchodzic;
s. pęknięcie; rozszczepienie;
rozdwojenie; odejscie
splitting ('splytyŋg) adj. roz-
sadzający; ostry; gwałtowny
splutter ('splater) v. pryskac;
opryskac; mowic bezładnie;
s. pryskanie; szybka gadanina;
zgiełk
spoil; spoilt; spoiled (spojl;
spojlt; spojld)
spoil (spojl) v. psuc (się);
zepsuc (się); (slang): krasc;
sprzątnąc; przetrącic
spoils (spojls) pl. łupy (też
w polityce)
spoilsport ('spojl'spo:rt) s.
psujący zabawę
spoilt ('spojlt) v. zob.spoil
spoke (spouk) v. zob. speak;
s. szczebel; szprycha
spoken ('spoukn) v. zob. speak
spokesman (spouksmen) s. rzecznik
sponge (spandż) s. gąbka; wycior; tampon; pieczeniarz; pasożyt; v. myc gąbką; chłonąc;
łowic gąbki; wyłudzac; wsysac;
pasożytowac

sponger ('spandżer) s. pasożyt;
pieczeniarz (slang)
sponge cake ('spandż'kejk) s.
biszkopt
spongy ('spandży) adj. gąbczasty
sponsor ('sponser) s. patron;
organizator; gwarant; ojciec
chrzestny; v. wprowadzac; byc
gwarantem; popierac; opłacac
(np. program telewizyjny)
spontaneous (spon'tejnjes)
adj. spontaniczny; samorzutny;
naturalny; odruchowy
spook (spuk) s. zjawa; duch;
upior
spool (spu:l) s. cewka; rolka;
szpulka; nawiajac na (rolkę
etc).
spoon (spu:n) s. łyżka; v. czerpac (łyżką); durzyc się w kims
spoon out ('spu:n,aut) v. drą-
życ; nabierac
spoon-fed ('spu:n,fed) adj. roz-
pieszczony; łyżką karmiony
spoonful ('spu:nful) s. łyżka
czegos
spore (spo:r) s. zarodnik;
v. wytwarzac zarodniki
sport (spo:rt) s. sport; zawody;
zabawa; rozrywka; sportowiec;
(slang): człowiek dobry, elegancki, lubiący zakładac się;
v. bawic się; uprawiac sport;
obnosic się z czyms; popisywac się; wysmiewac się
sportive ('spo:rtyw) adj. żartobliwy
sportsman ('spo:rtsmen) s.
sportowiec; mysliwy
sporty ('spo:rty) adj. (slang):
sportowy; krzykliwy (ubior);
modny
spot (spot) s. plama; skaza;
kropka; cętka; plamka; miejsce;
lokal; odrobina; punkt; dolar;
krotkie ogłoszenie; v. plamic
(sie); umiejscowic (np. zepsucie); poznawac; wyrozniac;
rozmieszczac; adj. gotowy;
gotowkowy; dorywczy
spotless ('spotlys) adj. bez
skazy

spotlight ('spotlajt) s. reflektor szczelinowy; v. rzucać światło (na coś)

spout (spaut) s. wylot; rynna; wylew; dziobek; strumień; pochyłe koryto; v. wyrzucać z siebie płyn; tryskać; chlusnąć; recytować

sprain (sprejn) s. bolesne wykręcenie (nie zwichnięcie); v. wykręcić

sprang (spraeng) v. zob. spring

sprat (spraet) s. szprotka (śledź); v. łowić szproty

sprawl (spro:l) v. rozwalać się; gramolić się; rozłazić się; rozrzucać; być rozrzuconym; s. rozwalenie się; rozłazenie się; rozkrzewianie się

spray (sprej) s. rozpylony płyn; krople z rozpylacza; płyn do rozpryskiwania; spryskiwacz; grad (kul); gałązka; v. opryskiwać; rozpryskiwać (się)

spread; spread; spread (spred; spred; spred)

spread (spred) v. rozpościerać (się); rozszerzać (się); posiać; rozsmarowywać; rozkładać; pokrywać; nakrywać; rozklepywać; s. rozpostarcie; rozpiętość; zasięg; szerokość; pasta; narzuta; (slang): smarowidło na chleb

sprig (spryg) s. gałązka; latorośl; młokos; szyft; v. ozdabiać gałązkami

sprightly ('sprajtly) adj. żywy; dziarski; wesoły

spring; sprang; sprung (spryng; spraeng; sprang)

spring (spryng) v. skakać; sprężynować; wypłynąć; puścić pędy (pąki); zaskoczyć; spowodować wybuch; paczyć się; puszczać oczko.; pękać; s.wiosna; skok; sprężyna; źródło; zdrój; prężność; adj. wiosenny; sprężynowy; źródlany

springboard ('spryng,bo:rd) s. trampolina; odskocznia

springtime ('spryngtajm) s. wiosna

sprinkle ('sprynkl) v. posypać; pokropić; s. deszczyk

sprint (sprynt) s. krótki bieg; krótki zrywny wysiłek; v.bieg na krótki dystans

sprinter (sprynter) s. sprinter; biegacz krótkodystansowy

sprout (spraut) s. pęd; odrośl; v. puszczać pędy; wyrastać

spruce (spru:s) s. świerk; smrek; adj. elegancki; schludny; v. stroić się

sprung (sprang) v. zob. spring

spun (span) v. zob. spin

spur (spe:r) v. pogardliwie odtrącać; pospieszyć; popędzać; s. odtrącenie z pogardą

sputter ('spater) v. pryskać (śliną); bełkotać; s. pryskanie; plwociny; bełkot

spy (spaj) s. szpieg; tajniak; szpiegowanie; v. szpiegować; wybadać; czatować; wypatrzeć

squabble ('skłobl) s. sprzeczka; sprzeczać się

squad (skłod) s. oddział; grupka; (lotny) patrol; wóz patrolowy; v. formować grupki

squall (skłó:l) s. szkwał; kłopot; wrzask; v. wiać gwałtownie; wrzeszczeć

squander ('skłonder) s. marnotrawstwo; v. trwonić; marnotrawić

square ('skłeer) s. kwadrat; czworobok (budynków); plac; kątownik; węgielnica; adj. kwadratowy; prostokątny; prostopadły; uporządkowany; zupełny; uczciwy; v. robić kwadratowym prostym; podnosić do kwadratu; płacić (dług); adv. w sedno; rzetelnie; wprost

squash (skłosz) v. ubijać (się); gnieść (się); miażdżyć; s. miazga; tłok; rodzaj tenisa; napój owocowy; mała dynia

squat; squat; squat (skłót; skłot; skłot)

squat (skłot) v. kucać; przycupnąć; nielegalnie koczować
na gruncie; adj. przysadzisty;
niski; szeroki; s. osoba przy-
sadzista; kucki
squeak (skłi:k) v. piszczeć;
skrzypieć; mówić piskliwie;
(slang): zdradzać (sekrety);
sypać; przepychać się z trudnością; s. pisk; trudne osiągnięcie czegoś
squeal (skłi:l) v. piszczeć;
kwiczeć; (slang): awanturować
się; sypać; wydawać (kogoś);
s. pisk; kwik; sypanie (kogoś, czegoś)
squeamish ('skłi:mysz) adj.
wybredny; pruderyjny; przesadny; wrażliwy
squeegee ('skłi:dźi:) s. przyrząd w kształcie litery T do
usuwania wody z mytych szyb
squeeze (skłi:z) v. ściskać;
wyciskać; wygniatać; wciskać;
odciskać; ścieśnić; s. ucisk;
nacisk; odcisk; tłok; ścis-
nięcie
squeezer ('skłi:zer) s. wy-
ciskacz (soku)
squid (skłyd) s. przynęta
z mątwy; kałamarnica (ryba)
squint (skłynt) s. zez; ukosne
spojrzenie; zerknięcie; skłonność; v. mrużyć oczy; wysiłać
wzrok; zezować; skłaniać się;
adj. zezowaty; zerkający
squirm (skłe:rm) v. wić się
(z bólu); płonąć (ze wstydu);
kręcić się niespokojnie;
s. skręcanie się
squirrel ('skło:rel) s. wiewiórka
squirt (skłe:rt) v. strzykać;
tryskać; s. strzykawka; struga; pętak
stab (staeb) v. dźgnąć; pchnąć;
ugodzić; ranić; s. pchnięcie;
dźgnięcie; rana kłuta
stability (ste'bylyty) s.sta-
łość; stateczność; stabil-
ność; równowaga
stabilize ('stejbylajz) v.
ustalać; stabilizować

stable ('stejbl) s. stajnia;
stadnina; v. trzymać konie
w stajni; adj. stały; stanowczy; trwały
stack (staek) s. stóg; stos;
sterta; komin; kupa; v. układać w stogi; ustawiać w kozły;
układać podstępnie przeciwko
komuś
stadium('stejdjem) s. stadion;
faza; stadium (czegoś)
staff (staef) s. laska; drzewce; sztab; personel; adj.
sztabowy; v. obsadzać persone-
lem
stag (staeg) s. rogacz; jeleń;
samotny mężczyzna
stage (stejdż) s. scena; stadium; etap; rusztowanie; pomost; postój; v. wystawiać;
odegrać (sztukę); urządzać;
inscenizować; adj. teatralny;
sceniczny
stagecoach ('stejdż-koucz) s.
dyliżans
stage-manager ('stejdż'maenydżer) s. reżyser
stagflation ('staegflejszyn)
s. stagnacja, rosnące bezrobocie i inflacja jednocześnie
stagger ('staeger) v. zataczać
się; wahać się; chwiać się;
układać w zygzak lub w odstę-
pach; porażać; s. układ skosny; zachodzący na siebie w od-
stępach lub zygzakowaty; zataczanie się; pl. zawroty głowy
staggering ('staegeryng) adj.
przerażający; oszałamiający;
rozbrajający
stagnant ('staegnent) adj. za-
stały; stojący; będący w za-
stoju
stain (stejn) v. plamić (się);
brudzić; szargać; barwić; ko-
lorować; farbować; drukować
tapety; s. plama;barwik; bej-
ca do drzewa
stained ('stejnd) adj. zabar-
wiony (np. szkło)
stainless ('stejnlys) adj. nierdzewny (stal); nieskalany

stair (steer) s. stopień; pl.
schody

stair case ('steer,kejs) s.
klatka schodowa

stair way ('steerłej) s. schody

stake (stejk) s. słup; słupek;
kołek; palik; stawka; kowa-
dełko blacharskie; v. przy-
twierdzać kołkami; wytaczać;
przywiązywać do słupa; stawiać na coś

stake out ('stejk,aut) v.
wziąć pod obserwację; wyznaczać granicę

stake-out ('stejkaut) s. zasadzka (slang)

stale ('stejl) adj. stęchły;
nieświeży; zwietrzały;
czerstwy; przestarzały;
v. czuć nieświeżym

stalk (sto:k) v. kroczyć; podkradać się; podchodzić; s.(majestatyczny) chód; podkrada-
nie się; podchodzenie; wysoki komin; łodyga; nóżka (kie-
liszka)

stall (sto:l) v. działać opóź-
niająco; zwlekać; przewlekać;
kręcić; zwodzić; przetrzymy-
wać; dławić motor; utykać;
grzęznąć; trzymać bydło w obo-
rze; zaopatrywać w przegrody
s. stajnia; obora; stragan;
kiosk; przegroda; komora
(w kopalni); (slang): trik;
kruczek

stallion ('staeljen) s. ogier

stalwart ('sto:lłert) s. bojownik partyjny; adj. dzielny;
krzepki; stanowczy

stammer ('staemer) v. jąkać się;
s. jąkanie się

stamp (staemp) v. stemplować;
wytłaczać; tupać; kruszyć;
wbijać (w pamięć); przylepiać
znaczki pocztowe; s. stempel;
pieczątka; znaczek; piętno;
cecha; pokrój; tupnięcie; ubijak do kruszenia (rudy)

stanch (staencz) v. tamować
krwotok; adj. wierny; stały;
krzepki; szczelny

stand; stood; stood (staend;
stud; stud)

stand (staend) v. stać; stanąc;
wytrzymać; znosić; przetrzymać;
zostać; utrzymywać się; stawiac
opór; znajdować się; być; postawić; (slang): płacić; s. stanie;
stanowisko; stojak; trybuna;
postój; łan; ława dla świadków;
unieruchomienie; umywalka

stand back ('staend,baek) v.
stać w tyle; zachowywać rezerwę

stand by ('staendbaj) v. popierać; być w stanie pogotowia

stand off ('staend,of) v. cofać
się

stand-off ('staend,of) s. nie-
rozegrana (równowaga sił)

stand out ('staend,aut) v. wyróżniać się; kontrastować;
wytrwać

stand up ('staend,ap) v. wstawać; powstawać; stawać w obro-
nie; nie ustępować; stawiac
czoło

standard ('staenderd) s. sztandar; norma; miernik; wzorzec;
wskaźnik; stopa (życiowa);
próba; słup; podpórka; adj.
znormalizowany; normalny; typowy; przeciętny; wzorcowy;
klasyczny; literacki (język)

standardize ('staenderdajz) v.
normalizować; dostosowywać do
normy; mierzyć wzorcem; porów-
nywać z wzorcem

standing ('staendyng) adj. stojący; na pniu; pionowy; stały;
s. stanie; stanowisko; znaczenie; poważanie; reputacja;
czas trwania

standing room ('staendyng,ru:m)
s. miejsce stojące

standoffish ('staend'ofysz) adj.
nieprzystępny; trzymający się
z dala

standpoint ('staend,poynt) s.
punkt widzenia; punkt obserwacyjny

standstill ('staendstyl) s. zastój; przerwa; martwy punkt;
unieruchomienie

stank (staenk) v. zob. stink
star (sta:r) s. gwiazda;
gwiazdor; gwiazdka; v. ozdabiać gwiazdkami; być gwiazdo-
rem; adj. gwiezdny; występu-
jący w głównej roli
starboard ('sta:rberd) s. prawa burta; v. sterować na prawo
starch (sta:rcz) s. skrobia;
sztywność; krochmal; v. na-
krochmalić;(slang):siła
starchy ('sta:rczy) adj. na-
krochmalony; skrobiowaty;
sztywny
stare (steer) v. patrzeć; gapić się; wpatrywać się; zwracać uwagę; s. nieruchomy
wzrok; wytrzeszczone oczy;
zagapione spojrzenie
stare at ('steer,aet) v. gapić
się na...
stark (sta:rk) adj. sztywny;
zupełny; czysty; wierutny;
ponury; posępny; adv. zupełnie; całkowicie
starling ('starlyng) s. szpak
starlit ('sta:rlyt) adj.
gwiaździsty; oświetlony
gwiazdami; wygwieżdżony
starry ('sta:ry) adj. gwiaździsty; usiany gwiazdami; promienny; marzycielski; rozmarzony
stars-spangled ('sta:r-spaengld)
adj. usiany gwiazdami (flaga
USA)
start (sta:rt) v. zacząć; ru-
szyc; startować; zerwać się;
podskoczyć; wyruszyć; zabierać się; uruchamiać; obsuwać;
rozpoczynać; wszczynać; s.po-
czątek; start; wymarsz; poderwanie się; obsunięcie się;
zdobywanie przewagi
starter ('sta:rter) s. starter;
rozrusznik; startujący zawodnik; pierwsze danie; kierownik ruchu
startle ('sta:rtl) v. zaskoczyć; zaniepokoić; podrywać;
wzdrygać się; przestraszać;

s. zaniepokojenie; poderwanie
się
startling ('sta:rtlyng) adj.
sensacyjny; zdumiewający; niepokojący
staryation (sta:r'wejszyn) s.
głód; głodowanie; głodzenie;
przymieranie głodem
starve (sta:rw) v. głodować;
zagłodzić; przymierać z głodu,
zimna; łaknąć; zmuszać (głodem, brakiem)
stash (staesz) v. (slang): chować na potem; s.schowanie;
schowek
state (stejt) s. państwo; stan;
zajęcie; parada; pompa; cere-
moniał; stan prac; adj. państwowy; stanowy; uroczysty;
paradny; formalny; v. stwierdzać; wyrażać; określać; wyrażać (też symbolami)
state department ('stejt,dy'-
'pa:rtment) w USA ministerstwo spraw zagranicznych
stately ('stejtly) adj. uroczysty; okazały; adv. uroczys-
cie; okazale
statement ('stejtment) s. wyrażenie; twierdzenie; sprawozdanie; wyciąg; oświadczenie;
deklaracja; zeznanie
state room ('stejt,rum) s. prywatny pokój; kabina; przedział
state side ('stejt,sajd) adj.
amerykański; w stanach
statesman('stejtsmen) s. mąż
stanu
statesmanship ('stejtsmenszyp)
s. rozum polityczny
static ('staetyk) adj. statycz-
ny; nieruchomy
station ('stejszyn) s. stacja;
stanowisko; stan; pozycja życiowa; godność; punkt; stacja
telewizyjna; radiowa, etc.
stationary ('stejsznery) adj.
niezmienny; stały; nieruchomy;
pozycyjny
stationmaster ('stejszyn,ma:-
ster) s. naczelnik stacji

station wagon ('stejszyn,ŧaegn)
s. samochód typu kombi
statistics (ste'tystyks) s.
statystyka
statue ('staeczu:) s. posąg
statute ('staetju) s. ustawa;
prawo; statut; nakaz
staunch (sto:ncz) v. tamowac
krwotok; tamponowac; adj. oddany; wierny; zagorzały
stay; stayed; staid (stej;
stejed; stejd)
stay (stej) s. pobyt; zwłoka;
odroczenie; opóźnienie; zawieszenie; podpora; wanta;
zatrzymanie; przerwa; wytrzymałosc; v. zostac; przebywac;
wytrzymac; odraczac; kłasc
kres; zaspakajac (głod)
stay away ('stej,ełej) v.
trzymac się z dala
stay up ('stej,ap) v. nie sia-
dac
stay with ('stej,łys) v. miesz-
kac u kogos
stead (sted) s. miejsce; na
miejsce; pożytecznosc
steadfast ('sted,fa:st) adj.
stały; nieruchomy; niezachwiany; niewzruszony; mocny;
pewny
steady ('stedy) adj. mocny;
silny; pewny; stały; rzetelny;
rowny; stateczny; excl.: powoli ! prosto ! naprzod ! stoj!
v. dawac rownowagę; odzyskiwac
rownowagę; s. podpora; (slang):
ukochany
steak (stejk) s. stek; befsztyk; płat (np. mięsa)
steal; stole; stolen (sti:l:
stoul; stoulen)
steal (sti:l) v. krasc; wykrasc;
wejsc ukradkiem; zakradac się;
skradac się; s. kradziez;
rzecz ukradziona; rzecz ku-
piona prawie że za darmo; dar-
mocha (slang)
stealth (stels) s. tajemniczosc; ukradkowosc
stealthy ('stelsy) adj. ukrad-
kowy; tajemny

steam (sti:m) s. para; v. parowac; dymic; płynąc pod parą;
gotowac w parze; umieszczac
pod parą
steam up ('sti:m,ap) v. zamglic
(się); zajsc mgłą lub parą
steamer ('sti:mer) s. parowiec
steamship ('sti:m,szyp) s. parowiec
steel (sti:l) s. stal; pręt
stalowy; adj. stalowy; ze
stali; v. pokrywac stalą; kar-
towac
steelworks ('sti:l,łe:rks) s.
stalowania
steep (sti:p) v. moczyc się;
rozmiękczac; impregnowac; po-
grażyc się; rozpijac się;
adj. stromy; nieprawdopodobny;
wygorowany; przesadny
steepen ('sti:pn) v. nagle
podnosic ceny; robic stromym
steeple ('sti:pl) s. strzelista
wieża; ostra wieżyczka
steer (stier) v. sterowac; kierowac; prowadzic; s. wskazowka; młody woł na mięso
steering wheel ('stieryng,hłi:l)
s. kierownica; koło sterowe
stem (stem) s. pien; łodyga;
szpulka; trzon; trzonek; noz-
ka; v. pochodzic; tamowac; powstrzymywac; isc pod prąd;
zwalczac
stench (stencz) s. smrod; odor;
fetor
stenographer ('stenegraefer) s.
stenograf; stenografistka
step (step) s. krok; stopien;
takt; szczebel; schodek;
v. stąpac; kroczyc; isc; tanczyc; podnosic; wzmagac; przy-
ciskac nogą; mierzyc (krokami)
stepchild ('step,czajld) s.
pasierb
stepfather ('step,fa:dzer) s.
ojczym
stepmother ('step,madzer) s.
macocha
stereo ('steriou) s. stereoskop;
dwugłosnikowe radio-adapter;
adj. stereofoniczny

sterile ('sterajl) adj. wyjałowiony; jałowy; sterylny;
bezpłodny
sterilize ('stery,lajz) v. wyjałowic; wysterylizowac
sterling (,ste:rlyŋg) s. pieniądz pełnowartosciowy; adj.
solidny; niezawodny
stern (ste:rn) adj. surowy;
srogi; s. rufa; zad; zadek;
tył; posladki
sternness ('ste:rnys) s. suro-
wosc; srogosc
stew (stu:) v. gotowac; dusic
(się); martwic się; wkuwac
się; s. potrawa duszona; kłopot; staw na ryby
steward ('stu:erd) s. zarządca;
ekonom; kelner; v. zarządzac;
byc stewardem
stewardess ('stu:erdys) s.
stewardesa
stewpan ('stu:,paen) s. rondel; garnek
stick; stuck;stuck (styk;
stak; stak)
stick (styk) v. wtykac; przekłuwac; kłuc; wbijac; zarzy-
nac; przyklejac; naklejac;
utkwic; utknąc; ugrzęznąc;
przyczepiac (się); trzymac
się (tematu); oszukiwac;
s. pałka; patyk; laska; kij;
tyczka; żerdź
stick out ('styk,aut) v. wystawiac; sterczec; zadac
stick to ('styk,tu) v. trzymac się (tematu); przylepiac
stick up ('styk,ap) v. terroryzowac (bronią); brac w obro-
nę; podnosic; przeciwstawiac
się
sticky ('styky) adj. lepki;
kleisty; grząski; parny;
(slang): marny; nieprzyjemny
stiff (styf) adj. sztywny;
twardy; kategoryczny; zdręt-
wiały; "słony"; wygorowany;
trudny; ciężki; silny;
s. (slang): trup; umrzyk;
niedojda; włoczęga; facet;
pedant

stiffen ('styfn) v. usztywniac;
podniesc (wymagania); zgęszczac;
zesztywniec
stifle (stajfl) v. dusic (się);
tłumic; przygaszac; tuszowac
stile (stajl) s. przełaz; kołowrot; pionowa rama drzwi
still (styl) adj. spokojny; cichy; nieruchomy; martwy (przedmiot); milczący; adv. jeszcze;
jednak; wciąż; dotąd; niemniej;
mimo to; v. uspokoic (się); uciszyc; destylowac; s. destylar-
nia (też wodki)
stillness ('stylnys) s. cisza;
spokoj; bezruch
stilt (stylt) s. szczudło
stilted ('styltyd) adj. na
szczudłach; nienaturalny;
sztuczny; na wspornikach
stimulant ('stymjulent) s. bodziec; podnieta; alkohol;
srodek podniecający; zachęta;
adj. pobudzający
stimulate ('stymjulejt) v. pobudzac; zachęcac
stimulating ('stymjulejtyŋg)
adj. podniecający; pobudzający
stimulation ('stymjulejszyn)
s. podnieta; zachęta; podniecenie
stimulus ('stymjules) s. bodziec;
zachęta; podnieta
sting; stung; stung (styŋg;
staŋg; staŋg)
sting (styŋg) v. kłuc; parzyc;
kąsac; szczypac; palic; rwac;
gryzc; s. żadło; ukłucie; poparzenie; piekący bol; uszczyp-
liwosc; zjadliwosc
stingy ('styndży) adj. skąpy
stink; stank; stunk (styŋk;
staeŋk; staŋk)
stink (styŋk) v. cuchnąc; smier-
dziec; zasmradzac; wyganiac
smrodem; (slang): poczuc smrod
s. smrod
stipulate ('stypjulejt) v. za-
żądac; uwarunkowac; zastrzegac
w umowie
stir (ste:r) v. ruszac; poruszac;
grzebac; mieszac; wzniecac; podniecac; s. poruszenie; podniecenie; ruch; (slang): więzienie

stirrup ('styrep) s. strzemię;
pocięgiel; okucie do wspinania się
stitch (stycz) s. szew; ścieg;
oczko; kłucie; v. szyc; zaszyc; zeszywac
stoat (stout) s. gronostaj; v.
zaszywac niewidocznym ście-
giem
stock (stok) s. zapas; zasób;
bydło; pień; strzon; kłoda;
łożysko; ród; rasa; surowiec;
kapitał udziałowy; akcje giełdowe; obligacje; wywar; v. zaopatrywac; zagospodarowac; za-
rybiac; miec na składzie;
adj. typowy; seryjny; w stałym zapasie; repertuarowy
stockade (sto'kejd) s. palisada;
częstokół; obóz
stockbroker ('stok,brouker) s.
makler giełdowy
stock exchange ('stok,eks'-
'czejndż) s. giełda
stockholder ('stok,houlder) s.
akcjonariusz; udziałowiec
stocking ('stokyŋg) s. ponczo-
cha
stocky ('stoky) adj. krępy
stock market ('stok-'ma:rkyt)
s. giełda
stole (stoul) v. zob. steal;
s. stuła; etola
stolen ('stouln) v. zob. steal
stolid ('stolyd) adj. obojętny;
flegmatyczny
stomach ('stamek) s. żołądek;
brzuch; apetyt; ochota;
v. jesc; przełykac (obelgę);
znosic
stone (stoun) s. kamień; głaz;
skała; pestka; adj. kamienny;
v. ukamieniowac; obkładac
(mur) kamieniem; wyjmowac
pestki; upijac (się) na umór
stonewall ('stoun-ło:l) v. odmówic zaciekle jakiejkolwiek
kooperacji
stoneware ('stoun-łeer) s. naczynia kamionkowe
stony ('stouny) adj. kamienny;
kamienisty; skamieniały;
pestkowy

stood (stud) v. zob. stand
stool (stu:l) s. stołek; sedes;
taboret; stolec; klęcznik; podnóżek; pniak puszczający pędy;
wabik; v. puszczac pędy
stoop (stu:p) v. schylac się;
ugiąc się; poniżyc się; raczyc;
garbic się; s. pochylenie;
przygarbione plecy; weranda;
taras (przy domu)
stooping ('stu:pyŋg) adj. przy-
garbiony
stop (stop) v. zatrzymywac;
powstrzymywac; wstrzymywac;
zatykac; zaplombowac; zagrodzic;
zablokowac; zamknąc; zaprzesta-
wac; niedopuscic; stanąc; prze-
stac; exp.:przstan ! stój !
dosyc tego !; s. zatrzymanie
(się); stop; postój; przystanek; zatkanie; zator; zatyczka;
zderzak; ogranicznik
stop by ('stop,baj) v. wstąpic
do kogos na chwilę
stopover ('stop'ouwer) s. zatrzymanie się w podróży
stoppage ('stopydż) s. wstrzymanie; zatrzymanie (się); zatwardzenie
stopper ('stoper) s. korek; zatyczka; v. zatykac; umocowac
liną
stopping ('stopyŋg) s. plomba
(w zębie); zatrzymanie; zatkanie
storage ('sto:rydż) s. skład;
przechowywanie; magazynowanie
store ('sto:r) s. zapas; sklep;
skład; mnóstwo; składnica;
v. magazynowac; miescic w sobie; zaopatrywac; wyposażac
store up ('sto:r,ap) v. zama-
gazynowac; zachowac
storehouse ('sto:rhaus) s.
skład; magazyn; skarbnica; kopalnia
storekeeper ('sto:r,ki:per) s.
sklepikarz; kupiec
storey ('sto:ry) s. piętro
storeyed ('sto:rjed) adj. pięt-
rowy (angielska pisownia)
storied ('sto:rjed) adj. pięt-
rowy

stork (sto:rk) s. bocian
storm (sto:rm) s. burza; wichura; sztorm; zawierucha;
szturm; v. szaleć (burza etc.)
wpaść do pokoju; wypaść z pokoju (jak burzą); rzucać gromy; szturmować; brać szturmem
stormy ('sto:rmy) adj. burzliwy; zwiastujący burzę
story ('sto:ry) s. opowiadanie; opowieść; powiastka; historia; bajka; anegdota; gawęda; zmyślanie; nowela;
piętro
story teller ('sto:ry,teler)
s. gawędziarz; kłamczuch
stout (staut) adj. dzielny;
krzepki; gruby; s, mocny np.
porto (wino); mocne piwo;
tęga osoba
stove (stouw) s. piec (też kuchenny); cieplarnia; v. zob.
stave; hodować w cieplarni
stow (stou) v. wypełniać; układać szczelnie; mieścić; wsuwać; chować; przesłać (slang)
stow away ('stou,e'łej) v.
jechać na gapę
stowaway ('stouełej) s. pasażer na gapę
straggling ('straeglyng) adj.
sporadyczny; rozpościerają-
cy się; rzadki
straight (strejt) adj. prosty;
bezpośredni; celny; szczery;
otwarty; rzetelny; zwykły;
s. prosta linia; prosty odcinek (toru); adv. prosto;
wprost; na przełaj; po prostu;
pod rząd; należycie; nieprzer-
wanie; ciągiem
straightaway ('strejt,ełej)
adv. natychmiast ;bez zwłoki
straight ahead ('strejt,ehed)
adv. na wprost
straighten ('strejtn) v. wy-
prostować(się); poprawić (się)
straightforward (strejt'fo:r-
łerd) adj. łatwy; jasny; prosty; prostolinijny; szczery;
uczciwy
strain (strejn) v. prężyć; na-

prężać; naciągać; wytężać; od-
kształcać; nadużywać; nadwerę-
żać; przeciążać; robić gwałtowne wysiłki; cedzić; przecedzać;
s. naprężenie; napięcie; obciążenie; przemęczenie; zwichnięcie; nadwerężenie; wysiłek; od-
kształcenie; rasa; odmiana;
rys
strainer ('strejner) s. sito;
sączek; cedzidło; rozciągacz;
napinacz
strait (strejt) v. ścieśniać;
być w trudnościach
straited circumstances ('strej-
tyd,ser'kamstenses) s. kłopoty pieniężne
straiten ('strejtn) v. zbied-
nieć; zubożeć
strait jacket ('strejt'dżaekyt)
s. kaftan bezpieczeństwa
straits (strejts) pl. cieśnina
morska; kłopoty finansowe;
braki czegoś
strand (straend) s.skręt; zwitek; pasmo; nitka; warkocz;
sznur; rys; kosmyk; brzeg; plaża; v. splatać; osadzać na
mieliźnie; osiąść na mieliźnie
strange (strejndż) adj. obcy;
dziwny; niezwykły; nieznany;
niewprawny
stranger ('strejndżer) s. obcy;
nieznajomy; człowiek nieobeznany; exp.:panie tego !
strangle ('straengl) v. dusić;
trzymać za gardło; zadusić
strap (straep) s. rzemień; pasek; rzemyk; taśma; uchwyt;
rączka; chłosta; bicie;
v. na pasku umocowywać;
ostrzyć; bić paskiem; zalepiać
plastrem
strategic (stre'ti:dżyk) adj.
strategiczny
strategy ('straetydży) s.
strategia; taktyka
straw (stro:) s. słoma
strawberry ('stro:bery) s.
truskawka
stray (strej)v. zabłądzić; za-
błąkać się; schodzić na manowce; s. zbłąkane zwierzę; dziecko bez opieki; adj.zabłąkany

strays (strejs) pl. zaburzenia
atmosferyczne (np. w radiu)
streak (stri:k) s. smuga; pasek; pasmo; prążek; rys;
pierwiastek;passa; v. rysować paski, prążki; błyskawicznie poruszać się; wpadać
nagle dokądś
streaky ('stri:ky) adj. prążko-
wany; w paski; zmienny; nierówny (slang)
stream (stri:m) s. strumień;
potok; rzeka; struga; prąd;
v. płynąć (strumieniami);
ociekać; tryskać; powiewać
street (stri:t) s. ulica
streetcar ('stri:tka:r) s.
tramwaj
strength (strenks) s. moc; siła; stężenie; natężenie;
ilość; skład (ludzi)
strengthen ('strenksn) v.
wzmocnić (się); wzmagać; dać
przewagę
strenuous (strenjues) adj.
męczący; żmudny; mozolny; wy-
tężony; zawzięty; pracowity;
energiczny; silny
stress (stres) s. nacisk; akcent; napór; wysiłek;
v. kłaść nacisk; podkreslać;
naciskać
stretch (strecz) s. naciągać
(się); naprężać; napinać; nadużywać; przeciągać; rozciągać (się); ciągnąć się; sięgać; powiesić (kogoś); s. napięcie; rozciąganie; przeciąganie się; nadużycie; połać;
okres służby; przeciąg czasu;
prosty odcinek toru; (slang):
pobyt w więzieniu
stretcher ('streczer) s. nosze
strew; strewed; strewn (stru:,
stru:d; stru:n)
strew (stru:) s. posypać; roz-
rzucić; porozrzucać
strewn (stru:n) v. zob. strew
stricken (stri:ken) v. zob.
strike; adj. dotknięty; nawie-
dzony; rażony; udręczony
stride; strode; stridden
(strajd; stroud; stridn)

stride (strajd) v. kroczyć;
przekroczyć; stać okrakiem
(nad czymś); s. krok; rozkrok
strife (stajf) s. spór; walka;
współzawodnictwo
strike; struck; stricken (strajk;
strak; strykn)
strike (strajk) v. uderzać; bić
(monetę); walić; kuć; wykrze-
sać; zapalić (zapałkę); natrafić; zastrajkować; porzucać
robotę; chwytać (przynętę);
s. strajk; strychulec; wybicie
monety; natrafienie (żyły, np.
złotodajnej); chwycenie przy-
nęty; nieudane uderzenie palan-
tem; zwalenie wszystkich kręgli
naraz
strike off ('strajk off) v. od-
rapywać; ścinać; wykreślać;
drukować kilka egzemplarzy
strike out ('strajk,aut) v.
uderzać na odlew; zacząć; ukuć;
wymyślić
striker ('strajker) s. strajku-
jący; młotek (w dzwonku)
striking ('strajkyng) adj.
uderzający
string; strung; strung (stryng;
strang; strang)
string (stryng) v.zawiązać;
przywiązać; zaopatrzyć w struny; stroić; napinać; podniecać;
powiesić kogoś; ciągnąć sie
(klej); obwieszać; s. sznurek;
szpagat; powróz; sznurowadło;
tasiemka; cięciwa; struna;
żyła; włókno; rząd; stek
(głupstw)
strip (stryp) v. obdzierać;
ogałacać; obnażać; zdzierać;
rozbierać (się); wydobyć do
końca; ścierać (gwint); ciąć
na paski; s. pasek; skrawek;
seria komiksów
strip-tease ('strypti:z) s.
rozbieranie się na scenie
stripes (strajps) pl. paski;
prążki; naszywki; chłosta;
cięgi
striped ('strajpt) adj. pa-
siasty; w pasy

strive; strove; striven
('strajw; strouw; strywn)
strive (strajw) v. starac się;
usiłowac; dążyc; borykac się;
zwalczac
striven ('strywn) v. zob.strive
strode (stroud) v. zob. stride
stroke (strouk) s. uderzenie;
cios; cięcie; raz; porażenie;
ciąg; pociagnięcie (pióra);
rys; kreska; ruch (wiosła);
wysiłek; suw; skok (tłoka);
takt; głaskanie; v. znaczyc;
przekreślac; nadawac' tempo;
głaskac; ugłaskac
stroke of luck ('strouk,ow'lak)
exp.: los szczęścia
stroll (stroul) v. przechadzac
się; spacerowac; wędrowac;
s. przechadzka
stroller ('strouler) s. space-
rowicz; włóczęga; aktor
wędrowny; wózek (dziecięcy)
strong (strong) adj. mocny;
silny; będacy w liczbie...;
mocarstwowy; potężny; trwały;
solidny; wyskokowy; przekonywujący; ordynarny
strongbox ('strong,boks) s.
sejf; kasa ogniotrwała
strongroom ('strong,rum) s.
skarbiec
strove (strouw) v. zob.strive
struck (strak) v.zob. strike
structure ('strakczer) s. budowa; struktura; budowla; wiązanie; splot; v. nadawac
kształt
struggle ('strągl) v. szarpac
się; szamotac się; walczyc;
usiłowac; s. walka;borykanie
strum (stram) v. rzępolic;
brzdąkac; s. brzdęk; brzdąkanie
strung (strąng) v. zob. string;
adj. napięty
strut (strat) v. kroczyc ma-
jestatycznie; rozpierac;
s. krok majestatyczny; zastrzał; rozpora
stub (stab) s. pniak; korzen:
resztka; niedopałek; grzbiet

(biletu); v. karczowac; gasic (papierosa)
stubble ('stabl) s. rżysko;
ściernisko; twardy zarost
stubborn ('stabern) adj. uparty
stuck (stak) v. zob. stick
stud (stad) s. sworzen; gwóźdz;
guz; trzon; słup; rozporka;
ogier; stadnina; v. nabijac
(np. gwoździami; guzami);
usiewac czyms; byc rozsianym;
podpierac (słupami)
student ('stu:dent) s. student;
badający coś; znawca czegoś
studio ('stju:djou) s. studio;
pracownia
studio couch ('stju:djou,kaucz)
s. tapczan
studious ('stu:djes) adj. pilny; staranny; dbały; wyszukany
study ('stady) s. pracownia;
gabinet; nauka; przedmiot nauki, staran, troski, zadumy,
marzenia; v. badac; studiowac;
dociekac; uczyc się
stuff (staf) v. napychac; opychac (się); tuczyc (się); fa-
szerowac; wpychac; wkuwac;
s. materia; materiał; glina;
rzecz; rupiecie (brednie)
stuffing ('stafyng) s. nadzienie; farsz; nadziewka; wyściółka
stuffy ('stafy) adj. zatęchły;
duszny; ciężki; nudny; zatka-
ny (nos); (slang): ważny;
tępy; skwaszony; zły; purytan-
ski
stumble ('stambl) v. potykac
(się); utykac; natknąc się;
zawahac (kogoś); miec skrupuły; czuc się dotkniętym;
s. potknięcie się
stumblebum ('stambl,bam) s.
(slang): zawalidroga; próżniak
stump (stamp) s. pniak; głąb;
kikut; ogarek; resztka; niedopałek; kulas; krzykactwo; agitacja (polityczna); kuc; klocek;
przysądkowaty człowiek; v. karczowac; obcinac; zdumiec (się);
agitowac; wyzwac kogoś; chodzic na protezie

stun (stan) v. ogłuszyć; oszo-
łomić; s. oszołomienie (uderzenie hukiem)
stung (stang) v. zob. sting
stunk (stank) v. zob . stink
stunning ('stanyŋg) adj. nadzwyczajny; szlagierowy; ka-
pitalny
stupefy ('stu:pyfaj) v. ogłu-
piać; odurzać; wprawiać
w osłupienie
stupid ('stu:pyd) adj. głupi;
odurzony; nudny; s. głupiec
stupidity ('stu:pydyty) s.
głupota; głupstwo
stupor ('stu:per) s. osłupienie; odurzenie; apatia
sturdy ('ste:rdy) adj. krzepki; dzielny; solidny; s. motylica
stutter ('stater) v. jąkać (się)
s. jąkanie się
sty (staj) s. chlew; burdel;
jęczmień (w oku); v. żyć w
chlewie; trzymać w chlewie
style (stajl) s. styl; maniera;
sposób; fason; wzór; kształt;
rylec; szyjka; tytuł; nazwa;
format; wskazówka; v. formować stylowo; określać mianem
stylish (stajlysh) adj. szykowny; stylowy; wytworny
suave (sła:w) adj. gładki; łagodny; uprzejmy
subdivision (,sabdy'wyżyn) s.
dzielnica (miasta; osiedla);
podział
subdue (seb'du:) s. ujarzmiać;
poskramiać; przyciszać; tłumić; łagodzić; podbijać
subject ('sabdżykt) s. podmiot;
przedmiot; temat; treść; tworzywo; (sab'dżekt) motyw;
poddany; osobnik; v. podporządkować; ujarzmić; podbić;
narazić; poddać czemuś; adj.
poddany; uległy; podległy;
narażony; podatny; podlegający; ujarzmiony; adv. pod warunkiem; z zastrzeżeniem;
z uwzględnieniem czegoś
subjective('sabdżektyw) adj.
subiektywny; podmiotowy

subjunctive mood (seb'dżanktyw,
,mu:d) s. tryb warunkowy
sublime (se'blajm) adj. wzniosły; wyniosły; podniosły
submachine-gun ('sabme'szi:ngan)
s. (automatyczny) pistolet maszynowy
submarine (sabme'ri:n) s. łódź
podwodna
submariners (sabme'ri:ners) pl.
załoga łodzi podwodnej
submerge (seb'me:rdż) v. zalewać; zatapiać; zanurzać (się);
zakrywać
submission (seb'myszyn) s.
uległość; poddanie się; przed-
łożenie (opinii)
submissive (seb'mysyw) adj.
uległy
submit (seb'myt) v. poddawać
(się); przedkładać
subnormal (sab'no:rmel) adj.
niżej normy; cofnięty w roz-
woju
subordinate(se'bo:rdnyt) adj.
zależny; podporządkowany;
s. podwładny; (se'bo:rdnejt)
v. podporządkowywać
subordinate clause (se'bo:rd-
nyt,klo:z) s. zdanie podrzędne
subscribe (seb'skrajb) v. za-
prenumerować; podpisywać (np.
obraz); pisać się na coś; dawać na cel
subscribe for (seb'skrajb,fo:r)
v. zapisywać się na (nową)
książkę
subscribe to (seb'skrajb,tu) v.
abonować gazetę
subscriber (seb'skrajber) s.
abonent; człowiek popierający
subscription (seb'skrypszyn) s.
prenumerata; przedpłata; pod-
pisanie; zgoda pisemna; podpis dołączony
subsequent ('sabsykłent) adj.
następny
subsequently ('sabsykłently)
adv. następnie
subside (seb'sajd) v. klęsnąć;
opadać; osadzać się; osiadać;
uspokajać się

subsidiary (seb'sydjery) adj.
pomocniczy; subsydiowany (zależny); s. pomocnik
subsidiary company (seb'sydjery'kampeny) s. firma zależna
od innej firmy
subsidize ('sabsydajz) v. zasiłkować; zasilać; opłacać;
przekupywać
subsidy ('sabsydy) s. zasiłek
(państwowy); subwencja; danina
subsist (seb'syst) s. istnieć;
egzystować; utrzymywać się
przy życiu; żyć czyms
subsistence (seb'systens) s.
utrzymanie; istnienie
substance ('sabstens) s. istota; tresć; sens; sedno; substancja; znaczenie; rzeczywistosć; majątek
substandard (sab'staenderd)
adj. poniżej poziomu; ordynarny (język)
substantial (sab'staenszel)
adj. materialny; rzeczywisty;
solidny; zasadniczy; ważny;
bogaty; wpływowy; konkretny;
tresciwy
substantive ('sabstentyw) adj.
rzeczywisty; niezależnie
istniejący; zasadniczy; poważny; rzeczownikowy; wyrażający
istnienie; s. rzeczownik
substitute ('sabstytut) s. namiastka; zastępca
substitution (,sabsty'tuszyn)
s. zastepstwo; zastąpienie
subtitle ('sabtajtl) s. podtytuł; napis na filmie
subtle ('sabtl) s. subtelny;
delikatny; cienki; rzadki;
chytry; bystry
subtract (sab'traekt) v. odejmować
suburb ('sabe:rb) s. przedmiescie
suburban ('sabe:rben) adj.
podmiejski
subway ('sabłej) s. kolejka
podziemna
succeed (sek'si:d) v. miec po-

wodzenie; udawać się; następować po kims
success (sek'ses) s. powodzenie;
sukces; rzecz udana; człowiek
majacy sukces
successful (sek'sesful) adj.
udały; mający powodzenie
succession (sek'seszyn) s. następstwo; kolej; kolejnosć;
sukcesja; spadkobiercy; szereg
successive (sek'sesyw) adj.
kolejny
successor (sek'seser) s. następca; dziedzic; spadkobierca
succumb (se'kam) v. ulegać (pokusie); poddawać się; umierać
such (sacz) adj. taki; tego
rodzaju; pron. taki; tym podobny
suck (sak) v. ssac; korzystać;
wyzyskiwać; wchłaniac; wciągać;
(slang): nabierac; dac się nabrać; podlizywac się komus;
s. ssanie; wciąganie; (slang):
łyk
suckle ('sakel) v. karmic piersią; dawac piers; ssac piers
suckling ('saklyng) s. osesek;
młode w okresie ssania
sudden ('sadn) adj. nagły
sudden death ('sadn,det) s.
nagła smierc; rozstrzygnięcie
w nastepnej rozgrywce
suddenly ('sadnly) adv. nagle;
raptowanie; nieoczekiwanie
suds (sadz) pl. mydliny; (slang):
piwo
sue (su:) v. skarżyc; zaskarżać;
pozywac; upraszac; ubiegać się
suede (slejd) s. zamsz
suet ('su:yt) s. łoj; adj. łojowy
suffer ('safer) v. cierpiec;
ucierpiec; scierpiec; doznac
(czegos); zostać straconym
suffer from ('safer,from) v.
być chorym(na cos)
sufferable ('saferebl) adj.
znosny
sufferer ('saferer) s. cierpiący
cy

suffice (se'fajs) v. wystarczyc

sufficiency (se'fyszensy) s. wystarczająca ilosc; zapasy

sufficient (se'fyszent) adj. dostateczny; wystarczający

suffix ('safyks) s. przyrostek

suffocate ('safokejt) v. udusic; zadusic

sugar ('szuger) s. cukier; slodkie dziecko; (slang): forsa; v. slodzic

sugar-cane ('szugerkejn) s. trzcina cukrowa

suggest (se'dzest) v. sugerowac; proponowac; nasuwac; podsuwac; poddawac (mysl)

suggestion (se'dzestszyn) s. sugestia; wskazowka; mysl; poddawanie; podsuwanie; slad (czegos)

suggestive (se'dzestyw) adj. przypominający; nasuwający (mysl). dwuznaczny

suicide (,su:y'sajd) s. samobojstwo; samobojca; v. popelnic samobojstwo

suit (su:t) v. dostosowac; odpowiadac; sluzyc; wybrac; byc odpowiednim; zadowalac; pasowac; s. garnitur; ubranie; komplet; skarga; proces; prosba; zaloty; staranie się; zestaw

suit yourself ('su:tjor,self) exp.:rob co chcesz

suitable ('su:tebl) adj. wlasciwy; stosowny; odpowiedni

suitcase ('su:tkejs) s. walizka

suite (sli:t) s. swita; orszak; szereg; zestaw (mebli); apartament; garnitur; komplet; suita

suitor ('su:ter) s. zalotnik; petent; pretendent; strona; konkurent

sulfate ('salfejt)s. siarczan; v. zakwaszac; zamieniac na siarczan

sulfur ('salfer) s. siarka; v. siarkowac

sulk (salk) v. byc w zlym humorze; s. zly humor; czlowiek w zlym humorze

sulky ('salky) adj. w zlym humorze; ponury; s. jednokonny dwukolowy wozek

sullen ('salen) adj. ponury; posępny; flegmatyczny; powolny

sulphur ('salfer) s. siarka; v. siarkowac

sultry ('saltry) adj. parny; duszny; gwaltowny; gorący; namiętny

sum (sam) s. suma; w sumie; rachunek; v. dodawac; zbierac; podsumowywac

sum up ('sam,ap) v. dodawac; zbierac; podsumowywac

summarize ('samerajz) v. streszczac; zbierac; podsumowywac

summary ('samery) s. streszczenie; skrot; adj. pobieżny; dorazny; krotki

Summer ('samer) s. lato; v. spędzac lato

Summer resort ('samer ry'so:rt) s. letnisko

Summer school ('samer,sku:l) s. szkola w lecie, w czasie wakacji

summit ('samyt) s. szczyt, summon ('samen) v. wzywac (oficjalnie); zdobywac się(na odwagę)

summons ('samens) pl. wezwanie urzędowe; v. doręczac wezwanie urzędowe

sun (san) s. slonce; v. naslonecznic (się)

sunbath ('sanba:s) s. kąpiel sloneczna

sunbathe ('sanbejz) v. opalac się

sunbeam ('sanbi:m) s. promien slonca

sunburn ('sanbe:rn) s. opalenizna

Sunday ('sandy) s. niedziela

sundial ('sandajel) s. zegar sloneczny

sundries ('sandryz) s. różności;
rozmaitości
sundry ('sandry) adj. różny;
rozmaity
sung (sang) v. zob. sing
sunglasses (san,gla:sys) pl.
okulary od słońca
sunk (sank) v. zob. sink
sunken ('sanken) v. zob. sink;
adj. zapadnięty; zatopiony;
podwodny
sunny ('sany) adj. słoneczny
sunny side up ('sany,sajd ap)
exp.: jaja sadzone
sunrise ('san-rajz) s. wschód
słońca
sunshade ('sanshejd) s. parasol
od słońca
sunset ('sanset) s. zachód
słońca
sunshine ('sanszajn) s. blask
słońca; pogoda. wesołość
sunstroke ('sanstrouk) s. porażenie słoneczne
sup (sap) s. łyk; v. częstować
kolacją; zjeść kolacje; pić
małymi łykami
super ('su:per) adj. pierwszorzędny; wspaniały; kwadratowy;
prefix: nad-; prze-; s. statysta; nadzorca; szlagier;
przebój (filmowy); najlepszy
gatunek
superabundant ('su:per,e'bandent) adj. nadmierny; przebo-
gaty
superb (se:'pe:rb) adj. wspaniały
super-duper (,su:per-'du:per)
adj. (slang): b. dobry; luksusowy; bardzo elegancki
superficial (,su:per'fyszel)
adj. powierzchowny; powierzchniowy
superfluous (su'pe:rflues)
adj. zbędny; zbyteczny
super-highway (su'per-hajłej)
s. (m.in. 4-pasmowa) autostrada
superhuman(,su:per'hju:man)
adj. nadludzki

superintend (,su:peryn'tend)
v. nadzorować; doglądac; kierować
superintendent (,su:peryn'tendent) s. nadzorca; dozorca;
nadinspektor
superior (su:'pierjer) adj.
wyższy; nieprzeciętny;
pierwszorzędny; przewyższa-
jący; lepszy; nadęty; wyniosły;
s. zwierzchnik; przełożony;
starszy rangą
superiority (su:,pie:ry'oryty)
s. wyższość
superlative (su:'pe:rlatyw)
adj. najwyższy; s. szczyt;
superlatyw; stopien najwyższy
superman ('su:permen) s. nadczłowiek
supermarket ('su:per'ma:rkyt)
s. supersam; duży sklep samo-
obsługowy (żywnosciowy)
supernatural (,su:per'naeczerel) adj. nadprzyrodzony
supernumerary (,su:per'nju:me-
ryry) adj. nadliczbowy; nie-
etatowy; statysta
superscription (,su:per'skrypszyn) s.napis u góry; nadpis;
adres; napis
supersede (sju:per'si:d) v.
zastąpic; wypierać; zajmować
miejsce
supersonic (,su:per'sonyk)
adj. ultradźwiękowy; ponad-
dzwiękowy
superstition (su:per'styszyn)
s. zabobon; przesądy
supervise ('su:perwajz) v.
nadzorować; doglądać
supervisor ('su:perwajzer)
s. inspektor; nadzorca
supper ('saper) s. wieczerza;
kolacja
supple ('sapl) adj. giętki;
gibki; v. stawać się gibkim
supplement ('saplyment) s.
dodatek; uzupełnienie;
v. uzupełniac
supplementary ('saplymentery)
adj. dodatkowy; uzupełniają-
cy

supplication (,saply'kejszyn)
s. błaganie; prosba
supplier (se'plajer) s. dostawca
supply (se'plaj) s. zapas;
aprowizacja; zaopatrzenie;
dostarczenie; dostawy; kredyty; podaż; dopływ; zasilanie;
v. dostarczac; zaopatrywać;
zaradzic; zastępowac
support (se'po:rt) s. utrzymanie; podtrzymanie; podpora;
poparcie; pomoc; wspornik;
dzwigar; rama; łożysko; podłoże; ostoja; v. podtrzymy-
wać; utrzymywać; podpierac;
popierac; wytrzymywać; znosic; tolerowac
suppose (se'pouz) v. przypuszczac; zakładac; sądzic
supposed (se'pouzd) adj. domniemany; przypuszczalny;
rzekomy
supposedly (se'pouzdly) adv.
rzekomo; przypuszczalnie
supposition (sape'zeszyn) s.
przypuszczenie; domniemanie
suppress (se'pres) v. tłumic;
zgniatac; znosic; zatrzymywac (krwawienie); usuwać;
taic
suppression (se'preszyn) s.
stłumienie; zgniecenie;
zniesienie; usunięcie; prze-
milczenie; zatajenie
suppurate ('sapjurejt) v. ro-
piec
supremacy (se'premesy) s.
zwierzchnictwo; przewaga; najwyższa władza; supremacja
supreme (se'pri:m) adj. najwyższy; doskonały; ostateczny
surcharge (se:r'cza:rdż) s.
nadpłata; nadmierny ciężar;
dodatkowy ciężar; opłata (kar-
na); przeładowanie; v. ścią-
gac opłatę podatkową; nakładac grzywnę; przeładowac;
przedrukować (znaczek)
sure (szuer) adj. pewny; niezawodny; niemylny; bezpieczny;
exp.: napewno !; zgadza się !

adv. z pewnoscią; pewnie; napewno; niezawodnie; niechybnie
sure enough ('szuer,y'naf) adv.
faktycznie
surely ('szuerly) adv. pewnie;
z pewnoscią
surety ('szuerty) s. ręczyciel;
gwarancja; zabezpieczenie;
kaucja; pewnosc
surf (se:rf) s. (łamiące się)
fale przybrzeżne
surface (se:rfys) s. powierzchnia; v. wypływac na powierzchnię; wykańczac powierzchnię
surfboard ('se:rfbo:rd) s. po-
jedyńcza (deska); narta wodna;
v. jeździc na desce na falach
ku brzegowi
surfriding ('se:rf,rajdyng) v.
zjeżdżac z fal ku brzegowi
surge (se:rdż) s. gwałtowny
impuls; fala uskokowa; falowanie; fala; v. nagle wzbierac;
drgac; popuscic; kołysac;
hustac; zeslizgiwac się
surgeon ('se:rdżen) s. chirurg
surgery ('se:rdżery) s. chi-
rurgia; operacja; sala opera-
cyjna
surgical ('se:rdżykel) adj.
chirurgiczny
surly ('se:rly) adj. grubiański;
zgryzliwy
surmise ('se:rmajz) s. domysł;
v. domyslac się czegos
surmount (ser'maunt) v. pokony-
wac; wychodzic na (górę);
przechodzic przez; pokrywac;
wznosic się
surmounted by (ser'mauntyd baj)
adj. pokonany przez
surname ('se:rnejm) s. nazwisko;
przydomek; (se:r'nejm) v.
przezywac; nadawac przydomek
surpass (se:r'paes) v. przewyższac; przechodzic (oczekiwania)
surpassing (se:r'paesyng) adj.
nieprzescigniony; niezrównany
surplus (se:r'plas) s. nadwyżka; nadmiar; superata; nadwyżka
produkcyjna; wartosc dodatkowa;
adj. stanowiący nadwyżkę; nadwyżko-
wy; zbywający

surprise (ser'prajz) s. niespodzianka; zaskoczenie; zdziwienie; v. zaskoczyc; zdziwic; zmuszac; złapac na gorącym uczynku; adj. nieoczekiwany; niespodziewany

surprised (ser'prajzd) adj.zaskoczony; złapany na gorącym uczynku

surrender (se'render) s. poddanie się; wyrzeczenie się; v. poddawac się; oddawac się; wyrzekac się czegos

surround (se'raund) v. otaczac; okrążac

surroundings (se'raundyngs) pl. otoczenie

survey (se:r'wej) s. przegląd; oględziny; inspekcja; pomiary; plan (topograficzny); opis; ankieta; statystyka; v. przeglądac; robic pomiary; wymierzac; oglądać

surveying (se:r'wejyng) s. miernictwo

surveyor (se:r'wejer) s. mierniczy; inspektor celny

survival (ser'wajwel) s. przeżycie; przeżytek

survive (ser,wajw) v. przeżyc; dalej życ

survivor (ser'wajwer) s. człowiek pozostały przy życiu

susceptible (se'septybl) adj. wrażliwy; drażliwy; podatny; dopuszczający

suspect (ses'pekt) v. podejrzewac kogos; ('saspekt) adj. podejrzany

suspected (ses'pektyd) adj. podejrzany

suspend (ses'pend) v. zawiesic; powstrzymac (się chwilowo)

suspended (ses'pendyd) adj. zawieszony w czynnosciach

suspenders (ses'penders) pl. podwiązki; szelki

suspense (ses'pens) s. niepewnosc; zawieszenie; nierozstrzygnięcie

suspension (ses'penszyn) s. zawieszenie; zawiesina; wstrzymanie

suspension bridge (ses'penszyn,brydż) s. wiszący most

suspicion (ses'pyszyn) s. podejrzenie; v. podejrzewac

suspicious (ses'pyszes) adj. podejrzany; nieufny

sustain (ses'tejn) v. podtrzymywac; dzwigac; cierpiec; doznawac; ponosic; potwierdzac; utrzymywac; uznawac (słusznosć)

sustenance ('sastynens) s. pożywienie; utrzymanie

swab (słob) s. wycior; wacik chłonący; scierka na kiju; gamoń; epoleta; v. wycierac; scierac; wuszorowac

swab up ('słob,ap) v. wytrzec

swagger (słaeger) v. paradowac; dumnie chodzi-; chełpic się; pysznic się;odstraszyc; nakłaniac strachem

swallow ('słolou) v. połykac (np. zniewagę); przełykac; dac się nabrac; odwołac (słowa); s. przełykanie; łyk; kęs; przełyk; jaskółka

swam (słaem) v. zob. swim

swamp (słomp) s. bagno; v. zalewac; pochłaniac; przysłaniac; grzęznąc

swampy (słompy) adj. bagnisty; błotnisty

swan (słon) s. łabędz

swap (słop) v. zamieniac (się); wymieniac (się); s. zamiana; wymiana

swarm (sło:rm) s. mrowie; mnostwo; rój; v. roic (się); wyroic; obfitowac (w cos); wspinac się; wdrapywac się

swarthy ('sło:rty) adj. sniady; smagły

swathe (słejz) v. spowijac; s. zawinięcie; bandaż

sway (słej) v. kołysac (się); chwiac (się); zachwiac (się); rządzic czyms; władac; s. chwianie się; władza

swear; sware; sworn (słeer; sło:r; sło:rn)

swear (słeer) v. przysięgac; poprzysiąc

sweat (słet) s. poty; pot; harówka; v. pocić się; pracować
ciężko; (slang): harować;
szwejsować; fermentować; wy-
świechtywać monety; wydzielać
(żywicę)

sweat out (słet,aut) v. wypacać (się); (slang): ciężko
pracować; wyduszać z kogoś
coś; wyciągać pieniądze szan-
tażem; wyciągać odpowiedzi
torturami; odsiadywać więzienie

sweater ('słeter) s. sweter;
wyzyskiwacz robotników

sweatshop ('słet,szop) s. zakład wyzyskujący robotników

sweatshirt ('slet,sze:rt) s.
koszula trykotowa

Swedish ('słi:dysz) adj.
szwedzki

sweep; swept; swept (słi:p;
słept; słept)

sweep (słi:p) v. zamiatać; wy-
miatać; zmiatać; oczyszczać;
wygrywać (np. wszystkie me-
dale); porywać (słuchaczy);
przewalić się przez coś (burza; wichura; powódź); ogarniać; obejmować; rozciągać
się; sunać uroczyście; ślizgać się; śmigać; zwalać (kogoś
z nóg); ostrzeliwać; etc.
s. zamiatanie; zdobycie; zagarnięcie; ogołocenie; śmieci;
śmignięcie; machnięcie; zasięg; robienie zakrętu; etc.

sweeper ('słi:per) s. zamia-
tacz; zamiataczka; zmiotka

sweeping ('słi:pyng) adj. szeroki; wspaniały; rozległy;
daleko idący

sweepings ('słi:pyngs) pl.
śmieci

sweepstake ('słi:pstejk) s.
wyścigi; loteria; nagroda
(zbiorowa) w wyścigach

sweet (słi:t) adj. słodki;
przyjemny; miły; rozkoszny;
dobrze osłodzony; deserowy;
melodyjny; świeży; łagodny;
zakochany

sweeten ('słi:tn) v. słodzić;
osładzać; stawać się słodkim;
(slang): zwiększać stawkę;
zwiększać zastaw

sweetheart ('słi:t-ha:rt) s.
ukochana; ukochany

sweetness ('słi:tnys) s. sło-
dycz

sweetpea ('słi:tpi:) s. groszek
pachnący

swell; swollen; swelled (słel;
słoulen; słeld)

swell (słel) v. puchnąć; wzdymać (się); nadymać (się); wydymać (się); rozdymać; wzbierać;
wzrastać; potęgować się;
s. wydęcie; zgrubienie; na-
brzmienie; wzbieranie; wzburzo-
na fala (morze); (slang): wy-
tworniak; gruba ryba

swelling ('słelyng) s. spuchlizna; wzdęcie; obrzęk; wezbranie
(rzeki)

swept (słept) v. zob. sweep

swerve (słe:rw) s. odchylenie;
zboczenie; v. zbaczać; odchylać (się)

swift (słyft) adj. prędki; rączy; chyży; żywy; s. nawijak
przędzy; traszka; jaszczurka;
jerzyk

swiftness ('słyftnys) s. prędko-
kość; chyżość

swim; swam; swum (słym; słaem;
słam)

swim (słym) v. płynąć; przepłynąć; pływać (w wyścigach); pławić; ociekać czymś; unosić się
na powierzchni; iść z prądem;
kręcić się (w głowie); s. pływanie; nurt (życia); woda (do
pływania); głębia; pęcherz
pławny

swimmer ('słymer) s. pływak

swimming ('słymyng) s. pływanie

swimming pool ('słymyng,pu:l)
s, pływanlnia

swimming suit ('słymyng,sju:t)
s. kostium kąpielowy

swindle (słyndl) s. oszustwo;
v. oszukiwać

swine (słajn) s. świnia

swing ; swung; swang (słyng;
slang;słaeng)
swing (słyng) v. huśtać (się);
kołysać (się); wahać (się);
bujac (się); machać; wywijać;
przerzucać (się) na cos; porywać (za sobą); pociągać
(za sobą); s. huśtanie (się);
kołysanie (się); ruch wahadłowy; zmiana pracy; objazd (te-
renu); rytm; przerzucanie się;
kołyszący chód; taniec (swing)
swing bridge ('słyng,brydż) s.
most wahadłowy
swing door ('słyng,do:r) s.
drzwi wahadłowe
swing wheel ('słyng,hłi:l) s.
koło rozpędowe (zamachowe)
swirl (słe:rl) s. wir; wirowanie; skręt; lok; v. wirować;
kręcic się; unosić się (wiru-
jąc)
Swiss (słys) adj. szwajcarski
switch (słycz) s. pręt; zwrotnica; przekładnia; wyłącznik;
przełącznik; kontakt; śmignięcie; v. bic prętem; machać;
wyrywać; zmieniać; przełączać;
włączać; rozłączac (się); wyłączac (się); włączac (np.
światło)
switch off ('słycz,of) v. wyłączac
switch on ('słycz,on) v. włączać
switchboard ('słyczbo:rd) s.
tablica rozdzielcza; łącznica
(telefoniczna etc.)
swollen ('słoulen) v. zob.swell
adj. opuchnięty; wzdęty;
wezbrany
swoon (słu:n) v. zemdlec; omdlec; zamierac; s. omdlenie
swoop down on ('słu:p,dałn on)
v. zaatakować z góry; runąc
na cos
swoop up ('słu:p,ap) v. porywać; s. spadnięcie; porwanie
swop (słop) v. zamieniać; wymieniać; s. zamiana; wymiana
sword (so:rd) s. pałasz; szpada;
miecz; szabla; bagnet (slang)

swore (sło:r) v. zob. swear
sworn (sło:rn) v. zob. swear;
adj. zaprzysiężony; przy-
sięgły
swum (słam) v. zob. swim
swung (słang)v. zob. swing
sycamore ('sykemo:r) s. jawor;
klon; figowiec
syllable ('syleble) s. sylaba;
zgłoska
symbol ('symbel) s. symbol;
v. symbolizowac
symbolic (,sym'bolyk) adj.
symboliczny
symbolism ('symbelyzem) s.
symbolizm
symmetric (sy'metryk) adj. symetryczny
symmetry ('symytry) s. symetria
sympathetic (,sympe'tetyk) adj.
współczujący; życzliwy; sympatyczny; współbrzmiący;
s. współczulny; łatwy do za-
hipnotyzowania
sympathize ('sympetajz) v.
współczuc; miec zrozumienie;
sympatyzowac z kims
sympathy ('sympety) s. współczucie; solidarnosc; sympatia
symphony ('symfeny) s. symfonia
symptom (sympten) s. symptom
synagogue ('synegog) s. bożni-
ca; synagoga
synchronize ('synkrenajz) s.
działac równoczesnie; synchro-
nizowac; pokazywać jednakowo
(czas); uzgadniac (zegary)
synonym ('synenym) s. synonim
synonymous (sy'nonymes) adj.
równoznaczny z czyms
syntax ('syntaeks) s. składnia
synthesis ('syntysys) s. synteza
syntheses ('syntysi:s) pl. syn-
tezy
synthetic (syn'tetyk) adj.
sztuczny; syntetyczny
syphilis ('syfylys) s. kiła; sy-
filis
syringe ('syryndż) s. strzykawka; v. strzykać (wodą)

syrup ('syrep) s. syrop
system ('systym) s. system
systematic (,systy'maetyk)
adj. systematyczny
t (ti:) dwudziesta litera
alfabetu angielskiego
tab (taeb) s. patka; wieszak
(przyszyty); język (buta);
naszywka; języczek; ucho;
przywieszka; rachunek; kontrola; pilnowanie; v. prowadzic
ewidencję; tabelowac; zaopatrywac w (języczek lub
ucho etc.)
table ('tejbl) s. stół; stolik; tablica; tabela; tabliczka (np. mnożenia); płyta;
płaskowyż; blat; v. kłasc
na stole; odraczac (na długo);
wciągac na agendę; adj.stołowy
tablecloth ('tejbl,kloś) s.
obrus
tableland ('tejbl-laend) s.
płaskowyż
tablespoon ('tejbl-spu:n) s.
łyżka stołowa (do zupy)
tablespoonful ('tejblspu:nful)
s. pełna łyżka (pół uncji)
tablet ('taeblyt) s. tabletka;
tabliczka (do pisania)
taboo (te'bu:) s. tabu; v.zakazywac; adj. zakazany
tacit ('taesyt) adj. milczący;
cichy; niemy
taciturn ('taesyte:rn) adj.
małomówny
tack (taek) s. gwoźdź tapicerski; papiak; pluskiewka;
fastryga; kurs (polityki);
taktyka; stan lepki; prowiant;
żywnosc; jedzenie; v. przyczepiac; przybijac (lekko); fastrygowac; zmieniac kurs; lawirowac; hałasowac
tackle ('taekl) s. zestaw przyborów (do łowienia, golenia);
wielokrążek; takielunek; złapanie i trzymanie; v. zewrzec
się; borykac (się); złapac
i trzymac; zmagac (się); brac
się do czegoś (ostro); umocowywac; porac (się)

tacky ('taeky) adj. lepki; niemodny; marny
tact (taekt) s. takt; wyczucie;
dotyk
tactful ('taektful) adj. taktowny
tactics ('taektyks) pl. taktyka
tactile ('taektajl) adj. dotykowy; dotykalny
tactless ('taektlys) adj. nietaktowny
tad (taed) s. berbec
tadpole ('taedpoul) s. kijanka
tag (taeg) s. skuwka; etykieta;
kartka; strzęp; przywieszka;
znaczek tożsamości; marka;
mandat karny (pisany);ucho;
igliczka; wieszadło (przyszyte);
błyszczka; dodatek; morał; frazes; banał; cytat; refren;
ogon; zabawa w gonionego;
v. przyczepiac: skuwkę; kartkę;
znaczek, markę; ucho; wieszadło, igliczkę, ogon; dawac:
mandat karny, morał, bawic się
w gonionego; tańczyc odbijanego;
wymierzac wyrok; przeznaczac;
włoczyc się za kims; dołączyc
do czegos
tail (tejl) s. ogon; tył; koniec;
tren; poła; posladki; buńczuk;
warkocz; swita; cień (chodzący za kims); v. dodawac ogon;
obrywac ogonki; sledzic (krok
w krok); zamykac pochód
tailcoat (,tejl'kout) s. frak
taillight ('tejl,lajt) s.
tylne swiatło (wozu)
tailor ('tejler) s. krawiec;
v. szyc odzież
tailor-made ('tejlermejd) adj.
uszyty na zamówienie
tail wind ('tejlłynd) s. wiatr
w plecy
taint (tejnt) s. skaza; zaraza;
plama; v. plamic; kazic; zepsuc; plugawic
taintless ('teintlys)adj. bez
skazy
take; took; taken (tejk; tuk;
'tejkn)

take (tejk) s. brać; wziąć; łapać; chwytać; zdobywać (twierdzę); zajmować (miejsce); rezerwować; zażywać; pić; jeść; odczuwać; rozumiec; pojechać; notować; zrobić (zdjęcie); zadać sobie (trud); dostawać (napadu); przyjmować (radę; karę; etc.); mierzyć swoją temperaturę; godzić się (na traktowanie); nabierać (połysku); isć (za przykładem) s. połów; zdjęcie; wpływy (do kasy)
take along (,tejke'long) v. zabrać ze sobą
take down ('tejk,dałn) v. zdejmować; rozmontowywać
take-in ('tejk'yn) s. oszukanie; naciąganie
take off ('tejk,of) v. rozbierać; kasować; małpować; wystartować; odjąć; usunąć
takeoff (tejkof) s. start; skok; skocznia; karykatura; parodia; naśladowanie; odbicie; lista materiałów
take out (tejk aut) v. podejmować (poza domem); wyprowadzać; wynieść;wyrywać; wykupić; odjąć; oddzielić
takeover ('tejkouwer) s. opanowanie firmy przez manipulacje giełdowe lub finansowe
take over ('tejk,ouwer) v. przejmować (firmę); przyjmować (obowiązki);dominować
take up ('tejk,ap) v. ponosic; wchłonąć; wziąć (miejsce); zacząć (uczyć się); zadawać się;brać;zcieśniać; besztać
taken ('tejkn) v. zob. take;
adj. zabrany; porwany; zdobyty; nabrany; oszukany
talc(taelk) s. talk; v. posypywać talkiem
tale (tejl) s. opowiadanie; plotka; wymysł
talent ('taelent) s. talent (do czegoś); dar; uzdolnienie
talk (to:k) v. mówić; rozmawiać; plotkować; namawiać;

s. rozmowa; dyskusja; pogadanka; plotka: gadanie; mowa
talkative ('to:ketyw) adj. rozmowny; gadatliwy
talk-to ('to:k,tu) s. bura
tall (to:l) adj. wysoki; (slang): nieprawdopodobny
tall talk ('to:l,to:k) s. przechwałki
tallow ('taelou) s. łój; v. tuczyć; smarować łojem
talon ('taelen) s. szpon; pazur; rygiel; łapa ludzka; palec
tame ('tejm) v. oswajać; poskramiać; ujarzmić; okiełzać; łagodzić; przytłumić; upokorzyć
tamper ('taemper) s. ubijak; v. majstrować; manipulować; zmieniać coś nielegalnie
tan (taen) s. opalenizna; kolor (brązowy) brunatny; kora garbarska; v. garbować; opalać się (na słońcu); brązowiec; wyłoic komus skórę
tangent ('taendżent) adj. styczny; s. styczna; szczegół oderwany; zmiana tematu (od rzeczy); zmiana kierunku rozmowy
tangerine (taendże'ri:n) s. mandarynka
tangle ('taengl) s. plątanina; v. plątać (się); wikłać (się); (slang): pobic się z kims
tank (taenk) s. tank; zbiornik; cysterna; czołg; (slang): więzienie; v. nabierać do zbiornika; (slang): popic sobie
tankard ('taenkerd) s. kufel
tanner ('taener) s. garbarz
tantalize ('tae ntalajż)v. dręczyć (zwodną) nadzieją; łudzić
tantrum ('taentrem) s. napad złości
tap (taep) v. stukąc; odszpuntowac; napoczynąc; robic; punkcje; naciąc; ciągnąc sok; wykorzystywac; gwintowac; podsłuchiwac (telefon); s. czop: szpunt; kurek; zawór; gwintownik; zaczep; odczep

tape (tejp) s. taśma; tasiemka; tasiemiec; (slang): wódka; v. wiązać taśmą (przylepcem); mierzyć; (slang):oceniać kogoś

tape measure ('tejp,mežer) s. miara na taśmie (krawiecka)

taper ('tejper) s. stopniowe zwężanie (się); stożek; ubytek; osłabianie; stoczek; świeczka

taper off ('tejper,of) v. zwężać się stopniowo; cichnąc stopniowo; kończyć się spiczasto

tape recorder ('tejp-ry,ko:rder) s. magnetofon

tape recording ('tejp;ry,ko:rdyng) s. nagranie na taśmę

tapestry ('taepystry) s. gobelin; arras; v. zdobić gobelinami

tapeworm ('tejpłor:m) s. soliter; tasiemiec

tar (ta:r) s. smoła; dziegieć; ter; v. smołowac; terowac

target ('ta:rgyt) s. cel; obiekt; tarcza strzelnicza; v. kierować do celu; celowac; ustalac cel

tariff ('taeryf) s. cło; taryfa; cennik; c. clic wg taryfy; układac taryfę celną

tarnish ('ta:rnysz) v. matowiec; przycmiewac; brudzic (się); brukac (się); tracic połysk; s, matowienie; skaza

tart ('ta:rt) adj. cierpki; zgryźliwy; s. ciastko owocowe; (slang): kurewka

tartan ('ta:rten) s. materiał w kratę szkocką

task ('taesk) s. zadanie (specjalne); lekcja zadana; przedsięwzięcie; v. wyznaczac zadanie; wystawiac na probę; rugac

taskforce ('taesk,fo:rs) s. oddział (grupa) do specjalnego zadania

taskmaster ('taesk,ma:ster) s. nadzorca (kontrolujący wykonanie zadania)

tassel ('taesel) s. kutas; kitka; v. ozdabiac kutasami; kitkami

taste (tejst) s. smak; gust; posmak; zamiłowanie; v. smakowac; kosztowac; czuc smak; miec smak; doznawac (czegoś)

tasteful ('tejstful) adj. gustowny; w dobrym smaku

tasteless ('tejstlys) adj. bez gustu; bez smaku

tasty ('tejsty) adj. smakowity; smaczny

ta-ta (tae'-ta:) exp. do widzenia; pa ! pa !

tattoo (te'tu:) v. bębnic palcami; tatuowac; s. capstrzyk; tatuaž

taught(to:t) v. zob. teach

taunt (to:nt) v. urągac; wymyslac komus; zwymyslac kogos; s. urąganie; wymyslanie; adj. wysoki (np, maszt)

taut (to:t) adj. napięty; naprężony; w dobrej formie; w dobrym stanie

tax (taeks) s. podatek; wysiłek; ciężar; obciążenie; v. opodatkowac; obarczac; obciążac; naweręžac; sprawdzac; wymagac wysiłku; zarzucac cos

taxation (taek'sejszyn) s. opodatkowanie

tax collector ('taekske,lekter) s. poborca podatkowy

taxi ('taeksy\ s. taksówka; v. jechac taksówką;wiezc taksówką

taxidriver ('taeksydrajwer) s. taksówkarz

taximeter ('taeksy,mi:ter) s. licznik (w taksówce); taksometr

taxpayer ('taeks,pejer) s. podatnik

tax return ('taeks,ry'te:rn)s. podatek (zapłata ze sprawozdaniem)

tea (ti:) s. herbata; herbatka; podwieczorek; v. pic i częstowac herbatą

teabag ('ti:baeg) s. woreczek papierowy z herbatą

teach; taught; taught (ti:cz;
to:t; to:t)
teach (ti:cz) v. uczyc (się);
nauczac; wykładac
teacher (ti:czer) s. nauczyciel
teacup ('ti:kap) s. filiżanka
na herbatę
teakettle ('ti:,ketl) s. imbryk; czajnik
team (ti:m) s. zespół; drużyna; zaprzęg; v. zaprzęgać;
jeździc zaprzęgiem
team up ('ti:map) v. łączyc
się razem (do pracy etc.)
teamwork ('ti:młe:rk) s. praca zespołowa
teapot ('ti:pot) s. mały czajnik
tear; tore; torn (teer; to:r;
to:rn)
tear (teer) v. drzec; targac;
rwac; kaleczyc; wydrzec (ranę)
pędzic; s. dziura; rozdarcie;
wybuch pasji; kropla; łza;
(slang) hulanka
tearoom ('ti:ru:m) s. herbaciarnia
tease (ti:z) v. drażnic; nu-
dzic; s. dokuczanie; nudziarstwo
teat (tyt) s. cycek (wulg.:ko-
biecy)
technical ('teknykel) adj.
techniczny; formalny; spekula-
cyjny
technician ('teknyszyn) s.
technik
technique (tek'ni:k) s. technika malowania, rzeźby etc.
tedious ('ti:dies) adj. nudny
teem (ti:m) v. roic się; obfitowac; opróżniac; wylewac
teen (ti:n) s. szkoda; zgryzota
teens (ti:nz) pl. wiek 12 do
18 lat
teeny ('ti:ny) adj. maleńki
teeth (ti:s) pl. zęby; zob.
tooth
teethe (ti:s) v. ząbkowac
teetotaler (ti:'toutler) s.
abstynent
telegram('telygraem)s. telegram

telegraph ('telygra:f) s. telegraf
telephone ('telyfoun) s. telefon; v. telefonowac
telephone booth('telyfoun,bu:s)
s. kabina telefoniczna
telephone call('telyfoun,ko:l)
s. rozmowa telefoniczna
telephone directory ('telyfoun,
dyrektory) s. książka telefoniczna
telephone exchange ('telyfoun-
eksczendż) s. centrala telefoniczna na zagranicę
telephone kiosk ('telyfoun-
kiosk) s. kiosk telefoniczny
teleprinter ('tely,prynter) s.
dalekopis
telescope ('telyskoup) s. teleskop
teletypewriter (,tely'tajpraj-
ter) s. dalekopis
televise ('telywajz) v. nadawac przez telewizję
television ('telywyżyn) v. telewizja
television set('telywyżyn,set)
s. telewizor; odbiornik telewizyjny
televisor ('telywajzer) s.
telewizor
tell;told; told (tel; tould;
tould)
tell (tel) v. (o kims; o czyms):
mowic; opowiadac; powiedziec;
wskazywac; pokazywac; kazac;
poznac; sprawdzic; policzyc;
poznawac; wiedziec; doniesc;
oskarżyc; skarżyc; miec znaczenie; odbijac się na kims;
odróżniac
teller ('teler) s. narrator;
kasjer; liczący głosy
telltale ('teltejl) s. plotkarz; okolicznosc ostrzegaw-
cza; wskaźnik odchylenia
(steru); aparat sprawdzający,
ostrzegawczy; adj. ostrzegawczy; wymowny
temper ('temper) s. usposobienie; humor; gniew; złosc; domieszka;mieszanka; stan; har-
townosc; v.łagodzic; hartowac

temperament ('temprement) s.
temperament; usposobienie;
skala temperowana; temperatura skali
temperance ('temperens) s.
umiarkowanie; powsciągliwosc;
obstynencja; wstrzemięźliwość
temperate ('temperyt) adj.
umiarkowany; powsciągliwy;
wstrzemięźliwy
temperature ('tempereczer) s.
temperatura; ciepłota
tempest ('tempyst) s. burza;
v. zaburzać
tempestuous (tem'pestjues) adj.
burzliwy
temple ('templ) s. świątynia;
skroń; ucho od okularów; rozciągacz tkacki
temporal ('temperel) adj. doczesny; czasowy; skroniowy;
s. kość skroniowa
temporary ('temperery) adj.
chwilowy; tymczasowy
tempt (tempt) v. kusic; nęcic
temptation (temp'tejszyn) s.
pokusa; kuszenie
tempting ('temptyng) adj. ponętny; nęcący; kuszący
ten (ten) num. dziesięc; s.
dziesiątka
tenacious (ty'nejszes) adj.
wytrwały; nieustępliwy; trwa
ły; wierny; czepny; ciągliwy;
mocny; spoisty
tenant ('tenent) s. lokator;
dzierżawca; v. zamieszkiwac;
dzierżawic
tend (tend) v. skłaniac się:
zmierzac; służyc; doglądac;
obsługiwac
tendency ('tendensy) s. skłonnosc; tendencja
tender ('tender) adj. delikatny; miękki; kruchy; wrażliwy;
czuły; niedojrzały; młody;
młodociany; uważający; dba
ły; łamliwy; drażliwy; wywrotny; v. oferowac; przedło
życ; założyc; s. oferta; środek płatniczy; dozorca; tender; statek pomocniczy-zaopatrzeniowy

tenderloin ('tenderloyn) s.
polędwica
tenderness ('tendernyss) s. czu
łosc; dbałosc; delikatnosc
tendon (tenden) s. ścięgno
tendril (tendryl) s. wąs; wic
tenement house (tenymenthaus) s.
dom czynszowy
tennis ('tenys) s. tenis
tennis court ('tenys'ko:rt) s.
kort tenisowy
tense (tens) s. czas (np. przyszły) adj. naprężony; napięty
tension (tenszyn) s. naprężenie;
napięcie; prężnosc
tent (tent) s. namiot
tentacle (tentekl) s. macka;
czułek
tenth (teng) adj. dziesiąty
tenthly (tengly) adv. po dziesiąte
tepee ('ti:pi:) s. namiot indiański (stożkowy)
tepid ('tepyd) adj. letni; ciepławy; bez zapału
term (te:rm) s. okres; czas
trwania; przeciąg; semestr; kadencja; termin; wyrażenie;
okreslenie; kres; v. okreslac;
nazywac;
terms (te:rms) pl. warunki
(kontraktu, porozumienia) stosunki wzajemne
terminal ('te:rmynel) adj. końcowy; terminowy; ostateczny;
s. zakończenie; koncówka;
uchwyt; koncowa stacja
terminate ('te:rmynejt) v. skończyc; zakończyc; kończyc (sie);
ograniczac; upływac; rozwiązywac (umowę); ustawac; wygasac;
upływac; wymawiac pracę
termination (,te:rmy'n ejszyn)
s. koniec; wypowiedzenie (pracy); wygasnięcie; zakończenie;
koncówka
terminus (te:rmynes) s. końcowa stacja; kres; koniec; granica
termite ('te:rmajt) s. termit
terrace ('teres) s. taras; terasa; ulica wzdłuż zbocza;
v. robic terasy

terraced ('terest) adj uformowany w terasy

terrible ('terybl) adj. straszliwy; straszny; okropny

terrific ('te'ryfyk) adj. przerażający; (slang): fantastyczny; pierwszej klasy

terrify ('teryfaj) v. przerażać

territorial (,tery'torjel) adj. terytorialny

territory ('teryto:ry) s. obszar; rejon; (terytorium bez praw stanu np. w USA)

terror ('terer) s. terror; przerażenie; postrach

terrorize ('tereraiz) v. siac strach; przerażać; terroryzowac

test (test) s. proba; sprawdzian; test; egzamin; odczynnik; skorupa; v. sprawdzać; poddawać próbie; oczyszczac (metal)

testament ('testement) s. testament

testify ('testyfaj) v. świadczyć; dawać świadectwo; zaświadczać; poswiadczac

testimonial (,testy'mounjel) s. świadectwo (moralności); polecenie; nagroda w uznaniu zasług

testimony ('testymouny) s. świadectwo

testy ('testy) adj. drażliwy; popędliwy; pobudliwy

tetanus ('tetenes) s. tężec

text (tekst) s. tekst

textbook ('tekstbuk) s. podręcznik

textile ('tekstail) s. tkanina; adj. tkacki; tekstylny

texture ('teksczer) s. budowa; tkanina; struktura; tkanie

than (dzaen) con, aniżeli; niż; od

thank (taenk) v. dziękowac; s. podziękowanie; dzięki

thank you ('taenkju:) exp.; dziękuję

thank you very much ('taenkju:-'wery,macz) exp.:bardzo dziękuję

thankful ('taenkful) adj. wdzięczny; dziękczynny

thankless ('taenklys) adj. niewdzięczny

thanks ('taenks) pl. podziękowanie; dzięki

Thanksgiving Day ('taenksgywyng,dej) s. dzień święta dziękczynienia (USA)

that (daet) adj. & pron. pl. thouse (dzous); tamten; tamta; tamto; ten; ta; to; ów; owa; owo; pl. tamci; tamte; ci; te; owi; owe; adv. tylu; tyle; conj. że; żeby; aby; skoro

thatch (taecz) s. strzecha; v. pokrywac strzechą

thaw (tso:) s. odwilż; rozkrochmalenie się; v. tajac; odtajac; taje; jest odwilż

the (przed samogłoską dy; przed spółgłoską de:, z naciskiem dy:) przyimek okreslony rzadko kiedy tłumaczony; ten; ta; to; pl. ci; te; ten własnie , etc. adv. tym; im...tym

theater ('tieter) s. teatr; kino; widownia; amfiteatr

theatrical (ti:aetrykel) adj. teatralny; sceniczny; aktorski

theatricals (ti:'aetrykels) pl. przedstawienie (amatorskie)

theatrics (ti:'aetryks) s. sztuka teatralna

thee (di:) archaiczna forma; ty używana przez kwakrów

theft (teft) s. kradzież

their (dzeer) zaimek; ich

theirs (dzeers) zaimek dzierzawczy: ich

them (dzem) przypadek zależny od: they , (np.: im; nimi; nich)

theme (ti:m) s. temat; zadanie; wypracowanie

themselves (dzem'selwz) pl.oni sami; one same

then (dzen) adv. wtedy; wówczas; po czym; potem; następnie; później; zatem; zaraz; poza tym; ponadto; conj.a więc; no to;wobec tego; ale przecież; adj.ówczesny;s.przedtem;uprzednio; dotąd; odtąd;

theologian (tie'loudżjen) s.
teolog

theology (tie'oledży) s. teologia

theoretic(al) (tie'retyk-el)
adj. teoretyczny

theory (tiery) s. teoria

therapy (terepy) s. leczenie;
terapia

there (dzeer) adv. tam; w tym;
co do tego; oto; właśnie; potem; tędy; dlatego; z tego;
na to; s. ta miejscowość; to
miasto; to miejsce

thereabout ('dzeerebaut) adv.
w tych stronach; gdzieś tam
mniej więcej; coś około tego

thereafter ('dzeera:fter) adv.
później; odtąd

there are (dzeer'a:r) exp.; są

thereby ('dzeer'baj) adv. przez
to; w ten sposób; skutkiem
tego

therefore ('dzeer,fo:r) adv.
dlatego; zatem więc

therein (,dzeer'yn) adv. w tym;
w nim; w niej

there is (,dzeer'ys) exp.; jest

thereupon ('dzeer,e'pon) adv.
skutkiem tego

therewith (,dzeer'łys) adv.
tym; z tym; w następstwie tego

there you are (,dzeer'ju:,a:r)
exp.; proszę; tu jest to !
tu pan to ma ! etc.

thermometer (ter'momyter) s.
termometr

thermos ('termos) s. termos

these (di:z) pl. od this

thesis ('ti:sys) s. teza; praca dyplomowa; pl. theses
('ti:syz)

they (dzej) pl. pron. oni; one
(ci; którzy)

they say (dzej sej) exp.;podob-
no (mówią)

thick (tyk) adj. gruby; gęsty;
zbity; rzęsisty; stłumiony;
niewyraźny; mętny; ponury;
tępy; ochrypły; (slang): blat-
ny; spoufalony; s. gruba część;
duren; głuptas; adv. gęsto;
grubo; ochryple; tępo

thicken ('tykn) v. pogrubiać
(sie); zagęszczac (się)

thicket ('tykyt) s. gaszcz;
gęstwina

thickness ('tyknys) s. grubość;
warstwa; gęstość

thief (ti:f) s. złodziej;
pl. thieves (ti:ws)

thigh (taj) s. udo

thimble ('tymbl) s. naparstek;
końcówka (metalowa liny)

thimbleful ('tymblful) s. odrobina; naparstek

thin (tyn) adj.cienki (sos;
głos etc). rzadki; szczupły;
słaby (kolor.etc.); (slang):
paskudny; v. rozcieńczać;
szczuplec;przerzedzac(się)

thine (tajn) sob. thy; stara
forma: twój; twoje

thing (tyng) s. rzecz; przedmiot;
uczynek; coś; krzyk mody; warunek; urojenia; przywidzenia;
pl. zwierzęta; rzęczy; odzież;
ubrania; ruchomości; sytuacja;
koniunktura;wszystko; nieruchomości; głupstwa

think; thought; thought (tynk;
'to:t;'to:t)

think (tynk) v. myśleć; pomyśleć;
zastanawiac się; rozważać; rozmyślać (się); wymyślić; wyobrażac sobie; uważać za; mieć zdanie; mieć za; zapomnieć (rozmyślnie); mieć na myśli; rozwiązywać; etc.

think over ('tynk'ouwer) v. przemyśliwać; zastanawiac się

think up ('tynk,ap) v. wymyślać;
wykombinować; rozwiązać

third (te:rd) adj. trzeci

third degree (,te:rd,dy'gri:)
exp.; trzeci stopień(przesłuchi-
wania na policji—głupi, przykry i męczący)

thirdly ('te:rdly) adv. po trzecie

third party (,te:rd'pa:rty) s.
strona trzecia; osoby trzecie

thirdrate ('te:rd'rejt) adj.
trzeciorzędny

Third World ('te:rd'╱e:rld) s.
trzeci swiat (poza Europą ,
Chinami, Indią oraz Ameryką)
thirst ('te:rst) s. pragnienie;
żądza; v. pragnąc
thirsty ('te:rsty) adj. spragniony; żadny; suchy; wyschnię-
ty; (slang): ciężki
this (tys) adj. & pron. pl.
these (ti:z) ten; ta; to; tak;
w ten sposob; tyle; obecny;
bieżący; adv. tak; tak daleko; tyle; tak dużo
thistle ('tysl) s. oset
thorn ('to:rn) s. kolec; ciern;
krzak cierniowy; v. kłuc;
draźnic
thorny ('to:rny)adj. kolczasty;
ciernisty; drazliwy
thorough (terou) adj. dokładny;
zupełny; całkowity; sumienny;
adv. na wskros; na wylot
thoroughbred ('te:rou,bred)
adj. rasowy; czystej krwi;
s. koń rasowy
thoroughfare ('te:rou,feer)
s. arteria komunikacyjna;
przejazd; ulica
thoroughly (te:rouly) adv. zupełnie; dokładnie; całkowicie;
na wskros; sumiennie; gruntownie
those (douz) pl. od that
thou (dau) biblijne: ty
though (tou) conj. chociaż;
chocby; gdyby; adv. jednak;
pomimo tego; przeciez
thought (to:t) v. zob. think;
s, mysl; namysł; zastanowienie
się; pomysł; oczekiwanie; rozwaga; zamiar; pl. zdanie; pogląd; odrobina;troszkę
thoughtful ('to:tful) adj. za-
myslony; zadumany; rozważny;
uważający; dbały; uprzejmy;
(oryginalnie) myslący
thoughtless ('to:tlys) adj.bez-
myslny; nieuważający; nierozważny
thousand ('tauzend) num.tysiąc
thousandth ('tauzendt) adj.
tysięczny

thrash (traesz) s. młocic; walic; bic; prac; dyskutowac;
s. młocenie; walenie
thrashing (traeszyng) s, młocka;
lanie
thread (tred) s. nic; nitka;
przędza; sznurek; wątek; żyłka;
krok (sruby); zwojnik (nici);
gwint; v. nawlekac (igłę);
przetykac; nacinac gwint (zwojnik); przepychac się
threadbare (tredbeer) adj. wytarty; wyswiechtany; wyszarza-
ły
threat (tret) s. grozba; pogrozka
threaten ('tretn) v. grozic;
zagrazac; odgrazac się
threatening ('tretnyng) adj.
grożący; zagrażający; groźny
three (tri:) num. trzy; s.trój-
ka
threefold ('tri:fold) adj.
potrojny
threescore ('tri:sko:r) num.
szescdziesiat
threestage ('tri:stejdż) adj.
trojfazowy; trzystopniowy
thresh (tresz) v. młocic; roz-
trzasac; obgadac szczegołowo;
omowic gruntownie; s. młocka
thresher ('treszer) s. młockarnia
threshing ('treszyng) s. młocenie
threshing machine ('treszyng,me-
'szi:n) s. młockarnia
threshold ('treszould) s. prog
threw (tru:) v. zob. throw
thrice (trajs) adj. trzykrotnie
thriftlees (tryftlys) adj. rozrzutny
thrifty (tryfty) adj. oszczędny; rozrastający się; kwitnący
thrill (tryl) v. przejmowac
(sie); drgac; s. dreszcz;
dreszczyk; drganie; powiesc
sencacyjna; szmer (serca)
thriller (tryler) s. dreszczowiec; powiesc sensacyjna (kry-
minalna); sztuka sensacyjna;
opowiesc sensacyjna

thrilling (trylyŋg) adj. podniecający; przejmujący; sensacyjny
thrive; throve; thriven
(trajw; trouw; trywn)
thrive (trajw) v. dobrze : rosnąc, chowac się, rozwijac się,
miewać się, kwitnąc, prospe-
rowac
thro(tru:) = through
throat (trout) s. gardło; szyja; wlot; gardziel; waskie
przejscie; v. żłobic; żłobko-
wac; mówic gardłowo
throb (trob) v. pulsowac; drgac;
bic; tętnic; rwac; s. pulsowa-
nie; drganie; bicie serca;
dreszcz; warkot maszyny
thrombosis (trom'bousys) s.
skrzep
throne (troun) s. tron; v. tro-
nowac; wprowadzac na tron
throng (tro:ng)s. tłum; tłok;
rzesza; masa; v. tłoczyc się;
zatłaczac; napierac na
throstle (trosl) s. drozd;
przędzarka
throttle ('trotl) s. gardziel;
dławik; przepustnica; zawor
dławiący; v. dusic; regulowac
dławikiem
through (tru:) prep. przez; po-
przez; po; wskros; na wylot;
ze; z; skutkiem; na skutek;za;
dzięki; z powodu; adv. na
wskros; na wylot; adj. przelo-
towy; bezposredni; skończony
(np. życiowo)
throughout ('tru:,aut) prep. po-
przez; przez cały; od początku
do konca; wszędzie; całkowicie;
adv. na wskros
throw (trou) v. zob. thrive
throw; threw; thrown (trou;
tru:, troun)
throw (trou) v. rzucac; ciskac;
zarzucac; zrzucac; skręcac;
powalic; narzucac; modelowac
na kole; odrzucac; marnowac;
s. rzut; ryzyko; szal; narzuta;
uskok

throw up ('trou,ap) v. wymiotowac; rzucac w górę; podrzucac
thrown ('troun) v. zob. throw
thru (tru:) = through
thrum (tram) v. rzępolic; beb-
nic; robic z nitek; odcinac
luzne nitki; s. brzdąkanie;
odcięta nitka; krajka
thrush (trasz) s. drozd; choroba strzałki kopyta końskiego;
plesniawka
thrust; thrust; thrust (trast;
trast; trast)
thrust (trast) v. wpychac;
wsadzac; wtykac; wrazic; pchac
(się); przepychac się; wysuwac (się); szturchac; przebijac; wepchnąc; narzucac (się);
wtracac (się); zadawac pchnięcie; pchnąc; s. pchnięcie;
dzgnięcie; wypad; wypchnięcie;
nacisk; siła : napędu, ciągu,
pędu; zrzut; parcie; uwaga;
przytyk
thud (tad) s. łomot; łoskot
(głuchy); v. łomotac; upadac
z łoskotem
thug (tag) s. bandyta; zbir
thumb (tam) s. kciuk; duży palec; władza (domowa); talent
ogrodniczy; zasada (praktyczna); v. kartkowac; brudzic
palcami; niszczyc; walac; grac
niezgrabnie; prosic o podwiezienie; wyprosic (gestem)
thumb a lift (tam a lyft) v.
prosic o podwiezienie (autostopem)
thumbtack ('tam-taek) s. pi-
neska; pluskiewka
thump ('tamp) s. grzmotnięcie;
v. grzmocic; walic; isc ciężko
thunder ('tander) s. grzmot;
burza; grom; piorun; v.
grzmiec; rzucac gromy; pioru-
nowac; miotac (grozby)
thunderstorm ('tander-sto:rm)
s. burza z piorunami
thunderstruck ('tander-strak)
adj. rażony piorunem; oszołomiony

Thursday ('te:r-zdej) s. czwartek

thus (tas) adv. tak; w ten sposób; tak więc; a zatem

thus far ('tas,fa:r) adv. jak dotąd

thus much ('tas,mach) adv. tyle

thwart ('tło:rt) v. udaremnić; pokrzyżować; psuć szyki; adj. poprzeczny; przeciwny; niepomyślny; s. poprzeczna ławka wioślarska

thy (taj) pron. twój; twoje; zob. thine

tick (tyk) s. kleszcz; tykanie; moment; wsyp; kredyt; sprawne działanie; v. tykać; kupować na kredyt; sprzedawać na kredyt (slang); ustalać sprawne działanie

tick away ('tyke'łej) v. znaczyć tykaniem

tick off ('tykof) v. odliczać; besztać; odfajkować

ticker ('tyker) s. telegraf; zegarek; serce (slang)

ticket ('tykyt) s. bilet; kwit; znaczek; wywieszka; lista kandydatów (USA); v. zaopatrywać w bilet, etykietkę; umieszczać na liście kandydatów

ticket office ('tykyt'ofys) s. kasa biletowa

tickle ('tykl) v. łaskotać; łechtać; swędzić; rozśmieszać; bawić; cieszyć; s. łaskotanie; łechtanie; swędzenie

tidal wave ('tajdelłejw) s. olbrzymia fala przypływu skutkiem trzęsienia ziemi

tide (tajd) n. przypływ & odpływ morza; fala; okres; v. przypływać falą; płynąć z falą; wybrnąć

tidy ('tajdy) adj. schludny; czysty; niemały; spory; s. zbiornik na odpadki; pokrowiec na mebel; v. oporządzić; sporządzać; oporządzać (się); porządkować

tie (taj) v. wiązać; zawiązać;

przywiązać; łączyć; sznurować; remisować; zawrzeć ślub; unieruchomić; s. węzeł; krawat; podkład kolejowy; próg; remis; sznur; rozgrywka; półbucik

tie up ('taj,ap) v. zawiązywać; unieruchamiać

tier (tier) s. piętro; rząd; węzeł; zwój; kondygnacja; rzecz wiążąca; fartuszek; v. spiętrzać się (też warstwami)

tiger ('tajger) s. tygrys; jaguar; kugar; zawadiaka; pracujący zapamiętale

tight (tajt) adj. zaciśnięty; mocny; zwarty; szczelny; spoisty: obcisły; wąski; nabity; wstawiony; zalany; skąpy; niewystarczający; silny; mocny; uparty; adv. zwarcie; ciasno; szczelnie; obciśle; mocno; silnie

tighten ('tajtn) v. zaciskać (się); uszczelniać; napinać (się)

tightfisted ('tajt-,tystyd) adj. sknera; kutwa

tight fitting ('tajt-fytyng) adj. obcisły; opięty

tightrope ('tajt-roup) s. lina akrobatyczna

tights (tajts) pl. trykot baletnicy, akrobaty etc.; w Anglii rajstopy

tigress ('tajgrys) s. tygrysica

tile (tajl) n. dachówka; kafelek; dren; (slang): cylinder; v. pokrywać dachówkami; wykładać kaflami (płytami)

till (tyl) prep. aż do; dopiero; dotychczas; aż; dopóki nie; dotąd; v. uprawiać (ziemię); s. szufladka na pieniądze; kasa podręczna

tilt (tylt) s. przechylenie; przechylr; nachylenie; natarcie kopią; plandeka; daszek; v. przechylać (się); nachylać (się); nacierać kopią; (pełnym) pędem lecieć; zaopatrywać w daszek

timber ('tymber) s. drzewo; budulec; drewno; belka; wręga; las; charakter; v. zaopatrywać w budulec; podpierać belką
timberland ('tymber'laend) s. obszar lasu budulcowego
timberwork ('tymber:če:rk) s. konstrukcja drewniana
timber yard ('tymber,ja:rd) s. skład (drzewa) budulca
time (tajm) s. czas; pora; raz; takt; v. obliczać czas zużyty; ustalać czas; wybierać czas; robić we właściwym czasie; nastawiać (przyrząd); regulować (zegar); synchronizować; harmonizować; trzymać takt; excl.:czas ! (zamykać lokal etc.)
time and again ('tajm end,e'- 'gen) exp.:ciągle; ustawicznie
time bomb ('tajm,bom) s. bomba zegarowa
time is up ('tajm'ys,ap) exp.: koniec (zabawy; rozmowy etc)
timely ('tajmly) adv. na czasie; w porę; adj. aktualny; odpowiedni; właściwy; punktualny
timetable ('tajm,tejbl) s. rozkład jazdy, zajęć etc.
timeless ('tajmlys) adj. wieczny; ponadczasowy (niekończący się)
timid ('tymyd) adj. niesmiały; bojaźliwy
timidity (ty'mydyty) s. bojaźliwość
timorous ('tymeres) adj, bojaźliwy
tin (tyn) s. cyna; blacha; puszka blaszana; blaszanka; folia cynowa; pieniądze; adj. cynowany; blaszany; dziadowski (kubek); v. cynować
tinfoil ('tynfojl) s. folia metalowa; cynfolia; staniol
tinge (tyndż) s. odcień; lekkie zabarwienie;v. zabarwiać lekko
tingle ('tyngl) s. mrowienie; swierzbienie; kłucie; v. czuć kłucie; mrowienie; kłuc

tinkle ('tynkl) v. dzwonić; brzęczec;(siusiać) s. dzwonienie
tinned (tynd) adj. cynowany
tinopener ('tyn,oupner) s. otwieracz puszek (narzędzie)
tint (tynt) s. odcień;zabarwienie; v. zabarwiać
tinware ('tynčeer) s. wyroby blaszane
tiny ('tajny) adj. drobny; malusieński; malutki
tip (typ) s. koniec (np. palca); koniuszek; szczyt; zakończenie; skuwka; okucie; napiwek; poufna informacja; wiadomosć; rada; wskazówka; trącenie; przechylenie; skład śmieci; v. wykańczać koniec; okuwać; przechylać (się);,ważyc; przewracać (się); dać napiwek; informować (poufnie); trącać lekko; dotykać; uderzać ukosem (piłkę); przeważać
tip off ('typ,of) v. ostrzegać
tip-off ('typof) s. poufne ostrzeżenie (informacja)
tipster ('typster) s. człowiek udzielający poufnych informacji (o wyścigach etc.)
tipsy ('typsy) adj. podchmielony; pijany; chwiejny; niepewny
tiptoe ('typtou) s. koniec palca u nogi; v. chodzic na palcach; adv. na palcach (u nóg)
tire ('tajer) v. męczyc (się); nudzić (się); nakładać obręcz, oponą; przystroic; s. obręcz; opona; strój
tired ('tajerd) adj. znęczony; znużony; znudzony
tireless ('tajerlys) adj. niestrudzony
tiresome ('tajersem) adj. męczący; nudny
tissue ('tyszu:) s. tkanka; tkanina; siatka; bibułka
tissue paper (tyszu:,pejper) s. bibułka; papier toaletowy; papier płótnowany

tit (tyt) s. sikora

tit for tat ('tyt,fo:r taet)
exp.: wet za wet

titbit ('tytbyt) s. smakołyk

titilate ('tytylejt) s. łechtac

title ('tajtl) s. tytuł; nagłowek; napis; tytuł rodowy; tytuł prawny; prawo; czystosc złota w karatach

titled ('tajtld) adj. utytułowany

titter ('tyter) v. chichotac; s. chichot

tittle-tattle ('tytl-'taetl) v. plotkowac; s. plotkowanie

to (tu:; tu) prep. do; aż do; ku; przy; w stosunku do; w porównaniu z; w stosunku jak; stosownie do; dla; wobec; względem; za (zależnie od ustalen zwyczajowych)

toad (toud) s. ropucha

to and fro ('tu:end,rou) exp.: tam i z powrotem

toast (toust) s. grzanka; toast; v. robic granki;wznosic toast

tobacco (te'baekou) s. tyton

tobacconist (te'baekounyst) s. sprzedawca wyrobów tytoniowych

toboggan (te'bogen) s. saneczki; v. sankowac sie; spadac (ceny)

today (te'dej) adv. dzisiaj; dzis; s. dzien dzisiejszy

toddle ('todl) v. dreptac; drobic nóżkami; s. drobienie nóżkami; dreptanie; pedrak

toddler ('todler) s. pedrak; berbec

to-do (te'du:) s. zamieszanie; rwetes

toe (tou) s. palec u nogi; nosek; szpic; stopa wału (tamy); wystep z przodu; przednia czesc kopyta; hacel; dno odwiertu; v. kopnac; cerowac palec u ponczochy; podporzadkowac sie; stawac na starcie; stosowac sie do linii (też partyjnej); ukosnie wbijac gwoździe; krzywo chodzic (palcami zbyt do wewnatrz lub na zewnatrz)

toffee ('tofi) s. karmelek

toffy ('tofy) s. karmelek (śmietankowy)

together (te'gedzer) adv. razem; wspólnie; naraz; rownoczesnie

toil (tojl) s. znoj; mozoł; trud; mozolic sie; trudzic sie; harowac

toilet ('tojlyt) s. ustep; toaleta; ubranie; adj. toaletowy

toilet paper ('tojlyt,pejper) s. papier toaletowy

toils (tojlz) s. sidła; matnia

token ('toukn) s. znak; dowod autentycznosci; symbol; pamiątka; żeton; bon; adj. symboliczny; niewiążący

told (tould) v. zob. tell

tolerable ('tolerebl) adj. znosny; nienajgorszy; dosyc zdrowy

tolerance ('tolerens) s. tolerancja; luz; wyrozumiałosc

tolerant ('tolerent) adj. tolerancyjny; wyrozumiały; tolerancki

tolerate ('tolerate) v. znosic; tolerowac; cierpiec

toleration (,tole'rejszyn) s. znoszenie; tolerancja; tolerowanie

toll (toul) s. opłata (np. telefoniczna); myto: mostowe; drogowe; miejski podatek; trybut; danina; dzwonienie; v. uiszczac opłate; wydzwaniac; dzwonic jednostajnie; wabic (zwierzyne)

toll bar ('toulba:r) s. szlaban

tollgate ('toulgejt) s. rogatka wjazdowa na płatny most lub autostrade

tomato (te'mejtou) s. pomidor

tomatoes (te'mejtouz) pl. pomidory

tomb (tu:m) s. grób; grobowiec; v. pochowanie

tombstone (tu:m-stoun) s. kamien nagrobny; nagrobek

tomcat ('tom'kaet) s. kocur

tomorrow (te'mo:rou) s.& adv. jutro

ton (tan) s. tona (2000 funtów) (slang): mnóstwo

tone (toun) s. ton; normalny stan (np. ciała; organizmu); brzmienie; v. stonować się; stroic; harmonizować

tone down ('toun,dałn) v. złagodzic; stonować

tongs (tonz) s. szczypce; kleszcze; obcęgi

tongue (tan) s. język; mowa; ozór; v. dotykać językiem; łajac; mlec językiem

tonic ('tonyk) adj. wzmacniający; elastyczny; krzepiący; s. środek tonizujacy

tonight (te'najt) s. dziś wieczór; dzisiejsza noc; adv. dziś wieczorem; gwara: ubiegłej nocy; wczoraj wieczór

tonnage ('tanydż) n. tonaż; opłata od tony ładunku

tonsil ('tonsel) s. migdałek

tonsillitis (,tonsy'lajtys) s. zapalenie migdałków

tony (touny) adj.(slang):szykowny

too (tu:) adv. tak; także; ponadto; do tego; zbytnio; zanadto; zbyt; za; na dodatek; też

took (tuk) v. zob. take

tool (tu:l) s. narzędzie; obrabiarka; v. obrabiac; oporządzac

tool up ('tu:l,ap) v. oprzyrządzac

tools (tu:ls) pl. przybory; sprzęt

tooth (tu:s) s. ząb; pl. teeth (ti:s) v. uzębiac; wcinac zęby; ząbkować; szczepiac zębami trybów

tooth ache ('tu:s ejk) s. ból zęba

tooth brush ('tu:s,brasz) s. szczotka do zębów

toothless('tu:slys) adj. bezzębny

toothpaste ('tu:spejst) s. pasta do zębów

toothpick ('tu:spyk) s. wykałaczka

top (top) s. wierzchołek; czubek; szczyt; wierzch; powierzchnia; góra; bocianie gniazdo; przykrywka; bąk; fryga; adj. wierzchni; zewnętrzny; górny; wyższy; najwyższy; szczytowy; maksymalny; v. nakrywać; wieńczyc; uwieńczać; przewyższać; stanowic wierzch; osiągnąć szczyt; ścinać szczyt; przeskoczyc (przez cos); położyc kres; mierzyc wysokosc; wznosic się

topaz ('toupez) s. topaz

topic ('topyk) s. temat (rozmowy)

topple ('topl) v. przechylać; wywracac

topple down ('topldałn) v. przewrócic

top secret (,topsi:kryt) adj. ściśle tajny

topsy-turvy ('topsy'te:rwy) adj. do góry nogami; v. przewracac do góry nogami; s. rozgardiasz; bałagan; galimatias

torch (to:rcz) s. pochodnia; znicz; kaganek; palnik (do lutowania etc.)

tore (to:r) v. zob. tear

torment ('to:rment) s. męka; udręka; (to:r'ment) v. męczyc; dręczyc

torn (to:rn) v. zob. tear

tornado (,to:r'nejdou) s. trąba powietrzna; tornado

torrent ('to:rent) s. potok (rwacy); ulewny deszcz; burza

torsion ('to:rszyn) s. skręt; skręcanie

tortoise ('to:rtes) s. żółw (słodkowodny)

torture ('to:rczer) s. tortura; męka; v. torturować; męczyc; dręczyc; wykręcać; przekręcac

tosh (tosz) s. bzdury; brednie; banialuki

toss (to:s) v. rzucać się;
podrzucać; zarzucać; podnosić;
niepokoić; kłopotać; przewracać się (w łóżku); podbijać
(piłkę); wypaść z pokoju;
kołysać się na boki; s. rzut;
losowanie; upadek (z konia)
toss about (,to:s e'baut) v.
przewracać się (po czyms)
toss up ('to:s,ap) v. przewracać; grać w orła i reszkę
toss-up ('to:sap) s. 50%
prawdopodobieństwa; orzeł
czy reszka ?;rzecz wątpliwa
total ('total) a. ogólny; zupełny; całkowity; totalny;
kompletny; v. zliczać; wynosić ogółem; (slang): niszczyc
całkowicie (np. samochód
w wypadku)
totalitarian (tou,taely'tear-
jen) adj. totalitarny; tota-
listyczny; s. totalista
totter ('toter) v. chwiać się;
zataczać się; s. chwianie
się; zataczanie się (dziecka)
touch (tacz) v. dotykać; stykać (się); wzruszac (się);
poruszać (coś); brać; wydobywać; zabarwiać;lekko uszka-
dzać; cechować; mierzyć; retuszować; rabnąć kogoś na
pieniądze (slang); s. dotyk;
dotknięcie; pociągnięcie;
odrobina; kontakt; lekka (choroba); rys; nuta (np.złości);
obmacywanie;cecha; probierz;
naciąganie na pieniądze(slang)
touch down ('tacz,dałn) v. lądować;uzyskiwać 6 punktów
touch down (taczdałn) s. lądowanie;gol w futbolu(6 punktów)
touching ('taczyng) adj. wzruszający; rozrzewniający; adv.
odnośnie (do czegoś)
touchy ('taczy) adj. drażliwy;
obraźliwy; przewrażliwiony
tough (taf) adj. twardy;trudny;
ciężki; łobuzerski; adv. trudno; s. człowiek: trudny, twardy; łobuz; chuligan

tour (tuer) s. objazd; wycieczka; tura; przechadzka; służba
(wojskowa); v. objeżdżać; ob-
wozić
tourist ('tueryst) s. turysta;
klasa turystyczna
tourist-agency ('tueryst'ejdżensy) s. biuro podróży
tournament ('tuernement) s.
turniej
tousle ('tauzl) v. szarpać;
mierzwić; czochrać; targać;
s. rozczochrane włosy;rozczo-
chranie
tow (tou) v. holować; ciągnąć;
s. holowanie; lina holownicza;
przedmiot holowany; włókna
lniane; paździory
towards (to:rdz; 'tołerdz) prep.
ku; w kierunku; dla; w celu;
na (coś)
tow-boat ('taubout) s. holownik
towel ('tauel) s. ręcznik;
v. wycierać ręcznikiem
tower ('tauer) s. wieża; wznosić (się); sterczeć; wzbijać
się
town (tałn) s. miasto
town councilor (,tałn'kaunsyler)
s. radny miejski
town hall ('tałn,ho:l) s. ratusz
towrope ('touroup) s. lina
holownicza
toy (toj) s. zabawka; cacko;
v. bawić się; cackać się; robić niedbale; flirtować (też
np. z pomysłem)
toxic ('toksyk) adj. trujący;
jadowity
trace (trejs) s. ślad;postronek;
drążek przekaznikowy; v. iść
śladami; kopiować rysunek;
przypisywać czemuś; wytyczać;
nakreślać; kreślić
track (traek) s.tor; koleina;
ślad; trop; bieżnia; rozstaw
kół; v. śledzic; tropić; zostawiać ślady; zabłocić; zawalać; zakładać tor; mieć
rozstęp kół; ciągnąć liną
z brzegu

track down ('traek,dałn) v.
wytropic; wysledzic; schwytac
track and field events ('traek-
,end-fi:ldy'wents) s. lekkoatletyka
track events (traek y'wents)
s. biegi; zawody na bieżni
traction engine (traekszyn-
endżyn) s. lokomotywa; pociągowy
motor; traktor
tractor ('traekter) s. ciągnik;
traktor
trade (trejd) s. zawód; zajęcie;
rzemiosło; handel; wymiana;
klientela; branża; kupiectwo;
v. handlowac; wymieniac; frymarczyc; przewozic towary;
kupczyc; przehandlowac
trademark ('trejd,ma:rk) s.
znak ochronny; v. przybijac
znak ochronny; rejestrowac
znak ochronny
trader ('trejder) s. handlowiec;
statek handlowy; spekulator
giełdowy
trade-union ('trejd'ju:njen)
s. związek zawodowy
trade unionist ('trejd'ju:n-
jenyst) s. działacz związku
zawodowego
tradition (tre'dyszyn) s. tradycja
traditional (tre'dyszynel) adj.
tradycyjny
traffic ('traefyk) s. ruch(kołowy, pasażerski,towarowy,
telegraficzny, telefoniczny,
drogowy, etc.); v. handel
czyms; frymarczyc; kupczyc
traffic island ('traefyk-aj-
lend) s. wysepka na jezdni
traffic jam('traefyk-dżaem)
s. zator ruchu
traffic lights ('traefyk-
lajts) pl. semafory uliczne
traffic regulation ('traefyk,re-
gju'lejszyn) s. przepisy ruchu
traffic sign ('traefyk,sajn)
s. znak drogowy
traffic-cop ('traefyk,kop) s.
policjant ruchu (drogowego)

tragedy ('traedżydy) s. tragedia
tragic ('traedżyk) adj. tragiczny
tragical ('traedżykel) = tragic
trail (trejl) v. pociągnąc (się);
powlec (się);holowac; wlec (się)
pozostawac w tyle; isc za tro-
pem; scigac; wydeptywac (sciez-
kę); nosic (karabin poziomo
przy boku); s. szlak; scieżka;
trop; ogon; smuga; struga;
bruzda; koleina
trailer ('trejler) s. przyczepa
(do samochodu); przyczepa to-
warowa, mieszkalna, turystyczna, etc.; maruder; pnąca (się)
roslina
train (trejn) v. szkolic; kształcic; przyuczac; wytresowac;
cwiczyc (się); trenowac (się);
kierowac na kogos (np. wzrok);
wlec; s. pociąg; tren; ogon;
sznur; szereg; następstwo;
orszak; swita; porządek; wątek;
łańcuch
trainer ('trejner) s. trener;
instruktor; samolot szkolny
training ('trejnyng) s. zaprawa; trening; cwiczenie; szkolenie
trait (trejt) s. cecha
traitor ('trejtor) s. zdrajca
tram (traem) s. tramwaj
tramp (traemp) v. stąpac; włó-
czyc się; wędrowac pieszo;
isc pieszo; s. włóczęga;tramp;
wędrowiec; statek (nieregular-
nej żeglugi)
trample ('traempl) v. deptac
trance (tra:ns) s. trans; uniesienie; ekstaza
tranquil ('traenkłyl) adj. spokojny
tranquility ('traen'kłylyty) s.
spokój
tranquilize ('traenkłylajz) v.
uspokajac
tranquilizer ('traenkłylajzer)
s. srodek uspakajający
transact (traen'saekt) v. załatwiac; pertraktowac; przeprowadzac

transaction (traen'saekszyn)
s. transakcja; przeprowadze-
nie sprawy; pl. sprawozdania
naukowe; rozprawy
transalpine (traens'aelpajn)
adj. transalpejski
transatlantic (traenzet'laentyk) adj. transatlantycki
transcend (traen'send) v.,
przewyższać; prześcignąć;
górować
transcribe (traens'krajb) v.
nagrywać na taśmie; przepisywać
transcript ('traenskrypt) s.
kopia; transkrypcja
transfer (traens'fe:r) y.
przemieścić; przenieść (się);
przewozić; przekazać; s.prze-
niesienie; przewóz; przedruk;
przekaz; przelew; odstąpienie
transferable (traens'fe:rebl)
adj. przenośny
transform (traens'fo:rm) v.
przekształcić; zmienić postać
transformation (,traensfer'-
'mejszyn) s. przekształcanie;
przeobrażenie
transfuse (traens'fjuz) v.
przelać; przetoczyć (krew)
transfusion (traens'fjużyn) s.
transfuzja
transgress (traens'gres) v.
naruszyć; zgrzeszyć
transgression (traens'greszyn)
s. naruszenie; grzech; wykroczenie
transgressor (traens'greser)
s. grzesznik
transient ('traenzjent) adj.
przechodni; przejeżdżający;
przelotny
transistor (traen'syster) s.
tranzystor
transit ('traensyt) s.przejazd;
przelot; przewóz; tranzyt;
teodolit
transition (traen'syszyn) s.
przejście; zmiana
transitive ('traensytyw) adj.
przechodni

translate (traens'lejt) v. przetłumaczyć; przełożyć
translation (traens'lejszyn)
s. tłumaczenie; przekład
translator (traens'lejter) s.
tłumacz
translucent (traenz'lu:sent)
adj. przeswiecający; pół-
przezroczysty
transmission (traenz'myszyn) s.
przekładnia; transmisja
transmit (traenz'myt) v. przekazywać; nadawać; transmitować
transmitter (traenz'myter) s.
nadajnik; przekaźnik
transparent (traens'peerent)
adj. przezroczysty
transpire (traens'pajer) v. pocić się; wyparować; okazywać
się; zdarzyć się
transplant (traens'pla:nt) v.
przeszczepiać; przesadzać;
s. przesadzanie; przeszczep
transport (traens'po:rt) v.
przewozić; zachwycać; s.prze-
wóz; zachwyt; uniesienie
transportation (,traenpo:r'tejszyn) s. przewóz; transport;
deportacja; zesłanie
trap (traep) s. pułapka; potrzask; sidła; zasadzka; podstęp; syfon; skała wylewna;
(slang): jadaczka; pl.:manatki;
v. złapać w pułapkę; zaopatrywać w pułapkę; zatrzymywać
(w czymś); przykrywać czapra-
kiem; puszczać rzutki
trap-door ('traep'do:r) s.
drzwi zapadowe; zapadnia
trapeze (tre'pi:z) s. trapez
trapper ('traeper) s. traper;
myśliwy; zastawiający pułapki;
nadzorca szybów powietrznych
w kopalni
trappings (traepyŋgz) s.ozdoby;
strój ozdobny; czaprak
trash (traesz) s. śmieci; ru-
pieci; tandeta; odpadki; bzdury; hołota; v. obdzierać (z
liści, gałązek)

travel ('traewl) v. podróżować
(też za interesem); poruszać
się (części maszyny); przesuwać się; biec (w terenie);
przechodzic (oczami po czyms);
poruszać się żwawo; błądzić;
s. (daleka) podróż; ruch (po-
jazdów); suw (maszynowy);
przesunięcie
travel agency ('traewl'ejdżensy)
s. biuro podróży
traveler ('traewler) s. podróżnik; wodzik nitkowy; komiwojażer
traveler's check ('traewlers,-
,czek) s. z góry wykupiony
czek do użytku w podróży
traveling bag ('traewlyng,baeg)
s. torba podrożna
traverse (trae'we:rs)v. przecinać; przesuwać na bok; przechodzic; omawiać; pokrzyżować;
zaprzeczyc formalnie; nakiero-
wywać (działo); obracać (się)
jak na osi
travesty ('traewysty) s. trawe-
stia; parodia; v. trawestować;
parodiować
trawl (tro:l) s. włok; włok;
trał; niewód; siec - worek do
holowania;v.ciagnąć niewód; łowic niewodem, włókiem, wędką
ciagnioną za łodzią
trawler ('tro:ler) s. trawler
tray (trej) s, taca; szufladka
(też wkładowa)
treacherous ('treczeres) adj.
zdradziecki; niebezpieczny;
zdradliwy; zawodny; perfidny
treachery ('treczery) s. zdrada; zdradzieckość; zdradliwość;
perfidia
treacle ('tri:kl) s. syrop; melasa; sok (drzewny)
tread; trod; tro(den), (tred;
trod; 'trodn)
tread (tred) v. deptać; stapać
(po czyms); nadepnąć; tłoczyc;
wdeptywać; isc (ścieżką); wydeptać (ścieżkę) ; gniesć;
s. stąpanie; krok; podnóżek;

guma opony dotykająca jezdni;
szyna; bieżnik; podeszwą (dotykająca ziemi); stopień
treadle ('tredl) s. pedał;
v. pedałować
treadmill ('tredmyl) s. kierat
(cylindryczny ze stopniami)
treason('tri:zn) s. zdrada
treasure ('treżer) s. skarb;
v. zaskarbiac; cenić; strzec
skarbu
treasure up ('treżer,ap) v.
przechowywać jak skarb
treasurer ('treżerer) s. skarbnik
treasury ('treżery) s. urząd
skarbowy; skarbnica
Treasury Department ('treżery,-
,dy'pa:rtment) s. ministerstwo
skarbu (USA)
treat (tri:t) v. traktować; po-
traktować; obchodzić się z
kims; uważać kogos za; brać
cos (za żart); leczyc cos; poddawac działaniu; pertraktować;
fundować (komus); s. przyjęcie;
uczta; majówka; poczęstunek;
zabawa; przyjemność; rozkosz
treatise ('tri:tys) s. traktat;
rozprawa
treatment ('tri:tment) s. traktowanie; leczenie
treaty ('tri:ty) s. traktat;
układ; umowa
treble ('trebl) adj. potrójny;
wysoki; ostry; przenikliwy;
sopranowy; s. sopran; wysoki
dzwięk; v. potrajać (się)
tree (tri:) s. drzewo; forma;
kopyto; rama siodła; belka;
nadproże; krokiew; szubienica;
v. zapędzić (na drzewo); wsa-
dzic (na kopyto)
treeless ('tri:lys) adj. bez-
drzewny
tree-trunk ('tri:,trank) s.
pien roslina trójlistna;
trefoil ('trefojl) s. koniczyna trójlistna;adj.trójlistny
trellis ('trely) s, krata; altana; v, kratować winorosl;
nadawać forme kraty

tremble ('trembl) v. trząść
się; drżec; dygotac; s.drże-
nie; drżączka
tremendous (try'mendes) adj.
straszny; olbrzymi
tremor ('tremer) s. drżenie;
drganie; trzęsienie (ziemi)
tremulous ('tremjules) adj.
drżący
trench (trencz) s.rów; okop;
bruzda; cięcie; rów strzelec-
ki; v. kopac rów; okopywac
się; kłasc do rowu; żłobic;
ciąc; przecinac; podkopywac
się; graniczyc
trench up ('trencz,ap) v.
wdzierac się (bezczelnie)
w cudze (prawa etc.)
trend (trend) s. dążnosc; ogól-
na tendencja; ogólny kierunek;
v. dążyc; miec tendencję;
kształtowac się; ciągnąc się
trespass ('trespas) v. wdzierac się w cudze; naduzywac;
naruszac; wykraczac; grze-
szyc; v. przekroczenie; wykroczenie; grzech; szkoda wy-
rządzona na cudzym terenie
trespasser ('trespaser) s.
człowiek naruszający przepisy,prawo (czyjes)
tress (tres) s. warkocz; v.za-
platac warkocz
trestle ('tresl) s. kozioł;
kobylica; most filarowy
trial ('trajel) s. próba; proces sądowy; zmartwienie; zawody eliminacyjne; adj. próbny; doswiadczalny
trial and error ('trajel end'-
'erer) exp.: chaotyczne próby
(w nieznane)
triangle ('trajaengl) s. trój-
kąt
triangular (traj'aengjular) adj.
trójkątny
triangulate (traj'aengjulejt)
v. mierzyc (trójkatami) przy
pomocy triangulacji
tribe (trajb) s. plemię; szczep
tribunal (traj'bju:nl) s. try-
bunał ; sąd

tribune ('trybju:n) s. trybuna;
mównica; gazeta; trybun (ludu)
tributary ('trybjutery) adj.
pomocniczy; płacący daninę;
haracz; s. dopływ; kraj płac-
cący daninę
tribute ('trybju:t) s. haracz;
danina
trick (tryk) s. podstęp; chwyt;
sztuczka; sposób; nawyk; maniera; psota; fortel; (slang):
dziecko; dziewczynka; v. oszukac; okpic; wyłudzic; płatac
figla; zawodzic; zaskakiwac
trick up ('tryk,ap) s. wystroic
trickle ('trykl) v. sączyc (się);
przeciekac; przesączyc; puszczac ciurkiem; kroplami;
s. struga (mała)
tricky ('tryky) adj. podstępny;
chytry; sprytny; trudny; zawiły; zręczny
tricycle ('trajsykl) s. rower
na trzech kołach
trifle ('trajfl) s. drobiazg;
drobnostka; błachostka; bagatela; odrobina; głupstewko; byle
co; stop cyny i ołowiu; biszkopt z kremem; v. nie brac po-
ważnie; poflirtowac; baraszko-
wac; paplac; bagatelizowac
trifling ('trajflyng) adj. płoc-
chy; błachy; znikomy
trigger ('tryger) s. spust;
cyngiel; zapadka; v. pociągac
za spust; wywoływac; dawac początek; zaczynac (akcję)
trill (tryl) s. trel; wibrująca
spółgłoska; v. wymawiac z wi-
bracją; trząść głosem; trelo-
wac; wymawiac wibrując
trillion ('tryljen) = USA billion ('byljen) num. trylion
trim (trym) v. oporządzac;
usuwac niepotrzebne (gałęzie;
tłuszcz etc.); przybierac (li-
stwą; tasmą etc); rozkładac
poprawnie ładunek; poprawiac
(opinię); byc oportunista;
zmyc komus głowę; dac komus lanie; wyprowadzic w pole; besztac; rugac; s. stan; forma;

nastrój; gotowosc; porządek;
strój; ozdoby; listwy; tasmy;
wstążki do poprawienia wyglądu; dekoracja wystawy; oporzą-
dzenie; obcięcie; równowaga
lotu; wyposażenie wnętrza
(np. samochodu, domu etc,)
adj. schludny; porządny;
uporządkowany; wysprzątany
trimming ('trymyŋg) s. ozdoby;
uporządkowanie; przystrzyżenie;
garnirowanie
trimmings ('trymyŋgs) s. zrzyn-
ki i obrzynki z przybierania;
dodatki do potraw; obcinki
Trinity ('trynyty) s.Trójca Sw.
trinket ('tryŋkyt) s. ozdóbka
(na suknie); swiecidełko;
błahostka
trip (tryp) s. podróż; wycieczka; jazda; trans narkomana;
potknięcie; podstawienie nogi;
zgrabny krok; wyzwalanie za-
padkowe lub wychwytowe; błąd;
pomyłka; v. potknąc się; isc
lekkim krokiem; drobic nóżkami;
tanczyc (lekko); pomylic się;
podstawiac noge; złapac na błędzie; wyzwalac; odczepiac kotwicę; przesuwac wychwytem kot-
wicowym; obracac reje; spuszczac nagle częsc maszyny
tripe (trajp) s. flaki (też potrawa); byle co; paskudztwo;
lichota
triple (tripl) adj. potrójny;
s. potrójna ilosc; trójka;
v. potrajac (się)
triplets ('tryplyts) pl. trojacz-
ki
tripod ('trajpod) s. trójnóg;
statyw
triumph ('trajemf) s. triumf;
v. triumfowac
triumphal (traj'amfel) adj.
triumfalny
triumphant (traj'amfent) adj.
zwycięski; triumfalny
trivial ('trywiel) adj. trywialny; błahy; płytki; banalny;
znikomy
trod (trod) v. zob. tread

trodden ('trodn) v. zob. tread
trolley car ('troly car) s.
tramwaj; wywrotka (woz)
trombone (trom'boun) s. puzon
troop (tru:p) s. grupa; gromada; trupa teatralna; rota;
pół szwadronu; s. isc gromadą;
gromadzic się; formowac w ro-
ty (pułk)
trophy ('troufy) s. trofeum
tropic ('tropyk) adj. podzwrotnikowy; tropikalny; s. zwrotnik
tropical ('tropykel) adj. tropikalny; gorący; namiętny
trot (trot) s. kłus; trucht;
bryk (szkolny); (slang): biegunka
trouble ('trabl) s. kłopot;
zmartwienie; zaburzenie; niepokój; trud; dolegliwosc; fatyga; bieda; awaria; uszkodzenie; defekt; v. martwic (się);
dręczyc (się); dokuczac; niepokoic (się); kłopotac (się)
troublesome ('trablsem) adj.
kłopotliwy
trough (trof) s. koryto; rynna;
rów (też między falami); niec-
ka; łęk; synklina
trouser leg ('trauserleg) s.
nogawka
trousers ('trauzez) pl. spodnie
trouseau ('tru:sou) s. wyprawa
(slubna)
trout (traut) s. pstrąg; v. łowic pstrągi
truant ('tru:ent) s. wagarowicz;
opuszczający pracę; adj. próz-
niacki; wałęsajacy (się); v.
chodzic na wagary; opuszczac
pracę
truce (tru:s) s. rozejm; zawieszenie broni
truck (trak) s. ciężarowka;
taczki; wózek; podwozie na kołach; lora; drobne towary; warzywa; wymiana; interes; smieci; brednie; stosunki z kims;
v. przewozic wozem; ładowac na
wóz; wymieniac się z kims; obnosic towar; utrzymywac stosunki z kims

truck farm ('trak,fa:rm) s.
gospodarstwo warzywne
trudge (tradż) s. trudny marsz;
v. trudzić się marszem; odbywać z trudem drogę
true (tru:) adj. prawdziwy;
wierny; ścisły; dokładny; prawdomówny; czysty; faktyczny;
szczery; lojalny; dobrze dopasowany; s. prawda; właściwe
położenie; v. regulować; wyregulować; adv. prawdziwie; dokładnie; exp.:to jest prawda !
truly ('tru:ly) adv. prawdziwie;
dokładnie
true-blue ('tru:blu:) adj. bezkompromisowy; prawdziwie oddany
trump (tramp) s. atut; as; zuch;
złoty człowiek; trąba; v. bić
atutem; roztrąbić
trump up ('tramp,ap) v. wyssać
z palca; zmyślać (zarzuty);
preparować (zarzuty)
trumpet ('trampyt) s. trąbka;
dźwięk; trębacz; v. grać na
trąbie; trąbić; roztrąbić
truncheon ('tranczen) s. pałka
policjanta; buława marszałka
trunk (trank) s. pień; trzon;
tułów; tors; kadłub; główny kanał; główna linia; trąba słoniowa; kufer; bagażnik;
pl. spodnie (krótkie)
trunk line ('trank-lajn) s.
linia międzymiastowa (też telefoniczna w Anglii)
trunk road ('trank-roud) s.
szosa główna
truss (tras) s. wieżba; wspornik;
kratownica; wiązanie dachowe;
wiązka (siana); pas przepuklinowy; v. związać (np. dach);
przywiązać; wieszać (zbrodniarza)
trust (trast) s. pewność; zaufanie; wiara; nadzieja; kredyt;
opieka; powiernictwo; trust;
v. zaufać; mieć zaufanie; ufać;
wierzyć; polegać (na pamięci
swojej etc.) powierzać; kredytować

trustful ('trastful) adj. ufny
trusting ('trastyng) adj. ufny;
pełen zaufania
trustworthy ('trast,łe:rty) adj.
godny zaufania; pewny
truth (tru:s) s. prawda; prawdziwość; rzetelność
truthful ('tru:sful) adj. prawdomówny; prawdziwy (np. opis)
truths (tru:sz) pl. prawdy
try (traj) v. próbować; wypróbować; sądzić; sprawdzić; kosztować; doświadczyć; starać się;
męczyć; s. próba. usiłowanie;
wysiłek
trying (trajyng) adj. przykry;
męczący; nieznośny; irytujący;
ciężki
try on ('traj,on) s. przymierzać
try out ('traj,aut) v. wypróbowywać
T-square ('ti:,skłeer) s. węgielnica
tub (tab) s. balia; ceber; kadź;
wanna; kąpiel; łódź terningowa
(wiosłowa); oszalowanie;
v. wsadzać do wanny; prać;
szalować
tube (tju:b) s. rura; wąż; dętka; tubka; tunel (kolei podziemnej); v. zamykać w rurze;
zaopatrywać w rury; nadawać
kształt rury
tuberculosis (tjube:rkju:lousys) s. gruźlica
tuck (tak) v. wtykać; wsuwać;
podwijać; zawijać (rąbek);
otulać; zbierać w fałdy; obrębiać; schować; (slang): pałaszować; wcinać; wieszać
(skazańca); s. fałd; fałda;
obręb; koncha
tuck (takyn) v. otulać
(w łóżku)
tuck up ('tak,ap) v. podkasać
Tuesday ('tju:zdy) s. wtorek
tuft (taft) s. pęk; pęczek;
kiść; kępa; kitka; bródka;
pikowanie; v. robić pęki; dawać pęki; rosć pękami; pikować

tug (tag) v. ciągnąć (z trudem)
holować; wciągać; s. holownik;
gwałtowne pociągnięcie
tug-of-war ('tag,ow łor) s.
przeciąganie liny (próba sił;
zawody); zażarta walka o przewagę
tuition (tju'yszyn) s. czesne;
nauczanie; lekcje (płatne)
tulip ('tju:lyp) s. tulipan
tumble ('tambl) v. upaść; zwalić (się); potknąć się; ząta-
czać się; kołysać się; hustać
się; wywalić się; gramolić się;
rzucać się; biegać na oślep;
cisnąć; zwichrzyć; (slang):
kapować; iść do łóżka; v.zwa-
lenie; pobicie rekordu; upadek;
sztuka akrobatyczna; bałagan
tummy ('tamy) s. żołądek;
brzuch (dziecka)
tumor ('tu:mer) s. tumor;
obrzęk; guz ; nowotwór
tumult ('tu:malt) s. zgiełk;
wrzawa; tumult; podniecenie;
zaburzenie
tumultuous ('tu:altjues) adj.
burzliwy; podniecony; hałasliwy
tun (tan) s. beczka; kadź (252
galonów); v. wlewać do beczki;
przechowywać w beczce
tuna ('tu:na) s. tuńczyk
tune (tu:n) s. melodia; nastrój;
harmonia; v. stroić; dostroić;'
harmonizować; nucić
tune in ('tu:n,yn) v. nastawiać
(radio etc.)
tune up ('tu:n,ap) v. nastrajać
(np. motor)
tunnel ('tanl) s. tune;; nora;
v. przekopywać tunel, korytarz,
norę; przekopywać się
turbine ('te:rbyn) s. turbina
turbot ('te:rbet) s. skarptur-
bot (ryba)
turbulent ('te:rbjulent) adj.
wzburzony; burzliwy; gwałtowny;
buntowniczy
turf (te:rf) s. torf; darń;
v. pokrywać darniną; (slang):
drałować (piechotą)
Turk (te:rk) adj. turecki

turkey ('te:rky) s. indyk;
v.mówić bez ogródek
Turkish ('te:rkysz) adj. turecki
Turkish bath ('te:kysz,ba:s)
s. parówka; kąpiel parowa;
łaźnia
turmoil (te:rmojl) s. zamieszanie; zgiełk; niepokój; podniecenie
turn (te:rn) v. odwrócić (się);
odkręcić (się); przekręcać
(się); skręcać (się); zwracać
(się); odwracać (się); odpierać
(atak); napadać; zmieniać się;
nawracać (się); popełniać
(zdradę); stawać się (np. kato-
likiem); wyświadczać; obracać;
kierować; robić skręt; wyprawiać; odprawiać; toczyć (na
kole); puścić w ruch; okazać
się; zdarzać się; zwolnić; wyganiać; wyrzucać etc.
s. obrót; kolej; z kolei; po
kolei; tura; zakręt; zwrot;
skręt; punkt zwrotny; przełom;
kształt; forma; przechadzka;
transakcja; wstrząs; atak;
przysługa; numer (popisowy);
kolejność; postępowanie wobec
kogoś
turn away ('te:rn,e'łej) v. odwracać się od ; porzucić
turn back ('te:rn,baek) v. za-
wrócić (z drogi)
turn down ('te:rn,dałn) v. od-
mówić; przyciszać; odrzucać
turn off ('te:rn,of) v. zakręcić (kurek); skręcić; wyłączac
(światło). odprawić
turn on ('te:rn,on) v. puszczać
(wodę); włączać (światło); od-
kręcać (kurek)
turn out ('te:rn,aut) v. wyrzucać (za drzwi); wyrabiać; zwalniać (z pracy)
turn over ('te:rn'ouwer) v. odwracać; rozważać; mieć obrót;
wydawać (policji);przekazywać
turn round ('te:rn raund) v.
przekręcać; odwracać; zmieniać
przekonania ;przekabacić

turn to ('te:rn,tu) v. zabrać
się (do czegoś)
turn up ('te:rn,ap) v. odwracać;
zawinąć (rękawy); podkręcać;
przychodzić; zgłosić się;
przytrafić (się)
turncoat ('te:rn,kout) s. zdrajca
turning point ('te:rnyng,poynt)
s. punkt zwrotny
turnip ('te:rnyp) s. rzepa
turnout ('te:rnaut) s. stawie-
nie się; ilość obecnych;ekwipunek
turnover ('te:rn,ouwer) s. zmiana; kapotaż; przewrócenie; placek; przemieszczanie (ludzi,rzeczy
turnpike ('te:rn,pajk) s. kołowrót; rogatka;autostrada(płatna)
turnstile ('te:rnstajl) s. koło-
wrot(do wchodzenia pojedyńczo)
turnup ('te:rnap) s. traf; zamieszanie; część wywrócona;
coś podwiniętego; podwinięcie
turpentine ('te:rpentajn) s.
terpentyna; v. terpentynować;
zbierać terpentynę
turret ('te:ryt) s. wieżyczka;
imak wielonożowy
turtle ('te:rtl) s. żółw (morski)
turtledove ('te:rtl,daw) s.
turkawka
tusk (task) s. kieł; ząb (u bro-
ny); v. bość; kłuć; rozdzierać
kłami
tutor ('tu:ter) s. nauczyciel
prywatny; korepetytor; opiekun
(studentów); v. uczyć kogoś;
mieć opiekę nad kims; powsciagać
(się); być korepetytorem; uczyć
się pod nadzorem nauczyciela
tutorial ('tu:terjel) adj. wychowawczy; opiekuńczy
TV (ti:wi:) s. telewizja
tuxedo (tak'si:dou) s. smoking
(USA)
twang (tłaeng) s. brzęk (struny);
mówienie przez nos; v. brzęczec;
rzępolic; brzdąkać; mówic przez
nos
tweed(tłi:d) s. materiał wełniany lub wełniano-bawełniany z
szorską powierzchnią

tweet (tłi:t) s. ćwierkanie;
v. ćwierkać
tweezers (tli-zez) s. szczypczyki (kosmetyczne itp.)
twelfth (tłelfs) adj. dwunasty
twelve (tłelw) num. dwanaście;
s. dwunastka
twentieth ('tłentyjes) adj.
dwudziesty
twenty (tłenty) num. dwadzies-
cia; s. dwudziestka
twice (tłajs) adv. dwa razy;
podwojnie; dwukrotnie
twiddle ('tłydl) s. obracanie;
v. kręcić; obracać; przebierać palcami; próżnować
twig (tłyg) v. zrozumiec; po-
łapać się; spostrzec; zauważyć; rozpoznawać; s. gałązka;
różdżka czarodziejska
twilight ('tłajlajt) s. zmrok;
półcień; półmrok; zmierzch
twin (tłyn) s. bliźniak; adj.
bliźniaczy; v. rodzić się jako bliźnieta; łączyć (się)
ściśle ze sobą
twin-engined ('tłyn'endżynd)
adj. dwumotorowy
twinkle (tłynkl) v. migotać;
błyszczeć; mrugać; s. migotanie; błysk; mrugnięcie
twirl (tłe:rl) v. wirować;
kręcić (się); s. wirowanie;
kręcenie się; zakrętas; piruet
twist (tłyst) v. skręcać (się);
zwijać (się); zwichnąć (się);
zawirować; wykrzywiać (twarz);
przekręcać; pokręcić (się);
wic (się); powikłać (się);
tańczyć (twista); wykręcać;
przewijać się (przez tłum)
s. skręt; szpagat; przędza;
lina (skręcona); splot; obrót;
przekręcenie (znaczenia);
zwichnięcie; skłonność;
strucla
twitch(tłytcz)v. szarpać; wyrwać; wydrzec; wykrzywić (się);
poruszyć się gwałtownie;
s. skurcz; szarpnięcie;pociag-
nięcie(za rękaw);drgawka; tik;
drganie(powieki);spazm;kurcz

twitter ('tłyter) v. ćwierkać;
świergotać; chichotać; drżeć
(ze strachu etc.); s. świergot; chichot; podniecenie;
zdenerwowanie
two (tu:) num. dwa; s. dwójka
two-bit ('tu:byt) adj. tandetny;
marny; (slang): wart 25 centów;
rzecz mała; rzecz bez znaczenia
twofold ('tu:fould) adj. podwójny; adv. podwójnie; dwojako
two-piece ('tu:pi:s) adj. dwu-
częściowy
two stroke ('tu:,strouk) adj.
dwutaktowy; dwusuwowy
two-way ('tu:,łej) adj. dwukie-
runkowy (np. ruch); dwutorowy;
dwuwartościowy
type (tajp) s. typ; wzór; przykład; symbol; klasa; okaz;
czcionka; kaszta (drukarska);
v. pisać na maszynie; ustalać
typ; symbolizować; wyznaczać
role
typewriter('tajp,rajter) s. maszyna do pisania
typhoid ('tajfoyd) adj. tyfusowy; s. tyfus; dur brzuszny
typhoon (taj'fu:n) s. tajfun;
burza (morska) w układzie
wielkiego wiru
typhus ('tajfes) adj. tyfusowy
typical ('typykel) adj. typowy;
charakterystyczny
typify ('typyfaj) v. uosabiać;
stanowić typ; zapowiadać
typist ('tajpyst) s. maszynistka
tyrannical (ty'raenykel) adj.
tyrański
tyrannize ('tyrenajz) v. tyranizować
tyranny ('tyreny) s. tyrania
tyrant ('tajerent) s. tyran
tyre ('tajer) s. opona; obręcz;
v. nakładać opone (obręcz)
u (ju:) dwudziesta pierwsza litera alfabetu angielskiego
ubiquity (ju'byklyty) s. wszech-
obecność
U-boat ('ju:bout) s. łódz podwodna (niemiecka)
udder ('ader) s. wymię

ugly ('agly) adj. brzydki; paskudny
uhlan ('u:la:n) s. ułan
ulan ('u:la:n s. ułan
ulcer ('alser) s. wrzód
ultimate ('altymyt) adj. ostateczny; ostatni; końcowy; podstawowy; s. ostateczny wynik;
podstawowy fakt
ultimatum (alty'mejtem) s. ultimatum
umbrella (am'brela) s. parasol
umpire ('ampajer) s. sędzia
sportowy; rozjemca; v. sędzio-
wać; rozstrzygać jako arbiter
unabashed ('ane'baeszt) adj.
niespeszony; niezmieszany;
nie zbity z tropu
unabated ('an,e'bejtyd) adj.
niesłabnący; niezmniejszony
unable ('an'ejbl) adj. niezdolny; nieudolny
unacceptable ('ane'kseptebl)
adj. nie do przyjęcia
unaccountable ('ane'kauntebl)
adj. niewytłumaczony; niezrozumiały; dziwny; nie
tłumaczący się nikomu
unaccustomed ('ane'kastemd)
adj. niezwykły; nie przyzwyczajony
unacquainted ('ane'kłejntyd)
adj. nie obznajomiony
unaffected (,ane'fektyd) adj.
niekłamany; naturalny
unanimous (ju'naenymes) adj.
jednogłosny
unapproachable (,ane'prouczebl)
adj. niedostępny; niezrównany
unarmed ('an'a:rmd) adj. bezbronny; nie uzbrojony
unashamed ('an,e'szejmd) adj.
bezwstydny
unassisted ('an,e'systyd)adj.
nie wspomagany
unassuming ('an,e'sju:myŋg)
adj. skromny; bezpretensjonalny
unauthorized ('an'o:terajzd)
adj. nieupoważniony
unavoidable ('an,e'wojdebl) adj.
nieunikniony; niechybny

unaware ('ane,e'Ker) adj.nie-
świadomy; niepoinformowany
unawares ('ane'Keerz) adv.nie-
świadomie; znienacka; niespo-
dziewanie ;nic nie wiedząc
unbalanced ('an'baelensd) adj.
niezrównoważony
unbar ('an'ba:r) v. odryglować
unbearable (an'beerebl) adj.
nieznośny; nie do wytrzymania
unbecoming ('an,by'kamyng)adj.
niestosowny; niewłaściwy;
nieodpowiedni; nietwarzowy
unbelievable (,anby'li:webl)
adj. niewiarygodny; nieprawdopodobny
unbelieving (.anby'li:wyng)
adj. niewierzący; niedowierzający
unbending ('an'bendyng) adj.
nieugięty; niezłomny
unbiased ('an'bajest) adj.
bezstronny
unbidden ('an'bydn) adj. nieproszony
unborn baby ('an'bo:rn'bejby)
adj. przyszłe dziecko; nie-
urodzone (jeszcze) dziecko
unbounded (an'naundyd) adj.
bez granic; bezgraniczny
unbroken (an'brouken) adj.
nieprzerwany; niezbity; nie
ujeżdżony (koń)
unbutton ('an'batn) v. odpiać;
rozpiać (sie)
uncalled-for (an'ko:ld,fo:r)
adj. niewłaściwy; niezasłużony;
niczym nie usprawiedliwiony
uncanny (an'kaeny) adj. niesamowity
uncared-for ('an'keerd,fo:r)
adj. porzucony; zaniedbany
unceasing (an'si:syng) adj.
bezustanny; nieprzerwany
uncertain (an'se:rtn) adj. niepewny; wątpliwy
unchallenged (an'chaelyndżd)
adj. niekwestionowany
unchangeable (an'chejndżebl)
adj. stały; niezmienny
unchanged (an'chejndżd) adj.
niezmieniony

unchecked (an'czekt) adj. niepowstrzymany; niepohamowany;
nieposkromiony
uncivil ('an'sywyl) adj. niegrzeczny; nieuprzejmy; nieokrzesany; grubiański
uncivilized ('an'sywylajzd)
adj. dziki; niecywilizowany;
barbarzyński
uncle ('ankl) s. wujek; stryjek
unclean ('an'kli:n) adj. nieczysty; plugawy; sprośny
uncomparable ('an'komperebl) adj.
nieporownywalny
uncommon ('an'komen) adj. niezwykły; rzadki; adv. niezwykle;
nadzwyczaj
uncommunicative ('an-ke'mju:ny-
ketyw); adj. małomówny; skryty;
niekomunikatywny
uncomplaining ('an-kem'plejnyng)
adj. cierpliwy; nienarzekający
unconcern ('anken'se:rn) s.
beztroska; niefrasobliwość;
obojętność
unconcerned ('anken'se:rnd) adj.
obojętny; niefrasobliwy; beztroski
unconditional ('an-ken'dyszynl)
adj. bezwarunkowy
unconfirmed ('an-ken'fe:rmd) adj.
nie potwierdzony
unconscious (an'kouszes) adj.
nieprzytomny; zemdlony; nieświadomy; s. podświadomość
unconsciousness (an'konszesnys)
omdlenie; nieprzytomność
unconstitutional ('an,konsty'-
'tju:szynl) adj. niezgodny
z konstytucja
uncontrollable ('an,kon'troulebl)
adj. nieposkromiony; niepohamowany
unconventional ('an-ken'wenszynl)
adj. niekonwencjonalny; oryginalny
unconvinced ('an-ken'wynst) adj.
nieprzekonany
unconvincing ('an-ken'wynsyng)
adj. nieprzekonywujący
uncouth (an'ku:s) adj. nieokrzesany; niezręczny; niezgrabny

uncover (an'kawer) v. odkryć;
demaskować
uncultivated ('an'kaltywejtyd)
adj. nieuprawny; leżący odłogiem; niekulturalny
uncultured ('an'kalczerd) adj.
niewykształcony; niekulturalny
undamaged ('an'daemydżd) adj.
nieuszkodzony
undecided ('an-dy'sajdyd) adj.
niezdecydowany; niepewny;
nieokreślony; nierozstrzygnięty
undefined ('andy'fajnd) adj.
nieokreślony; mglisty
undeniable (,andy'najebl) adj.
niezaprzeczalny
under ('ander) prep. pod; poniżej; w; w trakcie; zgodnie
z; z; adv. poniżej; pod spodem; adj. spodni; niższy;
dolny; podrzędny; podwładny
underbid ('ander'byd) v. zob.
bid; składać niższą ofertę
w przetargu
undercarriage ('ander,kaerydż)
s. podwozie
underclothes ('ander;klouz)
pl. bielizna
underclothing ('ander-klouzyng)
s. bielizna
underdeveloped (ander,dy'we-
lept) adj. zacofany; nie wywołany poprawnie; niedorozwinięty
underdone ('ander'dan) adj.
półsurowy; niedogotowany
underestimate ('ander'estymejt)
v. niedoceniać; za nisko
oszacować
underfed ('ander'fed) v. niedo-
żywiony
undergo (,ander'gou) v. zob.go;
doznawać czegoś; przechodzić
coś; doświadczyć; poddawać się
(operacji)
undergraduate (,ander'graedjuit)
s. student bez stopnia bachelor
underground ('ander,graund) adj.
podziemny; zaskórny; tajny;
s. kolej podziemna; ruch oporu;

adv. (,ander'graund)pod ziemią;
skrycie; tajnie
undergrowth ('ander-grous) s.
poszycie (lasu)
underline ('anderlajn) v. podkreślać; s. podkreślenie; podpis pod ilustracją; zawiadomienie (u spodu afisza teatralne-
go) o następnej sztuce
undermine (,ander'majn) v. podkopywać (zdrowie etc.) podmywać (brzegi etc.)
undermost ('andermoust) adj.
najniższy
underneath (,ander'ni:s) adv.
pod spodem; poniżej; na dole;
pod spód
underpass (,ander'pa:s) s.
przejazd poniżej poziomu (w
skrzyżowaniu bezkolizyjnym)
underpay ('ander'pej) v. za mało płacić
underprivileged ('ander'prywylydżd) adj. upośledzony
undershirt ('andersze:rt) s.
podkoszulek
undersigned ('ander'sajnd) adj.
(niżej) podpisany
undersized ('ander'sajzd) adj.
zbyt mały; małego wzrostu
under soil ('ander,sojl) s.
podglebie
understaffed ('ander'sta:ft)
adj. mający zbyt mały personel
understand; understood; understood (,ander'staend; ander'-
stud; ,ander'stud)
understand (,ander'staend) v.
rozumieć; domyślać się; orien-
tować się; znać; wywnioskować;
wiedzieć jak; umieć dobrze
understandable (,ander'staend-
ebl) adj. zrozumiały
understanding (,ander'staendyng)
adj. pełen zrozumienia; s. zrozumienie; warunek; (wyższa)
inteligencja; porozumienie;
rozum
understatement (,ander'stejtment) s. zbyt skromne wyraża-
nie się; niedomówienie

undertake (,ander'tejk) v.zob.
take; przedsiębrać; podejmować się; ręczyć; zobowiązywać się do czegoś; być przed-
siębiorcą pogrzebowym
undertaker (,ander'tejker) s.
przedsiębiorca pogrzebowy
undertaking (,ander'tejkyŋg) s.
przedsięwzięcie; zobowiązanie;
obietnica; przyrzeczenie;
przedsiębiorstwo pogrzebowe
undervalue (,ander'waelju) v.
niedoceniać; za nisko szacować
underwear ('anderłeer) s. bielizna
underwood ('ander,łu:d) s. poszycie (lasu)
underworld ('ander,łe:rld) s.
podziemie; świat podziemny;
pl. antypody
underwrite ('ander-rajt) v.
zob. write; zakontraktować
(ubezpieczenie); podpisać(się);
wydawać (polisę ubezpieczenio-
wą); zobowiazywać się
underwriter ('ander-rajter) s.
ajent ubezpieczeniowy
undeserved ('andy'ze:rwd) adj.
niezasłużony; niesłuszny
undesirable (andy'zajerebl)
adj. niepożądany; niedogodny;
s. człowiek niepożądany
undeveloped (andy'welopt) adj.
nierozwinięty; niewywołany
undies (andyz) pl. bielizna
(damska i dziecięca)
undignified (an'dygnyfajd) adj.
niegodny; bez godności
undiminished (an'dymynszt) adj.
niezmniejszony
un-disciplined (an'dysyplind)
adj. niezdyscyplinowany; nie-
karny
undisputed (,andys'pju:tyd)
adj. bezsporny; niezaprzeczony
undisturbed ('andys'te:rbd) adj.
niezakłócony
undo; undid; undone ('an'du;
'an'dyd, an'dan)
undo ('an'du:) v. robić nieby-
łym; unieważniac; usuwać;
niszczyć; rujnować; rozpakowac;

rozwiązać; otwierać; rozpinać;
przekreślać
undreamt-of ('an'dremt,ow)
adj. nieprawdopodobny; nie do
pomyślenia; niesłychany
undress (an'dres) v. rozbierać
(się); odbandażowywać; s. negliż; zwykłe ubranie
undressed (an'drest) adj. nie
przyrządzony; chropowaty; nie
opatrzona (rana); rozebrany
undue (an'dju:) adj. przesadny;
nadmierny; postronny; niewłas-
ciwy; jeszcze niepłatny (np.
rachunek)
undutiful (an'djutyful) adj.
nieobowiązkowy
uneasy (an'i:zy) adj. niespokojny; niepokojący; nieswój;
zażenowany; nieprzyjemny;
krępujacy; budzący niepokój
uneducated (an'edjukejtyd)
adj. niewykształcony; bez
wykształcenia
unemployed (an'emplojd) adj.
bez pracy; bezrobotny; nie-
wykorzystany; nie zużytkowany
unemployment (an'emplojment)
s. bezrobocie
unendurable ('anyn'djuerebl)
adj. nie do zniesienia
unenviable ('an'enwjebl) adj.
nie do pozazdroszczenia
unequal ('an'i:kłol) adj. nie-
rowny; nie na wysokości (zadania)
unequaled ('an'i:kłold) adj.
niezrównany
unequivocal ('any'kływokel) adj.
niedwuznaczny; wyraźny; jasny
unerring ('an'e:ryŋg) adj.
nieomylny; niezawodny
uneven ('an'i:wen) adj. nieparzysty; niejednolity; nierówny
uneventful ('an,y'wentful)
adj. nieurozmaicony; spokojny;
jednostajny
unexpected ('anyks'pektyd)
adj. niespodziewany; nieoczekiwany
unfailing (an'fejlyŋg) adj.
niezawodny; niewyczerpany

unfair (an'feer) adj. niesprawiedliwy; krzywdzący; nieuczciwy; nieprzepisowy

unfaithful (an'fejsful) adj.
niewierny; wiarołomny; nieścisły

unfamiliar ('anfe'myljer) adj.
nieznany; nieobznajomiony;
obcy

unfashionable ('an'faeszenebl)
adj. niemodny

unfasten ('an'fa:sn) v. odczepić (się); odpiąć (się); od-
wiązywać (się); odryglowac
(się); rozluźnic (się)

unfavorable ('an'fejwerebl)
adj. niepomyślny; nieżyczliwy;
niesprzyjający; nieprzychylny

unfeasible (an'fi:sebl) adj.
niewykonalny

unfeeling (an'fi:lyng) adj.
bez uczucia; bez serca; okrutny

unfinished ('an'fynyszt) adj.
niewykończony; niedokończony

unfit ('an'fyt) adj. nie nadający się; niezdatny; niezdolny; nieodpowiedni; v. czynic
niezdolnym do czegoś

unflappable ('an'flaepebl) adj,
nie do wytrącenia z równowagi

unfold ('an'fould) v. ujawniać
(się); rozwijać (się); otwierać; odsłonić

unforseen ('an'fer,si:n) adj.
nieprzewidziany; niespodziewa-
wany

unforgettable ('an-fer'getebl)
adj. pamiętny; niezapomniany

unforgiving ('an-fer'gywyng)
adj. niewybaczający; nieprzejednany

unforgotten ('an-fer'gotn)adj.
niezapomniany

unfortunate (an'fo:rcznyt) adj.
niefortunny; pechowy; niepomyślny; nieszczęśliwy

unfortunately (an'fo:rcznytly)
adv. niestety; nieszczęśliwie

unfounded (an'faundyd) adj.
bezpodstawny

unfriendly (an'frendly) adj.
nieprzyjazny; nieprzychylny

unfurnished (an'fe:rnyszt) adj.
nieumeblowany

ungainly (an'gejnly) adj. niezdarny; niezgrabny

ungenerous (an'dżeneres) adj.
małostkowy; nie szczodry

ungentle (an'dżentl) adj. nie-
łagodny

unget-at-able ('anget'aetbl)
adj. niedostępny (slang)

ungovernable (an'gawernebl)adj.
dziki; niesforny; krnąbrny;
nieopanowany

ungraceful (an'grejsful) adj.
niewdzięczny; nieuprzejmy

ungrateful (an'grejful) adj.
niewdzięczny

unguarded ('an'ga:rdyd) adj.
niebaczny;nieopatrzny; nierozważny; niestrzeżony

unhappy (an'haepy) adj. nieszczęśliwy; pechowy; zmartwiony;nieudany

unharmed ('an'ha:rmd) adj. nietknięty

unharness ('an'ha:rnys) v. wyprzęgać; zdejmować zbroję; etc.

unhealthy (an'helsy) adj. niezdrowy

unheard-of (an'he:rd,ow) adj.
niesłychany; niebywały; nieprawdopodobny

unheeded (an'hi:dyd) adj. niezauważony; niedostrzeżony

unheeding (an'di:dyng) adj. nieuważający; niedostrzegający

unhesitating (an'hezytejtyng)
adj. nie wahający się

unhoped-for (an'hopt,fo:r) adj.
niespodziewany; nieoczekiwany

unhurt (an'he:rt) adj. nieuszkodzony; bez szwanku

unicorn ('ju:nyko:rn) s. jedno-
rożec; jednoróg

unification (,ju:nyfy'kejszyn)
s. zjednoczenie; zcalenie;
ujednolicenie

uniform ('ju:nyfo:rm) adj.
jednolity; równomierny; jednostajny; s, mundur; uniform

uniformity ('ju:ny'fo:rmyty)
s. jednolitość; jednostajność;
ujednolicenie;ujednostajnienie

unilateral ('ju:ny'laeterel)
adj. jednostronny
unimaginable (any'maedżynebl)
adj. nie do pomyslenia
unimaginative (any'maedżynejtyw)
adj. bez wyobraźni; bez polotu
unimportant ('anym'po:rtent)
adj. nieważny; błahy; mało
ważny
uninhabitable('anyn'haebytebl)
adj. nie do mieszkania; nie
do życia
uninhabited ('anyn'haebytyd)
adj. niezamieszkały
uninjured ('an'yndżerd) adj.
bez szwanku; nie uszkodzony;
bez obrażeń
uninspired ('anyn'spajerd) adj.
banalny
unintelligible ('anyn'telydżebl)
adj. niezrozumiały
unintentional ('anyn'tenszynl)
adj. mimowolny; nie zamierzony
uninteresting ('anyn'terestyŋg)
adj. nudny; nieciekawy; nie-
interesujący
uninterrupted ('anyn'teraptyd)
adj. nieprzerwany; ciągły;
bezustanny
uninvited ('anyn'wajtyd) adj.
nieproszony
uninviting ('anyn'wajtyŋg) adj.
nie zachęcający; odpychający;
nieapetyczny
union ('ju:njen) s. połączenie;
złącze; łączność; związek;
zjednoczenie; małżeństwo; zgoda; łącznik; złączka; godło
unionist ('ju:njenyst) s.
związkowiec; zwolennik związku
union Jack ('ju:njen'dżaek) s.
flaga angielska
unique (ju:'ni:k) adj. wyjątkowy; jedyny; niezrównany
unisex ('ju:ny'seks) adj. styl
(wyrobów) do użytku obu płci;
odzież, przybory toaletowe,
zakład fryzjerski etc.
unison ('ju:nyzn) adj. zgodnie
(razem)
unit ('ju:nyt) s. jednostka;
zespół

unite (ju:'najt) v. łączyć; jednoczyc; zjednoczyć
united (ju:'najtyd) adj. połączony; zjednoczony; łączny
unity ('ju:nyty) s. jedność
(czasu, miejsca, działania, etc);
jednostka; jednolitość; harmonia; zgoda
universal (ju:ny've:rsel) adj.
powszechny; ogólny; uniwersalny
universe ('ju:nyvers) s. wszechświat; świat; ludzkość; kosmos
university (,ju:ny'wersyty) s.
uniwersytet; wszechnica; uczelnia
unjust ('an'dżast) adj. niesprawiedliwy
unkempt ('an'kempt) adj. nie-
uczesany; rozczochrany; niechlujny
unkind (an'kajnd) adj. niedobry;
okrutny
unknown ('an'noun) adj. nieznany;
niewiadomy
unlace ('an'lejs) v. rozsznurowac
unlawful ('an'lo:ful) adj. bezprawny; nielegalny
unlearn ('an'le:rn) v. oduczac
(się); zob, learn
unless (an'les) conj. jeżeli
nie; chyba że
unlike ('an'lajk) adj. niepodobny; odmienny; prep. odmiennie;
inaczej; w przeciwieństwie
unlikely (an'lajkly) adj. nieprawdopodobny; nieoczekiwany;
nie rokujący
unlimited (an'lymytyd) adj.
nieograniczony; bezgraniczny;
dowolny
unload ('an'loud) v. rozładowy-
wać; zrzucać ciężar
unlock ('an'lok) v. otwierać
zamek; otworzyć
unlocked ('an'lokt) adj. otwarty; niezamknięty
unlooked-for (an'lukt,fo:r)
adj. nieoczekiwany; niespodziewany; nieprzewidziany
unloosen ('an'lu:sn) adj. rozluźniony; rozwiązany; rozsznu-
rowany

unlucky (an'laky) adj. pechowy; niefortunny; niepomyślny;
nieszczęśliwy
unmanageable (an'maenydżebl)
adj. niesforny; krnąbrny
unmanly (an'maenly)adj. znie-
checający; odbierający odwagę; adv. zniechecająco
unmarried (an'maeryd) adj. nieżonaty; niezamężna
unmistakabe ('anmys'tejkbl)
adj. niewątpliwy; wyraźny;
niedwuznaczny
unmoved ('an'm:wd) adj. niewzruszony
unnatural (an'naeczrel) adj.
sztuczny; nienaturalny;
wbrew naturze; nienormalny
unnecessary (an'nesysery)
adj. zbędny; zbyteczny; niepotrzebny
unnoticed ('an'noutyst) adj.
niezauważony; (pominięty)
unobtainable ('aneb'tejnebl)
adj. nie do nabycia(otrzyma-
nia)
unobtrusive ('aneb'tru:syw)
adj. skromny; dyskretny; nie
narzucający się
unoccupied ('an'okjupajd) adj.
wolny; nie zajęty
unoffending ('ane'fendyng)
adj. nieszkodliwy; (niewinny)
unofficial ('ane'fyszel) adj.
nie urzędowy; nieoficjalny
unpack ('an'paek) v. rozpako-
wywać (się)
unpaid ('an'pejd) adj. niezapłacony; (bezinteresowny)
unparalleled (an'paereleld)adj.
niezrównany; niespotykany;
bezprzykładny; niesłychany
unpardonable (an'pa:rdnebl)
adj. niewybaczalny
unperceived (an'per'si:wd)adj.
niespostrzeżony
unperturbed ('an-per'te:rbd)
adj. spokojny; nie zaniepokojony; nie przejmujący się
unpleasant (an'plezent) adj.
nieprzyjemny; przykry; niemiły

_wyciągnąć z kontaktu
unplug (an'plag) v. odczopować;
unpolished ('an'polyszt) adj.
niewyczyszczony; niewygładzony
unpopular (an'popjuler) adj. m.
niepopularny; niemile widziany
unpopularity ('an,popju'laeryty)
s. niepopularność; złe przyjęcie
unpractical ('an'praektykel) adj.
niepraktyczny; nierealny
unpracticed (an'praektyst) adj.
nie wypraktykowany; niewprawny
unprecedented (an'presydentyd)
adj. bezprzykładny; bez pre-
cedensu; niesłychany
unprejudiced (an'predżudyst)
adj. bezstronny; nie mający
przesądów
un-premeditated ('anpry:'medy-
tejtyd) adj. bez premedytacji;
nienaumyślny
unprepared ('anpry'peerd) adj.
nieprzygotowany; nieprzyrzą-
dzony
unprincipled (an'prynsepld) adj.
bez skrupułów; niegodziwy
unproductive (an'prodaktyw) adj.
niewydajny; nie wytwórczy;
niepłodny;
unprofitable (an'profytebl) adj.
niepopłatny; niekorzystny; nie-
rentowny
unprovided-for ('an-pre'wajdyd-
,fo:r) adj. niezabezpieczony;
bez srodków do życia
unqualified ('an'kłolyfajd) adj.
niewykwalifikowany; bez kwali-
fikacji; niesprecyzowany; nieograniczony (np. zaufanie)
unquestionable (an'kłesczynebl)
adj. bezsporny; niewątpliwy
unquestioned (an'kłesczynd)
adj. niezaprzeczony; niepytany
unreasonable (an'ri:znebl) adj.
nierozsądny; niedorzeczny; wygorowany (w cenie)
unrefined ('anry'faind) adj.
niesubtelny; niewyrafinowany;
niewykształcony
unreliable ('anry'lajebl) adj.
niepewny; niesolidny

unreserved ('anry'ze:rwd) adj.
otwarty; szczery; bez zastrże-
zeń; całkowity; niezarezerwo-
wany
unresisting ('anry'zystyŋg)
adj. nieodporny; nieopierają-
cy się
unrest ('an'rest) s. niepokój;
zamieszki; niepokoje
unrestrained ('anrys'trejnd)
adj. niepowstrzymany; niepohamowany; nieopanowany
unrestricted ('anrys'tryktyd)
adj. nieograniczony; (niedostępny)
unrip ('an'ryp) v. porozpruwac
unripe ('an'rajp) adj. niedojrzały
unrivaled (an'rajweld) adj.
niezrównany; bezkonkurencyjny
unroll ('an'roul) v. rozwinąć
(zwój; rolkę)
unruffled (an'rafld) adj. niezmącony; niezakłócony; zachowujący równowagę
unruly (an'ru:ly) adj. niesforny
unsafe ('an'sejf) adj. niepewny;
ryzykowny; niebezpieczny
unsanitary ('an'saenytery) adj.
niehigieniczny; szkodliwy;nie-
zdrowy
unsatisfactory ('an,saetys'faektery) adj. niezadawalający;
niedostateczny
unsatisfied (an'saetysfajd) adj.
niezadowolony; niezaspokojony
unsavory ('an'sejwery) adj.
niesmaczny; przykry
unscrew('an'skru:) v. odśrubo-
wac; rozśrubowac; odkręcic
(gwint)
unscrupulous ('an'skru:pjules)
adj. bez skrupułów; niegodziwy
unseen (an'si:n) adj. nie widziany; niewidoczny
unselfish (an'selfysz) adj.bez-
interesowny
unsettled ('an'setld) adj. za-
burzony; zakłócony; nieustalo-
ny; niezapłacony; rozstrojony
unshaven (an'szejwn) adj. nie-
ogolony

unshrinkable (an'szrynkebl)
adj. nie kurczący się (w praniu)
unshrinking (an'szrynkiŋg) adj.
nie wahający się; nie wzdry-
gający się
unskilled (an'skyld) adj. niewprawny; niewykwalifikowany
unskilful (an'skylful) adj.
niewprawny; niezręczny
unsociable ('an'souszebl) adj.
nietowarzyski
unsocial (an'souszel) adj. nie-
socjalny; niespołeczny
unsolvable (an'salwebl) adj.
nierozwiązalny; nierozpuszczalny
unsolved (an'solwd) adj. nie-
rozwiązany; nierozpuszczony
unsophisticated (,anso'fystykejtyd) adj. prosty; naturalny; prawdziwy
unsound (an'saund) adj. niezdrowy; sprochniały; słaby;
niepewny; ryzykowny; błędny;
niesolidny
unspeakable (an'spi:kebl) adj.
niewypowiedziany;nie do opisania
unspoiled (an'spojld) adj.
niezepsuty; nierozpieszczony
(dziecko)
unspoken ('an'spouken) adj.
nie mówiony (np. prawo)
unspoken-for (an'spoukn;fo:r)
adj. niezamówiony
unspoken-of (an'spoukn) adj.
nie omawiany
unstable (an'stejbl) adj. niepewny; chwiejny;niezrównowa-
żony
unsteady ('an'stedy) adj.
chwiejny; chwiejący się; niezdecydowany; nieustabilizowany;
zmienny; niepewny
unstressed ('an'strest) adj.
nieakcentowany; niepodkreslony;
nieobciążony
unsuccessful ('an-sek'sesful)
adj. nieudany; bez powodzenia;
nieudały; nie mający powodzenia; bezowocny

unsuitable ('an'sju:tebl) adj.
niewłaściwy; niestosowny;
nieodpowiedni
unsure (an'szuer) adj. niepewny; zawodny
unsurpassed ('an-ser'pa:st)
adj. nieprześcigniony; niezrównany
unsuspected ('an-ses'pekyd)
adj. (zupełnie) niepodejrzany
unsuspecting('an-ses'pektyng)
adj. nieczego nie podejrzewa-
jący
unsuspicious ('an-ses'pyszes)
adj. ufny; niepodejrzliwy
unthinkable ('an'tynkebl) adj.
nie do pomyślenia; nieprawdopodobny
unthinking ('an'tynkyng) adj.
bezmyślny
untidy (an'tajdy) adj. niechlujny;niestaranny; rozczor-
rany; zaniedbany; nie posprzą-
tany
untie(an'taj) v. rozwiązywać
(się); rozsupłać; uwalniać
(się) z więzów; usuwać (trudności)
until (an'tyl) prep. & conj.
do; dotychczas; dopiero; aż
untimely (an'tajmly) adj. nie
w porę; przedwczesny; nie na
czasie; wczesny; adv. przedwcześnie; w nieodpowiedniej
chwili
untiring (an'tajeryng) adj.
niezmordowany
unto ('antu:) prep.,= to; do;
ku; aż do
untold (an'told) adj. niewypowiedziany; nieprzeliczony
untouchable (an'taczebl) adj.
niedotykalny
untouched (an'taczt) adj. nietknięty; nieskazitelny; nieczuły
untried (an'trajd) adj. niewy-
próbowany
untroubled (an'trabld) adj.
spokojny; beztroski

untrue ('an'tru:) adj. nieprawdziwy; fałszywy; niewierny;
sprzeniewierzający się
untrustworthy ('an'trast,łe:rsy)
adj. niegodny zaufania; niepewny
untruth ('an'tru:s) s. nieprawda;
kłamstwo
unused ('an'ju:zd) adj. nie używa-
wany; nie przyzwyczajony; nie
stosowany
unusual (an'ju:żuel) adj. niezwykły; wyjątkowy
unutterable (an'aterebl) adj.
niewysłowiony; niewypowiedziany
unvarying (an'weery-yng) adj.
jednostajny; nieurozmaicony;
nie zmieniający (się)
unvoiced (an'woist) adj. bez-
głosny; bezdźwięczny
unwanted (an'łontyd) adj. niepożądany; niepotrzebny; zbędny; zbyteczny
unwarranted ('an'łorentyd) adj.
nieusprawiedliwiony; bezpodstawny
unwholesome ('an'houlsem) adj.
niezdrowy; szkodliwy
unwilling ('an'łylyng) adj.
niechętny
unwind ('an'łajnd) v. zob,wind;
rozwijać (się); odprężać (się);
(slang): odpoczywać sobie
unwise ('an'łajz) adj. niemądry;
nieostrożny; nieroztropny
unworthy (an'łe:rsy) adj. niegodny; niegodziwy; niewart;
niezasługujący; ujemny
unwrap ('an'raep) v. rozwijać
(się); rozpakować; odsłonic
(się); odwijać (się)
unyielding ('an'ji:ldyng) adj.
nieustępliwy; twardy; nieugięty
up (ap) adv. do góry; w górę;
w zwyż; w górze; wyżej; na;
tam (gdzie); na górze; wysoko;
wyżej; aż (do); aż (po); na
(piętro); pod (górę); v. podnosić; zrywać się; podbijać
(cenę); zaczynać

up-and-about ('apend,ebaut)
exp.:(znowu) na nogach (po
chorobie)
up-and-coming ('ap,end'komyng)
exp.;(slang): obiecujący;
rzutki; przedsiębiorczy (człowiek)
up-and-doing ('ap,end'duyng)
exp.;(slang): czynny; ruchliwy
up-and-up ('ap,end'ap)być uczciwym
up to('ep,tu)adv.aż do pogodny
upbeat('apbi:t)adj.optymistyczny;
upbringing (' p,bryngyng) s.
wychowanie ; wychowywanie
uphill ('ap'hyl) adj. wznoszą-
cy (się); stromy; trudny;
uciążliwy; adv. stromo; pod
górę; w górę
upholster (ap'houlster) v.
obijać (meble); wyścielać;
pokrywać; urządzać
upholsterer (ap'houlsterer)
s. tapicer; dekorator
upholstery(ap'houlstry) s.
tapicerstwo; meble wyścielane
upkeep ('apki:p) s. utrzymanie;
koszty utrzymania szanie się
upmanship('apmen,szyp)s.wywyż-
upon (e'pon)prep.=on; na; po
upper ('aper) adj. wyższy; górny; wierzchni; s. przyszwa
uppermost ('aper,moust) adj.
najwyższy; adv. na górze; na
górę
uppish ('apysh) adj. zadziera-
jący nos do góry (slang)
upright ('ap'rajt) adj. wypro-
stowany; prosty; uczciwy; prawy; adv. pionowo; s. pionowy
słup; podpora; pianino; pozycja pionowa
uprising (ap'rajzyng) s. powstanie; wstawanie
uproar ('ap,ro:) s. zgiełk;
wrzawa; harmider; tumult
upset ('apset) v. zob. set;
przewracać (się), pokonywać;
wzburzać; rozstrajać; rozku-
wać; pogrubiać; skręcać; rozklepywać; s. wywrócenie (się);
porażka; podniecenie; zaburzenie; rozstrój; niepokój;

bałagan; sztanca do kucia
upside-down ('apsajd'dałn)adv.
do góry nogami; do góry dnem;
adj. odwrócony do góry nogami
upstairs ('ap'steerz) adv. na
górę; na górze
upstart ('ap-sta:rt) s. par-
wenjusz
upstream ('ap'stri:m) adv. pod
prąd; w górę rzeki
uptight ('ap'tajt) adj. (slang);
napięty; naprężony (nerwowo)
up-to-date ('ap-tu-'dejt) adj.
bieżący; nowoczesny
upwards (apłerdz) adv. w górę;
ku górze; na wierzch; wyżej;
powyżej (czegoś)
uranium (ju'rejnjem) s. uran
urbane (e:r'bejn) adj. grzeczny; układny; wytworny
urchin ('e:rczyn) s. ulicznik;
urwis; łobuz; smyk; jeżowiec;
jeżak; czesak
urge (e:rdż) v. poganiać; popędzać; ponaglać; przyspieszać; nalegać; pilić; namawiać; s. pragnienie; impuls;
tęsknota; pociąg; bodziec
urge on ('e:rdż,on) v. namawiać
na coś
urgent (e:rdżent) adj. pilny;
naglący; gwałtowny; natarczywy; nalegający
urine ('jueryn) s. mocz; uryna
urn (e:rn) s. urna
usage ('ju:sydż) s. zwyczaj;
praktyka; obchodzenie (się);
używanie (zwrotów, języka po-
prawnego)
use (ju:s) s. użytek; używanie;
użycie; posługiwanie; zastosowanie; pożytek; korzyść; zwyczaj; praktyka; obrządek; przyzwyczajenie; v. używać; korzystać; wykorzystać; zużywać; zużyć; wyczerpać; traktować;
obejść się; mieć zwyczaj
used (ju:zd) adj. przyzwyczajony; używany; stosowany
useful ('ju:zful) adj. użyteczny;
pożyteczny; dogodny; wygodny;
(slang):doskonały; sprawny;
biegły; zdolny

useless ('ju:zlys) adj. niepotrzebny; bezużyteczny; zbyteczny; bezcelowy; nieużyteczny; do niczego

use up ('ju:s,ap) v. zużyć
(wszystko); wyczerpać (np.
pracą

usher ('aszer) s, odźwierny;
woźny; bileter; rozprowadzaj-
jący na miejsca (w kinie;
w kościele etc.) v. wprowadzać; zapoczątkować

usher in ('aszer,yn) v. wprowadzać do

usherette (,asze'ret) s. bi-
leterka (rozprowadzająca)

usual ('ju:zuel) adj. zwykły;
zwyczajny; normalny; zwyczajowy; utarty

usually ('ju:żuely) adv. zwykle; zazwyczaj

usurer ('ju:żerer) s. lichwiarz

usury ('ju:żury) s. lichwa

utensil (ju'tensyl) s. sprzęt;
naczynie; narzędzie

utility (ju'tylyty) s. pożytek;
użyteczność; firma dostarcza-
jąca gaz, elektryczność lub
wodę ludności w USA

utilize ('ju:tylajz) v. zużytkować; spożytkować; wykorzystać

utmost ('atmoust) adj. najwyższy; ostateczny; skrajny; największy; najdalszy; ostatni

utter ('ater) adj. całkowity;
zupełny; kompletny; skończony; skrajny; ostatni; v. wydawać (głos); powiedzieć; wy-
powiedzieć (hasło itp.); wyrażać; wystawiać (czeki); podrabiać (np. dokumenty); puszczać (w obieg)

utterance ('aterens) s. wypo-
wiedź; wymowa; wyrażenie;
zeznanie; oświadczenie

uvula ('ju:wjula) s. języczek
miękkiego podniebienia

v (wi:) dwudziesta druga litera
alfabetu angielskiego

vacancy ('wejkensy) s. wolne
mieszkanie; wolne pokoje mote-
lowe; wakans; próżnia; pustka;
bezczynność

vacant ('wejkent) adj. pusty;
próżny; wolny; wakujący;bez-
czynny; bezmyślny; obojętny

vacate (we'kejt) v. opróżniać;
opuszczać; unieważniać

vacation (we'kejszyn) s. wakacje
ferie; opróżnienie; zwolnienie
(mieszkania); ewakuacja

vaccinate ('waeksynejt) v.
szczepić

vaccination ('waeksynejszyn)
s. szczepienie

vaccine ('waeksi:n) s. szczepionka

vacuum ('waekjuem) s. próżnia

vacuum bottle ('waekjuem'botl)
s. termos

vacuum cleaner ('waekjuem'kli:-
ner)s. odkurzacz

vacuum flask ('waekjuem,fla:sk)
s. termos

vagabond ('waegebond) adj.
włóczęgowski; wędrowny;
s. włóczęga; nierób; próżniak

vagary ('wejgery) s. kaprys;
chimera

vague (wejg) adj. niejasny; niewyraźny; nieokreślony; nieuchwytny; niewyraźny; wymijający; niezdecydowany

vain (wejn) adj. próżny; zarozumiały; czczy; pusty; gołosłowny; daremny; bezcelowy

valance ('waelens) s. krótka
podłużna zasłona (światła);
rodzaj adamaszku

vale ('wejl) s. dolina; pożegnanie; excl.;żegnajcie !

valerian (we'lerjen) s. waleria-
na

valet ('waelyt) s. służący;
v. usługiwać

valiant ('waeljent) adj. dzielny;
s. zuch

valid ('waelyd) adj. słuszny;
ważny; uzasadniony

valley ('waely) s. dolina; koryto fali; wewnętrzny kąt płaszczyzn dachu

valor ('waeler) s. dzielność

valuable ('waeljuebl) adj.
wartościowy; cenny; kosztowny;
s.(pl)kosztowności;biżuteria

valuables ('waljuebls) pl.
kosztownosci
valuation (,walju'ejszyn) s.
oszacowanie; cena
value ('waelju;) s. wartosc;
cena; stopien jasnosci barwy
(w obrazie); v. szacowac; cenic; oceniac
valueless ('waelju:lys) adj.
bezwartosciowy
valuer ('waelju:er) s. taksa-
tor
valve (waelw) s. zawor; wentyl;
klapa; zastawka
van (waen) s. kryty woz (cię-
żarowy); czoło armii; v. przewozic krytym wozem; badac rudę pukaniem
vane (wejn) s. chorągiewka (od
wiatru); łopatka śmigła;
brzechwa bomby; skrzydło wiatraka
vanilla (we'nyle) s. wanilia
vanish ('waenysz) v. znikac;
zanikac
vanity ('waenyty) s. próżnosc;
pycha; marnosc; czczość; toaleta; źródło próżnosci; rzecz
bez wartosci
vanitycase ('waenyty,kejs) s.
kosmetyczka
vantage ('waentydż) s. korzyst-
na pozycja; przewaga (w tenisie)
vaporize ('wejporajz) v. wypa-
rowac; zamieniac sie w parę
vapor (wejpor) s. para; mgła;
v. parowac; ględzic
vaporous ('wejperes) adj.
mglisty; zamglony
variable ('weerjebl) adj. zmienny; niestały; s, zmienny wiatr
variance ('weerjens) s. rozbieżnosc; niezgodność
variant ('weerent) s. odmiana;
wariant; adj. odmienny; rozny
variation (,weery'ejszyn) s,
zmiana; odmiana; wariant;
wariacja
varicose vein ('waerykous,wejn)
s. żylak
varied ('waeryd) adj. rożnorodny;
rozny; urozmaicony

variety (we'rajety) s. rozmai-
tosc; urozmaicenie; rożnorod-
nosc; wielostronnosc; teatr
rozmaitosci; kabaret; szereg;
odmiana
various ('weerjes) adj. rozny;
rozmaity; urozmaicony; wiele;
kilka; kilkakrotnie
varnish ('wa:rnysz) s. pokost;
politura; werniks; polewa;
v. pokostowac; werniksowac
Varsovian (wa:r'souwjen) adj.
warszawski; s.warszawiak
vary ('weery) v, zmieniac (się);
urozmaicac; rożnic się; nie podzielac zdania
vase (wejz) s. waza; wazon
vat (waet) s. zbiornik; kadz;
cysterna
vault (wo:lt) s. sklepienie;
podziemie; piwnica; grobowiec;
skok o tyczce; v. przesklepiac;
osklepic; przeskoczyc; skoczyc
o tyczce
vaulting horse ('wo:ltyng,ho:rs)
s. kozioł (przyrząd gimnastyczny)
veal(wi:l) s. cielęcina
vegetable ('wedżytebl) s. jarzyna
vegetarian (,wedży'teerjen) adj.
jarski; s. jarosz; wegetarianin
vegetate ('wedżytejt) v. wegeto-
wac; rosnąc
vehemence ('wi:ymens) s. gwał-
townosc; porywczosc; wybucho-
wosc
vehement ('wi:yment) adj. gwałtowny; porywczy; wybuchowy
vehicle ('wi:ykl) s. pojazd;
srodek; narzędzie; przymieszka
do farby
veil (wejl) s. welon; woalka;
wstąpienie do klasztoru; zasłona (maska); chrypka; v. zasłaniac; ukrywac
vein (wejn) s. żyła (też złota);
usposobienie; natura; nastroj;
wena; v. żyłkowac
velocity (wy'losyty) s. szyb-
kosc

velvet ('welwyt) s. aksamit;
delikatna skórka; (slang);
zarobek; forsa; adj. aksamit-
ny

venal ('wi:nl) adj. sprzedajny

vend (wend) v. sprzedawać

vender ('wender) s. (uliczny)
sprzedawca; automat do sprzedaży

vending machine ('wendyng,me'-
'szi:n) s. automat do sprzedaży

venerable ('wenerebl) adj.
czcigodny; wielebny

venerate ('wenerejt) v. czcić

venereal (wy'njerjel) adj.
weneryczny; chory wenerycznie;
przeciwwenervczny; płciowy

Venetian blind (wy'ni:szyn,-
,blajnd)s. żaluzja (wenecka)

vengeance ('wendżens) s. zem-
sta; pomsta

venison ('wenzn) s. dziczyzna

venom ('wenem) s. jad

venomous('wenemes) adj. jadowity

vent (went) s. odwietrznik;
wentyl; otwór wentylacyjny;
rozcięcie w tyle marynarki;
ujście; upust; v. dawać upust
czemuś; wyładowywać (złość);
rozgłaszać; wietrzyć; wiercić
otwór wentylacyjny

ventilate ('wentylejt) v.
wentylować; wietrzyć; prze-
dyskutować

ventilator ('wentylejtor) s.
wentylator; wietrznik

ventriloquist (wen'trylokłyst)
s. brzuchomówca

venture ('wenczer) s. ryzyko;
stawka; spekulacja; impreza;
interes; próba; v. odważać
się; ośmielać się; ryzykować;
śmieć; narazić się

veranda (we'raende) s. weranda

verb (we:rb) s. czasownik;
słowo

verbal ('we:rbel) adj. ustny;
słowny; werbalny; czasownikowy

verdict ('we:rdykt) s. wyrok;
werdykt; osąd; orzeczenie

verdure ('we:rdżer) s. zieleń

verge ('we:rdż) s. skraj; brzeg;
krawędź; v. graniczyć; zbliżać
się; chylić się; skłaniać się;

verge on ('we:rdż,on) v. graniczyć

verification (,weryfy'kejszyn)
s. uwierzytelnienie; sprawdzenie

verify ('weryfaj) v. sprawdzać;
potwierdzać; udowadniać

vermicelli (we:rmy'sely) s. cienki makaron

vermiform appendix (we:rmy'fo:rm-
e'pendyks) s. ślepa kiszka;
wyrostek robaczkowy

vermin ('we:rmyn) s. robactwo;
świat przestępczy

vernacular (we:r'naekjuler) adj.
rodzimy; miejscowy; krajowy;
s. gwara; język rodzinny; do-
sadne powiedzenie

versatile ('we:rsetail) adj.
wszechstronny

verse (we:rs) s. wiersz; strofa

versed ('we:rst) adj. doświadczony; wprawiony (w czymś)

version ('we:rżyn) s. wersja;
przekład; przekręcenie macicy

vertebra ('we:rtybre) s. krąg

vertebrae ('we:rtybri:) pl.
kręgi

vertical ('we:rtykel) adj. pionowy; szczytowy; s. pionowa
płaszczyzna; linia

very ('wery) adv. bardzo; absolutnie; zaraz; własnie; adj.
prawdziwy; sam; skończony(drań)

vessel ('wesl) s. naczynie; pojemnik; statek; okręt

vest (west) s. kamizelka; v. nadawać; przekazać; przysługiwać
komuś; przypadać komuś; odziewać w szaty; przykrywać ołtarz

vestry ('westry) s. zakrystia

vet ('wet) s. weterynarz

veteran ('weteran) s. weteran

veterinary ('weterynery) s.
weterynarz

veto ('wi:tou) s. weto; v. zakładać weto

vex (weks) v. złościć; dręczyc;
dokuczac
vexation (wek'sejszyn) s. dokuczanie; drażnienie; zniecierpliwienie; irytacja; udręka;
przykrosc; zaniepokojenie
vexatious (wek'sejszes) adj.
dokuczliwy; irytujący; przykry; nieznosny
via ('waje) prep. przez; wia
vibrate (waj'brejt) v. zadrgac;
zadrzec; oscylowac; wprawiac
w drganie lub ruch wahadłowy
vibration (waj'brejszyn) s.
drganie; drżenie; wibracja;
oscylacja; ruch wahadłowy
vibrator (waj'brejter) s. wi-
brator; oscylator
vicar ('wyker) s. wikary; wi-
kariusz; zastępca
vice (wajs) imadło; zacisk;
rozpusta; występek; nałog;
narów; wada; v. zaciskać w
imadle
vice versa ('wajsy'we:rsa)
adv. odwrotnie
vicinity (wy'synyty) s. sąsiedztwo; pobliże
vicious ('wy'szes) adj. błędny;
występny; złosliwy; wadliwy;
zepsuty; dokuczliwy; narowisty;
rozpustny
victim ('wyktym) s. ofiara
victor ('wykter) s. zwycięzca
victorian (wyk'to:rjan) adj.
wiktorjański
victorious (wyk'to:rjes) adj.
zwycięski
victory ('wyktery) s. zwycięstwo
victuals ('wytlz) s. prowianty; wiktuały
video ('wydjou) s. telewizja;
adj. telewizyjny
view (wju:) v. oglądac; rozpatrywac; zbadac; zapatrywać się;
s. obejrzenie; spojrzenie;
wizja; zasięg wzroku; widok;
przegląd umysłowy; pogląd;
zapatrywanie; intencja; zamiar;
cel; ocena
viewer ('wju:er) s. widz (telewizyjny etc.)

viewpoint ('wju:,pojnt) s.
punkt widzenia; zapatywanie
vigil ('wydżyl) s. czuwanie;
wigilia
vigilance ('wydżylens) s. czuj-
nosc; bezsennosc
vigilant ('wydżylent) adj.
czujny
vigor ('wyger) s. krzepkosc;
tężyzna; rzeskosc; energia;
siła; moc
vigorous ('wygeres) adj.krzep-
ki; mocny; jędrny; energiczny
vile (wajl) adj. podły; nędzny;
marny
village ('wylydż) s. wies
villager ('wylydżer) s. wiesniak (raczej nieokrzesany)
villain ('wylen) s. łajdak;
łotr; nikczemnik; łobuziak
villainous ('wylenes) adj.
łajdacki; niegodziwy
villainy ('wyleny) s. łajdactwo
vim (wym) s. tężyzna
vincible ('wynsybl) adj. prze-
zwyciężalny
vindicate ('wyndykejt) v.
oczyszczac z zarzutu, oskarżenia, podejrzenia; rehabilitowac;
usprawiedliwiac; bronic; docho-
dzic; dowodzic
vindication (,wyndy'kejszyn) s.
obrona; windykacja; usprawiedliwienie: oczyszczenie się (z
zarzutu); rehabilitacja
vindictive (wyn'dyktyw) adj.
msciwy; karzący
vine (wajn) s. winna latorosl;
winorosl
vinegar ('wynyger) s. ocet;
v. kwasic
vineyard ('wynjerd) s. winnica
vintage ('wyntydż) s. rocznik
wina; winobranie; robienie
wina; model (roczny)
violate ('wajelejt) v. gwałcic;
zgwalcic (kobietę)
violation (,waje'lejszyn) s.
pogwałcenie; zgwałcenie; gwałt;
zbeszczeszczenie; naruszenie
(też praw ruchu)

violence ('wajelens) s. gwał-
towność; gwałt; przemoc
violent ('wajelent) adj. gwałtowny; niepohamowany; wściekły
violet ('wajelyt) s. fiołek;
adj. fioletowy (np. promień)
violin (,waje'lyn) s. skrzypce
violinist (,waje'lynyst) s.
skrzypek
viper ('wajper) s. żmija
virgin ('we:rdżyn) s. dziewica
virginity (we:r'dżynyty) s.
dziewictwo
virile ('wyrajl) adj. męski
virility (wy'rylyty) s. męskość;
wiek męski; cechy męskie
virtual ('we:rczuel) adj. zasadniczy; właściwy; faktyczny;
prawdziwy; rzeczywisty
virtually ('we:rczuely) adv.
rzeczywiście; faktycznie;
praktycznie biorąc
virtue ('we:rczju:) s. cnota;
prawość; czystość; skuteczność;
siła; moc
virtuoso (,we:rczju'ouzou) s.
wirtuoz; miłośnik- znawca
sztuki
virtuous (,we:rczjues) adj.
cnotliwy; prawy
virulent ('wyrulent) adj. jadowity; złośliwy; zjadliwy
virus ('wajeres) s. wirus;
jad (chorobowy)
visa ('wi:za) s. wiza; v. wiza;
v. wizować   skleistość
viscosity(wys'kosyty)s.lepkość;
visibility (wyzy'bylyty) s.
widoczność
visible (wyzybl) adj. widoczny;
wyraźny; widzialny
vision ('wyżyn) s. widzenie;
wzrok; wizja; dar przewidywa-
nia; v. okazywać wizję; mieć
wizję
visit('wyzyt) v. odwiedzać; wi-
zytować zwiedzać; nawiedzać;
karać; udzielać się; gawędzić;
s. wizyta; odwiedziny; pobyt
visitor ('wyzyter) s. gość;
przyjezdny; zwiedzający; inspektor

vista ('wysta) s. perspektywa;
wizja; widok
visual ('wyżjuel) adj. wzrokowy; optyczny
visualize ('wyżjuelajz) v. wyobrażać sobie; uwidaczniać;
uzmysławiać
vital ('wajtl) adj. witalny;
życiowy; żywotny; zasadniczy;
śmiertelny
vitality (waj'taelyty) s. żywotność; żywość
vitamin ('wajtemyn) s. witamina
vivacious (wy'wejszes) adj.
żywy
vivacity (wy'waesyty) s. żywość
vivid ('wywyd) adj. żywy
vivify ('wywyfaj) v. ożywiać
vivisection ('wywysekszyn) s.
wiwisekcja
vixen ('wyksen) s. liszka; li-
sica; jędza
vixenish ('wyksenysz) adj.
jędzowaty
vocabulary (wou'kaebjulery) s.
słownik (specjalny); słownictwo
vocal ('woukel) s. samogłoska;
adj. głosowy; wokalny; głośny;
natarczywy
vocalist ('woukelyst) s. śpiewak; wokalista
vocation (wou'kejszyn) s. zawód; zamiłowanie; powołanie;
skłonność
vogue (woug) s. moda; popularność
voice (wois) s. głos; dźwięk
samogłoskowy; strona (czasownika); v. wymawiać; wyrażać;
dawać wyraz czemuś; wymawiać
dźwięcznie; udźwięczniać; pisać partie głosowe do muzyki;
stroić
void (woid) s. próżnia; pustka;
adj, próżny; pusty; pozbawiony
czegoś; wolny od czegoś; wakujący; nieważny; v. unieważniać;
wydalać; wypróżniać (się); oddawać (mocz)
void of ('woid,ow) exp.: bez

volatile ('woletyl) adj. lotny;
ulatniający się; zmienny
volcano (wol'kejnou) s. wulkan
volley ('woly) s. salwa; potok;
odbicie (piłki); wolej;
v. dać salwę; wypuszczać salwę; podawać wolejem; miotać
potokiem (przekleństw);leciec
salwą; odbijać w locie
volleyball ('woly,bo:l) s.
siatkówka
volt (woult) s. wolt (elektr.)
wolta; v. robić woltę
voltage ('woultydż) s. napięcie
prądu; woltaż
voluble ('woljubl) adj. gładki;
potoczysty; ze swadą
volume ('wolju:m) s. tom; objętość; masa; ilość; pojemność;
rozmiar; siła
voluntary ('wolentery) adj.
ochotniczy; dobrowolny; wolą
kontrolowany; spontaniczny;
samorzutny; s. specjalny wyczyn z wyboru sportowca; gra
solo na organie
volunteer ('wolentier) s. ochotnik (bezpłatnie pracujący);
v. robić z własnej ochoty;
zgłaszać się na ochotnika;
podejmować cos dobrowolnie;
być ochotnikiem
voluptuous (we'lapczues) adj.
zmysłowy; lubieżny
vomit ('womyt) v. wymiotować;
wyrzucać; pobudzać do wymiotów; s. wymioty; środek wymiotny
voodoo ('wu:du:) s. wiara w
czary; czarownik;v.zaczarować
voracious (we'rejszes) adj.
żarłoczny
voracity (we'raesyty) s. żarłoczność
vote (wout) s. głos; głosy;
głosowanie; prawo głosowania;
uchwała; wotum (zaufania);
v. głosować; uchwalać; orzekać; uznawać powszechnie za
cos
vote down ('wout,dałn) v. odrzucać w głosowaniu

voting paper ('woutyŋg'pejper)
s. kartka wyborcza
vouch (waucz) v. ręczyc; gwarantować; potwierdzać; zapewnic
voucher ('wauczer) s. dowód
kasowy
vouch for ('waucz,fo:r) v. ręczyc za kogoś
vouch safe (waucz'sejf) v. (łaskawie) raczyc
vow (wau) s. ślub (też zakonny);
przymierze; v. przysięgać;
ślubować; składać śluby
vowel ('wałel) s. samogłoska
voyage ('wojydż) s. podróż
(statkiem)
voyager ('wojedżer) s. podróżnik
vulcanize ('walkenajz) s. wulkanizowac
vulgar ('walger) adj. ordynarny;
wulgarny; prostacki; gminny;
pospolity; powszechny
vulgarity (wal'gaeryty) s.
wulgarność; wyrażenie wulgarne
vulnerable ('walnerebl) adj.
czuły; wrażliwy; mający słabe
miejsce; narażony na cios; poddatny na zranienie; niezabezpieczony
vulpine ('walpajn) adj. lisi;
przebiegły; chytry
vulture ('walczer) s. sęp; (slang)
szakal
vulturine (walczeryn) adj. sępi
w ('dablju:) dwudziesta trzecia
litera alfabetu angielskiego
wabble ('łobl) v. (slang); rozklekotac; roztrząsnąć; rozchwiać;
s. rozchwianie; rozklekotanje;
wack (łaek) s. (slang); oryginał;
dziwak
wacky ('łaeky) adj.(slang):
zwariowany;zdziwaczały; nieobliczalny
wad (łod) s. tampon; wałek (zwinięty); wata (w uszach); przybitka naboju w strzelbie;
(slang): forsa; plik (banknotów);
v. zatykać (tamponem); watowac;
przybijać (nabój); wypychać;
zwijać w wałek
wadding ('łodyŋg) s. watowanie;
watolina; wata; wełna (do utykania); podkład; przybitka

waddle ('łódl) v. chodzic kołysząc się w biodrze jak
kaczka; s. kaczy krok
wade (łejd) y. brodzic; brnąc;
przechodzic w bród; brodze-
nie
wafer ('łejfer) s. wafel;
opłatek; naklejka urzędowa
(pieczątkowa); v. zapieczę-
towywac naklejką
waffle ('łofl) s. wafel z ciasta nalesnikowego
waft ('łaeft) v. popychac (lekko); posuwac; posyłac (cału-
sa); przepędzac; unosic (w
powietrzu). s. smignięcie
skrzydła; powiew; podmuch;
tchnienie; przelotne uczucie;
smuga (swiatła)
wag (łaeg) v. kiwac (ogonem);
poruszac się; wahac się; chodzic tam i spowrotem; merdac
wage (łejdż) s. płaca; zarobek;
zapłata; v. prowadzic (np.
wojnę)
wage earner ('łejdż,e:rner) s.
człowiek zarobkujący
wages ('łejdżyz) s. zapłata
wager ('łejdżer) s. zakład;
v. zakładac się o cos
wagon ('łaegen) s. ciężki woz
(kryty); lora; woz policyjny;
furgon
wail (łejl) v. zawodzic; lamentowac; opłakiwac; v. zawodze-
nie; lament; płacz
wainscot ('łejnsket) s. boazeria;
ozdobne obicie scian drzewem
waist (łejst) s. talia; stan;
pas; kibic; stanik; srodokrę-
cie; zwężenie
waistcoat ('łeiskout) s. kamizelka
wait (łejt) v. czekac; oczekiwac;
czyhac; czatowac; czaic się;
obsłużyc; obsługiwac kogos;
s. czekanie; oczekiwanie; zasadzka; czaty
wait at table('łejtettejbl) v.
usługiwac przy stole
waiter ('łejter) s. kelner
wait on('łejton) v.obsługiwac

waiting (łejtyŋg) s. czekanie;
oczekiwanie; wyczekiwanie; zasadzka
waiting list (łejtyŋg,lyst) s.
lista kolejnosci (kandydatow,
klientow)
waiting room(łejtyŋrum) s.po-
czekalnia
waitings (łejtyns) pl. kolędni-
cy
waitress (łejtryss) s. kelnerka
wake; woke; woken (łejk; łouk;
łoukn)
wake (łejk) v. obudzic (się);
nie spac; pobudzic; rozbudzic;
wzbudzic; wskrzesic; czuwac
przy (zwłokach); s. niespanie;
czuwanie przy zwłokach; kilwater; fala w slad za statkiem
(motorowką); slad (po kims, po
czyms)
wake up ('łejk,ap) v. obudzic
(się); ocknąc się; oprzytomniec; zdawac sobie sprawę;
zbudzic
wakeful ('łejkful) adj. czuwa-
jący; bezsenny; czujny
waken ('łejkn) = woken (łouken)
v. zob. wake
waken ('łejkn) v. zbudzic;
obudzic; ożywiac; wzbudzic;
wskrzesic (np. zmarłego)
walk (ło:k) v. isc; przechadzac się; chodzic; kroczyc;
isc stępa; jechac stępa;
wejsc; zejsc; s. chod; krok;
przechadzka; spacer; marsz;
deptak; aleja; odległosc prze-
byta
walk about ('ło:ke,baut) v.
włoczyc się; łazic
walk along ('ło:ke,loŋg) v.
chodzic sobie
walk away ('ło:ke,łej) v. odchodzic; (w zawodach): łatwo
wygrywac
walk back ('ło:k,baek) v. wracac
walk down ('ło:k,dałn) v. schodzic
walk in ('ło:k,yn) v. wchodzic

walk off ('ło:k,of) v. odchodzic; zniknąc; ulotnic się (z czyms)

walk out ('ło:k,aut) v. wyjsc; opuscic

walk over ('ło:k,ouwer) v. wygrywac łatwo; traktować pogardliwie

walk up ('ło:k,ap) v. podejsc; wejsc na gorę

walker ('ło:ker) s. piechur

walkie-talkie ('ło:ky-'to:ky) s. przenosny, mały odbiornik-nadajnik radiowy

walking (ło:kyng) s. chodzenie; marsz; wycieczka piesza; adj. chodzący; wędrowny

walking papers ('ło:kyn'pejpers) pl. zwolnienie z pracy na pismie

walking stick ('ło:kyng,styk) s. laska

walking-tour ('ło:kyng,tu:r) s. wycieczka piesza; zwiedzanie piechotą

walk-out ('ło:kaut) s. strajk

walk-over ('ło:k-over ('ło:k-ouwer) s. walkower (sport)

wall (ło:l) s. sciana; mur; przepierzenie; wał; v. obmurowac

wall in ('ło:l,yn) v. otaczac

wall up ('ło:,ap) v. zamurowac

wallboard ('ło:l,bo:rd) s. licówka (sciany)

wallet ('łolyt) s. portfel

wallop ('łolep) v. walic; łoic; prac; pobic na głowę; galopowac; łazic ciężko i niezgrabnie; s. wyrznięcie (cios); galop; ruch ciężki i niezgrabny

wallow ('łolou) v. tarzac się; kłębic się; kołysac się; s. tarzanie się

wallpaper ('łol,pejper) s. tapety; v. tapetowac

Wall Street ('łolstri:t) s. osrodek finansowy (USA)

walnut ('ło:lnat) s. orzech włoski

walrus ('ło:lres) s. mors

waltz ('ło:ls) s. walc; v.tan-czyc walca; (slang): ruszac się żwawo

wan (łon) adj. blady; wybladły; blednąc

wand (łond) s. laseczka; pałeczka; pręt; buława

wander ('łonder) v. wędrowac;

wanderer ('łonderer) s. wędrowiec

wane (łejn) v. zanikac; gasnąc; s. zanik

wangle ('łaengl) v. (slang): wycyganic; wyłudzic; sfałszowac; s. krętactwo; kant

want (ło:nt) s. brak; potrzeba; niedostatek; niedopatrzenie; bieda; nędza; v. pragnąc; chciec; brakowac; potrzebowac; pożądac

wanted ('ło:ntyd) adj. poszukiwany

wanting ('ło:ntyng) adj. brakujący; kiepski; niedokładny; pozbawiony; nie na poziomie; słaby na umysle; prep. bez; mniej;przy braku

want in ('ło:nt,yn) v. chciec wejsc

wanton ('łonten) adj. złosliwy; krzywdzący; bez powodu; bezmyslny; samowolny; bezczelny; nieokiełzany; wyuzdany; lubiezny; bujny; zbytkowny; s. lubieznik; lubieznica; y. oddawac się rozpuscie; używac sobie; swawolic; rosc bujnie; trwonic; psocic; figlowac; bawic się

want out ('ło:nt,aut) v. chciec wyjsc

war (łor) s. wojna; v. wojowac; zawojowac

warble ('łorbl) v. nucic; jodłowac; s. nucący głos; nucona piesn; guz od siodła na grzbiecie konia; guz wywołany larwą gza bydlęcego

ward (ło:rd) s. dzielnica; cela; sala; oddział; podopieczny; opieka; kuratela; postawa obronna; parada; straż; v.odparowywac (cios); odsuwac (niebezpieczenstwo);umieszczac na oddziale

ward off ('ɫo:rd,of) v. odparowywać cios; odsuwać (zagro-
żenie)
warden ('ɫo:rdn) s. dyrektor
więzienia; dozorca; nadzorca;
gatunek twardej gruszki
warder ('ɫo:rder) s. strażnik
więzienny; posterunek; buława
ward heeler('ɫo:rd,hi:ler) s.
naganiacz partyjny
wardrobe ('ɫo:droub) s. garderoba; szafa na ubranie
ware (ɫeer) s. towar; wyrób;
ceramika; v. uwaga na coś;
trzymać się z dala od czegoś;
excl.:strzeż się !
warehouse ('ɫeerhaus) s. magazyn; składnica; dom składowy;
v. magazynować; składować
warm (ɫo:rm) adj. ciepły; świeży (trop); bliski znalezienia;
zadomowiony (na posadzie);
zamożny
warm up ('ɫo:rm,ap) v. ożywiać
(się); podgrzewać (się); ogrze-
wać (się); rozgrzewać (się)
warmup ('ɫo:rmap) s. ćwiczenia
rozluźniające (przed zawodami
etc); zagrzanie się
warmth ('ɫo:rms) s. ciepło;
serdeczność; zapał
warn (ɫo:rn) v. ostrzegać;
przypominać; wzywać; zapowiadać; uprzedzać
warn against(ɫo:negejnst) v.
ostrzegać przed czymś
warning ('ɫo:rnyŋg) adj. ostrzegawczy; s. ostrzeżenie; przestroga; znak ostrzegawczy;
wypowiedzenie (posady)
warp ('ɫo:rp) v. wypaczyć (się);
zwichrować (się); wykrzywić
(się); spaczyć (się); przyholo-
wywać do miejsca utwierdzenia
liny lub łańcucha; użyźniać
(przez zalewanie osadem);
s. spaczenie; wypaczenie; osnowa; szew skośny; lina holownicza; osad
warrant ('ɫorent) v. usprawiedliwiać; uzasadniać; gwarantować; s. upoważnienie; gwarancja;

nakaz prawny (aresztu; rewizji,
etc). pełnomocnictwo dla ad-
wokatów; patent starszego pod-
oficera (USA)
warranty ('ɫorenty) s. gwarancja; poręka; rękojmia; podstawa; usprawiedliwienie; upoważnienie; dokument sądowy
warren ('ɫo:ryn) s. królikarnia
warrior ('ɫo:rjor) s. wojownik;
żołnierz; adj. wojowniczy
wart (ɫo:rt) s. brodawka; ku-
rzawka
wary ('ɫeery) adj. ostrożny
was (ɫoz) v. zob. be
wash (ɫo:sz) v. myć (się); prać;
prać (się); oczyszczać; zraszać; lekko barwić; lawować;
umyć się; sunąć; płynąć z
pluskiem; płukać (rudę);
s. mycie; pranie; płyn (czyszczący); fale; plusk; pomyje;
lura; wypłukane miejsce w ziemi; ględzenie; zaburzenie wody za statkiem; zaburzenie powietrza za samolotem; ziemia
na tacy zawierająca złoto; pod-
mywanie przez fale; mielizna;
kanał wyżłobiony przez wodę;
mielizna naniesiona wodą; la-
wowanie; cienka warstwa metalu;
kilwater; ślad wodny
wash away (ɫo:sze,ɫej) v. spłukać; zmyć; unosić
wash down ('ɫo:sh,daɫn) v. zmywać strumieniem wody; popić
jedzenie
wash off (ɫo:sh,of) v. odeprać;
wymywać
wash out ('ɫo:sh,aut) v. wypłu-
kiwać (się) (z pieniędzy etc.)
wash up ('ɫo:sh,ap) v. zmywać
naczynia; wymyć się
wash and wear ('ɫo:sz,end'ɫeer)
s. bielizna i odzież gotowa
do noszenia po praniu bez pra-
sowania
washbowl ('ɫo:sz,boul) s.mied-
nica; umywalka; umywalnia
washcloth ('ɫo:sz,cloś) s. zmy-
wak; szmatka do zmywania

washer ('ło:szer) s. uszczelka; podkładka; maszyna do prania
washing ('łoszyŋg)s. mycie; pranie; przemywanie; woda z prania; popłuczyny; wypłukane złoto; wypłukany żwir; bielizna do prania
washing machine ('ło:szyŋg,me'szi:n) s. pralka; maszyna do prania
washing powder ('ło:szyn'pał der) s. proszek do prania
washing up ('ło:szyng,ap) v. obmycie się
washleather ('ło:sz,ledzer) s. ircha; zamsz
washout ('ło:szaut) s. zapadnięcie się; podmycie; (slang): klapa; niepowodzenie
washtub ('ło:sztab) s. balia
washy ('ło:szy) adj. wodnisty; rzadki; blady; cienki; wypłowiały
wasn't = was not
wasp (łosp) n. osa; (slang): biały-anglosaksonin-protestant
waspish ('łospysh) adj. zjadliwy; cienki w pasie (jak osa)
wastage ('łejstydż) s. strata; zużycie
waste (łejst) adj. pustynny; pusty; nieużyty (ziemia); opustoszały; wyludniony; leżący odłogiem; zużyty; niepotrzebny; zbyteczny; odpadowy; v. pustoszyc; psuć; niszczyć (się); stracić (też zabić); zmarnować; ginąć; zużywac (się); zapuscic; zaniedbać; s. pustynia; marnowanie; trwonienie; zniszczenie; ubytek; zużycie; odpady; bezmiar (np. wody); zaniedbanie; marnotrawstwo
waste away ('łejst,e'łey) v. marniec
wasteful ('łejstful) adj. rozrzutny; marnotrawny
wastepaper basket ('łejst-pej-per-ba:skyt) s. kosz na śmieci

waste pipe ('łejstpajp) s. rura odpływowa; rura ściekowa
waster ('łejster) s. marnotrawca; zepsuty materiał; artykuł wybrakowany; nicpoń
watch (ło:cz) s. czuwanie; pilnowanie; czaty; czujność; wachta; zegarek; miec się na baczności; oczekiwanie na coś; wygladanie czegoś; v. czuwac; oczekiwac; czatowac; pilnowac; opiekowac się; uważać; mieć na oku; miec się na baczności; wygladac czegoś; obserwowac; szpiegowac; przyglądac się; patrzyc; oczekiwać sposobności; sledzic
watch out ('ło:czaut) v. uważac; strzec się; uwaga !; uważaj !
watchdog ('ło:czdog) s. pies podwórzowy
watchful ('ło:czful) adj. czujny; baczny
watchmaker ('ło:cz,mejker) s. zegarmistrz
watchman ('ło:czmen) s. stróż; dozorca
watchtower ('ło:cz,tauer) s. strażnica; wieża strażnicza
watchword ('ło:człe:rd) s. hasło; slogan
watch your step ('ło:cz,jo:r'-'step) exp.: uważaj !; pilnuj się !
water (ło:ter) s. woda; wysięk; przypływ; odpływ; pl. zdrój; wody lecznicze; ocean; morze; jezioro; rzeka; v. polewać; podlewac; pokropic; poic; isc do wodopoju; nawadniac; rozwadniac; rozcienczac; skrapiac; łzawic się; ślinic się
water anchor ('ło:ter'aenker) s. kotwica dryfująca
water blister ('ło:ter,blyster) s. pęcherzyk z wodą
waterborne ('ło:ter,born) adj. przenoszony lub przekazywany przez wodę
water bottle ('ło:ter,botl) s. karafka; manierka

water brush ('ło:ter,brasz) s.
zgaga
water but ('ło:ter,bąt) s.
zbiornik na deszczówkę
water-cart ('ło:ter,ca:rt) s.
beczkowóz
water closet ('ło:ter'klozet)
s. ustęp
watercolor ('ło:ter'kaler) s.
akwarela
water cool ('ło:ter,ku:l) v.
chłodzić wodą
watercourse ('ło:ter,ko:rs)
s. strumień; rzeka ; kanał
watercress ('ło:ter,kres) s.
rzeżucha wodna
water-cure ('ło:ter,kjuer) s.
kuracja wodna
water-dog ('ło:ter,dog) s. pies
myśliwski aportujący z wody;
(slang): amator pływania, etc)
water down ('ło:ter,dałn) v.
rozwadniać
waterfall ('ło:ter,fo:l) s.
wodospad
waterfowl ('ło:ter,faul) s.
ptactwo wodne
waterfront ('ło:ter,frant) s.
wybrzeże; doki; dzielnica
portowa
watergap ('ło:ter,gaep) s.
przełom rzeki
water gate('ło:ter,gejt) s.
śluza
water gauge('ło:ter,gejdż) s.
wodowskaz; licznik wodny
water-glass ('ło:ter,gla:s) s.
szklanka; naczynie; kubek;
szklany wodowskaz; przeziernik podwodny
water hammer ('ło:ter,haemer)
s. silny wstrząs wywołany na-
głym zatrzymaniem wody w rurze
water hen ('ło:ter,hen) s. kur-
ka wodna
water hole ('ło:terhol) s. stojąca woda (w suchym łożysku
rzeki); wodopój
water ice ('ło:ter,ajs) s. sor-
bet

watering place ('ło:teryng-
plejs) s. wodopój; kąpielisko;
zdrojowisko
waterless ('ło:terłys) adj.
bezwodny; pozbawiony wody
water lily ('ło:ter,lyly) s.
grzybień biały; lilia wodna
water level ('ło:ter'lewl) s.
poziom wody
waterline ('ło:terlajn) s.
linia zanurzenia statku
waterlogged ('ło:ter,logd) adj.
przesycony wodą
watermain ('ło:ter,mejn) s.
główna rura wodociągów
waterman ('ło:termen) s. prze-
woźnik; wioślarz
watermark ('ło:terma:rk) s.
znak wodny; wodowskaz; v. robić znak wodny
watermelon ('ło:ter,melen) s.
arbuz; kawon
water meter('ło:ter'mi:ter) s.
wodomierz; licznik wodny
water mill ('ło:ter,myl) s.
młyn
water mocassin ('ło:ter,mokesyn)
s. żmija wodna w USA
water motor ('ło:ter'mouter) s.
motor wodny
water plane ('ło:ter'plejn) s.
hydroplan
waterpower ('ło:ter'pałer) s.
siła wodna; prawo do używania
wody
water pot ('ło:ter,pot) s.ko--
newka; polewaczka
waterproof ('ło:ter,pru:f)
adj. nieprzemakalny; v. robić
nieprzemakalnym
water-rat ('ło:ter,raet) s.
szczur wodny
water rate ('ło:ter,rejt) s.
opłata za wodę; cena wody
waterscape ('ło:ter,skejp) s.
krajobraz morski
watershed ('ło:ter,szed) s,
dział wodny; (slang): ważna
granica
water-ski ('ło:ter,ski:) s.
narta wodna

water spout('łó:ter,spaut) s.
trąba wodna; rynna pionowa
water supply ('łó:terse,plaj)
s. zaopatrzenie w wodę; sieć
wodociągowa
water table ('łó:ter,tejbl) s.
poziom (w ziemi) wody zaskórnej
watertight ('łó:ter,tajt)
adj. wodoszczelny
water tower ('łoter,tauer) s.
wieża ciśnień
water wave ('łó:ter,łejw) s.
ondulacja wodna
waterway ('łó:ter,łej) s.
droga wodna; kanał; rzeka
spławna
waterwheel ('łó:ter,hłi:l) s.
koło (młyńskie) wodne
water witch ('łó:ter,łycz) s.
różdżkarz
waterworks ('łó:ter,łe:rks) s.
wodociągi; fontanna
watery ('łó:tery) adj. wodnisty;
zalzawiony; śliniący się; wróżący deszcz
watt (łot) s. (electr.) wat
waul (ło:l) v. miałczeć ostro
i przeciągle
wave (łejw) s. fala; falistość;
ondulacja; pokiwanie ręką;
gest ręką; v. falować; ondulować; machać do kogoś
wave away ('łejwe'łej) v. odprawiać machnięciem ręki
wave back ('łejw,baek) v. przywoływać (spowrotem) machnięciem ręki
wavelength ('łejw,lenks) s.
długość fali
wave meter('łejwmi:ter) s. falomierz
waver ('łejwer) v. zachwiać(się);
zamigotać; być niezdecydowanym;
załamywać się; drzeć; zawahać
się; kołysać się; trzepotać
się;szchwianie (się)
wavy ('łejwy) adj. falisty; sfalowany; drżący; migocący;
karbowany
wawl ('ło:l) v. wrzeszczeć jak
kot

wax (łaeks) s. wosk; adj. woskowy; v. woskować; stawać się
waxen ('łaeksn) adj. woskowy;
miękki jak wosk
wax paper ('łaeks'pejper) s.
papier woskowy
waxwork ('łaeksłe:rk) s. figura woskowa; v, modelować
z wosku
waxy ('łaeksy) adj. woskowy;
woskowaty; (slang): wściekły;
zły; okrutny
way (łej) s. droga; szlak;
trakt; przejście; wolna droga;
odległość; kierunek; strona;
sposób; zwyczaj; bieg; tok;
sens; stan; położenie
way back (łej baek) adv. dawno
temu; daleko w tyle; dawno
waybill ('łejbyl) s. list
przewozowy; fracht
wayfarer ('łej,feerer) s. podróżnik (pieszy)
waylay (łejlej) v.zob. lay;
zaskoczyć kogoś; czyhać na
kogoś; czatować
way of life ('łej ow,lajf) s.
styl życia; sposób życia
way-out ('łej,aut) s. wyjście;
rozwiązanie; adj. (slang):
nadzwyczajny; nadzwyczaj;
dobrze zrobiony; nadzwyczaj
zdolny; (zob.: far-out)
wayside ('łej,sajd) s. skraj
drogi; adj. przydrożny
way station (,łej'stejszyn) s.
przystanek
-ways (łejz) (przyrostek)
w taki sposób (np:sideways)
wayward ('łejłerd) adj. przewrotny; uparty; kaprysny;
nieobliczalny; chimeryczny
we (łi:) pron. my
weak (łi:k) adj. słaby
weaken ('łi:kn) v. osłabiać;
słabnąć; rozcieńczać
weak-kneed ('łi:kni:d) adj.
słaby
weakling ('łi:klyng) s. słabeusz; cherlak; człowiek słaby; adj. słaby

weakly ('łi:kly) adj. słabowity; adv. słabo
weak-minded ('łi:k,majndyd)
adj. słaby na umyśle; słabe-
go charakteru
weakness (łi:knys) s. słabość;
słabostka
wealth (łels) s. bogactwo; dobrobyt
wealthy ('łelsy) adj. bogaty
wean (łi:n) v. odłączać od
piersi; oduczać; odrywać
weanling ('łi:nlyng) s. dziecko świeżo odsunięte od piersi
weapon ('łepon) s. broń
wear; wore; worn (łeer; ło:r;
ło:rn)
wear (łeer) v. nosić; chodzić
w czyms; ścierać się; wycierać się; żłobić; zacierać się;
przechodzić; mijać; zdzierać;
nużyć; męczyć; wyczerpywać;
długo trwać; długo służyć;
s. noszenie; rzeczy noszone;
moda; zużycie; wytrzymałość
wear away ('łeer,e'łej) v.
zużywać; wlec się
wear off ('łeer,of) v. ze-
trzeć (się); zacierać (się);
mijać
wear on ('łeer,on) v. wlec się
wear out ('łeer,aut) v. zdzierać (się); wyczerpywać (się)
wearing ('łieryng)adj.przezna-
czony do noszenia na sobie
wearisome ('łierysem) adj.
męczący; nużący; nudny
weary ('łiery) adj. zmęczony;
znużony; znudzony; męczący;
nużący; nudny; v. męczyć;
nudzić; naprzykrzać się;
uprzykrzać sobie
weasel ('łi:zl) s. łasica
weather ('łedzer) s. pogoda;
adj. atmosferyczny; odwietrz-
ny; pogodny; v. zwietrzać;
okrywać się patyna (śniedzią)
weather-beaten ('łedzer,bi:tn)
adj. zaharowany; skołatany
przez burze
weather-bound ('łedzer,baund)
adj. zatrzymany przez pogodę
(statek)

weather bureau ('łedzer,bjuerou)
s. instytut meteorologiczny
weather chart ('łedzer,cza:rt)
s. wykres meteorologiczny
weathercock ('łedzer,kok) s.
chorągiewka na dachu; kurek
na dachu; człowiek niestały
weather forecast ('łedz,fo:r-
ka:st) s. komunikat meteorologiczny
weather vane ('łedzer,wejn) s.
wiatrowskaz; chorągiewka na
dachu
weave; wove; woven (łi:w; łouw;
łouwn)
weave (łi:w) v. tkać (tkaninę);
knuć (spisek); układać (intry-
gę; opowiadanie) spleść; splatać; zajmować się tkactwem
weaver ('łi:wer) s. tkacz
weaving ('łi:wyng) s. tkactwo
web (łeb) s. tkanina; sztuka
(materiału); stek (kłamstw);
pajęczyna; błona (nietoperza);
tkanka łączna; usztywnienie
wed (łed) v. zaślubiać; łączyć
się; pobrać się; adj. zaślubiony
wedded ('łedyd) adj. zaślubiony; ślubny; oddany (sprawie)
wedding ('łedyng) s. ślub; wesele; adj. ślubny; weselny
wedding ring ('łedyng,ryng) s.
obrączka ślubna
we'd (łi:d) = we had; we would;
we should
wedge (łedż) s. klin; trójkatny
kawałek (tortu); golfowy kijek
z klinowym zakończeniem; v.kli-
nować; zaklinować; rozklinować;
łupać
wedge in ('łedż,yn) v. wpychać
(się); wcisnąć (się)
wedge off ('łedż,of) v. wypychać (się)
wedlock ('łedlok) s. małżeństwo
Wednesday ('łenzdy) s. środa
weed (łi:d) s. chwast; zielsko;
cygaro; (slang): chuchro; cherlak; mizerak; szkapa; v. pie-
lić; odchwaszczać
weeder ('łi:der) s. pielnik;
wypielacz

weed grown ('łi:dgroun)adj.
zachwaszczony
weed out ('łi:d,aut) v. wypie-
lac; usuwac
weeds ('łi:ds) pl. krepa żałobna; stroj żałobny
weedy ('łi:dy) adj. zachwaszczony; chudy; wysoki
weed killer ('łi:d,kyler) s.
trucizna na chwasty
week (łi:k) s. tydzien
weekday ('łi:kdej) s. dzien
powszedni
weekend ('łi:kend) s. niedziela oraz części wolne
soboty i poniedziałku;
v. spędzac weekend
week in-week out ('łi:k,yn-
'łi:k,aut) adv. exp.: co tydzien
weekly ('łi:kly) adj. tygodniowy; adv. tygodniowo; s.
tygodnik
weep; wept; wept (łi:p; łept;
łept)
weep (łi:p) v. płakac; opłakiwac; zapłakac; lamentowac;
cieknąc; wyciekac; ociekac;
s. płacz; cieknięcie
weeper ('łi:per) s. płaczek;
płaczka; welon żałobny; krepa żałobna
weep away ('łi:pe,łej) v. wy-
płakac się
weeping willow ('łi:pyng,ły-
lou) s. wierzba płacząca
weep for joy ('łi:p-fo:r-dżoj)
v. płakac z radosci
weep out ('łi:p,aut) v. powiedziec z płaczem
weigh (łej) v. ważyc (się);
rozważac; mierzyc; równoważyc;
podnosic (kotwicę); s. waże-
nie
weigh in ('łej,yn) v. ważyc
(boksera; dżokeja przed zawodami)
weigh out ('łej,aut) v. wywa-
życ człowieka przed zawodami
weigh up ('łej,ap) v. rozważyc
weigh upon ('łej,apon) v. przygniatac; ciążyc na kims

weight (łejt) s. ciężar; waga;
obciążenie; ciężarek; odważnik;
przycisk; grubosc (odziezy);
znaczenie; doniosłosc; odpowiedzialnosc; v. obciążac; pogru-
biac sztucznie tkaninę
weight lifting ('łejt lyftyng)
s. (sport) podnoszenie ciężarow
weightless ('łejtlys) adj. lekki;
bez ciężaru
weighted-with(łejyd,łys) adj.
obarczony (np. wiekiem)
weighty ('łejty) adj. ciężki;
ważki; doniosły; ważny; poważny ; przekonywujący; rozważony;
przemyslany
weir (łier) s. jaz; grobla
weird (łierd) adj. niesamowity;
tajemniczy; nadprzyrodzony;
dziwny; dziwaczny; s. los
welcome ('łekem) exp.: witaj !
witajcie ! s. powitanie; adj.
mile widziany; mający pozwolenie; mogący korzystac; v. powitac; witac (z radoscią)
weld (łeld) v. spawac (się);
spajac; zespalac; zgrzewac;
s. spoina; spawanie; spojenie;
miejsce spojenia
welder (łelder) s. spawacz;
spawarka; przyrząd do spawania
welfare ('łelfeer) s. dobro;
dobrobyt; powodzenie; pomysl-
nosc; szczęscie
welfare-state ('łelfeer'stejt)
s. panstwo o bardzo wysokich
swiadczeniach społecznych
welfare-work ('łelfeer,łe:rk)
s. praca społeczna; społecz-
nictwo; praca dobroczynna
well; better; best (łel; beter;
best) adv. dobrze; lepiej; najlepiej
well (łel) s. studnia; otwor
wiertniczy; odwiert; zrodło;
klatka (schodowa); adv. dobrze;
należycie; porządnie; mocno; so-
lidnie; szczęsliwie; całkiem;
wyraznie; łatwo; lekko; słusznie; adj. dobry; zdrowy; zadawalający; pomyslny; w porządku;
exp.: dobrze ! a więc ?

well-balanced ('łel'baelenst)
adj. zrównoważony
well-behaved ('łelby'hejwd)
adj. dobrze wychowany
well-being ('łel'bi:yŋg)s.
dobrobyt; powodzenie; po-
myślność
well-born ('łel'bo:rn) adj.
dobrze urodzony
well-bred ('łel'bred) adj.
rasowy; dobrze wychowany
well-connected ('łel'konektyd)
adj. dobrze skoligacony
well-disposed ('łeldys'pouzd)
adj. życzliwie usposobiony
well done ('łeldan) exp.:
brawo ! dobrze zrobione !
well-fed ('łelfed) adj. dobrze
odżywiony
well-founded ('łelfaundyd)
adj. uzasadniony
wellhead ('łel'hed) s. źródło
well-heeled ('łel'hi:ld) adj.
slang): forsisty (ma forsę)
Wellingtons ('łelyntenz) s.
buty z wysokimi holewami
(też z gumy)
well-informed ('łel-ynfo:rmd)
adj. dobrze poinformowany;
wykształcony
well-intended ('łel-'yntendyd)
adj. dobrze pomyślany
well-judged ('łel-'dżadżd) adj.
rozsądny; roztropny; dobrze
pomyślany
well-knit ('łel'nyt) adj.
zwarty; dobrze zbudowany;
jędrny
well-known ('łel'nołn) adj.
dobrze znany
well-meant ('łel'ment) adj.
zrobiony w najlepszej intencji
well-nigh ('łel'naj) adv. nieledwie; o mało co; o mało nie
well-off ('łel'o:f) adj. dobrze sytuowany; zamożny
well point('łel'poynt) s. rura
do usuwania wody podskórnej
(przed kopaniem)
well-read ('łel'red) adj.
oczytany
well-sinker ('łel'syŋker)s.
studniarz

well-spoken ('łel'spouken) adj.
uprzejmy; pięknie mówiący;
dobrze powiedziany
wellspring (łel'spryŋg)s.
źródło
well-timed ('łel'tajmd) adj.
na czasie; odpowiedni
well-to-do ('łel-te'du:) adj.
zamożny; dobrze sytuowany
well-wisher ('łel'łyszer) s.
sympatyk
well-worn ('łel'ło:rn) adj.
wytrwały; wyświechtany; oklepany; dobrze noszony
welsh (łelsz) adj. walijski;
s. wykręcanie się od płacenia;
v. uciekać nie zapłaciwszy
welter ('łelter) v. falować;
tarzać się; s. falowanie;
powódź; zamęt; kolos; silne
uderzenie
wench (łencz) s. dziewucha;
ulicznica; v. latać za dziew-
kami
Wendish (łendysz) adj. łużycki
went (łent) v. zob. go
wept (łept) v. zob. weep
were (łe:r) v. zob. be
we're (łier) = we are
werewolf('łe:rłuf) s. wilkołak
west (łest) s. zachód; adj.
zachodni; adv. na zachód; ku
zachodowi
westerly ('łesterly) adj. zachodni; adv. na zachód
western ('łestern) adj. zachodni; pochodzący z zachodu
westward ('łestłerd) adj. zachodni; ku zachodowi; na zachód
wet (łet) adj. mokry; wilgotny;
zmoczony; przemoczony; słotny;
deszczowy; dżdżysty; (slang):
w błędzie; s. wilgoć; wilgot-
ność; trunek; v. moczyć (się);
zwilżać; zraszać
wet nurse ('łet,ne:rse) s.
mamka; v. karmić
wether ('łedzer) s.skop (ka-
strowany baran)
wet through ('łet'tru:) v.
przemoczyć (na wylot)
we've (łi:w) = we have

whack (hłaek) v. walic; grzmocic; (slang): dzielic się
czyms; s. walnięcie; trzas-
nięcie; (slang): część; próba;
stan (rzeczy)
whacker ('hłaeker) s. kolor
whacking ('hłaekyng) adj. kolosalny
whale (hłejl) s. wieloryb;
rzecz wspaniała; v. polowac
na wieloryby; (slang): bic
whale-boat ('hłejl,bout) s.
łódz do połowu wielorybów;
łódz strażnicza; ratunkowa
whalebone ('hłejlboun) s, fisz-
bin
whale-fin ('hłejlfyn) s. fisz-
bin
whale-oil ('hłejl,ojl) s. tran
wielorybi
whaler ('hłejler) s. statek do
połowu wielorybów
whammy ('hłaemy) s. (slang):
urok (rzucony na kogos)
whang (hłaeng) s. grzmotnięcie;
huczenie; v. walic; grzmocic;
huczec
wharf (hło:rf) s. przystan (wy-
ładunkowa); nabrzeże; v. cumo-
wac do wyładunku; wyładowywac
w przystani
wharves (hło:rfs) pl. nabrzeża
wyładunkowe
what (hłot) adj. jaki; jaki
tylko; ten; który; ten...co;
taki... jaki; tyle.., ile;
pron. co; to co; cos;
excl.: co ? czego ? jak to !
what about ('hłote,baut) exp.:
a co z... ?; co powiesz o...?
whatever ('hłot'ewer) adj.
jakikolwiek; pron. cokolwiek;
wszystko co; co tylko; bez
względu; obojętnie co
what for('hłotfo:r) s. (slang):
bura; lanie; exp.:za co ?
what next ('hłot,nekst) exp.:
co dalej ?
whatnot ('hłotnot) s. etażerka;
cacka; (slang): cokolwiek;
obojętnie co; wszystko

whatsit ('hłotsyt) s. jak się
to nazywa; ten (przedmiot)
whatsoever ('hłotsou'ewer) adj.
jakikolwiek by; cokolwiek by;
co tylko by; pron. wszystko
co tylko
wheat (hłi:t) s. pszenica
wheaten ('hłi:tn) adj. prze-
niczny
wheel ('hłi:l) s. koło; kółko;
ster; kierownica; v. obracac
(się); wrócic (się); prowadzic
taczki (rower); wozic taczkami
etc.
wheelbarrow ('hłi:l,baerou) s.
taczki
wheel chair('hłi:l,czeer) s. fotel na kółkach
wheeler-dealer ('hłi:ler,di:ler)
s. cwaniak; politykier
wheelwright ('hłi:lrajt) s.
kołodziej
wheeze ('hłi:z) v. sapac; s. sa-
panie; (slang); dowcip; komunał
wheezy ('hłi:zy) adj. sapiący;
zasapany
when (hłen) adv. kiedy; kiedyż;
wtedy; kiedy to; gdy; przy;
podczas gdy;
s. czas (zdarzenia)
whenas (,hłen'aez) conj. kiedy;
podczas gdy
whence (hłens) adv. & conj. skąd
whenever ('hłenewer) adv. kiedy
tylko; skoro tylko
whensoever ('hłensou'ever) adv.
skoro tylko; skądkolwiek
where (hłeer) adv. & conj. gdzie;
dokąd
whereabout ('hłeere'baut) adv.
gdzie ?
whereabouts ('hłeere'bauts) adv.
zważywszy; gdzie; mniej więcej;
s. miejsce zamieszkania;(pobytu)
whereas('hłeer'aez) conj. podczas
gdy
whereat ('hłeer,et) conj. podczas
gdy
whereby ('hłeer,baj) adv. po
czym ? po kim ? po którym; za
pomocą którego? jak?którym

wherefore('hₑerfo:r) adj.
dlaczego; dlatego; z tego
powodu
wherefrom (hₑer'fro:m) adv.
skąd; z czego
wherein (hₑer'yn) adv. w czym;
w którym
whereof (hₑer'ow) adv. z czego; z którego
whereon (hₑer'on) adv. na
czym; na ktorym
wheresoever (,hₑersou'ever)
adv. wszędzie by; dokądkolwiek
by; gdzie tylko by
whereupon (,hₑere'pon) adv.
na czym; po czym
wherever (,hₑer'ever) adv.
dokądkolwiek; wszędzie; gdzie
tylko
wherewith (,hₑer'łyz) adv.
(z) czym ?
wherewithal (,hₑerły'so:l) s.
potrzebne środki (fundusze,
przybory)
whet (,hₑet) v. naostrzyć;
zaostrzyć (też apetyt);
s. ostrzenie; zakąska
whether ('hₑedzer) conj. czy-
czy; czy tak, czy owak
whetstone ('hₑet,stoun)s. osełka; kamień szlifierski
whey (hₑej) s. serwatka
which (hₑycz) pron. który; co;
którędy; dokąd; w jaki (sposób)
whichever (hₑycz,ewer) adj.
którykolwiek; jaki; każdy...
jaki; który tylko; pron.
którykowiek; każdy
whichsoever (,hₑyczsou'ewer)
adj. pron. = whichever (z naciskiem)
whiff (hₑyf) s. powiew; podmuch; tchnienie; zapach; dym;
lekki wybuch gniewu; v. dmuchać; dymić; palić; lekko
wiać
while (hₑajl) s. chwila; pewien czas; po chwili; niebawem; wkrótce; conj. podczas
gdy; jak długo; dopóki; póki;
natychmiast; chociaż co prawda

while ago ('hₑajl'egou) adv.
(nie)dawno
while away ('hₑajle'łej) v.
spędzać czas; skracać sobie
czas
whim ('hₑym) s. kaprys; zachcianka; fantazja; fanaberia;
kołowrot górniczy
whimper ('hₑymper) v. piszczeć;
kwilić; skomleć; skowyczeć;
s. kwilenie; skowyt; skamlanie
whimsical ('hₑymzykel) adj.
kapryśny; dziwaczny; cudaczny
whimsy ('hₑymzy) s. kaprys
whim-wham('hₑymhłaem) s. cacko
whine ('hₑajn) v. skomleć; je-
czeć; powiedzieć jękliwie;
s. skomlenie; jęk
whip (hₑyp) s. bat; bicz; pomocnik; woźnica; naganiacz;
uderzenie biczem; bita śmietana; v. chłostać; zacinać (batem); ubijać (śmietanę); smagać; przyrządzać na prędce;
zwyciężyć; zakasować (kogoś);
owijać; windować; śmigać;
zbierać; wyjechać (pośpiesznie)
whip in ('hₑyp,yn) v. zapędzać
batem
whip off ('hₑyp'o:f) v. zerwać
coś; czmychnąc z czyms
whip on ('hₑyp'on) v. popędzać
batem
whip out ('hₑyp,aut) v. wyciąg-
nąć błyskawicznie
whip round ('hₑyp,raund) v. od-
wrocic się znienacka
whip together ('hₑyp te'gedzer)
v. zganiać batem; zwalać na
kupę; montować na gwałt
whipped cream ('hₑypt'kri:m) s.
bita śmietana
whipper-snapper ('hₑyper'snae-
per) s. chłystek; smarkacz
whipping boy ('hₑypyng,boj) s.
kozioł ofiarny (chłopak chło-
stany za innego)
whipping top ('hₑypyng,top) s.
bąk do podbijania
whippy (,hₑypy) adj. giętki;
elastyczny

whipsaw (,hłyp'so) s. wąska
piłeczka; v. ciąc piłką;
wygrac podwojnie; pobic podwojnie
whipstock (,hłyp'stok) s. biczysko
whirl (hłe:rl) v. kręcic (się);
wirowac; zawirowac; porywac
w wir; s. wirowanie; ruch
wirowy; wir; (slang): proba
(czegos)
whirlpool ('hłe:rl'pu:l) s.
wir
whirlwind ('hłe:rl'łynd) s.
trąba powietrzna; wir po-
wietrzny
whirlybird (hłe:rly'be:rd) s.
helikoper (USA)
whirr (hłe:r) v. furgotac;
warkotac; s. furgot; warkot
(maszyny)
whisk (hłysk) s. wiechec;
smignięcie; trzepaczka (do
jajek etc.); miotełka;
v. otrzepac; odpędzac; porywac; szybko odwozic; przywozic; czmychac; wymachiwac;
smigac
whisk away ('hłyske'łej) s.
strzepnąc; przewiezc lotem
strzały; czmychnac
whiskers ('hłyskers) pl. baki;
bokobrody; wąsy
whisky ('hłysky) s. (wodka)
whiskey
whisper ('hłysper) v. szeptac;
mowic cicho; szmerac; szelescic; s. szeptanie; szmer
whistle ('hłysl) v. gwizdac;
swistac; zagwizdac; s. gwizdanie; gwizd; swist; gwizdek;
gardło
whistle away ('hłysle'łej) v.
pogwizdywac sobie
white (hłajt) adj. biały; bezbarwny; blady; czysty; niepokalany; uczciwy; rzetelny;
niewinny; s. biel; biały (człowiek); białko; białe wino
white coffee (hłajt'kofi) v.
kawa z mlekiem
white-collar('lajt,koler) adj.
zajęci biurowo(urzędnicy etc.)

white elephant (hłajt'elyfent)
s. towary wybrakowane; buble
white collar worker ('hłajt,ko-
ler łerker) s. pracownik
umysłowy
white frost ('hłajt'fro:st) s.
szron
white-headed ('hłajt'hedyd) adj.
siwowłosy
white heat (hłajt'hi:t) biały
zar
white lie (hłajt'laj) s. kłamstwo; wykręt towarzyski
white paper ('hłajt,pejper) s.
oficjalna publikacja wykazują-
ca, ze rząd ma zawsze rację
(USA)
whiten ('hłajtn) y. wybielac;
pobielac; bielic; zbielec
whiteness ('hłajtness) s. biel
whitewash (,hłajt'łosz) s.
wapno; wybielanie czegos lub
kogos; v. wybielac; wymywac
na czysto; uniewinnic; uspra-
wiedliwic; pobic na sucho
(na zero)
Whitsuntide ('hłajtsntajd) s.
Zielone Swięta
whittle down ('hłytl,dałn) v.
strugac; zestrugac; wystrugac;
obstrugac
whity ('hłajty) adj. białawy
whizz (hłyz) s. swist; (slang):
mistrz; rzecz wspaniała;
v. swistac; suszyc
who (hu:) pron. kto; ktory
whodunit (hu:danyt) s. (slang):
"kryminał"; powiesc detekty-
wistyczna
whoever (hu:'ewer) pron. ktokolwiek
whole (houl) adj. cały; pełnowartosciowy; zdrowy; s. całosc
wholehearted ('houl'ha:rtyd)
adj. serdeczny; szczery
whole hogger ('houl'hoger) s.
człowiek idący na całego
whole length ('houl'lenks) s.
(portret) w całosci
wholesale ('houl,sejl) s. hurt;
handel hurtowy; adj. hurtowy;
masowy; adv.hurtem; masowo

wholesaler ('houl,sejler) s.
hurtownik

wholesale trade ('houlsejl-
,trejd) s. handel hurtowy

wholesome ('houlsem) s. zdrowy;
zdrowotny

whole-time ('houltajm) adj.
pełno-etatowy (czasowy)

whole-wheat ('houl'hłi:t) adj.
pełno-ziarnisty (chleb)

who'll (hu:l) = who shall;
who will

wholly ('houly) adv. całkowicie

whoom (hu:m) pron. kogo ?
zob. who

whoop (hu:p) s. okrzyk (wesoły
np.)

whooping ('hu:pyŋg) adj.(slang):
ogromny

whooping cough ('hu:pyŋ,kof)
s. koklusz

whore (ho:r) s. wulg.: kurwa;
dziwka; v. kurwic się; gonic
za dziwkami

whorelet ('ho:rlyt) s. wulg.:
kurewka

whose (hu:z) pron.,& adj. czyj;
czyja; czyje; ktorego

why (hłaj) adv. dlaczego; czemu;czemuż; dlatego; własnie;
s. przyczyna; powod; exp.: jak
to ! właśnie ! patrzcie;
no wiesz !;no to co !

why so ('hłaj'sou) adv. dlaczego

wick (łyk) s. knot; tampon

wicked ('łykyd) adj. niegodziwy; niedobry; frywolny; paskudny; złosliwy; zły; nikczemny

wickedness ('łykydnys) s.
nikczemnosc; niegodziwosc

wicker basket ('łyker,ba:skyt)
s, pleciony kosz

wicker chair (łyker,czeer) s.
plecione krzesło

wicket (łykyt) s. furka; kołowrot; okienko kasowe; bramka;
cel; drzwi na poł wysokości
(otworu)

wide (łajd) adj. szeroki; rozległy; szeroko otwarty; ob-

szerny; wielki; pokażny; znaczny; duży; daleki; szeroko otwarty; adv. szeroko; z dala
(od czegoś)

wide-awake ('łajde,e'łejk) adj.
czujny; rozbudzony; bystry;
z szeroko otwartymi oczami,
widen ('łajdn) v. poszerzyc;
rozszerzac

wideness ('łajdnys) s. szerokosc;
rozległość; bezmiar

wide-open (,łajd'oupen) adj.
szeroko otwarty

widespread (,łajd'spred) adj.
rozprzestrzeniony; szeroko
rozpostarty

widow ('łydou) s. wdowa; v. wdowiec

widower ('łydouer) s. wdowiec

width (łyds) s. szerokosc

wife (łajf) s. żona; pl. wives
(łajwz)

wig (łyg) s. peruka; v. zaopatrywać w perukę

wild (łajld) adj. dziki; dziko
rosnący; gwałtowny; wsciekły;
szalony; burzliwy; rozwichrzo-
ny; pustynny;zdziczały; rozwydrzony; fantastyczny; nierealny; podniecony; s. pustynia;
dziki teren; adv. na chybił
trafił

wildcat ('łajld,kaet) adj. porywczy; awanturniczy; nadzwyczajny (np. pociąg); s. żbik;
szyb naftowy na nowym terenie;
awanturnicze przedsiębiorstwo;
spekulacja; samotna lokomotywa;
porywcza osoba; v. szukac nafty na niesprawdzonych terenach

wilderness(łajldernys) s.
pustynia; puszcza; odludzie

wildfire (,łajld'fajer) s.
błyskawicznie rozprzestrzenia-
jący się ogien; ogien grecki;
błędny ognik

willful('łylful) adj. rozmyslny;
umyslny; zamierzony; swiadomy;
samowolny; uparty

will (łyl) s. wola; testament;
siła woli; v. postanowic; zarządzac; zapisywac (w testamencie)
zmuszac; chciec

willing (,łylyŋg) adj. skłonny
(coś zrobić); chętny; pełen
dobrej woli
willow ('łylou) s. wierzba
willowy ('łyloły) adj. smukły;
gibki; giętki; obfitujący
w wierzby
will power ('łyl,pałer) s.
siła woli
willy-nilly ('łyly'nyly) adv.
chcąc nie chcąc
will you ? ('łyl,ju:) exp.: czy
zrobisz; czy zechcesz ?;czy
obiecasz ?
wilt (łylt) v. więdnąc; opadać;
oklapnąc; powodowac zwięd-
nięcie; opadac z sił; s. więdnięcie; osłabienie; depresja
wily (łajly) adj. chytry
win; won; won (łyn; łon; łon)
win (łyŋ) v. wygrywac; zwy-
ciężac; zdobywac; zarabiac;
osiągac; pozyskac; przedostac
się; przezwyciężac; s. wygrana; zwycięstwo
win over (łynouwer) v. pozyskac sobie; przekonac
wince (łyns) v. skrzywic się
(z bólu) drgac; s. drgnięcie;
skrzywienie
winch (łyncz) s. korba; wyciąg; kołowrot; v. podnosic;
wyciągac kołowrotem lub korbą
wind; wound; wound (łajnd;
łaund; łaund)
wind (łajnd) v. nawijac; zwijac; zwinąc; owinąc (się);
wic (się); zakonczyc
(łynd) s. wiatr; podmuch; oddech; dech; zapach; puste
słowa; gadanie; v. trąbic;
dąc w róg; przewietrzyc;
zwietrzyc; poczuc; zmęczyc;
dac wytchnąc
windbag ('łyndbaeg) s. czczy
gaduła
windfall ('łynd fo:l) s.
gratka; owoc zrzucony wiatrem
winding (łajndyŋg) adj. kręcony; kręcący się
winding-stairs (łajdyŋsteers)
s. kręcące się schody

wind-instrument (łynd,ynstru-
ment) s. intrument dęty
windlass (łyndles) s. wyciąg;
kołowrot
windmill ('łynmyl) s. wiatrak
wind off(łajnd,o:f) v. odwinąc
(się)
wind up (łajnd,ap) v. nakręcac
(zegar); konczyc (mowę; zamykac zebranie)
window ('łyndou) s. okno; okienko
window dressing ('łyndou,dres-
syŋg) s. dekoracja wystawy
sklepowej
windowpane ('łyndou,pejn) s.
szyba okienna
window shade ('łyndou,szejd)
s. żaluzja
window shopping ('łyndou-
szopyŋg) v. oglądac wystawy
(a nie kupowac)
window-sill ('łyndou,syl) s.
parapet
windpipe ('łynd,pajp) s. tchawica
windshield ('łyndszyld) s.
szyba ochronna (przednia) w
samochodzie
windshield wiper ('łundszyld-
'łajper) s. wycieraczka
szyby ochronnej
windy ('łyndy) adj. wystawiony
na wiatr; wietrzny; gadatliwy
wine ('łajn) s. wino
wineglass ('łajngla:s) s. kieliszek do wina
wine-press ('łajnpres) s. wy-
tłaczarka do winogron
wing (łyŋg) s. skrzydło; ramię
kulisa; dywizjon; lot;
v. uskrzydlac; przewozic na
skrzydłach; przeleciec (przez
cos); leciec; szybowac
wing commander ('łyŋg-ke,ma:n-
der) s. dowódca dywizjonu
lotnictwa (podpułkownik)
wink ('łyŋk) s. mrugac (na kogos); przymykac oczy; s.mrug-
nięcie
winner ('łyner) s. zdobywca nagrody; człowiek wygrywający;
laureat

winning ('łynyŋg) s. otwór do
wydobywania węgla; adj. ujmujący; zwycięski
winning post ('łynyŋg,poust)
s. meta
winnings ('łynyŋgs) pl. wygrana
winsome ('łynsem) adj. ujmujący; pociągający
winter ('łynter) s. zima; adj.
zimowy; v. zimować
winter crop('łynter,krop) s.
ozimina
winterize ('łynterajz) v. dostosowywać, przygotowywać do
zimy
wintry ('łyntry) adj. zimowy;
chłodny; obojętny
winy ('łajny) adj. podchmielony; winny
wipe (łajp) v. wycierać; ocierać; ścierać; wymazać; za-
machnąć się; s. starcie; wy-
tarcie; bicie
wipe away ('łejpe,łej) v. wycierać; wymazać
wipe off ('łajp,o:f) v. ze-
trzeć (plamę etc.)
wipe out ('łajp,aut) v. wytrzeć; wymazać; wyniszczyć;
zgładzać
wipe up ('łajp,ap) v. wytrzeć
(podłogę etc,)
wire (łajer) s. drut; przewód;
telegram; kabel; struna metalowa; sidła; v. drutować;
zadrutować; złapać (w sidła);
założyć przewody (w domu);
zatelegrafować; ciągnąć za
sznurki zakulisowe
wire cutter ('łajer,kater) s.
szczypce do cięcia drutu
wire haired ('łajer,heerd)
adj. ostrowłosy (pies)
wireless ('łajerlys) adj. radiowy; bez drutu
wireless set ('łajerlys,set)
s. radio
wire netting ('łajer,netyŋg)
s. siatka druciana
wire-pulling ('łajer,pulyŋg)
s. używanie protekcji; wpły-
wów

wire rope ('łajer,roup) s. lina
stalowa
wiry ('łajery) adj. twardy; żylasty; muskularny; druciany
wisdom ('łyzdem) s. mądrość
wisdom tooth ('łyzdem.tu:s) s.
ząb mądrości
wise (łajz) s. sposób; adj. mądry; roztropny
wiseacre ('łajz,ejker) s. mądra-
la; mędrek
wise after('łajz,a:fter) adj.
mądry po...
wisecrack ('łajzkra:k) s. dowcip-
na uwaga; v. robić dowcipy
wise guy('łajzgaj) s. nadęta
wielkość
wise saw('łajzso:) s. przysłowie
wish (łysz) v. życzyć (sobie);
pragnąć; chcieć; s. pragnienie;
życzenie; chęć; powinszowanie;
ochota; rzecz upragniona
wishbone ('łyszboun) s. kość
widełkowa (ptaków)
wish for ('łysz fo:r) v. życzyć
sobie (np. pogody)
wishful ('łyszful) adj. pragnący
wishful thinking ('łyszful-
tynkyŋg) s. pobożne życzenie
wish well ('łysz,łel) v. dobrze
życzyć
wishy-washy ('łyszy,łoszy) adj.
bez treści; wodnisty; lurowaty
wisp (łysp) s. wiązka; garść;
pęczek; kosmyk; wstęga (dymu)
wistful ('łystful) adj. smutny;
zadumany; pełen tęsknoty
wit (łyt) s. umysł; rozum; dowcip; człowiek dowcipny; inteligencja; olej w głowie
witch (łycz) s. czarownica;
czarodziejka; v. zaczarować;
oczarować
witchcraft ('łycz.kra:ft) s.
czary; czarnoksięstwo
witch doctor ('łycz,dakter) s.
czarownik; znachor
witchery ('łyczery) = witchcraft
witch hunt('łyczhant) s. tro-
pienie czarownic; polityczne
głośne śledztwo (propagandowe)
w celu udowadniania działalności wywrotowej

with (łys) prep. z (kims; czyms)
u (kogos); przy (kims); za pomocą); (stosownie) do; (cierpliwosc) dla
withdraw (łys'dro:) v. zob.
draw; cofac (się); wycofywac
(się); odwołac (cos); ode-
brac (ze szkoły); odsuwac
(zasłonę)
withdrawál (łys'dro:el) s.
wycofanie
wither ('łydzer) v. powodowac
więdnięcie, usychanie; zabijac (spojrzeniem); usychac;
usuwac się (w cien itp)
withers ('łydzers) pl. kłęby
(u konia między łopatkami)
withhold (łys'hould) v.zob.
hold; wstrzymywac; odmawiac;
wycofac
within (łys'yn) adv. wewnątrz;
w domu; u siebie; w (czyms):
w duchu; do wnętrza; w obrę-
bie; w odległosci (np. mili);
w ciągu (np..dnia); w zasie-
gu (wzroku); s. wnętrze
without (łysaut) prep. bez;
poza; na zewnątrz; adv. na
zewnątrz; poza domem; s. strona zewnętrzna
withstand (łys'staend) v. zob.
stand; opierac się; przeciwstawiac się; byc wytrzymałym;
wytrzymywac
witling ('łytlyng) s. dowcipnis
witness ('łytnys) s. swiadek;
widz; swiadectwo; v. byc
swiadkiem; swiadczyc (tez
podpisem)
witness box ('łytnys,boks) s.
miejsce dla swiadka w sądzie
(USA)
witness stand ('łytnys,staend)
s. miejsce dla zeznawania
w sądzie (USA)
witticism ('łytysyzem) s. złosliwy dowcip; dowcipkowanie
witty (łyty) adj. dowcipny
witty at someone's expense
('łyty et'somłans,yks,pens)
exp.:dowcipny cudzym kosztem

wives (łajwz) pl. żony; zob.
wife
wiz (łyz) s. (slang): znawca;
mistrz; rzecz wspaniała
wizard ('łyzerd) s. czarownik;
czarodziej; adj. czarodziejski;
(slang): wspaniały
wo (ło:u) exp.:prrr (na konia,
żeby stanął)
wobble ('łobl) v. chwiac się;
ruszac się chwiejnie; chodzic
chwiejnie; jechac kołysząc się;
mowic drżąco; grac drżąco (me-
lodię); drgac; wahac się; byc
niezdecydowanym
wobbler ('łobler) s. człowiek
chwiejny
wobbly (łobly) s. chwiejący
się; chwiejny
woe (łou) s. nieszczęscie
woebegone ('łoubi,go:n) adj.
nieszczęsny
woeful ('łouful) adj. bolesny;
żałosny
woke (łouk) v. zob . wake
woken (łoukn) v. zob. wake
wolf (łulf) s. pl. wolves
(łulvz); wilk; (slang):kobie-
ciarz; v. żrec; pożerac; połykac jak wilk; polowac na
wilki
wolf down ('łulf,dałn) v. pożerac jak wilk
wolfcall ('łulf,ko:l) s. (slang):
gwizdanie na kobietę (z po-
dziwem, zaczepką etc.)
wolf-cub ('łulf,kab) s. wilczek;
wilczę; młodszy harcerz
wolf-dog ('łulfdog) s. wilczur
wolfhound ('łulfhaund) s.
wilczur rosyjski lub alzacki
wolfish ('łulfysz) adj.wilczy
wolf skin('łulf'skyn) s. wilcza
skora (na podłogę etc.);
wilczura (okrycie)
wolf whistle('łulfhłysl) =
wolfcall
wolverene (,łulve'ri:n) s.
rosomak; mieszkaniec stanu
Michigan

woman ('łumen) s. pl. women
('łymyn); kobieta; baba; żona; v. mówić per "kobieta";
umieszczać między kobietami
woman doctor ('łumen'dakter)
s. lekarka
womanhood ('łumenhud) s. kobiety; kobiecość (dojrzała)
womanish ('łumenysz) adj. bab-
ski; zniewieściały
womanize ('łumenajz) v. ba-
biec; niewieściec; gonić za
kobietami
womankind ('łumen,kajnd) s.
kobiety; ród niewieści
womanlike ('łumen,lajk) adj.
kobiecy
womanly ('łumenly) adj. kobiecy
womb (łu:m) s. macica; łono;
żywot
women (łymyn) pl. zob, woman
womenfolk ('łymynfouk) =
womankind
won (łan) v. zob. win
wonder ('łander) s. zdumienie;
cud; v. dziwić się; być cie-
kaw; zastanawiać się
wonderful ('łanderful) adj.
cudowny
wonderland ('łanderlaend) s.
kraina cudów (czarów)
wonderment ('łanderment) s.
zdziwienie; zdumienie
wondering ('łanderyng) adj.
zdumiony; niedowierzający
wonderwork ('łanderłe:rk)
s. cud
wonder-worker ('łanderłe:rker)
s. cudotwórca
wonder-working ('łanderłe:rkyng)
adj. sprawiający cuda
wondrous ('łandres) adj. cudowny; adv. cudownie
wont; wont; wonted (łont;
łont; łantyd)
wont (łant) v. przyzwyczajać;
mieć zwyczaj; s. zwyczaj;
przyzwyczajenie
won't (łount) = will not
wonted ('łantyd) adj. zwykły

woo (łu:) v. zalecać się (do
kobiety): umizgać się; ubiegać
się; namawiać do czegoś
wood (łud) s. drzewo; drewno;
lasek; pl; lasy; puszcza;
v. obsadzać drzewami; dostarczać drzewo
woodbine ('łudbajn) s. powój
wonny; wiciokrzew pomorski
woodblock ('łudblok) s. drzeworyt (do odciskania)
wood carving ('łudka:rwyng) s.
drzeworytnictwo
woodchuck ('łudczak) s. świstak
wood coal ('łudkoul) s. węgiel
drzewny
woodcock ('łudkok) s. słomka
woodcraft ('łudkra:ft) s. znajomość lasu
woodcraftsman ('łudkra:ftsmen)
s. myśliwy; traper
woodcut ('łudkat) s. drzeworyt
woodcutter ('łudkater) s.
drwal; drzeworytnik
wooded ('łudyd) adj. lesisty;
zalesiony
wooden ('łudn) adj. drewniany;
tępy
wood engraver (,łudyn'grejwer)
s. drzeworytnik
wood engraving(,łudyn'grejwyng)
s. drzeworytnictwo
wooden head ('łudn,hed) s. głupiec
woodland ('łudlaend) s. las;
lesisty okręg; adj. lesisty
leśny
woodman ('łudmen) s. drwal;
leśnik
wood notes('łudnouts) s. dźwię-
ki lasu
woodpecker ('łud,peker) s. dzięcioł
wood pulp ('łud,palp) s. miazga
drzewna
woodruff ('łudraf) s. marzan-
na (wonna)
woodshed ('łud,szed) s. drwal-
nia; drewutnia
woodsman ('łudsmen) s. mieszkaniec lasu; drwal

wood sorrel('łudserel) s. szcza-
wik zajęczy
woodsy (łudzy) adj. leśny
wood wind ('łud,łynd) s.(dęty)
instrument drewniany
woodwork (łudłe:rk) s. wyroby
drzewne; części drewniane (np.
ramy okien etc.); drewniana
częśc budowy; budowa drewniana; stolarka; ciesiołka
woody ('łudy) adj. lesisty;
drewniany
wooer ('łu:er) s. zalotnik
woof (łu:f) s. wątek
wool (łul) s. wełna (czesana,
strzyżona, zgrzebna); czupryna; włosy (wełniste); owcze
runo; wełniane rzeczy
wool-bal ('łulbo:l) s. kłębek
wełny
woolen ('łuln) adj. wełniany;
s. wyrób wełniany
wool fat ('łulfaet) s. lanolina
woolfell, ('łulfel) s. barani-
ca; skóra owcza
woolgathering ('łul,gaedzeryng)
adj. głupio rozmarzony (roztargniony); s. głupie marzy-
cielstwo
woollen ('łulyn) adj. wełniany;
pl, tkanina wełniana
woolly ('łuly) adj. wełnisty;
oschły (głos); mętny umysł;
nie soczysty; mączasty;
włókniasty (owoc); zamazany;
(slang): surowy i niekulturalny; s. wełniana odzież; (slang):
owca
wooly ('łuly) = woolly
woozy ('łu:zy) adj. (slang):
wstawiony; otumaniony; niezdrów
word (łe:rd) s. słowo; wyraz;
słówko; komplement; przechwał-
ka; obelga; mowa; wieść; rozkaz; adv. ustnie; słownie;
adj. słowami wyrażony; v. wy-
razic; redagować; sformułować;
ubierać w szatę słowną; przybierać w słowa
wordage ('łe:rdydż) s. ilość
słów

word-blind('łe:rd,blajnd) adj.
niezdolny do rozumienia pisma
wordbook ('łe:rd,buk) s. słownik
wording ('łe:rdyng) s. ujęcie,
wyrażenie słowami
wordplay, ('łe:rd,plej) s.
gra słów
word-splitter('łe:rd,splyter)
s. pedant słowny
word-splitting ('łe:rd,splytyng)
s. sofistyka; dzielenie włosa
na czworo
wordy ('łe:rdy) adj. rozwlekły;
gadatliwy; słowny (wojna słów)
wore (łe:r) v. zob. wear
work ; worked; worked (łe:rk;
łe:rkt; łe:rkt)
work (łe:rk) s. praca; robota;
zajęcie; energia; zadanie;
dzieło; utwór; uczynek;
pl. fabryka; huta; fortyfika-
cje; ozdoby; v. pracować;
działać; funkcjonować; skutkować; oddziaływać; wywoływać;
sprawiać; wykonywać; kazać
robić; prowadzić; obsługiwać;
poruszać (motor); posuwać (się);
przesuwać (się); wprawiać w
(pasję); nadawać kształt;
przeprowadzać przez coś; obrabiac; urabiac (się); wyszywać; robić robótkę; (slang):
wykorzystywać (znajomości);
drgać; burzyć; falować; fermentować; trzeszczeć (statek);
źle działać (maszyna); wyczerpac się; odrabiać; wypracować;
wytwarzać; uzyskiwać z trudem;
podniecać (się) stopniowo; za-
znajamiać się z czymś; mieszać
w całość; dokazywać (cudów);
wywierać (wpływ); urabiac; fasonować; exploatować (kopalnie itp.)
work away ('łe:rke,łej) v.
pracować zawzięcie
work in ('łe:rkyn) v. pasować;
wprowadzać cos
work off ('łe:rko:f) v. pozbywać się czegos

work on ('łe:rkon) v. pracować dalej

work out ('łe:rkaut) v. przeprowadzać; realizować; obliczać; rozwiązywać; wyczerpywać; wyeksploatować; skończyć; wynosić (w sumie)

work up ('łe:rkap) v. podniecać (się); doprowadzać (się); opracowywać; wyrabiać; rozwijać; wspinać się; podnosić (się)

workable ('łe:rkebl) adj. możliwy (do obróbki, uprawy etc.); opłacalny; wykonalny; realny; możliwy do przeprowadzenia; w stanie używalności

workaday ('łe:rkedej) adj. codzienny; roboczy; powszedni

work-basket ('łe:rk,ba:skyt) s. koszyk z robótką

workbook ('łe:rk,buk) s. podręcznik ze wskazówkami; dziennik pracy

workbox ('łe:rkboks) s. pudełko z przyborami do szycia

workday ('łe:rkdej) adj. dzień roboczy; dzień powszedni

worker ('łe:rker) s. pracownik; robotnik

workhouse ('łe:rk,haus) s. dom poprawczy; przytułek

working ('łe:rkyng) adj. pracujący; pracowniczy; roboczy; praktyczny; działający; czynny; ruchomy; powszedni; s. praca; robota; działanie; ruch; roboczodniówka; obróbka

working capital ('łe:rkyng - kaepytl) s. kapitał obrotowy

working knowledge ('łe:rkyng-'nolydż) s. wiedza praktyczna

working-class ('łe:rkyng'- kla:s) s. klasa robotnicza

working day ('łe:rkyngdej) s. dzień pracy

working hours ('łe:rkyng,auers) s. godziny pracy

working load ('łe:rkyng,loud) s. ciężar użyteczny; nośność

workingman ('łe:rkyng,men) s. robotnik

working pressure ('łe:rkyng,preszer) s. ciśnienie robocze

workless ('łe:rklys) adj. & s. bezrobotny

worklike ('łe:rklajk) adj. dobrze wykonany; dobrze nastawiony do pracy

workman ('łe:rkmen) s. pl. workmen ('łe:rkmen); robotnik (fizyczny); fachowiec

workmanship ('łe:rkmanszyp) s. wykonanie; jakość wykonania; faktura; twór

work of art ('łe:rk-ow,a:rt) s. dzieło sztuki

workout ('łe:rkaut) s. trening; zaprawa; danie komuś szkoły

workroom ('łe:rk'rum) s. pracownia

works council ('łe:rks'kansl) s. rada zakładowa

workshop ('łe:rkszop) s. pracownia; warsztat; zakład; posiedzenie

workshy ('łe:rkszaj) s. próżniak

worktable ('łe:rktejbl) s. biurko

workup ('łe:rkap) s. podniecenie (się); powalanie podczas druku

workwoman ('łe:rkłumen) s. pl. workwomen ('łe:rkłymyn) ; robotnica; pracownica fizyczna

world (łe:rld) s. świat; ziemia; kula ziemska; sfery; masa; mnóstwo; zatrzęsienie czegoś; bezmiar; wielka ilość adj. światowy

worldling ('łe:rldlyng) s. człowiek oddany sprawom doczesnym

worldly ('łe:rldly) adj. światowy; ziemski; doczesny

worldminded ('łe:rld'majndyd) adj. oddany sprawom doczesnym

world old ('łe:rld,old) adj. stary jak świat

world power ('łe:rld'pałer)
s. potęga światowa; wielkie
mocarstwo
world-series ('łe:rld'sieri:z)
s. mistrzostwa palanta
(baseball) USA
world-war ('łe:rld'łor) s. wojna światowa
world-weary ('łe:rld'łeery)
adj. zmęczony życiem
world-wide ('łe:rld,łajd) adj.
światowy
world wise ('łe:rld,łajz) adj.
obyty; doświadczony
worm (łe:rm) s. robak; roba-
czek; glisda; dżdżownica;
gwint; zwojnik; śruba (nie
ostra); wężownica; v. wkradać się; wykradać; czołgać
się; wyciągać(tajemnicę z
kogoś); czyscić (zwierzę)
z robaków; czyscić (grządkę)
z robaków
wormcast ('łe:rm,ka:st) s.
gleba wydalana przez dżdżow-
nicę
worm-eaten ('łe:rm,i:tn) adj.
robaczywy; stłoczony przez
robaki; (slang); przestarzały
worm-fishing ('łe:rm,fyszyŋ)
s. łowienie ryb na robaki
worm gear('łe:rm,gier) s.
przekładnia ślimakowa
wormhole ('łe:rm,houl) s.
dziura wygryziona przez roba-
ka
wormseed ('łe:rm.si:d) s.
rośliny stosowane przeciw
robakom
worm wheel ('łe:rm,hłi:l) s.
koło przekładni ślimakowej
wormwood ('łe:rm,łud) s. pio-
łun;(też) przykrosć
wormy ('łe:rmy) adj. robaczywy
worn (ło:rn) v. zob. wear;
adj. używany; noszony; pomarszczony
worn-out ('ło:rn,aut) adj. zużyty; zniszczony; wynoszony
worried ('łe:ryd) adj. zatros-
kany; zaniepokojony

worriment (łe:ryment) s. zmartwienie
worrisome (łe:rysem) adj. tra-
piący; lubiący się martwić
worry (łe:ry) v. dręczyć (się);
martwić (się); trapić (się);
zadręczać; zamartwiać; naprzykrzać (się); narzucać (się);
napastować; kąsać; szarpać zębami; s. zmartwienie; troska;
kłopot; kąsanie (zdobyczy przez
psa)
worry along ('łe:rye,long) v.
uporać się z trudnościami
worry dawn ('łe:ry,dałn) v. połykać łapczywie
worry out ('łe:ry,aut) v. rozwiązać z wysiłkiem (np. problem)
worse (łe:rs) adj. gorszy (niż:
bad; evil; ill); podniszczony;
słabszy; bardziej chory;
s. coś gorszego; to co najgor-
sze; najgorszy stan; najgorszy
wypadek; v. pogarszać się;
adv. gorzej; bardziej
worsen ('łe:rsn) v. pogorszyć
(się)
worship ('łe:rszyp) s. cześć;
kult; uwielbienie; nabożeństwo;
bałwochwalstwo; v. czcić;
wielbić; uwielbiać; brać udział
w nabożeństwie
woshipful ('łe:rszypful) adj.
pełen czci; czcigodny
worship(p)er ('łe:rszyper) s.
czciciel
worst (łe:rst) adj. najgorszy;
s. coś najgorszego; najgorszy
wypadek; adj. najgorzej; najbardziej; (slang) : bardzo
v. pokonać; wziąć nad kims górę; zadać klęskę; pobić
worsted ('łustyd) adj. czesan-
kowy; s. kamgarn; przędza wełniana czesana; czesanka
worth (łe:rs) s. wartość; cena;
adj. wart; opłacający się
worthless ('łe:rslys) adj. bezwartościowy
worth reading ('łe:rs'ri:dyŋg)
adj. wart czytania

worth seeing ('łe:rz'si:yŋg)
adj. wart widzenia
worthwhile ('łe:rzhłajl) adj.
wart zachodu; opłacający się
worthy ('łe:rzy) adj. godny;
wartościowy; poczciwy;
s. godny człowiek; wybitny
człowiek (też żartem)
would (łud) v. zob. will
(forma warunkowa)
would be ('łud,bi:) adj. rzekomy; niedoszły; adv. rzekomo;
niby to
wound (łu:nd) s. rana; v. ranić; zob.: v. wind
wounded ('łu:ndyd) adj. ranny;
urażony
wove (łouw) v. zob.: weave
woven ('łouwn) v. zob.: weave
wow (łau) (slang): s. szlagier;
świetna rzecz; v. miec powodzenie; wywoływać zachwyt
excl.: au !;cudownie !
wrack (raek) s. = wreck (age);
chwasty morskie wyrzucone na
brzeg; używane na nawoz
wraith (rejs) s. sobowtór;
cien (duch)
wrangle ('raeŋgl) s. kłotnia;
burda; v. kłocic się; (slang):
pilnowac koni
wrangler ('raeŋgler) s. kłotnik;
pastuch koński (kowboj)
wrap; wrapt; wrapt (raep;
raept; raept)
wrap (raep) v. zawijac; owijac;
zapakowywac; spowijac; otulac
się; okrywac (się); zachodzic
na siebie; s. szal; chusta;
okrycie
wrap up ('raepap) v. owijac
(się); pakowac
wrapper ('raeper) s. opakowanie; opaska; obwoluta; bande-
rola; papierek; bibułka; osłona; podomka (damska); pako-
wacz
wrapping ('raepyŋg) s. opakowanie
wrapping paper ('raepyŋg pejper) s. papier do pakowania

wrapt (raept) v. zob. wrap
wrasse (raes) s. (ryba) wargacz
wrath (ra:s) s. gniew; oburzenie
wrathful (ra:sful) adj. gniewny
wreak (ri:k) v. wywierac (zem-
stę); dawac upust; wyładowac
(gniew)
wreath(ri:s) s. wieniec
wreathe (ri:z) v. wienczyc; wic
się; splatac; spowijac; plesc
się; kłębic się (dym etc.)
wreck (rek) s. ruina; wrak;
rozbicie się (np.statku); katastrofa; szczątki (np. na wodzie); zniszczenie; rozbitek
życiowy; kaleka; wypadek;
v. rozbic (pojazd); zniweczyc
(nadzieje); burzyc; byc roz-
bitym; spowodowac rozbicie;
zrujnowac; miec wypadek
wreckage ('rekydż) s. rozbicie;
szczątki; gruzy
wrecked ('rekt) adj. rozbity;
zniszczony; zepsuty
wrecking company ('rekyŋg'kampeny) s. przedsiębiorstwo
rozbiorki budynkow
wrecking service ('rekyŋg'se:r-
wys) s. przewóz zepsutych samochodów
wrecker ('reker) s. sprawca wypadku; ciężarowka (z dźwigiem)
do przewozu zepsutych samochodów; kierowca przewożący ze-
psute samochody; przedsiębiorca rozbiorki budynkow; przedsiębiorca wydobywania zatopio-
nych statkow; człowiek kradnący
szczątki statku; szkodnik; roz-
bijacz małżenstwa
wren (ren) s. strzyżyk
wrench (rencz) s. gwałtowne
skręcenie; ukręcenie; szarpnięcie; wykręcenie; zwichnięcie; przekręcenie (faktow);
ból (rozstania); klucz maszynowy; klucz nasadowy; klucz
nakrętkowy; v. szarpnąc;
skręcic; wykręcic; zwichnąc
(nogę); przekręcac(fakty);
ukręcac

wrench open ('rencz'oupen) v.
odkręcić; otwierać; odsrubo-
wywać

wrench off ('rencz,o:f) v. wyrywać; wykręcić; ukręcić
(głowę)

wrest (rest) v. wykręcać; wyrywać; przekręcać (fakty);
wydobywać zeznania; s. wykręcanie; wyrywanie; klucz
do strojenia (harfy)

wrest from ('restfrom) v. wyrwać komuś

wrestle ('resl) v. mocować
się; zmagać się; borykać się;
walczyć; s. zapasy; walka

wrestler ('resler) s. zapaśnik

wrestling ('reslyng) s. za-
paśnictwo

wrestpins ('rest,pynz) pl. koł-
ki na struny fortepianowe

wretch (recz) s. nieszczęśnik;
biedaczysko; biedak; nędzarz;
łajdak; łotr; nikczemnik

wretched ('reczyd) adj. nieszczęśliwy; pechowy; biedny;
nędzny; marny; fatalny;
ochydny; wstrętny; nadzwyczajny (łotr)

wrick (ryk) v. lekko zwichnąć;
nadwyrężyć; s. zwichnięcie;
lekkie naderwanie

wriggle ('rygl) v. wić się;
wkręcać (się); kręcić; wy-
winąć się; s. ruch wijący
się; wicie

wriggle along ('rygle'long)
v. posuwać się wijąc

wriggle in ('rygl,yn) v. wkręcać się

wriggle out ('ryglaut) v. wykręcać się

wright (rajt) s. robotnik;
twórca

wring; wrung; wrung (ryng;
rang; rang)

wring (ryng) v. wyżymać; wykręcać; ukręcić (łeb); przekręcać (słowa); ściskać (serce); uściskać (rękę); wymóc
(coś na kimś); zniekształcić;
s. wyżymanie; uścisk; ścis-
kanie; wyżęcie; wyciśnięcie;

wringer (rynger) s. wyżymaczka

wrinkle ('rynkl) s. zmarszczka;
fałda; zmarszczenie; (slang):
ciekawy pomysł; rada
v. marszczyć (się); być pomar-
szczonym; zmiąć (się)

wrinkle up ('rynkl ap) v. po-
marszczyć

wrinkly (rynkly) adj. pomarszczony

wrist (ryst) s. przegub; ruch
ręki w przegubie

wristband ('rystbaend) s. mankiet u koszuli

wristwatch ('ryst,łocz) s.
zegarek na rękę

writ (ryt) s. nakaz pisemny;
prawny

writ for ('ryt,fo:r) s. rozpi-
sanie (wyborów)

write; wrote; written (rajt;
rout; rytn)

write (rajt) v. pisać; napisać;
zapisać; wypisać; komponować;
wstawiąc (czek); spisywać;
sławić (piórem)

write back ('rajt,baek) v. odpisywać (komuś)

write down ('rajtdałn) v. spisywać; notować; określać (ujem-
nie)

write home ('rajt,houm) v. pisać do domu

write-in ('rajt,yn) v. wpisy-
wać; dopisywać

write-off ('rajt,of) v. odpisywać (na straty); pisać na
prędce

write out ('rajt,aut) v. wypisywać; sporządzać

write-up ('rajt,ap) v. zapisywać; opisywać; przesadnie szacować; pochwalić

writer ('rajter) s. pisarz;
niżej podpisany; powieścio-
pisarz

writhe (rajs) v. wić się (z bo-
lu); cierpieć (zniewagę);
skręcać się (ze wstydu)

writing ('rajtyng) s. pismo;
utwór; artykuł; pisanie;
piśmiennictwo; sztuka pisania;
praca literacka;napisana rzecz

writing desk ('rajtyng,desk)
s. biurko; pulpit
writing ink ('rajtyng,ynk)
s. atrament
writing paper ('rajtyng,pej-
per) s. papier listowy; papier do pisania
writing table ('rajtyng,tejbl)
s. biurko
written ('rytn) v. zob.: rite;
adj. pisany
wrong (ro:ng) adj. zły; niewłaściwy; błędny; nie w porządku; mylny; niekorzystny;
niesprawiedliwy; s. zło; wykroczenie; krzywda; wina; pomyłka; grzech; strata; niesprawiedliwość; v. skrzyw-
dzic; niesłusznie posądzac;
byc niesprawiedliwym;
adv. mylnie; niewłasciwie;
błędnie; źle; zdrożnie; nie-
korzystnie
wrongdoer ('ro:ng'du:er) s.
krzywdziciel; grzesznik;
winowajca
wrongdoing ('ro:ng'duyng) s.
nadużycia; wykroczenia;
grzechy; przestępstwa
wrongful ('ro:ngful) adj.zły;
krzywdzący; niesprawiedliwy;
bezprawny
wronghead ('ro:ng'hed) v.
przekręcac (słowa etc.)
wrongheaded ('ro:ng'hedyd)
adj. uparty; przewrotny
wrote (rout) v. zob. write
wroth (ro:s) adj. gniewny
wrought (ro:t) v. zob. work
wrought iron ('ro:t'ajern)
s. kute żelazo
wrought-up ('ro:t,ap) adj.
napięty; zdenerwowany
wrung ('rang) v. zob. wring
wry (raj) adj. krzywy; okrzy-
wiony
wryneck ('rajnek) s. zastrzał
szyi; kręcz karku
wynd (łajnd) s. (kręta) uliczka
x (eks) dwudziesta czwarta litera angielskiego alfabetu;
rzymska cyfra 10; niewiadoma

xenon ('zenon) s. ksenon
xenophobia (,zene'foubje) s.
ksenofobia
Xmas ('krysmes) = Christmas
x-ray ('eks'rej) adj. rentge-
nowski; v. prześwietlac; robic
zdjęcie rentgenowskie
x-ray diagnosis ('eks'rej,da-
jeg'nouzys) s. rozpoznanie
rentgenowskie
x-ray examination ('eks'rej-
yg'zaemynejszyn) s. badanie
rentgenowskie
x-ray picture ('eks'rej'pykczer)
s. zdjecie rentgenowskie
x-rays ('eks'rejs) pl. promienie rentgenowskie
xylem ('zajlem) s. drewno
xylophagous (zaj'lofeges) adj.
drzewożerny
xylophone ('zylefoun) s. ksylo-
fon
y (łaj) dwudziesta piąta litera
angielskiego alfabetu
yabber ('jaeber) v. gadac
yacht (jot) s. jacht; y. płynąc
jachtem; urządząc wyscigi jach-
towe
yachting ('jotyng) s. sport
żeglarski
yak (jaek) s. jak; (slang): gadanie; śmiech; v. gadac; smiac
się
yap (jaep) v. ujadac; (slang);
paplac; s. ujadanie; paplanina;
krzykacz; jadaczka
yard (ja:rd) s. jard (91.44 cm);
podwórze; dziedziniec; v. umieszczac w ogrodzeniu
yarn (ja:rn) s. włokno; przędza;
historyjka; v. opowiadac histo-
ryjki
yawn (jo:n) v. ziewac; ziąc; zionąc; s. ziewnięcie; ziewanie
ye (ji:) pron. wy (biblijne)
yea (jej) adv. tak; s. głosowanie "tak"
yeah (jej) (slang): tak; excl.:
tak !; nie wierzę !
year (je:r) s. rok
yearly (je:rly) adj. roczny;
coroczny; adv. corocznie;
s. rocznik;adv.raz na rok

yearn (je:rn) v. tęsknić
yeast (ji:st) s. drożdże; ferment; piana; v. fermentować;
pienić (się)
yell (jel) v. wrzeszczeć;
s.wrzask; dopingowanie
yellow ('jelou) adj. żółty;
(slang): tchórzliwy; zawistny;
żółty z zazdrości; n. żółty
kolor; żółtko; v. żółknąć;
powodować zóźknięcie
yelp (jelp) s. skowyt; v. skowyczeć
yeomen ('joumen) s. podoficer
marynarki; (dawniej) wolny
chłop
yep (jep) adv. (slang): tak
yes (jes) adv. tak; v.potakiwać
yesterday ('jesterdy) adv. &
s. wczoraj
yet (jet) adv. & conj. dotąd;
jeszcze do tej pory; na razie;
jak dotąd; jednak; ani też;
mimo to
yew (ju:) s. cis
Yiddish (jydysz) s. język żydowski
yield (ji:ld) v. wydawać; dawać; rodzić; przynosić; oddawać (się); porzucać; ustępować; s. plon; zysk; wydajność
yielding(ji:ldyng) s. wydajność; adj. ustępliwy
yogurt ('jouguert) s. jogurt
yoke (jouk) s. jarzmo; v. zaprzęgać; nakładać jarzmo;
(slang): zaskakiwać (prze-
chodnia) w celu rabunku
yolk (jouk) s. żółtko; rodzaj
żółtko
yonder ('jonder) adj. & adv.
tam dalej; tamten
you (ju:) pron. ty; wy; pan;
pani; panowie; panie
you'd (ju:d) = you would;
you had
you'll (ju:l) = you shall;
you will
young (jang) adj. młody; młodzieńczy; młodociany

youngster ('jaŋster) s. dziecko;
młodzik
your (ju:r) adj. twój; wasz;
pański
you're (jo:r) = you are
yours (juers) pron. twój; wasz;
pański (z poważaniem)
yourself (,juer'self) pron. ty
sam
yourselves (,juer'selvz) pron.
wy sami
youth (ju:s) s. młodość
youths (ju:dz) pl. młodzież;
młodzieniec
youthful ('ju:sful) adj, młody;
młodzieńczy
youth-hostel ('ju:s'hostl) s,
schronisko młodzieżowe
you've ('ju:w) = you have
Yugoslav ('ju:gou'sla:w) adj.
jugosłowiański
z (zi:) dwudziesta szósta litera alfabetu angielskiego
zany ('zejny) adj. pocieszny;
błazeński; s. błazen; głupek
zeal (zi:l) s. gorliwość
zealous ('zeles) adj. gorliwy
zebra ('zi:bre) s. zebra;
(slang): mulat; adj.pręgowany
zebra crossing ('zi:bre'krosyng)
s. pasami znaczone przejście
jezdni dla pieszych
zenith ('senit) s. zenit; szczyt
(sławy)
zero ('zierou) s. zero; v. ustawiać na zero; brać na cel
zest (zest) s. smak; pikanteria;
rozkosz; zamiłowanie; v. dodawać pikanterii
zigzag ('zygzaeg) s. zygzak;
adj. zygzakowaty; adv. zygza-
kiem
zinc (zynk) s. cynk; v. cynko-
wać
zip (zyp) s. świst; wigor;
v. śmigać; gnać; zapinać zamek
błyskawiczny
zip code ('zyp,koud) s. numera-
cja pocztowa miejscowości
zipper ('zyper) s. zamek błyskawiczny

zippy ('zypy) adj. żywy; zgrabny

zloty ('zlouty) s. złoty (pieniądz polski); adj. golden

zodiac ('zoudjaek) s. zodiak

zombie ('zomby) s. bóg-pyton; (slang); bałwan; tuman

zone (zoun) s. strefa; zona; v. opasywać; dzielić na zony

zoo (zu:) s. ogród zoologiczny

zoology (zou'oledźy) s. zoologia

zoom (zu:m) v. buczec; wzlatywać; wzbijac się szybko; śmigac; s. poderwanie (samolotu); soczewka zbliżająca w aparacie do filmowania oraz w aparacie do fotografowania

ABBREVIATIONS - SKRÓTY

a.	– attribute	– przydawka
adj.	– adjective	– przymiotnik
adj. f.	– adjective feminine	– przymiotnik żeński
adj. m.	– adjective masculine	– przymiotnik męski
adj. n.	– adjective neuter	– przymiotnik nijaki
adv.	– adverb	– przysłówek
am.	– American	– amerykański
chem.	– chemistry	– chemia
conj.	– conjunction	– spójnik
constr.	– construction	– budowa
etc.	– and so on	– i tak dalej
excl.	– exclamation	– wykrzyknik
expr.	– expression	– wyrażenie
f.	– substantive feminine	– rzeczownik żeński
gram.	– grammar	– gramatyka
hist.	– history	– historia
hyp.	– hyphen	– łącznik
indecl.	– indeclinable	– nieodmienny
inf.	– infinitive	– bezokolicznik
m.	– substantive musculine	– rzeczownik męski
m.in.	– among others	– między innymi
n.	– substantive neuter	– rzeczownik nijaki
num.	– numeral	– liczebnik
part.	– particle	– partykuła
pl.	– substantive plural	– rzeczownik liczba mnoga
poet.	– poetry	– poezja
polit.	– politics	– polityka
p.p.	– past participle	– imiesłów czasu przeszłego
prep.	– preposition	– przyimek
pron.	– pronoun	– zaimek
s.	– substantive	– rzeczownik
sb.	– somebody	– ktoś
slang	– slang	– gwara, żargon
v.	– verb	– czasownik
vulg.	– vulgarity	– ordynarność
wg	– according to	– według
W.W. II	– World War II	– druga wojna światowa
zob.	– see	– zobacz

CZĘSTO UŻYWANE PRZEDROSTKI I CZŁONY WYRAZÓW ZŁOŻONYCH
COMMON PREFIXES, SUFFIXES AND COMPONENT WORDS

Polish	English
a- (a-)	= no- (nou-); non- (non-)
anty- (anti-)	= anti- ('aentaj-)
arcy- (ar-tsi-)	= arch- (a:rcz-)
auto- ('aw-to-)	= auto- (,o:te'-)
bez- (bez-)	= -less (-lys)
beze- (be-ze-)	= -less (-lys)
bi- (bee-)	= bi- (baj-)
centy- (cen-ti-)	= centi- (senty-)
ćwierc- (chvyerch-)	= quarter- ('kło:ter-)
daleko- (da-le-ko-)	= far (fa:r-)
de- (de-)	= de- (dy-)
długo-(dwoo-go-)	= long- (long-)
do- (do-)	= to- (tu-)
	till- (tyl-)
drobno- (drob-no-)	= small- (smol-)
dwu- (dvoo-)	= two- (tu-)
eks- (eks-)	= ex- (eks-)
ekstra- (eks-tra-)	= extra- ('ekstre-)
gorzko- (gosh-ko-)	= bitter- ('byter-)
hetero- (khe-te-ro-)	= hetero- (hetere-)
homo- (kho-mo-)	= homo- (houmo-)
hydro- (khi-dro-)	= hydro- (,hajdre'-)
inno- (een-no-)	= other- (odzer-)
	else- (els-)
jasno- (yas-no-)	= fair- (feer-)
	clear- (klier-)
	light- (lajt-)
	bright- (brajt-)
jedno- (yed-no-)	= single- (syngl-)
	one- (łan-)
kilko- (keel-ko-)	= some- (som-)
	▬ few- (fju-)
kilku- (keel-ku-)	= some- (som-)
	= few- (fju-)
ko- (ko-)	= co- (ko-)
kontr- (kontr-)	= counter- (kaunter-)
kontra- (kon-tra-)	= counter- (kaunter-)
krótko- (kroot-ko-)	= short- (szort-)
	curt- (ke:rt-)
lewo- (le-vo-)	= left- (left-)
mało- (ma-wo-)	= few- (fju-)
	little- (lytl-)
między- (myań-dzi-)	= between- (by'twi:n)
	amont- (e'mang-)
	inter- ('ynter-)
mili- (mee-lee-)	= milli- (myly-)
multi- (mool-tee-)	= multi- (malty-)

```
na- (na-)              = on- (on-)
                         onto- (ontu-)
                         up- (ap-)
nad- (nad-)            = over- (ouver-)
                         above- (e'bav-)
                         on- (on-)
nade- (na-de-)         = over- (ouver-)
                         above- (e'bav-)
                         on- (on-)
naj- (nay-)            = most- (moust-)
neo- (ne-o-)           = neo- (ni:e-)
neuro- (neu-ro-)       = neuro- (nju'rou-)
niby- (ñee-bi-)        = as if- (es yf-)
                         would-be- ('łud-bi:-)
nie- (ñe-)             = no- (nou-)
                         non- (non-)
nisko- (ñees-ko-)      = low- (lou-)
nowo- (no-vo-)         = new- nju:-)
o- (o-)                = un- (an-)
                         re- (ry-)
                         de- (dy-); (de-)
ob- (ob-)              = off- (of-)
obco- (ob-tso-)        = foreign- ('foryn)
obe- (o-be-)           = off- (of-)
od- (od-)              = from- (from-)
                         since- (syns-)
ode- (o-de-)           = from- (from- )
                         since- (syns-)
ogólno- (o-gool-no-)   = wide- (łajd-)
około- (o-ko-wo-)      = about  (e-baut-)
ostro- (os-tro-)       = sharp- (szarp-)
pan- (pan-)            = pan- (paen-)
paro- (pa-ro-)         = couple- (-kapl)
                         two-  (tu:-)
pełno- (pew-no-)       = ful- (-ful)
pierwszo- (pyerw-sho-) = first- (fe:rst-)
płasko- (pwas-ko-)     = flat- (flaet-)
po- (po-)              = after- ('a:fter-)
pod- (pod-)            = under- (ander-)
pode- (po-de-)         = under- (ander-)
poli- (po-lee-)        = poli- (poly-)
polsko- (pol-sko-)     = Polish- (poulysz-)
ponad- (po-nad-)       = above- (e'bav-)
post- (post-)          = post- (post-)
poza- (po-za-)         = out- (aut-)
pół- (poow-)           = half- (ha:f-)
prawo- (pra-vo-)       = ortho- (orgo-)
                         right- (rajt-)
                         law- (lou-)
pre- (pre-)            = pre- (pry-)
pro- (pro-)            = pro- (pro-)
                         (pre-)
```

prosto- (pros-to-)	= straight- (strejt-)
proto- (pro-to-)	= proto- (proute-)
prze- (pzhe-)	= across- (e'kros)
	over- (ouwer)
przeciw- (pzhe-cheev-)	= counter- ('kaunter-)
przed- (pzhed-)	= before- (by'fo:r-)
przeszło- (pzhe-shwo-)	= over- (ouwer-)
przy- (pzhi-)	▪ by- (baj-)
	near- (nier-)
pseudo- (pseu-do-)	= pseudo- ('sju:dou-)
psycho- (psi-kho-)	= psycho- ('sajke-)
radio- (ra-dyo-)	▪ radio- ('rejdjou-)
roz- (roz-)	= de- (dy-)
	ex- (y'gs-) (,egz-)
roze- (roze-)	▪ de- (dy-)
	ex- (y'gs-), (,egz-)
równo- (roov-no-)	= equi- (,i:kły'-)
różno- (roozh-no-)	= many- ('meny-)
s- (s-)	= over- (ouwer-)
	off- (-of), etc.
samo- (sa-mo-)	= self- (self-)
słodko- (swod-ko-)	▪ sweet- (sli:t-)
spektro- (spektro-)	= spectro- (spectrou-)
staro- (sta-ro-)	= old- (ould-)
stereo- (ste-re-o-)	= stereo- ('stjery,ou-)
sub- (soob-)	= sub- (sab-)
super- (soo-per-)	= super- (super-)
szeroko- (she-ro-ko-)	= wide- (łajd-)
szybko- (shib-ko·)	= quick- (kłyk-)
średnio- (shred-no-)	= average- (aewrydż-)
	tolerably- (tolerebly-)
środkowo- (shrod-ko-vo-)	= center- ('senter-)
	middle- (mydl-)
	mean- (mi:n-)
śród- (shrood-)	= center- ('senter-), etc.
tele- (te-le-)	= tele- (tely-)
termo- (ter-mo-)	= thermo- (te:rmo-)
trans- (trans-)	= trans- (traens'-)
trój- (trooy-)	= three- (tri:-)
u- (oo-)	= at-(et-)
	de- (dy-), etc.
ultra- (ool-tra-)	= ultra- (altre-)
w- (v-)	= in- (yn-)
wąsko- (vown-sko-)	= narrow- ('naerou-)
wczesno- (vches-no-)	= rearly- ('e:rly-)
we- (ve-)	= in- (yn-)
wice- (vee-tse-)	= vice- (wajs-)
wielko- (vyel-ko-)	= great- (grejt-)
wodo- (vo-do-)	= water- (ło:ter-)
wolno- (vol-no-)	▪ free- (fri:-)
wpół- (vpoow-)	= half- (ha:f-)

```
ws- (vs-)                        = co- (kou-)
                                      (ko-)
wspóŁ- (vspoow-)                 = co- (kou-)
                                      (ko-)
wy- (vi-)                        = out- (aut-)
wysoko- (vi-so-ko-)              = high- (haj-)
wz- (vz-)                        = up- (ap-)
z- (z-)                          = out- (aut-)
za- (za-)                        = behind- (by'hajnd-)
zeszŁo- (zesh-wo-)               = past- (pa:st-)
zielono- (źhe-lo-no-)            = green- (gri;n-)
zŁoto- (zwo-to-)                 = gold- (gould-)
żóŁto- (zhoow-to-)               = yellow- ('jelou-)
```

GEOGRAPHIC NAMES	NAZWY GEOGRAFICZNE
Abyssinia (,aeby'synje)	- Abisynia (a-bee-sí-ńa)
Adriatic (,ejdry'aetyk)	- Adriatyk (ad-ryá-tik)
Africa ('aefryke)	- Afryka (áf-ri-ka)
Alabama (aele'baeme)	- Alabama (a-la-bá-ma)
Alaska (e'laeske)	- Alaska (a-láś-ka)
Albania (ael'bejnje)	- Albania (al-bá-ńa)
Albany ('o:lbeny)	- Albany (al-bá-ni)
Alberta (ael'be:rta)	- Alberta (al-bér-ta)
Algeria (ael'dźierje)	- Algeria (al-gér-ya)
Alps (aelp)	- Alpy (ál-pi)
Amazon ('aemezen)	- Amazonka (a-ma-zón-ka)
America (e'meryke)	- Ameryka (a-mé-ri-ka)
Arabia (e'rejbje)	- Arabia (a-ráb-ya)
Argentina (,a:dźen'ti:ne)	- Argentyna (ar-gen-tí-na)
Arizona (,aery'zoune)	- Arizona (a-ree-zó-na)
Arkansas ('a:ken,so:)	- Arkansas (ar-kán-sas)
Armenia (a:'mi:nje)	- Armenia (ar-mé-ńa)
Asia ('ejsze)	- Azja (áz-ya)
Atlanta (et'laente)	- Atlanta (at-lán-ta)
Atlantic (et'laentyk)	- Atlantyk (at-lán-ţik)
Auschwitz ('ouszwyc)	- Oświęcim (osh-vyáń-ćheem)
Australia (os'trejlje)	- Australia (aws-trál-ya)
Balkans ('bo:lkens)	- Bałkany (baw-ká-ni)
Baltic ('bo:ltyk)	- Bałtyk (báw-tik)
Baltimore ('bo:lty,mo:r)	- Baltimore (bal-ti-mó-re)
Belgium ('beldźem)	- Belgia (bél-gya)
Belgrade (bel'grejd)	- Belgrad (bél-grad)
Benelux ('beny,laks)	- Beneluks (be-ne-looks)
Berlin (be:r'lyn)	- Berlin (bér-leen)
Bermuda (be:r'mju:de)	- Bermudy (ber-moó-di)
Birmingham ('be:rmynem)	- Birmingham (beer-meéng-ham)
Black Sea ('blaek'si:)	- Morze Czarne (mó-she chár-ne)
Bolivia (be'lywje)	- Boliwia (bo-leév-ya)
Brazil (bre'zyl)	- Brazylia (bra-zíl-ya)
Britain ('brytn)	- Brytania (bri-tá-ńa),
British Isles ('brytysz'ajlz)	- Wyspy Brytyjskie (vis-pi bri-tíy-skye)
Bronx (bronks)	- Bronx (bronks)
Brussels ('braslz)	- Bruksela (broo-ksé-la)
Budapest ('bju:de'pest)	- Budapeszt (boo-dá-pesht)
Bulgaria (bal'geerje)	- Bułgaria (boow-gár-ya)
Byelorussia (by,elou'rasze)	- Białorus (bya-wó-roosh)
Cairo ('kaje,rou)	- Kair (ká-eer)
California (kaely'fo:rnje)	- Kalifornia (ka-lee-fór-ńa)
Cambodia (kaem'boudje)	- Kambodża (kam-bó-ja)
Canada ('kaenede)	- Kanada (ka-ná-da)
Caribbean Sea (,kaery'bjen'-si:)	- Morze Karaibskie (mó-zhe ka-ra-eéb-skye)
Carolina (,kaere'lajne)	- Karolina (ka-ro-leé-na)
Carpathians (ka:r'pejtjenz)	- Karpaty (kar-pá-ti)

Caspian Sea ('kaespjen'si:)   – Morze Kaspijskie (mó-zhe kas-
peéy-skye)
Caucasus ('ko:keses)   – Kaukaz (kaw-kaz)
Chicago (szy'ka:gou)   – Chicago (chee-ka-go)
Chile ('czyly)   – Chile (cheé-le)
China ('czajna)   – Chiny (kheé-ni)
Cincinnati (,synsy'naety)   – Cincinnati (tseen-tseen-ná-tee)
Cleveland ('kli:wlend)   – Cleveland (kle-ve-land)
Colorado (,kole'ra:dou)   – Kolorado (ko-lo-ra-do)
Congo ('kongou)   – Kongo (kón-go)
Connecticut (ke'netyket)   – Connecticut (kon-nek-teé-koot)
Copenhagen (,koupn'hejgen)   – Kopenhaga (ko-pen-khá-ga)
Corsica (ko:rsyke)   – Korsyka (kor-si-ka)
Cracow ('kraekou)   – Kraków (krá-koov)
Crimea (kraj'mje)   – Krym (krim)
Croatia (krou'ejsze)   – Chorwacja (khor-váts-ya)
Cuba ('kju:be)   – Kuba (koó-ba)
Czechoslovakia ('czekou-slou'waekje)   – Czechosłowacja (che-kho-swo-váts-ya)
Dakota (de'koute)   – Dakota (da-kó-ta)
Dalmatia (dael'mejszje)   – Dalmacja (dal-máts-ya)
Danzig ('daentsyg)   – Gdańsk (gdáńsk)
Delaware ('dele,ʒeer)   – Delaware (de-la-vá-re)
Denmark ('denma:rk)   – Dania (dá-ña)
Detroit (dy'troit)   – Detroit (de-tro-eet)
Drezden ('drezden)   – Drezno (dréz-no)
East Prussia ('i:st'prasza)   – Prusy Wschodnie (proó-si vskhód-ñe)
Edinburgh ('edynbere)   – Edynburg (e-din-boorg)
Egypt ('i:dżypt)   – Egipt (e-geept)
Eire ('eere)   – Irlandia (eer-lánd-ya)
England ('ynglend)   – Anglia (áng-lya)
Europe ('juerep)   – Europa (e-oo-ró-pa)
Eurasia (jue'rejzje)   – Eurazja (e-oor-áz-ya)
Finland ('fynlend)   – Finlandia (feen-lánd-ya)
Florida ('floryda)   – Floryda (flo-rí-da)
France (fra:ns)   – Francja (fránts-ya)
Gdansk (gdaensk)   – Gdańsk (gdáńsk)
Geneva (dży'ni:wa)   – Genewa (ge-né-va)
Georgia ('dżo:rdżje)   – Georgia (ge-órg-ya)
   – Gruzja (groóz-ya)
Germany ('dże:rmeny)   – Niemcy (ñem-tsi)
Great Britain ('grejt brytn)   – Wielka Brytania (vyél-ka bri-tá-ña)
Greece (gri:s)   – Grecja (grets-ya)
Hague (hejg)   – Haga (khá-ga)
Haiti ('hej-ty)   – Haiti (khá-ee-tee)
Hamburg ('haembe:rg)   – Hamburg (khám-boorg)
Havana (he'waena)   – Hawana (kha-vá-na)
Hawaii (ha:ʒai:)   – Hawaje (kha-vá-ye)
Helsinki ('helsynky)   – Helsinki (khel-seén-kee)

Himalayas (,hyme'lejez)   – Himalaje (khee-ma-la-ye)
Holland ('holend)   – Holandia (kho-land-ya)
Hollywood ('holyłud)   – Hollywood (kho-lee-vood)
Honolulu (,hone'lu:lu:)   – Honolulu (kho-no-loo-loo)
Hungary ('hangery)   – Węgry (van-gri)
Iceland ('ajslend)   – Islandia (ees-land-ya)
Idaho ('ajde,hou)   – Idaho (ee-da-kho)
Illinois (,yly'noj)   – Illinois (ee-lee-no-ees)
India ('yndje)   – India (eend-ya)
Indiana (,yndy'aena)   – Indiana (een-dya-na)
Indianapolis (,yndje'naepolys)   – Indianapolis (een-dya-no-po-lees)
Iowa ('ajoue)   – Iowa (ee-o-va)
Iraq (y'ra:k)   – Irak (ee-rak)
Ireland ('ajerlend)   – Irlandia (eer-land-ya)
Israel ('izrejel)   – Izrael (eez-ra-el)
Italy ('ytely)   – Włochy (vwo-khi)
Jamaica (dże'meike)   – Jamajka (ya-may-ka)
Japan (dże'paen)   – Japonia (ya-po-na)
Java ('dża:wa)   – Jawa (ya-va)
Jericho ('dżery,kou)   – Jerycho (ye-ri-kho)
Jersey ('dże:rzy)   – Jersey (yer-sey)
Jerusalem (dże'ru:selem)   – Jerozolima (ye-ro-zo-lee-ma)
Jordan ('dżo-rdn)   – Jordania (yor-da-ña)
Jugoslavia ('ju:gou'sla:wja)   – Jugosławia (yoo-go-swav-ya)
Kansas ('kaenzes)   – Kansas (kan-sas)
Kentucky (ken'taky)   – Kentucky
Kiev ('ki:ew)   – Kijów (kee-yoov)
Klondike ('klondajk)   – Klondike (klon-dee-ke)
Korea (ko'rje)   – Korea (ko-re-a)
Laos (lauz)   – Laos (la-os)
Latvia (lat-wja)   – Łotwa (wot-va)
Lebanon ('lebenon)   – Liban (lee-ban)
Leipzig ('lajpzig)   – Lipsk (leepsk)
Leningrad (,lenyn,graed)   – Leningrad (le-ñeen-grad)
Libya ('lybje)   – Libia (leeb-ya)
Lithuania (,lyŧju'ejnje)   – Litwa (leet-va)
Lodz (lodz)   – Łódź (woodzh)
London ('landen)   – Londyn (lon-din)
Los Angeles (los'aendży,li:z)   – Los Angeles (los an-ge-les)
Louisiana (lu,i:zy'aena)   – Louisiana (loo-ee-sya-na)
Lublin ('lablyn)   – Lublin (loob-leen)
Lvov (lwow)   – Lwów (lvooy)
Madrid (me'dryd)   – Madryt (ma-drit)
Main (mejn)   – Men (men)
Maine (mejn)   – Maine (ma-ee-n)
Manhattan (maen'haetn)   – Manhattan (man-kha-tan)
Maryland ('meerylaend)   – Maryland (ma-ri-land)
Massachusetts (,maese'czu:sets) – Massachusetts (ma-sa-choo-sets)
Masuria (me'sjuerje)   – Mazury (ma-zoo-ri)
Mediterranean (,medite'rejnjen) – Śródziemne (shrood-zhem-ne)

Memel ('mejmel)	– Kłajpeda (kway-pé-da)
Mexico ('meksy,kou)	– Meksyk (mek-sik)
Miami (maj'aemy)	– Miami (mya-mee)
Michigan ('myszygen)	– Michigan (mee-cheé-gan)
Milwaukee (myl'ƚo:ky)	– Milwaukee (meel-wó-ki)
Minneapolis (,myny'aepelys)	– Minneapolis (mee-ne-a-pó-lees)
Minnesota(,myny'soute)	– Minnesota (mee-ne-só-ta)
Mississippi (,mysy'sypy)	– Mississippi
Missouri (my'suery)	– Missouri
Montana (mon'taena)	– Montana (mon-ta-na)
Montreal (,montry'o:l)	– Montreal (monƒ-ré-al)
Moravia (mo'rejwje)	– Morawy (mo-rá-vi)
Morocco (me'rokou)	– Maroko (ma-ró-ko)
Moscow ('moskou)	– Moskwa (mós-kva)
Nebraska (ny'braeske)	– Nebraska (ne-bras-ka)
Neisse ('najsy)	– Nysa (ni-sa)
Nevada (ne'wa:de)	– Newada (ne-vá-da)
New England (nju:ynglend)	– Nowa Anglia (nó-va áng-lya)
New Hampshire (nju'haempszier)	– New Hampshire
New Jersey (nju:'dże:rzy)	– New Jersey
New Mexico (nju:'meksy,kou)	– Nowy meksyk (nó-vy mék-sik)
New Orleans (nju:'o:rlienz)	– Nowy Orlean (nó-vy or-le-an)
New York City (nju:'jo:rk'- syty)	– Nowy Jork (nó-vy york)
Niagara(naj'aegere)	– Niagara (ñee-a-gá-ra)
North Carolina ('no:rt,kaere'- lajne)	– Karolina Północna (ka-ro-lee-na poow-nóts-na)
North Dakota ('no:rt-de'koute)	– Dakota Północna
North Sea ('no:rt'si:)	– Morze Północne (mó-zhe poow-nóts-ne)
Norway ('no:rƚej)	– Norwegia (nor-vég-ya)
Oder ('ouder)	– Odra (ód-ra)
Odessa (ou'dese)	– Odessa (o-dés-sa)
Ohio (ou'hajou)	– Ohio (ókh-yo)
Oklahoma (,oukle'houme)	– Oklahoma (o-kla-khó-ma)
Ontario (on'teery,ou)	– Ontario (on-tár-yo)
Oregon (o'rygen)	– Oregon (o-ré-gon)
Oslo ('ozlou)	– Oslo (ós-lo)
Ottawa ('otele)	– Ottawa (o-ta-va)
Palestine ('paelys,tain)	– Palestyna (pa-les-ti-na)
Panama (,paene'ma:)	– Panama (pa-na-ma)
Paris (paerys)	– Paryż (pá-rizh)
Peking ('pi:kyŋ)	– Pekin (pe-keen)
Pennsylvania (,pensyl'venje)	– Pensylwania (pen-sil-vá-ña)
Persia ('pe:rsze)	– Persja (pér-sya)
Pittsburgh('pytsbe:rg)	– Pittsburg (peéts-boorg)
Podolia (pe'doulje)	– Podole (po-dó-le)
Poland (,poulend)	– Polska (pól-ska)
Pomerania (,pome'rejnje)	– Pomorze (po-mo-zhe)
Posen ('pouzn)	– Poznań (póz-nań)
Prague (pra:g)	– Praga (prá-ga)

Prussia ('prasze) — Prusy (proó-si)
Quebec (kɪ́y'bek) — Quebek (ke-bek)
Red Sea ('red'si:) — Morze Czerwone (mó-zhe cher-
vo-ne)
Reykjavik ('rejkje,wi:k) — Reykjawik
Rhine (rajn) — Ren (ren)
Rhode Island ('roud,ajlend) — Rhode Island
Riga ('ri:ga) — Ryga (ri-ga)
Rockies('rokyz) — Góry Skaliste (goó-ri ska-
leés-te)
Rome (roum) — Rzym (zhim)
Rumania (ru'mejnje) — Rumunia (roo-moó-ńa)
Russia ('rasze) — Rosja (rós-ya)
Salt Lake City ('so:lt,lejk'- — Salt Lake City
syty)
San Francisco (,saen-fren'- — San Francisco (sán-fran-tseés-
syskou) ko)
Saskatchewan (ses'kaeczy,ʈan) — Saskatchewan
Saudi Arabia ('saudy-e'rejbje)— Arabia Saudyjska (a-rab-ya
saw-diy-ska)
Savannah (se'waene) — Savannah
Saxony ('saekseny) — Saksonia (sak-só-ńa)
Scandinavia (,skaendy'nejwje) — Skandynawia (skan-di-náv-ya)
Scotland ('skotlend) — Szkocja (shkóts-ya)
Seattle (sy'aetl) — Seattle
Serbia ('se:rbje) — Serbia (sér-bya)
Siberia (saj'bierie) — Syberia (si-bér-ya)
Sicily ('sysyly) — Sycylia (si-tsil-ya)
Silesia (saj'li:zje) — Śląsk (śhlówńsk)
Sinai ('sajny,aj) — Synaj (si-nay)
Slavonia (sle'wounje) — Slawonia (sla-vo-ńa)
Slovakia (slou'waekje) — Słowacja (swo-váts-ya)
Slovenia (slou'wi:nje) — Słowenia (swo-ve-ńa)
Sofia ('soufje) — Sofia (sóf-ya)
South Carolina ('sous,kaere'- — Karolina Południowa (ka-ro-leé-
lajne) na po-wood-ńó-va)
South Dakota ('sous de'koute) — Dakota Południowa (da-kó-ta
po-wood-ńó-va)
Soviet Russia ('souwjet'rasze)— Rosja Sowiecka (rós-ya so-
vyéts-ka)
Spain (spejn) — Hiszpania (kheesh-pa-ńa)
Stettin ('stetyn) — Szczecin (shché-cheen)
Stockholm ('stokhoulm) — Sztokholm (sztók-kholm)
Sudetes (su:'di:ti:z) — Sudety (su-dé-ty)
Suez ('su:yz) — Suez (soó-ez)
Sweden ('słi:dn) — Szwecja (shvets-ya)
Switzerland ('słytserlend) — Szwajcaria (shvay-tsar-ya)
Syria ('syrje) — Syria (sír-ya)
Tahiti (ta:hyty) — Tahiti (ta-khee-tee)
Taiwan (taj'ʈaen) — Taiwan (táy-van)
Tallin ('taelyn) — Tallinn (tá-leen)

Tangier (taen'dźjer)	– Tanger (tán-ger)
Tannenberg ('taenen'be:rg)	– Stębark (stań-bark)
Tatra ('ta:tre)	– Tatry (tát-ri)
Teheran (te'ra:n)	– Teheran (te-khe-ran)
Tel Aviv (tel'a:wyw)	– Tel Awiw (te-la-veev)
Tennessee (,tene'si:)	– Tennessee
Teschen ('teszn)	– Cieszyn (che-shin)
Texas ('tekses)	– Teksas (tęk-sas)
Tibet (ty'bet)	– Tybet (ti-bet)
Tyrol ('tyrel)	– Tyrol (ti-rol)
Tokyo ('toukj,ou)	– Tokio (tók-yo)
Toledo (to'lejdou)	– Toledo (to-le-do)
Toronto (te'rontou)	– Toronto (to-ron-to)
Transylvania (,traensyl'-wejnje)	– Siedmiogród (shed-myo-grood)
Trieste (try'est)	– Triest (tree-est)
Tunis ('tju:nys)	– Tunis (too-ňees)
Turkey ('te:rky)	– Turcja (toor-tsya)
Turkestan (,te:rkys'ta:n)	– Turkiestan (toor-kyes-tan)
Ukraine (ju'kreyn)	– Ukraina (ook-ra-ee-na)
Ulster ('alster)	– Ulster (ools-ter)
Union of Soviet Socialist Republics ('ju:njenew'-souwjet'souszelyst-ry'-pablyks)	– Związek Socjalistycznych Republik Radzieckich (zvyown-zek sots-ya-lees-tich-nykh re-poob-leek ra-dzhets-keekh)
United Kingdom of Great Britain (ju'najtyd'kyndemew'-grejt'bryten)	– Zjednoczone Królestwo Wielkiej Brytanii (zyed-no-cho-ne kroo-les-tvo vyel-kyey bry-ta-ňee)
United States of America (ju'najtyd,stejts,owe'meryka)	– Stany Zjednoczone Ameryki (sta-ni zyed-no-cho-ne a-me-ri-kee)
Upper Silesia ('apersaj'li:z-je)	– Górny Śląsk (goor-ny shlownzk)
Ural ('juerel)	– Ural (oo-ral)
Utah ('ju:ta:)	– Utah
Vancouver (waen'ku:wer)	– Vancouver (van-koo-ver)
Varna ('wa:rna)	– Warna (var-na)
Vatican ('waetyken)	– Watykan (va-ti-kan)
Venezuela ('wene'zuejle)	– Wenezuela (ve-ne-zoo-e-la)
Venice ('wenys)	– Wenecja (ve-nets-ya)
Vermont (we:rmont)	– Vermont
Versailles (weer'saj)	– Wersal (ver-sal)
Vienna (wy'ene)	– Wiedeń (vye-deň)
Vietnam (wjet'na:m)	– Wietnam (wyet-nam)
Vilna ('wylne)	– Wilno (veel-no) Wilnius (veel-noos)
Virginia (wer'dźynje)	– Wirginia (veer-źee-ňa)
Vistula ('wystjule)	– Wisła (vees-wa)
Volga ('wolga)	– Wołga (vow-ga)
Volhynia (wol'hynje)	– Wołyń (vo-wiň)

Walachia (Łe'lejkje)	– Wołoszczyzna (vo-wosh-chíz-na)
Wales (Łejlz)	– Walia (vál-ya)
Warsaw ('Ło:rso:)	– Warszawa (var-shá-va)
Washington ('Łoszynten)	– Waszyngton (va-shíng-ton)
Waterloo (,Łó:ter'lu:)	– Waterloo (va-tér-lo)
West Virginia ('Łestve:r'-dżynje)	– Wirginia Zachodnia (veér-gee-ña za-khód-ña)
White Russia ('Łajt'rasza)	– Białoruś (bya-wó-roosh)
Winchester ('Łynczyster)	– Winchester
Winnipeg ('Łyny,peg)	– Winnipeg
Wyoming (Łah'oumyŋg)	– Wyoming
Yalta ('jaelte)	– Jalta (yáw-ta)
Yellowstone ('jelou,stoun)	– Yellowstone
Yugoslavia (ju:gou'sla:wje)	– Jugoslawia (yoo-go-swáv-ya)
Yukon ('ju:kon)	– Yukon
Zagreb ('za:greb)	– Zagrzeb (zág-zheb)
Zakopane ('za:kop ane)	– Zakopane (za-ko-pa-ne)
Zealand ('zi:lend)	– Zelandia (ze-land-ya)
Zurich ('zjueryk)	– Zurych (zoó-rikh)

CHRISTIAN NAMES	IMIONA WŁASNE
Abel ('ejbel) m.	– Abel (a-bel)
Abraham (ejbre,haem) m.	– Abraham (ab-ra-kham)
Ada ('ejde) f.	– Ada (a-da)
Adalbert ('aedel,be:rt) m.	– Wojciech (voy-chekh)
Adam ('aedem) m.	– Adam (a-dam)
Adela ('aedyle) f.	– Adela (a-dela)
Agnes ('aegnys) f.	– Agnieszka (ag-nesh-ka)
Albert ('aelbert) m.	– Albert (al-bert)
Alec ('aelyk) m.	– Lech (lekh)
Alexander (,aelyg'za:nder) m.	– Aleksander (a-lek-san-der)
Alfred (aelfred) m.	– Alfred (al-fred)
Alice ('aelys) f.	– Alicja (a-leets-ya)
Aloïs (e'louys) m.	– Alojzy (a-loy-zi)
Andrew ('aendru:) m.	– Andrzej (and-zhey)
Ann (aen) f.	– Anna (an-na)
Antony ('aenteny) m.	– Antoni (an-to-nee)
Antonia (aen'tounje) f.	– Antonina (an-to-nee-na)
Arnold ('a:rnld) m.	– Arnold (ar-nold)
Arthur ('a:rter) m.	– Artur (ar-toor)
Augustine (o:'gastyn) m.	– Augustyn (au-goos-tin)
Avis ('aewys) f.	– Awia (av-ya)
Barbara ('ba:rbere) f.	– Barbara (bar-ba-ra)
Benedict (benydykt) m.	– Benedykt (be-ne-dikt)
Benjamin ('bendżmyn) m.	– Benjamin (ben-ya-meen)
Bernard ('be:rnerd) m.	– Bernard (ber-nard)
Bill (byl) m.	– William (veel-yam)
Blanch (bla:ncz) f.	– Blanka (blan-ka)
Bob (bob) m.	– Robert (ro-bert)
Boris ('borys) m.	– Borys (bo-ris)
Bridget ('brydżyt) f.	– Brygida (bri-gee-da)
Camilia (ke'mylje) f.	– Kamila (ka-mee-la)
Carlotta (ka:r'lote) f.	– Karolina (ka-ro-lee-na)
Carol ('kaerel) f.	– Karolina (ka-ro-lee-na)
Casimir ('kaesymjer) m.	– Kazimierz (ka-zhee-myezh)
Catherine ('kaeteryn) f.	– Katarzyna (ka-ta-zhi-na)
Cecil ('sesl) m.	– Cecil (tse-tseel)
Cecilia (sy'sylje) f.	– Cecylia (tse-tsil-ya)
Charles (cza:rlz) m.	– Karol (ka-rol)
Charlie ('cza:rly) m.	– Karolek (ka-ro-lek)
Christina (krys'ti:ne) f.	– Krystyna (kris-ti-na)
Christopher ('krystefer) m.	– Krzysztof (kzhish-tof)
Clara (kleer) f.	– Klara (kla-ra)
Claud (klo:d) m.	– Klaudiusz (klawd-yoosh)
Claudia ('klo:dje) f.	– Klaudia (klawd-ya)
Clement ('klement) m.	– Klemens (kle-mens)
Clementine (,klemen,tajn)	– Klementyna (kle-men-ti-na)
Conrad ('konraed) m.	– Konrad (kon-rad)
Cyprian ('syprien) m.	– Cyprian (tsip-ryan)
Cyril ('syryl) m.	– Cyryl (tsi-ril)

Damian ('dejmjen) m.	– Damian (dám-yan)
Daniel ('dejnjel) m.	– Daniel (da-ñel)
David ('dejwyd) m.	– Dawid (da-veed)
Dennis('denys) m.	– Dionizy (dyo-ñee-zi)
Denise (dy'ni:z) f.	– Dioniza (dyo-ñee-za)
Dick (dyk) m.	= Richard
Dominic (do'mynyk) m.	– Dominik (do-mee-ñeek)
Dorothy ('dorety) f.	– Dorota (do-ró-ta)
Edmund ('edmend) m.	– Edmund (éd-moond)
Edward ('edłerd) m.	– Edward (éd-vard)
Edwin (edłyn) m.	– Edwin (éd-veen)
Eleanor ('elyner) f.	– Eleonora (e-le-o-nó-ra)
Elias (y'lajes) m.	– Eliasz (él-yash)
Elvira (el'wajere) f.	– Elwira (el-vee-ra)
Emily ('emyly) f.	– Emilia (e-meel-ya)
Eric ('eryk) m.	– Eryk (e-rik)
Erica ('eryka) f.	– Eryka (e-ri-ka)
Eugene (ju:zejn) m.	– Eugeniusz (ew-ge-ñoosh)
Eugenia (ju:dzi:nje) f.	– Eugenia (ew-ge-ña)
Eva ('i:we) f.	– Ewa (e-va)
Evan ('even) m.	– Jan (yan)
Eve ('i:w) f.	– Ewa (é-va)
Felicia (fy'lysie) f.	– Felicja (fe-leets-ya)
Felix ('fi:lyks) m.	– Feliks (fé-leeks)
	– Szczęsny (shchańs-ni)
Frances ('fra:nsys) f.	– Franciszka (fran-cheesh-ka)
Francis ('fra:nsys) m.	– Franciszek (fran-chee-shek)
Frank ('fraenk) m.	= Francis
Frederic ('fredrik) m.	– Fryderyk (fri-de-rik)
Gabriel ('gejbrjel) m.	– Gabriel (gáb-ryel)
George (dżo:rdż) m.	– Jerzy (ye-zhi)
Gervase ('dże:rwes) m.	– Gerwazy (ger-vá-zi)
Gregory ('gregeri) m.	– Grzegorz (gzhe-gozh)
Gustavus (,gus'ta:wes)	– Gustaw (goós-tav)
Guy (gaj) m.	– Wit (veet)
Harold ('haereld) m.	– Harold (khá-rold)
Hedwig ('hedlyg) f.	– Jadwiga (yad-vee-ga)
Helen ('helyn) f.	– Helena (he-le-na)
Henrietta (,henry'eta) f.	– Henryka (hen-rí-ka)
Henry ('henry) m.	– Henryk (hén-rik)
Herbert ('he:rbert) f.	– Herbert (hér-bert)
Hilary ('hylery) m.	– Hilary (hee-lá-ri)
Hubert ('hju:bert) m.	– Hubert (hoó-bert)
Ian ('yen) m.	= John
Igor ('i:go:r) m.	– Igor (eé-gor)
Irene (aj'ri:n) f.	– Irena (ee-ré-na)
Isabella (,yze'bele) f.	– Izabella (ee-za-bé-la)
Isidora (,yzy'do:re) f.	– Izydora (ee-zi-dó-ra)
Isidore ('yzy,do:r) m.	– Izydor (ee-zi-dor)
Ivan ('ajwen) m.	= John
Ivo (ajwou) m.	– Iwo (ee-vo)
Ivor (ajwo:r) m.	= Ivo
Jack (dżaek) m.	= John

Jacob ('dżejkeb) m.	- Jakub (ya-koob)
James (dżejmz) m.	= Jacob
Jane (dżejn) f.	- Janina (ya-ńee-na)
Jeane (dżi:n) f.	= Jane
Jenny (dżeny) f.	= Jane
Jerome ('dżerem) m.	- Hieronim (khye-ro-ńeem)
Jill (dżyl) f.	- Juliana
Jim (dżym) m.	- James
Jimmie ('dżymy) m.	- James
Joanna (dżou'aene) f.	- Joanna (yo-ań-na)
Joe (dżou) m.	- Joseph
John (dżon) m.	- Jan (yan)
Jonas (dżounes) m.	- Jonasz (yo-nash)
Joseph ('dżouzyf) m.	- Jozef (yoo-zef)
Josepha (,dżou'zefa) f.	- Jozefa (yoo-ze-fa)
Julia (dżu:lje) f.	- Julia (yool-ya)
Julian (dżu:ljen) m.	- Julian (yool-yan)
Kate (kejt) f.	= Catherine
Keith (ki:s) m.	- Keith
Kenneth ('kenys) m.	= Kenneth
Laura ('lo:re) f.	- Laura (law-ra)
Laurence ('lo:rens) m.	- Wawrzyniec (vav-zhi-ńets)
Leo ('liou) m.	- Leon (le-on)
Leonard ('lenerd) m.	- Leonard (le-o-nard)
Leopold ('lje,pould) m.	- Leopold (le-o-pold)
Lewis ('luys) m.	- Ludwik (lood-veek)
Lily ('lyly) f.	- Lilia (leel-ya)
Lilian ('lyljen) f.	- Lilianna (leel-yán-na)
Louisa (lu'i:ze) f.	- Ludwika (lood-vee-ka)
Lucas ('lu:kes) m.	- Łukasz (woo-kash)
Luther ('lu:ter) m.	- Luter (loo-ter)
Lydia ('lydje) f.	- Lidia (lyd-ya)
Marian ('meeryen) f.	- Marianna (mar-yań-na)
Mark (ma:rk) m.	- Marek (ma-rek)
Martha ('ma:rte) f.	- Marta (mar-ta)
Martin ('ma:rtyn) m.	- Marcin (mar-cheen)
Mary ('meery) f.	- Maria (mar-ya)
Mathilda (me'tylde) f.	- Matylda (ma-til-da)
Matthew ('maetju:) m.	- Mateusz (ma-te-oosh)
Maurice ('morys) m.	- Maurycy (maw-ri-tsi)
Maximilian (,maeksy'myljen)	- Maksymilian (mak-si-mil-yan)
Michael ('majkl) m.	- Michał (mee-khaw)
Monica ('monyke) f.	- Monika (mo-ńee-ka)
Moses ('mouzyz) m.	- Mojżesz (moy-shesh)
Natalia (ne'ta:lje) f.	- Natalia (na-tal-ya)
Natalie ('naetely) f.	- Natalia (na-tal-ya)
Nathan ('nejten) m.	- Natan (na-tan)
Nicholas ('nykeles) m.	- Mikołaj (mee-ko-way)
Nicola ('nykele) f.	- Michalina (mee-kha-lee-na)
Olga ('olge) f.	- Olga (ol-ga)
Olivia ('olywje) f.	- Oliwia (o-leew-ya)
Ophelia (o'fi:lje) f.	- Ofelia (o-fel-ya)

Oscar ('osker) m.	– Oskar (oś-kar)
Otto ('otou) m.	– Otton (ót-ton)
Pamela ('paemyle)	– Pamela (pa-mé-la)
Patricia (pe'trysze) f.	– Patrycja (pat-ríts-ya)
Patrick ('paetryk) m.	– Patrycy (pat-rí-tsi)
Paul ('po:l) m.	– Paweł (pa-vew)
Paula ('po:le) f.	– Paulina (paw-leé-na)
Pepe (pi:p)	= Joseph
Peter ('pi:ter) m.	– Piotr (pyotr)
Philip ('fylyp) m.	– Filip (feé-leep)
Rachel ('rejczel) f.	– Rachela (ra-khé-la)
Ralph (raelf) m.	– Ralf (ralf)
Randolph ('raendolf) m.	– Randolf (rán-dolf)
Raphael ('rejfel) m.	– Rafael (ra-fá-el)
Ray (rej) m.	– Ray (raj)
Rebecca (ry'beka)	– Rebeka (re-bé-ka)
Ricarda (ry'ka:rde) f.	– Ryszarda (ri-shár-da)
Richard ('ryczerd) m.	– Ryszard (ri-shard)
Robert ('robert) m.	– Robert (ro-bert)
Roberta (rou'be:rte) f.	– Roberta (ro-bér-ta)
Roger ('rodżer) m.	– Roger (ro-dżer)
Roland ('roulend) m.	– Roland (ro-land)
Rolf (rolf) m.	– Rudolf (rú-dolf)
Rose (rouz) f.	– Róża (roó-zha)
Rosemary ('rouzmery) f.	– Róża Maria (roó-zha mar-ya)
Samuel ('saemjuel) m.	– Samuel (sa-moó-el)
Sean (szo:n) m.	= John
Shane (szejn) m.	= John
Sigismund ('sygysmend) m.	– Zygmunt (zíg-moont)
Simon ('sajmen) m.	– Szymon (szí-mon)
Sophia (se'faje) f.	– Zofia (zof-ya)
Stanislaus (staenys,lo:s) m.	– Stanisław (sta-neés-wav)
Stephana ('stefene) f.	– Stefania (ste-fań-ya)
Stephen ('sti:wen) m.	– Stefan (sté-fan)
Teresa (te'ri:ze) f.	– Teresa (te-ré-sa)
Thaddeus ('taedjes) m.	– Tadeusz (ta-dé-oosh)
Theodore ('tje,do:r) m.	– Teodor (te-ó-dor)
Theophilus (ty'ofyles) m.	– Teofil (te-ó-feel)
Thomas ('tomas) m.	– Tomasz (to-mash)
Titus ('tajtes) m.	– Tytus (ti-toos)
Tobias (te'bajes) m.	– Tobiasz (to-byasz)
Ulric ('ulryk) m.	– Ulrych (oól-rikh)
Ursula ('e:rsele) f.	– Urszula (oor-shoo-la)
Valentine ('vaelen,tajn) m.	– Walenty (va-len-ti)
Valerian (ve'ljerjen) m.	– Walerian (va-ler-yan)
Vera ('vjere) f.	– Wera (vé-ra)
Victor ('vykter) m.	– Wiktor (veék-tor)
Vincent ('vynsent) m.	– Wincenty (veen-tsén-ti)
Virginia (ver'dżynje) f.	– Wirginia (veer-geé-ña)
Walter ('ło:lter) m.	– Walter (vál-ter)
Will (łyl) m.	– Wiliam (veél-yam)

William ('Iyljem) m.	- Wilhelm (veél-khelm)
Winston ('Iynsten) m.	= Winston
Xavier ('zaevjer) m.	- Ksawery (ksa-veˊri)
Yve (i:w) m.	= Ivo
Yves (i:w) m.	= Ivo
Yvonne (y'won) f.	- Ivona (ee-voˊna)
Zach (zaek) m.	= Zachariah
Zachariah (,zaeke'raje) m.	- Zachariasz (za-kháˊr-yash)
Zenobia (zy'noubje) f.	- Zenobia (ze-nóˊb-ya)

CARDINAL NUMBERS		–	LICZEBNIKI GŁÓWNE
0	nought, zero, cipher	–	zero
1	one	–	jeden, raz
2	two	–	dwa
3	three	–	trzy
4	four	–	cztery
5	five	–	pięć
6	six	–	sześć
7	seven	–	siedem
8	eight	–	osiem
9	nine	–	dziewieć
10	ten	–	dziesięć
11	eleven	–	jedenaście
12	twelve	–	dwanaście
13	thirteen	–	trzynaście
14	fourteen	–	czternaście
15	fifteen	–	piętnaście
16	sixteen	–	szesnaście
17	seventeen	–	siedemnaście
18	eighteen	–	osiemnaście
19	nineteen	–	dziewiętnaście
20	twenty	–	dwadzieścia
21	twenty-one	–	dwadzieścia jeden
22	twenty-two	–	dwadzieścia dwa
23	twenty-three	–	dwadzieścia trzy
24	twenty-four	–	dwadzieścia cztery
30	thirty	–	trzydzieści
40	forty	–	czterdzieści
50	fifty	–	pięćdziesiąt
60	sixty	–	sześćdziesiąt
70	seventy	–	siedemdziesiąt
80	eighty	–	osiemdziesiąt
90	ninety	–	dziewięćdziesiąt
100	one hundred	–	sto
101	one hundred and one	–	sto jeden
110	one hundred and ten	–	sto dziesięć
200	two hundred	–	dwieście
777	seven hundred seventy seven	–	siedemset siedemdziesiąt siedem
1,000.	one thousand	–	tysiąc
1,500.	fifteen hundred	–	tysiąc pięćset
1978	nineteen hundred and seventy eight	–	tysiąc dziewięćset siedemdziesiąt osiem
500,000.	five hundred thousand	–	pięćset tysięcy
1,000,000.	one million	–	milion
3,000,000.	three million	–	trzy miliony
1,000,000,000.	one billion	–	miliard

ORDINAL NUMBERS		—	LICZEBNIKI PORZĄDKOWE
1st	first		– pierwszy
2nd	second		– drugi
3rd	third		– trzeci
4th	fourth		– czwarty
5th	fifth		– piąty
6th	sixth		– szósty
7th	seventh		– siódmy
8th	eighth		– ósmy
9th	ninth		– dziewiąty
10th	tenth		– dziesiąty
11th	eleventh		– jedenasty
12th	twelfth		– dwunasty
13th	thirteenth		– trzynasty
14th	fourteenth		– czternasty
15th	fifteenth		– piętnasty
16th	sixteenth		– szesnasty
17th	seventeenth		– siedemnasty
18th	eighteenth		– osiemnasty
19th	nineteenth		– dziewiętnasty
20th	twentieth		– dwudziesty
21st	twenty-first		– dwudziesty pierwszy
22nd	twenty-second		– dwudziesty drugi
23rd	twenty-third		– dwudziesty trzeci
24th	twenty-fourth		– dwudziesty czwarty
30th	thirtieth		– trzydziesty
40th	fortieth		– czterdziesty
50th	fiftieth		– pięćdziesiąty
60th	sixtieth		– sześćdziesiąty
70th	seventieth		– siedemdziesiąty
80th	eightieth		– osiemdziesiąty
90th	ninetieth		– dziewięćdziesiąty
100th	(one) hundredth		– setny
101st	(one) hundred and first		– sto pierwszy
102nd	(one) hundred and second		– sto drugi
103rd	(one) hundred and third		– sto trzeci
104th	(one) hundred and fourth		– sto czwarty
200th	two hundredth		– dwusetny
500th	five hundredth		– pięćsetny
1,000th	(one) thousandth		– tysięczny
3,000th	three thousandth		– trzytysięczny
1978th	nineteen hundred and seventy eighth		– tysiąc dziewięćset siedemdziesiąty ósmy
500,000th	five hundred thousandth		– pięćsettysięczny
1,000,000th	millionth		– milionowy
3,000,000th	three millionth		– trzy milionowy

FRACTIONAL NUMBERS, ARITHMETIC EXPRESSIONS AND TIME
UŁAMKI, WYRAŻENIA : DZIAŁANIA ARYTMETYCZNE I CZAS

$\frac{1}{2}$ one half, a half — pół, połowa
   half a mile — pół mili
   half way — pół drogi, w połowie

$1\frac{1}{2}$ one and a half — półtora, jeden i pół

$3\frac{1}{2}$ three and a half — trzy i pół

$\frac{1}{3}$ one third, a third — jedna trzecia, trzecia część

$\frac{1}{4}$ one fourth, quarter — jedna czwarta, ćwierć

$\frac{3}{4}$ three fourths, three quarters — trzy czwarte, trzy ćwierci

$1\frac{1}{4}$ one and a quarter — jeden i ćwierć, jeden i jedna czwarta

$\frac{1}{5}$ one fifth, a fifth — jedna piąta

$2\frac{4}{5}$ two and four fifths — dwa i cztery piąte

.3 point three — 0,3 zero przecinek trzy
3.5 three point five — 3,5 trzy przecinek pięć
result in 100% — wynik stuprocentowy
single — pojedyńczy
double
twofold — podwójny
   — dwukrotny
threefold — potrójny
treble — trzykrotny
triple — trzykrotny
fourfold — poczwórny
quadruple — czterokrotny
fivefold — pięciokrotny
quintuple — pięciokrotny
sixfold — sześciokrotny

once — raz
twice — dwa razy
three times — trzy razy
twice as much — dwa razy więcej

first(ly) — po pierwsze
secondly — po drugie
thirdly — po trzecie
fourthly — po czwarte
in the first place — po pierwsze

3 x 3 = 9 three times three — trzy razy trzy równa się
      make nine,   dziewięć
      three multiplied
      by three are (make)
      nine

2 + 3 = 5 two plus three are   – dwa plus trzy równa się pięć,
     five   dwa dodac trzy równa się pięć

7— 4 = 3 seven minus four   – siedem minus cztery równa się
     are three   trzy,
                         siedem odjąc cztery równa się
                         trzy

8 ÷ 2 = 8 : 2 = 4   – osiem podzielone przez dwa
     eight divided by   równa się cztery
     two make four

TIME   –   CZAS

an hour	godzina
half an hour	pół godziny
a quarter of an hour	kwadrans
a minute	minuta
what time is it, please?	Przepraszam, która godzina?
it is exactly three o'clock	punktualnie trzecia
it is only two o'clock	dopiero druga
it is past seven	po siódmej
it has struck five	piąta wybiła
it is a quarter to one	za kwadrans pierwsza
	za piętnascie pierwsza
it is a quarter past two	kwadrans na trzecia,
	piętnascie po drugiej
it is three minutes before one	pierwsza za trzy minuty
it starts at six a.m.	zaczyna się o szóstej rano
it ends at one p m.	kończy się o pierwszej
	kończy się o trzynastej
at eight p.m.	o ósmej wieczór
	o dwudziestej
the morning	rano , przedpołudnie
noon. midday	południe
the afternoon	popołudnie
the evening	wieczór
tonight	dziś wieczorem
the night	noc
midnight	północ
a day	dzień
a week	tydzień
a month	miesiąc
a year	rok
a leap year	rok przestępny
a century	wiek, stulecie
today	dziś
tomorrow	jutro
the day after tomorrow	pojutrze
yesterday	wczoraj
the day before yesterday	przedwczoraj
a year and half	półtora roku
good night	dobranoc
good morning, sir	dzień dobry panu

POLISH WEIGHTS AND MEASURES
MIARY I WAGI

1. Lineal measure - miary długości

    1 mm milimetr - millimeter
      = 0.039 inch
    1 cm centymetr - centimeter
      = 10 mm = 0.394 inch
    1 m metr - meter (metre)
      = 100 cm = 1.094 yards =
      3.281 feet
    1 km kilometr - kilometer
      = 1000 m = 0.621 mile

2. Square measure - miary powierzchni

    1 mm² milimetr kwadratowy -
      - square millimeter
      = 0.002 square inch
    1 cm² centymetr kwadratowy -
      - square centimeter
    1 m² metr kwadratowy - square
      meter
      = 10,000 cm² = 1.196
      square yards
      = 10.764 square feet
    1 a - ar = 100 m²
      = 119.599 square yards
    1 ha - hektar - hectare
      = 100 a = 2.471 acres

3. Cubic measure - miary objętości

    1 cm³ centymetr sześcienny -
      cubic centimeter
      = 1000 mm³
      = 0.061 cubic inch
    1 RT tona rejestrowa -
      register ton
      = 100 feet³
      = 2,832. m³

4. Measure of capacity - miary pojemności

    1 l litr - liter (litre)
      = 1.760 pints
      = 1.057 U.S. liquid
      quarts
      = 0.906 dry quarts

    1 hl hektolitr - hectoliter
      = 100 l
      = 2.75 bushels
      = 26.418 U.S. gallons

5. Weights- wagi

    1 g gram - gram
      = 15.432 grains

    1 kg kilogram - kilogram
      = 1000 g
      = 2.205 pounds ardp
      = 2.677 pounds troy

    1 q = kwintal
      = 100 kg
      = 1.968 hundred-
      weights
      = 2.204 U.S. hundred-
      weights

    1 t tona - ton
      = 1000 kg
      = 0.984 long ton
      = 1.102 U.S. short
      tons

AMERICAN AND BRITISH WEIGHTS AND MEASURES
AMERYKAŃSKIE I BRYTYJSKIE WAGI I MIARY

1. Measures of length - Miary długości

```
1 mile (majl) = 1760 yards (ja:rdz)      = 1609,3 m
1 yard (ja:rd) = 3 feet (fi:t)           = 91,44 cm
1 foot (fut) = 12 inches ('ynczyz)       = 30,48 cm
1 inch (yncz)                            = 2,54 cm
```

2. Measures of surface - Miary powierzchni

```
1 square mile (skłeer majl) = 640 acres ('ejkerz)
                                         = 258,99 ha
1 acre ('ejker) = 4840 square yards (skłeer ja:rdz)
                                         = 0,40 ha
1 square yard (skleer ja:rd) = 9 square feet (skłeer fi:t)
                                         = 0,836 m²
1 square foot (skłeer fut) = 144 square inches
                       (,skłeer'ynczyz) = 929 cm²
1 square inch (skleer yncz)             = 6,45 cm²
```

3. Measures of capacity - Miary pojemności

	BR.	AM.
1 quarter ('kło:rter) (BR.)		
= 8 bushels (buszlz) =	290,94 l	-
1 bushel (buszl) = 8 gallons		
('gaelenz) =	36,368 l	35,238 l
1 gallon ('gaelen) = 4 quarts		
(kło:rts) =	4,546 l	4,405 l
1 quart (kło:rt) = 2 pints (paints) =	1,136 l	1,101 l
1 pint (paint) =	0,568 l	0,5306 l

4. Weights (avoirdupois) - Wagi
   (and apothecary)

```
1 pound (paund) = 16 ounces ('aunsyz)       =    453,59 g
1 ounce (auns) = 16 drams (draemz)          =     28,35 g
1 dram (draem) = 3 scruples (skru:plz)      =      4,00 g
1 scruple (skru:pl)= 20 grains(grejns)      =      1,33 g
1 grain (grejn)                             =     64,7989 mg
1 ton (tan) (U.S.) = 20 hundredweight ('handredłejt) (U.S.)
               = 2000 pounds (paundz)       =    907,185 kg
1 hundredweight (U.S.) = 100 pounds (paundz) =    45,359 kg
1 ton (tan) (Br.) = 20 hundredweight ('handredłejt) (Br.)
               = 2240 pounds (paundz)       =   1016,047 kg
1 hundredweight (Br.) = 112 pounds (paundz) =     50,802 kg
```

NOTE: Metric system in Poland since 1918, now is gradually
      introduced in the United States and in Great Britain

UWAGA: System metryczny jest obecnie stopniowo wprowadzany
       w U.S.A. i w Anglii.

AMERICAN, BRITISH AND POLISH CURRENCY

PIENIĄDZE W OBIEGU W U.S.A., ANGLII I POLSCE

American coins - monety

$ 1	dollar ('doler)	= 100 cents (sents)
1	half dollar ('ha:f,doler)	= 50 cents
1	quarter ('kło:ter)	= 25 cents
1	dime (dajm)	= 10 cents
1	nickel (nykl)	= 5 cents
1 ¢	penny ('peny)	- 1 cent (cent)

Banknotes:one dollar and up (1; 2; 5; 10; 20; 50; 100 etc.)
Banknoty: jednodolarowe i wyższe.

British: 1 pound sterling - funt
(,paund'ste:rlyŋg) = 100 pence (pens)

coins (koynz)	50 pence
monety (mone⁴ti)	10 pence
	5 pence
	2 pence
	1 penny ('peny)
	$\frac{1}{2}$ halfpenny ('hejpny)

Banknotes: 1 pound notes and up.
Banknoty: jednofuntowe i wyższe.

Polish: zl. złoty (zwó-ti) = 100 groszy (gróshi)

coinz (koynz)	20 zł - złotych (zwo-tikh)
monety (monéti)	10 zł
	5 zł
	2 zł
	1 zł. - złoty (zwó-ti)
	50 gr. - groszy (gró-shi)
	20 gr
	10 gr

Banknotes: 50 zł; 100; 200; 500; 1000; 2000 etc.
Banknoty: pięćdziesiąt złotowe i wyższe.

$-$NOTES$-$

—NOTES—

—NOTES—

—NOTES—

– NOTES –

—NOTES—

Also by Iwo Cyprian Pogonowski, from Hippocrene:

POLISH-ENGLISH/ENGLISH-POLISH CONCISE DICTIONARY
Over 6,500 entries. Perfect for travelers.
408 pages   *ISBN 0-87052-589-1*   *$5.95 paper*

POLISH-ENGLISH/ENGLISH-POLISH PRACTICAL DICTIONARY
Over 30,000 entries.
398 pages   *ISBN 0-87052-064-4*   *$7.95 paper*

ENGLISH CONVERSATIONS FOR POLES
3,300 expressions to meet every situation in modern American life.
Full pronunciation guide, and concise dictionary included.
250 pages   *ISBN 0-87052-873-4*   *$8.95 paper*

POLAND—A HISTORICAL ATLAS (Revised)
Over 160 maps covering topics ranging from relations with Russia,
Polish-Jewish history, and social developments, to linguistic evolution
and cultural achievement. "A model of clarity." —J. J. Maciuszko,
Choice, American Library Association
325 pages   *ISBN 0-87052-282-5*   *$27.50*

More Polish Interest titles from Hippocrene:

THE JEWS AND POLES IN WORLD WAR II
STEFAN KORBONSKI
"A valuable statement by a leading participant." —*Library Journal*
240 pages   *ISBN 0-87052-632-4*   *$14.95*

THE FORGOTTEN HOLOCAUST:
The Poles under German Occupation, 1939-1944
RICHARD C. LUKAS
"Richard Lukas tells this story with an outrage properly contained
within the framework of a scholarly narrative." —*Washington Post*
300 pages   *ISBN 0-87052-632-4*   *$9.95 paper*

PILSUDSKI:
A Life for Poland
WACLAW JEDRZEJEWICZ
Now in paperback, this masterly biography by a soldier and a colleague of Pilsudski, portrays the life and message of the charismatic
personality who epitomizes the history of independent Poland.
385 pages   *ISBN 0-87052-747-9*   *$11.95 paper*